THE CHRONICLES OF
THOMAS COVENANT,
THE UNBELIEVER

BOOK ONE: LORD FOUL'S BANE
BOOK TWO: THE ILLEARTH WAR
BOOK THREE: THE POWER THAT PRESERVES

Stephen Donaldson

HARPER
Voyager

Voyager
An imprint of HarperCollins*Publishers*
1 London Bridge Street,
London SE1 9GF
www.voyager-books.com

This paperback edition 1996
31

Previously published in paperback by HarperCollins
Science Fiction & Fantasy 1994, reprinted twice,
and by Fontana 1993

First published in Great Britain in three volumes:

Lord Foul's Bane published by Fontana 1978
Copyright © Stephen R. Donaldson 1977

The Illearth War published by Fontana 1978
Copyright © Stephen R. Donaldson 1977

The Power That Preserves published by Fontana 1978
Copyright © Stephen R. Donaldson 1977

This one-volume edition copyright © Stephen R. Donaldson 1993

The Author asserts the moral right to
be identified as the author of this work

ISBN 13: 978 0 00 647329 9

Set in Meridien

Printed and bound by
CPI Group (UK) Ltd, Croydon, CR0 4YY

MIX
Paper from
responsible sources
FSC
www.fsc.org **FSC® C007454**

STEPHEN DONALDSON

Stephen Donaldson was born in 1947 in Cleveland, Ohio. From the age of three until he was sixteen he lived in India, where his father, an orthopaedic surgeon, worked extensively with lepers. It was after hearing one of his father's speeches on the subject of leprosy that he conceived the character of Thomas Covenant. He now lives in New Mexico.

Stephen Donaldson made his publishing debut in 1977 with *The Chronicles of Thomas Covenant, the Unbeliever*. This bestselling trilogy was named Best Novel of the Year by the British Fantasy Society, and earned the author the John W. Campbell Award as best new writer in 1979. This success was followed by a second trilogy – *The Second Chronicles of Thomas Covenant* (which is also available in a one-volume edition); a collection of short stories – *Daughter of Regals*; and the two books in the bestselling *Mordant's Need* series – *The Mirror of Her Dreams* and *A Man Rides Through*. He is also the editor of *Strange Dreams*, a personal selection of favourite fantasy short stories.

His most recent series is the *Gap* sequence, the acclaimed five-volume space opera that begins in *The Real Story* and continues in *Forbidden Knowledge, A Dark and Hungry God Arises, Chaos and Order* and *This Day All Gods Die*.

His latest book, which marks a return to fantasy after more than ten years, is *Reave the Just*, a new collection of fantasy stories – available now from *Voyager*.

THE CHRONICLES OF
THOMAS COVENANT, THE UNBELIEVER

'In this enormous fantasy, the timeless battle of good and evil is played out against a stunningly detailed and imaginative alternate-world background – giants, cave-dwellers, intelligent horses, strange beasts, potent talismans, and men with incomprehensible powers. The hero, a modern American transported mysteriously to this strange environment, manages to make it all believable because he has trouble believing it himself. Donaldson has created a classic.'   *Washington Post*

Works by Stephen Donaldson

The Chronicles of Thomas Covenant, the Unbeliever

1. LORD FOUL'S BANE
2. THE ILLEARTH WAR
3. THE POWER THAT PRESERVES

The Second Chronicles of Thomas Covenant

1. THE WOUNDED LAND
2. THE ONE TREE
3. WHITE GOLD WIELDER

Short Stories

DAUGHTER OF REGALS AND OTHER TALES
STRANGE DREAMS (editor)
REAVE THE JUST

Mordant's Need

1. THE MIRROR OF HER DREAMS
2. A MAN RIDES THROUGH

The Gap Series

1. THE GAP INTO CONFLICT: THE REAL STORY
2. THE GAP INTO VISION: FORBIDDEN KNOWLEDGE
3. THE GAP INTO POWER: A DARK AND HUNGRY GOD ARISES
4. THE GAP INTO MADNESS: CHAOS AND ORDER
5. THE GAP INTO RUIN: THIS DAY ALL GODS DIE

For James R. Donaldson, M.D.,
whose life expressed compassion and commitment
more eloquently than any words

CONTENTS

Map   10–11

BOOK ONE: LORD FOUL'S BANE

1   Golden Boy   15
2   'You Cannot Hope'   21
3   Invitation to a Betrayal   37
4   Kevin's Watch   43
5   Mithil Stonedown   53
6   Legend of Berek Halfhand   61
7   Lena   77
8   The Dawn of the Message   84
9   Jehannum   102
10 The Celebration of Spring   122
11 The Unhomed   141
12 Revelstone   161
13 Vespers   178
14 The Council of Lords   195
15 The Great Challenge   215
16 Blood-Bourne   229
17 End in Fire   244
18 The Plains of Ra   271
19 Ringthane's Choice   290
20 A Question of Hope   302
21 Treacher's Gorge   313
22 The Catacombs of Mount Thunder   327
23 Kiril Threndor   344
24 The Calling of Lions   359
25 Survived   375

BOOK TWO: THE ILLEARTH WAR

Part I *Revelstone*

1	'The Dreams of Men'	383
2	Halfhand	390
3	The Summoning	403
4	'May Be Lost'	415
5	*Dukkha*	425
6	The High Lord	436
7	Korik's Mission	450
8	'Lord Kevin's Lament'	462
9	Glimmermere	483
10	Seer and Oracle	497

Part II *The Warmark*

11	War Council	509
12	Forth to War	527
13	The Rock Gardens of the Maerl	537
14	Runnik's Tale	547
15	Revelwood	563
16	Forced March	583
17	Tull's Tale	603
18	Doom's Retreat	624
19	The Ruins of the Southron Wastes	651
20	Garroting Deep	669

Part III *The Blood of the Earth*

21	Lena's Daughter	691
22	*Anundivian Yajña*	705
23	Knowledge	718
24	Descent to Earthroot	735
25	The Seventh Ward	754
26	Gallows Howe	768
27	Leper	779

BOOK THREE: THE POWER THAT PRESERVES

1	The Danger in Dreams	785
2	Variol-son	804
3	The Rescue	830
4	Siege	837
5	*Lomillialor*	854
6	The Defence of Mithil Stonedown	867
7	Message to Revelstone	889
8	Winter	910
9	Ramen Covert	923
10	Pariah	945
11	The Ritual of Desecration	958
12	*Amanibhavam*	988
13	The Healer	997
14	Only Those Who Hate	1009
15	'Lord Mhoram's Victory'	1025
16	Colossus	1057
17	The Spoiled Plains	1073
18	The Corrupt	1093
19	Ridjeck Thome	1112
20	The Unbeliever	1126
21	Leper's End	1144
	Glossary	*1153*

Outer Earth

North Plains

Grimmerdhore
Forest

Westron Mountains

Revelstone

Guards
Gap

North R.

White R.

Trothgard

Gray R.

Lintrollin R.

Soulsease River

Rill R.

Revelwood

Andelainian
Hills

Last Hills

Center Plains

Garroting Deep

Black River

Melenkurion
Skyweir

South Plains

Mithil R.

Kevin's
Watch

Rivenrock

Doom's
Retreat

Mithil
Stonedown

Cravenhaw

THE
LAND

Doriendor
Corishev

Southron Wastes

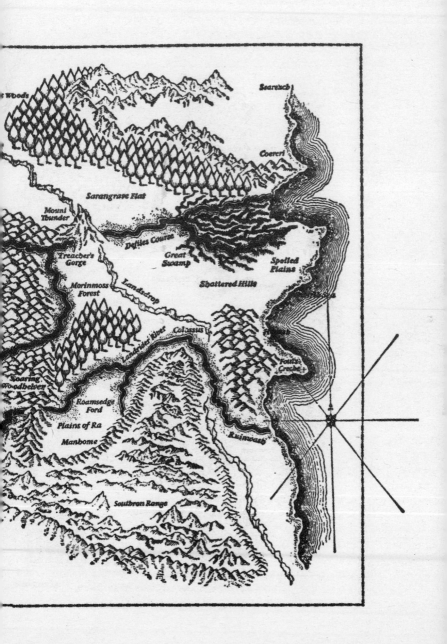

LORD FOUL'S
BANE

Something there is in beauty

1

GOLDEN BOY

She came out of the store just in time to see her young son playing on the sidewalk directly in the path of the grey, gaunt man who strode down the centre of the walk like a mechanical derelict. For an instant, her heart quailed. Then she jumped forward, gripped her son by the arm, snatched him out of harm's way.

The man went by without turning his head. As his back moved away from her, she hissed at it, 'Go away! Get out of here! You ought to be ashamed!'

Thomas Covenant's stride went on, as unfaltering as clockwork that had been wound to the hilt for just this purpose. But to himself he responded, *Ashamed? Ashamed?* His face contorted in a wild grimace. *Beware! Outcast unclean!*

But he saw that the people he passed, the people who knew him, whose names and houses and handclasps were known to him – he saw that they stepped aside, gave him plenty of room. Some of them looked as if they were holding their breath. His inner shouting collapsed. These people did not need the ancient ritual of warning. He concentrated on restraining the spasmodic snarl which lurched across his face, and let the right machinery of his will carry him forward step by step.

As he walked, he flicked his eyes up and down himself, verifying that there were no unexpected tears or snags in his clothing, checking his hands for scratches, making sure that nothing had happened to the scar which stretched from the heel of his right palm across where his last two fingers had been. He could hear the doctors saying, 'VSE, Mr Covenant. Visual Surveillance of Extremities. Your health depends upon it. Those dead nerves will never grow back – you'll never know when you've hurt yourself unless you get in the habit of checking. Do it all the time – think about it all the time. The next time you might not be so lucky.'

VSE. Those initials comprised his entire life.

Doctors! he thought mordantly. But without them, he might not have survived even this long. He had been so ignorant of his danger. Self-neglect might have killed him.

Watching the startled, frightened or oblivious faces – there were many oblivious faces, though the town was small – that passed around him, he wished he could be sure that his face bore a proper expression of disdain. But the nerves in his cheeks seemed only vaguely alive, though the doctors had assured him that this was an illusion at the present stage of his illness, and he could never trust the front which he placed between himself and the world. Now, as women who had at one time chosen to discuss his novel in their literary clubs recoiled from him as if he were some kind of minor horror or ghoul, he felt a sudden treacherous pang of loss. He strangled it harshly, before it could shake his balance.

He was nearing his destination, the goal of the affirmation or proclamation that he had so grimly undertaken. He could see the sign two blocks ahead of him: Bell Telephone Company. He was walking the two miles into town from Haven Farm in order to pay his phone bill. Of course, he could have mailed in the money, but he had learned to see that act as a surrender, an abdication to the mounting bereavement which was being practised against him.

While he had been in treatment, his wife, Joan, had divorced him – taken their infant son and moved out of the state. The only thing in which he, Thomas Covenant, had a stake that she had dared handle had been the car; she had taken it as well. Most of her clothing she had left behind. Then his nearest neighbours, half a mile away on either side, had complained shrilly about his presence among them; and when he refused to sell his property, one of them moved from the county. Next, within three weeks of his return home, the grocery store – he was walking past it now, its windows full of frenetic advertisements – had begun delivering his supplies, whether or not he ordered them – and, he suspected, whether or not he was willing to pay.

Now he strode past the courthouse, its old grey columns looking proud of their burden of justice and law – the building in which, by proxy, of course, he had been reft of his family. Even its front steps were polished to guard against the stain of human need which prowled up and down them, seeking restitution. The divorce had been granted because no compassionate law could force a woman to raise her child in the company of a man like him. *Were there tears?* he asked Joan's memory. *Were you brave? Relieved?* Covenant resisted an urge to run out of danger. The gaping giant heads which topped the courthouse columns looked oddly nauseated, as if they were about to vomit on him.

In a town of no more than five thousand, the business section was not large. Covenant crossed in front of the department store, and through the glass front he could see several high-school girls pricing cheap jewellery. They leaned on the counters in provocative poses, and Covenant's throat tightened involuntarily. He found himself resenting the hips and breasts of the girls – curves for other men's caresses, not his. He was impotent. In the decay of his nerves, his sexual capacity was just another amputated member. Even the release of lust was denied to him; he could conjure up desires until insanity threatened, but he could do nothing about them. Without warning, a memory of his wife flared in his mind, almost blanking out the sunshine and the sidewalk and the people in front of him. He saw her in one of the opaque nightgowns he had bought for her, her breasts tracing circles of invitation under the thin fabric. His heart cried, *Joan! How could you do it? Is one sick body more important than everything?*

Bracing his shoulders like a strangler, he suppressed the memory. Such thoughts were a weakness he could not afford; he had to stamp them out. Better to be bitter, he thought. Bitterness survives. It seemed to be the only savour he was still able to taste.

To his dismay, he discovered that he had stopped moving. He was standing in the middle of the sidewalk with his fists clenched and his shoulders trembling. Roughly, he forced himself into motion again. As he did so, he collided with someone.

Outcast unclean!

He caught a glimpse of ochre; the person he had bumped seemed to be wearing a dirty, reddish-brown robe. But he did not stop to apologize. He stalked on down the walk so that he would not have to face that particular individual's fear and loathing. After a moment, his stride recovered its empty, mechanical tick.

Now he was passing the offices of the Electric Company – his last reason for coming to pay his phone bill in person. Two months ago, he had mailed in a cheque to the Electric Company – the amount was small; he had little use for power – and it had been returned to him. In fact, his envelope had not even been opened. An attached note had explained that his bill had been anonymously paid for at least a year.

After a private struggle, he had realized that if he did not resist this trend, he would soon have no reason at all to go among his fellow human beings. So today he was walking the two miles into town to pay his phone bill in person – to show his peers that he did not intend to be shriven of his humanity. In rage at his outcasting, he sought to defy it, to assert the rights of his common mortal blood.

In person, he thought. What if he were too late? If the bill had already been paid? What did he come in person for then?

The thought caught his heart in a clench of trepidation. He clicked rapidly through his VSE, then returned his gaze to the hanging sign of the Bell Telephone Company, half a block away. As he moved forward, conscious of a pressure to surge against his anxiety, he noticed a tune running in his mind along the beat of his stride. Then he recollected the words:

> Golden boy with feet of clay,
> Let me help you on your way.
> A proper push will take you far —
> But what a clumsy lad you are!

The doggerel chuckled satirically through his thoughts, and its crude rhythm thumped against him like an insult, accompanied by slow stripper's music. He wondered if there were an overweight goddess somewhere in the mystical heavens of the universe, grinding out his burlesque fate: A proper push *leer* will take you far — but what a clumsy lad you are! *mock pained dismay*. Oh, right, golden boy.

But he could not sneer his way out of that thought, because at one time he had been a kind of golden boy. He had been happily married. He had had a son. He had written a novel in ecstasy and ignorance, and had watched it spend a year on the best-seller lists. And because of it, he now had all the money he needed.

I would be better off, he thought, if I'd known I was writing that kind of book.

But he had not known. He had not even believed that he would find a publisher, back in the days when he had been writing that book — the days right after he had married Joan. Together, they did not think about money or success. It was the pure act of creation which ignited his imagination; and the warm spell of her pride and eagerness kept him burning like a bolt of lightning, not for seconds or fractions of seconds, but for five months in one long wild discharge of energy that seemed to create the landscape of the earth out of nothingness by the sheer force of its brilliance — hills and crags, trees bent by the passionate wind, night-ridden people, all rendered into being by that white bolt striking into the heavens from the lightning rod of his writing. When he was done, he felt as drained and satisfied as all of life's love uttered in one act.

That had not been an easy time. There was an anguish in the perception of heights and abysses that gave each word he wrote the shape of dried, black blood. And he was not a man who liked heights; unconstricted emotion did not come easily to him. But it had been glorious. The focusing to that pitch of intensity had struck him as the cleanest thing that had ever happened to him. The stately frigate of his soul had sailed well over a deep and dangerous ocean. When he mailed his manuscript away, he did so with a kind of calm confidence.

During those months of writing and then of waiting, they lived on her income. She, Joan Macht Covenant, was a quiet woman who expressed more of herself with her eyes and the tone of her skin than she did with words. Her flesh had a hue of gold which made her look as warm and precious as a sylph or succuba of joy. But she was not large or strong, and Thomas Covenant felt constantly amazed at the fact that she earned a living for them by breaking horses.

The term *breaking*, however, did not do justice to her skill with animals. There were no tests of strength in her work, no bucking stallions with mad eyes and foaming nostrils. It seemed to Covenant that she did not break horses; she seduced them. Her touch spread calm over their twitching muscles. Her murmuring voice relaxed the tension in the angle of their ears. When she mounted them bareback, the grip of her legs made the violence of their brute fear fade. And whenever a horse burst from her control, she simply slid from its back and left it alone until the spasm of its wildness had worn away. Then she began with the animal again. In the end, she took it on a furious gallop around Haven Farm, to show the horse that it could exert itself to the limit without surpassing her mastery.

Watching her, Covenant had felt daunted by her ability. Even after she taught him to ride, he could not overcome his fear of horses.

Her work was not lucrative, but it kept her and her husband from going hungry until the day a letter of acceptance arrived from the publisher. On that day, Joan decided that the time had come to have a child.

Because of the usual delays of publication, they had to live for nearly a year on an advance on Covenant's royalties. Joan kept her job in one way or another for as long as she could without threatening the safety of the child conceived in her. Then, when her body told her that the time had come, she quit working. At that point, her life turned inward, concentrated on the task of growing her baby with a single-mindedness that often left her outward eyes blank and tinged with expectation.

After he was born, Joan announced that the boy was to be named Roger, after her father and her father's father.

Roger! Covenant groaned as he neared the door of the phone company's office. He had never even liked that name. But his son's infant face, so meticulously and beautifully formed, human and complete, had made his heart ache with love and pride — yes, pride, a father's participation in mystery. And now his son was gone — gone with Joan he did not know where. Why was he so unable to weep?

The next instant, a hand plucked at his sleeve. 'Hey, mister,' a thin voice said fearfully, urgently. 'Hey, mister.' He turned with a yell in his throat – Don't touch me! Outcast unclean! – but the face of the boy who clutched his arm stopped him, kept him from pulling free. The boy was young, not more than eight or nine years old – surely he was too young to be so afraid? His face was mottled pale-and-livid with dread and coercion, as if he were somehow being forced to do something which terrified him.

'Hey, mister,' he said, thinly supplicating. 'Here. Take it.' He thrust an old sheet of paper into Covenant's numb fingers. 'He told me to give it to you. You're supposed to read it. Please, mister?'

Covenant's fingers closed involuntarily around the paper. He? he thought dumbly, staring at the boy. He?

'Him.' The boy pointed a shaking finger back up the sidewalk.

Covenant looked, and saw an old man in a dirty ochre robe standing half a block away. He was mumbling, almost singing a dim nonsense tune; and his mouth hung open, though his lips and jaw did not move to shape his mutterings. His long, tattered hair and beard fluttered around his head in the light breeze. His face was lifted to the sky; he seemed to be staring directly at the sun. In his left hand he held a wooden beggar-bowl. His right hand clutched a long wooden staff, to the top of which was affixed a sign bearing one word: 'Beware.'

Beware?

For an odd moment, the sign itself seemed to exert a peril over Covenant. Dangers crowded through it to get at him, terrible dangers swam in the air toward him, screaming like vultures. And among them, looking toward him through the screams, there were eyes – two eyes like fangs, carious and deadly. They regarded him with a fixed, cold and hungry malice, focused on him as if he and he alone were the carrion they craved. Malevolence dripped from them like venom. For that moment, he quavered in the grasp of an inexplicable fear.

Beware!

But it was only a sign, only a blind placard attached to a wooden staff. Covenant shuddered, and the air in front of him cleared.

'You're supposed to read it,' the boy said again.

'Don't touch me,' Covenant murmured to the grip on his arm. 'I'm a leper.'

But when he looked around, the boy was gone.

2

'YOU CANNOT HOPE'

In his confusion, he scanned the street rapidly, but the boy had escaped completely. Then, as he turned back toward the old beggar, his eyes caught the door, gilt-lettered: Bell Telephone Company. The sight gave him a sudden twist of fear that made him forget all distractions. Suppose – This was his destination; he had come here in person to claim his human right to pay his own bills. But suppose –

He shook himself. He was a leper; he could not afford suppositions. Unconsciously, he shoved the sheet of paper into his pocket. With grim deliberateness, he gave himself a VSE. Then he gripped himself, and started toward the door.

A man hurrying out through the doorway almost bumped into him, then recognized him and backed away, his face suddenly grey with apprehension. The jolt broke Covenant's momentum, and he almost shouted aloud, Leper outcast unclean! He stopped again, allowed himself a moment's pause. The man had been Joan's lawyer at the divorce – a short, fleshy individual full of the kind of bonhomie in which lawyers and ministers specialize. Covenant needed that pause to recover from the dismay of the lawyer's glance. He felt involuntarily ashamed to be the cause of such dismay. For a moment, he could not recollect the conviction which had brought him into town.

But almost at once he began to fume silently. Shame and rage were inextricably bound together in him. I'm not going to let them do this to me, he rasped. By hell! They have no right. Yet he could not so easily eradicate the lawyer's expression from his thoughts. That revulsion was an accomplished fact, like leprosy – immune to any question of right or justice. And above all else a leper must not forget the lethal reality of facts.

As Covenant paused, he thought, I should write a poem.

> These are the pale deaths
> which men miscall their lives:
> for all the scents of green things growing,
> each breath is but an exhalation of the grave.

Bodies jerk like puppet corpses,
and hell walks laughing –

Laughing – now there's a real insight. Hellfire.

Did I do a whole life's laughing in that little time?

He felt that he was asking an important question. He had laughed when his novel had been accepted – laughed at the shadows of deep and silent thoughts that had shifted like sea currents in Roger's face – laughed over the finished product of his book – laughed at its presence on the best-seller lists. Thousands of things large and small had filled him with glee. When Joan had asked him what he found so funny, he was only able to reply that every breath charged him with ideas for his next book. His lungs bristled with imagination and energy. He chuckled whenever he had more joy than he could contain.

But Roger had been six months old when the novel had become famous, and six months later Covenant still had somehow not begun writing again. He had too many ideas. He could not seem to choose among them.

Joan had not approved of this unproductive luxuriance. She had packed up Roger, and had left her husband in their newly purchased house, with his office newly settled in a tiny, two-room hut overlooking a stream in the woods that filled the back of Haven Farm – left him with strict orders to start writing while she took Roger to meet his relatives.

That had been the pivot, the moment in which the rock had begun rolling toward his feet of clay – begun with rumbled warnings the stroke which had cut him off as severely as a surgeon attacking gangrene. He had heard the warnings, and had ignored them. He had not known what they meant.

No, rather than looking for the cause of that low thunder, he had waved goodbye to Joan with regret and quiet respect. He had seen that she was right, that he would not start to work again unless he were alone for a time; and he had admired her ability to act even while his heart ached under the awkward burden of their separation. So when he had waved her plane away over his horizons, he returned to Haven Farm, locked himself in his office, turned on the power to his electric typewriter, and wrote the dedication of his next novel:

'For Joan, who has been my keeper of the possible.'

His fingers slipped uncertainly on the keys, and he needed three tries to produce a perfect copy. But he was not seawise enough to see the coming storm.

The slow ache in his wrists and ankles he also ignored; he only stamped his feet against the ice that seemed to be growing in them. And when he found the numb purple spot on his right hand near the base of his little finger, he put it out of his mind. Within twenty-four hours of Joan's departure, he was deep into the plotting of his book. Images cascaded through his imagination. His fingers fumbled, tangled themselves around the simplest words, but his imagination was sure. He had no thought to spare for the suppuration of the small wound which grew in the centre of that purple stain.

Joan brought Roger home after three weeks of family visits. She did not notice anything wrong until that evening, when Roger was asleep, and she sat in her husband's arms. The storm windows were up, and the house was closed against the chill winter wind which prowled the Farm. In the still air of their living-room, she caught the faint, sweet, sick smell of Covenant's infection.

Months later, when he stared at the antiseptic walls of his room in the leprosarium, he cursed himself for not putting iodine on his hand. It was not the loss of two fingers that galled him. The surgery which amputated part of his hand was only a small symbol of the stroke which cut him out of his life, excised him from his own world as if he were some kind of malignant infestation. And when his right hand ached with the memory of its lost members, that pain was no more than it should be. No, he berated his carelessness because it had cheated him of one last embrace with Joan.

But with her in his arms on that last winter night, he had been ignorant of such possibilities. Talking softly about his new book, he held her close, satisfied for that moment with the press of her firm flesh against his, with the clean smell of her hair and the glow of her warmth. Her sudden reaction had startled him. Before he was sure what disturbed her, she was standing, pulling him up off the sofa after her. She held his right hand up between them, exposed his infection, and her voice crackled with anger and concern.

'Oh, Tom! Why don't you take care of yourself?'

After that, she did not hesitate. She asked one of the neighbours to sit with Roger, then drove her husband through the light February snow to the emergency room of the hospital. She did not leave him until he had been admitted to a room and scheduled for surgery.

The preliminary diagnosis was gangrene.

Joan spent most of the next day with him at the hospital, during the time when he was not being given tests. And the next morning, at six o'clock, Thomas Covenant was taken from his room for surgery on his right hand. He regained consciousness three hours later back in his hospital bed with two fingers gone. The grogginess of the drugs clouded him for a time, and he did not miss Joan until noon.

But she did not come to see him at all that day. And when she arrived in his room the following morning, she was changed. Her skin was pale, as if her heart was hoarding blood, and the bones of her forehead seemed to press against the flesh. She had the look of a trapped animal. She ignored his outstretched hand. Her voice was low, constrained; she had to exert force to make even that much of herself reach toward him. Standing as far away as she could in the room, staring emptily out the window at the slushy streets, she told him her news.

The doctors had discovered that he had leprosy.

His mind blank with surprise, he said, 'You're kidding.'

Then she spun and faced him, crying, 'Don't play stupid with me now! The doctor said he would tell you, but I told him no, I would do it. I was thinking of you. But I can't – I can't stand it. You've got leprosy! Don't you know what that means? Your hands and feet are going to rot away, and your legs and arms will twist, and your face will turn ugly like a fungus. Your eyes will get ulcers and go bad after a while, and I can't stand it – it won't make any difference to you because you won't be able to feel anything, damn you! And – oh, Tom, Tom! It's catching.'

'Catching?' He could not seem to grasp what she meant.

'Yes!' she hissed. 'Most people get it because – ' for a moment she choked on the fear which impelled her outburst – 'because they were exposed when they were kids. Children are more susceptible than adults. Roger – I can't risk – I've got to protect Roger from that!'

As she ran, escaped from the room, he answered. 'Yes, of course.' Because he had nothing else to say. He still did not understand. His mind was empty. He did not begin to perceive until weeks later how much of him had been blown out by the wind of Joan's passion. Then he was simply appalled.

Forty-eight hours after his surgery, Covenant's surgeon pronounced him ready to travel, and sent him to the leprosarium in Louisiana. On their drive to the leprosarium, the doctor who met his plane talked flatly about various superficial aspects of leprosy. *Mycobacterium leprae* was first identified by Armauer Hansen in 1874, but study of the bacillus has been consistently foiled by the failure of the researchers to meet two of Koch's four steps of analysis: no one had been able to grow the microorganism artificially, and no one had discovered how it is transmitted. However, certain modern research by Dr O. A. Skinsnes of Hawaii seemed promising. Covenant listened only vaguely. He could hear abstract vibrations of horror in the word *leprosy*, but they did not carry conviction. They affected him like a threat in a foreign language. Behind the intoxi-

24

cation of menace, the words themselves communicated nothing. He watched the doctor's earnest face as if he were staring at Joan's incomprehensible passion, and made no response.

But when Covenant was settled in his room at the leprosarium – a square cell with a white blank bed and antiseptic walls – the doctor took another tack. Abruptly, he said, 'Mr Covenant, you don't seem to understand what's at stake here. Come with me. I want to show you something.'

Covenant followed him out into the corridor. As they walked, the doctor said, 'You have what we call a primary case of Hansen's disease – a native case, one that doesn't seem to have a – a genealogy. Eighty per cent of the cases we get in this country involve people – immigrants and so on – who were exposed to the disease as children in foreign countries – tropical climates. At least we know where they contracted it, if not why or how.

'Of course, primary or secondary, they can take the same general path. But as a rule people with secondary cases grew up in places where Hansen's disease is less arcane than here. They recognize what they've got when they get it. That means they have a better chance of seeking help in time.

'I want you to meet another of our patients. He's the only other primary case we have here at present. He used to be a sort of hermit – lived alone away from everyone in the West Virginian mountains. He didn't know what was happening to him until the army tried to get in touch with him – tell him his son was killed in the war. When the officer saw this man, he called in the Public Health Service. They sent the man to us.'

The doctor stopped in front of a door like the one to Covenant's cell. He knocked, but did not wait for an answer. He pushed open the door, caught Covenant by the elbow, and steered him into the room.

As he stepped across the threshold, Covenant's nostrils were assaulted by a pungent reek, a smell like that of rotten flesh lying in a latrine. It defied mere carbolic acid and ointments to mask it. It came from a shrunken figure sitting grotesquely on the white bed.

'Good afternoon,' the doctor said. 'This is Thomas Covenant. He has a primary case of Hansen's disease, and doesn't seem to understand the danger he's in.'

Slowly, the patient raised his arms as if to embrace Covenant.

His hands were swollen stumps, fingerless lumps of pink, sick meat marked by cracks and ulcerations from which a yellow exudation oozed through the medication. They hung on thin, hooped arms like awkward sticks. And even though his legs were covered by his hospital pyjamas, they looked like gnarled wood. Half of one foot was gone, gnawed away, and in the place of the other was nothing but an unhealable wound.

Then the patient moved his lips to speak, and Covenant looked up at his face. His dull, cataractal eyes sat in his face as if they were the centre of an eruption. The skin of his cheeks was as white-pink as an albino's; it bulged and poured away from his eyes in waves, runnulets, as if it had been heated to the melting point; and these waves were edged with thick tubercular nodules.

'Kill yourself,' he rasped terribly. 'Better than this.'

Covenant broke away from the doctor. He rushed out into the hall and the contents of his stomach spattered over the clean walls and floor like a stain of outrage.

In that way, he decided to survive.

Thomas Covenant lived in the leprosarium for more than six months. He spent his time roaming the corridors like an amazed phantasm, practising his VSE and other survival drills, glaring his way through hours of conferences with the doctors, listening to lectures on leprosy and therapy and rehabilitation. He soon learned that the doctors believed patient psychology to be the key to treating leprosy. They wanted to counsel him. But he refused to talk about himself. Deep within him, a hard core of intransigent fury was growing. He had learned that by some bitter trick of his nerves the two fingers he had lost felt more alive to the rest of his body than did his remaining digits. His right thumb was always reaching for those excised fingers, and finding their scar with an awkward, surprised motion. The help of the doctors seemed to resemble this same trick. Their few sterile images of hope struck him as the gropings of an unfingered imagination. And so the conferences, like the lectures, ended as long speeches by experts on the problems that he, Thomas Covenant, faced.

For weeks the speeches were pounded into him until he began to dream them at night. Admonitions took over the ravaged, playground of his mind. Instead of stories and passions, he dreamed perorations.

'Leprosy,' he heard night after night, 'is perhaps the most inexplicable of all human afflictions. It is a mystery, just as the strange, thin difference between living and inert matter is a mystery. Oh, we know some things about it: it is not fatal; it is not contagious in any conceivable way; it operates by destroying the nerves, typically in the extremities and in the cornea of the eye; it produces deformity, largely because it negates the body's ability to protect itself by feeling and reacting against pain; it may result in complete disability, extreme deformation of the face and limbs, and blindness; and it is irreversible, since the nerves that die cannot be restored. We also know that, in almost all cases, proper treatment using DDS – diamino-diphenyl-sulfone – and some of the new synthetic antibiotics can arrest the spread of the disease, and that, once the neural deterioration has been halted, the proper medication and therapy can keep the affliction under control for the rest of the patient's life. What we do not know is why or how any specific person contracts the illness. As far as we can prove, it comes out of nowhere for no reason. And once you get it, you cannot hope for a cure.'

The words he dreamed were not exaggerated – they could have come verbatim from any one of a score of lectures or conferences – but their tolling sounded like the tread of something so unbearable that it should never have been uttered. The impersonal voice of the doctor went on: 'What we have learned from our years of study is that Hansen's disease creates two unique problems for the patient – interrelated difficulties that do not occur with any other illness, and that make the mental aspect of being a leprosy victim more crucial than the physical.

'The first involves your relationships with your fellow human beings. Unlike leukaemia today, or tuberculosis in the last century, leprosy is not, and has never been, a "poetic" disease which can be romanticized. Just the reverse. Even in societies that hate their sick less than we Americans do, the leper has always been despised and feared – outcast even by his most-loved ones, because of a rare bacillus no one can predict or control. Leprosy is not fatal, and the average patient can look forward to as much as thirty or fifty years of life as a leper. That fact, combined with the progressive disability which the disease inflicts, makes leprosy patients, of all sick people, the ones most desperately in need of human support. But virtually all societies condemn their lepers to isolation and despair – denounced as criminals and degenerates, as traitors and villains – cast out of the human race because science has failed to unlock the mystery of this affliction. In country after country, culture after culture around the world, the leper has been considered the personification of everything people, privately and communally, fear and abhor.

'People react this way for several reasons. First, the disease produces an ugliness and a bad smell that are undeniably unpleasant. And second, generations of medical research notwithstanding, people fail to believe that something so obvious and ugly and so mysterious is not contagious. The fact that we cannot answer questions about the bacillus reinforces their fear – we cannot be sure that touch or air or food or water or even compassion do not spread the disease. In the absence of any natural, provable explanation of the illness, people account for it in other ways, all bad – as proof of

27

crime or filth or perversion, evidence of God's judgment, as the horrible sign of some psychological or spiritual or moral corruption or guilt. And they insist it's catching, despite evidence that it is minimally contagious, even to children. So many of you are going to have to live without one single human support to bear the burden with you.

'That is one reason why we place such an emphasis on counselling here; we want to help you learn to cope with loneliness. Many of the patients who leave this institution do not live out their full years. Under the shock of their severance, they lose their motivation; they let their self-treatments slide, and become either actively or passively suicidal; few of them come back here in time. The patients who survive find someone somewhere who is willing to help them want to live. Or they find somewhere inside themselves the strength to endure.

'Whichever way you go, however, one fact will remain constant: from now until you die, leprosy is the biggest single fact of your existence. It will control how you live in every particular. From the moment you awaken until the moment you sleep, you will have to give your undivided attention to all the hard corners and sharp edges of life. You can't take vacations from it. You can't try to rest yourself by daydreaming, lapsing. Anything that bruises, bumps, burns, breaks, scrapes, snags, pokes, or weakens you can maim, cripple, or even kill you. And thinking about all the kinds of life you can't have can drive you to despair and suicide. I've seen it happen.'

Covenant's pulse was racing, and his sweat made the sheets cling to his limbs. The voice of his nightmare had not changed – it made no effort to terrify him, took no pleasure in his fear – but now the words were as black as hate, and behind them stretched a great raw wound of emptiness.

'That brings us to the other problem. It sounds simple, but you will find it can be devastating. Most people depend heavily on their sense of touch. In fact, their whole structure of responses to reality is organized around their touch. They may doubt their eyes and ears, but when they touch something they know it's real. And it is not an accident that we describe the deepest parts of ourselves – our emotions – in terms of the sense of touch. Sad tales *touch* our *feelings*. Bad situations *irritate* us or *hurt* us. This is an inevitable result of the fact that we are biological organisms.

'You must fight and change this orientation. You're intelligent creatures – each of you has a brain. Use it. Use it to recognize your danger. Use it to train yourself to stay alive.'

Then he woke up alone in his bed drenched with sweat, eyes staring, lips taut with whimpers that tried to plead their way between

28

his clenched teeth. Dream after dream, week after week, the pattern played itself out. Day after day, he had to lash himself with anger to make himself leave the ineffectual sanctuary of his cell.

But his fundamental decision held. He met patients who had been to the leprosarium several times before – haunted recidivists who could not satisfy the essential demand of their torment, the requirement that they cling to life without desiring any of the recompense which gave life value. Their cyclic degeneration taught him to see that his nightmare contained the raw materials for survival. Night after night, it battered him against the brutal and irremediable law of leprosy; blow by blow, it showed him that an entire devotion to that law was his only defence against suppuration and gnawing rot and blindness. In his fifth and sixth months at the leprosarium, he practised his VSE and other drills with manic diligence. He stared at the blank antiseptic walls of his cell as if to hypnotize himself with them. In the back of his mind, he counted the hours between doses of his medication. And whenever he slipped, missed a beat of his defensive rhythm, he excoriated himself with curses.

In seven months, the doctors were convinced that his diligence was not a passing phase. They were reasonably sure that the progress of his illness had been arrested. They sent him home.

As he returned to his house on Haven Farm in late summer, he thought that he was prepared for everything. He had braced himself for the absence of any communication from Joan, the dismayed revulsions of his former friends and associates – though these assaults still afflicted him with a vertiginous nausea of rage and self-disgust. The sight of Joan's and Roger's belongings in the house, and the desertion of the stables where Joan had formerly kept her horses, stung his sore heart like a corrosive – but he had already set his heels against the pull of such pains.

Yet he was not prepared, not for everything. The next shock surpassed his readiness. After he had double- and triple-checked to be sure he had received no mail from Joan, after he had spoken on the phone with the lawyer who handled his business – he had heard the woman's discomfort throbbing across the metallic connection – he went to his hut in the woods and sat down to read what he had written on his new book.

Its blind poverty left him aghast. To call it ridiculously naïve would have been a compliment. He could hardly believe that he was responsible for such supercilious trash.

That night, he reread his first novel, the best-seller. Then, moving with extreme caution, he built a fire in his hearth and burned both the novel and the new manuscript. Fire! he thought. Purgation. If I do not write another word, I will at least rid my life of these lies.

Imagination! How could I have been so complacent? And as he watched the pages crumble into grey ash, he threw in with them all thought of further writing. For the first time, he understood part of what the doctors had been saying; he needed to crush out his imagination. He could not afford to have an imagination, a faculty which could envision Joan, joy, health. If he tormented himself with unattainable desires, he would cripple his grasp on the law which enabled him to survive. His imagination could kill him, lead or seduce or trick him into suicide: seeing all the things he could not have would make him despair.

When the fire went out, he ground the ashes underfoot as if to make their consummation irrevocable.

The next morning, he set about organizing his life.

First, he found his old straight razor. Its long, stainless-steel blade gleamed like a leer in the fluorescent light of his bathroom; but he stropped it deliberately, lathered his face, braced his timorous bones against the sink, and set the edge to his throat. It felt like a cold line of fire across his jugular, a keen threat of blood and gangrene and reactivated leprosy. If his half-unfingered hand slipped or twitched, the consequences might be extreme. But he took the risk consciously to discipline himself, enforce his recognition of the raw terms of his survival, mortify his recalcitrance. He instituted shaving with that blade as a personal ritual, a daily confrontation with his condition.

For the same reason, he began carrying around a sharp penknife. Whenever he felt his discipline faltering, felt threatened by memories or hopes or love, he took out the knife and tested its edge on his wrist.

Then, after he had shaved, he worked on his house. He neatened it, rearranged the furniture to minimize the danger of protruding corners, hard edges, hidden obstacles; he eliminated everything which could trip, bruise, or deflect him, so that even in the dark his rooms would be navigable, safe; he made his house as much like his cell in the leprosarium as possible. Anything that was hazardous, he threw into the guest room; and when he was done he locked the guest room and threw away the key.

After that he went to his hut and locked it also. Then he pulled its fuses, so that there would be no risk of fire in the old wiring.

Finally he washed the sweat off his hands. He washed them grimly, obsessively; he could not help himself — the physical impression of uncleanness was too strong.

Leper outcast unclean.

He spent the autumn stumbling around the rims of madness. Dark violence throbbed in him like a *picar* thrust between his ribs, goading him aimlessly. He felt an insatiable need for sleep, but could not heed it because his dreams had changed to nightmares of gnawing; despite his numbness, he seemed to feel himself being eaten away. And wakefulness confronted him with a vicious and irreparable paradox. Without the support or encouragement of other people, he did not believe he could endure the burden of his struggle against horror and death; yet that horror and death explained, made comprehensible, almost vindicated the rejection which denied him support or encouragement. His struggle arose from the same passions which produced his outcasting. He hated what would happen to him if he failed to fight. He hated himself for having to fight such a winless and interminable war. But he could not hate the people who made his moral solitude so absolute. They only shared his own fear.

In the dizzy round of his dilemma, the only response which steadied him was vitriol. He clung to his bitter anger as to an anchor of sanity; he needed fury in order to survive, to keep his grip like a stranglehold on life. Some days he went from sun to sun without any rest from rage.

But in time even that passion began to falter. His outcasting was part of his law; it was an irreducible fact, as totally real and compulsory as gravity and pestilence and numbness. If he failed to crush himself to fit the mould of his facts, he would fail to survive.

When he looked out over the Farm, the trees which edged his property along the highway seemed so far away that nothing could bridge the gap.

The contradiction had no answer. It made his fingers twitch helplessly, so that he almost cut himself shaving. Without passion he could not fight – yet all his passions rebounded against him. As the autumn passed, he cast fewer and fewer curses at the impossibilities imprisoning him. He prowled through the woods behind Haven Farm – a tall, lean man with haggard eyes, a mechanical stride, and two fingers gone from his right hand. Every cluttered trail, sharp rock, steep slope reminded him that he was keeping himself alive with caution, that he had only to let his surveillance slip to go quietly unmourned and painless out of his troubles.

It gave him nothing but an addition of sorrow to touch the bark of a tree and feel nothing. He saw clearly the end that waited for him; his heart would become as effectless as his body, and then he would be lost for good and all.

Nevertheless, he was filled with a sudden sense of focus, of crystallization, as if he had identified an enemy, when he learned that someone had paid his electric bill for him. The unexpected gift made him abruptly aware of what was happening. The townspeople were not only shunning him, they were actively cutting off every excuse he might have to go among them.

When he first understood his danger, his immediate reaction was to throw open a window and shout into the winter, 'Go ahead! By hell, I don't need you!' But the issue was not simple enough to be blown away by bravado. As winter scattered into an early March spring, he became convinced that he needed to take some kind of action. He was a person, human like any other; he was kept alive by a personal heart. He did not mean to stand by and approve this amputation.

So when his next phone bill came, he gathered his courage, shaved painstakingly, dressed himself in clothes with tough fabrics, laced his feet snugly into sturdy boots, and began the two-mile walk into town to pay his bill in person.

That walk brought him to the door of the Bell Telephone Company with trepidation hanging round his head like a dank cloud. He stood in front of the gilt-lettered door for a time, thinking.

These are the pale deaths . . .

and wondering about laughter. Then he collected himself, pulled open the door like the gust of a gale, and stalked up to the girl at the counter as if she had challenged him to single combat.

He put his hands palms down on the counter to steady them. Ferocity sprang across his teeth for an instant. He said, 'My name is Thomas Covenant.'

The girl was trimly dressed, and she held her arms crossed under her breasts, supporting them so that they showed to their best advantage. He forced himself to look up at her face. She was staring blankly past him. While he searched her for some tremor of revulsion, she glanced at him and asked, 'Yes?'

'I want to pay my bill,' he said, thinking, She doesn't know, she hasn't heard.

'Certainly, sir,' she answered. 'What is your number?'

He told her, and she moved languidly into another room to check the files.

The suspense of her absence made his fear pound in his throat. He needed some way to distract himself, occupy his attention. Abruptly, he reached into his pocket and brought out the sheet of paper the boy had given him. *You're supposed to read it.* He smoothed it out on the counter and looked at it.

The old printing said:

A real man – real in all the ways that we recognize as real – finds himself suddenly abstracted from the world and deposited in a physical situation which could not possibly exist: sounds have aroma, smells have colour and depth, sights have texture, touches have pitch and timbre. There he is informed by a disembodied voice that he has been brought to that place as a champion for his world. He must fight to the death in single combat against a champion from another world. If he is defeated, he will die, and his world – the real world – will be destroyed because it lacks the inner strength to survive.

The man refuses to believe that what he is told is true. He asserts that he is either dreaming or hallucinating, and declines to be put in the false position of fighting to the death where no 'real' danger exists. He is implacable in his determination to disbelieve his apparent situation, and does not defend himself when he is attacked by the champion of the other world.

Question: is the man's behaviour courageous or cowardly? This is the fundamental question of ethics.

Ethics! Covenant snorted to himself. Who the hell makes these things up?

The next moment, the girl returned with a question in her face. 'Thomas Covenant? Of Haven Farm? Sir, a deposit has been made on your account which covers everything for several months. Did you send us a large cheque recently?'

Covenant staggered inwardly as if he had been struck, then caught himself on the counter, listing to the side like a reefed galleon. Unconsciously he crushed the paper in his fist. He felt light-headed, heard words echoing in his ears: Virtually all societies condemn, denounce, cast out – you cannot hope.

He focused his attention on his cold feet and aching ankles while he fought to keep the violence at bay. With elaborate caution, he placed the crumpled sheet on the counter in front of the girl. Striving to sound conversational, he said, 'It isn't catching, you know. You won't get it from me – there's nothing to worry about. It isn't catching. Except for children.'

The girl blinked at him as if she were amazed by the vagueness of her thoughts.

His shoulders hunched, strangling fury in his throat. He turned away with as much dignity as he could manage, and strode out into the sunlight, letting the door slam behind him. Hellfire! he swore to himself. Hellfire and bloody damnation.

Giddy with rage, he looked up and down the street. He could see the whole ominous length of the town from where he stood. In the direction of Haven Farm, the small businesses stood close together like teeth poised on either side of the road. The sharp sunlight made him feel vulnerable and alone. He checked his hand quickly for scratches or abrasions, then hurried down the gauntlet. As he moved, his numb feet felt unsure on the sidewalk, as if the cement were slick with despair. He believed that he displayed courage by not breaking into a run.

In a few moments the courthouse loomed ahead of him. On the sidewalk before it stood the old beggar. He had not moved. He was still staring at the sun, still muttering meaninglessly. His sign said, Beware, uselessly, like a warning that came too late.

As Covenant approached, he was struck by how dispossessed the old man looked. Beggars and fanatics, holy men, prophets of the apocalypse did not belong on that street in that sunlight; the frowning, belittling eyes of the stone columns held no tolerance for such preterite exaltation. And the scant coins he had collected were not enough for even one meal. The sight gave Covenant an odd pang of compassion. Almost in spite of himself, he stopped in front of the old man.

The beggar made no gesture, did not shift his contemplation of the sun; but his voice altered, and one clear word broke out of the formless hum:

'Give.'

The order seemed to be directed at Covenant personally. As if on command, his gaze dropped to the bowl again. But the demand, the effort of coercion, brought back his anger. *I don't owe you anything*, he snapped silently.

Before he could pull away, the old man spoke again.

'I have warned you.'

Unexpectedly, the statement struck Covenant like an insight, an intuitive summary of all his experiences in the past year. Through his anger, his decision came immediately. With a twisted expression on his face, he fumbled for his wedding ring.

He had never before removed his white gold wedding band; despite his divorce, and Joan's unanswering silence, he had kept the ring on his finger. It was an icon of himself. It reminded him of where he had been and where he was − of promises made and broken, companionship lost, helplessness − and of his vestigial humanity. Now he tore it off his left hand and dropped it in the bowl. 'That's worth more than a few coins,' he said, and stamped away.

'Wait.'

The word carried such authority that Covenant stopped again. He stood still, husbanding his rage, until he felt the man's hand on his arm. Then he turned and looked into pale blue eyes as blank as if they were still studying the secret fire of the sun. The old man was tall with power.

A sudden insecurity, a sense of proximity to matters he did not understand, disturbed Covenant. But he pushed it away. 'Don't touch me. I'm a leper.'

The vacant stare seemed to miss him completely, as if he did not exist or the eyes were blind; but the old man's voice was clear and sure.

'You are in perdition, my son.'

Moistening his lips with his tongue, Covenant responded, 'No, old man. This is normal – human beings are like this. Futile.' As if he were quoting a law of leprosy, he said to himself, Futility is the defining characteristic of life. 'That's what life is like. I just have less bric-à-brac cluttering up the facts than most people.'

'So young – and already so bitter.'

Covenant had not heard sympathy for a long time, and the sound of it affected him acutely. His anger retreated, leaving his throat tight and awkward. 'Come on, old man,' he said. 'We didn't make the world. All we have to do is live in it. We're all in the same boat – one way or another.'

'Did we not?'

But without waiting for an answer the beggar went back to humming his weird tune. He held Covenant there until he had reached a break in his song. Then a new quality came into his voice, an aggressive tone that took advantage of Covenant's unexpected vulnerability.

'Why not destroy yourself?'

A sense of pressure expanded in Covenant's chest, cramping his heart. The pale blue eyes were exerting some kind of peril over him. Anxiety tugged at him. He wanted to jerk away from the old face, go through his VSE, make sure that he was safe. But he could not; the blank gaze held him. Finally, he said, 'That's too easy.'

His reply met no opposition, but still his trepidation grew. Under the duress of the old man's will, he stood on the precipice of his future and looked down at jagged, eager dangers – rough damnations multiplied below him. He recognized the various possible deaths of lepers. But the panorama steadied him. It was like a touchstone of familiarity in a fantastic situation; it put him back on known ground. He found that he could turn away from his fear to say, 'Look, is there anything I can do for you? Food? A place to stay? You can have what I've got.'

As if Covenant had said some crucial password, the old man's eyes lost their perilous cast.

'You have done too much. Gifts like this I return to the giver.'

He extended his bowl toward Covenant.

'Take back the ring. Be true. You need not fail.'

35

Now the tone of command was gone. In its place, Covenant heard gentle supplication. He hesitated, wondering what this old man had to do with him. But he had to make some kind of response. He took the ring and replaced it on his left hand. Then he said, 'Everybody fails. But I am going to survive – as long as I can.'

The old man sagged, as if he had just shifted a load of prophecy or commandment on to Covenant's shoulders. His voice sounded frail now.

'That is as it may be.'

Without another word, he turned and moved away. He leaned on his staff like an exhausted prophet, worn out with uttering visions. His staff rang curiously on the sidewalk, as if the wood were harder than cement.

Covenant gazed after the wind-swayed ochre robe and the fluttering hair until the old man turned a corner and vanished. Then he shook himself, started into his VSE. But his eyes stopped on his wedding ring. The band seemed to hang loosely on his finger, as if it were too big for him. *Perdition*, he thought. *A deposit has been made.* I've got to do something before they barricade the streets against me.

For a while, he stood where he was and tried to think of a course of action. Absently, he looked up the courthouse columns to the stone heads. They had careless eyes and on their lips a spasm of disgust carved into perpetual imminence, compelling and forever incomplete. They gave him an idea. Casting a silent curse at them, he started down the walk again. He had decided to see his lawyer, to demand that the woman who handled his contracts and financial business find some legal recourse against the kind of black charity which was cutting him off from the town. Get those payments revoked, he thought. It's not possible that they can pay my debts – without my consent.

The lawyer's office was in a building at the corner of a cross street on the opposite side of the road. A minute's brisk walking brought Covenant to the corner and the town's only traffic light. He felt a need to hurry, to act on his decision before his distrust of lawyers and all public machinery convinced him that his determination was folly. He had to resist a temptation to cross against the light.

The signal changed slowly, but at last it was green his way. He stepped out on to the crosswalk.

Before he had taken three steps, he heard a siren. Red lights flaring, a police car sprang out of an alley into the main street. It skidded and swerved with the speed of its turn, then aimed itself straight at Covenant's heart.

He stopped as if caught in the grip of an unseen fist. He wanted to move, but he could only stand suspended, trapped, looking down the muzzle of the hurtling car. For an instant, he heard the frantic scream of brakes. Then he crumbled.

As he dropped, he had a vague sense that he was falling too soon, that he had not been hit yet. But he could not help himself; he was too afraid, afraid of being crushed. After all his self-protections, to die like this! Then he became aware of a huge blackness which stood behind the sunlight and the gleaming store windows and the shriek of tyres. The light and the asphalt against his head seemed to be nothing more than paintings on a black background; and now the background asserted itself, reached in and bore him down. Blackness radiated through the sunlight like a cold beam of night.

He thought that he was having a nightmare. Absurdly, he heard the old beggar saying, *Be true. You need not fail.*

The darkness poured through, swamping the day, and the only thing that Covenant was sure he could see was a single red gleam from the police car – a red bolt hot and clear and deadly, transfixing his forehead like a spear.

3

INVITATION TO A BETRAYAL

For a time that he could only measure in heartbeats, Covenant hung in the darkness. The red, impaling light was the only fixed point in a universe that seemed to seethe around him. He felt that he might behold a massive moving of heaven and earth, if only he knew where to look; but the blackness and the hot red beam on his forehead prevented him from turning away, and he had to let the currents that whirled around him pass unseen.

Under the pressure of the ferocious light, he could feel every throb of his pulse distinctly in his temples, as if it were his mind which hammered out his life, not his heart. The beats were slow – too slow for the amount of apprehension he felt. He could not conceive what was happening to him. But each blow shook him as if the very structure of his brain were under assault.

Abruptly, the bloody spear of light wavered, then split in two. He was moving toward the light – or the light was approaching him. The two flaming spots were eyes.

The next instant, he heard laughter – high, shrill glee full of triumph and old spite. The voice crowed like some malevolent rooster heralding the dawn of hell, and Covenant's pulse trembled at the sound.

'Done it!' the voice cackled. 'I! Mine!' It shrilled away into laughter again.

Covenant was close enough to see the eyes clearly now. They had no whites or pupils; red balls filled the sockets, and light moiled in them like lava. Their heat was so close that Covenant's forehead burned.

Then the eyes flared, seemed to ignite the air around them. Flames spread out, sending a lurid glow around Covenant.

He found himself in a cavern deep in stone. Its walls caught and held the light, so that the cave stayed bright after the single flare of the eyes. The rock was smooth, but broken into hundreds of irregular facets, as if the cavern had been carved with an erratic knife. Entrances gaped in the walls around the circumference of the cave. High above his head, the roof gathered into a thick cluster of stalactites, but the floor was flat and worn as if by the passing of many feet. Reflections sprang through the stalactites above, so that the cluster swarmed with red gleamings.

The chamber was full of a rank stench, an acrid odour with a sickly sweet under-smell – burning sulphur over the reek of rotting flesh. Covenant gagged on it, and on the sight of the being whose eyes had held him.

Crouched on a low dais near the centre of the cave was a creature with long, scrawny limbs, hands as huge and heavy as shovels, a thin, hunched torso, and a head like a battering ram. As he crouched, his knees came up almost to the level of his ears. One hand was braced on the rock in front of him; the other gripped a long wooden staff shod with metal and intricately carved from end to end. His grizzled mouth was rigid with laughter, and his red eyes seemed to bubble like magma.

'Ha! Done it!' he shrieked again. 'Called him. My power. Kill them all!' As his high voice ranted, he slavered hungrily. 'Lord Drool! Master! Me!'

The creature leaped to his feet, capering with mad pride. He strode closer to his victim, and Covenant recoiled with a loathing he could not control.

Holding his staff near the centre with both hands, the creature shouted, 'Kill you! Take your power! Crush them all! Be Lord Drool!' He raised his staff as if to strike Covenant with it.

Then another voice entered the cavern. It was deep and resonant, powerful enough to fill the air without effort, and somehow deadly, as if an abyss were speaking. 'Back, Rockworm!' it commanded.

'This prey is too great for you. I claim him.'

The creature jabbed his face toward the ceiling and cried, 'Mine! My staff! You saw. I called him. You saw!'

Covenant followed the red eyes upward, but he could see nothing there except the dizzy chiaroscuro of the clustered stone spikes.

'You had aid,' the deep voice said. 'The Staff was too hard a matter for you. You would have destroyed it in simple irritation, had I not taught you some of its uses. And my aid has a price. Do whatever else you wish. I claim this prize. It belongs to me.'

The creature's rage subsided, as if he had suddenly remembered some secret advantage. 'My Staff,' he muttered darkly. 'I have it. You are not safe.'

'You threaten me?' The deep voice bristled, and its dangers edged closer to the surface. 'Watch and ward, Drool Rockworm! Your doom grows upon you. Behold! I have begun!'

There was a low, grinding noise, as of great teeth breaking against each other, and a chilling mist intervened between Covenant and Drool, gathered and swirled and thickened until Drool was blocked from Covenant's sight. At first, the mist glowed with the light of the burning stones; but as it swirled the red faded into the dank, universal grey of fogs. The vile reek melted into a sweeter smell — attar, the odour of funerals. Despite the blindness of the mist, Covenant felt that he was no longer in Drool's cavern.

The change gave him no relief. Fear and bewilderment sucked at him as if he were sinking in nightmare. That unbodied voice dismayed him. As the fog blew around him his legs shuddered and bent, and he fell to his knees.

'You do well to pray to me,' the voice intoned. Its deadliness shocked Covenant like a confrontation with grisly murder. 'There are no other hopes or helps for a man amid the wrack of your fate. My Enemy will not aid you. It was he who chose you for this doom. And when he has chosen, he does not give; he takes.' A raw timbre of contempt ran through the voice, scraping Covenant's nerves as it passed. 'Yes, you would do well to pray to me. I might ease you of your burden. Whatever health or strength you ask is mine to give. For I have begun my attack upon this age, and the future is mine. I will not fail again.'

Covenant's mind lay under the shock of the voice. But the offer of health penetrated him, and his heart jumped. He felt the beat clearly in his chest, felt his heart labouring against the burden of his fear. But he was still too stricken to speak.

Over his silence, the voice continued, 'Kevin was a fool — fey, anile, and gutless. They are all fools. Look you, groveller. The mighty High Lord Kevin, son of Loric and great-grandson of Berek Lord-

Fatherer whom I hate, stood where you now kneel, and he thought to destroy me. He discovered my designs, recognized some measure of my true stature – though the dotard had set me on his right side in the Council for long years without sensing his peril – saw at the last who I was. Then there was war between us, war that blasted the west and threatened his precious Keep itself. The feller fist was mine and he knew it. When his armies faltered and his power waned, he lost himself in despair – he became mine in despair. He thought that he still might utterly undo me. Therefore he met me in that cavern from which I have rescued you – Kiril Threndor, Heart of Thunder.

'Drool Rockworm does not know what a black rock it is on which he stands. And that is not his only ignorance – but of my deeper plans I say nothing. He serves me well in his way, though he does not intend service. Likewise will you and those timid Lords serve me, whether you choose or no. Let them grope through their shallow mysteries for a time, barely fearing that I am alive. They have not mastered the seventh part of dead Kevin's Lore, and yet in their pride they dare to name themselves Earthfriends, servants of Peace. They are too blind to perceive their own arrogance. But I will teach them to see.

'In truth it is already too late for them. They will come to Kiril Threndor, and I will teach them things to darken their souls. It is fitting. There Kevin met and dared me in his despair. And I accepted. The fool! I could hardly speak the words for laughing. He thought that such spells might unbind me.

'But the Power which upholds me has stood since the creation of Time. Therefore when Kevin dared me to unleash the forces that would strike the Land and all its accursed creations into dust, I took the dare. Yes, and laughed until there was doubt in his face before the end. That folly brought the age of the Old Lords to its ruin – but I remain. I! Together we stood in Kiril Threndor, blind Kevin and I. Together we uttered the Ritual of Desecration. Ah, the fool! He was already enslaved to me and knew it not. Proud of his Lore, he did not know that the very Law which he served preserved me through that cataclysm, though all but a few of his own people and works were stricken into death.

'True, I was reduced for a time. I have spent a thousand years gnawing my desires like a beaten cur. The price of that has yet to be paid – for it and other things I shall exact my due. But I was not destroyed. And when Drool found the Staff and recognized it, and could not use it, I took my chance again. I will have the future of this life, to waste or hold as I desire. So pray to me, groveller. Reject the doom that my Enemy has created for you. You will not have many chances to repent.'

The fog and the attar-laden air seemed to weaken Covenant, as if the strength were being absorbed from his blood. But his heart beat on, and he clung to it for a defence against the fear. He wrapped his arms about his chest and bent low, trying to shelter himself from the cold. 'What doom?' he forced himself to say. His voice sounded pitiful and lost in the mist.

'He intends you to be my final foe. He chose you – you, groveller, with a might in your hands such as no mortal has ever held before – chose you to destroy me. But he will find that I am not so easily mastered. You have might – wild magic which preserves your life at this moment – but you will never know what it is. You will not be able to fight me at the last. No, you are the victim of his expectations, and I cannot free you by death – not yet. But we can turn that strength against him, and rid him of the Earth entirely.'

'Health?' Covenant looked painfully up from the ground. 'You said health.'

'Whatever health you lack, groveller. Only pray to me, while I am still patient.'

But the voice's contempt cut too deep. Covenant's violence welled up in the wound. He began to fight. Heaving himself up off his knees, he thought, No. I'm not a groveller. With his teeth gritted to stop his trembling, he asked, 'Who are you?'

As if sensing its mistake, the voice became smoother. 'I have had many names,' it said. 'To the Lords of Revelstone, I am Lord Foul the Despiser; to the Giants of Seareach, Satansheart and Soulcrusher. The Ramen name me Fangthane. In the dreams of the Bloodguard, I am Corruption. But the people of the Land call me the Grey Slayer.'

Distinctly, Covenant said, 'Forget it.'

'Fool!' ground the voice, and its force flattened Covenant on the rock. Forehead pressed against the stone, he lay and waited in terror for the anger of the voice to annihilate him. 'I do not take or eschew action at your bidding. And I will not forget this. I see that your pride is offended by my contempt. Groveller! I will teach you the true meaning of contempt before I am done. But not now. That does not meet my purpose. Soon I will be strong enough to wrest the wild magic from you, and then you will learn to your cost that my contempt is without limit, my desires bottomless.

'But I have wasted time enough. Now to my purpose. Heed me well, groveller. I have a task for you. You will bear a message for me to Revelstone – to the Council of Lords.

'Say to the Council of Lords, and to High Lord Prothall son of Dwillian, that the uttermost limit of their span of days upon the Land is seven time seven years from the present time. Before the end of those days are numbered, I will have the command of life and death in my hand. And as a token that what I say is the one word of truth, tell them this: Drool Rockworm, Cavewight of Mount Thunder, has found the Staff of Law, which was lost ten times a hundred years ago by Kevin at the Ritual of Desecration. Say to them that the task appointed to their generation is to regain the Staff. Without it, they will not be able to resist me for seven years, and my complete victory will be achieved six times seven years earlier than it would be else.

'As for you, groveller: do not fail with this message. If you do not bring it before the Council, then every human in the Land will be dead before ten seasons have passed. You do not understand – but I tell you Drool Rockworm has the Staff, and that it is a cause for terror. He will be enthroned at Lord's Keep in two years if the message fails. Already, the Cavewights are marching to his call; and wolves, and ur-viles of the Demondim, answer the power of the Staff. But war is not the worst peril. Drool delves ever deeper into the dark roots of Mount Thunder – Gravin Threndor, Peak of the Fire-Lions. And there are banes buried in the deeps of the Earth too potent and terrible for any mortal to control. They would make of the universe a hell forever. But such a bane Drool seeks. He searches for the Illearth Stone. If he becomes its master, there will be woe for low and high alike until Time itself falls.

'Do not fail with my message, groveller. You have met Drool. Do you relish dying in his hands?'

The voice paused, and Covenant held his head in his arms, trying to silence the echo of Foul's threats. This is a dream, he thought. A dream! But the blindness of the mist made him feel trapped, encapsulated in insanity. He shuddered with the force of his desire for escape and warmth. 'Go away! Leave me alone!'

'One word more,' Foul said, 'a final caution. Do not forget whom to fear at the last. I have had to be content with killing and torment. But now my plans are laid, and I have begun. I shall not rest until I have eradicated hope from the Earth. Think on that, and be dismayed!'

Dismayed hung prolonged in the air, while around it grew the noise of grinding, great boulders crushing lesser rocks between them. The sound rushed down on to Covenant, then passed over him and away, leaving him on his knees with his head braced between his arms and his mind blank with panic. He remained rigid there until the grinding was gone, and a low hum of wind rose through the new silence. Then he opened his eyes fearfully, and saw sunlight on the rock before his face.

4

KEVIN'S WATCH

He stretched himself flat and lay still for a long time, welcoming the sun's warmth into his fog-chilled bones. The wind whistled a quiet monody round him, but did not touch him; and soon after the trouble of Foul's passing had ended, he heard the call of faraway birds. He lay still and breathed deeply, drawing new strength into his limbs – grateful for sunshine and the end of nightmare.

Eventually, however, he remembered that there had been several people nearby during his accident in the street. They were strangely silent; the town itself seemed hushed. The police car must have injured him worse than he realized. Leper's anxiety jerked him up on to his hands and knees.

He found himself on a smooth stone slab. It was roughly circular, ten feet broad, and surrounded by a wall three feet high. Above him arched an unbroken expanse of blue sky. It domed him from rim to rim of the wall as if the slab were somehow impossibly afloat in the heavens.

No. His breath turned to sand in his throat. Where – ?

Then a panting voice called, 'Hail!' He could not locate it; it sounded vague with distance, like a hallucination. 'Hail!'

His heart began to tremble. What is this?

'Kevin's Watch! Are you in need?'

What the hell is this?

Abruptly, he heard a scrambling noise behind him. His muscles jumped; he dove to the wall and flipped around, put his back to it.

Opposite him, across a gap of open air beyond the wall, stood a mountain. It rose hugely from cliffs level with his perch to a sun-bright peak still tipped with snow high above him, and its craggy sides filled nearly half the slab's horizons. His first impression was one of proximity, but an instant later he realized that the cliff was at least a stone's throw away from him.

Facing squarely toward the mountain, there was a gap in the wall. The low, scrambling sound seemed to come from this gap.

He wanted to go across the slab, look for the source of the noise. But his heart was labouring too hard; he could not move. He was afraid of what he might see.

The sound came closer. Before he could react, a girl thrust her head and shoulders up into the gap, braced her arms on the stone. When she caught sight of him, she stopped to return his stare.

Her long full hair – brown with flashes of pale honey scattered through it – blew about her on the breeze; her skin was deeply shaded with tan, and the dark blue fabric of her dress had a pattern of white leaves woven into the shoulders. She was panting and flushed as if she had just finished a long climb, but she met Covenant's gaze with frank wonder and interest.

She did not look any older than sixteen.

The openness of her scrutiny only tightened his distress. He glared at her as if she were an apparition.

After a moment's hesitation, she panted, 'Are you well?' Then her words began to hurry with excitement. 'I did not know whether to come myself or to seek help. From the hills, I saw a grey cloud over Kevin's Watch, and within it there seemed to be a battle. I saw you stand and fall. I did not know what to do. Then I thought, better a small help soon than a large help late. So I came.' She stopped herself, then asked again, 'Are you well?'

Well?

He had been hit – !

His hands were only scraped, bruised, as if he had used them to absorb his fall. There was a low ache of impact in his head. But his clothing showed no damage, no sign that he had been struck and sent skidding over the pavement.

He jabbed his chest with numb fingers, jabbed his abdomen and legs, but no sharp pain answered his probing. He seemed essentially uninjured.

But that car must have hit him somewhere.

Well?

He stared at the girl as if the word had no meaning.

Faced with his silence, she gathered her courage and climbed up through the gap to stand before him against the background of the mountain. He saw that she wore a dark blue shift like a long tunic, with a white cord knotted at the waist. On her feet she had sandals which tied around her ankles. She was slim, delicately figured; and her fine eyes were wide with apprehension, uncertainty, eagerness. She took two steps toward him as if he were a figure of peril, then knelt to look more closely at his aghast incomprehension.

What the bloody hell is this?

Carefully, respectfully, she asked, 'How may I aid you? You are a stranger to the Land – that I see. You have fought an ill cloud. Command me.' His silence seemed to daunt her. She dropped her eyes. 'Will you not speak?'

What's happening to me?

The next instant, she gaped with excitement, pointed in awe at his right hand. 'Halfhand! Do legends live again?' Wonder lit her face. 'Berek Halfhand!' she breathed. 'Is it true?'

Berek? At first, he could not remember where he had heard that name before. Then it came back to him. Berek! In cold panic he realized that the nightmare was not over, that this girl and Lord Foul the Despiser were both part of the same experience.

Again he saw darkness crouching behind the brilliant blue sky. It loomed over him, beat toward his head like vulture wings.

Where – ?

Awkwardly, as if his joints were half frozen with dread, he lurched to his feet.

At once, an immense panorama sprang into view below him, attacked his sight like a bludgeon of exhilaration and horror. He was on a stone platform four thousand feet or more above the earth. Birds glided and wheeled under his perch. The air was as clean and clear as crystal, and through it the great sweep of the landscape seemed immeasurably huge, so that his eyes ached with trying to see it all. Hills stretched away directly under him; plains unrolled toward the horizons on both sides; a river angled silver in the sunlight out of the hills on his left. All was luminous with spring, as if it had just been born in that morning's dew.

Bloody hell!

The giddy height staggered him. Vulture wings of darkness beat at his head. Vertigo whirled up at him, made the earth veer.

He did not know where he was. He had never seen this before. How had he come here? He had been hit by a police car, and Foul had brought him here. Foul had brought him here?

Brought me here?

Uninjured.

He reeled in terror toward the girl and the mountain. Three dizzy steps took him to the gap in the parapet. There he saw that he was on the top of a slim splinter of stone – at least five hundred feet long – that pointed obliquely up from the base of the cliff like a rigid finger accusing the sky. Stairs had been cut into the upper surface of the shaft, but it was as steep as a ladder.

For one spinning instant, he thought dumbly, I've got to get out of here. None of this is happening to me.

Then the whole insanity of the situation recoiled on him, struck at him out of the vertiginous air like the claws of a condor. He stumbled; the maw of the fall gaped below him. He started to scream silently:

No!

45

As he pitched forward, the girl caught his arm, heaved at him. He swung and toppled to the stone within the parapet, pulled his knees up against his chest, covered his head.

Insane! he cried as if he were gibbering.

Darkness writhed like nausea inside his skull. Visions of madness burned across his mindscape.

How?

Impossible!

He had been crossing the street. He insisted upon that desperately. The light had been green.

Where?

He had been hit by a police car.

Impossible!

It had aimed itself straight for his heart, and it had hit him.

And not injured him?

Mad. I'm going mad mad mad.

And not injured him?

Nightmare. None of this is happening, is happening, is happening. Through the wild whirl of his misery, another hand suddenly clasped his. The grip was hard, urgent; it caught him like an anchor.

Nightmare! I'm dreaming. Dreaming!

The thought flared through his panic like a revelation. Dreaming! Of course he was dreaming. Juggling furiously, he put the pieces together. He had been hit by a police car — knocked unconscious. Concussion. He might be out for hours — days. And while he was out, he was having this dream.

That was the answer. He clutched it as if it were the girl's grip on his straining hand. It steadied him against his vertigo, simplified his fear. But it was not enough. The darkness still swarmed at him as if he were carrion Foul had left behind.

How?

Where do you get dreams like this?

He could not bear to think about it; he would go mad. He fled from it as if it had already started to gnaw on his bones.

Don't think about it. Don't try to understand. Madness — madness is the only danger. Survive! Get going. Do something. Don't look back.

He forced his eyes open; and as he focused on the sunlight, the darkness receded, dropped away into the background and came hovering slowly behind him as if it were waiting for him to turn and face it, fall prey to it.

The girl was kneeling beside him. She had his maimed right hand clamped in both of hers, and concern stood like tears in her eyes. 'Berek,' she murmured painfully as he met her gaze, 'oh, Berek.

What ill assails you? I know not what to do.'

She had already done enough – helped him to master himself, resist the pull of the dangerous questions he could not answer. But his fingers were numb; parts of her clasp on his hand he could not feel at all. He dredged himself into a sitting position, though the exertion made him feel faint. 'I'm a leper,' he said weakly. 'Don't touch me.'

Hesitantly, she loosened her grip, as if she were not sure he meant what he said, not sure he knew what he was saying.

With an effort that seemed harsh because of his weakness, he withdrew his hand.

She caught her lower lip between her teeth in chagrin. As if she feared she had offended him, she moved back and sat down against the opposite wall.

But he could see that she was consumed with interest in him. She could not remain silent long. After a moment, she asked softly, 'Is it wrong to touch you? I meant no harm. You are Berek Halfhand, the Lord-Fatherer. An ill I could not see assailed you. How could I bear to see you tormented so?'

'I'm a leper,' he repeated, trying to conserve his strength. But her expression told him that the word conveyed nothing to her. 'I'm sick – I have a disease. You don't know the danger.'

'If I touch you, will I become – "sick"?'

'Who knows?' Then, because he could hardly believe the evidence of his eyes and ears, he asked, 'Don't you know what leprosy is?'

'No,' she answered with a return of her earlier wonder. 'No.' She shook her head, and her hair swung lightly about her face. 'But I am not afraid.'

'Be afraid!' he rasped. The girl's ignorance or innocence made him vehement. Behind her words, he heard wings beating like violence. 'It's a disease that gnaws at you. It gnaws at you until your fingers and toes and hands and feet and arms and legs turn rotten and fall off. It makes you blind and ugly.'

'May it be healed? Perhaps the Lords – '

'There's no cure.'

He wanted to go on, to spit out some of the bitterness Foul had left in him. But he was too drained to sustain anger. He needed to rest and think, explore the implications of his dilemma.

'Then how may I aid you? I know not what to do. You are Berek Ha – '

'I'm not,' he sighed. The girl started, and into her surprise he repeated, 'I'm not.'

'Then who? You have the omen of the hand, for the legends say that Berek Earthfriend may come again. Are you a Lord?'

47

With a tired gesture he held her question at bay. He needed to think. But when he closed his eyes, leaned his head back against the parapet, he felt fear crowding up in him. He had to move, go forward – flee along the path of the dream.

He pulled his gaze back into focus on the girl's face. For the first time, he noticed that she was pretty. Even her awe, the way she hung on his words, was pretty. And she had no fear of lepers.

After a last instant of hesitation, he said, 'I'm Thomas Covenant.'

'Thomas Covenant?' His name sounded ungainly in her mouth. 'It is a strange name – a strange name to match your strange apparel. Thomas Covenant.' She inclined her head in a slow bow to him.

Strange, he thought softly. The strangeness was mutual. He still had no conception of what he would have to deal with in this dream. He would have to find out where he stood. Following the girl's lead, he asked, 'Who are you?'

'I am Lena,' she replied formally, 'daughter of Atiaran. My father is Trell, Gravelingas of the *rhadhamaerl*. Our home is in Mithil Stonedown. Have you been to our Stonedown?'

'No.' He was tempted to ask her what a *Stonedown* was, but he had a more important question in mind. 'Where – '. The word caught in his throat as if it were a dangerous concession to darkness. 'Where are we?'

'We are upon Kevin's Watch.' Springing lightly to her feet, she stretched her arms to the earth and the sky. 'Behold.'

Gritting his resolve, Covenant turned and knelt against the parapet. With his chest braced on the rim, he forced himself to look.

'This is the Land,' Lena said joyfully, as if the outspread earth had a power to thrill her. 'It reaches far beyond seeing to the north, west, and east, though the old songs say that High Lord Kevin stood here and saw the whole of the Land and all its people. So this place is named Kevin's Watch. Is it possible that you do not know this?'

Despite the coolness of the breeze, Covenant was sweating. Vertigo knuckled his temples, and only the hard edge of the stone against his heart kept it under control. 'I don't know anything,' he groaned into the open fall.

Lena glanced at him anxiously, then after a moment turned back to the Land. Pointing with one slim arm to the north-west, she said, 'There is the Mithil River. Our Stonedown stands beside it, but hidden behind this mountain. It flows from the Southron Range behind us to join the Black River. That is the northern bound of the South Plains, where the soil is not generous and few people live. There are only five Stonedowns in the South Plains. But in this north-going line of hills live some Woodhelvennin.

'East of the hills are the Plains of Ra.' Her voice sparkled as she went: 'That is the home of the wild free horses, the Ranyhyn, and their tenders the Ramen. For fifty leagues across the Plains they gallop, and serve none that they do not themselves choose.

'Ah, Thomas Covenant,' she sighed, 'it is my dream to see those horses. Most of my people are too content – they do not travel, and have not seen so much as a Woodhelven. But I wish to walk the Plains of Ra, and see the horses galloping.'

After a long pause, she resumed: 'These mountains are the Southron Range. Behind them are Wastes, and the Grey Desert. No life or passage is there; all the Land is north and west and east from us. And we stand on Kevin's Watch, where the highest of the Old Lords stood at the last battle, before the coming of the Desolation. Our people remember that, and avoid the Watch as the place of ill omen. But Atiaran my mother brought me here to teach me of the Land. And in two years I will be old enough to attend the Loresraat and learn for myself, as my mother did. Do you know,' she said proudly, 'my mother has studied with the Lorewardens?' She looked at Covenant as if she expected him to be impressed. But then her eyes fell, and she murmured, 'But you are a Lord, and know all these things. You listen to my talk so that you may laugh at my ignorance.'

Under the spell of her voice, and the pressure of his vertigo, he had a momentary vision of what the Land must have looked like after Kevin had unleashed the Ritual of Desecration. Behind the luminous morning, he saw hills ripped barren, soil blasted, rank water trickling through vile fens in the riverbed, and over it all a thick gloom of silence – no birds, no insects, no animals, no people, nothing living to raise one leaf or hum or growl or finger against the damage. Then sweat ran into his eyes, blurred them like tears. He pulled away from the view and seated himself again with his back to the wall. 'No,' he murmured to Lena, thinking. You don't understand. 'I did all my laughing – long ago.'

Now he seemed to see the way to go forward, to flee the dark madness which hovered over him. In that brief vision of Desolation, he found the path of the dream. Skipping transitions so that he would not have to ask or answer certain questions, he said, 'I've got to go to the Council of Lords.'

He saw in her face that she wanted to ask him why. But she seemed to feel that it was not her place to question his purpose. His mention of the Council only verified his stature in her eyes. She moved toward the stair. 'Come,' she said. 'We must go to the Stonedown. There a way will be found to take you to Revelstone.' She looked as if she wanted to go with him.

But the thought of the stair hurt him. How could he negotiate that descent? He could not so much as look over the parapet without dizziness. When Lena repeated, 'Come,' he shook his head. He lacked the courage. Yet he had to keep himself active somehow. To Lena's puzzlement, he said, 'How long ago was this Desolation?'

'I do not know,' she replied soberly. 'But the people of the South Plains came back across the mountains from the bare Wastes twelve generations past. And it is said that they were forewarned by High Lord Kevin – they escaped, and lived in exile in the wilderness by nail and tooth and *rhadhamaerl* lore for five hundred years. It is a legacy we do not forget. At fifteen, each of us takes the Oath of Peace, and we live for the life and beauty of the Land.'

He hardly heard her; he was not specifically interested in what she said. But he needed the sound of her voice to steady him while he searched himself for strength. With an effort, he found another question he could ask. Breathing deeply, he said, 'What were you doing in the mountains – why were you up where you could see me here?'

'I was stone-questing,' she answered. 'I am learning *suru-pa-maerl*. Do you know this craft?'

'No,' he said between breaths. 'Tell me.'

'It is a craft I am learning from Acence my mother's sister, and she learned it from Tomal, the best Craftsmaster in our Stonedown. He also studied for a time in the Loresraat. But *suru-pa-maerl* is a craft of making images from stones without binding or shaping. I walk the hills and search out the shapes of rocks and pebbles. And when I discover a form that I understand, I take it home and find a place for it, balancing or interlocking with other forms until a new form is made.

'Sometimes, when I am very brave, I smooth a roughness to make the joining of the stones steadier. In this way, I remake the broken secrets of the Earth, and give beauty to the people.'

Vaguely, Covenant murmured, 'It must be hard – think of a shape and then find the rocks to fit it.'

'That is not the way. I look at the stones, and seek for the shapes that are already in them. I do not ask the Earth to give me a horse. The craft is in learning to see what it is the Earth chooses to offer. Perhaps it will be a horse.'

'I would like to see your work.' Covenant paid no attention to what he was saying. The stairs beckoned him like the seductive face of forgetfulness, in which lepers lost their self-protective disciplines, their hands and feet, their lives.

But he was dreaming. The way to endure a dream was to flow with it until it ended. He had to make that descent in order to survive. That need outweighed all other considerations.

Abruptly, convulsively, he hauled himself to his feet. Planting himself squarely in the centre of the circle, he ignored the mountain and the sky, ignored the long fall below him, and gave himself a thorough examination. Trembling, he probed his still-living nerves for aches or twinges, scanned his clothing for snags, rents, inspected his numb hands.

He had to put that stair behind him.

He could survive it because it was a dream – it could not kill him – and because he could not stand all this darkness beating about his ears.

'Now, listen,' he snapped at Lena. 'I've got to go first. And don't give me that confused look. I told you I'm a leper. My hands and feet are numb – no feeling. I can't grip. And I'm – not very good at heights. I might fall. I don't want you below me. You – ' He balked, then went on roughly, 'You've been decent to me, and I haven't had to put up with that for a long time.'

She winced at his tone. 'Why are you angry? How have I offended you?'

By being nice to me! he rasped silently. His face was grey with fear as he turned, dropped to his hands and knees, and backed out through the gap.

In the first rush of trepidation, he lowered his feet to the stairs with his eyes closed. But he could not face the descent without his eyes; the leper's habit of watching himself, and the need to have all his senses alert, were too strong. Yet with his eyes open the height made his head reel. So he strove to keep his gaze on the rock in front of him. From the first step, he knew that his greatest danger lay in the numbness of his feet. Numb hands made him feel unsure of every grip, and before he had gone fifty feet he was clenching the edges so hard that his shoulders began to cramp. But he could see his hands, see that they were on the rock, that the aching in his wrists and elbows was not a lie. His feet he could not see – not unless he looked down. He could only tell that his foot was on a stair when his ankle felt the pressure of his weight. In each downward step he lowered himself on to a guess. If he felt an unexpected flex in his arch, he had to catch himself with his arms and get more of his foot on to the unseen stair. He tried kicking his feet forward so that the jar of contact would tell him when his toes were against the edge of the next stair; but when he misjudged, his shins or knees struck the stone corners, and that sharp pain nearly made his legs fold.

Climbing down stair by stair, staring at his hands with sweat streaming into his eyes, he cursed the fate which had cut away two of his fingers – two fingers less to save himself with if his feet failed.

In addition, the absence of half his hand made him feel that his right hold was weaker than his left, that his weight was pulling leftward off the stair. He kept reaching his feet to the right to compensate, and kept missing the stairs on that side.

He could not get the sweat out of his eyes. It stung him like blindness, but he feared to release one hand to wipe his forehead, feared even to shake his head because he might lose his balance. Cramps tormented his back and shoulders. He had to grit his teeth to keep from crying for help.

As if she sensed his distress, Lena shouted, 'Halfway!'

He crept on downward, step by step.

Helplessly, he felt himself moving faster. His muscles were failing — the strain on his knees and elbows was too great — and with each step he had less control over his descent. He forced himself to stop and rest, though his terror screamed for him to go on, get the climb over with. For a wild instant, he thought that he would simply turn and leap, hoping he was close enough to land on the mountain slope and live. Then he heard the sound of Lena's feet approaching his head. He wanted to reach up and grab her ankles, force her to save him. But even that hope seemed futile, and he hung where he was, quivering.

His breath rattled harshly through his clenched teeth, and he almost did not understand Lena's shout:

'Thomas Covenant! Be strong! Only fifty steps remain!'

With a shudder that almost tore him loose from the rock, he started down again.

The last steps passed in a loud chaos of cramps and sweat blindness — and then he was down, lying flat on the level base of the Watch and gasping at the cries of his limbs. For a long time, he covered his face and listened to the air lurching in and out of his lungs like sobs — listened until the sound relaxed and he could breathe more quietly.

When he finally looked up, he saw the blue sky, the long black finger of Kevin's Watch pointing at the noon sun, the towering slope of the mountain, and Lena bending over him so low that her hair almost brushed his face.

5

MITHIL STONEDOWN

Covenant felt strangely purged, as if he had passed through an ordeal, survived a ritual trial by vertigo. He had put the stair behind him. In his relief, he was sure that he had found the right answer to the particular threat of madness, the need for a real and comprehensible explanation to his situation, which had surrounded him on Kevin's Watch. He looked up at the radiant sky, and it appeared pure, untainted by carrion eaters.

Go forward, he said to himself. Don't think about it. Survive.

As he thought this, he looked up into Lena's soft brown eyes and found that she was smiling.

'Are you well?' she asked.

'Well?' he echoed. 'That's not an easy question.' It drew him up into a sitting position. Scanning his hands, he discovered blood on the heels and fingertips. His palms were scraped raw, and when he probed his knees and shins and elbows they burned painfully.

Ignoring the ache of his muscles, he pushed to his feet. 'Lena, this is important,' he said, 'I've got to clean my hands.'

She stood also, but he could see that she did not understand. 'Look!' He brandished his hands in front of her. 'I'm a leper. I can't feel this. No pain.' When she still seemed confused, he went on, 'That's how I lost my fingers. I got hurt and infected, and they had to cut my hand apart. I've got to get some soap and water.'

Touching the scar on his right hand, she said, 'The sickness does this?'

'Yes!'

'There is a stream on the way toward the Stonedown,' said Lena, 'and hurtloam near it.'

'Let's go.' Brusquely, Covenant motioned for her to lead the way. She accepted his urgency with a nod, and started at once down the path.

It went west from the base of Kevin's Watch along a ledge in the steep mountain slope until it reached a cluttered ravine. Moving awkwardly because of the clenched stiffness of his muscles, Covenant followed Lena up the ravine, then stepped gingerly behind her down a rough-hewn stair in the side of a sharp cut which branched away into the mountain. When they reached the bottom of the cut, they continued along it, negotiating its scree-littered floor while the slash of sky overhead narrowed and the sides of the cut leaned together. A rich, damp smell surrounded them, and the cool shadows deepened until Lena's dark tunic became dim in the gloom ahead of Covenant. Then the cut turned sharply to the left and opened without warning into a small, sun-bright valley with a stream sparkling through the centre and tall pines standing over the grass around the edges.

'Here,' said Lena with a happy smile. 'What could heal you more than this?'

Covenant stopped to gaze, entranced, down the length of the valley. It was no more than fifty yards long, and at its far end the stream turned left again and filed away between two sheer walls. In this tiny pocket in the vastness of the mountain, removed from the overwhelming landscapes below Kevin's Watch, the earth was comfortably green and sunny, and the air was both fresh and warm – pine-aromatic, redolent with springtime. As he breathed the atmosphere of the place, Covenant felt his chest ache with a familiar grief at his own sickness.

To ease the pressure in his chest, he moved forward. The grass under his feet was so thick and springy that he could feel it through the strained ligaments of his knees and calves. It seemed to encourage him toward the stream, toward the cleansing of his hurts.

The water was sure to be cold, but that did not concern him. His hands were too numb to notice cold very quickly. Squatting on a flat stone beside the stream, he plunged them into the current and began rubbing them together. His wrists felt the chill at once, but his fingers were vague about the water; and it gave him no pain to scrub roughly at his cuts and scrapes.

He was marginally aware that Lena had moved away from him up the stream, apparently looking for something, but he was too preoccupied to wonder what she was doing. After an intense scrubbing he let his hands rest, and rolled up his sleeves to inspect his elbows. They were red and sore, but the skin was not broken.

When he pulled up his pant legs, he found that his shins and knees were more battered. The discoloration of his bruises were already darkening, and would be practically black before long: but the tough fabric of his trousers had held, and again the skin was unbroken. In their way, bruises were as dangerous to him as cuts, but he could not treat them without medication. He made an effort to stifle his anxiety, and turned his attention back to his hands.

Blood still oozed from the heels and fingertips, and when he washed it off he could see bits of black grit lodged deep in some of the cuts. But before he started washing again, Lena returned. Her cupped hands were full of thick brown mud. 'This is hurtloam,' she said reverently, as if she were speaking of something rare and powerful. 'You must put it on all your wounds.'

'Mud?' His leper's caution quivered. 'I need soap, not more dirt.'

'This is hurtloam,' repeated Lena. 'It is for healing.' She stepped closer and thrust the mud toward him. He thought he could see tiny gleams of gold in it.

He stared at it blankly, shocked by the idea of putting mud in his cuts.

'You must use it,' she insisted. 'I know what it is. Do you not understand? This is hurtloam. Listen. My father is Trell, Gravelingas of the *rhadhamaerl*. His work is with the fire-stones, and he leaves healing to the Healers. But he is a *rhadhamaerl*. He comprehends the rocks and soils. And he taught me to care for myself when there is need. He taught me the signs and places of hurtloam. This is healing earth. You must use it.'

Mud? He glared. In my cuts? Do you want to cripple me?

Before he could stop her, Lena knelt in front of him and dropped a handful of the mud on to his bare knee. With that hand free, she spread the brown loam down his shin. Then she scooped up the remainder and put it on his other knee and shin. As it lay on his legs, its golden gleaming seemed to grow stronger, brighter.

The wet earth was cool and soothing, and it seemed to stroke his legs tenderly, absorbing the pain from his bruises. He watched it closely. The relief that it sent flowing through his bones gave him a pleasure that he had never felt before. Bemused, he opened his hands to Lena, let her spread hurtloam over all his cuts and scrapes.

At once, the relief began to run up into him through his elbows and wrists. And an odd tingling started in his palms, as if the hurtloam were venturing past his cuts into his nerves, trying to reawaken them. A similar tingling danced across the arches of his feet. He stared at the glittering mud with a kind of awe in his eyes.

It dried quickly; its light vanished into the brown. In a few moments Lena rubbed it off his legs. Then he saw that his bruises were almost gone – they were in the last, faded yellow stages of healing. He slapped his hands into the stream, washed away the mud, looked at his fingers. They had become whole again. The heels of his hands were healed as well, and the abrasions on his forearms had disappeared completely. He was so stunned that for a moment he could only gape at his hands and think, Hellfire. Hellfire and bloody damnation. What's happening to me?

After a long silence, he whispered, 'That's not possible.'

In response, Lena grinned broadly.

'What's so funny?'

Trying to imitate his tone, she said, '"I need soap, not more dirt."' Then she laughed, a teasing sparkle in her eyes.

But Covenant was too full of surprise to be distracted. 'I'm serious. How can this happen?'

Lena dropped her eyes and answered quietly. 'There is power in the Earth – power and life. You must know this. Atiaran my mother says that such things as hurtloam, such powers and mysteries, are in all the Earth – but we are blind to them because we do not share enough, with the Land and with each other.'

'There are – other things like this?'

'Many. But I know only a few. If you travel to the Council, it may be that the Lords will teach you everything. But come – ' she swung lightly to her feet – 'here is another. Are you hungry?'

As if cued by her question, an impression of emptiness opened in his stomach. How long had it been since he had eaten? He adjusted his pant legs, rolled down his sleeves, and shrugged himself to his feet. His wonder was reinforced to find that almost every ache was gone from his muscles. Shaking his head in disbelief, he followed Lena toward one side of the valley.

Under the shade of the trees, she stopped beside a gnarled, waist-high shrub. Its leaves were spread and pointed like a holly's, but it was scattered with small viridian blooms, and nestled under some of the leaves were tight clusters of a blue-green fruit the size of blueberries.

'This is *aliantha*,' said Lena. 'We call them treasure-berries.' Breaking off a cluster, she ate four or five berries, then dropped the seeds into her hand and threw them behind her. 'It is said that a person can walk the whole length and breadth of the Land eating only treasure-berries, and return home stronger and better fed than before. They are a great gift of the Earth. They bloom and bear fruit in all seasons. There is no part of the Land in which they do not grow – except, perhaps, in the east, on the Spoiled Plains. And they are the hardiest of growing things – the last to die and the first to grow again. All this my mother told me, as part of the lore of our people. Eat,' she said, handing Covenant a cluster of the berries, 'eat, and spread the seeds over the Earth, so that the *aliantha* may flourish.'

But Covenant made no move to take the fruit. He was lost in wonder, in unanswerable questions about the strange potency of this Land. For the moment, he neglected his danger.

Lena regarded his unfocused gaze, then took one of the berries and put it in his mouth. By reflex, he broke the skin with his teeth; at once, his mouth was filled with a light, sweet taste like that of a ripe peach faintly blended with salt and lime. In another moment he was eating greedily, only occasionally remembering to spit out the seeds.

He ate until he could find no more fruit on that bush, then looked about him for another. But Lena put her hand on his arm to stop him. 'Treasure-berries are strong food,' she said. 'You do not need many. And the taste is better if you eat slowly.'

But Covenant was still hungry. He could not remember ever wanting food as much as he now wanted that fruit – the sensations of eating had never been so vivid, so compulsory. He snatched his arm away as if he meant to strike her, then abruptly caught himself.

What is this? What's happening?

Before he could pursue the question, he became aware of another feeling – overpowering drowsiness. In the space of one instant, he passed almost without transition from hunger to a huge yawn that made him seem top-heavy with weariness. He tried to turn, and stumbled.

Lena was saying, 'The hurtloam does this, but I did not expect it. When the wounds are very deadly, hurtloam brings sleep to speed the healing. But cuts on the hands are not deadly. Do you have hurts that you did not show me?'

Yes, he thought through another yawn. *I'm sick to death.*

He was asleep before he hit the grass.

When he began to drift slowly awake, the first thing that he became conscious of was Lena's firm thighs pillowing his head. Gradually, he grew aware of other things – the tree shade bedizened with glints of declining sunlight, the aroma of pine, the wind murmuring, the grass thickly cradling his body, the sound of a tune, the irregular tingling that came and went from his palms like an atavism – but the warmth of his cheek on Lena's lap seemed more important. For the time, his sole desire was to clasp Lena in his arms and bury his face in her thighs. He resisted it by listening to her song.

In a soft and somehow naïve tone, she sang:

> Something there is in beauty
> which grows in the soul of the beholder
> like a flower:
> fragile –
> for many are the blights
> which may waste
> the beauty
> or the beholder –
> and imperishable –

57

for the beauty may die,
or the beholder may die,
or the world may die,
but the soul in which the flower grows
survives.

Her voice folded him in a comfortable spell which he did not want to end. After a pause full of the scent of pine and the whispering breeze, he said softly, 'I like that.'

'Do you? I am glad. It was made by Tomal the Craftmaster, for the dance when he wed Imoiran Moiran-daughter. But oft-times the beauty of a song is in the singing, and I am no singer. It may be that tonight Atiaran my mother will sing for the Stonedown. Then you will hear a real song.'

Covenant gave no answer. He lay still, only wishing to nestle in his pillow for as long as he could. The tingling in his palms seemed to urge him to embrace Lena, and he lay still, enjoying the desire and wondering where he would find the courage.

Then she began to sing again. The tune sounded familiar, and behind it he heard the rumour of dark wings. Suddenly he realized that it was very much like the tune that went with 'Golden Boy'.

He had been walking down the sidewalk toward the offices of the phone company – the Bell Telephone Company; that name was written in gilt letters on the door – to pay his bill in person.

He jerked off Lena's lap, jumped to his feet. A mist of violence dimmed his vision. 'What song is that?' he demanded thickly.

Startled, Lena answered, 'No song. I was only trying to make a melody. Is it wrong?'

The tone of her voice steadied him – she sounded-so abandoned, so made forlorn by his quick anger. Words failed him, and the mist passed. No business, he thought. I've got no business taking it out on her. Extending his hands, he helped her to her feet. He tried to smile, but his stiff face could only grimace. 'Where do we go now?'

Slowly the hurt faded from her eyes. 'You are strange, Thomas Covenant,' she said.

Wryly, he replied, 'I didn't know it was this bad.'

For a moment, they stood gazing into each other's eyes. Then she surprised him by blushing and dropping his hands. There was a new excitement in her voice as she said, 'We will go to the Stonedown. You will amaze my mother and father.' Gaily, she turned and ran away down the valley.

She was lithe and light and graceful as she ran, and Covenant watched her, musing on the strange new feelings that moved in him. He had an unexpected sense that this Land might offer him some spell with which he could conjure away his impotence, some rebirth to which he could cling even after he regained consciousness, after the Land and all the insane implications faded into the miasma of half-remembered dreams. Such hope did not require that the Land be real, physically actual and independent of his own unconscious, uncontrolled dream-weaving. No, leprosy was an incurable disease, and if he did not die for his accident, he would have to live with that fact. But a dream might heal other afflictions. It might. He set off after Lena with a swing in his stride and eagerness in his veins.

The sun was down far enough in the sky to leave the lower half of the valley in shadow. Ahead of him, he could see Lena beckoning, and he followed the stream toward her, enjoying the spring of the turf under his feet as he walked. He felt somehow taller than before, as if the hurtloam had done more to him than simply heal his cuts and scrapes. Nearing Lena, he seemed to see parts of her for the first time – the delicacy of her ears when her hair swung behind them – the way the soft fabric of her shift hung on her breasts and hips – her slim waist. The sight of her made the tingling in his palms grow stronger.

She smiled at him, then led the way along the stream and out of the valley. They moved down a crooked file between the sheer walls of rock which climbed above them until the narrow slit of the sky was hundreds of feet away. The trail was rocky, and Covenant had to watch his feet constantly to keep his balance. The effort made the file seem long, but within a couple hundred yards he and Lena came to a crevice that ascended to the right away from the stream. They climbed into and along the crevice. Soon it levelled, then sloped gradually downward for a long way, but it bent enough so that Covenant could not see where he was headed.

At last, the crevice took one more turn and ended, leaving Lena and Covenant on the mountainside high above the river valley. They were facing due west into the declining sun. The river came out of the mountains to their left, and flowed away into the plains on their right. There was a branch of the mountain range across the valley, but it soon shrank into the plains to the north.

'Here is the Mithil,' said Lena. 'And there is Mithil Stonedown.' Covenant saw a tiny knot of huts north of him on the east side of the river. 'It is not a great distance,' Lena went on, 'but the path travels up the valley and then back along the river. The sun will be gone when we reach our Stonedown. Come.'

Covenant had an uneasy moment looking down the slope of the mountain – still more than two thousand feet above the valley – but he mastered it, and followed Lena to the south. The mountainside relaxed steadily, and soon the path lay along grassy slopes and behind stern rock buttresses, through dells and ravines, among mazes of fallen boulders. And as the trail descended, the air became deeper, softer and less crystalline. The smells slowly changed, grew greener; pine and aspen gave way to the loam of the grasslands. Covenant felt that he was alive to every gradation of the change, every nuance of the lowering altitude. Through the excitement of his new alertness, the descent passed quickly. Before he was ready to leave the mountains, the trail rolled down a long hill, found the river, and then swung north along it.

The Mithil was narrow and brisk where the path first joined it, and it spoke with wet rapidity in a voice full of resonances and rumours. But as the river drew toward the plains, it broadened and slowed, became more philosophical in its low, self-communing mutter. Soon its voice no longer filled the air. Quietly it told itself its long tale as it rolled away on its quest for the sea.

Under the spell of the river, Covenant became slowly more conscious of the reassuring solidity of the Land. It was not an intangible dreamscape; it was concrete, susceptible to ascertainment. This was an illusion, of course – a trick of his racked and smitten mind. But it was curiously comforting. It seemed to promise that he was not walking into horror, chaos – that this Land was coherent, manageable, that when he had mastered its laws, its peculiar facts, he would be able to travel unscathed the path of his dream, retain his grip on his sanity. Such thoughts made him feel almost bold as he followed Lena's lithe back, the swaying appeal of her hips.

While Covenant wandered in unfamiliar emotions, the Mithil valley dropped into shadow. The sun crossed behind the western mountains, and though light still glowed on the distant plains, a thin veil of darkness thickened in the valley. As he watched, the rim of the shadow stretched itself high up the mountain on his right, climbing like a hungry tide the shores of day. In the twilight, he sensed his peril sneaking furtively closer to him, though he did not know what it was.

Then the last ridge of the mountains fell into dusk, and the glow on the plains began to fade.

Lena stopped, touched Covenant's arm, pointed. 'See,' she said, 'here is Mithil Stonedown.'

They stood atop a long, slow hill, and at its bottom were gathered the buildings of the village. Covenant could see the houses quite clearly, although lights already shone faintly behind some of the windows. Except for a large, open circle in the centre of the village, the Stonedown looked as erratically laid out as if it had fallen off the mountain not long ago. But this impression was belied by the smooth sheen of the stone walls and the flat roofs. And when he looked more closely, Covenant saw that the Stonedown was not in fact unorganized. All the buildings faced in toward the centre.

None of them had more than one storey, and all were stone, with flat slabs of rock for roofs; but they varied considerably in size and shape – some were round, others square or rectangular, and still others so irregular from top to bottom that they seemed more like squat hollow boulders than buildings.

As she and Covenant stared down toward the Stonedown, Lena said, 'Five times a hundred people of the South Plains live here – *rhadhamaerl*, Shepherds, Cattleherds, Farmers, and those who Craft. But Atiaran my mother alone has been to the Loresraat.' Pointing, she added, 'The home of my family is there – nearest the river.'

Walking together, she and Covenant skirted the Stonedown toward her home.

6

LEGEND OF BEREK HALFHAND

Dusk was deepening over the valley. Birds gathered to rest for the night in the trees of the foothills. They sang and called energetically to each other for a while, but their high din soon relaxed into a quiet, satisfied murmur. As Lena and Covenant passed behind the outer houses of the Stonedown, they could again hear the river contemplating some excitement or agitation, and Covenant was too immersed in the twilight sounds around him to say anything. The swelling night seemed full of soft communions – anodynes for the loneliness of the dark. So they came quietly toward Lena's home.

It was a rectangular building, larger than most in the Stonedown, but with the same polished sheen on the walls. A warm yellow light radiated from the windows. As Lena and Covenant approached, a large figure crossed one of the windows and moved toward a farther room.

At the corner of the house, Lena paused to take Covenant's hand and squeeze it before she led him up to the doorway.

The entry was covered with a heavy curtain. She held it aside and drew him into the house. There she halted. Looking around swiftly, he observed that the room they had entered went the depth of the house, but it had two curtained doors in either wall. In it, a stone table and benches with enough space to seat six or eight people occupied the middle of the floor. But the room was large enough so that the table did not dominate it.

Cut into the rock walls all around the room were shelves, and these were full of stoneware jars and utensils, some obviously for use in cooking and eating, others with functions which Covenant could not guess. Several rock stools stood against the walls. And the warm yellow light filled the chamber, glowing on the smooth surfaces and reflecting off rare colours and textures in the stone.

The light came from fires in several stone pots, one in each corner of the room and one in the centre of the table; but there was no flicker of flames – the light was as steady as its stone containers. And with the light came a soft smell as of newly broken earth.

After only a cursory glance around the chamber, Covenant's attention was drawn to the far end of the room. There on a slab of stone against the wall sat a huge granite pot, half as tall as a man. And over the pot, peering intently at its contents, stood a large man, a great pillar of a figure, as solid as a boulder. He had his back to Lena and Covenant, and did not seem to be aware of them. He wore a short brown tunic with brown trousers under it, but the leaf pattern woven into the fabric at his shoulders was identical to Lena's. Under the tunic, his massive muscles bunched and stretched as he rotated the pot. It looked prodigiously heavy, but Covenant half expected the man to lift it over his head to pour out its contents.

There was a shadow over the pot which the brightness of the room did not penetrate, and for some time the man stared into the darkness, studying it while he rotated the pot. Then he began to sing. His voice was too low for Covenant to make out the words, but as he listened he felt a kind of invocation in the sound, as if the contents of the pot were powerful. For a moment, nothing happened. Then the shadow began to pale. At first, Covenant thought that the light in the room had changed but soon he saw a new illumination starting from the pot. The glow swelled and deepened, and at last shone out strongly, making the other lights seem thin.

With a final mutter over his work, the man stood upright and turned round. In the new brightness, he seemed even taller and broader than before, as if his limbs and shoulders and deep chest drew strength, stature, from the light; and his forehead was ruddy from the heat of the pot. Seeing Covenant, he stared in surprise. An uneasy look came into his eyes, and his right hand touched his thick reddish hair. Then he extended the hand, palm forward, toward Covenant, and said to Lena, 'Well, daughter, you bring a guest. But I remember that our hospitality is in your charge today.' The strange potency of a moment before was gone from his voice. He sounded like a man who did not speak much with people. But though he was treating his daughter sternly, he seemed essentially calm. 'You know I promised more graveling today, and Atiaran your mother is helping deliver the new child of Odona Murrin-mate. The guest will be offended by our hospitality – with no meal ready to welcome the end of his day.' Yet while he reprimanded Lena, his eyes studied Covenant cautiously.

Lena bowed her head, trying, Covenant felt sure, to look ashamed for her father's benefit. But a moment later she hurried across the room and hugged the big man. He smiled softly at her upturned face. Then, turning toward Covenant, she announced, 'Trell my father, I bring a stranger to the Stonedown. I found him on Kevin's Watch.' A lively gleam shone in her eyes, although she tried to keep her voice formal.

'So,' Trell responded. 'A stranger – that I see. And wonder what business took him to that ill-blown place.'

'He fought with a grey cloud,' answered Lena.

Looking at this bluff, hale man, whose muscle-knotted arm rested with such firm gentleness on Lena's shoulder, Covenant expected him to laugh at the absurd suggestion – a man fighting a cloud. Trell's presence felt imperturbable and earthy, like an assertion of common sense that reduced the nightmare of Foul to its proper unreality. So Covenant was put off his balance by hearing Trell ask with perfect seriousness, 'Which was the victor?'

The question forced Covenant to find a new footing for himself. He was not prepared to deal with the memory of Lord Foul – but at the same time he felt obscurely sure that he could not lie to Trell. He found that his throat had gone dry, and he answered awkwardly, 'I lived through it.'

Trell said nothing for a moment, but through the silence Covenant felt that his answer had increased the big man's uneasiness. Trell's eyes shifted away, then came back as he said, 'I see. And what is your name, stranger?'

Promptly, Lena smiled at Covenant and answered for him, 'Thomas Covenant. Covenant of Kevin's Watch.'

'What, girl?' asked Trell. 'Are you a prophet, that you speak for someone higher than you?' Then to Covenant he said, 'Well, Thomas Covenant of Kevin's Watch – do you have other names?'

Covenant was about to respond negatively when he caught an eager interest in the question from Lena's eyes. He paused. In a leap of insight, he realized that he was as exciting to her as if he had in fact been Berek Halfhand – that to her yearning toward mysteries and powers, all-knowing Lords and battles in the clouds, his strangeness and his unexplained appearance on the Watch made him seem like a personification of great events out of a heroic past. The message of her gaze was suddenly plain; in the suspense of her curiosity she was hanging from the hope that he would reveal himself to her, give her some glimpse of his high calling to appease her for her youth and ignorance.

The idea filled him with strange reverberations. He was not used to such flattery; it gave him an unfamiliar sense of possibility. Quickly, he searched for some high-sounding title to give himself, some name by which he could please Lena without falsifying himself to Trell. Then he had an inspiration. 'Thomas Covenant,' he said as if he were rising to a challenge, 'the Unbeliever.'

Immediately, he felt that with that name he had committed himself to more than he could measure at present. The act made him feel pretentious, but Lena rewarded him with a beaming glance, and Trell accepted the statement gravely. 'Well, Thomas Covenant,' he replied, 'you are welcome to Mithil Stonedown. Please accept the hospitality of this home. I must go now to take my graveling as I promised. It may be that Atiaran my wife will return soon. And if you prod her, Lena may remember to offer you refreshment while I am gone.'

While he spoke, Trell turned back to his stone pot. He wrapped his arms about it, lifted it from its base. With red-gold flames reflecting a dance in his hair and beard, he carried the pot toward the doorway. Lena hurried ahead of him to hold open the curtain, and in a moment Trell was gone, leaving Covenant with one glimpse of the contents of the pot. It was full of small, round stones like fine gravel, and they seemed to be on fire.

'Damnation,' Covenant whispered. 'How heavy is that thing?'

'Three men cannot lift the pot alone,' replied Lena proudly. 'But when the graveling burns, my father may lift it easily. He is a Gravelingas of the *rhadhamaerl*, deep with the lore of stone.'

Covenant stared after him for a moment, appalled by Trell's strength.

Then Lena said, 'Now, I must not fail to offer you refreshment. Will you wash or bathe? Are you thirsty? We have good springwine.'

Her voice brought back the scintillation of Covenant's nerves. His instinctive distrust of Trell's might dissipated under the realization that he had a power of his own. This world accepted him; it accorded him importance. People like Trell and Lena were prepared to take him as seriously as he wanted. All he had to do was keep moving, follow the path of his dream to Revelstone – whatever that was. He felt giddy at the prospect. On the impetus of the moment, he determined to participate in his own importance, enjoy it while it lasted.

To cover his rush of new emotions, he told Lena that he would like to wash. She took him past a curtain into another room, where water poured continuously from a spout in the wall. A sliding stone valve sent the water into either a wash-basin or a large tub, both formed of stone. Lena showed him some fine sand to use as soap, then left him. The water was cold, but he plunged his hands and head into it with something approaching enthusiasm.

When he was done, he looked around for a towel, but did not see one. Experimentally, he eased a hand over the glowing pot that lit the room. The warm yellow light dried his fingers rapidly, so he leaned over the pot, rubbing the water from his face and neck, and soon even his hair was dry. By force of habit, he went through his VSE, examining the nearly invisible marks where his hands had been cut. Then he pushed the curtain out of his way and re-entered the central chamber.

He found that another woman had joined Lena. As he returned, he heard Lena say, 'He says he knows nothing of us.' Then the other woman looked at him, and he guessed immediately that she was Atiaran. The leaf pattern at the shoulders of the long brown robe seemed to be a kind of family emblem; he did not need such hints to see the long familiarity in the way the older woman touched Lena's shoulder, or the similarities in their posture. But where Lena was fresh and slim of line, full of unbroken newness, Atiaran appeared complex, almost self-contradictory. Her soft surface, her full figure, she carried as if it were a hindrance to the hard strength of experience within her, as if she lived with her body on the basis of an old and difficult truce. And her face bore the signs of that truce; her forehead seemed prematurely lined, and her deep spacious eyes appeared to open inward on a weary battleground of doubts and uneasy reconciliations. Looking at her over the stone table, Covenant received a double impression of a frowning concern – the result of knowing and fearing more than other people realized – and an absent beauty that would rekindle her face if only she would smile.

After a brief hesitation, the older woman touched her heart and raised her hand toward Covenant as Trell had done. 'Hail, guest, and welcome. I am Atiaran Trell-mate. I have spoken with Trell, and with Lena my daughter – you need no introduction to me, Thomas Covenant. Be comfortable in our home.'

Remembering his manners – and his new determination – Covenant responded. 'I'm honoured.'

Atiaran bowed slightly. 'Accepting that which is offered honours the giver. And courtesy is always welcome.' Then she seemed to hesitate again, uncertain of how to proceed. Covenant watched the return of old conflicts to her eyes, thinking that gaze would have an extraordinary power if it were not so inward. But she reached her decision soon, and said, 'It is not the custom of our people to worry a guest with hard questions before eating. But the food is not ready – ' she glanced at Lena – 'and you are strange to me, Thomas Covenant, strange and disquieting. I would talk with you if I may, while Lena prepares what food we have. You seem to bear a need that should not wait.'

Covenant shrugged noncommittally. He felt a twinge of anxiety at the thought of her questions, and braced himself to try to answer them without losing his new balance.

In the pause, Lena began moving around the room. She went to the shelves to get plates, and bowls for the table, and prepared some dishes on a slab of stone heated from underneath by a tray of graveling. She turned her eyes toward Covenant often as she moved, but he did not always notice. Atiaran compelled his attention.

At first, she murmured uncertainly, 'I hardly know where to begin. It has been so long, and I learned so little of what the Lords know. But what I have must be enough. No one here can take my place.' She straightened her shoulders. 'May I see your hands?'

Remembering Lena's initial reaction to him, Covenant held up his right hand.

Atiaran moved around the table until she was close enough to touch him, but did not. Instead, she searched his face. 'Halfhand. It is as Trell said. And some say that Berek Earthfriend, Heartthew and Lord-Fatherer, will return to the Land when there is need. Do you know these things?'

Covenant answered gruffly, 'No.'

Still looking into his face, Atiaran said, 'Your other hand?'

Puzzled, he raised his left. She dropped her eyes to it.

When she saw it, she gasped, and bit her lip and stepped back. For an instant, she seemed inexplicably terrified. But she mastered herself, and asked with only a low tremble in her voice, 'What metal is that ring?'

'What? This?' Her reaction startled Covenant, and in his surprise he gaped at a complicated memory of Joan saying. *With this ring I thee wed*, and the old ochre-robed beggar replying. *Be true, be true.* Darkness threatened him. He heard himself answer as if he were someone else, someone who had nothing to do with leprosy and divorce, 'It's white gold.'

Atiaran groaned, clamped her hands over her temples as if she

66

were in pain. But again she brought herself under control, and a bleak courage came into her eyes. 'I alone,' she said, 'I alone in Mithil Stonedown know the meaning of this. Even Trell has not the knowledge. And I know too little. Answer, Thomas Covenant – is it true?'

I should've thrown it away, he muttered bitterly. A leper's got no right to be sentimental.

But Atiaran's intensity drew his attention toward her again. She gave him the impression that he knew more about what was happening to him than he did – that he was moving into a world which, in some dim, ominous way, had been made ready for him. His old anger mounted. 'Of course it's true,' he snapped. 'What's the matter with you? It's only a ring.'

'It is white gold,' Atiaran's reply sounded as forlorn as if she had just suffered a bereavement.

'So what?' He could not understand what distressed the woman. 'It doesn't mean a thing. Joan – ' Joan had preferred it to yellow gold. But that had not prevented her from divorcing him.

'It is white gold,' Atiaran repeated. 'The Lords sing an ancient lore-song concerning the bearer of white gold. I remember only part of it, thus:

> And he who wields white wild magic gold
> is a paradox –
> for he is everything and nothing,
> hero and fool,
> potent, helpless –
> and with the one word of truth or treachery,
> he will save or damn the Earth
> because he is mad and sane,
> cold and passionate,
> lost and found.

Do you know the song, Covenant? There is no white gold in the Land. Gold has never been found in the Earth, though it is said that Berek knew of it and made the songs. You come from another place. What terrible purpose brings you here?'

Covenant felt her searching him with her eyes for some flaw, some falsehood which would give the lie to her fear. He stiffened. *You have might*, the Despiser had said, *wild magic – You will never know what it is*. The idea that his wedding band was some kind of talisman nauseated him like the smell of attar. He had a savage desire to shout. None of this is happening! But he only knew of one workable response: don't think about it, follow the path, survive. He met Atiaran on her own ground. 'All purposes are terrible. I have a message for the Council of Lords.'

'What message?' she demanded.

After only an instant's hesitation, he grated, 'The Grey Slayer has come back.'

When she heard Covenant pronounce that name, Lena dropped the stoneware bowl she was carrying, and fled into her mother's arms.

Covenant stood glowering at the shattered bowl. The liquid it had contained gleamed on the smooth stone floor. Then he heard Atiaran pant in horror. 'How do you know this?' He looked back at her, and saw the two women clinging together like children threatened by the demon of their worst dreams. Leper outcast unclean! he thought sourly. But as he watched, Atiaran seemed to grow solider. Her jaw squared, her broad glance hardened. For all her fear, she was a strong woman comforting her child – and bracing herself to meet her danger. Again she asked, 'How do you know?'

She made him feel defensive, and he replied, 'I met him on Kevin's Watch.'

'Ah, alas!' she cried, hugging Lena. 'Alas for the young in this world! The doom of the Land is upon them. Generations will die in agony, and there will be war and terror and pain for those who live! Alas, Lena my daughter. You were born into an evil time, and there will be no peace or comfort for you when the battle comes. Ah, Lena, Lena.'

Her grief touched an undefended spot in Covenant, and his throat thickened. Her voice filled his own image of the Land's Desolation with a threnody he had not heard before. For the first time, he sensed that the Land held something precious which was in danger of being lost.

This combination of sympathy and anger tightened his nerves still further. He vibrated to a sharper pitch, trembled. When he looked at Lena, he saw that a new awe of him had already risen above her panic. The unconscious offer in her eyes burned more disturbingly than ever.

He held himself still until Atiaran and Lena slowly released each other. Then he asked, 'What do you know about all this? About what's happening to me?'

Before Atiaran could reply, a voice called from outside the house, 'Hail! Atiaran Tiaran-daughter. Trell Gravelingas tells us that your work is done for this day. Come and sing to the Stonedown!'

For a moment, Atiaran stood still, shrinking back into herself. Then she sighed, 'Ah, the work of my life has just begun,' and turned to the door. Holding aside the curtain, she said into the night,

'We have not yet eaten. I will come later. But after the gathering I must speak with the Circle of elders.'

'They will be told,' the voice answered.

'Good,' said Atiaran. But instead of returning to Covenant, she remained in the doorway, staring into the darkness for a while. When she closed the curtain at last and faced Covenant, her eyes were moist, and they held a look that he at first thought was defeat. But then he realized that she was only remembering defeat. 'No, Thomas Covenant,' she said sadly, 'I know nothing of your fate. Perhaps if I had remained at the Loresraat longer – if I had had the strength. But I passed my limit there, and came home. I know a part of the old Lore that Mithil Stonedown does not guess, but it is too little. All that I can remember for you are hints of a wild magic which destroys peace –

> wild magic graven in every rock,
> contained for white gold to unleash or control –

but the meaning of such lines, or the courses of these times, I do not know. That is a double reason to take you to the Council.' Then she looked squarely into his face, and added, 'I tell you openly, Thomas Covenant – if you have come to betray the Land, only the Lords may hope to stop you.'

Betray? This was another new thought. An instant passed before he realized what Atiaran was suggesting. But before he could protest, Lena put in for him, 'Mother! He fought a grey cloud on Kevin's Watch. I saw it. How can you doubt him?' Her defence controlled his belligerent reaction. Without intending to, she had put him on false ground. He had not gone so far as to fight Lord Foul.

Trell's return stopped any reply Atiaran might have made. The big man stood in the doorway for a moment, looking between Atiaran and Lena and Covenant. Abruptly, he said, 'So. We are come on hard times.'

'Yes, Trell my husband,' murmured Atiaran. 'Hard times.'

Then his eye caught the shards of stoneware on the floor. 'Hard times, indeed,' he chided gently, 'when stoneware is broken, and the pieces left to powder underfoot.'

This time, Lena was genuinely ashamed. 'I am sorry, Father,' she said. 'I was afraid.'

'No matter.' Trell went to her and placed his big hands, light with affection, on her shoulders. 'Some wounds may be healed. I feel strong today.'

At this, Atiaran gazed gratefully at Trell as if he had just undertaken some heroic task.

To Covenant's incomprehension, she said, 'Be seated, guest. Food will be ready soon. Come, Lena.' The two of them began to bustle around the cooking stone.

Covenant watched as Trell started to pick up the pieces of the broken pot. The Gravelingas's voice rumbled softly, singing an ancient subterranean song. Tenderly, he carried the shards to the table and set them down near the lamp. Then he seated himself. Covenant sat beside him, wondering what was about to happen.

Singing his cavernous song between clenched teeth, Trell began to fit the shards together as if the pot were a puzzle. Piece after piece he set in place, and each piece held where he left it without any adhesive Covenant could see. Trell moved painstakingly, his touch delicate on every fragment, but the pot seemed to grow quickly in his hands, and the pieces fit together perfectly, leaving only a network of fine black lines to mark the breaks. Soon all the shards were in place.

Then his deep tone took on a new cadence. He began to stroke the stoneware with his fingers, and everywhere his touch passed, the black fracture marks vanished as if they had been erased. Slowly, he covered every inch of the pot with his caress. When he had completed the outside, he stroked the inner surface. And finally he lifted the pot, spread his touch over its base. Holding the pot between the fingers of both hands, he rotated it carefully, making sure he had missed nothing. Then he stopped singing, set the pot down gently, took his hands away. It was as complete and solid as if it had never been dropped.

Covenant pulled his awed stare away from the pot to Trell's face. The Gravelingas looked haggard with strain, and his taut cheeks were streaked with tears. 'Mending is harder than breaking,' he mumbled. 'I could not do this every day.' Wearily, he folded his arms on the table and cradled his head in them.

Atiaran stood behind her husband, massaging the heavy muscles of his shoulders and neck, and her eyes were full of pride and love. Something in her expression made Covenant feel that he came from a very poor world, where no one knew or cared about healing stonework pots. He tried to tell himself that he was dreaming, but he did not want to listen.

After a silent pause full of respect for Trell's deed, Lena started to set the table. Soon Atiaran brought bowls of food from the cooking stone. When everything was ready, Trell lifted his head, climbed tiredly to his feet. With Atiaran and Lena, he stood beside the table. Atiaran said to Covenant, 'It is the custom of our people to stand before eating, as a sign of our respect for the Earth, from which life and food and power come.' Covenant stood as well, feeling awkward

70

and out of place. Trell and Atiaran and Lena closed their eyes, bowed their heads for a moment. Then they sat down. When Covenant had followed them to the bench, they began to pass around the food.

It was a bountiful meal: there was cold salt beef covered with a steaming gravy, wild rice, dried apples, brown bread, and cheese; and Covenant was given a tall mug of a drink which Lena called springwine. This beverage was as clear and light as water, slightly effervescent, and it smelled dimly of *aliantha*; but it tasted like a fine beer which had been cured of all bitterness. Covenant had downed a fair amount of it before he realized that it added a still keener vibration to his already thrumming nerves. He could feel himself tightening. He was too full of unusual pressures. Soon he was impatient for the end of the meal, impatient to leave the house and expand in the night air.

But Lena's family ate slowly, and a pall hung over them. They dined as deliberately as if this meal marked the end of all their happiness together. In the silence, Covenant realized that this was a result of his presence. It made him uneasy.

To ease himself, he tried to increase what he knew about his situation. 'I have a question,' he said stiffly. With a gesture, he took in the whole Stonedown. 'No wood. There's plenty of trees all over this valley, but I don't see you using any wood. Are the trees sacred or something?'

After a moment, Atiaran replied, 'Sacred? I know the word, but its meaning is obscure to me. There is Power in the Earth, in trees and rivers and soil and stone, and we respect it for the life it gives. So we have sworn the Oath of Peace. Is that what you ask? We do not use wood because the wood-lore, the *lillianrill*, is lost to us, and we have not sought to regain it. In the exile of our people, when Desolation was upon the Land, many precious things were lost. Our people clung to the *rhadhamaerl* lore in the Southron Range and the Wastes, and it enabled us to endure. The wood-lore seemed not to help us, and it was forgotten. Now that we have returned to the Land, the stone-lore suffices for us. But others have kept the *lillianrill*. I have seen Soaring Woodhelven, in the hills far north and east of us, and it is a fair place – their people understand wood, and flourish. There is some trade between Stonedown and Woodhelven, but wood and stone are not traded.'

When she stopped, Covenant sensed a difference in the new silence. A moment passed before he was sure that he could hear a distant rumour of voices. Shortly, Atiaran confirmed this by saying to Trell, 'Ah, the gathering. I promised to sing tonight.'

She and Trell stood together, and he said, 'So. And then you will speak with the Circle of elders. Some preparations for tomorrow I will make. See – ' he pointed at the table – 'it will be a fine day – there is no shadow on the heart of the stone.'

Almost in spite of himself, Covenant looked where Trell pointed. But he could see nothing.

Noticing his blank look, Atiaran said kindly, 'Do not be surprised, Thomas Covenant. No one but a *rhadhamaerl* can foretell weather in such stones as this. Now come with me, if you will, and I will sing the legend of Berek Halfhand.' As she spoke, she took the pot of graveling from the table to carry with her. 'Lena, will you clean the stoneware?'

Covenant got to his feet. Glancing at Lena, he saw her face twisted with unhappy obedience; she clearly wanted to go with them. But Trell also saw her expression and said, 'Accompany our guest, Lena my daughter. I will not be too busy to care for the stoneware.'

Pleasure transformed her instantly, and she leaped up to throw her arms around her father's neck. He returned her embrace for a moment, then lowered her to the floor. She straightened her shift, trying to look suddenly demure, and moved to her mother's side.

Atiaran said, 'Trell, you will teach this girl to think she is a queen.' But she took Lena's hand to show that she was not angry, and together they went past the curtain. Covenant followed promptly, went out of the house into the starry night with a sense of release. There was more room for him to explore himself under the open sky.

He needed exploration. He could not understand, rationalize, his mounting excitement. The springwine he had consumed seemed to provide a focus of his energies; it capered in his veins like a raving satyr. He felt inexplicably brutalized by inspiration, as if he were the victim rather than the source of his dream. White gold! he sputtered at the darkness between the houses. Wild magic! Do they think I'm crazy?

Perhaps he was crazy. Perhaps he was at this moment wandering in dementia, tormenting himself with false griefs and demands, the impositions of an illusion. Such things had happened to lepers.

I'm not! he shouted, almost cried out aloud. I know the difference – I know I'm dreaming.

His fingers twitched with violence, but he drew cool air deep into his lungs, put everything behind him. He knew how to survive a dream. Madness was the only danger.

As they walked together between the houses, Lena's smooth arm brushed his. His skin felt lambent at the touch.

The murmur of people grew quickly louder. Soon Lena, Atiaran, and Covenant reached the circle, moved into the gathering of the Stonedown.

72

It was lit by dozens of hand-held graveling pots, and in the illumination Covenant could see clearly. Men, women, and children clustered the rim of the circle. Covenant guessed that virtually the entire Stonedown had come to hear Atiaran sing. Most of the people were shorter than he was – and considerably shorter than Trell – and they had dark hair, brown or black, again like Trell. But they were a stocky, broad-shouldered breed, and even the women and children gave an impression of physical strength; centuries of stone-work had shaped them to suit their labour. Covenant felt the same dim fear of them that he had of Trell. They seemed too strong, and he had nothing but his strangeness to protect him if they turned against him.

They were busy talking to each other, apparently waiting for Atiaran, and they gave no sign of noticing Covenant. Reluctant to call attention to himself, he hung back at the outer edges of the gathering. Lena stopped with him. Atiaran gave her the graveling pot, then moved away through the crowd toward the centre of the circle.

After he had scanned the assembly, Covenant turned his attention to Lena. She stood by his right side, the top of her head an inch or two higher than his shoulder, and she held the graveling pot at her waist with both hands, so that the light emphasized her breasts. She was clearly unconscious of the effect, but he felt it intensely, and his palms itched again with eager and fearful desire to touch her.

As if she felt his thoughts, she looked up at him with a solemn softness in her face that made his heart lurch as if it were too big for his constraining ribs. Awkwardly, he took his eyes away, stared around the circle without seeing anything. When he glanced back at her, she seemed to be doing just what he had done – pretending to look elsewhere. He tightened his jaw and forced himself to wait for something to happen.

Soon the gathering became still. In the centre of the open circle, Atiaran stood up on a low stone platform. She bowed her head to the gathering, and the people responded silently raising their graveling pots. The lights seemed to focus around her like a penumbra.

When the pots were lowered, and the last ripple of shuffling had passed through the gathering, Atiaran began: 'I feel I am an old woman this night – my memory seems clouded, and I do not remember all the song I would like to sing. But what I remember I will sing, and I will tell you the story, as I have told it before, so that you may share what lore I have.' At this, low laughter ran through the gathering – a humorous tribute to Atiaran's superior knowl-edge. She remained silent, her head bowed to hide the fear that knowledge had brought her, until the people were quiet again. Then

73

she raised her eyes and said, 'I will sing the legend of Berek Halfhand.'

After a last momentary pause, she placed her song into the welcoming silence like a rough and rare jewel.

> In war men pass like shadows that stain the grass,
>> Leaving their lives upon the green:
>> While Earth bewails the crimson sheen,
> Men's dreams and stars and whispers all helpless pass,

> In one red shadow by woe and wicked cast,
>> In one red pool about his feet,
>> Berek mows the vile like ripe wheat,
> Though of all of Beauty's guarders he is last:

> Last to pass into the shadow of defeat,
>> And last to feel the full despair,
>> And leave his weapons lying there —
> Take his half unhanded hand from battle seat.

> Across the plains of the Land they all swept —
>> Treachers lust at faltering stride
>> As Berek fled before the tide,
> Till on Mount Thunder's rock-mantled side he wept.

> Berek! Earthfriend! — Help and weal,
> Battle-aid against the foe!
>> Earth gives and answers Power's peal,
>> Ringing, Earthfriend! Help and heal!
> Clean the Land from bloody death and woe!

The song made Covenant quiver, as if it concealed a spectre which he should have been able to recognize. But Atiaran's voice enthralled him. No instruments aided her singing, but before she had finished her first line, he knew that she did not need them. The clean thread of her melody was tapestried with unexpected resonances, implied harmonies, echoes of silent voices, so that on every rising motif she seemed about to expand into three or four singers, throat separate and unanimous in the song.

It began in a minor mode that made the gold-hued, star-gemmed night throb like a dirge; and through it blew a black wind of loss, in which things cherished and consecrated throughout the Stonedown seemed to flicker and go out. As he listened, Covenant felt that the entire gathering wept with the song, cried out as one in silent woe under the wide power of the singer.

But grief did not remain long in that voice. After a pause that opened in the night like a revelation, Atiaran broke into her brave refrain – 'Berek! Earthfriend!' – and the change carried her high in a major modulation that would have been too wrenching for any voice less rampant with suggestions, less thickly woven, than hers. The emotions of the gathering continued, but it was reborn in an instant from grief to joy and gratitude. And as Atiaran's long, last high note sprang from her throat like a salute to the mountains and the stars, the people held up their graveling pots and gave a resounding shout:

Berek! Earthfriend! Hail!

Then, slowly, they lowered their lights and began to press forward, moving close to Atiaran to hear her story. The common impulse was so simple and strong that Covenant took a few steps as well before he could recollect himself. Abruptly, he looked about him – focused his eyes on the faint glimmering stars, smelled the pervasive aroma of the graveling. The unanimous reaction of the Stonedown frightened him; he could not afford to lose himself in it. He wanted to turn away, but he needed to hear Berek's story, so he stayed where he was.

As soon as the people had settled themselves, Atiaran began.

'It came to pass that there was a great war in the eldest days, in the age that marks the beginning of the memory of mankind – before the Old Lords were born, before the Giants came across the Sunbirth Sea to make the alliance of Rockbrothers – a time before the Oath of Peace, before the Desolation and High Lord Kevin's last battle. It was a time when the Viles who sired the Demondim were a high and lofty race, and the Cavewights smithed and smelted beautiful metals to trade in open friendship with all the people in the Land. In that time, the Land was one great nation, and over it ruled a King and Queen. They were a hale pair, rich with love and honour, and for many years they held their sway in unison and peace.

'But after a time a shadow came over the heart of the King. He tasted the power of life and death over those who served him, and learned to desire it. Soon mastery became a lust with him, as necessary as food. His nights were spent in dark quests for more power, and by day he exercised that power, becoming hungrier and more cruel as the lust overcame him.

'But the Queen looked on her husband and was dismayed. She desired only that the health and fealty of the past years should return. But no appeal, no suasion or power of hers, could break the grip of cruelty that degraded the King. And at last, when she saw that the good of the Land would surely die if her husband were not halted, she broke with him, opposed his might with hers.

'Then there was war in the Land. Many who had felt the cut of the King's lash stood with the Queen. And many who hated murder and loved life joined her also. The chiefest of these was Berek – strongest and wisest of the Queen's champions. But the fear of the King was upon the Land, and whole cities rose up to fight for him, killing to protect their own slavery.

'Battle was joined across the Land, and for a time it seemed that the Queen would prevail. Her heroes were mighty of hand, and none were mightier than Berek, who was said to be a match for any King. But as the battle raged, a shadow, a grey cloud from the east, fell over the hosts. The Queen's defenders were stricken at heart, and their strength left them. But her enemies found a power of madness in the shadow. They forgot their humanity – they chopped and trampled and clawed and bit and maimed and defiled until their grey onslaught whelmed the heroes, and Berek's comrades broke one by one into despair and death. So the battle went until Berek was the last hater of the shadow left alive.

'But he fought on, heedless of his fate and the number of his foes, and souls fell dead under his sword like autumn leaves in a gale. At last, the King himself, filled with the fear and madness of the shadow, challenged Berek, and they fought. Berek stroked mightily, but the shadow turned his blade. So the contest was balanced until one blow of the King's axe cleft Berek's hand. Then Berek's sword fell to the ground, and he looked about him – looked and saw the shadow, and all his brave comrades dead. He cried a great cry of despair, and, turning, fled the battleground.

'Thus he ran, hunted by death, and the memory of the shadow was upon him. For three days he ran – never stopping, never resting – and for three days the King's host came behind him like a murderous beast, panting for blood. At the last of his strength and the extremity of his despair, he came to Mount Thunder. Climbing the rock-strewn slope, he threw himself down atop a great boulder and wept, saying, "Alas for the Earth. We are overthrown, and have no friend to redeem us. Beauty shall pass utterly from the Land."

'But the rock on which he lay replied, "There is a Friend for a heart with the wisdom to see it."

'"The stones are not my friends," cried Berek. "See, my enemies ride the Land, and no convulsion tears earth from under their befouling feet."

'"That may be," said the rock. "They are alive as much as you, and need the ground to stand upon. Yet there is a Friend for you in the Earth, if you will pledge your soul to its healing."

'Then Berek stood upon the rock, and beheld his enemies close upon him. He took the pledge, sealing it with the blood of his riven hand. The Earth replied with thunder; from the heights of the mountain came great stone Fire-Lions, devouring everything in their path. The King and all his host were laid waste, and Berek alone stood above the rampage on his boulder like a tall ship in the sea.

'When the rampage had passed, Berek did homage to the Lions of Mount Thunder, promising respect and communion and service for the Earth from himself and all the generations which followed him upon the Land. Wielding the first Earthpower, he made the Staff of Law from the wood of the One Tree, and with it began the healing of the Land. In the fullness of time, Berek Halfhand was given the name Heartthew, and he became the Lord-Fatherer, the first of the Old Lords. Those who followed his path flourished in the Land for two thousand years.'

For a long moment, there was silence over the gathering when Atiaran finished. Then together, as if their pulses moved to a single beat, the Stonedownors began to surge forward, stretching out their hands to touch her in appreciation. She spread her arms to hug as many of her friends as she could, and those who could not reach her embraced each other, sharing the oneness of their communal response.

7

LENA

Alone in the night – alone because he could not share the spontaneous embracing impulse of the Stonedown – Covenant felt suddenly trapped, threatened. A pressure of darkness cramped his lungs; he could not seem to get enough air. A leper's claustrophobia was on him, a leper's fear of crowds, of unpredictable behaviour. Berek! he panted with mordant intensity. These people wanted him to be a hero. With a stiff jerk of repudiation, he swung away from the gathering, went stalking in high dudgeon between the houses as if the Stonedownors had dealt him a mortal insult.

Berek! His chest heaved at the thought. Wild magic! It was ridiculous. Did not these people know he was a leper? Nothing could be less possible for him than the kind of heroism they saw in Berek Halfhand.

But Lord Foul had said, *He intends you to be my final foe. He chose you to destroy me.*

In stark dismay, he glimpsed the end toward which the path of the dream might be leading him; he saw himself drawn ineluctably into a confrontation with the Despiser.

He was trapped. Of course he could not play the hero in some dream war. He could not forget himself that much; forgetfulness was suicide. Yet he could not escape this dream without passing through it, could not return to reality without awakening. He knew what would happen to him if he stood still and tried to stay sane. Already, only this far from the lights of the gathering, he felt dark night beating toward him, circling on broad wings out of the sky at his head.

He lurched to a halt, stumbled to lean against a wall, caught his forehead in his hands.

I can't – he panted. All his hopes that this Land might conjure away his impotence, heal his sore heart somehow, fell into ashes.

Can't go on.

Can't stop.

What's happening to me?

Abruptly, he heard steps running toward him. He jumped erect, and saw Lena hurrying to join him. The swing of her graveling pot cast mad shadows across her figure as she moved. In a few more strides, she slowed, then stopped, holding her pot so that she could see him clearly. 'Thomas Covenant?' she asked tentatively. 'Are you not well?'

'No,' he lashed at her. 'I'm not *well*. Nothing's *well*, and it hasn't been since – ' the words caught in his throat for an instant – 'since I was divorced.' He glared at her, defying her to ask what a *divorce* was.

The way she held her light left most of her face in darkness; he could not see how she took his outburst. But some inner sensitivity seemed to guide her. When she spoke, she did not aggravate his pain with crude questions or condolences. Softly, she said, 'I know a place where you may be alone.'

He nodded sharply. Yes! He felt that his distraught nerves were about to snap. His throat was thick with violence. He did not want anyone to see what happened to him.

Gently, Lena touched his arm, led him away from the Stonedown toward the river. Under the dim starlight they reached the banks of the Mithil, then turned downriver. In half a mile, they came to an old stone bridge that gleamed with a damp, black reflection, as if it had just arisen from the water for Covenant's use. The suggestiveness of that thought made him stop. He saw the span as a kind of threshold; crises lurked in the dark hills beyond the far riverbank. Abruptly, he asked, 'Where are we going?' He was afraid that if he crossed that bridge he would not be able to recognize himself when he returned.

'To the far side,' Lena said. 'There you may be alone. Our people do not often cross the Mithil — it is said that the western mountains are not friendly, that the ill of Doom's Retreat which lies behind them has bent their spirit. But I have walked over all the western valley, stone-questing for *suru-pa-maerl* images, and have met no harm. There is a place nearby where you will not be disturbed.'

For all its appearance of age, the bridge had an untrustworthy look to Covenant's eyes. The unmortared joints seemed tenuous, held together only by dim, treacherous, star-cast shadows. When he stepped on to the bridge, he expected his foot to slip, the stones to tremble. But the arch was steady. At the top of the span, he paused to lean on the low side wall of the bridge and gaze down at the river.

The water flowed blackly under him, grumbling over its long prayer for absolution in the sea. And he looked into it as if he were asking it for courage. Could he not simply ignore the things that threatened him, ignore the opposing impossibilities, madnesses, of his situation — return to the Stonedown and pretend with blithe guile that he was Berek Halfhand reborn?

He could not. He was a leper; there were some lies he could not tell.

With a sharp twist of nausea, he found that he was pounding his fists on the wall. He snatched his hands up, tried to see if he had injured himself, but the dim stars showed him nothing.

Grimacing, he turned and followed Lena down to the western bank of the Mithil.

Soon they reached their destination. Lena led Covenant directly west for a distance, then up a steep hill to the right, and down a splintered ravine toward the river again. Carefully, they picked their way along the ragged bottom of the ravine as if they were balancing on the broken keel of a ship; its shattered hull rose up on either side of them, narrowing their horizons. A few trees stuck out of the sides like spars, and near the river the hulk lay aground on a swath of smooth sand which faded toward a flat rock promontory jutting into the river. The Mithil complained around this rock, as if annoyed by the brief constriction of its banks, and the sound blew up the ravine like a sea breeze moaning through a reefed wreck.

Lena halted on the sandy bottom. Kneeling, she scooped a shallow basin in the sand and emptied her pot of graveling into it. The fire-stones gave more light from the open basin, so that the ravine bottom was lit with yellow, and shortly Covenant felt a quiet warmth from the graveling. The touch of the stones' glow made him aware that the night was cool, a pleasant night for sitting around a fire. He squatted beside the graveling with a shiver like the last keen quivering of imminent hysteria.

After she had settled the graveling in the sand, Lena moved away toward the river. Where she stood on the promontory, the light barely reached her, and her form was dark; but Covenant could see that her face was raised to the heavens.

He followed her gaze up the black face of the mountains, and saw that the moon was rising. A silver sheen paled the stars along the rim of rock, darkening the valley with its shadow; but the shadow soon passed down the ravine, and moonlight fell on the river, giving it the appearance of old argent. And as the full moon arose from the mountains, it caught Lena, cast a white haze like a caress across her head and shoulders. Standing still by the river, she held her head up to the moon, and Covenant watched her with an odd grim jealousy, as if she were poised on a precipice that belonged to him.

Finally, when the moonlight had crossed the river into the eastern valley, Lena lowered her head and returned to the circle of the graveling. Without meeting Covenant's gaze, she asked softly, 'Shall I go?'

Covenant's palms itched as if he wanted to strike her for even suggesting that she might stay. But at the same time he was afraid of the night; he did not want to face it alone. Awkwardly, he got to his feet, paced a short distance away from her. Scowling up the hulk of the ravine, he fought to sound neutral as he said, 'What do you want?'

Her reply, when it came, was quiet and sure. 'I want to know more of you.'

He winced, ducked his head as if claws had struck at him out of the air. Then he snatched himself erect again.

'Ask.'

'Are you married?'

At that, he whirled to face her as if she had stabbed him in the back. Under the hot distress of his eyes and his bared teeth, she faltered, lowered her eyes and turned her head away. Seeing her uncertainty, he felt that his face had betrayed him again. He had not willed the snarling contortion of his features. He wanted to contain himself, not give way like this – not in front of her. Yet she aggravated his distress more than anything else he had encountered. Striving for self-control, he snapped, 'Yes. No. It doesn't matter. Why ask?'

Under his glare, Lena dropped to the sand, sat on her feet by the graveling, and watched him obliquely from beneath her eyebrows. When she said nothing immediately, he began to pace up and down the swath of sand. As he moved, he turned and pulled fiercely at his wedding ring.

After a moment, Lena answered with an air of irrelevance, 'There is a man who desires to marry me. He is Triock son of Thuler. Though I am not of age he woos me, so that when the time comes I will make no other choice. But if I were of age now I would not marry him. Oh, he is a good man in his way – a good Cattleherd, courageous in defence of his kine. And he is taller than most. But there are too many wonders in the world, too much power to know and beauty to share and to create – and I have not seen the Ranyhyn. I could not marry a Cattleherd who desires no more than a *suru-pa-maerl* for wife. Rather, I would go to the Loresraat as Atiaran my mother did, and I would stay and not falter no matter what trials the Lore put upon me, until I became a Lord. It is said that such things may happen. Do you think so?'

Covenant scarcely heard her. He was pacing out his agitation on the sand, enraged and undercut by an unwanted memory of Joan. Beside his lost love, Lena and the silver night of the Land failed of significance. The hollowness of his dream became suddenly obvious to his inner view, like an unveiled wilderland, a new permutation of the desolation of leprosy. This was not real – it was a torment that he inflicted upon himself in subconscious, involuntary revolt against his disease and loss. To himself, he groaned, Is it being out-cast that does this? Is being cut off such a shock? By hell! I don't need any more. He felt that he was on the edge of screaming. In an effort to control himself, he dropped to the sand with his back to Lena and hugged his knees as hard as he could. Careless of the unsteadiness of his voice, he asked, 'How do your people marry?'

In an uncomplicated tone, she said, 'It is a simple thing, when a man and a woman choose each other. After the two have become friends, if they wish to marry they tell the Circle of elders. And the elders take a season to assure themselves that the friendship of the two is secure, with no hidden jealousy or failed promise behind them to disturb their course in later years. Then the Stonedown gathers in the centre, and the elders take the two in their arms and ask, "Do you wish to share life, in joy and sorrow, work and rest, peace and struggle, to make the Land new?"

'The two answer, "Life with life, we choose to share the blessings and the service of the Earth." '

For a moment, her star-lit voice paused reverently. Then she went on, 'The Stonedown shouts together, "It is good! Let there be life and joy, and power while the years last!" Then the day is spent in joy and the new mates teach new games and dances and songs to the people, so that the happiness of the Stonedown is renewed, and communion and pleasure do not fail in the Land.'

She paused again shortly before continuing, 'The marriage of Atiaran my mother with Trell my father was a bold day. The elders who teach us have spoken of it many times. Everyday in the season of assurance, Trell climbed the mountains, searching forgotten paths and lost caves, hidden falls and new-broken crevices, for a stone of *orcrest* – a precious and many-powdered rock. For there was a drought upon the South Plains at that time, and the life of the Stonedown faltered in famine.

'Then, on the eve of the marriage, he found his treasure – a piece of *orcrest* smaller than a fist. And in the time of joy, after the speaking of the rituals, he and Atiaran my mother saved the Stonedown. While she sang a deep prayer to the Earth – a song known in the Loresraat but long forgotten among our people – he held the *orcrest* in his hand and broke it with the strength of his fingers. As the stone fell into dust, thunder rolled between the mountains, though there were no clouds, and one bolt of lightning sprang from the dust in his hand. Instantly, the blue sky turned black with thunderheads, and the rain began to fall. So the famine was broken, and the Stonedownors smiled on the coming days like a people reborn.'

Though he clenched his legs with all his strength, Covenant could not master his dizzy rage. Joan! Lena's tale struck him like mockery of his pains and failures.

I can't –

For a moment, his lower jaw shuddered under the effort he made to speak. Then he leaped up and dashed toward the river. As he covered the short distance, he bent and snatched a stone out of the sand. Springing onto the promontory, he hurled the stone with all the might of his body at the water.

Can't! –

A faint splash answered him, but at once the sound died under the heedless plaint of the river, and the ripples were swept away.

Softly at first, Covenant said to the river, 'I gave Joan a pair of riding boots for a wedding present.' Then, shaking his fists wildly, he shouted, 'Riding boots! Does my impotence surprise you?'

Unseen and incomprehending, Lena arose and moved toward Covenant, one hand stretched out as if to soothe the violence knotted in his back. But she paused a few steps away from him, searching for the right thing to say. After a moment, she whispered, 'What happened to your wife?'

Covenant's shoulders jerked. Thickly, he said, 'She's gone.'

'How did she die?'

'Not her – me. She left me. Divorced. Terminated. When I needed her.'

Indignantly, Lena wondered, 'Why would such a thing happen while there is life?'

'I'm not alive.' She heard fury climbing to the top of his voice. 'I'm a leper. Outcast unclean. Lepers are ugly and filthy. And abominable.'

His words filled her with horror and protest. 'How can it be?' she moaned. 'You are not – abominable. What world is it that dares treat you so?'

His muscles jumped still higher in his shoulders, as if his hands were locked on the throat of some tormenting demon. 'It's real. That is reality. Fact. The kind of thing that kills you if you don't believe it.' With a gesture of rejection toward the river, he gasped, 'This is a nightmare.'

Lena flared with sudden rage. 'I do not believe it. It may be that your world – but the Land – ah, the Land is real.'

Covenant's back clenched abruptly still, and he said with preter-natural quietness, 'Are you trying to drive me crazy?'

His ominous tone startled her, chilled her. For an instant, her courage stumbled; she felt the river and the ravine closing around her like the jaws of a trap. Then Covenant whirled and struck her a stinging slap across the face.

The force of the blow sent her staggering back into the light of the graveling. He followed quickly, his face contorted in a wild grin. As she caught her balance, got one last, clear, terrified look at him, she felt sure that he meant to kill her. The thought paralysed her. She stood dumb and helpless while he approached.

Reaching her, he knotted his hands in the front of her shift and rent the fabric like a veil. She could not move. For an instant, he stared at her, at her high, perfect breasts and her short slip, with grim triumph in his eyes, as though he had just exposed some foul plot. Then he gripped her shoulder with his left hand and tore away her slip with his right, forcing her down to the sand as he uncovered her.

Now she wanted to resist, but her limbs would not move; she was helpless with anguish.

A moment later, he dropped the burden of his weight on her chest, and her loins were stabbed with a wild, white fire that broke her silence, made her scream. But even as she cried out she knew that it was too late for her. Something that her people thought of as a gift had been torn from her.

But Covenant did not feel like a taker. His climax flooded him as if he had fallen into a Mithil of molten fury. Suffocating in passion, he almost swooned. Then time seemed to pass him by, and he lay still for moments that might have been hours for all he knew – hours during which his world could have crumbled, unheeded.

At last he remembered the softness of Lena's body under him, felt the low shake of her sobbing. With an effort, he heaved himself up and to his feet. When he looked down at her in the graveling light, he saw the blood on her loins. Abruptly, his head became giddy, unbalanced, as though he were peering over a precipice. He turned and hurried with a shambling, unsteady gait toward the river, pitched himself flat on the rock, and vomited the weight of his guts into the water. And the Mithil erased his vomit as cleanly as if nothing had happened.

He lay still on the rock while the exhaustion of his exacerbated nerves overcame him. He did not hear Lena rise, gather the shreds of her clothing, speak, or climb away out of the shattered ravine. He heard nothing but the long lament of the river – saw nothing but the ashes of his burnt-out passion – felt nothing but the dampness of the rock on his cheeks like tears.

8

THE DAWN OF THE MESSAGE

The hard bones of the rock slowly brought Thomas Covenant out of dreams of close embraces. For a time, he drifted on the rising current of the dawn – surrounded on his ascetic, sufficient bed by the searching self-communion of the river, the fresh odours of day, the wheeling cries of birds as they sprang into the sky. While his self-awareness returned, he felt at peace, harmonious with his context; and even the uncompromising hardness of the stone seemed apposite to him, a proper part of a whole morning.

His first recollections of the previous night were of orgasm, heart-rending, easing release and satisfaction so precious that he would have been willing to coin his soul to make such things part of his real life. For a long moment of joy, he re-experienced that sensation. Then he remembered that to get it he had hurt Lena.

Lena!

He rolled over, sat up in the dawn. The sun had not yet risen above the mountains, but enough light reflected into the valley from the plains for him to see that she was gone.

She had left her fire burning in the sand up the ravine from him. He lurched to his feet, scanned the ravine and both banks of the Mithil for some sign of her – or, his imagination leaped, of Stonedownors seeking vengeance. His heart thudded; all those rock-strong people would not be interested in his explanations or apologies. He searched for evidence of pursuit like a fugitive.

But the dawn was as undisturbed as if it contained no people, no crimes or desires for punishment. Gradually, Covenant's panic receded. After a last look around, he began to prepare for whatever lay ahead of him.

He knew that he should get going at once, hurry along the river toward the relative safety of the plains. But he was a leper, and could not undertake solitary journeys lightly. He needed to organize himself.

He did not think about Lena; he knew instinctively that he could not afford to think about her. He had violated her trust, violated the trust of the Stonedown; that was as close to his last night's rage as he could go. It was past, irrevocable – and illusory, like the dream itself. With an effort that made him tremble, he put it behind him. Almost by accident on Kevin's Watch, he had discovered the answer to all such insanity: keep moving, don't think about it, survive. That answer was even more necessary now. His 'Berek' fear of the previous evening seemed relatively unimportant. His resemblance to a legendary hero was only part of a dream, not a compulsory fact or demand. He put it behind him also. Deliberately, he gave himself a thorough scrutiny and VSE.

When he was sure that he had no hidden injuries, no dangerous purple spots, he moved out to the end of the promontory. He was still trembling. He needed more discipline, mortification; his hands shook as if they could not steady themselves without his usual shaving ritual. But the penknife in his pocket was inadequate for shaving. After a moment, he took a deep breath, gripped the edge of the rock, and dropped himself, clothes and all, into the river for a bath.

The current tugged at him seductively, urging him to float off under blue skies into a spring day. But the water was too cold; he could only stand the chill long enough to duck and thrash in the stream for a moment. Then he hauled himself on to the rock and stood up, blowing spray off his face. Water from his hair kept running into his eyes, blinding him momentarily to the fact that Atiaran stood on the sand by the graveling. She contemplated him with a grave, firm glance.

Covenant froze, dripping as if he had been caught in the middle of a flagrant act. For a moment, he and Atiaran measured each other across the sand and rock. When she started to speak, he cringed inwardly, expecting her to revile, denounce, hurl imprecations. But she only said, 'Come to the graveling. You must dry yourself.'

In surprise, he scrutinized her tone with all the high alertness of his senses, but he could hear nothing in it except determination and quiet sadness. Suddenly he guessed that she did not know what had happened to her daughter.

Breathing deeply to control the labour of his heart, he moved forward and huddled down next to the graveling. His mind raced with improbable speculations to account for Atiaran's attitude; but he kept his face to the warmth and remained silent, hoping that she would say something to let him know where he stood with her.

Almost at once, she murmured, 'I knew where to find you. Before I returned from speaking with the Circle of elders, Lena told Trell that you were here.'

She stopped, and Covenant forced himself to ask, 'Did you see her?'

He knew that it was a suspicious question. But Atiaran answered simply, 'No. She went to spend the night with a friend. She only called out her message as she passed our home.'

Then for several long moments Covenant sat still and voiceless, amazed by the implications of what Lena had done. Only called out! At first, his brain reeled with thoughts of relief. He was safe – temporarily, at least. With her reticence, Lena had purchased precious time for him. Clearly, the people of this Land were prepared to make sacrifices –

After another moment, he understood that she had not made her sacrifice for him. He could not imagine that she cared for his personal safety. No, she chose to protect him because he was a Berek-figure, a bearer of messages to the Lords. She did not want his purpose to be waylaid by the retribution of the Stonedown. This was her contribution to the defence of the Land from Lord Foul the Grey Slayer.

It was a heroic contribution. In spite of his discipline, his fear, he sensed the violence Lena had done herself for the sake of his message. He seemed to see her huddling naked behind a rock in the foothills throughout that bleak night, shunning for the first time in her young life the open arms of her community – bearing the pain and shame of her riven body alone so that he would not be required to answer for it. An unwanted memory of the blood on her loins writhed in him.

His shoulders bunched to strangle the thought. Through locked teeth, he breathed to himself, I've got to go to the Council.

When he had steadied himself, he asked grimly, 'What did the elders say?'

'There was little for them to say,' she replied in a flat voice. 'I told them what I know of you – and of the Land's peril. They agreed that I must guide you to Lord's Keep. For that purpose I have come to you now. See – ' she indicated two packs lying near her feet – 'I am ready. Trell my husband has given me his blessing. It grieves me to go without giving my love to Lena my daughter, but time is urgent. You have not told me all your message, but I sense that from this day forward each delay is hazardous. The elders will give thought to the defence of the plains. We must go.'

Covenant met her eyes, and this time he understood the sad determination in them. She was afraid, and did not believe that she would live to return to her family. He felt a sudden pity for her. Without fully comprehending what he said, he tried to reassure her. 'Things aren't as bad as they might be. A Cavewight has found the Staff of Law, and I gather he doesn't really know how to use it. Somehow, the Lords have got to get it away from him.'

But his attempt miscarried. Atiaran stiffened and said, 'Then the life of the Land is in our speed. Alas that we cannot go to the Ranyhyn for help. But the Ramen have little countenance for the affairs of the Land, and no Ranyhyn has been ridden, save by Lord or Bloodguard, since the age began. We must walk, Thomas Covenant, and Revelstone is three hundred long leagues distant. Is your clothing dry? We must be on our way.'

Covenant was ready; he had to get away from this place. He gathered himself to his feet and said, 'Fine. Let's go.'

However, the look that Atiaran gave him as he stood held something unresolved. In a low voice as if she were mortifying herself, she said, 'Do you trust me to guide you, Thomas Covenant? You do not know me. I failed in the Loresraat.'

Her tone seemed to imply not that she was undependable, but that he had the right to judge her. But he was in no position to judge anyone. 'I trust you,' he rasped. 'Why not? You said yourself – ' He faltered, then forged ahead. 'You said yourself that I come to save or damn the Land.'

'True,' she returned simply. 'But you do not have the sting of a servant of the Grey Slayer. My heart tells me that it is the fate of the Land to put faith in you, for good or ill.'

'Then let's go.' He took the pack that Atiaran lifted toward him and shrugged his shoulders into the straps. But before she put on her own pack, she knelt to the graveling in the sand. Passing her hand over the fire-stones, she began a low humming – a soft tune that sounded ungainly in her mouth, as if she were unaccustomed to it – and under her waving gestures the yellow light faded. In a moment, the stones had lapsed into a pale, pebbly grey, as if she had lulled them to sleep, and their heat dissipated. When they were cold, she scooped them into their pot, covered it, and stored it in her pack.

The sight reminded Covenant of all the things he did not know about this dream. As Atiaran got to her feet, he said, 'There's only one thing I need. I want you to talk to me – tell me all about the Loresraat and the Lords and everything I might be interested in.' Then because he could not give her the reason for his request, he concluded lamely, 'It'll pass the time.'

With a quizzical glance at him, she settled her pack on her shoulders. 'You are strange, Thomas Covenant. I think you are too eager to know my ignorance. But what I know I will tell you – though without your raiment and speech it would pass my belief to think you an utter stranger to the Land. Now come. There are treasure-berries aplenty along our way this morning. They will serve as breakfast. The food we carry must be kept for the chances of the road.'

Covenant nodded, and followed her as she began climbing out of the ravine. He was relieved to be moving again, and the distance passed quickly. Soon they were down by the river, approaching the bridge.

Atiaran strode straight on to the bridge, but when she reached the top of the span she stopped. A moment after Covenant joined her, she gestured north along the Mithil toward the distant plains. 'I tell you openly, Thomas Covenant,' she said, 'I do not mean to take a direct path to Lord's Keep. The Keep is west of north from us, three hundred leagues as the eye sees across the Centre Plains of the Land. There many people live, in Stonedown and Woodhelven, and it might chance that both road and help could be found to take us where we must go. But we could not hope for horses. They are rare in the Land, and few folk but those of Revelstone know them.

'It is in my heart that we may save time by journeying north, across the Mithil when it swings east, and so into the land of Andelain, where the fair Hills are the flower of all the beauties of the Earth. There we will reach the Soulsease River, and it may be that we will find a boat to carry us up that sweet stream, past the westland of Trothgard, where the promises of the Lords are kept, to great Revelstone itself, the Lord's Keep. All travellers are blessed by the currents of the Soulsease, and our journey will end sooner if we find a carrier there. But we must pass within fifty leagues of Mount Thunder – Gravin Threndor.' As she said the ancient name, a shiver seemed to run through her voice. 'It is there or nowhere that the

Staff of Law has been found, and I do not wish to go even as close as Andelain to the wrong wielder of such might.'

She paused for a moment, hesitating, then went on: 'There would be rue unending if a corrupt Cavewight gained possession of the ring you bear – the evil ones are quick to unleash such forces as wild magic. And even were the Cavewight unable to use the ring, I fear that ur-viles still live under Mount Thunder. They are lore-wise creatures, and white gold would not surpass them.

'But time rides urgently on us, and we must save it where we may. And there is another reason for seeking the passage of Andelain at this time of year – if we hasten. But I should not speak of it. You will see it and rejoice, if no ill befall us on our way.'

She fixed her eyes on Covenant, turning all their inward strength on him, so that he felt, as he had the previous evening, that she was searching for his weakness. He feared that she would discover his night's work in his face, and he had to force himself to meet her gaze until she said, 'Now tell me, Thomas Covenant. Will you go where I lead?'

Feeling both shamed and relieved, he answered, 'Let's get on with it. I'm ready.'

'That is well.' She nodded, started again toward the east bank. But Covenant spent a moment looking down at the river. Its soft plaint sounded full of echoes, and they seemed to moan at him with serene irony, *Does my impotence surprise you?* A cloud of trouble darkened his face, but he clenched himself, rubbed his ring, and stalked away after Atiaran, leaving the Mithil to flow on its way like a stream of forgetfulness or a border of death.

As the sun climbed over the eastern mountains, Atiaran and Covenant were moving north, downstream along the river toward the open plains. At first, they travelled in silence. Covenant was occupied with short forays into the hills to his right, gathering *aliantha*. He found their tangy peach flavour as keenly delicious as before; a fine essence in their juice made hunger and taste into poignant sensations. He refrained from taking all the berries off any one bush – he had to range away from Atiaran's sternly forward track often to get enough food to satisfy him – and he scattered the seeds faithfully, as Lena had taught him. Then he had to trot to catch up with Atiaran. In this way, he passed nearly a league, and when he finished eating, the valley was perceptibly broader. He made one last side trip – this time to the river for a drink – then hurried to take a position beside Atiaran.

Something in the set of her features seemed to ask him not to talk, so he disciplined himself to stillness with survival drills. Then he strove to regain the mechanical ticking stride which had carried him so far from Haven Farm. Atiaran appeared resigned to a trek of three hundred leagues, but he was not. He sensed that he would need all his leper's skills to hike for even a day without injuring himself. In the rhythm of his steps, he struggled to master the unruliness of his situation.

He knew that eventually he would have to explain his peculiar danger to Atiaran. He might need her help, at least her comprehension. But not yet – not yet. He did not have enough control.

But after a while, she changed direction, began angling away from the river up into the north-eastern foothills. This close to the mountains, the hills were steep and involuted, and she seemed to be following no path. Behind her, Covenant scrambled up and staggered down the rocky, twisting slopes, though the natural lay of the land tried constantly to turn them eastward. The sides of his neck started to ache from the weight of his pack, and twitches jumped like incipient cramps under his shoulder blades. Soon he was panting heavily, and muttering against the folly of Atiaran's choice of directions.

Toward midmorning, she stopped to rest on the downward curve of a high hill. She remained standing, but Covenant's muscles were trembling from exertion, and he dropped to the ground beside her, breathing hard. When he had regained himself a little, he panted, 'Why didn't we go around, north past these hills, then east? Save all this up and down?'

'Two reasons,' she said shortly. 'Ahead there is a long file north through the hills – easy walking so that we will save time. And again – ' she paused while she looked around – 'we may lose something. Since we left the bridge, there has been a fear in me that we are followed.'

'Followed?' Covenant jerked out. 'Who?'

'I do not know. It may be that the spies of the Grey Slayer are already abroad. It is said that his highest servants, his Ravers, cannot die while he yet lives. They have no bodies of their own, and their spirits wander until they find living beings which they can master. Thus they appear as animals or humans, as chance allows, corrupting the life of the Land. But it is my hope that we will not be followed through these hills. Are you rested? We must go.'

After adjusting her robe under the straps of her pack, she set off again down the slope. A moment later, Covenant went groaning after her.

For the rest of the morning, he had to drive himself to persevere in the face of exhaustion. His legs grew numb with fatigue, and the weight on his back seemed to constrict his breathing so that he panted as if he were suffocating. He was not conditioned for such work; lurching unsteadily, he stumbled up and down the hills. Time and again, only his boots and tough trousers saved him from damage. But Atiaran moved ahead of him smoothly, with hardly a wasted motion or false step, and the sight of her drew him onward.

But finally she turned down into a long ravine that ran north as far as he could see, like a cut in the hills. A small stream flowed down the centre of the file, and they stopped beside it to drink, bathe their faces, and rest. This time, they both took off their packs and dropped to the ground. Groaning deeply, Covenant lay flat on his back with his eyes closed.

For a while he simply relaxed, listened to his own hoarse respiration until it softened and he could hear behind it the wind whistling softly. Then he opened his eyes to take in his surroundings.

He found himself looking up four thousand feet at Kevin's Watch.

The view was unexpected; he sat up as if to look at it more closely. The Watch was just east and south from him, and it leaned out into the sky from its cliff face like an accusing finger. At that distance, the stone looked black and fatal, and it seemed to hang over the file down which he and Atiaran would walk. It reminded him of the Despiser and darkness.

'Yes,' Atiaran said, 'that is Kevin's Watch. There stood Kevin Landwaster, High Lord and wielder of the Staff, direct descendant of Berek Halfhand, in the last battle against the Grey Slayer. It is said that there he knew defeat, and mad grief. In the blackness which whelmed his heart he – the most powerful champion in all the ages of the Land – even he, High Lord Kevin, sworn Earthfriend, brought down the Destruction, the end of all things in the Land for many generations. It is not a good omen that you have been there.'

As she spoke, Covenant turned toward her, and saw that she was gazing, not up at the rock, but inward, as if she were considering how badly she would have failed in Kevin's place. Then, abruptly, she gathered herself and stood up. 'But there is no help for it,' she said. 'Our path lies under the shadow of the Watch for many leagues. Now we must go on.' When Covenant moaned, she commanded, 'Come. We dare not go slowly, for fear that we will be too late at the end. Our way is easiest now. And if it will help your steps, I will talk to you of the Land.'

Reaching for his pack, Covenant asked, 'Are we still being followed?'

'I do not know. I have neither heard nor seen any sign. But my heart misgives me. I feel some wrong upon our path this day.'

Covenant pulled on his pack and staggered wincing to his feet. His heart misgave him also, for reasons of its own. Here under Kevin's Watch, the humming wind sounded like the thrum of distant vulture wings. Settling the pack straps on his raw shoulders, he bent under the weight, and went with Atiaran down the bottom of the file.

For the most part, the cut was straight and smooth-floored, though never more than fifteen feet across. However, there was room beside the narrow stream for Atiaran and Covenant to walk together. As they travelled, pausing at every rare *aliantha* to pick and eat a few berries, Atiaran sketched in a few of the wide blanks in Covenant's knowledge of the Land.

'It is difficult to know how to speak of it,' she began. 'Everything is part of everything, and each question which I can answer raises three more which I cannot. My lore is limited to what all learn quickly in their first years in the Loresraat. But I will tell you what I can.

'Berek Heartthew's son was Damelon Giantfriend, and his son was Loric Vilesilencer, who stemmed the corruption of the Demondim, rendering them impotent.' As she spoke, her voice took on a cadence that reminded Covenant of her singing. She did not recite dry facts; she narrated a tale that was of sovereign importance to her, to the Land. 'And Kevin, whom we name Landwaster more in pity than in condemnation of his despair, was the son of Loric, and High Lord in his place when the Staff was passed on. For a thousand years, Kevin stood at the head of the Council, and he extended the Earthfriendship of the Lords beyond anything known before in the Land, and he was greatly honoured.

'In his early years, he was wise as well as mighty and knowledgeable. When he saw the first hints that the ancient shadow was alive, he looked far into the chances of the future, and what he saw gave him cause to fear. Therefore he gathered all his Lore into Seven Wards –

> Seven Wards of ancient Lore
> For Land's protection, wall and door –

and hid them, so that his knowledge would not pass from the Land even if he and the Old Lords fell.

'For many long years the Land lived on in peace. But during that time, the Grey Slayer rose up in the guise of a friend. In some ways, the eyes of Kevin were blinded, and he accepted his enemy as a friend and Lord. And for that reason, the Lords and all their works passed from the Earth.

'But when Kevin's betrayal had brought defeat and Desolation, and the Land had lain under the bane for many generations, and had begun to heal, it called out to the people who lived in hiding in the Wastes and the Northern Climbs. Slowly, they returned. As the years passed, and the homes and villages became secure, some folk travelled, exploring the Land in search of half-remembered legends. And when they finally braved Giant Woods, they came to the old land of Seareach, and found that the Giants, Rockbrothers of the people of the Land, had survived the Ritual of Desecration.

'There are many songs, old and new, praising the fealty of the Giants – with good reason. When the Giants learned that people had returned to the Land, they began a great journey, sojourning over all the Land to every new Stonedown and Woodhelven, teaching the tale of Kevin's defeat and renewing the old Rockbrotherhood. Then, taking with them those people who chose to come, the Giants ended their journey at Revelstone, the ageless castle-city which they had riven out of the rock of the mountain for High Lord Damelon, as surety of the bond between them.

'At Revelstone, the Giants gave a gift to the gathered people. They revealed the First Ward, the fundamental store of the beginning of Kevin's Lore. For he had trusted it to the Giants before the last battle. And the people accepted that Ward and consecrated themselves, swearing Earthfriendship and loyalty to the Power and beauty of the Land.

'One thing more they swore – Peace, a calmness of self to protect the Land from destructive emotions like those that maddened Kevin. For it was clear to all there gathered that power is a dreadful thing, and that the knowledge of power dims the seeing of the wise. When they beheld the First Ward, they feared a new Desecration. Therefore they swore to master the Lore, so that they might heal the Land – and to master themselves, so that they would not fall into the anger and despair which made Kevin his own worst foe.

'These oaths were carried back to all the people of the Land, and all the people swore. Then the few who were chosen at Revelstone for the great work took the First Ward to Kurash Plenethor, Stricken Stone, where the gravest damage of the last battle was done. They named the land Trothgard, as a token of their promise of healing, and there they founded the Loresraat – a place of learning where they sought to regain the knowledge and power of the Old Lords, and to train themselves in the Oath of Peace.'

Then Atiaran fell silent, and she and Covenant walked down the file in stillness textured by the whispering of the stream and by the occasional calls of the birds. He found that her tale did help him to keep up their pace. It caused him to forget himself somewhat, forget the raw ache of his shoulders and feet. And her voice seemed to give him strength; her tale was like a promise that any exhaustion borne in the Land's service would not be wasted.

After a time, he urged her to continue. 'Can you tell me about the Loresraat?'

The bitter vehemence of her reply surprised him. 'Do you remind me that I am of all people the least worthy to talk of these matters? You, Thomas Covenant, Unbeliever and white gold wielder – do you reproach me?'

He could only stare dumbly at her, unable to fathom the years of struggling that filled her spacious eyes.

'I do not need your reminders.'

But a moment later she faced forward again, her expression set to meet the north. 'Now you reproach me indeed,' she said. 'I am too easily hurt that the whole world knows what I know so well myself. Like a guilty woman, I fail to believe the innocence of others. Please pardon me – you should receive better treatment than this.'

Before he could respond, she forged ahead. 'In this way I describe the Loresraat. It stands in Trothgard in the Valley of Two Rivers, and it is a community of study and learning. To that place go all who will, and there they consecrate themselves to Earthfriendship and the Lore of the Old Lords.

'This Lore is a deep matter, not mastered yet despite all the years and effort that have been given to it. The chiefest problem is translation, for the language of the Old Lords was not like ours, and the words which are simple at one place are difficult at another. And after translation, the Lore must be interpreted, and then the skills to use it must be learned. When I – ' she faltered briefly ' – when I studied there, the Lorewardens who taught me said that all the Loresraat had not yet passed the surface of Kevin's mighty knowledge. And that knowledge is only a seventh part of the whole, the First Ward of Seven.'

Covenant heard an unwitting echo of Foul's contempt in her words, and it made him listen to her still more closely.

'Easiest of translation,' she went on, 'has been the Warlore, the arts of battle and defence. But there much skill is required. Therefore one part of the Loresraat deals solely with those who would follow the Sword, and join the Warward of Lord's Keep. But there have been no wars in our time, and in my years at the Loresraat the Warward numbered scarcely two thousand men and women.

'Thus the chief work of the Loresraat is in teaching and studying the language and knowledge of the Earthpower. First, the new learners are taught the history of the Land, the prayers and songs and legends – in time, all that is known of the Old Lords and their struggles against the Grey Slayer. Those who master this become Lorewardens. They teach others, or search out new knowledge and power from the First Ward. The price of such mastery is high – such purity and determination and insight and courage are required by Kevin's Lore – and there are some,' she said as if she were resolved not to spare her own feelings, 'who cannot match the need. I failed when that which I learned made my heart quail – when the Lorewardens led me to see, just a little way, into the Despite of the Grey Slayer. That I could not bear, and so I broke my devotion, and returned to Mithil Stonedown to use the little that I knew for my people. And now, when I have forgotten so much, my trial is upon me.'

She sighed deeply, as if it grieved her to consent to her fate. 'But that is no matter. In the Loresraat, those who follow and master both Sword and Staff, who earn a place in the Warward among the Lorewardens, and who do not turn away to pursue private dreams in isolation, as do the Unfettered – those brave hearts are named Lords, and they join the Council which guides the healing and protection of the Land. From their number, they choose the High Lord, to act for all as the Lore requires:

> And one High Lord to wield the Law
> To keep all uncorrupt Earth's Power's core.

'In my years at the Loresraat, the High Lord was Variol Tamarantha-mate son of the Pentil. But he was old, even for a Lord, and the Lords live longer than other folk – and our Stonedown has had no news of Revelstone or Loresraat for many years. I do not know who leads the Council now.'

Without thinking, Covenant said, 'Prothall son of Dwillian.'

'Ah!' Atiaran gasped. 'He knows me. As a Lorewarden he taught me the first prayers. He will remember that I failed, and will not trust my mission.' She shook her head in pain. Then, after a moment's reflection, she added, 'And you have known this. You know all. Why do you seek to shame the rudeness of my knowledge? That is not kind.'

'Hellfire!' Covenant snapped. Her reproach made him suddenly angry. 'Everybody in this whole business, you and – ' but he could not bring himself to say Lena's name – 'and everyone keep accusing me of being some sort of closet expert. I tell you, I don't know one damn thing about this unless someone explains it to me. I'm not your bloody Berek.'

Atiaran gave him a look full of scepticism – the fruit of long, harsh self-doubt – and he felt an answering urge to prove himself in some way. He stopped, pulled himself erect against the weight of his pack. 'This is the message of Lord Foul the Despiser: "Say to the Council of Lords, and to High Lord Prothall son of Dwillian, that the uttermost limit of their span of days upon the Land is seven times seven years from the present time. Before the end of those days are numbered, I will have the command of life and death in my hand."'

Abruptly, he caught himself. His words seemed to beat down the file like ravens, and he felt a hot leper's shame in his cheeks, as though he had defiled the day. For an instant, complete silence surrounded him – the birds were as silent as if they had been stricken out of the sky, and the stream appeared motionless. In the noon heat, his flesh was slick with sweat.

For that instant, Atiaran gaped aghast at him. Then she cried, '*Melenkurion abatha!* Do not speak it until you must! I cannot preserve us from such ills.'

The silence shuddered, passed; the stream began chattering again, and a bird swooped by overhead. Covenant wiped his forehead with an unsteady hand. 'Then stop treating me as if I'm something I'm not.'

'How can I?' she responded heavily. 'You are closed to me, Thomas Covenant. I do not see you.'

She used the word *see*, as if it meant something he did not understand. 'What do you mean, you don't see me?' he demanded sourly. 'I'm standing right in front of you.'

'You are closed to me,' she repeated. 'I do not know whether you are well or ill.'

He blinked at her uncertainly, then realized that she had unwittingly given him a chance to tell her about his leprosy. He took the opportunity; he was angry enough for the job now. Putting aside his incomprehension, he grated, 'Ill, of course. I'm a leper.'

At this, Atiaran groaned as if he had just confessed to a crime. 'Then woe to the Land, for you have the wild magic and can undo us all.'

'Will you cut that out?' Brandishing his left fist, he gritted, 'It's just a ring. To remind me of everything I have to live without. It's got no more – wild magic – than a rock.'

'The Earth is the source of all power,' whispered Atiaran.

With an effort, Covenant refrained from shouting his frustration at her. She was talking past him, reacting to him as if his words meant something he had not intended. 'Back up a minute,' he said. 'Let's get this straight. I said I was ill. What does that mean to you? Don't you even have diseases in this world?'

For an instant, her lips formed the word *diseases*. Then a sudden fear tightened her face, and her gaze sprang up past Covenant's left shoulder.

He turned to see what frightened her. He found nothing behind him; but as he scanned the west rim of the file, he heard a scrabbling noise. Pebbles and shale fell into the cut.

'The follower!' Atiaran cried. 'Run! Run!'

Her urgency caught him; he spun and followed her as fast as he could go down the file.

Momentarily, he forgot his weakness, the weight of his pack, the heat. He pounded after Atiaran's racing heels as if he could hear his pursuer poised above him on the rim of the file. But soon his lungs seemed to be tearing under the exertion, and he began to lose his balance. When he stumbled, his fragile body almost struck the ground.

Atiaran shouted, 'Run!' but he hauled up short, swung trembling around to face the pursuit.

A leaping figure flashed over the edge of the cut and dropped toward him. He dodged away from the plummet, flung up his arms to ward off the figure's swinging arm.

As the attacker passed, he scored the backs of Covenant's fingers with a knife. Then he hit the ground and rolled, came to his feet with his back to the east wall of the cut, his knife weaving threats in front of him.

The sunlight seemed to etch everything starkly in Covenant's vision. He saw the unevenness of the wall, the shadows stretched under them like rictus.

The attacker was a young man with a powerful frame and dark hair – unmistakably a Stonedownor, though taller than most. His knife was made of stone, and woven into the shoulders of his tunic was his family insignia, a pattern like crossed lightning. Rage and hate strained his features as if his skull were splitting. 'Raver!' he yelled. 'Ravisher!'

He approached swinging his blade. Covenant was forced to retreat until he stood in the stream, ankle-deep in cool water.

Atiaran was running toward them, though she was too far away to intervene between Covenant and the knife.

Blood welled from the backs of his fingers. His pulse throbbed in the cuts, throbbed in his fingertips.

He heard Atiaran's commanding shout: 'Triock!'

The knife slashed closer. He saw it as clearly as if it were engraved on his eyeballs.

His pulse pounded in his fingertips.

The young man gathered himself for a killing thrust.

Atiaran shouted again, 'Triock! Are you mad? You swore the Oath of Peace!'

In his fingertips?

He snatched up his hand, stared at it. But his sight was suddenly dim with awe. He could not grasp what was happening.

That's impossible, he breathed in the utterest astonishment. Impossible.

His numb, leprosy-ridden fingers were aflame with pain.

Atiaran neared the two men and stopped, dropped her pack to the ground. She seemed to place a terrible restraint on Triock; he thrashed viciously where he stood. As if he were choking on passion, he spat out, 'Kill him! Raver!'

'I forbid!' cried Atiaran. The intensity of her command struck Triock like a physical blow. He staggered back a step, then threw up his head and let out a hoarse snarl of frustration and rage.

Her voice cut sharply through the sound. 'Loyalty is due. You took the Oath. Do you wish to damn the Land?'

Triock shuddered. In one convulsive movement, he flung down his knife so that it drove itself to the hilt in the ground by his feet. Straightening fiercely, he hissed at Atiaran, 'He has ravished Lena. Last night.'

Covenant could not grasp the situation. Pain was a sensation, a splendour, his fingers had forgotten; he had no answer to it except, Impossible. Impossible. Unnoticed, his blood ran red and human down his wrist.

A spasm twitched across his face. Darkness gathered in the air about him; the atmosphere of the file seethed as if it were full of beating wings, claws which flashed toward his face. He groaned, 'Impossible.'

But Atiaran and Triock were consumed with each other, their eyes avoided him as if he were a plague spot. As Triock's words penetrated her, she crumbled to her knees, covered her face with her hands, and dropped her forehead to the ground. Her shoulders shook as if she were sobbing, though she made no sound; and over her anguish he said bitterly, 'I found her in the hills when this day's sun first touched the plains. You know my love for her. I observed her at the gathering, and was not made happy by the manner in which this fell stranger dazzled her. It wrung my heart that she should be so touched by a man whose comings and goings no one could ever know. So, late at night, I enquired of Trell your husband, and learned that she said she meant to sleep with a friend – Terass daughter of Annoria. Then I enquired of Terass – and she knew nothing of Lena's purpose. Then a shadow of fear came upon me – for when have any of the people been liars? I spent the whole of the night searching for her. And at first light I found her, her shift rent and blood about her. She strove to flee from me, but she was weak from cold and pain and sorrow, and in a moment she clung in my arms and told me what – what this Raver had done.

'Then I took her to Trell her father. While he cared for her I went away, purposing to kill the stranger. When I saw you, I followed, believing that my purpose was yours also – that you led him into the hills to destroy him. But you mean to save him – him, the ravisher of Lena your daughter! How has he corrupted your heart? You forbid? Atiaran Trell-mate! She was a child fair enough to make a man weep for joy at seeing her – broken without consent or care. Answer me. What have Oaths to do with us?'

The wild, rabid swirl of dark wings forced Covenant down until he huddled in the stream. Images reeled across his brain – memories of the leprosarium, of doctors saying, *You cannot hope.* He had been hit by a police car. He had walked into town to pay his phone bill – to pay his phone bill in person. In a voice abstract with horror, he murmured, 'Can't happen.'

Slowly, Atiaran raised her head and spread her arms, as if opening her breast to an impaling thrust from the sky. Her face was carved with pain, and her eyes were dark craters of grief, looking inward on her compromised humanity. 'Trell, help me,' she breathed weakly. Then her voice gathered strength, and her anguish seemed to make the air about her ache. 'Alas! Alas for the young in the world! Why is the burden of hating ill so hard to bear? Ah, Lena my daughter! I see what you have done. I understand. It is a brave deed, worthy of praise and pride! Forgive me that I cannot be with you in this trial.'

But after a while, her gaze swung outward again. She climbed unsteadily to her feet, and stood swaying for a moment before she rasped hoarsely, 'Loyalty is due. I forbid your vengeance.'

'Does he go unpunished?' protested Triock.

'There is peril in the Land,' she answered. 'Let the Lords punish him.' A taste of blood sharpened her voice. 'They will know what to think of a stranger who attacks the innocent.' Then her weakness returned. 'The matter is beyond me. Triock, remember your Oath.' She gripped her shoulders, knotted her fingers in the leaf pattern of her robe as if to hold her sorrow down.

Triock turned toward Covenant. There was something broken in the young man's face – a shattered or wasted capacity for contentment, joy. He snarled with the force of an anathema, 'I know you, Unbeliever. We will meet again.' Then abruptly he began moving away. He accelerated until he was sprinting, beating out his reproaches on the hard floor of the file. In a moment, he reached a place where the west wall sloped away, and then he was out of sight, gone from the cut in the hills.

'Impossible,' Covenant murmured. 'Can't happen. Nerves don't regenerate.' But his fingers hurt as if they were being crushed with pain. Apparently nerves did regenerate in the Land. He wanted to scream against the darkness and the terror, but he seemed to have lost all control of his throat, voice, self.

As if from a distance made great by abhorrence or pity, Atiaran said, 'You have made of my heart a wilderland.'

'Nerves don't regenerate.' Covenant's throat clenched as if he were gagging, but he could not scream. 'They don't.'

'Does that make you free?' she demanded softly, bitterly. 'Does it justify your crime?'

'Crime?' He heard the word like a knife thrust through the beating wings. 'Crime?' His blood ran from the cuts as if he were a normal man, but the flow was decreasing steadily. With a sudden convulsion, he caught hold of himself, cried miserably, 'I'm in pain!'

The sound of his wail jolted him, knocked the swirling darkness back a step. *Pain!* The impossibility bridged a gap for him. Pain was for healthy people, people whose nerves were alive.

Can't happen. Of course it can't. That proves it – proves this is all a dream.

All at once, he felt an acute desire to weep. But he was a leper, and had spent too much time learning to dam such emotional channels. Lepers could not afford grief. Trembling feverishly, he plunged his cut hand into the stream.

'Pain is pain,' Atiaran grated. 'What is your pain to me? You have done a black deed, Unbeliever – violent and cruel, without commitment or sharing. You have given me a pain that no blood or time will wash clean. And Lena my daughter – ! Ah, I pray that the Lords will punish – punish!'

The running water was chill and clear. After a moment, his fingers began to sting in the cold, and an ache spread up through his knuckles to his wrist. Red plumed away from his cuts down the stream, but the cold water soon stopped his bleeding. As he watched the current rinse clean his injury, his grief and fear turned to anger. Because Atiaran was his only companion, he growled at her, 'Why should I go? None of this matters – I don't give a damn about your precious Land.'

'By the Seven!' Atiaran's hard tone seemed to chisel words out of the air. 'You will go to Revelstone if I must drag you each step of the way.'

He lifted his hand to examine it. Triock's knife had sliced him as neatly as a razor; there were no jagged edges to conceal dirt or roughen the healing. But the cut had reached bone in his middle two fingers, and blood still seeped from them. He stood up. For the first time since he had been attacked, he looked at Atiaran.

She stood a few paces from him, with her hands clenched together

100

at her heart as if its pulsing hurt her. She glared at him abominably, and her face was taut with intimations of fierce, rough strength. He could see that she was prepared to fight him to Revelstone if necessary. She shamed him, aggravated his ire. Belligerently, he waved his injury at her. 'I need a bandage.'

For an instant her gaze intensified as if she were about to hurl herself at him. But then she mastered herself, swallowed her pride. She went over to her pack, opened it, and took out a strip of white cloth, which she tore at an appropriate length as she returned to Covenant. Holding his hand carefully, she inspected the cut, nodded her approval of its condition, then bound the soft fabric firmly around his fingers. 'I have no hurtloam,' she said, 'and cannot take the time to search for it. But the cut looks well, and will heal cleanly.'

When she was done, she went back to her pack. Swinging it on to her shoulders, she said, 'Come. We have lost time.' Without a glance at Covenant, she set off down the file.

He remained where he was for a moment, tasting the ache of his fingers. There was a hot edge to his hurt, as if the knife were still in the wound. But he had the answer to it now. The darkness had receded somewhat, and he could look around him without panic. Yet he was still afraid. He was dreaming healthy nerves; he had not realized that he was so close to collapse. Helpless, lying unconscious somewhere, he was in the grip of a crisis – a crisis of his ability to survive. To weather it he would need every bit of discipline or intransigence he could find.

On an impulse, he bent and tried to pull Triock's knife from the ground with his right hand. His half-grip slipped when he tugged straight up on the handle, but by working it back and forth he was able to loosen it, draw it free. The whole knife was shaped and polished out of one flat sliver of stone, with a haft leather-bound for a secure hold, and an edge that seemed sharp enough for shaving. He tested it on his left forearm, and found that it lifted off his hair as smoothly as if the blade were lubricated.

He slipped it under his belt. Then he hitched his pack higher on his shoulders and started after Atiaran.

9

JEHANNUM

Before the afternoon was over, he had lapsed into a dull, hypnotized throb of pain. His pack straps constricted the circulation in his arms, multiplied the aching of his hand; his damp socks gave him blisters to which his toes were acutely and impossibly sensitive; weariness made his muscles as awkward as lead. But Atiaran moved constantly, severely, ahead of him down the file, and he followed her as if he were being dragged by the coercion of her will. His eyes became sightless with fatigue; he lost all sense of time, of movement, of everything except pain. He hardly knew that he had fallen asleep, and he felt a detached, impersonal sense of surprise when he was finally shaken awake.

He found himself lying in twilight on the floor of the file. After rousing him, Atiaran handed him a bowl of hot broth. Dazedly, he gulped it. When the bowl was empty, she took it and handed him a large flask of springwine. He gulped it also.

From his stomach, the springwine seemed to send long, soothing fingers out to caress and relax each of his raw muscles, loosening them until he felt that he could no longer sit up. He adjusted his pack as a pillow, then lay down to sleep again. His last sight before his eyes fell shut was of Atiaran, sitting enshadowed on the far side of the graveling pot, her face set relentlessly toward the north.

The next day dawned clear, cool, and fresh. Atiaran finally succeeded in awakening Covenant as darkness was fading from the sky. He sat up painfully, rubbed his face, as if it had gone numb during the night. A moment passed before he recollected the new sensitivity of his nerves; then he flexed his hands, stared at them as if he had never seen them before. They were alive, alive.

He pushed the blanket aside to uncover his feet. When he squeezed his toes through his boots, the pain of his blisters answered sharply. His toes were as alive as his fingers.

His guts twisted sickly. With a groan, he asked himself, How long – how long is this going to go on? He did not feel that he could endure much more.

Then he remembered that he had not had on a blanket when he

went to sleep the night before. Atiaran must have spread it over him.

He winced, avoided her eyes by shambling woodenly to the stream to wash his face. Where did she find the courage to do such things for him? As he splashed cold water on his neck and cheeks, he found that he was afraid of her again.

But she did not act like a threat. She fed him, checked the bandage on his injured hand, packed up the camp as if he were a burden to which she had already become habituated. Only the lines of sleeplessness around her eyes and the grim set of her mouth showed that she was clenching herself.

When she was ready to go, he gave himself a deliberate VSE, then forced his shoulders into the straps of his pack and followed her down the file as if her stiff back were a demand he could not refuse.

Before the day was done, he was an expert on that back. It never compromised; it never submitted a doubt about its authority, never offered the merest commiseration. Though his muscles tightened until they became as inarticulate as bone – though the aching rictus of his shoulders made him hunch his pack like a cripple – though the leagues aggravated his sore feet until he hobbled along like a man harried by vultures – her back compelled him like an ultimatum: keep moving or go mad; I permit no other alternatives. And he could not deny her. She stalked ahead of him like a nightmare figure, and he followed as if she held the key to his existence.

Late in the morning, they left the end of the file, and found themselves on a heathered hillside almost directly north of the high, grim finger of Kevin's Watch. They could see the South Plains off to the west; and as soon as the file ended, the stream turned that way, flowing to some distant union with the Mithil. But Atiaran led Covenant still northward, weaving her way along fragmentary tracks and across unpathed leas which bordered the hills on her right.

To the west, the grasslands of the plains were stiff with bracken, purplish in the sunlight. And to the east, the hills rose calmly, cresting a few hundred feet higher than the path which Atiaran chose along their sides. In this middle ground the heather alternated with broad swaths of blue-grass. The hillsides wore flowers and butterflies around thick copses of wattle and clusters of taller trees – oaks and sycamores, a few elms, and some gold-leaved trees – Atiaran called them 'Gilden' – which looked like maples. All the colours – the trees, the heather, the bracken, the *aliantha*, the flowers, and the infinite azure sky – were vibrant with the eagerness of spring, lush and exuberant rebirth of the world.

But Covenant had no strength to take in such things. He was blind and deaf with exhaustion, pain, incomprehension. Like a penitent, he plodded on through the afternoon at Atiaran's behest.

At last the day came to an end. Covenant covered the final league staggering numbly, though he did not pass out on his feet as he had the previous day; and when Atiaran halted and dropped her pack, he toppled to the grass like a felled tree. But his overstrained muscles twitched as if they were appalled; he could not hold them still without clenching. In involuntary restlessness, he helped Atiaran by unpacking the blankets while she cooked supper. During their meal, the sun set across the plains, streaking the grasslands with shadows and lavender; and when the stars came out he lay and watched them, trying with the help of springwine to make himself relax.

At last he faded into sleep. But his slumbers were troubled. He dreamed that he was trudging through a desert hour after hour, while a sardonic voice urged him to enjoy the freshness of the grass. The pattern ran obsessively in his mind until he felt that he was sweating anger. When the dawn came to wake him, he met it as if it were an affront to his sanity.

He found that his feet were already growing tougher, and his cut hand had healed almost completely. His overt pain was fading. But his nerves were no less alive. He could feel the ends of his socks with his toes, could feel the breeze on his fingers. Now the immediacy of these inexplicable sensations began to infuriate him. They were evidence of health, vitality − a wholeness he had spent long, miserable months of his life learning to live without − and they seemed to inundate him with terrifying implications. They seemed to deny the reality of his disease.

But that was impossible. It's one or the other, he panted fiercely. Not both. Either I'm a leper or I'm not. Either Joan divorced me or she never existed. There's no middle ground.

With an effort that made him grind his teeth, he averred, I'm a leper. I'm dreaming. That's a fact.

He could not bear the alternative. If he were dreaming, he might still be able to save his sanity, survive, endure. But if the Land were real, actual − ah, then the long anguish of his leprosy was a dream, and he was mad already, beyond hope.

Any belief was better than that. Better to struggle for a sanity he could at least recognize than to submit to a 'health' which surpassed all explanation.

He chewed the gristle of such thoughts for leagues as he trudged along behind Atiaran, but each argument brought him back to the same position. The mystery of his leprosy was all the mystery he could tolerate, accept as fact. It determined his response to every other question of credibility.

It made him stalk along at Atiaran's back as if he were ready to attack her at any provocation.

Nevertheless, he did receive one benefit from his dilemma. Its immediate presence and tangibility built a kind of wall between him and the particular fears and actions which had threatened him earlier. Certain memories of violence and blood did not recur. And without shame to goad it, his anger remained manageable, discrete. It did not impel him to rebel against Atiaran's uncompromising lead.

Throughout the next day, her erect, relentless form did not relax its compulsion. Up slopes and down hillsides, across glens, around thickets — along the western margin of the hills — she drew him onward against his fuming mind and recalcitrant flesh. But early in the afternoon she stopped suddenly, looked about her as if she had heard a distant cry suddenly. Her unexpected anxiety startled Covenant, but before he could ask her what was the matter, she started grimly forward again.

Some time later she repeated her performance. This time, Covenant saw that she was smelling the air as if the breeze carried an erratic scent of evil. He sniffed, but smelled nothing. 'What is it?' he asked. 'Are we being followed again?'

She did not look at him. 'Would that Trell were here,' she breathed distractedly. 'Perhaps he would know why the Land is so unquiet.' Without explanation she swung hastening away northward once more.

That evening she halted earlier than usual. Late in the afternoon, he noticed that she was looking for something, a sign of some kind in the grass and trees; but she said nothing to explain herself, and so he could do nothing but watch and follow. Then without warning she turned sharply to the right, moved into a shallow valley between two hills. They had to skirt the edge of the valley to avoid a large patch of brambles which covered most of its bottom; and in a few hundred yards they came to a wide, thick copse in the northern hill. Atiaran walked around the copse, then unexpectedly vanished into it.

Dimly wondering, Covenant went to the spot where she had disappeared. There he was able to pick out a thin sliver of path leading into the copse. He had to turn sideways to follow this path around some of the trees, but in twenty feet he came to an open space like a chamber grown into the centre of the woods.

The space was lit by light filtering through the walls, which were formed of saplings standing closely side by side in a rude rectangle; and a faint rustling breeze blew through them. But interwoven branches and leaves made a tight roof for the chamber. It was comfortably large enough for three or four people, and along each of its walls were grassy mounds like beds. In one corner stood a large tree with a hollow centre, into which shelves had been built, and these were laden with pots and flasks made of both wood and stone. The whole place seemed deliberately welcoming and cozy.

As Covenant looked around, Atiaran set her pack on one of the beds, and said abruptly, 'This is a Waymeet.' When he turned a face full of questions toward her, she sighed and went on, 'A resting place for travellers. Here is food and drink and sleep for any who pass this way.'

She moved away to inspect the contents of the shelves and her busyness forced Covenant to hold on to his questions until a time when she might be more accessible. But while she replenished the supplies in her pack and prepared a meal, he sat and reflected that she was not ever likely to be accessible to him; and he was in no mood to be kept in ignorance. So after he had eaten, and Atiaran had settled herself for the night, he said with as much gentleness as he could manage, 'Tell me more about this place. Maybe I'll need to know some time.'

She kept her face away from him, and lay silent in the gathering darkness for a while. She seemed to be waiting for courage, and when at last she spoke, she sighed only, 'Ask.'

Her delay made him abrupt. 'Are there many places like this?'

'There are many throughout the Land.'

'Why? Who sets them up?'

'The Lords caused them to be made. Revelstone is only one place, and the people live in many — therefore the Lords sought a way to help travellers, so that people might come to Revelstone and to each other more easily.'

'Well, who takes care of them? There's fresh food here.'

Atiaran sighed again, as if she found talking to him arduous. The night had deepened; he could see nothing of her but a shadow as she explained tiredly, 'Among the Demondim-spawn that survived the Desolation, there were some who recalled Loric Vilesilencer with gratitude. They turned against the ur-viles, and asked the Lords to give them a service to perform, as expiation for the sins of their kindred. These creatures, the Waynhim, care for the Waymeets — helping the trees to grow, providing food and drink. But the bond between men and Waynhim is fragile, and you will not see one. They serve for their own reasons, not for love of us — performing simple tasks to redeem the evil of their mighty lore.'

The darkness in the chamber was now complete. In spite of his irritation, Covenant felt ready to sleep. He asked only one more question. 'How did you find this place? Is there a map?'

'There is no map. A Waymeet is a blessing which one who travels accepts wherever it is found – a token of the health and hospitality of the Land. They may be found when they are needed. The Waynhim leave signs in the surrounding land.'

Covenant thought he could hear a note of appreciation in her voice which clashed with her reluctance. The sound reminded him of her constant burden of conflicts – her sense of personal weakness in the face of the Land's strong need, her desires to both punish and preserve him. But he soon forgot such things as the image of Waymeets filled his reverie. Enfolded by the smell of the fresh grass on which he lay, he swung easily into sleep.

During the night, the weather changed. The morning came glowering under heavy clouds on a ragged wind out of the north, and Covenant met it with a massive frown that seemed to weigh down his forehead. He awoke before Atiaran called him. Though he had slept soundly in the security of the Waymeet, he felt as tired as if he had spent the whole night shouting at himself.

While Atiaran was preparing breakfast, he took out Triock's knife, then scanned the shelves and found a basin for water and a small mirror. He could not locate any soap – apparently the Waynhim relied on the same fine sand which he had used in Atiaran's home. So he braved himself to shave without lather. Triock's knife felt clumsy in his right hand, and he could not shake lurid visions of slitting his throat.

To marshal his courage, he studied himself in the mirror. His hair was tousled wildly; with his stubbled beard he looked like a rude prophet. His lips were thin and tight, like the chiselled mouth of an oracle, and there was grit in his gaunt eyes. All he needed to complete the picture was a touch of frenzy. Muttering silently, All in good time, he brought the knife to his cheek.

To his surprise, the blade felt slick on his chin, and it cut his whiskers without having to be scraped over them repeatedly. In a short time, he had given himself a shave which appeared adequate, at least by contrast, and he had not damaged himself. With a sardonic nod towards his reflection, he put the blade away in his pack and began eating his breakfast.

Soon he and Atiaran were ready to leave the Waymeet. She motioned for him to precede her; he went ahead a few steps along the path, then stopped to see what she was doing. As she left the chamber, she raised her head to the leafy ceiling, and said softly, 'We give thanks for the Waymeet. The giving of this gift honours us, and in accepting it we return honour to the giver. We leave in Peace.' Then she followed Covenant out of the copse.

When they reached the open valley, they found dark clouds piling over them out of the north. Tensely, Atiaran looked at the sky, smelled the air; she seemed distraught by the coming rain. Her reaction made the boiling thunderheads appear ominous to Covenant, and when she turned sharply down the valley to resume her northward path, he hurried after her, calling out, 'What's the matter?'

'Ill upon evil,' she replied. 'Do you not smell it? The Land is unquiet.'

'What's wrong?'

'I do not know,' she murmured so quietly that he could barely hear her. 'There is a shadow in the air. And this rain − ! Ah, the Land!'

'What's wrong with rain? Don't you get rain in the spring?'

'Not from the north,' she answered over her shoulder. 'The spring of the Land arises from the southwest. No, this rain comes straight from Gravin Threndor. The Cavewight Staff wrong-wielder tests his power − I feel it. We are too late.'

She stiffened her pace into the claws of the wind, and Covenant pressed on behind her. As the first raindrops struck his forehead, he asked, 'Does this Staff really run the weather?'

'The Old Lords did not use it so − they had no wish to violate the Land. But who can say what such power may accomplish?'

Then the full clouts of the storm hit them. The wind scourged the rain southward as if the sky were lashing out at them, at every defenceless living thing. Soon the hillsides were drenched with ferocity. The wind rent at the trees, tore, battered the grass; it struck daylight from the hills, buried the earth in preternatural night. In moments, Atiaran and Covenant were soaked, gasping through the torrent. They kept their direction by facing the dark fury, but they could see nothing of the terrain; they staggered down rough slopes, wandered helplessly into hip-deep streams, lurched headlong through thickets; they forced against the wind as if it were the current of some stinging limbo, some abyss running from nowhere mercilessly into nowhere. Yet Atiaran lunged onward erect, with careless determination, and the fear of losing her kept Covenant lumbering at her heels.

But he was wearying rapidly. With an extra effort that made his chest ache, he caught up with Atiaran, grabbed her shoulder, shouted in her ear. 'Stop! We've got to stop!'

'No!' she screamed back. 'We are too late! I do not dare!'

Her voice barely reached him through the howl of the wind. She started to pull away, and he tightened his grip on her robe, yelling, 'No choice! We'll kill ourselves!' The rain thrashed brutally; for an instant he almost lost his hold. He got his other arm around her, tugged her streaming face close to his. 'Shelter!' he cried. 'We've got to stop!'

Through the water, her face had a drowning look as she answered, 'Never! No time!' With a quick thrust of her weight and a swing of her arms, she broke his grip, tripped him to the ground. Before he could recover, she snatched up his right hand and began dragging him on through the grass and mud, hauling him like an unsupportable burden against the opposition of the storm. Her pull was so desperate that she had taken him several yards before he could heave upward and get his feet under him.

As he braced himself, her hold slipped off his hand, and she fell away from him. Shouting, 'By hell, we're going to stop!' he leapt after her. But she eluded his grasp, ran unevenly away from him into the spite of the storm.

He stumbled along behind her. For several long moments, he slipped and scrambled through the flailing rain after her untouchable back, furious to get his hands on her. But some inner resource galvanized her strength beyond anything he could match; soon he failed at the pace. The rain hampered him as if he were trying to run on the bottom of a breaking wave.

Then a vicious skid sent him sledding down the hill with his face full of mud. When he looked up again through the rain and dirt, Atiaran had vanished into the dark storm as if she were in terror of him, dreaded his touch.

Fighting his way to his feet, Covenant roared at the rampant clouds, 'Hellfire! You can't do this to me!'

Without warning, just as his fury peaked, a huge white flash exploded beside him. He felt that a bolt of lightning had struck his left hand.

The blast threw him up the hill to his right. For uncounted moments, he lay dazed, conscious only of the power of the detonation and the flaming pain in his hand. His wedding ring seemed to be on fire. But when he recovered enough to look, he could see no mark on his fingers, and the pain faded away while he was still hunting for its source.

He shook his head, thrust himself into a sitting position. There were no signs of the blast anywhere around him. He was numbly aware that something had changed, but in his confusion he could not identify what it was.

He climbed painfully to his feet. After only a moment, he spotted Atiaran lying on the hillside twenty yards ahead of him. His head felt unbalanced with bewilderment, but he moved cautiously toward her, concentrating on his equilibrium. She lay on her back, apparently unhurt, and stared at him as he approached. When he reached her, she said in wonderment, 'What have you done?'

The sound of her voice helped focus his attention. He was able to say without slurring, 'Me? I didn't – nothing.'

Atiaran came slowly to her feet. Standing in front of him, she studied him gravely, uncertainly, as she said, 'Something has aided us. See, the storm is less. And the wind is changed – it blows now as it should. Gravin Threndor no longer threatens. Praise the Earth, Unbeliever, if this is not your doing.'

'Of course it's not my doing,' murmured Covenant. 'I don't run the weather.' There was no asperity in his tone. He was taken aback by his failure to recognize the change in the storm for himself.

Atiaran had told the simple truth. The wind had shifted and dropped considerably. The rain fell steadily, but without fury; now it was just a good solid, spring rain.

Covenant shook his head again. He felt strangely unable to understand. But when Atiaran said gently, 'Shall we go?' he heard a note of unwilling respect in her voice. She seemed to believe that he had in fact done something to the storm.

Numbly, he mumbled, 'Sure,' and followed her onward again.

They walked in clean rain for the rest of the day. Covenant's sense of mental dullness persisted, and the only outside influences that penetrated him were wetness and cold. Most of the day passed without his notice in one long, drenched push against the cold. Toward evening, he had regained enough of himself to be glad when Atiaran found a Waymeet, and he checked over his body carefully for any hidden injuries while his clothes dried by the graveling. But he still felt dazed by what had happened. He could not shake the odd impression that whatever force had changed the fury of the storm had altered him also.

The next day broke clear, crisp, and glorious, and he and Atiaran left the Waymeet early in the new spring dawn. After the strain of the previous day, Covenant felt keenly alert to the joyous freshness of the air and the sparkle of dampness on the grass, the sheen on the heather and the bursting flavour of the treasure-berries. The Land around him struck him as if he had never noticed its beauty before. Its vitality seemed curiously tangible to his senses. He felt that he could see spring fructifying within the trees, the grass, the flowers, hear the excitement of the calling birds, smell the newness of the buds and the cleanliness of the air.

Then abruptly Atiaran stopped and looked about her. A grimace of distaste and concern tightened her features as she sampled the breeze. She moved her head around intently, as if she were trying to locate the source of a threat.

Covenant followed her example, and as he did so, a thrill of recognition ran through him. He could tell that there was indeed something wrong in the air, something false. It did not arise in his immediate vicinity – the scents of the trees and turf and flowers, the lush afterward of rain, were all as they should be – but it lurked behind those smells like something uneasy, out of place, unnatural in the distance. He understood instinctively that it was the odour of ill – the odour of premeditated disease.

A moment later, the breeze shifted; the odour vanished. But that ill smell had heightened his perceptions; the contrast vivified his sense of the vitality of his surroundings. With an intuitive leap, he grasped the change which had taken place within him or for him. In some way that completely amazed him, his senses had gained a new dimension. He looked at the grass, smelled its freshness – and *saw* its verdancy, its springing life, its fitness. Jerking his eyes to a nearby *aliantha*, he received an impression of potency, health, that dumbfounded him.

His thoughts reeled, groped, then suddenly clarified around the image of *health*. He was seeing health, smelling natural fitness and vitality, hearing the true exuberance of spring. *Health* was as vivid around him as if the spirit of the Land's life had become palpable, incarnate. It was as if he had stepped without warning into an altogether different universe. Even Atiaran – she was gazing at his entrancement with puzzled surprise – was manifestly healthy, though her life was complicated by uneasiness, fatigue, pain, resolution.

By hell, he mumbled. Is my leprosy this obvious to her? Then why doesn't she understand – ? He turned away from her stare, hunted for some way to test his eyes and hers. After a moment, he spotted near the top of a hill a Gilden tree that seemed to have something wrong with it. In every respect that he could identify, specify, the tree appeared normal, healthy, yet it conveyed a sense of inner rot, an unexpected pang of sorrow, to his gaze. Pointing at it, he asked Atiaran what she saw.

Soberly, she replied, 'I am not one of the *lillianrill*, but I can see that the Gilden dies. Some blight has stricken its heart. Did you not see such things before?'

He shook his head.

'Then how does the world from which you come live?' She sounded dismayed by the prospect of a place in which *health* itself was invisible.

He shrugged off her question. He wanted to challenge her, find out what she saw in him. But then he remembered her saying, *You are closed to me*. Now he understood her comment, and the comprehension gave him a feeling of relief. The privacy of his own illness was intact, safe. He motioned her northward again, and when after a moment she started on her way, he followed her with pleasure. For a long time he forgot himself in the sight of so much healthiness.

Gradually, as the day moved through afternoon into gloaming and the onset of night, he adjusted to seeing health behind the colours and forms which met his eyes. Twice more his nostrils had caught the elusive odour of wrongness, but he could not find it anywhere near the creek by which Atiaran chose to make camp. In its absence he thought that he would sleep peacefully.

But somehow a rosy dream of soul health and beauty became a nightmare in which spirits threw off their bodies and revealed themselves to be ugly, rotten, contemptuous. He was glad to wake up, glad even to take the risk of shaving without the aid of a mirror.

On the sixth day, the smell of wrong became persistent, and it grew stronger as Atiaran and Covenant worked their way north along the hills. A brief spring shower dampened their clothes in the middle of the morning, but it did not wash the odour from the air. That smell made Covenant uneasy, whetted his anxiety until he seemed to have a cold blade of dread poised over his heart.

Still he could not locate, specify, the odour. It keened in him behind the bouquet of the grass and the tangy bracken and the *aliantha*, behind the loveliness of the vital hills, like the reek of a rotting corpse just beyond the range of his nostrils.

Finally he could not endure it any longer in silence. He drew abreast of Atiaran, and asked, 'Do you smell it?'

Without a glance at him, she returned heavily, 'Yes, Unbeliever. I smell it. It becomes clear to me.'

'What does it mean?'

'It means that we are walking into peril. Did you not expect it?'

Thinking, Hellfire! Covenant rephrased his question. 'But what does it come from? What's causing it?'

'How can I say?' she countered. 'I am no oracle.'

Covenant caught himself on the edge of an angry retort. With an effort, he kept his temper. 'Then what is it?'

'It is murder,' Atiaran replied flatly, and quickened her pace to pull away from him. Do not ask me to forget, her back seemed to say, and he stumped fuming after it. Cold anxiety inched closer to his heart.

By mid-afternoon, he felt that his perception of wrongness was sharpening at almost every step. His eyes winced up and down the hills, as though he expected at any moment to see the source of the smell. His sinuses ached from constantly tasting the odour. But there was nothing for him to perceive – nothing but Atiaran's roaming

112

path through the dips and hollows and valleys and outcroppings of the hills – nothing but healthy trees and thickets and flowers and verdant grass, the blazonry of the Earth's spring and nothing but the intensifying threat of something ill in the air. It was a poignant threat, and he felt obscurely that the cause would be worth bewailing.

The sensation of it increased without resolution for some time. But then a sudden change in the tension of Atiaran's back warned Covenant to brace himself scant instants before she hissed at him to stop. She had just rounded the side of a hill far enough to see into the hollow beyond it. For a moment she froze, crouching slightly and peering into the hollow. Then she began running down the hill.

At once, Covenant followed. In three strides, he reached the spot where she halted. Beyond him, in the bottom of the hollow, stood a single copse like an eyot in a broad glade. He could see nothing amiss. But his sense of smell jabbered at him urgently, and Atiaran was dashing straight toward the copse. He sprinted after her.

She stopped short just on the east side of the trees. Quivering feverishly, she glared about her with an expression of terror and hatred, as if she wanted to enter the copse and did not have the courage. Then she cried out, aghast, 'Waynhim? *Melenkurion!* Ah, by the Seven, what evil!'

When Covenant reached her side, she was staring a silent scream at the trees. She held her hands clasped together at her mouth, and her shoulders shook.

As soon as he looked at the copse, he saw a thin path leading into it. Impulsively, he moved forward, plunged between the trees. In five steps, he was in the open space much like the other Waymeets he had seen. This chamber was round, but it had the same tree walls, branch-woven roof, beds, and shelves.

But the walls were spattered with blood, and a figure lay in the centre of the floor.

Covenant gasped as he saw that the figure was not human.

Its outlines were generally manlike, though the torso was inordinately long, and the limbs were short, matched in length, indicating that the creature could both stand erect and run on its hands and feet. But the face was entirely alien to Covenant. A long, flexible neck joined the hairless head to the body; two pointed ears perched near the top of the skull on either side; the mouth was as thin as a mere slit in the flesh. And there were no eyes. Two gaping nostrils surrounded by a thick, fleshy membrane filled the centre of the face. The head had no other features.

Driven through the centre of the creature's chest – pinning it to the ground – was a long iron stake.

The chamber stank of violence so badly that in a few breaths Covenant felt about to suffocate. He wanted to flee. He was a leper; even dead things were dangerous to him. But he forced himself to remain still while he sorted out one impression. On seeing the creature, his first thought had been that the Land was rid of something loathsome. But as he gritted himself, his eyes and nose corrected him. The wrongness which assailed his senses came from the killing – from the spike – not from the creature. Its flesh had a hue of ravaged health; it had been natural, right – a proper part of the life of the Land.

Gagging on the stench of the crime, Covenant turned and fled.

As he broke out into the sunlight, he saw Atiaran already moving away to the north, almost out of the hollow. He needed no urging to hurry after her; his bones ached to put as much distance as possible between himself and the desecrated Waymeet. He hastened in her direction as if there were fangs snapping at his heels.

For the rest of the day, he found relief in putting leagues behind him. The edge of the unnatural smell was slowly blunted as they hurried forward. But it did not fade below a certain level. When he and Atiaran were forced by fatigue and darkness to stop for the night, he felt sure that there was uneasiness still ahead – that the killer of the Waynhim was moving invidiously to the north of them. Atiaran seemed to share his convictions; she asked him if he knew how to use the knife he carried.

After sleep had eluded him for some time, he made himself ask her, 'Shouldn't we have – buried it?'

She answered softly from her shadowed bed across the low light of the graveling. 'They would not thank our interference. They will take care of their own. But the fear is on me that they may break their bond with the Lords – because of this.'

That thought gave Covenant a chill he could not explain, and he lay sleepless for half the night under the cold mockery of the stars.

The next day dawned on short rations for the travellers. Atiaran had been planning to replenish her supplies at a Waymeet the previous day, so now she had no springwine left and little bread or staples. However, they were in no danger of going hungry – treasure-berries were plentiful along their path. But they had to start without warm food to steady them after the cold, uncomforting night. And they had to travel in the same direction that the killer of the Waynhim had taken. Covenant found himself stamping angrily into the dawn as if he sensed that the murder had been intended for him. For the first time in several days, he allowed himself to think of Drool and Lord Foul. He knew that either of them was capable of killing a Waynhim, even of killing it gratuitously. And the Despiser,

114

at least, might easily know where he was.

But the day passed without mishap. The dim, constant uneasiness in the air grew no worse, and *aliantha* abounded. As the leagues passed, Covenant's anger lost its edge. He relaxed into contemplation of the health around him, looked with undiminished wonder at the trees, the magisterial oaks and dignified elms, the comforting spread of the Gilden, the fine filigree of the mimosa, the spry saplings of wattle – and at the calm old contours of the hills, lying like slumberous heads to the reclining earth of the Western Plains. Such things gave him a new sense of the pulse and pause, the climbing sap and the still rock of the Land. In contrast, the trailing ordure of death seemed both petty – insignificant beside the vast abundant vitality of the hills – and vile, like an act of cruelty done to a child.

The next morning, Atiaran changed her course, veering somewhat eastward, so that she and Covenant climbed more and more into the heart of the hills. And when the sun was low enough to cast the eastern hillsides into shadow, the travellers came in sight of Soaring Woodhelven.

Their approach gave Covenant a good view of the tree village from some distance away across a wide glade. He judged the tree to be nearly four hundred feet high, and a good thirty broad at the base. There were no branches, then abruptly huge limbs spread out horizontally from the stem, forming in outline a half-oval with a flattened tip. The whole tree was so thickly branched and leaved that most of the village was hidden; but Covenant could see a few ladders between the branches and along the trunk; and in some tight knots on the limbs he thought he could make out the shapes of dwellings. If any people were moving through the foliage, they were so well camouflaged that he could not discern them.

'That is Soaring Woodhelven,' said Atiaran, 'a home for the people of the *lillianrill*, as Mithil Stonedown is a home for those of the *rhadhamaerl*. I have been here once, on my returning from the Loresraat. The Woodhelvennin are a comely folk, though I do not understand their wood-lore. They will give us rest and food, and perhaps help as well. It is said, "To to the *rhadhamaerl* for truth, and the *lillianrill* for counsel." My need for counsel is sore upon me. Come.'

She led Covenant across the glade to the base of the great tree. They had to pass around the rough-barked tree to the northwest curve, and there they found a large natural opening in the hollow stem. The inner cavity was not deep; it was only large enough to hold a spiral stairway. Above the first thick limb was another opening, from which ladders began their way upward.

The sight gave Covenant a quiver of his old fear of heights, almost forgotten since his ordeal on the stairs of Kevin's Watch. He did not want to have to climb those ladders.

But it appeared that he would not have to climb. The opening to the trunk was barred with a heavy wooden gate, and there was no one to open it. In fact, the whole place seemed too quiet and dark for a human habitation. Dusk was gathering, but no home glimmers broke through the overhanging shadow, and no gloaming calls between families interrupted the silence.

Covenant glanced at Atiaran, and saw that she was puzzled. Resting her hands on the bars of the gate, she said, 'This is not well, Thomas Covenant. When last I came here, there were children in the glade, people on the stair, and no gate at the door. Something is amiss. And yet I sense no great evil. There is no more ill here than elsewhere along our path.'

Stepping back from the gate, she raised her head and called, 'Hail! Soaring Woodhelven! We are travellers, people of the Land! Our way is long – our future dark! What has become of you?' When no answering shout came, she went on in exasperation, 'I have been here before! In those days, it was said that Woodhelvennin hospitality had no equal! Is this your friendship to the Land?'

Suddenly, they heard a light scattering fall behind them. Spinning around, they found themselves encircled by seven or eight men gripping smooth wooden daggers. Instinctively, one of them said, 'The meaning of friendship changes with the times. We have seen darkness, and heard dark tidings. We will be sure of strangers.'

A torch flared in the hands of the man who had spoken. Through the glare, Covenant got his first look at the Woodhelvennin. They were all tall, slim, and lithe, with fair hair and light eyes. They dressed in cloaks of woodland colours, and the fabric seemed to cling to their limbs, as if to avoid snagging on branches. Each man held a pointed dagger of polished wood which gleamed dully in the torchlight.

Covenant was at a loss, but Atiaran gathered her robe about her and answered with stern pride, 'Then be sure, I am Atiaran Trellmate of Mithil Stonedown. This is Thomas Covenant, Unbeliever and message-bearer to the Lords. We come in friendship and need, seeking safety and help. I did not know that it is your custom to make strangers prisoner.'

The man who held the torch stepped forward and bowed seriously.

'When we are sure, we will ask your pardon. Until that time, you must come with me to a place where you may be examined. We have seen strange tokens, and see more now.' He nodded at Covenant. 'We would make no mistake, either in trust or in doubt. Will you accompany me?'

'Very well,' Atiaran sighed. 'But you would not be treated so in Mithil Stonedown.'

The man replied, 'Let the Stonedownors taste our troubles before they despise our caution. Now, come behind me.' He moved forward to open the gate.

At the command, Covenant balked. He was not prepared to go climbing around a tall tree in the dark. It would have been bad enough in the light, when he could have seen what he was doing, but the very thought of taking the risk at night made his pulse hammer in his forehead. Stepping away from Atiaran, he said with a quaver he could not repress, 'Forget it.'

Before he could react, two of the men grabbed his arms. He tried to twist away, but they held him, pulled his hands up into the torchlight. For one stark moment, the Woodhelvennin stared at his hands – at the ring on his left and the scar on his right – as if he were some kind of ghoul. Then the man with the torch snapped, 'Bring him.'

'No!' Covenant clamoured. 'You don't understand. I'm not good at heights. I'll fall.' As they wrestled him toward the gate, he shouted. 'Hellfire! You're trying to kill me!'

His captors halted momentarily. He heard a series of shouts, but in his confused, angry panic he did not understand. Then the leader said, 'If you do not climb well, you will not be asked to climb.'

The next moment, the end of a rope fell beside Covenant. Instantly, two more men lashed his wrists to the line. Before he realized what was happening, the rope sprang taut. He was hauled into the air like a sack of miscellaneous helplessness.

He thought he heard a shout of protest from Atiaran, but he could not be sure. Crying silently, Bloody hell! he tensed his shoulders against the strain and stared wildly up into the darkness. He could not see anyone drawing up the rope – in the last glimmering of the torch, the line seemed to stretch up into an abyss – and that made him doubly afraid.

Then the light below him vanished.

The next moment, a low rustling of leaves told him that he had reached the level of the first branches. He saw a yellow glow through the upper opening of the tree's stairwell. But the rope hauled him on upward into the heights of the village.

His own movements made him swing slightly, so that at odd intervals he brushed against the leaves. But that was his only contact with the tree. He saw no lights, heard no voices; the deep black weights of the mighty limbs slid smoothly past him as if he were being dragged into the sky.

Soon both his shoulders throbbed sharply, and his arms went

numb. With his head craned upward, he gaped into a lightless terror and moaned as if he were drowning. Hellfire! Ahh!

Then without warning his movement stopped. Before he could brace himself, a torch flared, and he found himself level with three men who were standing on a limb. In the sudden light, they looked identical to the men who had captured him, but one of them had a small circlet of leaves about his head. The other two considered Covenant for a moment, then reached out and gripped his shirt, pulling him toward their limb. As the solid branch struck his feet, the rope slackened, letting his arms drop.

His wrists were still tied together, but he tried to get a hold on one of the men, keep himself from falling off the limb. His arms were dead; he could not move them. The darkness stretched below him like a hungry beast. With a gasp, he lunged toward the men, striving to make them save him. They grappled him roughly. He refused to bear his own weight, forced them to carry and drag him down the limb until they came to a wide gap in the trunk. There the centre of the stem was hollowed out to form a large chamber, and Covenant dropped heavily to the floor, shuddering with relief.

Shortly, a rising current of activity began around him. He paid no attention to it; he kept his eyes shut to concentrate on the hard stability of the floor, and to the pain of blood returning to his hands and arms. The hurt was excruciating, but he endured it in clenched silence. Soon his hands were tingling, and his fingers felt thick, hot. He flexed them, curled them into claws. Through his teeth, he muttered to the fierce rhythm of his heart. Hellfire. Hell and blood.

He opened his eyes.

He was lying on polished wood at the centre of the myriad concentric circles of the tree trunk. The age rings made the rest of the room seem to focus toward him as if he were sprawled on a target. His arms felt unnaturally inarticulate, but he forced them to thrust him into a sitting position. Then he looked at his hands. His wrists were raw from the cut of the rope, but they were not bleeding.

Bastards!

He raised his head and glowered around him.

The chamber was about twenty feet wide, and seemed to fill the whole inside diameter of the trunk. The only opening was the one through which he had stumbled, and he could see darkness outside; but the room was brightly lit by torches set into the walls – torches which burned smokelessly, and did not appear to be consumed. The polished walls gleamed as if they were burnished, but the ceiling, high above the floor, was rough, untouched wood.

Five Woodhelvennin stood around Covenant in the hollow – three men, including the one wearing the circlet of leaves, and two women. They all were dressed in similar cloaks which clung to their outlines, though the colours varied, and all were taller than Covenant. Their tallness seemed threatening, so he got slowly to his feet, lowering the pack from his shoulders as he stood.

A moment later, the man who had led Covenant's captors on the ground entered the chamber, followed by Atiaran. She appeared unharmed, but weary and depressed, as though the climb and the distrust had sapped her strength. When she saw Covenant, she moved to take her stand beside him.

One of the women said, 'Only two, Soranal?'

'Yes,' Atiaran's guard answered. 'We watched, and there were no others as they crossed the south glade. And our scouts have not reported any other strangers in the hills.'

'Scouts?' asked Atiaran. 'I did not know that scouts were needed among the people of the Land.'

The woman took a step forward and replied, 'Atiaran Trell-mate, the folk of Mithil Stonedown have been known to us since our return to the Land in a new age. And there are those among us who remember your visit here. We know our friends, and the value of friendship.'

'Then in what way have we deserved this treatment?' Atiaran demanded. 'We came in search of friends.'

The woman did not answer Atiaran's question directly. 'Because we are all people of the Land,' she said, 'and because our peril is a peril for all, I will attempt to ease the sting of our discourtesy by explaining our actions. We in this heartwood chamber are the Heers of Soaring Woodhelven, the leaders of our people. I am Llaura daughter of Annamar. Here also – ' she indicated each individual with a nod – 'are Omournil daughter of Mournil, Soranal son of Thiller, Padrias son of Mill, Malliner son of Veinnin, and Baradakas, Hirebrand of the *lillianrill*.' This last was the man wearing the circlet of leaves. 'We made the decision of distrust, and will give our reasons.

'I see that you are impatient.' A taste of bitterness roughened her voice. 'Well, I will not tire you with the full tale of the blighting wind which has blown over us from time to time from Gravin Threndor. I will not describe the angry storms, or show you the body of the three-winged bird that died atop our Woodhelven, or discuss the truth of the rumours of murder which have reached our ears. By the Seven! There are angry songs that should be sung – but I will not sing them now. This I will tell you: all servants of the Grey Slayer are not dead. It is our belief that a Raver has been among us.'

That name carried a pang of danger that made Covenant look rapidly about him, trying to locate the peril. For an instant, he did not comprehend. But then he noticed how Atiaran stiffened at Llaura's words – saw the jumping knot at the centre of her jaw, felt the heightened fear in her, though she said nothing – and he understood. The Woodhelvennin feared that he and she might be Ravers.

Without thinking, he snapped, 'That's ridiculous.'

The Heers ignored him. After a short pause, Soranal continued Llaura's explanation. 'Two days past, in the high sun of afternoon, when our people were busy at their crafts and labours, and the children were playing in the upper branches of the Tree, a stranger came to Soaring Woodhelven. Two days earlier, the last ill storm out of Mount Thunder had broken suddenly and turned into good – and on the day the stranger came our hearts were glad, thinking that a battle we knew not of had been won for the Land. He wore the appearance of a Stonedownor, and said his name was Jehannum. We welcomed him with the hospitality which is the joy of the Land. We saw no reason to doubt him, though the children shrank from him with unwonted cries and fears. Alas for us – the young saw more clearly than the old.

'He passed among us with dark hints and spite in his mouth, casting sly ridicule on our crafts and customs. And we could not answer him. But we remembered Peace, and did nothing for a day.

'In that time, Jehannum's hints turned to open foretelling of doom. So at last we called him to the heartwood chamber and the meeting of the Heers. We heard the words he chose to speak, words full of glee and the reviling of the Land. Then our eyes saw more deeply, and we offered him the test of the *lomillialor*.'

'You know of the High Wood, *lomillialor* – do you not, Atiaran?' Baradakas spoke for the first time. 'There is much in it like the *orcrest* of the *rhadhamaerl*. It is an offspring of the One Tree, from which the Staff of Life itself was made.'

'But we had no chance to make the test,' Soranal resumed. 'When Jehannum saw the High Wood, he sprang away from us and escaped. We gave pursuit, but he had taken us by surprise – we were too full of quiet, not ready for such evils – and his fleetness far surpassed ours. He eluded us, and made his way toward the east.'

He sighed as he concluded, 'In the one day which has passed since that time, we have begun relearning the defence of the Land.'

After a moment, Atiaran said quietly, 'I hear you. Pardon my anger – I spoke in haste and ignorance. But surely now you can see that we are no friends of the Grey Slayer.'

'We see much in you, Atiaran Trell-mate,' said Llaura, her eyes fixed keenly on the Stonedownor, 'much sorrow and much courage.

But your companion is closed to us. It may be that we will need to imprison this Thomas Covenant.'

'*Melenkurion!*' hissed Atiaran. 'Do not dare! Do you not know? Have you not looked at him?'

At this, a murmur of relief passed among the Heers, a murmur which accented their tension. Stepping toward Atiaran, Soranal extended his right hand, palm forward, in the salute of welcome, and said, 'We have looked – looked and heard. We trust you, Atiaran Trell-mate. You have spoken a name which no Raver would call upon to save a companion.' He took her by the arm and drew her away from Covenant, out of the centre of the chamber.

Without her at his shoulder, Covenant felt suddenly exposed, vulnerable. For the first time, he sensed how much he had come to depend upon her presence, her guidance, if not her support. But he was in no mood to meet threats passively. He poised himself on the balls of his feet, ready to move in any direction, and his eyes shifted quickly among the faces that stared at him from the gleaming walls of the chamber.

'Jehannum predicted many things,' said Llaura, 'but one especially you should be told. He said that a great evil in the semblance of Berek Halfhand walked the hills toward us out of the south. And here – ' she pointed a pale arm at Covenant, her voice rising sternly as she spoke. 'Here is an utter stranger to the Land – half unhanded on his right, and on his left bearing a ring of white gold. Beyond doubt carrying messages to the Lords – messages or doom!'

With a pleading intensity, Atiaran said, 'Do not presume to judge. Remember the Oath. You are not Lords. And dark words may be warnings as well as prophecies. Will you trust the word of a Raver?'

Baradakas shrugged slightly. 'It is not the message we judge. Our test is for the man.' Reaching behind him, he lifted up a smooth wooden rod three feet long from which all the bark had been stripped. He held it by the middle gently, reverently. 'This is *lomillialor*.' As he said the name, the wood glistened as if its clear grain were moist with dew.

What the hell is this? Covenant tried to balance himself for whatever was coming.

But the Hirebrand's next move caught him by surprise. Baradakas swung his rod and lofted it toward the Unbeliever.

He jerked aside and clutched at the *lomillialor* with his right hand. But he did not have enough fingers to get a quick grip on it; it slipped away from him, dropped to the floor with a wooden click that seemed unnaturally loud in the hush of the chamber.

For an instant, everyone remained still, frozen while they

absorbed the meaning of what they had seen. Then, in unison, the Heers uttered their verdict with all the finality of a death sentence.

'The High Wood rejects him. He is a wrong in the Land.'

10

THE CELEBRATION OF SPRING

In one fluid motion, Baradakas drew a club from his cloak and raised it as he moved toward Covenant.

Covenant reacted instinctively, defensively. Before the Hirebrand could reach him, he stooped and snatched up the *lomillialor* rod with his left hand. As Baradakas swung the club at his head, he slashed the Hirebrand's arm with the rod.

In a shower of white sparks, the club sprang into splinters. Baradakas was flung back as if he had been blasted away by an explosion.

The force of the hit vibrated through Covenant's hand to his elbow, and his fingers were struck momentarily numb. The rod started to slip from his hand. He gaped at it, thinking, What the hell – ?

But then the mute astonishment of the Heers, and the Hirebrand's crumpled form, steadied him. Test me? he rasped. Bastards. He took the rod in his right hand, holding it by the middle as Baradakas had done. Its glistening wood felt slick; it gave him a sensation of slippage, as if it were oozing from his grasp, though the wood did not actually move. As he gripped it, he glared around at the Heers, put all the anger their treatment had sparked in him into his gaze. 'Now why don't you tell me one more time about how this thing rejects me.'

Soranal and Llaura stood on either side of Atiaran, with Malliner opposite them against the wall. Omournil and Padrias were bent over the fallen Hirebrand. As Covenant surveyed them, Atiaran faced him grimly. 'In the older age,' she said, 'when High Lord Kevin trusted the Grey Slayer, he was given priceless gifts of *orcrest* and *lomillialor*. The tale says that these gifts were soon lost – but while the Grey Slayer possessed them they did not reject him. It is possible for Despite to wear the guise of truth. Perhaps the wild magic surpasses truth.'

Thanks a lot! Covenant glared at her. What're you trying to do to me?

In a pale voice, Llaura replied, 'That is the tale. But we are only Woodhelvennin – not Lords. Such matters are beyond us. Never in the memory of our people has a test of truth struck down a Hirebrand of the *lillianrill*. What is the song? – "he will save or damn the Earth." Let us pray that we will not find damnation for our distrust.' Extending an unsteady hand toward Covenant in the salute of welcome, she said, 'Hail, Unbeliever! Pardon our doubts, and be welcome in Soaring Woodhelven.'

For an instant Covenant faced her with a bitter retort twisting his lips. But he found when he met her eyes that he could see the sincerity of her apology. The perception abashed his vehemence. With conflicting intentions, he muttered, 'Forget it.'

Llaura and Soranal both bowed as if he had accepted her apology. Then they turned to watch as Baradakas climbed dazedly to his feet. His hands pulled at his face as if it were covered with cobwebs, but he assured Omournil and Padrias that he was unharmed. With a mixture of wonder and dismay in his eyes, he also saluted Covenant.

Covenant responded with a dour nod. He did not wait for the Hirebrand to ask: he handed the *lomillialor* to Baradakas, and was glad to be rid of its disquieting, insecure touch.

Baradakas received the rod and smiled at it crookedly, as if it had witnessed his defeat. Then he slipped it away into his cloak. Turning his smile toward Covenant, he said, 'Unbeliever, our presences are no longer needed here. You have not eaten, and the weariness of the journey lies heavily upon you. Will you accept the hospitality of my house?'

The invitation surprised Covenant; for a moment he hesitated, trying to decide whether or not he could trust the Hirebrand. Baradakas appeared calm, unhostile, but his smile was more complex than Llaura's apology. But then Covenant reflected that if the question were one of trust, he would be safer with Baradakas alone than with all the Heers together. Stiffly, he said, 'You honour me.'

The Hirebrand bowed. 'In accepting a gift you honour the giver.' He looked around at the other Woodhelvennin, and when they nodded their approval, he turned and bowed out of the heartwood chamber.

Covenant glanced toward Atiaran, but she was already talking softly to Soranal. Without further delay, he stepped out onto the broad limb beside Baradakas.

The night over the great tree was now scattered with lights – the home fires of the Woodhelvennin. They illuminated the fall far down through the branches, but did not reach to the ground.

Involuntarily, Covenant clutched at Baradakas's shoulder.

'It is not far,' the Hirebrand said softly. 'Only up to the next limb. I will come behind you – you will not fall.'

Cursing softly through his teeth, Covenant gripped the rungs of the ladder. He wanted to retreat, go back to the solidity of the heartwood chamber, but pride and anger prevented him. And the rungs felt secure, almost adhesive, to his fingers. When Baradakas placed a reassuring hand on his back, he started awkwardly upward.

As Baradakas had promised, the next limb was not far away. Soon Covenant reached another broad branch. A few steps out from the trunk, it forked, and in the fork sat the Hirebrand's home. Holding Baradakas's shoulders for support, he gained the doorway, crossed the threshold as if he were being blown in by a gust of relief.

He was in a neat, two-roomed dwelling formed entirely from the branches of the tree. Interwoven limbs made part of the floor and all the walls, including the partition between the rooms. And the ceiling was a dome of twigs and leaves. Along one wall of the first room, broad knees of wood grew into the chamber like chairs, and a bunk opposite them. The place had a warm, clean atmosphere, an ambience of devotion to lore, that Covenant found faintly disturbing, like a reminder that the Hirebrand could be a dangerous man.

While Covenant scanned the room, Baradakas set torches in each of the outer walls and lit them by rubbing his hands over their ends and murmuring softly. Then he rummaged around in the far room for a moment, and returned carrying a tray laden with slabs of bread and cheese, a large bunch of grapes, and a wooden jug. He set a small, three-legged table between two of the chairs, put the tray on it, and motioned for Covenant to sit down.

At the sight of the food, Covenant discovered that he was hungry; he had eaten nothing but *aliantha* for the past two days. He watched while Baradakas bowed momentarily over the food. Then he seated himself. Following his host's example, he made sandwiches with cheese and grapes between slices of fresh bread, and helped himself liberally to the jug of springwine. In the first rush of eating, he said nothing, saving his attention for the food.

But he did not forget who his host was, what had happened between them.

Leaving the springwine with Covenant, Baradakas cleared away the remains of the meal. When he returned after storing his food in the far room, he said, 'Now, Unbeliever. In what way may I give you comfort?'

Covenant took a deep draught of springwine, then replied as casually as he could, 'Give an answer. You were ready to split my head open – back there. And it looked as if you got quite a jolt from that – from that High Wood. Why did you invite me here?'

For a moment, Baradakas hesitated, as if pondering how much he should say. Then he reached into his back room, picked up a smooth staff nearly six feet long, and sat down on the bed across from Covenant. As he spoke, he began polishing the white wood of the staff with a soft cloth. 'There are many reasons, Thomas Covenant. You required a place to sleep, and my home is nearer to the heartwood chamber than any other – for one who dislikes heights. And neither you nor I are necessary for the consideration of counsel and help which will be done this night. Atiaran knows the Land – she will say all that need be said concerning your journey. And both Soranal and Llaura are able to give any help she may ask.'

As he looked across the room at the Hirebrand's working hands and light, penetrating eyes, Covenant had the odd feeling that his test was being resumed – that the encounter with the *lomillialor* had only begun Baradakas's examining. But the springwine unknotted his fears and tensions; he was not anxious. Steadily, he said, 'Tell me more.'

'I also intended that my offer of hospitality should be an apology. I was prepared to injure you, and that violation of my Oath of Peace needs reparation. Had you shown yourself to be a servant of the Grey Slayer, it would have sufficed to capture you. And injury might have deprived the Lords of a chance to examine you. So in that way I was wrong. And became more wrong still when you lifted the *lomillialor*, and its fire struck me. I hope to amend my folly.'

Covenant recognized the Hirebrand's frankness, but his sense of being probed sharpened rather than faded. He held his host's eyes as he said, 'You still haven't answered my question.'

In an unsurprised tone, Baradakas countered, 'Are there other reasons? What do you see in me?'

'You're still testing me,' Covenant growled.

The Hirebrand nodded slowly. 'Perhaps. Perhaps I am.' He got to his feet and braced one end of the staff against the floor as he gave a last touch to its polish. Then he said, 'See, Thomas Covenant – I have made a staff for you. When I began it, I believed it was for myself. But now I know otherwise. Take it. It may serve you when help and counsel fail.' To the brief question in Covenant's eyes, he replied, 'No, this is not High Wood. But it is good nonetheless. Let me give it to you.'

Covenant shook his head. 'Finish your testing.'

Suddenly, Baradakas raised the staff and struck the wood under his feet a hard blow. For an instant, the entire limb shook as if a gale had come up; the smaller branches thrashed, and the dwelling tossed like a chip on an angry wave. Covenant feared that the tree was falling, and he gripped his chair in apprehension. But almost immediately the violence passed. Baradakas levelled his pale eyes at Covenant and whispered, 'Then hear me, Unbeliever. Any test of truth is no greater than the one who gives it. And I have felt your power. In all the memory of the *lillianrill*, no Hirebrand has ever been struck by the High Wood. We are the friends of the One Tree, not its foes. But beside you I am as weak as a child. I cannot force the truth from you. In spite of my testing, you might be the Grey Slayer himself, come to turn all the life of the Land to ashes.'

Incensed by the suggestion, Covenant spat, 'That's ridiculous.'

Baradakas stepped closer, drove his probing gaze deep into Covenant's eyes. Covenant squirmed; he could feel the Hirebrand exploring parts of him that he wanted to protect, keep hidden. What has that bastard Foul to do with me? he demanded bitterly. I didn't exactly choose to be his errand boy.

Abruptly, Baradakas's eyes widened, and he fell back across the room as if he had seen something of astonishing power. He caught himself on the bed, sat there for a moment while he watched his hands tremble on the staff. Then he said carefully, 'True. One day I may be wise enough to know what can be relied upon. Now I need time to understand. I trust you, my friend. At the last trial, you will not abandon us to death.

'Here.' He proffered the staff again. 'Will you not accept my gift?'

Covenant did not reply at once. He was trembling also, and he had to clench himself before he could say without a tremor, 'Why? Why do you trust me?'

The Hirebrand's eyes gleamed as if he were on the verge of tears, but he was smiling as he said, 'You are a man who knows the value of beauty.'

Covenant stared at that answer for a moment, then looked away. A complex shame came over him; he felt unclean, tainted, in the face of Baradakas's trust. But then he stiffened. Keep moving. Survive. What does trust have to do with it? Brusquely, he reached out and accepted the staff.

It felt pure in his hands, as if it had been shaped from the healthiest wood by the most loving devotion. He gripped it, scrutinized it, as if it could provide him with the innocence he lacked.

A short time later, he surprised himself with a wide yawn. He had not realized that he was so tired. He tried to suppress his weariness, but the effort only produced another yawn.

Baradakas responded with a kindly smile. He left the bed and motioned for Covenant to lie down.

Covenant had no intention of going to sleep, but as soon as he was horizontal, all the springwine he had consumed seemed to rush to his head, and he felt himself drifting on the high tree breeze. Soon he was fast in slumber.

He slept soundly, disturbed only by the memory of the Hirebrand's intense, questioning eyes, and by the sensation that the *lomillialor* was slipping through his fingers, no matter how hard he clenched it. When he awoke the next morning, his arms ached as if he had been grappling with an angel all night.

Opening his eyes, he found Atiaran sitting across the room from him, waiting. As soon as she saw that he was awake, she stood and moved closer to him. 'Come, Thomas Covenant,' she said. 'Already we have lost the dawn of this day.'

Covenant studied her for a moment. The background of her face held a deepening shadow of fatigue, and he guessed that she had spent much of the night talking with the Heers. But she seemed somehow comforted by what she had shared and heard, and the brightness of her glance was almost optimistic. Perhaps she now had some sort of hope.

He approved of anything that might reduce her hostility toward him, and he swung out of bed as if he shared her optimism. Despite the soreness of his arms, he felt remarkably refreshed, as if the ambience of the Woodhelven had been exerting its hospitality, its beneficence, to help him rest. Moving briskly, he washed his face, dried himself on a thick towel of leaves, then checked himself for injuries and adjusted his clothing. A loaf lay on the three-legged table, and when he broke off a hunk for his breakfast, he found that it was made of bread and meat baked together. Munching it, he went to look out one of the windows.

Atiaran joined him, and together they gazed through the branches northward. In the far distance, they saw a river running almost directly east, and beyond it the hills spread on to the horizon. But something more than the river separated these northern hills from those beside which the travellers had been walking since they left Mithil Stonedown. The land beyond the river seemed to ripple in the morning sunshine, as if the quiet earth were flowing over shoals – as if there the secret rock of the Land ruffled the surface, revealing itself to those who could read it. From his high Woodhelven vantage, Covenant felt he was seeing something that surpassed even his new perceptions.

'There,' said Atiaran softly, as if she were speaking of a holy place, 'there is Andelain. The Hirebrand has chosen his home well for such a view. Here the Mithil River runs east before turning north again toward Gravin Threndor and the Soulsease. And beyond are the Andelainian Hills, the heart-healing richness of the Land. Ah, Covenant, the seeing of them gives me courage. And Soranal has taught me a path which may make possible my fondest dream — With good fortune and good speed, we may see that which will turn much of my folly to wisdom. We must go. Are you prepared?'

No, Covenant thought. Not to go climbing around this tree. But he nodded. Atiaran had brought his pack to him, and while she stepped out of the Hirebrand's home on to the broad branch, he pulled the straps on to his shoulders, ignoring the ache of his arms. Then he took up the staff Baradakas had given him, and braced himself to risk his neck on the descent of the Woodhelven.

The trunk was only three or four steps away, but the two-hundred-foot drop to the ground made him freeze, hesitate apprehensively while the first reels of vertigo gnawed at his resolve. But as he stood in the Hirebrand's doorway, he heard the shouting of young voices, and saw children scampering through the branches overhead. Some of them pursued others, and in the chase they sprang from limb to limb as blithely as if the fall were helpless to hurt them.

The next instant, two children, a boy and a girl, dropped on the limb before Covenant from a branch nearly twenty feet above. The girl was in merry pursuit of the boy, but he eluded her touch and darted around behind Covenant. From this covert, he shouted gleefully, 'Safe! Chase another! I am safe!'

Without thinking, Covenant said, 'He's safe.'

The girl laughed, faked a lunge forward, and sprang away after someone else. At once, the boy dashed to the trunk and scurried up the ladder toward higher playgrounds.

Covenant took a deep breath, clutched the staff for balance, and stepped away from the door. Teetering awkwardly, he struggled to the relative safety of the trunk.

After that, he felt better. When he slid the staff through his pack straps, he could grip the ladder with both hands, and then the secure touch of the rungs reassured him. Before he had covered half the distance, his heart was no longer pounding, and he was able to trust his hold enough to look about him at the dwellings and people as he passed.

Finally, he reached the lowest branches, and followed Atiaran down the stair to the ground. There the Heers were gathered to say their farewells. When he saw Baradakas, Covenant took the staff in his hands to show that he had not forgotten it, and grimaced in response to the Hirebrand's smile.

'Well, message-bearers,' said Llaura after a pause, 'you have told us that the fate of the Land is on your shoulders, and we believe. It sorrows us that we cannot ease the burden — but we judge that no one can take your place in this matter. What little help we can give we have given. All which remains for us is to defend our homes, and to pray for you. We wish you good speed for the sake of all the Land. And for your own sake we urge you to be in time for the Celebration. There are great omens of hope for any who view that festival.

'Atiaran Trell-mate, go in Peace and fealty. Remember the path Soranal taught you, and do not turn aside.

'Thomas Covenant, Unbeliever, and stranger to the Land – be true. In the hour of darkness, remember the Hirebrand's staff. Now be on your way.'

Atiaran replied as formally as if she were completing a ritual. 'We go, remembering Soaring Woodhelven for home and help and hope.' She bowed, touching her palms to her forehead and then spreading her arms wide. Uncertainly, Covenant followed her example. The Heers returned the heart-opening gesture of farewell with ceremonial deliberateness. Then Atiaran strode off northward, and Covenant scudded along behind her like a leaf in the wake of her determination.

Neither of them looked back. The rest and restoration of the fair tree village made them brisk, gave them a forward air. They were both in their separate ways eager for Andelain, and they knew that Jehannum had left Soaring Woodhelven toward the east, not the north. They hastened ahead among the richening hills, and reached the banks of the Mithil River early that afternoon.

They crossed by wading a wide shallows. Before she entered the water, Atiaran removed her sandals, and some half-conscious insight urged Covenant to take off his boots and socks, roll up his pant legs. As he smelled the first lush scents of the Hills, he felt somehow that he needed to wade the Mithil barefoot in order to be ready, that the foot-washing of the stream was necessary to transubstantiate his flesh into the keener essence of Andelain. And when he stepped on to the north bank, he found that he could feel its vitality through his feet; now even his soles were sensitive to the Land's health.

He so liked the strong sensation of the Hills under his toes that he was loath to put his boots back on, but he denied himself that pleasure so that he would be able to keep up with Atiaran's pace. Then he followed her along the path which Soranal had taught her – an easy way through the centre of Andelain – walked and wondered at the change that had come over the Earth since they had crossed the river.

He felt the change distinctly, but it seemed to go beyond the details which composed it. The trees were generally taller and broader than their southern relations; abundant and prodigal *aliantha* sometimes covered whole hillsides with viridian; the rises and vales luxuriated in deep aromatic grass; flowers bobbed in the breeze as spontaneously as if just moments before they had gaily burst from the nurture of the soil; small woodland animals – rabbits, squirrels, badgers, and the like – scampered around, only vaguely remembering that they were wary of humans. But the real difference was transcendent. The Andelainian Hills carried a purer impression of health to all Covenant's senses than anything else he had experienced. The aura of rightness here was so powerful that he began to regret he belonged in a world where health was impalpable, indefinite, discernible only by implication. For a time, he wondered how he would be able to endure going back, waking up. But the beauty of Andelain soon made him forget such concerns. It was a dangerous loveliness – not because it was treacherous or harmful, but because it could seduce. Before long, disease, VSE, Despite, anger, all were forgotten, lost in the flow of health from one vista to another around him.

Enclosed in the Hills, surrounded by such tangible and specific vitality, he became more and more surprised that Atiaran did not wish to linger. As they hiked over the lambent terrain, penetrating league after league deeper into Andelain, he wanted to stop at each new revelation, each new valley or avenue or dale, to savour what he saw – grip it with his eyes until it was part of him, indelible, secure against any coming bereavement. But Atiaran pushed on – arising early, stopping little, hurrying late. Her eyes were focused far away, and the fatigue mounting behind her features seemed unable to reach the surface. Clearly, even these Hills paled for her beside her anticipation of the unexplained 'Celebration'. Covenant had no choice but to urge himself after her; her will tolerated no delay.

Their second night away from Soaring Woodhelven was so bright and clear that they did not have to stop with the setting of the sun, and Atiaran kept going until nearly midnight. After supper, Covenant sat for a while looking at the sky and the piquant stars. The ageing crescent of the moon stood high in the heavens, and its white silver sent down only a suggestion of the eldritch light which had illuminated his first night in the Land. Casually, he remarked, 'The moon'll be dark in a few days.'

At that, Atiaran looked at him sharply, as if she suspected that he had discovered some secret of hers. But she said nothing, and he did not know whether she reacted to a memory or to an anticipation.

The next day began as splendidly as the previous one. Sunshine begemmed the dew, sparkled like diamonds among the grass and leaves; air as fresh as the Earth's first breath carried the tang of *aliantha* and larch, the fragrance of Gilden and peony, across the Hills. Covenant beheld such things with something like bliss in his heart, and followed Atiaran northward as if he were content. But early in the afternoon something happened which darkened all his joy, offended him to the marrow of his bones. As he travelled down a natural lane between tree-thick hills, walking with a fine sense of the springy grass under his feet, he stepped without warning on a patch of turf that felt as dangerous as a pit of quicksand.

Instinctively, he recoiled, jerked back three steps. At once, the threatening sensation vanished. But his nerves remembered it from the sole of his foot up the whole length of his leg.

He was so surprised, so insulted, that he did not think to call Atiaran. Instead, he cautiously approached the spot on which he had felt the danger, and touched it with one tentative toe. This time, however, he felt nothing but the lush grass of Andelain. Bending down, he went over the grass for a yard in all directions with his hands. But whatever had fired his senses of wrongness was gone now, and after a moment of perplexity he started forward again. At first he took each step gingerly, expecting another jolt. But the Earth seemed as full of pure, resonant vitality as before. Shortly, he broke into a trot to catch up with Atiaran.

Toward evening, he felt the sting of wrong again, as if he had stepped into acid. This time, he reacted in violent revulsion; he pitched forward as if diving away from a blast of lightning, and a yell ripped past his teeth before he could stop himself. Atiaran came back to him at a turn, and found him pawing over the grass, tearing up the blades in handfuls of outrage.

'Here!' he gritted, thumping the turf with his fist. 'By hell! It was here.'

Atiaran blinked at him blankly. He jumped to his feet, pointed an accusing finger at the ground. 'Didn't you feel it? It was there. Hellfire!' His finger quivered. 'How did you miss it?'

'I felt nothing,' she replied evenly.

He shuddered and dropped his hand. 'It felt as if I – as if I stepped in quicksand – or acid – or – ' he remembered the slain Waynhim – 'or murder.'

Slowly, Atiaran knelt beside the spot he indicated. For a moment, she studied it, then touched it with her hands. When she stood up, she said, 'I feel nothing – '

'It's gone,' he interrupted.

' – but I have not the touch of a *rhadhamaerl*,' she went on. 'Have you felt this before?'

'Once. Earlier.'

'Ah,' she sighed, 'would that I were a Lord, and knew what to do. There must be an evil working deep in the Earth – a great evil, indeed, if the Andelainian Hills are not altogether safe. But the ill is

131

new yet, or timid. It does not remain. We must hope to outrun it. Ah, weak! Our speed becomes less sufficient with each passing day.'

She pulled her robe tightly about her, strode away into the evening. She and Covenant travelled on without a halt until night was thick around them, and the waning moon was high in its path among the stars.

The next day, Covenant felt convulsions of ill through the grass more often. Twice during the morning, and four times during the afternoon and evening, one foot or the other recoiled with sudden ferocity from the turf, and by the time Atiaran stopped for the night, his nerves from his legs to the roots of his teeth were raw and jangling. He felt intensely that such sore spots were an affront to, even a betrayal of, Andelain, where every other touch and line and hue of sky and tree and grass and hill was redolent with richness. Those attacks, pangs, stings made him involuntarily wary of the ground itself, as if the very foundation of the Earth had been cast into doubt.

On the fifth day since Soaring Woodhelven, he felt the wrongness of the grass less often, but the attacks showed an increase in virulence. Shortly after noon, he found a spot of ill that did not vanish after he first touched it. When he set his foot on it again, he felt a quiver as if he had stepped on an ache in the ground. The vibration rapidly numbed his foot, and his jaws hurt from clenching his teeth, but he did not back away. Calling to Atiaran, he knelt on the grass and touched the Earth's sore with his hands.

To his surprise, he felt nothing.

Atiaran explored the ground herself, then considered him with a frown in her eyes. She also felt nothing.

But when he probed the spot with his foot, he found that the pain was still there. It scraped his brain, made sweat bead on his forehead, drew a snarl from his throat. As the ache spread through his bones, sending cold numbness up his leg, he bent to slide his fingers under the sole of his boot. But his hands still felt nothing; only his feet were sensitive to the peril.

On an impulse, he threw off one boot, removed his sock, and placed his bare foot on the spot of ill. This time, the discrepancy was even more surprising. He could feel the pain with his booted foot, but not with his bare one. And yet his sensations were perfectly clear; the wrong arose from the ground, not from his boot.

Before he could stop himself, he snatched off his other boot and sock, and cast them away from him. Then he dropped heavily to sit on the grass, and clutched his throbbing head in both hands.

'I have no sandals for you,' Atiaran said stiffly. 'You will need footwear before this journey has reached its end.'

Covenant hardly heard her. He felt acutely that he had recognized a danger, identified a threat which had been warping him for days without his knowledge.

Is that how you're going to do it, Foul? he snarled. First my nerves come back to life. Then Andelain makes me forget – Then I throw away my boots. Is that it? Break down all my defences one at a time so that I won't be able to protect myself? Is that how you're going to destroy me?

'We must go on,' Atiaran said. 'Decide what you will do.'

Decide? Bloody hell! Covenant jerked himself to his feet. Fuming, he grated through his teeth, 'It's not that easy.' Then he stalked over to retrieve his boots and socks.

Survive.

He laced his feet into his boots as if they were a kind of armour.

For the rest of the day, he shied away from every hint of pain in the ground, and followed Atiaran grimly, with a clenched look in his eyes, striving against the stinging wrong to preserve his sovereignty, his sense of himself. And toward evening his struggle seemed to find success. After a particularly vicious attack late in the afternoon, the ill pangs stopped. He did not know whether or not they would return, but for a while at least he was free of them.

That night was dark with clouds, and Atiaran was forced to make camp earlier than usual. Yet she and Covenant got little rest. A light, steady rain soaked their blankets, and kept them awake most of the night, huddling for shelter under the deeper shadow of an enshrouding willow.

But the next morning – the sixth of their journey from Soaring Woodhelven – dawned bright and full of Andelainian cheer. Atiaran met it with haste and anticipation in her every move; and the way she urged Covenant along seemed to express more friendliness, more companionship, than any thing she had done since the beginning of their sojourn. Her desire for speed was infectious; Covenant was glad to share it because it rescued him from thinking about the possibility of further attacks of wrong. They began the day's travel at a lope.

The day was made for travelling. The air was cool, the sun clean and encouraging; the path led straight and level; springy grass carried Atiaran and Covenant forward at every stride. And her contagious eagerness kept him trotting behind her league after league. Toward midday, she slowed her pace to eat treasure-berries along the way; but even then she made good speed, and as evening neared she pushed their pace into a lope again.

Then the untracked path which the Woodhelvennin had taught her brought them to the end of a broad valley. After a brief halt while she verified her bearings, she started straight up a long, slow hillside that seemed to carry on away eastward for a great distance. She chose a plumb-line direction which took her directly between two matched Gilden trees a hundred yards above the valley, and Covenant followed her toiling lope up the hill without question. He was too tired and out of breath to ask questions.

So they ascended that hillside — Atiaran trotting upward with her head held high and her hair fluttering, as if she saw fixed before her the starry gates of heaven, and Covenant plodding, pumping behind her. At their backs, the sun sank in a deep exhalation like the release of a long-pent sigh. And ahead of them the slope seemed to stretch on into the sky.

Covenant was dumbfounded when Atiaran reached the crest of the hill, stopped abruptly, grabbed his shoulders, and spun him around in a circle, crying joyfully, 'We are here! We are in time!'

He lost his balance and fell to the turf. For a moment he lay panting, with hardly enough energy to stare at her. But she was not aware of him. Her eyes were fixed down the eastern slope of the hill as she called in a voice short-breathed by fatigue and exultation and reverence. '*Banas Nimoram!* Ah, glad heart! Glad heart of Andelain. I have lived to this time.'

Caught by the witchery in her voice, Covenant levered himself to his feet and followed her gaze as if he expected to behold the soul of Andelain incarnate.

He could not refrain from groaning at the first sag of his disappointment. He could see nothing to account for Atiaran's rapture, nothing that was more healthy or precious than the myriad vistas of Andelain past which she had rushed unheeding. Below him, the grass dipped into a smooth wide bowl set into the Hills like a drinking cup for the night sky. With the sun gone, the outlines of the bowl were not clear, but starlight was enough to show that there were no trees, no bushes, no interruptions to the smoothness of the bowl. It looked as regular as if the surface of the grass had been sanded and burnished. On this night, the stars seemed especially gay, as if the darkness of the moon challenged them to new brightness. But Covenant felt that such things were not enough to reward his bone-deep fatigue.

However, Atiaran did not ignore his groan. Taking his arm, she said, 'Do not judge me yet,' and drew him forward. Under the branches of the last tree on the bowl's lip, she dropped her pack and sat against the trunk, facing down the hill. When Covenant had joined her, she said softly, 'Control your mad heart, Unbeliever. We are here in time. This is *Banas Nimoram*, the dark of the moon on the middle night of spring. Not in my generation has there been such a

134

night, such a time of rareness and beauty. Do not measure the Land by the standard of yourself. Wait. This is *Banas Nimoram*, the Celebration of Spring – finest rite of all the treasures of the Earth. If you do not disturb the air with anger, we will see the Dance of the Wraiths of Andelain.' As she spoke, her voice echoed with rich harmonica as if she were singing; and Covenant felt the force of what she promised, though he did not understand. It was not a time for questions, and he set himself to wait for the visitation.

Waiting was not difficult. First Atiaran passed bread and the last of her springwine to him, and eating and drinking eased some of his weariness. Then, as the night deepened, he found that the air which flowed up to them from the bowl had a lush, restful effect. When he took it far into his lungs, it seemed to unwind his cares and dreads, setting everything but itself behind him and lifting him into a state of calm suspense. He relaxed in the gentle breeze, settled himself more comfortably against the tree. Atiaran's shoulder touched his with warmth, as if she had forgiven him. The night deepened, and the stars gleamed expectantly, and the breeze shifted the cobwebs and dust from Covenant's heart – and waiting was not difficult.

The first flickering light came like a twist of resolution which brought the whole night into focus. Across the width of the bowl, he saw a flame like the burn of a candle – tiny in the distance, and yet vivid, swaying yellow and orange as clearly as if he held the candlestick in his hands. He felt strangely sure that the distance was meaningless; if the flame were before him on the grass, it would be no larger than his palm.

As the Wraith appeared, Atiaran's breath hissed intently between her teeth, and Covenant sat up straighter to concentrate more keenly.

With a lucid, cycling movement, the flame moved down into the bowl. It was not halfway to the bottom when a second fire arrived on the northern rim. Then two more Wraiths entered from the south – and then, too sudden to be counted, a host of flames began tracing their private ways into the bowl from all directions. Some passed within ten feet of Atiaran and Covenant on either side, but they seemed unconscious of the observers; they followed their slow cycles as if each were alone in the Hills, independent of every gleam but its own. Yet their lights poured together, casting a dome of gold through which the stars could barely be seen; and at moments particular Wraiths seemed to bow and revolve around each other, as if sharing a welcome of their way toward the centre.

Covenant watched the great movement that brought thousands of flames, bobbing at shoulder height, into the bowl, and he hardly dared to breathe. In the excess of his wonder, he felt like an unpermitted spectator beholding some occult enactment which was not meant for human eyes. He clutched his chest as if his chance to see the Celebration to its end rode on the outer silence of his respiration, as if he feared that any sound might violate the fiery conclave, scare the Wraiths away.

Then a change came over the gathered flames. Up to the sky rose a high, scintillating, wordless song, an arching melody. From the centre of the bowl, the private rotations of the Wraiths resolved themselves into a radiating, circling Dance. Each Wraith seemed finally to have found its place in a large, wheel-like pattern which filled the bowl, and the wheel began to turn on its centre. But there were no lights in the centre; the wheel turned on a hub of stark blackness which refused the flow of the Wraiths.

As the song spread through the night, the great circle revolved – each flame dancing a secret, independent dance, various in moves and sways – each flame keeping its place in the whole pattern as it turned. And in the space between the inner hub and the outer rim, more circles rolled, so that the whole wheel was filled with many wheels, all turning. And no Wraith kept one position long. The flames flowed continuously through their moving pattern, so that as the wheel turned, the individual Wraiths danced from place to place, now swinging along the outer rim, now gyring through the middle circles, now circling the hub. Every Wraith moved and changed places constantly, but the pattern was never broken – no hiatus of misstep gapped the wheel, even for an instant – and every flame seemed both perfectly alone, wandering mysteriously after some personal destiny through the Dance, and perfectly part of the whole. While they danced, their steps grew stronger, until the stars were paled out of the sky, and the night was withdrawn, like a distant spectator of the Celebration.

And the beauty and wonder of the Dance made Covenant's suspense a yearning ache.

Then a new change entered the festival. Covenant did not realize it until Atiaran touched his arm; her signal sent a thrill of awareness through him, and he saw that the wheel of the Wraiths was slowly bending. The rest of the wheel retained its shape, and the black core did not move. Gradually, the turning circle became lopsided as the outer Wraiths moved closer to the onlookers. Soon the growing bulge pointed unmistakably at Covenant.

In response, he seemed to feel their song more intensely – a keening, ecstatic lament, a threnody as thoroughly passionate as a dirge and as dispassionate as a sublime, impersonal affirmation. Their nearing flames filled him with awe and fascination, so that he shrank within himself but could not move. Cycle after cycle, the

Wraiths reached out toward him, and he clasped his hands over his knees and held himself still, taut-hearted and utterless before the fiery Dancers.

In moments, the tip of this long extension from the circle stood above him, and he could see each flame bowing to him as it danced by. Then the rim of the extension dipped, and the pace of the Dance slowed, as though to give each Wraith a chance to linger in his company. Soon the fires were passing within reach of his hand. Then the long arm of the Dance flared, as if a decision had run through the Dancers. The nearest Wraith moved forward to settle on his wedding band.

He flinched, expecting the fire to burn him, but there was no pain. The flame attached itself to the ring as to a wick, and he felt faintly the harmonies of the Celebration song through his finger. As the Wraith held to his ring, it danced and jumped as if it were feeding excitedly there. And slowly its colour turned from flaming yellow-orange to silver-white.

When the transformation was complete, the Wraith flashed away, and the next took its place. A succession of fires followed, each dancing on his ring until it became argent; and as his anxiety relaxed, the succession grew faster. In a short time, the line of glistening white Wraiths had almost reached back to the rest of the Dance. Each new flame presented itself swiftly, as if eager for some apotheosis, some culmination of its being, in the white gold of Covenant's ring.

Before long, his emotion became too strong to let him remain seated. He surged to his feet, holding out his ring so that the Wraiths could light on it without lowering themselves.

Atiaran stood beside him. He had eyes only for the transformation which his ring somehow made possible, but she looked away across the Dance.

What she saw made her dig her fingers like claws of despair into his arm. 'No! By the Seven! This must not be!'

Her cry snatched at his attention; his gaze jumped across the bowl.

'There! That is the meaning of the ill your feet have felt!'

What he saw staggered him like a blow to the heart.

Coming over the northeast rim of the bowl into the golden light was an intruding wedge of darkness, as pitch-dark and unilluminable as the spawning ground of night. The wedge cut its narrow way down toward the Dance, and through the song of the flames, it carried a sound like a host of bloody feet rushing over clean grass. Deliberately, agonizingly, it reached inward without breaking its formation. In moments, the tip of darkness sliced into the Dance and began plunging towards its centre.

In horror, Covenant saw that the Dance did not halt or pause. At the wedge's first touch, the song of the Wraiths dropped from the air as if it had been ripped away by sacrilege, leaving no sound behind it but a noise like running murder. But the Dance did not stop. The flames went on revolving as if they were unconscious of what was happening to them, helpless. They followed their cycles into the wedge's path and vanished as if they had fallen into an abyss. No Wraith emerged from that darkness.

Swallowing every light that touched it, the black wedge gouged its way into the Celebration.

'They will all die!' Atiaran groaned. 'They cannot stop – cannot escape. They must dance until the Dance is done. All dead – every Wraith, every bright light of the Land! This must not be. Help them! Covenant, help them!'

But Covenant did not know how to help. He was paralysed. The sight of the black wedge made him feel as nauseated as if he were observing across a gulf of numbness his fingers being eaten by a madman – nauseated and enraged and impotent, as if he had waited too long to defend himself, and now had no hands with which to fight back. The knife of Triock slipped from his numb fingers and disappeared in darkness.

How – ?

For an instant, Atiaran dragged furiously at him. 'Covenant! Help them!' she shrieked into his face. Then she turned and raced down the valley to meet the wedge.

The Wraiths – !

Her movement broke the freeze of his horror. Snatching up the staff of Baradakas, he ducked under the flames and sped after her, holding himself bent over to stay below the path of the Wraiths. A madness seemed to hasten his feet; he caught Atiaran before she was halfway to the hub. Thrusting her behind him, he dashed on toward the penetrating wedge, spurred by a blind conviction that he had to reach the centre before the blackness did.

Atiaran followed, shouting after him, 'Ware and ward! They are ur-viles! Demondim corruption!'

He scarcely heard her. He was focused on the furious need to gain the centre of the Dance. For better speed, he ran more upright, flicking his head aside whenever a Wraith flashed near the level of his eyes.

With a last burst, he broke into the empty core of the wheel.

He halted. Now he was close enough to see that the wedge was composed of tall, crowded figures, so black-fleshed that no light could gleam or glisten on their skin. As the helpless Wraiths swung into the wedge, the attackers ate them.

The ur-viles drew nearer. The tip of their wedge was a single figure, larger than the rest. Covenant could see it clearly. It looked like one of the Waynhim grown tall and evil – long torso, short limbs of equal length, pointed ears high on its head, eyeless face almost filled by gaping nostrils. Its slit mouth snapped like a trap whenever a Wraith came near. Mucus trailed from its nostrils back along either side of its head. When Covenant faced it, its nose twitched as if it smelled new game, and it snarled out a cadenced bark like an exhortation to the other creatures. The whole wedge thrust eagerly forward.

Atiaran caught up with Covenant and shouted in his ear, 'Your hand! Look at your hand!'

He jerked up his left hand. A Wraith still clung to his ring – burning whitely – obliviously dancing.

The next instant, the leading ur-vile breached the core of the Dance, and stopped. The attackers stood packed against each other's shoulders behind their leader. Dark, roynish, and cruel, they slavered together and bit at the helpless Wraiths.

Covenant quailed as if his heart had turned to sand. But Atiaran raged, 'Now! Strike them now!'

Trembling, he stepped forward. He had no idea what to do.

At once, the first ur-vile brandished a long knife with a seething, blood-red blade. Fell power radiated from the blade; in spite of themselves, Covenant and Atiaran recoiled.

The ur-vile raised its hand to strike.

Impulsively, Covenant shoved the white, burning Wraith at the ur-vile's face. With a snarl of pain, the creature jumped back.

A sudden intuition gripped Covenant. Instantly, he touched the end of his staff to the burning Wraith. With a flash, bold white flame bloomed from the staff, shading the gold of the Dance and challenging the force of the ur-viles. Their leader retreated again.

But at once it regained its determination. Springing forward, it stabbed into the heart of the white fire with its blood-red blade.

Power clashed to the core of the Dance. The ur-vile's blade seethed like hot hate, and the staff blazed wildly. Their conflict threw sparks as if the air were aflame in blood and lightning.

But the ur-vile was a master. Its might filled the bowl with a deep, crumbling sound, like the crushing of a boulder under huge pressure. In one abrupt exertion, Covenant's fire was stamped out.

The force of the extinguishing threw him and Atiaran to their backs on the grass. With a growl of triumph, the ur-viles poised to leap for the kill.

Covenant saw the red knife coming, and cowered with a pall of death over his mind.

139

But Atiaran scrambled back to her feet, crying, '*Melenkurion!*
Melenkurion abatha!' Her voice sounded frail against the victory of
the ur-viles, but she met them squarely, grappled with the leader's
knife-hand. Momentary, she withheld its stroke.

Then, from behind her to the west, her cry was answered. An iron
voice full of fury shouted, '*Melenkurion abatha! Binas mill Banas
Nimoram khabaal! Melenkurion abatha! Abatha Nimoram!*' The sound
broke through Covenant's panic, and he lurched up to Atiaran's aid.
But together they could not hold back the ur-vile; it flung them to
the ground again. At once, it pounced on them.

It was stopped halfway by a hulking form that leaped over them
to tackle it. For a moment, the two wrestled savagely. Then the
newcomer took the blood-red blade and drove it into the heart of
the creature.

A burst of snarls broke from the ur-viles. Covenant heard a
sweeping noise like the sound of many children running. Looking
up, he saw a stream of small animals pour into the bowl – rabbits,
badgers, weasels, moles, foxes, a few dogs. With silent determination, they hurled themselves at the ur-viles.

The Wraiths were scattering. While Covenant and Atiaran stumbled to their feet, the last flame passed from the bowl.

But the ur-viles remained, and their size made the animals' attack
look a mere annoyance. In the sudden darkness, the creatures
seemed to expand, as if the light had hindered them, forced them to
keep their close ranks. Now they broke away from each other.
Dozens of blades that boiled like lava leaped out at once, and in
horrible unison began to slaughter the animals.

Before Covenant could take in all that was happening, the hulking
figure who had saved them turned and hissed, 'Go! North to the
river. I have released the Wraiths. Now we will make time for your
escape. Go!'

'No!' Atiaran panted. 'You are the only man. The animals are not
enough. We must help you fight!'

'Together we are not enough!' he cried. 'Do you forget your task?
You must reach the Lords – must! Drool must pay for this Desecration! Go! I cannot give you much time!' Shouting, '*Melenkurion
abatha!*' he whirled and jumped into the thick of the fray, felling ur-
viles with his mighty fists.

Pausing only to pick up the staff of Baradakas, Atiaran fled
northward. And Covenant followed her, running as if the ur-vile
blades were striking at his back. The stars gave them enough light.
They drove themselves up the slope, not looking to see if they were
pursued, not caring about the packs they left behind – afraid to
think of anything except their need for distance. As they passed over

the rim of the bowl, the sounds of slaughter were abruptly dimmed. They heard no pursuit. But they ran on – ran, and still ran, and did not stop until they were caught in midstride by a short scream, full of agony and failed strength.

At the sound, Atiaran fell to her knees, and dropped her forehead to the earth, weeping openly. 'He is dead!' she wailed. 'The Unfettered One, dead! Alas for the Land! All my paths are ill, and destruction fills all my choices. From the first, I have brought wrong upon us. Now there will be no more Celebration, and the blame is mine.' Raising her face to Covenant, she sobbed, 'Take your staff and strike me, Unbeliever!'

Blankly, Covenant stared into the pooled hurt of her eyes. He felt benumbed with pain and grief and wasted rage, and did not understand why she castigated herself. He stooped for the staff, then took her arm and lifted her to her feet. Stunned and empty, he led her onward into the night until she had cried out her anguish and could stand on her own again. He wanted to weep himself, but in his long struggle with the misery of being a leper he had forgotten how, and now he could only keep on walking. He was aware as Atiaran regained control of herself and pulled away from him that she accused him of something. Throughout the sleepless night of their northward trek, he could do nothing about it.

11

THE UNHOMED

Gradually, night stumbled as if stunned and wandering aimlessly into an overcast day – limped through the wilderland of transition as though there were no knowing where the waste of darkness ended and the ashes of light began. The low clouds seemed full of grief – tense and uneasy with accumulated woe – and yet affectless, unable to rain, as if the air clenched itself too hard for tears. And through the dawn, Atiaran and Covenant moved heavily, unevenly, like pieces of broken lament.

The coming of day made no difference to them, did not alter the way they fled – terrorless because their capacity for fear was exhausted – into the north. Day and night were nothing but disguises, motley raiment, for the constant shadow on the Land's heart. To that heart they could not guess how much damage had been done. They could only judge their own hurt – and so throughout the long, dismal night and day which followed the defilement of the Celebration, they walked on haunted by what they had witnessed and numb to everything else, as though even hunger and thirst and fatigue were extinguished in them.

That night, their flesh reached the end of its endurance, and they pitched blindly into sleep, no longer able to care what pursuit was on their trail. While they slept, the sky found some release for its tension. Blue lightning flailed the Hills; thunder groaned in long-suppressed pain. When the travellers awoke, the sun stood over them, and their clothes were drenched with the night's rain. But sunshine and morning could not unscar their wounded memories. They clambered like corpses to their feet – ate *aliantha*, drank from a stream – set off again walking as if they were stiff with death.

Yet time and *aliantha* and Andelainian air slowly worked their resuscitation. Slowly, Covenant's weary thoughts shifted; the trudging horror of slaughter receded, allowed a more familiar pain to ache in him. He could hear Atiaran crying, *Covenant, help them!* and the sound made his blood run cold with impotence.

The Wraiths, the Wraiths! he moaned dimly, distantly, to himself. They had been so beautiful – and he had been so unable to save them.

Yet Atiaran had believed him capable of saving them; she had expected some putting forth of power – Like Lena and Baradakas and everyone else he met, she saw him as Berek Halfhand reborn, the master of wild magic. *You have might*, the Despiser had said. *You will never know what it is*. He did not know; how could he? What did magic, or even dreams, have to do with him?

And yet the Wraiths had paid homage to his ring as if they recognized his lost humanity. They had been changed by it.

After a time, he said without meaning to speak aloud, 'I would have saved them if I could.'

'You have the power.' Atiaran's voice was dull, inert, as if she were no longer capable of grief or anger.

'What power?' he asked painfully.

'Do you wear the white gold for nothing?'

'It's just a ring, I wear it – I wear it because I'm a leper. I don't know anything about power.'

She did not look at him. 'I cannot see. You are closed to me.'

At that, he wanted to protest, cry out, grab her by the shoulders and shout into her face. Closed? Look – look at me! I'm no Berek! No hero. I'm too sick for that. But he lacked the strength. And he

142

had been too badly hurt – hurt as much by Atiaran's impossible demand as by his powerlessness.

How – ?

The Wraiths!

How can this happen to me?

A moment passed while he groaned over the question. Then he sighed to himself, I should have known – He should have heard his danger in Atiaran's singing of the Berek legend, seen it in Andelain, felt it in the revulsion in his boots. But he had been deaf, blind, numb. He had been so busy moving ahead, putting madness behind him, that he had ignored the madness toward which the path of his dream tended. This dream wanted him to be a hero, a saviour; therefore it seduced him, swept him along – urging him forward so that he would run heedless of himself to risk his life for the sake of Wraiths, the Land, illusion. The only difference between this Atiaran and Lord Foul was that the Despiser wanted him to fail.

You will never know what it is. Of course he would never know. A visceral anger writhed under his fatigue. He was dreaming – that was the answer to everything, to the Land's impossible expectations of him as well as to the Land's impossibility. He knew the difference between reality and dream; he was sane.

He was a leper.

And yet the Wraiths had been so beautiful. They had been slaughtered –

I'm a leper!

Trembling, he began to give himself a VSE. Hellfire! What do Wraiths and wild magic and Berek bloody Halfhand have to do with me? His body appeared whole – he could see no injuries, his clothing was rumpled but unrent – but the end of the Hirebrand's staff had been blackened by the power of the ur-viles. By hell! They can't do this to me.

Fuming against his weariness, he shambled along at Atiaran's side. She did not look at him, did not seem to recognize his presence at all, and during the day he left her alone as if he feared how he would respond if he gave her an opportunity to accuse him. But when they halted that evening, the cold night and the brittle stars made him regret the loss of their blankets and graveling. To distract himself from his hollow discomfort, he resumed his half-forgotten efforts to learn about the Land. Stiffly, he said, 'Tell me about that – whoever saved us. Back there.'

A long silence passed before she said, 'Tomorrow.' Her voice was lightless, unillumined by anything except torpor or defeat. 'Let me be. Until tomorrow.'

Covenant nodded in the darkness. It felt thick with cold and beating wings, but he could answer it better than he could reply to Atiaran's tone. For a long time he shivered as if he were prepared to resent every dream that afflicted a miserable mankind, and at last he fell into fitful slumber.

The next day, the ninth from Soaring Woodhelven, Atiaran told Covenant about the Unfettered One in a voice as flat as crushed rock, as if she had reached the point where what she said, how she exposed herself, no longer mattered to her. 'There are those from the Loresraat,' she said, 'who find that they cannot work for the Land or the Lore of the Old Lords in the company of their fellows – Lords or Lorewardens, the followers of Sword or Staff. Those have some private vision which compels them to seek it in isolation. But their need for aloneness does not divide them from the people. They are given the Rites of Unfettering, and freed from all common demands, to quest after their own lore with the blessing of the Lords and the respect of all who love the Land. For the Lords learned long ago that the desire for aloneness need not be a selfish desire, if it is not made so by those who do not feel it.

'Many of the Unfettered have never returned into knowledge. But stories have grown up around those Ones who have not vanished utterly. Some are said to know the secrets of dreams, others to practise deep mysteries in the arts of healing, still others to be the friends of the animals, speaking their language and calling on their help in times of great need.

'Such a One saved us – ' her voice thickened momentarily – 'a learner of the Wraiths and a friend to the small beasts of the woods. He knew more of the Seven Words than my ears have ever heard.' She groaned softly. 'A mighty man, to have been so slain. He released the Wraiths, and saved our lives. Would that I were worth so much. By the Seven! No evil has ever before been aimed at the Wraiths of Andelain. The Grey Slayer himself never dared – And it is said that the Ritual of Desecration itself had no power to touch them. Now it is in my heart that they will not dance again.'

After a heavy pause, she went on: 'No matter. All things end, in perversion and death. Sorrow belongs to those who also hope. But that Unfettered One gave his life so that you and your message and your ring might reach the Lords. This we will accomplish, so that such sacrifices may have meaning.'

She fell silent again for a moment, and Covenant asked himself, Is that why? Is that what living is for? To vindicate the deaths of others? But he said nothing, and shortly Atiaran's thoughts limped back to her subject. 'But the Unfettered. Some are dreamers, some healers, some share the life of the animals. Some delve the earth to

144

uncover the secrets of the Cavewights, others learn the lore of the Demondim — whatever knowledge guides the One's private prophecy. I have even heard it whispered that some Unfettered follow the legend of Caerroil Wildwood of Garroting Deep, and become Forestals. But that is a perilous thought, even when whispered.

'Never before have I seen one of the Unfettered. But I have heard the Rites of Unfettering. A hymn is sung.' Dully, she recited:

> Free
> Unfettered
> Shriven
> Free —
> Dream that what is dreamed will be:
> Hold eyes clasped shut until they see,
> And sing the silent prophecy
> And be
> Unfettered
> Shriven
> Free

'There is more, but my weakness will not recall — It may be that I will not sing any song again.' She pulled her robe tight around her shoulders as if a wind were chilling through her, and said nothing more for the rest of the day.

That night, when they had camped, Covenant again could not sleep. Unwillingly he lay awake and watched for the sliver of the new moon. When it finally rose over the Hills, he was appalled to see that it was no longer silver-white, but red — the colour of blood and Drool's laval eyes.

It hued the Hills with wrongness, gave the night a tinge of crimson like blood sweat sheening the shrubs and trees and grass and slopes, as if the whole of Andelain were in torment. Under it, the violated ground shimmered as if it were shuddering.

Covenant stared at it, could not close his eyes. Though he badly wanted company, he clamped his teeth together, refused to awaken Atiaran. Alone and shivering, with the staff of Baradakas clutched in his sweating hands, he sat up until moonset, then slept on the edge of consternation until dawn.

And on the fourth day after the night of the Dance, it was he who set the pace of their travelling. He pushed their speed more and more as the day passed, as though he feared that the bloody moon were gaining on them.

When they halted for the night, he gave Atiaran his staff and made her sit awake to see the moon. It came over the horizon in a crimson haze, rising like a sickle of blood in the heavens. Its crescent was noticeably fuller than it had been the previous night. She stared at it rigidly, clenched the staff, but did not cry out. When she had tasted all its wrong, she said tonelessly, 'There is no time,' and turned her face away.

But when morning came, she once more took charge of their pace. Under the pall of the despoiled moon she seemed to have reached a resolution, and now she drove herself forward as if she were spurred by some self-curse or flagellation which rejected through naked determination the logic of defeat. She seemed to believe that she had lost everything for herself and for the Land, yet the way she walked showed that pain could be as sharp a goad as any. Again Covenant found himself hurrying as hard as he could to keep up with her fierce back.

He accepted her pace in the name of his complex dread: he did not want to be caught by the forces that could attack Wraiths and render moons incarnadine. But he was scrupulous about his VSE and other self-protection. If he could have found a blade other than his penknife, he would have shaved with it.

They spent that day, part of the night, and the morning of the next day stumbling forward on the verge of a run. Covenant sustained their rate as best he could, but long days and restless nights had drained his stamina, made his stride ragged and his muscles irresilient. He came to lean more and more on his staff, unable to keep his balance without it. And even with it he might have fallen if he had been pursuing such a pace in some other region. But the keen essence of Andelain supported him. Healthy air salved his lungs, thick grass cushioned his sore joints, Gilden shaded him, treasure-berries burst with energy in his mouth. And at last, near noon on the sixth day, he and Atiaran staggered over the crest of a hill and saw at the bottom of the slope beyond them the Soulsease River.

Blue under the azure sky, it meandered broad, quiet and slow almost directly eastward across their path like a demarcation or boundary of achievement. As it turned and ran among the Hills, it had a glitter of youth, a sparkle of contained exuberance which could burst into laughter the moment it was trickled by other shoals. And its water was as clean, clear and fresh as an offer of baptism. At the sight of it, Covenant felt a rushing desire to plunge in, as if the stream had the power to wash away his mortality.

But he was distracted from it almost immediately. Some distance away to the west, and moving upstream in the centre of the river, was a boat like a skiff with a tall figure in the stern. The instant she saw it, Atiaran cried out sharply, waved her arms, then began pelting down the slope, calling with a frantic edge of her voice, 'Hail! Help! Come back! Come back!'

Covenant followed less urgently. His gaze was fixed on the boat.

With a swing of its prow, it turned in their direction.

Atiaran threw her arms into the air again, gave one more call, then dropped to the ground. When Covenant reached her, she was sitting with her knees clasped to her chest, and her lips trembled as if her face were about to break. She stared feverishly at the approaching boat.

As it drew nearer, Covenant began to see with growing surprise just how tall the steering figure was. Before the boat was within a hundred feet of them, he was sure that the steersman was twice his own height. And he could see no means of propulsion. The craft appeared to be nothing more than an enormous rowboat, but there were no oarlocks, no oars, no poles. He gaped widely at the boat as it glided closer.

When it was within thirty feet of them, Atiaran thrust herself to her feet and called out, 'Hail, Rockbrother! The Giants of Seareach are another name for friendship! Help us!' The boat kept gliding towards the bank, but its steersman did not speak; and shortly Atiaran added in a whisper that only Covenant could hear, 'I beg you.'

The Giant kept his silence as he approached. For the last distance, he swung the tiller over so that the boat's prow aimed squarely at the riverbank. Then, just before the craft struck, he drove his weight down in the stern. The prow lifted out of the water and grounded itself securely a few yards from Atiaran and Covenant. In a moment, the Giant stood before them on the grass, offering them the salute of welcome.

Covenant shook his head in wonder. He felt that it was impossible for anyone to be so big; the Giant was at least twelve feet tall. But the rocky concreteness of the Giant's presence contradicted him. The Giant struck his perceptions as tangibly as stumbling on rough stone.

Even for a being twelve feet tall, he appeared gnarled with muscles, like an oak come to life. He was dressed in a heavy leather jerkin and leggings, and carried no weapons. A short beard, as stiff as iron, jutted from his face. And his eyes were small, deep-set and enthusiastic. From under his brows, massed over his sockets like the wall of a fortress, his glances flashed piercingly, like gleams from his cavernous thoughts. Yet, in spite of his imposing appearance, he gave an impression of incongruous geniality, of immense good humour.

'Hail, Rocksister,' he said in a soft, bubbling tenor voice which sounded too light and gentle to come from his bemuscled throat.

'What is your need? My help is willing, but I am a legate, and my embassy brooks little delay.'

Covenant expected Atiaran to blurt out her plea; the hesitation with which she met the Giant's offer disturbed him. For a long moment, she gnawed her lips as if she were chewing over her rebellious flesh, searching for an utterance which would give direction, one way or another, to a choice she hated. Then, with her eyes downcast as if in shame, she murmured uncertainly, 'Where do you go?'

At her question, the Giant's eyes flashed, and his voice bubbled like a spring of water from a rock as he said, 'My destination? Who is wise enough to know his own goal? But I am bound for – No, that name is too long a story for such a time as this. I go to Lord's Keep, as you humans call it.'

Still hesitating, Atiaran asked, 'What is your name?'

'That is another long story,' the Giant returned, and repeated, 'What is your need?'

But Atiaran insisted dully, 'Your name.'

Again a gleam sprang from under the Giant's massive brows. 'There is power in names. I do not wish to be invoked by any but friends.'

'Your name!' Atiaran groaned.

For an instant, the Giant paused, indecisive. Then he said, 'Very well. Though my embassy is not a light one, I will answer for the sake of the loyalty between my people and yours. To speak shortly, I am called Saltheart Foamfollower.'

Abruptly, some resistance, some hatred of her decision, crumbled in Atiaran as if it had been defeated at last by the Giant's trust. She raised her head, showing Covenant and Foamfollower the crushed landscape behind her eyes. With grave deliberation, she gave the salute of welcome. 'Let it be so. Saltheart Foamfollower, Rockbrother and Giants' legate, I charge you by the power of your name, and by the great Keep of faith which was made between Damelon Giant-friend and your people, to take this man, Thomas Covenant, Unbeliever and stranger to the Land, in safety to the Council of Lords. He bears messages to the Council from Kevin's Watch. Ward him well, Rockbrother. I can go no farther.'

What? Covenant gaped. In his surprise, he almost protested aloud. And give up your revenge? But he held himself still with his thoughts reeling, and waited for her to take a stance he could comprehend.

'Ah, you are too quick to call on such bold names,' the Giant said softly. 'I would have accepted your charge without them. But I urge you to join us. There are rare healings at Lord's Keep. Will you not

148

come? Those who await you would not begrudge such a sojourn – not if they could see you as I do now.'

Bitterness twisted Atiaran's lips. 'Have you seen the new moon? That comes of the last healing I looked for.' As she went on, her voice grew grey with self-despite. 'It is a futile charge I give you. I have already caused it to fail. There has been murder in all my choices since I became this man's guide, such murder – ' She choked on the bile of what she had seen, and had to swallow violently before she could continue. 'Because my path took us too close to Mount Thunder. You passed around that place. You must have seen the evil working there.'

Distantly, the Giant said, 'I saw.'

'We went into the knowledge of that wrong, rather than make our way across the Centre Plains. And now it is too late for anyone. He – The Grey Slayer has returned. I chose that path because I desired healing for myself. What will happen to the Lords if I ask them to help me now?'

And give up your revenge? Covenant wondered. He could not comprehend. He turned completely toward her and studied her face, trying to see her health, her spirit.

She looked as if she were in the grip of a ravaging illness. Her mien had thinned and sharpened; her spacious eyes were shadowed, veiled in darkness; her lips were drained of blood. And vertically down the centre of her forehead lay a deep line like a rift in her skull – the tool work of unblinkable despair. Etched there was the vastness of the personal hurt which she contained by sheer force of will, and the damage she did herself by containing it.

At last Covenant saw clearly the moral struggle that wasted her, the triple conflict between her abhorrence of him, her fear of the Land, and her dismay at her own weakness – a struggle whose expense exhausted her resources, reduced her to penury. The sight shamed his heart, made him drop his gaze. Without thinking, he reached toward her and said in a voice full of self-contradicting pleas, 'Don't give up.'

'Give up?' she gasped in virulence, backing away from him. 'If I gave up, I would stab you where you stand!' Suddenly, she thrust a hand into her robe and snatched out a stone knife like the one Covenant had lost. Brandishing it, she spat, 'Since the Celebration – since you permitted Wraiths to die – this blade has cried out for your blood. Other crimes I could set aside. I speak for my own. But that – ! To countenance such desecration – !'

She hurled the knife savagely to the ground, so that it stuck hilt-deep in the turf by Covenant's feet. 'Behold!' she cried, and in that instant her voice became abruptly gelid, calm. 'I wound the Earth instead of you. It is fitting. I have done little else since you entered the Land.

'Now hear my last word, Unbeliever. I let you go because these decisions surpass me. Delivering children in the Stonedown does not fit me for such choices. But I will not intrude my desires on the one hope of the Land – barren as that hope is. Remember that I have withheld my hand – I have kept my Oath.'

'Have you?' he asked, moved by a complex impulse of sympathy and nameless ire.

She pointed a trembling finger at her knife. 'I have not harmed you. I have brought you here.'

'You've hurt yourself.'

'That is my Oath,' she breathed stiffly. 'Now farewell. When you have returned in safety to your own world, remember what evil is.'

He waited to protest, argue, but her emotion mastered him, and he held himself silent before the force of her resolve. Under the duress of her eyes, he bent, and drew her knife out of the grass. It came up easily. He half expected to see blood ooze from the slash it had made in the turf, but the thick grass closed over the cut, hiding it as completely as an absolution. Unconsciously, he tested the blade with his thumb, felt its acuteness.

When he looked up again, he saw that Atiaran was climbing up the hill and away, moving with the unequal stride of a cripple.

This isn't right! he shouted at her back. Have mercy! – pity! But his tongue felt too thick with the pain of her renunciation; he could not speak. At least forgive yourself. The tightness of his face gave him a nasty impression that he was grinning. Atiaran! he groaned. Why are we so unable?

Into his aching, the Giant's voice came gently. 'Shall we go?'

Dumbly, Covenant nodded. He tore his eyes from Atiaran's toiling back, and shoved her knife under his belt.

Saltheart Foamfollower motioned for him to climb into the boat. When Covenant had vaulted over the gunwale and taken a seat on the thwart in the prow – the only seat in the thirty-foot craft small enough for him – the Giant stepped aboard, pushing off from the bank at the same time. Then he went to the broad, shallow stern. Standing there, he grasped the tiller. A surge of power flowed through the keel. He swung his craft away from the riverbank into mid-stream, and shortly it was moving westward among the Hills.

As soon as he had taken his seat, Covenant had turned with failure in his throat to watch Atiaran's progress up the hillside. But the surge of power which moved the boat gave it a brisk pace as fast as running, and in moments distance had reduced her to a brown mite in the lush, oblivious green of Andelain. With a harsh effort, he forced his eyes to let her go, compelled himself to look instead for the source of the boat's power.

But he could locate no power source. The boat ran smoothly up against the current as if it were being towed by fish. It had no propulsion that he could discern. Yet his nerves were sensitive to the energy flowing through the keel. Dimly he asked, 'What makes this thing move? I don't see any engine.'

Foamfollower stood in the stern, facing upstream, with the high tiller under his left arm and his right held up to the river breezes; and he was chanting something, some plain-song in a language Covenant could not understand – a song with a wave-breaking, salty timbre like the taste of the sea. For a moment after Covenant's question, he kept up his rolling chant. But soon its language changed, and Covenant heard him sing:

> Stone and Sea are deep in life,
> two unalterable symbols of the world;
> permanence at rest, and permanence in motion;
> participants in the Power that remains.

Then Foamfollower stopped, and looked down at Covenant with humour sparkling under his unbreachable brows. 'A stranger to the Land,' he said. 'Did that woman teach you nothing?'

Covenant stiffened in his seat. The Giant's tone seemed to demean Atiaran, denigrate the cost she had borne; his bland, impregnable forehead and humorous glance appeared impervious to sympathy. But her pain was vivid to Covenant. She had been dispossessed of so much normal human love and warmth. In a voice rigid with anger, he retorted, 'She is Atiaran Trell-mate, of Mithil Stonedown, and she did better than teach me. She brought me safely past Ravers, murdered Waynhim, a bloody moon, ur-viles – Could you have done it?'

Foamfollower did not reply, but a grin spread gaily over his face, raising the end of his beard like a mock salute.

'By hell!' Covenant flared. 'Do you think I'm lying. I wouldn't condescend to lie to you.'

At that, the Giant's humour burst into high, headback, bubbling laughter.

Covenant watched, stifling with rage, while Foamfollower laughed. Briefly, he bore the affront. Then he jumped from his seat and raised his staff to strike the Giant.

Foamfollower stopped him with a placating gesture. 'Softly, Unbeliever,' he said. 'Will you feel taller if I sit down?'

'Hell and blood!' Covenant howled. Swinging his arms savagely,

151

he struck the floorboards, with the ur-vile blackened end of his staff.

The boat pitched as if his blow had sent the river into convulsions. Staggering, he clutched a thwart to save himself from being thrown overboard. In a moment, the spasm ceased, leaving the sun-glittered stream as calm as before. But he remained gripping the thwart for several long heartbeats, while his nerves jangled and his ring throbbed heavily.

Covenant, he snarled to steady himself, you would be ridiculous if you weren't so – ridiculous. He drew himself erect, and stood with his feet braced until he had a stranglehold on his emotions. Then he bent his gaze toward Foamfollower, probed the Giant's aura. But he could perceive no ill; Foamfollower seemed as hale as native granite. Ridiculous! Covenant repeated, 'She deserves respect.'

'Ah, forgive me,' said the Giant. With a twist, he lowered the tiller so that he could hold it under his arm in a sitting position. 'I meant no disrespect. Your loyalty relieves me. And I know how to value what she has achieved.' He seated himself in the stern and leaned back against the tiller so that his eyes were only a foot above Covenant's. 'Yes, and how to grieve for her as well. There are none in the Land, not men or Giants or Ranyhyn, who would bear you to – to Lord's Keep faster than I will.'

Then his smile returned. 'But you, Thomas Covenant, Unbeliever and stranger in the Land – you burn yourself too freely. I laughed when I saw you because you seemed like a rooster threatening one of the Ranyhyn. You waste yourself, Thomas Covenant.'

Covenant took a double grip on his anger, and said quietly, 'Is that a fact? You judge too quickly, Giant.'

Another fountain of laughter bubbled out of Foamfollower's chest. 'Bravely said! Here is a new thing in the Land – a man accusing a Giant of haste. Well, you are right. But did you not know that men consider us a – ' he laughed again – 'a deliberate people? I was chosen as legate because short human names, which bereave their bearers of so much history and power and meaning, are easier for me than for most of my people. But now it appears that they are too easy.' Once more he threw back his head and let out a stream of deep gaiety.

Covenant glared at the Giant as if all this humour were incomprehensible to him. Then with an effort he pulled himself away, dropped his staff into the bottom of the boat, and sat down on the thwart facing forward, into the west and the afternoon sun. Foamfollower's laughter had a contagious sound, a colouration of uncomplicated joy, but he resisted it. He could not afford to be the victim of any more seductions. Already he had lost more of himself than he could hope to regain.

Nerves don't regenerate. He tolled the words as if they were a private litany, icons of his embattled self. Giants don't exist. I know the difference.

Keep moving, survive.

He chewed his lips as if that pain could help him keep his balance, keep his rage under command.

At his back, Saltheart Foamfollower softly began to chant again. His song rolled through its channel like a long inlet to the sea, rising and falling like a condensation of the tides, and the winds of distance blew through the archaic words. At intervals, they returned to their refrain –

Stone and Sea are deep in life –

then voyaged away again. The sound of long sojourning reminded Covenant of his fatigue, and he slumped in the prow to rest.

Foamfollower's question caught him wandering, 'Are you a storyteller, Thomas Covenant?'

Absently, he replied, 'I was, once.'

'And you gave it up? Ah, that is as sad a tale in three words as any you might have told me. But a life without a tale is like a sea without salt. How do you live?'

Covenant folded his arms across the gunwales and rested his chin on them. As the boat moved, Andelain opened constantly in front of him like a bud; but he ignored it, concentrated instead on the plaint of water past the prow. Unconsciously, he clenched his fist over his ring. 'I live.'

'Another?' Foamfollower returned. 'In two words, a story sadder than the first. Say no more – with one word you will make me weep.'

If the Giant intended any umbrage, Covenant could not hear it. Foamfollower sounded half teasing, half sympathetic. Covenant shrugged his shoulders, and remained silent.

In a moment, the Giant went on: 'Well, this is a bad pass for me. Our journeying will not be easy, and I had hoped that you could lighten the leagues with a story. But no matter. I judge that you will tell no happy tales in any case. Ravers. Waynhim and Andelainian Wraiths slain. Well, some of this does not surprise me – our old ones have often guessed that Soulcrusher would not die as easily as poor Kevin hoped. Stone and Sea! All that Desecration – ravage and rapine – for a false hope. But we have a saying, and it comforts our children – few as they are – when they weep for the nation, the homes, and company of our people, which we lost – we say, Joy is in the ears that hear, not in the mouth that speaks. The world has few stories glad in themselves, and we must have gay ears to defy Despite. Praise the Creator! Old Lord Damelon Giantfriend knew the value of a good laugh. When we reached the Land, we were too grieved to fight for the right to live.'

A good laugh. Covenant sighed morosely. Did I do a whole life's laughing in that little time?

'You humans are an impatient lot, Thomas Covenant. Do you think that I ramble? Not a bit – I have come hastening to the point. Since you have given up the telling of stories, and since it appears that neither of us is happy enough to withstand the recital of your adventures – why, I must do the telling myself. There is strength in stories – heart rebirth and thew binding – and even Giants need strength when they face such tasks as mine.'

He paused, and Covenant, not wishing him to stop – the Giant's voice seemed to weave the rush of water past the boat into a soothing tapestry – said into the silence, 'Tell.'

'Ah,' Foamfollower responded, 'that was not so bad. You recover despite yourself, Thomas Covenant. Now, then. Gladden your ears, and listen gaily, for I am no purveyor of sorrows – though in times of action we do not wince from facts. If you asked me to resail your path here, I would require every detail of your journey before I took three steps into the Hills. Resailing is perilous, and too often return is impossible – the path is lost, or the traveller changed, beyond hope of recovery.

'But you must understand, Unbeliever, that selecting a tale is usually a matter for deliberation. The old Giantish is a wealth of stories, and some take days in the telling. Once, as a child, I heard three times in succession the tale of Bahgoon the Unbearable and Thelma Twofist, who tamed him – now that was a story worth the laughter – but nine days were gone before I knew it. However, you do not speak Giantish, and translation is a long task, even for Giants, so the problem of selection is simplified. But the lore of our life in Seareach since our ships found the Land contains many times many stories – tales of the reigns of Damelon Giantfriend and Loric Vilesilencer and Kevin, who is now called Landwaster – tales of the building, the carving out of the mountain, of Revelstone, revered rock, "a handmark of allegiance and fealty in the eternal stone of time," as Kevin once sang it, the mightiest making that the Giants have done in the Land, a temple for our people to look upon and remember what can be achieved – tales of the voyage which saved us from the Desecration, and of the many healings of the new Lords. But again selection is made easy because you are a stranger. I will tell you the first story of the Seareach Giants – the Song of the Unhomed.'

Covenant looked about him at the shining blue tranquillity of the Soulsease, and settled himself to hear Foamfollower's story. But the narration did not begin right away. Instead of starting his tale, the Giant went back to his antique plain-song, spinning the melody meditatively so that it unrolled like the sea path of the river. For a long time, he sang, and under the spell of his voice Covenant began to drowse. He had too much exhaustion dripping through his bones to keep his attention ready. While he waited, he rested against the prow like a tired swimmer.

But then a modulation sharpened the Giant's chant. The melody took on keener edges, and turned itself to the angle of a lament. Soon Foamfollower was singing words that Covenant could understand.

> We are the Unhomed –
>> lost voyagers of the world.
> In the land beyond the Sunbirth Sea
>> we lived and had our homes and grew –
>> and set our sails to the wind,
>> unheeding of the peril of the lost.
>
> We are the Unhomed.
> From home and hearth,
>> stone sacred dwellings crafted by our reverent hands,
>> we set our sails to the wind of the stars,
>> and carried life to lands across the earth,
>> careless of the peril of our loss.
>
> We are the Unhomed –
>> lost voyagers of the world.
> From desert shore to high cliff crag,
>> home of men and sylvan sea-edge faery lands –
>> from dream to dream we set our sails,
>> and smiled at the rainbow of our loss.
>
> Now we are Unhomed,
>> bereft of root and kith and kin.
> From other mysteries of delight,
>> we set our sails to resail our track;
>> but the winds of life blew not the way we chose,
>> and the land beyond the Sea was lost.

'Ah, Stone and Sea! Do you know the old lore-legend of the Wounded Rainbow, Thomas Covenant? It is said that in the dimmest past of the Earth, there were no stars in our sky. The heavens were a blackness which separated us from the eternal universe of the Creator. There he lived with his people and his myriad bright children, and they moved to the music of play and joy.

'Now, as the ages spired from forever to forever, the Creator was moved to make a new thing for the happy hearts of his children. He descended to the great forges and cauldrons of his power, and brewed and hammered and cast rare theurgies. And when he was done, he turned to the heavens, and threw his mystic creation to the sky – and, behold! A rainbow spread its arms across the universe.

'For a moment, the Creator was glad. But then he looked closely at the rainbow – and there, high in the shimmering span, he saw a wound, a breach in the beauty he had made. He did not know that his Enemy, the demon spirit of murk and mire that crawled through the bowels of even his universe, had seen him at work, and had cast spite into the mortar of his creating. So now, as the rainbow stood across the heavens, it was marred.

'In vexation, the Creator returned to his works, to find a cure for his creation. But while he laboured, his children, his myriad bright children, found the rainbow, and were filled with rejoicing at its beauty. Together, they climbed into the heavens and scampered happily up the bow, dancing gay dances across its bright colours. High on the span, they discovered the wound. But they did not understand it. Chorusing joy, they danced through the wound, and found themselves in the sky. This new unlighted world only gladdened them the more, and they spun through the sky until it sparkled with the glee of play.

'When they tired of this sport, they sought to return to their universe of light. But their door was shut. For the Creator had discovered his Enemy's handiwork – the cause of the wound – and in his anger his mind had been clouded. Thoughtless, he had torn the rainbow from the heavens. Not until his anger was done did he realize that he had trapped his children in our sky. And there they remain, stars to guide the sojourners of our nights, until the Creator can rid his universe of his Enemy, and find a way to bring his children Home.

'So it was with us, the Unhomed. In our long-lost rocky land, we lived and flourished among our own kind, and when we learned to travel the seas we only prospered the more. But in the eagerness of our glee and our health and our wandering, we betrayed ourselves into folly. We built twenty fine ships, each large enough to be a castle for you humans, and we made a vow among ourselves to set sail and discover the whole Earth. Ah, the whole Earth! In twenty ships, two thousand Giants said high farewells to their kindred, promising to bring back in stories every face of the multitudinous world – and they launched themselves into their dream.

'Then from sea to sea, through tempest and calm, drought and famine and plenty, between reef and landfall, the Giants sailed, glorying in the bite of the salt air, and the stench of sailors' thews, and the perpetual contest with the ocean, "permanence in motion" – and in the exaltation of binding together new peoples in the web of their wandering.

'Three ships they lost in half a generation. One hundred Giants chose to remain and live out their lot with the sylvan faery *Elohim*. Two hundred died in the war service of the *Bhrathair*, who were nearly destroyed by the Sandgorgons of the great Desert. Two ships were reefed and wrecked. And when the first children born on the voyage were old enough to be sailors themselves, the fifteen vessels held council, and turned their thoughts toward Home – for they had learned the folly of their vow, and were worn from wrestling with the seas.

'So they set their sails by the stars, and sought for Home. But they were prevented. Familiar paths led them to unknown oceans and unencountered perils. Tempests drove them beyond their reckoning until their hands were stripped to the bone by the flailing ropes, and the waves rose up against them as if in hatred. Five more ships were lost – though the wreckage of one was found, and the sailors of another were rescued from the island on which they had been cast. Through ice that held them in its clutch for many seasons, killing scores of them – through calms that made them close comrades of starvation – they endured, struggling for their lives and Home. But disasters erased every vestige of knowledge from their bearings, until they knew not where they were or where to go. When they reached the Land, they cast their anchors. Less than a thousand Giants stepped down to the rocky shore of Seareach. In disconsolation, they gave up their hope of Home.

'But the friendship of High Lord Damelon Heartthewson renewed them. He saw omens of promise in his mighty Lore, and at his word the Giants lifted up their hearts. They made Seareach their place, and swore fealty to the Lords – and sent three vessels out in quest of Home. Since that time – for more than three times a thousand years – there have always been three Giant ships at sea, seeking our land turn by turn, three new standing out when the old return, their hands empty of success. Still we are Unhomed, lost in the labyrinth of a foolish dream.

'Stone and Sea! We are a long-lived people, compared to you humans – I was born on the shipboard during the short voyage which saved us from the Desecration, and my great-grandparents were among the first wanderers. And we have so few children. Rarely does any woman bear more than one child. So now there are only five hundred of us, and our vitality narrows with each generation.

'We cannot forget.

'But in the old lore-legend, the children of the Creator had hope. He put rainbows in our sky after cleansing rains, as a promise to the stars that somehow, some day, he would find a way to bring them Home.

'If we are to survive, we must find the Home that we have lost, the heartland beyond the Sunbirth Sea.'

During Foamfollower's tale, the sun had declined into late afternoon; and as he finished, sunset began on the horizon. Then the Soulsease ran out of the west with fiery, orange-gold glory reflected flame for flame in its burnished countenance. In the fathomless heavens the fire radiated both loss and prophecy, coming night and promised day, darkness which would pass; for when the true end of day and light came, there would be no blazonry to make it admirable, no spectacle or fine fire or joy, nothing for the heart to behold but decay and grey ashes.

In splendour, Foamfollower lifted up his voice again, and sang with a plummeting ache:

> We set our sails to resail our track;
> but the winds of life blew not the way we chose,
> and the land beyond the Sea was lost.

Covenant pushed himself around to look at the Giant. Foamfollower's head was held high, with wet streaks of gleaming gold-orange fire drawn delicately down his cheeks. As Covenant watched, the reflected light took on a reddish shade and began to fade.

Softly, the Giant said, 'Laugh, Thomas Covenant – laugh for me. Joy is in the ears that hear.'

Covenant heard the subdued, undemanding throb and supplication in Foamfollower's voice, and his own choked pain groaned in answer. But he could not laugh; he had no laughter of any kind in him. With a spasm of disgust for the limitations that crippled him, he made a rough effort in another direction. 'I'm hungry.'

For an instant, Foamfollower's shadowed eyes flared as if he had been stung. But then he put back his head and laughed for himself. His humour seemed to spring straight from his heart, and soon it had banished all tension and tears from his visage.

When he had relaxed into quiet chuckling, he said, 'Thomas

Covenant, I do not like to be hasty – but I believe you are my friend. You have toppled my pride, and that would be fair service even had I not laughed at you earlier.

'Hungry? Of course you are hungry. Bravely said. I should have offered you food earlier – you have the transparent look of a man who has eaten only *aliantha* for days. Some old seers say that privation refines the soul – but I say it is soon enough to refine the soul when the body has no other choice.

'Happily, I am well supplied with food.' He pushed a prodigious leather sack toward Covenant with his foot, and motioned for him to open it. When Covenant loosened its drawstrings, he found salt beef, cheese, old bread, and more than a dozen tangerines as big as his two fists, as well as a leather jug which he could hardly lift. To postpone this difficulty, he tackled the staples first, washing the salt out of his throat with sections of tangerine. Then he turned his attention to the jug.

'That is *diamondraught*,' said Foamfollower. 'It is a vital brew. Perhaps I should – No, the more I look at you, my friend, the more weariness I see. Just drink from the jug. It will aid your rest.'

Tilting the jug, Covenant sipped the *diamondraught*. It tasted like light whisky, and he could smell its potency; but it was so smooth that it did not bite or burn. He took several relishing swallows, and at once felt deeply refreshed.

Carefully, he closed the jug, replaced the food in the sack, then with an effort pushed the sack back into Foamfollower's reach. The *diamondraught* glowed in his belly, and he felt that in a little while he would be ready for another story. But as he lay down under the thwarts in the bow, the twilight turned into crystal darkness in the sky, and the stars came out lornly, like scattered children. Before he knew that he was drowsing, he was asleep.

It was an uneasy slumber. He staggered numbly through plague-ridden visions full of dying moons and slaughter and helpless ravaged flesh, and found himself lying in the street near the front bumper of the police car. A circle of townspeople had gathered around him. They had eyes of flint, and their mouths were stretched in one uniform rictus of denunciation. Without exception, they were pointing at his hands. When he lifted his hands to look at them, he saw that they were rife with purple, leprous bruises.

Then two white-clad, brawny men came up to him and man-handled him on to a stretcher. He could see the ambulance nearby. But the men did not carry him to it immediately. They stood still, holding him at waist-level like a display to the crowd.

A policeman stepped into the circle. His eyes were the colour of contempt. He bent over Convenant and said grimly, 'You got in my way. That was wrong. You ought to be ashamed.' His breath covered Covenant with the smell of attar.

Behind the policeman, someone raised his voice. It was as full of unction as that of Joan's lawyer. It said, 'That was wrong.'

In perfect unison, all the townspeople vomited gouts of blood on to the pavement.

I don't believe this, Covenant thought.

At once, the unctuous voice purred, 'He doesn't believe us.' A silent howl of reality, rabid assertion of fact, sprang up from the crowd. It battered Covenant until he cowered under it, abject and answerless.

Then the townspeople chorused, 'You are dead. Without the community, you can't live. Life is in the community, and you have no community. You can't live if no one cares.' The unison of their voices made a sound like crumbling, crushing. When they stopped, Covenant felt that the air in his lungs had been turned to rubble.

With a sigh of satisfaction, the unctuous voice said, 'Take him to the hospital. Heal him. There is only one good answer to death. Heal him and throw him out.'

The two men swung him into the ambulance. Before the door slammed shut, he saw the townspeople shaking hands with each other, beaming their congratulations. After that, the ambulance started to move. He raised his hands and saw that the purple spots were spreading up his forearms. He stared at himself in horror, moaning, Hellfire hellfire hellfire!

But then a bubbling tenor voice said kindly, 'Do not fear. It is a dream.' The reassurance spread over him like a blanket. But he could not feel it with his hands, and the ambulance kept on moving. Needing the blanket, he clenched the empty air until his knuckles were white with loneliness.

When he felt that he could not ache any more, the ambulance rolled over, and he fell out of the stretcher into blankness.

12

REVELSTONE

The pressure against his left cheek began slowly to wear his skin raw, and the pain nagged him up off the bottom of his slumber. Turbulence rushed under his head, as if he were pillowed on shoals. He laboured his way out of sleep. Then his cheek was jolted twice in rapid succession, and his resting place heaved. Pushing himself up, he smacked his head on a thwart of the boat. Pain throbbed in his skull. He gripped the thwart, swung himself away from the rib which had been rubbing his cheek, and sat up to look over the gunwales.

He found that the situation of the boat had changed radically. No shade or line or resonance of Andelainian richness remained in the surrounding terrain. On the northeast, the river was edged by a high, bluff rock wall. And to the west spread a grey and barren plain, a crippled wilderness like a vast battleground where more than men had been slain, where the fire that scorched and the blood that drenched had blighted the ground's ability to revitalize itself, bloom again – an uneven, despoiled lowland marked only by the scrub trees clinging to life along the river which poured into the Soulsease a few hundred yards ahead of the boat. The eastering wind carried an old burnt odour, and behind it lay the fetid memory of a crime.

Already, the river joining ahead troubled the Soulsease – knotted its current, stained its clarity with flinty mud – and Covenant had to grip the gunwales to keep his balance as the pitching of the boat increased.

Foamfollower held the boat in the centre of the river, away from the turmoil against the northeast rock wall. Covenant glanced back at the Giant. He was standing in the stern – feet widely braced, tiller clamped under his right arm. At Covenant's glance he called over the mounting clash of the rivers, 'Trothgard lies ahead! Here we turn north – the White River! The Grey comes from the west!' His voice had a strident edge to it, as if he had been singing as strongly as he could all night; but after a moment he sang out a fragment of a different song:

> For we will not rest – ,
> not turn aside,

lose faith,
or fail –
until the Grey flows Blue,
and Rill and Maerl are as new and clean
as ancient Llurallin.

The heaving of the river mounted steadily. Covenant stood in the bottom of the boat – bracing himself against one of the thwarts, gripping the gunwale – and watched the forced commingling of the clean and tainted water. Then Foamfollower shouted, 'One hundred leagues to the Westron Mountains – Guards Gap and the high spring of the Llurallin – and one hundred fifty southwest to the Last Hills and Garroting Deep! We are seventy from Lord's Keep!'

Abruptly, the river's moiling growl sprang louder, smothered the Giant's voice. An unexpected lash of the current caught the boat and tore its prow to the right, bringing it broadside to the stream. Spray slapped Covenant as the boat heeled over; instinctively, he threw his weight on to the left gunwale.

The next instant, he heard a snatch of Foamfollower's plain-song, and felt power thrumming deeply along the keel. Slowly, the boat righted itself, swung into the current again.

But the near-disaster had carried them dangerously close to the northeast wall. The boat trembled with energy as Foamfollower worked it gradually back into the steadier water flowing below the main force of the Grey's current. Then the sensation of power faded from the keel.

'Your pardon!' the Giant shouted. 'I am losing my seamanship!' His voice was raw with strain.

Covenant's knuckles were white from clenching the gunwales. As he bounced with the pitch of the boat, he remembered, *There is only one good answer to death.*

One good answer, he thought. This isn't it.

Perhaps it would be better if the boat capsized, better if he drowned – better if he did not carry Lord Foul's message halfhanded and beringed to Revelstone. He was not a hero. He could not satisfy such expectations.

'Now the crossing!' Foamfollower called. 'We must pass the Grey to go on north. There is no great danger – except that I am weary. And the rivers are high.'

This time, Covenant turned and looked closely at the Giant. He saw now that Saltheart Foamfollower was suffering. His cheeks were sunken, hollowed as if something had gouged the geniality out of his face; and his cavernous eyes burned with taut, febrile volition. Weary? Covenant thought. More like exhausted. He lurched awkwardly from thwart to thwart until he reached the Giant. His eyes were no higher than Foamfollower's waist. He tipped his head back to shout, 'I'll steer! You rest!'

A smile flickered on the Giant's lips. 'I thank you. But no – you are not ready. I am strong enough. But please lift the *diamondraught* to me.'

Covenant opened the food sack and put his hands on the leather jug. Its weight and suppleness made it unwieldy for him, and the tossing of the boat unbalanced him. He simply could not lift the jug. But after a moment he got his arms under it. With a groan of exertion, he heaved it upward.

Foamfollower caught the neck of the jug neatly in his left hand. 'Thank you, my friend,' he said with a ragged grin. Raising the jug to his mouth, he disregarded the perils of the current for a moment to drink deeply. Then he put down the jug and swung the boat toward the mouth of the Grey River.

Another surge of power throbbed through the craft. As it hit the main force of the Grey, Foamfollower turned downstream and angled across the flow. Energy quivered in the floorboards. In a smooth manoeuvre, Foamfollower reached the north side of the current, pivoted upstream with the backwash along the wall, and let it sling him into the untroubled White. Once he had rounded the northward curve, the roar of the joining began to drop swiftly behind the boat.

A moment later, the throb of power faded again. Sighing heavily, Foamfollower wiped the sweat from his face. His shoulders sagged, and his head bowed. With laboured slowness, he lowered the tiller, and at last dropped into the stern of the boat. 'Ah, my friend,' he groaned, 'even Giants are not made to do such things.'

Covenant moved to the centre of the boat and took a seat in the bottom, leaning against one of the sides. From that position, he could not see over the gunwales, but he was not at present curious about the terrain. He had other concerns. One of them was Foamfollower's condition. He did not know how the Giant had become so exhausted.

He tried to approach the question indirectly by saying, 'That was neatly done. How did you do it? You didn't tell me what powers this thing.' And he frowned at the tactless sound of his voice.

'Ask for some other story,' Foamfollower sighed wearily. 'That one is nearly as long as the history of the Land. I have no heart to teach you the meaning of life here.'

'You don't know any short stories,' responded Covenant.

At this, the Giant managed a wan smile. 'Ah, that is true enough. Well, I will make it brief for you. But then you must promise to tell a story for me – something rare, that I will never guess for myself. I will need that, my friend.'

Covenant agreed with a nod, and Foamfollower said, 'Well. Eat, and I will talk.'

Vaguely surprised at how hungry he was, Covenant tackled the contents of Foamfollower's sack. He munched meat and cheese rapidly, satisfied his thirst with tangerines. And while he ate, the Giant began in a voice flat with fatigue: 'The time of Damelon Giantfriend came to an end in the Land before my people had finished the making of *Coercri*, their home in Seareach. They carved Lord's Keep, as men called it, out of the mountain's heart before they laboured on their own Lord-given land, and Loric was High Lord when *Coercri* was done. Then my forebearers turned their attention outward – to the Sunbirth Sea, and to the friendship of the Land.

'Now, both *lillianrill* and *rhadhamaerl* desired to study the lore of the Giants, and the time of High Lord Loric Vilesilencer was one of great growth for the *lillianrill*. To help in this growth, it was necessary for the Giants to make many sojourns to Lord's Keep – ' he broke into a quiet chant, singing for a while as if an invocation of the old grandeur of Giantish reverence – 'to mighty Revelstone. This was well, for it kept Revelstone bright in their eyes.

'But the Giants are not great lovers of walking – no more so then than now. So my forebearers bethought them of the rivers which flow from the Westron Mountains to the Sea, and decided to build boats. Well, boats cannot come here from the Sea, as you may know – Landsdrop, on which stands Gravin Threndor, blocks the way. And no one, Giant or otherwise, would willingly sail the Defiles Course from Lifeswallower, the Great Swamp. So the Giants built docks on the Soulsease, up-river from Gravin Threndor and the narrows called Treacher's Gorge. There they kept such boats as this – there, and at Lord's Keep at the foot of Furl Falls, so that at least two hundred leagues of the journey might be on the water which we love.

'In this journeying, Loric and the *lillianrill* desired to be of aid to the Giants. Out of their power they crafted Gildenlode – a strong wood which they named *lor-liarill* – and from this wood they made rudders and keels for our riverboats. And it was the promise of the Old Lords that, when their omens of hope for us came to pass, then Gildenlode would help us.

'Ah, enough,' Foamfollower sighed abruptly. 'In short, it is I who impel this craft.' He lifted his hand from the tiller, and immediately the boat began to lose headway. 'Or rather, it is I who call out the power of the Gildenlode. There is life and power in the Earth – in stone and wood and water and earth. But life in them is somewhat hidden – somewhat slumberous. Both knowledge and strength are needed – yes, and potent vital songs – to awaken them.' He grasped the tiller again, and the boat moved forward once more.

'So I am weary,' he breathed. 'I have not rested since the night before we met.' His tone reminded Covenant of Trell's fatigue after the Gravelingas had healed the broken pot. 'For two days and two nights I have not allowed the Gildenlode to stop or slow, though my bones are weak with the expense.' To the surprise in Covenant's face, he added, 'Yes, my friend – you slept for two nights and a day. From the west of Andelain across the Centre Plains to the marge of Trothgard, more than a hundred leagues.' After a pause, he concluded, '*Diamondraught* does such things to humans. But you had need of rest.'

For a moment, Covenant sat silent, staring at the floorboards as if he were looking for a place to hit them. His mouth twisted sourly when he raised his head and said, 'So now I'm rested. Can I help?'

Foamfollower did not reply immediately. Behind the buttress of his forehead, he seemed to weigh his various uncertainties before he muttered, 'Stone and Sea! Of course you can. And yet the very fact of asking shows that you cannot. Some unwillingness or ignorance prevents.'

Covenant understood. He could hear dark wings, see slaughtered Wraiths. Wild magic! he groaned. Heroism! This is unsufferable. With a jerk of his head, he knocked transitions aside and asked roughly, 'Do you want my ring?'

'Want?' Foamfollower croaked, looking as if he felt he should laugh but did not have the heart for it. 'Want?' His voice quavered painfully, as if he were confessing to some kind of aberration. 'Do not use such a word, my friend. *Wanting* is natural, and may succeed or fail without wrong. Say *covet*, rather. To covet is to desire something which should not be given. Yes, I covet your un-Earth, wild magic, peace-ending white gold.

> There is wild magic graven in every rock,
> contained for white gold to unleash or control –

I admit the desire. But do not tempt me. Power has a way of revenging itself upon its usurpers. I would not accept this ring if you offered it to me.'

'But you do know how to use it?' Covenant enquired dully, half dazed by his inchoate fear of the answer.

This time Foamfollower did laugh. His humour was emaciated, a mere wisp of its former self, but it was clean and gay. 'Ah, bravely said, my friend. So covetousness collapses of its own folly. No, I do not know. If the wild magic may not be called up by the simple decision of use, then I do not understand it at all. Giants do not have such lore. We have always acted for ourselves – though we gladly use such tools as Gildenlode. Well, I am rewarded for unworthy thoughts. Your pardon, Thomas Covenant.'

Covenant nodded mutely, as if he had been given an unexpected reprieve. He did not want to know how wild magic worked: he did not want to believe in it any way. Simply carrying it around was dangerous. He covered it with his right hand and gazed dumbly, helplessly, at the Giant.

After a moment, Foamfollower's fatigue quenched his humour. His eyes dimmed, and his respiration sighed wearily between his slack lips. He sagged on the tiller, as if laughing had cost him vital energy. 'Now, my friend,' he breathed. 'My courage is nearly spent. I need your story.'

Story? Covenant thought. I don't have any stories. I burned them.

He had burned them – both his new novel and his bestseller. They had been so complacent, so abjectly blind to the perils of leprosy, which lurked secretive and unpredictable behind every physical or moral existence – and so unaware of their own sightlessness. They were carrion – like himself, like himself – fit only for flames. What story could he tell now?

But he had to keep moving, act, survive. Surely he had known that before he had become the victim of dreams. Had he not learned it at the leprosarium, in putrefaction and vomit? Yes, yes! Survive! And yet his dream expected power of him, expected him to put an end to slaughter – Images flashed through him like splinters of vertigo, mirror shards: Joan, police car, Drool's laval eyes. He reeled as if he were falling.

To conceal his sudden distress, he moved away from Foamfollower, went to sit in the prow facing north. 'A story,' he said thickly. In fact, he did know one story – one story in all its grim and motley disguises. He sorted quickly, vividly, until he found one which suited the other things he needed to articulate. 'I'll tell you a story. A true story.'

He gripped the gunwales, fought down his dizziness. 'It's a story about culture shock. Do you know what culture shock is?' Foamfollower did not reply. 'Never mind. I'll tell you about it. Culture shock is what happens when you take a man out of his own world and put him down in a place where the assumptions, the – the standards of being a person – are so different that he can't possibly understand them. He isn't built that way. If he's – facile – he can pretend to be someone else until he gets back to his own world. Or he can just collapse and let himself be rebuilt – however. There's no other way.

'I'll give you an example. While I was at the leprosarium, the doctors talked about a man – a leper – like me. Outcast. He was a classic case. He came from another country – where leprosy is a lot more common – he must have picked up the bacillus there as a child, and years later when he had a wife and three kids of his own and was living in another country, he suddenly lost the nerves in his toes and started to go blind.

'Well, if he had stayed in his own country, he would have been – The disease is common – it would have been recognized early. As soon as it was recognized, he – and his wife – and the kids – and everything he owned – and his house – and his animals – and his close relatives – they would have all been declared *unclean*. His property and house and animals would have been burned to the ground. And he and his wife and his kids and his close relatives would have been sent away to live in the most abject poverty in a village with other people who had the same disease. He would have spent the rest of his life there – without treatment – without hope – while hideous deformity gnawed his arms and legs and face – until he and his wife and his kids and his close relatives all died of gangrene.

'Do you think that's cruel? Let me tell you what did happen to the man. As soon as he recognized his disease, he went to his doctor. His doctor sent him to the leprosarium – alone – without his family – where the spread of the disease was arrested. He was treated, given medicine and training – rehabilitated. Then he was sent home to live a "normal" life with his wife and kids. How nice. There was only one problem. He couldn't handle it.

'To start with, his neighbours gave him a hard time. Oh, at first, they didn't know he was sick – they weren't familiar with leprosy, didn't recognize it – but the local newspaper printed a story on him, so that everyone in town knew he was *the leper*. They shunned him, hated him because they didn't know what to do about him. Then he began to have trouble keeping up his self-treatments. His home country didn't have medicine and leper's therapy – in his bones he believed that such things were magic, that once his disease was arrested he was *cured*, pardoned – given a stay of something worse than execution. But, lo and behold! When he stops taking care of himself, the numbness starts to spread again. Then comes the clincher. Suddenly he finds that behind his back – while he wasn't even looking, much less alert – he has been cut off from his family. They don't share his trouble, far from it. They want to get rid of him, go back to living the way they were before.

'So they pack him off to the leprosarium again. But after getting on the plane – they didn't have planes in his home country, either – he goes into the bathroom as if he had been disinherited without anyone ever telling him why and slits his wrists.'

He gaped wide-eyed at his own narration. He would have been willing, eager, to weep for the man if he had been able to do so without sacrificing his own defences. But he could not weep. Instead, he swallowed thickly, and let his momentum carry him on again.

'And I'll tell you something else about culture shock. Every world has its own ways of committing suicide, and it is a lot easier to kill yourself using methods that you are not accustomed to. I could never slit my wrists. I've read too much about it – talked about it too much. It's too vivid. I would throw up. But I could go to that man's world and sip belladonna tea without nausea. Because I don't know enough about it. There's something vague about it, something obscure – something not quite fatal.

'So that poor man in the bathroom sat there for over an hour, just letting his lifeblood run into the sink. He didn't try to get help until all of a sudden, finally, he realized that he was going to die just as dead as if he had sipped belladonna tea. Then he tried to open the door – but he was too weak. And he didn't know how to push the button to get help. They eventually found him in this grotesque position on the floor with his fingers broken, as if he – as if he had tried to crawl under the door. He – '

He could not go on. Grief choked him into silence, and he sat still for a time while water lamented dimly past the prow. He felt sick, desperate for survival; he could not submit to these seductions. Then Foamfollower's voice reached him. Softly, the Giant said, 'Is this why you abandoned the telling of stories?'

Covenant sprang up, whirled in instant rage. 'This Land of yours is trying to kill me!' he spat fiercely. 'It – you're pressuring me into suicide! White gold! – Berek! – Wraiths! You're doing things to me that I can't handle. I'm not that kind of person – I don't live in that kind of world. All these – seductions! Hell and blood! I'm a leper! Don't you understand that?'

For a long moment, Foamfollower met Covenant's hot gaze, and the sympathy in the Giant's eyes stopped his outburst. He stood glaring with his fingers clawed while Foamfollower regarded him sadly, wearily. He could see that the Giant did not understand; *leprosy* was a word that seemed to have no meaning in the Land. 'Come on,' he said with an ache. 'Laugh about it. Joy is in the ears that hear.'

But then Foamfollower showed that he did understand something. He reached into his jerkin and drew out a leather packet, which he unfolded to produce a large sheet of supple hide. 'Here,' he said, 'you will see much of this before you are done with the Land. It is *clingor*. The Giants brought it to the Land long ages ago — but I will spare us both the effort of telling.' He tore a small square from the corner of the sheet and handed the piece to Covenant. It was sticky on both sides, but transferred easily from hand to hand, and left no residue of glue behind. 'Trust it. Place your ring upon that piece and hide it under your raiment. No one will know that you bear a talisman of wild magic.'

Covenant grasped at the idea. Tugging his ring from his finger, he placed it on the square of *clingor*. It stuck firmly; he could not shake the ring loose, but he could peel the *clingor* away without difficulty. Nodding sharply to himself, he placed his ring on the leather, then opened his shirt and pressed the *clingor* to the centre of his chest. It held there, gave him no discomfort. Rapidly, as if to seize an opportunity before it passed, he rebuttoned his shirt. To his surprise, he seemed to feel the weight of the ring on his heart, but he resolved to ignore it.

Carefully, Foamfollower refolded the *clingor*, replaced it within his jerkin. Then he studied Covenant again briefly. Covenant tried to smile in response, express his gratitude, but his face seemed only capable of snarls. At last, he turned away, reseated himself in the prow to watch the boat's progress and absorb what Foamfollower had done for him.

After musing for a time, he remembered Atiaran's stone knife. It made possible a self-discipline that he sorely needed. He leaned over the side of the boat to wet his face, then took up the knife and painstakingly shaved his whiskers. The beard was eight days old, but the keen, slick blade slid smoothly over his cheeks and down his neck, and he did a passable job of shaving without cutting himself. But he was out of practice, no longer accustomed to the risk; the prospect of blood made his heart tremble. Then he began to see how urgently he needed to return to his real world, needed to recover himself before he altogether lost his ability to survive as a leper.

Later that day came rain, a light drizzle which spattered the surface of the river, whorling the sky mirror into myriad pieces. The drops brushed his face like spray, seeped slowly into his clothes until he was as soaked and uncomfortable as if he had been drenched. But he endured it in a grey, dull reverie, thinking about what he gained and lost by hiding his ring.

At last, the day ended. Darkness dripped into the air as if the rain were simply becoming blacker, and in the twilight Covenant and Foamfollower ate their supper glumly. The Giant was almost too weak to feed himself, but with Covenant's help he managed a decent meal, drank a great quantity of *diamondraught*. Then they returned to their respective silences. Covenant was glad for the dusk; it spared him sight of Foamfollower's exhaustion. Unwilling to lie down on the damp floorboards, he huddled cold and wet against the side of the boat and tried to relax, sleep.

After a time, Foamfollower began to chant faintly:

> Stone and Sea are deep in life,
> two unalterable symbols of the world:
> permanence at rest, and permanence in motion;
> participants in the Power that remains.

He seemed to gather strength from the song, and with it he impelled the boat steadily against the current, drove northward as if there were no fatigue that could make him falter.

Finally, the rain stopped; the cloud cover slowly broke open. But Covenant and Foamfollower found no relief in the clear sky. Over the horizon, the red moon stood like a blot, an imputation of evil, on the outraged background of the stars. It turned the surrounding terrain into a dank bloodscape, full of crimson and evanescent forms like uncomprehended murders. And from the light came a putrid emanation, as if the Land were illuminated by a bane. Then Foamfollower's plain-song sounded dishearteningly frail, futile, and the stars themselves seemed to shrink away from the moon's course.

But dawn brought a sunlight-washed day unriven by any taint or memory of taint. When Covenant raised himself to look around, he saw mountains directly to the north. They spread away eastward, where the tallest of them were still snow-crested; but the range ended abruptly at a point in line with the White River. Already the mountains seemed near at hand.

'Ten leagues,' Foamfollower whispered hoarsely. 'Half a day against this current.'

The Giant's appearance filled Covenant with sharp dismay. Dull-eyed and slack-lipped, Foamfollower looked like a corpse of himself. His beard seemed greyer, as if he had aged several years overnight, and a trail of spittle he was helpless to control ran from the corner of his mouth. The pulse in his temples limped raggedly. But his grip on the tiller was as hard as a gnarled knot of wood, and the boat ploughed stiffly up the briskening river.

Covenant moved to the stern to be of help. He wiped the Giant's lips, then held up the jug of *diamondraught* so that Foamfollower could drink. The fragments of a smile cracked the Giant's lips, and he breathed, 'Stone and Sea. It is no easy thing to be your friend.

Tell your next ferryman to take you downstream. Destinations are for stronger souls than mine.'

'Nonsense,' said Covenant gruffly. 'They're going to make up songs about you for this. Don't you think it's worth it?'

Foamfollower tried to respond, but the effort made him cough violently, and he had to retreat into himself, concentrate the fading fire of his spirit on the clench of his fist and the progress of the boat.

'That's all right,' Covenant said softly. 'Everyone who helps me ends up exhausted – one way or another. If I were a poet, I would make up your song myself.' Cursing silently at his helplessness, he fed the Giant sections of tangerine until there was no fruit left. As he looked at Foamfollower, the tall being shriven of everything except the power to endure, self-divested, for reasons Covenant could not comprehend, of every quality of humour or even dignity as if they were mere appurtenances, he felt irrationally in debt to Foamfollower, as if he had been sold – behind his back and with blithe unregard for his consent – into the usury of his only friend. 'Everyone who helps me,' he muttered again. He found the prices the people of the Land were willing to pay for him appalling.

Finally he was no longer able to stand the sight. He returned to the bow, where he stared at the looming mountains with deserted eyes and grumbled, I didn't ask for this.

Do I hate myself so much? he demanded. But his only answer was the rattle of Foamfollower's breath.

Half the morning passed that way, measured in butchered hunks out of the impenetrable circumstance of time by the rasp of Foamfollower's respiration. Around the boat the terrain stiffened, as if preparing for a leap into the sky. The hills grew higher and more ragged, gradually leaving behind the heather and banyan trees of the plains for a stiffer scrub grass and a few scattered cedars. And ahead the mountains stood taller beyond the hills with every curve of the river. Now Covenant could see that the east end of the range dropped steeply to a plateau like a stair into the mountains – a plateau perhaps two or three thousand feet high that ended in a straight cliff to the foothills. From the plateau came a waterfall, and some effect of the light on the rock made the cascade gleam pale blue as it tumbled. Furl Falls, Covenant said to himself. In spite of the rattle of Foamfollower's breathing, he felt a stirring in his heart, as if he were drawing near to something grand.

But the drawing near lost its swiftness steadily. As the White wound between the hills, it narrowed; and as a result, the current grew increasingly stiff. The Giant seemed to have passed the end of his endurance. His respiration sounded stertorous enough to strangle him at any time; he moved the boat hardly faster than a walk.

Covenant did not see how they could cover the last leagues.

He studied the riverbanks for a place to land the boat; he intended somehow to make the Giant take the boat to the shore. But while he was still looking, he heard a low rumble in the air like the running of horses. What the hell – ? A vision of ur-viles flared in his mind. He snatched up his staff from the bottom of the boat and clenched it, trying to control the sudden drum of his trepidation.

The next moment, like a breaking wave over the crest of a hill upstream and east from the boat, came cantering a score of horses bearing riders. The riders were human, men and women. The instant they saw the boat, one of them shouted, and the group broke into a gallop, sweeping down the hill to rein in at the edge of the river.

The riders looked like warriors. They wore high, soft-soled boots over black leggings, black sleeveless shirts covered by breastplates moulded of a yellow metal, and yellow headbands. A short sword swung from each belt, a bow and quiver of arrows from each back. Scanning them rapidly, Covenant saw the characteristic features of both Woodhelvennin and Stonedownor; some were tall and fair, light-eyed and slim, and others, square, dark and muscular.

As soon as their horses were stopped, the riders slapped their right fists in unison to their hearts, then extended their arms, palms forward, in a gesture of welcome. A man distinguished by a black diagonal line across his breastplate shouted over the water, 'Hail, Rockbrother! Welcome and honour and fealty to you and your people! I am Quaan, Warhaft of the Third Eoman of the Warward of Lord's Keep!' He paused for a reply, and when Covenant said nothing, he went on in a more cautious tone, 'Lord Mhoram sent us. He saw that important matters were moving on the river today. We are come as escort.'

Covenant looked at Foamfollower, but what he saw only convinced him that the Giant was past knowing what happened round him. He slumped in the stern, deaf and blind to everything except his failing effort to drive the boat. Covenant turned back toward the Eoman and called out, 'Help us! He's dying!'

Quaan stiffened, then sprang into action. He snapped an order, and the next instant he and two other riders plunged their horses into the river. The two others headed directly for the west bank, but Quaan guided his horse to intercept the boat. The mustang swam powerfully, as if such work were part of his training. Quaan soon neared the boat. At the last moment, he stood up on his mount's back and vaulted easily over the gunwales. On command, his horse started back toward the east bank.

Momentarily, Quaan measured Covenant with his eyes, and Covenant saw in his thick black hair, broad shoulders, and transparent face that he was a Stonedownor. Then the Warhaft moved toward Foamfollower. He gripped the Giant's shoulders and shook them, barking words which Covenant could not understand.

At first, Foamfollower did not respond. He sat sightless, transfixed, with his hand clamped like a death grip on to the tiller. But slowly Quaan's voice seemed to penetrate him. The cords of his neck trembled as he lifted his head, torturously brought his eyes into focus on Quaan. Then with a groan that seemed to spring from the very marrow of his bones, he released the tiller and fell over sideways.

The craft immediately lost headway, began drifting back downriver. But by this time the two other riders were ready on the west bank. Quaan stepped past Covenant into the bow of the boat, and when he was in position, one of the two riders threw the end of a long line to him. He caught it neatly and looped it over the prow. It stuck where he put it; it was not rope, but *clingor*. At once, he turned toward the east bank. Another line reached him, and he attached it also to the prow. The lines pulled taut; the boat stopped drifting. Then Quaan waved his arm, and the riders began moving along the banks, pulling the boat upstream.

As soon as he understood what was being done, Covenant turned back to Foamfollower. The Giant lay where he had fallen, and his breathing was shallow, irregular. Covenant groped momentarily for some way to help, then lifted the leather jug and poured a quantity of *diamondraught* over Foamfollower's head. The liquid ran into his mouth; he sputtered at it, swallowed heavily. Then he took a deep, rattling breath, and his eyes slitted open. Covenant held the jug to his lips, and after drinking from it, he stretched out flat in the bottom of the boat. At once, he fell into deep sleep.

In relief, Covenant murmured over him, 'Now that's a fine way to end a song – "and then he went to sleep." What good is being a hero if you don't stay awake until you get congratulated?'

He felt suddenly tired, as if the Giant's exhaustion had drained his own strength, and sighing he sat down on one of the thwarts to watch their progress up the river, while Quaan went to the stern to take the tiller. For a while, Covenant ignored Quaan's scrutiny. But finally he gathered enough energy to say, 'He's Saltheart Foamfollower, a – a legate from the Seareach Giants. He hasn't rested since he picked me up in the centre of Andelain – three days ago.' He saw comprehension of Foamfollower's plight spread across Quaan's face. Then he turned his attention to the passing terrain.

The towing horses kept up a good pace against the White's tightening current. Their riders deftly managed the variations of the riverbanks, trading haulers and slackening one rope or the other whenever necessary. As they moved north, the soil became rockier, and the scrub grass gave way to bracken. Gilden trees spread their broad boughs and leaves more and more thickly over the foothills, and the sunlight made the gold foliage glow warmly. Ahead, the plateau now appeared nearly a league wide, and on its west the mountains stood erect as if they were upright in pride.

By noon, Covenant could hear the roar of the great falls, and he guessed that they were close to Revelstone, though the high foothills now blocked most of his view. The roaring approached steadily. Soon the boat passed under a wide bridge. And a short time later, the riders rounded the last curve, drew the boat into a lake at the foot of Furl Falls.

The lake was round and rough in shape, wide, edged along its whole western side by Gilden and pine. It stood at the base of the cliff – more than two thousand feet of sheer precipice – and the blue water came thundering down into it from the plateau like the loud heart's-blood of the mountains. In the lake, the water was clean and cool as rain-washed ether, and Covenant could clearly see the depths of its bouldered bottom.

Knotted jacarandas with delicate blue flowers clustered on the wet rocks at the base of the falls, but most of the lake's eastern shore was clear of trees. There stood two large piers and several smaller loading docks. At one pier rested a boat much like the one Covenant rode in, and smaller craft – skiffs and rafts – were tied to the docks. Under Quaan's guidance, the riders pulled the boat up to one of the piers, where two of the Eoman made it fast. Then the Warhaft gently awakened Foamfollower.

The Giant came out of his sleep with difficulty, but when he pried his eyes open they were calm, unhaggard, though he looked as weak as if his bones were made of sandstone. With help from Quaan and Covenant, he climbed into a sitting position. There he rested, looking dazedly about him as if he wondered where his strength had gone.

After a time, he said thinly to Quaan, 'Your pardon, Warhaft. I am – a little tired.'

'I see you,' Quaan murmured. 'Do not be concerned. Revelstone is near.'

For a moment, Foamfollower frowned in perplexity as he tried to remember what had happened to him. Then a look of recollection tensed his face. 'Send riders,' he breathed urgently. 'Gather the Lords. There must be a Council.'

Quaan smiled. 'Times change, Rockbrother. The newest Lord, Mhoram son of Variol, is a seer and oracle. Ten days ago he sent riders to the Loresraat, and to High Lord Prothall in the north. All will be at the Keep tonight.'

'That is well,' the Giant sighed. 'These are shadowed times. Terrible purposes are abroad.'

'So we have seen,' responded Quaan grimly. 'But Saltheart Foamfollower has hastened enough. I will send the fame of your brave journey ahead to the Keep. They will provide a litter to bear you, if you desire it.'

Foamfollower shook his head, and Quaan vaulted up to the pier to give orders to one of his Eoman. The Giant looked at Covenant and smiled faintly. 'Stone and Sea, my friend,' he said, 'did I not say that I would bring you here swiftly?'

That smile touched Covenant's heart like a clasp of affection. Thickly, he replied, 'Next time take it easier. I can't stand – watching – Do you always keep promises – this way?'

'Your messages are urgent. How could I do otherwise?'

From his leper's perspective, Covenant countered, 'Nothing's *that* urgent. What good does anything do you if you kill yourself in the process?'

For the moment, Foamfollower did not respond. He braced a heavy hand on Covenant's shoulder, and heaved himself, tottering, to his feet. Then he said as if he were answering Covenant's question, 'Come. We must see Revelstone.'

Willing hands helped him on to the pier, and shortly he was standing on the shore of the lake. Despite the toll of his exertion, he dwarfed even the men and women on horseback. And as Covenant joined him, he introduced his passenger with a gesture like an according of dominion. 'Eoman of the Warward, this is my friend, Thomas Covenant, Unbeliever and message-bearer to the Council of Lords. He partakes of many strange knowledges, but he does not know the Land. Ward him well, for the sake of friendship, and for the semblance which he bears of Berek Heartthew, Earthfriend and Lord-Fatherer.'

In response, Quaan gave Covenant the salute of welcome. 'I offer you the greetings of Lord's Keep, Giant-wrought Revelstone,' he said. 'Be welcome in the Land – welcome and true.'

Covenant returned the gesture brusquely, but did not speak, and a moment later Foamfollower said to Quaan, 'Let us go. My eyes are hungry to behold the great work of my forebearers.'

The Warhaft nodded, spoke to his command. At once, two riders galloped away to the east, and two more took positions on either side of the Giant so that he could support himself on the backs of their horses. Another warrior, a young fair-haired Woodhelvennin woman, offered Covenant a ride behind her. For the first time, he noticed that the saddles of the Eoman were nothing but *clingor*, neither horned nor padded, forming broad seats and tapering on either side into stirrup loops. It would be like riding a blanket glued to both horse and rider. But though Joan had taught him the rudiments of riding, he had never overcome his essential distrust of horses. He refused the offer. He got his staff from the boat and took a place beside one of the horses supporting Foamfollower, and the Eoman started away from the lake with the two travellers.

They passed around one foothill on the south side, and joined the road from the bridge below the lake. Eastward, the road worked almost straight up the side of a traverse ridge. The steepness of the climb made Foamfollower stumble several times, and he was barely strong enough to catch himself on the horses. But when he had laboured up the ridge, he stopped, lifted up his head, spread his arms wide, and began to laugh. 'There, my friend. Does that not answer you?' His voice was weak, but gay with refreshed joy.

Ahead over a few lower hills was Lord's Keep.

The sight caught Covenant by surprise, almost took his breath away. Revelstone was a masterwork. It stood in granite permanence like an enactment of eternity, a timeless achievement formed of mere lasting rock by some pure, supreme Giantish participation in skill.

Covenant agreed that *Revelstone* was too short a name for it.

The eastern end of the plateau was finished by a broad shaft of rock, half as high as the plateau and separate from it except at the base, the first several hundred feet. This shaft had been hollowed into a tower which guarded the sole entrance to the Keep, and circles of windows rose up past the abutments to the fortified crown. But most of Lord's Keep was carved into the mountain gut-rock under the plateau.

A surprising distance from the tower, the entire cliff face had been worked by the old Giants – sheered and crafted into a vertical wall for the city, which, Covenant later learned, filled this whole, wedge-shaped promontory of the plateau. The wall was intricately laboured – lined and coigned and serried with regular and irregular groups of windows, balconies, buttresses – orieled and parapeted – wrought in a prolific and seemingly spontaneous multitude of details which appeared to be on the verge of crystallizing into a pattern. But light flashed and danced on the polished cliff face, and the wealth of variation in the work overwhelmed Covenant's senses, so that he could not grasp whatever pattern might be there.

But with his new eyes he could see the thick, bustling communal life of the city. It shone from behind the wall as if the rock were almost translucent, almost lit from within like a chiaroscuro by the life-force of its thousands of inhabitants. The sight made the whole

Keep swirl before him. Though he looked at it from a distance, and could encompass it all – Furl Falls roaring on one side and the expanse of the plains reclining on the other – he felt that the old Giant's had outdone him. Here was a work worthy of pilgrimages, ordeals. He was not surprised to hear Foamfollower whisper like a vestal, 'Ah, Revelstone! Lord's Keep! Here the Unhomed surpass their loss.'

The Eoman responded in litany:

> Giant-troth Revelstone, ancient ward –
> Heart and door of Earthfriend's main:
> Preserve the true with Power's sword,
> Thou ages-Keeper, mountain-reign!

Then the riders started forward again. Foamfollower and Covenant moved in wonder towards the looming walls, and the distance passed swiftly, unmarked except by the beat of their uplifted hearts. The road ran parallel to the cliff to its eastern edge, then turned up towards the tall doors in the southeast base of the tower. The gates – a mighty slab of rock on either side – were open in the free welcome of peace; but they were notched and bevelled and balanced so that they could swing shut and interlock, closing like teeth. The entrance they guarded was large enough for the whole Eoman to ride in abreast.

As they approached the gates, Covenant saw a blue flag flying on the crown of a tower – an azure oriflamme only a shade lighter than the clear sky. Beneath it was a smaller flag, a red pennant the colour of the bloody moon and Drool's eyes. Seeing the direction of Covenant's gaze, the woman near him said, 'Do you know the colours? The blue is High Lord's Furl, the standard of the Lords. It signifies their Oath and guidance to the peoples of the Land. And the red is the sign of our present peril. It will fly there while the danger lasts.'

Covenant nodded without taking his eyes off the Keep. But after a moment he looked away from the flags down toward the entrance to Revelstone. The opening looked like a cave that plunged straight into the mountain, but he could see sunlight beyond it.

Three sentries stood in an abutment over the gates. Their appearance caught Covenant's attention; they did not resemble the riders of the Warward. They were like Stonedownors in size and build, but they were flat-faced and brown-skinned, with curly hair cropped short. They wore short ochre tunics belted in blue that appeared to be made of vellum, and their lower legs and feet were bare. Simply standing casual and unarmed on the abutment, they bore themselves with an almost feline balance and alertness; they seemed ready to do battle at an instant's notice.

When his Eoman was within call of the gate, Quaan shouted to the sentries, 'Hail! First Mark Tuvor! How is it that the Bloodguard have become guest welcomers?'

The foremost of the sentries responded in a voice that sounded foreign, awkward, as if the speaker were accustomed to a language utterly unlike the speech of the Land. 'Giant and message-bearer have come together to the Keep.'

'Well, Bloodguard,' Quaan returned in a tone of camaraderie, 'learn your duties. The Giant is Saltheart Foamfollower, legate from Seareach to the Council of Lords. And the man, the message-bearer, is Thomas Covenant, Unbeliever and stranger to the Land. Are their places ready?'

'The orders are given. Bannor and Korik await.'

Quaan waved in acknowledgement. With his warriors, he rode into the stone throat of Lord's Keep.

13

VESPERS

As he stepped between the balanced jaws, Covenant gripped his staff tightly in his left hand. The entrance was like a tunnel leading under the tower to an open courtyard between the tower and the main Keep, and it was lit only by the dim, reflected sunlight from either end. There were no doors or windows in the stone. The only openings were dark shafts directly overhead, which appeared to serve some function in Revelstone's defences. The hooves of the horses struck echoes off the smooth stone, filling the tunnel like a rumour of war, and even the light click of Covenant's staff pranced about him as if shadows of himself were walking one hesitation step behind him down the Keep's throat.

Then the Eoman entered the sunlit courtyard. Here the native stone had been hollowed down to the level of the entrance so that a space nearly as wide as the tower stood open to the sky between high sheer walls. The court was flat and flagged, but in its centre was a broad plot of soil out of which grew one old Gilden, and a small fountain sparkled on either side of the hoary tree. Beyond were more stone gates like those in the base of the tower, and they also were open. That was the only ground-level entrance to the Keep, but at intervals above the court, wooden crosswalks spanned the open space from the tower to crenellated coigns on the inner face of the Keep. In addition two doors on either side of the tunnel provided access to the tower.

Covenant glanced up the main Keep. Shadows lay within the south and east walls of the court, but the heights still gleamed in the full shine of the afternoon sun, and from his angle, Revelstone seemed tall enough to provide a foundation for the heavens. For a moment as he gazed, his awe made him wish that he were, like Foamfollower, an inheritor of Lord's Keep – that he could in some way claim its grandeur for himself. He wanted to belong here. But as Revelstone's initial impact on him passed, he began to resist the desire. It was just another seduction, and he had already lost too much of his fragile, necessary independence. He shut down his awe with a hard frown, pressed his hand against his ring. The fact that it was hidden steadied him.

There lay the only hope he could imagine, the only solution to his paradoxical dilemma. As long as he kept his ring secret, he could deliver his message to the Lords, satisfy his exigent need to keep moving, and still avoid dangerous expectations, demands of power that he could not meet. Foamfollower – and Atiaran, too, perhaps involuntarily – had given him a certain freedom of choice. Now he might be able to preserve himself – if he could avoid further seductions, and if the Giant did not reveal his secret.

'Foamfollower,' he began, then stopped. Two men were approaching him and the Giant from the main Keep. They resembled the sentries. Their flat, unreadable faces showed no signs of youth or age, as if their relationship with time was somehow ambivalent; and they conveyed such an impression of solidarity to Covenant's eyes that he was distracted from the Giant. They moved evenly across the courtyard as if they were personified rock. One of them greeted Foamfollower, and the other strode toward Covenant.

When he reached Covenant, he bowed fractionally and said, 'I am Bannor of the Bloodguard. You are in my charge. I will guide you to the place prepared!' His voice was awkward, as if his tongue could not relax in the language of the Land, but through his tone Covenant heard a stiffness that sounded like distrust.

It and the Bloodguard's hard, imposing aura made him abruptly uneasy. He looked toward Foamfollower, saw him give the other Bloodguard a salute full of respect and old comradeship. 'Hail, Korik!' Foamfollower said. 'To the Bloodguard I bring honour and fealty from the Giants of Seareach. These are consequential times,

179

and in them we are proud to name the Bloodguard among our friends.'

Flatly, Korik responded, 'We are the Bloodguard. Your chambers have been made ready, so that you may rest. Come.'

Foamfollower smiled. 'That is well. My friend, I am very weary.' With Korik, he walked toward the gates.

Covenant started after them, but Bannor barred his way with one strong arm. 'You will accompany me,' the Bloodguard said without inflection.

'Foamfollower!' Covenant called uncertainly. 'Foamfollower! Wait for me.'

Over his shoulder, the Giant replied, 'Go with Bannor. Be at Peace.' He seemed to have no awareness of Covenant's misapprehension; his tone expressed only grateful relief, as if rest and Revelstone were his only thoughts. 'We will meet again — tomorrow.' Moving as if he trusted the Bloodguard implicitly, he went with Korik into the main keep.

'Your place is in the tower,' Bannor said.

'In the tower? Why?'

The Bloodguard shrugged. 'If you question this, you will be answered. But now you must accompany me.'

For a moment, Covenant met Bannor's eyes, and read there the Bloodguard's competence, his ability and willingness to enforce his commands. The sight sharpened Covenant's anxiety still further. Even the eyes of Soranal and Baradakas when they had first captured him, thinking him a Raver, had not held such a calm and committed promise of coercion, violence. The Woodhelvennin had been harsh because of their habitual gentleness, but Bannor's gaze gave no hint of any Oath of Peace. Daunted, Covenant looked away. When Bannor started toward one of the tower doors, he followed in uncertainty and trepidation.

The door opened as they approached, and closed behind them, though Covenant could not see who or what moved it. It gave into an open-centred, spiral stairwell, up which Bannor climbed steadily until after a hundred feet or more he reached another door. Beyond it, Covenant found himself in a jumbled maze of passageways, stairs, doors that soon confused his sense of direction completely. Bannor led him this way and that at irregular intervals, up and down unmeasured flights of steps, along broad and then narrow corridors, until he feared that he would not be able to make his way out again without a guide. From time to time, he caught glimpses of other people, primarily Bloodguard and warriors, but he did not encounter any of them. At last, however, Bannor stopped in the middle of what appeared to be a blank corridor. With a short gesture, he opened a hidden door. Covenant followed him into a large living chamber with a balcony beyond it.

Bannor waited while Covenant gave the room a brief look, then said, 'Call if there is anything you require,' and left, pulling the door shut behind him.

For a moment, Covenant continued to glance around him; he took a mental inventory of the furnishings so that he would know where all the dangerous corners, projections, edges were. The room contained a bed, a bath, a table arrayed with food, chairs – one of which was draped with a variety of apparel – and an arras on one wall. But none of these presented any urgent threat, and shortly his gaze returned to the door.

It had no handle, knob, latch, draw line – no means by which he could open it.

What the hell – ?

He shoved at it with his shoulder, tried to grip it by the edges and pull; he could not budge the heavy stone.

'Bannor!' With a wrench, his mounting fear turned to anger. 'Bloody damnation! Bannor. Open this door!'

Almost immediately, the stone swung inward. Bannor stood impassively in the doorway. His flat eyes were expressionless.

'I can't open the door,' Covenant snapped. 'What is this? Some kind of prison?'

Bannor's shoulders lifted fractionally. 'Call it what you choose. You must remain here until the Lords are prepared to send for you.'

' "Until the Lords are prepared." What am I supposed to do in the meantime? Just sit here and *think*?'

'Eat. Rest. Do whatever you will.'

'I'll tell you what I will. I will not stay here and go crazy waiting for the good pleasure of those Lords of yours. I came here all the way from Kevin's Watch to talk to them. I risked my – ' With an effort, he caught himself. He could see that his fuming made no impression on the Bloodguard. He gripped his anger with both hands, and said stiffly, 'Why am I a prisoner?'

'Message-bearers may be friends or foes,' Bannor replied. 'Perhaps you are a servant of Corruption. The safety of the Lords is in our care. The Bloodguard will not permit you to endanger them. We will be sure of you before we allow you to move freely.'

Hellfire! Covenant swore. Just what I need. The room behind him seemed suddenly full of the dark, vulturine thoughts on which he had striven so hard to turn his back. How could he defend himself against them if he did not keep moving? But he could not bear to stand where he was with all his fears exposed to Bannor's dispassionate scrutiny. He forced himself to turn around. 'Tell them I don't like to wait.' Trembling, he moved to the table and picked up a stoneware flask of springwine.

When he heard the door close, he took a long draught like a gesture of defiance. Then, with his teeth clenched on the fine beery flavour of the springwine, he looked around the room again, glared about him as if he were daring dark spectres to come out of hiding and attack.

This time, the arras caught his attention. It was a thick, varicoloured weaving, dominated by stark reds and sky blues, and after a moment's incomprehension he realized that it depicted the legend of Berek Halfhand.

Prominent in the centre stood the figure of Berek in a stylized stance which combined striving and beatitude. And around this foreground were worked scenes encapsulating the Lord-Fatherer's history – his pure loyalty to his Queen, the King's greedy pursuit of power, the Queen's repudiation of her husband, Berek's exertions in the war, the cleaving of his hand, his despair on Mount Thunder, the victory of the Fire-Lions. The effect of the whole was one of salvation, of redemption purchased on the very brink of ruin by rectitude – as if the Earth itself had intervened, could be trusted to intervene, to right the moral imbalance of the war.

Oh, bloody hell! Covenant groaned. Do I have to put up with this?

Clutching the stoneware flask as if it were the only solid thing in the room, he went toward the balcony.

He stopped in the entryway, braced himself against the stone. Beyond the railing of the balcony was a fall of three or four hundred feet to the foothills. He did not dare step out to the railing; already a premonition of giddiness gnawed like nausea in his guts. But he made himself look outward long enough to identify his surroundings.

The balcony was in the eastern face of the tower, overlooking a broad reach of plains. The late afternoon sun cast the shadow of the promontory eastward like an aegis, and in the subdued light beyond the shadow the plains appeared various and colourful. Bluish grasslands and ploughed brown fields and new-green crops intervaled each other into the distance, and between them sun-silvered threads of streams ran east and south; the clustered spots of villages spread a frail web of habitation over the fields; purple heather and grey bracken lay in broadening swaths toward the north. To his right, Covenant could see far away the White River winding in the direction of Trothgard.

The sight reminded him of how he had come to this place – of Foamfollower, Atiaran, Wraiths, Baradakas, a murdered Waynhim – A vertigo of memories gyred up out of the foothills at him. Atiaran had blamed him for the slaughter of the Wraiths. And yet she had forsworn her own just desire for retribution, her just rage. He had done her so much harm –

He recoiled back into the chamber, stumbled to sit down at the table. His hands shook so badly that he could not drink from the flask. He set it down, clenched both fists, and pressed his knuckles against the hard ring hidden over his heart.

I will not think about it.

A scowl like a contortion of the skull gripped his forehead.

I am not Berek.

He locked himself there until the sound of dangerous wings began to recede, and the giddy pain in his stomach eased. Then he unclawed his stiff fingers. Ignoring their impossible sensitivity, he started to eat.

On the table he found a variety of cold meats, cheeses and fruits, with plenty of brown bread, he ate deliberately, woodenly, like a puppet acting out the commands of his will, until he was no longer hungry. Then he stripped off his clothes and bathed, scrubbing himself thoroughly and scrutinizing his body to be sure he had no hidden wounds. He sorted through the clothing provided for him, finally donned a pale blue robe which he could tie closed securely to conceal his ring. Using Atiaran's knife, he shaved meticulously. Then, with the same wooden deliberateness, he washed his own clothes in the bath and hung them on chair backs to dry. All the time, his thoughts ran to the rhythm of,

I will not –

I am not –

While he worked, evening drifted westward over Revelstone, and when he was done he set a chair in the entrance to the balcony so that he could sit and watch the twilight without confronting the height of his perch. But darkness appeared to spread outward from the unlit room behind him into the wide world, as if his chamber were the source of night. Before long, the empty space at his back seemed to throng with carrion eaters.

He felt in the depths of his heart that he was becoming frantic to escape this dream.

The knock at his door jolted him, but he yanked his way through the darkness to answer it. 'Come – come in.' In momentary confusion, he groped for a handle which was not there. Then the door opened to a brightness that dazzled him.

At first, all he could see were three figures, one back against the wall of the outer corridor and two directly in the doorway. One of them held a flaming wooden rod in either hand, and the other had each arm wrapped around a pot of graveling. The dazzle made them appear to loom toward him out of penumbra, and he stepped back, blinking rapidly.

As if his retreat were a welcome, the two men entered his room. From behind them a voice curiously rough and gentle said, 'May we come in? I am Lord Mhoram – '

'Of course,' the taller of the two men interrupted in a voice veined and knuckled with age. 'He requires light, does he not? Darkness withers the heart. How can he receive light if we do not come in? Now if he knew anything, he could not fend for himself. Of course. And he will not see much of us. Too busy. There is yet Vespers to attend to. The High Lord may have special instructions. We are late as it is. Because he knows nothing. Of course. But we are swift. Darkness withers the heart. Pay attention, young man. We cannot afford to return merely to redeem your ignorance.'

While the man spoke, jerking the words like lazy servants up off the floor of his chest, Covenant's eyes cleared. Before him, the taller man resolved into an erect but ancient figure, with a narrow face and a beard that hung like a tattered flag almost to his waist. He wore a Woodhelvennin cloak bordered in blue, and a circle of leaves about his head.

His immediate companion appeared hardly older than a boy. The youth was clad in a brown Stonedownor tunic with blue woven like epaulettes into the shoulders, and he had a clean, merry face. He was grinning at the old man in amusement and affection.

As Covenant studied the pair, the man behind them said admonishingly, 'He is a guest, Birinair.' The old man paused as if he were remembering his manners, and Covenant looked past him at Lord Mhoram. The Lord was a lean man about Covenant's height. He wore a long robe the colour of High Lord's Furl, with a pitch-black sash, and held a long staff in his right hand.

Then the old man cleared his throat. 'Ah, very well,' he fussed. 'But this uses time, and we are late. There is Vespers to be made ready. Preparation for the Council. Of course. You are a guest. Be welcome. I am Birinair, Hirebrand of the *lillianrill* and Hearthrall of Lord's Keep. This grinning whelp is Tohrm, Gravelingas of the *rhadhamaerl* and likewise Hearthrall of Lord's Keep. Now harken. Attend.' In high dignity, he moved toward the bed. Above it in the wall was a torch socket. Birinair said, 'These are made for ignorant young men like yourself,' and set the burning end of one rod in the socket. The flame died; but when he removed the rod, its fire returned almost at once. He placed the unlit end in the socket, then moved across the chamber to fix his other rod in the opposite wall.

While the Hirebrand was busy, Tohrm set one of his graveling pots down on the table and the other on the stand by the washbasin.

'Cover them when you wish to sleep,' he said in a light voice.

When he was done, Birinair said, 'Darkness withers the heart. Beware of it, guest.'

'But courtesy is like a drink at a mountain stream,' murmured Tohrm, grinning as if at a secret joke.

'It is so.' Birinair turned and left the room. Tohrm paused to wink at Covenant and whisper, 'He is not as hard a taskmaster as you might think.' Then he, too, was gone, leaving Covenant alone with Lord Mhoram.

Mhoram closed the door behind him, and Covenant got his first good look at one of the Lords. Mhoram had a crooked, humane mouth, and a fond smile for the Hearthralls lingered on his lips. But the effect of the smile was counter-balanced by his eyes. They were dangerous eyes — grey-blue irises flecked with gold — that seemed to pierce through subterfuge to the secret marrow of premeditation in what they beheld — eyes that seemed themselves to conceal something potent and unknown, as if Mhoram were capable of surprising fate itself if he were driven to his last throw. And between his perilous eyes and kind mouth, the square blade of his nose mediated like a rudder, steering his thoughts.

Then Covenant noticed Mhoram's staff. It was metal-shod like the Staff of Law, which he had glimpsed in Drool's spatulate fingers, but it was innocent of the carving that articulated the Staff. Mhoram held it in his left hand while he gave Covenant the salute of welcome with his right. Then he folded his arms on his chest, holding the staff in the crook of his elbow.

His lips twisted through a combination of amusement, diffidence and watchfulness as he spoke. 'Let me begin anew. I am Lord Mhoram son of Variol. Be welcome in Revelstone, Thomas Covenant, Unbeliever and message-bearer. Birinair is Hearthrall and chief *lillianrill* of Lord's Keep — but nevertheless there is time before Vespers. So I have come for several reasons. First to bid you welcome, second to answer the questions of a stranger in the Land — and last to enquire after the purpose which brings you to the Council. Pardon me if I seem formal. You are a stranger, and I know not how to honour you.'

Covenant wanted to respond. But he still felt confused by darkness; he needed time to clear his head. He blinked at the Lord for a moment, then said to fill the silence, 'That Bloodguard of yours doesn't trust me.'

Mhoram smiled wryly. 'Bannor told me that you believe you have been imprisoned. That is also why I determined to speak with you this evening. It is not our custom to examine guests before they have rested. But I must say a word or two concerning the Bloodguard. Shall we be seated?' He took a chair for himself, sitting with his staff across his knees as naturally as if it were part of him.

Covenant sat down by the table without taking his eyes off Mhoram. When he was settled, the Lord continued: 'Thomas Covenant, I tell you openly – I assume that you are a friend – or at least not an enemy – until you are proven. You are a guest, and should be shown courtesy. And we have sworn the Oath of Peace. But you are as strange to us as we to you. And the Bloodguard have spoken a Vow which is not in any way like our Oath. They have sworn to serve the Lords and Revelstone – to preserve us against any threat by the strength of their fidelity.' He sighed distantly. 'Ah, it is humbling to be so served – in defiance of time and death. But let that pass. I must tell you two things. Left to the dictates of their Vow, the Bloodguard would slay you instantly if you raised your hand against any Lord – yes, against any inhabitant of Revelstone. But the Council of Lords has commanded you to their care. Rather than break that command – rather than permit any harm to befall you – Bannor or any Bloodguard would lay down his life in your defence.'

When Covenant's face reflected his doubt, the Lord said, 'I assure you. Perhaps it would be well for you to question Bannor concerning the Bloodguard. His distrust may not distress you – when you have come to understand it. His people are the *Haruchai*, who live high in the Westron Mountains beyond the passes which we now name Guards Gap. In the first years of Kevin Loricson's High Lordship they came to the Land – came, and remained to make a Vow like that swearing which binds even the gods.' For a moment he seemed lost in contemplation of the Bloodguard. 'They were a hot-blooded people, strong loined and prolific, bred to tempest and battle – and now made by their pledged loyalty ascetic, womanless and old. I tell you, Thomas Covenant – their devotion has had such unforeseen prices – Such one-mindedness does not come easily to them, and their only reward is the pride of unbroken, pure service. And then to learn the bitterness of doubt – ' Mhoram sighed again, then smiled diffidently. 'Enquire of Bannor. I am too young to tell the tale aright.'

Too young? Covenant wondered. How old are they? But he did not ask the question; he feared that the story Mhoram could tell would be as seductive as Foamfollower's tale of the Unhomed. After a moment, he pulled the loose ends of his attention together, and said, 'I've got to talk to the Council.'

Mhoram's gaze met him squarely. 'The Lords will meet tomorrow to hear both you and Saltheart Foamfollower. Do you wish to speak now?' The Lord's gold-flecked eyes seemed to flame with concentration. Unexpectedly, he asked, 'Are you an enemy, Unbeliever?'

Covenant winced inwardly. He could feel Mhoram's scrutiny as if its heat burned his mind. But he was determined to resist. Stiffly, he countered, 'You're the seer and oracle. You tell me.'

'Did Quaan call me that?' Mhoram's smile was disarming. 'Well, I showed prophetic astuteness when I let a mere red moon disquiet me. Perhaps my oracular powers amaze you.' Then he set aside his quiet self-deprecation, and repeated intently, 'Are you an enemy?'

Covenant returned the Lord's gaze, hoping that his own eyes were hard, uncompromising. I will not — he thought. Am not — 'I'm not anything to you by choice. I've got — a message for you. One way or another, I've been pressured into bringing it here. And some things happened along the way that might interest you.'

'Tell me,' Mhoram said in soft urgency.

But his look reminded Covenant of Baradakas — of Atiaran — of times they had said, *You are closed* — he could see Mhoram's health, his dangerous courage, his vital love for the Land. 'People keep asking me that,' he murmured. 'Can't you tell?'

An instant later, he answered himself, Of course not. What do they know about leprosy? Then he grasped the reason behind Mhoram's question. The Lord wanted to hear him talk, wanted his voice to reveal his truth or falsehood. Mhoram's ears could discern the honesty or irrectitude of the answer.

Covenant glanced at the memory of Foul's message, then turned away in self-defence. 'No — I'll save it for the Council. Once is enough for such things. My tongue'll turn to sand if I have to say it twice.'

Mhoram nodded as if in acceptance. But almost immediately he asked, 'Does your message account for the befouling of the moon?'

Instinctively, Covenant looked out over his balcony.

There, sailing tortuously over the horizon like a plague ship, was the bloodstained moon. Its glow rode the plains like an incarnadine phantasm. He could not keep the shudder out of his voice as he replied, 'He's showing off — that's all. Just showing us what he can do.' Deep in his throat, he called, Hellfire! Foul! The Wraiths were helpless! What do you do for an encore, rape children?

'Ah,' Lord Mhoram groaned, 'this comes at a bad time.' He stepped away from his seat and pulled the wooden partition shut across the entrance to the balcony. 'The Warward numbers less than two thousand. The Bloodguard are only five hundred — a pittance for any task but the defence of Revelstone. And there are only five Lords. Of those, two are old, at the limit of their strength, and none have mastered more than the smallest part of Kevin's First Ward. We are weaker than any other Earthfriends in all the ages of the Land. Together we can hardly make scrub grass grow in Kurash Plenethor.

'There have been more,' he explained, returning to his seat. 'But in the last generation nearly all the best at the Loresraat have chosen the Rites of Unfettering. I am the first to pass the tests in fifteen years. Alas, it is in my heart that we will want other power now.' He clenched his staff until his knuckles whitened, and for a moment his eyes did not conceal his sense of need.

Gruffly, Covenant said, 'Then tell your friends to brace themselves. You're not going to like what I've got to say.'

But Mhoram relaxed slowly, as if he had not heard Covenant's warning. One finger at a time, he released his grip until the staff lay untouched in his lap. Then he smiled softly. 'Thomas Covenant, I am not altogether reasonless when I assume that you are not an enemy. You have a *lillianrill* staff and a *rhadhamaerl* knife – yes, and the staff has seen struggle against a strong foe. And I have already spoken with Saltheart Foamfollower. You have been trusted by others. I do not think you would have won your way here without trust.'

'Hellfire!' retorted Covenant. 'You've got it backward.' He threw his words like stones at a false image of himself. 'They coerced me into coming. It wasn't my idea. I haven't had a choice since this thing started.' With his fingers he touched his chest to remind himself of the one choice he did have.

'Unwilling,' Mhoram replied gently. 'So there is good reason for calling you "Unbeliever". Well, let it pass. We will hear your tale at the Council tomorrow.

'Now. I fear I have given your questions little opportunity. But the time for Vespers has come. Will you accompany me? If you wish we will speak along the way.'

Covenant nodded at once. In spite of his weariness, he was eager for a chance to be active, keep his thoughts busy. The discomfort of being interrogated was only a little less than the distress of the questions he wanted to ask about white gold. To escape his complicated vulnerabilities, he stood up and said, 'Lead the way.'

The Lord bowed in acknowledgement, and at once preceded Covenant into the corridor outside his room. There they found Bannor. He stood against the wall near the door with his arms folded stolidly across his chest, but he moved to join them as Mhoram and Covenant entered the passageway. On an impulse, Covenant intercepted him. He met Bannor's gaze, touched the Bloodguard's chest with one rigid finger, and said, 'I don't trust you either.' Then he turned in angry satisfaction back to the Lord.

Mhoram paused while Bannor went into Covenant's room to pick up one of the torches. Then the Bloodguard took a position a step behind Covenant's left shoulder, and Lord Mhoram led them down the corridor. Soon Covenant was lost again; the complexities of the tower confused him as quickly as a maze. But in a short time they reached the hall which seemed to end in a dead wall of stone. Mhoram touched the stone with an end of his staff, and it swung inward, opening over the courtyard between the tower and the Main Keep. From this doorway, a crosswalk stretched over to a buttressed coign.

Covenant took one look at the yawning gulf of the courtyard and backed away. 'No,' he muttered, 'forget it. I'll just stay here if you don't mind.' Blood rushed like shame into his face, and a rivulet of sweat ran coldly down his back. 'I'm no good at heights.'

The Lord regarded him curiously for a moment, but did not challenge his reaction. 'Very well,' he said simply. 'We will go another way.'

Sweating half in relief, Covenant followed as Mhoram retraced part of their way, then led a complex descent to one of the doors at the base of the tower. There they crossed the courtyard.

Then for the first time Covenant was in the main body of Revelstone.

Around him, the Keep was brightly lit with torches and graveling. Its walls were high and broad enough for Giants, and their spaciousness contrasted strongly with the convolution of the tower. In the presence of so much wrought, grand and magisterial granite, such a weight of mountain rock spanning such open, illuminated hills, he felt acutely his own meagreness, his mere frail mortality. Once again, he sensed that the makers of Revelstone had surpassed him.

But Mhoram and Bannor did not appear meagre to him. The Lord strode forward as if these halls were his natural element, as if his humble flesh flourished in the service of this old grandeur. And Bannor's personal solidity seemed to increase, as if he bore within him something that almost equalled Revelstone's permanence. Between them, Covenant felt half disincarnate, void of some essential actuality.

A snarl jumped across his teeth, and his shoulders hunched as he strangled such thoughts. With a grim effort, he forced himself to concentrate on the superficial details around him.

They turned down a hallway which went straight but for gradual undulations, as if it were carved to suit the grain of the rock – into the heart of the mountain. From it, connecting corridors branched out at various intervals, some cutting directly across between cliff and cliff, and some only joining the central hall with the outer passages. Through these corridors, a steadily growing number of men and women entered the central hall, all, Covenant guessed, going toward Vespers. Some wore breastplates and headbands of warriors;

others, Woodhelvennin and Stonedownor garb with which Covenant was familiar. Several struck him as being related in some way to the *lillianrill* or *rhadhamaerl*; but many more seemed to belong to the more prosaic occupations of running a city – cooking, cleaning, building, repairing, harvesting. Scattered through the crowd were a few Bloodguard. Many of the people nodded and beamed respectfully at Lord Mhoram, and he returned salutations in all directions, often hailing his greeters by name. But behind him, Bannor carried the torch and walked as inflexibly as if he were alone in the Keep.

As the throng thickened, Mhoram moved toward the wall on one side, then stopped at a door. Opening it, he turned to Bannor and said, 'I must join the High Lord. Take Thomas Covenant to a place among the people in the sacred enclosure.' To Covenant, he added, 'Bannor will bring you to the Close at the proper time tomorrow.' With a salute, he left Covenant with the Bloodguard.

Now Bannor led Covenant ahead through Revelstone. After some distance, the hall ended, split at right angles to arc left and right around a wide wall, and into this girdling corridor the people poured in all directions. Doors large enough to admit Giants marked the curved wall at regular intervals; through them the people passed briskly, but without confusion or jostling.

On either side of each door stood a Gravelingas and a Hirebrand; and as Covenant neared one of the doors, he heard the door wardens intoning, 'If there is ill in your heart, leave it here. There is no room for it within.' Occasionally one of the people reached out and touched a warden as if handing over a burden.

When he reached the door, Bannor gave his torch to the Hirebrand. The Hirebrand quenched it by humming a snatch of song and closing his hand over the flame. Then he returned the rod to Bannor, and the Bloodguard entered the enclosure with Covenant behind him.

Covenant found himself on a balcony circling the inside of an enormous cavity. It held no lights, but illumination streamed into it from all the open doors, and there were six more balconies above the one on which Covenant stood, all accessed by many open doors. He could see clearly. The balconies stood in vertical tiers, and below them, more than a hundred feet down, was the flat bottom of the cavity. A dais occupied one side, but the rest of the bottom was full of people. The balconies also were full, but relatively uncrowded; everyone had a full view of the dais below.

Sudden dizziness beat out of the air at Covenant's head. He clutched at the chest-high railing, braced his labouring heart against it. Revelstone seemed full of vertigoes; everywhere he went, he had to contend with cliffs, gulfs, abysms. But the rail was reassuring granite. Hugging it, he fought down his fear, looked up to take his eyes away from the enclosure bottom.

He was dimly surprised to find that the cavity was not open to the sky; it ended in a vaulted dome several hundred feet above the highest balcony. The details of the ceiling were obscure, but he thought he could make out figures carved in the stone, giant forms vaguely dancing.

Then the light began to fail. One by one, the doors were being shut; as they closed, darkness filled the cavity like recreated night. Soon the enclosure was sealed free of light, and into the void the soft moving noises and breathing of people spread like a restless spirit. The blackness seemed to isolate Covenant. He felt as anchorless as if he had been cast adrift in deep space, and the massive stone of the Keep impended over him as if its sheer brute tonnage bore personally on the back of his neck. Involuntarily, he leaned toward Bannor, touched the solid Bloodguard with his shoulder.

Then a flame flared up on the dais – two flames, a *lillianrill* torch and a pot of graveling. Their lights were tiny in the huge cavity, but they revealed Birinair and Tohrm standing on either side of the dais, holding their respective fires. Behind each Hearthrall were two blue-robed figures – Lord Mhoram with an ancient woman on his arm behind Birinair, and a woman and an old man robed in blue. His erect carriage denied the age of his white hair and beard. Intuitively, Covenant guessed, That's him – High Lord Prothall.

The man raised his staff and struck its metal three times on the stone dais. He held his head high as he spoke, but his voice remembered that he was old. In spite of bold carriage and upright spirit, there was a rheumy ache of age in his tone as he said, 'This is the Vespers of Lord's Keep – ancient Revelstone, Giant-wrought bourne of all that we believe. Be welcome, strong heart and weak, light and dark, blood and bone and thew and mind and soul, for good and all. Set Peace about you and within you. This time is consecrate to the services of the Earth.'

His companions responded, 'Let there be healing and hope, heart and home, for the Land, and for all people in the services of the Earth – for you before us, you direct participants in Earthpower and Lore, *lillianrill* and *rhadhamaerl*, learners, Lorewardens, and warriors – and for you above us, you people and daily carers of the hearth and harvest of life – and for you among us, you Giants, Bloodguards, strangers – and for you absent Ranyhyn and Ramen and Stonedownors and Woodhelvennin, all brothers and sisters of the common troth. We are the Lords of the Land. Be welcome and true.'

Then the Lords sang into the darkness of the sacred enclosure. The Hearthrall fires were small in the huge, high, thronged sanctuary

– small, and yet for all their smallness distinct, cynosural, like uncorrupt courage. And in that light the Lords sang their hymn.

> Seven Wards of ancient Lore
> For Land's protection, wall and door;
> And one High Lord to wield the Law
> To keep all uncorrupt Earth's Power's core.
>
> Seven Words for ill's despite –
> Banes for evil's dooming wight:
> And one pure Lord to hold the Staff
> To bar the Land from Foul's betraying sight.
>
> Seven hells for failed faith,
> For Land's betrayers, man and wraith:
> And one brave Lord to deal the doom
> To keep the blacking blight from Beauty's bloom.

As the echo of their voices faded, High Lord Prothall spoke again. 'We are the new preservers of the Land – votaries and handservants of the Earthpower; sworn and dedicated to the retrieval of Kevin's Lore, and to the healing of the Earth from all that is barren or unnatural, ravaged, foundationless, or perverse. And sworn and dedicated as well, in equal balance with all other consecrations and promises – sworn despite any urging of the importunate self – the Oath of Peace. For serenity is the only promise we can give that we will not desecrate the Land again.'

The people standing before the dais replied in unison, 'We will not redesecrate the Land, though the effort of self-mastery wither us on the vine of our lives. Nor will we rest until the shadow of our former folly is lifted from the Land's heart, and the darkness is whelmed in growth and life.'

And Prothall returned, 'But there is no withering in the service of the Land. Service enables service, just as servility perpetuates debasement. We may go from knowledge to knowledge, and to still braver knowledge, if courage holds, and commitment holds, and wisdom does not fall under the shadow. We are the new preservers of the Land – votaries and handservants to the Earthpower.

> 'For we will not rest –
>   not turn aside,
>   lose faith,
>   or fail –
> until the Grey flows Blue,

and Rill and Maerl are as new and clean
as ancient Llurallin.'

To this the entire assembly responded by singing the same words,
line by line, after the High Lord; and the massed communal voice
reverberated in the sacred enclosure as if his rheumy tone had
tapped some pent, subterranean passion. While the mighty sound
lasted, Prothall bowed his head in humility.

But when it was over, he threw back his head and flung his arms
wide as if baring his breast to a denunciation. 'Ah, my friends!' he
cried. 'Handservants, votaries of the Land – why have we so failed
to comprehend Kevin's Lore? Which of us has in any way advanced
the knowledge of our predecessors? We hold the First Ward in our
hands – we read the script, and in much we understand the words –
and yet we do not penetrate the secrets. Some failure in us, some
false inflection, some mistaken action, some base alloy in our
intention, prevents. I do not doubt that our purpose is pure – it is
High Lord Kevin's purpose – and before him Loric's and Damelon's
and Heartthew's – but wiser, for we will never lift our hands against
the Land in mad despair. But what, then? Where are we wrong, that
we cannot grasp what is given to us?'

For a moment after his voice faltered and fell, the sanctuary was
silent, and the void throbbed like weeping, as if in his words the
people recognized themselves, recognized the failure he described as
their own. But then a new voice arose. Saltheart Foamfollower said
boldly, 'My Lord, we have not reached our end. True, the work of
our lifetime has been to comprehend and consolidate the gains of
our forebearers. But our labour will open the doors of the future.
Our children and their children will gain because we have not lost
heart, for faith and courage are the greatest gift that we can give to
our descendants. And the Land holds mysteries of which we know
nothing – mysteries of hope as well as of peril. Be of good heart,
Rockbrothers. Your faith is precious above all things.'

But you don't have time! Covenant groaned. Faith! Children! Foul
is going to destroy you. Within him, his conception of the Lords
whirled, altered. They were not superior beings, fate-shapers; they
were mortals like himself, familiar with impotence. Foul would
reave them –

For an instant, he released the railing as if he meant to cry out his
message of doom to the gathered people. But at once vertigo broke
through his resistance, pounced at him out of the void. Reeling, he
stumbled against the rail, then fell back to clutch at Bannor's
shoulder.

– that the uttermost limit of their span of days upon the Land –

He would have to read them their death warrant.

'Get me out of here,' he breathed hoarsely. 'I can't stand it.'

Bannor held him, guided him. Abruptly, a door opened into the brilliance of the outer corridor. Covenant half fell through the doorway. Without a word, Bannor relit his torch at one of the flaming brands set into the wall. Then he took Covenant's arm to support him.

Covenant threw off his hand. 'Don't touch me,' he panted inchoately. 'Can't you see I'm sick?'

No flicker of expression shaded Bannor's flat countenance. Dispassionately, he turned and led Covenant away from the sacred enclosure.

Covenant followed, bent forward and holding his stomach as if he were nauseated – *that the uttermost limit* – How could he help them? He could not even help himself. In confusion and heart distress, he shambled back to his room in the tower, stood dumbly in the chamber while Bannor replaced his torch in the tower, closing the door like a judgment behind him. Then he gripped his temples as if his mind were being torn in two.

None of this is happening, he moaned. How are they doing this to me?

Reeling inwardly, he turned to look at the arras as if it might contain some answer. But it only aggravated his distress, incensed him like a sudden affront. Bloody hell! Berek, he groaned. Do you think it's that easy? Do you think that ordinary human despair is enough, that if you just feel bad enough something cosmic or at least miraculous is bound to come along and rescue you? Damn you! he's going to destroy them! You're just another leper outcast unclean, and you don't even know it!

His fingers curled like feral claws, and he sprang forward, ripping at the arras as if he were trying to rend a black lie off the stone of the world. The heavy fabric refused to tear in his half-unfingered grasp, but he got it down from the wall. Throwing open the balcony, he wrested the arras out into the crimson-tainted night and heaved it over the railing. It fell like a dead leaf of winter.

I am not Berek!

Panting at his effort, he returned to the room, slammed the partition shut against the bloody light. He threw off his robe, put on his own underwear, then extinguished the fires and climbed into bed. But the soft, clean touch of the sheets on his skin gave him no consolation.

14

THE COUNCIL OF LORDS

He awoke in a dull haze which felt like the presage of some thunderhead, some black boil and white fire blaring. Mechanically he went through the motions of readying himself for the Council — washed, inspected himself, dressed in his own clothes, shaved again. When Bannor brought him a tray of food, he ate as if the provender were made of dust and gravel. Then he slipped Atiaran's knife into his belt, gripped the staff of Baradakas in his left hand, and sat down facing the door to await the summons.

Finally, Bannor returned to tell him that the time had come. For a few moments, Covenant sat still, holding the Bloodguard in his half-unseeing gaze, and wondering where he could get the courage to go on with this dream. He felt that his face was twisted, but he could not be sure.

— that the uttermost limit —

Get it over with.

He touched the hard, hidden metal of his ring to steady himself, then levered his reluctant bones erect. Glaring at the doorway as if it were a threshold into peril, he lumbered through it and started down the corridor. At Bannor's commanding back, he moved out of the tower, across the courtyard, then inward and down through the ravelled and curiously wrought passages of Revelstone.

Eventually they came through bright-lit halls deep in the mountain to a pair of arching wooden doors. These were closed, sentried by Bloodguard; and lining both walls were stone chairs, some man-sized and others large enough for Giants. Bannor nodded to the sentries. One of them pulled open a door while the other motioned for Bannor and Covenant to enter. Bannor guided Covenant into the council chamber of the Lords.

The Close was a huge, sunken, circular room with a ceiling high and groined, and tiers of seats set around three-quarters of the space. The door through which Covenant entered was nearly level with the highest seats, as were the only two other doors — both of them small — at the opposite side of the chamber. Below the lowest tier of seats were three levels: on the first, several feet below the gallery, stood a curved stone table, three-quarters round, with its gap toward the large doors and many chairs around its outer edge; below this, contained within the C of the table, was the flat floor of the Close; and finally, in the centre of the floor, lay a broad, round pit of graveling. The yellow glow of the fire-stones was supported by four huge *lillianrill* torches, burning without smoke or consumption in their sockets around the upper wall.

As Bannor took him down the steps toward the open end of the table, Covenant observed the people in the chamber. Saltheart Foamfollower lounged nearby at the table in a massive stone chair; he watched Covenant's progress down the steps and grinned a welcome for his former passenger. Beyond him, the only people at the table were the Lords. Directly opposite Covenant, at the head of the table, sat High Lord Prothall. His staff lay on the stone before him. An ancient man and woman were several feet away on either side of him; an equal distance from the woman on her left was Lord Mhoram; and opposite Mhoram, down the table from the old man, sat a middle-aged woman. Four Bloodguard had positioned themselves behind each of the Lords.

There were only four other people in the Close. Beyond the High Lord near the top of the gallery sat the Hearthralls, Birinair and Tohrm, side by side as if they complemented each other. And just behind them were two more men, one a warrior with a double black diagonal on his breastplate, and the other Tuvor, First Mark of the Bloodguard. With so few people in it, the Close seemed large, hollow, and cryptic.

Bannor steered Covenant to the lone chair below the level of the Lords' table and across the pit of graveling from the High Lord. Covenant seated himself stiffly and looked around. He felt that he was uncomfortably far from the Lords; he feared he would have to shout his message. So he was surprised when Prothall stood and said softly, 'Thomas Covenant, be welcome to the Council of Lords.' His rheumy voice reached Covenant as clearly as if they had been standing side by side.

Covenant did not know how to respond; uncertainly he touched his right fist to his chest, then extended his arm with his palm open and forward. As his senses adjusted to the Close, he began to perceive the presence, the emanating personality and adjudication, of the Lords. They gave him an impression of stern vows gladly kept, of wide-ranging and yet single-minded devotion. Prothall stood alone, meeting Covenant's gaze. The High Lord's appearance of white age was modified by the stiffness of his beard and the erectness of his carriage; clearly, he was strong yet. But his eyes were worn with the experience of an asceticism, an abnegation, carried so far that it seemed to abrogate his flesh — as if he had been old for so long that now only the power to which he devoted himself preserved him from decrepitude.

The two Lords who flanked him were not so preserved. They had dull, age-marked skin and wispy hair; and they bowed at the table as if striving against the antiquity of their bones to distinguish between meditation and sleep. Lord Mhoram Covenant already knew, though now Mhoram appeared more incisive and dangerous, as if the companionship of his fellow Lords whetted his capacities. But the fifth Lord Covenant did not know; she sat squarely and factually at the table, with her blunt, forthright face fixed on him like a defiance.

'Let me make introduction before we begin,' the High Lord murmured. 'I am Prothall son of Dwillian, High Lord by the choice of the Council. At my right are Variol Tamarantha-mate and Pentil-son, once High Lord – ' as he said this, the two ancient Lords raised their time latticed faces and smiled privately at each other – 'and Osondrea daughter of Sondrea. At my left, Tamarantha Variol-mate and Enesta-daughter, and Mhoram son of Variol. You know the Seareach Giant, Saltheart Foamfollower, and have met the Hearthralls of Lord's Keep. Behind me also are Tuvor, First Mark of the Bloodguard, and Garth, Warmark of the Warward of Lord's Keep. All have the right of presence at the Council of Lords. Do you protest?'

Protest? Covenant shook his head dumbly.

'Then we shall begin. It is our custom to honour those who come before us. How may we honour you?'

Again, Covenant shook his head. I don't want any honour. I made that mistake once already.

After an enquiring pause, the High Lord said, 'Very well.' Turning toward the Giant, he raised his voice. 'Hail and welcome, Giant of Seareach, Saltheart Foamfollower, Rockbrother and inheritor of Land's loyalty. The Unhomed are a blessing to the Land.

Stone and Sea are deep in life.

Welcome whole or hurt, in boon or bane – ask or give. To any requiring name we will not fail while we have life or power to meet the need. I am High Lord Prothall; I speak in the presence of Revelstone itself.'

Foamfollower stood to return the salutation. 'Hail, Lord and Earthfriend. I am Saltheart Foamfollower, legate from the Giants of Seareach to the Council of Lords. The truth of my people is in my mouth, and I hear the approval of the ancient sacred ancestral stone –

raw Earth rock –
pure friendship –
a handmark of allegiance and fealty in the
eternal stone of time.

Now is the time for proof and power of troth. Through Giant Woods
and Sarangrave Flat and Andelain, I bear the name of the ancient
promises.' Then some of the formality dropped from his manner,
and he added with a gay glance at Covenant, 'And bearing other
things as well. My friend Thomas Covenant has promised that a song
will be made of my journey.' He laughed gently. 'I am a Giant of
Seareach. Make no short songs for me.'

His humour drew a chuckle from Lord Mhoram, and Prothall
smiled softly; but Osondrea's dour face seemed incapable of laughter,
and neither Variol nor Tamarantha appeared to have heard the
Giant. Foamfollower took his seat and almost at once Osondrea said
as if she were impatient, 'What is your Embassy?'

Foamfollower sat erect in his chair, and his hands stroked the
stone of the table intently. 'My Lords – Stone and Sea! I am a Giant.
These matters do not come easily, though easier to me than to any
of my kindred – and for that reason I was chosen. But I will
endeavour to speak hastily.

'Please understand me. I was given my embassy in a Giantclave
lasting ten days. There was no waste of time. When comprehension
is needed, all tales must be told in full. Haste is for the hopeless, we
say – and hardly a day has passed since I learned that there is truth
in sayings. So it is that my embassy contains much that you would
not choose to hear at present. You must know the history of my
people – all the sojourn and the loss which brought us ashore here,
all the interactions of our peoples since that age – if you are to hear
me. But I will forgo it. We are the Unhomed, adrift in soul and
lessened by an unreplenishing seed. We are hungry for our native
land. Yet since the time of Damelon Giantfriend we have not
surrendered hope, though Soulcrusher himself contrives against us.
We have searched the seas, and have waited for the omens to come
to pass.'

Foamfollower paused to look thoughtfully at Covenant, then went
on. 'Ah, my Lords, omening is curious. So much is said – and so
little made clear. It was not Home that Damelon foretold for us, but
rather an end, a resolution, to our loss. Yet that sufficed for us –
sufficed.

'Well. One hope we have found for ourselves. When spring came
to Seareach, our questing ships returned, and told that at the very
limit of their search they came upon an isle that borders the ancient

oceans on which we once roamed. The matter is not sure, but our next questers can go directly to this isle and look beyond it for surer signs. Thus across the labyrinth of the seas we unamaze ourselves.'

Prothall nodded, and through the perfect acoustics of the Close, Covenant could hear the faint rustle of the High Lord's robe.

With an air of nearing the crux of his embassy, Foamfollower continued, 'Yet another hope we received from Damelon Giant-friend, High Lord and Heartthew's son. At the heart of his omening was this word: our exile would end when our seed regained its potency, and the decline of our offspring was reversed. Thus hope is born of hope, for without any foretelling we would gain heart and courage from any increase in our rare, beloved children. And behold! On the night that our ships returned, Wavenhair Haleall, wived to Sparlimb Keelsetter, was taken to her bed and delivered – ah, Stone and Sea, my Lords! It cripples my tongue to tell this without its full measure of long Giantish gratitude. How can there be joy for people who say everything briefly? Proud-wife, clean-limbed Wav-enhair gave birth to three sons.' No longer able to restrain himself, he broke into a chant full of the brave crash of breakers and tang of salt.

To his surprise, Covenant saw that Lord Osondrea was smiling, and her eyes caught the golden glow of the graveling damply – eloquent witness to the gladness of the Giant's news.

But Foamfollower abruptly stopped himself. With a gesture toward Covenant, he said, 'Your pardon – you have other matters in your hands. I must bring myself to the bone of my embassy. Ah, my friend,' he said to Covenant, 'will you still not laugh for me? I must remember that Damelon promised us an end, not a return Home – though I cannot envision any end but Home. It may be that I stand in the gloaming of the Giants.'

'Hush, Rockbrother,' Lord Tamarantha interrupted. 'Do not make evil for your people by uttering such things.'

Foamfollower responded with a hearty laugh. 'Ah, my thanks, Lord Tamarantha. So the wise old Giants are admonished by young women. My entire people will laugh when I tell them of this.'

Tamarantha and Variol exchanged a smile, and returned to their semblance of meditation or dozing.

When he was done laughing, the Giant said, 'Well, my Lords. To the bone, then. Stone and Sea! Such haste makes me giddy. I have come to ask the fulfilment of the ancient offers. High Lord Loric Vilesilencer promised that the Lords would give us a gift when our hope was ready – a gift to better the chances of our Homeward way.'

'Birinair,' said Lord Osondrea.

High in the gallery behind Prothall, old Birinair stood and replied, 'Of course. I am not asleep. Not as old as I look, you know. I hear you.'

With a broad grin, Foamfollower cried, 'Hail, Birinair! Hearthrall of Lord's Keep and Hirebrand of the *lillianrill*. We are old friends, Giants and *lillianrill*.'

'No need to shout,' Birinair returned. 'I hear you. Old friends from the time of High Lord Damelon. Never otherwise.'

'Birinair,' Osondrea cut in, 'does your lore recall the gift promised by Loric to the Giants?'

'Gift? Why not? Nothing amiss with my memory. Where is that whelp my apprentice? Of course. *Lorliarill*. Gildenlode, they call it. There. Keels and rudders for ships. True course – never becalmed. And strong as stone,' he said to Tohrm, 'you grinning *rhadhamaerl* to the contrary. I remember.'

'Can you accomplish this?' Osondrea asked quietly.

'Accomplish?' Birinair echoed, apparently puzzled.

'Can you make Gildenlode keels and rudders for the Giants? Has that lore been lost?' Turning to Foamfollower, Lord Osondrea asked, 'How many ships will you need?'

With a glance at Birinair's upright dignity, Foamfollower contained his humour, and replied simply, 'Seven. Perhaps five.'

'Can this be done?' Osondrea asked Birinair again, distinctly but without irritation. Covenant's blank gaze followed from speaker to speaker as if they were talking in a foreign language.

The Hearthrall pulled a small tablet and stylus from his robe and began to calculate, muttering to himself throughout the Close until he raised his head and said stiffly, 'The lore remains. But not easily. The best we can do. Of course. And time – it will need time. *Bodach glas*, it will need time.'

'How much time?'

'The best we can do. If we are left alone. Not my fault. I did not lose all the proudest lore of the *lillianrill*. Forty years.' In a sudden whisper, he added to Foamfollower, 'I am sorry.'

'Forty years?' Foamfollower laughed gently. 'Ah, bravely said, Birinair, my friend. Forty years? That does not seem a long time to me.' Turning to High Lord Prothall, he said, 'My people cannot thank you. Even in Giantish, there are no words long enough. Three millennia of our loyalty have not been enough to repay seven Gildenlode keels and rudders.'

'No,' protested Prothall. 'Seventy times seven Gildenlode gifts are nothing compared to the great friendship of our Seareach Giants. Only the thought that we have aided your return Home can fill the emptiness your departure will leave. And our help is forty years distant. But we will begin at once and it may be that some new understanding of Kevin's Lore will shorten the time.'

Echoing, 'At once,' Birinair reseated himself.

Forty years? Covenant breathed. You don't have forty years.

Then Osondrea said, 'Done?' She looked first at Foamfollower, then at High Lord Prothall. When they both nodded to her, she turned on Covenant and said, 'Then let us get to the matter of this Thomas Covenant.' Her voice seemed to whet the atmosphere like a distant thunderclap.

Smiling to ameliorate Osondrea's forthrightness, Mhoram said, 'A stranger called the Unbeliever.'

'And for good reason,' Foamfollower added.

The Giant's words rang an alarm in Covenant's clouded trepidations, and he looked sharply at Foamfollower. In the Giant's cavernous eyes and buttressed forehead, he saw the import of the comment. As clearly as if he were pleading outright, Foamfollower said, *Acknowledge the white gold and use it to aid the Land.* Impossible, Covenant replied. The backs of his eyes felt hot with helplessness and belligerence, but his face was as stiff as a marble slab.

Abruptly, Lord Osondrea, demanded, 'The tapestry from your room was found. Why did you cast it down?'

Without looking at her, Covenant answered, 'It offended me.'

'Offended?' Prothall admonished gently. 'He is a stranger.'

She kept the defiance of her face on Covenant, but fell silent. For a moment, no one moved or spoke; Covenant received the unsettling impression that the Lords were debating mentally with each other about how to treat him. Then Mhoram stood, walked around the end of the stone table, and moved back inside the circle until he was again opposite Osondrea. There he seated himself on the edge of the table with his staff across his lap, and fixed his eyes on Covenant.

Covenant felt more exposed than ever to Mhoram's scrutiny. At the same time, he sensed that Bannor had stepped closer to him, as if anticipating an attack on Mhoram.

Wryly, Lord Mhoram said, 'Thomas Covenant, you must pardon our caution. The desecrated moon signifies an evil in the Land which we hardly suspected. Without warning, the sternest test of our age appears in the sky, and we are utterly threatened. Yet we do not prejudge you. You must prove you're ill – if ill you are.' He looked at Covenant for some response, some acknowledgement, but Covenant only stared back emptily. With a slight shrug, the Lord went on, 'Now. Perhaps it would be well if you began with your message.'

Covenant winced, ducked his head like a man harried by vultures. He did not want to recite that message, did not want to remember

Kevin's Watch, Mithil Stonedown, anything. His guts ached at visions of vertigo. Everything was impossible. How could he retain his outraged sanity if he thought about such things?

But Foul's message had a power of compulsion. He had borne it like a wound in his mind too long to repudiate it now. Before he could muster any defence, it came over him like a convulsion. In a tone of irremediable contempt, he said, 'These are the words of Lord Foul the Despiser.

'"Say to the Council of Lords, and to High Lord Prothall son of Dwillian, that the uttermost limit of their span of days upon the Land is seven times seven years from the present time. Before the end of those days are numbered, I will have the command of life and death in my hand. And as a token that what I say is the one word of truth, tell them this: Drool Rockworm, Cavewight of Mount Thunder, has found the Staff of Law, which was lost ten times a hundred years ago by Kevin at the Ritual of Desecration. Say to them that the task appointed to their generation is to regain the Staff. Without it, they will not be able to resist me for seven years, and my complete victory will be achieved six times seven years earlier than it would be else.

'"As for you, groveller: do not fail with this message. If you do not bring it before the Council, then every human in the Land will be dead before ten seasons have passed. You do not understand – but I tell you Drool Rockworm has the Staff, and that is a cause for terror. He will be enthroned at Lord's Keep in two years if the message fails. Already, the Cavewights are marching to his call; and wolves, and ur-viles of the Demondim, answer the power of the Staff. But war is not the worst peril. Drool delves ever deeper into the dark roots of Mount Thunder – Gravin Threndor, Peak of the Fire-Lions. And there are banes buried in the deeps of the Earth too potent and terrible for any mortal to control. They would make of the universe a hell forever. But such a bane Drool seeks. He searches for the Illearth Stone. If he becomes its master, there will be woe for low and high alike until Time itself falls.

'"Do not fail with my message, groveller. You have met Drool. Do you relish dying in his hands?"' Covenant's heart lurched with the force of his loathing for the words, the tone. But he was not done. '"One word more, a final caution. Do not forget whom to fear at the last. I have had to be content with killing and torment. But now my plans are laid, and I have begun. I shall not rest until I have eradicated hope from the Earth. Think on that, and be dismayed!"'

As he finished, he heard fear and abhorrence flare in the Close as if ignited by his involuntary peroration. Hellfire hellfire! he moaned, trying to clear his gaze of the darkness from which Foul's contempt had sprung. Unclean!

Prothall's head was bowed, and he clenched his staff as if he were trying to wring courage from it. Behind him, Tuvor and Warmark Garth stood in attitudes of martial readiness., Oddly, Variol and Tamarantha doddered in their seats as if dozing, unaware of what had been said. But Osondrea gaped at Covenant as if he had stabbed her in the heart. Opposite her, Mhoram stood erect, head high and eyes closed, with his staff braced hard against the floor, and where his metal met the stone, a hot blue flame burned. Foamfollower hunched in his seat; his huge hands clutched a stone chair. His shoulders quivered, and suddenly the chair snapped.

At the noise, Osondrea covered her face with her hands, gave one stricken cry, *'Melenkurion abatha!'* The next instant, she dropped her hands and resumed her stony, amazed stare at Covenant. And he shouted, *Unclean!* As if he were agreeing with her.

'Laugh, Covenant,' Foamfollower whispered hoarsely. 'You have told us the end of all things. Now help us. Laugh.'

Covenant replied dully, 'You laugh. "Joy is in the ears that hear." I can't do it.'

To his astonishment, Foamfollower did laugh. He lifted his head and made a strangled, garish noise in his throat that sounded like sobbing; but in a moment the sound loosened, clarified, slowly took on the tone of indomitable humour. The terrible exertion appalled Covenant.

As Foamfollower laughed, the first shock of dismay passed from the Council. Gradually, Prothall raised his head. 'The Unhomed are a blessing to the Land,' he murmured. Mhoram sagged, and the fire between his staff and the floor went out. Osondrea shook her head, sighed, passed her hands through her hair. Again, Covenant sensed a kind of mental melding from the Lords; without words, they seemed to join hands, share strength with each other.

Sitting alone and miserable, Covenant waited for them to question him. And as he waited, he struggled to recapture all the refusals on which his survival depended.

Finally, the Lords returned their attention to him. The flesh of Prothall's face seemed to droop with weariness, but his eyes remained steady, resolute. 'Now, Unbeliever,' he said softly. 'You must tell us all that has happened to you. We must know how Lord Foul's threats are embodied.'

Now, Covenant echoed, twisting in his chair. He could hardly resist a desire to clutch at his ring. Dark memories beat at his ears, trying to break down his defences. Shortly, everyone in the Close was looking at him. Tossing his words down as if he were discarding flawed bricks, he began.

'I come from – some place else. I was brought to Kevin's Watch – I don't know how. First I got a look at Drool – then Foul left me on the Watch. They seemed to know each other.'

'And the Staff of Law?' Prothall asked.

'Drool had a staff – all carved up, with metal ends like yours. I don't know what it was.'

Prothall shrugged the doubt away; and grimly Covenant forced himself to describe without any personal mention of himself, any reference to Lena or Triock or Baradakas, the events of his journey. When he spoke of the murdered Waynhim, Osondrea's breath hissed between her teeth, but the Lords made no other response.

Then, after he mentioned the visit to Soaring Woodhelven of a malicious stranger, possibly a Raver, Mhoram asked intently, 'Did the stranger use a name?'

'He said his name was Jehannum.'

'Ah. And what was his purpose?'

'How should I know?' Covenant rasped, trying to conceal his falsehood with belligerence. 'I don't know any Ravers.'

Mhoram nodded noncommittally, and Covenant went on to relate his and Atiaran's progress through Andelain. He avoided gruffly any reference to the wrong which had attacked him through his boots. But when he came to the Celebration of Spring, he faltered.

The Wraiths – ! he ached silently. The rage and horror of that night were still in him, still vivid to his raw heart. *Covenant, help them!* How could I? It's madness! I'm not – I am not Berek.

With an effort that made his throat hurt as if his words were too sharp to pass through it, he said, 'The Celebration was attacked by ur-viles. We escaped. Some of the Wraiths were saved by – by one of the Unfettered, Atiaran said. The the moon turned red. Then we got to the river and met Foamfollower. Atiaran decided to go back home. How the hell much longer do I have to put up with this?'

Unexpectedly, Lord Tamarantha raised her nodding head. 'Who will go?' she asked toward the ceiling of the Close.

'It has not yet been determined that anyone will go,' Prothall replied in a gentle voice.

'Nonsense,' she sniffed. Tugging at a thin wisp of hair behind her ear, she coaxed her old bones erect. 'This is too high a matter for caution. We must act. Of course I trust him. He has a Hirebrand's staff, does he not? What Hirebrand would give his staff without sure reason? And look at it – one end blackened. He has fought with it – at the Celebration, if I do not mistake. Ah, the poor Wraiths. That was ill, ill.' Looking across at Variol, she said, 'Come. We must prepare.'

Variol worked himself to his feet. Taking Tamarantha's arm, he left the Close through one of the doors behind the High Lord.

After a respectful pause for the old Lords, Osondrea levelled her stare at Covenant and demanded, 'How did you gain that staff?'

'Baradakas – the Hirebrand – gave it to me.'

'Why?'

Her tone sparked his anger. He said distinctly, 'He wanted to apologize for distressing me.'

'How did you teach him to trust you?'

Damnation! 'I passed his bloody test of truth.'

Carefully, Lord Mhoram asked, 'Unbeliever – why did the Hirebrand of Soaring Woodhelven desire to test you?'

Again, Covenant felt compelled to lie. 'Jehannum made him nervous. He tested everyone.'

'Did he also test Atiaran?'

'What do you think?'

'I think,' Foamfollower interposed firmly, 'that Atiaran Trell-mate of Mithil Stonedown would not require any test of truth to demonstrate her fidelity.'

This affirmation produced a pause, during which the Lords looked at each other as if they had reached an impasse. Then High Lord Prothall said sternly, 'Thomas Covenant, you are a stranger, and we have no time to learn your ways. But we will not surrender our sense of what is right to you. It is clear that you have spoken falsehood. For the sake of the Land, you must answer our questions. Please tell us why the Hirebrand Baradakas gave you the test of truth, but not to Atiaran your companion.'

'No.'

'Then tell us why Atiaran Trell-mate chose not to accompany you here. It is rare for a person born of the Land to stop short of Revelstone.'

'No.'

'Why do you refuse?'

Covenant glared seething up at his interrogators. They sat above him like judges with the power of outcasting in their hands. He wanted to defend himself with shouts, curses; but the Lords' intent eyes stopped him. He could see no contempt in their faces. They regarded him with anger, fear, disquietude, with offended love for the Land, but with no contempt. Very softly, he said, 'Don't you understand? I'm trying to get out of telling you an even bigger lie. If you keep pushing me – we'll all suffer.'

The High Lord met his irate, supplicating gaze for a moment, then said catarrhally, 'Very well. You make matters difficult for us. Now we must deliberate. Please leave the Close. We will call for you in a short time.'

Covenant stood, turned on his heel, started up the steps toward the big doors. Only the sound of his boots against the stone marked the silence until he had almost reached the doors. Then he heard Foamfollower say as clearly as if his own heart uttered the words, 'Atiaran Trell-mate blamed you for the slaughter of the Wraiths.'

He froze, waiting in blank dread for the Giant to continue. But Foamfollower said nothing more. Trembling, Covenant passed through the doors and moved awkwardly to sit in one of the chairs along the wall. His secret felt so fragile within him that he could hardly believe it was still intact.

I am not –

When he looked up, he found Bannor standing before him. The Bloodguard's face was devoid of expression, but it did not seem uncontemptuous. Its flat ambiguity appeared capable of any response, and now it implied a judgment of Covenant's weakness, his disease.

Impelled by anger and frustration, Covenant muttered to himself, Keep moving. Survive. 'Bannor,' he growled, 'Mhoram seems to think we should get to know each other. He told me to ask you about the Bloodguard.'

Bannor shrugged as if he were impervious to any question.

'Your people – the *Haruchai* – ' Bannor nodded – 'live up in the mountains. You came to the Land when Kevin was High Lord. How long ago was that?'

'Centuries before the Desecration.' The Bloodguard's alien tone seemed to suggest that units of time like years and decades had no significance. 'Two thousand years.'

Two thousand years. Thinking of the Giants, Covenant said, 'That's why there's only five hundred of you left. Since you came to the Land you've been dying off.'

'The Bloodguard have always numbered five hundred. That is the Vow. The *Haruchai* – are more.' He gave the name a tonal lilt that suited his voice.

'More?'

'They live in the mountains as before.'

'Then how do you – You say that as if you haven't been back there for a long time.' Again Bannor nodded slightly. 'How do you maintain your five hundred here? I haven't seen any – '

Bannor interrupted dispassionately. 'When one of the Bloodguard is slain, his body is sent into the mountains through Guards Gap, and another of the *Haruchai* comes to take his place in the Vow.'

Is slain? Covenant wondered. 'Haven't you been home since? Don't you visit your – Do you have a wife?'

'At one time.'

Bannor's tone did not vary, but something in his inflectionlessness made Covenant feel that the question was important. 'At one time?' he pursued. 'What happened to her?'

'She has been dead.'

An instinct warned Covenant, but he went on, spurred by the fascination of Bannor's alien, inflexible solidity. 'How – long ago did she die?'

Without a flicker of hesitation, the Bloodguard replied, 'Two thousand years.'

What! For a long moment, Covenant gaped in astonishment, whispering to himself as if he feared that Bannor could hear him, That's impossible. That's impossible. In an effort to control himself, he blinked dumbly. Two – ? What is this?

Yet in spite of his amazement, Bannor's claim carried conviction. That flat tone sounded incapable of dishonesty, of even misrepresentation. It filled Covenant with horror, with nauseated sympathy. In sudden vision he glimpsed the import of Mhoram's description, *made by their pledged loyalty ascetic, womanless, and old.* Barren – how could there be any limit to a bareness which had already lasted for two thousand years? 'How,' he croaked, 'how old are you?'

'I came to the Land with the first *Haruchai*, when Kevin was young in High Lordship. Together we first uttered the Vow of service. Together we called upon the Earthpower to witness our commitment. Now we do not return home until we have been slain.'

Two thousand years, Covenant mumbled. *Until we have been slain.* That's impossible. None of this is happening. In his confusion, he tried to tell himself that what he heard was like the sensitivity of his nerves, further proof of the Land's impossibility. But it did not feel like proof. It moved him as if he had learned that Bannor suffered from a rare form of leprosy. With an effort, he breathed, 'Why?'

Flatly, Bannor said, 'When we came to the Land, we saw wonders – Giants, Ranyhyn, Revelstone – Lords of such power that they declined to wage war with us lest we be destroyed. In answer to our challenge, they gave to the *Haruchai* gifts so precious – ' He paused, appeared to muse for a moment over private memories. 'Therefore we swore the Vow. We could not equal that generosity in any other way.'

'Is that your answer to death?' Covenant struggled with his sympathy, tried to reduce what Bannor said to manageable proportions. 'Is that how things are done in the Land? Whenever you're in trouble you just do the impossible? Like Berek?'

'We have sworn the Vow. The Vow is life. Corruption is death.'

'But for two thousand years?' Covenant protested. 'Damnation! It isn't even decent. Don't you think you've done enough?'

Without expression, the Bloodguard replied, 'You cannot corrupt us.'

'Corrupt you? I don't want to corrupt you. You can go on serving those Lords until you wither for all I care. I'm talking about your life, Bannor! How long do you go on serving without just once asking yourself if it's worth it? Pride or at least sanity requires that. Hellfire!' He could not conceive how even a healthy man remained unsuicidal in the face of so much existence. 'It isn't like salad dressing – you can't just spoon it around. You're human. You weren't born to be immortal.'

Bannor shrugged impassively. 'What does immortality signify? We are Bloodguard. We know only life or death – the Vow or Corruption.'

An instant passed before Covenant remembered that *Corruption* was the Bloodguard name for Lord Foul. Then he groaned, 'Well of course I understand. You live forever because your pure, sinless service is utterly indomitably unballasted by any weight or dross of mere human weakness. Ah, the advantage of clean living.'

'We do not know.' Bannor's awkward tone echoed strangely. 'Kevin saved us. How could we guess what was in his heart? He sent us all into the mountains – into the mountains. We questioned, but he gave the order. He charged us by our Vow. We knew no reason to disobey. How could we know? We would have stood by him at the Desecration – stood by or prevented. But he saved us – the Bloodguard. We who swore to preserve his life at any cost.'

Saved, Covenant breathed painfully. He could feel the unintended cruelty of Kevin's act. 'So now you don't know whether all these years of living are right or wrong,' he said distantly. *How do you stand it?* 'Maybe your Vow is mocking you.'

'There is no accusation which can raise its finger against us,' Bannor averred. But for an instant his dispassion sounded a shade less immaculate.

'No, you do all that yourself.'

In response, Bannor blinked slowly, as if neither blame nor exculpation carried meaning to the ancient perspective of his devotion.

A moment later, one of the sentries beckoned Covenant toward the Close. Trepidation constricted his heart. His horrified sympathy for Bannor drained his courage; he did not feel able to face the Lords, answer their demands. He climbed to his feet as if he were tottering, then hesitated. When Bannor motioned him forward, he said in a rush, 'Tell me one more thing. If your wife were still alive, would you go to visit her and then come back here? Could you – ' He faltered. 'Could you bear it?'

The Bloodguard met his imploring gaze squarely, but thoughts seemed to pass like shadows behind his countenance before he said softly, 'No.'

Breathing heavily as if he were nauseated, Covenant shambled through the door and down the steps toward the yellow immolation of the graveling pit.

Prothall, Mhoram, and Osondrea, Foamfollower, the four Bloodguard, the four spectators – all remained as he had left them. Under the ominous expectancy of their eyes, he seated himself in the lone chair below the Lords' table. He was shivering as if the fire-stones radiated cold rather than heat.

When the High Lord spoke, the age rattle in his voice seemed worse than before. 'Thomas Covenant, if we have treated you wrongly we will beg your pardon at the proper time. But we must resolve our doubt of you. You have concealed much that we must know. However, on one matter we have been able to agree. We see your presence in the Land in this way.

'While delving under Mount Thunder, Drool Rockworm found the lost Staff of Law. Without aid, he would require many years to master it. But Lord Foul the Despiser learned of Drool's discovery, and agreed for his own purposes to teach the Cavewight the uses of the Staff. Clearly he did not wrest the Staff from Drool. Perhaps he was too weak. Or perhaps he feared to use the tool not made for his hand. Or perhaps he has some terrible purpose which we do not grasp. But again it is clear that Lord Foul induced Drool to use the Staff to summon you to the Land – only the Staff of Law has such might. And Drool could not have conceived or executed that task without deep-lored aid. You were brought to the Land at Lord Foul's behest. We can only pray that there were other powers at work as well.'

'But that does not tell us why,' said Mhoram intently. 'If the carrying of messages were Lord Foul's only purpose, he had no need of someone from beyond the Land – and no need to protect you from Drool, as he did when he bore you to Kevin's Watch, and as I believe he attempted to do by sending his Raver to turn you from your path towards Andelain. No, you are our sole guide to the Despiser's true intent. Why did he call someone from beyond the Land? And why you? In what way do you serve his designs?'

Panting, Covenant locked his jaws and said nothing.

'Let me put the matter another way,' Prothall urged. 'The tale you have told us contains evidence of truth. Few living know that the Ravers were at one time named Herem, Sheol, and Jehannum. And we know that one of the Unfettered has been studying the Wraiths of Andelain for many years.'

Unwillingly, Covenant remembered the hopeless courage of the animals that had helped the Unfettered One to save him in Andelain. They had hurled themselves into their own slaughter with desperate and futile ferocity. He gritted his teeth, tried to close his ears to the memory of their dying.

Prothall went on without pause, 'And we know that the *lomillialor* test of truth is sure – if the one tested does not surpass the tester.'

'But the Despiser also knows,' snapped Osondrea. 'He could know that an Unfettered One lived and studied in Andelain. He could have prepared this tale and taught it to you. If he did,' she enunciated darkly, 'then the matters on which you have refused to speak are precisely those on which your story would fail. Why did the Hirebrand of Soaring Woodhelven test you? How was the testing done? Who have you battled with that staff? What instinct turned Atiaran Trell-mate against you? You fear to reply because then we will see the Despiser's handiwork.'

Authoritatively, High Lord Prothall rattled, 'Thomas Covenant, you must give us some token that your tale is true.'

'Token?' Covenant groaned.

'Give us proof that we should trust you. You have uttered doom upon our lives. That we believe. But perhaps it is your purpose to lead us from the true defence of the Land. Give us some token, Unbeliever.'

Through his quavering, Covenant felt the impenetrable circumstances of his dream clamp shut on him, deny every desire for hope or independence. He climbed to his feet, strove to meet the crisis erect. As a last resort, he grated to Foamfollower, 'Tell them. Atiaran blamed herself for what happened to the Celebration. Because she ignored the warnings. Tell them.'

He burned at Foamfollower, willing the Giant to support his last chance for autonomy, and after a grave moment the Giant said, 'My friend Thomas Covenant speaks truth, in his way. Atiaran Trell-mate believed the worst of herself.'

'Nevertheless!' Osondrea snapped. 'Perhaps she blamed herself for guiding him to the Celebration – for enabling – Her pain does not approve him.' And Prothall insisted in a low voice, 'Your token, Covenant. The necessity for judgment is upon us. You must choose between the Land and the Land's Despiser.'

Covenant, help them!

'No!' he gasped hoarsely, whirling to face the High Lord. 'It wasn't my fault. Don't you see that this is just what Foul wants you to do?'

Prothall stood, braced his weight on his staff. His stature seemed to expand in power as he spoke. 'No, I do not see. You are closed to me. You ask to be trusted, but you refuse to show your trustworthiness. No. I demand the token by which you refuse us. I am Prothall son of Dwillian, High Lord by the choice of the Council. I demand.'

For one long instant, Covenant remained suspended in decision. His eyes fell to the graveling pit. *Covenant, help them!* With a groan, he remembered how much Atiaran had paid to place him where he stood now. *Her pain does not approve.* In counterpoint he heard Bannor saying. *Two thousand years. Life or death. We do not know.* But the face he saw in the fire-stones was his wife's. *Joan!* he cried. Was one sick body more important than everything?

He tore open his shirt as if he were trying to bare his heart. From the patch of *clingor* on his chest, he snatched his wedding band jammed it on to his ring finger, raised his left fist like a defiance. But he was not defiant. 'I can't use it!' he shouted lornly, as if the ring were still a symbol of marriage, not a talisman of wild magic. 'I'm a leper!'

Astonishment rang in the Close, clanging changes in the air. The Hearthralls and Garth were stunned. Prothall shook his head as if he were trying to wake up for the first time in his life. Intuitive comprehension broke like a bow wave on Mhoram's face, and he snapped to his feet in stiff attention. Grinning gratefully, Foamfollower stood as well. Lord Osondrea also joined Mhoram, but there was no relief in her eyes. Covenant could see her shouldering her way through a throng of confusions to the crux of the situation — could see her thinking, *Save or damn, save or damn.* She alone among the Lords appeared to realize that even this token did not suffice.

Finally the High Lord mastered himself. 'Now at last we know how to honour you,' he breathed. 'Ur-Lord Thomas Covenant, Unbeliever and white gold wielder, be welcome and true. Forgive us, for we did not know. Yours is the wild magic that destroys peace. And power is at all times a dreadful thing.'

The Lords saluted Covenant as if they wished to both invoke and ward against him, then together began to sing:

> There is wild magic graven in every rock
> contained for white gold to unleash or control —
> gold, rare metal, not born of the Land,
> nor ruled, limited, subdued
> by the Law with which the Land was created
> (for the Land is beautiful,
> as if it were a strong soul's dream of peace and

harmony,
and Beauty is not possible without discipline –
and the Law which gave birth to Time
is the Land's Creator's self-control) –
but keystone rather, pivot, crux
for the anarchy out of which Time was made,
and with Time Earth,
and with Earth those who people it:
wild magic restrained in every particle of life,
and unleashed or controlled by gold
(not born of the Land)
because that power is the anchor of the arch of life
that spans and masters Time:
and white – white gold,
not ebon, ichor, incarnadine, viridian –
because white is the hue of bone;
structure of flesh,
discipline of life.

This power is a paradox,
because Power does not exist without Law,
and wild magic has no Law;
and white gold is a paradox,
because it speaks for the bone of life,
but has no part of the Land.
And he who wields white wild magic gold
is a paradox –
for he is everything and nothing,
hero and fool,
potent, helpless –
and with the one word of truth or treachery
he will save or damn the Earth
because he is mad and sane,
cold and passionate,
lost and found.

It was an involuted song, curiously harmonized, with no resolving cadences to set the hearers at rest. And in it Covenant could hear the vulture wings of Foul's voice saying, *You have might, but you will never know what it is. You will not be able to fight me at the last.* As the song ended, he wondered if his struggling served or denied the Despiser's manipulations. He could not tell. But he hated and feared the truth in Foul's words. He cut into the silence which followed the Lords' hymning. 'I don't know how to use it. I don't want to know.

That's not why I wear it. If you think I'm some kind of personified redemption – it's a lie. I'm a leper.'

'Ah, ur-Lord Covenant,' Prothall sighed as the Lords and Foamfollower reseated themselves, 'let me say again, please forgive us. We understand much now – why you were summoned – why the Hirebrand Baradakas treated you as he did – why Drool Rockworm attempted to ensnare you at the Celebration of Spring. Please understand in turn that knowledge of the ring is necessary to us. Your semblance to Berek Halfhand is not gratuitous. But, sadly, we cannot tell you how to use the white gold. Alas, we know little enough of the Lore we already possess. And I fear that if we held and comprehended all Seven Wards and Words, the wild magic would still be beyond us. Knowledge of white gold has come down to us through the ancient prophecies – foretellings, as Saltheart Foamfollower has observed, which say much but clarify little – but we comprehend nothing of the wild magic. Still, the prophecies are clear about your importance. So I name you "ur-Lord", a sharer of all the matters of the Council until you depart from us. We must trust you.'

Pacing back and forth now on the spur of his conflicting needs, Covenant growled, 'Baradakas said just about the same thing. By hell! You people terrify me. When I try to be responsible, you pressure me – and when I collapse you – You're not asking the right questions. You don't have the vaguest notion of what a leper is, and it doesn't even occur to you to enquire. *That's* why Foul chose me for this. Because I can't – Damnation! Why don't you ask me about where I come from? I've got to tell you. The world I come from doesn't allow anyone to live except on its own terms. Those terms – those terms contradict yours.'

'What are its terms?' the High Lord asked carefully.

'That your world is a dream.'

In the startled stillness of the Close, Covenant grimaced, winced as images flashed at him – courthouse columns, an old beggar, the muzzle of the police car. A dream! he panted feverishly. A dream! None of this is happening – !

Then Osondrea shot out, 'What? A dream? Do you mean to say that you are dreaming? Do you believe that you are asleep?'

'Yes!' He felt weak with fear; his revelation bereft him of a shield, exposed him to attack. But he could not recant it. He needed it to regain some kind of honesty. 'Yes.'

'Indeed!' she snapped. 'No doubt that explains the slaughter of the Celebration. Tell me, Unbeliever – do you consider that a nightmare, or does your world relish such dreams?'

Before Covenant could retort, Lord Mhoram said, 'Enough, sister

213

Osondrea. He torments himself – sufficiently.'

Glaring, she fell silent, and after a moment Prothall said, 'It may be that gods have such dreams as this. But we are mortals. We can only resist ill or surrender. Either way, we perish. Were you sent to mock us for this?'

'Mock you?' Covenant could not find the words to respond. He chopped dumbly at the thought with his halfhand. 'It's the other way around. He's mocking me.' When all the Lords looked at him in incomprehension, he cried abruptly, 'I can feel the pulse in my fingertips! But that's impossible. I've got a disease. An incurable disease. I've – I've got to figure out a way to keep from going crazy. Hell and blood! I don't want to lose my mind because some perfectly decent character in a dream needs something from me that I can't produce.'

'Well, that may be,' Prothall's voice held a note of sadness and sympathy, as if he were listening to some abrogation or repudiation of sanity from a revered seer. 'But we will trust you nonetheless. You are bitter, and bitterness is a sign of concern. I trust that. And what you say also meets the old prophecy. I fear the time is coming when you will be the Land's last hope.'

'Don't you understand?' Covenant groaned, unable to silence the ache in his voice. 'That's what Foul wants you to think.'

'Perhaps,' Mhoram said thoughtfully. 'Perhaps.' Then, as if he had reached a decision, he turned the peril of his gaze straight at Covenant. 'Unbeliever, I must ask you if you have resisted Lord Foul. I do not speak of the Celebration. When he bore you from Drool Rockworm to Kevin's Watch – did you oppose him?'

The question made Covenant feel abruptly frail, as if it had snapped a cord of his resistance. 'I didn't know how.' Wearily, he reseated himself in the loneliness of his chair. 'I didn't know what was happening.'

'You are ur-Lord now,' murmured Mhoram. 'There is no more need for you to sit there.'

'No need to sit at all,' amended Prothall, with sudden briskness. 'There is much work to be done. We must think and probe and plan – whatever action we will take in this trial must be chosen quickly. We will meet again tonight. Tuvor, Garth, Birinair, Tohrm – prepare yourselves and those in your command. Bring whatever thoughts of strategy you have to the Council tonight. And tell all the Keep that Thomas Covenant has been named ur-Lord. He is a stranger and a guest. Birinair – begin your work for the Giants at once. Bannor, I think the ur-Lord need no longer stay in the tower.' He paused and looked about him, giving everyone a chance to speak. Then he turned and left the Close. Osondrea followed him, and after giving

Covenant another formal salute, Mhoram also departed.

Numbly, Covenant moved behind Bannor up through the high passages and stairways until they reached his new quarters. The Bloodguard ushered him into a suite of rooms. They were high-ceilinged, lit by reflected sunlight through several broad windows, abundantly supplied with food and springwine, and unadorned. When Bannor had left, Covenant looked out one of the windows, and found that his rooms were perched in the north wall of Revelstone, with a view of the rough plains and the northward-curving cliff of the plateau. The sun was overhead, but a bit south of the Keep, so that the windows were in shadow.

He left the window, moved to the tray of food, and ate a light meal. Then he poured out a flask of springwine, which he carried into the bedroom. There he found one orieled window. It had an air of privacy, of peace.

Where did he go from here? He did not need to be self-wise or prophetic to know that he could not remain at Revelstone. He was too vulnerable here.

He sat down in the stone alcove to brood over the Land below and wonder what he had done to himself.

15

THE GREAT CHALLENGE

That night, when Bannor entered the suite to call Thomas Covenant to the evening meeting of the Lords, he found Covenant still sitting within the oriel of his bedroom window. By the light of Bannor's torch, Covenant appeared gaunt and spectral, as if half seen through shadows. The sockets of his eyes were dark with exhausted emotion; his lips were grey, bloodless; and the skin of his forehead had an ashen undertone. He held his arms across his chest as if he were trying to comfort a pain in his heart – watched the plains as if he were waiting for moonrise. Then he noticed the Bloodguard, and his lips pulled back, bared his teeth.

'You still don't trust me,' he said in a spent voice.

Bannor shrugged. 'We are the Bloodguard. We have no use for white gold.'

'No use?'

'It's a knowledge – a weapon. We have no use for weapons.'

'No use?' Covenant repeated dully. 'How do you defend the Lords without weapons?'

'We – ' Bannor paused as if searching the language of the Land for a word to match his thoughts – 'suffice.'

Covenant brooded for a moment, then swung himself out of the oriel. Standing in front of Bannor, he said softly, 'Bravo.' Then he picked up his staff and left the rooms.

This time, he paid more attention to the route Bannor chose, and did not lose his sense of direction. Eventually he might be able to dispense with Bannor's guidance. When they reached the huge wooden doors of the Close, they met Foamfollower and Korik. The Giant greeted Covenant with a salute and a broad grin, but when he spoke his voice was serious. 'Stone and Sea, ur-Lord Covenant! I am glad you did not choose to make me wrong. Perhaps I do not comprehend all your dilemma. But I believe you have taken the better risk – for the sake of all the Land.'

'You're a fine one to talk,' replied Covenant wanly. His sarcasm was a defensive reflex; he had lost so much other armour. 'How long have you Giants been lost? I don't think you would know a good risk if it kicked you.'

Foamfollower chuckled. 'Bravely said, my friend. It may be that the Giants are not good advisers – all our years notwithstanding. Still you have lightened my fear for the Land.'

Grimacing uselessly, Covenant went on into the Close.

The council chamber was as brightly lit and acoustically perfect as before, but the number of people in it had changed. Tamarantha and Variol were absent, and scattered through the gallery were a number of spectators – *rhadhamaerl*, *lillianrill*, warriors, Lorewardens. Bloodguard sat behind Mhoram and Osondrea; and Tuvor, Garth, Birinair, and Tohrm were in their places behind the High Lord.

Foamfollower took his former seat, gesturing Covenant into a chair near him at the Lords' table. Behind them, Bannor and Korik sat down in the lower tier of the gallery. The spectators fell silent almost at once; even the rustle of their clothing grew still. Shortly, everyone was waiting for the High Lord to begin.

Prothall sat as if wandering in thought for some time before he climbed tiredly to his feet. He held himself up by leaning on his staff, and when he spoke his voice rattled agedly in his chest. But he went without omission through the ceremonies of honouring Foamfollower and Covenant. The Giant responded with a gaity which disguised the effort he made to be concise. But Covenant rejected the formality with a scowl and a shake of his head.

When he was done, Prothall said without meeting the eyes of his fellow Lords, 'There is a custom among the new Lords – a custom which began in the days of High Lord Vailant, a hundred years ago. It is this: when a High Lord doubts his ability to meet the needs of the Land, he may come to the Council and surrender his High Lordship. Then any Lord who so chooses may claim the place for himself.' With an effort, Prothall continued firmly, 'I now surrender my leadership. Rock and root, the trial of these times is too great for me. Ur-Lord Thomas Covenant, you are permitted to claim the High Lordship if you wish.'

Covenant held Prothall's eyes, trying to measure the High Lord's intentions. But he could find no duplicity in Prothall's offer. Softly, he replied, 'You know I don't want it.'

'Yet I ask you to accept it. You bear the white gold.'

'Forget it,' Covenant said. 'It isn't that easy.'

After a moment, Prothall nodded slowly. 'I see.' He turned to the other Lords. 'Do you claim the High Lordship?'

'You are the High Lord,' Mhoram averred. And Osondrea added, 'Who else? Do not waste more time in foolishness.'

'Very well.' Prothall squared his shoulders. 'The trial and the doom of this time are on my head. I am High Lord Prothall, and by consent of the Council my will prevails. Let none fear to follow me, or blame another if my choices fail.'

An involuntary twitch passed across Covenant's face, but he said nothing; and shortly Prothall sat down, saying, 'Now let us consider what we must do.'

In silence the Lords communed mentally with each other. Then Osondrea turned to Foamfollower. 'Rockbrother, it is said, "When many matters press you, consider friendship first." For the sake of your people, you should return to Seareach as swiftly as may be. The Giants must be told all that has transpired here. But I judge that the waterway of Andelain will no longer be safe for you. We will provide an escort to accompany you through Grimmerdhore Forest and the North Plains until you are past Landsdrop and Sarangrave Flat.'

'Thank you, my Lords,' replied Foamfollower formally, 'but that will not be needed. I have given some thought myself to this matter. In their wandering, my people learned a saying from the *Bhrathair*: "He who waits for the sword to fall upon his neck will surely lose his head." I believe that the best service which I can do for my people is to assist whatever course you undertake. Please permit me to join you.'

High Lord Prothall smiled and bowed his head in acknowledgment. 'My heart hoped for this. Be welcome in our trial. Peril or plight, the Giants of Seareach strengthen us, and we cannot sing our gratitude enough. But your people must not be left unwarned. We will send other messengers.'

Foamfollower bowed in turn, and then Lord Osondrea resumed by calling on Warmark Garth.

Garth stood and reported, 'Lord, I have done as you requested. Furl's Fire now burns atop Revelstone. All who see it will warn their folk, and will spread the warning of war south and east and north. By morning, all who live north of the Soulsease and west of Grimmerdhore will be forearmed, and those who live near the river will send runners into the Centre Plains. Beyond that, the warning will carry more slowly.

'I have sent scouts in relays toward Grimmerdhore and Andelain. But six days will pass before we receive clear word of the Forest. And though you did not request it, I have begun preparations for a siege. In all, one thousand three hundred of my warriors are now at work. Twenty Eoman remain ready.'

'That is well,' said Osondrea. 'The warning which must be taken to Seareach we entrust to you. Send as many warriors as you deem necessary to ensure the embassy.'

Garth bowed and sat down.

'Now.' She nodded her head as if to clear it of other considerations. 'I have given my time to the study of ur-Lord Covenant's tale of his journey. The presence of white gold explains much. But still many things require thought – south-running storms, a three-winged bird, an abominable attack on the Wraiths of Andelain, the bloodying of the moon. To my mind, the meaning of these signs is clear.'

Abruptly, she slapped the table with her palm as if she needed the sound and the pain to help her speak. 'Drool Rockworm has already found his bane – the Illearth Stone or some other deadly evil. With the Staff of Law, he has might enough to blast the seasons in their course!'

A low groan arose from the gallery, but Prothall and Mhoram did not appear surprised. Still, a dangerous glitter intensified in Mhoram's eyes as he said softly, 'Please explain.'

'The evidence of power is unmistakable. We know that Drool has the Staff of Law. But the Staff is not a neutral tool. It was carved from the One Tree as a servant of the Earth and the Earth's Law. Yet all that has occurred is unnatural, wrong. Can you conceive the strength of will which could corrupt the Staff even enough to warp one bird? Well, perhaps madness gives Drool that will. Or perhaps the Despiser now controls the Staff. But consider – birthing a three-winged bird is the smallest of these ill feats. At his peak in the former age, Lord Foul did not dare attack the Wraiths. And as for the

218

desecrated moon – only the darkest and most terrible of ancient prophecies bespeak such matters.

'Do you call this proof conclusive that Lord Foul indeed possesses the Staff? But consider – for less exertion than corrupting the moon requires, he could surely stamp us into death. We could not fight such might. And yet he spends himself so – so vainly. Would he employ his strength to so little purpose – against the Wraiths first when he could easily destroy us? And if he would, could he corrupt the moon using the Staff of Law – a tool not made for his hand, resisting his mastery at every touch?

'I judge that if Lord Foul controlled the Staff, he would not and perhaps could not do what has been done – not until we were destroyed. But if Drool still holds the Staff, then it alone does not suffice. No Cavewight is large enough to perform such crimes without the power of both Staff and Stone. The Cavewights are weak-willed creatures, as you know. They are easily swayed, easily enslaved. And they have no heaven-challenging lore. Therefore they have always been the fodder of Lord Foul's armies.

'If I judge truly, then the Despiser himself is as much at Drool's mercy as we are. The doom of this time rides on the mad whim of a Cavewight.

'This I conclude because we have not been attacked.'

Prothall nodded glumly to Osondrea, and Mhoram took up the line of her reasoning. 'So Lord Foul relies upon us to save him and damn ourselves. In some way, he intends that our response to ur-Lord Covenant's message will spring upon ourselves a trap which holds both us and him. He has pretended friendship to Drool to preserve himself until his plans are ripe. And he has taught Drool to use his new-found power in ways which will satisfy the Cavewight's lust for mastery without threatening us directly. Thus he attempts to ensure that we will make trial to wrest the Staff of Law from Drool.'

'And therefore,' Osondrea barked, 'it would be the utterest folly for us to make trial.'

'How so?' Mhoram objected. 'The message said, "Without it, they will not be able to resist me for seven years." He foretells a sooner end for us if we do not make the attempt, or if we attempt and fail, than if we succeed.'

'What does he gain by such foretelling? What but our immediate deaths? His message is only a lure of false hope to lead us into folly.'

But Mhoram replied by quoting, '"Drool Rockworm has the Staff, and that is a cause for terror. He will be enthroned at Lord's Keep in two years if the message fails."'

'The message has not failed!' Osondrea insisted. 'We are forewarned. We can prepare. Drool is mad, and his attacks will be flawed by madness. It may be that we will find his weakness and prevail. By the Seven! Revelstone will never fall while the Bloodguard remain. And the Giants and Ranyhyn will come to our aid.' Turning toward the High Lord, she urged, 'Prothall, do not follow the lure of this quest. It is chimera. We will fall under the shadow, and the Land will surely die.'

'But if we succeed,' Mhoram countered, 'if we gain the Staff, then our chance is prolonged. Lord Foul's prophecy notwithstanding, we may find enough Earthpower in the Staff to prevail in war. And if we do not, still we will have that much more time to search for other salvations.'

'How can we succeed? Drool has both the Staff of Law and the Illearth Stone.'

'And is master of neither.'

'Master enough! Ask the Wraiths the extent of his might. Ask the moon.'

'Ask me,' growled Covenant, climbing slowly to his feet. For a moment he hesitated, torn between a fear of Drool and a dread of what would happen to him if the Lords did not go in search of the Staff. He had a vivid apprehension of the malice behind Drool's laval eyes. But the thought of the Staff decided him. He felt that he had gained an insight into the logic of his dream. The Staff had brought him to the Land: he would need the Staff to escape. 'Ask me,' he said again. 'Don't you think I have a stake in this?'

The Lords did not respond, and Covenant was forced to carry the argument forward himself. In his brooding, he had been able to find only one frail hope. With an effort, he broached the subject. 'According to you, Foul chose me. But he talked about me on Kevin's Watch as if I had been chosen by someone else – "my Enemy", he said. Who was he talking about?'

Thoughtfully, the High Lord replied, 'I do not know. We said earlier that we hoped there were other forces at work in your selection. Perhaps there were. A few of our oldest legends speak of a Creator – the Creator of the Earth – but we know nothing of such a being. We only know that we are mortal, but Lord Foul is not – in some way, he surpasses flesh.'

'The Creator,' Covenant muttered. 'All right.' A disturbing memory of the old beggar who had accosted him outside the courthouse flared momentarily. 'Why did he choose me?'

Prothall's abnegate eyes did not waver. 'Who can say? Perhaps for the very reasons that Lord Foul chooses you.'

That paradox angered Covenant, but he went on as if inspired by the contradiction, 'Then this – Creator – also wanted you to hear Foul's message. Take that into account.'

'There!' Osondrea pounced. 'There is the lie I sought – the final bait. By raising the hope of unknown help, Lord Foul seeks to ensure that we will accept this mad quest.'

Covenant did not look away from the High Lord. He held Prothall's eyes, tried to see beyond the wear of long asceticisms into his mind. But Prothall returned the gaze unflinchingly. The lines at the corners of his eyes seemed etched there by self-abrogation. 'Lord Osondrea,' he said evenly, 'does your study reveal any signs of hope?'

'Signs? Omens?' Her voice sounded reluctant in the Close. 'I am not Mhoram. If I were, I would ask Covenant what dreams he has had in the Land. But I prefer practical hopes. I see but one: so little time has been lost. It is in my heart that no other combination of chance and choice could have brought Covenant here so swiftly.'

'Very well,' Prothall replied. His look, locked with Covenant's, sharpened momentarily, and in it Covenant at last saw that the High Lord had already made his decision. He only listened to the debate to give himself one last chance to find an alternative. Awkwardly, Covenant dropped his eyes, slumped in his chair. How does he do it? he murmured pointlessly to himself. Where does all this courage come from?

Am I the only coward – ?

A moment later, the High Lord pulled his blue robe about him and rose to his feet. 'My friends,' he said, his voice thick with rheum, 'the time has come for decision. I must choose a course to meet our need. If any have thoughts which must be uttered, speak now.' No one spoke, and Prothall seemed to draw dignity and stature from the silence. 'Hear then the will of Prothall son of Dwillian, High Lord by the choice of the Council – and may the Land forgive me if I mistake or fail. In this moment, I commit the future of the Earth.

'Lord Osondrea, to you and to the Lords Variol and Tamarantha I entrust the defences of the Land. I charge you do all which wisdom or vision suggest to preserve the life in our sworn care. Remember that there is always hope while Revelstone stands. But if Revelstone falls, then all the ages and works of the Lords, from Berek Heartthew to our generation, shall come to an end, and the Land will never know the like again.

'Lord Mhoram and I will go in search of Drool Rockworm and the Staff of Law. With us will go the Giant Saltheart Foamfollower, ur-Lord Thomas Covenant, as many of the Bloodguard as First Mark Tuvor deems proper to spare from the defence of Revelstone, and one Eoman of the Warward. Thus we will not go blithe or unguarded into doom – but the main might of Lord's Keep will be left for the defence of the Land if we fail.

'Hear and be ready. The Quest departs at first light.'

'High Lord!' protested Garth, leaping to his feet. 'Will you not wait for some word from my scouts? You must brave Grimmerdhore to pass toward Mount Thunder. If the Forest is infested by the servants of Drool or the Grey Slayer, you will have little safety until my scouts have found out the movements of the enemy.'

'That is true, Warmark,' Prothall said. 'But how long will we be delayed?'

'Six days, High Lord. Then we will know how much force the crossing of Grimmerdhore requires.'

For some time, Mhoram had been sitting with his chin in his hands, staring absently into the graveling pit. But now he roused himself and said, 'One hundred Bloodguard. Or every warrior that Revelstone can provide. I have seen it. There are ur-viles in Grimmerdhore – and wolves by the thousand. They hunt in my dreams.' His voice seemed to chill the air in the Close like a wind of loss.

But Prothall spoke at once, resisting the spell of Mhoram's words. 'No, Garth. We cannot delay. And the peril of Grimmerdhore is too great. Even Drool Rockworm must understand that our best road to Mount Thunder leads through the Forest and along the north of Andelain. No, we will go south – around Andelain, then east through Morinmoss to the Plains of Ra, before moving north to Gravin Threndor. I know – that seems a long way, full of needless leagues, for a Quest which must rue the loss of each day. But this southward way will enable us to gain the help of the Ramen. Thus all the Despiser's olden foes will share in our Quest. And perhaps we will throw Drool out of his reckoning.

'No, my choice is clear. The Quest will depart tomorrow, riding south. That is my word. Let any who doubt speak now.'

And Thomas Covenant, who doubted everything, felt Prothall's resolution and dignity so strongly that he said nothing.

Then Mhoram and Osondrea stood, followed immediately by Foamfollower; and behind them the assembly rushed to its feet. All turned toward High Lord Prothall, and Osondrea lifted up her voice to say, '*Melenkurion* Skyweir watch over you, High Lord. *Melenkurion abatha!* Preserve and prevail! Seed and rock, may your purpose flourish. Let no evil blind or ill assail – no fear or faint, no rest or joy or pain, assuage the grief of wrong. Cowardice is inexculpate, corruption unassailed. Skyweir watch and Earthroot anneal. *Melenkurion abatha! Minas mill khabaal!*'

Prothall bowed his head, and the gallery and the Lords responded with one unanimous salute, one extending of arms in mute benediction.

Then in slow order the people began to leave the Close. At the same time, Prothall, Mhoram, and Osondrea departed through their private doors.

Once the Lords were gone, Foamfollower joined Covenant, and they moved together up the steps, followed by Bannor and Korik. Outside the Close, Foamfollower hesitated, considering something, then said, 'My friend, will you answer a question for me?'

'You think I've got something left to hide?'

'As to that, who knows? The faery *Elohim* had a saying – "The heart cherishes secrets not worth the telling." Ah, they were a laughing people. But – '

'No,' Covenant cut in. 'I've been scrutinized enough.' He started away toward his rooms.

'But you have not heard my question.'

He turned. 'Why should I? You were going to ask what Atiaran had against me.'

'No, my friend,' replied Foamfollower, laughing softly. 'Let your heart cherish that secret to the end of time. My question is this. What dreams have you had since you came to the Land? What did you dream that night in my boat?'

Impulsively, Covenant answered, 'A crowd of my people – real people – were spitting blood at me. And one of them said, "There is only one good answer to death."'

'Only one? What answer is that?'

'Turn your back on it,' Covenant snapped as he strode away down the corridor. 'Outcast it.' Foamfollower's good-natured humour echoed in his ears, but he marched on until he could no longer hear the Giant. Then he tried to remember the way to his rooms. With some help from Bannor, he found the suite and shut himself in, only bothering to light one torch before closing the door on the Bloodguard.

He found that in his absence someone had shuttered his windows against the fell light of the moon. Perversely, he yanked one of them open. But the bloodscape hurt his eyes like the stink of a corpse, and he slammed the shutter closed again. Then for a long time before he went to bed he paced the floor, arguing with himself until fatigue overcame him.

When morning neared, and Bannor began shaking him awake, he resisted. He wanted to go on sleeping as if in slumber he could find absolution. Dimly, he remembered that he was about to start on a journey far more dangerous than the one he had just completed, and his tired consciousness moaned in protest.

'Come,' said Bannor. 'If we delay, we will miss the call of the Ranyhyn.'

'Go to hell,' Covenant mumbled. 'Don't you ever sleep?'

'The Bloodguard do not sleep.'

'What?'

'No Bloodguard has slept since the *Haruchai* swore their Vow.'

With an effort, Covenant pulled himself into a sitting position. He peered blearily at Bannor for a moment, then muttered, 'You're already in hell.'

The alien flatness of Bannor's voice did not waver as he replied, 'You have no reason to mock us.'

'Of course not,' Covenant growled, climbing out of bed. 'Naturally, I'm supposed to enjoy having my integrity judged by someone who doesn't even need sleep.'

'We do not judge. We are cautious. The Lords are in our care.'

'Like Kevin — who killed himself. And took just about everything else with him.' But as he made this retort, he felt suddenly ashamed of himself. In the firelight, he remembered the costliness of the Bloodguard's fidelity. Wincing at the coldness of the stone floor, he said, 'Forget it. I talk like that in self-defence. Ridicule seems to be — my only answer.' Then he hurried away to wash, shave and get dressed. After a quick meal, he made sure of his knife and staff, and at last nodded his readiness to the Bloodguard.

Bannor led him down to the courtyard of the old Gilden tree. A haze of night still dimmed the air, but the stars were gone, and sunrise was clearly imminent. Unexpectedly, he felt that he was taking part in something larger than himself. The sensation was an odd one, and he tried to reason it away as he followed Bannor through the tunnel, between the huge, knuckled tower gates, and out into the dawn.

There, near the wall a short distance to the right of the gate, was gathered the company of the Quest. The warriors of the Third Eoman sat astride their horses in a semicircle behind Warhaft Quaan, and to their left stood nine Bloodguard led by First Mark Tuvor. Within the semicircle were Prothall, Mhoram, and Saltheart Foamfollower. The Giant carried in his belt a quarterstaff as tall as a man, and wore a blue neck-scarf that fluttered ebulliently in the morning breeze. Nearby were three men holding three horses saddled in *clingor*. Above them all, the face of Revelstone was crowded with people. The dwellers of the mountain city thronged every balcony and terrace, every window. And facing the gathered company was Lord Osondrea. She held her head high as if she defied her responsibility to make her stoop.

Then the sun crested the eastern horizon. It caught the upper rim of the plateau, where burned the blue flame of warning; it moved down the wall until it lifted High Lord's Furl out of the gloaming like the lighting of a torch. Next it revealed the red pennant, and then a new white flag.

Nodding up at the new flag, Bannor said, 'That is for you, ur-Lord. The sign of white gold.' Then he went to take his place among the Bloodguard.

Silence rested on the company until the sunlight touched the ground, casting its gold glow over the Questers. As soon as the light reached her feet, Osondrea began speaking as if she had been waiting impatiently for this moment, and she covered the ache in her heart with a scolding tone. 'I am in no mood for the ceremony, Prothall. Call the Ranyhyn and go. The folly of this undertaking will not be made less by delay and brave words. There is nothing more for you to say. I am well suited for my task, and the defence of the Land will not falter while I live. Go – call the Ranyhyn.'

Prothall smiled gently, and Mhoram said with a grin, 'We are fortunate in you, Osondrea. I could not entrust any other with Variol my father and Tamarantha my mother.'

'Taunt me at your peril!' she snapped. 'I am in no mood – no mood, do you hear?'

'I hear. You know that I do not taunt you. Sister Osondrea, be careful.'

'I am always careful. Now go, before I lose patience altogether.'

Prothall nodded to Tuvor, the ten Bloodguard turned and spread out, so that each faced the rising sun with no one to obscure the view. One at a time, each Bloodguard raised his hand to his mouth and gave a piercing whistle which echoed off the walls of the Keep into the dawn air.

They whistled again, and then a third time, and each call sounded as fierce and lonely as a heart cry. But the last whistle was answered by a distant whinny and a low thunder of distant hooves. All eyes turned expectantly eastward, squinted into the morning glory. For a long moment, nothing appeared, and the rumble of the earth came disembodied to the company, a mystic manifestation. But then the horses could be seen within the sun's orb, as if they had materialized in skyfire.

Soon the Ranyhyn passed out of the direct line of the sun. There were ten of them – wild and challenging animals. They were great craggy beasts, deep-chested, proud-necked, with some of the rough angularity of mustangs. They had long flying manes and tails, gaits as straight as plumb lines, eyes full of restless intelligence. Chestnuts, bays, roans, they galloped toward the Bloodguard.

Covenant knew enough about horses to see that the Ranyhyn were as individual as people, but they shared one trait: a white star marked the centre of each forehead. As they approached, with the dawn burning on their backs, they looked like the Land personified – the essence of health and power.

Nickering and tossing their heads, they halted before the Bloodguard. And the Bloodguard bowed deeply to them. The Ranyhyn stamped their feet and shook their manes as if they were laughing affectionately at a mere human show of respect. After a moment Tuvor spoke to them. 'Hail, Ranyhyn! Land-riders and proud-bearers. Sun-flesh and sky-mane, we are glad that you have heard our call. We must go on a long journey of many days. Will you bear us?'

In response, a few of the horses nodded their heads, and several others pranced in circles like colts. Then they moved forward, each approaching a specific Bloodguard and nuzzling him as if urging him to mount. This the Bloodguard did, though the horses were without saddle or bridle. Riding bareback, the Bloodguard trotted the Ranyhyn in a circle around the company, and arrayed themselves beside the mounted warriors.

Covenant felt that the departure of the company was imminent, and he did not want to miss his chance. Stepping close to Osondrea, he asked, 'What does it mean? Where did they come from?'

The Lord turned and answered almost eagerly, as if glad for any distraction, 'Of course – you are a stranger. Now, how can I explain such a deep matter briefly? Consider – the Ranyhyn are free, untamed, and their home is in the Plains of Ra. They are tended by the Ramen, but they are never ridden unless they choose a rider for themselves. It is a free choice. And once a Ranyhyn selects a rider, it is faithful to that one though fire and death interdict.

'Few are chosen. Tamarantha is the only living Lord to be blessed with a Ranyhyn mount – Hynaril bears her proudly – though neither Prothall nor Mhoram have yet made the trial. Prothall has been unwilling. But I suspect that one of his reasons for journeying south is to give Mhoram a chance to be chosen.

'No matter. Since the age of High Lord Kevin, a bond has grown up between the Ranyhyn and the Bloodguard. For many reasons, only some of which I can guess, no Bloodguard has remained unchosen.

'As to the coming here of the Ranyhyn today – that surpasses my explaining. They are creatures of Earthpower. In some way, each Ranyhyn knows when its rider will call – yes, knows, and never fails to answer. Here are Huryn, Brabha, Marny, and others. Ten days ago they heard the call which only reached our ears this morning – and after more than four hundred leagues, they arrive as fresh as the dawn. If we could match them, the Land would not be in such peril.'

As she had been speaking, Prothall and Mhoram had mounted their horses, and she finished while walking Covenant toward his mustang. Under the influence of her voice, he went up to the animal without hesitation. But when he put his foot in the stirrup of the *clingor* saddle he felt a spasm of reluctance. He did not like horses, did not trust them; their strength was too dangerous. He backed away, and found that his hands were trembling.

Osondrea regarded him curiously; but before she could say anything a bustle of surprise ran through the company. When he looked up, Covenant saw three old figures riding forward – the Lords Variol and Tamarantha, and Hearthrall Birinair. Tamarantha sat astride a great roan Ranyhyn mare with laughing eyes.

Bowing toward them from the back of his horse, High Lord Prothall said, 'I am glad that you have come. We need your blessing before we depart, just as Osondrea needs your help.'

Tamarantha bowed in return, but there was a sly half-smile on her wrinkled lips. She scanned the company briefly. 'You have chosen well, Prothall.' Then she brought her old eyes back to the High Lord. 'But you mistake us. We go with you.'

Prothall began to object, but Birinair put in stoutly, 'Of course. What else? A Quest without a Hirebrand, indeed!'

'Birinair,' said Prothall reprovingly, 'surely our work for the Seareach Giants requires you.'

'Requires? Of course. As to that, why,' the Hirebrand huffed, 'as to that – no. Shames me to say it. I have given all the orders. No. The others are abler. Have been for years.'

'Prothall,' Tamarantha urged, 'do not forbid. We are old – of course we are old. And the way will be long and hard. But this is the great challenge of our time – the only high and bold enterprise in which we will ever be able to share.'

'Is the defence of Revelstone then such a little thing?'

Variol jerked up his head as if Prothall's question had been a gibe. 'Revelstone remembers we have failed to retrieve any of Kevin's Lore. What possible help can we be here? Osondrea is more than enough. Without this Quest, our lives will be wasted.'

'No, my Lords – no. Not wasted,' Prothall murmured. With a baffled expression, he looked to Mhoram for support. Smiling crookedly, Mhoram said, 'Life is well designed. Men and women grow old so that someone will be wise enough to teach the young. Let them come.'

After another moment's hesitation, Prothall decided. 'Come then. You will teach us all.'

Variol smiled up at Tamarantha, and she returned his gaze from the high back of the Ranyhyn. Their faces were full of satisfaction and calm expectancy, which they shared in the silent marriage of their eyes. Watching them, Covenant abruptly snatched up his horse's reins and climbed into the saddle. His heart thudded anxiously, but almost at once the *clingor* gave him a feeling of security which eased his trepidation. Following the example of Prothall and Mhoram, he slid the staff under his left thigh, where it was held by the *clingor*. Then he gripped the mustang with his knees and tried not to fret.

The man who had been holding the horse touched Covenant's knee to get his attention. 'Her name is Dura – Dura Fairflank. Horses are rare in the Land. I have trained her well. She is as good as a Ranyhyn,' he boasted, then lowered his eyes as if embarrassed by his exaggeration.

Covenant replied gruffly, 'I don't want a Ranyhyn.'

The man took this as approval, he touched his palms to his forehead and spread his arms wide in salute.

From this new vantage, Covenant surveyed the company. There were no packhorses, but attached to every saddle were bags of provisions and tools, and Birinair had a thick bundle of *lillianrill* rods behind him. The Bloodguard were unencumbered, but Foamfollower carried his huge sack over his shoulder, and looked ready to travel as fast as any horse.

Shortly, Prothall rose in his stirrups and called out over the company, 'My friends, we must depart. The Quest is urgent, and the time of our trial presses upon us. I will not try to stir your hearts with long words, or bind you with awesome oaths. But I give you two charges. Be true to the limit of your strength. And remember the Oath of Peace. We go into danger, and perhaps into war – we will fight if need be. But the Land will not be served by angry bloodshed. Remember the Code:

> Do not hurt where holding is enough;
> do not wound where hurting is enough;
> do not maim where wounding is enough;
> and kill not where maiming is enough;
> the greatest warrior is one who does not need to kill.'

Then the High Lord wheeled his mount to face Revelstone. He drew out his staff, swung it three times about his head, and raised it to the sky. From its end, a blue incandescent flame burst. And he cried to the Keep:

'Hail, Revelstone!'

The entire population of the Keep responded with one mighty, heart-shaking shout:

'Hail!'

That myriad-throated paean sprang across the hills; the dawn air itself seemed to vibrate with praise and salutation. Several of the Ranyhyn nickered joyously. In answer, Covenant clenched his teeth against a sudden thickening in his throat. He felt unworthy.

Then Prothall turned his horse and urged it into a canter down the hillside. Swiftly, the company swung into place around him. Mhoram guided Covenant to a position behind Prothall, ahead of Variol and Tamarantha. Four Bloodguard flanked the Lords on either side. Quaan, Tuvor, and Korik rode ahead of Prothall, and behind came Birinair and the Eoman. With a long, loping stride, Foamfollower pulled abreast of Mhoram and Covenant, where he jogged as easily as if such travelling were natural to him.

Thus the Quest for the Staff of Law left Lord's Keep in the sunlight of a new day.

16

BLOOD-BOURNE

Thomas Covenant spent the next three days in one long, acute discovery of saddle soreness. Sitting on thin leather, he felt as if he were riding bareback; the hard, physical fact of Dura's spine threatened to saw him open. His knees felt as if they were being twisted out of joint; his thighs and calves ached and quivered with the strain of gripping his mount – a pain which slowly spread into and up his back; and his neck throbbed from the lash of Dura's sudden lurchings as she crossed the obstacles of the terrain. At times, he remained on her back only because the *clingor* saddle did not let him fall. And at nights his clenched muscles hurt so badly that he could not sleep without the benefit of *diamondraught*.

As a result, he noticed little of the passing countryside, or the weather, or the mood of the company. He ignored or rebuffed every effort to draw him into conversation. He was consumed by the painful sensation of being broken in half. Once again, he was forced to recognize the suicidal nature of this dream, of what the subconscious darkness of his mind was doing to him.

But the Giant's *diamondraught* and the Land's impossible health worked in him regardless of his suffering. His flesh grew tougher to meet the demands of Dura's back. And without knowing it he had been improving as a rider. He was learning to move with instead of resisting his mount. When he woke up after the third night, he found that the physical hurting no longer dominated him.

By that time, the company had left behind the cultivated region around Revelstone, and had moved out into rough plains. They had camped in the middle of a rude flatland; and when Covenant began to look about him, the terrain that met his eyes was rocky and unpromising.

Nevertheless, the sense of moving forward reasserted itself in him, gave him once again the illusion of safety. Like so many other things, Revelstone was behind him. When Foamfollower addressed him, he was able to respond without violence.

At that, the Giant remarked to Mhoram, 'Stone and Sea, my Lord! I believe that Thomas Covenant has chosen to rejoin the living. Surely this is the work of *diamondraught*. Hail, ur-Lord Covenant. Welcome to our company. Do you know, Lord Mhoram, there is an ancient Giantish tale about a war which was halted by *diamondraught*? Would you like to hear? I can tell it in half a day.'

'Indeed?' Mhoram chuckled. 'And will it take only half a day if you tell it on the run, while we ride?'

Foamfollower laughed broadly. 'Then I can be done by sunset tomorrow. I, Saltheart Foamfollower, say it.'

'I have heard that tale,' High Lord Prothall said. 'But the teller assured me that *diamondraught* did not in fact end the conflict. The actual rein was Giantish talk. When the Giants were done asking after the causes of war, the combatants had been listening so long that they had forgotten the answer.'

'Ah, High Lord,' Foamfollower chortled, 'you misunderstand. It was the Giants who drank the *diamondraught*.'

Laughter burst from the listening warriors, and Prothall smiled as he turned to mount his horse. Soon the Quest was on its way, and Covenant fell into place beside Mhoram.

Now as he rode, Covenant listened to the travelling noises of the company. The Lords and Bloodguard were almost entirely silent, preoccupied; but over the thud of hooves, he could hear talk and snatches of song from the warriors. In Quaan's leadership, they sounded confident and occasionally eager, as if they looked forward to putting their years of Sword training to the test.

Some time later, Lord Mhoram surprised Covenant by saying without preamble, 'Ur-Lord, as you know there were questions which the Council did not ask you. May I ask them now? I should like to know more concerning your world.'

'My world.' Covenant swallowed roughly. He did not want to talk about it; he had no desire to repeat the ordeal of the Council. 'Why?'

Mhoram shrugged. 'Because the more I know of you, the better I will know what to expect from you in times of peril. Or because an understanding of your world may teach me to treat you rightly. Or because I have asked the question in simple friendship.'

Covenant could hear the candour in Mhoram's voice, and it disarmed his refusals. He owed the Lords and himself some kind of honesty. But that debt was bitter to him, and he could not find any easy way to articulate all the things which needed saying. Instinctively, he began to make a list. We have cancer, heart failure, tuberculosis, multiple sclerosis, birth defects, leprosy – we have alcoholism, venereal disease, drug addiction, rape, robbery, murder, child beating, genocide – but he could not bear to utter a catalogue of woes that might run on forever. After a moment, he stood in his stirrups and gestured out over the ruggedness of the plains.

'You probably see it better than I do – but even I can tell that this is beautiful. It's alive – it's alive the way it should be alive. This kind of grass is yellow and stiff and thin – but I can see that it's healthy. It belongs here, in this kind of soil. By hell! I can even see what time of year this is by looking at the dirt. I can see *spring*.

'Where I come from we don't see – If you don't know the annual cycles of plants, you can't tell the difference between spring and summer. If you don't have a – have a standard of comparison, you can't recognize – But the world is beautiful – what's left of it, what we haven't damaged.' Images of Haven Farm sprang irrefusably across his mind. He could not restrain the mordancy of his tone as he concluded, 'We have beauty too. We call it "scenery".'

'"Scenery",' Mhoram echoed. 'The word is strange to me – but I do not like the sound.'

Covenant felt oddly shaken, as if he had just looked over his shoulder and found himself standing too close to a precipice. 'It means that beauty is something extra,' he rasped. 'It's nice, but we can live without it.'

'Without?' Mhoram's gaze glittered dangerously.

And behind him Foamfollower breathed in astonishment, 'Live without beauty? Ah, my friend! How do you resist despair?'

'I don't think we do,' Covenant muttered. 'Some of us are just stubborn.' Then he fell silent. Mhoram asked him no more questions and he rode on chewing the gristle of his thoughts until High Lord Prothall called a rest halt.

As the day progressed, Covenant's silence seemed to infect the company. The travelling banter and singing of the Eoman faded gradually into stillness; Mhoram watched Covenant curiously askance, but made no effort to renew their conversation; and Prothall looked as night-faced as the Bloodguard. After a time, Covenant guessed the cause of their reticence. Tonight would be the first full of the bloody moon.

A shiver ran through him. The night would be a kind of test of Drool's power. If the Cavewight could maintain his red hold even when the moon was full, then the Lords would have to admit that his might had no discernible limit. And such might would be spawning armies, would almost certainly have produced marauders to feed Drool's taste for pillage. Then the company would have to fight for passage. Covenant remembered with a shudder his brief meeting with Drool in the cavern of Kiril Threndor. Like his companions, he fell under the pall of what the night might reveal.

Only Variol and Tamarantha seemed untouched by the common mood. She appeared half-asleep, and rode casually, trusting the Ranyhyn to keep her on its back. Her husband sat erect, with a steady hand on his reins, but his mouth was slack and his eyes unfocused. They looked frail; Covenant felt that he could see the brittleness of their bones. But they alone of all the company were blithe against the coming night – blithe or uncomprehending.

The riders camped before dusk on the north side of a rough hill, partially sheltered from the prevailing southwest breeze. The air had turned cold like a revisitation of winter, and the wind carried chill to the hearts of the travellers. In silence, some of the warriors fed and rubbed down the horses, while others cooked a spare meal over a fire that Birinair coaxed from one of his *lillianrill* rods and some scrub wood. The Ranyhyn galloped away together to spend the night in some secret play or rite, leaving the horses hobbled and the Bloodguard standing sentinel and the rest of the company huddled in their cloaks around the fire. As the last of the sunlight scudded from the air, the breeze stiffened into a steady wind.

Covenant found himself wishing for some of the camaraderie that had begun the day. But he could not supply the lack himself; he had to wait until High Lord Prothall rose to meet the apprehension of the Quest.

Planting his staff firmly, he began to sing the Vespers hymn of Revelstone. Mhoram joined him, followed by Variol and Tamarantha, and soon the whole Eoman was on its feet, adding its many-throated voice to the song. There they stood under the stern sky, twenty-five souls singing like witnesses:

> Seven hells for failed faith,
> For Land's betrayers, man and wraith;
> And one brave Lord to deal the doom
> To keep the blacking blight from Beauty's bloom.

They raised their voices bravely, and their melody was counter-pointed by the tenor roll of Foamfollower's plain-song. When they were done, they reseated themselves and began to talk together in low voices, as if the hymn were all they needed to restore their courage.

Covenant sat staring at his knotted hands. Without taking his eyes off them, he knew when moonrise came; he felt the sudden stiffening around him as the first crimson glow appeared on the horizon. But he gnawed his lip and did not look up. His companions breathed tensely; a red cast slowly deepened in the heart of the fire; but he clenched his gaze as if he were studying the way his knuckles whitened.

Then he heard Lord Mhoram's agonized whisper, '*Melenkurion*,' and he knew that the moon was full red, stained as if its defilement were complete — as bloody as if the night sky had been cut to the heart. He felt the light touch his face, and his cheek twitched in revulsion.

The next moment, there came a distant wail like a cry of protest. It throbbed like desolation in the chill air. In spite of himself, Covenant looked over the blood-hued plain; for an instant, he expected the company to leap to the relief of that call. But no one moved. The cry must have come from some animal. Glancing briefly at the full violated moon, he changed his grip and lowered his eyes again.

When his gaze reached his fingers, he saw in horror that the moonlight gave his ring a reddish cast. The metal looked as if it had been dipped in blood. Its inner silver struggled to show through the crimson, but the blood-light seemed to be soaking inward, slowly quenching, perverting the white gold.

He understood instinctively. For one staggering heartbeat, he sat still, howled silent and futile warnings at his unsuspecting self. Then he sprang to his feet, erect and rigid as if he had been yanked upright by the moon — arms tight at his sides, fists clenched.

Behind him, Bannor said, 'Do not fear, ur-Lord. The Ranyhyn will warn us if the wolves are any danger.'

Covenant turned his head. The Bloodguard reached a restraining hand toward him.

'Don't touch me!' Covenant hissed.

He jerked away from Bannor. For an instant while his heart laboured, he observed how the crimson moon made Bannor's face look like old lava. Then a vicious sense of wrong exploded under his feet, and he pitched toward the fire.

As he struck the earth he flung himself onward, careless of everything but his intense visceral need to escape the attack. After one roll, his legs crashed among the flaming brands.

But as Covenant fell, Bannor sprang forward. When Covenant hit the fire, the Bloodguard was only a stride away. He caught Covenant's wrist in almost the same instant, heaved him child-light out of the flames and on to his feet.

Even before he had regained his balance, Covenant spun on Bannor and yelled into the Bloodguard's face, 'Don't touch me!'

Bannor released Covenant's wrist, backed away a step.   Prothall, Mhoram, Foamfollower, and all the warriors were on their feet. They stared at Covenant in surprise, confusion, outrage.

He felt suddenly weak. His legs trembled; he dropped to his knees beside the fire. Thinking, Hellfire and bloody Foul has done it to me, he's taking me over damnation! he pointed an unsteady finger at the ground that had stung him. 'There,' he gasped. 'It was there. I felt it.'

The Lords reacted immediately. While Mhoram shouted for Birinair, Prothall hurried forward and stooped over the spot Covenant indicated. Mumbling softly to himself, he touched the spot with the tips of his fingers like a physician testing a wound. Then he was joined by Mhoram and Birinair. Birinair thrust the High Lord aside, took his *lillianrill* staff and placed its end on the sore place. Rotating the staff between his palms, he concentrated imperiously on his beloved wood.

'For one moment,' Prothall murmured, 'for one moment I felt something – some memory in the Earth. Then it passed beyond my touch.' He sighed. 'It was terrible.'

Birinair echoed, 'Terrible,' talking to himself in his concentration. Prothall and Mhoram watched him as his hands trembled with either age or sensitivity. Abruptly, he cried, 'Terrible! The hand of the Slayer! He dares do this?' He snatched himself away so quickly that he stumbled, and would have fallen if Prothall had not caught him.

Momentarily, Prothall and Birinair met each other's eyes as if they were trying to exchange some knowledge that could not be voiced. Then Birinair shook himself free. Looking about him as if he could see the shards of his dignity scattered around his feet, he mumbled gruffly, 'Stand on my own. Not that old yet.' After a glance at Covenant, he went on more loudly, 'You think I am old. Of course. Old and foolish. Push himself into a Quest when he should be resting his bones by the hearth. Like a lump.' Pointing toward the Unbeliever, he concluded, 'Ask him. Ask.'

Covenant had climbed to his feet while the attention of the company was on the Hirebrand, and had pushed his hands into his pockets to hide the hue of his ring. As Birinair pointed at him, he raised his eyes from the ground. A sick feeling of presage twisted his stomach as he remembered his attacks in Andelain, and what had followed them.

Prothall said firmly, 'Step there again, ur-Lord.'

Grimacing, Covenant strode forward and stamped his foot on the spot. As his heel hit the ground, he winced in expectation, tried to brace himself for the sensation that at this one point the earth had become insecure, foundationless. But nothing stung him. As in Andelain, the ill had vanished, leaving him with the impression that a veneer of trustworthiness had been replaced over a pit.

In answer to the silent question of the Lords, he shook his head.

After a pause, Mhoram said evenly, 'You have felt this before.'

With an effort, Covenant forced himself to say, 'Yes. Several times – in Andelain. Before that attack on the Celebration.'

'The hand of the Grey Slayer touched you,' Birinair spat. But he could not sustain his accusation. His bones seemed to remember their age, and he sagged tiredly, leaned on his staff. In an odd tone of self-reproach, as if he were apologizing, he mumbled, 'Of course. Younger. If I were younger.' He turned from the company and shuffled away to his bed beyond the circle.

'Why did you not tell us?' Mhoram asked severely.

The question made Covenant feel suddenly ashamed, as if his ring were visible through the fabric of his pants. His shoulders hunched, drove his hands deeper into his pockets. 'I didn't – at first I didn't want you to know what – how important Foul and Drool think I am. After that – ' he referred to his crisis in the Close with his eyes – 'I was thinking about other things.'

Mhoram accepted this with a nod, and after a moment Covenant went on: 'I don't know what it is. But I only get it through my boots. I can't touch it – with my hands or my feet.'

Mhoram and Prothall shared a glance of surprise. Shortly the High Lord said, 'Unbeliever, the cause of these attacks surpasses me. Why do your boots make you sensitive to this wrong? I do not know. But either Lord Mhoram or myself must remain by you at all times, so that you may respond without delay.' Over his shoulder, he said,

'First Mark Tuvor. Warhaft Quaan. Have you heard?'

Quaan came to attention and replied, 'Yes, High Lord.' And from behind the circle Tuvor's voice carried softly, 'There will be an attack. We have heard.'

'Readiness will be needed,' said Mhoram grimly, 'and stout hearts to face an onslaught of ur-viles and wolves and Cavewights without faltering.'

'That is so,' the High Lord said at last. 'But such things will come in their own time. Now we must rest. We must gather strength.'

Slowly, the company began the business of bedding down. Humming his Giantish plain-song, Foamfollower stretched out on the ground with his arm around his leather flask of *diamondraught*. While the Bloodguard set watches, the warriors spread their blankets for themselves and the Lords. Covenant went to bed self-consciously, as if he felt the company studying him, and he was glad of the blankets that helped him hide his ring. Then he lay awake long into the night, feeling too cold to sleep; the blankets did not keep out the chill which emanated from his ring.

But until he finally fell asleep, he could hear Foamfollower's humming and see Prothall sitting by the embers of the fire. The Giant and the High Lord kept watch together, two old friends of the Land sharing some vigil against their impending doom.

The next day dawned grey and cheerless – overcast with clouds like ashes in the sky – and into it Covenant rode bent in his saddle as if he had a weight around his neck. His ring had lost its red stain with the setting moon; but the colour remained in his mind and the ring seemed to drag him down like a meaningless crime. Helplessly, he perceived that an allegiance he had not chosen, could not have chosen, was being forced upon him. The evidence seemed irrefutable. Like the moon, he was falling prey to Lord Foul's machinations. His volition was not required; the strings which dangled him were strong enough to overbear any resistance.

He did not understand how it could happen to him. Was his death wish, his leper's weariness or despair, so strong? What had become of his obdurate instinct for survival? Where was his anger, his violence? Had he been victimized for so long that now he could only respond as a victim, even to himself?

He had no answers. He was sure of nothing but the fear which came over him when the company halted at noon. He found that he did not want to get down from Dura's back.

He distrusted the ground, dreaded contact with it. He had lost a fundamental confidence: his faith that the earth was stable – a faith so obvious and constant and necessary that it had been unconscious until now – had been shaken. Blind silent soil had become a dark hand malevolently seeking out him and him alone.

Nevertheless, he swung down from the saddle, forced himself – set foot on the ground and was stung. The virulence of the sensation made all his nerves cringe, and he could hardly stand as he watched Prothall and Mhoram and Birinair try to capture what he had felt. But they failed completely; the misery of that ill touch withdrew the instant he jumped away from it.

That evening during supper he was stung again. When he went to bed to hide his ring from the moon, he shivered as if he were feverish. On the morning of the sixth day, he arose with a grey face and a crippled look in his eyes. Before he could mount Dura he was stung again.

And again during one of the company's rest halts.

And again the instant he mustered enough despair to dismount at the end of the day's ride. The wrong felt like another spike in his coffin lid. This time, his nerves reacted so violently that he tumbled to the ground like a demonstration of futility. He had to lie still for a long time before he could coax his arms and legs under control again, and when he finally regained his feet, he jerked and winced with fear at every step. Pathetic, pathetic, he panted to himself. But he could not find the rage to master it.

With keen concern in his eyes, Foamfollower asked him why he did not take off his boots. Covenant had to think for a moment before he could remember why. Then he murmured, 'They're part of me – they're part of the way I have to live. I don't have – very many parts left. And besides,' he added wanly, 'if I don't keep having these fits, how is Prothall going to figure them out?'

'Do not do such a thing for us,' Mhoram replied intently. 'How could we ask it?'

But Covenant only shrugged and went to sit by the fire. He could not face food that night – the thought of eating made his raw nerves nauseous – but he tried a few *aliantha* from a bush near the camp, and found that they had a calming effect. He ate a handful of the berries, absentmindedly tossing away the seeds as Lena had taught him, and returned to the fire.

When the company had finished its meal, Mhoram seated himself beside Covenant. Without looking at him, the Lord asked, 'How can we help you? Should we build a litter so that you will not have to touch the earth? Or are there other ways? Perhaps one of Foamfollower's tales would ease your heart. I have heard Giants that boast that the Despiser himself would become an Earthfriend if he could be made to listen to the story of Bahgoon the Unbearable and Thelma Twofist – such healing there is in stories.' Abruptly, Mhoram turned squarely toward Covenant, and Covenant saw that the Lord's face was full of sympathy. 'I see your pain, ur-Lord.'

Covenant hung his head to avoid Mhoram's gaze, made sure his left hand was securely in his pocket. After a moment, he said distantly, 'Tell me about the Creator.'

'Ah,' Mhoram sighed, 'we do not know that a Creator lives. Our only lore of such a being comes from the most shadowy reaches of our oldest legends. We know the Despiser. But the Creator we do not know.'

Then Covenant was vaguely startled to hear Lord Tamarantha cut in, 'Of course we know. Ah, the folly of the young. Mhoram my son, you are not yet a prophet. You must learn that kind of courage.' Slowly, she pulled her ancient limbs together and got to her feet, leaning on her staff for support. Her thin white hair hung in wisps about her face as she moved into the circle around the fire, muttering frailly, 'Oracles and prophecy are incompatible. According to Kevin's Lore, only Heartthew the Lord-Fatherer was both seer and prophet. Lesser souls lose the paradox. Why, I do not know. But when Kevin Landwaster decided in his heart to invoke the Ritual of Desecration, he saved the Bloodguard and the Ranyhyn and the Giants because he was an oracle. And because he was no prophet he failed to see that Lord Foul would survive. A lesser man than Berek. Of course the Creator lives.'

She looked over at Variol for confirmation, and he nodded, but Covenant could not tell whether he was approving or drowsing. But Tamarantha nodded in return as if Variol had supported her. Lifting her head to the night sky and the stars, she spoke in a voice fragile with age.

'Of course the Creator lives,' she repeated. 'How else? Opposites require each other. Otherwise the difference is lost, and only chaos remains. No, there can be no Despite without Creation. Better to ask how the Creator can have forgotten that when he made the Earth. For if he did not forget, then Creation and Despite existed together in his one being, and he did not know it.

'This the elder legends tell us: into the infinity before Time was made came the Creator like a worker into his workshop. And since it is the nature of creating to desire perfection, the Creator devoted all himself to the task. First he built the arch of Time, so that his creation would have a place in which to be – and for the keystone of that arch he forged the wild magic, so that Time would be able to resist chaos and endure. Then within the arch he formed the Earth. For ages he laboured, formed and uniformed, trialled and tested and rejected and trialled and tested again, so that when he was done his creation would have no cause to reproach him. And when the Earth was fair to his eye, he gave birth to the inhabitants of the Earth, beings to act out in their lives his reach for perfection – and he did not neglect to give them the means to strive for perfection themselves. When he was done, he was proud as only those who create can be.

'Alas, he did not understand Despite, or had forgotten it. He understood his task thinking that perfect labour was all that he required to create perfection. But when he was done, and his pride had tasted its first satisfaction, he looked closely at the Earth, thinking to gratify himself with the sight – and he was dismayed. For, behold! Buried deep in the Earth through no will or forming of his were banes of destruction, powers virile enough to rip his masterwork into dust.

'Then he understood or remembered. Perhaps he found Despite itself beside him, misguiding his hand. Or perhaps he saw the harm in himself. It does not matter. He became outraged with grief and torn pride. In his fury he wrestled with Despite, either within him or without, and in his fury he cast the Despiser down, out of the infinity of the cosmos on to the Earth.

'Alas! thus the Despiser was emprisoned within Time. And thus the Creator's creation became the Despiser's world, to torment as he chose. For the very Law of Time, the principle of power which made the arch possible, worked to preserve Lord Foul, as we now call him. That Law requires that no act may be undone. Desecration may not be undone – defilement may not be recanted. It may be survived or healed, but not denied. Therefore Lord Foul has afflicted the Earth, and the Creator cannot stop him – for it was the Creator's act which placed Despite here.

'In sorrow and humility, the Creator saw what he had done. So that the plight of Earth would not be utterly without hope, he sought to help his creation in indirect ways. He guided the Lord-Fatherer to the fashioning of the Staff of Law – a weapon against Despite. But the very Law of the Earth's creation permits nothing more. If the Creator were to silence Lord Foul, that act would destroy Time – and then the Despiser would be free in infinity again, free to make whatever befoulments he desired.'

Tamarantha paused. She had told her tale simply, without towering rhetoric or agitation or any sign of passion beyond her agedness. But for a moment, her thin old voice convinced Covenant that the universe was at stake – that his struggle was only a microcosm of a far larger conflict. During that moment, he waited in suspense for what she would say next.

Shortly, she lowered her head and turned her wrinkled gaze full on him. Almost whispering, she said, 'Thus we are come to the greatest test. The wild magic is here. With a word our world could be riven to the core. Do not mistake,' she quavered. 'If we cannot win this Unbeliever to our cause, then the Earth will end in rubble.' But Covenant could not tell whether her voice shook because she was old, or because she was afraid.

Moonrise was near; he went to his bed to avoid exposing the alteration of his ring. With his head under the blankets, he stared into the blackness, saw when the moon came up by the bloody glow which grew in his wedding band. The metal seemed more deeply stained than it had two nights ago. It held his covered gaze like a fixation; and when he finally slept, he was as exhausted as if he had been worn out under an interrogation.

The next morning, he managed to reach Dura's back without being attacked – and he groaned in unashamed relief. Then Prothall broke his usual habit and did not call for a halt at noon. The reason became clear when the riders topped a rise and came in sight of the Soulsease River. They rode down out of the harsh plains and swam their horses across the river before stopping to rest. And there again Covenant was not attacked when he set foot on the ground.

But the rest of the day contrasted grimly with this inexplicable respite. A few leagues beyond the Soulsease, the Quest came upon a Waymeet for the first time. Remembering Covenant's tale of a murdered Waynhim, Prothall sent two Bloodguard, Korik and Terrel (who warded Lord Mhoram), into the Waymeet. The investigation was only necessary for confirmation. Even Covenant in his straitened condition could see the neglect, smell the disuse; the green travellers' haven had gone brown and sour. When Korik and Terrel returned, they could only report what the company had already perceived; the Waymeet was untended.

The Lords met this discovery with stern faces. Clearly, they had feared that the murder Covenant had described would lead the Waynhim to end their service. But several of the warriors groaned in shock and dismay, and Foamfollower ground his teeth. Covenant glanced around at the Giant, and for a moment saw Foamfollower's face suffused with fury. The expression passed quickly, but it left Covenant feeling shaken. Unexpectedly, he sensed that the unmarred loyalty of the Giants of the Land was dangerous; it was quick to judge.

So there was a gloom on the company at the end of the seventh day, a gloom which could only be aggravated by the moon, incarnadine and corrupt, as it coloured the night like a conviction of disaster. Only Covenant received any relief; once again, his private, stalking ill left him alone. But the next day brought the riders in sight of Andelain. Their path lay along the outskirts of the Hills on the southwest side, and even through the hanging grey weather, the richness of Andelain glistened like the proudest gem of the Earth. It made the company feel light-boned, affected the Quest like a living view of what the Land had been like before Desecration.

Covenant needed that quiet consolation as much as anyone, but it was denied him. While eating breakfast, he had been bitten again by the wrong in the earth. The previous day's respite seemed only to multiply the virulence of the attack; it was compact with malevolence, as if that respite had frustrated it, intensified its spite. The sensation of wrong left him foundering.

During one of the rest halts, he was struck again.

And that evening, while he made himself a supper of *aliantha*, he was struck again. This time the wrong lashed him so viciously that he passed out for some time. When he regained consciousness, he was lying in Foamfollower's arms like a child. He felt vaguely that he had had convulsions.

'Take off your boots,' Foamfollower urged intently.

Numbness filled Covenant's head like mist, clouded his reactions. But he mustered the lucidity to ask, 'Why?'

'Why? Stone and Sea, my friend! When you ask like that, how can I answer? Ask yourself. What do you gain by enduring such wrong?'

'Myself,' he murmured faintly. He wanted simply to recline in the Giant's arms and sleep, but he fought the desire, pushed himself away from Foamfollower until the Giant set him on his feet by Birinair's *lillianrill* fire. For a moment, he had to cling decrepitly to Foamfollower's arm to support himself, but then one of the warriors gave him his staff, and he braced himself on it. 'By resisting.'

But he knew in his bones that he was not resisting. They felt weak, as if they were melting under the strain. His boots had become a hollow symbol for an intransigence he no longer felt.

Foamfollower started to object, but Mhoram stopped him. 'It is his choice,' the Lord said softly.

After a while, Covenant fell into a feverish sleep. He did not know that he was carried tenderly to bed, did not know that Mhoram watched over him during the night, and saw the bloody stain on his wedding band.

He reached some sort of crisis while he slept, and awoke with the feeling that he had lost, that his ability to endure had reached the final either-or of a toss which had gone against him. His throat was parched like a battleground. When he forced his eyes open, he found himself again prostrated in Foamfollower's arms. Around him, the company was ready to mount for the day's ride.

When he saw Covenant's eyes open, Foamfollower bent over him and said quietly, 'I would rather bear you in my arms than see you suffer. Our journey to Lord's Keep was easier for me than watching you now.'

Part of Covenant rallied to look at the Giant. Foamfollower's face showed strain, but it was not the strain of exhaustion. Rather, it seemed like a pressure building up in his mind – a pressure that made the fortress of his forehead appear to bulge. Covenant stared at it dumbly for a long moment before he realized that it was sympathy. The sight of his own pain made Foamfollower's pulse throb in his temples.

Giants? Covenant breathed to himself. Are they all like this? Watching that concentration of emotion, he murmured, 'What's a "foamfollower"?'

The Giant did not appear to notice the irrelevance of the question. 'A "follower" is a compass,' he answered simply. 'So "foamfollower" – "sea-compass".'

Covenant began weakly moving, trying to get out of the Giant's arms. But Foamfollower held him, forbade him in silence to set his feet on the ground.

Lord Mhoram intervened. With grim determination in his voice, he said, 'Set him down.'

'Down,' echoed Covenant.

Several retorts passed under Foamfollower's heavy brows, but he only said, 'Why?'

'I have decided,' Mhoram replied. 'We will not move from this place until we understand what is happening to ur-Lord Covenant. I have delayed this risk too long. Death gathers around us. Set him down.' His eyes flashed dangerously.

Still Foamfollower hesitated until he saw High Lord Prothall nod support for Mhoram. Then he turned Covenant upright and lowered him gently to the ground. For an instant, his hands rested protectively on Covenant's shoulders. Then he stepped back.

'Now, ur-Lord,' said Mhoram. 'Give me your hand. We will stand together until you feel the ill, and I feel it through you.'

At that, a coil of weak panic writhed in Covenant's heart. He saw himself reflected in Mhoram's eyes, saw himself standing lornly with what he had lost written in his face. That loss dismayed him. In that tiny, reflected face he perceived abruptly that if the attacks continued he would inevitably learn to enjoy the sense of horror and loathing which they gave him. He had discovered a frontier into the narcissism of revulsion, and Mhoram was asking him to risk crossing over.

'Come,' the Lord urged, extending his right hand. 'We must understand this wrong if we are to resist it.'

In desperation or despair, Covenant thrust out his hand. The heels of their palms met; they gripped each other's thumbs. His two fingers felt weak, hopeless for Mhoram's purpose, but the Lord's grasp was sturdy. Hand to hand like combatants, they stood there as though they were about to wrestle with some bitter ghoul.

The attack came almost at once. Covenant cried out, shook as if his bones were gibbering, but he did not leap away. In the first instant, Mhoram's hard grip sustained him. Then the Lord threw his arm around Covenant, clasped him to his chest. The violence of Covenant's distress buffeted Mhoram, but he held his ground, gritted his embrace.

As suddenly as it had come, the attack passed. With a groan, Covenant sagged in Mhoram's arms.

Mhoram held him up until he moved and began to carry his own weight. Then, slowly, the Lord released him. For a moment, their faces appeared oddly similar; they had the same haunted expression, the same sweat-damp hollow gaze. But shortly Covenant gave a shuddering sigh, and Mhoram straightened his shoulders – and the similarity faded.

'I was a fool,' Mhoram breathed. 'I should have known – That ill is Drool Rockworm, reaching out with the power of the Staff to find you. He can sense your presence by the touch of your boots on the earth, because they are unlike anything made in the Land. Thus he knows where you are, and so where we are.

'It is my guess that you were untouched the day we crossed the Soulsease because Drool expected us to move toward him on the River, and was searching for us on water rather than on land. But he learned his mistake, and regained contact with you yesterday.'

The Lord paused, gave what he was saying a chance to penetrate Covenant. Then he concluded, 'Ur-Lord, for the sake of us all – for the sake of the Land – you must not wear your boots. Drool already knows too much of our movements. His servants are abroad.'

Covenant did not respond. Mhoram's words seemed to sap the last of his strength. The trial had been too much for him; with a sigh he fainted into the Lord's arms. So he did not see how carefully his boots and clothes were removed and packed in Dura's saddlebags – how tenderly his limbs were washed by the Lords and dressed in a robe of white samite – how sadly his ring was taken from his finger and placed on a new patch of *clingor* over his heart – how gently he was cradled in Saltheart Foamfollower's arms throughout the long march of that day. He lay in darkness like a sacrifice; he could hear the teeth of his leprosy devouring his flesh. There was a smell of contempt around him insisting on his impotence. But his lips were bowed in a placid smile, a look of fondness, as if he had come at last to approve his disintegration.

He continued to smile when he awoke late that night and found himself staring into the wide ghoul-grin of the moon. Slowly, his smile stretched into a taut grimace, a look of happiness or hatred. But then the moon was blocked out of his vision by Foamfollower's great bulk. The Giant's huge palms, each as large as Covenant's face, stroked his head tenderly and in time the caress had its effect on him. His eyes lost their ghastly appearance, and his face relaxed, drifted away from torment into repose. Soon he was deep in a less perilous slumber.

The next day – the tenth of the Quest – he awoke calmly, as if he were held in numb truce or stasis between irreconcilable demands. A feeling of affectlessness pervaded him, as if he no longer had the heart to care about himself. Yet he was hungry. He ate a large breakfast, and remembered to thank the Woodhelvennin woman who seemed to have assigned herself the task of providing for him. His new apparel he accepted with a rueful shrug, noticing in silent, dim sarcasm how easily after all he was able to shed himself – and how the white robe flattered his gaunt form as if he were born to it. Then, dumbly, he mounted Dura.

His companions watched him as if they feared he would fall. He was weaker than he had realized; he needed most of his concentration to keep his seat, but he was equal to the task. Gradually the Questers began to believe that he was out of danger. Among them, he rode through the sunshine and the warm spring air along the flowered marge of Andelain – rode attenuated and careless, as if he were locked between impossibilities.

17

END IN FIRE

That night, the company camped in a narrow valley between two rocky hillsides half a league from the thick grasses of Andelain. The warriors were cheery, recovering their natural spirits after the tensions of the past few days, and they told stories and sang songs to the quiet audience of the Lords and Bloodguard. Though the Lords did not participate, they seemed glad to listen, and several times Mhoram and Quaan could be heard chuckling together.

But Covenant did not share the ebullience of the Eoman. A heavy hand of blankets held shut the lid of his emotions, and he felt separate, untouchable. Finally he went to his bed before the warriors were done with their last song.

He was awakened some time later by a hand on his shoulder. Opening his eyes, he found Foamfollower stooping beside him. The moon had nearly set. 'Arise,' the Giant whispered. 'The Ranyhyn have brought word. Wolves are hunting us. Ur-viles may not be far behind. We must go.'

Covenant blinked sleepily at the Giant's benighted face for a moment. 'Why? Won't they follow?'

'Make haste, ur-Lord. Terrel, Korik, and perhaps a third of Quaan's Eoman will remain here in ambush. They will scatter the pack. Come.'

But Covenant persisted. 'So what? They'll just fall back and follow again. Let me sleep.'

'My friend, you try my patience. Arise, and I will explain.'

With a sigh, Covenant rolled from his blankets. While he tightened the sash of his robe, settled his sandals on his feet, and assured himself of his staff and knife, his Woodhelvennin helper snatched up his bedding and packed it away. Then she led Dura toward him.

Amid the silent urgency of the company, he mounted, then went with Foamfollower toward the centre of the camp, where the Lords and Bloodguard were already mounted. When the warriors were ready, Birinair extinguished the last embers of the fire, and climbed stiffly on to his horse. A moment later, the riders turned and fled the narrow valley, picking their way across the rough terrain by the last red light of the moon.

The ground under Dura's hooves looked like blood slowly clotting, and Covenant clutched his ring to preserve it from the crimson light. Around him, the company moved in a tight suspense of silence; every low, metal clatter of sword was instantly muffled, every breath covered. The Ranyhyn were as noiseless as shadows, and on their broad backs the Bloodguard sat like statues, eternally alert and insentient.

Then the moon set. Darkness was a relief, though it seemed to increase the hazard of their escape. But the whole company was surrounded, guided, by the Ranyhyn, and the mighty horses chose a path which kept the other mounts safe between them.

After two or three leagues had passed, the mood of the Quest relaxed somewhat. They heard no pursuit, sensed no danger. Finally, Foamfollower gave Covenant the explanation he had promised.

'It is simple,' the Giant whispered. 'After scattering the wolves, Korik and Terrel will lead a trail away from ours. They will go straight into Andelain, east toward Mount Thunder, until pursuit has been confused. Then they will turn and rejoin us.'

'Why?' Covenant asked softly.

Lord Mhoram took up the explanation. 'We doubt that Drool can understand our purpose.' Covenant could not feel the Lord's presence as strongly as Foamfollower's, so Mhoram's voice sounded disembodied in the darkness, as if the night were speaking. That impression seemed to belie his words, as if without the verification of physical presence what the Lord said was vain. 'Much of our Quest may seem foolhardy or foolish to him. Since he holds the Staff, we are mad to approach him. But if we mean to approach nonetheless, then our southward path is folly, for it is long, and his power grows – daily. He will expect us to turn east toward him, or south toward Doom's Retreat and escape. Korik and Terrel will give Drool's scouts reason to believe that we have turned to attack. If he becomes unsure of where we are, he will not guess our true aim. He will search for us in Andelain, and will seek to strengthen his defences in Mount Thunder. Believing that we have turned to attack him, he will also believe that we have mastered the power of your white gold.'

Covenant considered momentarily before asking, 'What's Foul going to be doing during all this?'

'Ah,' Mhoram sighed, 'that is a question. There hangs the fate of our Quest – and of the Land.' He was silent for a long time. 'In my dreams, I see him laughing.'

Covenant winced at the memory of Foul's crushing laughter, and fell silent. So the riders crept on through the dark, trusting themselves to the instincts of the Ranyhyn. When dawn came, they had left their ambush for the wolves far behind.

It took the company four more days of hard riding, fifteen leagues a day, to reach the Mithil River, the southern boundary of Andelain. For sixty leagues, the Quest drove to the southeast without a hint of what had befallen Korik's group. In all, only eight people had left the company. But somehow without them the Quest seemed shrunken and puny. The concern of the High Lord and his companions rumbled in the hoofbeats of their mounts, and echoed in the silence that lay between them like an empty bier.

Gone now was the gladness of eye with which the warriors had beheld Andelain never more than a league to the left. From dawn to dusk every glance studied the eastern horizons; they saw nothing but a void in which Korik's riders had not appeared. Time and again, Foamfollower broke away from the company to trot up the nearest hill and peer into the distance; time and again, he returned panting and comfortless, and the company was left to conceive nightmares to explain Korik's absence.

The unspoken consensus was that no number of wolves was large enough to conquer two Bloodguard, mounted as they were on Huryn and Brabha of the Ranyhyn. No, Korik's group must have fallen into the hands of a small army of ur-viles – so the company reasoned, though Prothall argued that Korik might have had to ride many leagues to find a river or other means to throw the wolves off his trail. The High Lord's words were sound, but somehow under the incarnadine moon they seemed hollow. In spite of them, Warhaft Quaan went about his duties with the death of six warriors in his face.

All the riders were shrouded in gloom when, near twilight on the fourth day, they reached the banks of the Mithil.

Immediately on their left as they neared the river stood a steep hill like a boundary of Andelain. It guarded the north bank; the company could only cross its base into Andelain by riding single file along the river edge. But Prothall chose that path in preference to swimming the stiff current of the Mithil. With only Tuvor before him, he led the way east along the scant bank. The Questers followed one by one. Soon the entire company was traversing the boundary of the hill.

Spread out as they were, they were vulnerable. As the hill rose beside them, its slope became almost sheer, and its rocky crown commanded the path along the river like a fortification. The riders moved with their heads craned upward; they were keenly conscious of the hazard of their position.

They were still in the traverse when they heard a hail from the hilltop. Among the rocks, a figure rose into view. It was Terrel.

The riders returned his hail joyfully. Hurrying, they crossed the base of the hill, and found themselves in a broad, grassy valley where horses – two Ranyhyn and five mustangs – grazed up away from the river.

The mustangs were exhausted. Their legs quivered weakly, and their necks drooped; they barely had strength enough to eat.

Five, Covenant repeated. He felt numbly sure that he had miscounted.

Korik was on his way down from the hilltop. He was accompanied by five warriors.

With an angry shout, Quaan leaped from his horse and ran toward the Bloodguard. 'Irin!' he demanded. 'Where is Irin? By the Seven! What has happened to her?'

Korik did not answer until he stood with his group before High Lord Prothall. They struck Covenant as a strange combination: five warriors full of conflicting excitement, courage, grief; and one

Bloodguard as impassive as a patriarch. If Korik felt any satisfaction or pain, he did not show it.

He held a bulging pack in one hand, but did not refer to it immediately. Instead, he saluted Prothall, and said, 'High Lord. You are well. Have you been pursued?'

'We have seen no pursuit,' Prothall replied gravely.

'That is good. It appeared to us that we were successful.'

Prothall nodded, and Korik began his tale. 'We met the wolves and sought to scatter them. But they were *kresh* – ' he made a spitting sound – 'not easily turned aside. So we led them eastward. They would not enter Andelain. They howled on our track, but would not enter. We watched from a distance until they turned away to the north. Then we rode east.

'After a day and a night, we broke trail and turned south. But we came upon marauders. They were mightier than we knew. There were ur-viles and Cavewights together, and with them a *griffin*.'

Korik's audience murmured with surprise and chagrin, and the Bloodguard paused to utter what sounded like a long curse in the tonal native tongue of the *Haruchai*. Then he continued: 'Irin purchased our escape. But we were driven far from our way. We reached this place only a short time before you.'

With a revolted flaring of his nostrils, he lifted the pack. 'This morning we saw a hawk over us. It flew strangely. We shot it.' Reaching into the pack, he drew out the body of the bird. Above its vicious beak, it had only one eye, a large mad orb centred in its forehead.

It struck the company with radiated malice. The hawk was ill, incondign, a thing created by wrong for purposes of wrong – bent away from its birth by a power that dared to warp nature. The sight stuck in Covenant's throat, made him want to retch. He could hardly hear Prothall say, 'This is the work of the Illearth Stone. How could the Staff of Law perform such a crime, such an outrage? Ah, my friends, this is the outcome of our enemy. Look closely. It is a mercy to take such creatures out of life.' Abruptly, the High Lord turned away, burdened by his new knowledge.

Quaan and Birinair cremated the ill-formed hawk. Soon the warriors who had gone with Korik began to talk, and a fuller picture of their past four days emerged. Attention naturally centred on the fight which had killed Irin of the Eoman.

The Ranyhyn Brabha had first smelled danger, and had given the warning to Korik. At once, he had hidden his group in a thick copse to await the coming of the marauders. Listening with his ear to the ground, he had judged that they were a mixed force of unmounted ur-viles and Cavewights – Cavewights had not the ur-viles' ability to step softly – totalling no more than fifteen. So Korik had asked himself which way his service lay: to preserve his companions as defenders of the Lords, or to damage the Lords' enemies. The Bloodguard were sworn to the protection of the Lords, not of the Land. He had elected to fight because he judged that his force was strong enough, considering the element of surprise, to meet both duties without loss of life.

His decision had saved them. They learned later that if they had not attacked they would have been trapped in the copse; the panic of the horses would have given away their hiding.

It was a dark night after moonset, the second night after Korik's group had left the company, and the marauders were moving without lights. Even the Bloodguard's keen eyes discerned nothing more than the shadowy outlines of the enemy. And the wind blew between the two forces, so that the Ranyhyn were prevented from smelling the extent of their peril.

When the marauders reached open ground, Korik signalled to his group; the warriors swept out of the copse behind him and Terrel. The Ranyhyn outdistanced the others at once, so Korik and Terrel had just engaged the enemy when they heard the terror screams of the horses. Wheeling around, the Bloodguard saw all six warriors struggling with their panicked steeds – and the *griffin* hovering over them. The *griffin* was a lionlike creature with sturdy wings that enabled it to fly for short distances. It terrified the horses, swooped at the riders. Korik and Terrel raced towards their comrades. And behind them came the marauders.

The Bloodguard hurled themselves at the *griffin*, but aloft, with its clawed feet downward, it had no vulnerable spots that they could reach without weapons. Then the marauders fell on the group. The warriors rallied to defend their horses. In the mêlée, Korik poised himself on Brabha's back to spring up at the *griffin* at the first opportunity. But when his chance came, Irin cut in front of him. Somehow, she had captured a long Cavewightish broadsword. The *griffin* snatched her up in its claws, and as it ripped her apart she beheaded it.

The next moment, another party of marauders charged forward. The warriors' horses were too terrified to do anything but run. So Korik's group fled, dashed east and north with the enemy on their heels. By the time they lost the pursuit, they had been driven so far into Andelain that they had not been able to rejoin Prothall until the fourth day.

Early in the evening, the reunited company set up camp. While they prepared supper, a cool wind slowly mounted out of the north. At first it felt refreshing, full of Andelainian scents. But as moonrise neared, it stiffened with a palpable wrench until it was scything straight through the valley. Covenant could taste its unnaturalness; he had felt something like it before. Like a whip, it drove dark cloud banks southward.

As the evening wore on, no one seemed inclined toward sleep. Depression deepened in the company as if the wind were taut with dismay. On opposite sides of the camp, Foamfollower and Quaan paced out their uneasiness. Most of the warriors squatted around in dejected attitudes, fiddling aimlessly with their weapons. Birinair poked in unrelieved dissatisfaction at the fire. Prothall and Mhoram stood squarely in the wind as if they were trying to read it with the nerves of their faces. And Covenant sat with his head bowed under a flurry of memories.

Only Variol and Tamarantha remained ungloomed. Arm in arm, the two ancient Lords sat and stared with a dreaming, drowsy look into the fire, and the firelight flickered like writing on their foreheads.

Around the camp, the Bloodguard stood as solid as stone.

Finally, Mhoram voiced the feeling of the company. 'Something happens – something dire. This is no natural wind.'

Under the clouds, the eastern horizon glowed red with moonlight. From time to time, Covenant thought he saw an orange flicker in the crimson, but he could not be sure. Covertly, he studied his ring, and found the same occasional orange cast under the dominating blood. But he said nothing. He was too ashamed of Drool's hold on him.

Still no storm came. The wind blew on, rife with red mutterings and old ice, but it brought nothing but clouds and discouragement to the company. At last, most of the warriors dozed fitfully, shivering against the cut of the wind as it bore its harvest of distress toward Doom's Retreat and the Southron Wastes.

There was no dawn; clouds choked the rising sun. But the company was roused by a change in the wind. It dropped and warmed, swung slowly toward the west. But it did not feel healthier – only more subtle. Several of the warriors rolled out of their blankets, clutching their swords.

The company ate in haste, impelled by the indefinite apprehension of the breeze. The old Hirebrand, Birinair, was the first to understand. While chewing a mouthful of bread, he suddenly jerked erect as if he had been slapped. Quivering with concentration, he glowered at the eastern horizon, then spat the bread to the ground. 'Burning!' he hissed. 'The wind. I smell it. Burning. What? I can smell – Burning – a tree!

'A tree!' he wailed. 'Ah, they dare!'

For an instant, the company stared at him in silence. Then Mhoram ejaculated, 'Soaring Woodhelven is in flames!'

His companions sprang into action. Shrilly, the Bloodguard whistled for the Ranyhyn. Prothall snapped orders which Quaan echoed in a raw shout. Some of the warriors sprinted to saddle the horses, while others broke camp. By the time Covenant was dressed and mounted on Dura, the Quest was ready to ride. At once, it galloped away eastward along the Mithil.

Before long, the horses began to give trouble. Even the freshest one could not keep pace with the Ranyhyn, and the mustangs which had been with Korik in Andelain had not recovered their strength. The terrain did not allow for speed; it was too uneven. Prothall sent two Bloodguard ahead as scouts. But after that he was forced to move more slowly; he could not afford to leave part of his force behind. Still, he kept the pace as fast as possible. It was a frustrating ride — Covenant seemed to hear Quaan grinding his teeth — but it could not be helped. Grimly, Prothall held the fresher horses back.

By noon, they reached the ford of the Mithil. Now they could see smoke due south of them, and the smell of burning was powerful in the air. Prothall commanded a halt to water the horses. Then the riders pushed on, urging their weakest mounts to find somewhere new resources of strength and speed.

Within a few leagues, the High Lord had to slow his pace still more; the scouts had not returned. The possibility that they had been ambushed clenched his brow, and his eyes glittered as if the orbs had facets of granite. He held the riders to a walk while he sent two more Bloodguard ahead.

These two returned before the company had covered a league. They reported that Soaring Woodhelven was dead. The area around it was deserted; signs indicated that the first two scouts had ridden away to the south.

Muttering, '*Melenkurion!*' under his breath, Prothall led the riders forward at a canter until they reached the remains of the tree village.

The destruction was a fiendish piece of work. Fire had reduced the original tree to smouldering spars less than a hundred feet tall, and the charred trunk had been split from top to bottom, leaving the two halves leaning slightly away from each other. Occasionally flames still flickered near the tips. And all around the base of the tree, corpses littered the ground as if the earth were already too full of dead to contain the population of the village. Other Woodhelvennin bodies, unburned, were scattered generally in a line to the south across the glade.

Along this southward line, a few dead Cavewights sprawled in battle contortion. But near the tree there was only one body which was not human – one dead ur-vile. It lay on its long back on the south of the tree, facing the split trunk; and its soot-black frame was as twisted as the iron stave still clutched in its hands. Nearby lay a heavy iron plate nearly ten feet across.

The stench of dead, burned flesh appalled the surrounding glade. A memory of Woodhelvennin children writhed in Covenant's guts. He felt like vomiting.

The Lords seemed stupefied by the sight, stunned to realize that people under their care could be so murdered. After a moment, First Mark Tuvor reconstructed the battle for them.

The folk of Soaring Woodhelven had not had a chance.

Late the previous day, Tuvor judged, a large party of Cavewights and ur-viles – the trampling of the glade attested that the party was very large – had surrounded the tree. They had kept out of effective arrow range. Instead of assaulting the Woodhelvennin directly, they sent a few of their number – almost certainly ur-viles – forward under cover of the iron plate. Thus protected, the ur-viles set flame to the tree.

'A poor fire,' Birinair inserted. Approaching the tree, he tapped it with his staff. A patch of charcoal fell away, showing white wood underneath. 'Strong fire consumes everything,' he muttered. 'Almost, they survived. This is good wood. Make the flame a little weaker – and the wood survives. Those who dared – only strong enough by a little. Numbers are nothing. Strength counts. Of course. A narrow chance. Or if the Hirebrand had known. Been ready. He could have prepared the tree – given it strength. They could have lived. Ah! I should have been here. They would not do this to wood in my care.'

Once the fire began, Tuvor explained, the attackers simply shot arrows to prevent the flames from being put out – and waited for the desperate Woodhelvennin to attempt escape. Hence the line of unburned bodies running southward; that was the direction taken by the sortie. Then, when the fire was too great for the Woodhelvennin to resist further, the ur-vile loremaster split the tree to destroy it utterly, and to shake any survivors from its limbs.

Again Birinair spoke: 'He learned. Retribution. The fool – not master of his own power. The tree struck him down. Good wood. Even burning, it was not dead. The Hirebrand – a brave man. Struck back. And – and before the Desecration the *lillianrill* could have saved what life is left.' He scowled as if he dared anyone to criticize him. 'No more. This I cannot.' But a moment later his imperiousness faded, and he turned sadly back to gaze on the ruined tree as if silently asking it to forgive him.

Covenant did not question Tuvor's analysis; he felt too sickened by the blood-thick reek around him. But Foamfollower did not seem affected in that way. Dully, he asserted, 'This is not Drool's doing. No Cavewight is the master of such strategy. Wind and clouds to disguise the signs of attack, should any help be near. Iron protection carried here from who knows what distance. An attack with so little waste of resource. No, the hand of Soulcrusher is here from first to last. Stone and Sea!' Without warning, his voice caught, and he turned away, groaning his Giantish plain-song to steady himself.

Into the silence, Quaan asked, 'But why here?' There was an edge like panic in his voice. 'Why attack this place?'

Something in Quaan's tone, some hint of hysteria among brave but inexperienced, appalled young warriors, called Prothall back from the wilderland where his thoughts wandered. Responding to Quaan's emotion rather than to his question, the High Lord said sternly, 'Warhaft Quaan, there is much work to be done. The horses will rest, but we must work. Burial must be dug for the dead. After their last ordeal, it would be unfitting to set them to the pyre. Put your Eoman to the task. Dig graves in the south glade – there.' He indicated a spread of grass about a hundred feet from the riven tree. 'We – ' he referred to his fellow Lords. 'We will carry the dead to their graves.'

Foamfollower interrupted his plain-song. 'No. I will carry. Let me show my respect.'

'Very well,' Prothall replied. 'We will prepare food and consider our situation.' With a nod, he sent Quaan to give orders to the Eoman. Then, turning to Tuvor, he asked that sentries be posted. Tuvor observed that eight Bloodguard were not enough to watch every possible approach to an open area as large as the glade, but if he sent the Ranyhyn roaming separately around the bordering hills, he might not need to call on the Eoman for assistance. After a momentary pause, the First Mark asked what should be done about the missing scouts.

'We will wait,' Prothall responded heavily.

Tuvor nodded, and moved away to communicate with the Ranyhyn. They stood in a group nearby, looking with hot eyes at the burned bodies around the tree. When Tuvor joined them, they clustered about him as if eager to do whatever he asked, and a moment later they charged out of the glade, scattering in all directions.

The Lords dismounted, unpacked the sacks of food, and set about preparing a meal on a small *lillianrill* fire Birinair built for them. Warriors took all the horses upwind from the tree, unsaddled and tethered them. Then the Eoman went to begin digging.

Taking great care not to step on any of the dead, Foamfollower moved toward the tree, reached the iron plate. It was immensely heavy, but he lifted it and carried it beyond the ring of bodies. There he began gently placing corpses on the plate, using it as a sled to move the bodies to their graves. Knots of emotion jumped and bunched across his buttressed forehead, and his eyes flared with a dangerous enthusiasm.

For a while, Covenant was the only member of the company without an assigned task. The fact disturbed him. The stench of the dead – Baradakas included somewhere among them, he thought achingly, Baradakas and Llaura and children, children! – made him remember Soaring Woodhelven as he had left it days ago: tall and proud, lush with the life of a fair people.

He needed something to do to defend himself.

As he scanned the company, he noticed that the warriors lacked digging tools. They had brought few picks and shovels with them; most of them were trying to dig with their hands or their swords. He walked over to the tree. Scattered around the trunk were many burned branches, some of them still solid in the core. Though he had to pick his way among the dead – though the close sight of all that flesh smeared like mouldering wax over charred bones hurt his guts – he gathered branches that he could not break across his knee. These he carried away from the tree, then used his Stonedownor knife to scrape them clean and cut them into stakes. The work blackened his hands, his white robe, and the knife twisted awkwardly in his half-fingered grip, but he persisted.

The stakes he gave to the warriors, and with them they were able to dig faster. Instead of individual graves, they dug trenches, each deep and long enough to hold a dozen or more of the dead. Using Covenant's stakes, the warriors began to finish their graves faster than Foamfollower could fill them.

Late in the afternoon, Prothall called the company to eat. By that time, nearly half the bodies had been buried. No one felt like consuming food with their lungs full of acrid air and their eyes sore of tormented flesh, but the High Lord insisted. Covenant found this strange until he tasted the food. The Lords had prepared a stew unlike anything he had eaten in the Land. Its savour quickened his hunger, and when he swallowed it, it soothed his distress. It was the first meal he had had since the previous day, and he surprised himself by eating ravenously.

Most of the warriors were done eating, and the sun was about to set, when their attention was snatched erect by a distant hail. The southmost sentry answered, and a moment later the two missing Bloodguard came galloping into the glade. Their Ranyhyn were soaked with sweat.

254

They brought two people with them: a woman, and a boy-child the size of a four-year-old, both Woodhelvennin, both marked as if they had survived a battle.

The tale of the scouts was quickly told. They had reached the deserted glade, and had found the southward trail of the Woodhelvennin's attempted escape. And they had seen some evidence that all the people might not have been killed. Since the enemy had gone – so there was no compelling need to ride back to warn the Lords – they had decided to search for survivors. They had erased the signs, so that any returning marauders might not find them, and had ridden south.

Early in the afternoon, they found the woman and child fleeing madly without thought or caution. Both appeared injured; the child gave no sign of awareness at all, and the woman vacillated between lucidity and incoherence. She accepted the Bloodguard as friends, but was unable to tell them anything. However, in a lucid moment, she insisted that an Unfettered Healer lived a league or two away. Hoping to gain knowledge from the woman, the scouts took her to the cave of the Healer. But the cave was empty – and appeared to have been empty for many days. So the scouts brought the two survivors back to Soaring Woodhelven.

The two stood before the Lords, the woman clutching the child's unresponsive hand. The boy gazed incuriously about him, but did not notice faces or react to voices. When his hand slipped from the woman's, his arm fell limply to his side; he neither resisted nor complied when she snatched it up again. His unfocused eyes seemed preternaturally dark, as if they were full of black blood.

The sight of him jabbed Covenant. The boy could have been the future of his own son, Roger – the son of whom he had been dispossessed, reft as if even his fatherhood had been abrogated by leprosy. Children! Foul? he panted. Children?

As if in oblique answer to his thoughts, the woman suddenly said, 'He is Pietten son of Soranal. He likes the horses.'

'It is true,' one of the scouts responded. 'He rode before me and stroked the Ranyhyn's neck.'

But Covenant was not listening. He was looking at the woman. Confusedly, he sorted through the battle wreckage of her face, the cuts and burns and grime and bruises. Then he said hesitantly, 'Llaura?'

The sun was setting, but there was no sunset. Clouds blanked the horizon, and a short twilight was turning rapidly into night. But as the sun fell, the air became thicker and more sultry, as if the darkness were sweating in apprehension.

'Yes, I know you,' the woman said in a flagellated voice. 'You are Thomas Covenant, Unbeliever and white gold wielder. In the semblance of Berek Halfhand, Jehannum spoke truth. Great evil has come.' She articulated with extreme care, as if she were trying to balance her words on the edge of a sword. 'I am Llaura daughter of Annamar, of the Heers of Soaring Woodhelven. Our scouts must have been slain. We had no warning. Be – '

But as she tried to say the words, her balance failed, and she collapsed into a hoarse, repeating moan – 'Uhn, uhn, uhn, uhn – ' as if the connection between her brain and her throat broke, leaving her struggling frantically with her inability to speak. Her eyes burned with furious concentration, and her head shook as she tried to form words. But nothing came between her juddering lips except, 'Uhn, uhn, uhn.'

The Bloodguard scout said, 'So she was when we found her. At one moment, she can speak. A moment later, she cannot.'

Hearing this, Llaura clenched herself violently and pushed down her hysteria, rejecting what the scout said. 'I am Llaura,' she repeated, 'Llaura – of the Heers of Soaring Woodhelven. Our scouts must have been slain. I am Llaura, I am Llaura,' she insisted. 'Beware – ' Again her voice broke into moaning, 'Uhn, uhn.'

Her panic mounted. 'Be – uhn, uhn, uhn. Be – uhn, uhn. I am Llaura. You are the Lords. You must I – uhn, uhn. Amb – uhn, uhn, uhn.' As she fought, Covenant glanced around the company. Everyone was staring intently at Llaura, and Variol and Tamarantha had tears in their eyes. 'Somebody do something,' he muttered painfully. 'Somebody.'

Abruptly, Llaura seemed to collapse. Clutching her throat with her free hand, she shrieked, 'You must hear me!' and started to fall.

As her knees gave way, Prothall stepped forward and caught her. With fierce strength, he gripped her upper arms and held her erect before him. 'Stop,' he commanded. 'Stop. Do not speak any more. Listen, and use your head to answer me.'

A look of hope flared across Llaura's eyes, and she relaxed until Prothall set her on her feet. Then she regained the child's hand.

'Now,' the High Lord said levelly, staring deep into her ravaged eyes. 'You are not mad. Your mind is clear. Something has been done to you.'

Llaura nodded eagerly, *Yes.*

'When your people attempted to escape, you were captured.'

She nodded, *Yes.*

'You and the child.'

Yes.

'And something was done to him as well?'

Yes.

'Do you know what it was?'

She shook her head, *No.*

256

'Was the same done to you both?'

No.

'Well,' Prothall sighed. 'Both were captured instead of slain. And the ur-vile loremaster afflicted you.'

Llaura nodded, *Yes,* shuddering.

'Damaged you.'

Yes.

'Caused the difficulty that you now have when you speak.'

Yes!

'Now your ability to speak comes and goes.'

No!

'No?'

Prothall paused to consider for a moment, and Covenant interjected, 'Hellfire! Get her to write it down.'

Llaura shook her head, raised her free hand. It trembled uncontrollably.

Abruptly, Prothall said, 'Then there are certain things that you cannot say.'

Yes!

'There is something that the attackers do not wish you to speak.'

Yes!

'Then – ' The High Lord hesitated as if he could hardly believe his thoughts. 'Then the attackers knew that you would be found – by us or others who came too late to the aid of Soaring Woodhelven.'

Yes!

'Therefore you fled south, toward Banyan Woodhelven and the Southron Stonedowns.'

She nodded, but her manner seemed to indicate that he had missed the point.

Observing her, he muttered, 'By the Seven! This cannot do. Such questioning requires time, and my heart tells me we have little. What has been done to the boy? How could the attackers know that we – or anyone – would come this way? What knowledge could she have? Knowledge that an ur-vile loremaster would fear to have told? No, we must find other means.'

At the edge of his sight, Covenant saw Variol and Tamarantha setting out their blankets near the campfire. Their action startled him away from Llaura for a moment. Their eyes held a sad and curiously secret look. He could not fathom it, but for some reason it reminded him that they had known what Prothall's decision for the Quest would be before that decision was made.

'High Lord,' said Birinair stiffly.

Concentrating on Llaura, Prothall replied, 'Yes?'

'That young whelp of a Gravelingas, Tohrm, gave me a *rhadha-*

maerl gift. I almost thought he mocked me. Laughed because I am not a puppy like himself. It was hurtloam.'

'Hurtloam?' Prothall echoed in surprise. 'You have some?'

'Have it? Of course. No fool, you know. I keep it moist. Tohrm tried to teach me. As if I knew nothing.'

Mastering his impatience, Prothall said, 'Please bring it.'

A moment later, Birinair handed to the High Lord a small stoneware pot full of the damp, glittering clay – hurtloam. 'Watch out,' Covenant murmured with complex memories in his voice, 'it'll put her to sleep.' But Prothall did not hesitate. In darkness lit only by Birinair's *lillianrill* fire and the last coals of the riven tree, he scooped out some of the hurtloam. Its golden flecks caught the firelight and gleamed. Tenderly, he spread the mud across Llaura's forehead, cheeks, and throat.

Covenant was marginally aware that Lord Mhoram no longer attended Prothall and Llaura. He had joined Variol and Tamarantha, and appeared to be arguing with them. They lay side by side on their backs, holding hands, and he stood over them as if he were trying to ward off a shadow. But they were unmoved. Through his protests, Tamarantha said softly, 'It is better thus, my son.' And Variol murmured, 'Poor Llaura. This is all we can do.'

Covenant snapped a look around the company. The warriors seemed entranced by the questioning of the Heer, but Foamfollower's cavernous eyes flicked without specific focus over the glade as if they were weaving dangerous visions. Covenant turned back toward Llaura with an ominous chill scrabbling along his spine.

The first touch of the hurtloam only multiplied her distress. Her face tightened in torment, and a rictus like a foretaste of death stretched her lips into a soundless scream. But then a harsh convulsion shook her, and the crisis passed. She fell to her knees and wept with relief as if a knife had been removed from her mind.

Prothall knelt beside her and clasped her in the solace of his arms, waiting without a word for her self-control to return. She needed a moment to put aside her weeping. Then she snatched herself up, crying, 'Flee! You must flee! This is an ambush! You are trapped!'

But her warning came too late. At the same moment, Tuvor returned from his lookout at a run, followed almost at once by the other Bloodguard. 'Prepare for attack,' the First Mark said flatly. 'We are surrounded. The Ranyhyn were cut off, and could not warn us. There will be battle. We have only little time to prepare.'

Covenant could not grasp the immediacy of what he heard. Prothall barked orders; the camp began to clear. Warriors and Bloodguard dove into the still-empty trenches, hid themselves in the hollow base of the tree. 'Leave the horses,' Tuvor commanded. 'The

Ranyhyn will break through to protect them if it is possible.' Prothall consigned Llaura and the child to Foamfollower, who placed them alone in a grave and covered them with the iron plate. Then Prothall and Mhoram jumped together into the southmost trench. But Covenant stood where he was. Vaguely, he watched Birinair reduce the campfire to its barest embers, then position himself against the burned trunk of the tree. Covenant needed time to comprehend what had been done to Llaura. Her plight numbed him.

First she had been given knowledge which might have saved the Lords – and then she had been made unable to communicate that knowledge. And her struggles to give the warning only ensured her failure by guaranteeing that the Lords would attempt to understand her rather than ride away. Yet what had been done to her was unnecessary, gratuitous; the trap would have succeeded without it. In every facet of her misery, Covenant could hear Lord Foul laughing.

Bannor's touch on his shoulder jarred him. The Bloodguard said as evenly as if he were announcing the time of day, 'Come, ur-Lord. You must conceal yourself. It is necessary.'

Necessary? Silently, Covenant began to shout, *Do you know what he did to her?*

But when he turned, he saw Variol and Tamarantha still lying by the last embers of the fire, protected by only two Bloodguard. What – ? he gaped. They'll be killed!

At the same time, another part of his brain insisted, He's doing the same thing to me. Exactly the same thing. To Bannor he groaned, 'Don't touch me. Hellfire and bloody damnation. Aren't you ever going to learn?'

Without hesitation, Bannor lifted Covenant, swung him around, and dropped him into one of the trenches. There was hardly room for him; Foamfollower filled the rest of the grave, squatting to keep his head down. But Bannor squeezed into the trench after Covenant, positioned himself with his arms free over the Unbeliever.

Then a silence full of the aches and quavers of fear fell over the camp. At last, the apprehension of the attack caught up with Covenant. His heart lurched; sweat bled from his forehead; his nerves shrilled as if they had been laid bare. A grey nausea that filled his throat like dirt almost made him gag. He tried to swallow it away, and could not. No! he panted. Not like this. I will not!

Exactly the same, exactly what happened to Llaura.

A hungry shriek ripped the air. After it came the tramp of approach. Covenant risked a glance over the rim of the grave, and saw the glade surrounded by black forms and hot laval eyes. They moved slowly, giving the encamped figures a chance to taste their own end. And flapping heavily overhead just behind the advancing line was the dark shape of a beast.

Covenant recoiled. In fear, he watched the attack like an outcast, from a distance.

As the Cavewights and ur-viles contracted their ring around the glade – centred their attack on the helpless campsite – the wall of them thickened, reducing at every step the chance that the company might be able to break through their ranks. Slowly their approach became louder; they stamped the ground as if they were trying to crush the grass. And a low wind of mutterings became audible – soft snarls, hissings through clenched teeth, gurgling, gleeful salivations – blew over the graves like an exhalation littered with the wreckage of mangled lives. The Cavewights gasped like lunatics tortured into a love of killing; the nasal sensing of the ur-viles sibilated wetly. And behind the other sounds, terrible in their quietness, came the wings of a *griffin*, drumming a dirge.

The tethered horses began to scream. The stark terror of the sound pulled Covenant up, and he looked long enough to see that the mustangs were not harmed. The tightening ring parted to bypass them, and a few Cavewights dropped from the attack to unfetter them, lead them away. The horses fought hysterically, but the strength of the Cavewights mastered them.

Then the attackers were less than a hundred feet from the graves. Covenant cowered down as far as he could. He hardly dared to breathe. The whole company was helpless in the trenches.

The next moment, a howl went up among the attackers. Several Cavewights cried, 'Only five?'

'All those horses?'

'Cheated!'

In rage at the puny number of their prey, nearly a third of them broke ranks and charged the campfire.

Instantly, the company seized its chance.

The Ranyhyn whinnied. Their combined call throbbed in the air like the shout of trumpets. Together they thundered out of the east toward the captured horses.

Birinair stepped away from the riven tree. With a full swing of his staff and a cry, he struck the burned wood. The tree erupted in flames, threw dazzling light at the attackers.

Prothall and Mhoram sprang together from the southmost trench. Their staffs flared with blue Lords-fire. Crying, *'Melenkurion!'* they drove their power against the creatures. The nearest Cavewights and ur-viles retreated in fear from the flames.

Warriors and Bloodguard leaped out of the graves, sprinted from the hollow of the tree.

And behind them came the towering form of Saltheart Foamfollower, shouting a rare Giantish war call.

With cries of fear and rage, fire, swift blows and clashing weapons, the battle began.

The company was outnumbered ten to one.

Jerking his gaze from scene to scene, Covenant saw how the fighting commenced. The Bloodguard deployed themselves instantly, two to defend each Lord, with one standing by Birinair and another, Bannor, warding the trench where Covenant stood. The warriors rapidly formed groups of five. Guarding each other's backs, they strove to cut their way in and out of the line of the attackers. Mhoram charged around the fight, trying to find the commanders or loremasters of the enemy. Prothall stood in the centre of the battle to give the company a rallying point. He shouted warnings and orders about him.

But Foamfollower fought alone. He rampaged through the attack like a berserker, pounding with his fists, kicking, throwing anything within reach. His war call turned into one long piercing snarl of fury; his huge strides kept him in the thick of the fighting. At first, he looked powerful enough to handle the entire host alone. But soon the great strength of the Cavewights made itself felt. They jumped at him in bunches; four of them were able to bring him down. He was up again in an instant, flinging bodies about him like dolls. But it was clear that, if enough Cavewights attacked him together, he would be lost.

Variol and Tamarantha were in no less danger. They lay motionless under the onslaught, and their four Bloodguard strove extravagantly to preserve them. Some of the attackers risked arrows; the Bloodguard knocked the shafts aside with the backs of their hands. Spears followed, and then the Cavewights charged with swords and staves. Weaponless and unaided, the Bloodguard fought back with speed, balance, skill, with perfectly placed kicks and blows. They seemed impossibly successful. Soon a small ring of dead and unconscious Cavewights encircled the two Lords. But like Foamfollower they were vulnerable, would have to be vulnerable to a concerted assault.

At Prothall's order, one group of warriors moved to help the four Bloodguard.

Covenant looked away.

He found Mhoram waging a weird contest with thirty or forty ur-viles. All the ur-viles in the attack – they were few in proportion to the Cavewights – had formed a fighting wedge behind their tallest member, their loremaster – a wedge which allowed them to focus their whole power in the leader. The loremaster wielded a scimitar with a flaming blade, and against it Mhoram opposed his fiery staff. The clashing of power showered hot sparks that dazzled and singed the air.

Then a swirl of battle swept towards Covenant's trench. Figures leaped over him; Bannor fought like a dervish to ward off spears. A moment later, a warrior came to his aid. She was the Woodhelvennin who had assigned herself to Covenant. She and Bannor struggled to keep him alive.

He clutched his hands to his chest as if to protect his ring. His fingers unconsciously took hold of the metal.

Through the dark flash of legs, he caught a glimpse of Prothall, saw that the High Lord was under attack. Using his blazing staff like a lance, he strove with the *griffin*. The beast's wings almost buffeted him from his feet, but he kept his position and jabbed his blue fire upward. But astride the *griffin* sat another ur-vile loremaster. The creature used a black stave to block the High Lord's thrusts.

As Covenant watched, the desperation of the conflict mounted. Figures fell and rose and fell again. Blood spattered down on him. Across the glade, Foamfollower heaved to his feet from under a horde of Cavewights, and was instantly deluged. Prothall fell to one knee under the combined force of his assailants. The ur-vile wedge drove Mhoram steadily backwards; the two Bloodguard with him were hard pressed to protect his back.

Covenant's throat felt choked with sand.

Already, two warriors had fallen among the Cavewights around Variol and Tamarantha. At one instant, a Bloodguard found himself, and Tamarantha behind him, attacked simultaneously by three Cavewights with spears. The Bloodguard broke the first spear with a chop of his hand, and leaped high over the second to kick its wielder in the face. But even his great speed was not swift enough. The third Cavewight caught him by the arm. Grappling at once, the first latched his long fingers on to the Bloodguard's ankle. The two stretched their captive between them, and their companion jabbed his spear at the Bloodguard's belly.

Covenant watched, transfixed with helplessness, as the Bloodguard strained against the Cavewights, pulled them close enough together to wrench himself out of the path of the spear. Its tip scored his back. The next instant, he groined both his captors. They dropped him, staggered back. He hit the ground and rolled. But the middle Cavewight caught him with a kick so hard that it flung him away from Tamarantha.

Yelling his triumph, the Cavewight lunged forward with his spear raised high in both hands to impale the recumbent Lord.

Tamarantha!

Her peril overwhelmed Covenant's fear. Without thinking, he vaulted from the safety of his trench and started toward her. She was so old and frail that he could not restrain himself.

The Woodhelvennin yelled, 'Down!' His sudden appearance above the ground distracted her, gave her opponents a target. As a result, she missed a parry, and a sword thrust opened her side. But Covenant did not see her. He was already running toward Tamarantha – and already too late.

The Cavewight drove his spear downward.

At the last moment, the Bloodguard saved Tamarantha by diving across her and catching the spear in his own back.

Covenant hurled himself at the Cavewight and tried to stab it with his stone knife. The blade twisted in his half-hand; he only managed to scratch the creature's shoulder blade.

The knife fell from his wrenched fingers.

The Cavewight whirled and struck him to the ground with a slap. The blow stunned him for a moment, but Bannor rescued him by attacking the creature. The Cavewight countered as if elevated, inspired, by his success against the dead Bloodguard. He shrugged off Bannor's blows, caught him in his long strong arms and began to squeeze. Bannor struck at the Cavewight's ears and eyes, but the maddened creature only tightened his grip.

Inchoate rage roared in Covenant's ears. Still half dazed, he stumbled towards Tamarantha's still form and snatched her staff from her side. She made no movement, and he asked no permission. Turning, he wheeled the staff wildly about his head and brought it down with all his strength on the back of the Cavewight's skull.

White and crimson power flashed in a silent explosion. The Cavewight fell instantly dead.

The ignition blinded Covenant for a moment. But he recognized the sick red hue of the flare. As his eyes cleared he gaped at his hands, at his ring. He could not remember having removed it from the *clingor* on his chest. But it hung on his wedding finger and throbbed redly under the influence of the cloud-locked moon.

Another Cavewight loomed out of the battle at him. Instinctively, he hacked with the staff at the creature. It collapsed in a bright flash that was entirely crimson.

At the sight, his old fury erupted. His mind went blank with violence. Howling, 'Foul!' as if the Despiser were there before him, he charged into the thick of the fray. Flailing about him like madness, he struck down another Cavewight, and another, and another. But he did not watch where he was going. After the third blow he fell into one of the trenches. Then for a long time he lay in the grave like a dead man. When he finally climbed to his feet, he was trembling with revulsion.

Above him, the battle burned feverishly. He could not judge how many of the attackers had been killed or disabled. But some turning point had been reached; the company had changed its tactics. Prothall fled from the *griffin* to Foamfollower's aid. And when the Giant regained his feet, he turned, dripping blood, to fight the *griffin* while Prothall joined Mhoram against the ur-viles. Bannor held himself over Covenant; but Quaan marshalled the survivors of his Eoman to make a stand around Variol and Tamarantha.

A moment later, the Ranyhyn gave a ringing call. Having freed the horses, they charged into the battle. And as their hooves and teeth crashed among the Cavewights, Prothall and Mhoram together swung their flaming staffs to block the loremaster's downstroke. Its hot scimitar shattered into fragments of lava, and the backlash of power felled the ur-vile itself. Instantly, the creatures shifted their wedge to present a new leader. But their strongest had fallen, and they began to give way.

On the other side of the battle, Foamfollower caught the *griffin* by surprise. The beast was harrying the warriors around Variol and Tamarantha. With a roar, Foamfollower sprang into the air and wrapped his arms in a death hug around the body of the *griffin*. His weight bore it to the ground; they rolled and struggled on the blood-slick grass. The riding ur-vile was thrown off, and Quaan beheaded it before it could raise its stave.

The *griffin* yowled hideously with rage and pain, tried to twist in Foamfollower's grip to reach him with its claws and fangs. But he squeezed it with all his might, silently braced himself against its thrashings and strove to kill it before it was able to turn and rend him.

For the most part, he succeeded. He exerted a furious jerk of pressure, and heard bones retort loudly in the beast's back. The *griffin* spat a final scream, and died. For a moment, he rested beside its body, panting hoarsely. Then he lumbered to his feet. His forehead had been clawed open to the bone.

But he did not stop. Dashing blood from his eyes, he ran and threw himself full-length on to the tight wedge of the ur-viles. Their formation crumbled under the impact.

At once, the ur-viles chose to flee. Before Foamfollower could get to his feet, they were gone, vanished into the darkness.

Their defection seemed to drain the Cavewights' mad courage. The gangrel creatures were no longer able to brave the Lords-fire. Panic spread among them from the brandished staffs, flash-firing in the sudden tinder of their hearts.

A cry of failure broke through the attack. The Cavewights began to run.

Howling their dismay, they scattered away from the blazing tree. They ran with grotesque jerkings of their knuckled joints, but their strength and length of limb gave them speed. In moments, the last of them had fled the glade.

Foamfollower charged after them. Yelling Giantish curses, he chased the fleers as if he meant to crush them all underfoot. Swiftly, he disappeared into the darkness, and soon he could no longer be heard. But from time to time there came faint screams through the night, as he caught escaping Cavewights.

Tuvor asked Prothall if some of the Bloodguard should join Foamfollower, but the High Lord shook his head. 'We have done enough,' he panted. 'Remember the Oath of Peace.'

For a time of exhaustion and relief, the company stood in silence underscored by the gasp of their breathing and the groans of the disabled Cavewights. No one moved; to Covenant's ears, the silence sounded like a prayer. Unsteadily, he pulled himself out of the trench. Looking about him with glazed eyes, he took the toll of the battle.

Cavewights sprawled around the camp in twisted heaps – nearly a hundred of them, dead, dying and unconscious – and their blood lay everywhere like a dew of death. There were ten ur-viles dead. Five warriors would not ride again with their Eoman, and none of Quaan's command had escaped injury. But of the Bloodguard only one had fallen.

With a groan that belied his words, High Lord Prothall said, 'We are fortunate.'

'Fortunate?' Covenant echoed in vague disbelief.

'We are fortunate.' An accent of anger emphasized the old rheumy rattle of Prothall's voice. 'Consider that we might all have died. Consider such an attack during the full of the moon. Consider that while Drool's thoughts are turned here, he is not multiplying defences in Mount Thunder. We have paid – ' his voice choked for a moment – 'paid but little for our lives and hope.'

Covenant did not reply for a moment. Images of violence dizzied him. All the Woodhelvennin were dead – Cavewights – ur-viles – the warrior who had chosen to watch over him. He did not even know her name. Foamfollower had killed – he himself had killed five – five –

He was trembling, but he needed to speak, needed to defend himself. He was sick with horror.

'Foamfollower's right,' he rasped hoarsely. 'This is Foul's doing.'

No one appeared to hear him. The Bloodguard went to the

Ranyhyn and brought their fallen comrade's mount close to the fire. Lifting the man gently, they set him on the Ranyhyn's back and bound him in place with *clingor* thongs. Then together they gave a silent salute, and the Ranyhyn galloped away, bearing its dead rider toward the Westron Mountains and Guards Gap – home.

'Foul planned the whole thing.'

When the Ranyhyn had vanished into the night, some of the Bloodguard tended the injuries of their mounts, while others resumed their sentry duty.

Meanwhile, the warriors began moving among the Cavewights, finding the living among the dead. All that were not mortally wounded were dragged to their feet and chased away from the camp. The rest were piled on the north side of the tree for a pyre.

'It means two things.' Covenant strove to master the quaver in his voice. 'It's the same thing that he's doing to me. It's a lesson – like what happened to Llaura. Foul is telling us what he's doing to us because he's sure that knowing won't help. He wants to milk us for all the despair we're worth.'

With the aid of two warriors, Prothall released Llaura and Pietten from their tomb. Llaura looked exhausted to the limit; she was practically prostrate on her feet. But little Pietten ran his hands over the blood-wet grass, then licked his fingers.

Covenant turned away with a groan. 'The other thing is that Foul really wants us to get at Drool. To die or not. He tricked Drool into this attack so that he wouldn't be busy defending himself. So Foul must know what we're doing, even if Drool doesn't.'

Prothall seemed troubled by the occasional distant screams, but Mhoram did not notice them. While the rest of the company set about their tasks, the Lord went and knelt beside Variol and Tamarantha. He bent over his parents, and under his red-stained robe his body was rigid.

'I tell you, this is all part of Foul's plan. Hellfire! Aren't you listening to me?'

Abruptly, Mhoram stood and faced Covenant. He moved as if he were about to hurl a curse at Covenant's head. But his eyes bled with tears, and his voice wept as he said, 'They are dead. Variol and Tamarantha my parents – father and mother of me, body and soul.'

Covenant could see the hue of death on their old skin.

'It cannot be!' one of the warriors cried. 'I saw. No weapon touched them. They were kept by the Bloodguard.'

Prothall hastened to examine the two Lords. He touched their hearts and heads, then sagged and sighed, 'Nevertheless.'

Both Variol and Tamarantha were smiling.

The warriors stopped what they were doing; in silence, the Eoman put aside their own fatigue and grief to stand bowed in respect before Mhoram and his dead. Stooping, Mhoram lifted both Variol and Tamarantha in his arms. Their thin bodies were light in his embrace, as if they had lost the weight of mortality. On his cheeks, tears gleamed orangely, but his shoulders were steady, un-sob-shaken, to uphold his parents.

Covenant's mind was beclouded. He wandered in mist, and his words were wind-torn from him. 'Do you mean to tell me that we – that I – we – ? For a couple of corpses?'

Mhoram showed no sign of having heard. But a scowl like a spasm passed across Prothall's face, and Quaan stepped to the Unbeliever's side at once, gripped his elbow, whispered into his ear, 'If you speak again, I will break your arm.'

'Don't touch me,' Covenant returned. But his voice was forceless. He submitted, swirling in lost fog.

Around him, the company took on an attitude of ritual. Leaving his staff with one of the warriors, High Lord Prothall retrieved the staffs of the dead Lords and held them like an offering across his arms. And Mhoram turned toward the blaze of the tree with Variol and Tamarantha clasped erect in his embrace. The silence quivered painfully. After a long moment, he began to sing. His rough song sighed like a river, and he sang hardly louder than the flow of water between quiet banks.

> Death reaps the beauty of the world –
> bundles old crops to hasten new.
> Be still, heart:
> hold peace.
> Growing is better than decay:
> I hear the blade which severs life from life.
> Be still, peace:
> hold heart.
> Death is passing on –
> the making way of life and time for life.
> Hate dying and killing, not death.
> Be still, heart:
> make no expostulation.
> Hold peace and grief
> and be still.

As he finished, his shoulders lurched as if unable to bear their burden without giving at least one sob to the dead. 'Ah, Creator!' he cried in a voice full of bereavement. 'How can I honour them? I am stricken at heart, and consumed with the work that I must do. You must honour them – for they have honoured you.'

At the edge of the firelight, the Ranyhyn Hynaril gave a whinny like a cry of grief. The great roan mare reared and pawed the air with her forelegs, then whirled and galloped away eastward.

Then Mhoram murmured again,

> Be still, heart:
> make no expostulation.
> Hold peace and grief
> and be still.

Gently, he laid Variol on the grass and lifted Tamarantha in both arms. Calling hoarsely, 'Hail!' he placed her into the cleft of the burning tree. And before the flames could blacken her age-etched skin, he lifted Variol and set him beside her, calling again, 'Hail!' Their shared smile could be seen for a moment before the blaze obscured it. So they lay together in consummation.

Already dead, Covenant groaned. That Bloodguard was killed. Oh, Mhoram! In his confusion, he could not distinguish between grief and anger.

His eyes now dry, Mhoram turned to the company, and his gaze seemed to focus on Covenant. 'My friends, be still at heart,' he said comfortingly. 'Hold peace for all your grief. Variol and Tamarantha are ended. Who could deny them? They knew the time of their death. They read the close of their lives in the ashes of Soaring Woodhelven, and were glad to serve us with their last sleep. They chose to draw the attack upon themselves so that we might live. Who will say that the challenge which they met was not great? Remember the Oath, and hold peace.'

Together, the Eoman made the heart-opening salute of farewell, arms spread wide as if uncovering their hearts to the dead. Then Quaan cried, 'Hail!' and led the warriors back to the work of piling Cavewights and burying Woodhelvennin.

After the Eoman had left, High Lord Prothall said to Mhoram, 'Lord Variol's staff. From father to son. Take it. If we survive this Quest to reach a time of peace, master it. It has been the staff of a High Lord.'

Mhoram accepted it with a bow.

Prothall paused for a moment, irresolute, then turned to Covenant. 'You have used Lord Tamarantha's staff. Take it for use again. You will find it readier to aid your ring than your Hirebrand's staff. The *lillianrill* work in other ways than the Lords, and you are ur-Lord, Thomas Covenant.'

Remembering the red blaze which had raged out of that wood to kill and kill, Covenant said, 'Burn it.'

A touch of danger tightened Mhoram's glance. But Prothall shrugged gently, took Lord Tamarantha's staff to the fire, and placed it into the cleft of the tree.

For an instant, the metal ends of the staff shone as if they were made of verdigris. Then Mhoram cried, 'Ware the tree!' Quickly, the company moved away from the fiery spars.

The staff gave a sharp report like the bursting of bonds. Blue flame detonated in the cleft, and the riven tree dropped straight to the ground in fragments, collapsing as if its core had been finally killed. The heap of wood burned furiously.

From a distance, Covenant heard Birinair snort, 'The Unbeliever's doing,' as if that were a calumny.

Don't touch me, he muttered to himself.

He was afraid to think. Around him, darkness lurked like vulture wings made of midnight. Horrors threatened; he felt ghoul-begotten. He could not bear the bloodiness of his ring, could not bear what he had become. He searched about him as if he were looking for a fight.

Unexpectedly, Saltheart Foamfollower returned.

He shambled out of the night like a massacre metaphored in flesh – an icon of slaughter. He was everywhere smeared in blood, and much of it was his own. The wound on his forehead covered his face with a dark, wet sheen, and through the stain his deep eyes looked sated and miserable. Shreds of Cavewight flesh still clung to his fingers.

Pietten pointed at the Giant, and twisted his lips in a grin that showed his teeth. At once, Llaura grabbed his hand, pulled him away to a bed which the warriors had made for them.

Prothall and Mhoram moved solicitously toward the Giant, but he pushed past them to the fire. He knelt near the blaze as if his soul needed warming, and his groan as he sank to his knees sounded like a rock cracking.

Covenant saw his chance, approached the Giant. Foamfollower's manifest pain brought his confused angry grief to a pitch that demanded utterance. He himself had killed five Cavewights, five – ! His ring was full of blood. 'Well,' he snarled, 'that must've been fun. I hope you enjoyed it.'

From the other side of the camp, Quaan hissed threateningly. Prothall moved to Covenant's side, said softly, 'Do not torment him. Please. He is a Giant. This is the *caamora* – the fire of grief. Has there not been enough pain this night?'

I killed five Cavewights! Covenant cried in bereft fury.

But Foamfollower was speaking as if entranced by the fire and unable to hear them. His voice had a keening sound; he knelt before the fire in an attitude of lament.

'Ah, brothers and sisters, did you behold me? Did you see, my people? We have come to this. Giants, I am not alone. I feel you in me, your will in mine. You would not have done differently – not felt other than I felt, not grieved apart from my grief. This is the result. Stone and Sea! We are diminished. Lost Home and weak seed have made us less than we were. Do we remain faithful, even now? Ah, faithful? My people, my people, if steadfastness leads to this? Look upon me! Do you find me admirable? I stink of hate and unnecessary death.' A chill blew through his words. Tilting back his head, be began a low chant.

His threnody went on until Covenant felt driven to the brink of screaming. He wanted to hug or kick the Giant to make him cease. His fingers itched with mounting frenzy. Stop! he moaned. I can't stand it!

A moment later, Foamfollower bowed his head and fell silent. He remained still for a long time as if he were preparing himself. Then he asked fiercely, 'Who has been lost?'

'Very few,' Prothall answered. 'We were fortunate. Your valour served us well.'

'Who?' Foamfollower ached.

With a sigh, Prothall named the five warriors, the Bloodguard, Variol and Tamarantha.

'Stone and Sea!' the Giant cried. With a convulsion of his shoulders, he thrust his hands into the fire.

The warriors gasped; Prothall stiffened at Covenant's side. But this was the Giantish *caamora*, and no one dared interfere.

Foamfollower's face stretched in agony, but he held himself still. His eyes seemed to bulge in their sockets; yet he kept his hands in the fire as if the blaze could heal, or at least sear, the blood on them, cauterize if it could not assuage the stain of shed life. But his pain showed in his forehead. The hard heart-pulse of hurt broke the crust on his wound; new blood dripped around his eyes and down his cheeks into his eyes.

Panting, Hellfire hellfire! Covenant pushed away from Prothall. Stiffly, he went close to the kneeling Giant. With a fierce effort that made him sound caustic in spite of his intent, he said, 'Now somebody really ought to laugh at you.' His jutting head was barely as high as the Giant's shoulder.

For a moment, Foamfollower gave no sign of having heard. But then his shoulders slumped. With a slow exertion almost as though he were reluctant to stop torturing himself, he withdrew his hands. They were unharmed – for some reason, his flesh was impervious to

270

flame – but the blood was gone from them; they looked as clean as if they had been scrubbed by exoneration.

His fingers were still stiff with hurt, and he flexed them painfully before he turned his bloody face toward Covenant. As if he were appealing a condemnation, he met the Unbeliever's impacted gaze and asked, 'Do you feel nothing?'

'Feel?' Covenant groaned. 'I'm a leper.'

'Not even for tiny Pietten? A child?'

His appeal made Covenant want to throw his arms around the Giant, accept this terrible sympathy as some kind of answer to his dilemma. But he knew it was not enough, knew in the deepest marrow of his leprosy that it did not suffice. 'We killed them too,' he croaked. 'I killed – I'm no different than they are.'

Abruptly he turned, walked away into the darkness to hide his shame. The battleground was a fit and proper place for him; his nostrils were numb to the stink of death. After a time, he stumbled, then lay down among the dead, on blood surrounded by graves and pyres.

Children! He was the cause of their screams and their agony. Foul had attacked the Woodhelven because of his white gold ring. Not again – I won't – His voice was empty of weeping.

I will not do any more killing.

18

THE PLAINS OF RA

Despite the battleground – despite the acrid smoke of flame and flesh and power – despite the nearby trenches, where the dead were graved like lumps of charred agony, piled wearily into the earth like accumulated pain for which only the ground could now find use or surcease – despite his own inner torn and trampled ground – Covenant slept. For what was left of the night, the other survivors of the battle laboured to bury or burn the various dead, but Covenant slept. Restless unconsciousness arose from within him like a perpetually enumerated VSE, and he spent his repose telling in dreams that rigid round: left arm shoulder to wrist, left hand palm and back, each finger, right arm, shirt, chest, left leg –

He awoke to meet a dawn which wore the aspect of an uncomfortable tomb. Shuddering himself to his feet, he found that all the work of burying was done; each of the trenches was filled, covered with dirt, and planted with a sapling which Birinair had found somewhere. Now most of the warriors lay awkwardly on the ground, in fatigue searching themselves for some kind of strength. But Prothall and Mhoram were busy cooking a meal, and the Bloodguard were examining and readying the horses.

A spate of disgust crossed Covenant's face – disgust that he had not done his share of the work. He looked at his robe; the samite was stiff and black with encrusted blood. Fit apparel for a leper, he thought, an outcast.

He knew that it was past time for him to make a decision. He had to determine where he stood in his impossible dilemma. Propped on his staff in the sepulchred dawn, he felt that he had reached the end of his evasions. He had lost track of his self-protective habits, lost the choice of hiding his ring, lost even his tough boots – and he had shed blood. He had brought down doom on Soaring Woodhelven. He had been so preoccupied with his flight from madness that he had not faced the madness toward which his fleeing took him.

He had to keep moving; he had learned that. But going on posed the same impenetrable problem. Participate, and go mad. Or refuse to participate, and go mad. He had to make a decision, find bedrock somewhere and cling to it. He could not accept the Land – and could not deny it. He needed an answer. Without it, he would be trapped like Llaura – forced to the tune of Foul's glee to lose himself in order to avoid losing himself.

Then Mhoram looked up from his stirring and saw the disgust and dismay on Covenant's face. Gently, the Lord said, 'What troubles you, my friend?'

For a moment, Covenant stared at Mhoram. The Lord looked as if he had become old overnight. The smoke and dirt of battle marked his face, accentuating the lines on his forehead and around his eyes like a sudden aggravation of wear and decay. His eyes seemed dulled by fatigue. But his lips retained their kindness, and his movements, though draped in such a rent and bloodied robe, were steady.

Covenant flinched instinctively away from the tone in which Mhoram said, *my friend*. He could not afford to be anyone's friend. And he flinched away, too, from his impulse to ask what had caused Tamarantha's staff to become so violent in his hands. He feared the answer to that question. To cover his wincing, he turned roughly away, and went in search of Foamfollower.

The Giant was sitting with his back to the last standing, extinguished fragment of Soaring Woodhelven. Grime and blood darkened his face; his skin had the colour of a flaw in the heart of a tree. But the wound on his forehead dominated his appearance. Ripped flesh hung over his brows like a foliage of pain, and through the wound, drops of new blood seeped as if red thoughts were making their way from a crack in his skull. He had his right arm wrapped around his great jug of *diamondraught*, and his eyes followed Llaura as she tended little Pietten.

Covenant approached the Giant; but before he could speak, Foamfollower said, 'Have you considered them? Do you know what has been done to them?'

The question raised black echoes in Covenant's mind. 'I know about her.'

'And Pietten? Tiny Pietten? A child?'

Covenant shrugged awkwardly.

'Think, Unbeliever!' His voice was full of swirling mists. 'I am lost. You can understand.'

With an effort, Covenant replied, 'The same thing. Just exactly what's been done to us. And to Llaura.' A moment later he added mordantly, 'And to the Cavewights.' Foamfollower's eyes shied, and Covenant went on, 'We're all going to destroy – whatever we want to preserve. The essence of Foul's method. Pietten is a present to us – an example of what we're going to do to the Land when we try to save it. Foul is that confident. And prophecies like that are self-fulfilling.'

At this, Foamfollower stared at Covenant as if the Unbeliever had just laid a curse on him. Covenant tried to hold the Giant's eyes, but an unexpected shame made him drop his head. He looked at the power-scorched grass. The burning of the grass was curious. Some patches did not look as wrong as others – apparently Lords-fire did less essential damage than the might of the ur-viles.

After a moment, Foamfollower said, 'You forget that there is a difference between a prophet and a seer. Seeing the future is not prophecy.'

Covenant did not want to think about it. To get away from the subject, he demanded, 'Why didn't you get some of that hurtloam for your forehead?'

This time, Foamfollower's eyes turned away. Distantly, he said, 'There was none left.' His hands opened and closed in a gesture of helplessness. 'Others were dying. And others needed the hurtloam to save their arms or legs. And – ' His voice stumbled momentarily. 'And I thought tiny Pietten might be helped. He is only a child,' he insisted, looking up suddenly with an appeal that Covenant could not understand. 'But one of the Cavewights was dying slowly – in such pain.' A new trickle of blood broke open in his forehead and began to drip from his brow. 'Stone and Sea!' he moaned. 'I could not endure it. Hearthrall Birinair kept aside a touch of hurtloam for me, from all the wounds to be treated. But I gave it to the Cavewight. Not Pietten – to the Cavewight. Because of the pain.'

Abruptly, he put back his head and took a long pull of *diamondraught*. With the heel of his palm he wiped roughly at the blood on his brows.

Covenant gazed intently at the Giant's racked visage. Because he could find no other words for his sympathy, he asked, 'How're your hands?'

'My hands?' Foamfollower seemed momentarily confused, but then he remembered. 'Ah, the *caamora*. My friend, I am a Giant,' he explained. 'No ordinary fire can harm me. But the pain – the pain teaches many things.' A flinch of self-disgust crossed his lips. 'It is said that the Giants are made of granite,' he mumbled. 'Do not be concerned for me.'

On an impulse, Covenant responded, 'In parts of the world where I come from, there are little old ladies who sit by the side of the road pounding away all day on hunks of granite with little iron hammers. It takes a long time – but eventually they turn big pieces into little pieces.'

Foamfollower considered briefly before asking, 'Is that prophecy, ur-Lord Covenant?'

'Don't ask me. I wouldn't know a prophecy if it fell on me.'

'Nor would I,' said Foamfollower. A dim smile tinged his mouth.

Shortly, Lord Mhoram called the company to the meal he and Prothall had prepared. Through a haze of suppressed groans, the warriors pried themselves to their feet and moved toward the fire. Foamfollower lurched upright. He and Covenant followed Llaura and Pietten to get something to eat.

The sight and smell of food suddenly brought Covenant's need for decision to a head. He was empty, hollow with hunger, but when he reached out to take some bread, he saw how his arm was befouled with blood and ashes. He had killed – The bread dropped from his fingers. This is all wrong, he murmured. Eating was a form of acquiescence – a submission to the physical actuality of the Land. He could not afford it.

I've got to think.

The emptiness in him ached with demands, but he refused them. He took a drink of springwine to clear his throat, then turned away from the fire with a gesture of rejection. The Lords and Foamfollower looked after him enquiringly, but made no comment.

He needed to put himself to the test, discover an answer that would restore his ability to survive. With a grimace, he resolved to go hungry until he found what he required. Perhaps in hunger he would become lucid enough to solve the fundamental contradiction of his dilemma.

All the abandoned weapons had been cleared from the glade, gathered into a pile. He went to it and searched until he found Atiaran's stone knife. Then, on an obscure impulse, he walked over to the horses to see if Dura had been injured. When he learned that she was unscathed, he felt a vague relief. He did not want under any circumstances to be forced to ride a Ranyhyn.

A short time later, the warriors finished their meal. Wearily, they moved to take up the Quest again.

As Covenant mounted Dura, he heard the Bloodguard whistle sharply for the Ranyhyn. The call seemed to hang in the air for a moment. Then, from various directions around the glade, the great horses came galloping – manes and tails flaring as if afire, hooves pounding in long, mighty, trip-rhythmed strides – nine star-browed chargers as swift and elemental as the life-pulse of the Land. Covenant could hear in their bold nickering the excitement of going home, toward the Plains of Ra.

But the Questers who left dead Soaring Woodhelven that morning had little of the bold or home-going in their attitudes. Quaan's Eoman was now six warriors short, and the survivors were gaunt with weariness and battle. They seemed to carry their shadows in their faces as they rode north toward the Mithil River. The riderless horses they took with them to provide relief for the weaker mounts. Among them, Saltheart Foamfollower trudged as if he were carrying the weight of all the dead. In the crook of one arm he cradled Pietten, who had fallen asleep as soon as the sun cleared the eastern horizon. Llaura rode behind Lord Mhoram, gripping the sides of his robe. She appeared bent and frail behind his grim-set face and erect posture, but he shared with her an eroded expression, an air of inarticulate grief. Ahead of them moved Prothall, and his shoulders bespoke the same kind of inflexible will which Atiaran had used to make Covenant walk from Mithil Stonedown to the Soulsease River.

Vaguely, Covenant wondered how much further he would have to follow other people's choices. But he let the thought go and looked at the Bloodguard. They were the only members of the company who did not appear damaged by the battle. Their short robes hung in tatters; they were as filthy as anyone; one of their number had been killed, and several were injured. They had defended the Lords, especially Variol and Tamarantha, to the utmost; but the Bloodguard were unworn and undaunted, free of rue. Bannor rode his prancing, reinless Ranyhyn beside Covenant, and gazed about him with an impervious eye.

The horses of the company could manage only a slow, stumbling walk, but even that frail pace brought the riders to the ford of the Mithil before noon. Leaving their mounts to drink and graze, all of them except the Bloodguard plunged into the stream. Scrubbing at themselves with fine sand from the river bottom, they washed the blood and grit and pain of death and long night into the wide current of the Mithil. Clear skin and eyes reappeared from under the smears of battle; minor unhurtloamed wounds opened and bled clean; scraps of shredded clothing floated out of reach. Among them, Covenant beat his robe clean, rubbed and scratched stains from his flesh as if he were trying to rid himself of the effects of killing. And he drank quantities of water in an effort to appease the aching hollowness of his hunger.

Then, when the warriors were done, they went to their horses to get new clothing from their saddlebags. After they had dressed and regained command of their weapons, they posted themselves as sentries while First Mark Tuvor and the Bloodguard bathed.

The Bloodguard managed to enter and leave the river without splashing, and they washed noiselessly. In a few moments, they were dressed in new robes and mounted on the Ranyhyn. The Ranyhyn had refreshed themselves by crossing into Andelain and rolling on the grass while their riders bathed. Now the company was ready to travel. High Lord Prothall gave the signal, and the company rode away eastward along the south bank of the river.

The rest of the day was easy for the riders and their mounts. There was soft grass underhoof, clean water at one side, a tang of vitality in the air, and a nearby view of Andelain itself, which seemed to pulse with robust sap. The people of the Land drew healing from the ambience of the Hills. But the day was hard for Covenant. He was hungry, and the vital presence of Andelain only made him hungrier.

He kept his gaze away from it as best he could, refusing the sight as he had refused food. His gaunt face was set in stern lines, and his eyes were hollow with determination. He followed a double path: his flesh rode Dura doggedly, keeping his position in the company; but in his mind, he wandered in chasms, and their dark, empty inanition hurt him.

I will not —

He wanted to survive.

I am not —

From time to time, *aliantha* lay directly in his path like a personal appeal from the Land, but he did not succumb.

Covenant, he thought. Thomas Covenant. Unbeliever. Leper outcast unclean. When a pang from his hunger made him waver, he remembered Drool's bloody grip on his ring, and his resolve steadied.

From time to time, Llaura looked at him with the death of Soaring

Woodhelven in her eyes, but he only clenched himself harder and rode on.

I won't do any more killing.

He had to have some other answer.

That night, he found that a change had come over his ring. Now all evidence that it resisted red encroachments was gone. His wedding band burned completely crimson under the dominion of the moon, flaming coldly on his hand as if in greedy response to Drool's power. The next morning, he began the day's riding like a man torn between opposing poles of insanity.

But there was a foretaste of summer in the noon breeze. The air turned warm and redolent with the ripeness of the earth. The flowers had a confident bloom, and the birds sang languidly. Gradually, Covenant grew full of lassitude. Languor loosened the strings of his will. Only the habit of riding kept him on Dura's back; he became numb to such superficial considerations. He hardly noticed when the river began to curve northward away from the company, or when the hills began to climb higher. He moved blankly on the warm currents of the day. That night he slept deeply, dreamlessly, and the next day he rode on in numbness and unconcern.

Waking slumber held him. It was a wilderland that he wandered unaware; he was in danger without knowing it. Lassitude was the first step in an inexorable logic, the law of leprosy. The next was gangrene, stink of rotting live flesh so terrible that even some physicians could not bear it – a stench which ratified the outcasting of lepers in a way no mere compassion or unprejudice could oppose. But Covenant travelled his dream with his mind full of sleep.

When he began to recover – early in the afternoon of the third day from Soaring Woodhelven, the eighteenth since the company had left Revelstone – he found himself looking over Morinmoss Forest. The company stood on the last hilltop before the land fell under the dark aegis of the trees.

Morinmoss lay at the foot of the hill like a lapping sea; its edges gripped the hillsides as if the trees had clenched their roots in the slopes and refused to be driven back. The dark, various green of the Forest spread to the horizon north and east and south. It had a forbidding look; it seemed to defy the Quest to pass through it. High Lord Prothall stopped on the crest of the hill, and gazed for a long time over the Forest, weighing the time needed to ride around Morinmoss against the obscure dangers of the trees.

Finally, he dismounted. He looked over the riders, and his eyes were full of potential anger as he spoke. 'We will rest now. Then we will ride into Morinmoss, and will not stop until we have reached the far side – a journey of nearly a day and night. During that ride, we must show neither blade nor spark. Hear you? All swords sheathed, all arrows quivered, all knives cloaked, all spear tips bound. And every spark or gleam of fire quenched. I will have no mistake. Morinmoss is wilder than Grimmerdhore – and none go unanxious into that wood. The trees have suffered for ages, and they do not forget their kinship with Garroting Deep. Pray that they do not crush us all, regardless.' He paused, scanning the company until he was sure that all understood him. Then he added more gently, 'It is possible that there is still a Forestal in Morinmoss – though that knowledge has been lost since the Desecration.'

Several of the warriors tensed at the word *Forestal*. But Covenant, coming slowly out of his languor, felt none of the awe which seemed to be expected of him. He asked as he had once before, 'Do you worship trees?'

'Worship?' Prothall seemed puzzled. 'The word is obscure to me.'

Covenant stared.

A moment later, the High Lord went on, 'Do you ask if we reverence the forests? Of course. They are alive, and there is Earthpower in all living things, all stone and earth and water and wood. Surely you understand that we are the servants of that Power. We care for the life of the Land.' He glanced back at the Forest, then continued, 'The Earthpower takes many forms between wood and stone. Stone bedrocks the world, and to the best of our comprehension – weak as it is – that form of power does not know itself. But wood is otherwise.

'At one time, in the dimmest, lost distance of the past, nearly all the land was One Forest – one mighty wood from Trothgard and *Melenkurion* Skyweir to Sarangrave Flat and Seareach. And the Forest was awake. It knew and welcomed the new life which people brought to the Land. It felt the pain where mere men – blind, foolish moments in the ancientness of the Land – cut down and burned out the trees to make space in which to breed their folly. Oh, it's hard to take pride in human history. Before the slow knowledge spread throughout the Forest, so that each tree knew its peril, hundreds of leagues of life had been decimated. By our reckoning, the deed took time – more than a thousand years. But it must have seemed a rapid murder to the trees. At the end of that time, there were only four places left in the Land where the soul of the Forest lingered – survived, and shuddered in its awesome pain – and took resolve to defend itself. Then for many ages Giant Woods and Grimmerdhore and Morinmoss and Garroting Deep lived, and their awareness endured in the care of the Forestals. They remembered, and no human or Vile or Cavewight who dared enter them survived.

'Now even those ages are past. We know not if the Forestals yet live – though only a fool would deny that Caerroil Wildwood still walks in Garroting Deep. But the awareness which enabled the trees to strike back is fading. The Lords have defended the Forests since Berek Halfhand first took up the Staff of Law – we have not let the trees diminish. Yet their spirit fails. Cut off from each other, the collective knowledge of the Forests dies. And the glory of the world becomes less than it was.'

Prothall paused sadly for a moment before concluding, 'It is in deference to the remaining spirit, and in reverence for the Earth-power, that we ask permission for so many to enter the Forest at one time. And it is in simple caution that we offer no offence. The spirit is not dead. And the power of Morinmoss could crush a thousand thousand men if the trees were pained into wakefulness.'

'Are there other dangers?' Quaan asked. 'Will we need our weapons?'

'No. Lord Foul's servants have done great harm to the Forests in ages past. Perhaps Grimmerdhore has lost its power, but Morinmoss remembers. And tonight is the dark of the moon. Even Drool Rockworm is not mad enough to order his forces into Morinmoss at such a time. And the Despiser has never been such a fool.'

Quietly, the riders dismounted. Some of the Eoman fed the horses, while others prepared a quick meal. Soon all the company except Covenant had eaten. And after the meal, while the Bloodguard watched, the Questers laid themselves down to rest before the long passage of the Forest.

When they were roused again and ready to travel, Prothall strode up to the edge of the hillcrest. The breeze was stronger there; it fluttered his black-sashed blue robe as he raised his staff and cried loudly, 'Hail, Morinmoss! Forest of the One Forest! Enemy of our enemies! Morinmoss, hail!' His voice fell into the expanse of the woods forlornly, without echo. 'We are the Lords – foes to your enemies, and learners of the *lillianrill* lore! We must pass through!

'Harken, Morinmoss! We hate the axe and flame which hurt you! Your enemies are our enemies. Never have we brought edge of axe or flame of fire to touch you – nor ever shall. Morinmoss, harken! Let us pass!'

His call disappeared into the depths of the Forest. At last, he lowered his arms, then turned and came back to the company. He mounted his horse, looked once more sternly over the riders. At his signal, they rode down toward the knuckled edges of Morinmoss.

They seemed to fall like a stone into the Forest. One moment, they were still winding down the hillside above the trees; the next they had penetrated the gloomy deep, and the sunlight closed behind them like an unregainable door. Birinair went at the head of the company, with his Hirebrand's staff held across his mount's neck; and behind him rode First Mark Tuvor on the Ranyhyn stallion Marny – for the Ranyhyn had nothing to fear from the old anger of Morinmoss, and Marny could guide Birinair if the aged Hearthrall went astray. Behind Tuvor came Prothall and Mhoram, with Llaura at Mhoram's back; and behind them came Covenant and Foamfollower. The Giant still carried the sleeping child. Then followed Quaan and his Eoman, bunched together among the Bloodguard.

There was room for them to pass. The trees with their dark-mingled ebony and russet trunks were widely placed, leaving space between them for undergrowth and animals; and the riders found their way without difficulty. But the trees were not tall. They rose for fifteen or twenty feet on squat trunks, then spread outward in gnarled, drooping branches heavy with foliage, so that the company was completely enshrouded in the gloom of Morinmoss. The branches interwove until each tree seemed to be standing with its arms braced heavily on the shoulders of its kindred. And from the limbs hung great curtains and strands of moss – dark, thick, damp moss falling from the branches like slow blood caught and frozen as it bled. The moss dangled before the riders as if it were trying to turn them aside, deflect them from their path. And on the deep, mossy ground the hooves of the horses made no sound. The riders went their way as silently as if they had been translated into an illusion.

Instinctively dodging away from the dark touch of the moss, Covenant peered into the Forest's perpetual gloaming. As far as he could see in all directions, he was surrounded by the grotesque ire of moss and branch and trunk. But beyond the limit of his explicit senses he could see more – see, and smell, and in the silence of the Forest hear, the brooding heart of the woods. There the trees contemplated their grim memories – the broad, budding burst of self-awareness, when the spirit of the wood lay grandly over hundreds of leagues of rich earth; and the raw plummet of pain and horror and disbelief, spreading like ripples on an ocean until the farthest leaves in the Land shivered, when the slaughter of the trees began, root and branch and all cut and consumed by axe and flame, and stumps dragged away; and the scurry and anguish of the animals, slaughtered too or bereft of home and health and hope; and the clear song of the Forestal, whose tune taught the secret, angry pleasure of crushing, of striking back at tiny men and tasting their blood at the roots; and the slow weakness which ended even that fierce joy, and left the trees with nothing but their stiff memories and their despair as they watched their rage fall into slumber.

Covenant sensed that the trees knew nothing of Lords or friendship; the Lords were too recent in the Land to be remembered.

No, it was weakness, the failure of spirit, that let the riders pass – weakness, sorrow, helpless sleep. Here and there, he could hear trees that were still awake and aching for blood. But they were too few, too few. Morinmoss could only brood, bereft of force by its own ancient mortality.

A hand of moss struck him, and left moisture on his face. He wiped the wet away as if it were acid.

Then the sun set beyond Morinmoss, and even that low light was gone. Covenant leaned forward in his saddle, alert now, and afraid that Birinair would lose his way, or stumble into a curtain of moss and be smothered. But as darkness seeped into the air as if it were dripping from the enshrouding branches, a change came over the wood. Gradually, a silver glow grew on the trunks – grew and strengthened as night filled the Forest, until each tree stood shimmering like a lost soul in the gloom. The silver light was bright enough to show the riders their way. Across the shifting patterns of the glow, the moss sheets hung like shadows of an abyss – black holes into emptiness – giving the wood a blotched, leprous look. But the company huddled together, and rode on through a night illuminated only by the gleam of the trees, and by the red burn of Covenant's ring.

He felt that he could hear the trees muttering in horror at the offence of his wedding band. And its pulsing red glow appalled him. Moss fingers flicked his face with a wet, probing touch. He clenched his hands over his heart, trying to pull himself inward, reduce himself and pass unnoticed – rode as if he carried an axe under his robe, and was terrified lest the trees discover it.

That long ride passed like the hurt of a wound. Acute throbs finally blurred together, and at last the company was again riding through the dimness of day. Covenant shivered, looked about within himself. What he saw left him mute. He felt that the cistern of his rage was full of darkness.

But he was caught in toils of insoluble circumstance. The darkness was a cup which he could neither drink nor dash aside.

And he was trembling with hunger.

He could hardly restrain himself from striking back at the damp clutch of the moss.

Still the company travelled the perpetual twilight of Morinmoss. They were silent, stifled by the enshrouding branches; and in the cloying quiet, Covenant felt as lost as if he had missed his way in the old Forest which had covered all the Land. With vague fury, he ducked and dodged the grasping of the moss. Time passed, and he had a mounting desire to scream.

Then, finally, Birinair waved his staff over his head and gave a weak shout. The horses understood; they stumbled into a tired run beside the strong step of the Ranyhn. For a moment, the trees seemed to stand back, as if drawing away from the company's madness. Then the riders broke out into sunshine. They found themselves under a noon sky on a slope which bent gradually down to a river lying squarely across their way. Birinair and Marny had brought them unerringly to Roamsedge Ford.

Hoarsely shouting their relief, the warriors set heels to their mounts, and the company swept down the slope at a brave gallop. Shortly, the horses splashed into the stream, showering themselves and their glad riders with the cool spray of the Roamsedge. On the southern bank, Prothall called a halt. The passage of Morinmoss was over.

Once halted, the company tasted the toll of the passage. Their foodless vigil had weakened the riders. But the horses were in worse condition. They quivered with exhaustion. Once their last run was over, their necks and backs sagged; they scarcely had the strength to eat or drink. Despite the nickering encouragement of the Ranyhn, two of the Eoman mustangs collapsed on their sides on the grass, and the others stood around with unsteady knees like foals. 'Rest — rest,' Prothall said in rheumy anxiety. 'We go no farther this day.' He walked among the horses, touching them with his old hands and humming a strengthening song.

Only the Ranyhn and the Bloodguard were unmarred by fatigue. Foamfollower lowered the child Pietten into Llaura's arms, then dropped himself wearily on his back on the stiff grass. Since the company had left Soaring Woodhelven, he had been unnaturally silent; he had avoided speaking as if he feared his voice would betray him. Now he appeared to feel the strain of travelling without the support of stories and laughter.

Covenant wondered if he would ever hear the Giant laugh again.

Sourly, he reached a hand up to get his staff from Dura's saddle, and noticed for the first time what Morinmoss had done to his white robe. It was spattered and latticed with dark green stains — the markings of the moss.

The stains offended him. With a scowl, he looked around the company. The other riders must have been more adept at dodging; they showed none of the green signature of the moss. Lord Mhoram was the only exception; each shoulder of his robe bore a dark stripe like an insignia.

Roughly, Covenant rubbed at the green. But it was dry and set. Darkness murmured in his ears like the distant rumour of an avalanche. His shoulders hunched like a strangler's. He turned away from the Questers, stamped back into the river. Knotting his fingers in his robe, he tried to scrub out the stains of the Forest.

But the marks had become part of the fabric, immitigable; they clung to his robe, signing it like a chart, a map to unknown regions. In a fit of frustration, he pounded the river with his fists. But its current erased his ripples as if they had never existed.

He stood erect and dripping in the stream. His heart laboured in his chest. For a moment, he felt that his rage must either overflow or crack him to the bottom.

None of this is happening – His jaw quivered. I can't stand it.

Then he heard a low cry of surprise from the company. An instant later, Mhoram commanded quietly, 'Covenant. Come.'

Spitting protests against so many things that he could not name them all, he turned around. The Questers were all facing away from him, their attention bent on something which he could not see because of the water in his eyes.

Mhoram repeated, 'Come.'

Covenant wiped his eyes, waded to the bank, and climbed out of the river. He made his dripping way through the Eoman until he reached Mhoram and Prothall.

Before them stood a strange woman.

She was slim and slight – no taller than Covenant's shoulder – and dressed in a deep brown shift which left her legs and arms free. Her skin was sun-darkened to the colour of earth. Her long black hair she wore tied into one strand by a heavy cord. The effect was severe, but this was relieved by a small necklace of yellow flowers. Despite her size, she stood proudly, with her arms folded and her legs slightly apart, as if she could deny the company entrance to the Plains of Ra if she chose. She watched Covenant's approach as if she had been waiting for him.

When he stopped, joining Mhoram and Prothall, she raised her hand and gave him the salute of welcome awkwardly, as if it were not a natural gesture for her. 'Hail, Ringthane,' she said in a clear, nickering voice. 'White gold is known. We homage and serve. Be welcome.'

He shook the water from his forehead and stared at her.

After greeting him, she turned with a ritual precision toward each of the others. 'Hail, High Lord Prothall. Hail, Lord Mhoram. Hail, Saltheart Foamfollower. Hail, First Mark Tuvor. Hail, Warhaft Quaan.' In turn, they saluted her gravely, as if they recognized her as a potentate.

Then she said, 'I am Manethrall Lithe. We see you. Speak. The Plains of Ra are not open to all.'

Prothall stepped forward. Raising his staff, he held it in both hands level with his forehead and bowed deeply. At this, the woman smiled faintly. Holding her own palms beside her head, she matched his bow. This time, her movement was smooth, natural. 'You know us,' she said. 'You come from afar, but you are not unknowing.'

Prothall replied, 'We know that the Manethralls are the first tenders of the Ranyhyn. Among the Ramen, you are most honoured. And you know us.'

He stood close to her now, and the slight stoop of his agedness inclined him over her. Her brown skin and his blue robe accentuated each other like earth and sky. But still she withheld her welcome. 'No,' she returned. 'Not know. You come from afar. Unknown.'

'Yet you speak our names.'

She shrugged. 'We are cautious. We have watched since you left Morinmoss. We heard your talk.'

We? Covenant wondered blankly.

Slowly, her eyes moved over the company. 'We know the sleepless ones – the Bloodguard.' She did not appear pleased to see them. 'They take the Ranyhyn into peril. But we serve. They are welcome.' Then her gaze settled on the two collapsed horses, and her nostrils flared. 'You have urgency?' she demanded, but her tone said that she would accept few justifications for the condition of the mustangs. At that, Covenant understood why she hesitated to welcome the Lords, though they must have been known to her, at least by legend or reputation; she wanted no one who mistreated horses to enter the Plains of Ra.

The High Lord answered with authority. 'Yes. Fangthane lives.'

Lithe faltered momentarily. When her eyes turned to Covenant, they swarmed with hints of distant fear. 'Fangthane,' she breathed. 'Enemy of Earth and Ranyhyn. Yes. White gold knows. The Ringthane is here.' Abruptly, her tone became hard. 'To save the Ranyhyn from rending.' She looked at Covenant as if demanding promises from him.

He had none to give her. He stood angrily dripping, too soaked with hunger to respond in repudiation or acquiescence or shame. Soon she retreated in bafflement. To Prothall, she said, 'Who is he? What manner of man?'

With an ambivalent smile, Prothall said, 'He is ur-Lord Thomas Covenant, Unbeliever and white gold wielder. He is a stranger to the Land. Do not doubt him. He turned the battle for us when we were beset by the servants of Fangthane – Cavewights and ur-viles, and a *griffin* spawned in some unknown pit of malice.'

Lithe nodded noncommittally, as if she did not understand all his words. But then she said, 'There is urgency. No action against Fangthane must be hindered or delayed. There have been other signs. Rending beasts have sought to cross into the Plains. High Lord Prothall, be welcome in the Plains of Ra. Come with all speed to Manhome. We must take counsel.'

'Your welcome honours us,' the High Lord responded. 'We return honour in accepting. We will reach Manhome the second day from today – if the horses live.'

His cautious speech made Lithe laugh lightly. 'You will rest in the hospitality of the Ramen before the sun sets a second time from this moment. We have not served the Ranyhyn knowledgeless from the beginning. Cords! Up! Here is a test for your Maneing.'

At once, four figures appeared; they suddenly stood up from the grass in a loose semicircle around the company as if they had risen out of the ground. The four, three men and a woman, were as slight as Manethrall Lithe, and dressed like her in brown over their tanned skin; but they wore no flowers, and had short lengths of rope wrapped around their waists.

'Come, Cords,' said Lithe. 'Stalk these riders no longer. You have heard me welcome them. Now tend their horses and their safety. They must reach Manhome before nightfall of the next day.' The four Ramen stepped forward, and Lithe said to Prothall, 'Here are my Cords – Thew, Hurn, Grace, and Rustah. They are hunters. While they learn the ways of the Ranyhyn and the knowing of the Manethralls, they protect the Plains from dangerous beasts. I have spent much time with them – they can care for your mounts.'

With courteous nods to the company, the Cords went straight to the horses and began examining them.

'Now,' Lithe continued, 'I must depart. The word of your coming must cross the Plains. The Winhomes must prepare for you. Follow Rustah. He is the nearest to his Maneing. Hail, Lords! We will eat together at nightfall of the new day.'

Without waiting for a reply, the Manethrall turned southward and sprinted away. She ran with surprising speed; in a few moments, she had crested a hill and vanished from sight.

Watching her go, Mhoram said to Covenant, 'It is said that a Manethrall can run with the Ranyhyn – for a short time.'

Behind them, Cord Hurn muttered, 'It is said – and it is true.'

Mhoram faced the Cord. He stood as if waiting to speak. His appearance was much like Lithe's, though his hair had not been permitted to grow as long as hers, and his features had a dour cast. When he had Mhoram's attention, he said, 'There is a grass which will heal your horses. I must leave you to bring it.'

Gently, the Lord responded, 'The knowing is yours. Do what is best.'

Hurn's eyes widened, as if he had not expected soft words from people who mistreated horses. Then, uncertain of his movements, he saluted Mhoram in Lords' fashion. Mhoram returned a Ramen bow. Hurn grinned, and was about to gallop away when Covenant abruptly asked, 'Why don't you ride? You've got all those Ranyhyn.'

Mhoram moved swiftly to restrain Covenant. But the damage was already done. Hurn stared as if he had heard blasphemy, and his strong fingers twitched the rope about his waist, holding it between his fist like a garrote. 'We do not ride.'

'Have a care, Hurn,' said Cord Rustah softly. 'The Manethrall welcomed him.'

Hurn glanced at his companion, then roughly reknotted his rope around his waist. He spun away from the company, and soon vanished as if he had disappeared into the earth.

Gripping Covenant's arm, Mhoram said sternly, 'The Ramen serve the Ranyhyn. That is their reason for life. Do not affront them, Unbeliever. They are quick to anger – and the deadliest hunters in the Land. There might be a hundred of them within the range of my voice, and you would never know. If they chose to slay you, you would die ignorant.'

Covenant felt the force of the warning. It seemed to invest the surrounding grass with eyes that peered balefully. He felt conspicuous, as if his green-mapped robe were a guide for deadly intentions hidden in the ground. He was trembling again.

While Hurn was away, the rest of the Cords worked on the horses – caressing, cajoling them into taking water and food. Under their hands, most of the mustangs grew steadier. Satisfied that their mounts were in good hands, the Lords went to talk with Quaan and Tuvor; and around them, the warriors began preparing food.

Covenant cursed the aroma. He lay on the stiff grass and tried to still his gnawing emptiness by staring at the sky. Fatigue caught up with him, and he dozed for a while. But soon he was roused by a new smell which made his hunger sting in his guts. It came from clumps of rich, ferny flowers that the horses were munching – the healing herbs which Cord Hurn had brought for them. All the horses were on their feet now, and they seemed to gain strength visibly as they ate. The piquant odour of the flowers gave Covenant a momentary vision of himself on his hands and knees, chewing like the horses, and he muttered in suppressed savagery, 'Damn horses eat better than we do.'

Cord Rustah smiled oddly, and said, 'This grass is poison to humans. It is *amanibhavam*, the flower of health and madness. Horses it heals, but men and women – ah, they are not enough for it.'

Covenant answered with a glare, and tried to stifle the groan of his hunger. He felt a perverse desire to taste the grass; it sang to his senses delectably. Yet the thought that he had been brought so low was bitter to him, and he savoured its sourness instead of food.

Certainly, the plants worked wonders for the horses. Soon they were feeding and drinking normally – and looked sturdy enough to bear riders again. The Questers finished their meal, then packed away their supplies. The Cords pronounced the horses ready to travel. Shortly, the riders were on their way south over the swift hills of Ra, with the Ramen trotting easily beside them.

Under the hooves of the horses, the grasslands rolled and passed like mild billows, giving the company an impression of speed. They rode over the hardy grass up and down short low slopes, along shallow valleys between copses and small woods beside thin streams, across broad flats. It was a rough land. Except for the faithful *aliantha*, the terrain was unrefined by fruit trees or cultivation or any flowers other than *amanibhavam*. But still the Plains seemed full of elemental life, as if the low, quick hills were formed by the pulse of the soil, and the stiff grass were rich enough to feed anything strong enough to bear its nourishment. When the sun began to set, the bracken on the hillsides glowed purple. Herds of nilgai came out of the woods to drink at the streams, and ravens flocked clamorously to the broad chintz trees which dotted the flats.

But the riders gave most of their attention to the roaming Ranyhyn. Whether galloping by like triumphal banners or capering together in evening play, the great horses wore an aura of majesty, as if the very ground they thundered on were proud of their creation. They called in fierce joy to the bearers of the Bloodguard, and these chargers did little dances with their hooves, as if they could not restrain exhilaration of their return home. Then the unmounted Ranyhyn dashed away, full of gay blood and unfetterable energy, whinnying as they ran. Their calls made the air tingle with vitality.

Soon the sun set in the west, bidding farewell to the Plains with a flare of orange. Covenant watched it go with dour satisfaction. He was tired of horses – tired of Ranyhyn and Ramen and Bloodguard and Lords and quests, tired of the unrest of life. He wanted darkness and sleep, despite the blood burn of his ring, the newcoming crescent of the moon, and the vulture wings of horror.

But when the sun was gone, Rustah told Prothall that the company would have to keep on riding. There was danger, he said. Warnings had been left in the grass by other Ramen. The company would have to ride until they were safe – a few leagues more. So they travelled onward. Later, the moon rose, and its defiled silver turned the night to blood, calling up a lurid answer from Covenant's ring and his hungry soul.

Then Rustah slowed the riders, warned them to silence. With as much stealth as they could muster, they angled up the south side of a hill, and stopped just below its crest. The company dismounted, left a few of the Bloodguard to watch over the horses, and followed the Cords to the hilltop.

Low, flat ground lay to the north. The Cords peered across it for some time, then pointed. Covenant fought the fatigue of his eyes and the crimson dimness until he thought he saw a dark patch moving southward over the flat.

'*Kresh*,' whispered Hurn. 'Yellow wolves – Fangthane's brood. They have crossed Roamsedge.'

'Wait for us,' Rustah breathed. 'You will be safe.'

He and the other Cords faded into the night.

Instinctively, the company drew closer together, and stared with throbbing eyes through the thin red light which seemed to ooze like sweat from the moving darkness on the flat. In suspense, they stood hushed, hardly breathing.

Pietten sat in Llaura's arms, as wide awake as a vigil.

Covenant learned later that the pack numbered fifteen of the great yellow wolves. Their fore-shoulders were waist-high on a man; they had massive jaws lined with curved, ripping fangs, and yellow omnivorous eyes. They were drooling on the trail of two Ranyhyn foals protected only by a stallion and his mare. The legends of the Ramen said that the breath of such *kresh* was hot enough to scorch the ground, and they left a weal of pain across the grass wherever their plundering took them. But all Covenant saw now was an approaching darkness, growing larger moment by moment.

Then to his uncertain eye the rear of the pack appeared to swirl in confusion briefly; and as the wolves moved on he thought he could see two or three black dots lying motionless on the flat.

The pack swirled again. This time, several short howls of surprise and fear broke the silence. One harsh snarl was suddenly choked off. The next instant, the pack started a straight dash toward the company, leaving five more dots behind. But now Covenant was sure that the dots were dead wolves.

Three more *kresh* dropped. Now he could see three figures leap away from the dead and sprint after the survivors.

They vanished into shadows at the foot of the hill. From the darkness came sounds of fighting – enraged snarls, the snap of jaws that missed their mark, bones cracking.

Then silence flooded back into the night. The apprehension of the company sharpened, for they could see nothing; the shadow reached almost to the crest of the hill where they stood.

Abruptly, they heard the sound of frantic running. It came directly toward them.

Prothall sprang forward. He raised his staff, and blue fire flared from its tip. The sudden light revealed a lone *kresh* with hatred in its eyes pelting at him.

Tuvor reached Prothall's side an instant before Foamfollower. But the Giant went ahead to meet the wolf's charge.

Then, without warning, Cord Grace rose out of hiding squarely in front of the wolf. She executed her movement as smoothly as if she were dancing. As she stood, a swift jerk freed her rope. When the *kresh* sprang at her, she flipped a loop of the rope around its neck, and stepped neatly aside, turning as she did so to brace her feet. The force of the wolf's charge as it hit her noose broke its neck. The yank pulled her from her feet, but she rolled lightly to one side, keeping pressure on the rope, and came to her feet in a position to finish the *kresh* if it were still alive.

The Eoman met her performance with a low murmur of admiration. She glanced toward them and smiled diffidently in the blue light of Prothall's staff. Then she turned to greet the other Cords as they loped out of the shadow of the hill. They were uninjured. All the wolves were dead.

Lowering his staff, Prothall gave the Cords a Ramen bow. 'Well done,' he said. They bowed in acknowledgement.

When he extinguished his staff, red darkness returned to the hilltop. In the bloodlight, the riders began moving back to their horses. But Bannor stepped over to the dead wolf and pulled Grace's rope from around its neck. Holding the cord in a fighting grip, he stretched it taut.

'A good weapon,' he said with his awkward inflectionlessness. 'The Ramen did mighty work with it in the days when High Lord Kevin fought Corruption openly.' Something in his tone reminded Covenant that the Bloodguard were lusty men who had gone unwived for more than two thousand years.

Then, on the spur of an obscure impulse, Bannor tightened his muscles, and the rope snapped. Shrugging slightly, he dropped the pieces on the dead *kresh*. His movement had the finality of a prophecy. Without a glance at Cord Grace, he left the hilltop to mount the Ranyhyn that had chosen him.

19

RINGTHANE'S CHOICE

Cord Rustah informed Prothall that, according to Ramen custom, dead renders of the Ranyhyn were left for the vultures. The Ramen had no desire to honour *kresh*, or to affront the earth, by burying them, and pyres raised the danger of fire on the Plains. So the riders could rest as soon as their horses were away from the smell of death. The Cord led the company on southward for nearly a league until he was satisfied that no night breeze would carry unrest to the animals. Then the Quest camped.

Covenant slept fitfully, as if he lay with the point of a spike against his stomach; and when the dawn came, he felt as ineffectual as if he had spent the night trying to counter-punch hunger. And when his nose tasted again the tangy smell of the poison *amanibhavam*, the sensation made his eyes water as if he had been struck.

He did not believe that he could hold himself upright much longer. But he still did not have the answer he needed. He had found no new insight, and the green handiwork of Morinmoss on his robe seemed illegible. A sure instinct told him that he could find what he lacked in the extremity of hunger. When his companions had eaten, and were ready to travel again, he climbed dully on to Dura's back and rode with them. His eyes dripped senselessly from time to time, but he was not weeping. He felt charged with passion, but could not let it out. The grief of his leprosy did not permit any such release.

In contrast to the cold ash of his mood, the day was cheery, full of bright, unclouded sun and a warm northward breeze, of deep sky and swift hills. Soon the rest of the company had surrendered to the spell of the Plains – an incantation woven by the proud roaming of the Ranyhyn. Time and again, mighty horses cantered or raced by, glancing aside at the riders with laughter in their eyes and keen shimmering calls in their throats. The sight of them added a spring to the strides of the Cords, and as the morning passed, Grace and Thew sang together:

> Run, Ranyhyn:
> gallop, play –
> feed, and drink, and coat-gloss gleam.

You are the marrow of the earth.
No rein will curb, or bit control –
no claw or fang unpunished rend;
no horse-blood drop without the healing grass.
We are the Ramen, born to serve:
Manethrall curry,
Cord protect,
Winhome hearth and bed anneal –
our feet do not bear our hearts away.
Grass-grown hooves, and forehead stars;
hocks and withers earth-wood bloom:
regal Ranyhyn, gallop, run –
we serve the Tail of the Sky,
Mane of the World.

Hearing the song, Ranyhyn pranced around the company and away, running as smoothly as if the ground flowed in their strides.

In Foamfollower's arms, Pietten stirred and shook off his day sleep for a while to watch the Ranyhyn with something like longing in his blank eyes. Prothall and Mhoram sat relaxed in their saddles, as if for the first time since leaving Revelstone they felt that the company was safe. And tears ran down Covenant's face as if it were a wall.

In his emptiness, the heat of the sun confused him. His head seemed to be fulminating, and the sensation made him feel that he was perched on an unsteady height, where great gulfs of vertiginous grass snapped like wolves at his heels. But the *clingor* of his saddle held him on Dura's back. After a time, he dozed into a dream where he danced and wept and made love at the commands of a satirical puppeteer.

When he awoke, it was mid-afternoon, and there were mountains across most of the horizon ahead. The company was making good time. In fact, the horses were cantering now, as if the Plains gave them more energy than they could contain. For a moment, he looked ahead to Manhome, where, he foresaw, a misguided and valueless respect for his wedding ring would offer him to the Ranyhyn as a prospective rider. This was surely one of Prothall's reasons for choosing to visit the Plains of Ra before approaching Mount Thunder. Honour the ur-Lord, the Ringthane. Ah, hell! He tried to envision himself riding a Ranyhyn, but his imagination could not make the leap; more than anything else except Andelain, the great, dangerous, Earthpowerful horses quintessenced the Land. And Joan had been a breaker of horses. For some reason, the thought made his nose sting, and he tried to hold back his tears by gritting his teeth.

The rest of the afternoon he passed by watching the mountains. They grew ahead of the company as if the peaks were slowly clambering to their feet. Curving away southwest and northeast, the range was not as high as the mountains behind Mithil Stonedown, but it was rugged and raw, as if high pinnacles had been shattered to make those forbidding, impenetrable. Covenant did not know what lay behind the mountains, and did not want to know. Their impenetrability gave him an obscure comfort, as if they came between him and something he could not bear to see.

They stood up more swiftly now as the company rode at a slow run toward them. The sun was dipping into the western plains as the riders entered the foothills of a precipitous outcropping of the range. And their backs were hued in orange and pink as they crossed a last rise, and reached a broad flat glade at the foot of the cliff.

There, at last, was Manhome.

The bottom of the cliff face for the last two hundred fifty or three hundred feet inclined sharply inward along a broad, half-oval front, leaving a cave like a deep, vertical bowl in the rock. Far back in the cave, where they were protected from the weather, and yet still exposed to the open air, were the hooped tents of the Ramen families. And in the front under the shelter of the cliff was the communal area, the open space and fires where the Ramen cooked and talked and danced and sang together when they were not out on the Plains with the Ranyhyn. The whole place seemed austere, as if generations of Ramen had not worn a welcome for themselves in the stone; for Mahome was only a centre, a beginning for the Plains-roaming of a nomadic people.

Perhaps seventy Ramen gathered to watch the company approach. They were nearly all Winhomes, the young and old of the Ramen, and others who needed safety and a secure bed. Unlike the Cords and Manethralls, they had no fighting ropes.

But Lithe was there, and she walked lightly out to meet the company with three other Ramen whom Covenant took to be Manethralls also; they wore necklets of yellow flowers like hers, and carried their cords in their hair rather than at their waists. The company halted, and Prothall dismounted before the Manethralls. He bowed to them in the Ramen fashion, and they gestured their welcome in return. 'Hail again, Lords from afar,' said Lithe. 'Hail Ringthane and High Lord and Giant and Bloodguard. Be welcome to the hearth and bed at Manhome.'

At her salutation, the Winhomes surged forward from under the cliff. As the riders got down from their horses, each was greeted by a smiling Winhome bearing a small band of woven flowers. With gestures of ritual stateliness, they fastened the bands to the right wrists of their guests.

Covenant climbed off Dura, and found a shy-bold Ramen girl no more than fifteen or sixteen years old standing before him. She had fine black hair that draped her shoulders, and soft wide brown eyes. She did not smile: she seemed awed to find herself greeting the Ringthane, the wielder of the white gold. Carefully, she reached out to put her flowers around his wrist.

Their smell staggered him, and he nearly retched. The band was woven of *amanibhavam*. Its tang burned his nose like acid, made him so hungry that he felt about to vomit chunks of emptiness. He was helpless to stop the tears that ran from his eyes.

With a face full of solemnity, the Winhome girl raised her hands and touched his tears as if they were precious.

Behind him, the Ranyhyn of the Bloodguard were galloping off into the freedom of the Plains. The Cords were leading the company's horses away to be tended, and more Ramen cantered into the glade in answer to the news of the Quest's arrival. But Covenant kept his eyes on the girl, stared at her as if she were a kind of food. Finally she answered his gaze by saying, 'I am Winhome Gay. Soon I will share enough knowing to join the Cords.' After an instant of hesitation, she added, 'I am to care for you while you guest here.' When he did not respond, she said hurriedly, 'Others will gladly serve if my welcome is not accepted.'

Covenant remained silent for a moment longer, clenching his useless ferocity. But then he gathered his strength for one final refusal. 'I don't need anything. Don't touch me.' The words hurt his throat.

A hand touched his shoulder. He glanced around to find Foamfollower beside him. The Giant was looking down at Covenant, but he spoke to the pain of rejection in Gay's face. 'Do not be sad, little Winhome,' he murmured. 'Covenant Ringthane tests us. He does not speak his heart.'

Gay smiled gratefully up at Foamfollower, then said with sudden sauciness, 'Not so little, Giant. Your size deceives you. I have almost reached Cording.'

Her gibe appeared to take a moment to penetrate Foamfollower. Then his stiff beard twitched. Abruptly, he began to laugh. His glee mounted; it echoed off the cliff from Manhome until the mountain seemed to share his elation, and the infectious sound spread until everyone near him was laughing without knowing why. For a long moment, he threw out gales as if he were blowing debris from his soul.

But Covenant turned away, unable to bear the loud weight of the Giant's humour. Hellfire, he growled. Hell and blood. What are you doing to me? He had made no decision, and now his capacity for self-denial seemed spent.

So when Gay offered to guide him to his seat for the feast which the Winhomes had prepared, he followed her numbly. She took him under the ponderous overhang of the cliff to a central, clear space with a campfire burning in the middle. Most of the company had already entered Manhome. There were two other fires, and the Ramen divided the company into three groups: the Bloodguard sat around one of the fires; Quaan and his fourteen warriors around another; and in the centre, the Ramen invited Prothall, Mhoram, Foamfollower, Llaura, Pietten, and Covenant to join the Manethralls. Covenant let himself be steered until he was sitting cross-legged on the smooth stone floor, across the circle from Prothall, Mhoram, and Foamfollower. Four Manethralls made places for themselves beside the Lords, and Lithe seated herself near Covenant. The rest of the circle was filled with Cords who had come in from the Plains with their Manethrall teachers.

Most of the Winhomes bustled around cooking fires farther back in the cave, but one stood behind each guest, waiting to serve. Gay attended Covenant, and she hummed a light melody which reminded him of another song he had once heard.

> Something there is in beauty
> which grows in the soul of the beholder
> like a flower.

Under the wood smoke and the cooking odours, he thought that he could smell Gay's clean, grassy fragrance.

As he sat lumpishly on the stone, the last glow of the sunset waved orange and gold on the roof like an affectionate farewell. Then the sun was gone. Night spread over the Plains; campfire flames gave the only light in Manhome. The air was full of bustle and low talk like a hill breeze rich in Ranyhyn scent. But the food Covenant dreaded did not come immediately. First, some of the Cords danced.

Three of them performed within the circle where Covenant sat. They danced around the fire with high prancing movements and sang a nickering song to the beat of complex clapping from the Winhomes. The smooth flow of their limbs, the sudden eruptions of the dance, the dark tan of their skins, made them look as if they were enacting the pulse of the Plains – dancing the pulse by making it fast enough for human eyes to see. And they repeatedly bent their bodies so that the firelight cast horselike shadows on the walls and ceiling.

Occasionally, the dancers leaped close enough to Covenant for him to hear their song:

> Grass-grown hooves, and forehead stars;
> hocks and withers earth-wood bloom:
> regal Ranyhyn, gallop, run —
> we serve the Tail of the Sky,
> Mane of the World.

The words and the dance made him feel that they expressed some secret knowledge, some vision that he needed to share. The feeling repelled him; he tore his eyes away from the dancers to the glowing coals of the fire. When the dance was done, he went on staring into the fire's heart with a gaze full of vague trepidations.

Then the Winhomes brought food and drink to the circles. Using broad leaves for plates, they piled stew and wild potatoes before their guests. The meal was savoury with rare herbs which the Ramen relished in their cooking, and soon the Questers were deep in the feast. For a long time the only sounds in Manhome were those of serving and eating.

In the midst of the feast, Covenant sat like a stunted tree. He did not respond to anything Gay offered him. He stared at the fire; there was one coal in it which burned redly, like the night glow of his ring. He was doing a kind of VSE in his mind, studying his extremities from end to end; and his heart ached in the conviction that he was about to find some utterly unexpected spot of leprosy. He looked as if he were withering.

After a time, people began to talk again. Prothall and Mhoram handed their leaf plates back to the Winhomes, and turned their attention to the Manethralls. Covenant caught glimpses of their conversation. They were discussing him — the message he had brought to them, the role he played in the fate of the Land. Their physical comfort contrasted strangely with the seriousness of their words.

Near them, Foamfollower described the plight of Llaura and Pietten to one of the Manethralls.

Covenant scowled into the fire. He did not need to look down to see the blood change which came over his ring; he could feel the radiation of wrong from the metal. He concealed the band under his fist and trembled.

The stone ceiling seemed to hover over him like a cruel wing of revelation, awaiting the moment of his greatest helplessness to plunge on to his exposed neck. He was abysmally hungry.

I'm going crazy, he muttered into the flames.

Winhome Gay urged him to eat, but he did not respond.

Across the circle, Prothall was explaining the purpose of his Quest. The Manethralls listened uncertainly, as if they had trouble seeing the connection between evils far away and the Plains of Ra. So the High Lord told them what had been done to Andelain.

Pietten gazed with blank unfocus out into the night, as if he were looking forward to moonrise. Beside him, Llaura spoke quietly with the Cords around her, grateful for the Ramen hospitality.

As Foamfollower detailed the horrors which had been practised on the two survivors of Soaring Woodhelven, his forehead knotted under the effort he made to contain his emotion.

The fire shone like a door with an intolerable menace waiting behind it. The back of Covenant's neck was stiff with vulnerability, and his eyes stared blindly, like knotholes.

The green stains on his robe marked him like a warning that said, Leper outcast unclean.

He was nearing the end of his VSE. Behind him was the impossibility of believing the Land true. And before him was the impossibility of believing it false.

Abruptly, Gay entered the circle, and confronted him, with her hands on her hips and her eyes flashing. She stood with her legs slightly apart, so that he saw the bloody coals of the fire between her thighs.

He glanced up at her.

'You must take food,' she scolded. 'Already you are half dead.' Her shoulders were squared, drawing her shift tight over her breasts. She reminded him of Lena.

Prothall was saying, 'He has not told us all that occurred at the Celebration. The ravage of the Wraiths was not prevented – yet we believe he fought the ur-viles in some way. His companion blamed both herself and him for the ill which befell the Dance.'

Covenant trembled. Like Lena, he thought. Lena?

Darkness pounced at him like claws of vertigo. Lena?

For an instant, his vision was obscured by roaring and black waters. Then he crashed to his feet. He had done that to Lena – done *that*? He flung the girl aside and jumped toward the fire. Lena! Swinging his staff like an axe, he chopped at the blaze. But he could not fight off the memory, could not throw it back. The staff twisted with the force of the blow, fell from his hands. Sparks and coals shattered, flew in all directions. He had done *that* to her! Shaking his half-fist at Prothall, he cried, 'She was wrong! I couldn't help it!' – thinking, Lena! What have I done? – 'I'm a leper!'

Around him, people sprang to their feet. Mhoram came forward quickly, stretched out a restraining hand. 'Softly, Covenant,' he said. 'What is wrong? We are guests.'

But even while he protested, Covenant knew that Atiaran had not been wrong. He had seen himself kill at the battle of Soaring Woodhelven, and had thought in his folly that being a killer was something new for him, something unprecedented. But it was not something he had recently become; he had been that way from the beginning of the dream, from the beginning. In an intuitive leap, he saw that there was no difference between what the ur-viles had done to the Wraiths and what he had done to Lena. He had been serving Lord Foul since his first day in the Land.

'No!' he spat as if he were boiling in acid. 'No. I won't do it any more. I'm not going to be the victim any more. I will not be waited on by children.' He shook with the ague of his rage as he cried at himself, You raped her! You stinking bloody bastard!

He felt as weak as if the understanding of what he had done corroded his bones.

Mhoram said intently, 'Unbeliever! What is wrong?'

'No!' Covenant repeated. 'No!' He was trying to shout, but his voice sounded distant, crippled. 'I will not – tolerate – this. It isn't right. I am going to survive! Do you hear me?'

'Who are you?' Manethrall Lithe hissed through taut lips. With a quick shake of her head, a flick of her wrist, she pulled the cord from her hair and held it battle-ready.

Prothall caught her arm. His old voice rattled with authority and supplication. 'Forgive, Manethrall. This matter is beyond you. He holds the wild magic that destroys peace. We must forgive.'

'Forgive?' Covenant tried to shout. His legs failed under him, but he did not fall. Bannor held him erect from behind. 'You can't forgive.'

'Do you ask to be punished?' Mhoram said incredulously. 'What have you done?'

'Ask?' Covenant struggled to recollect something. Then he found it. He knew what he had to do. 'No. Call the Ranyhyn.'

'What?' snapped Lithe in indignation. And all the Ramen echoed her protest.

'The Ranyhyn! Call them.'

'Are you mad? Have a care, Ringthane. We are the Ramen. We do not call – we serve. They come as they will. They are not for your calling. And they do not come at night.'

'Call, I tell you! I! Call them!'

Something in his terrible urgency confounded her. She hesitated, stared at him in confused anger and protest and unexpected compassion, then turned on her heel and strode out of Manhome.

Supported by Bannor, Covenant tottered out from under the oppressive weight of the mountain. The company and the Ramen trailed after him like a wake of dumbfounded outrage. Behind them, the red moon had just crested the mountain; and the distant Plains, visible beyond the foothills in front of Manhome, were already awash with crimson. The incarnadine flood seemed to untexture the earth, translate rock and soil and grass into decay and bitter blood.

The people spread out on either side of the flat so that the open ground was lit by the campfires.

Into the night walked Lithe, moving toward the Plains until she stood near the far edge of the glade. Covenant stopped and watched her. Unsteadily, but resolutely, he freed himself from Bannor's support – stood on his own like a wrecked galleon left by the tide, perched impossibly high on a reef. Moving woodenly, he went toward Lithe.

Before him, the bloody vista of the moonlight lay like a dead sea, and it tugged at him as it flowed closer with each degree of the moonrise. His ring smouldered coldly. He felt that he was the lodestone. Sky and earth were alike hued scarlet, and he walked outward as if he were the pole on which the red night turned – he and his ring the force which compelled that tide of violated night. Soon he stood in the centre of the open flat.

A widening-sheet of silence enwrapped the onlookers.

Ahead of him, Manethrall Lithe spread her arms as if she were beckoning the darkness toward her. Abruptly, she gave a shrill cry. *'Kelenbhrabanal marushyn! Rushyn hynyn kelenkoor rillynarunal! Ranyhyn Kelenbhrabanal!'* Then she whistled once. It echoed off the cliff like a shriek.

For a long moment, silence choked the flat. Striding defiantly, Lithe moved back toward Manhome. As she passed Covenant, she snapped, 'I have called.' Then she was behind him, and he faced the siege of the moonlight alone.

But shortly there came a rumbling of hooves. Great horses pounded the distance; the sound swelled as if the hills themselves were rolling Manhome-ward. Scores of Ranyhyn approached. Covenant locked his knees to keep himself upright. His heart felt too weak to go on beating. He was dimly conscious of the hushed suspense of the spectators.

Then the outer edge of the flat seemed to rise up redly, and a wave of Ranyhyn broke into the open – nearly a hundred chargers galloping abreast like a wall at Covenant.

A cry of amazement and admiration came from the Ramen. Few

of the oldest Manethralls had ever seen so many Ranyhyn at one time.

And Covenant knew that he was looking at the proudest flesh of the Land. He feared that they were going to trample him.

But the pounding wall broke away to his left, ran around him until he was completely encircled. Manes and tails tossing, forehead stars catching the firelight as they flashed past, fivescore Ranyhyn thundered on the turf and enclosed him. The sound of their hooves roared in his ears.

Their circle drew tighter as they ran. Their reeling strength snatched at his fear, pulled him around with them as if he were trying to face them all at once. His heart laboured painfully. He could not turn fast enough to keep up with them. The effort made him stumble, lose his balance, fall to his knees.

But the next instant, he was erect again, with his legs planted against the vertigo of their circling, and his face contorted as if he were screaming – a cry lost in the thunder of Ranyhyn hooves. His arms spread as if they were braced against opposing walls of night.

Slowly, tortuously, the circle came stamping and fretting to a halt. The Ranyhyn faced inward toward Covenant. Their eyes rolled, and several of them had froth on their lips. At first, he failed to comprehend their emotion.

From the onlookers came a sudden cry. He recognized Llaura's voice. Turning, he saw Pietten running toward the horses, with Llaura struggling after him, too far behind to catch him. The child had caught everyone by surprise; they had been watching Covenant. Now Pietten reached the circle and scrambled among the frenzied feet of the Ranyhyn.

It seemed impossible that he would not be trampled. His head was no larger than one of their hooves, and the chargers were stamping, skittering. Then Covenant saw his chance. With an instinctive leap, he snatched Pietten from under one of the horses.

His half-unfingered hand could not retain its grip; Pietten sprawled away from him. Immediately, the child jumped to his feet. He dashed at Covenant and struck as hard as he could.

'They hate you!' he raged. 'Go away!'

Moonlight fell into the flat as if it had sprung from the sides of the mountain. In the crimson glow, Pietten's little face looked like a wasteland.

The child struggled, but Covenant lifted him off the ground, gripped him to his chest with both arms. Restraining Pietten in his hug, he looked up at the Ranyhyn.

Now he understood. In the past, he had been too busy avoiding them to notice how they reacted to him. They were not threatening him. These great chargers were terrified – terrified of him. Their eyes shied off his face, and they scattered foam flecks about them. The muscles of their legs and chests quivered. Yet they came agonized forward. Their old role was reversed. Instead of choosing their riders, they were submitting themselves to his choice.

On an impulse, he unwrapped his left arm from Pietten and flourished his cold red ring at one of the horses. It flinched and ducked as if he had thrust a serpent at it, but it held its ground.

He gripped Pietten again. The child's struggles were weaker now, as if Covenant's hug slowly smothered him. But the Unbeliever clung. He stared wildly at the Ranyhyn, and wavered as if he could not regain his balance.

But he had already made his decision. He had seen the Ranyhyn recognize his ring. Clenching Pietten to his heart like a helm, he cried, 'Listen!' in a voice as hoarse as a sob. 'Listen, I'll make a bargain with you. Get it right. Hellfire! Get it right. A bargain. Listen. I can't stand – I'm falling apart. Apart.' He clenched Pietten. 'I see – I see what's happening to you. You're afraid of me. You think I'm some kind of – All right. You're free. I don't choose any of you.'

The Ranyhyn watched him fearfully.

'But you've got to do things for me. You've got to *back off*!' That wail almost took the last of his strength. 'You – the Land – ' he panted, pleaded, *Let me be*! 'Don't ask so much.' But he knew that he needed something more from them in return for his forbearance, something more than their willingness to suffer his Unbelief.

'Listen – listen. If I need you, you had better come. So that I don't have to be a hero. Get it right.' His eyes bled tears, but he was not weeping.

'And – and there's one more thing. One more. Lena – ' Lena! 'A girl. She lives in Mithil Stonedown. Daughter of Trell and Atiaran. I want – I want one of you to go to her. Tonight. And every year. At the last full moon before the middle of spring. Ranyhyn are – are what she dreams about.'

He shook the tears out of his eyes, and saw the Ranyhyn regarding him as if they understood everything he had tried to say.

'Now go,' he gasped, 'have mercy on me.'

With a sudden, bursting, united neigh, all the Ranyhyn reared around him, pawing the air over his head as if they were delivering promises. Then they wheeled, whinnying with relief, and charged away from Manhome. The moonlight did not appear to touch them. They dropped over the edge of the flat and vanished as if they were being welcomed into the arms of the earth.

Almost at once, Llaura reached Covenant's side. Slowly, he released Pietten to her. She gave him a long look that he could not read, then turned away. He followed her, trudging as if he were overburdened with the pieces of himself. He could hear the amazement of the Ramen – amazement too strong for them to feel any offence at what he had done. He was beyond them; he could hear it. 'They reared to him,' the whispers ran. But he did not care. He was perversely sick with the sense that he had mastered nothing, proved nothing, resolved nothing.

Lord Mhoram came out to join him. Covenant did not meet Mhoram's gaze, but he heard complex wonder in the Lord's voice as he said, 'Ur-Lord – ah! Such honour has never been done to mortal man or woman. Many have come to the Plains, and have been offered to the Ranyhyn – and refused. And when Lord Tamarantha my mother was offered, five Ranyhyn came to consider her – five. It was a higher honour than she had dreamed possible. We could not hear. Have you refused them? Refused?'

'Refused,' Covenant groaned. They hate me.

He pushed past Mhoram and shambled into Manhome. Moving unsteadily, like a ship with a broken keel, he headed toward the nearest cooking fire. The Ramen made way for him, watched him pass with awe in their faces. He did not care. He reached the fire and grabbed the first food he saw. The meat slipped in his halfhand, so he held it with his left fist and devoured it.

He ate blankly, swallowing food in chunks and taking more by the fistful. Then he wanted something to drink. He looked around, discovered Foamfollower standing nearby with a flagon of *diamondraught* dwarfed in his huge hand.

Covenant took the flagon and drained it. Then he stood numbly still, waiting for the *diamondraught*'s effect.

It came swiftly. Soon mist began to fill his head. His hearing seemed hollow, as if he were listening to Manhome from the bottom of a well. He knew that he was going to pass out – wanted hungrily to pass out – but before he lost consciousness, the hurt in his chest made him say, 'Giant, I – I need friends.'

'Why do you believe you have none?'

Covenant blinked, and saw everything that he had done in the Land. 'Don't be ridiculous.'

'Then you do believe that we are real.'

'What?' Covenant groped for the Giant's meaning with hands which had no fingers.

'You think us capable of not forgiving you,' Foamfollower explained. 'Who would forgive you more readily than your dream?'

'No,' the Unbeliever said. 'Dreams – never forgive.'

Then he lost the firelight and Foamfollower's kind face, and stumbled into sleep.

20

A QUESTION OF HOPE

He wandered wincing in sleep, expecting nightmares. But he had none. Through the vague rise and fall of his drifting – as if even asleep his senses were alert to the Land – he felt that he was being distantly watched. The gaze on him was anxious and beneficent; it reminded him of the old beggar who had made him read an essay on 'the fundamental question of ethics'.

When he woke up, he found that Manhome was bright with sunshine.

The shadowed ceiling of the cave was dim, but light reflecting off the village floor seemed to dispel the oppressive weight of the stone. And the sun reached far enough into Manhome to tell Covenant that he had awakened early in the afternoon of a warm presummer day. He lay near the back of the cave in an atmosphere of stillness. Beside him sat Saltheart Foamfollower.

Covenant closed his eyes momentarily. He felt he had survived a gauntlet. And he had an unfocused sense that his bargain was going to work. When he looked up again, he asked, 'How long have I been asleep?' as if he had just been roused from the dead.

'Hail and welcome, my friend,' returned the Giant. 'You make my *diamondraught* appear weak. You have slept for only a night and a morning.'

Stretching luxuriously, Covenant said, 'Practice. I do so much of it – I'm becoming an expert.'

'A rare skill,' Foamfollower chuckled.

'Not really. There're more of us lepers than you might think.' Abruptly he frowned as if he had caught himself in unwitting violation of his promised forbearance. In order to avoid being taken seriously, he added in a lugubrious tone, 'We're everywhere.'

But his attempt at humour only appeared to puzzle the Giant. After a moment, Foamfollower said slowly, 'Are the others – "Leper" is not a good name. It is too short for such as you. I do not know the word, but my ears hear nothing in it but cruelty.'

Covenant sat up and pushed off his blankets. 'It's not cruel exactly.' The subject appeared to shame him. While he spoke, he could not meet Foamfollower's gaze. 'It's either a meaningless accident . . . or a "just desert". If it were cruel, it would happen more often.'

'More often?'

'Sure. If leprosy were an act of cruelty – by God or whatever – it wouldn't be so rare. Why be satisfied with a few thousand abject victims when you could have a few million?'

'Accident,' Foamfollower murmured. 'Just. My friend, you bewilder me. You speak with such haste. Perhaps the Despiser of your world has only a limited power to oppose its Creator.'

'Maybe. Somehow I don't think my world works that way.'

'Yet you said – did you not? – that lepers are everywhere.'

'That was a joke. Or a metaphor.' Covenant made another effort to turn his sarcasm into humour. 'I can never tell the difference.'

Foamfollower studied him for a long moment, then asked carefully, 'My friend, do you jest?'

Covenant met the Giant's gaze with a sardonic scowl. 'Apparently not.'

'I do not understand this mood.'

'Don't worry about it.' Covenant caught his chance to escape this conversation. 'Let's get some food, I'm hungry.'

To his relief, Foamfollower began laughing gently. 'Ah, Thomas Covenant,' he chuckled, 'do you remember our river journey to Lord's Keep? Apparently there is something in my seriousness which makes you hungry.' Reaching down to one side, he brought up a tray of bread and cheese and fruit and a flask of springwine. And he went on laughing quietly while Covenant pounced on the food.

Covenant ate steadily for some time before he began looking around. Then he was taken aback to find that the cave was profuse with flowers. Garlands and bouquets lay everywhere, as if overnight each Ramen had raised a garden thick with white columbines and greenery. The white and green eased the austerity of Manhome, covered the stone like a fine robe.

'Are you surprised?' asked Foamfollower. 'These flowers honour you. Many of the Ramen roamed all night to gather blooms. You have touched the hearts of the Ranyhyn, and the Ramen are not unamazed – or ungrateful. A wonder has come to pass for them – fivescore Ranyhyn offering to one man. The Ramen would not exchange such a sight for Andelain itself, I think. So they have returned what honour is in their power.'

Honour? Covenant echoed.

The Giant settled himself more comfortably, and said as if he were beginning a long tale, 'It is sad that you did not see the Land before the Desecration. Then the Ramen might have shown you honour that would humble all your days. All matters were higher in that age, but even among the Lords there were few beauties to equal the great craft of the Ramen. "Marrowmeld", they called it – *anundivian yajña*, in the tongue of the Old Lords. Bonesculpting it was. From vulture – and time-cleaned skeletons on the Plains of Ra, the Ramen formed figures of rare truth and joy. In their hands – under the power of their songs – the bones bent and flowed like clay, and were fashioned curiously, so that from the white core of lost life the Ramen made emblems for the living. I have never beheld these figures, but the tale of them is preserved by the Giants. In the destitution and diminishment, the long generations of hunger and hiding and homelessness, which came to the Ranyhyn and the Ramen with the Desecration, the skill of marrowmeld was lost.'

His voice faded as he finished, and after a moment he began to sing softly:

Stone and Sea are deep in life –

A silence of respectful attention surrounded him. The Winhomes near him had stopped to listen.

A short time later, one of them waved out toward the glade, and Covenant, following the gesture, saw Lithe striding briskly across the flat. She was accompanied by Lord Mhoram astride a beautiful roan Ranyhyn. The sight gladdened Covenant. He finished his springwine in a salute to Mhoram.

'Yes,' said Foamfollower, noticing Covenant's gaze, 'much has occurred this morning. High Lord Prothall chose not to offer himself. He said that his old bones would better suit a lesser mount – meaning, I think, that he feared his "old bones" would give affront to the Ranyhyn. But it would be well not to underestimate his strength.'

Covenant heard a current of intimations running through Foamfollower's words. Distantly, he said, 'Prothall is going to resign after this Quest – if it succeeds.'

The Giant's eyes grinned. 'Is that prophecy?'

Covenant shrugged. 'You know as well as I do. He spends too much time thinking about how he hasn't mastered Kevin's Lore. He thinks he's a failure. And he's going to go on thinking that even if he gets the Staff of Law back.'

'Prophecy, indeed.'

'Don't laugh.' Covenant wondered how he could explain the

resonance of the fact that Prothall had refused a chance at the Ranyhyn. 'Anyway, tell me about Mhoram.'

Happily, Foamfollower said, 'Lord Mhoram son of Variol was this day chosen by Hynaril of the Ranyhyn, who also bore Tamarantha Variol-mate. Behold! She is remembered with honour among the great horses. The Ramen say that no Ranyhyn has ever before borne two riders. Truly, an age of wonders has come to the Plains of Ra.'

'Wonders,' Covenant muttered. He did not like to remember the fear with which all those Ranyhyn had faced him. He glared into his flask as if it had cheated him by being empty.

One of the nearest Winhomes started toward him carrying a jug. He recognized Gay. She approached among the flowers, then stopped. When she saw that he was looking at her, she lowered her eyes. 'I would refill your flagon,' she said, 'but I fear to offend. You will consider me a child.'

Covenant scowled at her. She affected him like a reproach, and he stiffened where he sat. With an effort that made him sound coldly formal, he said, 'Forget last night. It wasn't your fault.' Awkwardly, he extended the flask toward her.

She came forward, and poured out springwine for him with hands that shook slightly.

He said distinctly, 'Thank you.'

She gazed at him widely for a moment. Then a look of relief filled her face, and she smiled.

Her smile reminded him of Lena. Deliberately, as if she were a burden he refused to shirk, he motioned for her to sit down. She placed herself cross-legged at the foot of his bed, gleaming at the honour the Ringthane did her.

Covenant tried to think of something to say to her; but before he found what he wanted, he saw Warhaft Quaan striding into Manhome. Quaan came toward him squarely, as if he were forging against Covenant's gaze, and when he neared the Unbeliever, he waited only an instant before asking his question. 'We were concerned. Life needs food. Are you well?'

'Well?' Covenant felt that he was beginning to glow with his second flask of springwine. 'Can't you see? I can see you. You're as sound as an oak.'

'You are closed to us,' said Quaan, stolid with disapproval. 'What we see is not what you are.'

This ambiguous statement seemed to invite a mordant retort, but Covenant restrained himself. He shrugged, then said, 'I'm eating,' as if he did not want to lay claim to too much health.

Quaan seemed to accept this reply for what it was worth. He nodded, bowed slightly, and left.

Watching him go, Winhome Gay breathed, 'He dislikes you.' Her tone expressed awe at the Warhaft's audacity and foolishness. She seemed to ask how he dared to feel as he did – as if Covenant's performance the previous night had exalted him in her eyes to the rank of a Ranyhyn.

'He has good reason,' answered Covenant flatly.

Gay looked unsure. As if she were reaching out for dangerous knowledge, she asked quickly, 'Because you are a – a "leper"?'

He could see her seriousness. But he felt that he had already said too much about lepers. Such talk compromised his bargain. 'No,' he said, 'he just thinks I'm obnoxious.'

At this, she frowned as if she could hear his complex dishonesty. For a long moment, she studied the floor as if she were using the stone to measure his duplicity. Then she got to her feet, filled Covenant's flask to the brim from her jug. As she turned away, she said in a low voice, 'You do consider me a child.' She walked with a defiant and fearful swing to her hips, as if she believed she was risking her life by treating the Ringthane so insolently.

He watched her young back, and wondered at the pride of people who served others – and at the inner conditions which made telling the truth so difficult.

From Gay, his gaze shifted to the outer edge of Manhome, where Mhoram and Lithe stood together in the sunlight. They were facing each other – she nut-brown and he blue-robed – and arguing like earth and sky. When he concentrated on them, he could make out what they were saying.

'I will,' she insisted.

'No, hear me,' Mhoram replied. 'He does not want it. You will only cause pain for him – and for yourself.'

Covenant regarded them uneasily out of the cool, dim cave. Mhoram's rudder nose gave him the aspect of a man who faced facts squarely; and Covenant felt sure that indeed he did not want whatever Mhoram was arguing against.

The dispute ended shortly. Manethrall Lithe swung away from Mhoram and strode into the recesses of the village. She approached Covenant and surprised him entirely by dropping to her knees, bowing her forehead to the stone before him. With her palms on the floor beside her head, she said, 'I am your servant. You are the Ringthane, master of the Ranyhyn.'

Covenant gaped at the back of her head. For an instant, he did not understand her; in his surprise, he could not conceive of any emotion powerful enough to make a Manethrall bow so low. His face felt suddenly full of shame. 'I don't want a servant,' he grated. But then he saw Mhoram frowning unhappily behind Lithe. He steadied himself, went on more gently, 'The honour of your service is beyond me.'

'No!' she averred without raising her head. 'I saw. The Ranyhyn reared to you.'

He felt trapped. There seemed to be no way to stop her from humiliating herself without making her aware of the humiliation. He had lived without tact or honour for such a long time. But he had promised to be forbearant. And in the distance he had travelled since Mithil Stonedown, he had tasted the consequences of allowing the people of the Land to treat him as if he were some kind of mythic figure. With an effort, he replied gruffly, 'Nevertheless. I'm not used to such things. In my own world, I'm – just a little man. Your homage makes me uneasy.'

Softly, Mhoram sighed his relief, and Lithe raised her head to ask in wonder, 'Is it possible? Can such worlds be, where you are not among the great?'

'Take my word for it.' Covenant drank deeply from his flask.

Cautiously, as if fearful that he did not mean what he had said, she climbed to her feet. She threw back her head and shook her knotted hair. 'Covenant Ringthane, it shall be as you choose. But we do not forget that the Ranyhyn reared to you. If there is any service we may do, only let it be known. You may command us in all things that do not touch the Ranyhyn.'

'There is one thing,' he said, staring at the mountain stone of the ceiling. 'Give Llaura and Pietten a home.'

When he glanced at Lithe, he saw that she was grinning. He snapped fiercely, 'She's one of the Heers of Soaring Woodhelven. And he's just a kid. They've been through enough to earn a little kindness.'

Gently, Mhoram interposed. 'Foamfollower has already spoken to the Manethralls. They have agreed to care for Llaura and Pietten.'

Lithe nodded. 'Such commands are easy. If the Ranyhyn did not challenge us more, we would spend most of our days in sleep.' Still smiling, she left Covenant and cantered out into the sun.

Mhoram also was smiling. 'You look – better, ur-Lord. Are you well?'

Covenant returned his attention to his springwine. 'Quaan asked me the same thing. How should I know? Half the time these days I can't even remember my name. I'm ready to travel, if that's what you're getting at.'

'Good. We must depart as soon as may be. It is pleasant to rest here in safety. But we must go if we are to preserve such safeties. I will tell Quaan and Tuvor to make preparation.'

But before the Lord could leave, Covenant said, 'Tell me something. Exactly why did we come here? You got yourself a Ranyhyn – but we lost four or five days. We could've skipped Morinmoss.'

'Do you wish to discuss tactics? We believe we will gain an advantage by going where Drool cannot expect us to go, and by allowing him time to respond to his defeat at Soaring Woodhelven. Our hope is that he will send out an army. If we arrive too swiftly, the army may still be in Mount Thunder.'

Covenant resisted the plausibility of this. 'You planned to come here long before we were attacked at Soaring Woodhelven. You planned it all along. I want to know why.'

Mhoram met Covenant's demands squarely, but his face tensed as if he did not expect Covenant to like his answer. 'When we made our plans at Revelstone, I saw that good would come of this.'

'You saw?'

'I am an oracle. I see – occasionally.'

'And?'

'And I saw rightly.'

Covenant was not ready to push the question further. 'It must be fun.' But there was little sarcasm in his tone, and Mhoram laughed. His laughter emphasized the kindness of his lips. A moment later, he was able to say without bitterness, 'I would rather see more such good. There is so little in these times.'

As the Lord walked away to ready the company, Foamfollower said, 'My friend, there is hope for you.'

'Forsooth,' Covenant sneered. 'Giant, if I were as big and strong as you, there would always be hope for me.'

'Why? Do you believe that hope is a child of strength?'

'Isn't it? Where do you get hope if you don't get it from power? If I'm wrong – by hell! There's a lot of lepers running around the world confused.'

'How is power judged?' Foamfollower asked with a seriousness Covenant had not expected.

'What?'

'I do not like the way in which you speak of lepers. Where is the value of strength if your enemy is stronger?'

'You assume there is some kind of enemy. I think that's a little too easy. I would like nothing better than – than to blame it on someone else – some enemy who afflicted me. But that's just another kind of suicide. Abdicate the responsibility to keep myself alive.'

'Ah, alive,' Foamfollower countered. 'No, consider further, Covenant. What value has power at all if it is not power over death? If you place hope on anything less, then your hope may mislead you.'

'So?'

'But the power over death is a decision. There cannot be life without death.'

Covenant recognized that this was a fact. But he had not expected such an argument from the Giant. It made him want to get out of the cave into the sunlight. 'Foamfollower,' he muttered, climbing out of his bed, 'you've been thinking again.' But he felt the intensity of Foamfollower's gaze. 'All right. So you're right. Tell me, just where the hell do you get hope?'

Slowly, the Giant rose to his feet. He towered over Covenant until his head nearly touched the ceiling. 'From faith.'

'You've been dealing with humans too long – you're getting hasty. "Faith" is too short a word. What do you mean?'

Foamfollower began picking his way among the flowers. 'I mean the Lords. Consider, Covenant. Faith is a way of living. They have dedicated themselves wholly to the services of the Land. And they have sworn the Oath of Peace – committed themselves to serve the great goal of their lives in only certain ways, to choose death rather than submit to the destruction of passion which blinded High Lord Kevin and brought the Desecration. Come – Can you believe that Lord Mhoram will ever despair? That is the essence of the Oath of Peace. He will never despair, nor ever do what despair commands – murder, desecrate, destroy. And he will never falter, because his Lordship, his service to the Lord, will sustain him. Service enables service.'

'That's not the same thing as hope.' With the Giant, Covenant moved out of Manhome to stand in the sunny flat. The bright light made him duck his head, and as he did so he noticed again the moss stains which charted his robe. Abruptly, he looked back into the cave. There the greenery was arranged among the columbines to resemble moss lines on white samite.

He stifled a groan. As if he were articulating a principle, he said, 'All you need to avoid is irremediable stupidity or unlimited stubbornness.'

'No,' insisted Foamfollower. 'The Lords are not stupid. Look at the Land.' He gestured broadly with his arm as if he expected Covenant to view the whole country from border to border.

Covenant's gaze did not go so far. But he looked blinking beyond the green flat toward the Plains. He heard the distant whistles of the Bloodguard call to the Ranyhyn, and the nickering answer. He noticed the fond wonder of the Winhomes who came out of the cave because they were too eager to wait in Manhome until the Ranyhyn appeared. After a moment, he said, 'In other words, hope comes from the power of what you serve, not from yourself. Hellfire, Giant – you forget who I am.'

'Do I?'

'Anyway, what makes you such an expert on hope? I don't see that you've got anything to despair about.'

'No?' The Giant's lips smiled, but his eyes were hard under his buttressed brows, and his forehead's scar shone vividly. 'Do you forget that I have learned to hate? Do – But let that pass. How if I tell you that I serve you? I, Saltheart Foamfollower, Giant of Seareach and legate of my people?'

Covenant heard echoes in the question, like the distant rack of timbers barely perceived through a high, silent wind, and he recoiled. 'Don't talk like a damned mystic. Say something I can understand.'

Foamfollower reached down to Covenant's chest with one heavy finger, as if he marked a spot on Covenant's mapped robe. 'Unbeliever, you hold the fate of the Land in your hands. Soulcrusher moves against the Lords at the very time when our dreams of Home have been renewed. Must I explain that you have the power to save us, or orphan us until we share whatever doom awaits the Land?'

'Hellfire!' Covenant snapped. 'How many times have I told you that I'm a leper? It's all a mistake. Foul's playing tricks on us.'

The Giant responded simply and quietly. 'Then are you so surprised to learn that I have been thinking about hope?'

Covenant met Foamfollower's eyes under the scarred overhang of his forehead. The Giant watched him as if the hope of the Unhomed were a sinking ship, and Covenant ached with the sense of his own helplessness to save that hope. But then Foamfollower said as if he were coming to Covenant's rescue, 'Be not concerned, my friend. This tale is yet too brief for any of us to guess its ending. As you say, I have spent too much time with hastening humans. My people would laugh greatly to see me – a Giant who has not patience enough for a long story. And the Lords contain much which may yet surprise Soulcrusher. Be of good heart. It may be that you and I have already shared our portion of the terrible purpose of these times.'

Gruffly, Covenant said, 'Giant, you talk too much.' Foamfollower's capacity for gentleness surpassed him. Muttering, Hellfire, to himself, he turned away, went in search of his staff and knife. He could hear the noises of preparations from beyond the flat; and in the village the Winhomes were busy packing food in saddlebags. The company was readying itself, and he did not want to be behind-hand. He found his staff and knife with the bundle of his clothes laid out on a slab of stone amid the flowers, as if on display. Then he got a flustered, eager Winhome to provide him with water, soap, and a mirror. He felt that he owed himself a shave.

But when he had set the mirror so that he could use it, and had doused his face in water, he found Pietten standing solemnly in front of him; and in the mirror he saw that Llaura was behind him. Pietten stared at him as if the Unbeliever were as intangible as a wisp of smoke. And Llaura's face seemed tight, as if she were forcing herself to do something she disliked. She pushed her hand unhappily through her hair, then said, 'You asked the Ramen to make a home for us here.'

He shrugged. 'So did Foamfollower.'

'Why?'

His hearing picked out whole speeches of meaning behind her question. She held his gaze in the mirror, and he saw the memory of a burning tree in her eyes. He asked carefully, 'Do you really think you might get a chance to hit back at Foul? Or be able to use it if you got it?' He looked away at Pietten. 'Leave it to Mhoram and Prothall. You can trust them.'

'Of course.' Her tone said as clearly as words that she was incapable of distrusting the Lords.

'Then take the job you already have. Here's Pietten. Think about what's going to happen to him – more of what you've already been through. He needs help.'

Pietten yawned as if he were awake past his bedtime, and said, 'They hate you.' He sounded as sober as an executioner.

'How?' Llaura returned defiantly. 'Have you observed him? Have you seen how he sits awake at night? Have you seen how his eyes devour the moon? Have you seen his relish for the taste of blood? He is no child – no more.' She spoke as if Pietten were not there listening to her, and Pietten listened as if she were reciting some formula of no importance. 'He is treachery concealed in a child's form. How can I help him?'

Covenant wet his face again and began lathering soap. He could feel Llaura's presence bearing on the back of his neck as he rubbed lather into his beard. Finally, he muttered, 'Try the Ranyhyn. He likes them.'

When she reached over him to take Pietten's hand and draw the child away, Covenant sighed and set the knife to his beard. His hand was unsteady; he had visions of cutting himself. But the blade moved over his skin as smoothly as if it could remember that Atiaran had refused to injure him.

By the time he was done, the company had gathered outside Manhome. He hurried out to join the riders as if he feared that the Quest would leave without him.

The last adjustments of saddles, and saddlebags were in progress, and shortly Covenant stood beside Dura. The condition of the horses surprised him. They all gleamed with good grooming, and looked as well-fed and rested as if they had been under the care of the Ramen since the middle of spring. Some of the Eoman mounts which had been exhausted were now pawing the ground and shaking their manes eagerly.

The whole company seemed to have forgotten where they were going. The warriors were laughing together. Old Birinair chuckled and scolded over the way the Ramen handled his *lillianrill* brands. He treated the Ramen like spoiled children, and appeared to enjoy himself almost too much to hide it behind his dignity. Mhoram sat smiling broadly on Hynaril. And High Lord Prothall stood relaxed by his mount as if he had shed years of care. Only the Bloodguard, already mounted and waiting on their Ranyhyn, remained stern.

The company's good spirits disturbed Covenant like a concealed threat. He understood that it arose in part from rest and reassurance. But he felt sure that it also arose from his meeting with the Ranyhyn. Like the Ramen, the warriors had been impressed; their desire to see in him a new Berek had been vindicated. The white gold wielder had shown himself to be a man of consequence.

The Ranyhyn were terrified! he snapped to himself. They saw Foul's hold on me, and they were terrified. But he did not remonstrate aloud. He had made a promise of forbearance in return for his survival. Despite the tacit dishonesty of allowing his companions to believe what they wished of him, he held himself still.

As the riders laughed and joked, Manethrall Lithe came to stand before them, followed by several other Manethralls and a large group of Cords. When she had the company's attention, she said, 'The Lords have asked for the help of the Ramen in their fight against Fangthane the Render. The Ramen serve the Ranyhyn. We do not leave the Plains of Ra. That is life, and it is good – we ask for nothing else until the end, when all the Earth is Andelain, and man and Ranyhyn live together in peace without wolves or hunger. But we must aid the foes of Fangthane as we can. This we will do. I will go with you. My Cords will go with you if they choose. We will care for your horses on the way. And when you leave them to see Fangthane's hiding in the ground, we will keep them safe. Lords, accept this service as honour among friends and loyalty among allies.'

At once, the Cords Hurn, Thew, Grace, and Rustah stepped forward and avowed their willingness to go wherever Manethrall Lithe would lead them.

Prothall bowed to Lithe in the Ramen fashion. 'The service you offer is great. We know that your hearts are with the Ranyhyn. As friends we would refuse this honour if our need as allies were not so great. The doom of these times compels us to refuse no aid or succour. Be welcome among us. Your hunter skill will greatly ease the hazards of our way. We hope to do honour in return – if we survive our Quest.'

'Kill Fangthane,' said Lithe. 'That will do us honour enough to the end of our days.' She returned Prothall's bow, and all the assembled Ramen joined her.

Then the High Lord spoke to his companions. In a moment, the Quest for the Staff of Law was mounted and ready to ride. Led by Manethrall Lithe and her Cords, the company cantered away from Manhome as if in the village of the Ramen they had found abundant courage.

21

TREACHER'S GORGE

They crossed the Plains northward in confidence and good spirits. No danger or report of danger appeared anywhere along their way. And the Ranyhyn rode the grasslands like live blazonry, challenges uttered in flesh. Foamfollower told gay tales as if he wished to show that he had reached the end of a passing travail. Quaan and his warriors responded with ripostes and jests. And the Ramen entertained them with displays of hunting skill. The company rode late into the first night, in defiance of the dismal moon. And the second night, they camped on the south bank of Roamsedge Ford.

But early the next morning they crossed the Ford and turned northeast up a broad way between Roamsedge and Morinmoss. By mid-afternoon, they reached the east-most edge of the Forest. From there, the Roamsedge, the northern border of the Plains, swung more directly eastward, and the company went on northeast, away from both Morinmoss and the Plains of Ra. That night they slept on the edge of a stark, unfriendly flatland where no people lived and few willingly travelled. The whole region north of them was cut and scarred and darkened like an ancient battleground, a huge field that had been ruined by the shedding of too much blood. Scrub grass, stunted trees, and a few scattered *aliantha* took only slight hold on the uncompromising waste. The company was due south of Mount Thunder.

As the Quest angled northeastward across the land, Mhoram told Covenant some of its history. It spread east to Landsdrop, and formed the natural front of attack for Lord Foul's armies in the ancient wars. From the Fall of the River Landrider to Mount Thunder was open terrain along the great cliff of Landsdrop. The hordes issuing from Foul's Creche could ascend in scores of places to bring battle to the Upper Land. So it was that the first great battles in all the Land's wars against the Despiser occurred across this ravaged plain. Age after age, the defenders strove to halt Lord Foul at Landsdrop, and failed because they could not block all the ways up from the Spoiled Plains and Sarangrave Flat. Then Lord Foul's armies passed westward along the Mithil, and struck deep into the Centre Plains. In the last war, before Kevin Landwaster had been finally driven to invoke the Ritual of Desecration, Lord Foul had crushed through the heart of the Centre Plains, and had turned north to force the Lords to their final battle at Kurash Plenethor, now named Trothgard.

In the presence of so much old death, the riders did not travel loudly. But they sang songs during the first few days, and several times they returned to the legend telling of Berek Halfhand and the Fire-Lions of Mount Thunder. On this wilderland Berek had fought, suffering the deaths of his friends and the loss of his fingers in battle. Here he had met despair, and had fled to the slopes of Gravin Threndor, the Peak of the Fire-Lions. And there he had found both Earthfriendship and Earthpower. It was a comforting song, and the riders sang its refrain together as if they sought to make it true for themselves:

> Berek! Earthfriend! – Help and weal,
> Battle-aid against the foe!
>   Earth gives and answers Power's peal,
>   Ringing, Earthfriend! Help and heal!
>   Clean the Land from bloody death and woe!

They needed its comfort. The hard, reft and harrowed warland seemed to say that Berek's victory was an illusion – that all his Earthfriendship and his Staff of Law and his lineage of Lords, his mighty works and the works of his descendants, amounted to so much scrub grass and charred rock and dust – that the true history of the Land was written here, in the bare topsoil and stone which lay like a litter of graves from the Plains of Ra to Mount Thunder, from Andelain to Landsdrop.

The atmosphere of the region agitated Foamfollower. He strode at Covenant's side with an air of concealed urgency, as if he were repressing desire to break into a run. And he talked incessantly, striving to buoy up his spirits with a constant stream of stories and legends and songs. At first, his efforts pleased the riders, appeased their deepening, hungry gloom like treasure-berries of entertainment. But the Questers were on their way toward the bleak, black prospect of Drool Rockworm, crouched like a bane in the catacombs of Mount Thunder. By the fourth day from Roamsedge Ford, Covenant felt that he was drowning in Giantish talk; and the voices of the warriors when they sang sounded more pleading than confident – like whistling against inexorable night.

With the Ramen to help him, Prothall found rapid ways over the rough terrain. Long after sunset on the fourth day – when the growing moon stood high and baleful in the night sky – the Quest made a weary camp on the edge of Landsdrop.

The next dawn, Covenant resisted the temptation to go and look over the great cliff. He wanted to catch a glimpse of the Lower Land, of the Spoiled Plains and Sarangrave Flat – regions which had filled Foamfollower's talk in the past days. But he had no intention of exposing himself to an attack of vertigo. The fragile stability of his bargain did not cover gratuitous risks. So he remained in the camp when most of his companions went to gaze out over Landsdrop. But later, as the company rode north within a stone's throw of the edge, he asked Lord Mhoram to tell him about the great cliff.

'Ah, Landsdrop,' Mhoram responded quietly. 'There is talk, unfounded even in the oldest legends, that the cleft of Landsdrop was caused by the sacrilege which buried immense banes under Mount Thunder's roots. In a cataclysm that shook its very heart, the Earth heaved with revulsion at the evils it was forced to contain. And the force of that dismay broke the Upper Land from the Lower, lifted it toward the sky. So this cliff reaches from deep in the Southron Range, past the Fall of the River Landrider, through the heart of Mount Thunder, at least half a thousand leagues into the mapless winter of the Northron Climbs. It varies in height from place to place. But it stands across all the Land, and does not allow us to forget.'

The Lord's rough voice only sharpened Covenant's anxiety. As the company rode, he held his gaze away to the west, trusting the wilderland to anchor him against his instinctive fear of heights.

Before noon, the weather changed. Without warning, a sharp wind bristling with grim, preternatural associations sprang out of the north. In moments, black clouds seethed across the sky. Lightning ripped the air; thunder pounded like a crushing of boulders. Then, out of the bawling sky, rain struck like a paroxysm of rage – hit with savage force until it stung. The horses lowered their heads as if they were wincing. Torrents battered the riders, drenched, blinded them. Manethrall Lithe sent her Cords scouting ahead to keep the company from plunging over Landsdrop. Prothall raised his staff with bright fire flaring at its tip to help keep his companions from losing each other. They huddled together, and the Bloodguard positioned the Ranyhyn around them to bear the brunt of the attack.

In the white revelations of the lightning, Prothall's flare appeared dim and frail, and thunder detonated hugely over it as if exploding at the touch of folly. Covenant crouched low on Dura's back, flinched away from the lightning as if the sky were stone which the thunder shattered. He could not see the Cords, did not know what was happening around him; he was constantly afraid that Dura's next step would take him over the cliff. He clenched his eyes to Prothall's flame as if it could keep him from being lost.

The skill and simple toughness of the Ramen preserved the company, kept it moving toward Mount Thunder. But the journey seemed like wandering in the collapse of the heavens. The riders could only be sure of their direction because they were always forcing their way into the maw of the storm. The wind flailed the rain at their faces until their eyes felt lacerated and their cheeks shredded. And the cold drenching stiffened their limbs, paralysed them slowly like the rigour of death. But they kept on as if they were trying to beat down a wall of stone with their foreheads.

For two full days, they pushed onward – felt themselves crumbling under the onslaught of the rain. But they knew neither day nor night, knew nothing but one continuous, pummelling, dark, savage, implacable storm. They rode until they were exhausted – rested on their feet knee-deep in water and mud, gripping the reins of their horses – ate sopping morsels of food half warmed by *lillianrill* fires which Birinair struggled to keep half alive – counted themselves to be sure no one had been lost – and rode again until they were forced by exhaustion to stop again. At times, they felt that Prothall's wan blue flame alone sustained them. Then Lord Mhoram moved among the company. In the lurid lightning, his face appeared awash with water like a foundering wreck; but he went to each Quester, shouted through a howl of wind and rain, the devastating thunder, 'Drool – storm – for us! But he – mistaken! Main force – passes – west! Take heart! Augurs – for us!'

Covenant was too worn and cold to respond. But he heard the generous courage behind Mhoram's words. When the company started forward again, he squinted ahead toward Prothall's flame as if he were peering into a mystery.

The struggle went on, prolonged itself far beyond the point where it felt unendurable. In time, endurance itself became abstract – a mere concept, too impalpable to carry conviction. The lash and riot of the storm reduced the riders to raw, quivering flesh hardly able to cling to their mounts. But Prothall's fire burned on. At each new flash and blast, Covenant reeled in his seat. He wanted nothing in life but a chance to lie down in the mud. But Prothall's fire burned on. It was like a manacle, emprisoning the riders, dragging them forward. In the imminent madness of the torrents, Covenant gritted his gaze as if that manacle were precious to him.

Then they passed the boundary. It was as abrupt as if the wall against which they had thrown themselves like usurped titans had suddenly fallen into mud. Within ten stumbling heartbeats, the end of the storm blew over them, and they stood gasping in a sun-bright noon. They could hear the tumult rushing blindly away. Around them were the remains of the deluge – broken pools and streams and fens, thick mud like wreckage on the battle plain. And before them stood the great ravaged head of Mount Thunder: Gravin Threndor, Peak of the Fire-Lions.

For a long moment, it held them like an aegis of silence – grim, grave and august, like an outcropping of the Earth's heart. The Peak was north and slightly west of them. Taller than Kevin's Watch, above the Upper Land, it seemed to kneel on the edge of the Sarangrave, with its elbows braced on the plateau and its head high over the cliff, fronting the sky in a strange attitude of pride and prayer; and it rose twelve thousand feet over the Defiles Course, which flowed eastward from its feet. Its sides from its crumpled foothills to the raw rock of its crown were bare, not cloaked or defended from storms, snows, besieging time by any trees or grasses, but instead wearing sheer, fragmented cliffs like facets, some as black as obsidian and others as grey as the ash of a granite fire – as if the stone of the Mount were too thick, too charged with power, to bear any gentle kind of life.

There, deep in the hulky chest of the mountain, was the destination of the Quest: Kiril Threndor, Heart of Thunder.

They were still ten leagues from the Peak, but the distance was deceptive. Already that scarred visage dominated the northern horizon; it confronted them over the rift of Landsdrop like an irrefusable demand. Mount Thunder! There Berek Halfhand had found his great revelation. There the Quest for the Staff of Law hoped to regain the future of the Land. And there Thomas Covenant sought release from the impossibility of his dreams. The company stared at the upraised rock as if it searched their hearts, asked them questions which they could not answer.

Then Quaan grinned fiercely, and said, 'At least now we have been washed clean enough for such work.'

That incongruity cracked the trance which held the riders. Several of the warriors burst into laughter as if recoiling from the strain of the past two days, and most of the others chuckled, daring Drool or any enemy to believe that the storm had weakened them. Though nearly prostrated by the exertion of finding a path through the torrents on foot, the Ramen laughed as well, sharing a humour they did not fully understand.

Only Foamfollower did not respond. His eyes were fixed on Mount Thunder, and his brows overhung his gaze as if shielding it from something too bright or hot to be beheld directly.

The Questers found a relatively dry hillock on which to rest and eat, and feed their mounts; and Foamfollower went with them absently. While the company made itself as comfortable as possible for a time, he stood apart and gazed at the mountain as if he were reading secrets in its scored crevices and cliffs. Softly he sang to himself:

> Now we are Unhomed,
>   bereft of root and kith and kin.
> From other mysteries of delight,
>   we set our sails to resail our track;
>   but the winds of life blew not the way we chose,
>   and the land beyond the Sea was lost.

High Lord Prothall let the company rest for as long as he dared in the open plain. Then he moved on again for the remainder of the afternoon, clinging to the edge of Landsdrop as if it were his only hope. Before the storm, Covenant had learned that the sole known entrance to the catacombs of Mount Thunder was through the western chasm of the Soulsease – Treacher's Gorge, the rocky maw which swallowed the river, only to spit it out again eastward on the Lower Land, transmogrified by hidden turbulent depths into the Defiles Course, a stream grey with the sludge and waste of the Wightwarrens. So Prothall's hope lay in his southeastern approach. He believed that by reaching Mount Thunder on the south and moving toward Treacher's Gorge from the east, the company could arrive unseen and unexpected at the Gorge's western exposure. But he took no unnecessary risks. Gravin Threndor stood perilously large against the sky, and seemed already to lean looming toward the company as if the Peak itself were bent to the shape of Drool's malice. He urged the tired Ramen to their best cunning in choosing a way along Landsdrop; and he kept the riders moving until after the sun had set.

But all the time he rode slumped agedly in his saddle, with his head bowed as if he were readying his neck for the stroke of an axe. He seemed to have spent all his strength in pulling his companions through the storm. Whenever he spoke, his long years rattled in his throat.

The next morning, the sun came up like a wound into ashen skies. Grey clouds overhung the earth, and a shuddering wind fell like a groan from the slopes of Mount Thunder. Across the wasteland, the pools of rainwater began to stagnate, as if the ground refused to drink the moisture, leaving it to rot instead. And as they prepared to ride, the Questers heard a low rumble like the march of drums deep in the rock. They could feel the throb in their feet, in their knee joints.

It was the beat of mustering war.

The High Lord answered as if it were a challenge. 'Melenkurion!' he called clearly. 'Arise, champions of the Land! I hear the drums of the Earth! This is the great work of our time!' He swung on to his horse with his blue robe fluttering.

Warhaft Quaan responded with a cheer, 'Hail, High Lord Prothall! We are proud to follow!'

Prothall's shoulders squared. His horse lifted its ears, raised its head, took a few prancing steps as grandly as a Ranyhyn. The Ranyhyn nickered humorously at the sight, and the company rode after Prothall boldly, as if the spirits of the ancient Lords were in them.

They made their way to the slopes of Mount Thunder through the constant buried rumble of the drums. As they found a path across the thickening rubble which surrounded the mountain, the booming subterranean call accompanied them like an exhalation of Despite. But when they started up the first battered sides of the Peak, they forgot the drums; they had to concentrate on the climb. The foothills were like a gnarled stone mantle which Mount Thunder had shrugged from its shoulders in ages long past, and the way westward over the slopes was hard. Time and again, the riders were forced to dismount to lead their mounts down tricky hills or over grey piles of tumbled, ashen rock. The difficulty of the terrain made their progress slow, despite all the Ramen could do to search out the easiest trails. The Peak seemed to lean gravely over them as if watching their small struggles. And down on to them from the towering cliffs came a chilling wind, as cold as winter.

At noon, Prothall halted in a deep gully which ran down the mountainside like a cut. There the company rested and ate. When they were not moving, they could hear the drums clearly, and the cold wind seemed to pounce on them from the cliffs above. They sat in the straight light of the sun and shivered – some at the cold, others at the drums.

During the halt, Mhoram came over to Covenant and suggested that they climb a way up the gully together. Covenant nodded; he was glad to keep himself busy. He followed the Lord up the cut's contorted spine until they reached a break in its west wall. Mhoram entered the break; and when Covenant stepped in behind the Lord, he got a broad, sudden view of Andelain.

From the altitude of the break – between the stone walls – he felt that he was looking down over Andelain from a window in the side of Mount Thunder. The Hills lay richly over all the western horizon, and their beauty took his breath away. He stared hungrily with a feeling of stasis, of perfect pause in his chest, like a quick grip of eternity. The lush, clear health of Andelain shone like a country of stars despite the grey skies and the dull battle roll. He felt obscurely unwilling to breathe. To break the trance, but after a moment his lungs began to hurt for air.

'Here is the Land,' Mhoram whispered. 'Grim, powerful Mount Thunder above us. The darkest banes and secrets of the Earth in the catacombs beneath our feet. The battleground behind. Sarangrave Flat below. And there – priceless Andelain, the beauty of life. Yes. This is the heart of the Land.' He stood reverently, as if he felt himself to be in an august presence.

Covenant looked at him. 'So you brought me up here to convince me that this is worth fighting for.' His mouth twisted on the bitter taste of shame. 'You want something from me – some declaration of allegiance. Before you have to face Drool.' The Cavewights he had slain lay hard and cold in his memory.

'Of course,' the Lord replied. 'But it is the Land itself which asks for your allegiance.' Then he said with sudden intensity, 'Behold, Thomas Covenant. Use your eyes. Look upon it all. Look and listen – hear the drums. And hear me. This is the heart of the Land. It is not the home of the Despiser. He has no place here. Oh, he desires the power of the banes, but his home is in Foul's Creche – not here. He has not depth or sternness or beauty enough for this place, and when he works here it is through ur-viles or Cavewights. Do you see?'

'I see.' Covenant met the Lord's gaze flatly. 'I've already made my bargain – my "peace", if you want to call it that. I'm not going to do any more killing.'

'Your "peace"?' Mhoram echoed in a complex tone. Slowly, the danger dimmed in his eyes. 'Well, you must pardon me. In times of trouble, some Lords behave strangely.' He passed Covenant and started back down the gully.

Covenant remained in the window for a moment, watching Mhoram go. He had not missed the Lord's oblique reference to Kevin; but he wondered what kinship Mhoram saw between himself and the Landwaster. Did the Lord believe himself capable of that kind of despair?

Muttering silently, Covenant returned to the company. He saw a measuring look in the eyes of the warriors; they were trying to assess what had occurred between him and Lord Mhoram. But he did not care what portents they read into him. When the company moved on, he led Dura up the side of the gully, blank to the shifting shale which more than once dropped him to his hands and knees, scratching and bruising him dangerously. He was thinking about the Celebration of Spring, about the battle of Soaring Woodhelven, about children and Llaura and Pietten and Atiaran and the nameless Unfettered One and Lena and Triock and the warrior who had died defending him – thinking, and striving to tell himself that his bargain was secure, that he was not angry enough to risk fighting again.

That afternoon, the company struggled on over the arduous ground, drawing slowly higher as they worked westward. They caught no glimpses of their destination. Even when the sun fell low in the sky, and the roar of waters became a distinct accompaniment to the buried beat of the drums, they were still not able to see the Gorge. But then they entered a sheer, sheltered ravine in the mountainside. From this ravine a rift too narrow for the horses angled away into the rock, and through it they could hear a snarling current. In the ravine the riders left their mounts under the care of the Cords. They went ahead on foot down the rift as it curved into the mountain and then broke out of the cliff no more than a hundred feet directly above Treacher's Gorge.

They no longer heard the drums; the tumult of the river smothered every sound but their own half-shouts. The walls of the chasm were high and sheer, blocking the horizon on either side. But through the spray that covered them like a mist, they could see the Gorge itself – the tight rock channel constricting the river until it appeared to scream, and the wild, white, sunset-flame-plumed water thrashing as if it fought against its own frantic rush. From nearly a league away to the west, the river came writhing down the Gorge, and sped below the company into the guts of the mountain as if sucked into an abyss. Above the Gorge, the setting sun hung near the horizon like a ball of blood in the leaden sky; and the light gave a shade of fire to the few hardy trees that clung to the rims of the chasm as if rooted by duty. But within Treacher's Gorge was nothing but spray and sheer stone walls and tortured waters.

The roar inundated Covenant's ears, and the mist-wet rock seemed to slip under his feet. For an instant, the cliffs reeled; he could feel the maw of Mount Thunder gaping for him. Then he snatched himself back into the rift, stood with his back pressed against the rock, hugged his chest and fought not to gasp.

There was activity around him. He heard shouts of surprise and fear from the warriors at the end of the rift, heard Foamfollower's strangled howl. But he did not move. He clenched himself against the rock in the mist and roar of the river until his knees steadied, and the scream of slippage eased in his feet. Only then did he go to find out what caused the distress of his companions. He kept one hand braced on the wall and moved the other from shoulder to shoulder among the company as he went forward.

Between Covenant and the cliff, Foamfollower struggled. Two Bloodguard clung to his arms, and he battered them against the sides of the rift, hissing rapaciously, 'Release me! Release – ! I want them!' as if he wished to leap down into the Gorge.

'No!' Abruptly, Prothall stood before the Giant. The backlight of the sunset dimmed his face as he stood silhouetted against the glow with his arms wide and his staff held high. He was old, and only half the Giant's size. But the orange-red fire seemed to expand him, make him taller, more full of authority. 'Rockbrother! Master yourself! By the Seven! Do you rave?'

At that, Foamfollower threw off the Bloodguard. He caught the front of Prothall's robe, heaved the High Lord into the air, pinned him against the wall. Into his face, the Giant wheezed as if he were choking with rage, 'Rave? Do you accuse me?'

The Bloodguard sprang toward Foamfollower. But a shout from Mhoram stopped them. Prothall hung clamped against the stone like a handful of old rags, but his eyes did not flinch. He repeated, 'Do you rave?'

For one horrible moment, Foamfollower held the High Lord as if he meant to murder him with one huge squeeze of his fist. Covenant tried to think of something to say, some way to intervene, but could not. He had no conception of what had happened to Foamfollower.

Then from behind Covenant First Mark Tuvor said clearly, 'A Rave? In one of the Seareach Giants? Impossible.'

As if impaled by Tuvor's assertion, Foamfollower broke into a convulsion of coughing. The violence of his reaction knotted his gnarled frame. He lowered Prothall, then collapsed backward, falling with a thud against the opposite wall. Slowly, his paroxysm changed into a low chuckle like the glee of hysteria.

Heard through the groaning of the river, that sound made Covenant's skin crawl like a slimy caress. He could not abide it. Driven by a need to learn what had befallen Foamfollower, he moved forward to look into the Gorge.

There, braced now against his vertigo and the inundation of the river roar, he saw what had ignited Foamfollower. Ah, Giant! he groaned. To kill – ! Below him and barely twenty feet above the level of the river was a narrow roadway like a ledge in the south wall of the Gorge. And along the roadway to the beat of unheard drums marched an army of Cavewights out of Mount Thunder. Captained by a wedge of ur-viles, file after file of the gangrel creatures jerked out of the mountain and tramped along the ledge with a glare of lust in their laval eyes. Thousands had already left their Wightwarrens; and behind them the files continued as if Mount Thunder were spewing all the hordes of its inhabiting vermin on to the undefended Earth.

Foamfollower!

For a moment, Covenant's heart beat to the rhythm of the Giant's pain. He could not bear to think that Foamfollower and his people might lose their hope of Home because of creatures like those.

Is killing the only answer?

Numbly, half blindly, he began looking for the way in which Foamfollower had meant to reach the ledge and the Cavewights.

He found it easily enough; it looked simple for anyone not timorous of heights. There was a rude, slick stair cut into the rock of the south wall from the rift down to the roadway. Opposite it were steps which went from the rift up to the top of the Gorge. They were as grey, sprayworn and old as native stone.

Lord Mhoram had come up behind Covenant. His voice reached dimly through the river roar. 'This is the ancient Look of Treacher's Gorge. That part of the First Ward which tells of this place is easily understood. It was formed for the watch and concealment of the betrayers. For here at Treacher's Gorge, Lord Foul the Despiser revealed his true self to High Lord Kevin. Here was struck the first blow of the open war which ended in the Ritual of Desecration.

'Before that time, Kevin Landwaster doubted Lord Foul without knowing why – for the Despiser had enacted no ill which Kevin could discover – and he showed trust for Lord Foul out of shame for his unworthy doubt. Then, through the Despiser's plotting, a message came to the Council of Lords from the Demondim in Mount Thunder. The message asked the Lords to come to the Demondim loreworks, the spawning crypts where the ur-viles were made, to meet with the loremasters, who claimed knowledge of a secret power.

'Clearly, Lord Foul intended for Kevin to go to Mount Thunder. But the High Lord doubted, and did not go. Then he was ashamed of his doubt, and sent in his stead some of his truest friends and strongest allies. So a high company of the Old Lords rafted as was their wont down the Soulsease through Andelain to Mount Thunder. And here, in the roar and spray and ill of Treacher's Gorge, they were ambushed by ur-viles. They were slaughtered, and their bodies sent to the abyss of the mountain. Then marched armies like these out of the catacombs, and the Land was plunged all unready into war.

'That long conflict went on battle after death-littered battle without hope. High Lord Kevin fought bravely. But he had sent his friends into ambush. Soon he began his midnight meetings with despair – and there was no hope.'

The seductive, dizzy rush of the river drained Covenant's resistance. Spray beaded on his face like sweat.

Foamfollower had wanted to do the same thing – leap into the writhing allure of the Gorge – fall on the Cavewights from ambush.

With an effort that made him moan through his clenched teeth, Covenant backed away from the Look. Gripping himself against the wall, he asked without apparent emotion, 'Is he still laughing?'

Mhoram appeared to understand. 'No. Now he sits and quietly sings the song of the Unhomed, and gives no sign.'

Foamfollower! Covenant breathed. 'Why did you stop the Bloodguard? He might've hurt Prothall.'

The Lord turned his back on Treacher's Gorge to face Covenant. 'Saltheart Foamfollower is my friend. How could I interfere?' A moment later, he added, 'The High Lord is not defenceless.'

Covenant persisted. 'Maybe a Raver – '

'No.' Mhoram's flat assertion acknowledged no doubt. 'Tuvor spoke truly. No Raver has the might to master a Giant.'

'But something – ' Covenant groped – 'something is hurting him. He – he doesn't believe those omens. He thinks – Drool – or something – is going to prevent the Giants from going Home.'

Mhoram's reply was so soft that Covenant was forced to read it on his crooked lips. 'So do I.'

Foamfollower!

Covenant looked down the rift at the Giant. In the darkness Foamfollower sat like a lump of shale against one wall, singing quietly and staring at invisible visions on the stone before him. The sight brought up a surge of sympathetic anger in Covenant, but he clamped it down, clutched his bargain. The walls of the rift leaned in toward him, like suffocating fear, dark wings. He thrust himself past the Giant and out toward the ravine.

Before long, the company gathered there for supper. They ate by the light of one dim *lillianrill* torch; and when the meal was done, they tried to get some sleep. Covenant felt that rest was impossible; he sensed the army of Cavewights unrolling like a skein of destruction for the weaving of the Land's death. But the ceaseless roar of the river lulled him until he relaxed against the ground. He dozed slightly, with the drums of war throbbing in the rock under him.

Later, he found himself sharply awake. The red moon had passed the crest of Mount Thunder, and now glared straight down on the ravine. He guessed that midnight was past. At first, he thought that the moon had roused him with its nearly full stare. But then he realized that the vibration of the drums was gone from the rock. He glanced around the camp, and saw Tuvor whispering with High Lord Prothall. The next moment, Tuvor began waking the sleepers.

Soon the warriors were alert and ready. Covenant had his knife in the belt of his robe, his staff in his hand. Birinair held aloft a rod with a small flame flickering its tip, and in that uncertain light Mhoram and Prothall stood together with Manethrall Lithe, Warhaft Quaan, and the First Mark. Dim shadows shifted like fear and resolution across Prothall's face. His voice sounded weak with age as he said, 'Now is our last hour of open sky. The outpouring of Drool's army has ended. Those of us who will must go into the catacombs of Mount Thunder. We must take this chance to enter, while Drool's attention is still with his army – before he can perceive that we are not where he thinks us to be.

'Now is the time for those who would to lay down the Quest. There can be no retreat, or escape after failure, in the Wightwarrens. The Quest has already been bravely served. None who now lay it down need feel shame.'

Carefully, Quaan said, 'Do you turn back, High Lord?'

'Ah, no,' sighed Prothall. 'The hand of these times is upon me. I dare not falter.'

Then Quaan replied, 'Can a Eoman of the Warward of Lord's Keep turn back when the High Lord leads? Never!'

And the Eoman echoed, 'Never!'

Covenant wondered where Foamfollower was, what the Giant would do. For himself, he felt intuitively sure that he had no choice, that his dream would only release him by means of the Staff of Law. Or by death.

The next moment, Manethrall Lithe spoke to Prothall. Her head was back, and her slim form was primed as if she were prepared to explode. 'I gave my word. Your horses will be tended. The Cords will preserve them in hope of your return. But I – ' She shook her bound hair as if she were defying herself. 'I will go with you. Under

325

the ground.' Prothall's protest she stopped with a sharp gesture. 'You set an example I must follow. How could I stand before a Ranyhyn again, if I come so far only to turn away when the peril becomes great? And I feel something more. The Ramen know the sky, the open earth. We know air and grass. We do not lose our way in darkness – the Ranyhyn have taught our feet to be sure. I feel that I will always know my way – outward. You may have need of me, though I am far from the Plains of Ra, and from myself.'

The shadows formed Prothall's face into a grimace, but he responded quietly, 'I thank you, Manethrall. The Ramen are brave friends of the Land.' Casting his eyes over the whole company, he said, 'Come, then. The outcome of our Quest awaits. Whatever may befall us – as long as there are people to sing, they will sing that in this dark hour the Land was well championed. Now be true to the last.' Without waiting for an answer, he went out of the bloody moonlight into the rift.

The warriors let Covenant follow behind the two Lords as if according him a position of respect. Prothall and Mhoram walked side by side; and when they neared the Look, Covenant could see from between them Foamfollower standing at the edge of the cliff. The Giant had his palms braced above his head on either wall. His back was to the Lords; he stared into the bleak, blood-hued writhing of the river. His huge form was dark against the vermilion sky.

When the Lords came near him, he said as if he were speaking back to them from the Gorge, 'I remain here. My watch. I will guard you. Drool's army will not trap you in Mount Thunder while I live.' A moment later, he added as if he had recognized the bottom of himself, 'From here I will not smell the Wightwarrens.' But his next words carried an echo of old Giantish humour. 'The catacombs were not made to accommodate creatures the size of Giants.'

'You choose well,' murmured Prothall. 'We need your protection. But do not remain here after the full moon. If we do not return by that time, we are lost, and you must go to warn your people.'

Foamfollower answered as if in reply to some other voice, 'Remember the Oath of Peace. In the maze where you go, it is your lifeline. It preserves you against Soulcrusher's purposes, hidden and savage. Remember the Oath. It may be that hope misleads. But hate – hate corrupts. I have been too quick to hate. I become like what I abhor.'

'Have some respect for the truth,' Mhoram snapped. The sudden harshness of his tone startled Covenant. 'You are Saltheart Foamfollower of the Seareach Giants, Rockbrother to the men of the Land. That name cannot be taken from you.'

But Covenant had heard no self-pity in the Giant's words – only recognition and sorrow. Foamfollower did not speak again. He stood as still as the walls against which he braced himself – stood like a statue carved to occupy the Look.

The Lords spent no more time with him. Already the night was waning, and they wanted to enter the mountain before daylight.

The Questers took positions. Prothall, Birinair, and two Blood-guard followed First Mark Tuvor. Then came Mhoram, Lithe, Bannor, Covenant, and Korik. Then came Warhaft Quaan, his fourteen warriors, and the last four Bloodguard.

They were only twenty-nine against all of Drool Rockworm's unknown might.

They strung a line of *clingor* from Tuvor to the last Bloodguard. In single file, they started down the slick stair into Treacher's Gorge.

22

THE CATACOMBS OF MOUNT THUNDER

Drool's moon embittered the night like a consummation of gall. Under it, the river thrashed and roared in Treacher's Gorge as if it were being crushed. Spray and slick-wet moss made the stair down from the Look as treacherous as a quagmire.

Covenant bristled with trepidations. At first, when his turn to begin the descent had come, his dread had paralysed him. But when Bannor had offered to carry him, he had found the pride to make himself move. In addition to the *clingor* line, Bannor and Korik held his staff like a railing for him. He went torturously down into the Gorge as if he were striving to lock his feet on the stone of each step.

The stair dropped irregularly from the cliff into the wall of the Gorge. Soon the company was creeping into the loud chasm, led only by the light of Birinair's torch. The crimson froth of the river seemed to leap up at them like a hungry plague as they neared the roadway. Each step was slicker than the one before. Behind him, Covenant heard a gasp as one of the warriors slipped. The low cry carried terror like the quarrel of a crossbow. But the Bloodguard anchoring the line were secure; the warrior quickly regained his footing.

The descent dragged on. Covenant's ankles began to ache with the increasing uncertainty of his feet. He tried to think his soles into the rock, make them part of the stone through sheer concentration.

And he gripped his staff until his palms were so slick with sweat that the wood seemed to be pulling away from him. His knees started to quiver.

But Bannor and Korik upheld him. The distance to the roadway shrank. After several long, bad moments, the threat of panic receded.

Then he reached the comparative safety of the ledge. He stood in the midst of the company between the Gorge wall and the channel of the river. Above them, the slash of sky had begun to turn grey, but that lightening only emphasized the darkness of the Gorge. Birinair's lone torch flickered as if it were lost in a wilderland.

The Questers had to yell to make themselves understood over the tumult of the current. Briskly, Quaan gave marching orders to his Eoman. The warriors checked over their weapons. With a few gestures and a slight nod or two, Tuvor made his last arrangements with the Bloodguard. Covenant gripped his staff, and assured himself of his Stonedownor knife – Atiaran's knife. He had a vague impression that he had forgotten something. But before he could try to think what it was, he was distracted by shouts.

Old Birinair was yelling at High Lord Prothall. For once, the Hearthrall seemed careless of his gruff dignity. Against the roar of the river, he thrust his seamed and quivering face at Prothall, and barked, 'You cannot! The risk!'

Prothall shook his head negatively.

'You cannot lead! Allow me!'

Again, Prothall silently refused.

'Of course!' shouted Birinair, struggling to make his determination carry over the howl of water. 'You must not! I can! I know the ways! Of course. Are you alone old enough to study? I know the old maps. No fool, you know – if I look old, and – ' he faltered momentarily – 'and useless. You must allow me!'

Prothall strove to shout without sounding angry. 'Time is short! We must not delay, Birinair, old friend, I cannot put the first risk of this Quest on to another. It is my place.'

'Fool!' spat Birinair, daring any insolence to gain his point. 'How will you see?'

'See?'

'Of course!' The Hearthrall quivered with sarcasm. 'You will go before! Risk all! Light the way with Lords-fire! Fool! Drool will see you before you reach Warrenbridge!'

Prothall at last understood. 'Ah, that is true.' He sagged as if the realization hurt him. 'Your light is quieter than mine. Drool will surely sense our coming if I make use of my staff.' Abruptly, he turned to one side, angry now. 'Tuvor!' he commanded. 'Hearthrall Birinair leads! He will light our way in my place. Ward him well,

328

Tuvor! Do not let this old friend suffer my perils.'

Birinair drew himself up, rediscovering dignity in his responsibility. He extinguished the rod he carried, and gave it to a warrior to pack away with the rest of his brands. Then he stroked the end of his staff, and a flame sprang up there. With a brusque beckon, he raised his fire and started stiffly down the roadway toward the maw of Mount Thunder.

At once, Terrel and Korik passed the Hirebrand and took scouting positions twenty feet ahead of him. Two other Bloodguard placed themselves just behind him, and after them went Prothall and Mhoram together, then two more Bloodguard followed singly by Manethrall Lithe, Covenant, and Bannor. Next marched Quaan with his Eoman in files of three, leaving the last two Bloodguard to bring up the rear. In that formation, the company moved toward the entrance to the catacombs.

Covenant looked upward briefly to try to catch a last glimpse of Foamfollower in the Look. But he did not see the Giant; the Gorge was too full of darkness. And the roadway demanded his attention. He went into the rock under Foamfollower without any wave or sign of farewell.

Thus the company strode away from daylight – from sun and sky and open air and grass and possibility of retreat – and took their Quest into the gullet of Mount Thunder.

Covenant went into that demesne of night as if into a nightmare. He was not braced for the entrance to the catacombs. He had approached it without fear; the relief of having survived the descent from the Look had rendered him temporarily immune to panic. He had not said farewell to Foamfollower; he had forgotten something; but these pangs were diffused by a sense of anticipation, a sense that his bargain would bring him out of the dream with his ability to endure intact.

But the sky above – an openness of which he had hardly been aware – was cut off as if by an axe, and replaced by the huge stone weight of the mountain, so heavy that its aura alone was crushing. In his ears, its mass seemed to rumble like silent thunder. The river's roaring mounted in the gullet of the cave, adumbrated itself as if the constricted pain of the current were again constricted into keener and louder pain. The spray was as thick as rain; ahead of the company, Birinair's flame burned dim and penumbral, nearly quenched by the wet air. And the surface of the roadway was hazardous, littered with holes and rocks and loose shale. Covenant strained his attention as if he were listening for a note of sense in the gibberish of his experience, and under this alertness he wore his hope of escape like a buckler.

In more ways than one, he felt that it was his only protection. The company seemed pathetically weak, defenceless against the dark-dwelling Cavewights and ur-viles. Stumbling through night broken only at the solitary point of Birinair's fire, he predicted that the company would be observed soon. Then a report would go to Drool, and the inner forces of the Wightwarrens would pour forth, and the army would be recalled – what chance had Foamfollower against so many thousands of Cavewights? – and the company would be crushed like a handful of presumptuous ants. And in that moment of resolution or death would come his own rescue or defeat. He could not envision any other outcome.

With these thoughts, he walked as if he were listening for the downward rush of an avalanche.

After some distance, he realized that the sound of the river was changing. The roadway went inward almost horizontally, but the river was falling into the depths of the rock. The current was becoming a cataract, an abysmal plummet like a plunge into death. The sound of it receded slowly as the river crashed farther and farther away from the lip of the chasm.

Now there was less spray in the air to dim Birinair's flame. With less dampness to blur it, the stone wall showed more of its essential granite. Between the wall and the chasm, Covenant clung to the reassurance of the roadway. When he put a foot down hard, he could feel the solidity of the ledge jolt from his heel to the base of his spine.

Around him, the cave had become like a tunnel except for the chasm on the left. He fought his apprehension by concentrating on his feet and the Hirebrand's flame. The river fell helplessly, and its roar faded like fingers scraping for a lost purchase. Soon he began to hear the moving noises of the company. He turned to try to see the opening of the Gorge, but either the road had been curving gradually, or the opening had been lost in the distance; he saw nothing behind him but night as unmitigated as the blackness ahead.

But after a time he felt that the looming dark was losing its edge. Some change in the air attenuated the midnight of the catacombs. He stared ahead, trying to clarify the perception. No one spoke; the company hugged its silence as if in fear that the walls were capable of hearing.

Shortly, however, Birinair halted. Covenant, Lithe, and the Lords quickly joined the old Hirebrand. With him stood Terrel.

'Warrenbridge lies ahead,' said the Bloodguard. 'Korik watches. There are sentries.' He spoke softly, but after the long silence his voice sounded careless of hazards.

'Ah, I feared that,' whispered Prothall. 'Can we approach?'

'Rocklight makes dark shadows. The sentries stand atop the span. We can approach within bowshot.'

Mhoram called quietly for Quaan while Prothall asked, 'How many sentries?'

Terrel replied, 'Two.'

'Only two?'

The Bloodguard shrugged fractionally. 'They suffice. Between them lies the only entrance to the Wightwarrens.'

But Prothall breathed again. 'Only two?' He seemed to be groping to recognize a danger he could not see.

While the High Lord considered, Mhoram spoke rapidly to Quaan. At once, the Warhaft turned to his Eoman, and shortly two warriors stood by Terrel, unslinging their bows. They were tall, slim Wood-helvennin, and in the pale light their limbs hardly looked brawny enough to bend their stiff bows.

For a moment longer, Prothall hesitated, pulling at his beard as if he were trying to tug a vague impression into consciousness. But then he thrust his anxiety down, gave Terrel a sharp nod. Briskly, the Bloodguard led the two warriors away toward the attenuated night ahead.

Prothall whispered intently to the company, 'Have a care. Take no risk without my order. My heart tells me there is peril here – some strange danger which Kevin's Lore names – but now I cannot recall it. Ah, memory! That knowledge is so dim and separate from what we have known since the Desecration. Think, all of you. Take great care.'

Walking slowly, he went forward beside Birinair, and the company followed.

Now the light became steadily clearer – an orange-red, rocky glow like that which Covenant had seen long ago in his brief meeting with Drool in Kiril Threndor. Soon the Questers could see that in a few hundred yards the cave took a sharp turn to the right, and at the same time the ceiling of the tunnel rose as if there were a great vault beyond the bend.

Before they had covered half the distance, Korik joined them to guide them to a safe vantage. On the way, he pointed out the position of Terrel and the two warriors. They had climbed partway up the right wall, and were kneeling on a ledge in the angle of the bend.

Korik led the company close to the river cleft until they reached a sheer stone wall. The chasm appeared to leave them – vanish straight into the rock which turned the road toward the night – but light shone over this rock as well as through the chasm. The rock was not a wall, but rather a huge boulder sitting like a door ajar before the entrance to an immense chamber. Terrel had taken the two warriors to a position from which they could fire their shafts over this boulder.

Korik guided Prothall, Mhoram, and Covenant across the shadow cast by the boulder until they could peer to the left around its edge. Covenant found himself looking into a high, flat-floored cavern. The chasm of the river swung around behind the boulder, and cut at right angles to its previous direction straight through the centre of the vault, then disappeared into the far wall. So the roadway went no farther along the river's course. But there were no other openings in the outer half of the cavern.

At that point, the chasm was at least fifty feet wide. The only way across it was a massive bridge of native stone which filled the middle of the vault.

Carefully, Mhoram whispered, 'Only two. They are enough. Pray for a true aim. There will be no second chance.'

At first, Covenant saw no guards. His eyes were held by two pillars of pulsing, fiery rocklight which stood like sentries on either side of the bridge crest. But he forced himself to study the bridge, and shortly he discerned two black figures on the span, one beside each pillar. They were nearly invisible so close to the rocklight.

'Ur-viles,' the High Lord muttered. 'By the Seven! I must remember! Why are they not Cavewights? Why does Drool waste ur-viles on such duty?'

Covenant hardly listened to Prothall's uneasiness. The rocklight demanded his attention; it seemed to hold affinities for him that he could not guess. By some perverse logic of its pulsations, he felt himself made aware of his wedding band. The Droolish, powerful glow made his hand itch around his ring like a reminder that its promise of cherishing had failed. Grimly, he clenched his fist.

Prothall gripped himself, said heavily to Korik, 'Make the attempt. We can only fail.'

Without a word, Korik nodded up at Terrel.

Together, two bowstrings thrummed flatly.

The next instant, the ur-viles were gone. Covenant caught a glimpse of them dropping like black pebbles into the chasm.

The High Lord sighed his relief. Mhoram turned away from the vault, threw a salute of congratulations toward the two archers, then hurried back to give explanations and orders to the rest of the company. From the Eoman came low murmured cheers, and the noises of a relaxation of battle tension.

'Do not lower your guard!' Prothall hissed. 'The danger is not past. I feel it.'

Covenant stood where he was, staring into the rocklight, clenching his fist. Something that he did not understand was happening.

'Ur-Lord,' Prothall asked softly, 'what do you see?'

'Power.' The interruption irritated him. His voice scraped roughly in his throat. 'Drool's got enough to make you look silly.' He raised his left fist. 'It's daylight outside.' His ring burned blood-red, throbbed to the pulse of the rocklight.

Prothall frowned at the ring, concentrating fiercely. His lips were taut over his teeth as he muttered, 'This is not right. I must remember. Rocklight cannot do this.'

Mhoram approached, and said before he saw what was between Covenant and Prothall, 'Terrel has rejoined us. We are ready to cross.' Prothall nodded inattentively. Then Mhoram noticed the ring. Covenant heard a sound as if Mhoram were grinding his teeth. The Lord reached out, clasped his hand over Covenant's fist.

A moment later, he turned and signalled to the company. Quaan led his Eoman forward with the Bloodguard. Prothall looked distracted, but he went with Birinair into the vault. Automatically, Covenant followed them toward Warrenbridge.

Tuvor and another Bloodguard went ahead of the High Lord. They neared the bridge, inspecting it to be sure that the span was truly safe before the Lords crossed.

Covenant wandered forward as if in a trance. The spell of the rocklight grew on him. His ring began to feel hot. He had to make an effort of consciousness to wonder why his ring was bloody rather than orange-red like the glowing pillars. But he had no answer. He felt a change coming over him that he could not resist or measure or even analyse. It was as if his ring were confusing his senses, turning them on their pivots to peer into unknown dimensions.

Tuvor and his comrade started up the bridge. Prothall held the company back, despite the inherent danger of remaining in the open light. He stared after Tuvor and yanked at his beard with a hand which trembled agedly.

Covenant felt the spell mastering him. The cavern began to change. In places, the rock walls seemed thinner, as if they were about to become transparent. Quaan and Lithe and the warriors grew transparent as well, approached the evanescence of wraiths. Prothall and Mhoram appeared solider, but Prothall flickered where Mhoram was steady. Only the Bloodguard showed no sign of dissipating, of losing their essence in mist – the Bloodguard and the ring. Covenant's own flesh now looked so vague that he feared his ring would fall through it to the stone. At his shoulder, Bannor stood – hard, implacable and dangerous, as if the Bloodguard's mere touch might scatter his beclouded being to the winds.

He was drifting into transience. He tried to clench himself; his fingers came back empty.

Tuvor neared the crest of the span. The bridge seemed about to crumble under him – he appeared so much solider than the stone.

Then Covenant saw it – a loop of shimmering air banded around the centre of the bridge, standing flat across the roadway and around under the span and back. He did not know what it was, understood nothing about it, except that it was powerful.

Tuvor was about to step into it.

With an effort like a convulsion, Covenant started to fight, resist the spell. Some intuition told him that Tuvor would be killed. Even a leper! he adjured himself. This was not his bargain; he had not promised to stand silent and watch men die. Hellfire! Then, with recovered rage, he cried again, Hellfire!

'Stop!' he gasped. 'Can't you see?'

At once, Prothall shouted, 'Tuvor! Do not move!' Wheeling on Covenant, he demanded, 'What is it? What do you see?'

The violence of his rage brought back some of the solidity to his vision. But Prothall still appeared dangerously evanescent. Covenant jerked up his ring, spat, 'Get them down. Are you blind? It's not the rocklight. Something else up there.'

Mhoram recalled Tuvor and his companion. But for a moment Prothall only stared in blank fear at Covenant. Then, abruptly, he struck his staff on the stone and ejaculated, 'Ur-viles! And rocklight just there – as anchors! Ah, I am blind, blind! They tend the power!'

Incredulously, Mhoram whispered, 'A Word of Warning?'

'Yes!'

'Is it possible? Has Drool entirely mastered the Staff? Can he speak such might?'

Prothall was already on his way toward the bridge. Over his shoulder, he replied, 'He has Lord Foul to teach him. We have no such help.' A moment later, he strode up the span with Tuvor close behind him.

The spell reached for Covenant again. But he knew it better now, and held it at bay with curses. He could still see the shimmering loop of the Word as Prothall neared it.

The High Lord approached slowly, and at last halted a step before the Word. Gripping his staff in his left hand, he held his right arm up with the palm forward like a gesture of recognition. With a rattling cough, he began to sing. Constantly repeating the same motif, he sang cryptically in a language Covenant did not understand – a language so old that it sounded grizzled and hoary. Prothall sang it softly, intimately, as if he were entering into private communion with the Word of Warning.

Gradually, vaguely, like imminent mist, the Word became visible to the company. In the air opposite Prothall's palm, an indistinct shred of red appeared, coalesced, like a fragment of an unseen tapestry. The pale, hanging red expanded until a large, rough circle was centred opposite his palm. With extreme caution – singing all the while – he raised his hand to measure the height of the Word, moved sideways to judge its configuration. Thus in tatters the company saw the barrier which opposed them. And as Covenant brought more of himself to the pitch of his stiff rage, his own perception of the Word paled until he saw only as much of it as the others did.

At last, Prothall lowered his hand and ceased his song. The shreds vanished. He came tightly down the bridge as if he were only holding himself erect by the simple strength of his resolution. But his gaze was full of comprehension and the measure of risks.

'A Word of Warning,' he reported sternly, 'set here by the power of the Staff of Law to inform Drool if his defences were breached – and to break Warrenbridge at the first touch.' His tone carried a glimpse of a plunge into the chasm. 'It is a work of great power. No Lord since the Desecration has been capable of such a feat. And even if we had the might to undo it, we would gain nothing, for Drool would be warned. Still, there is one sign in our favour. Such a Word cannot be maintained without constant attention. It must be tended, else it decays – though not speedily enough for our purpose. That Drool set ur-viles here as sentries perhaps shows that his mind is elsewhere.'

Wonderful! Covenant growled corrosively. Terrific! His hands itched with an intense urge to throttle someone.

Prothall continued: 'If Drool's eyes are turned away, it may be that we can bend the Word without breaking.' He took a deep breath, then asserted, 'I believe it can be done. This Word is not as pure and dangerous as might be.' He turned to Covenant. 'But I fear for you, ur-Lord.'

'For me?' Covenant reacted as if the High Lord had accused him of something. 'Why?'

'I fear that the mere closeness of your ring to the Word may undo it. So you must come last. And even then we may be caught within the catacombs, with no bridge to bear us out again.'

Last? He had a sudden vision of being forsaken or trapped here, blocked by that deep cleft from the escape he needed. He wanted to protest. Let me go first. If I can make it, anybody can. But he saw the folly of that argument. Forbear, he urged himself. Keep the bargain. His fear made him sound bitter as he grated, 'Get on with it. They're bound to send some new guards one of these days.'

Prothall nodded. With a last measuring look at Covenant, he turned away. He and Mhoram went up on to the bridge to engage the Word.

Tuvor and Terrel followed carrying coils of *clingor* which they attached to the Lords' waists and anchored at the foot of the bridge. Thus secured against the collapse of the span, Prothall and Mhoram ascended cautiously until they were only an arm's length from the invisible Word. There they knelt together and started their song.

When the bottom of the Word became visible in crimson, they placed their staffs parallel to it on the stone before them. Then, with torturous care, they rolled their staffs directly under the iridescent power. For one bated moment, they remained still in an attitude of prayer as if beseeching their wood not to interrupt the current flowing past their faces. A heart-stopping flicker replied in the red shimmer. But the Lords went on singing – and shortly the Word steadied.

Bracing themselves, they started the most difficult part of their task. They began lifting the inner ends of their staffs.

With a quick intake of wonder and admiration, the company saw the lower edge of the Word bend, leaving a low, tented gap below it.

When the peak of the gap was more than a foot high, the Lords froze. Instantly, Bannor and two other Bloodguard dashed up the bridge, unrolling a rope as they ran. One by one, they crawled through the gap and took their end of the lifeline to safe ground beyond the span.

As soon as Bannor had attached his end of the rope. Mhoram took hold of Prothall's staff. The High Lord wormed through the gap, then held the staffs for Mhoram. By the time Mhoram had regained his position beside Prothall, old Birinair was there and ready to pass. Behind him in rapid single file went the Eoman, followed by Quaan and Lithe.

In turn, Tuvor and Terrel slipped under the Word and anchored their ropes to the two Lords beyond the chasm. Then, moving at a run, the last Bloodguard slapped the central lifeline around Covenant and made their way through the gap.

He was left alone.

In a cold sweat of anger and fear, he started up the bridge. He felt the two pillars of rocklight as if they were scrutinizing him. He went up the span fiercely, cursing Foul, and cursing himself for his fear. He did not give a glance to the chasm. Staring at the gap, he ground his rage into focus, and approached the shimmering tapestry of power. As he drew nearer, his ring ached on his hand. The bridge seemed to grow thinner as if it were dissolving under him. The Word became starker, dominating his vision more and more.

But he kept his hold on his rage. Even a leper! He reached the gap, knelt before it, looked momentarily through the shimmer at the Lords. Their faces ran with sweat, and their voices trembled in their song. He clenched his hands around the staff of Baradakas, and crawled into the gap.

As he passed under the Word, he heard an instant high keening like a whine of resistance. For that instant, a cold red flame burst from his ring.

Then he was through, and the bridge and the Word were still intact.

He stumbled down the span, flinging off the *clingor* lifeline. When he was safe, he turned long enough to see Prothall and Mhoram remove their staffs from under the Word. Then he stalked out of the vault of Warrenbridge into the dark tunnel of the roadway. He felt Bannor's presence at his shoulder almost at once, but he did not stop until the darkness against which he thrust himself was thick enough to seem impenetrable.

In frustration and congested fear, he groaned, 'I want to be alone. Why don't you leave me alone?'

With the repressed lilt of his *Haruchai* inflection, Bannor responded, 'You are ur-Lord Covenant. We are the Bloodguard. Your life is in our care.'

Covenant glared into the ineluctable dark around him, and thought about the unnatural solidity of the Bloodguard. What binding principle made their flesh seem less mortal than the gutrock of Mount Thunder? A glance at his ring showed him that its incarnadine gleam had almost entirely faded. He found that he was jealous of Bannor's dispassion; his own pervasive irrectitude offended him. On the impulse of a ferocious intuition, he returned, 'That isn't enough.'

He could envision Bannor's slight, eloquent shrug without seeing it. In darkness he waited defiantly until the company caught up with him.

But when he was again marching in his place in the Quest – when Birinair's wan flame had passed by him, treading as if transfixed by leadership the invisible directions of the roadway – the night of the catacombs crowded toward him like myriad leering spectators, impatient for bloodshed, and he suffered a reaction against the strain. His shoulders began to tremble, as if he had been hanging by his arms too long, and cold petrification settled over his thoughts.

The Word of Warning revealed that Lord Foul was expecting them, knew they would not fall victim to Drool's army. Drool could not have formed the Word, much less made it so apposite to white gold. Therefore it served the Despiser's purposes rather than Drool's. Perhaps it was a test of some kind – a measure of the Lords' strength and resourcefulness, an indication of Covenant's vulnerability. But whatever it was, it was Lord Foul's doing. Covenant felt sure that the Despiser knew everything – planned, arranged, made inevitable all that happened to the Quest, every act and decision. Drool was ignorant, mad, manipulated; the Cavewight probably failed to understand half of what he achieved under Lord Foul's hand.

But in his bones Covenant had known such things from the beginning. They did not surprise him; rather, he saw them as symptoms of another, a more essential threat. This central peril – a peril which so froze his mind that only his flesh seemed able to react by trembling – had to do with his white gold ring. He perceived the danger clearly because he was too numb to hide from it. The whole function of the compromise, the bargain, he had made with the Ranyhyn, was to hold the impossibility and the actuality of the Land apart, in equipoise – Back off! Let me be! – to keep them from impacting into each other and blasting his precarious hold on life. But Lord Foul was using his ring to bring crushing together the opposite madnesses which he needed so desperately to escape.

He considered throwing the ring away. But he knew he could not do it. The band was too heavy with remembered lost love and honour and mutual respect to be tossed aside. And an old beggar –

If his bargain failed, he would have nothing left with which to defend himself against the darkness – no power or fertility or coherence – nothing but his own capacity for darkness, his violence, his ability to kill. That capacity led – he was too numb to resist the conclusion – as inalterably as leprosy to the destruction of the Land.

There his numbness seemed to become complete. He could not measure his situation more than that. All he could do was trail behind Birinair's flame and tell over his refusals like some despairing acolyte, desperate for faith, trying to invoke his own autonomy.

He concentrated on his footing as if it were tenuous and the rock unsure – as if Birinair might lead him over the edge of an abyss.

Gradually the character of their benighted journey changed. First, the impression of the surrounding tunnel altered. Behind the darkness, the walls seemed to open from time to time into other tunnels, and at one point the night took on an enormous depth, as if the company were passing over the floor of an amphitheatre. In this blind openness, Birinair searched for his way. When the sense of vast empty space vanished, he led his companions into a stone corridor so low that his flame nearly touched the ceiling, so narrow that they had to pass in single file.

Then the old Hearthrall took them through a bewildering series of shifts in direction and terrain and depth. From the low tunnel, they turned sharply and went down a long steep slope with no discernible walls. As they descended, turning left and right at landmarks only Birinair seemed able to see, the black air became colder and somehow loathsome, as if it carried an echo of ur-viles. The cold came in sudden draughts and pockets, blowing through chasms and tunnels that opened unseen on either side into dens and coverts and passages and great Cavewightish halls, all invisible but for the timbre, the abrupt impression of space, which they gave the darkness.

Lower down the sudden draughts began to stink. The buried air seemed to flow over centuries of accumulated filth, vast hordes of unencrypted dead, long-abandoned laboratories where banes were made. At moments, the putrescence became so thick that Covenant could see it in the air. And out of the adjacent opening came cold, distant sounds – the rattle of shale dropping into immeasurable faults; occasional low complaints of stress; soft, crystalline, chinking noises like the tap of iron hammers; muffled sepulchral detonations; and long tired sighs, exhalations of fatigue from the ancient foundations of the mountain. The darkness itself seemed to be muttering as the company passed.

But at the end of the descent they reached a wavering stair cut into a rock wall, with lightless, hungry chasms gaping below them. And after that, they went through winding tunnels, along the bottom of crevices, over sharp rock ridges like arêtes within the mountain, around pits with the moan of water and the reek of decay in their depths, under arches like entryways to grotesque festal halls – turned and climbed and navigated in the darkness as if it were a perilous limbo, trackless and fatal, varying only in the kind and extremity of its dangers. Needing proof of his own reality, Covenant moved with the fingers of his left hand knotted in his robe over his heart.

Three times in broad, flat spaces which might have been halls or ledges or peak tops surrounded by plunges, the company stopped and ate cold food by the light of Birinair's staff. Each meal helped; the sight of other faces around the flame, the consumption of tangible provender, acted like an affirmation or a pooling of the company's capacity for endurance. Once, Quaan forced himself to attempt a jest, but his voice sounded so hollow in the perpetual midnight that no one had the heart to reply. After each rest, the

Questers set out again bravely. And each time, their pooled fortitude evaporated more rapidly, as if the darkness inhaled it with increasing voracity.

Later old Birinair led them out of cold and ventilated ways into close, musty, hot tunnels far from the main Wightwarrens. To reduce the risk of discovery, he chose a path through a section of the caves deader than the rest – silent and abandoned, with little fresh air left. But the atmosphere only raised the pitch of the company's tension. They moved as if they were screaming voicelessly in anticipation of some blind disaster.

They went on and on, until Covenant knew only that they had not marched for days because his ring had not yet started to glow with the rising of the moon. But after a time his white gold began to gleam like a crimson prophecy. Still they went on into what he now knew was night. They could not afford sleep or long rests. The peak of Drool's present power was only one day away.

They were following a tunnel with walls which seemed to stand just beyond the reach of Birinair's tottering fire. Abruptly, Terrel returned from his scouting position, loomed out of the darkness to appear before the old Hirebrand. Swiftly, Prothall and Mhoram, with Lithe and Covenant behind them, hastened to Birinair's side. Terrel's voice held a note like urgency as he said, 'Ur-viles approach – perhaps fifty. They have seen the light.'

Prothall groaned; Mhoram spat a curse. Manethrall Lithe drew a hissing breath, whipped her cord from her hair as if she were about to encounter the stuff of which Ramen nightmares were made.

But before anyone could take action, old Birinair seemed to snap like a dry twig. Shouting, 'Follow!' he spun to his right and raced away into the darkness.

At once, two Bloodguard sprinted after him. For an instant, the Lords hesitated. Then Prothall cried, '*Melenkurion!*' and dashed after Birinair. Mhoram began shouting orders; the company sprang into battle readiness.

Covenant fled after Birinair's bobbing fire. The Hirebrand's shout had not sounded like panic. The cry – *Follow!* – urged Covenant along. Behind him, he heard the first commands and clatters of combat. He kept his eyes on Birinair's light, followed him into a low, nearly airless tunnel.

Birinair raced down the tunnel, still a stride or two ahead of the Bloodguard.

Suddenly, there came a hot noise like a burst of lightning; without warning a sheet of blue flame enveloped the Hirebrand. Dazzling, coruscating, it walled the tunnel from top to bottom. It roared like a furnace. And Birinair hung in it, spread-limbed and transfixed, his frame contorted with agony. Beside him, his staff flared and became ash.

Without hesitation, the two Bloodguard threw themselves at the fire. It knocked them back like blank stone. They leaped together at Birinair, trying to force him through and past the flame sheet. But they had no effect; Birinair hung where he was, a charred victim in a web of blue fire.

The Bloodguard were poised to spring again when the High Lord caught up with them. He had to shout to make himself heard over the crackling of power. 'My place!' he cried, almost screaming. 'He will die! Aid Mhoram!'

He seemed to have fallen over an edge into distraction. His eyes had a look of chaos. Spreading his arms, he went forward and tried to embrace Birinair.

The fire kicked him savagely away. He fell, and for a long moment lay facedown on the stone.

Behind them, the battle mounted. The ur-viles had formed a wedge, and even with all the help of the Bloodguard and warriors, Mhoram barely held his ground. The first rush of the attack had driven the company back; Mhoram had retreated several yards into the tunnel where Birinair hung. There he made a stand. Despite Prothall's cries and the roar of the fire behind him, he kept his face toward the ur-viles.

Heavily, Prothall raised himself. His head trembled on his tired old neck. But his eyes were no longer wild.

He took a moment to recollect himself, knowing that he was already too late. Then, measuring his strength, he hurled his staff at the blue coruscation.

The shod wood struck with a blinding flash. For one blank instant, Covenant could see nothing. When his vision cleared, he found the staff hanging in the sheet of flame. Birinair lay in the tunnel beyond the fire.

'Birinair!' the High Lord cried. 'My friend!' He seemed to believe that he could help the Hirebrand if he reached him in time. Once again, he flung himself at the flame, and was flung back.

The ur-viles pressed their attack ferociously, in hungry silence. Two of Quaan's Eoman were felled as the company backed into the tunnel, and one more died now with an iron spike in his heart. A woman struck in too close to the wedge, and her hand was hacked off. Mhoram fought the loremaster with growing desperation. Around him, the Bloodguard battled skilfully, but they could find few openings in the wedge.

Covenant peered through the blue sheet at Birinair. The Hirebrand's face was unmarked, but it held a wide stare of agony, as if he had remained alive for one instant after his soul had been seared. The remains of his cloak hung about him in charred wisps.

Follow!

That call had not been panic. Birinair had had some idea. His shout echoed and compelled. His cloak hung about him —

Follow!

Covenant had forgotten something — something important. Wildly, he started forward.

Mhoram strove to strike harder. His strength played like lightning along his staff as he dealt blow after blow against the loremaster. Weakened by his losses, the wedge began to give ground.

Covenant stopped inches away from the sheet of power. Prothall's staff was suspended vertically within it like a landmark. The fire seemed to absorb rather than give off heat. Covenant felt himself growing cold and numb. In the dazzling blue force, he saw a chance for immolation, escape.

Abruptly, the ur-vile loremaster gave a barking shout, and broke formation. It ducked past Mhoram and dashed into the tunnel toward the fire, toward the kneeling High Lord. Mhoram's eyes flashed perilously, but he did not turn from the fight. He snapped an order to Quaan, and struck at the ur-viles with still fiercer force.

Quaan leaped from the fight. He raced to unsling his bow, nock an arrow, and shoot before the loremaster reached Prothall.

Vaguely, Covenant heard the High Lord gasp against the dead air, 'Ur-Lord! Beware!' But he did not listen. His wedding band burned as if the defiled moon were like the rocklight on Warrenbridge — a Word of Warning.

He reached out his left hand, hesitated momentarily, then grasped the High Lord's staff.

Power surged. Bloody fire burst from his ring against the coruscating blue. The roar of the flame cycled upward beyond hearing. Then came a mighty blast, a silent explosion. The floor of the tunnel jumped as if its keel had struck a reef.

The blue sheet fell in tatters.

Quaan was too late to save Prothall. But the ur-vile did not attack the High Lord. It sprang over him toward Covenant. With all his strength, Quaan bent his bow and fired at the creature's back.

For an instant, Covenant stood still, listing crazily to one side and staring in horror at the abrupt darkness. Dim orange fire burned on his hand and arm, but the brilliant blue was gone. The fire gave no pain, though at first it clung to him as if he were dry wood. It was cold and empty, and it died out in sputtering flickers, as if after all he did not contain enough warmth to feed it.

Then the loremaster, with Quaan's arrow squarely between its shoulders, crashed into him and scattered him across the stone.

A short time later, he looked up with his head full of mist. The only light in the tunnel came from Mhoram's Lords-fire as he drove back the ur-viles. Then that light was gone, too; the ur-viles were scattered. Tuvor and the Bloodguard started after them to prevent them from carrying reports to Drool, but Mhoram called, 'Let them go! We are already exposed. No reports of ur-viles matter now.' Voices gasped and groaned in the darkness; soon two or three of the warriors lit torches. The flames cast odd, dim shadows on the walls. The company drew together around Lord Mhoram and moved down to where Prothall knelt.

The High Lord held Birinair's charred form in his arms. But he brushed aside the sympathy and grief of the company. 'Go on,' he said weakly. 'Discover what he intended. I will be done with my farewells soon.' In explanation, he added, 'He led in my place.'

Mhoram laid a commiserating hand on the High Lord's shoulder. But the dangers of their situation did not allow him to remain still. Almost certainly, Drool now knew where they were; the energies they had released would point them out like an accusing finger. 'Why?' Mhoram wondered aloud. 'Why was such power placed here? This is not Drool's doing.' Carrying one of the torches, he started down the tunnel.

From his collapse on the stone, Covenant replied in a grotesque, stricken voice. But he was answering a different question. 'I forgot my clothes – left them behind.'

Mhoram bent over him. Lighting his face with the torch, the Lord asked, 'Are you injured? I do not understand. Of what importance are your old clothes?'

The question seemed to require a world of explanation, but Covenant responded easily, glib with numbness and fog. 'Of course I'm injured. My whole life is an injury.' He hardly listened to his own speech. 'Don't you see? When I wake up, and find myself dressed in my old clothes, not this moss-stained robe at all – why, that will prove that I really have been dreaming. If it wasn't so reassuring, I would be terrified.'

'You have mastered a great power,' Mhoram murmured.

'That was an accident. It happened by itself. I was – I was trying to escape. Burn myself.'

Then the strain overcame him. He lowered his head to the stone and went to sleep.

He did not rest long; the air of the tunnel was too uncomfortable, and there was too much activity in the company. When he opened his eyes, he saw Lithe and several warriors preparing a meal over a low fire. With a trembling song on his lips, and tears spilling from his eyes, Prothall was using his blue fire to sear the injured woman's wrist-stump.

Covenant watched as she bore the pain; only when her wrist was tightly bandaged did she let herself faint. After that he turned away, sick with shared pain. He lurched to his feet, reeled as if he could not find his footing, had to brace himself against the wall. He stood there hunched over his aching stomach until Mhoram returned, accompanied by Quaan, Korik, and two other Bloodguard.

The Warhaft was carrying a small iron chest.

When Mhoram reached the fire, he spoke in quiet wonder. 'The power was a defence placed here by High Lord Kevin. Beyond this tunnel lies a chamber. There we found the Second Ward of Kevin's Lore – the Second of the Seven.'

High Lord Prothall's face lit up with hope.

23

KIRIL THRENDOR

Reverently, Prothall took the chest. His fingers fumbled at the bindings. When he raised the lid, a pale, pearly glow like clean moonlight shone from within the cask. The radiance gave his face a look of beatitude as he ventured his hand into the chest to lift out an ancient scroll. When he raised it, the company saw that it was the scroll which shone.

Quaan and his Eoman half knelt before the Ward, bowed their heads. Mhoram and Prothall stood erect as if they were meeting the scrutiny of the master of their lives. After a moment of amazement, Lithe joined the warriors. Only Covenant and the Bloodguard showed no reverence. Tuvor's comrades stood casually alert, and Covenant leaned uncomfortably against the wall, trying to bring his unruly stomach under control.

But he was not blind to the importance of that scroll. A private hope wrestled with his nausea. He approached it obliquely. 'Did Birinair know – what you were going to find? Is that why?'

'Why he ran here?' Mhoram spoke absently; all of him except his voice was focused on the scroll which Prothall held up like a mighty talisman. 'Perhaps it is possible. He knew the old maps. No doubt they were given to us in the First Ward so that in time we might find our way here. It may be that his heart saw what our eyes did not.'

Covenant paused, then asked, obliquely again, 'Why did you let the ur-viles escape?'

This time, the Lords seemed to hear his seriousness. With a piercing glance at him, Prothall replaced the scroll in the cask. When the lid was closed, Mhoram answered stiffly, 'Unnecessary death, Unbeliever. We did not come here to slay ur-viles. We will harm ourselves more by unnecessary killing than by risking a few live foes. We fight in need, not in lust or rage. The Oath of Peace must not be compromised.'

But this also did not answer Covenant's question. With an effort, he brought out his hope directly. 'Never mind. This Second Ward – it doubles your power. You could send me back.'

Mhoram's face softened at the need for assurance, for consolation against impossible demands, in the question. But his reply denied Covenant. 'Ah, my friend, you forget. We have not yet mastered the First Ward – not in generations of study. The best of the Loresraat have failed to unveil the central mysteries. We can do nothing with this new Ward now. Perhaps, if we survive this Quest, we will learn from the Second in later years.'

There he stopped. His face held a look of further speech, but he said no more until Prothall sighed, 'Tell him all. We can afford no illusions now.'

'Very well,' Mhoram said hurriedly. 'In truth, our possession of the Second Ward at such a time is perilous. It is clear from the First that High Lord Kevin prepared the Seven in careful order. It was his purpose that the Second Ward remain hidden until all the First was known. Apparently, certain aspects of his Lore carry great hazard to those who have not first mastered certain other aspects. So he hid his Wards, and defended them with powers which could not be breached until the earlier Lore was mastered. Now his intent has been broken. Until we penetrate the First, we will risk much if we attempt the use of the Second.'

He pulled himself up and took a deep breath. 'We do not regret. For all our peril, this discovery may be the great moment of our age. But it may not altogether bless us.'

In a low voice, Prothall added, 'We raise no blame or doubt. How could any have known what we would find? But the doom of the Land is now doubly on our heads. If we are to defeat Lord Foul in the end, we must master powers for which we are not ready. So we learn hope and dismay from the same source. Do not mistake us –

this risk we accept gladly. The mastery of Kevin's Lore is the goal of our lives. But we must make clear that there is risk. I see hope for the Land, but little for myself.'

'Even that sight is dim,' said Mhoram tightly. 'It may be that Lord Foul has led us here so that we may be betrayed by powers we cannot control.'

At this, Prothall looked sharply at Mhoram. Then, slowly, the High Lord nodded his agreement. But his face did not lose the relief, the lightening of its burden, which his first sight of the Ward had given him. Under its influence, he looked equal to the stewardship of his age. Now the time of High Lord Prothall son of Dwillian would be well remembered — if the company survived its Quest. His resolve had a forward look as he closed the chest of the Second Ward; his movements were crisp and decisive. He gave the cask to Korik, who bound it to his bare back with strips of *clingor*, and covered it by knotting his tunic shut.

But Covenant looked at the remains of the brief structure of his own hope, collapsed like a child's toy house, and he had no solid ground on which to build them. He was too weak and tired to think about it. He stood leaning where he was for a long time, with his head bent as if he were trying to decipher the chart of his robe.

Despite the danger, the company rested and ate there in the tunnel. Prothall judged that remaining where they were for a time was as unpredictable as anything else they might do; so while the Bloodguard stood watch, he encouraged his companions to rest. Then he lay down, pillowed his head on his arms, and seemed at once to fall into deep sleep, so intensely calm and quiet that it looked more like preparation than repose. Following his example, most of the company let their eyes close, though they slept only fitfully. But Mhoram and Lithe remained watchful. He stared into the low fire as if he were searching for a vision, and she sat across from him with her shoulders hunched against the oppressive weight of the mountain — as unable to rest underground as if the lack of open sky and grasslands offended her Ramen blood. Reclining against the wall, Covenant regarded the two of them, and slept a little until the strain of his ring began to fade with moonset.

After that Prothall arose, awake and alert, and roused the company. As soon as everyone had eaten again, he put out the campfire. In its place, he lit one of the *lillianrill* torches. It guttered and jumped dangerously in the thick air, but he used it rather than his staff to light the tunnel. Soon the Quest was marching again. Helpless to do otherwise, they left their dead lying on the stone of the Ward chamber. It was the only tribute they could give Birinair and the slain warriors.

Again they went into darkness, led by the High Lord through interminable, black, labyrinthian passages in the deep rock of Mount Thunder. The air became thicker, hotter, deader. In spite of occasional ascents, their main progress was downward, toward the bottomless roots of the mountain, closer with every unseen, unmeasured league toward immense, buried, slumbering, grim ills, the terrible bones of the Earth. On and on they walked as if they were amazed by darkness, irremediable night. They made their way in hard silence, as if their lips were stiff with resisted sobs. They could not see. It affected them like a bereavement.

As they approached the working heart of the Wightwarrens, certain sounds became louder, more distinct – the battering of anvils, the groaning of furnaces, gasps of anguish. From time to time they crossed blasts of hot fetid air like forced ventilation for charnel pits. And a new noise crept into their awareness – a sound of bottomless boiling. For a long while, they drew nearer to this deep moil without gaining any hint of what it was.

Later they passed its source. Their path lay along the lip of a huge cavern. The walls were lit luridly by a seething orange sea of rocklight. Far below them was a lake of molten stone.

After the long darkness of their trek, the bright light hurt their eyes. The rising acrid heat of the lake snatched at them as if it were trying to pluck them from their perch. The deep, boiling sound thrummed in the air. Great gouts of magma spouted toward the ceiling, then fell back into the lake like crumbling towers.

Vaguely, Covenant heard someone say, 'The Demondim in the days of High Lord Loric discarded their failed breeding efforts here. It is said that the loathing of the Demondim – and of the Viles who sired them – for their own forms surpassed all restraint. It led them to the spawning which made both ur-viles and Waynhim. And it drove them to cast all their weak and faulty into such pits as this – so strongly did they abhor their unseen eyelessness.'

Groaning, he turned his face to the wall, and crept past the cavern into the passage beyond it. When he dropped his hands from the support of the stone, his fingers twitched at his sides as if he were testing the sides of a casket.

Prothall chose to rest there, just beyond the cavern of rocklight. The company ate a quick, cold meal, then pressed on again into darkness. From this passage, they took two turns, went up a long slope, and at length found themselves walking a ledge in a fault. Its crevice fell away to their left. Covenant made his way absently, shaking his head in an effort to clear his thoughts. Ur-viles reeled across his brain like images of self-hatred, premonitions. Was he doomed to see himself even in such creatures as that? No. He gritted his teeth. No. In the light of remembered bursts of lava, he began to fear that he had already missed his chance – his chance to fall –

In time, fatigue came back over him. Prothall called a rest halt on the ledge, and Covenant surprised himself by nearly falling asleep that close to a crevice. But the High Lord was pushing toward his goal now, and did not let the company rest long. With his guttering torch, he led the Quest forward again, through darkness into darkness.

As the trek dragged on, their moment-by-moment caution began to slip. The full of the moon was coming, and somewhere ahead Drool was preparing for them. Prothall moved as if he were eager for the last test, and led them along the ledge at a stiff pace. As a result, the lone ur-vile took them all by surprise.

It had hidden itself in a thin fissure in the wall of the crevice. When Covenant passed it, it sprang out at him, threw its weight against his chest. Its roynish, eyeless face was blank with ferocity. As it struck him, it grappled for his left hand.

The force of the attack knocked him backward toward the crevice. For one flicker of time, he was not aware of that danger. The ur-vile consumed his attention. It pulled his hand close to its face, sniffed wetly over his fingers as if searching for something, then tried to jam his ring finger into its ragged mouth.

He staggered back one more step; his foot left the ledge. In that instant, he realized the hungry fall under him. Instinctively, he closed his fist against the ur-vile and ignored it. Clinging to his staff with all the strength of his halfhand, he thrust its end toward Bannor. The Bloodguard was already reaching for him.

Bannor caught hold of the staff.

For one slivered moment, Covenant kept his grip.

But the full weight of the ur-vile hung on his left arm. His hold tore loose from the staff. With the creature struggling to bite off his ring, he plunged into the crevice.

Before he could shriek his terror, a force like a boulder struck him, knocked the air from his lungs, left him gasping sickly as he plummeted. With his chest constricted and retching, unable to cry out, he lost consciousness.

When he roused himself after the impact, he was struggling for air against a faceful of dirt. He lay head down on a steep slope of shale and loam and refuse, and the slide caused by his landing had covered his face. For a long moment, he could not move except to gag and cough. His efforts shook him without freeing him.

Then, with a shuddering exertion, he rolled over, thrust up his head. He coughed up a gout of dirt, and found that he could breathe. But he still could not see. The fact took a moment to penetrate his awareness. He checked his face, found that his eyes were uncovered and open. But they perceived nothing except an utter and desolate darkness. It was as if he were blind with panic – as if his optic nerves were numb with terror.

For a time he did panic. Without sight, he felt the empty air suck at him as if he were drowning in quicksand. The night beat about him on naked wings like vultures dropping toward dead meat.

His heart beat out heavy jolts of fear. He cowered there on his knees, abandoned, bereft of eyes and light and mind by the extremity of his dread, and his breath whimpered in his throat. But as the first rush of his panic passed, he recognized it. Fear – it was an emotion he understood, a part of the condition of his existence. And his heart went on beating. Lurching as if wounded, it still kept up his life.

Suddenly, convulsively, he raised his fists and struck at the shale on either side of his head, pounded to the rhythm of his pulse as if he were trying to beat rationality out of the dirt. No! No! I am going to *survive!*

The assertion steadied him. Survive! He was a leper, accustomed to fear. He knew how to deal with it. Discipline – discipline.

He pressed his hands over his eyeballs; spots of colour jerked across the black. He was not blind. He was seeing darkness. He had fallen away from the only light in the catacombs; of course he could not see.

Hell and blood.

Instinctively, he rubbed his hands, winced at the bruises he had given himself.

Discipline.

He was alone – alone – Lightless somewhere on the bottom of a ledge of the crevice long leagues from the nearest open sky. Without help, friends, rescue, for him the outside of the mountain was as unattainable as if it had ceased to exist. Escape itself was unattainable unless –

Discipline.

– unless he found some way to die.

Hellfire!

Thirst. Hunger. Injury – loss of blood. He iterated the possibilities as if he were going through a VSE. He might fall prey to some dark-bred bane. Might stumble over a more fatal precipice. Madness, yes. It would be as easy as leprosy.

Midnight wings beat about his ears, reeled vertiginously across the blind blackscape. His hands groped unconsciously around his head, seeking some way to defend himself.

Damnation!

None of this is happening to me.

349

Discipline!

A fetal fancy came over him. He caught hold of it as if it were a vision. Yes! Quickly, he changed his position so that he was sitting on the shale slope. He fumbled over his belt until he found Atiaran's knife. Poising it carefully in his half fingerless grip, he began to shave.

Without water or a mirror, he was perilously close to slitting his throat, and the dryness of his beard caused him pain as if he were using the knife to dredge his face into a new shape. But this risk, this pain, was part of him; there was nothing impossible about it. If he cut himself, the dirt on his skin would make infection almost instantaneous. It calmed him like a demonstration of his identity.

In that way, he made the darkness draw back, withhold its talons.

When he was done, he mustered his resolution for an exploration of his situation. He wanted to know what kind of place he was in. Carefully, tentatively, he began searching away from the slopes on his hands and knees.

Before he had moved three feet across flat stone, he found a body. The flesh yielded as if it had not been dead long, but its chest was cold and slick, and his hand came back wet, smelling of rotten blood.

He recoiled to the slope, gritted himself into motionlessness while his lungs heaved loudly and his knees trembled. The ur-vile – the ur-vile that had attacked him. Broken by the fall. He wanted to move, but could not. The shock of discovery froze him like a sudden opening of dangerous doors; he felt surrounded by perils which he could not name. How had that creature known to attack him? Could it actually smell white gold?

Then his ring began to gleam. The bloody radiation transformed it into a band of dull fire about his wedding finger, a crimson fetter. But it shed no light – did not even enable him to see the digit on which it hung. It shone balefully in front of him, exposed him to any eyes that were hidden in the dark, but it gave him nothing but dread.

He could not forget what it meant. Drool's bloody moon was rising full over the Land.

It made him quail against the shale slope. He had a gagging sensation in his throat, as if he were being force-fed terror. Even the uncontrollable wheeze of his respiration seemed to mark him for attack by claws and fangs so invisible in the darkness that he could not visualize them. He was alone, helpless, abject.

Unless he found some way to make use of the power of his ring.

He fell back in revulsion from that thought the instant it crossed his mind. No! Never! He was a leper; his capacity for survival depended on a complete recognition, acceptance, of his essential importance. That was the law of leprosy. Nothing could be as fatal to him – nothing could destroy him body and mind as painfully – as the illusion of power. Power in a dream. And before he died he would become as fetid and deformed as that man he had met in the leprosarium.

No!

Better to kill himself outright. Anything would be better.

He did not know how long he spun giddily before he heard a low noise in the darkness – distant, slippery and ominous, as if the surrounding midnight had begun breathing softly through its teeth. It stunned him like a blow to the heart. Flinching in blind fear, he tried to fend it off. Slowly, it grew clearer – a quiet, susurrous sound like a gritted exhalation from many throats. It infested the air like vermin, made his flesh crawl.

They were coming for him. They knew where he was because of his ring, and they were coming for him.

He had a quick vision of a Waynhim with an iron spike through its chest. He clapped his right hand over his ring. But he knew that was futile as soon as he did it. Frenetically, he began searching over the shale for some kind of weapon. Then he remembered his knife. It felt too weightless to help him. But he gripped it, and went on hunting with his right hand, hardly knowing what he sought.

For a long moment, he fumbled around him, regardless of the noise he made. Then his fingers found his staff. Bannor must have dropped it, and it had fallen near him.

The susurration drew nearer. It was the sound of many bare feet sliding over stone. They were coming for him.

The staff! – it was a Hirebrand's staff. Baradakas had given it to him. *In the hour of darkness, remember the Hirebrand's staff.* If he could light it –

But how?

The black air loomed with enemies. Their steps seemed to slide toward him from above.

How? he cried desperately, trying to make the staff catch fire by sheer force of will. *Baradakas!*

Still the feet came closer. He could hear hoarse breathing behind their sibilant approach.

It had burned for him at the Celebration of Spring. Shaking with haste, he pressed the end of the staff to his blood-embered ring. At once, red flame blossomed on the wood, turned pale orange and yellow, flared up brightly. The sudden light dazzled him, but he leaped to his feet and held the staff over his head.

He was standing at the bottom of a long slope which filled half the floor of the crevice. This loose-piled shale had saved his life by giving under the impact of his fall, rolling him down instead of holding him where he hit. Before and behind him, the crevice stretched upward far beyond the reach of his flame. Nearby, the ur-vile lay twisted on its back, its black skin wet with blood.

Shuffling purposefully toward him along the crevice floor was a disjointed company of Cavewights.

They were still thirty yards away, but even at that distance, he was surprised by their appearance. They did not look like other Cavewights he had seen. The difference was not only in costume, though these creatures were ornately and garishly caparisoned like a royal cadre, elite and obscene. They were physically different. They were old – old prematurely, unnaturally. Their red eyes were hooded, and their long limbs bent as if the bones had been warped in a short time. Their heads sagged on necks that still looked thick enough to be strong and erect. Their heavy, spatulate hands trembled as if with palsy. Together, they reeked of ill, of victimization. But they came forward with clenched determination, as if they had been promised the peace of death when this last task was done.

Shaking off his surprise, he brandished his staff threateningly. 'Don't touch me!' he hissed through his teeth. 'Back off! I made a bargain – !'

The Cavewights gave no sign that they had heard. But they did not attack him. When they were almost within his reach, they spread out on both sides, awkwardly encircled him. Then, by giving way on one side and closing toward him on the other, they herded him in the direction from which they had come.

As soon as he understood that they wished to take him some place without a fight, he began to co-operate. He knew intuitively where they were going. So through their torturous herding he moved slowly along the crevice until he reached a stair in the left wall. It was a rude way, roughly hacked out of rock, but it was wide enough for several Cavewights to climb abreast. He was able to control his vertigo by staying near the wall, away from the crevice.

They ascended for several hundred feet before they reached an opening in the wall. Though the stairs continued upward the Cavewights steered him through this opening. He found himself in a narrow tunnel with a glow of rocklight at its end. The creatures marched him more briskly now, as if they were hurrying him toward a scaffold.

Then a wash of heat and a stink of brimstone poured over him. He stepped out of the tunnel into Kiril Threndor.

He recognized the burnished stone gleam of the faceted walls, the fetid stench like sulphur consuming rotten flesh, the several entrances, the burning dance of light on the clustered stalactites high overhead. It was all as vivid to him as if it had just been translated from a nightmare. The Cavewights ushered him into the chamber, then stood behind him to block the entrance.

For the second time, he met Drool Rockworm.

Drool crouched on his low dais in the centre of the cave. He clenched the Staff of Law in both his huge hands, and it was by the Staff that Covenant first recognized him. Drool had changed. Some blight had fallen on him. As he caught sight of Covenant, he began laughing shrilly. But his voice was weak, and his laughter had a pitch of hysteria. He did not laugh long; he seemed too exhausted to sustain it. Like the Cavewights who had herded Covenant, he was old.

But whatever had damaged them had hurt him more. His limbs were so gnarled that he could hardly stand; saliva ran uncontrolled from his drooping lips; and he was sweating profusely, as if he could no longer endure the heat of his own domain. He gripped the Staff in an attitude of fierce possessiveness and desperation. Only his eyes had not changed. They shone redly, without iris or pupil, and seemed to froth like malicious lava, eager to devour.

Covenant felt a strange mixture of pity and loathing. But he had only a moment to wonder what had happened to Drool. Then he had to brace himself. The Cavewight began hobbling painfully toward him.

Groaning at the ache in his limbs, Drool stopped a few paces from Covenant. He released one hand from the intricately runed Staff to point a trembling finger at Covenant's wedding band. When he spoke, he cast continual, twitching leers back over his shoulder, as if referring to an invisible spectator. His voice was as gnarled and racked as his arms and legs.

'Mine!' he coughed. 'You promised. Mine. Lord Drool, Staff and ring. You promised. Do this, you said. Do that. Do not crush. Wait now.' He spat viciously. 'Kill later. You promised. The ring if I did what you said. You said.' He sounded like a sick child. 'Drool, Lord Drool! Power! Mine now.'

Slavering thickly, he reached a hand for Covenant's ring.

Covenant reacted in instant revulsion. With his burning staff, he struck a swift blow, slapped Drool's hand away.

At the impact, his staff broke into slivers as if Drool's flesh were vehement iron.

But Drool gave a coughing roar of rage, and stamped the heel of the Staff of Law on the floor. The stone jumped under Covenant's feet; he pitched backward, landed with a jolt that seemed to stop his heart.

He lay stunned and helpless. Through a throbbing noise in his ears, he heard Drool cry, 'Slay him! Give the ring!' He rolled over. Sweat blurred his vision; blearily, he saw the Cavewights converging toward him. His heart felt paralysed in his chest, and he could not get his feet under him. Retching for air, he tried to crawl out of reach.

The first Cavewight caught hold of his neck, then abruptly groaned and fell away to the side. Another Cavewight fell; the rest drew back in confusion. One of them cried fearfully, 'Bloodguard! Lord Drool, help us!'

'Fool!' retorted Drool, coughing as if his lungs were in shreds. 'Coward! I am power! Slay them!'

Covenant climbed to his feet, wiped the sweat from his eyes, and found Bannor standing beside him. The Bloodguard's robe hung tattered from his shoulders, and a large bruise on his brow closed one eye. But his hands were poised, alert. He carried himself on the balls of his feet, ready to leap in any direction. His flat eyes held a dull gleam of battle.

Covenant felt such a surge of relief that he wanted to hug Bannor. After his long, lightless ordeal, he felt suddenly rescued, almost redeemed. But his gruff voice belied his emotion. 'What the hell took you so long?'

The Cavewights came forward slowly, timorously, and surrounded Covenant and Bannor. Drool raged at them in hoarse gasps.

Overhead, the chiaroscuro of the stalactites danced gaily.

With startling casualness, Bannor replied that he had landed badly after killing the ur-vile, and had lost consciousness. Then he had been unable to locate Covenant in the darkness. Lashed by Drool's strident commands, a Cavewight charged Covenant from behind. But Bannor spun easily, felled the creature with a kick. 'The flame of your staff revealed you,' he continued. 'I chose to follow.' He paused to spring at two of the nearest attackers. They retreated hastily. When he spoke again, his foreign *Haruchai* tone held a note of final honesty. 'I withheld my aid, awaiting proof that you are not a foe of the Lords.'

Something in the selfless and casual face that Bannor turned toward death communicated itself to Covenant. He answered without rancour, 'You picked a fine time to test me.'

'The Bloodguard know doubt. We require to be sure.'

Drool mustered his strength to shriek furiously, 'Fools! Worms! Afraid of only two!' He spat. 'Go! Watch! Lord Drool kills.'

The Cavewights gave way, and Drool came wincing forward. He held the Staff of Law before him like an axe.

Bannor leaped, launched a kick at Drool's face.

But for all his crippled condition, Drool Rockworm was full of power. He did not appear to feel Bannor's attack. In ponderous fury, he raised the Staff to deal a blast which would incinerate Bannor and Covenant where they stood. Against the kind of might he wielded, they were helpless.

Still Bannor braced himself in front of Covenant to meet the blow. Flinching, Covenant waited for the pain that would set him free.

But Drool was already too late. He had missed his chance, neglected other dangers. Even as he raised the Staff, the company of the Quest, led by First Mark Tuvor and High Lord Prothall, broke into Kiril Threndor.

They looked battered, as if they had just finished a skirmish with Drool's outer defences, but they were whole and dourhanded, and they entered the chamber like a decisive wave. Prothall stopped Drool's blast with a shout full of authority. Before the Cavewights could gather themselves together, the Eoman fell on them, drove them from the cave. In a moment, Drool was surrounded by a wide ring of warriors and Bloodguard.

Slowly, with an appearance of confusion, he retreated until he was half-crouching on his dais. He looked around the circle as if unable to realize what had happened. But his spatulate hands held the Staff in a grip as grim as death.

Then, grotesquely, his laval eyes took on an angle of cunning. Twitching nods over his shoulder, he hissed in a raw voice, 'Here – this is fair. Fair. Better than promises. All of them – here. All little Lords and puny Bloodguard – humans. Ready for crushing.' He started to laugh, broke into a fit of coughing. 'Crush!' he spat when he regained control of himself. 'Crush with power.' He made a noise like a cracking of bones in his throat. 'Power! Little Lords. Mighty Drool. Better than promises.'

Prothall faced the Cavewight squarely. Giving his staff to Mhoram, he stepped forward to the dais with Tuvor at his side. He stood erect; his countenance was calm and clear. Supported by their years of abnegation, his eyes neither wavered nor burned. In contrast, Drool's red orbs were consumed with the experience of innumerable satiations – an addictive gluttony of power. When the High Lord spoke, even the rattle of his old voice sounded like authority and decision. Softly, he said, 'Give it up. Drool Rockworm, hear me. The Staff of Law is not yours. It is not meant for you. Its strength must only be used for the health of the Land. Give it to me.'

Covenant moved to stand near the High Lord. He felt that he had to be near the Staff.

But Drool only muttered, 'Power? Give it up? Never.' His lips went on moving, as if he were communing over secret plans.

Again, Prothall urged, 'Surrender it. For your own sake. Are you blind to yourself? Do you not see what has happened to you? This power is not meant for you. It destroys you. You have used the Staff wrongly. You have used the Illearth Stone. Such powers are deadly. Lord Foul has betrayed you. Give the Staff to me. I will strive to help you.'

But that idea offended Drool. 'Help?' he coughed. 'Fool! I am Lord Drool. Master! The moon is mine. Power is mine. You are mine. I can crush! Old man – little Lord. I let you live to make me laugh. Help? No, dance. Dance for Lord Drool.' He waved the Staff threateningly. 'Make me laugh. I let you live.'

Prothall drew himself up, and said in a tone of command, 'Drool Rockworm, release the Staff.' He advanced a step.

With a jerk like a convulsion of hysteria, Drool raised the Staff to strike.

Prothall rushed forward, tried to stop him. But Tuvor reached the Cavewight first. He caught the end of the Staff.

Slavering with rage, Drool jabbed the iron heel of the Staff against Tuvor's body. Bloody light flashed. In that instant the First Mark's flesh became transparent; the company could see his bones burning like dry sticks. Then he fell, reeling backward to collapse in Covenant's arms.

His weight was too great for the Unbeliever to hold; Covenant sank to the stone under it. Cradling Tuvor, he watched the High Lord.

Prothall grappled with Drool. He grasped the Staff with both hands to prevent Drool from striking him. They wrestled together for possession of it.

The struggle looked impossible for Prothall. Despite his decrepitude, Drool retained some of his Cavewightish strength. And he was full of power. And Prothall was old.

With Tuvor in his arms, Covenant could do nothing. 'Help him!' he cried to Mhoram. 'He'll be killed!'

But Lord Mhoram turned his back on Prothall. He knelt beside Covenant to see if he could aid Tuvor. As he examined the First Mark, he said roughly, 'Drool seeks to master the Staff with malice. The High Lord can sing a stronger song than that.'

Appalled, Covenant shouted, 'He'll be killed! You've got to help him!'

'Help him?' Mhoram's eyes glinted dangerously. Pain and raw restraint sharpened his voice as he said, 'He would not welcome my help. He is the High Lord. Despite my Oath – ' he choked momentarily on a throat full of passion – 'I would crush Drool.' He invested Drool's word, *crush*, with a potential for despair that silenced Covenant.

Panting, Covenant watched the High Lord's fight. He was horrified by the danger, by the price both Lords were willing to pay.

Then battle erupted around him. Cavewights charged into Kiril Threndor from several directions. Apparently Drool had been able to send out a silent call; his guards were answering. The first forces to reach the chamber were not large, but they sufficed to engage the whole company. Only Mhoram did not join the fight. He knelt beside Covenant and stroked the First Mark's face, as if he were transfixed by Tuvor's dying.

Shouting stertorously over the clash of weapons, Quaan ordered his warriors into a defensive ring around the dais and the Lords. Loss and fatigue had taken their toll on the Eoman, but stalwart Quaan led his command as if the Lords' need rendered him immune to weakness. Among the Bloodguard, his Eoman parried, thrust, fought on the spur of his exhortations.

The mounting perils made Covenant reel. Prothall and Drool struggled horribly above him. The fighting around him grew faster and more frenzied by the moment. Tuvor lay expiring in his lap. And he could do nothing about any of it, help none of them. Soon their escape would be cut off, and all their efforts would be in vain.

He had not foreseen this outcome to his bargain.

Drool bore Prothall slowly backward. 'Dance!' he raged.

Tuvor shuddered; his eyes opened. Covenant looked away from Prothall. Tuvor's lips moved, but he made no sound.

Mhoram tried to comfort him. 'Have no fear. This evil will be overcome – it is in the High Lord's hands. And your name will be remembered with honour wherever trust is valued.'

But Tuvor's eyes held Covenant, and he managed to whisper one word, 'True?' His whole body strained with supplication, but Covenant did not know whether he asked for a promise or a judgment.

Yet the Unbeliever answered. He could not refuse a Bloodguard, could not deny the appeal of such expensive fidelity. The word stuck in his throat, but he forced it out. 'Yes.'

Tuvor shuddered again, and died with a flat groan as if the cord of his Vow had snapped. Covenant gripped his shoulders, shook him; there was no response.

On the dais, Drool had forced Prothall to his knees, and was bending the High Lord back to break him. In futility and rage, Covenant howled, 'Mhoram!'

The Lord nodded, surged to his feet. But he did not attack Drool. Holding his staff over his head, he blared in a voice that cut through the clamour of the battle, *'Melenkurion abatha! Minas mill khabaal!'* From end to end, his staff burst into incandescent fire.

357

The power of the Words jolted Drool, knocked him back a step. Prothall regained his feet.

More Cavewights rushed into Kiril Threndor. Quaan and his Eoman were driven back toward the dais. At last, Mhoram sprang to their aid. His staff burned furiously as he attacked. Around him, the Bloodguard fought like wind devils, leaping and kicking among the Cavewights so swiftly that the creatures interfered with each other when they tried to strike back.

But Drool's defenders kept coming, pouring into the cave. The company began to founder in the rising onslaught.

Then Prothall cried over the din, 'I have it! The moon is free!'

He stood triumphant on the dais, with the Staff of Law upraised in his hands. Drool lay at his feet, sobbing like a piece of broken rock. Between spasms of grief, the creature gasped, 'Give it back. I want it.'

The sight struck fear into the Cavewights. They recoiled, quailed back against the walls of the chamber.

Released from battle, Quaan and his warriors turned toward Prothall and gave a raw cheer. Their voices were hoarse and worn, but they exulted in the High Lord's victory as if he had won the future of the Land.

Yet overhead the dancing lights of Kiril Threndor went their own bedizened way.

Covenant snapped a look at his ring. Its argent still burned with blood. Perhaps the moon was free; he was not.

Before the echoes of cheering died – before anyone could move – a new sound broke over them. It started softly, then expanded until it filled the chamber like a collapse of the ceiling. It was laughter – Lord Foul's laughter, throbbing with glee and immitigable hate. Its belittling weight dominated them, buried them in their helplessness; it paralysed them, seemed to cut them off from their own heartbeats and breathing. While it piled on to them, they were lost.

Even Prothall stood still. Despite his victory, he looked old and feeble, and his eyes had an unfocused stare as if he were gazing into his own coffin. And Covenant, who knew that laugh, could not resist it.

But Lord Mhoram moved. Springing on to the dais, he whirled his staff around his head until the air hummed, and blue lightning bolted upward into the clustered stalactites. 'Then show yourself, Despiser!' he shouted. 'If you are so certain, face us now! Do you fear to try your doom with us?'

Lord Foul's laughter exploded with fiercer contempt. But Mhoram's defiance had broken its transfixation. Prothall touched

Mhoram's shoulder. The warriors gripped their swords, placed themselves in grim readiness behind the Lords.

More Cavewights entered the chamber, though they did not attack. At the sight of them, Drool raised himself on his crippled arms. His bloody eyes bolted still, clinging to fury and malice to the end. Coughing as if he were about to heave up his heart, he gasped, 'The Staff. You do not know. Cannot use it. Fools. No escape. None. I have armies. I have the Stone.' With a savage effort, he made himself heard through the laughter. 'Illearth Stone. Power and power. I will crush. Crush.' Flailing one weak arm at his guards, he screamed in stricken command, 'Crush!'

Wielding their weapons, the Cavewights surged forward.

24

THE CALLING OF LIONS

They came in a mass of red eyes dull with empty determination. But Lord Foul's bodiless laughter seemed to slow them. They waded through it as if it were a quagmire, and their difficult approach gave the company time to react. At Quaan's command, the warriors ringed Mhoram and Prothall. The Bloodguard took fighting positions with the Eoman.

Mhoram called to Covenant.

Slowly, Covenant raised his head. He looked at his companions, and they seemed pitifully few to him. He tried to get to his feet. But Tuvor was too heavy for him to lift. Even in death, the massive devotion of the First Mark surpassed his strength.

He heard Manethrall Lithe shout, 'This way! I know the way!' She was dodging among the Cavewights toward one of the entrances. He watched her go as if he had already forsaken her. He could not lift Tuvor because he could not get a grip with his right hand; two fingers were not enough.

Then Bannor snatched him away from the fallen First Mark, thrust him toward the protective ring of the Eoman. Covenant resisted. 'You can't leave him!' But Bannor forced him among the warriors. 'What are you doing?' he protested. 'We've got to take him along. If you don't send him back, he won't be replaced.' He spun to appeal to the Lords. 'You can't leave him!'

Mhoram's lips stretched taut over his teeth. 'We must.'

From the mouth of the tunnel she had chosen, Lithe called, 'Here!' She clenched her cord around a Cavewight's neck, and used the creature's body to protect herself from attack. 'This is the way!' Other Cavewights converged on her, forced her backward.

In response, Prothall lit his old staff, swung it, and led a charge toward her. With Mhoram's help, he burned passage for his companions through the massed Cavewights.

Bright Lords-fire intimidated the creatures. But before the company had gained the tunnel Lithe had chosen, a wedge of ur-viles drove snarling into the chamber from a nearby entrance. They were led by a mighty loremaster, as black as the catacombs, wielding an iron stave that looked wet with power or blood.

Prothall cried, 'Run!' The Questers dashed for the tunnel.

The ur-viles raced to intercept them.

The company was faster. Prothall and Mhoram gained the passage, and parted to let the others enter between them.

But one of the warriors decided to help his comrades escape. He suddenly veered away from the Eoman. Whirling his sword fervidly, he threw himself at the ur-vile wedge.

Mhoram yelled, started back out into the chamber to help him. But the loremaster brushed the warrior aside with a slap of its stave, and he fell. Dark moisture covered him from head to foot; he screamed as if he had been drenched in acid. Mhoram barely evaded the stave's backstroke, retreated to Prothall's side in the mouth of the passage.

There they tried to stand. They opposed their blazing blue flame to the ur-viles. The loremaster struck at them again and again; they blocked each blow with their staffs; gouts of flaming fluid, igniting blue and then turning quickly black, spattered on all sides at every clash. But the wedge fought with a savagery which drove the Lords backward step by step into the tunnel.

Quaan tried to counter by having his strongest archers loose arrows at the loremaster. But the shafts were useless. They caught fire in the ur-viles' black power and burned to ashes.

Behind the company, Lithe was chafing to pursue the guide of her instinct for daylight. She called repeatedly for the Lords to follow her. But they could not; they did not dare turn their backs on the wedge.

Each clash drove them backward. For all their courage and resolve, they were nearly exhausted, and every blow of the loremaster's stave weakened them further. Now their flame had a less rampant blaze, and the burning gouts turned black more swiftly. It was clear that they could not keep up the fight. And no one in the company could take it for them.

Abruptly, Mhoram shouted, 'Back! Make room!' His urgency allowed no refusal; even the Bloodguard obeyed.

'Covenant!' Mhoram cried.

Covenant moved forward until he was only an arm's length from the searing battle.

'Raise your ring!'

Compelled by Mhoram's intensity, the Unbeliever lifted his left hand. A crimson cast still stained the heart of his wedding band.

The loremaster observed the ring as if suddenly smelling its presence. It recognized white gold, hesitated. The wedge halted, though the loremaster did not drop its guard.

'*Melenkurion abatha!*' Mhoram commanded. 'Blast them!'

Half intuitively, Covenant understood. He jabbed at the loremaster with his left fist as if launching a bolt.

Barking in strident fear, the whole wedge recoiled.

In that instant, the Lords acted. Shouting, '*Minas mill khabaal*' on different pitches in half-screamed harmony, they drew with their fire an X which barricaded the tunnel from top to bottom. The flame of the X hung in the air; and before it could die, Prothall placed his staff erect within it. At once, a sheet of blue flared in the passage.

Howling in rage at Mhoram's ruse, the ur-viles sprang forward. The loremaster struck hugely at the flame with its stave. The fiery wall rippled and fluttered – but did not let the wedge pass.

Prothall and Mhoram took only a moment to see how their power held. Then they turned and dashed down the tunnel.

Gasping for breath, Mhoram told the company, 'We have forbidden the tunnel! But it will not endure. We are not strong enough – the High Lord's staff was needed to make any forbidding at all. And the ur-viles are savage. Drool drives them mad with the Illearth Stone.' In spite of his haste, his voice carried a shudder. 'Now we must run. We must escape – must! All our work will go for nothing if we do not take both Staff and Ward to safety.'

'Come!' the Manethrall responded. 'I know grass and sky. I can find the way.'

Prothall nodded agreement, but his movements were slow, despite the need for alacrity. He was exhausted, driven far past the normal limits of his stamina. With his breath rattling deep in his chest as if he were drowning in the phlegm of his age, he leaned heavily on the Staff of Law. 'Go!' he panted. 'Run!'

Two Bloodguard took his arms, and between them he stumbled into a slow run down the passage. Rallying around him, the company started away after Lithe.

At first, they went easily. Their tunnel offered few branchings; at each of these, Lithe seemed instantly sure which held the greatest promise of daylight. Lit from behind by Mhoram's staff, she loped forward as if following a warm trail of freedom.

After the struggles of close combat, the company found relief in simple, single-minded running. It allowed them to focus and conserve their strength. Furthermore, they were passing, as if slowly liberated, out of the range of Lord Foul's laughter. Soon they could hear neither mockery nor threat of slaughter at their backs. For once, the silent darkness befriended them.

For nearly a league, they hastened onward. They began to traverse a section of the catacombs which was intricate with small caves and passages and turnings, but which appeared to contain no large halls, crevices, wightworks. Throughout these multiplied corridors, Lithe did not hesitate. Several times she took ways which inclined slowly upward.

But as the complex tunnels opened into broader and blacker ways, where Mhoram's flame illumined no cave walls or ceilings, the catacombs became more hostile. Gradually, the silence changed — lost the hue of relief, and became the hush of ambush. The darkness around Mhoram's light seemed to conceal more and more. At the turnings and intersections, night thickened in their choices, clouding Lithe's instinct. She began to falter.

Behind her, Prothall grew less and less able to keep up the pace. His hoarse, wheezing breath was increasingly laboured; even the weariest Questers could hear his gasps over their own hard panting. The Bloodguard were almost carrying him.

Still they pushed on into stark midnight. They bore the Staff of Law and the Second Ward, and could not afford surrender.

Then they reached a high cave which formed a crossroads for several tunnels. The general direction they had maintained since Kiril Threndor was continued by one passage across the cave. But Lithe stopped in the centre of the junction as if she had been reined to a halt. She searched about her uncertainly, confused by the number of her choices — and by some intuitive rejection of her only obvious selection. Shaking her head as if resisting a bit, she grated, 'Ah, Lords. I do not know.'

Mhoram snapped, 'You must! We have no other chance. The old maps do not show these ways. You have led us far beyond our ken.' He gripped her shoulder as if he meant to force her decision. But the next moment he was distracted by Prothall. With a sharp spasm of coughing, the High Lord collapsed to the floor.

One Bloodguard quickly propped him into a sitting position, and Mhoram knelt beside him, peering with intent concern into his old face. 'Rest briefly,' mumbled Mhoram. 'Our forbidding has long since broken. We must not delay.'

Between fits of coughing, the High Lord replied, 'Leave me. Take the Staff and go. I am done.'

His words appalled the company. Covenant and the warriors covered their own breathing to hear Mhoram's answer. The air was suddenly intense with a fear that Mhoram would accept Prothall's sacrifice.

But Mhoram said nothing.

'Leave me,' Prothall repeated. 'Give your staff to me, and I will defend your retreat as I can. Go, I say. I am old. I have had my time of triumph. I lose nothing. Take the Staff and go.' When the Lord still did not speak, he rattled in supplication, 'Mhoram, hear me. Do not let my old bones destroy this high Quest.'

'I hear you.' Mhoram's voice sounded thick and wounded in his throat. He knelt with his head bowed.

But a moment later he rose to his feet, and put back his head, and began to laugh. It was quiet laughter – unfeverish and unforced – the laughter of relief and indespair. The company gaped at it until they understood that it was not hysteria. Then, without knowing why, they laughed in response. Humour ran like a clean wind through their hearts.

Covenant almost cursed aloud because he could not share it.

When they had subsided into low chuckling, Mhoram said to the High Lord, 'Ah, Prothall son of Dwillian. It is good that you are old. Leave you? How will I be able to take pleasure in telling Osondrea of your great exploits if you are not there to protest my boasting?' Gaily, he laughed again. Then, as if recollecting himself, he returned to where Lithe stood bewildered in the centre of the cave.

'Manethrall,' he said gently, 'you have done well. Your instinct is true – remember it now. Put all doubt away. We do not fear to follow where your heart leads.'

Covenant had noticed that she, too, had not joined the laughter of the company. Her eyes were troubled; he guessed that her swift blood had been offended by Mhoram's earlier sharpness. But she nodded gravely to the Lord. 'That is well. My thoughts do not trust my heart.'

'In what way?'

'My thoughts say that we must continue as we have come. But my heart wishes to go there.' She indicated a tunnel opening back almost in the direction from which they had come. 'I do not know,' she concluded simply. 'This is new to me.'

But Mhoram's reply held no hesitation. 'You are Manethrall Lithe of the Ramen. You have served the Ranyhyn. You know grass and sky. Trust your heart.'

After a moment, Lithe accepted his counsel.

Two Bloodguard helped Prothall to his feet. Supporting him between them, they joined the company and followed Lithe's instinct into the tunnel.

This passage soon began to descend slowly, and they set a good pace down it. They were buoyed along by the hope that their pursuers would not guess what they were doing, and so would neither cut them off nor follow them directly. But in the universal darkness and silence, they had no assurances. Their way met no branchings, but it wavered as if it were tracing a vein in the mountain. Finally it opened into a vast impression of blank space, and began to climb a steep, serrated rock face through a series of switchbacks. Now the company had to toil upward.

The difficulties of the ascent slowed them as much as the climbing. The higher they went, the colder the air became, and the more there seemed to be a wind blowing in the dark gulf beside them. But the cold and the wind only accented their dripping sweat and the exhausted rack of their respiration. The Bloodguard alone appeared unworn by the long days of their exertion; they strode steadily up the slope as if it were just a variation of their restless devotion. But their companions were more death prone. The warriors and Covenant began to stagger like cripples in the climb.

Finally Mhoram called a halt. Covenant dropped to sit with his back to the rock, facing the black-blown, measureless cavern. The sweat seemed to freeze on his face. The last of the food and drink was passed around, but in this buried place, both appeared to have lost their capacity to refresh – as if at last even sustenance were daunted by the darkness of the catacombs. Covenant ate and drank numbly. Then he shut his eyes to close out the empty blackness for a time. But he saw it whether his eyes were open or not.

Some time later – Covenant no longer measured duration – Lord Mhoram said in a stinging whisper, 'I hear them.'

Korik's reply sounded as hollow as a sign from a tomb. 'Yes. They follow. They are a great many.'

Lurching as if stricken, the Questers began to climb again, pushing themselves beyond the limits of their strength. They felt weak with failure, as if they were moving only because Mhoram's blue flame pulled them forward, compelled them, beseeched, cajoled, urged, inspired, refused to accept anything from them except endurance and more endurance. Disregarding every exigency except the need for escape, they continued to climb.

Then the wind began to howl around them, and their way

changed. The chasm abruptly narrowed; they found themselves on a thin, spiral stair carved into the wall of a vertical shaft. The width of the rude steps made them ascend in single file. And the wind went yelling up the shaft as if it fled the catacombs in stark terror. Covenant groaned when he realized that he would have to risk yet another perilous height, but the rush of the wind was so powerful that it seemed to make falling impossible. Cycling dizzily, he struggled up the stair.

The shaft went straight upward, and the wind yowled in pain; and the company climbed as if they were being dragged by the air. But as the shaft narrowed, the force of the wind increased; the air began to move past them too fast for breathing. As they gasped upward, a light-headed vertigo came over them. The shaft seemed to cant precariously from side to side. Covenant moved on his hands and knees.

Soon the whole company was crawling.

After an airless ache which extended interminably around him, Covenant lay stretched out on the stairs. He was not moving. Dimly, he heard voices trying to shout over the roar of the wind. But he was past listening. He felt that he had reached the verge of suffocation, and the only thing he wanted to do was weep. He could hardly remember what prevented him even now from releasing his misery.

Hands grabbed his shoulders, hauled him up on to flat stone. They dragged him ten or fifteen feet along the bottom of a thin crevice. The howl of the wind receded.

He heard Quaan give a choked, panting cheer. With an effort, he raised his head. He was sprawled in the crevice where it opened on one of the eastern faces of Mount Thunder. Across a flat, grey expanse far below him, the sun rose redly.

To his stunned ears, the cheering itself sounded like sobs. It spread as the warriors one by one climbed out past him into the dawn. Lithe had already leaped down a few feet from the crevice, and was on her knees kissing the earth. Far away, across the Sarangrave and the gleaming line of the Defiles Course and the Great Swamp, the sun stood up regally, wreathed in red splendour.

Covenant pushed himself into a sitting position and looked over at the Lords to see their victory.

They had no aspect of triumph. The High Lord sat crumpled like a sack of old bones, with the Staff of Law on his knees. His head was bowed, and he covered his face with both hands. Beside him, Mhoram stood still and dour, and his eyes were as bleak as a wilderness.

Covenant did not understand.

Then Bannor said, 'We can defend here.'

365

Mhoram's reply was soft and violent. 'How? Drool knows many ways. If we prevent him here, he will attack from below – above. He can bring thousands against us.'

'Then close this gap to delay them.'

Mhoram's voice became softer still. 'The High Lord has no staff. I cannot forbid the gap alone – I have not the power. Do you believe that I am strong enough to bring down the walls of this crevice? No – not even if I were willing to damage the Earth in that way. We must escape. There – ' He pointed down the mountainside with a hand that trembled.

Covenant looked downward. The crevices opened into the bottom of a ravine which ran straight down the side of Mount Thunder like a knife wound. The spine of this cut was jumbled and tossed with huge rocks – fallen boulders, pieces of the higher cliffs like dead fragments of the mountain. And its walls were sheer, unclimbable. The Questers would have to pick their way torturously along the bottom of the cut for half a league. There the walls gave way, and the ravine dropped over a cliff. When the company reached the cliff, they would try to work around the mountainsides until they found another descent.

Still Covenant did not understand. He groaned at the difficulty of the ravine, but it was escape. He could feel sunlight on his face. Heaving himself to his feet, he muttered, 'Let's get going.'

Mhoram gave him a look thick with suppressed pain. But he did not voice it. Instead, he spoke stiffly to Quaan and Korik. In a few moments, the Questers started down the ravine.

Their progress was deadly slow. In order to make their way, they had to climb from rock to rock, swing themselves over rough boulders, squeeze on hands and knees through narrow gaps between huge fists of stone. And they were weak. The strongest of the warriors needed help time and again from the Bloodguard. Prothall had to be almost entirely carried. He clutched the Staff, and scrabbled frailly at the climbs. Whenever he jumped from a rock, he fell to his knees; soon the front of his robe was spattered with blood.

Covenant began to sense their danger. Their pace might be fatal. If Drool knew other ways on to the slope, his forces might reach the end of the ravine before the company did.

He was not alone in his perception. After their first relief, the warriors took on a haunted look. Soon they were trudging, clambering, struggling with their heads bowed and backs bent as if the weight of all they had ever known were tied around their necks. The sunlight did not allow them to be ignorant of their peril.

Like a prophecy, their fear was fulfilled before the company was halfway down the ravine. One of the Eoman gave a broken cry, pointed back up the mountain. There they saw a horde of ur-viles rushing out of the cleft from which they had come.

They tried to push faster down the littered spine of the cut. But the ur-viles poured after them like a black flood. The creatures seemed to spring over the rocks without danger of misstep, as if borne along by a rush of savagery. They gained on the company with sickening speed.

And the ur-viles were not alone. Near the end of the ravine, Cavewights suddenly appeared atop one wall. As soon as they spotted the Questers, they began throwing ropes over the edge, scaling down the wall.

The company was caught like a group of mites in the pincers of Drool's power.

They stopped where they were, paralysed by dismay. For a moment, even Quaan's sense of responsibility for his Eoman failed; he stared blankly about him, and did not move. Covenant sagged against a boulder. He wanted to scream at the mountain that this was not fair. He had already survived so much, endured so much, lost so much. Where was his escape? Was this the cost of his bargain, his forbearance? It was too great. He was a leper, not made for such ordeals. His voice shook uncontrollably – full of useless outrage. 'No wonder he – let us have the Staff. So it would hurt worse now. He knew we wouldn't get away with it.'

But Mhoram shouted orders in a tone that cut through the dismay. He ran a short way down the ravine and climbed on to a wide, flat rock higher than the others near it. 'There is space for us! Come!' he commanded. 'We will make our end here!'

Slowly, the warriors shambled to the rock as if they were overburdened with defeat. Mhoram and the Bloodguard helped them up. High Lord Prothall came last, propped between two Bloodguard. He was muttering, 'No. No.' But he did not resist Mhoram's orders.

When everyone was on the rock, Quaan's Eoman and the Bloodguard placed themselves around its edge. Lithe joined them, her cord taut in her hands, leaving Prothall and Mhoram and Covenant in the ring of the company's last defence.

Now the ur-viles had covered half the distance to the rock where the company stood. Behind them came hundreds of Cavewights, gushing out of the crevice and pouring down the ravine. And as many more worked upward from the place where they had entered the cut.

Surveying Drool's forces, Mhoram said softly, 'Take heart, my friends. You have done well. Now let us make our end so bravely that even our enemies will remember it. Do not despair. There are many chances between the onset of a war and victory. Let us teach

Lord Foul that he will never taste victory until the last friend of the Land is dead.'

But Prothall whispered, 'No. No.' Facing upward toward the crest of Mount Thunder, he planted his feet and closed his eyes. With slow resolution, he raised the Staff of Law level with his heart and gripped it in both fists. 'It must be possible,' he breathed. 'By the Seven! It must.' His knuckles whitened on the intricate runed and secret surface of the Staff. '*Melenkurion* Skyweir, help me. I do not accept this end.' His brows slowly knotted over his shut, sunken eyes, and his head bowed until his beard touched his heart. From between his pale lips came a whispered, wordless song. But his voice rattled so huskily in his chest that his song sounded more like a dirge than an invocation.

Drool's forces poured down and surged up at the company inexorably. Mhoram watched them with a rictus of helplessness on his humane lips.

Suddenly, a desperate chance blazed in his eyes. He spun, gripped Covenant with his gaze, whispered, 'There is a way! Prothall strives to call the Fire-Lions. He cannot succeed – the power of the Staff is closed, and we have not the knowledge to unlock it. But white gold can release that power. It can be done!'

Covenant recoiled as if Mhoram had betrayed him. No! he panted. I made a bargain – !

Then, with a sickening, vertiginous twist of insight, he caught a glimpse of Lord Foul's plan for him, glimpsed what the Despiser was doing to him. Here was the killing blow which had lain concealed behind all the machinations, all the subterfuge.

Hell and blood!

Here was the point of impact between his opposing madnesses. If he attempted to use the wild magic – if his ring had power – if it had no power – He flinched at the reel and strike of dark visions – the company slain – the Staff destroyed – thousands of creatures dead, all that blood on his head, his head.

'No,' he gasped thickly. 'Don't ask me. I promised I wouldn't do any more killing. You don't know what I've done – to Atiaran – to – I made a bargain so I wouldn't have to do any more killing.'

The ur-viles and Cavewights were almost within bow-shot now. The Eoman had arrows nocked and ready. Drool's hordes slowed, began to poise for the last spring of attack.

But Mhoram's eyes did not release Covenant. 'There will be still more killing if you do not. Do you believe that Lord Foul will be content with our deaths? Never! He will slay again until all life without exception is his to corrupt or destroy. All life, do you hear? Even these creatures that now serve him will not be spared.'

'No!' Covenant groaned again. 'Don't you see? This is just what he wants. The Staff will be destroyed – or Drool will be destroyed – or we'll – No matter what happens, he'll win. He'll be free. You're doing just what he wants.'

'Nevertheless!' Mhoram returned fervidly. 'The dead are dead – only the living may hope to resist Despite.'

Hellfire! Covenant groped for answers like a man incapable of his own distress. But he found none. No bargain or compromise met his need. In his pain, he cried out wildly, protested, appealed, 'Mhoram! It's suicide! You're asking me to go crazy!'

The peril in Mhoram's eyes did not waver. 'No, Unbeliever. You need not lose your mind. There are other answers – other songs. You can find them. Why should the Land be destroyed for your pain? Save or damn! Grasp the Staff!'

'Damnation!' Fumbling furiously for his ring, Covenant shouted, 'Do it yourself!' He wrenched the band from his finger and tried to throw it at Mhoram. But he was shaking madly; his fingers slipped. The ring dropped to the stone, rolled away.

He scrambled after it. He did not seem to have enough digits to catch it; it skidded past Prothall's feet. He lurched toward it again – then missed his footing, fell, and smacked his forehead on the stone.

Distantly, he heard the thrum of bowstrings; the battle had begun. But he paid no attention. He felt that he had cracked his skull. When he raised his head, he found that his vision was wrong; he was seeing double.

The moss-stain chart of his robe smeared illegibly on his sight. Now he had lost whatever chance he had to read it, decipher the cryptic message of Morinmoss. He saw two of Mhoram as the Lord held up the ring. He saw two Prothalls above him, clutching the Staff and trying with the last strength of his life-force to compel its power to his will. Two Bannors turned away from the fight toward the Lords.

Then Mhoram stooped to Covenant. The Lord lashed out, caught his right wrist. The grip was so fierce that he felt his bones grinding together. It forced his hand open, and when his two fingers were spread and vulnerable, Mhoram shoved the ring on to his index digit. It stuck after the first knuckle. 'I cannot usurp your place,' the double Lord grated. He stood and roughly pulled Covenant erect. Thrusting his double face at the Unbeliever, he hissed, 'By the Seven! You fear power more than weakness.'

Yes! Covenant moaned at the pain of his wrist and head. Yes! I want to survive!

The snap of bowstrings came now as fast as the warriors could ready their arrows. But their supply of shafts was limited. And the

369

ur-viles and Cavewights hung back, risking themselves only enough to draw the warriors' fire. Drool's forces were in no hurry. The ur-viles particularly looked ready to relish the slow slaughter of the company.

But Covenant had no awareness to spare for such things. He stared in a kind of agony at Mhoram. The Lord seemed to have two mouths — lips stretched over multiplied teeth — and four eyes, all aflame with compulsions. Because he could think of no other appeal, he reached his free hand to his belt, took out Atiaran's knife, and extended it toward Mhoram. Through his teeth, he pleaded, 'It would be better if you killed me.'

Slowly, Mhoram's grip eased. His lips softened; the fire of his eyes faded. His gaze seemed to turn inward, and he winced at what he beheld. When he spoke, his voice sounded like dust. 'Ah, Covenant — forgive me. I forget myself. Foamfollower — Foamfollower understood this. I should have heard him more clearly. It is wrong to ask for more than you give freely. In this way, we come to resemble what we hate.' He released Covenant's wrist and stepped back. 'My friend, this is not on your head. The burden is ours, and we bear it to the end. Forgive me.'

Covenant could not answer. He stood with his face twisted as if he were about to howl. His eyes ached at the duplicity of his vision. Mhoram's mercy affected him more than any argument or demand. He turned miserably toward Prothall. Could he not find somewhere the strength for that risk? Perhaps the path of escape lay that way — perhaps the horror of wild magic was the price he would have to pay for his freedom. He did not want to be killed by ur-viles. But when he raised his arm, he could not tell which of those hands was his, which of those two Staffs was the real one.

Then, with a flat thrum, the last arrow was gone. The Cavewights gave a vast shout of malice and glee. At the command of the ur-viles, they began to approach. The warriors drew their swords, braced themselves for their useless end. The Bloodguard balanced on the balls of their feet.

Trembling, Covenant tried to reach toward the Staff. But his head was spinning, and a whirl of darkness jumped dizzily at him. He could not overcome his fear; he was appalled at the revenge his leprosy would wreak on him for such audacity. His hand crossed half the distance and stopped, clutched in unfingered impotence at the empty air.

Ah! he cried lornly. *Help me!*

'We are the Bloodguard.' Bannor's voice was almost inaudible through the loud lust of the Cavewights. 'We cannot permit this end.'

Firmly, he took Covenant's hand and placed it on the Staff of Law, midway between Prothall's straining knuckles.

Power seemed to explode in Covenant's chest. A silent concussion, a shock beyond hearing, struck the ravine like a convulsion of the mountain. The blast knocked the Questers from their feet, sent all the ur-viles and Cavewights sprawling among the boulders. Only the High Lord kept his feet. His head jerked up, and the Staff bucked in his hands.

For a moment, there was stillness in the ravine – a quiet so intense that the blast seemed to have deafened all the combatants. And in that moment, the entire sky over Gravin Threndor turned black with impenetrable thunder.

Then came noise – one deep bolt of sound as if the very rock of the mountain cried out – followed by long waves of hot, hissing sputters. The clouds dropped until they covered the crest of Mount Thunder.

Great yellow fires began to burn on the shrouded peak.

For a time, the company and their attackers lay in the ravine as if they were afraid to move. Everyone stared up at the fires and the thunderheads.

Suddenly, the flames erupted. With a roar as if the air itself were burning, fires started charging like great, hungry beasts down every face and side of the mountain.

Shrieking in fear, the Cavewights sprang up and ran. A few hurled themselves madly against the walls of the ravine. But most of them swept around the company's rock and fled downward, trying to outrun the Fire-Lions.

The ur-viles went the other way. In furious haste, they scrambled up the ravine toward the entrance to the catacombs.

But before they could reach safety, Drool appeared out of the cleft above them. The Cavewight was crawling, too crippled to stand. But in his fist he clutched a green stone which radiated intense wrong through the blackness of the clouds. His scream carried over the roar of the Lions:

'Crush! Crush!'

The ur-viles stopped, caught between fears.

While the creatures hesitated, the company started down the ravine. Prothall and Covenant were too exhausted to support themselves, so the Bloodguard bore them, throwing them from man to man over the boulders, dragging them along the tumbled floor of the ravine.

Ahead, the Cavewights began to reach the end of the cut. Some of them ran so blindly that they plunged over the cliff; others scattered in either direction along the ridge, wailing for escape.

But behind the company, the ur-viles formed a wedge and again started downward. The Questers were barely able to keep their distance from the wedge.

The roar of the flaming air grew sharper, fiercer. Set free by the power of the Peak, boulders tumbled from the cliffs. The Fire-Lions moved like molten stone, sprang down the slopes as if spewed out of the heart of an inferno. Still far above the ravine, the consuming howl of their might seemed to double and treble itself with each downward lunge. A blast of scorched air blew ahead of them like a herald, trumpeting the progress of fire and volcanic hunger. Gravin Threndor shuddered to its roots.

The difficulty of the ravine eased as the company neared the lower end, and Covenant began to move for himself. Impelled by broken vision, overborne hearing, gaining rampage, he shook free of the Bloodguard. Moving stiff-kneed like a puppet, he jerked in a dogged, stumbling line for the cliff.

The other Questers swung to the south along the edge. But he went directly to the precipice. When he reached it, his legs barely had the strength to stop him. Tottering weakly, he looked down the drop. It was sheer for two thousand feet, and the cliff was at least half a league wide.

There was no escape. The Lions would get the company before they reached any possible descent beyond the cliff – long before.

People yelled at him, warning him futilely; he could hardly hear them through the roaring air. He gave no heed. That kind of escape was not what he wanted. And he was not afraid of the fall; he could not see it clearly enough to be afraid.

He had something to do.

He paused for a moment, summoning his courage. Then he realized that one of the Bloodguard would probably try to save him. He wanted to accomplish his purpose before that could happen.

He needed an answer to death.

Pulling off his ring, he held it firmly in his half-fingerless hand, cocked his arm to throw the band over the cliff.

His eyes followed the ring as he drew back his arm, and he stopped suddenly, struck by a blow of shame. The metal was clean. His vision still saw two rings, but both were flat argent; the stain was gone from within them.

He spun from the cliff, searched up the ravine for Drool.

He heard Mhoram shout, 'Bannor! It is his choice!' The Blood-guard was springing toward him. At Mhoram's command, Bannor pulled to a halt ten yards away, despite his Vow. The next instant, he rejected the command, leaped toward Covenant again.

Covenant could not focus his vision. He caught a glimpse of fiery

Lions pouncing toward the crevice high up the ravine. But his sight was dominated by the ur-vile wedge. It was only three strides away from him. The loremaster had already raised its stave to strike.

Instinctively, Covenant tried to move. But he was too slow. He was still leaning when Bannor crashed into him, knocked him out of the way.

With a mad, exulting bark as if they had suddenly seen a vision, the ur-viles sprang forward as one and plunged over the cliff. Their cries as they fell sounded ferociously triumphant.

Bannor lifted Covenant to his feet. The Bloodguard urged him toward the rest of the company, but he broke free and stumbled a few steps up the slope, straining his eyes toward the crevice. 'Drool! What happened to Drool?' His eyes failed him. He stopped, wavered uncertainly, raged, 'I can't see!'

Mhoram hastened to him, and Covenant repeated his question, shouting it into the Lord's face.

Mhoram replied gently, 'Drool is there, in the crevice. Power that he could not master destroys him. He no longer knows what he does. In a moment, the Fire-Lions will consume him.'

Covenant strove to master his voice by biting down on it. 'No!' he hissed. 'He's just another victim. Foul planned this all along.' Despite his clamped teeth, his voice sounded broken.

Comfortingly, Mhoram touched his shoulder. 'Be at peace, Unbeliever. We have done all we can. You need not condemn yourself.'

Abruptly, Covenant found that his rage was gone – collapsed into dust. He felt blasted and wrecked, and he sank to the ground as if his bones could no longer hold him. His eyes had a tattered look, like the sails of a ghost ship. Without caring what he did, he pushed his wedding band back on to his ring finger.

The rest of the company was moving toward him. They had given up their attempt at flight; together, they watched the progress of the Lions. The midnight clouds cast a gloom over the whole mountain, and through the dimness the pouncing fires blazed and coruscated like beasts of sun flame. They sprang down the walls into the ravine, and some of them bounded upward toward the crevice.

Lord Mhoram finally shook himself free of his entrancement. 'Call your Ranyhyn,' he commanded Bannor. 'The Bloodguard can save themselves. Take the Staff and the Second Ward. Call the Ranyhyn and escape.'

Bannor met Mhoram's gaze for a long moment, measuring the Lord's order. Then he refused stolidly. 'One of us will go. To carry the Staff and Ward to Lord's Keep. The rest remain.'

'Why? We cannot escape. You must live – to serve the Lords who must carry on this way.'

'Perhaps.' Bannor shrugged slightly. 'Who can say? High Lord Kevin ordered us away, and we obeyed. We will not do such a thing again.'

'But this death is useless!' cried Mhoram.

'Nevertheless.' The Bloodguard's tone was as blank as iron. Then he added, 'But you can call Hynaril. Do so, Lord.'

'No,' Mhoram sighed with a tired smile of recognition. 'I cannot. How could I leave so many to die?'

Covenant only half listened. He felt like a derelict, and he was picking among the wreckage of his emotions, in search of something worth salvaging. But part of him understood. He put the two fingers of his right hand between his lips and gave one short, piercing whistle.

All the company stared at him. Quaan seemed to think that the Unbeliever had lost his mind; Mhoram's eyes jumped at wild guesses. But Manethrall Lithe tossed her cord high in the air and crowed, 'The Ranyhyn! Mane of the World! He calls them!'

'How?' protested Quaan. 'He refused them.'

'They reared to him!' she returned with a nickering laugh. 'They will come.'

Covenant had stopped listening altogether. Something was happening to him, and he lurched to his feet to meet it upright. The dimensions of his situation were changing. To his blurred gaze, the comrades of the company grew slowly harder and solider – took on the texture of native rock. And the mountain itself became increasingly adamantine. It seemed as immutable as the cornerstone of the world. He felt veils drop from his perception; he saw the unclouded fact of Gravin Threndor in all its unanswerable power. He paled beside it; his flesh grew thin, transient. Air as thick as smoke blew through him, chilling his bones. The throat of his soul contracted in silent pain. 'What's happening to me?'

Around the cliff edge to the south, Ranyhyn came galloping. Like a blaze of hope, they raced the downrush of the Lions. At once, a hoarse cheer broke from the warriors. 'We are saved!' Mhoram cried. 'There is time enough!' With the rest of the company, he hurried forward to meet the swift approach of the Ranyhyn.

Covenant felt that he had been left alone. 'What's happening to me?' he repeated dimly toward the hard mountain.

But Prothall was still at his side. Covenant heard the High Lord say in a kind voice that seemed as loud as thunder, 'Drool is dead. He was your summoner, and with his death the call ends. That is the way of such power.

'Farewell, Unbeliever! Be true! You have wrought greatly for us. The Ranyhyn will preserve us. And with the Staff of Law and the

Second Ward, we will not be unable to defend against the Despiser's ill. Take heart. Despair and bitterness are not the only songs in the world.'

But Covenant wailed in mute grief. Everything around him – Prothall and the company and the Ranyhyn and the Fire-Lions and the mountains – became too solid for him. They overwhelmed his perceptions, passed beyond his senses into grey mist. He clutched about him and felt nothing. He could not see; the Land left the range of his eyes. It was too much for him, and he lost it.

25

SURVIVED

Grey mist swirled around him for a long convulsive moment. Then it began to smear, and he lost it as well. His vision blurred, as if some hard god had rubbed a thumb across it. He blinked rapidly, tried to reach up to squeeze his eyes; but something soft prevented his hand. His sight remained blank.

He was waking up, though he felt more as if he were dropping into grogginess.

Gradually, he became able to identify where he was. He lay in a bed with tubular protective bars on the sides. White sheets covered him to his chin. Grey curtains shut him off from the other patients in the room. A fluorescent light stared past him emptily from the ceiling. The air was faintly tinged with ether and germicide. A call button hung at the head of the bed.

All his fingers and toes were numb.

Nerves don't regenerate, of course they don't, they don't –

This was important – he knew it was important – but for some reason it did not carry any weight with him. His heart was too hot with other emotions to feel that particular ice.

What mattered to him was that Prothall and Mhoram and the Quest had survived. He clung to that as if it were proof of sanity – a demonstration that what had happened to him, that what he had done, was not the product of madness, self-destruction. They had survived; at least his bargain with the Ranyhyn had accomplished that much. They had done exactly what Lord Foul wanted them to do – but they had survived. At least he was not guilty of their deaths, too. His inability to use his ring, to believe in his ring, had not made Wraiths of them. That was his only consolation for what he had lost.

Then he made out two figures standing at the foot of the bed. One of them was a woman in white – a nurse. As he tried to focus on her, she said, 'Doctor – he's regaining consciousness.'

The doctor was a middle-aged man in a brown suit. The flesh under his eyes sagged as if he were weary of all human pain, but his lips under his greying moustache were gentle. He approached along the side of the bed, touched Covenant's forehead for a moment, then pulled up Covenant's eyelids and shined a small light at his pupils.

With an effort, Covenant focused on the light.

The doctor nodded, and put his flashlight away. 'Mr Covenant?'

Covenant swallowed at the dryness in his throat.

'Mr Covenant.' The doctor held his face close to Covenant's, and spoke quietly, calmly. 'You're in the hospital. You were brought here after your run-in with that police car. You've been unconscious for about four hours.'

Covenant lifted his head and nodded to show that he understood.

'Good,' said the doctor. 'I'm glad you're coming around. Now, let me talk to you for a moment.

'Mr Covenant, the police officer who was driving that car says that he didn't hit you. He claims that he stopped in time – you just fell down in front of him. From my examination, I would be inclined to agree with him. Your hands are scraped up a bit, and you have a bruise on your forehead – but things like that could have happened when you fell.' He hesitated momentarily, then asked, '*Did* he hit you?'

Dumbly, Covenant shook his head. The question did not feel important.

'Well, I suppose you could have knocked yourself out by hitting your head on the pavement. But why did you fall?'

That, too, did not feel important. He pushed the question away with a twitch of his hands. Then he tried to sit up in bed.

He succeeded before the doctor could help or hinder him; he was not as weak as he had feared he might be. The numbness of his fingers and toes still seemed to lack conviction, as if they would recover as soon as their circulation was restored.

Nerves don't –

After a moment, he regained his voice, and asked for his clothes.

The doctor studied him closely. 'Mr Covenant,' he said. 'I'll let you go home if you want to. I suppose I should keep you under observation for a day or two. But I really haven't been able to find anything wrong with you. And you know more about taking care of leprosy than I do.' Covenant did not miss the look of nausea that flinched across the nurse's face. 'And, to be perfectly honest – ' the doctor's tone turned suddenly acid – 'I don't want to have to fight the staff here to be sure that you get decent care. Do you feel up to it?'

In answer, Covenant began fumbling with awkward fingers at the dull white hospital gown he wore.

Abruptly, the doctor went to a locker, and came back with Covenant's clothes.

Covenant gave them a kind of VSE. They were scuffed and dusty from his fall in the street; yet they looked exactly as they had looked when he had last worn them, during the first days of the Quest.

Exactly as if none of it had ever happened.

When he was dressed, he signed the releases. His hand was so cold that he could hardly write his name.

But the Quest had survived. At least his bargain had been good for that.

Then the doctor gave him a ride in a wheelchair down to the discharge exit. Outside the building, the doctor suddenly began to talk as if in some oblique way he were trying to apologize for not keeping Covenant in the hospital. 'It must be hell to be a leper,' he said rapidly. 'I'm trying to understand. It's like – I studied in Heidelberg, years ago, and while I was there I saw a lot of medieval art. Especially religious art. Being a leper reminds me of statues of the Crucifixion made during the Middle Ages. There is Christ on the Cross, and his features – his body, even his face – are portrayed so blandly that the figure is unrecognizable. It could be anyone, man or woman. But the wounds – the nails in the hands and feet, the spear in the side, the crown of thorns – are carved and even painted in incredibly vivid detail. You would think the artist crucified his model to get that kind of realism.

'Being a leper must be like that.'

Covenant felt the doctor's sympathy, but he could not reply to it. He did not know how.

After a few minutes, an ambulance came and took him back to Haven Farm.

He had survived.

He walked up the long driveway to his house as if that were his only hope.

THE ILLEARTH
WAR

That beauty and truth should pass utterly

PART I

Revelstone

1

'THE DREAMS OF MEN'

By the time Thomas Covenant reached his house the burden of what had happened to him had already become intolerable.

When he opened the door, he found himself once more in the charted neatness of his living room. Everything was just where he had left it – just as if nothing had happened, as if he had not spent the past four hours in a coma or in another world where his disease had been abrogated despite the fact that such a thing was impossible, impossible. His fingers and toes were numb and cold; their nerves were dead. That could never be changed. His living room – all his rooms – were organized and carpeted and padded so that he could at least try to feel safe from the hazards of bumps, cuts, burns, bruises which could damage him mortally because he was unable to feel them, know that they had happened. There, lying on the coffee table in front of the sofa, was the book he had been reading the previous day. He had been reading it while he was trying to make up his mind to risk a walk into town. It was still open to a page which had had an entirely different meaning to him just four hours ago. It said, '. . . modelling the incoherent and vertiginous matter of which dreams are composed was the most difficult task a man could undertake . . .' And on another page it said, '. . . the dreams of men belong to God . . .'

He could not bear it.

He was as weary as if the Quest for the Staff of Law had actually happened – as if he had just survived an ordeal in the catacombs and on the mountainside, and had played his involuntary part in wresting the Staff from Lord Foul's mad servant. But it was suicide for him to believe that such things had happened, that such things, could happen. They were impossible, like the nerve-health he had felt while the events had been transpiring around him or within him. His survival depended on his refusal to accept the impossible.

Because he was weary and had no other defence, he went to bed and slept like the dead, dreamless and alone.

Then for two weeks he shambled through his life from day to day in a kind of somnolence. He could not have said how often his phone rang, how often anonymous people called to threaten or berate or vilify him for having dared to walk into town. He wrapped blankness about him like a bandage, and did nothing, thought nothing, recognized nothing. He forgot his medication, and neglected his VSE (his Visual Surveillance of Extremities — the discipline of constant self-inspection on which the doctors had taught him his life depended). He spent most of his time in bed. When he was not in bed, he was still essentially asleep. As he moved through his rooms, he repeatedly rubbed his fingers against table legs, door-frames, chair backs, fixtures, so that he had the appearance of trying to wipe something off his hands.

It was as if he had gone into hiding — emotional hibernation or panic. But the vulture wings of his personal dilemma beat the air in search of him ceaselessly. The phone calls became angrier and more frustrated; his mute irresponsiveness goaded the callers, denied them any effective release for their hostility. And deep in the core of his slumber something began to change. More and more often, he awoke with the dull conviction that he had dreamed something which he could not remember, did not dare remember.

After those two weeks, his situation suddenly reasserted its hold on him. He saw his dream for the first time. It was a small fire — a few flames without location or context, but somehow pure and absolute. As he gazed at them, they grew into a blaze, a conflagration. And he was feeding the fire with paper — the pages of his writings, both the published best-seller and the new novel he had been working on when his illness was discovered.

This was true; he had burned both works. After he had learned that he was a leper — after his wife, Joan, had divorced him and taken his young son, Roger, out of the state — after he had spent six months in the leprosarium — his books had seemed to him so blind and complacent, so destructive of himself, that he had burned them and given up writing.

But now, watching that fire in dreams, he felt for the first time the grief and outrage of seeing his handiwork destroyed. He jerked awake wide-eyed and sweating — and found that he could still hear the crackling hunger of the flames.

Joan's stables were on fire. He had not been to the place where she had formerly kept her horses for months, but he knew they contained nothing which could have started this blaze spontaneously. This was vandalism, revenge; this was what lay behind all those threatening phone calls.

The dry wood burned furiously, hurling itself up into the dark abyss of the night. And in it he saw Soaring Woodhelven in flames. He could smell in memory the smouldering dead of the tree village. He could feel himself killing Cavewights, incinerating them with an impossible power which seemed to rage out of the white gold of his wedding band.

Impossible!

He fled the fire, dashed back in his house and turned on the lights as if mere electric bulbs were his only shield against insanity and darkness.

Pacing there miserably around the safety of his living room, he remembered what had happened to him.

He had walked – leper outcast unclean! – into town from Haven Farm where he lived, to pay his phone bill, to pay it in person as an assertion of his common humanity against the hostility and revulsion and black charity of his fellow citizens. In the process, he had fallen down in front of a police car –

And found himself in another world. A place which could not possibly exist, and to which he could not possibly have travelled if it did exist: a place where lepers recovered their health.

That place had called itself 'the Land'. And it had treated him like a hero because of his resemblance to Berek Halfhand, the legendary Lord-Fatherer – and because of his white gold ring. But he was not a hero. He had lost the last two fingers of his right hand, not in combat, but in surgery; they had been amputated because of the gangrene which had come with the onset of his disease. And the ring had been given to him by a woman who had divorced him because he was a leper. Nothing could have been less true than the Land's belief in him. And because he was in a false position, he had behaved with a subtle infidelity which now made him squirm.

Certainly none of those people had deserved his irrectitude. Not the Lords, the guardians of the health and beauty of the Land; not Saltheart Foamfollower, the Giant who had befriended him; not Atiaran Trell-mate, who had guided him safely towards Revelstone, the mountain city where the Lords lived; and not, oh, not her daughter Lena, whom he had raped.

Lena! he cried involuntarily; beating his numb fingers against his sides as he paced. How could I do that to you?

But he knew how it had happened. The health which the Land gave him had taken him by surprise. After months of impotence and repressed fury, he had not been prepared for the sudden rush of his vitality. And that vitality had other consequences, as well. It had seduced him into a conditional cooperation with the Land, though he knew that what was happening to him was impossible, a dream. Because of that health, he had taken to the Lords at Revelstone a message of doom given to him by the Land's great enemy, Lord Foul the Despiser. And he had gone with the Lords on their Quest for the Staff of Law, Berek's rune staff which had been lost by High Lord

Kevin, last of the Old Lords, in his battle against the Despiser. This weapon the new Lords considered to be their only hope against their enemy; and he had unwillingly, faithlessly, helped them to regain it.

Then almost without transition he had found himself in a bed in the town's hospital. Only four hours had passed since his accident with the police car. His leprosy was unchanged. Because he appeared essentially uninjured, the doctor sent him back to his house on Haven Farm.

And now he had been roused from somnolence, and was pacing his lighted house as if it were an eyot of sanity in a night of darkness and chaos. Delusion! He had been deluded. The very idea of the Land sickened him. Health was impossible to lepers; that was the law on which his life depended. Nerves do not regenerate, and without a sense of touch there is no defence against injury and infection and dismemberment and death — no defence except the exigent law which he had learned in the leprosarium. The doctors there had taught him that his illness was the definitive fact of his existence, and that if he did not devote himself wholly, heart and mind and soul, to his own protection, he would ineluctably become crippled and putrescent before his ugly end.

That law had a logic which now seemed more infallible than ever. He had been seduced, however conditionally, by a delusion; and the results were deadly.

For two weeks now he had completely lost his grasp on survival, had not taken his medication, had not performed one VSE, or any other drill, had not even shaved.

A dizzy nausea twisted in him. As he checked himself over, he was trembling uncontrollably.

But somehow he appeared to have escaped harm. His flesh showed no scrapes, burns, contusions, none of the fatal purple spots of resurgent leprosy.

Panting as if he had just survived an immersion in horror, he set about trying to regain his hold on his life.

Quickly, urgently, he took a large dose of his medication — DDS, diamino-diphenyl-sulfone. Then he went into the white fluorescence of his bathroom, stropped his old straight razor, and set the long sharp blade to his throat.

Shaving this way, with the blade clutched in the two fingers and thumb of his right hand, was a personal ritual which he had taught himself in order to discipline and mortify his unwieldy imagination. It steadied him almost in spite of himself. The danger of that keen metal so insecurely held helped him to concentrate, helped to rid him of false dreams and hopes, the alluring and suicidal progeny of his mind. The consequences of a slip were acid-etched in his brain.

He could not ignore the law of his leprosy when he was so close to hurting himself, giving himself an injury which might reawaken the dormant rot of his nerves, cause infection and blindness, gnaw the flesh off his face until he was too loathsome to be beheld.

When he had shaved off two weeks of beard, he studied himself for a moment in the mirror. He saw a grey, gaunt man with leprosy riding the background of his eyes like a plague ship in a cold sea. And the sight gave him an explanation for his delusion. It was the doing of his subconscious mind – the blind despair-work or cowardice of a brain that had been bereft of everything which had formerly given it meaning. The revulsion of his fellow human beings taught him to be revolted at himself, and this self-despite had taken him over while he had been helpless after his accident with the police car. He knew its name: it was a death wish. It worked in him subconsciously because his conscious mind was so grimly devoted to survival, to avoiding the outcome of his illness.

But he was not helpless now. He was awake and afraid.

When morning finally came, he called his lawyer, Megan Roman – a woman who handled his contracts and financial business – and told her what had happened to Joan's stables.

He could hear her discomfort clearly through the connection. 'What do you want me to do, Mr Covenant?'

'Get the police to investigate. Find out who did it. Make sure it doesn't happen again.'

She was silent for a long, uncomfortable moment. Then she said, 'The police won't do it. You're in Sheriff Lytton's territory, and he won't do a thing for you. He's one of the people who thinks you should be run out of the county. He's been sheriff here a long time, and he gets pretty protective about "his" county. He thinks you're a threat. Just between you and me, I don't think he has any more humanity than he absolutely needs to get re-elected every two years.'

She was talking rapidly as if to keep him from saying anything, offering to do anything. 'But I think I can make him do something for you. If I threaten him – tell him you're going to come into town to press charges – I can make him make sure nothing like this happens again. He knows this county. You can bet he already knows who burned your stables.'

Joan's stables, Covenant answered silently. I don't like horses.

'He can keep those people from doing anything else. And he'll do it – if I scare him right.'

Covenant accepted this. He seemed to have no choice.

'Incidentally, some of the people around here have been trying to find some legal way to make you move. They're upset about that visit of yours. I've been telling them it's impossible – or at least more trouble than it's worth. So far, I think most of them believe me.'

He hung up with a shudder. He gave himself a thorough VSE, checking his body from head to foot for danger signs. Then he went about the task of trying to recover all his self-protective habits.

For a week or so, he made progress. He paced through the charted neatness of his house like a robot curiously aware of the machinery inside him, searching despite the limited function of his programming for one good answer to death. And when he left the house, walked out the driveway to pick up his groceries, or hiked for hours through the woods along Righters Creek in back of Haven Farm, he moved with an extreme caution, testing every rock and branch and breeze as if he suspected it of concealing malice.

But gradually he began to look about him, and as he did so some of his determination faltered. April was on the woods – the first signs of a spring which should have appeared beautiful to him. But at unexpected moments his sight seemed to go suddenly dim with sorrow as he remembered the spring of the Land. Compared to that, where the very health of the sap and buds was visible, palpable, discernible by touch and scent and sound, the woods he now walked looked sadly superficial. The trees and grass and hills had no savour, no depth of beauty. They could only remind him of Andelain and the taste of *aliantha*.

Then other memories began to disturb him. For several days, he could not get the woman who had died for him at the battle of Soaring Woodhelven out of his thoughts. He had never even known her name, never even asked her why she had devoted herself to him. She was like Atiaran and Foamfollower and Lena; she assumed that he had a right to such sacrifices.

Like Lena, about whom he could rarely bear to think, she made him ashamed; and with shame came anger – the old familiar leper's rage on which so much of his endurance depended. By hell! he fumed. They had no right. They had no right! But then the uselessness of his passion rebounded against him, and he was forced to recite to himself as if he were reading the catechism of his illness, Futility is the defining characteristic of life. Pain is the proof of existence. In the extremity of his moral solitude, he had no other answers.

At times like that, he found bitter consolation in psychological studies where a subject was sealed off from all sensory input, made blind, deaf, silent, and immobile, and as a result began to experience the most horrendous hallucinations. If conscious normal men and women could be placed so much at the mercy of their own inner chaos, surely one abject leper in a coma could have a dream that was worse than chaos – a dream specifically self-designed to drive him mad. At least what had happened to him did not altogether surpass comprehension.

Thus in one way or another he survived the days for nearly three weeks after the fire. At times he was almost aware that the unresolved stress within him was building towards a crisis; but repeatedly he repressed the knowledge, drove the idea down with anger. He did not believe he could endure another ordeal; he had handled the first one so badly.

But even the concentrated vitriol of his anger was not potent enough to protect him indefinitely. One Thursday morning, when he faced himself in the mirror to shave, the crisis abruptly surged up in him, and his hand began to shake so severely that he had to drop the razor in the sink in order to avoid cutting his jugular.

Events in the Land were not complete. By regaining the Staff of Law, the Lords had done exactly what Lord Foul wanted them to do. That was just the first step in Foul's plotting – machinations which had begun when he had summoned Covenant's white gold ring to the Land. He would not be done until he had gained the power of life and death over the entire Earth. And to do that, Foul needed the wild magic of the white gold.

Covenant stared desperately at himself in the mirror, trying to retain a grip on his own actuality. But he saw nothing in his own eyes capable of defending him.

He had been deluded once.

It could happen again.

Again? he cried, in a voice so forlorn that it sounded like the wail of an abandoned child. Again? He could not master what had happened to him in his first delusion: how could he so much as live through a second?

He was on the verge of calling the doctors at the leprosarium – calling them to beg! – when he recovered some of his leper's intransigence. He would not have survived this long if he had not possessed some kind of fundamental capacity to refuse defeat if not despair, and that capacity stopped him now. What could I tell them that they would believe? he rasped. I don't believe it myself.

The people of the Land had called him the Unbeliever. Now he found that he would have to earn that title whether the Land actually existed or not.

And for the next two days he strove to earn it with a grimness which was as close as he could come to courage. He only made one compromise: since his hand shook so badly, he shaved with an electric razor, pushing it roughly at his face as if he were trying to remould his features. Beyond that, he acknowledged nothing. At night, his heart quivered so tangibly in his chest that he could not sleep; but he clenched his teeth and did without sleep. Between himself and delusion he placed a wall of DDS and VSEs; and whenever delusion threatened to breach his defence, he drove it back with curses.

But Saturday morning came, and still he could not silence the dream which made his hands shake.

Then at last he decided to risk going among his fellow human beings once more. He needed their actuality, their affirmation of the reality he understood, even their revulsion towards his illness. He knew of no other antidote to delusion; he could no longer face his dilemma alone.

2

HALFHAND

But that decision itself was full of fear, and he did not act on it until evening. He spent most of the day cleaning his house as if he did not expect to return to it. Then, late in the afternoon, he shaved with the electric razor and showered meticulously. For the sake of prudence, he put on a tough pair of jeans, and laced his feet into heavy boots; but over his T-shirt he wore a dress shirt, tie, and sports coat, so that the informality of his jeans and boots would not be held against him. His wallet – generally so useless to him that he did not carry it – he placed in his coat pocket. And into a pocket of his trousers he stuffed a small, sharp penknife – a knife which he habitually took with him in case he lost control of his defensive concentration, and needed something dangerous to help him refocus himself. Finally, as the sun was setting, he walked down his long driveway to the road, where he extended his thumb to hitch a ride away from town.

The next place down the road was ten miles from Haven Farm, and it was bigger than the town where he had had his accident. He headed for it because he was less likely to be recognized there. But his first problem was to find a safe ride. If any of the local motorists spotted him, he was in trouble from the beginning.

In the first few minutes, three cars went by without stopping. The occupants stared at him in passing as if he were some kind of minor freak, but none of the drivers slowed down. Then, as the last sunlight faded into dusk, a large truck came towards him. He waved his thumb, and the truck rode to a halt just past him on the loud hissing of air brakes. He climbed up to the door, and was gestured into the cab by the driver.

The man was chewing over a black stubby cigar, and the air in the cab was thick with smoke. But through the dull haze, Covenant could see that he was big and burly, with a distended paunch, and one heavy arm that moved over the steering wheel like a piston, turning the truck easily. He had only that one arm; his right sleeve was empty, and pinned to his shoulder. Covenant understood dismemberment, and he felt a pang of sympathy for the driver.

'Where to, buddy?' the big man asked comfortably.

Covenant told him.

'No problem,' he responded to a tentative inflection in Covenant's tone. 'I'm going right through there.' As the automatic transmission whined upward through its gears, he spat his cigar out the window, then let go of the wheel to unwrap and light a new smoke. While his hand was busy, he braced the wheel with his belly. The green light of the instrument panel did not reach his face, but the glow of the cigar coal illuminated massive features whenever he inhaled. In the surging red, his face looked like a pile of boulders.

With his new smoke going, he rested his arm on the wheel like a sphinx, and abruptly began talking. He had something on his mind.

'You live around here?'

Covenant said noncommittally, 'Yes.'

'How long? You know the people.'

'After a fashion.'

'You know this leper – this Thomas something or other – Thomas Covenant?'

Covenant flinched in the gloom of the cab. To disguise his distress, he shifted his position on the seat. Awkwardly, he asked, 'What's your interest?'

'Me? I got no interest. Just passing through – hauling my ass where they give me a load to go. I never even been around here before. But where I et at back in town I heard talk about this guy. So I asked the broad at the counter and she damn near yaks my ear off. One question – and I get instant mouth with everything I eat. You know what a leper is?'

Covenant squirmed. 'After a fashion.'

'Well, it's a mess, let me tell you. My old lady reads about this stuff all the time in the Bible. Dirty beggars. Unclean. I didn't know there was creeps like that in America. But that's what we're coming to. You know what I think?'

'What do you think?' Covenant asked dimly.

'I think them lepers ought to leave decent folks alone. Like that broad at the counter. She's okay, even with that motor mouth, but there she is, juiced to the gills on account of some sick bastard. That Covenant guy ought to stop thinking of hisself. Other folks don't need that aggravation. He ought to go away with every other leper and stick to hisself, leave decent folks alone. It's just selfishness, expecting ordinary guys like you and me to put up with that. You know what I mean?'

The cigar smoke in the cab was as thick as incense, and it made Covenant feel light-headed. He kept shifting his weight, as if the falseness of his position gave him an uncomfortable seat. But the talk and his vague vertigo made him feel vengeful. For a moment, he forgot his sympathy. He turned his wedding ring forcefully around his finger. As they neared the city limits, he said, 'I'm going to a nightclub – just up the road here. How about joining me for a drink?'

Without hesitation, the trucker said, 'Buddy, you're on. I never pass up a free drink.'

But they were still several stoplights from the club. To fill the silence and satisfy his curiosity, Covenant asked the driver what had happened to his arm.

'Lost it in the war.' He brought the truck to a stop at a light while adjusting the cigar in his lips and steering with his paunch. 'We was on patrol, and walked right into one of them antipersonnel mines. Blew the squad to hell. I had to crawl back to camp. Took me two days – I sort of got unhinged, you know what I mean? Didn't always know what I was doing. Time I got to the doc, it was too late to save the arm.

'What the hell, I don't need it. Least my old lady says I don't – and she ought to know by now.' He chuckled. 'Don't need no two arms for that.'

Ingenuously, Covenant asked, 'Did you have any trouble getting a licence to drive this rig?'

'You kidding? I can handle this baby better with my gut than you can with four arms and sober.' He grinned around his cigar, relishing his own humour.

The man's geniality touched Covenant. Already he regretted his duplicity. But shame always made him angry, stubborn – a leper's conditioned reflex. When the truck was parked behind the night-club, he pushed open the door of the cab and jumped to the ground as if he were in a hurry to get away from his companion.

Riding in the darkness, he had forgotten how far off the ground he was. An instant of vertigo caught him. He landed awkwardly, almost fell. His feet felt nothing, but the jolt gave an added throb to the ache of his ankles.

Over his moment of dizziness, he heard the driver say, 'You know, I figured you got a head start on the booze.'

To avoid meeting the man's stony, speculative stare, Covenant went ahead of him around towards the front of the nightclub.

As he rounded the corner, Covenant nearly collided with a battered old man wearing dark glasses. The old man stood with his back to the building, extending a bruised tin cup towards the passers-by, and following their movements with his ears. He held his head high, but it trembled slightly on his thin neck; and he was singing 'Blessed Assurance' as if it were a dirge. Under one arm he carried a white-tipped cane. When Covenant veered away from him, he waved his cup vaguely in that direction.

Covenant was leery of beggars. He remembered the tattered fanatic who had accosted him like an introduction or preparation just before the onset of his delusion. The memory made him alert to a sudden tension in the night. He stepped close to the blind man and peered into his face.

The beggar's song did not change inflection, but he turned an ear towards Covenant, and poked his cup at Covenant's chest.

The truck driver stopped behind Covenant. 'Hell,' he growled, 'they're swarming. It's like a disease. Come on. You promised me a drink.'

In the light of the streetlamp, Covenant could see that this was not that other beggar, the fanatic. But still the man's blindness affected him. His sympathy for the maimed rushed up in him. Pulling his wallet out of his jacket, he took twenty dollars and stuffed them in the tin cup.

'Twenty bucks!' ejaculated the driver. 'Are you simple, or what? You don't need no drink, buddy. You need a keeper.'

Without a break in his song, the blind man put out a gnarled hand, crumpled the bills, and hid them away somewhere in his rags. Then he turned and went tapping dispassionately away down the sidewalk, secure in the private mysticism of the blind – singing as he moved about 'a foretaste of glory divine'.

Covenant watched his back fade into the night, then swung around towards his companion. The driver was a head taller than Covenant, and carried his bulk solidly on thick legs. His cigar gleamed like one of Drool Rockworm's eyes.

Drool, Covenant remembered, Lord Foul's mad, Cavewightish servant or pawn. Drool had found the Staff of Law, and had been destroyed by it or because of it. His death had released Covenant from the Land.

Covenant poked a numb finger at the trucker's chest, trying vainly to touch him, taste his actuality. 'Listen,' he said. 'I'm serious about that drink. But I should tell you – ' he swallowed, then forced himself to say it – 'I'm Thomas Covenant. That leper.'

The driver snorted around his cigar. 'Sure, buddy. And I'm Jesus Christ. If you blew your wad, say so. But don't give me that leper crap. You're just simple, is all.'

Covenant scowled up at the man for a moment longer. Then he said resolutely, 'Well, in any case, I'm not broke. Not yet. Come on.'

Together they went to the entrance of the nightclub. It was called The Door. In keeping with its name, the place had a wide iron gate like a portal into Hades. The gate was lit in a sick green, but spotlighted whitely at its centre was a large poster which bore the words:

Positively the last night
America's newest singing sensation
SUSIE THURSTON

Included was a photograph which tried to make Susie Thurston look alluring. But the flashy gloss of the print had aged to an ambiguous grey.

Covenant gave himself a perfunctory VSE, adjured his courage, and walked into the nightclub, holding his breath as if he were entering the first circle of hell.

Inside, the club was crowded; Susie Thurston's farewell performance was well attended. Covenant and his companion took the only seats they could find – at a small table near the stage. The table was already occupied by a middle-aged man in a tired suit. Something about the way he held his glass suggested that he had been drinking for some time. When Covenant asked to join him, he did not appear to notice. He stared in the direction of the stage with round eyes, looking as solemn as a bird.

The driver discounted him with a brusque gesture. He turned a chair around, and straddled it as if bracing the burden of his belly against the chair back. Covenant took the remaining seat and tucked himself close to the table, to reduce the risk of being struck by anyone passing between the tables.

The unaccustomed press of people afflicted him with anxiety. He sat still, huddling into himself. A fear of exposure beat on his pulse, and he gripped himself hard, breathing deeply as if resisting an attack of vertigo; surrounded by people who took no notice of him, he felt vulnerable. He was taking too big a chance. But they were people, superficially like himself. He repulsed the urge to flee.

Gradually, he realized that his companion was waiting for him to order.

Feeling vaguely ill and defenceless, he raised his arm and attracted the waiter's attention. The driver ordered a double Scotch on the rocks. Apprehension momentarily paralysed Covenant's voice, but then he forced himself to request a gin and tonic. He regretted that order at once; gin and tonic had been Joan's drink. But he did not change it. He could hardly help sighing with relief when the waiter moved away.

Through the clutch of his tension, he felt that the order came with almost miraculous promptitude. Swirling around the table, the waiter deposited three drinks, including a glass of something that looked like raw alcohol for the middle-aged man. Raising his glass, the driver downed half his drink, grimaced, and muttered, 'Sugar water.' The solemn man poured his alcohol past his jumping Adam's apple in one movement.

A part of Covenant's mind wondered if he were going to end up paying for all three of them.

Reluctantly, he tasted his gin and tonic, and almost gagged in sudden anger. The lime in the drink reminded him intensely of *aliantha*. Pathetic! he snarled at himself. For punishment, he drank off the rest of the gin, and signalled to the waiter for more. Abruptly he determined to get drunk.

When the second round came, the waiter again brought three drinks. Covenant looked stiffly at his companions. Then the three of them drank as if they had tacitly engaged each other in a contest.

Wiping his mouth with the back of his hand, the driver leaned forward and said, 'Buddy, I got to warn you. It's your dough. I can drink you under the table.'

To give the third man an opening, Covenant replied, 'I think our friend here is going to last longer than both of us.'

'What, a little guy like him?' There was humour in the trucker's tone, an offer of comradeship. 'No way. No way at all.'

But the solemn man did not recognize the driver's existence with even a flick of his eyes. He kept staring into the stage as if it were an abyss.

For a while, his gloom presided over the table. Covenant ordered again, and a few minutes later the waiter brought out a third round – three more drinks. This time, the trucker stopped him. In a jocose way as if he were assuming responsibility for Covenant, he jerked his thumb at the middle-aged man and said, 'I hope you know we ain't payin' for *him*.'

'Sure.' The waiter was bored. 'He has a standing order. Pays in advance.' Disdain seemed to tighten his face, pulling it together like the closing of a fist around his nose. 'Comes here every night just to watch her and drink himself blind.' Then someone else signalled to him, and he was gone.

For a moment, the third man said nothing. Slowly, the houselights went down, and an expectant hush dropped like a shroud over the packed club. Then into the silence the man croaked quietly, 'My wife.'

A spotlight centred on the stage, and the club MC came out of the wings. Behind him, musicians took their places – a small combo, casually dressed.

The MC flashed out a smile, started his spiel. 'It makes me personally sad to introduce our little lady tonight, because this is the last time she'll be with us – for a while, at least. She's going on from here to the places where famous people get famouser. We at The Door won't soon forget her. Remember, you heard her here first. Ladies and gentlemen, Miss Susie Thurston!'

The spotlight picked up the singer as she came out, carrying a hand microphone. She wore a leather outfit – a skirt that left most of her legs bare and a sleeveless vest with a fringe across her breasts, emphasizing their movement. Her blonde hair was bobbed short, and her eyes were dark, surrounded by deep hollow circles like bruises. She had a full and welcoming figure, but her face denied it; she wore the look of an abandoned waif. In a pure, frail voice that would have been good for supplication, she sang a set of love ballads defiantly, as if they were protest songs. The applause after each number was thunderous, and Covenant quaked at the sound. When the set was over and Susie Thurston retired for a break, he was sweating coldly.

The gin seemed to be having no effect on him. But he needed some kind of help. With an aspect of desperation, he signalled for another round. To his relief, the waiter brought the drinks soon.

After he had downed his Scotch, the driver hunched forward purposefully, and said, 'I think I got this bastard figured out.'

The solemn man was oblivious to his tablemates. Painfully, he croaked again, 'My wife.'

Covenant wanted to keep the driver from talking about the third man so openly, but before he could distract him, his guest went on, 'He's doing it out of spite, that's what.'

'Spite?' echoed Covenant helplessly. He missed the connection. As far as he could tell, their companion – no doubt happily or at least doggedly married, no doubt childless – had somehow conceived a hopeless passion for the waif-woman behind the microphone. Such things happened. Torn between his now grim fidelity and his obdurate need, he could do nothing but torment himself in search of release, drink himself into stupefaction staring at the thing he wanted and both could not and should not have.

With such ideas about their tablemate, Covenant was left momentarily at sea by the driver's comment. But the big man went on almost at once. 'Course. What'd you think, being a leper is fun? He's thinking he'll just sort of share it around. Why be the only one, you know what I mean? That's what this bastard thinks. Take my word, buddy. I got him figured out.' As he spoke, his cobbled face loomed before Covenant like a pile of thetic rubble. 'What he does, he goes round where he ain't known, and he hides it, like, so nobody knows he's sick. That way he spreads it; nobody knows so they don't take care, and all of a sudden we got us an epidemic. Which makes Covenant laugh hisself crazy. Spite, like I tell you. You take my word. Don't go shaking hands when you don't know the guy you're shaking with.'

Dully, the third man groaned, 'My wife.'

Gripping his wedding band as if it had the power to protect him, Covenant said intently, 'Maybe that isn't it. Maybe he just needs people. Do you ever get lonely – driving that rig all alone, hour after hour? Maybe this Thomas Covenant just can't stand to go on living without seeing other faces once in a while. Did you think about that?'

'So let him stick to lepers. What call is he got to bother decent folks? Use your head.'

Use my head? Covenant almost shouted. Hellfire! What do you think I'm doing? Do you think I like doing this, being here? A grimace that he could not control clutched his face. Fuming, he waved for more drinks. The alcohol seemed to be working in reverse, tightening his tension rather than loosening it. But he was too angry to know whether or not he was getting drunk. The air swarmed with the noise of The Door's patrons. He was conscious of the people behind him as if they lurked there like ur-viles.

When the drinks came, he leaned forward to refute the driver's arguments. But he was stopped by the dimming of the lights for Susie Thurston's second set.

Bleakly, their tablemate groaned, 'My wife.' His voice was starting to blur around the edges; whatever he was drinking was finally affecting him.

In the moment of darkness before the MC came on, the driver responded, 'You mean that broad's your wife?'

At that, the man moaned as though in anguish.

After a quick introduction, Susie Thurston reseated herself within the spotlight. Over a querulous accompaniment from her combo, she put some sting into her voice, and sang about the infidelities of men. After two numbers, there were slow tears running from the dark wounds of her eyes.

The sound of her angry laments made Covenant's throat hurt. He regretted fiercely that he was not drunk. He would have liked to forget people and vulnerability and stubborn survival – forget and weep.

But her next song burned him. With her head back so that her white throat gleamed in the light, she sang a song that ended,

> Let go my heart –
> Your love makes me look small to myself.
> Now, I don't want to give you any hurt,
> But what I feel is part of myself;
> What you want turns what I've got to dirt –
> So let go of my heart.

Applause leaped on the heels of her last note, as if the audience were perversely hungry for her pain. Covenant could not endure any more. Buffeted by the noise, he threw dollars – he did not count them – on the table, and shoved back his chair to escape.

But when he moved around the table, he passed within five feet of the singer. Suddenly she saw him. Spreading her arms, she exclaimed joyfully, 'Berek!'

Covenant froze, stunned and terrified. No!

Susie Thurston was transported. 'Hey!' she called, waving her arms to silence the applause. 'Get a spot out here ! On him! Berek! Berek, honey!'

From over the stage, a hot white light spiked down at Covenant. Impaled in the glare, he turned to face the singer, blinking rapidly and aching with fear and rage.

No!

'Ladies and gentlemen, kind people, I want you to meet an old friend of mine, a dear man.' Susie Thurston was excited and eager. 'He taught me half the songs I know. Folks, this is Berek.' She began clapping for him as she said, 'Maybe he'll sing for us.' Good-naturedly, the audience joined her applause.

Covenant's hand limped about him, searching for support. In spite of his efforts to control himself, he stared at his betrayer with a face full of pain. The applause reverberated in his ears, made him dizzy.

No!

For a long moment, he cowered under Susie Thurston's look. Then, like a wash of revelation, all the houselights came on. Over the bewildered murmurs and rustlings of the audience, a commanding voice snapped, 'Covenant.'

Covenant spun as if to ward off an attack. In the doorway he saw two men. They both wore black hats and khaki uniforms, pistols in black holsters, silver badges; but one of them towered over the other. Sheriff Lytton. He stood with his fists on his hips. As Covenant gaped at him, he beckoned with two fingers. 'You, Covenant. Come here.'

'Covenant?' the trucker yelped. 'You're really Covenant?'

Covenant heeled round awkwardly, as if under tattered canvas, to meet this fresh assault. As he focused his eyes on the driver, he saw that the big man's face was flushed with vehemence. He met the red glare as bravely as he could. 'I told you I was.'

'Now I'm going to get it!' the driver grated. 'We're all going to get it! What the hell's the matter with you?'

The patrons of The Door were thrusting to their feet to watch what was happening. Over their heads, the sheriff shouted, 'Don't touch him!' and began wading through the crowd.

Covenant lost his balance in the confusion. He tripped, caught something like a thumb or the corner of a chair in his eye, and sprawled under a table.

People yelled and milled around. The sheriff roared orders through the din. Then with one heave of his arm, he knocked away the table over Covenant.

Covenant looked gauntly up from the floor. His bruised eye watered thickly, distorting everything over him. With the back of his hand, he pushed away the tears. Blinking and concentrating fiercely, he made out two men standing above him – the sheriff and his former tablemate.

Swaying slightly on locked knees, the solemn man looked dispassionately down at Covenant. In a smudged and expended voice, he delivered his verdict. 'My wife is the finest woman in the world.'

The sheriff pushed the man away, then bent over Covenant, brandishing a face full of teeth. 'That's enough. I'm just looking for something to charge you with, so don't give me any trouble. You hear me? Get up.'

Covenant felt too weak to move, and he could not see clearly. But he did not want the kind of help the sheriff might give him. He rolled over and pushed himself up from the floor.

He reached his feet, listing badly to one side; but the sheriff made no move to support him. He braced himself on the back of a chair, and looked defiantly around the hushed spectators. At last, the gin seemed to be affecting him. He pulled himself erect, adjusted his tie with a show of dignity.

'Get going,' the sheriff commanded from his superior height.

But for one more moment Covenant did not move. Though he could not be sure of anything he saw, he stood where he was and gave himself a VSE.

'Get going,' Lytton repeated evenly.

'Don't touch me.' When his VSE was done, Covenant turned and stalked greyly out of the nightclub.

Out in the cool April night, he breathed deeply, steadying himself. The sheriff and his deputy herded him towards a squad car. Its red warning lights flashed balefully. When he was locked into the back seat behind the protective steel grating, the two officers climbed into the front. While the deputy drove away in the direction of Haven Farm, the sheriff spoke through the grating.

'Took us too long to find you, Covenant. The Millers reported you were trying to hitch a ride, and we figured you were going to try your tricks somewhere. Just couldn't tell where. But it's still my county, and you're walking trouble. There's no law against you − I can't arrest you for what you've done. But it sure was mean. Listen, you. Taking care of this county is my business, and don't you forget it. I don't want to hunt around like this for you. You pull this stunt again, and I'll throw you in the can for disturbing the peace, disorderly conduct, and everything else I can think of. You got that?'

Shame and rage struggled in Covenant, but he could find no way to let them out. He wanted to yell through the grate, It isn't catching! It's not my fault! But his throat was too constricted; he could not release the wail. At last, he could only mumble, 'Let me out. I'll walk.'

Sheriff Lytton regarded him closely, then said to his deputy, 'All right. We'll let him walk. Maybe he'll have an accident.' Already they were well out of town.

The deputy drove to a halt on the berm, and the sheriff let Covenant out. For a moment, they stood together in the night. The sheriff glared at him as if trying to measure his capacity to do harm. Then Lytton said, 'Go home. Stay home.' He got back into the car. It made a loud squealing turn and fled back towards town. An instant later, Covenant sprang into the road and cried after the tail-lights, 'Leper outcast unclean!' They looked as red as blood in the darkness.

His shout did not seem to dent the silence. Before long, he turned back towards Haven Farm, feeling as small as if the few stars in the dense black sky were deriding him. He had ten miles to walk.

The road was deserted. He moved in empty stillness like a hiatus in his surroundings; though he was retreating into open countryside, he could hear no sounds, no night talk of birds or insects. The silence

400

made him feel deaf and alone, vulnerable to the hurrying vultures at his back.

It was a delusion! He raised his protest like a defiance; but even to his ears, it had the hollow ring of despair, composed equally of defeat and stubbornness. Through it, he could hear the girl shouting *Berek!* like the siren of a nightmare.

Then the road went through a stand of trees which cut out the dim light of the stars. He could not feel the pavement with his feet; he was in danger of missing his way, of falling into a ditch or injuring himself against a tree. He tried to keep up his pace, but the risk was too great, and finally he was reduced to waving his arms before him and testing his footing like a blind man. Until he reached the end of the woods, he moved as if he were wandering lost in a dream, damp with sweat, and cold.

After that, he set a hard pace for himself. He was spurred on by the cries that rushed after him, *Berek! Berek!* When at last, long miles later, he reached the driveway into Haven Farm, he was almost running.

In the sanctuary of his house, he turned on all the lights and locked the doors. The organized chastity of his living space surrounded him with its unconsoling dogma. A glance at the kitchen clock told him that the time was just past midnight. A new day, Sunday – a day when other people worshipped. He started some coffee, threw off his jacket, tie and dress shirt, then carried his steaming cup into the living room. There he took a position on the sofa, adjusted Joan's picture on the coffee table so that it looked straight at him, and braced himself to weather the crisis.

He needed an answer. His resources were spent, and he could not go on the way he was.

Berek!

The girl's shout, and the raw applause of her audience, and the trucker's outrage, reverberated in him like muffled earth tremors. Suicide loomed in all directions. He was trapped between mad delusion and the oppressive weight of his fellow human beings.

Leper outcast unclean!

He gripped his shoulders and hugged himself to try to still the gasping of his heart.

I can't stand it! Somebody help me!

Suddenly, the phone rang – cut through him as stridently as a curse. Disjointedly, like a loose collection of broken bones, he jumped to his feet. But then he did not move. He lacked the courage to face more hostility, indemnification.

The phone shrilled again.

His breath shuddered in his lungs. Joan seemed to reproach him from behind the glass of the picture frame.

Another ring, as insistent as a fist.

He lurched towards the phone. Snatching up the receiver, he pressed it to his ear to hold it steady.

'Tom?' a faint, sad voice sighed. 'Tom – it's Joan. Tom? I hope I didn't wake you. I know it's late, but I had to call. Tom?'

Covenant stood straight and stiff, at attention, with his knees locked to keep him from falling. His jaw worked, but he made no sound. His throat felt swollen shut, clogged with emotions, and his lungs began to hurt for air.

'Tom? Are you there? Hello? Tom? Please say something. I need to talk to you. I've been so lonely. I – I miss you.' He could hear the effort in her voice.

His chest heaved fiercely, as if he were choking. Abruptly he broke through the block in his throat, and took a deep breath that sounded as if he were between sobs. But still he could not force up words.

'Tom! Please! What's happening to you?'

His voice seemed to be caught in a death grip. Desperate to shatter the hold, to answer Joan, cling to her voice, keep her on the line, he picked up the phone and started back towards the sofa – hoping that movement would ease the spasm that clenched him, help him regain control of his muscles.

But he turned the wrong way, wrapping the phone cord around his ankle. As he jerked forward, he tripped and pitched headlong towards the coffee table. His forehead struck the edge of the table squarely. When he hit the floor, he seemed to feel himself bounce.

Instantly, his sight went blank. But he still had the receiver clutched to his ear. During a moment of white stillness, he heard Joan's voice clearly. She was becoming upset, angry.

'Tom, I'm serious. Don't make this any harder for me than it already is. Don't you understand? I want to talk to you. I need you. Say something, Tom. Tom! Damn you, say something!'

Then a wide roaring in his ears washed out her voice. No! he cried. No! But he was helpless. The rush of sound came over him like a dark tide, and carried him away.

3

THE SUMMONING

The wide roar modulated slowly, changing the void of his sight. On the surge of the sound, a swath of grey-green spread upward until it covered him like a winding sheet. The hue of the green was noxious to him, and he felt himself smothering in its close, sweet, fetid reek – the smell of attar. But the note which filled his ears grew more focused, scaled up in pitch. Droplets of gold bled into view through the green. Then the sound turned softer and more plaintive, higher still in pitch, so that it became a low human wail. The gold forced back the green. Soon a warm, familiar glow filled his eyes.

As the sound turned more and more into a woman's song, the gold spread and deepened – cradled him as if it were carrying him gently along the flood of the voice. The melody wove the light, gave it texture and shape, solidity. Helpless to do otherwise, he clung to the sound, concentrated on it with his mouth stretched open in protest.

Slowly, the singing throat opened. Its harmonic pattern became sterner, more demanding. Covenant felt himself pulled forward now, hurried down the tide of the song. Arching with supplication, it took on words.

> Be true, Unbeliever –
> Answer the call.
> Life is the Giver:
> Death ends all.
> The promise is truth,
> And banes disperse
> With promise kept:
> But soul's deep curse
> On broken faith
> And faithless thrall,
> For doom of darkness
> Covers all.
> Be true, Unbeliever –
> Answer the call.
> Be true.

The song seemed to reach back into him, stirring memories, calling up people he had once, in one fey mood, thought had the right to make demands of him. But he resisted it. He kept silent, held himself in.

The melody drew him on into the warm gold.

At last, the light took on definition. He could locate its shape before him now; it washed out his vision as if he were staring into the sun. But on the last words of the song, the light dimmed, lost its brilliance. As the voice sang, 'Be true,' it was seconded by many throats: 'Be true!' That adjuration stretched him like the tightening of a string to its final pitch.

Then the source of the light fell into scale, and he could see beyond it.

He recognized the place. He was in the Close, the council chamber of the Lords in the heart of Revelstone. Its tiers of seats reached above him on all sides towards the granite ceiling of the hall.

He was surprised to find himself standing erect on the bottom of the Close. The stance confused his sense of balance, and he stumbled forward towards the pit of graveling, the source of the gold light. The fire-stones burned there before him without consumption, filling the air with the smell of newly broken earth.

Strong hands caught him by either arm. As his fall was halted, drops of blood spattered onto the stone floor at the edge of the graveling pit.

Regaining his feet, he cried hoarsely, 'Don't touch me!'

He was dizzy with confusion and rage, but he braced himself while he put a hand to his forehead. His fingers came away covered with blood. He had cut himself badly on the edge of the table. For a moment, he gaped at his red hand.

Through his dismay, a quiet, firm voice said, 'Be welcome in the Land, ur-Lord Thomas Covenant, Unbeliever and Ringthane. I have called you to us. Our need for your aid is great.'

'You called me?' he croaked.

'I am Elena,' the voice replied, 'High Lord by the choice of the Council, and holder of the Staff of Law. I have called you.'

'You called me?' Slowly, he raised his eyes. Thick wetness ran from the sockets as if he were weeping blood. 'You called me?' He felt a crumbling inside him like rocks breaking, and his hold over himself cracked. In a voice of low anguish, he said, 'I was talking to Joan.'

He saw the woman dimly through the blood in his eyes. She stood behind the stone table on the level above him, holding a long staff in her right hand. There were other people around the table, and behind them the gallery of the Close held many more. They were all watching him.

'To Joan, do you understand? I was talking to Joan. *She* called me. After all this time. When I needed – needed. You have no right.' He gathered force like a storm wind. 'You've got no right! I was talking to *Joan!*' He shouted with all his might, but it was not enough. His voice could not do justice to his emotion. 'To Joan! to Joan! do you hear me? She was my *wife!*'

A man who had been standing near the High Lord hurried around the broad open *C* of the table, and came down to Covenant on the lower level. Covenant recognized the man's lean face, with its rudder nose mediating between crooked, humane lips and acute, gold-flecked, dangerous eyes. He was Lord Mhoram.

He placed a hand on Covenant's arm, and said softly, 'My friend. What has happened to you?'

Savagely, Covenant threw off the Lord's hand. 'Don't touch me!' he raged in Mhoram's face. 'Are you deaf as well as blind?! I was talking to Joan! On the phone!' His hand jerked convulsively, struggling to produce the receiver out of the empty air. 'She needed' – abruptly his throat clenched, and he swallowed roughly – 'she said she needed me. Me!' But his voice was helpless to convey the crying of his heart. He slapped at the blood on his forehead, trying to clear his eyes.

The next instant, he grabbed the front of Mhoram's sky-blue robe in his fist, hissed, 'Send me back! There's still time! If I can get back fast enough!'

Above them, the woman spoke carefully. 'Ur-Lord Covenant, it grieves me to hear that our summoning has done you harm. Lord Mhoram has told us all he could of your pain, and we do not willingly increase it. But it is our doom that we must. Unbeliever, our need is great. The devastation of the Land is nearly upon us.'

Pushing away from Mhoram to confront her, Covenant fumed, 'I don't give a bloody damn about the Land!' His words came in such a panting rush that he could not shout them. 'I don't care what you need. You can drop dead for all I care. You're a delusion! A sickness in my mind. You don't exist! Send me back! You've got to send me back. While there's still time!'

'Thomas Covenant.' Mhoram spoke in a tone of authority that pulled Covenant around. 'Unbeliever. Listen to me.'

Then Covenant saw that Mhoram had changed. His face was still the same – the gentleness of his mouth still balanced the promise of peril in his gold-concentrated irises – but he was older, old enough now to be Covenant's father. There were lines of use around his eyes and mouth, and his hair was salted with white. When he spoke, his lips twisted with self-deprecation, and the depths of his eyes stirred uneasily. But he met the fire of Covenant's glare without flinching.

'My friend, if the choice were mine, I would return you at once to your world. The decision to summon you was painfully made, and I would willingly undo it. The Land has no need of service which is not glad and free. But, ur-Lord' – he gripped Covenant's arm again to steady him – 'my friend, we cannot return you.'

'Cannot?' Covenant groaned on a rising, half-hysterical note.

'We have no lore for the releasing of burdens. I know not how it is in your world – you appear unchanged to my eyes – but forty years have passed since we stood together on the slopes of Mount Thunder, and you freed the Staff of Law for our hands. For long years we have striven – '

'Cannot?' Covenant repeated more fiercely.

'We have striven with power which we fail to master, and Lore which we have been unable to penetrate. It has taken forty years to bring us here, so that we may ask for your aid. We have reached the limit of what we can do.'

'No!' He turned away because he could not bear the honesty he saw in Mhoram's face, and yelled up at the woman with the Staff, 'Send me back!'

For a moment, she looked at him squarely, measuring the extremity of his demand. Then she said, 'I entreat you to understand. Hear the truth of our words. Lord Mhoram has spoken openly. I hear the hurt we have done you. I am not unmoved.' She was twenty or thirty feet away from him, beyond the pit of graveling and behind the stone table, but her voice carried to him clearly through the crystal acoustics of the Close. 'But I cannot undo your summoning. Had I the power, still the Land's need would deny me. Lord Foul the Despiser – '

Head back, arms thrown wide, Covenant howled, 'I don't care!'

Stung into sharpness, the High Lord said, 'Then return yourself. You have the power. You wield the white gold.'

With a cry, Covenant tried to charge at her. But before he could take a step, he was caught from behind. Wrestling around, he found himself in the grasp of Bannor, the unsleeping Bloodguard who had warded him during his previous delusion.

'We are the Bloodguard,' Bannor said in his. toneless alien inflection. 'The care of the Lords is in our hands. We do not permit any offer of harm to the High Lord.'

'Bannor,' Covenant pleaded, 'she was my wife.'

But Bannor only gazed at him with unblinking dispassion.

Throwing his weight wildly, he managed to turn in the Bloodguard's powerful grip until he was facing Elena again. Blood scattered from his forehead as he jerked around. 'She was my wife!'

'Enough,' Elena commanded.

'Send me back!'

'Enough!' She stamped the iron heel of the Staff of Law on the floor, and at once blue fire burst from its length. The flame roared vividly, like a rent in the fabric of the gold light, letting concealed power shine through; and the force of the flame drove Covenant back into Bannor's arms. But her hand where she held the Staff was untouched. 'I am the High Lord,' she said sternly. 'This is Revelstone – Lord's Keep, not Foul's Creche. We have sworn the Oath of Peace.'

At a nod from her, Bannor released Covenant, and he stumbled backward, falling in a heap beside the graveling. He lay on the stone for a moment, gasping harshly. Then he pried himself into a sitting position. His head seemed to droop with defeat. 'You'll get Peace,' he groaned. 'He's going to destroy you all. Did you say forty years? You've only got nine left. Or have you forgotten his prophecy?'

'We know,' Mhoram said quietly. 'We do not forget.' With a crooked smile, he bent to examine Covenant's wound.

While Mhoram did this, High Lord Elena quenched the blaze of the Staff, and said to a person Covenant could not see, 'We must deal with this matter now, if we are to have any hope of the white gold. Have the captive brought here.'

Lord Mhoram mopped Covenant's forehead gently, peered at the cut, then stood and moved away to consult with someone. Left alone, with most of the blood out of his eyes, Covenant brought his throbbing gaze into focus to take stock of where he was. Some still-uncovered instinct for self-preservation made him try to measure the hazards around him. He was on the lowest level of the tiered chamber, and its high vaulted and groined ceiling arched over him, lit by the gold glow of the graveling, and by four large smokeless *lillianrill* torches set into the walls. Around the centre of the Close, on the next level, was the three-quarters-round stone council table of the Lords, and above and behind the table were the ranked seats of the gallery. Two Bloodguard stood at the high massive doors, made by Giants to be large enough for Giants, of the main entryway, above and opposite the High Lord's seat.

The gallery was diversely filled with warriors of the Warward of Lord's Keep, Lorewardens from the Loresraat, several Hirebrands and Gravelingases dressed respectively in their traditional cloaks and tunics, and a few more Bloodguard. High up behind the High Lord sat two people Covenant thought he recognized – the Gravelingas Tohrm, a Hearthrall of Lord's Keep; and Quaan, the Warhaft who had accompanied the Quest for the Staff of Law. With them were two others – one a Hirebrand, judging by his Woodhelvennin cloak and the circlet of leaves about his head, probably the other Hearthrall; and one the First Mark of the Bloodguard. Vaguely, Covenant wondered who had taken that position after the loss of Tuvor in the catacombs under Mount Thunder.

His gaze roamed on around the Close. Standing at the table were seven Lords, not counting the High Lord and Mhoram. Covenant recognized none of them. They must all have passed the tests and joined the Council in the last forty years. Forty years? he asked dimly. Mhoram had aged, but he did not look forty years older. And Tohrm, who had been hardly more than a laughing boy when Covenant had known him, now seemed far too young for middle age. The Bloodguard were not changed at all. Of course, Covenant groaned to himself, remembering how old they were said to be. Only Quaan showed a believable age: white thinning hair gave the former Warhaft the look of sixty or sixty-five summers. But his square commanding shoulders did not stoop. And the openness of his countenance had not changed; he frowned down on the Unbeliever with exactly the frank disapproval that Covenant remembered.

He did not see Prothall anywhere. Prothall had been the High Lord during the Quest, and Covenant knew that he had survived the final battle on the slopes of Mount Thunder. But he also knew that Prothall had been old enough to die naturally in forty years. In spite of his pain, he found himself hoping that the former High Lord had died as he deserved, in peace and honour.

With a sour mental shrug, he moved his survey to the one man at the Lords' table who was not standing. This individual was dressed like a warrior, with high, soft-soled boots over black leggings, a black sleeveless shirt under a breastplate moulded of a yellow metal, and a yellow headband; but on his breastplate were the double diagonal marks which distinguished him as the Warmark, the commander of the Warward, the Lords' army. He was not looking at anyone. He sat back in his stone chair, with his head down and his eyes covered with one hand, as if he were asleep.

Covenant turned away, let his gaze trudge at random around the Close. High Lord Elena was conferring in low tones with the Lords nearest her. Mhoram stood waiting near the broad stairs leading up to the main doors. The acoustics of the chamber carried the commingled voices of the gallery to Covenant, so that the air was murmurous about his head. He wiped the gathering blood from his brows, and thought about dying.

It would be worth it, he mused. After all it would be worth it to escape. He was not tough enough to persevere when even his dreams turned against him. He should leave living to the people who were potent for it.

Ah, hellfire, he sighed. Hellfire.

Distantly, he heard the great doors of the Close swing open. The murmuring in the air stopped at once; everyone turned and looked towards the doors. Forcing himself to spend some of his waning strength, Covenant twisted around to see who was coming.

The sight struck him cruelly, seemed to take the last rigour out of his bones.

He watched with bloodied eyes as two Bloodguard came down the stairs, holding upright between them a green-grey creature that oozed with fear. Though they were not handling it roughly the creature trembled in terror and revulsion. Its hairless skin was slick with sweat. It had a generally human outline, but its torso was unusually long, and its limbs were short, all equal in length, as if it naturally ran on four legs through low caves. But its limbs were bent and useless – contorted as if they had been broken many times and not reset. And the rest of its body showed signs of worse damage.

Its head was its least human feature. Its bald skull had no eyes. Above the ragged slit of its mouth, in the centre of its face, were two wide, wet nostrils that quivered fearfully around the edges as the creature smelled its situation. Its small pointed ears perched high on its skull. And the whole back of its head was gone. Over the gap was a green membrane like a scar, pulsing against the remaining fragment of a brain.

Covenant knew immediately what it was. He had seen a creature like it once before – whole in body, but dead, lying on the floor of its Waymeet with an iron spike through its heart.

It was a Waynhim. A Demondim-spawn, like the ur-viles. But unlike their black roynish kindred, the Waynhim had devoted their lore to the services of the Land.

This Waynhim had been lavishly tortured.

The Bloodguard brought the creature down to the bottom of the Close, and held it opposite Covenant. Despite his deep weakness, he forced himself to his feet, and kept himself up by leaning against the wall of the next level. Already, he seemed to be regaining some of the added dimension of sight which characterized the Land. He could see into the Waynhim, could feel with his eyes what had been done to it. He saw torment and extravagant pain – saw the healthy body of the Waynhim caught in a fist of malice, and crushed gleefully into this crippled shape. The sight made his eyes hurt. He had to lock his knees to brace himself up. A cold mist of hebetude and despair filled his head, and he was glad for the blood which clogged his eyes; it prevented him from seeing the Waynhim.

409

Through his fog, he heard Elena say, 'Ur-Lord Covenant, it is necessary to burden you with this sight. We must convince you of our need. Please forgive such a welcome to the Land. The duress of our plight leaves us little choice.

'Ur-Lord, this poor creature brought us to the decision of your summoning. For years we have known that the Despiser prepares his strength to march against the Land – that the time appointed in his prophecy grows short for us. You delivered that prophecy unto us, and the Lords of Revelstone have not been idle. From the day in which Lord Mhoram brought to Lord's Keep the Staff of Law and the Second Ward of Kevin's Lore, we have striven to meet this doom. We have multiplied the Warward, studied our defences, trained ourselves in all our skills and strengths. We have learned some of the uses of the Staff. The Loresraat has explored with all its wisdom and devotion the Second Ward. But in forty years, we have gained no clear knowledge of Lord Foul's intent. After the wresting of the Staff from Drool Rockworm, the Despiser's presence left Kiril Threndor in Mount Thunder, and soon reseated itself in the great thronehall of Ridjeck Thome, Foul's Creche, the Grey Slayer's ancient home. And since that time, our scouts have been unable to penetrate Lord Foul's demesne. Power has been at work there – power and ill – but we could learn nothing of it, though Lord Mhoram himself assayed the task. He could not breach the Despiser's forbidding might.

'But there have been dim and dark foreboding movements throughout the Land. *Kresh* from the east and ur-viles from Mount Thunder, *griffins* and other dire creatures from Sarangrave Flat, Cavewights, little-known denizens of Lifeswallower, the Great Swamp – we have heard them all wending towards the Spoiled Plains and Foul's Creche. They disappear beyond the Shattered Hills, and do not return. We need no great wisdom to teach us that the Despiser prepares his army. But still we have lacked clear knowledge. Then at last knowledge came to us. During the summer, our scouts captured this creature, this broken remnant of a Waynhim, on the western edges of Grimmerdhore Forest. It was brought here so that we might try to gain tidings from it.'

'So you tortured it to find out what it knows.' Covenant's eyes were sticky with blood, and he kept them shut, giving himself up to useless rage and mist.

'Do you believe that of us?' The High Lord sounded hurt. 'No. We are not Despisers. We would not so betray the Land. We have treated the Waynhim as gently as we could without releasing it. It has told us willingly all that we would know. Now it begs us to kill it. Unbeliever, hear me. This is Lord Foul's handiwork. He possesses the Illearth Stone. This is the work of that bane.'

Through the greyness in his mind, Covenant heard the doors open again. Someone came down the stairs and whispered with Lord Mhoram. Then Mhoram said, 'High Lord, hurtloam has been brought for the Unbeliever. I fear that his wound extends far beyond this simple cut. There is other ill at work in him. He must be tended without delay.'

'Yes, at once,' High Lord Elena responded promptly. 'We must do all that we can to heal him.'

With a steady stride, Mhoram came towards Covenant.

At the thought of hurtloam, Covenant pushed himself away from the wall, rubbed the caked blood out of his eyes. He saw Mhoram holding a small stoneware bowl containing a light mud spangled with gold gleams that seemed to throb in the glow of the Close.

'Keep that stuff away from me,' he whispered.

Mhoram was taken aback. 'This is hurtloam, ur-Lord. It is the healing soil of the Earth. You will be renewed by it.'

'I know what it does!' Covenant's voice was raw from all the shouting he had done, and it sounded spectral and empty, like the creaking of a derelict. 'I've had it before. You put that stuff on my head, and before you know it the feeling comes back into my fingers and toes, and I go around ra – ' He barely caught himself. 'Hurting people.'

He heard Elena say softly, 'I know,' but he disregarded her.

'That's the real lie,' he snarled at the bowl, 'that stuff there. That's what makes me feel so healthy I can't stand it.' He took a long breath, then said fervidly, 'I don't want it.'

Mhoram held Covenant in a gaze intense with questions. And when Covenant did not waver, the Lord asked in a low voice, a tone of amazement, 'My friend, do you wish to die?'

'Use it on that poor devil over there,' Covenant replied dully. 'It's got a right to it.'

Without bending the straitness of his look, Mhoram said, 'We have made the attempt. You have known us, Unbeliever. You know that we could not refuse the plea of such distress. But the Waynhim is beyond all our succour. Our Healers cannot approach its inner wound. And it nearly died at the touch of hurtloam.'

Still Covenant did not relent.

Behind him, High Lord Elena continued what Mhoram had been saying. 'Even the Staff of Law cannot match the power which has warped this Waynhim. Such is our plight, ur-Lord. The Illearth Stone surpasses us.

'This Waynhim has told us much. Much that was obscure is now clear. Its name was *dharmakshetra*, which in the Waynhim tongue

411

means "to brave the enemy". Now it calls itself *dukkha* – "victim". Because its people desired knowledge of the Despiser's plotting, it went to Foul's Creche. There it was captured, and – and wronged – and then set free – as a warning to its people, I think. It has told us much.

'Unbeliever, we know that when you first delivered the Despiser's prophecy to High Lord Prothall son of Dwillian and the Council of Lords forty years ago, many things were not understood concerning the Grey Slayer's intent. Why did he warn the Lords that Drool Rockworm had found the Staff of Law under Mount Thunder? Why did he seek to prepare us for our fate? Why did he aid Drool's quest for dark might, and then betray the Cavewight? These questions are now answered. Drool possessed the Staff, and with it unearthed the buried bane, the Illearth Stone. By reason of these powers, the Despiser was at Drool's mercy while the Cavewight lived.

'But with Lord Mhoram and High Lord Prothall, you retrieved the Staff and brought the threat of Drool Rockworm to an end. Thus the Stone fell into Lord Foul's hands. He knew that the Stone, joined with his own lore and power, is a greater strength than the Staff of Law. And he knew that we are no masters for even that little might which we possess.

'In forty years, we have not rested. We have spoken to all the people of the Land. The Loresraat has grown greatly, giving us warriors and Lorewardens and Lords to meet our need. The *rhadhamaerl* and *lillianrill* have laboured to the utmost. And all have given themselves to the study of the Two Wards, and of the Staff. Gains have been made. Trothgard, where the Lords swore their promise of healing to the Land, has flowered, and we have made there works undreamed by our forefathers. The Staff meets many needs. But the heart of our failure remains.

'For all our lore, all our knowledge of the Staff and the Earthpower, comes to us from Kevin, High Lord of the Old Lords. And he was defeated – yes, and worse than defeated. Now we face the same foe, made greatly stronger by the Illearth Stone. And we have recovered only Two of the Seven Wards in which Kevin left his Lore. And at their core these Two are beyond us. Some weakness of wisdom or incapacity of spirit prevents our grasp of their mystery. Yet without mastery of the Two we cannot gain the rest, for Kevin, wise to the hazards of unready knowledge and power, hid his Wards each in its turn, so that the comprehension of one would lead to the discovery of the next.

'For forty years, this failure has clung to us. And now we have learned that Lord Foul, too, has not been idle. We have learned from this Waynhim. The Land's enemy has grown power and armies until the region beyond the Shattered Hills teems with warped life — myriads of poor bent creatures like *dukkha*, held by the power of the Stone in soul chattelry to Lord Foul. He has built for himself a force more ill than any the Land has known, more fell than any we can hope to conquer. He has gathered his three Ravers, the servants of his right hand, to command his armies. It may be that his hordes are already afoot against us.

'So it is that we have called you, ur-Lord Covenant, Unbeliever and white gold wielder. You are our hope at the last. We summoned you, though we knew it might carry a cost hard for you to bear. We have sworn our service to the Land, and could not do otherwise. Thomas Covenant! Will you not help us?'

During her speech, her voice had grown in power and eloquence until she was almost singing. Covenant could not refuse to listen. Her tone reached into him, and made vivid all his memories of the Land's beauty. He recalled the bewitching Dance of the Celebration of Spring, and the lush, heart-soothing health of the Andelainian Hills, the uneasy eldritch gleaming of Morinmoss, the stern swift Plains of Ra and the rampant Ranyhyn, the great horses. And he remembered what it was like to feel, to have lively nerves in his fingers, capable of touching grass and stone. The poignancy of it made his heart ache.

'Your hope misleads you,' he groaned into the stillness after Elena's appeal. 'I don't know anything about power. It has something to do with life, and I'm as good as dead. Or what do you think life is? Life is feeling. I've lost that. I'm a leper.'

He might have started to rage again, but a new voice cut sharply through his protest. 'Then why don't you throw away your ring?'

He turned, and found himself confronting the warrior who had been sitting at the end of the Lords' table. The man had come down to the bottom of the Close, where he faced Covenant with his hands on his hips. To Covenant's surprise, the man's eyes were covered with dark, wrap-around sunglasses. Behind the glasses, his head moved alertly, as if he were studying everything. He seemed to possess a secret. Without the support of his eyes, the slight smile on his lips looked private and unfathomable, like an utterance in an alien tongue.

Covenant grasped the inconsistency of the sunglasses — they were oddly out of place in the Close — but he was too stung by the speaker's question to stop for discrepancies. Stiffly, he answered, 'It's my wedding ring.'

The man shrugged away this reply. 'You talk about your wife in the past tense. You're separated — or divorced. You can't have your life both ways now. Either get rid of the ring and stick to whatever it is you seem to think is real, or get rid of her and do your duty here.'

'My duty?' The affront of the man's judgment gave Covenant the energy to object. 'How do you know what my duty is?'

'My name is Hile Troy.' The man gave a slight bow. 'I'm the Warmark of the Warward of Lord's Keep. My job is to figure out how to meet Foul's army.'

'Hile Troy,' added Elena slowly, almost hesitantly, 'comes from your world, Unbeliever.'

What?

The High Lord's assertion seemed to snatch the ground from under Covenant. The enervation in his bones suddenly swamped him. Vertigo came over him as if he were on the edge of a cliff, and he stumbled. Mhoram caught him as he dropped heavily to his knees.

His movement distracted the Bloodguard holding *dukkha*. Before they could react, the Waynhim broke away from them and sprang at Covenant, screaming with fury.

To save Covenant, Mhoram spun and blocked *dukkha*'s charge with his staff. The next instant, the Bloodguard recaptured the Waynhim. But Covenant did not see it. When Mhoram turned away from him, he fell on his face beside the graveling pit. He felt weak, overburdened with despair, as if he were bleeding to death. For a few moments, he lost consciousness.

He awoke to the touch of cool relief on his forehead. His head was in Mhoram's lap, and the Lord was gently spreading hurtloam over his cut brow.

He could already feel the effect of the mud. A soothing caress spread from his forehead into the muscles of his face, relaxing the tension which gripped his features. Drowsiness welled up in him as the healing earth unfettered him, anodyned the restless bondage of his spirit. Through his weariness, he saw the trap of his delusion winding about him. With as much supplication as he could put into his voice, he said to Mhoram, 'Get me out of here.'

The Lord seemed to understand. He nodded firmly, then got to his feet, lifting Covenant with him. Without a word to the Council, he turned his back and went up the stairs, half carrying Covenant out of the Close.

4

'MAY BE LOST'

Covenant hardly heard the shutting of the great doors behind him; he was hardly conscious of his surroundings at all. His attention was focused inward on the hurtloam's progress. It seemed to spread around his skull and down his flesh, soothing as it radiated within him. It made his skin tingle, and the sensation soon covered his face and neck. He scrutinized it as if it were a poison he had taken to end his life.

When the touch of the loam reached past the base of his throat into his chest, he stumbled, and could not recover. Bannor took his other arm. The Lord and the Bloodguard carried him on through the stone city, working generally upward through the interlocking levels of Lord's Keep. At last, they brought him to a spacious suite of living quarters. Gently, they bore him into the bedroom, laid him on the bed, and undressed him enough to make him comfortable.

Then Mhoram bent close to him and said reassuringly, 'This is the power of the hurtloam. When it works upon a dire wound, it brings a deep sleep to speed healing. You will rest well now. You have done without rest too long.' He and Bannor turned to go.

But Covenant could feel the cool, tingling touch near his heart. Weakly, he called Mhoram back. He was full of dread; he could not bear to be alone. Without caring what he said – seeking only to keep Mhoram near him – he asked, 'Why did that – *dukkha* attack me?'

Again, Lord Mhoram appeared to understand. He brought a wooden stool near the head of the bed, and seated himself there. In a quiet steady voice, he said, 'That is a searching question, my friend. *Dukkha* has been tormented out of all recognition, and I can only guess at the sore impulses which drive it. But you must remember that it is a Waynhim. For many generations after the Desecration, when the new Lords began their work at Revelstone, the Waynhim served the Land – not out of allegiance to the Lords, but rather out of their desire to expiate to the Land for the dangerous works and dark lore of the ur-viles. Such a creature still lives, somewhere far within *dukkha*. Despite what has been done to it – even if its soul has been enslaved by the power of the Stone, so that now it serves the Despiser – it still remembers what it was, and hates what it is.

That is Lord Foul's way in all things − to force his foes to become that which they most hate, and to destroy that which they most love.

'My friend, this is not pleasant to say. But it is in my heart that *dukkha* attacked you because you refuse to aid the Land. The Waynhim knows the might you possess − it is of the Demondim, and in all likelihood comprehends more of the uses and power of white gold than any Lord. Now it is in pain too great to allow it to understand you. The last remnant of itself saw dimly that you − that you refuse. For a moment, it became its former self enough to act.

'Ah, ur-Lord. You have said that the Land is a dream for you − and that you fear to be made mad. But madness is not the only danger in dreams. There is also the danger that something may be lost which can never be regained.'

Covenant sighed. The Lord had given him an explanation he could grasp. But when Mhoram's steady voice stopped, he felt how much he needed it − how close he was to the brink of some precipice which appalled him. He reached a hand outward, into the void around him, and felt his fingers clasped firmly in Mhoram's. He tried once more to make himself understood.

'She was my wife,' he breathed. 'She needed me. She − she'll never forgive me for doing this to her.'

He was so exhausted that he could no longer see Mhoram's face. But as he ran out of consciousness, he felt the Lord's unfaltering hold on his hand. Mhoram's care comforted him, and he slept.

Then he hung under a broad sky of dreams, measurable only by the strides of stars. Out of the dim heavens, a succession of dark shapes seemed to hover and strike. Like carrion, he was helpless to fend them off. But always a hand gripped his and consoled him. It anchored him until he returned to consciousness.

Without opening his eyes, he lay still and probed himself tentatively, as if he were testing buboes. He was enfolded from his chest down in soft clean sheets. And he could feel the fabric with his toes. The cold numbness of dead nerves was gone from them, warmed away by a healing glow which reached into the marrow of his bones.

The change in his fingers was even more obvious. His right fist was knotted in the sheets. When he moved his fingers, he could feel the texture of the cloth with their tips. The grip on his left hand was so hard that he could feel the pulse in his knuckles.

But nerves do not regenerate − cannot −

Damnation! he groaned. The sensation of touch prodded his heart like fear. Involuntarily, he whispered, 'No. No.' But his tone was full of futility.

'Ah, my friend,' Mhoram sighed, 'your dreams have been full of such refusals. But I do not understand them. I hear in your breathing that you have resisted your own healing. And the outcome is obscure to me. I cannot tell whether your denials have brought you to good or ill.'

Covenant looked up into Mhoram's sympathetic face. The Lord still sat beside the bed; his iron-shod staff leaned against the wall within easy reach of his hand. But now there were no torches in the room. Sunlight poured through a large oriel beside the bed.

Mhoram's gaze made Covenant acutely conscious of their clasped hands. Carefully, he extricated his fingers. Then he propped himself up on his elbows, and asked how long he had been asleep. His rest after the shouting he had done in the Close made his voice rattle harshly in his throat.

'It is now early afternoon,' Mhoram replied. 'The summoning was performed in the evening yesterday.'

'Have you been here – all that time?'

The Lord smiled. 'No. During the night – How shall I say it? I was called away. High Lord Elena sat with you in my absence.' After a moment, he added, 'She will speak with you this evening, if you are willing.'

Covenant did not respond. The mention of Elena reawakened his outrage and fear at the act which had compelled him into the Land. He thought of the summoning as her doing; it was her voice which had snatched him away from Joan. Joan! he wailed. To cover his distress, he climbed out of bed, gathered up his clothes, and went in search of a place to wash himself.

In the next room, he found a stone basin and tub connected to a series of balanced stone valves which allowed him to run water where he wanted it. He filled the basin. When he put his hands into the water, its sharp chill thrilled the new vitality of his nerves. Angrily, he thrust his head down into the water, and did not raise it until the cold began to make the bones of his skull hurt. Then he went and stood dripping over a warm pot of graveling near the tub.

While the glow of the fire-stones dried him, he silenced the aching of his heart. He was a leper, and knew down to the core of his skeleton the vital importance of recognizing facts. Joan was lost to him; that was a fact, like his disease, beyond any possibility of change. She would become angry when he did not speak to her, and would hang up, thinking that he had deliberately rebuffed her appeal, her proud, brave effort to bridge the loneliness between them. And he could do nothing about it. He was trapped in his delusion again. If he meant to survive, he could not afford the

417

luxury of grieving over lost hopes. He was a leper; all his hopes were false. They were his enemies. They could kill him by blinding him to the lethal power of facts.

It was a fact that the Land was a delusion. It was a fact that he was trapped, caught in the web of his own weakness. His leprosy was a fact. He insisted on these things while he protested weakly to himself, No! I can't stand it! But the cold water dried from his skin, and was replaced by the kind, earthy warmth of the graveling. Sensations ran excitedly up his limbs from his fingers and toes. With a wild, stubborn look as if he were battering his head against a wall, he gave himself a VSE.

Then he located a mirror of polished stone, and used it to inspect his forehead. No mark was there – the hurtloam had erased his injury completely.

He called out, 'Mhoram!' But his voice had an unwanted beseeching tone. To counter it, he began shoving himself into his clothes. When the Lord appeared in the doorway, Covenant did not meet his eyes. He pulled on his T-shirt and jeans, laced up his boots, then moved away to the third room of his suite.

There he found a door opening onto a balcony. With Mhoram behind him, he stepped out into the open air. At once, perspectives opened, and a spasm of vertigo clutched at him. The balcony hung halfway up the southern face of Revelstone – more than a thousand feet straight above the foothills which rested against the base of the mountain. The depth of the fall seemed to gape unexpectedly under his feet. His fear of heights whirred in his ears; he flung his arms around the stone railing, clung to it, clutched it to his chest.

In a moment, the worst of the spasm passed. Mhoram asked him what was wrong, but he did not explain. Breathing deeply, he pushed himself erect, and stood with his back pressed against the reassuring stone of the Keep. From there, he took in the view.

As he remembered it, Revelstone filled a long wedge of the mountains which stood immediately to the west. It had been carved out of the mountain promontory by the Giants many centuries ago, in the time of Old Lord Damelon Giantfriend. Above the Keep was a plateau which went beyond it west and north, past Furl Falls for a distance of a league or two before rising up into the rugged Westron Mountains. The Falls were too far away to be seen, but in the distance the White River angled away south and slightly east from its head in the pool of Furl Falls.

Beyond the river to the southwest, Covenant made out the open plains and hills that led towards Trothgard. In that direction, he saw no sign of cultivation or habitation; but eastward from him were ripe fields, stands of trees, streams, villages – all glowing under the sun as if they were smiling with health. Looking over them, he sensed that the season was early autumn. The sun stood in the southern sky, the air was not as warm as it seemed, and the breeze which blew gently up the face of Revelstone was flavoured with the loamy lushness of fall.

The Land's season — so different from the spring weather from which he had been wrenched away — gave him a renewed sense of discrepancy, of stark and impossible translation. It reminded him of many things, but he forced himself to begin with the previous evening. Stiffly, he said, 'Has it occurred to you that Foul probably let that poor Waynhim go just to get you to call me here?'

'Of course,' Mhoram replied. 'That is the Despiser's way. He intends you to be the means of our destruction.'

'Then why did you do it? Hellfire! You know how I feel about this — I told you often enough. I don't want — I'm not going to be responsible for what happens to you.'

Lord Mhoram shrugged. 'That is the paradox of white gold. Hope and despair run together for us. How could we refuse the risk? Without every aid which we can find or make for ourselves, we cannot meet Lord Foul's might. We trust that at the last you will not turn your back on the Land.'

'You've had forty years to think about it. You ought to know by now how little I deserve or even want your trust.'

'Perhaps. Warmark Hile Troy argues much that way — though there is much about you that he does not know. He feels that faith in one who is so unwilling is folly. And he is not convinced that we will lose this war. He makes bold plans. But I have heard the Despiser laughing. For better or worse, I am seer and oracle for this Council. I hear — I approve the High Lord's decision of summoning. For many reasons.

'Thomas Covenant, we have not spent our years in seclusion here, dreaming sweet dreams of peace while Lord Foul grows and moves against us. From your last moment in the Land to this day, we have striven to prepare our defence. Scouts and Lords have ridden the Land from end to end, drawing the people together, warning them, building what lore we have. I have braved the Shattered Hills, and fought on the marge of Hotash Slay — but of that I do not speak. I brought back knowledge of the Ravers. *Dukkha* alone did not move us to summon you.'

Even in the direct beam of the sun, the word *Ravers* gave Covenant a chill he could not suppress. Remembering the other Waynhim he had seen, dead with an iron spike through its heart — killed by a Raver — he asked, 'What about them? What did you learn?'

'Much or little,' Mhoram sighed, 'according to the uses of the knowledge. The importance of this lore cannot be mistaken — and yet its value eludes us.

'While you were last in the Land, we learned that the Ravers were still abroad — that like their master they had not been undone by the Ritual of Desecration, which Kevin Landwaster wreaked in his despair. Some knowledge of these beings had come to us through the old legends, the Lore of the First Ward, and the teachings of the Giants. We knew that they were named Sheol, Jehannum, and Herem, and that they lived without bodies, feeding upon the souls of others. When the Despiser was powerful enough to give them strength, they enslaved creatures or people by entering their bodies, subduing their wills, and using the captured flesh to enact their master's purposes. Disguised in forms not their own, they were well hidden, and so could gain trust among their foes. By that means, many brave defenders of the Land were lured to their deaths in the age of the Old Lords.

'But I have learned more. There near Foul's Creche, I was beaten — badly overmastered. I fled through the Shattered Hills with only the staff of Variol my father between me and death, and could not prevent my foe from laying hands upon me. I had thought that I was in battle with a supreme loremaster of the ur-viles. But I learned — I learned otherwise.'

Lord Mhoram stared unseeing into the depths of the sky, remembering with grim, concentrated eyes what had happened to him. After a moment, he continued: 'It was a Raver I fought — a Raver in the flesh of an ur-vile. The touch of its hand taught me much. In the oldest time — beyond the reach of our most hoary legends, even before the dim time of the coming of men to the Land, and the cruel felling of the One Forest — the Colossus of the Fall had both power and purpose. It stood on Landsdrop like a forbidding fist over the Lower Land, and with the might of the Forest denied a dark evil from the Upper Land.'

Abruptly, he broke into a slow song like a lament, a quiet declining hymn which told the story of the Colossus as the Lords had formerly known it, before the son of Variol had gained his new knowledge. In restrained sorrow over lost glory, the song described the Colossus of the Fall — the huge stone monolith, upraised in the semblance of a fist, which stood beside the waterfall where the River Landrider of the Plains of Ra became the Ruinwash of the Spoiled Plains.

Since a time that was ancient before Berek Lord-Fatherer lost half his hand, the Colossus had stood in lone sombre guard above the cliff of Landsdrop; and the oldest hinted legends of the Old Lords told of a time, during the ages of the One Forest's dominion in the

Land, when that towering fist had held the power to forbid the shadow of Despite – held it, and did not wane until the felling of the Forest by that unsuspected enemy, man, had cut too deeply to be halted. But then, outraged and weakened by the slaughter of the trees, the Colossus had unclasped its interdict, and let the shadow free. From that time, from the moment of that offended capitulation, the Earth had slowly lost the power or the will or the chance to defend itself. So the burden of resisting the Despiser had fallen to a race which had brought the shadow upon itself, and the Earth lay under the outcome.

'But it was not Despite which the Colossus resisted,' Mhoram resumed when his song was done. 'Despite was the bane of men. It came with them into the Land from the cold anguish of the north, and from the hungry kingdom of the south. No, the Colossus of the Fall forbade another foe – three tree- and soil-hating brothers who were in the Spoiled Plains before Lord Foul first cast his shadow there. They were triplets, the spawn of one birth from the womb of their long-forgotten mother, and their names were *samadhi*, *moksha*, and *turiya*. They hated the Earth and all its growing things, just as Lord Foul hates all life and love. When the Colossus eased its interdict, they came to the Upper Land, and in their lust for ravage and dismay fell swiftly under the mastery of the Despiser. From that time, they have been his highest servants. They have performed treachery for him when he could not show his hand, and have fought for him when he would not lead his armies.

'It was *samadhi*, now named Sheol, who mastered the heart of Berek's liege – Sheol who slaughtered the champions of the Land, and drove Berek, half-unhanded and alone, to his extremity on the slopes of Mount Thunder. It was *turiya* and *moksha*, Herem and Jehannum, who lured the powerful and austere Demondim to their breeding dens, and to the spawning of the ur-viles. Now the three are united with Lord Foul again – united, and clamouring for the decimation of the Land. But alas – alas for my ignorance and weakness. I cannot foresee what they will do. I can hear their voices, loud with lust for the ripping of trees and the scorching of soil, but their intent eludes me. The Land is in such peril because its servants are weak.'

The rough eloquence of Mhoram's tone carried Covenant along, and under its spell the brilliant sunlight seemed to darken in his eyes. Grimly, unwilling, he caught a sense of the looming and cruel ill which crept up behind the Land's spirit, defying its inadequate defenders. And when he looked at himself, he saw nothing but omens of futility. Other people who had protested their weakness to him had suffered terribly at the hands of his own irreducible and immedicable impotence. Harshly – more harshly than he intended – he asked, 'Why?'

Mhoram turned away from his private visions, and cocked an inquiring eyebrow at Covenant.

'Why are you weak?'

The Lord met this with a wry smile. 'Ah, my friend – I had forgotten that you ask such questions. You lead me into long speeches. I think that if I could reply to you briefly, I would not need you so.' But Covenant did not relent, and after a pause Mhoram said, 'Well, I cannot refuse to answer. But come – there is food waiting. Let us eat. Then I will make what answer I can.'

Covenant refused. Despite his hunger, he was unwilling to make any more concessions to the Land until he knew better where he stood.

Mhoram considered him for a moment, then replied in a measured tone, 'If what you say is true – if Land and Earth and all are nothing more than a dream, a threat of madness for you – then still you must eat. Hunger is hunger, and need is need. How else – ?'

'No.' Covenant dismissed the idea heavily.

At that, the gold flecks in Mhoram's eyes flared, as if they reflected the passion of the sun, and he said levelly, 'Then answer yourself that question yourself. Answer it, and save us. If we are helpless and unfriended, it is your doing. Only you can penetrate the mysteries which surround us.'

'No,' Covenant repeated. He recognized what Mhoram was saying, and refused to tolerate it. No, he responded to the heat of Mhoram's look. That's too much like blaming me for being a leper. It's not my fault. 'You go too far.'

'Ur-Lord,' Mhoram replied, articulating each word distinctly, 'there is peril upon the Land. Distance will not restrain me.'

'That isn't what I meant. I meant you're taking what I said too far. I'm not the one – the shaper. I'm not in control. I'm just another victim. All I know is what you tell me.

'What I want to know is why you keep trying to make me responsible. What makes you any weaker than I am? You've got the Staff of Law. You've got the *rhadhamaerl* and *lillianrill*. What makes you so bloody weak?'

The heat slowly faded from the Lord's gaze. Folding his arms so that his staff was clasped across his chest, he smiled crookedly. 'Your question grows with each asking. If I require you to ask again, I fear that nothing less than a Giant's tale will suffice for answer. Forgive me, my friend. I know that our peril cannot be laid on your head. Dream or no – there is no difference for us. We must serve the Land.

'Now, I must first remind you that the *rhadhamaerl* and *lillianrill* are another question, separate from the weakness of the Lords. The stone-lore of the *rhadhamaerl*, and the woodlore of the *lillianrill*, have been preserved from past ages by the people of Stonedown and Woodhelven. In their exile after the Ritual of Desecration, the people of the Land lost much of the richness of their lives. They were sorely bereft, and could cling only to that lore which enabled them to endure. Thus, when they returned to the Land, they brought with them those whose work in exile was to preserve and use the lore — Gravelingases of the *rhadhamaerl*, and Hirebrands of the *lillianrill*. It is the work of Hirebrand and Gravelingas to make the lives of the villages bounteous — warm in winter and plentiful in summer, true to the song of the Land.

'The Lore of High Lord Kevin Landwaster is another matter. That knowledge is the concern of the Loresraat and the Lords.

'The age of the Old Lords, before Lord Foul broke into open war with Kevin son of Loric, was among the bravest and gladdest and strongest of all the times of the Land. Kevin's Lore was mighty with Earthpower, and pure with Landservice. Health and gaiety flowered in the Land, and the bright Earth jewel of Andelain bedizened the Land's heart with precious woods and stones. That was a time —

'Yet it came to an end. Despair darkened Kevin, and in the Ritual of Desecration he destroyed that which he loved, intending to destroy the Despiser as well. But before the end, he was touched with prophecy or foresight, and found means to save much of power and beauty. He warned the Giants and the Ranyhyn, so that they might flee. He ordered the Bloodguard into safety. And he left his Lore for later ages — hid it in Seven Wards so that it would not fall into wrong or unready hands. The First Ward he gave to the Giants, and when the exile was ended they gave it to the first of the new Lords, the forebearers of this Council. In turn, these Lords conceived the Oath of Peace and carried it to all the people of the Land — an Oath to guard against Kevin's destroying passion. And these Lords, our forebearers, swore themselves and their followers in fealty and service to the Land and the Earthpower.

'Now, my friend, you know we have found the Second Ward. The Two contain much knowledge and much power, and when they are mastered they will lead us to the Third Ward. In this way, mastery will guide us until all Kevin's Lore is ours. But we fail — we fail to penetrate. How can I say it? We translate the speech of the Old Lords. We learn the skills and rites and songs of the Lore. We study Peace, and devote ourselves to the life of the Land. And yet something lacks. In some way, we miscomprehend — we do not suffice. Only a part of the power of this knowledge answers to our touch. We can learn nothing of the other Wards – and little of the Seven Words which evoke the Earthpower. Something – ur-Lord, it is something in us which fails. I feel it in my heart. We lack. We have not the stature of mastery.'

The Lord fell silent, musing with his head down and his cheek pressed against his staff. Covenant watched him for a time. The warmth of the sun and the cool breeze seemed to underscore Mhoram's stern self-judgment. Revelstone itself dwarfed the people who inhabited it.

Yet the Lord's influence or example strengthened Covenant. At last, he found the courage to ask his most important question. 'Then why am I here? Why did he let you summon me? Doesn't he want the white gold?'

Without raising his head, Mhoram said, 'Lord Foul is not yet ready to defeat you. The wild magic still surpasses him. Instead, he strives to make you destroy yourself. I have seen it.'

'Seen it?' Covenant echoed softly, painfully.

'In grey visions I have caught glimpses of the Despiser's heart. In this matter, I speak from sure comprehension. Even now, Lord Foul believes that his might is not equal to the wild magic. He is not yet ready to battle you.

'Remember that forty years ago Drool Rockworm held both Staff and Stone. Desiring still more power – desiring all power – he exerted himself against you in ways which the Despiser would not have chosen – ways which were wasteful or foolish. Drool was mad. And Lord Foul had no wish to teach him wisdom.

'Matters are otherwise now. Lord Foul wastes no power, takes no risks which do not gain his ends. He seeks indirectly to make you do his bidding. If it comes to the last, and you are still unmastered, he will fight you – but only when he is sure of victory. Until that time, he will strive to bend your will so that you will choose to strike against the Land – or to withhold your hand from our defence, so that he will be free to destroy us.

'But he will make no open move against you now. He fears the wild magic. White gold is not bound by the law of Time, and he must prevent its use until he can know that it will not be used against him.'

Covenant heard the truth of Mhoram's words. The Despiser had told him much the same thing, high on Kevin's Watch, when he had first appeared in the Land. He shivered under the livid memory of Lord Foul's contempt – shivered and felt cold, as if behind the clean sunlight over Revelstone blew the dank mist of Despite, dampening his soul with the smell of attar, filling his ears on a level just beyond hearing with the rumble of an avalanche. Looking into

Mhoram's eyes, he knew that he had to speak truly as well, reply as honestly as he could.

'I don't have any choice.' Even this made him want to duck his head in shame, but he forced himself to hold the Lord's gaze. 'I'll have to do it that way. Even if that's not the one good answer — even if madness is not the only danger in dreams. Even if I believed in this wild magic. I haven't got one idea how to use it.'

With an effort, Mhoram smiled gently. But the sombreness of his glance overshadowed his smile. He met Covenant's eyes unwaveringly, and when he spoke, his voice was sad. 'Ah, my friend, what will you do?'

The uncritical softness of the question caught Covenant by the throat. He was not prepared for such sympathy. With difficulty, he answered, 'I'll survive.'

Mhoram nodded slowly, and a moment later he turned away, back towards the room. As he reached the door, he said, 'I am late. The Council waits for me. I must go.'

But before the Lord could leave, Covenant called after him, 'Why aren't you the High Lord?' He was trying to find some way to thank Mhoram. 'Don't they appreciate you around here?'

Over his shoulder, Mhoram replied simply, 'My time has not yet come.' Then he left the room, closing the door carefully after him.

5

DUKKHA

Covenant turned back to the southward view from Revelstone. He had many things to think about, and no easy way to grasp them. But already his senses seemed to be swinging into consonance with the Land. He could smell the crops in the fields east of him — they were nearly ready for harvesting — and see the inner ripeness of the distant trees. He found autumn in the way the sunlight stroked his face. Such sensations accented the excitement in his veins, but they confused his efforts to deal clearly with his situation. No leper, he thought painfully, no leper should be asked to live in such a healthy world.

Yet he could not deny it; he was moved by Mhoram's account of the dilemmas of the Lords. He was moved by the Land, and by the people who served it — though they made him look so small to himself. Sourly, he left the balcony, and scanned the tray of food which had been set for him on a stone table in the centre of his sitting room. The soup and the stew still steamed, reminding him how hungry he was.

No. He could not afford to make any more concessions. Hunger was like nerve-health — illusion, deception, dream. He could not —

A knock at the door interrupted him. For a moment, he stood still, irresolute. He did not want to talk to anyone until he had had more time to think. But at the same time he did not want to be alone. The threat of madness was always at its worst when he was alone.

Keep moving, don't look back, he muttered bitterly to himself, echoing a formula which had served him ambiguously at best.

He went to open the door.

Standing in the outer hallway was Hile Troy.

He was dressed as Covenant had seen him before, with his sunglasses firmly in place; and again the slight smile on his lips looked vaguely mysterious and apologetic. A sharp pang of anxiety joined the tingling of Covenant's blood. He had been trying not to think about this man.

'Come on,' Troy said. His tone was full of the power of command. 'The Lords are doing something you ought to see.'

Covenant shrugged to disguise a tremor in his shoulders. Troy was an adversary — Covenant could sense it. But he had made his decision when he had opened the door. Defiantly, he strode out into the hall.

In the hallway, he found Bannor standing watch by his door.

Hile Troy started away with a swift, confident stride, but Covenant turned towards the Bloodguard. Bannor met his look with a nod; for a moment they held each other's eyes. Bannor's flat, brown, unreadable face had not changed a whit, not aged a day that Covenant could discern. As he stood relaxed and ready, the Bloodguard radiated a physical solidity, a palpable competence, which intimidated or belittled Covenant; and yet Covenant sensed something extreme and sad in Bannor's timeless impenetrability.

The Bloodguard were said to be two thousand years old. They were clenched into immutability by a strait and consuming Vow of service to the Lords, while all the people they had ever known — including the long-lived Giants, and High Lord Kevin, who had inspired them to their Vow — fell into dust.

Looking now at Bannor, with his alien countenance and his bare feet and his short brown tunic, Covenant received a sudden intuitive impression, as if a previous subliminal perception had crystallized. How many times had Bannor saved his life? For an instant, he could not remember. He felt unexpectedly sure that the Bloodguard could tell him what he needed to know, that from the extravagance of his two-thousand-year perspective, bereft by the unforeseen power of his Vow of home and sleep and death, of everyone he had ever loved, he had gained the knowledge Covenant needed.

'Bannor – ' he began.

'Ur-Lord.' The Bloodguard's voice was as passionless as time.

But Covenant did not know how to ask; he could not put his need into words which would not sound like an attack on the Bloodguard's impossible fidelity. Instead, he murmured, 'So we're back to this.'

'The High Lord has chosen me to keep watch over you.'

'Come on,' called Troy peremptorily. 'You should see this.'

Covenant disregarded him for a moment longer. To Bannor he said, 'I hope – I hope it works out better than the last time.' Then he turned and moved down the hall after Troy. He knew that Bannor came behind him, though the Bloodguard walked without a sound.

Impatiently, Hile Troy guided Covenant inward through the levels of the Keep. They passed briskly across high vaulted halls, along connecting corridors, and down stairs until they reached a place that Covenant recognized: the long circular passage around the sacred enclosure, where the inhabitants of Revelstone worshipped.

He followed Troy in through one of the many doors onto a balcony which hung in the great cavern. The cavity was cylindrical in shape, with seven balconies cut into the walls, a flat floor with a dais on one side, and a domed ceiling too high above the balconies to be seen clearly. The enclosure was dim; the only illumination came from four large *lillianrill* torches set around the dais. Bannor closed the door, shutting out the light from the outer hallway; and in the gloom Covenant clung to the railing for security against the depth of the cavity. He was several hundred feet above the dais.

The balconies were nearly empty. Clearly, whatever ceremony was about to be enacted was not intended for the general population of Revelstone.

The nine Lords were already on the dais. They stood in a circle facing each other. With their backs to the torches, their faces were shadowed, and Covenant could not make out their features.

'This is your doing,' said Troy in an intent whisper. 'They have tried everything else. You shamed them into this.'

Two Bloodguard bearing some figure between them moved towards the dais. With a start, Covenant identified the injured Waynhim. *Dukkha* was struggling feebly, but it could not prevent the Bloodguard from placing it within the circle of the Lords.

'They're going to try to break the hold of the Illearth Stone,' Troy continued. 'This is risky. If they fail, it could spread to one of them. They'll be too exhausted to fight it.'

Clutching the railing with both hands, Covenant watched the scene below him. The two Bloodguard left *dukkha* cowering in the circle, and retreated to the wall of the enclosure. For a long moment, the Lords stood in silent concentration, preparing themselves. Then they lifted their heads, planted their staffs firmly before them on the stone, and began to sing. Their hymn echoed in the enclosure as if the domed gloom itself were resonating. They appeared small in the immense chamber, but their song stood up boldly, filling the air with authority and purpose.

As the echoes died, Troy whispered in Covenant's ear, 'If something goes wrong here, you're going to pay for it.'

I know, Covenant said like a prophet. I'm going to have to pay for everything.

When silence at last refilled the enclosure, High Lord Elena said in a clear voice, '*Dharmakshetra* Waynhim, if you can hear us through the wrong which has been done to you, listen. We seek to drive the power of the Illearth Stone from you. Please aid us. Resist the Despiser. *Dukkha*, hear! Remember health and hope, and resist this ill!'

Together, the Lords raised their staffs.

Troy's fingers reached out of the darkness and gripped Covenant's arm above the elbow.

Crying in one voice, '*Melenkurion abatha!*' the Lords struck their staffs on the stone. The metal rang through the sacred enclosure like a clashing of shields, and blue Lords-fire burst from the upheld end of each staff. The incandescent flames burned hotly, outshining the light of the torches. But the Staff of Law dazzled them all, flaring like a tongue of lightning. And the fire of the staffs made a low sound like the rush of distant storm winds.

Slowly, one of the lesser staffs bent towards the head of *dukkha*. It descended, then stopped with its flame well above the Waynhim's head, as if at that point the fire met resistance. When the wielding Lord pressed down, the air between *dukkha*'s skull and the staff ignited; the whole space burned. But the fire there was as green as cold emerald, and it devoured the Lords' blue power.

Troy's fingers dug like claws into the flesh of Covenant's arm. But Covenant hardly felt them.

To meet the green flame, the Lords broke into a stern antiphonal chant, using words that Covenant could not understand. Their voices pounded against the green, and the rushing wind of their power mounted. Yet through it could be heard the voice of *dukkha* Waynhim, gibbering.

One by one, the Lords added their fires to the struggle over *dukkha*'s head, until only the Staff of Law remained uncommitted. As each new power touched the green, a sound of hunger and the crushing of bones multiplied in the air, and the baleful emerald fire blazed up more mightily, expanding like an inferno of cruel ice to combat the Lords' strength.

Abruptly, the *lillianrill* torches went out, as if extinguished by a high wind.

Troy's fingers tightened.

Then High Lord Elena's voice sprang out over the song of the Lords. '*Melenkurion abatha! Duroc minas mill khabaal!*' With a sweeping stroke, she swung the Staff of Law into the fray.

For an instant, the force of her attack drove the conflicting fires together. Blue and green became one, and raged up over the circle of the Lords, ravening and roaring like a holocaust. But the next moment, *dukkha* shrieked as if its soul were torn in two. The towering flame ruptured like a thunderhead.

The detonation blew out all the fire in the enclosure. At once a darkness as complete as a grave closed over the Lords.

Then two small torches appeared in the hands of the Bloodguard. The dim light showed *dukkha* lying on the stone beside two prostrate Lords. The others stood in their places, leaning on their staffs as if stunned by their exertion.

Seeing the fallen Lords, Troy drew a breath that hissed fiercely through his teeth. His fingers seemed to be trying to bare Covenant's bone. But Covenant bore the pain, watched the Lords.

Swiftly, the Bloodguard relit the four torches around the dais. At the touch of the warm light, one of the Lords – Covenant recognized Mhoram – shook off his numbness, and went to kneel beside his collapsed comrades. He examined them for a moment with his hands, using his sense of touch to explore the damage done to them; then he turned and bent over *dukkha*. Around him vibrated a silence of hushed fear.

At last he climbed to his feet, bracing himself with his staff. He spoke in a low voice, but his words carried throughout the enclosure. 'The Lords Trevor and Amatin are well. They have only lost consciousness.' Then he bowed his head, and sighed. 'The Waynhim *dukkha* is dead. May its soul at last find peace.'

'And forgive us,' High Lord Elena responded, 'for we have failed.'

Breathing in his deep relief, Troy released Covenant. Covenant felt sudden stabs of pain in his upper arm. The throbbing made him aware that his own hands hurt. The intensity of his hold on the railing had cramped them until they felt crippled. The pain was sharp, but he welcomed it. He could see death in the broken limbs of the Waynhim. The bruises on his arms, the aching stiffness in his palms, were proof of life.

Dully, he said, 'They killed it.'

'What did you want them to do?' Troy retorted with ready indignation. 'Keep it captive, alive and in torment? Let it go, and disclaim responsibility? Kill it in cold blood?'

'No.'

'Then this is your only choice. This was the only thing left to try.'

'No. You don't understand.' Covenant tried to find the words to explain, but he could go no further. 'You don't understand what Foul is doing to them.' He pulled his cramped fingers away from the railing, and left the enclosure.

When he regained his rooms, he was still shaken. He did not think to close the door behind him, and the Warmark strode after him into the suite without bothering to ask admittance. But Covenant paid no attention to his visitor. He went straight to the tray of food, picked up the flask which stood beside the still-steaming bowls and drank deeply, as if he were trying to quench the heat of his blood. The springwine in the flask had a light, fresh, beery taste; it washed into him, clearing dust from his internal passages. He emptied the flask, then remained still for a moment with his eyes shut, experiencing the sensation of the draught. When its clear light had eased some of the constriction in his chest, he seated himself at the table and began to eat.

'That can wait,' Troy said gruffly. 'I've got to talk to you.'

'So talk,' Covenant said around a mouthful of stew. In spite of his visitor's insistent impatience, he kept on eating. He ate rapidly, acting on his decision before doubt could make him regret it.

Troy paced the room stiffly for a moment, then brought himself to take a seat opposite Covenant. He sat as he stood — with unbending uprightness. His gleaming, impenetrable, black sunglasses emphasized the tightness of the muscles in his cheeks and forehead. Carefully, he said, 'You're determined to make this hard, aren't you? You're determined to make it hard for everyone.'

Covenant shrugged. As the springwine unfurled within him, he began to recover from what he had seen in the sacred enclosure. At the same time, he remembered his distrust of Troy. He ate with increasing wariness, watched the Warmark from under his eyebrows.

'Well, I'm trying to understand,' Troy went on in a constrained tone. 'God knows I've got a better chance than anyone else here.'

Covenant put down the wooden fork and looked squarely at Troy.

'The same thing happened to us both.' To the obvious disbelief in Covenant's face, he responded, 'Oh, it's all clear enough. A white gold wedding ring. Books, jeans, and a T-shirt. You were talking on the phone with your wife. And the time before that – have I got this right? – you were hit by a car of some kind.'

'A police car,' Covenant murmured, staring at the Warmark.

'You see? I can recognize every detail. And you could do the same for my story. We both came here from the same place, the same world, Covenant. The real world.'

No, Covenant breathed thickly. None of this is happening.

'I've even heard of you,' Troy went on as if this argument would be incontrovertible. 'I've read – your book was read to me. It made an impression on me.'

Covenant snorted. But he was disturbed. He had burned that book too late; it continued to haunt him.

'No, hold on. Your damn book was a best-seller. Hundreds of thousands of people read it. It was made into a movie. Just because I know about it doesn't mean I'm a figment of your imagination. In fact, my presence here is proof that you are not going crazy. Two independent minds perceiving the same phenomenon.'

He said this with confident plausibility, but Covenant was not swayed. 'Proof?' he muttered. 'I would be amused to hear what else you call proof.'

'Do you want to hear how I came here?'

'No!' Covenant was suddenly vehement. 'I want to hear why you don't want to go back.'

For a moment, Troy sat still, facing Covenant with his sunglasses. Then he snapped to his feet, and started to pace again. Swinging tightly around on his heel at one end of the room, he said, 'Two reasons. First, I like it here. I'm useful to something worth being useful to. The issues at stake in this war are the only ones I've ever seen worth fighting for. The life of the Land is beautiful. It deserves preservation. For once, I can do some good. Instead of spending my time on troop deployment, first- and second-strike capabilities, super-ready status, demoralization parameters, nuclear induction of lethal genetic events,' he recited bitterly, 'I can help defend against a genuine evil. The world we came from – the "real" world – hasn't got such clear colours, no blue and black and green and red, "ebon ichor incarnadine viridian". Grey is the colour of "reality".

'Actually' – he dropped back into his chair, and his voice took on a more conversational tone – 'I didn't even know what grey was until I came here. That's my second reason.'

He reached up with both hands and removed his sunglasses.

'I'm blind.'

His sockets were empty, orbless, lacking even lids and lashes. Blank skin grew in the holes where his eyes should have been.

431

'I was born this way,' the Warmark said, as if he could see Covenant's astonishment. 'A genetic freak. But my parents saw fit to keep me alive, and by the time they died I had learned various ways to function on my own. I got myself into special schools, got special help. It took a few extra years because I had to have most things read to me, but eventually I got through high school and college. After which my only real skill was keeping track of spatial relationships in my head. For instance, I could play chess without a board. And if someone described a room to me, I could walk through it without bumping into anything. Basically I was good at that because it was how I kept myself alive.

'So I finally got a job in a think tank with the Department of Defence. They wanted people who could understand situations without being able to see them – people who could use language to deal with physical facts. I was the expert on war games, computer hypotheticals, that sort of thing. All I needed was accurate verbal information on topography, troop strength, hardware and deployment, support capabilities – then leave the game to me. I always won. So what did it all amount to? Nothing. I was the freak of the group, that's all.

'I took care of myself as well as I could. But for a place to live, I was pretty much at the mercy of what I could get. So I lived in this apartment house on the ninth floor, and one night it burned down. That is, I assume it burned down. The fire company still hadn't come when my apartment caught. There was nothing I could do. The fire backed me to the wall, and finally I climbed out the window. I hung from the window-sill while the heat blistered my knuckles. I was determined not to let go because I had a very clear idea of how far above the ground nine floors is. Made no difference. After a while, my fingers couldn't hold on any more.

'The next thing I knew, I was lying on something that felt like grass. There was a cool breeze – but with enough warmth behind it to make me think it must be daylight. The only thing wrong was a smell of burned flesh. I assumed it was me. Then I heard voices – urgent, people hurrying to try to prevent something. They found me.

'Later, I learned what had happened. A young student at the Loresraat had an inspiration about a piece of the Second Ward he was working on. All this was about five years ago. He thought he had figured out how to get help for the Land – how to summon you, actually. He wanted to try it, but the Lorewardens refused to let him. Too dangerous. They took his idea to study, and sent to Revelstone for a Lord to help them decide how to test his theory.

'Well, he didn't want to wait. He left the Loresraat and climbed a few miles up into the western hills of Trothgard until he thought he was far enough away to work in peace. Then he started the ritual. Somehow, the Lorewardens felt the power he was using, and went after him. But they were too late. He succeeded – in a manner of speaking. When he was done, I was lying there on the grass, and he – He had burned himself to death. Some of the Lorewardens think he caught the fire that should have killed me. As they said, it was too dangerous.

'The Lorewardens took me in, cared for me, put hurtloam on my hands – even on my eyesockets. Before long, I began having visions. Colours and shapes started to jump at me out of the – out of whatever it was I was used to. This round, white-orange circle passed over me every day – but I didn't know what it was. I didn't even know it was "round", I had no visual concept of "round". But the visions kept getting stronger. Finally, Elena – she was the Lord who came down from Revelstone, only she wasn't High Lord then – she told me that I was learning to see with my mind – as if my brain were actually starting to see through my forehead. I didn't believe it, but she showed me. She demonstrated how my sense of spatial relationships fitted what I was "seeing", and how my sense of touch matched the shapes around me.'

He paused for a moment, remembering. Then he said strongly, 'I'll tell you – I never think about going back. How can I? I'm here, and I can see. The Land's given me a gift I could never repay in a dozen lifetimes. I've got too big a debt – The first time I stood on the top of Revelwood and looked over the valley where the Rill and Llurallin rivers come together – the first time in my life that I had ever seen – the first time, Covenant, I had ever even known that such sights existed – I swore I was going to win this war for the Land. Lacking missiles and bombs, there are other ways to fight. It took me a little while to convince the Lords – just long enough for me to outsmart all the best tacticians in the Warward. Then they made me their Warmark. Now I'm just about ready. A difficult strategic problem – we're too far from the best line of defence, Landsdrop. And I haven't heard from my scouts. I don't know which way Foul is going to try to get at us. But I can beat him in a fair fight. I'm looking forward to it.

'Go back? No. Never.'

Hile Troy had been speaking in a level tone, as if he did not want to expose his emotions to his auditor. But Covenant could hear an undercurrent of enthusiasm in the words – a timbre of passion too unruly to be concealed.

Now Troy leaned towards Covenant intently, and his ready indignation came back into his voice. 'In fact, I can't understand you at all. Do you know that this whole place' – he indicated Revelstone with a brusque gesture – 'revolves around you? White gold. The wild magic that destroys peace. The Unbeliever who found the Second Ward and saved the Staff of Law – unwillingly, I hear. For forty years, the Loresraat and the Lords have worked for a way to get you back. Don't get me wrong – they've done everything humanly possible to try to find other ways to defend the Land. They've built up the Warward, racked their brains over the Lore, risked their necks on things like Mhoram's trip to Foul's Creche. And they're scrupulous. They insist that they accept your ambivalent position. They insist that they don't expect you to save them. All they want is to make it possible for the wild magic to aid the Land, so they won't have to reproach themselves for neglecting a possible hope. But I tell you – they don't believe there is any hope but you.

'You know Lord Mhoram. You should have some idea of just how tough that man is. He's got backbone he hasn't even touched yet. Listen. He screams in his sleep. His dreams are that bad. I heard him once. He – I asked him the next morning what possessed him. In that quiet, kind voice of his, he told me that the Land would die if you didn't save it.

'Well, I don't believe that – Mhoram or no Mhoram. But he isn't the only one. High Lord Elena eats, drinks, and sleeps Unbeliever. Wild magic and white gold, Covenant Ringthane. Sometimes I think she's obsessed. She – '

But Covenant could not remain silent any longer. He could not stand to be held responsible for so much commitment. Roughly, he cut in, 'Why?'

'I don't know. She doesn't even know you.'

'No. I mean, why is she High Lord – instead of Mhoram?'

'What does it matter?' said Troy irritably. 'The Council chose her. A couple of years ago – when Osondrea, the old High Lord, died. They put their minds together – you must have noticed when you were here before how the Lords can pool their thoughts, think together – and she was elected.' As he spoke, the irritation faded from his tone. 'They said she has some special quality, some inner mettle that makes her the best leader for this war. Maybe I don't know what they mean – but I know she's got something. She's impossible to refuse. I would fight with stew forks and soup spoons against Foul –

'So I don't understand you. You may be the last man alive who's seen the Celebration of Spring. And there she stands, looking like all the allure of the Land put together – practically begging you. And you!' Troy struck the table with his hand, brandished his empty sockets at Covenant. 'You refuse.'

Abruptly, he slapped his sunglasses back on, and flung away from the table to pace the room again, as if he could not sit still in the face of Covenant's perversity.

Covenant watched him, seething at the freedom of Troy's judgment – the trust he placed in his own rectitude. But Covenant had heard something else in Troy's voice, a different explanation. Probing bluntly, he asked, 'Is Mhoram in love with her, too?'

At that, Troy spun, pointed a finger rigid with accusation at the Unbeliever. 'You know what I think? You're too cynical to see the beauty here. You're too cheap. You've got it made in your "real" world, with all those royalties rolling in. So what if you're sick? That doesn't stop you from getting rich. Coming here just gets in the way of hacking out more best-sellers. Why should you fight the Despiser? You're just like him yourself.'

Before the Warmark could go on, Covenant rasped thickly, 'Get out. Shut up and get out.'

'Forget it. I'm not going to leave until you give me one – '

'Get out.'

' – one good reason for the way you're acting. I'm not going to walk away and let you destroy the Land just because the Lords are too scrupulous to lean on you.'

'That's enough!' Covenant was on his feet. His hurt blazed up before he could catch hold of himself. 'Don't you even know what a leper is?'

'What difference does that make? It's not worse than not having any eyes. Aren't you healthy here?'

Mustering all the force of his injury, his furious grief, Covenant averred, 'No!' He waved his hands. 'Do you call this health? It's a lie!'

That cry visibly stunned Troy. The black assertion of his sunglasses faltered; the inner aura of his spirit was confused by doubt. For the first time, he looked like a blind man.

'I don't understand,' he said softly.

He faced the onslaught of Covenant's glare for a moment longer. Then he turned and left the room, moving quietly, as if he had been humbled.

6

THE HIGH LORD

When evening came, Thomas Covenant sat on his balcony to watch the sun set behind the Westron Mountains. Though summer was hardly past, there was a gleam of white snow on many of the peaks. As the sun dropped behind them, the western sky shone with a sharing of cold and fire. White silver reflected from the snow across the bottom of a glorious sky, an orange-gold gallant display sailing with full canvas over the horizon.

Covenant watched it bleakly. A scowl knotted his forehead like a fist. He had spent the afternoon in useless rage, but after a time his anger at Troy had died down among the embers of his protest against being summoned to the Land. Now he felt cold at heart, desolate and alone. The resolve he had expressed to Mhoram, his determination to survive, seemed pretentious – fey and anile. And the frown clenched his forehead as if the flesh over his skull refused to admit that it had been healed.

He was thinking of jumping from the balcony. To quell his fear of heights, he would have to wait until the darkness of the night was complete, and he could no longer see the ground. But considered in that way, the idea both attracted and repelled him. It offended his leper's training, heaped ridicule on everything he had already endured to cling to life. It spoke of a defeat that was as bitter as starkest gall to him. But he yearned for relief from his dilemma. He felt as dry as a wasteland, and rationalizations came easy. Chiefest of these was the argument that since the Land was not real it could not kill him; a death here would only force him back into the reality that was the only thing which he could believe. In his aloneness, he could not tell whether that argument expressed courage or cowardice.

Slowly, the last of the sun fell behind the mountains, and its emblazonry faded from the sky. Gloaming spread out of the shadow of the peaks, dimming the plains below Covenant until he could only discern them as uneasy, recumbent shapes under the heavens. The stars came out and grew gradually brighter, as if to clarify trackless space; but the voids between them were too great, and the map they made was unreadable. In his dusty, unfertile gaze, they seemed to twinkle unconsolably.

When he heard the polite knock at his door, his need for privacy groaned at the intrusion. But he had other needs as well. He pushed himself to go answer the knock.

The stone door swung open easily on noiseless hinges, and light streamed into the room from the bright-lit hall, dazzling him so that for a moment he did not recognize either of the men outside. Then one of them said, 'Ur-Lord Covenant, we bid you welcome,' in a voice that seemed to bubble with good humour. Covenant identified Tohrm.

'Welcome and true,' said Tohrm's companion carefully, as if he were afraid he would make a mistake. 'We are the Hearthralls of Lord's Keep. Please accept welcome and comfort.'

As Covenant's eyes adjusted, he considered the two men. Tohrm's companion wore a grey-green Woodhelvennin cloak, and had a small wreath in his hair – the mark of a Hirebrand. In his hands he carried several smooth wooden rods for torches. Both the Hearthralls were clean-shaven, but the Hirebrand was taller and slimmer than his partner. Tohrm had the stocky, muscular frame of a Stonedownor, and he wore a loam-coloured tunic with soft trousers. His companion's cloak was bordered in Lords' blue; he had blue epaulettes woven into the shoulders of his tunic. Cupped in each of his hands was a small, covered, stone bowl.

Covenant scrutinized Tohrm's face. The Hearthrall's nimble eyes and swift smile were soberer than Covenant remembered them, but still essentially unchanged. Like Mhoram, he did not show enough years to account for the full forty.

'I am Borillar,' Tohrm's companion recited, 'Hirebrand of the *lillianrill* and Hearthrall of Lord's Keep. This is Tohrm, Gravelingas of the *rhadhamaerl* and likewise Hearthrall of Lord's Keep. Darkness withers the heart. We have brought you light.'

But as Borillar spoke, a look of concern touched Tohrm's face, and he said, 'Ur-Lord, are you well?'

'Well?' Covenant murmured vaguely.

'There is a storm on your brow, and it gives you pain. Shall I call a Healer?'

'What?'

'Ur-Lord Covenant, I am in your debt. I am told that at the hazard of your life you rescued my old friend Birinair from beyond the forbidding fire under Mount Thunder. That was bravely done – though it came too late to save his life. Do not hesitate to ask of me. For Birinair's sake, I will do all in my power for you.'

Covenant shook his head. He knew he should correct Tohrm, tell him that he had braved that fire in an effort to immolate himself, not to save Birinair. But he lacked the courage. Dumbly, he stepped aside and let the Hearthralls into his rooms.

Borillar immediately set about lighting his torches; he moved studiously to the wall sockets as if he were trying to create a good, grave impression. Covenant watched him for a moment, and Tohrm said with a covered smile, 'Good Borillar is in awe of you, ur-Lord. He has heard the legends of the Unbeliever from his cradle. And he has not been Hearthrall long. His former master in the *lillianrill* lore resigned this post to oversee the completion of the Gildenlode keels and rudders which they have been devising for the Giants – as High Lord Loric Vilesilencer promised. Borillar feels himself untimely thrust into responsibility. My old friend Birinair would have called him a whelp.'

'He's young,' Covenant said dully. Then he turned to Tohrm, forced himself to ask the question which most concerned him. 'But you – you're too young. You should be older. Forty years.'

'Ur-Lord, I have seen fifty-nine summers. Forty-one have passed since you came to Revelstone with the Giant, Saltheart Foamfollower.'

'But you're not old enough. You don't look more than forty now.'

'Ah,' said Tohrm, grinning broadly, 'the service of our lore, and of Revelstone, keeps us young. Without us, these brave Giant-wrought halls would be dark, and in winter – to speak truly – they would be cold. Who could grow old on the joy of such work?'

Happily, he moved off, set one of his pots on the table in the sitting room, and another in the bedroom by the bed. When he uncovered the pots, the warm glow of the graveling joined the light of the torches, and gave the illumination in the suite a richer and somehow kinder cast.

Tohrm breathed the graveling's aroma of newly broken earth with a glad smile. He finished while his companion was lighting the last of his torches in the bedroom. Before Borillar could return to the sitting room, the older Hearthrall stepped close to Covenant and whispered, 'Ur-Lord, say a word to good Borillar. He will cherish it.'

A moment later, Borillar walked across the room to stand stiffly by the door. He looked like a resolute acolyte, determined not to fail a high duty. Finally his young intentness, and Tohrm's appeal, moved Covenant to say, awkwardly, 'Thank you, Hirebrand.'

At once, pleasure transformed Borillar's face. He tried to maintain his gravity, to control his grin, but the man of legends, Unbeliever and Ringthane, had spoken to him, and he blurted out, 'Be welcome, ur-Lord Covenant. You will save the Land.'

Tohrm cocked an amused eyebrow at his fellow Hearthrall, gave Covenant a gay, grateful bow, and ushered the Hirebrand from the room. As they departed, Tohrm started to close the door, then stopped, nodded to someone in the hall, and went away leaving the door open,.

Bannor stepped into the room. He met Covenant's gaze with eyes that never slept – that only rarely blinked – and said, 'The High Lord would speak with you now.'

'Oh, hell,' Covenant groaned. He looked back with something like regret at his balcony and the night beyond. Then he went with the Bloodguard.

Walking down the hall, he gave himself a quick VSE. It was a pointless exercise, but he needed the habit of it, if for no other reason than to remind himself of who he was, what the central fact of his life was. He did it deliberately, as a matter of conscious choice. But it did not hold his attention. As he moved, Revelstone exerted its old influence over him again.

The high, intricate ways of the Keep had a strange power of suasion, an ability to carry conviction. They had been delved into the mountain promontory by Saltheart Foamfollower's laughing, story-loving ancestors; and like the Giants they had an air of bluff and inviolable strength. Now Bannor was taking Covenant deeper down into Revelstone than he had ever been before. With his awakening perceptions, he could feel the massive gut-rock standing over him; it was as if he were in palpable contact with absolute weight itself. And on a pitch of hearing that was not quite audible, or not quite hearing, he could sense the groups of people who slept or worked in places beyond the walls from him. Almost he seemed to hear the great Keep breathe. And yet all those myriad, uncountable tons of stone were not fearsome. Revelstone gave him an impression of unimpeachable security; the mountain refused to let him fear that it would fall.

Then he and Bannor reached a dim hall sentried by two Bloodguard standing with characteristic relaxed alacrity on either side of the entrance. There were no torches or other lights in the hall, but a strong glow illuminated it from its far end. With a nod to his comrades, Bannor led Covenant inward.

At the end of the hall, they entered a wide, round courtyard under a high cavern, with a stone floor as smooth as if it had been meticulously polished for ages. The bright pale-yellow light came from this floor; the stone shone as if a piece of the sun had gone into its making.

The courtyard held no other lights. But though it was not blinding at the level of the floor, the glow cast out all darkness. Covenant could survey the cave clearly from bottom to top. At intervals up the walls were railed coigns with doors behind them which provided access to the open space above the court.

Bannor paused for a moment to allow Covenant to look around. Then he walked barefoot out onto the shining floor. Tentatively, Covenant followed, fearing that his feet would be burned. But he felt nothing through his boots except a quiet resonance of power. It set up a tingling vibration in his nerves.

Only after he became accustomed to the touch of the floor did he notice that there were doors widely spaced around the courtyard. He counted fifteen. Bloodguard sentries stood at nine of them, and several feet into the shining floor from each of these nine was a wooden tripod. Three of these tripods held Lords' staffs – and one of the staffs was the Staff of Law. It was distinguished from the smooth wood of the other staffs by its greater thickness, and by the complex runes carved into it between its iron heels.

Bannor took Covenant to the door behind the Staff. The Bloodguard there stepped forward to meet them, greeted Bannor with a nod.

Bannor said, 'I have brought ur-Lord Covenant to the High Lord.'

'She awaits him.' Then the sentry levelled the impassive threat of his gaze at Covenant. 'We are the Bloodguard. The care of the Lords is in our hands. I am Morin, First Mark of the Bloodguard since the passing of Tuvor. The High Lord will speak with you alone. Think no harm against her, Unbeliever. We will not permit it.' Without waiting for an answer, Morin stepped aside to let him approach the door.

Covenant was about to ask what harm he could possibly do the High Lord, but Bannor forestalled him. 'In this place,' the Bloodguard explained, 'the Lords set aside their burdens. Their staffs they leave here, and within these doors they rest, forgetting the cares of the Land. The High Lord honours you greatly in speaking to you here. Without Staff or guard, she greets you as a friend in her sole private place. Ur-Lord, you are not a foe of the Land. But you give little respect. Respect this.'

He held Covenant's gaze for a moment as if to enforce his words. Then he went and knocked at the door.

When the High Lord opened her door, Covenant saw her clearly for the first time. She had put aside her blue Lord's robe, and instead wore a long, light brown Stonedownor shift with a white pattern woven into the shoulders. A white cord knotted at her waist emphasized her figure, and her thick hair, a rich brown with flashes of pale honey, fell to her shoulders, disguising the pattern there. She appeared younger than he had expected – he would have said that she was in her early thirties at most – but her face was strong, and the white skin of her forehead and throat knew much about sternness and discipline, though she smiled almost shyly when she saw Covenant.

But behind the experience of responsibility and commitment in her features was something strangely evocative. She seemed distantly familiar, as if in the background of her face she resembled someone he had once known. This impression was both heightened and denied by her eyes. They were grey like his own; but though they met him squarely they had an elsewhere cast, a disunion of focus, as if she were watching something else – as if some other, more essential eyes, the eyes of her mind, were looking somewhere else. Her gaze touched parts of him which had not responded for a long time.

'Please enter,' she said in a voice like a clear spring.

Moving woodenly, Covenant went past her into her rooms, and she shut the door behind him, closing out the light from the courtyard. Her antechamber was illumined simply by a pot of graveling in each corner. Covenant stopped in the centre of the room, and looked about him. The space was bare and unadorned, containing nothing but the graveling, a few stone chairs, and a table on which stood a white carving; but still the room seemed quiet and comfortable. The light gave this effect, he decided. The warm graveling glow made even flat stone companionable, enhanced the essential security of Revelstone. It was like being cradled – wrapped in the arms of the rock and cared for.

High Lord Elena gestured towards one of the chairs. 'Will you sit? There is much of which I would speak with you!'

He remained standing, looking away from her. Despite the room's ambience, he felt intensely uncomfortable. Elena was his summoner, and he distrusted her. But when he found his voice, he half surprised himself by expressing one of his most private concerns. Shaking his head, he muttered, 'Bannor knows more than he's telling.'

He caught her off guard. 'More?' she echoed, groping. 'What has he said that leaves more concealed?'

But he had already said more than he intended. He kept silent, watching her out of the corner of his sight.

'The Bloodguard know doubt,' she went on unsurely. 'Since Kevin Landwaster preserved them from the Desecration and his own end, they have felt a distrust of their own fidelity – though none would dare to raise any accusation against them. Do you speak of this?'

He did not want to reply, but her direct attention compelled him. 'They've already lived too long. Bannor knows it.' Then, to escape the subject, he went over to the table to look at the carving. The

441

white statuette stood on an ebony base. It was a rearing Ranyhyn mare made of a material that looked like bone. The work was blunt of detail, but through some secret of its art it expressed the power of the great muscles, the intelligence of the eyes, the oriflamme of the fluttering mane.

Without approaching him, Elena said, 'That is my craft – marrow-meld. Does it please you? It is Myrha, the Ranyhyn that bears me.'

Something stirred in Covenant. He did not want to think about the Ranyhyn, but he thought that he had found a discrepancy. 'Foamfollower told me that the marrowmeld craft had been lost.'

'So it was. I alone in the Land practise this Ramen craft. *Anundivian yajña*, also named marrowmeld or bone-sculpting, was lost to the Ramen during their exile in the Southron Range – during the Ritual of Desecration. I do not speak in pride – I have been blessed in many things. When I was a child, a Ranyhyn bore me into the mountains. For three days we did not return, so that my mother thought me dead. But the Ranyhyn taught me much – much – In my learning, I recovered the ancient craft. The lore to reshape dry bones came to my hands. Now I practise it here, when the work of the Lords wearies me.'

Covenant kept his back to her, but he was not studying her sculpture. He was listening to her voice as if he expected it to change at any moment into the voice of someone he knew. Her tone resonated with implicit meanings. But he could not make them out. Abruptly, he turned to meet her eyes. Again, though she faced him, she seemed to be looking at or thinking about something else, something beyond him. Her elsewhere glance disturbed him. Studying her, his frown deepened until he wore the healing of his forehead like a crown of thorns.

'What do you want?' he demanded.

'Will you sit?' she said quietly. 'There is much I would speak of with you.'

'Like what?'

The hardness of his tone did not make her flinch, but she spoke more quietly still. 'I hope to find a way to win your help against the Despiser.'

Thinking self-contemptuous thoughts, he retorted, 'How far are you willing to go?'

For an instant, the other focus of her eyes came close to him, touched him like a lick of fire. Blood rushed to his face, and he almost recoiled a step – so strongly did he feel for that instant that she had the capacity to go far beyond anything he could imagine. But the glimpse passed before he could guess at what it was. She turned unhurriedly away, went briefly into one of her other rooms.

When she returned, she bore in her hands a wooden casket bound with old iron.

Holding the casket as if it contained something precious, she said, 'The Council has been much concerned in this matter. Some said, "Such a gift is too great for anyone. Let it be kept and safe for as long as we may be able to endure." And others said, "It will fail of its purpose, for he will believe that we seek to buy his aid with gifts. He will be angered against us, and will refuse." So spoke Lord Mhoram, whose knowledge of the Unbeliever is more than any other's. But I said, "He is not our foe. He gives us no aid because he cannot give aid. Though he holds the white gold, its use is beyond him or forbidden him. Here is a weapon which surpasses us. It may be that he will be able to master it, and that with such a weapon he will help us, though he cannot use the white gold."

'After much thought and concern, my voice prevailed. Therefore the Council asks to give you this gift, so that its power will not lie idle, but will turn against the Despiser.

'Ur-Lord Covenant, this is no light offering. Forty years ago, it was not in the possession of the Council. But the Staff of Law opened doors deep in Revelstone – doors which had been closed since the Desecration. The Lords hoped that these chambers contained other Wards of Kevin's Lore – but no Wards were there. Yet among many things of forgotten use or little power this was found – this which we offer to you.'

She pressed curiously on the sides of the casket, and the lid swung open, revealing a cushioned velvet interior, on which lay a short silver sword. It was a two-edged blade, with straight guards and a ribbed hilt; and it was forged around a clear white gem, which occupied the junction of the blade, guards, and hilt. This gem looked strangely lifeless; it reflected no light from the graveling, as if it were impervious or dead to any ordinary flame.

With awe in her low voice, Elena said, 'This is the *krill* of Loric Vilesilencer son of Damelon son of Berek. With this he slew the Demondim guise of *moksha* Raver, and delivered the Land from the first great peril of the ur-viles. Ur-Lord Covenant, Unbeliever and Ringthane, will you accept it?'

Slowly, full of a leper's fascinated dread of things that cut, Covenant lifted the *krill* from its velvet rest. Hefting it, he found that its balance pleased his hand, though his two fingers and thumb could not grip it well. Cautiously, he tested its edges with his thumb. They were as dull as if they had never been honed – as dull as the white gem. For a moment, he stood still, thinking that a knife did not need to be sharp to harm him.

'Mhoram was right,' he said out of the dry, lonely hebetude of his heart. 'I don't want any gifts. I've had more gifts than I can bear.'

Gifts! It seemed to him that everyone he had ever known in the Land had tried to give him gifts – Foamfollower, the Ranyhyn, Lord Mhoram, even Atiaran. The Land itself gave him an impossible nerve-health. But the gift of Lena Atiaran-daughter was more terrible than all the others. He had raped her, raped! And afterward, she had gone into hiding so that her people would not learn what had happened to her and punish him. She had acted with an extravagant forbearance so that he could go free – free to deliver Lord Foul's prophecy of doom to the Lords. Beside that self-abnegation, even Atiaran's sacrifices paled.

Lena! he cried. A violence of grief and self-recrimination blazed up in him. 'I don't want any more.' Thunder blackened his face. He grasped the *krill* in both fists, its blade pointing downward. With a convulsive movement, he stabbed the sword at the heart of the table, trying to break its blunt blade on the stone.

A sudden flash of white blinded him like an instant of lightning. The *krill* wrenched out of his hands. But he did not try to see what had happened to it. He spun instantly back to face Elena. Through the white dazzle that confused his sight, he panted, 'No more *gifts!* I can't afford them!'

But she was not looking at him, not listening to him. She held her hands to her mouth as she stared past him at the table. 'By the Seven!' she whispered. 'What have you done?'

What – ?

He whirled to look.

The blade of the *krill* had pierced the stone; it was embedded halfway to its guards in the table.

Its white gem burned like a star.

Dimly, he became conscious of a throbbing ache in his wedding finger. His ring felt hot and heavy, almost molten. But he ignored it; he was afraid of it. Trembling, he reached out to touch the *krill*.

Power burned his fingers.

Hellfire!

He snatched his hand away. The fierce pain made him clasp his fingers under his other arm, and groan.

At once, Elena turned to him. 'Are you harmed?' she asked anxiously. 'What has happened to you?'

'Don't touch me!' he gasped.

She recoiled in confusion, then stood watching him, torn between her concern for him and her astonishment at the blazing gem. After a moment, she shook herself as if throwing off incomprehension, and said softly, 'Unbeliever – you have brought the *krill* to life.'

Covenant made an effort to match her, but his voice quavered as he said, 'It won't make any difference. It won't do you any good. Foul's got all the power that counts.'

'He does not possess the white gold.'

'To hell with the white gold!'

'No!' she retorted vehemently. 'Do not say such a thing. I have not lived my life for nothing. My mother, and her mother before her, have not lived for nothing!'

He did not understand her, but her sudden passion silenced him. He felt trapped between her and the *krill*; he did not know what to say or do. Helpless, he stared at the High Lord as her own emotions grew into speech.

'You say that this makes no difference – that it does no good. Are you a prophet? And if you are, what do you say that we should do? Surrender?' For an instant, her self-possession wavered, and she exclaimed furiously, 'Never!' He thought that he heard hatred in her words. But then she lowered her voice, and the sound of loathing faded. 'No! There is no one in the Land who could endure to stand aside and allow the Despiser to work his will. If we must suffer and die without hope, then we will do so. But we will not despair, though it is the Unbeliever himself who says that we must.'

Useless emotions writhed across his face, but he could not answer. His own conviction or energy had fallen into dust. Even the pain in his hand was almost gone. He looked away from her, then winced at the sharp sight of the *krill*. Slowly, as if he had aged in the past few moments, he lowered himself into a chair. 'I wish,' he murmured blankly, emptily, 'I wish I knew what to do.'

At the edge of his attention, he was aware that Elena had left the room. But he did not raise his head until she returned and stood before him. In her hands she held a flask of springwine which she offered to him.

He could see a concern he did not deserve in the complex otherness of her gaze.

He accepted the flask and drank deeply, searching for a balm to ease the splitting ache in his forehead – and for some way to support his failing courage. He dreaded the High Lord's intentions, whatever they were. She was too sympathetic, too tolerant of his violence; she allowed him too much leeway without setting him free. Despite the solidness of Revelstone under his sensitive feet, he was on unsteady ground.

When after a short silence she spoke again, she had an air of bringing herself to the point of some difficult honesty; but there was nothing candid in the unexplained disfocus of her eyes. 'I am lost in this matter,' she said. 'There is much that I must tell you, if I am to be open and blameless. I do not wish to be reproached with any lack

445

of knowledge in you – the Land will not be served by any concealment which might later be called by another name. Yet my courage fails me, and I know not what words to use. Mhoram offered to take this matter from me, and I refused, believing that the burden is mine. Yet now I am lost, and cannot begin.'

Covenant bent his frown towards her, refusing with the pain in his forehead to give her any aid.

'You have spoken with Hile Troy,' she said tentatively, unsure of this approach. 'Did he describe his coming to the Land?'

Covenant nodded without relenting. 'An accident. Some misbegotten kid – a young student, he says – was trying to get me.'

Elena moved as if she meant to pursue that idea, but then she stopped herself, reconsidered, and took a different tack. 'I do not know your world – but the Warmark tells me that such things do not happen there. Have you observed Lord Mhoram? Or Hiltmark Quaan? Or perhaps Hearthrall Tohrm? Any of those you knew forty years ago? Does it appear to you that – that they are young?'

'I've noticed.' Her question agitated him. He had been clinging to the question of age, trying to establish it as a discrepancy, a breakdown in the continuity of his delusion. 'It doesn't fit. Mhoram and Tohrm are too young. It's impossible. They are not forty years older.'

'I also am young,' she said intently, as if she were trying to help him guess a secret. But at the sight of his glowering incomprehension, she retreated from the plunge. To answer him, she said, 'This has been true for as long as there has been such lore in the Land. The Old Lords lived to great age. They were not long-lived as the Giants are – because that is the natural span of their people. No, it was the service of the Earthpower which preserved them, secured them from age long past their normal years. High Lord Kevin lived centuries as people live decades.

'So, too, it is in this present time, though in a lesser way. We do not bring out all the potency of the Lore. And the Warlore does not preserve its followers, so Quaan and his warriors alone of your former comrades carry their full burden of years. But those of the *rhadhamaerl* and the *lillianrill*, and the Lords who follow Kevin's Lore, age more slowly than others. This is a great boon, for it extends our strength. But also it causes grief – '

She fell silent for a moment, sighed quietly to herself as if she were remembering an old injury. But when she spoke again, her voice was clear and steady. 'So it has always been. Lord Mhoram has seen ten times seven summers – yet he hardly carries fifty of them. And – ' Once again, she stopped herself and changed directions. With a look that searched Covenant, she said, 'Does it surprise you to hear that I rode a Ranyhyn as a child? There is no other in the Land who has had such good fortune.'

He finished his springwine, and got to his feet to pace the room in front of her. The tone in which she recurred to the Ranyhyn was full of suggestions; he sensed wide possibilities of distress in it. More in anxiety than in irritation, he growled at her, 'Hellfire. Get on with it.'

She tensed as if in preparation for a struggle, and said, 'Warmark Hile Troy's account of his summoning to the Land may not have been altogether accurate. I have heard him tell his tale, and he confuses something which I – we – have not thought it well to correct. We have kept this matter secret between us.

'Ur-Lord Covenant.' She paused, steadying herself, then said carefully, 'Hile Troy was summoned by no young student, ignorant of the perils of power. The summoner was one whom you have known.'

Triock! Covenant almost missed his footing. Triock son of Thuler, of Mithil Stonedown, had reason to hate the Unbeliever. He had loved Lena – But Covenant could not bear to say that name aloud. Squirming at his cowardice, he avoided Triock by saying, 'Pietten. That poor kid – from Soaring Woodhelven. The ur-viles did something to him. Was it him?' He did not dare to meet the High Lord's eyes.

'No, Thomas Covenant,' she said gently. 'It was no man. You knew her well. She was Atiaran Trell-mate – she who guided you from Mithil Stonedown to your meeting with Saltheart Foamfollower at the Soulsease River.'

'Hellfire!' he groaned. At the sound of her name, he saw in his mind Atiaran's spacious eyes, saw the courage with which she had denied her passion against him in order to serve the Land. And he caught a quick visionary image of her face as she incinerated herself trying to summon him – entranced, bitter, livid with the conflagration of all the inner truces which he had so severely harmed. 'Ah, hell,' he breathed. 'Why? She needed – she needed to forget.'

'She could not. Atiaran Trell-mate returned to the Loresraat in her old age for many reasons, but two were uppermost. She desired to bring – no, desire is too small a word. She hungered for you. She could not forget. But whether she wanted you for the Land, or for herself, I do not know. She was a torn woman, and it is in my heart that both hungers warred in her to the last. How otherwise? She said that you permitted the ravage of the Celebration of Spring, though my mother taught me a different tale.'

No! moaned Covenant, pacing bent as if borne down by the weight of the darkness on his forehead. Oh, Atiaran!

'Her second reason touches on the grief of long years and extended strength. For her husband was Trell, Gravelingas of the *rhadhamaerl*. Their marriage was brave and glad in the memory of Mithil Stonedown, for though she had surpassed her strength during her youth in the Loresraat, and had left in weakness, yet was she strong enough to stand with Trell her husband.

'But her weakness, her self-distrust, remained. The grave test of her life came and passed, and she grew old. And to the pain you gave her was added another; she aged, and Trell Atiaran-mate did not. His lore sustained him beyond his years. So after so much hurt she began to lose her husband as well, though his love was steadfast. She was his wife, yet she became old enough to be his mother.

'So she returned to the Loresraat, in grief and pain – and in devotion, for though she doubted herself, her love for the Land did not waver. Yet at the last ill came upon her. Fleeing the restraint of the Lorewardens, she wrought death upon herself. In that way, she broke her Oath of Peace, and ended her life in despair.'

No! he protested. But he remembered Atiaran's anguish, and the price she had paid to repress it, and the wrong he had done her. He feared that Elena was right.

In a sterner voice that did not appear to match her words, the High Lord continued, 'After her death, Trell came to Revelstone. He is one of the mightiest of all the *rhadhamaerl*, and he remains here, giving his skill and lore to the defence of the Land. But he knows bitterness, and I fear that his Oath rests uneasily upon him. For all his gentleness, he has been too much made helpless. It is in my heart that he does not forgive. There was no aid he could give Atiaran – or my mother.'

Through the ache of his memories, Covenant wanted to protest that Trell, with his broad shoulders and his strange power, knew nothing about the true nature of helplessness. But this objection was choked off by the grip of Elena's voice as she said, *my mother*. He stood still, bent as if he were about to capsize, and waited for the last unutterable blackness to fall on him.

'So you must understand why I rode a Ranyhyn as a child. Every year at the last full moon before the middle night of spring, a Ranyhyn came to Mithil Stonedown. My mother understood at once that this was a gift from you. And she shared it with me. It was so easy for her to forget that you had hurt her. Did I not tell you that I also am young? I am Elena daughter of Lena daughter of Atiaran Trell-mate. Lena my mother remains in Mithil Stonedown, for she insists that you will return to her.'

For one more moment, he stood still, staring at the pattern woven into the shoulders of her shift. Then a flood of revelation crashed through him, and he understood. He stumbled, dropped into a chair as suddenly as if his spine had broken. His stomach churned, and he gagged, trying to heave up his emptiness.

'I'm sorry.' The words burst between his teeth as if torn out of his chest by a hard fist of contrition. They were as inadequate as stillborns, too dead to express what he felt. But he could do nothing else. 'Oh, Lena! I'm sorry.' He wanted to weep, but he was a leper, and had forgotten how.

'I was impotent.' He forced the jagged confession through his sore throat. 'I forgot what it's like. Then we were alone. And I felt like a man again, but I knew it wasn't true, it was false, I was dreaming, had to be, it couldn't happen any other way. It was too much. I couldn't stand it.'

'Do not speak to me of impotence,' she returned tightly. 'I am the High Lord. I must defeat the Despiser using arrows and swords.' Her tone was harsh; he could hear other words running through it, as if she were saying, Do you think that mere explanation or apology is sufficient reparation? And without the diseased numbness which justified him, he could not argue.

'No,' he said in a shaking voice. 'Nothing suffices.'

Slowly, heavily, he raised his head and looked at her. Now he could see in her the sixteen-year-old child he had known, her mother. That was her hidden familiarity. She had her mother's hair, her mother's figure. Behind her discipline, her face was much like her mother's. And she wore the same white leaf-pattern woven into the cloth at her shoulders which Lena had worn – the pattern of Trell's and Atiaran's family.

When he met her eyes, he saw that they too, were like Lena's. They glowed with something that was neither anger nor condemnation; they seemed to contradict the judgment he had heard a moment earlier.

'What are you going to do now?' he said weakly. 'Atiaran wanted – wanted the Lords to punish me.'

Abruptly, she left her seat, moved around behind him. She put her hands tenderly on his clenched brow and began to rub it, seeking to stroke away the knots and furrows. 'Ah, Thomas Covenant,' she sighed, with something like yearning in her voice. 'I am the High Lord. I bear the Staff of Law. I fight for the Land, and will not quail though the beauty may die, or I may die, or the world may die. But there is much of Lena my mother in me. Do not frown at me so. I cannot bear it.'

Her soft, cool, consoling touch seemed to burn his forehead. Mhoram had said that she had sat with him during his ordeal the previous night – sat, and watched over him, and held his hand.

Trembling, he got to his feet. Now he knew why she had summoned him. There was a world of implications in the air between them; her whole life was on his head, for good or ill. But it was too much; he was too staggered and drained to grasp it all, deal with it. His stiff face was only capable of grimaces. Mutely, he left her, and Bannor guided him back to his rooms.

In his suite, he extinguished the torches, covered the graveling pots. Then he went out onto his balcony.

The moon was rising over Revelstone. It was still new, and it came in silver over the horizon, tinting the plains with unviolated luminescence. He breathed the autumn air, and leaned on the railing, immune for the moment from vertigo. Even that had been drained out of him.

He did not think about jumping. He thought about how difficult Elena was to refuse.

7

KORIK'S MISSION

Sometime before dawn, an insistent pounding at his door woke him. He had been dreaming about the Quest for the Staff of Law – about his friend, Saltheart Foamfollower, whom the company of the Quest had left behind to guard their rear before they had entered the catacombs of Mount Thunder. Covenant had not seen him again, did not know whether the Giant had survived that perilous duty. When he awoke, his heart was labouring as if the clamour at the door were the beating of his dread.

Numbly, dazed with sleep, he uncovered a graveling pot, then shambled into the sitting room to answer the door.

He found a man standing in the brightness of the hall. His blue robe belted in black and his long staff identified him as a Lord.

'Ur-Lord Covenant,' the man began at once. 'I must apologize profusely for disturbing your rest. Of all the Lords, I am the one who most regrets such an intrusion. I have a deep love for rest. Rest and food, ur-Lord – sleep and sustenance. They are exquisite. Although there are some who would say that I have tasted so much sustenance that I should no longer require rest. No doubt some such argument caused me to be chosen for this arduous and altogether unsavoury journey.' Without asking for permission, he bustled past Covenant into the room. He was grinning.

Covenant blinked his bleary gaze into focus, and took a close look at the man.

He was short and corpulent, with a round, beatific face, but the serenity of his countenance was punctured by his gleeful eyes, so that he looked like a misbegotten cherub. His expression was constantly roiled; fleet smiles, smirks, frowns, grimaces chased each other across the surface of his essential good humour. Now he was regarding Covenant with a look of appraisal, as if he were trying to gauge the Unbeliever's responsiveness to jesting.

'I am Hyrim son of Hoole,' he said fluidly, 'a Lord of the Council, as you see, and a lover of all good cheer, as you have perhaps not failed to notice.' His eyes gleamed impishly. 'I would tell you of my parentage and history, so that you might know me better – but my time is short. There are consequences to this riding of Ranyhyn, but when I offered myself to their choice I did not know that the honour could be so burdensome. Perhaps you will consent to accompany me?'

Mutely, Covenant's lips formed the word, Accompany?

'To the courtyard, at least – if I can persuade you no farther. I will explain while you ready yourself.'

Covenant felt too groggy to understand what was being asked of him. The Lord wanted him to get dressed and go somewhere. Was that all? After a moment, he found his voice, and asked, 'Why?'

With an effort, Hyrim pulled an expression of seriousness onto his face. He studied Covenant gravely, then said, 'Ur-Lord, there are some things which are difficult to say to you. Both Lord Mhoram and High Lord Elena might have spoken. They do not desire that this knowledge should be withheld from you. But brother Mhoram is reluctant to describe his own pain. And the High Lord – it is in my heart that she fears to send you into peril.'

He grinned ruefully. 'But I am not so selfless. You will agree that there is much of me to consider – and every part is tender. Courage is for the lean. I am wiser. Wisdom is no more and no less deep than the skin – and mine is very deep. Of course, it is said that trial and hardship refine the spirit. But I have heard the Giants reply that there is time enough to refine the spirit when the body has no other choice.'

Covenant had heard that, too; Foamfollower had said it to him. He shook his head to clear away the painful memory. 'I don't understand.'

'You have cause,' said the Lord. 'I have not yet uttered anything of substance. Ah, Hyrim,' he sighed to himself, 'brevity is such a simple thing – and yet it surpasses you. Ur-Lord, will you not dress? I must tell you news of the Giants which will not please you.'

A pang of anxiety stiffened Covenant. He was no longer sleepy. 'Tell me.'

'While you dress.'

Cursing silently, Covenant hurried into the bedroom and began to put on his clothes.

Lord Hyrim spoke from the other room. His tone was careful, as if he were making a deliberate effort to be concise. 'Ur-Lord, you know of the Giants. Saltheart Foamfollower himself brought you to Revelstone. You were present in the Close when he spoke to the Council of Lords, telling them that the omens which High Lord Damelon had foreseen for the Giants' hope of Home had come to pass.'

Covenant knew; he remembered it vividly. Back in the age of the Old Lords, the Giants had been wanderers of the sea who had lost their way. For that reason, they called themselves the Unhomed. They had roamed for decades in search of their lost homeland, but had not found it. At last, they had come to the shores of the Land in the region known as Seareach, and there – welcomed and befriended by Damelon – they had made a place for themselves to live until they rediscovered their ancient Home.

Since that time, three thousand years ago, their search had been fruitless. But Damelon Giantfriend had prophesied for them; he had foreseen an end to their exile.

After, and perhaps because, they had lost their Home, the Giants had begun to decline. Though they dearly loved children, few children were born; their seed did not replenish itself. For many centuries, their numbers had been slowly shrinking.

Damelon had foretold that this would change, that their seed would regain its vitality. That was his omen, his sign that the exile was about to end, for good or ill.

In his turn, Damelon's son, Loric, had made a promise to support and affirm that prophecy. He had said that, when Damelon's omens were fulfilled, the Lords would provide the Giants with potent Gildenlode keels and rudders for the building of new ships for their homeward journey.

So it was that Foamfollower had reported to the Council that Wavenhair Haleall, the wife of Sparlimb Keelsetter, had given birth to triplets, three sons – an event unprecedented in Seareach. And at the same time, scouting ships had returned to say that they had found a way which might lead the Giants Home. Foamfollower had come to Revelstone to claim High Lord Loric's promise.

'For forty years,' Lord Hyrim went on, 'the *lillianrill* of Lord's Keep have striven to meet that promise. The seven keels and rudders are now nearly complete. But time hurries on our heels, driving us dangerously. When this war begins, we will be unable to transport the Gildenlode to Seareach. And we will need the help of the Giants to fight Lord Foul. Yet it may be that all such helps or hopes will fail. It may be – '

'Foamfollower,' Covenant interrupted. He fumbled at the laces of his boots. A keen concern made him impatient, urgent. 'What about him? Is he – ? What happened to him – after the Quest?'

The Lord's tone became still more careful. 'When the Quest for the Staff of Law made its way homeward, it found that Saltheart Foamfollower was alive and unharmed. He had gained the safety of Andelain, and so had escaped the Fire-Lions. He returned to his people, and since that time he has come twice to Revelstone to help in the shaping of the Gildenlode and to share knowledge. Many Giants came and went, full of hope.

'But now, ur-Lord – ' Hyrim stopped. There was sorrow and grimness in his voice. 'Ah, now.'

Covenant strode back into the sitting room, faced the Lord. 'Now?' His own voice was unsteady.

'Now for three years a silence has lain over Seareach. No Giant has come to Revelstone – no Giant has set foot on the Upper Land.' To answer the sudden flaring of Covenant's gaze, he continued, 'Oh, we have not been idle. For a year we did nothing – Seareach is near to four hundred leagues distant, and a silence of a year is not unusual. But after a year, we became concerned. Then for a year we sent messengers. None have ever returned. During the spring, we sent an entire Eoman. Twenty warriors and their Warhaft did not return.

'Therefore the Council decided to risk no more warriors. In the summer, Lord Callindrill and Lord Amatin rode eastward with the Bloodguard, seeking passage. They were thrown back by a dark and nameless power in Sarangrave Flat. Sister Amatin would have died when her horse fell, but the Ranyhyn of Callindrill bore them both to safety. Thus a shadow has come between us and our ancient Rockbrothers, and the fate of the Giants is unknown.'

Covenant groaned inwardly. Foamfollower had been his friend – and yet he had not even said goodbye to the Giant when they had parted. He felt an acute regret. He wanted to see Foamfollower again, wanted to apologize.

But at the same time he was conscious of Hyrim's gaze on him. The Lord's naturally gay eyes held a look of painful sombreness. Clearly, he had some reason for awakening Covenant before dawn like this. With a jerk of his shoulders, Covenant pushed down his regret, and said, 'I still don't understand.'

At first Lord Hyrim did not falter. 'Then I will speak plainly. During the night after your summoning, Lord Mhoram was called from your side by a vision. The hand of his power came upon him, and he saw sights which turned his blood to dread in his veins. He saw – ' Then abruptly he turned away. 'Ah, Hyrim,' he sighed, 'you are a fat, thistle-brained fool. What business had you to dream of Lords and Lore, of Giants and bold undertakings? When such thoughts first entered your childish head, you should have been severely punished and sent to tend sheep. Your thick, inept self does scant honour to Hoole Grenmate your father, who trusted that your foolish fancies would not lead you astray.' Over his shoulder, he said softly, 'Lord Mhoram saw the death of the Giants marching towards them. He could not make out the face of that death. But he saw that if they are not aided soon – soon, perhaps in a score of days! – they will surely be destroyed.'

Destroyed? Covenant echoed silently. Destroyed? Then he went a step further. Is that my fault, too? 'Why,' he began, then swallowed roughly. 'Why are you telling me? What do you expect me to do?'

'Because of brother Mhoram's vision, the Council has decided that it must send a mission to Seareach at once – now. Because of the war, we cannot spare much of our strength – but Mhoram says that speed is needed more than strength. Therefore High Lord Elena has chosen two Lords – two Lords who have been accepted by the Ranyhyn – Shetra Verement-mate, whose knowledge of Sarangrave Flat is greater than any other's, and Hyrim son of Hoole, who has a passing acquaintance with the lore of the Giants. To accompany us, First Mark Morin has chosen fifteen Bloodguard led by Korik, Cerrin, and Sill. The High Lord has given the mission to them as well as to us, so that if we fall they will go on to the Giants' aid.

'Korik is among the most senior of the Bloodguard.' The Lord seemed to be digressing, avoiding something that he hesitated to say. 'With Tuvor, Morin, Bannor, and Terrel, he commanded the original *Haruchai* army which marched against the Land – marched, and met High Lord Kevin, with the Ranyhyn and the Giants, and was moved by love and wonder and gratitude to swear the Vow of service which began the Bloodguard. Sill is the Bloodguard who holds me in his especial care, just as Cerrin holds Lord Shetra. I will require them to hold us well,' Hyrim growled with a return to humour. 'I do not wish to lose all flesh which I have so joyfully gained.'

In frustration, Covenant repeated sharply, 'What do you expect me to do?'

Slowly, Hyrim turned to face him squarely. 'You have known Saltheart Foamfollower,' he said. 'I wish you to come with us.'

Covenant gaped at the Lord in astonishment. He felt suddenly faint. From a distance, he heard himself asking weakly, 'Does the High Lord know about this?'

Hyrim grinned. 'Her anger will blister the skin of my face when she hears what I have said to you.' But a moment later, he was sober again. 'Ur-Lord, I do not say that you should accompany us. Perhaps I am greatly wrong in my asking. There is much that we do not know concerning the Despiser's intent for this war — and of these one of the greatest is our ignorance of the direction from which he will attack. Will he move south of Andelain as he has in past ages, and then strike northward through the Centre Plains, or will he march north along Landsdrop to approach us from the east? This ignorance paralyses our defence. The Warward cannot move until we know the answer. Warmark Troy is much concerned. But if Lord Foul chooses to assail us from the east, then our mission to Seareach will ride straight into his strength. For that reason, it would be unsurpassable folly for the white gold to accompany us.

'No, if it were wise for you to ride with us, Lord Mhoram would have spoken of it with you. Nevertheless I ask. I love the Giants deeply, ur-Lord. They are precious to all the Land. I would brave even High Lord Elena's wrath to give them any aid.'

The simple sincerity of the Lord's appeal touched Covenant. Though he had just met the man, he found that he liked Hyrim son of Hoole — liked him and wanted to help him. And the Giants were a powerful argument. He could not bear to think that Foamfollower, so full of life and laughter and comprehension, might be killed if he were not given aid. But that argument reminded Covenant bitterly that he was less capable of help than anyone in the Land. And Elena's influence was still strong on him. He did not want to do anything to anger her, anything that would give her additional cause to hate him. He was torn; he could not answer the candid question in Hyrim's gaze.

Abruptly the Lord's eyes filled with tears. He looked away, blinking rapidly. 'I have given you pain, ur-Lord,' he said softly. 'Forgive me.' Covenant expected to hear irony, criticism, in the words, but Hyrim's tone expressed only an uncomplex sorrow. When he faced Covenant again, his lips wore a lame smile. 'Well, then. Will you not at least come with me to the courtyard? The mission will soon meet there to depart. Your presence will say to all Revelstone that you act from choice rather than from ignorance.'

That Covenant could not refuse; he was too ashamed of his essential impotence, too angry. Kicking himself vehemently into motion, he strode out of his suite.

At once, he found Bannor at his elbow. Between the Bloodguard and the Lord, he stalked downward through the halls and passages towards the gates of Revelstone.

There was only one entrance to Lord's Keep, and the Giants had designed it well to defend the city. At the wedge tip of the plateau, they had hollowed out the stone to form a courtyard between the main Keep and the watchtower which protected the outer gates. Those gates – huge, interlocking stone slabs which could close inward to seal the entrance completely – led to a tunnel under the tower. The tunnel opened into the courtyard, and the entrance from the courtyard to the Keep was defended by another set of gates as massive and solid as the first. The main Keep was joined to the tower by a series of wooden crosswalks suspended at intervals above the court, but the only ground-level access to the tower was through two small doors on either side of the tunnel. Thus any enemy who accomplished the almost impossible task of breaking the outer gates would then have to attempt the same feat at the inner gates while under attack from the battlements of both the watchtower and the main Keep.

The courtyard was paved with flagstones except in the centre, where an old Gilden tree grew, nourished by springs of fresh water. Lord Hyrim, Bannor, and Covenant found the rest of the mission there beside the tree, under the waning darkness of the sky. Dawn had begun.

Shivering in the crisp air, Covenant looked around the court. In the light which reflected from within the Keep, he could see that all the people near the tree were Bloodguard except for one Lord, a tall woman. She stood facing into Revelstone; Covenant could see her clearly. She had stiff, iron-grey hair that she wore cropped short; and her face was like the face of a hawk – keen of nose and eye, lean of cheek. Her eyes held a sharp gleam like the hunting stare of a hawk. But behind the gleam, Covenant discerned something that looked like an ache of desire, a yearning which she could neither satisfy nor repress.

Lord Hyrim greeted her companionably, but she ignored him, stared back into the Keep as if she could not bear to leave it.

Behind her, the Bloodguard were busy distributing burdens, packing their supplies into bundles with *clingor* thongs. These they tied to their backs so that their movements would not be hampered. Soon one of them – Covenant recognized Korik – stepped forward and announced to Lord Hyrim that he was ready.

'Ready, friend Korik?' Hyrim's voice had a jaunty sound. 'Ah, would that I could say the same. But, by the Seven! I am not a man suited for great dangers – I am better made to applaud victories than to perform them. Yes, that is where my skills lie. Were you to bring me a victory, I could drink a pledge to it which would astound you. But this – riding at speed across the Land, into the teeth of who knows what ravenous perils – ! Can you tell us of these perils, Korik?'

'Lord?'

'I have given this matter thought, friend Korik – you may imagine how difficult it was for me. But I see that the High Lord gave this mission into your hands for good reason. Hear what I have thought – efforts like mine should not be wasted. Consider this. Of all the people of Revelstone, only the Bloodguard have known the Land before the Desecration. You have known Kevin himself. Surely you know far more of him than do we. And surely, also, you know far more of the Despiser. Perhaps you know how he wages war. Perhaps you know more than Lord Callindrill could tell us of the dangers which lie between us and Seareach.'

Korik shrugged slightly.

'It is in my heart,' Hyrim went on, 'that you can measure the dangers ahead better than any Lord. You should speak of them, so that we may prepare. It may be that we should not risk Grimmerdhore or the Sarangrave, but should rather ride north and around, despite the added length of days.'

'The Bloodguard do not know the future.' Korik's tone was impassive, yet Covenant heard a faint stress on the word *know*. Korik seemed to use that word in a different sense than Hyrim did, a larger or more prophetic sense.

And the Lord was unsatisfied. 'Perhaps not. But you did not share Kevin's reign and learn nothing. Do you fear we cannot endure the knowledge you bear?'

'Hyrim, you forget yourself,' Lord Shetra cut in abruptly. 'Is this your respect for the keepers of the Vow?'

'Ah, sister Shetra, you misunderstand. My respect for the Bloodguard is unbounded. How could I feel otherwise about men sworn beyond any human oath to keep me alive? Now if they were to promise me good food, I would be totally in their debt. But surely you see where we stand. The High Lord has given this mission into their hands. If the peril we ride to meet so blithely forces them to the choice, the Bloodguard will pursue the mission rather than defend us.'

For a moment, Lord Shetra fixed Hyrim with a hard glance like an expression of contempt. But when she spoke, her voice did not impugn him. 'Lord Hyrim, you are not blithe. You believe that the survival of the Giants rides on this mission, and you seek to conceal your fear for them.'

'*Melenkurion* Skyweir!' Hyrim growled to keep himself from laughing. 'I seek only to preserve my fine and hard-won flesh from inconsiderate assault. It would become you to share such a worthy desire.'

'Peace, Lord. I have no heart for jesting,' sighed Shetra, and turned away to resume her study of Revelstone.

Lord Hyrim considered her in silence briefly, then said to Korik, 'Well, she has less body to preserve than I have. It may be that fine spirit is reserved for neglected flesh. I must speak of this with the Giants – if we reach them.'

'We are the Bloodguard,' answered Korik flatly. 'We will gain Seareach.'

Hyrim glanced up at the night sky, and said in a soft, musing tone, 'Summon or succour. Would that there were more of us. The Giants are vast, and if they are in need the need will be vast.'

'They are the Giants. Are they not equal to any need?'

The Lord flashed a look at Korik, but did not reply. Soon he moved to Shetra's side, and said quietly, 'Come, sister. The journey calls. The way is long, and if we hope to end we must first begin.'

'Wait!' she cried softly, like the distant scream of a bird.

Hyrim studied her for another moment. Then he came back to Covenant. In a whisper so low that Covenant could hardly hear it, the Lord said, 'She desires to see Lord Verement her husband before we go. Theirs is a sad tale, ur-Lord. Their marriage is troubled. Both are proud – Together they made the journey to the Plains of Ra to offer themselves to the Ranyhyn. And the Ranyhyn – ah, the Ranyhyn chose her, but refused him.

'Well, they choose in their own way, and even the Ramen cannot explain them. But it has made a difference between these two. Brother Verement is a worthy man – yet now he has reason to believe himself unworthy. And sister Shetra can neither accept nor deny his self-judgment. And now this mission – Verement should rightly go in my place, but the mission requires the speed and endurance of the Ranyhyn. For her sake alone, I would wish that you might go in her stead.'

'I don't ride Ranyhyn,' Covenant replied unsteadily.

'They would come to your call,' answered Hyrim.

Again Covenant could not respond; he feared that this was true. The Ranyhyn had pledged themselves to him, and he had not released them. But he could not ride one of the great horses. They had reared to him out of fear and loathing. Again he had nothing to offer Hyrim but the look of his silent indecision.

Moments later, he heard movement in the throat of the Keep behind him. Turning, he saw two Lords striding out towards the courtyard – High Lord Elena and a man he had not met.

Elena's arrival made him quail; at once, the air seemed to be full of wings, vulturine implications. But the man at her side also compelled his attention. He knew immediately that this was Lord Verement. The man resembled Shetra too much to be anyone else. He had the same short stiff hair, the same hawklike features, the same bitter taste in his mouth. He moved towards her as if he meant to throw himself at her.

But he stopped ten feet away. His eyes winced away from her sharp gaze; he could not bring himself to look at her directly. In a low voice, he said, 'Will you go?'

'You know that I must.'

They fell silent. Heedless of the fact that they were being observed, they stood apart from each other. Some test of will that needed no utterance hung between them. For a time, they remained still, as if refusing to make any gestures which might be interpreted as compromise or abdication.

'He did not wish to come,' Hyrim whispered to Covenant, 'but the High Lord brought him. He is ashamed.'

Then Lord Verement moved. Abruptly, he tossed his staff upright towards Shetra. She caught it, and threw her own staff to him. He caught it in turn. 'Stay well, wife,' he said bleakly.

'Stay well, husband,' she replied.

'Nothing will be well for me until you return.'

'And for me also, my husband,' she breathed intensely.

Without another word, he turned on his heel and hastened back into Revelstone.

For a moment, she watched him go. Then she turned also, moved stiffly out of the courtyard into the tunnel. Korik and the other Bloodguard followed her. Shortly, Covenant was left alone with Hyrim and Elena.

'Well, Hyrim,' the High Lord said gently, 'your ordeal must begin. I regret that it will be arduous for you.'

'High Lord – ' Hyrim began.

'But you are capable of it,' she went on. 'You have not begun to take the measure of your true strength.'

'High Lord,' Hyrim said, 'I have asked ur-Lord Covenant to accompany us.'

She stiffened. Covenant felt a surge of tension radiate from her; she seemed suddenly to emanate a palpable tightness. 'Lord Hyrim,' she said in a low voice, 'you tread dangerous ground.' Her tone was hard, but Covenant could hear that she was not warning Hyrim, threatening him. She respected what he had done. And she was afraid.

Then she turned to Covenant. Carefully, as if she feared to express her own acute desire, she asked, 'Will you go?'

The light from Revelstone was at her back, and he could not see her face. He was glad of this; he did not want to know whether or not her strange gaze focused on him. He tried to answer her, but for a moment his throat was so dry that he could not make a sound.

'No,' he said at last. 'No.' For Hyrim's sake, he made an effort to tell the truth. 'There's nothing I can do for them.' But as he said it, he knew that that was not the whole truth. He refused to go because Elena daughter of Lena wanted him to stay.

Her relief was as tangible in the gloom as her tension had been. 'Very well, ur-Lord.' For a long moment, she and Hyrim faced each other, and Covenant sensed the current of their silent communication, their mental melding. Then Hyrim stepped close to her and kissed her on the forehead. She hugged him, released him. He bowed to Covenant, and walked away into the tunnel.

In turn, she moved away from Covenant, entered the tower through one of the small doors beside the mouth of the tunnel. Covenant was left alone. He breathed deeply, trying to steady himself as if he had just come through an interrogation. Despite the coolness of the dawn, he was sweating. For a moment, he remained in the courtyard, uncertain of what to do. But then he heard whistling from outside the Keep – shrill piercing cries that echoed off the wall of Revelstone. Korik's mission was calling the Ranyhyn.

At once, Covenant hurried into the tunnel.

Outside the shadowed court, the sky was lighter. In the east, the first rim of the sun had broken the horizon. Morning streamed westward, and in it fifteen Bloodguard and two Lords raised their call again. And again. While the echoes of the third cry faded, the air filled with the thunder of mighty hooves.

For a long moment, the earth rumbled to the beat of the Ranyhyn, and the air pulsed deeply. Then a shadow swept up through the foothills. Seventeen strong, clean-limbed horses came surging and proud to Revelstone. Their white forehead stars looked like froth on a wave as they galloped towards the riders they had chosen to serve. With keen whinnying and the flash of hooves, they slowed their pace.

In response, the Bloodguard and the two Lords bowed, and Korik shouted, 'Hail, Ranyhyn! Land-riders and proud-bearers! Sun-flesh and sky-mane, we are glad that you have heard our call. Evil and war are upon the Land! Peril and fatigue await the foes of Fangthane. Will you bear us?'

The great horses nodded and nickered as they came forward the last few steps to nuzzle their riders, urging them to mount. Instantly, all the Bloodguard leaped onto the backs of their Ranyhyn. They used no saddles or reins; the Ranyhyn bore their riders willingly, and replied to the pressure of a knee or the touch of a hand even to the command of a thought. The same strange power of hearing which made it possible for them to answer their riders at once, anywhere in the Land – allowed them to sense the call tens or scores of days before it was actually uttered, and to run from the Plains of Ra to answer as if mere moments, not three or four hundred leagues, separated the southeast corner of the Land from any other region – also enabled them to act as one with their riders, a perfect meeting of mind and bone.

The Lords Shetra and Hyrim mounted more slowly, and Covenant watched them with a thickness in his throat, as if they were accepting a challenge which rightly belonged to him. Foamfollower, please – he thought. Please – But he could not articulate the words, forgive me.

Then he heard a shout behind and above him. Turning back towards Revelstone, he saw a small, slim figure standing with arms raised atop the watchtower – the High Lord. As the mounted company swung around to face her, she flourished the Staff of Law, drew from its tip an intense blue blaze that flared and coruscated against the deep sky – a paean of power which in her hands burned with a core of interfused blue and white turning to purest azure along the flame. Three times she waved the Staff, and its blaze was so bright that its path seemed to linger against the heavens. Then she cried, 'Hail!' and thrust the Staff upward. For an instant the whole length of it flashed, so that an immense incandescent burst of Lords-fire sprang towards the sky. For that instant, she cast so much light over the feet of Revelstone that the dawn itself was effaced – as if to show the assembled company that she was strong enough to erase the fate written in the morning.

The Lords answered, wielding their own power and returning the vibrant cry, 'Hail!' And the Bloodguard shouted together as one, 'First and faith! Hail, High Lord!'

For a moment, all the staffs were upraised in fire. Then all the Lords silenced their flames. On that signal, the company of the mission wheeled in a smooth turn and galloped away into the sunrise.

8

'LORD KEVIN'S LAMENT'

The departure of the mission – and his meeting with High Lord Elena the previous evening – left Covenant deeply disturbed. He seemed to be losing what little independence or authenticity he possessed. Instead of determining for himself what his position should be, and then acting according to that standard, he was allowing himself to be swayed, seduced even more fundamentally than he had been during his first experience with the Land. Already, he had acknowledged Elena's claim on him, and only that claim had prevented him from acknowledging the Giants as well.

He could not go on in this fashion. If he did, he would soon come to resemble Hile Troy – a man so overwhelmed by the power of sight that he could not perceive the blindness of his desire to assume responsibility for the Land. That would be suicide for a leper. If he failed, he would die. And if he succeeded, he would never again be able to bear the numbness of his real life, his leprosy. He knew lepers who had died that way, but for them the death was never quick, never clean. Their ends lay beyond a fetid ugliness so abominable that he felt nauseated whenever he remembered that such putrefaction existed.

And that was not the only argument. This seduction of responsibility was Foul's doing. It was the means by which Lord Foul attempted to ensure the destruction of the Land. When inadequate men assumed huge burdens, the outcome could only serve Despite. Covenant had no doubt that Troy was inadequate. Had he not been summoned to the Land by Atiaran in her despair? And as for himself – he, Thomas Covenant, was as incapable of power as if such a thing did not exist. For him it could not. If he pretended otherwise, then the whole Land would become just another leper in Lord Foul's hands.

By the time he reached his rooms, he knew that he would have to do something, take some action to establish the terms on which he had to stand. He would have to find or make some discrepancy, some incontrovertible proof that the Land was a delusion. He could not trust his emotions; he needed logic, an argument as inescapable as the law of leprosy.

He paced the suite for a time as if he were searching the stone floor for an answer. Then, on an impulse, he jerked open the door and looked out into the hallway. Bannor was there, standing watch as imperturbably as if the meaning of his life were beyond question. Stiffly, Covenant asked him into the sitting room.

When Bannor stood before him, Covenant reviewed quickly what he knew about the Bloodguard. They came from a race, the *Haruchai*, who lived high in the Westron Mountains beyond Trothgard and the Land. They were a warlike and prolific people, so it was perhaps inevitable that at some time in their history they would send an army east into the Land. This they had done during the early years of Kevin's High Lordship. On foot and weaponless – the *Haruchai* did not use weapons, just as they did not use lore; they relied wholly on their own physical competence – they had marched to Revelstone and challenged the Council of Lords.

But Kevin had refused to fight. Instead, he had persuaded the *Haruchai* to friendship.

In return, they had gone far beyond his intent. Apparently the Ranyhyn, and the Giants, and Revelstone itself – as mountain dwellers, the *Haruchai* had an intense love of stone and bounty – had moved them more deeply than anything in their history. To answer Kevin's friendship, they had sworn a Vow of service to the Lords; and something extravagant in their commitment or language had invoked the Earthpower, binding them to their Vow in defiance of time and death and choice. Five hundred of their army had become the Bloodguard. The rest had returned home.

Now there were still nearly five hundred. For every Bloodguard who died in battle was sent on his Ranyhyn up through Guards Gap into the Westron Mountains, and another *Haruchai* came to take his place. Only those whose bodies could not be recovered, such as Tuvor, the former First Mark, were not replaced.

Thus the great anomaly of the Bloodguard's history was the fact that they had survived the Ritual of Desecration intact even though Kevin and his Council and all his works had been destroyed. They had trusted him. When he had ordered them all into the mountains without explaining his intent, they had obeyed. But afterward they had seen reason to doubt that their service was truly faithful. They had sworn the Vow; they should have died with Kevin in Kiril Threndor under Mount Thunder – or prevented him from meeting Lord Foul there in his despair, prevented him from uttering the Ritual which brought the age of the Old Lords to its destruction. They were faithful to an extreme that defied their own mortality, and yet they had failed in their promise to preserve the Lords at any cost to themselves.

Covenant wanted to ask Bannor what would happen to the Bloodguard if they ever came to believe that their extravagant fidelity was false, that in their Vow they had betrayed both Kevin and themselves. But he could not put such a question into words. Bannor deserved better treatment than that from him. And Bannor, too, had lost his wife – She had been dead for two thousand years.

Instead, Covenant concentrated on his search for a discrepancy.

But he soon knew he would not find one by questioning Bannor. In his flat, alien voice, the Bloodguard gave brief answers that told Covenant what he both wanted and did not want to hear concerning the survivors of the Quest for the Staff of Law. He had already learned what had happened to Foamfollower and Lord Mhoram. Now Bannor told him that High Lord Prothall, who had led the Quest, had resigned his Lordship even before his company had returned to Revelstone. He had not been able to forget that the old Hearthrall Birinair had died in his place. And he had felt that in regaining the Staff he had fulfilled his fate, done all that was in him. He had committed the Staff and the Second Ward to Lord Mhoram's care, and had ridden away to his home in the Northron Climbs. The inhabitants of Lord's Keep never saw him again.

So upon Mhoram's return Osondrea had assumed the High Lordship. Until her death, she had used her power to rebuild the Council, expand the Warward, and grow Revelwood, the new home of the Loresraat.

After returning to Revelstone, Quaan – the Warhaft of the Eoman that had accompanied Prothall and Mhoram – had also tried to resign. He had been ashamed to bring only half of his warriors back alive. But High Lord Osondrea, knowing his worth, had refused to release him, and soon he had returned to his duties. Now he was the Hiltmark of the Warward, Hile Troy's second-in-command. Though his hair was white and thin – though his gaze seemed rubbed smooth by age and use – still he was the same strong, honest man he had always been. The Lords respected him. In Troy's absence they would willingly have trusted Quaan to lead the Warward.

Covenant sighed sourly, and let Bannor go. Such information did not meet his need. Clearly, he was not going to find any easy solutions to his dilemma. If he wanted proof of delusion, he would have to make it for himself.

He faced the prospect with trepidation. Anything he might do would take a long time to bear fruit. It would not become proof, brookless and unblinkable, until his delusion ended – until he had returned to his real life. In the meantime, it would do little to sustain him. But he had no choice; his need was urgent.

He had available three easy ways to create a definitive discontinuity: he could destroy his clothes, throw away his penknife – the only thing he had in his pockets – or grow a beard. Then, when he awakened, and found himself clothed, or still possessed of his penknife, or clean-shaven, he would have his proof.

The obvious discrepancy of his healed forehead he did not trust. Past experience made him fear that he would be reinjured shortly before this delusion ended. But he could not bring himself to act on his first two alternatives. The thought of destroying his tough, familiar apparel made him feel too vulnerable, and the expedient of discarding his penknife was too uncertain. Cursing at the way his plight forced him to abandon all the strict habits upon which his survival depended, he decided to give up shaving.

When at last he summoned the courage to leave his rooms and go into the Keep in search of breakfast, he brandished the stubble on his cheeks as if it were a declaration of defiance.

Bannor guided him to one of the great refectories of Revelstone, then left him alone to eat. But before he was done, the Bloodguard came striding back to his table. There was an extra alertness in the spring of Bannor's steps – a tightness that looked oddly like excitement. But when he addressed Covenant, his flat, shrouded eyes expressed nothing, and the repressed lilt of his voice was as inflectionless as ever.

'Ur-Lord, the Council asks that you come to the Close. A stranger has entered Revelstone. The Lords will soon meet with him.'

Because of Bannor's heightened alertness, Covenant asked cautiously, 'What kind of stranger?'

'Ur-Lord?'

'Is it – is it someone like me? Or Troy?'

'No.'

In his confusion, Covenant did not immediately perceive the certitude of Bannor's reply. But as he followed the Bloodguard out of the refectory and down through Revelstone, he began to hear something extra in the denial, something more than Bannor's usual confidence. That *No* resembled Bannor's stride; it was tenser in some way. Covenant could not fathom it. As they descended a broad, curved stair through several levels of the Keep, he forced himself to ask, 'What's so urgent about this stranger? What do you know about him?'

Bannor ignored the question.

When they reached the Close, they found that High Lord Elena, Lord Verement, and four other Lords had already preceded them. The High Lord was at her place at the head of the curved table, and the Staff of Law lay on the stone before her. To her right sat two men, then two women. Verement was on her left beyond two empty seats. Eight Bloodguard sat behind them in the first row of the gallery, but the rest of the Close was empty. Only First Mark Morin and the Hearthralls Tohrm and Borillar occupied their positions in back of the High Lord.

An expectant hush hung over the chamber. For an instant, Covenant half expected Elena to announce the start of the war.

Bannor guided him to a seat at the Lords' table one place down from Lord Verement. The Unbeliever settled himself in the stone chair, rubbing the stubble of his new beard with one hand as if he expected the Council to know what it meant. The eyes of the Lords were on him, and their gaze made him uncomfortable. He felt strangely ashamed of the fact that his fingertips were alive to the touch of his whiskers.

'Ur-Lord Covenant,' the High Lord said after a moment, 'while we await Lord Mhoram and Warmark Troy, we should make introduction. We have been remiss in our hospitality. Let me present to you those of the Council whom you do not know.'

Covenant nodded, glad of anything that would turn her disturbing eyes away from him, and she began on her left. 'Here is Lord Verement Shetra-mate, whom you have seen.' Verement glowered at his hands, did not glance at Covenant.

Elena turned to her right. The man next to her was tall and broad; he had a wide forehead, a watchful face draped with a warm blond beard, and an expression of habitual gentleness. 'Here is Lord Callindrill Faer-mate. Faer his wife is a rare master of the ancient *suru-pa-maerl* craft.' Lord Callindrill smiled half shyly at Covenant, and bowed his head.

'At his side,' the High Lord went on, 'are the Lords Trevor and Loerya.' Lord Trevor was a thin man with an air of uncertainty, as if he were not sure that he belonged at the Lords' table; but Lord Loerya his wife looked solid and matronly, conscious that she contained power. 'They have three daughters who gladden all our hearts.' Both Lords replied with smiles, but where his was both surprised and proud, hers was calm, confident.

Elena concluded, 'Beyond them is Lord Amatin daughter of Matin. Only a year ago she passed the tests of the Sword and Staff at the Loresraat, and joined the Council. Now her work is with the schools of Revelstone – the teaching of the children.' In her turn, Lord Amatin bowed gravely. She was slight, serious, and hazel-eyed, and she watched Covenant as if she were studying him.

After a pause, the High Lord began the ritual ceremonies of welcoming the Unbeliever to Lord's Keep, but she stopped short when Lord Mhoram entered the Close. He came through one of the private doors behind the Lords' table. There was weariness in his step and febrile concentration in his eyes, as if he had spent all night wrestling with darkness. In his fatigue, he needed his staff to hold himself steady as he took his seat at Elena's left.

All the Lords watched him as he sat there, breathing vacantly, and a wave of support flowed from their minds to his. Slowly, their silent help strengthened him. The hot glitter faded from his gaze, and he began to see the faces around him.

'Have you met success?' Elena asked softly. 'Can you withdraw the *krill*?'

'No.' Mhoram's lips formed the word, but he made no sound.

'Dear Mhoram,' she sighed, 'you must take greater care of yourself. The Despiser marches against us. We will need all your strength for the coming war.'

Through his weariness, Mhoram smiled his crooked, humane smile. But he did not speak.

Before Covenant could muster the resolve to ask Mhoram what he hoped to accomplish with the *krill*, the main door of the Close opened, and Warmark Troy strode down the stairs to the table. Hiltmark Quaan came behind him. While Troy went to sit opposite Covenant, Quaan made his way to join Morin, Tohrm, and Borillar. Apparently, Troy and Quaan had just come from the Warward. They had not taken the time to set aside their swords, and their scabbards clashed dully against the stone as they seated themselves.

As soon as they were in their places, High Lord Elena began. She spoke softly, but her clear voice carried perfectly throughout the Close. 'We are gathered thus without forewarning because a stranger has come to us. Crowl, the stranger is in your care. Tell us of him.'

Crowl was one of the Bloodguard. He arose from his seat near the broad stairs of the chamber, and faced the High Lord impassively to make his report. 'He passed us. A short time ago, he appeared at the gate of Revelstone. No scout or sentry saw his approach. He asked if the Lords were within. When he was answered, he replied that the High Lord wished to question him. He is not as other men. But he bears no weapon, and intends no ill. We chose to admit him. He awaits you.'

In a sharp voice like the barking of a hawk, Lord Verement asked, 'Why did the scouts and sentries fail?'

'The stranger was hidden from our eyes,' Crowl replied levelly. 'Our watch did not falter.' His unfluctuating tone seemed to assert that the alertness of the Bloodguard was beyond question.

'That is well,' said Verement. 'Perhaps one day the whole army of the Despiser will appear unnoticed at our gates, and we will still be sleeping when Revelstone falls.'

He was about to say more, but Elena interposed firmly, 'Bring the stranger now.'

As the Bloodguard at the top of the stairs swung open the high wooden doors, Amatin asked the High Lord, 'Does this stranger come at your request?'

'No. But I do now wish to question him.'

Covenant watched as two more Bloodguard came into the Close with the stranger between them. He was slim, simply clad in a cream-coloured robe, and his movements were light, buoyant. Though he was nearly as tall as Covenant, he seemed hardly old enough to have his full growth. There was a sense of boyish laughter in the way his curly hair bounced as he came down the steps, as if he were amused by the precautions taken against him. But Covenant was not amused. With the new dimension of his sight, he could see why Crowl had said that the boy was 'not as other men'. Within his young, fresh flesh were bones that seemed to radiate oldness – not age – they were not weak or infirm – but rather antiquity. His skeleton carried this oldness, this aura of time, as if he were merely a vessel for it. He existed for it rather than in spite of it. The sight baffled Covenant's perception, made his eyes ache with conflicting impressions of dread and glory as he strained to comprehend.

When the boy reached the floor of the Close, he stepped near to the graveling pit, and made a cheerful obeisance. In a high, young voice, he exclaimed, 'Hail, High Lord!'

Elena stood and replied gravely, 'Stranger, be welcome in the Land – welcome and true. We are the Lords of Revelstone, and I am Elena daughter of Lena, High Lord by the choice of the Council, and holder of the Staff of Law. How may we honour you?'

'Courtesy is like a drink at a mountain stream. I am honoured already.'

'Then will you honour us in turn with your name?'

With a laughing glance, the boy said, 'It may well come to pass that I will tell you who I am.'

'Do not game with us,' Verement cut in. 'What is your name?'

'Among those who do not know me, I am named Amok.'

Elena controlled Verement with a swift look, then said to the youth, 'And how are you named among those who know you?'

'Those who know me have no need of my name.'

'Stranger, we do not know you.' An edge came into her quiet voice. 'These are times of great peril in the Land, and we can spend neither time nor delicacy with you. We require to know who you are.'

'Ah, then I fear I cannot help you,' replied Amok with an impervious gaiety in his eyes.

For a moment, the Lords met his gaze with stiff silence. Verement's thin lips whitened; Callindrill frowned thoughtfully; and Elena faced the boy with low anger flushing her cheeks, though her eyes did not lose their odd, dislocated focus. Then Lord Amatin straightened her shoulders and said, 'Amok, where is your home? Who are your parents? What is your past?'

Lightly, Amok turned and gave her an unexpected bow. 'My home is Revelstone. I have no parents. And my past is both wide and narrow, for I have wandered everywhere, waiting.'

A surge ran through the Council, but no one interrupted Amatin. Studying the boy, she said, 'Your home is Revelstone? How can that be? We have no knowledge of you.'

'Lord, I have been away. I have feasted with the *Elohim*, and ridden Sandgorgons. I have danced with the Dancers of the Sea, and teased brave *Kelenbhrabanal* in his grave, and traded apothegms with the Grey Desert. I have waited.'

Several of the Lords stirred, and a gleam came into Loerya's eyes, as if she recognized something potent in Amok's words. They all watched him closely as Amatin said, 'Yet everything that lives has ancestry, forebearers of its own kind. Amok, what of your parentage?'

'Do I live?'

'It appears not,' Verement growled. 'Nothing mortal would try our patience so.'

'Peace, Verement,' said Loerya. 'There is grave import here.' Without taking her eyes off Amok, she asked, 'Are you alive?'

'Perhaps. While I have purpose, I move and speak. My eyes behold. Is this life?'

His answer confused Lord Amatin. Thinly, as if her uncertainty pained her, she said, 'Amok, who made you?'

Without hesitation, Amok replied, 'High Lord Kevin son of Loric son of Damelon son of Berek Heartthew the Lord-Fatherer.'

A silent clap of surprise echoed in the Close. Around the table, the Lords gaped in astonishment. Then Verement smacked the stone with the flat of his hand, and barked, 'By the Seven! This whelp mocks us.'

'I think not,' answered Elena.

Lord Mhoram nodded wearily, and sighed his agreement. 'Our ignorance mocks us.'

Quickly, Trevor asked, 'Mhoram, do you know Amok? Have you seen him?'

Lord Loerya seconded the question, but before Mhoram could gather his strength to respond, Lord Callindrill leaned forward to ask, 'Amok, why were you made? What purpose do you serve?'

'I wait,' said the boy. 'And I answer.'

Callindrill accepted this with a glum nod, as if it proved an unfortunate point, and said nothing more. After a pause, the High Lord said to Amok, 'You bear knowledge, and release it in response to the proper questions. Have I understood you aright?'

In answer, Amok bowed, shaking his head so that his gay hair danced like laughter about his head.

'What knowledge is this?' she inquired.

'Whatever knowledge you can ask for, and receive answer.'

At this, Elena glanced ruefully around the table. 'Well, that at least was not the proper question,' she sighed. 'I think we will need to know Amok's knowledge before we can ask the proper questions.'

Mhoram looked at her and nodded.

'Excellent!' Verement's retort was full of suppressed ferocity. 'So ignorance increases ignorance, and knowledge makes itself unnecessary.'

Covenant felt the force of Verement's sarcasm. But Lord Amatin ignored it. Instead, she asked the youth, 'Why have you come to us now?'

'I felt the sign of readiness. The *krill* of Loric came to life. That is the appointed word. I answer as I was made to do.'

As he mentioned the *krill*, Amok's inner cradled glory and dread seemed to become more visible. The sight gave Covenant a pang. Is this my fault, too? he groaned. What have I gotten myself into now? But the glimpse was mercifully brief; Amok's boyish good humour soon veiled it again.

When it was past, Lord Mhoram climbed slowly to his feet, supporting himself on his staff like an old man. Standing beside the High Lord as if he were speaking for her, he said, 'Then you have – Amok, hear me, I am seer and oracle for this Council. I speak words of vision. I have not seen you. You have come too soon. We did not give life to the *krill*. That was not our doing. We lack the lore for such work.'

Amok's face became suddenly grave, almost frightened, showing for the first time some of the antiquity of his skull. 'Lack the lore? Then I have erred. I have misserved my purpose. I must depart; I will do great harm else.'

Quickly, he turned, slipped with deceptive speed between the Bloodguard, and darted up the stairs.

When he was halfway to the doors, everyone in the Close lost sight of him. He vanished as if they had all taken their eyes off him for an instant, allowing him to hide. The Lords jumped to their feet in amazement. On the stairs, the pursuing Bloodguard halted, looked rapidly about them, and gave up the chase.

'Swiftly!' Elena commanded. 'Search for him! Find him!'

'What is the need?' Crowl replied flatly. 'He is gone.'

'That I see! But where has he gone? Perhaps he is still in Revelstone.'

But Crowl only repeated, 'He is gone.' Something in his certitude reminded Covenant of Bannor's subdued, unusual excitement. Are they in this together? he asked himself. *My purpose?* The words repeated dimly in his mind. *My purpose?*

Through his mystification, he almost did not hear Troy whisper, 'I thought – for a minute – I thought I saw him.'

High Lord Elena paid no attention to the Warmark. The attitude of the Bloodguard seemed to baffle her, and she sat down to consider the situation. Slowly, she spread about her the melding of the Council, one by one bringing the minds of the other Lords into communion with her own. Callindrill shut his eyes, letting a look of peace spread over his face, and Trevor and Loerya held hands. Verement shook his head two or three times, then acquiesced when Mhoram touched him gently on the shoulder.

When they all were woven together, the High Lord said, 'Each of us must study this matter. War is near at hand, and we must not be taken unaware by such mysteries. But to you, Lord Amatin, I give the chief study of Amok and his secret knowledge. If it can be done, we must seek him out and learn his answers.'

Lord Amatin nodded with determination in her small face.

Then, like an unclasping of mental hands, the melding ended, and an intensity which Covenant could sense but not join faded from the air. In silence, the Lords took up their staffs, and began to leave.

'Is that it?' Covenant muttered in surprise. 'Is that all you're going to do?'

'Watch it, Covenant,' Troy warned softly.

Covenant shot a glare at the Warmark, but his black sunglasses seemed to make him impervious. Covenant turned towards the High Lord. 'Is that all?' he insisted. 'Don't you even want to know what's going on here?'

Elena faced him levelly. 'Do you know?'

'No. Of course not.' He wanted to add, to protest, But Bannor does. But that was something else he could not say. He had no right to make the Bloodguard responsible. Stiffly, he remained silent.

'Then do not be too quick to judge,' Elena replied. 'There is much here that requires explanation, and we must seek answers in our own way if we hope to be prepared.'

Prepared for what? he wanted to ask. But he lacked the resolution to challenge the High Lord; he was afraid of her eyes. To escape the situation, he brushed past Bannor and hurried out of the Close ahead of the Lords and Troy.

But back in his rooms he found no relief for his frustration. And in the days that followed, nothing happened to give him any relief. Elena, Mhoram, and Troy were as absent from his life as if they were deliberately avoiding him. Bannor answered his aimless questions courteously, curtly, but the answers shed no light. His beard grew until it was thick and full, and made him look to himself like an unravelled fanatic; but it proved nothing, solved nothing. The full of the moon came and went, but the war did not begin; there arrived no word from the scouts, no signs, no insights. Around him, Revelstone palpably trembled in the clench of its readiness; everywhere he went, he heard whispers of tension, haste, urgency, but no action was taken. Nothing. He roamed for leagues in Lord's Keep as if he were treading a maze. He drank inordinate quantities of springwine, and slept the sleep of the dead as if he hoped that he would never be resurrected. At times he was even reduced to standing on the northern battlements of the city to watch Troy and Quaan drill the Warward. But nothing happened.

His only oasis in this static and frustrated wilderland was given to him by Lord Callindrill and his wife, Faer. One day, Callindrill took the Unbeliever to his private quarters beyond the floor-lit courtyard, and there Faer provided him with a meal which almost made him forget his plight. She was a hale Stonedownor woman with a true gift for hospitality. Perhaps he would have been able to forget – but she studied the old *suru-pa-maerl* craft, as Lena had done, and that evoked too many painful memories in him. He did not visit long with Faer and her husband.

Yet before he left, Callindrill had explained to him some of the oddness of his current position in Revelstone. The High Lord had summoned him, Callindrill said, when the Council had agreed that the war could begin at any moment, when any further postponement of the call might prove fatal. But Warmark Troy's battle plans could not be launched until he knew which of two possible assault routes Lord Foul's army would take. Until the Warmark received clear word from his scouts, he could not afford to commit his Eowards. If he risked a guess, and guessed wrong, disaster would result. So Covenant had been urgently summoned, and yet now was left to himself, with no demands upon him.

In addition, the Lord went on, there was another reason why he had been summoned at a time which now appeared to have been premature. Warmark Troy had argued urgently for the summons. This surprised Covenant until Callindrill explained Troy's reasoning.

The Warmark had believed that Lord Foul would be able to detect the summons. So by means of Covenant's call Troy had hoped to put pressure on the Despiser, force him, because of his fear of the wild magic, to launch his attack before he was ready. Time favoured Lord Foul because his war resources far surpassed those of the Council, and if he prepared long enough he might well field an army that no Warward could defeat. Troy hoped that the ploy of summoning Covenant would make the Despiser cut his preparations short.

Lastly, Callindrill explained in a gentle voice, High Lord Elena and Lord Mhoram were in fact evading the Unbeliever. Covenant had not asked that question, but Callindrill seemed to divine some of the causes of his frustration. Elena and Mhoram, each in their separate ways, felt so involved in Covenant's dilemma that they stayed away from him in order to avoid aggravating his distress. They sensed, said Callindrill, that he found their personal appeals more painful than any other. The possibility that he might go to Seareach had jolted Elena. And Mhoram was consumed by his work on the *krill*. Until the war bereft them of choice, they refrained as much as possible from imposing upon him.

Well, Troy warned me, Covenant muttered to himself as he left Callindrill and Faer. He said that they're scrupulous. After a moment, he added sourly, I would be better off if all these people would stop trying to do me favours.

Yet he was grateful to Faer and her husband. Their companionly gestures helped him to get through the next few days, helped him to keep the vertiginous darkness at bay. He felt that he was rotting inside, but he was not going mad.

But he knew that he could not stand it much longer. The ambience of Revelstone was as tight as a string about to snap. Pressure was building inside him, rising towards desperation. When Bannor knocked at his door one afternoon, he was so startled that he almost cried out.

However, Bannor had not come to announce the start of the war. In his flat voice, he asked Covenant if the Unbeliever would like to go hear a song.

A song, he echoed numbly. For a moment, he was too confused to respond. He had not expected such a question, certainly not from the Bloodguard. But then he shrugged jerkily. 'Why not?' He did not stop to ask what had prompted Bannor's unusual initiative. With a scowl, he followed the Bloodguard out of his suite.

Bannor took him up through the levels of the Keep until they were higher in the mountain than he had ever been before. Then the wide passage they followed rounded a corner, and came unexpectedly into open sunlight. They entered a broad, roofless amphitheatre. Rows of stone benches curved downward to form a bowl around a flat centre stage; and behind the topmost row the stone wall rose straight for twenty or thirty feet, ending in the flat of the plateau, where the mountain met the sky. The afternoon sun shone into the amphitheatre, drenching the dull white stone of the stage and benches and wall with warmth and light.

The seats were starting to fill when Bannor and Covenant arrived. People from all occupations of the Keep, including farmers and cooks and warriors, and the Lords Trevor and Loerya with their daughters, came through several openings in the wall to take seats around the bowl. But the Bloodguard formed the largest single group. Covenant estimated roughly that there were a hundred of them on the benches. This vaguely surprised him. He had never seen more than a score of the *Haruchai* in one place before. After looking around for a while, he asked Bannor, 'What song is this, anyway?'

'Lord Kevin's Lament,' Bannor replied dispassionately.

Then Covenant felt that he understood. Kevin, he nodded to himself. Of course the Bloodguard wanted to hear this song. How could they be less than keenly interested in anything which might help them to comprehend Kevin Landwaster?

For it was Kevin who had summoned Lord Foul to Kiril Threndor to utter the Ritual of Desecration. The legends said that when Kevin had seen that he could not defeat the Despiser, his heart had turned black with despair. He had loved the Land too intensely to let it fall to Lord Foul. And yet he had failed; he could not preserve it. Torn by his impossible dilemma, he had been driven to dare the Ritual. He had known that the unleashing of that fell power would destroy the Lords and all their works, and ravage the Land from end to end, make it barren for generations. He had known that he would die. But he had hoped that Lord Foul would also die, that when at last life returned to the Land it would be life free of Despite. He chose to take that risk rather than permit Lord Foul's victory. Thus he dared the Despiser to join him in Kiril Threndor. He and Lord Foul spoke the Ritual, and High Lord Kevin Landwaster destroyed the Land which he loved.

And Lord Foul had not died. He had been reduced for a time, but he had survived, preserved by the law of Time which imprisoned him upon the Earth — so the legends said. So now all the Land and the new Lords lay under the consequences of Kevin's despair.

It was not surprising that the Bloodguard wanted to hear this song — or that Bannor had asked Covenant to come hear it also.

As he mused, Covenant caught a glimpse of blue from across the amphitheatre. Looking up, he saw High Lord Elena standing near one of the entrances. She, too, wanted to hear this song.

With her was Warmark Troy.

Covenant felt an urge to go join them, but before he could make up his mind to move, the singer entered the amphitheatre. She was a tall, resplendent woman, simply clad in a crimson robe, with golden hair that flew like sparks about her head. As she moved down the steps to the stage, her audience rose to its feet and silently gave her the salute of welcome. She did not return it. Her face bore a look of concentration, as if she were already feeling her song.

When she reached the stage, she did not speak, said nothing to introduce or explain or identify her song. Instead, she took her stance in the centre of the stage, composed herself for a moment as the song came over her, then lifted her face to the sun and opened her throat.

At first, her melody was restrained, arid and angular – only hinting at buried pangs and poignancies.

> I stood on the pinnacle of the Earth:
> Mount Thunder,
> its Lions in full flaming mane,
> raised its crest no higher
> than the horizons that my gaze commanded;
> the Ranyhyn,
> hooves unfettered since the Age began,
> galloped gladly to my will;
> iron-thewed Giants
> from the sun's birth in the sea
> came to me in ships as mighty as castles,
> and cleft my castle from the
> raw Earth rock
> and gave it to me out of pure friendship –
> a handmark of allegiance and fealty
> in the eternal stone of Time;
> the Lords under my Watch laboured
> to find and make manifest
> the true purpose of the Earth's Creator,
> barred from His creation by the very
> power of that purpose –
> power graven into the flesh and bone of the Land
> by the immutable Law of its creation:
> how could I stand so,
> so much glory and dominion comprehended

> by the outstretch of my arms —
> stand thus,
> eye to eye with the Despiser,
> and not be dismayed?

But then the song changed, as if the singer opened inner chambers to give her voice more resonance. In high, arching spans of song, she gave out her threnody — highlighted it and underscored it with so many implied harmonies, so many suggestions of other accompanying voices, that she seemed to have a whole choir within her, using her one throat for utterance.

> Where is the power that protects
> beauty from the decay of life?
> preserves truth pure of falsehood?
> secures fealty from that slow stain of chaos which
> corrupts?
> How are we so rendered small by Despite?
> Why will the very rocks not erupt
> for their own cleansing,
> or crumble into dust for shame?
> Creator!
> When You desecrated this temple,
> rid Yourself of this contempt by
> inflicting it upon the Land,
> did You intend
> that beauty and truth should pass utterly from the Earth?
> Have You shaped my fate into the Law of life?
> Am I effectless?
> Must I preside over,
> sanction,
> acknowledge with the bitter face of treachery,
> approve
> the falling of the world?

Her music ached in the air like a wound of song. And as she finished, the people came to their feet with a rush. Together they sang into the fathomless heavens:

> Ah Creator!
> Timelord and Landsire!
> Did You intend
> that beauty and truth should pass utterly
> from the Earth?

Bannor stood, though he did not join the song. But Covenant kept his seat, feeling small and useless beside the community of Revelstone. Their emotion climaxed in the refrain, expending sharp grief and then filling the amphitheatre with a wash of peace which cleansed and healed the song's despair, as if the united power of the singing alone were answer enough to Kevin's outcry. By making music out of despair, the people resisted it. But Covenant felt otherwise. He was beginning to understand the danger that threatened the Land.

So he was still sitting, gripping his beard and staring blankly before him, when the people filed out of the amphitheatre, left him alone with the hot brightness of the sun. He remained there, muttering grimly to himself, until he became aware that Hile Troy had come over to him.

When he looked up, the Warmark said, 'I didn't expect to see you here.'

Gruffly, Covenant responded, 'I didn't expect to see *you*.' But he was only obliquely thinking about Troy. He was still trying to grapple with Kevin.

As if he could hear Covenant's thoughts, the Warmark said, 'It all comes back to Kevin. He's the one who made the Seven Wards. He's the one who inspired the Bloodguard. He's the one who did the Ritual of Desecration. And it wasn't necessary – or it wasn't inevitable. He wouldn't have been driven that far if he hadn't already made his big mistake.'

'His big mistake,' Covenant murmured.

'He admitted Foul to the Council, made him a Lord. He didn't see through Foul's disguise. After that it was too late. By the time Foul declared himself and broke into open war, he'd had time for so much subtle treachery that he was unbeatable.

'In situations like that, I guess most ordinary men kill themselves. But Kevin was no ordinary man – he had too much power for that, even though it seemed useless. He killed the Land instead. All that survived were the people who had time to escape into exile.

'They say that Kevin understood what he'd done – just before he died. Foul was laughing at him. He died howling.

'Anyway, that's why the Oath of Peace is so important now. Everyone takes it – it's as fundamental as the Lords' oath of service to the Land. Together they all swear that somehow they'll resist the destructive emotions – like Kevin's despair. They – '

'I know,' Covenant sighed. 'I know all about it.' He was remembering Triock, the man who had loved Lena in Mithil Stonedown forty years ago. Triock had wanted to kill Covenant, but Atiaran had prevented him on the strength of the Oath of Peace. 'Please don't say any more. I'm having a hard enough time as it is.'

'Covenant,' Troy continued as if he were still on the same subject. 'I don't see why you aren't ecstatic about being here. How can the "real" world be any more important than this?'

'It's the only world there is.' Covenant climbed heavily to his feet. 'Let's get out of here. This heat is making me giddy.'

Moving slowly, they left the amphitheatre. The air in Revelstone welcomed them back with its cool, dim pleasance, and Covenant breathed it deeply, trying to steady himself.

He wanted to get away from Troy, evade the questions he knew Troy would ask him. But the Warmark had a look of determination. After a few moments, he said, 'Listen, Covenant. I'm trying to understand. Since the last time we talked, I've spent half my time trying. Somebody has got to have some idea what to expect from you. But I just don't see it. Back there, you're a leper. Isn't this better?'

Dully, answering as briefly as possible, Covenant said, 'It isn't real. I don't believe it.' Half to himself, he added, 'Lepers who pay too much attention to their own dreams or whatever don't live very long.'

'Jesus,' Troy muttered. 'You make it sound as if leprosy is all there is.' He thought for a moment, then demanded, 'How can you be so sure this isn't real?'

'Because life isn't like this. Lepers don't get well. People with no eyes don't suddenly start seeing. Such things don't happen. Somehow, we're being betrayed. Our own – our own needs for something that we don't have – are seducing us into this. It's crazy. Look at you. Come on – think about what happened to you. There you were, trapped between a nine-storey fall and a raging fire – blind and helpless and about to die. Is it so strange to think that you cracked up?

'That is,' he went on mordantly, 'assuming you exist at all. I've got an idea about you. I must've made you up subconsciously so that I would have someone to argue with. Someone to tell me I'm wrong.'

'Damn it!' Troy cried. Turning swiftly, he snatched up Covenant's right hand and gripped it at eye level between them. With his head thrust defiantly forward, he said intensely, 'Look at me. Feel my grip. I'm here. It's a fact. It's real.'

For a moment, Covenant considered Troy's hand. Then he said, 'I feel you. And I see you. I even hear you. But that only proves my point. I don't believe it. Now let go of me.'

'Why?!'

Troy's sunglasses loomed at him darkly, but Covenant glared back into them until they turned away. Gradually, the Warmark released the pressure of his grip. Covenant yanked his hand away, and walked on with a quiver in his breathing. After a few strides, he said, 'Because I *can* feel it. And I can't afford it. Now listen to me. Listen hard. I'm going to try to explain this so you can understand.

'Just forget that you know there's no possible way you could have come here. It's impossible – But just forget that for a while. Listen. I'm a leper. Leprosy is not a directly fatal disease, but it can kill indirectly. I can only – any leper can only stay alive by concentrating all the time every minute to keep himself from getting hurt – and to take care of his hurts as soon as they happen. The one thing – Listen to me. The one thing no leper can afford is to let his mind wander. If he wants to stay alive. As soon as he stops concentrating, and starts thinking about how he's going to make a better life for himself, or starts dreaming about how his life was before he got sick, or about what he would do if he only got cured, or even if people simply stopped abhorring lepers' – he threw the words at Troy's head like chunks of stone – 'then he is as good as dead.

'This – Land – is suicide to me. It's an escape, and I can't afford even thinking about escapes, much less actually falling into one. Maybe a blind man can stand the risk, but a leper can't. If I give in here, I won't last a month where it really counts. Because I'll have to go back. Am I getting through to you?'

'Yes,' Troy said. 'Yes. I'm not stupid. But think about it for a minute. If it should happen – if it should somehow be true that the Land is real – then you're denying your only hope. And that's – '

'I know.'

' – that's not all. There's something you're not taking into account. The one thing that doesn't fit this delusion theory of yours is power – your power. White gold. Wild magic. That damn ring of yours changes everything. You're not a victim here. This isn't being done to you. You're responsible.'

'No,' Covenant groaned.

'Wait a minute! You can't just deny this. You're responsible for your dreams, Covenant. Just like anybody else.'

No! Nobody can control dreams. Covenant tried to fill himself with icy confidence, but his heart was chilled by another cold entirely.

Troy pressed his argument. 'There's plenty of evidence that white gold is just exactly what the Lords say it is. How were the defences of the Second Ward broken? How did the Fire-Lions of Mount Thunder get called down to save you? White gold, that's how. You've already got the key to the whole thing.'

'No.' Covenant struggled to give his refusal some force. 'No. It isn't like that. What white gold does in the Land has nothing to do with me. It isn't me. I can't touch it, make it work, influence it. It's just another thing that's happened to me. I've got no power. For all I know or can do about it, this wild magic could turn on tomorrow or five seconds from now and blast us all. It could crown Foul king of the universe whether I want it to or not. It has nothing to do with me.'

'Is that a fact?' Troy said sourly. 'And since you don't have any power, no one can hold you to blame.'

Troy's tone gave Covenant something on which to focus his anger. 'That's right!' he flared. 'Let me tell you something. The only person in life who's free at all, ever, is a person who's impotent. Like me. Or what do you think freedom is? Unlimited potential? Unrestricted possibilities? Hellfire! Impotence is freedom. When you're incapable of anything, no one can expect anything from you. Power has its own limits — even ultimate power. Only the impotent are free.

'No!' he snapped to stop Troy's protest. 'I'll tell you something else. What you're really asking me to do is learn how to use this wild magic so I can go around butchering the poor, miserable creatures in Foul's army. Well, I'm not going to do it. I'm not going to do any more killing — and certainly not in the name of something that isn't even real!'

'Hooray,' muttered Troy in tight sarcasm. 'Sweet Jesus. Whatever happened to people who used to believe in things?'

'They got leprosy and died. Weren't you listening to that song?'

Before Troy could reply, they rounded a corner, and entered an intersection where several halls came together. Bannor stood in the junction as if he were waiting for them. He blocked the hall Covenant had intended to take. 'Choose another way,' he said expressionlessly. 'Turn aside. Now.'

Troy did not hesitate; he swung away to his right. While he moved, he asked quickly, 'Why? What's going on?'

But Covenant did not follow. The crest of his anger, his bone-deep frustration, still held him up. He stopped where he was and glared at the Bloodguard.

'Turn aside,' Bannor repeated. 'The High Lord desires that you should not meet.'

From the next hallway, Troy called, 'Covenant! Come on!'

For a moment, Covenant maintained his defiance. But Bannor's impervious gaze deflated him. The Bloodguard looked as immune to affront or doubt as a stone wall. Muttering uselessly under his breath, Covenant started after Troy.

But he had delayed too long. Before he was hidden in the next hallway, a man came into the intersection from the passage behind

Bannor. He was as tall, thick, and solid as a pillar; his deep chest easily supported his broad massive shoulders and brawny arms. He walked with his head down, so that his heavy, red-grey beard rested like a burden on his breast; and his face had a look of ruddy strength gone ominously rancid, curdled by some admixture of gall.

Woven into the shoulders of his brown Stonedownor tunic was a pattern of white leaves.

Covenant froze; a spasm of suspense and fear gripped his guts. He recognized the Stonedownor. In the still place at the centre of the spasm, he felt sorrow and remorse for this man whose life he had ruined as if he were incapable of regret.

Striding back into the intersection, Troy said, 'I don't understand. Why shouldn't we meet this man? He's one of the *rhadhamaerl*. Covenant, this is – '

Covenant cut Troy off. 'I know him.'

Trell's eyes held Covenant redly, as if after years of pressure they were charged with too much blood. 'And I know you, Thomas Covenant.' His voice came out stiffly; it sounded disused, cramped, as if he had kept it fettered for a long time, fearing that it would betray him. 'Are you not satisfied? Have you come to do more harm?'

Through a roar of pounding blood in his ears, Covenant heard himself saying for the second time, 'I'm sorry.'

'Sorry?' Trell almost choked on the word. 'Is that enough? Does it raise the dead?' For a moment, he shuddered as if he were about to break apart. His breath came in deep, hoarse gasps. Then, convulsively, he threw his strong arms wide like a man breaking bonds. Jumping forward, he caught Covenant around the chest, lifted him off the floor. With a fierce snarl, he hugged Covenant, striving to crush his ribs.

Covenant wanted to cry out, howl his pain, but he could make no sound. The vice of Trell's arm drove the air from his lungs, stunned his heart. He felt himself collapsing, destroying himself with his own pressure.

Dimly, he saw Bannor at Trell's back. Twice Bannor punched at Trell's neck. But the Gravelingas only increased his grip, growling savagely.

Someone, Troy, shouted, 'Trell! Trell!'

Bannor turned and stepped away. For one frantic instant, Covenant feared that the Bloodguard was abandoning him. But Bannor only needed space for his next attack. He leaped high in the air, and as he dropped towards Trell, he chopped the Gravelingas across the base of his neck with one elbow. Trell staggered; his grip loosened. Continuing the same motion, Bannor caught Trell under the chin with his other arm. The sharp backward jerk pulled Trell off balance. As he toppled, he lost his hold on Covenant.

Covenant landed heavily on his side, retching for air. Through his dizzy gasps, he heard Troy shouting, heard the warning in Troy's voice. He looked up in time to see Trell charge towards him again. But Bannor was swifter. As Trell lunged, Bannor met him head-on, butted him with such force that he reeled backward, crashed against the wall, fell to his hands and knees.

The impact stunned him. His massive frame writhed in pain, and his fingers gouged involuntarily at the stone, as if he were digging for breath.

They clenched into the floor as if it were only stiff clay. In a moment, both his fists were knotted in the rock.

Then he threw a deep shuddering breath, and snatched his hands out of the floor. He stared at the holes he had made; he was appalled to see that he had damaged stone. When he raised his head, he was panting hugely, so that his broad chest strained at the fabric of his tunic.

Bannor and Troy stood between him and Covenant. The Warmark held his sword poised. 'Remember your Oath!' he commanded sharply. 'Remember what you swore. Don't betray your own life.'

Tears started running soundlessly from Trell's eyes as he stared past the Warmark at Covenant. 'My Oath?' he rasped. 'He brings me to this. What Oath does he take?' With a sudden exertion, he heaved himself to his feet. Bannor stepped slightly ahead of Troy to defend against another attack, but Trell did not look at Covenant again. Breathing strenuously, as if there were not enough air for him in the Keep, he turned and shambled away down one of the corridors.

Hugging his bruised chest, Covenant moved over to sit with his back against the wall. The pain made him cough thickly. Troy stood nearby, tight-lipped and intense. But Bannor appeared completely unruffled; nothing surprised his comprehensive dispassion.

'Jesus! Covenant,' Troy said at last. 'What has he got against you?'

Covenant waited until he found a clear space between coughs. Then he answered, 'I raped his daughter.'

'You're joking!'

'No.' He kept his head down, but he was avoiding Bannor's eyes rather than Troy's.

'No wonder they call you the Unbeliever.' Troy spoke in a low voice to keep his rage under control. 'No wonder your wife divorced you. You must have been insufferable.'

No! Covenant panted. I was never unfaithful to her. Never. But he did not raise his head, made no effort to meet the injustice of Troy's accusation.

'Damn you, Covenant.' Troy's voice was soft, fervid. He sounded too furious to shout. As if he could no longer bear the sight of the Unbeliever, he turned on his heel and strode away. But as he moved he could no longer contain his rage. 'Good God!' he yelled. 'I don't know why you don't drop him in some dungeon and throw away the key! We've got enough trouble as it is!' Soon he was out of view down one of the halls, but his voice echoed after him like an anathema.

Sometime later, Covenant climbed to his feet, hugging the pains in his chest. His voice was weak from the effort of speaking around his hurt. 'Bannor.'

'Ur-Lord?'

'Tell the High Lord about this. Tell her everything – about Trell and me – and Troy.'

'Yes.'

'And, Bannor – '

The Bloodguard waited impassively.

'I wouldn't do it again – attack a girl like that. I would take it back if I could.' He said it as if it were a promise that he owed Bannor for saving his life.

But Bannor gave no sign that he understood or cared what the Unbeliever was saying.

After a while, Covenant went on, 'Bannor, you're practically the only person around here who hasn't at least tried to forgive me for anything.'

'The Bloodguard do not forgive.'

'I know. I remember. I should count my blessings.' With his arms wrapped around his chest to hold the pieces of himself together, he went back to his rooms.

9

GLIMMERMERE

Another evening and night passed away without any word or sign of Lord Foul's army – no glimmer of the fire warnings which the Lords had prepared across the Centre and North Plains, no returning scouts, no omens. Nevertheless Covenant felt an increase in the tension of Revelstone; as the suspense mounted, the ambient air almost audibly quivered with strain, and Lord's Keep breathed with a sharper intake, a more cautious release. Even the walls of his room expressed a mood of imminence. So he spent the evening on his balcony, drinking springwine to soothe the ache in his chest, and watching the vague shapes of the twilight as if they were incipient armies, rising out of the very ground to thrust bloodshed upon him. After a few flasks of the fine, clear beverage, he began to feel that only the tactile sensation of beard under his fingertips stood between him and actions – war and killing – which he could not stomach.

When he slept that night, he had dreams of blood – wounds glutted with death in a vindictive and profligate expenditure which horrified him because he knew so vividly that only a few drops from an untended scratch were enough; there was no need or use for this hacking and slaughtering of flesh. But his dreams went on, agitating his sleep until at last he threw himself out of bed and went to stand on his balcony in the dawn, groaning over his bruised ribs.

Wrapped in the Keep's suspense, he tried to compose himself to continue his private durance – waiting in mixed anxiety and defiance for a peremptory summons from the High Lord. He did not expect her to take his encounter with her grandfather calmly, and he had kept to his rooms since the previous afternoon so that she would know where to find him. Still, when it came, the knock at his door made his heart jump. His fingers and toes tingled – he could feel his pulse in them – and he found himself breathing hard again, in spite of the pain in his chest. He had to swallow down a quick sour taste before he could master his voice enough to answer the knock.

The door opened, and Bannor entered the room. 'The High Lord wishes to speak with you,' he said without inflection. 'Will you come?'

Yes, Covenant muttered grimly to himself. Of course. Do I have a choice? Holding his chest to keep himself from wincing, he strode out of his suite and down the hall.

He started in the direction of the Close. He expected that Elena would want to make her anger public – to make him writhe before the assembled disapproval of Revelstone. He could have avoided Trell; it would have cost him nothing more than one instant of simple trust or considerateness. But Bannor soon steered him into other corridors. They passed through a small, heavy door hidden behind a curtain in one of the meeting halls, and went down a long, twisting stairwell into a deep part of the Keep unfamiliar to Covenant. The stair ended in a series of passages so irregular and dim that they confused him until he knew nothing about where he was except that he was deep in the gut-rock of Revelstone – deeper than the private quarters of the Lords.

But before long Bannor halted, facing a blank wall of stone. In the dim light of one torch, he spread his arms to the wall as if he were invoking it, and spoke three words in a language that came awkwardly to his tongue. When he lowered his arms, a door became visible. It swung inward, admitting the Bloodguard and Covenant to a high, brilliant cavern.

The makers of Revelstone had done little to shape or work this spacious cave. They had given it a smooth floor, but had left untouched the raw rough stone of its walls and ceiling; and they had not altered the huge rude columns which stood thickly through it like massive tree trunks, reaching up from the floor to take the burden of the ceiling upon their shoulders. However, the whole cavern was lit by large urns of graveling placed between the columns so that all the surfaces of the walls and columns were clearly illumined.

Displayed on these surfaces everywhere were works of art. Paintings and tapestries hung on the walls; large sculptures and carvings rested on stands between the columns and urns; smaller pieces, carvings and statuettes and stoneware and *suru-pa-maerl* works, sat on wooden shelves cunningly attached to the columns.

In his fascination, Covenant forgot why he had been brought here. He began moving around the hall, looking avidly. The smaller works caught his attention first. Many of them appeared in some way charged with action, imminent heat, as if they had been captured in a moment of incarnation; but the differences in materials and emotions were enormous. Where an oaken figure of a woman cradling a baby wept protectively over the griefs and hurts of children, a similar granite subject radiated confident generative power; where a polished Gildenlode flame seemed to yearn upward, a *suru-pa-maerl* blaze expressed comfort and practical warmth. Studies of children and Ranyhyn and Giants abounded; but scattered among them were darker subjects – roynish ur-viles, strong, simple-minded Cavewights, and mad, valorous Kevin, reft of judgment and foresight but not courage or compassion by sheer despair. There was little copying of nature among them; the materials used were not congenial to mirroring or literalism. Instead, they revealed the comprehending hearts of their makers. Covenant was entranced.

Bannor followed him as he moved around the columns, and after a while the Bloodguard said, 'This is the Hall of Gifts. All these were made by the people of the Land, and given to the Lords. Or to Revelstone.' He gazed about him with unmoved eyes. 'They were given for honour or love. Or to be seen. But the Lords do not desire such gifts. They say that no one can possess such things. The treasure comes from the Land, and belongs to the Land. So all gifts given to the Lords are placed here, so that any who wish it may behold them.'

Yet Covenant heard something deeper in Bannor's voice. Despite its monotone, it seemed to articulate a glimpse of the hidden and unanswerable passion which bound the Bloodguard to the Lords. But Covenant did not pursue it, did not intrude on it.

From among the first columns, he was drawn to a large, thick arras hanging on one of the walls. He recognized it. It was the same work he had once tried to destroy. He had thrown it out of his room in the watchtower in a fit of outrage at the fable of Berek's life – and at the blindness which saw himself as Berek reborn. He could not be mistaken. The arras was tattered around the edges, and had a carefully repaired rent down its centre halfway through the striving, irenic figure of Berek Halfhand. In scenes around the central figure, it showed the hero's soul-journey to his despair on Mount Thunder, and to his discovery of the Earthpower. From it, Berek gazed out at the Unbeliever with portents in his eyes.

Roughly, Covenant turned away, and a moment later he saw High Lord Elena walking towards him from the opposite side of the Hall. He remained where he was, watched her. The Staff of Law in her right hand increased the stateliness and authority of her step, but her left hand was open in welcome. Her robe covered her without disguising either the suppleness or the strength of her movements. Her hair hung loosely about her shoulders, and her sandals made a whispering noise on the stone.

Quietly, she said, 'Thomas Covenant, be welcome to the Hall of Gifts. I thank you for coming.'

She was smiling as if she were glad to see him.

That smile contradicted his expectations, and he distrusted it. He studied her face, trying to discern her true feelings. Her eyes invited study. Even while they regarded him, they seemed to look beyond him or into him or through him, as if the space he occupied were shared by something entirely different. He thought fleetingly that perhaps she did not actually, concretely, see him at all.

As she approached, she said, 'Do you like the Hall? The people of the Land are fine artists, are they not?' But when she neared him, she stopped short with a look of concern, and asked, 'Thomas Covenant, are you in pain?'

He found that he was breathing rapidly again. The air in the Hall seemed too rarefied for him. When he shrugged his shoulders, he could not keep the ache of the movement off his face.

Elena reached her hand towards his chest. He half winced, thinking that she meant to strike him. But she only touched his bruised ribs gently with her palm for a moment, then turned away towards Bannor. 'Bloodguard,' she said sharply, 'the ur-Lord has been hurt. Why was he not taken to a Healer?'

'He did not ask,' Bannor replied stolidly.

'Ask? Should help wait for asking?'

Bannor met her gaze flatly and said nothing, as if he considered his rectitude to be self-evident. But the reproach in her tone gave Covenant an unexpected pang. In Bannor's defence, he said, 'I don't need – didn't need it. He kept me alive.'

She sighed without taking her eyes off the Bloodguard. 'Well, that may be. But I do not like to see you harmed.' Then, relenting, she said, 'Bannor, the ur-Lord and I will go upland. Send for us at once if there is any need.'

Bannor nodded, bowed slightly, and left the Hall.

When the hidden door was closed behind him, Elena turned back to Covenant. He tensed instinctively. Now, he muttered to himself. Now she'll do it. But to all appearances her irritation was gone. And she made no reference to the arras; she seemed unaware of the connection between him and that work. With nothing but innocence in her face, she said, 'Well, Thomas Covenant. Do you like the Hall? You have not told me.'

He hardly heard her. Despite her pleasant expression, he could not believe that she did not intend to task him for his encounter with Trell. But then he saw concern mounting in her cheeks again, and he hurried to cover himself.

'What? Oh, the Hall. I like it fine. But isn't it a little out of the way? What good is a museum if people can't get to it?'

'All Revelstone knows the way. Now we are alone, but in times of peace – or in times when war is more distant – there are always people here. And the children in the schools spend much time here, learning of the crafts of the Land. Craftmasters come from all the Land to share and increase their skills. The Hall of Gifts is thus deep and concealed because the Giants who wrought the Keep deemed such a place fitting – and because if ever Revelstone is whelmed the Hall may be hidden and preserved, in hope of the future.'

For an instant, the focus of her gaze seemed to swing closer to him, and her vision tensed as if she meant to burn her way through his skull to find out what he was thinking. But then she turned away with a gentle smile, and walked towards another wall of the cavern. 'Let me show you another work,' she said. 'It is by one of our rarest Craftmasters, Ahanna daughter of Hanna. Here.'

He followed, and stopped with her before a large picture in a burnished ebony frame. It was a dark work, but glowing bravely near its centre was a figure that he recognized immediately: Lord Mhoram. The Lord stood alone in a hollow tightly surrounded by black fiendish shapes which were about to fall on him like a flood, deluge him utterly. His only weapon was his staff, but he wielded it defiantly; and in his eyes was a hot, potent look of extremity and triumph, as if he had discovered within himself some capacity for peril that made him unconquerable.

Elena said respectfully, 'Ahanna names this "Lord Mhoram's Victory". She is a prophet, I think.'

The sight of Mhoram in such straits hurt Covenant, and he took it as a reproach. 'Listen,' he said. 'Stop playing around with me like this. If you've got something to say, say it. Or take Troy's advice, and lock me up. But don't do this to me.'

'Playing around? I do not understand.'

'Hellfire! Stop looking so innocent. You got me down here to let me have it for that run-in with Trell. Well, get it over with. I can't stand the suspense.'

The High Lord met his glare with such openness that he turned away, muttering under his breath to steady himself.

'Ur-Lord.' She placed an appealing hand on his arm. 'Thomas Covenant. How can you believe such thoughts? How can you understand us so little? Look at me. Look at me!' She pulled his arm until he turned back to her, faced the sincerity she expressed with every line of her face. 'I did not ask you here to torment you. I wished to share my last hour in the Hall of Gifts with you. This war is near – near – and I will not soon stand here again. As for the Warmark – I do not take counsel from him concerning you. If there is any blame in your meeting with Trell, it is mine. I did not give you clear warning of my fears. And I did not see the extent of the danger – else I would have told all the Bloodguard to prevent your meeting.

'No, ur-Lord. I have no hard words to speak to you. You should reproach me. I have endangered your life, and cost Trell Atiaran-mate my grandfather his last self-respect. He was helpless to heal his daughter and his wife. Now he will believe that he is helpless to heal himself.'

Looking at her, Covenant's distrust fell into dust. He took a deep breath to clean stale air from his lungs. But the movement hurt his ribs. The pain made him fear that she would reach towards him, and he mumbled quickly, 'Don't touch me.'

For an instant, she misunderstood him. Her fingers leaped from his arm, and the otherness of her vision flicked across him with a virulence that made him flinch, amazed and baffled. But what she saw corrected her misapprehension. The focus of her gaze left him; she extended her hand slowly to place her palm on his chest.

'I hear you,' she said. 'But I must touch you. You have been my hope for too long. I cannot give you up.'

He took her wrist with the two fingers and thumb of his right hand, but he hesitated a moment before he removed her palm. Then he said, 'What happens to Trell now? He broke his Oath. Is anything done to him?'

'Alas, there is little we can do. It lies with him. We will try to teach him that an Oath which has been broken may still be kept. But it was not his intent to harm you – he did not plan his attack. I know him, and am sure of this. He has known of your presence in Revelstone, yet he made no effort to seek you out. No, he was overcome by his hurt. I do not know how he will recover.'

As she spoke, he saw that once again he had failed to comprehend. He had been thinking about punishment rather than healing. Hugging his sore ribs, he said, 'You're too gentle. You've got every right to hate me.'

She gave him a look of mild exasperation. 'Neither Lena my mother nor I have ever hated you. It is impossible for us. And what would be the good? Without you, I would not be. It may be that Lena would have married Triock, and given birth to a daughter – but that daughter would be another person. I would not be who I am.' A moment later, she smiled. 'Thomas Covenant, there are few children in all the history of the Land who have ridden a Ranyhyn.'

'Well, at least that part of it worked out.' He shrugged aside her questioning glance. He did not feel equal to explaining the bargain he had tried to make with the Ranyhyn – or the way in which that bargain had failed him.

A mood of constraint came between them. Elena turned away from it to look again at 'Lord Mhoram's Victory'.

'This picture disturbs me,' she said. 'Where am I? If Mhoram is thus sorely beset, why am I not at his side? How have I fallen, that he is so alone?' She touched the picture lightly, brushed her fingertips over Mhoram's lone, beleaguered, invincible stance. 'It is in my heart that this war will go beyond me.'

The thought stung her. Suddenly she stepped back from the painting, stood tall with the Staff of Law planted on the stone before her. She shook her head so that her brown-and-honey hair snapped as if a wind blew about her shoulders, and breathed intensely, 'No! I will see it ended! Ended!'

As she repeated *Ended*, she struck the floor with the Staff's iron heel. An instant of bright blue fire ignited in the air. The stone lurched under Covenant's feet, and he nearly fell. But she quenched her power almost at once; it passed like a momentary intrusion of nightmare. Before he could regain his balance, she caught his arm and steadied him.

'Ah, you must pardon me,' she said with a look like laughter. 'I forgot myself.'

He braced his feet, tried to determine whether or not he could still trust the floor. The stone felt secure. 'Give me fair warning next time,' he muttered, 'so I can sit down.'

The High Lord broke into clear laughter, then subdued herself abruptly. 'Your pardon again, Thomas Covenant. But your expression is so fierce and foolish.'

'Forget it,' he replied. He found that he liked the sound of her laugh. 'Ridicule may be the only answer.'

'Is that a proverb from your world? Or are you a prophet?'

'A little of both.'

'You are strange. You transpose wisdom and jest – you reverse their meanings.'

'Is that a fact?'

'Yes, ur-Lord Covenant,' she said lightly, humorously. 'That is a fact.' Then she appeared to remember something. 'But we must go. I think we are expected. And you have never seen the upland. Will you come with me?'

He shrugged. She smiled at him, and he followed her towards the door of the Hall.

'Who's expecting us?' he asked casually.

She opened the door and preceded him through it. When it was closed behind them, she answered, 'I would like to surprise you. But perhaps that would not be fair warning. There is a man – a man who studies dreams – to find the truth in them. One of the Unfettered.'

His heart jumped again, and he wrapped his arms protectively around his sore chest. Hellfire, he groaned to himself. An interpreter of dreams. Just what I need. An Unfettered One had saved him and Atiaran from the ur-viles at the Celebration of Spring. By a perverse trick of recollection, he heard the Unfettered One's death cry in the wake of Elena's clear voice. And he remembered Atiaran's grim insistence that it was the responsibility of the living to make meaningful the sacrifices of the dead. With a brusque gesture, he motioned for Elena to lead the way, then walked after her, muttering Hellfire. Hellfire.

She guided him back up through the levels of Revelstone until he began to recognize his surroundings. Then they moved westward, still climbing, and after a while they joined a high, wide passage like a road along the length of the Keep, rising slowly. Soon the decreasing weight of the stone around him, and the growing autumnal tang of the air, told him that they were approaching the level of the plateau which topped the Keep. After two sharp switchbacks, the passage ended, and he found himself out in the open, standing on thick grass under the roofless heavens. A league or two west of him were the mountains.

A cool breeze hinting a fall crispness touched him through the late morning sunlight – a low blowing as full of ripe earth and harvests as if it were clairvoyant, foretelling bundled crops and full fruit and seeds ready for rest. But the trees on the plateau and the upland hills were predominantly evergreens, feathery mimosas and tall pines and wide cedars with no turning of leaves. And the hardy grass made no concessions to the changing season.

The hills of the upland were Revelstone's secret strength. They were protected by sheer cliffs on the east and south, by mountains on the north and west; and so they were virtually inaccessible except through Lord's Keep itself. Here the people of the city could get food and water to withstand a siege. Therefore Revelstone could endure as long as its walls and gates remained impregnable.

'So you see,' said Elena, 'that the Giants wrought well for the Land in all ways. While Revelstone stands, there remains one bastion of hope. In its own way, the Keep is as impervious to defeat as Foul's Creche is said to be – in the old legends. This is vital, for the legends also say that the shadow of Despite will never be wholly driven from the Land while Ridjeck Thome, Lord Foul's dire demesne, endures. So our debt to the Giants is far greater than for unfaltering friendship. It is greater than anything we can repay.'

Her tone was grateful, but her mention of the Giants cast a gloom over her and Covenant. She turned away from it, and led him northward along the curve of the upland.

In this direction, the plateau rose into rumpled hills; and soon, on their left, away from the cliff, they began to pass herds of grazing cattle. Cattleherds saluted the High Lord ceremoniously, and she responded with quiet bows. Later, she and Covenant crossed a hilltop from which they could see westward across the width of the upland. There, beyond the swift river that ran south towards the head of Furl Falls, were fields where crops of wheat and maize rippled in the breeze. And a league behind the grazeland and the river and the fields stood the mountains, rising rugged and grand out of the hills. The peaks were snow-clad, and their white bemantling made them look hoary and aloof – sheer, wild, and irreproachable. The *Haruchai* lived west and south in this same range.

Covenant and the High Lord continued northward, slowly winding away from the cliffs and towards the river as Elena chose an easy path among the hills. She seemed content with the silence between them, so they both moved without speaking. Covenant walked as if he were drinking in the upland with his eyes and ears. The sturdy health of the grass, the clean, hale soil and the inviolate rock, the ripeness of the wheat and maize – all were vivid to his sight. The singing and soaring of the birds sounded like joy in the air. And when he passed close to a particularly tall, magisterial pine, he felt that he could almost hear the climbing of its sap. For a league, he forgot himself in his enjoyment of the Land's late summer.

Then he began to wonder vaguely how far Elena meant to take him. But before he became willing to interrupt the quietness with a question, they crossed the rise of a high hill, and she announced that they had arrived. 'Ah,' she said with a sigh of gladness, 'Glimmermere! Lakespring and riverhead – hail, clean pool! It pleases my heart to see you again.'

They were looking down on a mountain lake, the headwater of the river which ran to Furl Falls. For all the swiftness of the current rushing from it, it was a still pool, with no inflowing streams; all its water came from springs within it. And its surface was as flat, clear, and reflective as polished glass. It echoed the mountains and the sky with flawless fidelity, imaging the world in every detail.

'Come,' Elena said suddenly. 'The Unfettered One will ask us to bathe in Glimmermere.' Throwing a quick smile at him she ran lightly down the hill. He followed her at a walk, but the springy grass seemed to urge him forward until he was trotting. On the edge of the lake, she dropped the Staff as if she were discarding it, tightened the sash of her robe, and with a last wave towards him dived into the water.

When he reached Glimmermere, he was momentarily appalled to find that she had vanished. From this range, the reflection was transparent, and behind it he could see the rocky bottom of the lake. Except for a darkness like a deep shadow at its centre, he could see the whole bottom in clear detail, as if the pool were only a few feet deep. But he could not see Elena. She seemed to have dived out of existence.

He leaned over the water to peer into it, then stepped back sharply as he noticed that Glimmermere did not reflect his image. The noon sun was repeated through him as if he were invisible.

The next instant, Elena broke water twenty yards out in the lake. She shook her head clear, and called for him to join her. When she saw the wide gape of his astonishment, she laughed gaily. 'Does Glimmermere surprise you?'

He stared at her. He could see nothing of her below the plane where she broke the water. Her physical substance seemed to terminate at the waterline. Above the surface, she bobbed as if she were treading water; below, the bottom of the pool was clearly visible through the space she should have occupied. With an effort, he pulled his mouth shut, then called to her, 'I told you to give me fair warning!'

'Come!' she replied. 'Do not be concerned. There is no harm.' When he did not move, she continued, 'This is water, like any other – but stronger. There is Earthpower here. Our flesh is too unsolid for Glimmermere. It does not see us. Come!'

Tentatively, he stooped and dipped his hand in the water. His fingers vanished as soon as they passed below the surface. But when he snatched them back, they were whole and wet, tingling with cold.

Impelled by a sense of surprise and discovery, he pulled off his boots and socks, rolled up his pant legs, and stepped into the pool.

At once, he plunged in over his head. Even at its edges, the lake was deep; the clarity with which he could see the bottom had misled him. But the cold, tangy water buoyed him up, and he popped quickly back to the surface. Treading water and spluttering, he looked around until he located Elena. 'Fair warning!' He tried to sound angry despite Glimmermere's fresh, exuberant chill. 'I'll teach you fair warning!' He reached her in a few swift strokes, and shoved her head down.

She reappeared immediately, laughing almost before she lifted her head above water. He lunged at her, but she slipped past him, and pushed him under instead. He grappled for her ankles and missed. When he came up she was out of sight.

He felt her tugging at his feet. Grabbing a deep breath, he upended himself and plunged after her. For the first time, he opened his eyes underwater, and found that he could see well. Elena swam near him, grinning. He reached her in a moment, and caught her by the waist.

Instead of trying to pull away, she turned, put her arms around his neck and kissed him on the mouth.

Abruptly, all the air burst from his lungs as if she had kicked his sore ribs. He thrust away from her, scrambled back to the surface. Coughing and gasping, he thrashed over to the edge of the pool where he had left his boots, and climbed out to collapse on the grass.

His chest hurt as if he had reinjured his ribs, but he knew he had not. The first touch of Glimmermere's potent water had effaced his bruises, simply washed them away, and they did not ache now. This was another pain; in his exertions underwater he seemed to have wrenched his heart.

He lay panting face down on the grass, and after a while, his breathing relaxed. He became aware of other sensations. The cold, tart touch of the water left his whole body excited; he felt cleaner than he had at any time since he had learned of his leprosy. The sun was warm on his back, and his fingertips tingled vividly. And his heart ached when Elena joined him on the grass.

He could feel her eyes on him before she asked quietly, 'Are you happy in your world?'

Clenching himself, he rolled over, and found that she sat close to him, regarding him softly. Unable to resist the sensation, he touched a strand of her wet hair, rubbed it between his fingers. Then he lifted his grey, gaunt eyes to meet her gaze. The way he held himself made his voice unintentionally harsh. 'Happiness has got nothing to do with it. I don't think about happiness. I think about staying alive.'

'Could you be happy here?'

'That's not fair. What would you say if I asked you that?'

'I would say yes.' But a moment later she saw what he meant and drew herself up. 'I would say that happiness lies in serving the Land. And I would say that there is no happiness in times of war.'

He lay back on the grass so that he would not have to look at her. Bleakly, he murmured, 'Where I come from, there is no "Land". Just "ground". Dead. And there's always war.'

After a short pause, she said with a smile in her voice, 'If I have heard rightly, it is such talk which makes Hiltmark Quaan angry with you.'

'I can't help it. It's the simple fact.'

'You have a great respect for facts.'

He breathed carefully around his sore heart before answering. 'No. I hate them. They're all I've got.'

A gentle silence came over them. Elena reclined beside him, and they lay still to let the sunlight dry them. The warmth, the smell of the grass, seemed to offer him a sense of well-being; but when he tried to relax and flow with it, his pulse throbbed uncomfortably in his chest. He was too conscious of Elena's presence. But gradually he became aware that a larger silence covered Glimmermere. All the birds and even the breeze had become quite hushed. For a time, he kept his breathing shallow and explored the ambience of the air with his ears.

Shortly, Elena said, 'He comes,' and went to retrieve the Staff. Covenant sat up and looked around. Then he heard it – a soft, clean sound like a flute, spreading over Glimmermere from no source that he could see, as if the air itself were singing. The tune moved, came closer. Soon he could follow the words.

Free
unfettered
Shriven
Free –
Dream that what is dreamed will be:
Hold eyes clasped shut until they see,
And sing the silent prophecy –
And be
Unfettered
Shriven
free

Lone
Unfriended
Bondless
Lone –
Drink of loss 'til it is done,
'Til solitude has come and gone,
And silence is communion –
And yet
Unfriended
Bondless
Lone

Deep
Unbottomed
Endless
Deep –
Touch the true mysterious Keep
Where halls of fealty laugh and weep;
While treachers through the dooming creep
In blood
Unbottomed
Endless
Deep.

'Stand to meet him,' the High Lord said quietly. 'He is One of the Unfettered. He has gone beyond the knowledge of the Loresraat, in pursuance of a private vision open to him alone.'

Covenant arose, still listening to the song. It had an entrancing quality which silenced his questions and doubts. He stood erect, with his head up as if he were eager. And soon the Unfettered One came into sight over the hills north of Glimmermere.

He stopped singing when he saw Covenant and Elena, but his

appearance sustained his influence over them. He wore a long flowing robe that seemed to have no colour of its own; instead it caught the shades around it, so that it was grass-green below his waist, azure on his shoulders, and the rock and snow of the mountains flickered on his right side. His unkempt hair flared, reflecting the sun.

He came directly towards Covenant and Elena, and soon Covenant could make out his face – soft androgynous features thickly bearded, deep eyes. When he stopped before them, he and the High Lord exchanged no rituals or greetings. He said to her simply, 'Leave us,' in a high, fluted voice like a woman's. His tone expressed neither rejection nor command, but rather something that sounded like necessity, and she bowed to it without question.

But before she left, she put her hand on Covenant's arm, looked searchingly into his face. 'Thomas Covenant,' she said with a low quaver in her voice as if she were afraid of him or for him. 'Ur-Lord. When I must leave for this war – will you accompany me?'

He did not look at her. He stood as if his toes were rooted in the grass, and gazed into the Unfettered One's eyes. When after a time he failed to reply, she bowed her head, squeezed his arm, then moved away towards Revelstone. She did not look back. Soon she was out of sight beyond the hill.

'Come,' said the Unfettered One in the same tone of necessity. Without waiting for a response, he started to return the way he had come.

Covenant took two uncertain steps forward, then stopped as a spasm of anxiety clenched his features. He tore his eyes off the Unfettered One's back, looked urgently around him. When he located his socks and boots, he hurried towards them, dropped to the grass and pulled them onto his feet. With a febrile deliberateness, as if he were resisting the tug of some current or compulsion, he laced his boots and tied them securely.

When his feet were safe from the grass, he sprang up and ran after the interpreter of dreams.

10

SEER AND ORACLE

Late the next evening, Lord Mhoram answered a knock at the door
of his private quarters, and found Thomas Covenant standing
outside, silhouetted darkly like a figure of distress against the light
of the glowing floor. He had an aspect of privation and fatigue, as if
he had tasted neither food nor rest since he had gone upland.
Mhoram admitted him without question to the bare room, and
closed the door while he went to stand before the stone table in the
centre of the chamber – the table Mhoram had brought from the
High Lord's rooms, with the *krill* of Loric still embedded and burning
in it.

Looking at the bunched muscles of Covenant's back, Mhoram
offered him food and drink or a bed, but Covenant shrugged them
away brusquely, despite his inanition. In a flat and strangely closed
tone, he said, 'You've been beating your brains out on this thing
ever since – since it started. Don't you ever rest? I thought you Lords
rested down here – in this place.'

Mhoram crossed the room, and stood opposite his guest. The *krill*
flamed whitely between them. He was uncertain of his ground; he
could see the trouble in Covenant's face, but its causes and implications were confused, obscure. Carefully, the Lord said, 'Why should
I rest? I have no wife, no children. My father and mother were both
Lords, and Kevin's Lore is the only craft I have known. And it is
difficult to rest from such work.'

'And you're driven. You're the seer and oracle around here.
You're the one who gets glimpses of the future whether you want
them or not, whether they make you scream in your sleep or not,
whether you can stand them or not.' Covenant's voice choked for a
moment, and he shook his head fiercely until he could speak again.
'No wonder you can't rest. I'm surprised you can stand to sleep at
all.'

'I am not a Bloodguard,' Mhoram returned calmly. 'I need sleep
like other men.'

'What have you figured out? Do you know what this thing is good
for? What was that Amok business about?'

Mhoram gazed at Covenant across the *krill*, then smiled softly.

'Will you sit down, my friend? You will hear long answers more comfortably if you ease your weariness.'

'I'm not tired,' the Unbeliever said with obvious falseness. The next moment, he dropped straight into a chair. Mhoram took a seat, and when he sat down he found that Covenant had positioned himself directly across the table, so that the *krill* stood between their faces. This arrangement disturbed Mhoram, but he could think of no other way to help Covenant than to listen and talk, so he stayed where he was, and focused his other senses to search for what was blocked from his sight by the gem of the *krill*.

'No, I do not comprehend Loric's sword – and I cannot draw it from the table. I might free it by breaking the stone, but that would serve no purpose. We would gain no knowledge – only a weapon we could not touch. If the *krill* were free, it would not help us. It is a power altogether new to us. We do not know its uses. And we do not like to break wood or stone, for any purpose.

'As to Amok – that is an open question. Lord Amatin could answer better.'

'I'm asking you.'

'It is possible,' Mhoram said steadily, 'that he was created by Kevin to defend against the *krill* itself. Perhaps the power here is so perilous that in unwise hands, or ignorant hands, it would do great harm. If that is true, then it may be that Amok's purpose is to warn us from any unready use of this power, and to guide our learning.'

'You shouldn't sound so plausible when you say things like that. That isn't right. Didn't you hear what he said? "I have misserved my purpose."'

'Perhaps he knows that if we are too weak to bring the *krill* to life, we are powerless to use it in any way, for good or ill.'

'All right. Forget it. Just forget that this is something else I did to you without any idea what in hell I was doing. Let it stand. What makes you think that good old Kevin Landwaster who started all this anyway is lurking in back of everything that happens to you like some kind of patriarch, making sure you don't do the wrong thing and blow yourselves to bits? No, forget it. I know better than that, even if I have spent only a few weeks going crazy over this and not forty years like the rest of you. Tell me this. What's so special about Kevin's Lore? Why are you so hot to follow it? If you need power, why don't you go out and find it for yourselves, instead of wasting whole generations of perfectly decent people on a bunch of incomprehensible Wards? In the name of sanity, Mhoram, if not for the sake of mere pragmatic usefulness.'

'Ur-Lord, you surpass me. I hear you, and yet I am left as if I were deaf and blind.'

'I don't care about that. Tell me why.'

'It is not difficult – the matter is clear. The Earthpower is here, regardless of our mastery or use. The Land is here. And the banes and the evil – the Illearth Stone, the Despiser – are here, whether or not we can defend against them.

'Ah, how shall I speak of it? At times, my friend, the most simple, clear matters are the most difficult to utter.' He paused for a moment to think. But through the silence he felt an upsurge of agitation from Covenant, as if the Unbeliever were clinging to the words between them, and could not bear to have them withdrawn. Mhoram began to speak again, though he did not have his answer framed to his satisfaction.

'Consider it in this way. The study of Kevin's knowledge is the only choice we can accept. Surely you will understand that we cannot expect the Earth to speak to us, as it did to Berek Halfhand. Such things do not happen twice. No matter how great our courage, or how imposing our need, the Land will not be saved that way again. Yet the Earthpower remains, to be used in Landservice – if we are able. But that Power – all power – is dreadful. It does not preserve itself from harm, from wrong use. As you say, we might strive to master the Earthpower in our own way. But the risk forbids.

'Ur-Lord, we have sworn an Oath of Peace which brooks no compromise. Consider – forgive me, my friend, but I must give you a clear example – consider the fate of Atiaran Trell-mate. She dared powers which were beyond her, and was destroyed. Yet the result could have been far worse. She might have destroyed others, or hurt the Land. How could we, the Lords – we who have sworn to uphold all health and beauty – how could we justify such hazards?

'No, we must work in other ways. If we are to gain the power to defend the Earth, and yet not endanger the Land itself, we must be the masters of what we do. And it was for this purpose that Lord Kevin created his Wards – so that those who came after him could hold power wisely.'

'Oh, right!' Covenant snapped. 'Look at the good it did him. Hellfire! Even supposing you're going to have the luck or the brains or even the chance to find all Seven Wards and figure them out, what – bloody damnation! – what's going to happen when dear, old, dead Kevin finally lets you have the secret of the Ritual of Desecration? And it's your last chance to stop Foul in a war – again! How're you going to rationalize that to the people who'll have to start from scratch a thousand years from now because you just couldn't get out of repeating history? Or do you think that when the crisis comes you're somehow going to do a better job than Kevin did?'

He spoke coldly, rapidly, but a smudged undercurrent in his voice told Mhoram that he was not talking about what was uppermost in his mind. He seemed to be putting the Lord through a ritual of questions, testing him. Mhoram responded carefully, hoping for Covenant's sake that he would not make a mistake.

'We know the peril now. We have known it since the Giants returned the First Ward to us. Therefore we have sworn the Oath of Peace — and will keep it — so that never again will life and Land be harmed by despair. If we are brought to the point where we must desecrate or be defeated, then we will fight until we are defeated. The fate of the Earth will be in other hands.'

'Which I'm doing nothing but make difficult for you. Just having this white gold raises prospects of eradication that never occurred to you before — not to mention the fact that it's useless. Before this there wasn't enough power around to make it even worth your while to worry about despair, since you couldn't damage the Land if you wanted to. But now Foul might get my ring — or I might use it against you — but it'll never save you.'

Covenant's hands twitched on the table as if he were fumbling for something. His fingers knotted together, tensed, then sprang apart to grope separately, aimlessly. 'All right. Forget that, too. I'm coming to that. How in the name of all the gods are you going to fight a war — a war, Mhoram, not just fencing around with a bunch of Cavewights and ur-viles! — when everyone you've got who's tall enough to hold a sword has sworn this Oath of Peace? Or are there special dispensations like fine print in your contracts exempting wars from moral strictures or even the simple horror of blood?'

It was in Mhoram's heart to tell Covenant that he went too far. But the fumbling, graspless jerks of his hands — one maimed, the other carrying his ring like a fetter — told Mhoram that the affront of the Unbeliever's language was directed inward at himself, not at the Lords or the Land. This perception increased Mhoram's concern, and again he replied with steady dignity.

'My friend, killing is always to be abhorred. It is a measure of our littleness that we cannot evade it. But I must remind you of a few matters. You have heard Berek's Code — it is part of our Oath. It commands us:

> Do not hurt where holding is enough;
> do not wound where hurting is enough;
> do not maim where wounding is enough;
> and kill not where maiming is enough;
> the greatest warrior is he who does not need to kill.

And you have heard High Lord Prothall say that the Land would not be served by angry bloodshed. There he touched upon the heart of the Oath. We will do all that might or mastery permits to defend the Land from Despite. But we will do nothing – to the Land, to our foes, to each other – which is commanded to us by our hearts' black passions or pain or lust for death. Is this not clear to you, ur-Lord? If we must fight and, yes, kill, then our only defence and vindication is to fight so that we do not become like our Enemy. Here Kevin Landwaster failed – he was weakened by that despair which is the Despiser's strength.

'No, we must fight – if only to preserve ourselves from watching the evil, as Kevin watched and was undone. But if we harm each other, or the Land, or hate our foes – ah, there will be no dawn to the night of that failure.'

'That's sophistry.'

'Sophistry? I do not know this word.'

'Clever arguments to finance what you've already decided to do. Rationalizations. War in the name of Peace. As if when you poke your sword into a foe you aren't slicing up ordinary flesh and blood that has as much right to go on living as you do.'

'Then do you truly believe that there is no difference between fighting to destroy the Land and fighting to preserve it?'

'Difference? What has that got to do with it? It's still killing. But never mind. Forget that, too. You're doing too good a job. If I can't pick holes in your answers any better than this, I'm going to end up – ' His hands began to shake violently, and he snatched them out of sight, shoved them below the table. 'I'll end up freezing to death, that's what.'

Slumped back in his chair, Covenant fell into an aching silence. Mhoram felt the pressure between them build, and decided that the time had come to ask questions of his own. Breathing to himself the Seven Words, he said kindly, 'You are troubled, my friend. The High Lord is difficult to refuse, is she not?'

'So?' Covenant snapped. But a moment later, he groaned, 'Yes. Yes, she is. But that isn't it. The whole Land is difficult to refuse. I've felt that way from the beginning. That isn't it.' After a tense pause, he went on: 'Do you know what she did to me yesterday? She took me upland to see that Unfettered One – the man who claims to understand dreams. I was there for a day or more – But you're the seer and oracle – I don't have to tell you about him. You've probably gone up there yourself more than anyone else, couldn't help it, if only because mere ordinary human ears can only stand to hear so much contempt and laughter and no more, regardless of whether you're asleep or not. So you know what it's like. You know how he latches onto you with those eyes, and holds you down, and dissects – But you're the seer and oracle. You probably even know what he said to me.'

'No,' Mhoram replied quietly.

'He said – Hellfire!' He shook his head as if he were dashing water from his eyes. 'He said that I dream the truth. He said that I am very fortunate. He said that people with such dreams are the true enemies of Despite – it isn't Law, the Staff of Law wasn't made to fight Foul with – no, it's wild magic and dreams that are the opposite of Despite.' For an instant, the air around him quivered with indignation. 'He also said that I don't believe it. That was a big help. I just wish I knew whether I am a hero or a coward.

'No, don't answer that. It isn't up to you.'

Lord Mhoram smiled to reassure Covenant, but the Unbeliever was already continuing, 'Anyway, I've got a belief – for what it's worth. It just isn't exactly the one you people want me to have.'

Probing again, Mhoram said, 'That may be. But I do not see it. You do not show us belief, but Unbelief. If this is believing, then it is not belief for, but rather belief against.'

Covenant jumped to his feet as if he had been stung. 'I deny that! Just because I don't affirm the Land or whatever, carry on like some unravelled fanatic and foam at the mouth for a chance to fight like Troy does, doesn't mean – Assuming that there's some kind of justice in the labels and titles which you people spoon around – assuming you can put a name at all to this gut-broken whatever that I can't even articulate much less prove to myself. That is not what Unbelief means.'

'What does it mean?'

'It means – ' For a moment, Covenant stopped, choking on the words as if his heart suffered some blockage. Then he reached forward and shaded the gem of the *krill* with his hands so that it did not shine in his eyes. In a voice suddenly and terribly suffused with the impossibility of any tears which would have eased him, he shouted, 'It means I've got to withhold – to discount – to keep something for myself! Because I don't know why!' The next instant, he dropped back into his chair and bowed his head, hiding it in his arms as if he were ashamed.

'Why?' Mhoram said softly. 'That is not so hard a matter here, thus distant from "how". Some of our legends hint at one answer. They tell of the beginning of the Earth, in a time soon after the birth of Time, when the Earth's Creator found that his brother and Enemy, the Despiser, had marred his creation by placing banes of surpassing evil deep within it. In outrage and pain, the Creator cast his Enemy down – out of the universal heavens onto the Earth –

502

and imprisoned him here within the arch of Time. Thus, as the legends tell it, Lord Foul came to the Land.'

As he spoke, he felt that he was not replying to Covenant's question – that the question had a direction he could not see. But he continued, offering Covenant the only answer he possessed.

'It is clear now that Lord Foul lusts to strike back at his brother, the Creator. And at last, after ages of bootless wars carried on out of malice, out of a desire to harm the creation because he could not touch the Creator, Lord Foul has found a way to achieve his end, to destroy the arch of Time, unbind his exile and return to his forbidden home, for spite and woe. When the Staff of Law, lost by Kevin at the Desecration, came within his influence, he gained a chance to bridge the gap between worlds – a chance to bring white gold into the Land.

'I tell you simply: it is Lord Foul's purpose to master the wild magic – "the anchor of the arch of life that spans and masters Time" – and with it bring Time to an end, so that he may escape his bondage and carry his lust throughout the universe. To do this, he must defeat you, must wrest the white gold from you. Then all the Land and all the Earth will surely fall.'

Covenant raised his head, and Mhoram tried to anticipate his next question. 'But how? – how does the Despiser mean to accomplish this purpose? Ah, my friend, that I do not know. He will choose ways which resemble our own desires so closely that we will not resist. We will not be able to distinguish between his service and our own until we are bereft of all aids but you, whether you choose to help us or no.'

'But why?' Covenant repeated. 'Why me?'

Again, Mhoram felt that his answer did not lie in the direction of Covenant's question. But still he offered it, humbly, knowing that it was all he had to give his tormented visitor.

'My friend, it is in my heart that you were chosen by the Creator. That is our hope. Lord Foul taught Drool to do the summoning because he desired white gold. But Drool's hands were on the Staff, not Lord Foul's. The Despiser could not control who was summoned. So if you were chosen, you were chosen by the Creator.

'Consider. He is the Creator, the maker of the Earth. How can he stand careless and see his making destroyed? Yet he cannot reach his hand to help us here. That is the law of Time. If he breaks the arch to touch the Land with his power, Time will end, and the Despiser will be free. So he must resist Lord Foul elsewhere. With you, my friend.'

'Damnation,' Covenant mumbled.

'Yet even this you must understand. He cannot touch you here, to teach or help you, for the same reason that he cannot help us. Nor can he touch or teach or help you in your own world. If he does, you will not be free. You will become his tool, and your presence will break the arch of Time, unbinding Despite. So you were chosen. The Creator believes that your uncoerced volition and strength will save us in the end. If he is wrong, he has put the weapon of his own destruction into Lord Foul's hands.'

After a long silence, Covenant muttered, 'A hell of a risk.'

'Ah, but he is the Creator. How could he do otherwise?'

'He could burn the place down, and try again. But I guess you don't think gods are that humble. Or do you call it arrogance – to burn – ? Never mind. I seem to remember that not all the Lords believe in this Creator as you do.'

'That is true. But you came to me. I answer as I can.'

'I know. Don't mind me. But tell me this. What would you do in my place?'

'No,' said Mhoram. At last he moved his chair to one side, so that he could see Covenant's face. Gazing into the Unbeliever's unsteady features, he replied, 'That I will not answer. Who can declare? Power is a dreadful thing. I cannot judge you with an answer. I have not yet judged myself.'

The instability of Covenant's expression momentarily resolved into seeking. But he did not speak, and after a time Mhoram decided to ask another question. 'Thomas Covenant, why do you take this so? Why are you so hurt? You say that the Land is a dream – a delusion – that we have no real life. Then do not be concerned. Accept the dream, and laugh. When you awaken, you will be free.'

'No,' Covenant said. 'I recognized something in what you said – I'm starting to understand this. Listen. This whole crisis here is a struggle inside me. By hell, I've been a leper so long, I'm starting to think that the way people treat lepers is justified. So I'm becoming my own enemy, my own Despiser – working against myself when I try to stay alive by agreeing with the people who make it so hard. That's why I'm dreaming this. Catharsis. Work out the dilemma subconsciously, so that when I wake up I'll be able to cope.'

He stood up suddenly, and began to pace Mhoram's ascetic chamber with a voracious gleam in his eyes. 'Sure. That's it. Why didn't I think of it before? I've been telling myself all the time that this is escapism, suicide. But that's not it – that's not it at all. Just forget that I'm losing every one of the habits that keep me alive. This is dream therapy.'

But abruptly a grimace of pain clutched his face. 'Hellfire!' he rasped intensely. 'That sounds like a story I should have burned – back when I was burning stories – when I still had stories to burn.'

Mhoram heard the anguished change, the turning to dust, in Covenant's tone, and he stood to reach out towards his visitor. But he did not need to move; Covenant came almost aimlessly in his direction, as if within the four walls of the chamber he had lost his way. He stopped at the table near Mhoram, and gazed miserably at the *krill*. His voice shook.

'I don't believe it. That's just another easy way to die. I already know too many of them.'

He seemed to stumble, though he was standing still. He lurched forward, and caught himself on Mhoram's shoulder. For a moment, he clung there, pressing his forehead into Mhoram's robe. Then Mhoram lowered him into a chair.

'Ah, my friend, how can I help you? I do not understand.'

Covenant's lips trembled, but with a visible effort he regained control of his voice. 'Just tired. I haven't eaten since yesterday. That Unfettered One – drained me. Some food would be very nice.'

The opportunity to do something for Covenant gave Mhoram a feeling of relief. Moving promptly, he brought his guest a flask of springwine. Covenant drank as if he were trying to break an inner drought, and Mhoram went to his back rooms to find some food.

While he was placing bread and cheese and grapes on a tray, he heard a sharp, distant shout; a voice cried his name with an urgency that smote his heart. He set the tray down, hastened to throw open the door of his chambers.

In the sudden wash of light from the courtyard, he saw a warrior standing in one of the coigns high above him. The warrior was a young man – too young for war meat, Mhoram thought grimly – who had lost command of himself. 'Lord Mhoram!' he blurted. 'Come! Now! The Close!'

'Stop!' The authority in Mhoram's tone caught the young man like a bit. He winced, stiffened, forced down a chaotic tumult of words. Then he recovered his self-possession. Seeing this, the Lord said more gently, 'I hear you. Speak.'

'The High Lord asks that you come to the Close at once. A messenger has come from the Plains of Ra. The Grey Slayer is marching.'

'War?' Mhoram spoke softly to conceal a sharp prevision of blood.

'Yes, Lord Mhoram.'

'Please say to the High Lord that – that I have heard you.'

Bearing himself carefully, Mhoram turned back towards Covenant. The Unbeliever met his gaze with a hot, oddly focused look, as if his skull were splitting between his eyes. Mhoram asked simply, 'Will you come?'

Covenant gripped the Lord's gaze, and said, 'Tell me something,

Mhoram. How did you get away – when that Raver caught you – near Foul's Creche?'

Mhoram answered with a conscious serenity, a refusal of dismay, which looked like danger in his gold-flecked eyes. 'The Bloodguard with me were slain. But when *samadhi* Raver touched me, he knew me as I knew him. He was daunted.'

For a moment, Covenant did not move. Then he dropped his glance. Wearily, he set the stoneware flask on the table, pushed it over so that it clicked against the *krill*. He tugged momentarily at his beard, then pulled himself to his feet. To Mhoram's gaze, he looked like a thin candle clogged with spilth – guttering, frail, and portionless.

'Yes,' he said. 'Elena asked me the same thing. For all the good it'll do any of us. I'm coming.'

Awkwardly, he shambled out onto the burning floor.

PART II

The Warmark

11

WAR COUNCIL

Hile Troy was sure of one thing; despite whatever Covenant said, the Land was no dream. He perceived this with an acuteness which made his heart ache.

In the 'real' world, he had not been simply blind, he had been eyeless from birth. He lacked even the organs of sight which could have given him a conception of what vision was. Until the mysterious event which had snatched him from between opposing deaths, and had dropped him on the sunlit grass of Trothgard, light and dark had been equally incomprehensible to him. He had not known that he lived in immitigable midnight. The tools with which he had handled his physical surroundings had been hearing and touch and language. His sense of ambience, his sensitivity to the auras of objects and the resonances of space, was translated by words until it became his sole measure of the concrete world. He had been a good strategist precisely because his perceptions of space and interacting force were pure, undistracted by any knowledge of day or night or colour or brilliance or illusion.

Therefore he could not be imagining the Land. His former mind had not contained the raw materials out of which such dreams were made. When he appeared in the Land – when Lord Elena taught him that the rush of sensations which confused him was sight – the experience was altogether new. It did not restore to him something that he had lost. It opened in front of him like an oracle.

He knew that the Land was real.

And he knew that its future hung by the thread of his strategy in this war. If he made a mistake, then more brightness and colour than he could ever take into account were doomed.

So when Ruel, the Bloodguard assigned to watch over him, came to him in his quarters and informed him that a Ramen Manethrall had arrived from the Plains of Ra, bringing word of Lord Foul's army, Troy felt an instant of panic. It had begun – the test of all his training, planning, hopes. If he had believed Mhoram's tales of a Creator, he would have dropped to his knees to pray –

But he had never learned to rely on anyone but himself. The Warward and the strategy were his; he was in command. He paused

509

just long enough to strap the traditional ebony sword of the Warmark to his waist and don his headband. Then he followed Ruel towards the Close.

As he moved, he was grateful for the brightness of the torches in the hallways. Even with their help, his sight was dim. In daylight, he could see clearly, with more grasp of detail and more distance than the far-eyed Giants. The sun brought distant things close to him; at times, he felt that he possessed more of the Land than anyone else. But night restored his blindness like an insistent reminder of where he had come from. While the sun was down, he was lost without torches or fires. Starlight did not touch his private darkness, and even a full moon cast no more than a grey smudge across his mind.

Sometimes in the middle of the night, his sightlessness scared him like a repudiation of sunlight and vision.

By force of habit, he adjusted his sunglasses. He had worn them for so long, out of consideration for the people with eyes who had to look at him, that they felt like a part of his face. But he never saw them; they had no effect on his vision. Nothing that came within six inches of his orbless sockets blocked his mental sight at all.

To control his tension, he strode towards the Close without hurrying. At one point, a group of Hafts, the commanders of Eoward, saluted him and then jogged ahead with their swords clattering; and later Lord Verement came hawklike down a broad staircase and rushed past him. But he did not vary his step until he reached the high doors of the council chamber. There he found Quaan waiting for him.

The sight of the old stalwart Hiltmark gave him a pang. In this dim light, Quaan's thin white hair made him look frail. But he saluted Troy briskly, and reported that all fifty Hafts were now in the Close.

Fifty. Troy recited the numbers to himself as if he were repeating a rite of command: Fifty Eoward, one thousand Eoman; a total of twenty-one thousand and fifty warriors; First Haft Amorine, Hiltmark Quaan, and himself. He nodded as if to assure Quaan that they would be enough. Then he marched down into the Close to take his seat at the Lords' table.

Around him, the chamber was almost filled, and most of the leaders were in their chairs. The space was so well-lit that now he could see clearly. The High Lord sat with quiet intensity at the head of the table; and between her and him were Callindrill, Trevor, Loerya, and Amatin, each keeping a private silence. But Troy knew them, and could guess something of their thoughts. Lord Loerya hoped despite the demands of her Lordship that she and Trevor would not be chosen to leave Revelstone and her daughters. And her husband seemed to be remembering that he had fallen under the strain of fighting the ill in *dukkha* Waynhim – remembering, and wondering if he had the strength for this war.

About Elena, Troy did not speculate. Her beauty confused him; he did not want to think that something might happen to her in this war. Deliberately, he kept his gaze away from her.

On her left beyond Mhoram's empty chair was Lord Verement and two more unoccupied seats – places for the Lords Shetra and Hyrim. For a moment, Troy paused to wonder how Korik's mission was doing. Four days after their departure, word had been brought to Revelstone by some of the scouts that they had passed into Grimmerdhore Forest. But after that, of course, Troy knew he could not expect to hear any more news until long days after the mission was over, for good or ill. In the privacy of his heart, he dreamed that sometime during the course of this war he would have the joy of seeing Giants march to his aid, led by Hyrim and Shetra. He missed them all, Shetra as much as Korik, Hyrim as much as the Giants. He feared that he would need them.

Above and behind the High Lord, the Hearthralls Tohrm and Borillar sat in their places with Hiltmark Quaan and First Mark Morin. And behind the Lords, spaced around the first rows of seats in the gallery, were other Bloodguard: Morril, Bann, Howor, Koral, and Ruel on Troy's side; Terrel, Thomin, and Bannor opposite him.

Most of the remaining people in the Close were his Hafts. As a group, they were restless, tense. Most of them had no experience of war, and they had been training rigorously under his demanding gaze. He found himself hoping that what they saw and heard at this Council would galvanize their courage, turn their tightness into fortitude. They had such an ordeal ahead of them –

The few Lorewardens visiting Revelstone were all present, as were the most skilled of the Keep's *rhadhamaerl* and *lillianrill*. But Troy noticed that the Gravelingas Trell was not among them. He felt vaguely relieved – more for Trell's sake than for Covenant's.

Shortly, Lord Mhoram entered the Close, bringing the Unbeliever with him. Covenant was tired – his hunger and weakness were plainly visible in the gaunt pallor of his face – but Troy could see that he had suffered no real harm. And his reliance upon Mhoram's support expressed how little he was a threat to the Lords at this moment. Troy frowned behind his sunglasses, tried not to let his indignation at Covenant surge back up again. As Mhoram seated Covenant, and then walked around to take his own place at Elena's left, Troy turned his attention to the High Lord.

She was ready to begin now; and as always her every movement, her every inflection, fascinated him. Slowly, she looked around the table, meeting the eyes of each of the Lords. Then in a clear, stately voice, she said, 'My friends, Lords and Lorewardens and servers of the Land, our time has come. For good or ill, weal or woe, the trial is upon us. The word of war is here. In our hands now is the fate of the Land, to keep or lose, as our strength permits. The time of preparation is ended. No longer do we build or plan against the future. Now we go to war. If our might is not potent to preserve the Land, then we fall, and whatever world is to come will be of the Despiser's making, not ours.

'Hear me, my friends. I do not speak to darken your hearts, but to warn against false hope and wishful dreams, which could unbind the thews of purpose. We are the chance of the Land. We have striven for worth. Now our worthiness meets its test. Harken, and make no mistake. This is the test which determines.' For a moment, she paused to gaze over all the attentive faces in the Close. When she had seen the resolution in their eyes, she gave a smile of approval, and said quietly, 'I am not afraid.'

Troy nodded to himself. If his warriors felt as he did, she had nothing to fear.

'Now,' said High Lord Elena, 'let us hear the bearer of these tidings. Admit the Manethrall.'

At her command, two Bloodguard opened the doors, and made way for the Ramen.

The woman wore a deep brown shift which left her arms and legs free, and her long black hair was knotted at her neck by a cord. This cord, and the small woven garland of yellow flowers around her neck, sadly wilted now after long days of wear, marked her as a Manethrall – a member of the highest rank of her people. She was escorted by an honour guard of four Bloodguard, but she moved ahead of them down the stairs, bearing the fatigue of her great journey proudly. Yet despite her brave spirit, Troy saw that she could hardly stand. The slim grace of her movements was dull, blunted. She was not young. Her eyes, long familiar with open sky and distance, nested in fine wrinkles of age, and the weariness of several hundred leagues lay like lead in the marrow of her bones, giving a pallid underhue to the dark suntan of her limbs.

With a sudden rush of anxiety, Troy hoped that she had not come too late.

As she descended to the lowest level of the Close, and stopped before the graveling pit, High Lord Elena rose to greet her, 'Hail, Manethrall, highest of the Ramen, the selfless tenders of the Rany-hyn! Be welcome in Lord's Keep – welcome and true. Be welcome whole or hurt, in boon or bane – ask or give. To any requiring name we will not fail while we have life or power to meet the need. I am

High Lord Elena. I speak in the presence of Revelstone itself.'

Troy recognized the ritual greeting of friends, but the Manethrall gazed up at Elena darkly, as if unwilling to respond. Then she turned to her right, and said in a low, bitter voice unlike the usual nickering tones of the Ramen, 'I know you, Lord Mhoram.' Without waiting for a response, she moved on. 'And I know you, Covenant Ringthane.' As she looked at him, the quality of her bitterness changed markedly. Now it was not weariness and defeat and old Ramen resentment of the Lords for presuming to ride the Ranyhyn, but something else. 'You demanded the Ranyhyn at night, when no mortal may demand them at all. Yet they answered – one hundred proud Manes, more than most Ramen have ever seen in one place. They reared to you, in homage to the Ringthane. And you did not ride.' Her voice made clear her respect for such an act, her awe at the honour which the Ranyhyn had done this man. 'Covenant Ringthane, do you know me?'

Covenant stared at her intensely, with a look of pain as if his forehead were splitting. Several moments passed before he said thickly, 'Gay. You're – you were Winhome Gay. You waited on – you were at Manhome.'

The Manethrall returned his stare. 'Yes. But you have not changed. Forty-one summers have ridden past me since you visited the Plains of Ra and Manhome, and would not eat the food I brought to you. But you are changeless. I was a child then, a Winhome then, barely near my Cording – and now I am a tired old woman, far from home, and you are young. Ah, Covenant Ringthane, you treated me roughly.'

He faced her with a bruised expression; the memories she called up were sore in him. After another moment, she raised her hands until her palms were turned outward level with her head, and bowed to him in the traditional Ramen gesture of greeting. 'Covenant Ringthane, I know you. But you do not know me. I am not Winhome Gay, who passed her Cording and studied the Ranyhyn in the days when Manhome was full of tales of your Quest – when Manethrall Lithe returned from the dark underground, and from seeing the Fire-Lions of Mount Thunder. And I am not Cord Gay, who became a Manethrall, and later heard the word of the Lords asking for Ramen scouts to search the Spoiled Plains between Landsdrop and the Shattered Hills. This requesting word was heard, though these same Lords knew that all the life of the Ramen is on the Plains of Ra, in the tending of the Ranyhyn – yes, heard, and accepted by Manethrall Gay, with the Cords in her watch. She undertook the task of scouting because she hated Fangthane the Render, and because she admired Manethrall Lithe, who dared to leave sunlight for the sake of the Lords, and because she honoured Covenant Ringthane, the bearer of white gold, who did not ride when the Ranyhyn reared to him. Now that Manethrall Gay is no more.'

As she said this, her fingers hooked into claws, and her exhausted legs bent into the semblance of a fighting crouch. 'I am Manethrall Rue — old bearer of the flesh of her who was named Gay. I have seen Fangthane marching, and all the Cords in my watch are dead.' Then she sagged, and her proud head dropped low. 'And I have come here — I, who should never have left the Plains of home. I have come here, to the Lords who are said to be the friends of the Ranyhyn, in no other name but grief.'

While she spoke, the Lords kept silence, and all the Close watched her in anxious suspense, torn between respect for her fatigue and desire to hear what she had to say. But Troy heard dangerous vibrations in her voice. Her tone carried a pitch of recrimination which she had not yet articulated clearly. He was familiar with the grim, suppressed outrage that filled all the Ramen when any human had the insolence, the almost blasphemous audacity, to ride a Ranyhyn. But he did not understand it. And he was impatient for the Manethrall's news.

Rue seemed to sense the increasing tension around her. She stepped warily away from Covenant, and addressed all her audience for the first time. 'Yes, it is said that the Lords are our friends. It is said. But I do not know it. You come to the Plains of Ra and give us tasks without thought for the pain we feel on hills which are not our home. You come to the Plains of Ra, and offer yourselves to the generosity of the Ranyhyn as if you were an honour for some Mane to accept. And when you are accepted, as the Bloodguard are accepted — five hundred Manes thralled like chattel to purposes not their own — you call the Ranyhyn away from us into danger, where none can protect, where the flesh is rent and the blood spilt, with no *amanibhavam* to stem the pain or forestall death. Ah, Ranyhyn!

'Do not flex your distrust at me. I know you all.'

In a soft, careful voice, containing neither protest nor apology, the High Lord said, 'Yet you have come.'

'Yes,' Manethrall Rue returned in tired bitterness, 'I have come. I have fled, and endured, and come. I know we are united against Fangthane, though you have betrayed us.'

Lord Verement stiffened angrily, but Elena controlled him with a glance, and said, still softly and carefully, to Rue, 'In what way betrayed?'

'Ah, the Ramen do not forget. In tales preserved in Manhome from the age of mighty *Kelenbhrabanal*, we know Fangthane, and the wars of the Old Lords. Always, when Fangthane built his armies in the Lower Land, the Old Lords came to the ancient battleground north of the Plains of Ra and the Roamsedge River, and fought at Landsdrop, to forbid Fangthane from the Upper Land. So the Ranyhyn were preserved, for the enemy could not turn his teeth to the Plains of Ra while fighting the Lords. And in recognition, the Ramen left their hills to fight with the Lords.

'But you – ! Fangthane marches, and your army is here. The Plains of Ra are left without defence or help.'

'That was my idea.' His impatience made Troy sound sharper than he intended.

'For what reason?' A dangerous challenge pulsed in her quiet tone.

'I think they were good reasons,' he responded. Impelled by an inner need to reassure himself that he had not been wrong, he spoke swiftly. 'Think about it. You're right – every time in the past Foul has built up an army, the Lords have gone to fight him at Landsdrop. And every time, they've lost. They've been pushed back. There are too many different ways up from the Lower Land. And the Lords have been too far from their supplies and support. Sure, they put up a good fight – and that takes some of the pressure off the Plains of Ra because Foul is occupied elsewhere. But the Lords lose. Whole Eoward get hacked to pieces, and the Warward has to retreat on the run just to stay alive long enough to regroup and fight the same fight all over again, farther west – closer to Revelstone.

'And that's not all. This time, Foul might be building his army farther north – in Sarangrave Flat north of the Defiles Course. He's never done that before. But back then the Giants always kept the north Sarangrave clear. This time' – he winced at the thought of the Giants – 'this time it's different. If we marched an army down to you while Foul was on his way north of Mount Thunder towards Revelstone, we'd be helpless to stop him from attacking the Keep. Revelstone might fall. So I made the decision. We wait here.

'Don't get me wrong – we're not abandoning you. The fact is, I don't think you're in that much danger. Look, suppose Foul has an army of fifty thousand – or even a hundred thousand. How long is it going to take him to conquer the Plains of Ra?'

'He will not,' Rue breathed between her teeth.

The Warmark nodded. 'And even if he does, it'll take him years. You're too good at hunting – he can't beat you on your own ground. You and the Ranyhyn will run circles around his troops, and every time they turn their backs, you'll throttle a few score of them. Even if he outnumbers you fifty to one, you'll just send the Ranyhyn into the mountains, and keep chipping away at him for God knows how long. He'll need years to do it. Even assuming we are not attacking his rear. No, until he's got the Lords beaten, he can't afford to tackle you. That's why I've been thinking all along that he would come north.'

He stopped and faced Rue squarely with his argument. The recital of his reasoning calmed him; he knew that his logic was sound. And the Manethrall was forced to acknowledge it. After considering his explanation for a time, she sighed, 'Ah, very well. I see your reasons. But I do not like such ideas. You juggle risk for the Ranyhyn too freely.'

Tiredly, she turned back towards Elena. 'Hear me, High Lord,' she said in a grey, empty voice. 'I will speak my message, for I am weary and must rest, come what may.

'I have journeyed here from the Shattered Hills which surround and defend Foul's Creche. I left that maimed place when I saw a great army issuing from the Hills. It marched as straight as the eye sees towards Landsdrop and the Fall of the River Landrider. It was an army dire and numberless − I could not guess its size, and did not wait to count. With the four Cords in my watch, I fled so that I might keep my word to the Lords.'

The south way, Troy breathed to himself. At once, his brain took hold of the information; concrete images of the Spoiled Plains and Landsdrop filled his mind. He began to calculate Lord Foul's progress.

'But some enemy knew my purpose. We were pursued. A black wind came upon us, and from it fearsome, abominable creatures fell like birds of prey. My Cords were lost so that I might escape − yet I was driven far from my way, north into the marge of the Sarangrave.

'I knew that the peril was great. Yet I knew that there was no waiting army of friends or Lords on the Upper Land to help the Ranyhyn. A shadow came over my heart. Almost I turned aside from my purpose, and left the Lords to a fate of their own devising. But I contended with the Sarangrave, so that the lives of my Cords would not have been lost in vain.

'Over the ancient battleground, through the rich joy of Andelain, then across a stern plain south of a great forest like unto Morinmoss, but darker and more slumberous − thus I made my way, so that your idea might have its chance. That is my message. Ask what questions you will, and then release me, for I must rest.'

With quiet dignity, the High Lord arose, holding the Staff of Law before her. 'Manethrall Rue, the Land is measureless in your debt. You have paid a grim price to bring your word to us, and we will do our utmost to honour that cost. Please hear me. We could not turn away from the Ranyhyn and their Ramen. To do so, we would cease to be what we are. Only one belief has kept us from your side. It is in our hearts that this is the final war against Fangthane. If we fall, there will be none left to fight again. And we have not the strength of the Old Lords. What force we have we must use cunningly. Please do not harden your heart against us. We will pay many prices to match your own.' Holding the Staff at the level of her eyes, she bent forward in a Ramen bow.

A faint smile flickered across Rue's lips – amusement at Elena's approximation of the fluid Ramen salute – and she returned it to show how it should be done. 'It is also said among the Ramen that the Lords are courteous. Now I know it. Ask your questions. I will answer as I can.'

The High Lord reseated herself. Troy was eager to speak, but she did not give him permission. To Manethrall Rue she said, 'One question is first in my heart. What of Andelain? Our scouts report no evil there, but they have not your eyes. Are the Hills free of wrong?'

A surge of frustration bunched the muscles of Troy's shoulders. He was eager, urgent, to begin probing the Manethrall. But he recognized the tact of Elena's inquiry. The Andelainian Hills rode through Ramen legend like an image of paradise; it would ease Rue's heart to speak of them.

In response, her grim bitterness relaxed for a moment. Her eyes filled with tears that ran down over the slight smile on her lips. 'The Hills are free,' she said simply.

A glad murmur ran through the Close, and several of the Lords nodded in satisfaction. This was not something about which a Manethrall could be mistaken. The High Lord sighed her gratitude. When she freed the Warmark to begin his questions, she did so with a look that urged him to be gentle.

'All right,' Troy said, rising to his feet. His heart laboured with anxiety, but he ignored it. 'I understand that you don't know the size of Foul's army. I accept that. But I've got to know how much head start he has. Exactly how many days ago did you see his army leave the Shattered Hills?'

The Manethrall did not need to count back. She replied promptly, 'Twenty days.'

For an instant, the Warmark regarded her eyelessly from behind his sunglasses, stunned into silence. Then he whispered, 'Twenty days?' His brain reeled. 'Twenty?' With a violence that wrenched his heart, his image of the Despiser's army surged forward thirty-five leagues – five days. He had counted on receiving word of Lord Foul's movements in fifteen days. He had studied the Ramen; he knew to a league how far a Manethrall could travel in a day. 'Oh, my God.' Rue should have been able to reach Revelstone in fifteen days.

He was five days short. Five days less in which to march over three hundred leagues – ! And Lord Foul's army would be in the Centre Plains ten days from now.

Without knowing how he had reached that position, he found himself sitting with his face in his hands as if he could not bear to look at the ruin of all his fine strategy. Numbly, as if it were a matter of no consequence, he realized that he had been right about one thing: Covenant's summons coincided with the start of Lord Foul's army. That ploy had triggered the Despiser's attack. Or did it work the other way around? Had Lord Foul somehow anticipated the call?

'How – ?' For a moment, he could not find what he wanted to ask, and he repeated stupidly, 'How – ?'

'Ask!' Rue demanded softly.

He heard the warning in her voice, the danger of offending her pride after an exhausting ordeal. It made him raise his head, look at her. She was glaring at him, and her hands twitched as if they yearned to snatch the fighting cord from her hair. But he had to ask the question, had to be sure – 'What happened to you? Why did it take so long?' His voice sounded small and lorn to himself.

'I was driven from my way,' she said through her teeth, 'north into the marge of the Sarangrave.'

'Dear God,' Troy breathed weakly. He felt the way Rue looked at him, felt all the eyes in the Close on him. But he could not think; his brain was inert. Lord Foul was only a three-day march from Morinmoss.

The Manethrall snorted disdainfully, and turned away towards the High Lord. 'Is this the man who leads your warriors?' she asked sourly.

'Please pardon him,' Elena replied. 'He is young in the Land, and in some matters does not see clearly. But he has been chosen by the Ranyhyn. In time he will show his true value.'

Rue shrugged. 'Do you have other questions?' she said wearily. 'I would end this.'

'You have told us much. We have no more doubt of Lord Foul's movements, and can guess his speed. Only one question remains. It concerns the composition of Fangthane's army. What manner of beings comprise it?'

Bitterness stiffened Rue's stance, and she said harshly, 'I have spoken of the wind, and the evil in the air which felled my Cords. In the army I saw ur-viles, Cavewights, a mighty host of *kresh*, great lion-like beasts with wings which both ran and flew, and many other ill creatures. They wore shapes like dogs or horses or men, yet they were not what they seemed. They shone with great wrong. To my heart, they appeared as the people and beasts of the Land made evil by Fangthane.'

'That is the work of the Illearth Stone,' the High Lord murmured.

But Manethrall Rue was not done. 'One other thing I saw. I could not be mistaken, for it marched near the forefront, commanding the movements of the horde. It controlled the creatures with baleful green light, and called itself Fleshharrower. It was a Giant.'

For an instant, a silence like a thunderclap broke over the Close. It snatched Troy's attention erect, lit a fire of dread in his chest. The Giants! Had Lord Foul conquered them? Already?

Then First Mark Morin came to his feet and said in a voice flat with certainty, 'Impossible. Rockbrother is another name for fealty and faith. Do you rave?'

At once, the chamber clamoured in protest against the very idea that a Giant could join the Despiser. The thought was too shocking to be admitted; it cast fundamental beliefs into hysteria. The Hafts burst out lividly, and several of them shouted through the general uproar that Rue was lying. Two Lorewardens took up Morin's question and made it an accusation: Rue was in the grip of a Raver. Confusion overcame even the Lords. Trevor and Loerya paled with fear; Verement barked at Mhoram; Elena and Callindrill were staggered; and Amatin burst into tears.

The noise aggravated swiftly in the clear acoustics of the Close, exacerbated itself, forced each voice to become rawer and wilder. There was panic in the din. If the Giants could be made to serve Despite, then nothing was safe, sure; betrayal lurked everywhere. Even the Bloodguard had an aspect of dismay in their flat faces.

Yet under the protesting and the abuse, Manethrall Rue stood firmly, holding up her head with a blaze of pride and fury in her eyes.

The next moment, Covenant reached her side. Shaking his fists at the assembly, he howled, 'Hellfire! Can't you see that she's telling the truth?'

His voice had no effect. But something in his yell penetrated Hiltmark Quaan. The old veteran knew the Ramen well; he had known Rue during her youth. He jumped to his feet and shouted, 'Order!!'

Caught in their trained military reactions, the Hafts sprang to attention.

Then High Lord Elena seemed to realize what was happening around her. She reasserted her control with a blast of blue fire from the Staff, and one hot cry:

'I am ashamed!'

A stung silence, writhing with fear and indignation, burned in answer to her shout. But she met it passionately, sternly, as if something precious were in danger. '*Melenkurion abatha!* Have we come to this? Does fear so belittle us? Look! Look at her. If you have not heard the truth in her voice, then look at her now. Remember your Oath of Peace, and look at her. By the Seven! What evil do you see? No – I will hear no protestations that ill can be disguised. We are in the Close of Revelstone. This is the Council of Lords. No Raver could utter falsehood and betrayal here. If there were any wrong in the Manethrall, you would have known it.'

When she saw that she had mastered the assembly, she continued more quietly. 'My friends, we are more than this. I do not know the meaning of Manethrall Rue's tidings. Perhaps the Despiser has captured and broken a Giant through the power of the Illearth Stone. Perhaps he can create ill wights in any semblance he desires, and showed a false Giant to Rue, knowing how the tale of a betraying Rockbrother would harm us. We must gain answers to these questions. But here stands Manethrall Rue of the Ramen, exhausted in the accomplishment of a help which we can neither match nor repay. Cleanse your hearts of all thoughts against her. We must not do such injustice.'

'Right.' Troy heaved himself to his feet. His brain was working again. He was ashamed of his weakness – and, by extension, ashamed of his Hafts as well. Belatedly, he remembered that the Lords Callindrill and Amatin had been unable to breach Sarangrave Flat – and yet Rue had survived it, so that she could come to warn Revelstone. And he did not like to think that Covenant had behaved better than he. 'You're right.' He faced the Ramen squarely. 'Manethrall, my Hafts and I owe you an apology. You deserve better – especially from us.' He put acid in his tone for the ears of the Hafts. 'War puts burdens on people without caring whether they're ready for them or not.'

He did not wait for any reply. Turning towards Quaan, he said, 'Hiltmark – my thanks for keeping your head. Let's make sure that nothing like this happens again.' Then he sat down and withdrew behind his sunglasses to try to think of some way to salvage his battle plans.

Quaan commanded, 'Rest!' The Hafts reseated themselves, looking abashed – and yet in some way more determined than before. That seemed to mark the end of an ugliness. Manethrall Rue and ur-Lord Covenant sagged, leaned tiredly towards each other as if for support. The High Lord started to speak, but Rue interrupted her in a low voice. 'I want no more apologies. Release me. I must rest.'

Elena nodded sadly. 'Manethrall Rue, go in Peace. All the hospitality Revelstone can provide is yours for as long as you choose to stay. We do not take the service you have done us lightly. But please hear me. We have never taken the Ramen lightly. And the value of the Ranyhyn to all the Land is beyond any measure. We do not forget. Hail, Manethrall! May the bloom of *amanibhavam* never fail. Hail, Ramen! May the Plains of Ra be forever swift under your feet. Hail, Ranyhyn! Tail of the Sky, Mane of the World.' Once again, she bowed to Rue in the Ramen fashion.

Manethrall Rue returned the gesture, and added the traditional salute of farewell; touching the heels of her hands to her forehead, she bent forward and spread her arms wide as if baring her heart. Together, the Lords answered her bow. Then she turned and started up towards the high doors. Covenant went with her, walking at her side awkwardly, as if he wanted and feared to take her arm.

At the top of the stairs, they stopped and faced each other. Covenant looked at her with emotions that seemed to make the bone between his eyes bulge. He had to strain to speak. 'What can I – is there anything I can do – to make you Gay again?'

'You are young and I am old. This journey has taken much from me. I have few summers left. There is nothing.'

'My time has a different speed. Don't covet my life.'

'You are Covenant Ringthane. You have power. How should I not covet?'

He ducked away from her gaze; and after a short pause she added, 'The Ranyhyn still await your command. Nothing is ended. They served you at Mount Thunder, and will serve you again – until you release them.' When she passed through the doors away from him, he was left staring down at his hands as if their emptiness pained him.

But after a moment he pulled himself up, and came back down the stairs to take his seat again.

For a time, there was silence in the Close. The gathered people watched the Lords, and the Lords sat still, bending their minds in towards each other to meld their purpose and strength. This had a calming effect on the assembly. It was part of the mystery of being a Lord, and all the people of the Land, Stonedownor and Woodhelvennin, trusted the Lords. As long as the Council was capable of melding and leadership, Revelstone would not be without hope. Even Warmark Troy gained a glimpse of encouragement from this communion he could not share.

At last, the contact broke with an almost audible snap from Lord Verement, and the High Lord raised her head to the assembly. 'My friends, warriors, servants of the Land,' she said, 'now is the time of decision. Deliberation and preparation are at an end. War marches towards us, and we must meet it. In this matter, the chief choice of action is upon Warmark Hile Troy. He will command the Warward, and we will support it with our best strength, as the need of the Land demands.

'But one matter compels us first – this Giant named Fleshharrower. The question of this must be answered.'

Roughly, Verement said, 'The Stone does not explain. It is not enough. The Giants are strong – yes, strong and wise. They would resist the Stone or evade it.'

'I agree,' said Loerya. 'The Seareach Giants understand the peril of the Illearth Stone. It is easier to believe that they have left the Land in search of their lost Home.'

'Without the Gildenlode?' Trevor countered uncomfortably. 'That is unlikely. And it is not – it is not what Mhoram saw.'

The other Lords turned to Mhoram, and after a moment he said, 'No, it is not what I have seen. Let us pray that I have seen wrongly – or wrongly understood what I have seen. But for good or ill, this matter is beyond us at present. We know that Korik and the Lords Hyrim and Shetra will do their uttermost for the Giants. And we cannot send more of our strength to Seareach now, to ask how a Giant has been made to lead Foul's army. It is in my heart that we will learn that answer sooner than any of us would wish.'

'Very well,' the High Lord sighed. 'I hear you. Then let us now divide among ourselves the burdens of this war.' She looked around the Council, measuring each member against the responsibilities which lay ahead. Then she said, 'Lord Trevor – Lord Loerya – to you I commit the keeping of Revelstone. It will be your task to care for the people made homeless by this war – to lay up stores and strengthen defences against any siege that may come – to fight the last battle of the Land if we fail. My friends, hear me. It is a grim burden I give you. Those who remain here may in the end require more strength than all others – for if we fall, then you must fight to the last without surrender or despair. You will be in a strait place like that which drove High Lord Kevin to his Desecration. I trust you to resist. The Land must not be doomed in that way again.'

Troy nodded to himself; her choice was a good one. Lord Loerya would fight extravagantly, and yet would never take any action that would imperil her daughters. And Lord Trevor would work far beyond his strength in the conviction that he did not do as much as others could. They accepted the High Lord's charge quietly, and she went on to other matters.

'After the defence of Revelstone, our concern must be for the Loresraat and Trothgard. The Loresraat must be preserved. And Trothgard must be held for as long as may be – as a sanctuary for the homeless, men or beasts – and as a sign that in no way do we bow to the Despiser. Within the Valley of Two Rivers, Trothgard is defensible, though it will not be easy. Lord Callindrill – Lord Amatin – this burden I place upon your shoulders. Preserve Trothgard, so that the ancient name of Kurash Plenethor, Stricken Stone, will not become the new name of our promise to the Land.'

'Just a minute,' Warmark Troy interrupted hesitantly. 'That leaves just you, Mhoram, and Verement to go with me. I think I'm going to need more than that.'

Elena considered for a moment. Then she said, 'Lord Amatin, will you accept the burden of Trothgard alone? Trevor and Loerya will give you all possible aid.'

'We fight a war,' Amatin replied simply. 'It is bootless to protest that I do not suffice. I must learn to suffice. The Lorewardens will support me.'

'You will be enough,' responded the High Lord with a smile. 'Very well. Those Lords who remain – Callindrill, Verement, Mhoram, and myself – will march with the Warward. Two other matters, and then the Warmark will speak. First Mark Morin.'

'High Lord.' Morin stood to receive her requests.

'Morin, you are the First Mark. You will command the Bloodguard as your Vow requires. Please assign to Warmark Troy every Bloodguard who can be spared from the defence of Revelstone.'

'Yes, High Lord. Two hundred will join the Warmark's command.'

'That is well. Now I have another task for you. Riders must be sent to every Stonedown and Woodhelven in the Centre and South Plains, and in the hills beyond. All the people who may live in the Despiser's path must be warned, and offered sanctuary at Trothgard if they choose to leave their homes. And all who dwell along the southward march of the Warward must be asked for aid – food for the warriors, so that they may march more easily, carrying less. *Aliantha* alone will not suffice for so many.'

'It will be done. The Bloodguard will depart before moonset.'

Elena nodded her approval. 'No thanks can repay the Bloodguard. You give a new name to unflawed service. While people endure in the Land, you will be remembered for faithfulness.'

Bowing slightly, the First Mark sat down.

The High Lord set the Staff of Law on the table before her, took her seat, and signed to Warmark Troy. He took a deep breath, then got stiffly to his feet. He was still groping, juggling. But he had regained a grip on his situation; he was thinking clearly again. Even as he started to speak, new ideas were coming into focus.

'I'm not going to waste time apologizing for this mess I've gotten us into. I built my strategy on the idea that we would get word of where Foul was marching in fifteen days. Now we're five days short. That's all there is to it.

'Most of you know generally what I had in mind. As far as I can learn, the Old Lords had two problems fighting Foul – the simple attrition of doing battle all the way from Landsdrop, and the terrain. The Centre Plains favour whichever army is fresher and larger. My idea was to let Foul get halfway here on his own, and meet him at the west end of the Mithil valley, where the Mithil River forms the south border of Andelain. Then we would retreat southwest, luring Foul after us across to Doom's Retreat. In all the legends, that's the place armies run to when they're routed. But in fact it's a hell of a place to take on armies that are bigger and faster than you are. The terrain – that bottleneck between the mountains – gives a tremendous advantage to the side that gets there first – if it gets there in time to dig in before the enemy arrives.

'Well, it was a nice idea. Now we're in a different war. We're five days short. Foul will be through the Mithil valley ten days from now. And he'll turn north, forcing us to fight him wherever he wants in the Centre Plains. If we have to retreat at all, we'll end up in Trothgard.'

He paused for a moment, half expecting groans of dismay. But most of the people simply watched him closely, and several of the Lords had confidence in their eyes. Their trust touched him. He had to swallow down a sudden lump in his throat before he could continue.

'There's one way we can still do it. It's going to be hell – but it's just about possible.'

Then for an instant he faltered. *Hell* was a mild word for what his warriors would have to endure. How could he ask them to do it, when he was to blame for the miscalculation which made it necessary? How – ?

But Elena was watching him steadily. From the beginning, she had supported his desire to command the Warward. And now he was the Warmark. He, Hile Troy. In a tone of anger at the extremity of what he was asking, he said, 'Here it is. First. We have nine days. I absolutely guarantee that Foul will hit the western end of the Mithil valley by the end of the ninth day from now. That's one of the things not having any eyes is good for. I can measure things like this. All right? Nine days. We've got to get there before that and block the valley.

'Morin, your two hundred Bloodguard have got to leave tonight. Callindrill, you go with them. On Ranyhyn you can get there in seven days. You've got to stop Foul right there.

524

'Borillar, how many of those big rafts have you got in the lake?'

Surprised, Hearthrall Borillar answered, 'Three, Warmark.'

'How many warriors and horses can they carry?'

Borillar glanced helplessly over at Quaan. The Hiltmark replied, 'Each raft will carry two Eoman and their Warhafts – forty-two warriors and horses. But the crowding will be dangerous.'

'If you ride a raft as far as Andelain, how fast can you get those Eoman to the Mithil valley?'

'If there is no mishap – in ten days. Four days may be saved through the use of rafts.'

'All right. We have twelve horse-mounted Eoward – two hundred and forty Eoman. Borillar, I need one hundred and twenty of those rafts. Quaan, you're in command of this. You've got to get all twelve mounted Eoward – and Verement – down to the Mithil valley as fast as possible – to help Callindrill and the Bloodguard keep Foul from coming through. You've got to buy us the time we need. Get on it.'

Hiltmark Quaan spoke a word to the Hafts, and twelve of them jumped up to form ranks behind him as he hastened out of the Close. Borillar looked at the High Lord with an expression of indecision, but she nodded to him. Rubbing his hands nervously as if to warm them, he left the chamber, taking all the *lillianrill* with him.

'Second,' Troy said. 'The rest of the Warward will march straight south from here to Doom's Retreat. That's something less than three hundred leagues.' He called the remaining Hafts to their feet, and addressed them directly. 'I think you should explain this to your commands. We've got to get to Doom's Retreat in twenty-eight days. And that's only enough if the Hiltmark can do everything I've got in mind for him. Tell your Eoward – ten leagues a day. That's going to be the easy part of this war.'

In the back of his mind, he was thinking, Ten leagues a day for twenty-eight days. Good God! Half of them will be dead before we reach the South Plains.

For a moment, he studied the Hafts, trying to judge their mettle. Then he said, 'First Haft Amorine.'

The First Haft stepped forward, and responded. 'Warmark.' She was a short, broad, dour woman with blunt features which appeared to have been moulded in a clay too hard and dry for detailed handiwork. But she was a seasoned veteran of the Warward – one of the few survivors of the Eoman which Quaan had commanded on the Quest for the Staff of Law.

'Ready the Warward. We march at dawn. Pay special attention to the packs. Make them as light as possible. Use all the rest of the horses for cartage if you have to. If we don't make it to Doom's Retreat in time, Revelstone won't have any use for the last few hundred horses. Get started.'

First Haft Amorine gave a stern command to the Hafts. Saluting the Lords altogether, they moved out of the Close behind her.

Troy watched until they were gone, and the doors were shut after them. Then he turned to the High Lord. With an effort, he forced himself to say, 'You know I've never commanded a war before. In fact, I've never commanded anything. All I know is theory — just mental exercises. You're putting a lot of faith in me.'

If she felt the importance of what he said, she gave no sign. 'Do not fear, Warmark,' she replied firmly. 'We see your value to the Land. You have given us no cause to doubt the rightness of your command.'

A rush of gratitude took Troy's voice away from him. He saluted her, then sat down and braced his arms on the table to keep himself from trembling.

A moment later, High Lord Elena said to the remaining assembly, 'Ah, my friends, there is much to be done, and the night will be all too short for our need. This is not the time for long talk or exhortation. Let us all go about our work at once. I will speak to the Keep, and to the Warward, at dawn.'

'Hearthrall Tohrm.'

'High Lord,' Tohrm responded with alacrity.

'I think that there are ways in which you may make the rafts more stable, safer for horses. Please do so. And send any of your people who may be spared to assist Hearthrall Borillar in the building.

'My friends, this war is upon us. Give your best strength to the Land now. If mortal flesh may do it, we must prevail.' She drew herself erect, and flourished the Staff. 'Be of good heart. I am Elena daughter of Lena, High Lord by the choice of the Council, and wielder of the Staff of Law. My will commands. I speak in the presence of Revelstone itself.' Bowing to the assembly, she swept from the Close through one of the private doors, followed variously by the other Lords.

The chamber emptied rapidly as the people hurried away to their tasks. Troy stood and started towards the stairs. But on the way, Covenant accosted him. 'Actually,' Covenant said as if he were telling Troy a secret, 'it isn't you they've got faith in at all. Just as they don't have faith in me. It's the student who summoned you. That's whom they've staked their faith on.'

'I'm busy,' Troy said stiffly. 'I've got things to do. Let me go.'

'Listen!' Covenant demanded. 'I'm trying to warn you. If you could hear it. It's going to happen to you, too. One of these days, you're going to run out of people who'll march their hearts out to make your ideas work. And then you'll see that you put them through all that for nothing. Three-hundred-league marches — blocked valleys — your ideas. Paid for and wasted. All your fine tactics won't be worth a rusty damn.

'Ah, Troy,' he sighed wearily. 'All this responsibility is going to make another Kevin Landwaster out of you.' Instead of meeting Troy's taut stare, he turned away and wandered out of the Close as if he hardly knew or cared where he was going.

12

FORTH TO WAR

Just before dawn, Troy rode away from the gates of Revelstone in the direction of the lake at the foot of Furl Falls. The predawn dimness obscured his sight, blinded him like a mist in his mind. He could not see where he was going, could hardly discern the ears of his mount. But he was in no danger; he was riding Mehryl, the Ranyhyn that had chosen to bear him.

Yet as he trotted westward under the high south wall of the Keep, he had a precarious aspect, like a man trying to balance himself on a tree limb that was too small. He had spent a good part of the night reviewing the decisions he had made in the war council, and they scared him. He had committed the Lords and the Warward to a path as narrow and fatal as a swaying tight-rope.

But he had no choice. He had either to go ahead or to abandon his command, leave the war in Quaan's worthy but unimaginative hands. So in spite of his anxiety he did not hesitate. He intended to show all the Land that he was the Warmark for good reason.

Time was urgent. The Warward had to begin its southward march as soon as possible. So he trusted Mehryl to carry him through his inward fog. Letting the Ranyhyn pick their way, he hastened towards the blue lake where the rafts were being built.

Before he rounded the last wide foothill, he moved among scattered ranks of warriors holding horses. Men and women saluted him as he passed, but he could recognize none of them. He held up his right hand in blank acknowledgement, and rode down the thronged road without speaking. If his strategy failed, these warriors – and the two hundred Bloodguard who had already followed Lord Callindrill towards the Mithil valley – would be the first to pay for his mistake.

He found the edge of the lake by the roar of the Falls and the working sounds of the raft builders, and slipped immediately off Mehryl's back. The first shadowy figure that came near him he sent in search of Hiltmark Quaan. Moments later, Quaan's solid form appeared out of the fog, accompanied by a lean man carrying a staff – Lord Verement. Troy spoke directly to the Hiltmark. He felt uneasy about giving orders to a Lord.

'How many rafts are ready?'

'Three and twenty are now in the water,' Quaan replied. 'Five yet lack the *rhadhamaerl* rudders, but that task will be accomplished by sunrise.'

'And the rest?'

'Hearthrall Borillar and the raft builders promise that all one hundred and twenty will be complete by dawn tomorrow.'

'Damn! Another day gone. Well, you can't wait for them. Lord Callindrill is going to need help faster than that.' He calculated swiftly, then went on: 'Send the rafts downriver in groups of twenty – two Eoman at a time. If there's any trouble, I want them to be able to defend themselves. You go first. And – Lord Verement, will you go with Quaan?'

Verement answered with a sharp nod.

'Good. Now, Quaan. Get your group going right away. Put whomever you want in command of the other Eoward – tell them to follow you in turn just as soon as another twenty rafts are ready to go. Have the warriors who are going last try to help the raft builders – speed this job up.'

His private fog was clearing now as the sun started to rise. Quaan's age-lined bulwark of a face drifted into better focus, and Troy fell silent for a moment, half dismayed by what he was asking his friend to do. Then he shook his head roughly, forced himself to continue.

'Quaan, you've got the worst job in this whole damn business. You and those Bloodguard with Callindrill. You have got to make this plan of mine work.'

'If it can be done, we will do it,' Quaan spoke steadily, almost easily, but his experience with grim, desperate undertakings gave his statement conviction.

Troy went on hurriedly, 'You've got to hold Foul's army in that valley. Even after you get your whole force there, you're going to be outnumbered ten to one. You've got to hold Foul back, and still keep enough of your force alive to lead him down to Doom's Retreat.'

'I understand.'

'No, you don't. I haven't told you the worst of it yet. You have got to hold Foul back for eight days.'

'Eight?' Verement snapped. 'You jest!'

Controlling himself sternly, Troy said, 'Figure it out for yourself. We've got to march all the way to Doom's Retreat. We need that much time just to get there. Eight days will hardly give us time to get in position.'

'You ask much,' Quaan said slowly.

'You're the man who can do it,' Troy replied. 'And the truth is, the warriors'll follow you better in a situation like that than they would me. You'll have two Lords working with you, plus all the Bloodguard Callindrill has left. There's nobody who can take your place.'

Quaan met this in silence. Despite the square set of his shoulders, he appeared to be hesitating. Troy leaned close to him, whispered intently through the noise of Furl Falls, 'Hiltmark, if you accomplish what I ask, I swear that I will win this war.'

'Swear?' Verement cut in again. 'Does the Despiser know that you bind him with your oaths?'

Troy ignored the Lord. 'I mean it. If you get the chance for me, I won't waste it.'

A low, war-ready grin touched Quaan's lips. 'I hear you,' he said. 'I felt the dour hand of your skill when you won the command of the Warward from me. Warmark, you will be given your eight days if they lie within the reach of human thew and will.'

'Good!' Quaan's promise gave Troy an obscure feeling of relief, as if he were no longer alone on his narrow limb. 'Now. When you engage Foul in the Mithil valley, what you've got to do is force him southward. Push him down into the southern hills – the farther the better. Hold the valley closed until he has enough of his army in the hills to attack you from that side. Then run like hell straight towards Doom's Retreat.'

'That will be costly.'

'Not as costly as letting that army go north when we're in the south.' Quaan nodded grimly, and Troy went on, 'And not as costly as letting Foul get to the Retreat ahead of us. Whatever else happens, we've got to avoid that. If you can't hold him back eight days' worth, you'll have to figure out where we are, and lead him to us instead of to the Retreat. We'll try to pull him the last way south ourselves.'

Quaan nodded again, and the lines of his face clenched. To relax him, Troy said dryly, 'Of course, it would be better if you just defeated him yourself, and saved us the trouble.'

The Hiltmark started to reply, but Lord Verement interrupted him. 'If that is your desire, you should choose someone other than an old warrior and a Ranyhyn-less Lord to do your bidding.'

Troy was about to respond when he heard hooves coming towards him from the direction of Revelstone. Now the sun had started to rise – light danced on the blue water pouring over the top of the Falls – and the fog over his vision had begun to fade. When he turned, he made out the Bloodguard Ruel riding towards him.

Ruel stopped his Ranyhyn with a touch of his hand, and said without dismounting, 'Warmark, the Warward is ready. High Lord Elena awaits you.'

'On my way,' Troy answered, and swung back to Quaan. For a moment, the Hiltmark's gaze replied firmly to his. Torn between affection and resolve, he muttered, 'By God, I will earn what you do for me.' Springing onto Mehryl's back, he started away.

He moved so suddenly that he almost ran into Manethrall Rue. She had been standing a short distance away, regarding Mehryl as if she expected to find that Troy had injured the Ranyhyn. Unintentionally he urged his mount straight towards her. But she stepped aside just as he halted the Ranyhyn.

Her presence surprised him. He acknowledged her, then waited for her to speak. He felt that she deserved any courtesy he could give her.

While she stroked Mehryl's nose with loving hands, she said as if she were explaining something, 'I have done my part in your war. I will do no more. I am old, and need rest. I will ride your rafts to Andelain, and from there make my own way homeward.'

'Very well.' He could not deny her permission to ride a raft, but he sensed that this was only a preparation for what she meant to say.

After a heavy pause, she went on: 'I will have no further use for this.' With a brusque movement, she twitched the fighting cord from her hair, hesitated, then handed it to Troy. Softly, she said, 'Let there be peace between us.'

Because he could think of no fit response, he accepted the cord. But it gave him a pang, as if he were not worthy of it. He tucked it into his belt, and with his hands free, he gave the Manethrall his best approximation of a Ramen bow.

She bowed in turn, gestured for him to move on. But as he started away, she called after him, 'Tell Covenant Ringthane that he must defeat Fangthane. The Ranyhyn have reared to him. They require him. He must not let them fall.' Then she was gone, out of sight in the mist.

The thought of Covenant gave him a bitter taste in his mouth, but he forced it down. With Ruel at his side, he left Quaan shouting orders, and urged Mehryl into a brisk trot up the road towards the gate of Revelstone. As he moved, the sunrise began to burn away the last dimness of his vision. The great wrought wall of the Keep became visible; it shone in the new light with a vivid glory that made him feel at once both small and resolute. In it, he caught a glimpse of the true depth of his willingness to sacrifice himself for the Land. Now he could only hope that what he had to offer would be enough.

There was only one thing for which he could not forgive Covenant. That was the Unbeliever's refusal to fight.

Then he topped the last rise, and found the Lords assembled before the gates, above the long, ranked massing of the Warward.

The sight of the Warward gave him a surge of pride. This army was his – a tool of his own shaping, a weapon which he had sharpened himself and knew how to wield. Each warrior stood in place in an Eoman; each Eoman held its position around the fluttering standard of its Eoward; and the thirty-eight Eoward spread out around the foot of Lord's Keep like a human mantle. More than fifteen thousand metal breastplates caught the rising fire of the sun.

All the warriors were on foot except the Hafts and a third of the Warhafts. These officers were mounted to bear the standards and the marching drums, and to carry messages and commands through the Warward. Troy was acutely aware that the one thing his army lacked was some instantaneous means of communication. Without such a resource, he felt more vulnerable than he liked to admit. To make up for it, he had developed a network of riders who could shuttle from place to place in battle. And he had trained his officers in complex codes of signals and flares and banners, so that under at least some circumstances messages could be communicated by sight. But he was not satisfied. Thousands upon thousands of lives were in his hands. As he gazed out over his command, his tree limb seemed to be shaking in the wind.

He swung away from the Warward, and scanned the mounted gathering before the gates. Only Trevor and Loerya were absent. The Lords Amatin and Mhoram were there, with twenty Bloodguard, a handful of Hirebrands and Gravelingases, all the visiting Lorewardens, and First Haft Amorine. Covenant sat on a *clingor* saddle astride one of the Revelstone mustangs. And at his side was the High Lord. Myrha, her golden Ranyhyn mare, made her look more than ever like a concentrated heroine, a noble figure like that legended Queen for whom Berek had fought his great war.

She was leaning towards Covenant, listening to him with interest – almost with deference – in every line of her form.

The sight galled Troy.

His own feelings for the High Lord were confused; he could not fit them into any easy categories. She was the Lord who had taught him the meaning of sight. And as he had learned to see, she had taught him the Land, introduced him to it with such gentle delight that he always thought of her and the Land together, as if she herself summarized it. When he came to understand the peril of the Land – when he began to search for a way to serve what he saw – she was the one who breathed life into his ideas. She recognized the potential value of his tactical skill, put faith in it; she gave his voice the power of command. Because of her, he was now giving orders of great risk, and leading the Warward in a cause for which he would not be ashamed to die.

Yet Covenant appeared insensitive to her, immune to her. He wore an aura of weary bitterness. His beard darkened his whole face, as if to assert that he had not one jot or tittle of belief to his name. He looked like an Unbeliever, an infidel. And his presence seemed to demean the High Lord, sully her Landlike beauty.

Various sour thoughts crossed Troy's mind, but one was uppermost. There was still something he had to say to Covenant – not because Covenant would or could profit from it, but because he, Troy, wanted to leave no doubt in Covenant's mind.

The Warmark waited until Elena had turned away to speak with Mhoram. Then he pulled Mehryl up to Covenant's side. Without preamble, he said bluntly, 'There's something I've got to tell you before we leave. I want you to know that I spoke against you to the Council. I told them what you did to Trell's daughter.'

Covenant cocked an eyebrow. After a pause, he said, 'And then you found out that they already knew all about it.'

'Yes.' For an instant, he wondered how Covenant had known this. Then he went on: 'So I demanded to know why they put up with you. I told them they can't afford to waste their time and strength rehabilitating people like you when they've got Foul to worry about.'

'What did they say?'

'They made excuses for you. They told me that not all crimes are committed by evil people. They told me that sometimes a good man does ill because of the pain in his soul. Like Trell. And Mhoram told me that the blade of your Unbelief cuts both ways.'

'And that surprises you?'

'Yes! I told them – '

'You should have expected it. Or what did you think this Oath of Peace is about? It's a commitment to the forgiving of lepers – of Kevin and Trell. As if forgiveness weren't the one thing no leper or criminal either could ever have any use for.'

Troy stared into Covenant's grey, gaunt face. Covenant's tone confused him. The words seemed to be bitter, even cynical, but behind them was a timbre of pain, a hint of self-judgment, which he had not expected to hear. Once again, he was torn between anger at the folly of the Unbeliever's stubbornness and amazement at the extent of Covenant's injury. An obscure shame made him feel that he should apologize. But he could not force himself to go that far. Instead, he gave a relenting sigh, and said, 'Mhoram also suggested that I should be patient with you. Patience. I wish I had some. But the fact is – '

'I know,' Covenant murmured. 'The fact is that you're starting to find out just how terrible all this responsibility is. Let me know when you start to feel like a failure. We'll commiserate together.'

That stung Troy. 'I'm not going to fail!' he snapped.

Covenant grimaced ambiguously. 'Then let me know when you succeed, and I'll congratulate you.'

With an effort, Troy swallowed his anger. He was in no mood to be tolerant of Covenant, but for his own sake – and Elena's – rather than for the Unbeliever's, he said, 'Covenant, I really don't understand what your trouble is. But if there's ever anything I can do for you, I'll do it.'

Covenant did not meet his gaze. Self-sarcastically, the Unbeliever muttered, 'I'll probably need it.'

Troy shrugged. He leaned his weight to send Mehryl towards First Haft Amorine. But then he saw Hearthrall Tohrm striding towards them from the gate of the Keep. He held Mehryl back, and waited for the Gravelingas.

When Tohrm stepped between their mounts, he saluted them both, then turned to Covenant. The usual playfulness of his expression was cloaked in sobriety as he said, 'Ur-Lord, may I speak?'

Covenant glowered at him from under his eyebrows, but did not refuse.

After a brief pause, Tohrm said, 'You will soon depart from Revelstone, and it may be that yet another forty years will pass before you return again. Perhaps I will live forty years more – but the chance is uncertain. And I am still in your debt. Ur-Lord Covenant, may I give you a gift?'

Reaching into his robe, he pulled out and held up a smooth, lopsided stone no larger than his palm. Its appearance struck the

Warmark. It gave the impression of being transparent, but he could not see through it; it seemed to open into unglimpsed depths like a hole in the visible fabric of Tohrm's hand and the air and the ground.

Startled, Covenant asked, 'What is it?'

'It is *orcrest*, a rare piece of the One Rock which is the heart of the Earth. The Earthpower is abundant in it, and it may serve you in many ways. Will you accept it?'

Covenant stared at the *orcrest* as if there were something cruel in Tohrm's offer. 'I don't want it.'

'I do not offer it for any want,' said Tohrm. 'You have the white gold, and need no gifts of mine. No, I offer it out of respect for my old friend Birinair, whom you released from the fire which consumed him. I offer it in gratitude for a brave deed.'

'Brave?' Covenant muttered thickly. 'I didn't do it for him. Don't you know that?'

'The deed was done by your hand. No one in the Land could do such a thing. Will you accept it?'

Slowly, Covenant reached out and took the stone. As his left hand closed around it, it changed colour, took on an argent gleam from his wedding ring. Seeing this, he quickly shoved it into the pocket of his pants. Then he cleared his throat, and said, 'If I ever – if I ever get a chance – I'll give it back to you.'

Tohrm grinned. 'Courtesy is like a drink at a mountain stream. Ur-Lord, it is in my heart that behind the thunder of your brow you are a strangely courteous man.'

'Now you're making fun of me,' Covenant replied glumly.

The Hearthrall laughed at this as if it were a high jest. With a sprightly step, he moved away to re-enter the Keep.

Warmark Troy frowned. Everyone in Revelstone seemed to see something in Covenant that he himself could not perceive. To escape that thought, he sent Mehryl trotting from Covenant's side towards his army.

First Haft Amorine joined him a short way down the hill, and together they spent a brief time speaking with the mounted Warhafts who carried the drums. Troy counted out the pace he wanted them to set, and made sure that they knew it by heart. It was faster than the beat he had trained into them, and he did not want the army to lag. In the back of his mind, he chafed at the delay which kept the march from starting. The sun was well up now; the Warward had already lost the dawn.

He was discussing the terrain ahead with his First Haft when a murmur ran through the army. All the warriors turned towards the great Keep. The Lords Trevor and Loerya had finally arrived.

They stood atop the tower which guarded Revelstone's gates. Between them they held a bundle of blue cloth.

As the Lords took their places, the inhabitants of the Keep began to appear at the south wall. In a rush, they thronged the balconies and ramparts, filled the windows, crowded out onto the edge of the plateau. Their voices rolled expectantly.

Leaving Amorine with the army, Warmark Hile Troy rode back up the hill to take his place with the Lords while Trevor and Loerya busied themselves around the tall flagpole atop the tower. His blood suddenly stirred with eagerness, and he wanted to shout some kind of cry, hurl some fierce defiance at the Despiser.

When Trevor and Loerya were ready, they waved to High Lord Elena. At their signal, she clapped Myrha with her heels, and galloped away from her mounted companions. A short distance away, between the wall of the Keep and the main body of the Warward, she halted. Swinging Myrha in a tight circle with the Staff of Law raised high over her head, she shouted to the warriors and the inhabitants of Revelstone, 'Hail!' Her clear cry echoed off the cliffs like a tantara, and was answered at once by one thrilling shout from a myriad of voices:

'Hail!'

'My friends, people of the Land!' she called out to them, 'the time has come. War is upon us, and we march to meet it. Hear me, all! I am the High Lord, holder of the Staff of Law – sworn and dedicate to the services of the Land. At my will, we march to do battle with the Grey Slayer – to pit our strength against him for the sake of the Earth. Hear me! It is I, Elena daughter of Lena, who say it: do not fear! Be of strong heart and bold hand. If it lies within our power, we will prevail!'

As she held high the Staff, she caught the early sunlight. Her hair shone about her like an anadem, and the golden Ranyhyn bore her up like an offering to the wide day. For a moment, she had a look of immolation, and Troy almost choked on the fear of losing her. But there was nothing sacrificial in the upright peal of her voice as she addressed the people of Revelstone.

'Do not mistake. This peril is severe – the gravest danger of our age. It may be that all we have ever seen or heard or felt will be lost. If we are to live – if the Land is to live – we must wrest life from the Despiser. It is a task that surpassed the Old Lords who came before us.

'But I say to you, do not fear! The coming battle is our great test, our soul measure. It is our opportunity to repudiate utterly the Desecration which destroys what it loves. It is our opportunity to shape courage and service and faith out of the very rock of doom. Even if we fall, we will not despair.

'Yet I do not believe that we shall fall.' Taking the Staff in one hand, she thrust it straight towards the heavens, and a bright flame burst from its end. 'Hear me, all!' she cried. 'Hear the Dedication in Time of War!' Then she opened her throat and began to sing a song that pulsed like the stalking of drums.

Friends! comrades!
Proud people of the Land!
There is war upon us;
blood and pain and killing are at hand.
Together we confront the test of death.

Friends and comrades,
remember Peace!
Repeat the Oath with every breath.
Until the end and Time's release,
we bring no fury or despair,
no passion of hatred, spite, or slaughter,
no Desecration to the service of the Land.
We fight to mend, anneal, repair —
to free the Earth of detestation;
for health and home and wood and stone,
for beauty's fragrant bloom and gleam,
and rivers clear and fair
we strike;
nor will we cease,
let fall our heads to ash and dust,
lose faith and heart and hope and bone.

We strike
until the Land is clean of wrong and pain,
and we have kept our trust.
Let no great whelm of evil wreak despair!
Remember Peace:
brave death!
We are the proud preservers of the Land!

As she finished, she turned Myrha, faced the watchtower. From the Staff of Law, she sent crackling into the sky a great, branched lightning tree. At this sign, Lord Loerya threw her bundle into the air, and Lord Trevor pulled strongly on the lines of the flagpole. The defiant war-flag of Revelstone sprang open and snapped in the mountain wind. It was a huge oriflamme, twice as tall as the Lords who raised it, and it was clear blue, the colour of High Lord's Furl, with one stark black streak across it. As it flapped and fluttered, a mighty cheer rose up from the Warward, and was repeated on the thronged wall of Revelstone.

For a moment, High Lord Elena kept the Staff blazing. Then she silenced her display of power. As the shouting subsided, she looked at the group of riders, and called firmly, 'Warmark Hile Troy! Let us begin!'

At once, Troy sent Mehryl prancing towards the Warward. When he was alone in front of the riders, he saluted his second-in-command, and said quietly, to control his excitement, 'First Haft Amorine, you may begin.'

She returned his salute, swung her mount towards the army.

'Warward!' she shouted. 'Order!'

With a wide surge, the warriors came to attention.

'Drummers ready!'

The pace-beaters raised their sticks. When she thrust her right fist into the air, they began their beat, pounding out together the rhythm Troy had taught them.

'Warriors, march!'

As she gave the command, she pulled down her fist. Nearly sixteen thousand warriors started forward to the cadence of the drums.

Troy watched their precision with a lump of pride in his throat. At Amorine's side, he moved with his army down the road towards the river.

The rest of the riders followed close behind him. Together, they kept pace with the Warward as it marched westward under the high south wall of Revelstone.

13

THE ROCK GARDENS OF THE MAERL

Together, the riders and the marching Warward passed down the road to the wide stone bridge which crossed the White River a short distance south of the lake. As they mounted the bridge, they received a chorus of encouraging shouts from the horsemen and raft builders at the lake; but Warmark Troy did not look that way. From the top of the span, he gazed downriver: there he could see the last rafts of

Hiltmark Quaan's first two Eoward moving around a curve and out of sight. They were only a small portion of Troy's army, but they were crucial. They were risking their lives in accordance with his commands, and the fate of the Land went with them. In pride and trepidation, he watched until they were gone, on their way to receive the measure of bloodshed he had assigned to them. Then he rode on precariously across the bridge.

Beyond it, the road turned southward, and began winding down away from the Keep's plateau towards the rough grasslands which lay between Revelstone and Trothgard. As he moved through the foothills, Troy counted the accompanying Hirebrands and Gravelingases, to be sure that the Warward had its full complement of support from the *lillianrill* and *rhadhamaerl*. In the process, he caught a glimpse of an extra Gravelingas mounted and travelling behind the group of riders.

Trell.

The powerful Gravelingas kept to the back of the group, but he made no attempt to hide his face or his presence. The sight of him gave Troy a twinge of anxiety. He stopped and waited for the High Lord. Motioning the other riders past him, he said to Elena in a low voice, 'Did you know that he's coming with us? Is it all right with you?' High Lord Elena met him with a questioning look which he answered by nodding towards Trell.

Covenant had stopped with Elena, and at Troy's nod he turned to look behind him. When he saw the Gravelingas, he groaned.

Most of the riders were past Elena, Troy, and Covenant now, and Trell could clearly see the three watching him. He halted where he was — still twenty-five yards away — and returned Covenant's gaze with a raw, bruised stare.

For a moment, they all held their positions, regarded each other intently. Then Covenant cursed under his breath, gripped the reins of his horse, and moved up the road towards Trell.

Bannor started after the Unbeliever, but High Lord Elena stopped him with a quick gesture. 'He needs no protection,' she said quietly. 'Do not affront Trell with your doubt.'

Covenant faced Trell, and the two men glared at each other. Then Covenant said something. Troy could not hear what he said, but the Gravelingas answered it with a red-rimmed stare. Under his tunic, his broad chest heaved as if he were panting. His reply was inaudible also.

There was violence in Trell's limbs, struggling for action; Troy could see it. He did not understand Elena's assertion that Covenant was safe. As he watched, he whispered to her, 'What did Covenant say?'

Elena responded as if she could not be wrong, 'The ur-Lord promises that he will not harm me.'

This surprised Troy. He wanted to know why Covenant would try to reassure Trell in that way, but he could not think of a way to ask Elena what the connection was between her and Trell. Instead, he asked, 'What's Trell's answer?'

'Trell does not believe the promise.'

Silently, Troy congratulated Trell's common sense.

A moment later, Covenant jerked his horse into motion, and came trotting back down the road. His free hand pulled insistently at his beard. Without looking at Elena, he shrugged his shoulders defensively as he said, 'Well, he has a good point.' Then he urged his mount into a canter to catch up with the rest of the riders.

Troy wanted to wait for Trell, but the High Lord firmly took him with her, as she followed Covenant. Out of respect for the Gravelingas, Troy did not look back.

But when the Warward broke march at midday for food and rest, Troy saw Trell eating with the other *rhadhamaerl*.

By that time, the army had wound out of the foothills into the more relaxed grasslands west of the White River. Troy gauged the distance they had covered, and used it as a preliminary measure of the pace he had set for the march. So far, the pace seemed right. But many factors influenced a day's march. The Warmark spent part of the afternoon with First Haft Amorine, discussing how to match the frequency and duration of rest halts with such variables as the terrain, the distance already traversed, and the state of the supplies. He wanted to prepare her for his absences.

He was glad to talk about his battle plan; he felt proud of it, as if it were a work of objective beauty. Traditionally, beaten people fled to Doom's Retreat, but he meant to remake it into a place of victory. His plan was the kind of daring strategic stroke that only a blind man could create. But after a time Amorine responded by gesturing over the Warward and saying dourly, 'One day of such a pace is no great matter. Even five days may give no distress to a good warrior. But twenty days, or thirty – In that time, this pace may kill.'

'I know,' Troy replied carefully. His trepidation returned in a rush. 'But we haven't got any choice. Even at this pace, too many warriors and Bloodguard are going to get killed buying us the time we need.'

'I hear you,' Amorine grated. 'We will keep the pace.'

When the army stopped for the night, Mhoram, Elena, and Amatin moved among the bright campfires, singing songs and telling gleeful Giantish stories to buttress the hearts of the warriors. As he watched them, Troy felt a keen regret that long days would pass

539

before the Lords could again help Amorine maintain the Warward's spirit.

But the separation was necessary. High Lord Elena had several reasons for visiting the Loresraat. But Revelwood was out of the way; the added distance was prohibitive for the marching warriors. So the Lords and the Warward parted company the next afternoon. The three Lords, accompanied by Covenant and Troy, the twenty Bloodguard, and the Lorewardens, turned with the road southwest towards Trothgard and Revelwood. And First Haft Amorine led the Warward, with its mounted Hirebrands and Gravelingases, almost due south in a direct line towards Doom's Retreat.

Troy had business of his own at the Loresraat, and he was forced to leave Amorine alone in command of his army. That afternoon, the autumn sky turned dim as rainclouds moved heavily eastward. When he gave the First Haft his final instructions, his vision was blurred; he had to peer through an ominous haze. 'Keep the pace,' he said curtly. 'Push it even faster when you reach easier ground past the Grey River. If you can gain a little time, we won't have to drive so hard around the Last Hills. If those Bloodguard the High Lord sent out were able to do their jobs, there should be plenty of supplies along the way. We'll catch up to you in the Centre Plains.' His voice was stiff with awareness of the difficulties she faced.

Amorine responded with a nod that expressed her seasoned resolve. A light rain started to fall. Troy's vision became so clouded that he could no longer make out individual figures in the massed Warward. He gave the First Haft a tight salute, and she turned to lead the warriors angling away from the road.

The Lords and Lorewardens gave a shout of encouragement, but Troy did not join in. He took Mehryl to the top of a bare knoll, and stood there with his ebony sword raised against the drizzle while the whole length of his army passed by like a shadow in the fog below him. He told himself that the Warward was not going into battle without him – that his warriors would only march until he rejoined them. But the thought did not ease him. The Warward was his tool, his means of serving the Land; and when he returned to the other riders he felt awkward, disjointed, almost dismembered, as if only the skill of the Ranyhyn kept him on balance. He rode on through the rest of the day wrapped in the familiar loneliness of the blind.

The drizzle continued throughout the remainder of the afternoon, all that night, and most of the next day. Despite the piled thickness of the clouds, the rain did not come down hard; but it kept out the sunlight, tormented Troy by obscuring his vision. In the middle of the night, sleeping in wet blankets that seemed to cling to him like winding sheets, he was snatched awake by a wild, inchoate conviction that the weather would be overcast when he went into battle at Doom's Retreat. He needed sunlight, clarity. If he could not see – !

He arose depressed, and did not recover his usual confidence until the rainclouds finally blew away to the east, letting the sun return to him.

Before midmorning the next day, the company of the Lords came in sight of the Maerl River. They had been travelling faster since they had left the Warward, and when they reached the river, the northern boundary of Trothgard, they were half-way to Revelwood. The Maerl flowed out of high places in the Westron Mountains, and ran first northeast, then southeast, until it joined the Grey, became part of the Grey, and went eastward to the Soulsease. Beyond the Maerl was the region where the Lords concentrated their efforts to heal the ravages of Desecration and war.

Trothgard had borne the name Kurash Plenethor, Stricken Stone, from the last years of Kevin Landwaster until it was rechristened when the new Lords first swore their oath of service after the Desecration. At that time, the region had been completely blasted and barren. The last great battle between the Lords and the Despiser had taken place there, and had left it burned, ruined, soaked in scorched blood, almost soilless. Some of the old tales said that Kurash Plenethor had smoked and groaned for a hundred years after that last battle. And forty years ago the Maerl River had still run thick with eroded and infertile mud.

But now there was only a trace of silt left in the current. For all the limitations of their comprehension, the Lords had learned much about the nurturing of damaged earth from the Second Ward, and on this day the Maerl carried only a slight haze of impurity. Because of centuries of past erosion, it lay in a ravine like a crack across the land. But the sides of the ravine were gentle with deep-rooted grasses and shrubs, and healthy trees lifted their boughs high out of the gully.

The Maerl was a vital river again.

Looking down into it from the edge of the ravine, the company paused for a moment of gladness. Together, Elena, Mhoram, and Amatin sang softly part of the Lords' oath. Then they galloped down the slope and across the road ford, so that the hooves of the Ranyhyn and the horses made a gay, loud splashing as they passed into Trothgard.

This region lay between the Westron Mountains and the Maerl, Grey, and Rill rivers. Within these borders, the effects of the Lords' care were everywhere, in everything. Generations of Lords had made Stricken Stone into a hale woodland, a wide hilly country of forests and glades and dales. Whole grassy hillsides were vivid with small blue and yellow flowers. For scores of leagues south and west of the riders, profuse *aliantha* and deep grasses were full of gold-leaved Gilden and other trees, cherry and apple and white linden, prodigious oaks and elms and maples anademed in autumn glory. And air that for decades after the battle had still echoed with the blasts and shrieks of war was now so clear and clean that it seemed to glisten with birdcalls.

This was what Troy had first seen when his vision began; this was what Elena had used to teach him the meaning of sight.

Riding now on Mehryl's back under brilliant sun in Trothgard's luminous ambience, he felt more free of care than he had for a long time.

As the company of the Lords moved through the early part of the afternoon, the country around them changed. Piles of tumbled rock began to appear among the trees and through the greensward; rugged boulders several times taller than the riders thrust their heads out of the ground, and smaller stones overgrown with moss and lichen lay everywhere. Soon the company seemed to be riding within the ancient rubble of a shattered mountain, a tall, incongruous peak which had risen out of the hills of Kurash Plenethor until some immense force had blasted it to bits.

They were approaching the rock gardens of the Maerl.

Troy had never taken the time to study the gardens, but he knew that they were said to be the place where the best *suru-pa-maerl* Craftmasters of the *rhadhamaerl* did their boldest work. Though in the past few years he had ridden along this road through the bristling rocks many times, he could not say where the gardens themselves began. Except for a steady increase in the amount of rubble lying on or sticking through the grass, he could locate no specific changes or boundaries until the company crested a hill above a wide valley. Then at least he was sure that he was in one of the gardens.

Most of the long, high hillside facing the valley was thickly covered with stones, as if it had once been the heart of the ancient shattered peak. The rocks clustered and bulged on all sides, raising themselves up in huge piles or massive single boulders, so that virtually the only clear ground on the steep slope was the roadway.

None of these rocks and boulders was polished or chipped or shaped in any way, though scattered individual stones and clusters of stones appeared to have had their moss and lichen cleaned away. And they all seemed to have been chosen for their natural grotesquerie. Instead of sitting or resting on the ground, they jutted and splintered and scowled and squatted and gaped, reared and cowered and blustered like a mad, packed throng of troglodytes terrified or ecstatic to be breathing open air. On its way to the valley, the road wandered among the weird shapes as if it were lost in a garish forest, so that as they moved downward the riders were constantly in the shadow of one tormented form or another.

Troy knew that the jumbled amazement of that hillside was not natural; it had been made by men for some reason which he did not grasp.

On past journeys, he had never been interested enough in it to ask about its significance. But now he did not object when High Lord Elena suggested that the company go to look at the work from a distance. Across the grassy bottom of the valley was another hill, even steeper and higher than the one it faced. The road turned left, and went away along the bottom of the valley, ignoring the plainer hill. Elena suggested that the riders climb this hill to look back at the gardens.

She spoke to her companions generally, but her gaze was on Covenant. When he acquiesced with a vague shrug, she responded as if he had expressed the willingness of all the riders.

The front of the hill was too steep for the horses, so they turned right and cantered up the valley until they found a place where they could swing around and mount the hill from behind. As they rode, Troy began to feel mildly expectant. The High Lord's eagerness to show the view to Covenant invested it with interest. He remembered other surprises – like the Hall of Gifts, which had not interested him until Mhoram had practically dragged him to it.

At the top, the hill bulged into a bare knoll. The riders left their mounts behind, and climbed the last distance on foot. They moved quickly, sharing Elena's mood, and soon reached the crest.

Across the valley, the rock garden lay open below them, displayed like a bas-relief. From this distance, they could easily see that all its jumbled rock formed a single pattern.

Out of tortured stone, the makers of the garden had designed a wide face – a broad countenance with lumped, gnarled and twisted features. The unevenness of the rock made the face appear bruised and contorted; its eyes were as ragged as deep wounds, and the roadway cut through it like an aimless scar. But despite all this, the face was stretched with a grin of immense cheerfulness. The unexpectedness of it startled Troy into a low, glad burst of laughter.

Though the Lords and Lorewardens were obviously familiar with the garden, all their faces shared a look of joy, as if the displayed hilarious grin were contagious. High Lord Elena clasped her hands together to contain a surge of happiness, and Lord Mhoram's eyes glittered with keen pleasure. Only Covenant did not smile or nod, or show any other sign of gladness. His face was gaunt as a shipwreck. His eyes held a restless, haggard look of their own, and his right hand fumbled at his ring in a way that emphasized his two missing fingers. After a moment, he muttered through the company's murmuring, 'Well, the Giants certainly must be proud of you.'

His tone was ambiguous, as if he were trying to say two contradictory things at once. But his reference to the Giants overshadowed anything else he might have meant. Lord Amatin's smile faltered, and a sudden scrutinizing gleam sprang from under Mhoram's brow. Elena moved towards him, intending to speak, but before she could begin, he went on, 'I knew a woman like that once.' He was striving to sound casual, but his voice was awkward. 'At the leprosarium.'

Troy groaned inwardly, but held himself still.

'She was beau – Of course, I didn't know her then. And she didn't have any pictures of herself, or if she did she didn't show them. I don't think she could even stand to look in the mirror any more. But the doctors told me that she used to be beautiful. She had a smile – Even when I knew her, she could still smile. It looked just like that.' He nodded in the direction of the rock garden, but he did not look at it. He was concentrating on his memory.

'She was a classic case.' As he continued, his tone became harsher and more bitter. He articulated each word distinctly, as if it had jagged edges. 'She was exposed to leprosy as a kid in the Philippines or somewhere – her parents were stationed there in the military, I suppose – and it caught up with her right after she got married. Her toes went numb. She should have gone to a doctor right then, but she didn't. She was one of those people whom you can't interrupt. She couldn't take time away from her husband and friends to worry about cold toes.

'So she lost her toes. She finally went to a doctor when her feet began to cramp so badly that she could hardly walk, and eventually he figured out what was wrong with her, and sent her to the leprosarium, and the doctors there had to amputate. That gave her some trouble – it's hard to walk when you don't have any toes – but she was irrepressible. Before long she was back with her husband.

'But she couldn't have any kids. It's just criminal folly for lepers who know better to have any kids. Her husband understood that – but he still wanted children, and so in due course he divorced her. That hurt her, but she survived it. Before long, she had a job and new friends and a new life. And she was back in the leprosarium. She was just too full of vitality and optimism to take care of herself. This time, two of her fingers were numb.

'That cost her her job. She was a secretary, and needed her fingers. And of course her boss didn't want any lepers working for him. But once her disease was arrested again, she learned how to type without using those dead fingers. Then she moved to a new area, got another job, more new friends, and went right on living as if absolutely nothing had happened.

'At about this time – or so they told me – she conceived a passion for folk dancing. She'd learned something about it in her travels as a kid, and now it became her hobby, her way of making new friends and telling them that she loved them. With her bright clothes and her smile, she was – '

He faltered, then went on almost at once. 'But she was back in the leprosarium two years later. She didn't have very good footing, and she took too many falls. And not enough medication. This time she lost her right leg below the knee. Her sight was starting to blur, and her right hand was pretty much crippled. Lumps were growing in her face, and her hair was falling out.

'As soon as she learned how to hobble around on her artificial limb, she started folk-dancing lessons for the lepers.

'The doctors kept her a long time, but finally she convinced them to let her out. She swore she was going to take better care of herself this time. She'd learned her lesson, she said, and she wasn't ever coming back.

'For a long time, she didn't come back. But it wasn't because she didn't need to. Bit by bit, she was whittling herself away. When I met her, she was back at the leprosarium because a nursing home had thrown her out. She didn't have anything left except her smile.

'I spent a lot of time in her room, watching her lie there in bed – listening to her talk. I was trying to get used to the stench. Her face looked as if the doctors hit her with clubs every morning, but she still had that smile. Of course, most of her teeth were gone – but her smile hadn't changed.

'She tried to teach me to dance. She'd make me stand where she could see me, and then she'd tell me where to put my feet, when to jump, how to move my legs.' Again he faltered. 'And in between she used to take hours telling me what a full life she'd had.

'She must have been all of forty years old.'

Abruptly, he stooped to the ground, snatched up a stone, and hurled it with all his strength at the grinning face of the rock garden. His throw fell far short, but he did not stop to watch the stone roll into the valley. Turning away from it, he rasped thickly, 'If I ever get my hands on her husband, I'll wring his bloody neck.' Then he strode down off the knoll towards the horses. In a moment, he was astride his mount and galloping away to rejoin the road. Bannor was close behind him.

Troy took a deep breath, trying to shake off the effect of Covenant's tale, but he could think of nothing to say. When he looked over at Elena, he saw that she was melding with Mhoram and Amatin as if she needed their support to bear what she had heard. After a moment, Mhoram said aloud, 'Ur-Lord Covenant is a prophet.'

'Does he foretell the fate of the Land?' Amatin asked painfully.

'No!' Elena's denial was fierce, and Mhoram breathed also, 'No.' But Troy could hear that Mhoram meant something different.

Then the melding ended, and the Lords returned to their mounts. Soon the company was back on the road, riding after Covenant in the direction of Revelwood.

For the rest of the afternoon, Troy was too disturbed by the Lords' reaction to Covenant to relax and enjoy the journey. But the next day, he found a way to soothe his vague distress. He envisioned in detail the separate progresses of the Warward – the Bloodguard riding with Lord Callindrill, the mounted Eoward rafting and galloping, the warriors marching behind Amorine. On his mental map of the Land, these various thrusts had a deliberate symmetry that pleased him in some fundamental way. Before long, he began to feel better.

And Trothgard helped him, also. South of the rock gardens, the Land's mantle of soil became thicker and more fertile, so that the hills through which the company rode had no bare stone jutting up among the grass and flowers. Instead, copses and broad swaths of woodland grew everywhere, punctuating the slopes and unfurling oratorically across the vales and valleys. Under the bright sky and the autumn balm of Trothgard, Troy put his uncertainty about Covenant behind him like a bad dream.

At that point, even the problem of communications did not bother him. Ordinarily, he was even more concerned by his inability to convey messages to Quaan than by his ignorance of what was happening to Korik's mission. But he was on his way to Revelwood. High Lord Elena had promised him that the Loresraat was working on his problem. He looked forward hopefully to the chance that the students of the Staff had found a solution for him.

That evening, he enjoyed the singing and talk of the Lords around the campfire. Mhoram was withdrawn and silent, with a strange look of foreboding in his eyes, and Covenant glowered glum and taciturn into the coals of the fire. But High Lord Elena was in vibrant good spirits. With Amatin, she spread a mood of humour and gaiety over the company until even the sombrest of the Lorewardens seemed to effervesce. Troy thought that she had never looked more lovely.

Yet he went to the blindness of his bed with an ache in his heart.

He could not help knowing that Elena exerted her brilliance for Covenant's sake, not for his.

He fell at once into sleep as if to escape his sightlessness. But in the darkest part of the moonless night, sharp voices and the stamping of hooves roused him. Through the obscure illumination of the fire embers, he saw a Bloodguard on a Ranyhyn standing in the centre of the camp. The Ranyhyn steamed in the cold air; it had galloped hotly to reach the Lords.

First Mark Morin and Lord Mhoram already stood by the Ranyhyn, and the High Lord was hurrying from her blankets with Lord Amatin behind her. Troy threw an armful of kindling on the fire. The sudden blaze gave him a better view of the Bloodguard.

The grime of hard fighting streaked his face, and among the rents there were patches of dried blood on his robe. He dismounted slowly, as if he were tired or reluctant.

Troy felt his balance suddenly waver, as if the tree limb of his efforts for the Land had jumped under his feet. He recognized the Bloodguard. He was Runnik, one of the members of Korik's mission to Seareach.

14

RUNNIK'S TALE

For a moment, Troy groped around him, trying to regain his balance. Runnik should not be here; it was too soon. Only twenty-three days had passed since the departure of Korik's mission. Even the mightiest Ranyhyn could not gallop to Seareach and back in that time. So Runnik's arrival here meant – meant – Even before the High Lord could speak, Troy found himself demanding in a constricted voice, 'What happened? What happened?'

But Elena stopped him with a sharp word. He could see that the implications of Runnik's presence were not lost on her. She stood with the Staff of Law planted firmly on the ground, and her face was full of fire.

At her side, Covenant had a look of nausea, as if he were already sickened by what he expected to hear. He had the aspect of a man who wanted to know whether or not he had a terminal illness as he rasped at the Bloodguard, 'Are they dead?'

Runnik ignored both Covenant and Troy. He nodded to First Mark Morin, then bowed slightly to the High Lord. Despite its flatness, his countenance had a reluctant cast, an angle of unwillingness, that made Troy groan in anticipation.

'Speak, Runnik,' Elena said sternly. 'What word have you brought to us?' And after her Morin said, 'Speak so that the Lords may hear you.'

Yet Runnik did not begin. Barely visible in the background of his unblinking gaze, there was an ache – a pang that Troy had never expected to see in any Bloodguard. 'Sweet Jesus,' he breathed. 'How bad *is* it?'

Then Lord Mhoram spoke. 'Runnik,' he said softly, 'the mission to Seareach was given into the hands of the Bloodguard. This is a difficult burden, for you are Vowed to the preservation of the Lords above all things. There is no blame for you if your Vow and the mission have come into conflict, requiring that one or the other must be set aside. There can be no doubt of the Bloodguard, whatever the doom that brings you to us thus battle-rent at the dark of the moon.'

For a moment longer, Runnik hesitated. Then he said, 'High Lord, I have come from the depths of Sarangrave Flat – from the Defiles Course and the mission to Seareach. To me, and to Pren and Porib with me, Korik said, "Return to the High Lord. Tell her all – all the words of Warhaft Hoerkin, all the struggles of the Ranyhyn, all the attacks of the lurker. Tell her of the fall of Lord Shetra."' Amatin moaned in her throat, and Mhoram stiffened. But Elena held Runnik with the intensity of her face. '"She will know how to hear this tale of Giants and Ravers. Tell her that the mission will not fail."

'"Fist and faith," we three responded. "We will not fail."

'But for four days we strove with the Sarangrave, and Pren fell to the lurker that has awakened. Then we won our way to the west of the Flat, and there regained our Ranyhyn. With our best speed we rode towards Revelstone. But when we entered Grimmerdhore, we were beset by wolves and ur-viles, though we saw no sign of them when we passed eastward. Porib and his Ranyhyn fell so that I might escape, and I rode onward.

'Then on the west of Grimmerdhore, I met with scouts of the Warward, and learned that Corruption was marching, and that the High Lord had ridden towards Revelwood. So I turned aside from Revelstone and came in pursuit to find you here.

'High Lord, there is much that I must say.'

'We will hear you,' Elena said. 'Come.' Turning, she moved to the campfire. There she seated herself with Mhoram and Amatin beside her. At a sign from her, Runnik sat down opposite her, and allowed one of the Lorewardens who had skill as a Healer to clean his cuts. Troy piled wood on the fire so that he could see better, then positioned himself near the Lords on the far side from Covenant. In a moment, Runnik began to speak.

At first, his narration was brief and awkward. The Bloodguard lacked the Giants' gift for storytelling; he skimmed crucial subjects, and ignored things his hearers needed to know. But the Lords questioned him carefully. And Covenant repeatedly insisted on details. At times, he seemed to be trying to stall the narrative, postpone the moment when he would have to hear its outcome. Gradually, the events of the mission began to emerge in a coherent form.

Troy listened intensely. He could see nothing beyond the immediate light of the campfire; nothing distracted his attention. Despite the flatness of Runnik's tone, the Warmark seemed to see what he was hearing as if the mission were taking place in the air before him.

The mission had made its way eastward through Grimmerdhore, and then for three days had ridden in rain. But no rain could halt the Ranyhyn, and this was no great storm. On the eighth day of the mission, when the clouds broke and let sunlight return to the earth, Korik and his party were within sight of Mount Thunder.

It grew steadily against the sky as they rode through the sunshine. They passed twenty-five leagues to the north of it, and reached the great cliff of Landsdrop late that afternoon. They were at one of its highest points, and could look out over the Lower Land from a vantage of more than four thousand feet. Here Landsdrop was as sheer as if the Lower Land had been cut away with an axe. And below it beyond a hilly strip of grassland less than five leagues wide lay Sarangrave Flat.

It was a wet land, latticed with waterways like exposed veins in the flesh of the ground, overgrown with fervid luxuriance, and full of subtle dangers – strange, treacherous, water-bred, and man-shy animals; cunning, old, half-rotten willows and cypresses that sang quiet songs which could bind the unwary; stagnant, poisonous pools, so covered with slime and mud and shallow plants that they looked like solid ground; lush flowers, beautifully bedewed with clear liquids that could drive humans mad; deceptive stretches of dry ground that turned suddenly to quicksand. All this was familiar to the Bloodguard. However ominous to human eyes, or unsuited to human life, Sarangrave Flat was not naturally evil. Rather, because of the darkness which slumbered beneath it, it was simply dangerous – a wild haven for the misborn of the Land, the warped fruit of evils long past. The Giants, who knew how to be wary, had always been able to travel freely through the Flat, and they had kept paths open for others, so that the crossing of the Sarangrave was not normally a great risk.

But now something else met the gaze of the mission. Slumbering evil stirred; the hand of Corruption was at work, awakening old wrongs.

The peril was severe, and Lord Hyrim was dismayed. But neither the Lords nor the Bloodguard were surprised. The Lords Callindrill and Amatin – the Bloodguard Morril and Koral – had spoken of this danger. And though he was dismayed, Lord Hyrim did not propose that the mission should evade the danger by riding north and around Sarangrave Flat, a hundred leagues from their way. Therefore in the dawn of the ninth day the mission descended Landsdrop, using a horse trail which the Old Lords had made in the great cliff, and rode eastward across the grassland foothills towards the main Giantway through the Sarangrave.

The air was noticeably warmer and thicker than it had been above Landsdrop. It breathed as if it were clogged with invisible, damp fibres, and it seemed to leave something behind in the lungs when it was exhaled.

Then shrubs and low, twisted bushes began to appear through the grass. And the grass itself grew longer, wetter. At odd intervals, stray, hidden puddles of water splashed under the hooves of the Ranyhyn. Soon gnarled, lichenous trees appeared, spread out moss-draped limbs. They grew thicker and taller as the mission passed into the Sarangrave. In moments, the riders entered a grassy avenue that lay between two unrippling pools and angled away just north of eastward into a jungle which already appeared impenetrable. The Ranyhyn slowed to a more cautious pace. Abruptly, they found themselves plunging through the chest-deep elephant grass.

When the riders looked behind them, they could see no trace of the Giantway. The Flat had closed like jaws.

But the Bloodguard knew that that was the way of the Sarangrave. Only the path ahead was visible. The Ranyhyn moved on, thrusting their broad chests through the grass.

As the jungle tightened, the Giantway narrowed until they could ride no more than three abreast – each of the Lords flanked by Bloodguard. But the elephant grass receded, allowing them to move with better speed.

Their progress was loud. They disturbed the Flat, and as they travelled they set waves and wakes and noise on both sides. Birds and monkeys gibbered at them; small, furry animals that yipped like hyenas broke out of the grass in front of them and scurried away;

and when the jungle gave way on either side to dark, rancid pools or sluggish streams, waterfowl with iridescent plumage clattered fearfully into the air. Sudden splashes echoed across the still ponds; pale, vaguely human forms darted away under the ripples.

Throughout the morning, the mission followed the winding trail which careful Giants had made in times long past. No danger threatened, but still the Ranyhyn grew tense. When the riders stopped beside a shallow lake to rest and eat, their mounts became increasingly restive. Several of them made low, blowing noises; their ears were up and alert, shifting directions in sharp jerks, almost quivering. One of them – the youngest stallion, bearing the Bloodguard Tull – stamped a hoof irrhythmically. The Lords and the Bloodguard increased their caution, and rode on down the Giantway.

They had covered only two more leagues when Sill called the Bloodguard to observe Lord Hyrim.

The Lord's face was flushed as if he had a high fever. Sweat rolled down his cheeks, and he was panting hoarsely, almost gasping for breath. His eyes glittered. But he was not alone. Lord Shetra, too, was flushed and panting.

Then even the Bloodguard found that they were having trouble breathing. The air felt turgid. It resisted being drawn into their lungs, and once within them it clung there with miry fingers, like the grasp of quicksand.

The sensation grew rapidly worse.

Suddenly, all the noise of the Flat ceased.

It was as Lord Callindrill had said.

But the Lord Amatin's mount had not been a Ranyhyn. Trusting to the great horses, the mission continued on its way.

The riders moved slowly. The Ranyhyn walked with their heads straining forward, ears cocked, nostrils flared. They were sweating, though the air was not warm.

They covered a few hundred yards this way – forcing passage through the stubborn, mucky air and the silence. After that, the jungle fell away on both sides. The Giantway lay along a grassy ridge like a dam between two still pools. One of them was blue and bright, reflecting the sky and the afternoon sunlight, but the other was dark and rank.

The mission was halfway down the ridge when the sound began.

It started low, wet, and weak, like the groan of a dying man. But it seemed to come from the dark pool. It transfixed the riders. As they listened to it, it slowly swelled. It scaled upward in pitch and volume – became a ragged scream – echoed across the pools. Higher and louder it went on. Through it, the Lords shouted together, 'Melenkurion abatha! Duroc minas mill khabaal!' But they could hardly make themselves heard.

Then the young Ranyhyn bearing Tull lost control. It whinnied in fear, whirled and sprang towards the blue pool. As it leaped, Tull threw himself to the safety of the grass.

The Ranyhyn crashed into the chest-deep water. At once, it gave a squeal of pain that almost matched the screaming in the air. Plunging frantically, it heaved itself out of the pool, and fled westward, back down the Giantway.

The howling mounted eagerly higher.

The other Ranyhyn broke and bolted. They reared, spun, pounded away after their fleeing brother. The jerk of their start unhorsed Lord Hyrim, and he only saved himself from the dark pool by a thrust of his staff. Immediately, Lord Shetra dropped off her mount to join him. Sill, Cerrin and Korik also dismounted. As he jumped, Korik ordered the other Bloodguard to protect the Ranyhyn.

Runnik and his comrades clung to their horses. The Ranyhyn followed the injured stallion. As they raced, the howling behind them faded, and the air began to thin. But for some distance, the Bloodguard could not regain control of their mounts. The Ranyhyn plunged along a side path which was unfamiliar; the Bloodguard knew that they had missed the Giantway.

Then the leading Ranyhyn crested a knoll, and blundered without warning into a quagmire. But the rest of the great horses were able to stop safely. The Bloodguard dismounted, and took *clingor* lines from their packs. By the time Korik, Cerrin, Sill, Tull, and the Lords reached them, the free Ranyhyn were busy pulling their trapped kindred from the quagmire.

Seeing that the other Ranyhyn were uninjured, the Lords turned to the stallion which had jumped into the pool. It stood to one side, champed its teeth and jerked its head from side to side in agony. Under its coat all the flesh of its limbs and belly was covered with blisters and boils. Blood streamed from its sores. Through some of them, the bone was visible. Despite the determination in its eyes, it whimpered at the pain.

The Lords were deeply moved. There were tears in Hyrim's eyes, and Shetra cursed bitterly. But they could do nothing. They were not Ramen. And they could find no *amanibhavam*, that potent, yellow-flowered grass which could heal horses but which drives humans mad. They could only close their ears to the stallion's pain, and try to consider what course the mission should take.

Soon all the other Ranyhyn were safe on solid ground. They shed the mud of the quagmire easily, but they could not rid themselves of the shame of their panic. Their eyes showed that they felt they had disgraced themselves.

But when they heard the whimpering of their injured brother, they pricked up their ears. They shuffled their feet and nudged each other. Slowly, their eldest went to face Tull's mount. For a moment, the two spoke together, nose to nose. Several times the younger Ranyhyn nodded its head.

Then the old Ranyhyn reared; he stretched high in the ancient Ranyhyn expression of homage. When he descended, he struck the head of his injured brother powerfully with both fore hooves. The younger horse shuddered once under the force of the blow, and fell dead.

The rest of the Ranyhyn watched in silence. When their eldest turned away from the fallen horse, they nickered their approval and sorrow softly.

In their own way, the Bloodguard were not unmoved. But High Lord Elena had given the need of the Giants into their hands. To the Lords, Korik said, 'We must go. The mission waits. Tull may ride with Doar.'

'No!' Lord Shetra cried. 'We will take the Ranyhyn no deeper into Sarangrave Flat.' And Lord Hyrim said, 'Friend Korik, surely you know as much as we of this force which forbids us to cross the Flat. Surely you know that to stop us this force must first see us. It must perceive us, and know where we are.'

Korik nodded.

'Then you must also know that it is no easy matter to sense the presence of human beings. We are mere ordinary life amid the multitudes of the Sarangrave. But the Ranyhyn are unordinary. They are stronger than we – the power of life burns more brightly in them. Their presence here is more easily seen than ours. It may be that the force against us is attuned to them. The Despiser is wise enough for such strategy. For this reason, we must travel without the Ranyhyn.'

'The mission requires their speed,' Korik said. 'We lack the time to walk.'

'I know,' Hyrim sighed. 'Without mishap, we would spend at least one full cycle of the moon at that journey. But to ride around the Sarangrave will take too long also.'

'Therefore we must ride through. We must fight.'

'Ride through, forsooth,' Shetra snapped. 'We do not know how to fight such a thing – or we would have given it battle already. I tell you plainly, Korik – if we encounter that forbidding again, we will lose more than Ranyhyn. No! We must go another way.'

'What way?'

For a moment, the Lords gazed into each other. Then Lord Shetra said, 'We will build a raft, and ride the Defiles Course.'

The Bloodguard were surprised. Even the boat-loving Giants chose to walk Sarangrave Flat rather than to put themselves in the hands of that river. Korik said, 'Can it be done?'

'We will do it,' Shetra replied.

Seeing the strength of her purpose, the Bloodguard responded to themselves, 'We will do it.' And Korik said, 'Then we must make great haste while the Ranyhyn are yet with us.'

So began the great run of the Ranyhyn, in which the horses of Ra redeemed their shame. When all the riders had remounted, they moved cautiously back to the true path of the Giantway. But then the Ranyhyn cast all but the simplest caution to the wind. First at a canter, then galloping, they ran westward out of the peril of the Sarangrave.

This was no gait for distance, no easy, strength-conserving pace. It was a gallop to surpass the best fleetness of ordinary horses. And it did not slow or falter. At full stretch, the Ranyhyn came out of Sarangrave Flat under the eaves of Landsdrop before moonrise. Then they veered away just east of southward along the line of the cliff.

On the open ground, their running became harder. The rough foothills of Landsdrop cut across their way like rumpled folds in the earth, forced them to plummet down and then labour up uncertain slopes twenty times a league. And southward the terrain worsened. The grass slowly failed from the hillsides, so that the Ranyhyn pounded over bare rock and shale and scree.

The moon was nearly full, and in its light Mount Thunder, ancient Gravin Threndor, was visible against the sky. Already it dominated the southern horizon, and as the mission travelled, it lifted its crown higher and higher.

Under its shadow, the Ranyhyn mastered both the night and the foothills. Breathing hoarsely, blowing foam, sweating and straining extremely, but never faltering, they struck daylight no more than five leagues from the Defiles Course. Now they began to stumble, and slip on the hillsides, scattering froth from their lips, tearing the skin of their knees. Yet they refused to fail.

In the middle of the morning on the tenth day, they lumbered over the crest of one ankle and dropped down into the narrow valley between Mount Thunder's legs – the valley of the Defiles Course.

To their right at the base of the mountain was the head of the river. There rank black water erupted roaring from under a sheer cliff. This was the Soulsease River of Andelain transformed. That fair river entered Mount Thunder through Treacher's Gorge, then plunged into the depths of the earth, where it ran through aban-

doned Wightwarrens and Demondim breeding dens, Cavewightish
slag and refuse pits, charnels and offal grounds and lakes of acid, the
excreta of the buried banes. When it broke out thick, oily, and fetid
at the base of Gravin Threndor, it carried the sewage of the
catacombs, the pollution of ages of filthy use.

From Mount Thunder to Lifeswallower, the Great Swamp,
nothing lived along the banks of the Defiles Course except Sarangrave Flat, which grew thickest on either side of the Course,
flourishing on the black water. But high in the sides of the valley
were two or three thin streams of clean water, which nourished
grass and shrubs and some trees, so that only the bottom of the
valley was barren. There the Ranyhyn rested at last. Quivering and
blowing, they put their noses in a stream to drink.

The Lords disregarded their own weariness, went immediately in
search of *amanibhavam*. Shortly Shetra returned with a double
handful of the horse-healing grass. With it she tended the Ranyhyn
while Hyrim brought more of it to her. Only when all the great
horses had eaten some of the *amanibhavam* did the Lords allow
themselves to rest.

Then the Bloodguard turned their attention to the task of building
a raft. The only trees hardy enough to grow in the valley were teaks,
and in one stand nearby three of the tallest were dead. Their
ironwood trunks showed what had happened to them; when they
had grown above a certain size, their roots had reached down deep
enough to touch soil soaked by the river, and so they had died.

Using hatchets and *clingor* ropes, the Bloodguard were able to
bring down these three trees. Each they sectioned into four logs of
roughly equal length. When they had rolled the logs down to the
dead bank of the Course, they began lashing them together with
clingor thongs.

The task was slow because of the size and weight of the ironwood
logs, and the Bloodguard worked carefully to make sure that the raft
was secure. But they were fifteen, and made steady progress. Shortly
after noon, the raft was complete. After they had prepared several
steering poles, they were ready to continue on their way.

The Lords readied themselves also. After a moment of melding,
they bid ceremonious farewell to the Ranyhyn. Then they came
down to the banks of the Defiles Course and bid Korik launch the
raft.

Two of the Bloodguard fastened ropes to their raft while the others
positioned themselves along its sides. Together, they lifted the
massive ironwood logs, heaved the raft into the river. It bucked in
the stiff current, but the two ropes secured it. Cerrin and Sill leaped
out onto it to see how it held together. When they gave their

approval, Korik signed for the Lords to precede him.

Lord Shetra sprang down to the raft, and at once set about wedging her staff between the centre logs so that she could use its power for a rudder. Lord Hyrim followed her, as did the other Bloodguard, until only the two who held the ropes remained on the bank. Lord Shetra began to sing quietly, calling up the Earthpower through her staff. When she was ready, she nodded to Korik.

At his command, the last two Bloodguard sprang for the raft as the current ripped it away.

The raft plunged, swirled; the boiling water spun it out into the middle of the river.

But then Lord Shetra caught her balance. The power of her staff took hold like a Gildenlode rudder in the hands of a Giant. The raft resisted her, but slowly it became steady. She piloted it down the torrent of the stream, and in moments the mission rushed out of the valley back into the grasp of Sarangrave Flat.

Free of the constriction of the valley, the Defiles Course gradually widened, slowed. Then it began to wind and spill out into the waterways of the Sarangrave, and the worst of the current was past.

For the rest of the afternoon, Lord Shetra remained in the stern of the raft, guided it along the black water. The riverbed bent and twisted as the Defiles Course became more and more woven into the fabric of Sarangrave Flat. Side currents ran into and away from the main stream, and rocky eyots topped with tufts of jungle began to dot the river. When the pace of the Course grew sluggish, she used her staff to propel the raft; she needed headway to navigate the channels. By evening she was greatly weary.

Then four of the Bloodguard took up the poles and began thrusting the raft through twilight into night, where only their dark-familiar eyes could see well enough to keep the raft moving safely. Lord Shetra ate the meal Hyrim prepared for her over a small *lillianrill* fire, then dropped into slumber despite the stink and spreading dampness of the river.

But at dawn she returned to work, plying the Defiles Course with her staff.

However, Lord Hyrim soon came to her aid. Alternately they propelled the raft throughout the day, and at night they rested while the Bloodguard used their poles. In this way, the mission travelled down the Defiles Course until the evening of the twelfth day. During the days, the sky was clear, and the sunlight was full of butterflies. The raft made good progress.

But that night dark clouds hid the moon, and rain soaked the Lords, damaging their sleep. When Korik called to them in the last blackness before dawn, they both threw off their blankets at once and came to their feet.

Korik pointed into the night. In the darkness of a jungled islet ahead of the raft, there was a faint light. It flickered and waned like a weak fire of wet wood, but revealed nothing.

As the raft approached the eyot, the Lords stared at it. Then Shetra whispered, 'That is a made light. It is not natural to the Sarangrave.'

The Bloodguard agreed. None of the Flat's light-bearing animals or insects were abroad in the rain.

'Pull in to the islet,' Shetra breathed. 'We must see the maker of this light.'

Korik gave the orders. The Bloodguard at the poles moved the raft so that it floated towards the head of the islet. When it was within ten yards of the edge, Doar and Pren slipped into the water. They swam to the eyot, then faded up into the underbrush. The steersman swung the raft so that it floated downstream within jumping distance of the bank.

The islet was long and narrow. As the mission floated by almost within reach of the low-hanging branches, the light came into clearer view. It was a thin flame – a weak flickering like the burn of a torch. But it revealed nothing around it except the tree shadows which passed between it and the raft.

When the raft was some distance past it, the light went out. Both the Lords started, raised their staffs, but they said nothing. The steering Bloodguard leaned on their poles until one side of the raft nudged the bank. Almost at once, Doar and Pren leaped out onto the logs, bearing between them the battered form of a man.

Immediately, the steersmen sent the raft swinging out into the main channel. Lord Hyrim bent to light a *lillianrill* rod.

In the rain the torch shone dimly, but it revealed the man. His face and limbs were streaked with dirt and grime, clotted with the blood of numerous small wounds, cuts, and scratches. Surrounded by dirt and blood, the whites of his eyes glistened. His clothes, like the wounds and mud on him, spoke of a long struggle to survive the Flat. The remains of a uniform hung about him in shreds.

Only one piece of his apparel was intact. He wore a scarred metal breastplate, yellow under the filth, with one black diagonal insignia across it.

'By the Seven!' Lord Shetra said. 'A Warhaft!'

She caught hold of the man's shoulders. But then she recoiled as if the man had burned her. '*Melenkurion*! Warhaft,' she cried, 'what has been done to you? Your flesh is ice!'

The man gave no sign that he heard her. He stood where Doar

and Pren had placed him, and his head hung to one side. His breathing was shallow. He did not move in any way, except to blink his eyes at long intervals.

But Shetra did not wait for answers. 'Hyrim,' she said, 'this man is freezing!' She snatched up her blanket, threw it over him. Lord Hyrim built his torch into a fire. There he boiled a stoneware pot of water until it was clean, while Shetra seated the man by the fire. She took hold of his head to force some springwine between his lips.

The cold of his flesh blistered her fingers.

She and Hyrim wrapped their hands in blankets for protection, then laid the man down by the fire and stripped him of his rags. They washed him with boiling water. When he was clean, Lord Shetra drew a stone vial of hurtloam from her robe, and spread some of the healing mud over the worst of his wounds.

Dawn came through the rain. In the light, the Bloodguard saw the result of the Lords' work. The man's skin looked like the flesh of a corpse. On his wounds, the hurtloam lay impotent. The cold in him was uneased.

Yet he breathed and blinked. When the Lords covered him and lifted him into a sitting posture, he squeezed his eyes, and water began to run from them like tears. It spread out over his cheeks and formed beads of ice in his beard.

'By the Seven. By the Seven!' Lord Shetra moaned. 'He is dead, and yet he lives. What has been done to him?'

Lord Hyrim made no answer.

After a time, Korik spoke for the Bloodguard. 'He is Hoerkin, a Warhaft of the Warward. He commanded the First Eoman of the Tenth Eoward. The High Lord sent his command to seek out the Giants in Seareach.'

'Yes,' Hyrim murmured. 'I remember. When his Eoman did not return, the High Lord sent Callindrill and Amatin to attempt the Sarangrave. Twenty-one warriors – Warhaft Hoerkin and his command – all lost, Callindrill and Amatin found no trace.'

Lord Shetra addressed herself to the man. 'Hoerkin. Warhaft Hoerkin. Do you hear me? Speak! I am Shetra Verement-mate, Lord of the Council of Revelstone. I adjure you to speak.'

At first, Hoerkin did not respond. Then his jaw moved, and a low noise came from his mouth.

'I am *ahamkara*, the Door. I am sent – '

His voice trailed off into the flow of his tears.

'Sent? Door?' Shetra said. 'Hoerkin, speak!'

The Warhaft did not seem to hear. He sat in silence, while his tears formed clusters of ice in his beard.

Then Lord Hyrim commanded, '*Ahamkara*, answer!'

Hoerkin swallowed, and spoke.

'I am *ahamkara*, the Door. I am sent to bear witness to – to – '

He faltered, but resumed a moment later.

'I am sent to bear witness to the downfall of Giants.'

For all the Bloodguard, Korik said, 'You lie!' And Lord Shetra sprang on Hoerkin. Regardless of the pain, she gripped his face between her hands, and shouted, 'Despiser!'

He gave a cry and tore himself from her grasp. Huddling with his face against the logs of the raft, he sobbed like a child.

Appalled, Shetra backed away from him. At Lord Hyrim's side, she stopped and waited. Long moments passed before Hoerkin moved. Then he pushed himself up into his former posture. Still his tears ran down into his beard.

' – the downfall of Giants. There were three, brothers of one birth. Omen of the end. They serve Satansheart Soulcrusher.'

He stopped again.

After a moment, Korik said, 'This cannot be. It is impossible. The Giants of Seareach are the Rockbrothers of the Land.'

Hoerkin did not respond. Staring at the logs of the raft, he sat like dead clay. But soon he spoke again.

' – crusher. They are named Fleshharrower, Satansfist – and one other not to be named.'

He swallowed once more.

'They are the three Ravers.'

For a time, all the mission was silent. Then both Hyrim and Shetra strove to compel Hoerkin to say more. But he remained beyond their reach, unspeaking.

At last, Lord Shetra said to Hyrim, 'How do you hear his words? What meaning do you see?'

'I hear truth,' Lord Hyrim said. 'Omen of the end.'

Korik said, 'No. By the Vow, it is impossible.'

Quickly, Lord Hyrim said, 'Do not swear by your Vow here.'

His reproof was just. The Bloodguard were not ignorant of his meaning. Korik did not speak again. But Lord Shetra said, 'I agree with Korik. It surpasses belief to think that a Raver could master any Giant. If the Despiser's power extended so far, why did he not enslave Giants in the past?'

Lord Hyrim answered her, 'That is true. The Ravers do not suffice. They do not explain. But now Lord Foul has possession of the Illearth Stone. That was not so in the age of the Old Lords. Perhaps the Ravers and the Stone together – '

'Hyrim, we are speaking of the Giants! If such an ill had come upon them, they would have sent word to us.'

'Yes,' Lord Hyrim said. 'How was it done?'

'Done?'

'How were they prevented? What has been done to them?'

'To them?' said Lord Shetra. 'Ask a more immediate question. What has been done to Hoerkin? What has been done to us?'

'It is the Despiser's way. In the battle of Soaring Woodhelven – we are told – he damaged the Heer Llaura and the child Pietten so that they would help destroy what they loved.'

'They were used to bait a trap. Hyrim, we are baited!'

She did not wait for an answer. She sprang to the rear of the raft, jammed her staff between the logs, began her song. Strength ran through the ironwood; the raft moved forward through the rain. 'Join me!' she called to Lord Hyrim. 'We must flee this place!'

Lord Hyrim climbed wearily to his feet. 'At Soaring Woodhelven, the trap was complete without Llaura and Pietten. They were an arrogance – a taunt – unnecessary.' As he spoke, his breath began to labour in his chest. The muscles of his neck corded with the strain of inhaling.

The Bloodguard, too, could not breathe easily.

In moments, Hyrim fell to his knees, clutching at his chest. Lord Shetra gasped at the effort of each breath.

The rain falling on the river seemed to make no sound.

Then Warhaft Hoerkin leaped to his feet. From between his lips came a low moan of pain. The sound was terrible. His head bent back, and his cry rose until it became a scream.

It was the same scream which had caused the Ranyhyn to panic.

Korik was the first of the Bloodguard to recover his strength. At once, he knocked the Warhaft from the raft.

Hoerkin sank like a stone. The voice was immediately silent.

Yet the thickness of the air only increased. It tightened around the mission like a fist.

Lord Hyrim struggled to his feet. To Doar, he panted, 'Did you put out his fire? Hoerkin's fire?'

'No,' Doar said. 'It fell when we laid hands upon him.'

'By the Seven!' Hyrim said. 'It was you! The Bloodguard! Not the Ranyhyn. This ill force listens to you! – to the power of the Vow!'

The Bloodguard had no answer. The Vow was not something which could be concealed or denied.

But Lord Shetra was surprised. Her strength dropped away from the raft.

At Korik's command, the four steersmen took up their poles, and thrust the raft towards the north bank of the Course. He wished to meet the attack on land, if he could. He made the steersmen responsible for the raft, then called the other Bloodguard to the defence of the Lords.

In that instant, the river erupted. Silently, water blasted upward, hurling the raft into the air, overturning it.

Behind the burst, a black tentacle licked out of the water. It twisted, coiled, caught Lord Shetra.

Most of the Bloodguard dived clear of the fall of the raft. But Sill and Lord Hyrim were directly under it.

With Pren and Tull, Korik swam for the place where Lord Shetra had been taken. But the dark water blinded them; they could see nothing, find nothing. The river seemed to have no bottom.

Korik made his decision. The mission to Seareach was in his hands. In a tone that allowed no refusal, he ordered the Bloodguard out of the Course.

Soon he stood on the north bank in the fringe of the jungle. Most of the other Bloodguard were with him. Sill and Lord Hyrim had preceded them. The Lord was uninjured; Sill had protected him from the raft.

Downriver, two of the steersmen were tying up the raft, while the other two dived for the company's supplies.

There was no sign of Cerrin and Lord Shetra.

Hyrim was coughing severely – he had swallowed some of the rank water – but he struggled to his feet, and gasped, 'Save her!'

But the Bloodguard made no move to obey. The mission to Seareach was in their hands. And they knew that Cerrin was still alive. He could call to them if their aid would be worth the cost.

'I tried,' Hyrim panted. 'But I cannot swim. Oh, worthless!' A convulsion came over him. He threw his arms wide, and cried out into the rain, 'Shetra!' A bolt of power struck from his staff down through the water towards the river bottom. Then he collapsed into Sill's arms.

His blast seemed to have an effect. The river around the point of Lord Shetra's disappearance started to boil. A turmoil in the water sent up gouts of blood and hunks of black flesh. Steam arose from the current. Deep down in the Defiles Course, a flash of blue was briefly visible.

Then a noise like a thunderclap shook the ground. The river hissed like a torment. And the thickness of the air broke. It was swept away as if it had been washed off the Sarangrave.

The Bloodguard knew that Cerrin was dead.

Only one sign came back from Lord Shetra's struggle. Porib saw it first, dived into the river to retrieve it. Silently, he put it into Lord Hyrim's hands – Lord Shetra's staff.

Between its metal-shod ends, it was completely burned and brittle. It snapped like kindling in Hyrim's grasp.

The Lord pulled away from Sill, and seated himself against a tree.

With tears running openly down his cheeks, he hugged the pieces of Shetra's staff to his chest.

But the peril was not ended. For the sake of his Vow, Korik said to the Lord, 'The lurker is not dead. It has only been cut back here. We must go on.'

'Go?' Hyrim said. 'Go on? Shetra is dead. How can I go on? I feared from the first that your Vow was a voice which the evil in the Sarangrave could hear. But I said nothing.' There was bitterness in him. 'I believed that you would speak of it if my fear were justified.'

Again the Bloodguard had no answer. They had not known beyond doubt or possibility of error that the lurker was alert to their presence. And so many manifestations of power were not what they appeared to be. In respect for the Lord's grief, the Bloodguard left him alone while they readied the raft to go on their way.

The steersmen had been able to salvage the poles and food, most of the *clingor* and the *lillianrill* rods, but none of the clothes or blankets. The raft itself was intact.

Then Korik spoke to Runnik, Pren, and Porib, charged them to bear word of the mission to High Lord Elena. The three accepted without question, but waited for the mission's departure before starting their westward trek.

When all things were prepared, Korik and Sill lifted Lord Hyrim between them, and guided him like a child down the bank onto the raft. He appeared to be unwell. Perhaps the river water he had swallowed was sickening him. As the steersmen thrust the raft out into the centre of the Defiles Course, he murmured to himself, 'This is not the end. There will be pain and death to humble this. Hyrim son of Hoole, you are a coward.' Then the mission was gone. Together, Runnik, Pren, and Porib started into the jungle of Sarangrave Flat.

The fire had died down to coals, and without its light Troy could see nothing – nothing to counteract the images of death and grief in his mind. He knew that there were questions he should ask Runnik, but in the darkness they did not seem important. He was dismayed to think that Shetra's fall had taken place ten days ago; it felt too immediate for such a lapse of time.

The Lords beside him sat still, as if they were stunned or melding; and Covenant was silent – too moved for speech. But after a time Elena said with a shudder of emotion in her voice, 'Ah, Verement! How will you bear it?' Her eyes were only visible as embers. In the darkness they had an aspect of focus and unendurable virulence.

Softly, Lord Mhoram sang:

Death is passing on —
the making way of life and time for life.
Hate dying and killing, not death.
Be still, heart:
make no expostulation.
Hold peace and grief,
and be still.

15

REVELWOOD

The High Lord's company reached the Loresraat by nightfall of the sixth day. During the last leagues, the road worked gradually down into the lowlands of Trothgard; and just as the sun started to dip into the Westron Mountains, the riders entered the wide Valley of Two Rivers.

There the Rill and Llurallin came together in a broad V, joined each other in the narrow end of the valley, to the left of the riders. The Llurallin River, which flowed almost due east below them, arose from clear springs high in the raw rock of the mountains beyond Guards Gap, and had a power of purity that had rendered it inviolate to all the blood and hacked flesh and blasted earth which had ruined Kurash Plenethor. Now, generations after the Desecration, it ran with the same crystal taintlessness which had given it its ancient name — the Llurallin.

Across the valley was the Rill River, the southern boundary of Trothgard. Like the Maerl, the Rill had been greatly improved by the long work of the Lords, and the water which flowed from the Valley of Two Rivers no longer deserved the name Grey.

In the centre of the valley, within the broad middle of the river V, was Revelwood, the tree city of the Loresraat.

It was an immense and expansive banyan. Invoked and strengthened by the new knowledge of the Second Ward, and by the Staff of Law, it grew to the height of a mighty oak, sent down roots as thick as hawsers from boughs as broad as walkways — roots which formed new trunks with new boughs and new roots — and spread out in the valley until the central core of the first tree was surrounded by six others, all intergrown, part of each other, the fruit of one seed.

Once these seven trunks were established, the shapers of the tree prevented any more of the hanging roots from reaching the ground, and instead wove the thick bundles into chambers and rooms – homes and places of study for the students and teachers of the Loresraat. Three of the outer trees had been similarly woven before their roots found the soil, and so now their trunks contained cavities large enough for meeting halls and libraries. On the sheltered acres of ground beneath the trees were gardens and practice fields, training areas for the students of both Staff and Sword. And above the main massive limbs of the trees, the lesser branches had been trained and shaped for leaf-roofed dwellings and open platforms.

Revelwood was a thriving city, amply supplied by the fertile lowlands of Trothgard; and the Loresraat was busier now than at any other time in its history. The Lorewardens and apprentices of the Sword and Staff did all the work of the city – all the cooking, farming, herding, cleaning – but they were not its only inhabitants. A band of *lillianrill* lived there to care for the tree itself. Visitors came from all over the Land. Villages sent emissaries to seek knowledge from the Lorewardens; Hirebrands came to study the Tree; and Gravelingases used Revelwood as a dwelling from which to visit the rock gardens. And the Lords worked there to keep their promises to the Land.

As the riders looked down at it, its broad glossy leaves caught the orange-red fire of the sun, so that it appeared to burn proudly above the shadows spreading down the valley. The company responded to the sight with a glad hail. Clapping their heels to their mounts, they galloped down the slope towards the ford of the Llurallin.

In the time when Revelwood was being grown, the Lords had been mindful of its defence. They had made only two fords for the valley, one across each river. And the ford beds were submerged; they had to be raised before they could be used. All the High Lord's company except Covenant had the necessary knowledge and skill, so Troy was vaguely surprised when Elena halted on the riverbank and gravely asked Trell to open the ford. Troy understood that she was doing the Gravelingas an honour, but he did not know why. Her gesture deepened the mystery of Trell.

Without meeting her gaze, Trell dismounted, and walked to the Llurallin's edge. At first, he did not appear to know the ford's secret. Troy had learned a few quick words in a strange language and two gestures to raise the bed, but Trell used none of them. He stood on the bank as if he were presenting himself to the deep current, and began to sing a rumbling, cryptic song. The rest of the company watched him in hushed stillness. Troy could not grasp the words of the song, but he felt their effect. They had an old, buried, cavernous sound, as if they were being sung by the bedrock of the valley. For a moment, they made him want to weep.

But soon, Trell's singing stopped. In silence, he lifted his arms – and the flat rock of the ford stood up out of the river bottom. It broke water in sections with channels between them so that it did not dam the current. By the time it was ready for crossing, it was as dry as if it had never been submerged.

With his head bowed, Trell walked back to his mount.

When the last horse had crossed the river, and all the company was within the valley, the ford closed itself without any of the usual signals.

Troy was impressed. Remembering Trell's attack on Covenant, he thought that the Unbeliever was lucky to be alive. And he began to feel that he would be well advised to solve the riddle of Trell before he left Trothgard.

But he could do nothing immediately. The last twilight was ebbing out of the valley as if the river currents carried the light away, and he had to concentrate to keep a grip on his own location. The Lorewardens lit torches, but torchlight could not take the place of the sun. Focusing himself sternly, he rode between Lord Mhoram and Ruel across the valley towards Revelwood.

The High Lord's company was met on the ground near the Tree by a welcoming group of Lorewardens. They greeted the Lords with solemn dignity, and embraced their comrades who returned from visiting Lord's Keep. To Warmark Troy, whom they knew well, they gave a special welcome. But when they caught sight of Covenant, they all turned towards him. Squaring their shoulders as if to meet an inspection, they saluted him, and said together, 'Hail, white gold wielder! – you who are named ur-Lord Thomas Covenant, Unbeliever and Ringthane. Be welcome in Revelwood! You are the crux and pivot of our age in the Land – the keeper of the wild magic which destroys peace. Honour us by accepting our hospitality.'

Troy expected some discomforting sarcasm from Covenant. But the Unbeliever replied in a gruff, embarrassed voice, 'Your hospitality honours me.'

The Lorewardens bowed in answer, and their leader stepped forward. He was an old, wrinkled man with hooded eyes and a stooped posture – the result of decades of back-bending study. His voice had a slight tremor of age. 'I am Corimini,' he said, 'the Eldest of the Loresraat. I speak for all the seekers of the Lore, both Sword and Staff. The accepting of a gift returns honour to the giver. Be welcome.' As he spoke, he held out his hand to help Covenant dismount.

But Covenant either misunderstood the gesture or went beyond it intuitively. Instead of swinging off his mount, he brusquely pulled his wedding band from his left hand and dropped it into Corimini's extended palm.

The Eldest caught his breath; a look of astonishment widened his eyes. Almost at once, he turned to show the ring to the other Lorewardens. With muted awed murmurings of invocation like low snatches of prayer, they crowded around Corimini to gaze at the white gold, and to handle it with fingers that trembled.

But their touches were brief. Shortly Corimini returned to Covenant. The Eldest's eyes were damp with emotion, and his hand shook as he passed the ring back up to the Unbeliever. 'Ur-Lord Covenant,' he said with a pronounced quaver, 'you exceed us. We will need many generations to repay this honour. Command us, so that we may serve you.'

'I don't need service,' Covenant replied bluntly. 'I need an alternative. Find some way to save the Land without me.'

'I do not wholly understand you,' said Corimini. 'All our strength is bent towards the preservation of the Land. If that may aid you also, we will be pleased.' Facing the company of the Lords more generally, he went on, 'Will you now enter Revelwood with us? We have prepared food and pleasure for you.'

High Lord Elena made a gracious answer, and dropped lightly from Myrha's back. The rest of the riders promptly dismounted. At once, a group of students hurried out of the shadows of the Tree to take charge of the horses. Then the company was escorted through the ring of trunks towards the central tree. Many lights had appeared throughout Revelwood, and their combined illumination ameliorated the dimness of Troy's sight. He was able to walk confidently with the Lords, and to look up with fondness into the branches of the familiar city. In some ways, he felt more at home here than in Lord's Keep. In Revelwood he had learned to see.

And he felt that Revelwood also suited the High Lord. The two were inextricably linked for him. He was gratified by her just pre-eminence, her glow of gentle authority, and her easy grace as she swung up the wide ladder of the central trunk. Under her influence, he found the fortitude to give Covenant a word of encouragement when the Unbeliever balked at climbing into the Tree.

'You don't understand,' Covenant responded vaguely. 'I'm afraid of heights.' With a look of rigid trepidation, he forced his hands to the rungs of the ladder.

Bannor took a position close behind Covenant, making himself responsible for the ur-Lord's safety. Soon they had climbed to the level of the first branches.

Troy moved easily up into the Tree after them. The smooth, strong wood of the rungs made him feel that he could not miss his grip; it almost seemed to lift him upward, as if Revelwood were eager for him. In moments, he was high up the trunk, stepping away from the ladder onto one of the main boughs of the city. The shapers of Revelwood had grown the banyan so that the upper surfaces of the branches were flat, and the level stretch down which Troy walked was wide enough for three or four people to stand safely abreast. As he moved, he waved greetings to the people he knew – most of the Sword Lorewardens, and a few students whose families lived in Lord's Keep.

The procession of the Lords crossed an intersection where several limbs came together, and passed beyond it towards one of the outer trunks. Formed in this trunk was a large hall, and when Troy entered it he found that the room had been set for a banquet. The chamber was brilliant with *lillianrill* torches; long tables with carpets of moss between them covered the floor; and students of all ages bustled around, carrying trays laden with steaming bowls and flagons.

There Troy was joined by Drinishok, Sword-Elder of the Lorewardens, and the Warmark's first battle-teacher. Except for his grizzled eyebrows, Drinishok did not look like a warrior; his thin, spidery limbs and fingers did not seem sturdy enough to handle either a sword or a bow. But three Lords and three-quarters of Troy's Warward had trained under the old Sword-Elder; and his tanned forearms were laced with many white battle scars. Troy greeted his mentor warmly, and after standing together in the Land's customary thanks for food, they sat down to the feast.

The fare of Revelwood was simple but excellent – it made up in convivial gusto what it lacked in complexity – and all the Lords and Lorewardens were bountifully supplied with meats, rice, cheeses, bread, fruit, and springwine. Warmed by the glow of Revelwood's welcome, the High Lord's company ate with enthusiasm, talking and joking all the while with their hosts and the busy students. Then, when the eating was done, High Lord Elena presided over an entertainment which the students had prepared. Champions of the Sword gave demonstrations of gymnastics and blade work, and the apprentices of the Staff told an intricate tale which they had distilled from the ancient Giantish story of Bahgoon the Unbearable and Thelma Twofist who tamed him. Troy had never heard it before, and it delighted him.

He was reluctant to lose this pleased and comfortable mood, so when the Lords left the hall with the Lorewardens to speak with them concerning the tidings which Runnik had brought from

Sarangrave Flat, Troy did not accompany them. Instead, he accepted Drinishok's invitation, and went to spend the night in the old Sword-Elder's home.

High in one of the outer trees, in a chamber of woven leaves and branches, he and Drinishok sat up for a long time, drinking spring-wine and discussing the war. Drinishok was excited by the prospect of the battle, and he avowed that only Revelwood's need for a strong defence kept him from marching with the Warward. As always, he showed a swift grasp of Troy's ideas, and when the Warmark finally went to bed the only immediate blot on his private satisfaction was the mystery of Trell.

The breeze in the branches lulled him into a fine sleep, and he awoke early the next morning feeling eager for the new day. He was amused but not surprised to find that his host was up and away before him; he knew the rigorous schedule of the Loresraat. He bathed and dressed, pulled his high boots over his black leggings, and carefully adjusted his headband and his sunglasses. After a quick breakfast, he spent a few moments polishing his breastplate and his gleaming ebony sword. When he was properly apparelled as the Warmark of the Lords' Warward, he left Drinishok's chambers, moved to the central tree, and started up it towards the lookout of Revelwood.

On a small platform in the uppermost branches of the Tree, he joined the two students on watch duty. While he exchanged pleasantries with them, he breathed the crisp autumn air and studied the whole length and breadth of the Valley of Two Rivers. In the west, he could see the snow crests of the mountains. He was not being cautious, looking for danger. He loved the fertile hills of Trothgard, and he wanted to fix them in his mind so that he would never forget them. If something were to strike him down during the coming war, he wanted to be sure to the very end, death or blindness, that he had in fact seen this place.

He was still in the lookout when he heard the signal for the gathering of the Loresraat.

At once, he took leave of the two students, and started down the Tree. Shortly, he reached the wide, roofless bowl of the gathering place. High in the city, on a frame of four heavy boughs radiating from the central trunk, the shapers of Revelwood had woven an immense net of banyan roots and hung it around the central trunk. It formed a wide basin supported by the four boughs and anchored by the roots themselves in each of the six outer trees. The result was the *viancome*, a meeting place large enough for half the population of the city. People sat on the roots and dangled their feet through the gaps of the net.

These gaps were rarely larger than a foot square, but they made the *viancome* an uneasy experience for novices. However, the people of Revelwood moved and even ran lightly over the net. Warmark Troy, with a blind man's alert, careful feet, was able to walk confidently away from the central trunk to join Drinishok and the other Sword Lorewardens where they stood partway up one side of the bowl.

Lord Amatin was already there, talking intently with a cluster of Staff Lorewardens and advanced students. Most of the Bloodguard were stationed around the edge of the net, and past them came a steady flow of Revelwood's inhabitants. As Troy joined Drinishok, he caught sight of Lord Mhoram moving across the bowl towards Amatin. If the *viancome* caused Mhoram any anxiety, he did not show it; he strode boldly from root to root with his staff held in the crook of his arm.

Soon High Lord Elena arrived in the company of the Staff-Elder, Asuraka. Troy was taken slightly aback; he had expected her to be with Corimini, the Eldest of the Loresraat. But when Corimini entered the bowl, he brought with him the ur-Lord Covenant. Troy saw what had happened. The Loresraat ranked Covenant above Elena, and so the highest honour of Revelwood's hospitality, the invitation of the Eldest, had gone to the Unbeliever. This nettled Troy; he did not like to see the High Lord slighted in favour of Covenant. But he consoled himself by watching the sick look with which Covenant regarded the net and the fall below it.

Shortly all the Lorewardens were in their places. The sides of the *viancome*, and the branches overhead, thronged with the people of Revelwood. Covenant clung to a root over one of the supporting boughs, and Bannor crouched protectively near him. The Lords and Warmark Troy sat in a fanned group with the Elder Lorewardens, facing south, and Corimini stood before them, looking out over the assembly with a dignified mien. When all the people were still, hushed and expectant, he began the ceremonies of the meeting.

He and the High Lord exchanged traditional salutations, and sang to each other the ritual invocations which they considered appropriate to the purpose of the meeting. Their stately alternation spun a mood of reverent seriousness over the *viancome*, wrapped all the people together as if it were weaving them into the grim and wondrous history of the Land. Under the influence of the ceremonies, Troy was almost able to forget that half of what was said and sung was intended to honour the white gold wielder.

But Covenant did not look as if he were being honoured. He sat there with an awkward stiffness, as if the point of a knife were pressed against his spine.

After the last song was done, Corimini gazed at Covenant in silence, giving the Unbeliever a chance to speak. But the glare which Covenant returned almost made the Eldest wince. He turned away, and said, 'High Lord Elena, Lord Mhoram, Lord Amatin, Warmark Troy, be welcome in the *viancome* of Revelwood. We are the Loresraat, the seekers and servants of Kevin's Lore. We gather to honour you – and to offer you the help of all our knowledge in the name of the approaching war. The preservation of Land and Lore is in your hands, as the mystery of Land and Lore is in ours. If there is any way in which we may aid you, only speak of it, and we will put forth all our strength to meet the need.'

With a deep bow, High Lord Elena replied formally, 'The gathering of the Loresraat honours us, and I am honoured to speak before the people of Revelwood.' Troy thought that he had rarely seen her look more radiant. 'Eldest, Elders, Lorewardens, students of the Sword and Staff, friends of the Land – my friends, in the name of all the Lords, I thank you. We will never be defeated while such faithfulness is alive in the Land.

'My friends, there are matters of which I would speak. I do not speak of the danger that war brings to Revelwood. The Lore of the Sword will not neglect your defence. And Lord Amatin will remain with you, to do all that a Lord may do to preserve the Valley of the Two Rivers.'

A cheer started up on the edges of the bowl, but she stopped it with a commanding glance, and went on. 'More, I do not speak of Stonedowns and Woodhelvens which will be destroyed by war – or of people made homeless. I know that the dispossessed of this war will find here all comfort and relief and restitution that human hearts may ask or give. This is sure, and requires no urging.

'More, I do not speak of any need for mastery of Kevin's Lore. You have given your best strength, and have achieved much. You will give and achieve more. All these matters are secure in your fidelity.

'But there are two questions of which I must speak.' A change in the cadence of her voice showed that she was approaching the heart of her reasons for coming to Revelwood. 'The second concerns a stranger who has visited Lord's Keep. But the first is one which was presented to you a year ago – at the request of Warmark Hile Troy.' She offered Troy a chance to speak, but he declined with a shake of his head, and she continued. 'It is our hope that the Loresraat has discovered a way to speak and hear messages across distances. The Warmark believes that such a way will be of great value in this war.'

Corimini's look of satisfaction revealed his answer before he spoke it. 'High Lord, we have learned a way.' Troy's heart surged at the news, and he gripped the handle of his sword. His battle plan appeared suddenly flawless. He was grinning broadly as the Eldest went on, 'Several of our best students and Lorewardens have devoted themselves to this need. And they were aided by Hirebrands of the *lillianrill*. With the Hirebrands and two students, Staff-Elder Asuraka learned that messages may be spoken and heard through *lomillialor*, the High Wood of the *lillianrill*. The task is difficult, and requires strength − but it will not surpass any Lord accustomed to the Earthpower.' Nodding at the Staff-Elder, he said, 'Asuraka will teach the knowledge to you. We have prepared three *lomillialor* rods for this purpose. More we could not do, for the High Wood is very rare.'

Lomillialor. Troy had heard of it. It was the *lillianrill* parallel to *orcrest* − a potent white wood descended from the One Tree from which Berek Halfhand had formed the Staff of Law. The Hirebrands used it − as the Gravelingases used *orcrest* − to give the test of truth. *Lomillialor* was said to be a sure test of fidelity − if the one tested did not far surpass the strength of the tester. Some of the old tales of Covenant's first visit to the Land said that the Unbeliever had passed a test of truth given to him at Soaring Woodhelven.

And Soaring Woodhelven had later been destroyed.

As Troy got up to join Elena in thanking the Loresraat for what it had achieved, he looked over to see how Covenant took Corimini's news.

For some reason, the Unbeliever was on his feet. Swaying uncertainly, afraid of falling, he muttered, '*Lomillialor*. The test of truth. Are you going to trust that?'

A hot retort leaped into Troy's mouth, but something about Covenant's appearance silenced it. Troy blocked his sight with his hand, adjusted his sunglasses, then looked again. The strangeness was still there.

Covenant's chest seemed to ripple like roiled water. He was solid, but something disturbed the centre of his chest, making it waver like a mirage.

Troy had seen an effect like this once before. He glanced quickly away towards the High Lord. She regarded him with a question in her face. Nothing distorted her. The rippling touched no one else in the *viancome*. And even Covenant seemed unaware of it. But the Bloodguard around the bowl stood as if at attention, and Bannor held himself at Covenant's side with a coiled poise that belied his blank expression.

Then Troy saw the area of distortion detach itself from Covenant and float lazily towards the High Lord.

The other time he had seen it, it had appeared so briefly, with such evanescence, that he had finally disregarded it as a trick of his vision, a misconception. But now he knew what it was.

He bowed deliberately to Corimini. 'Forgive the interruption. I forget what I was going to say.' Without waiting for an answer, he addressed Elena. He hoped that she would understand him through the careful nonchalance of his tone. 'Why don't you go ahead? There was something else you wanted to talk to the Loresraat about.' While he spoke, he took a few steps in her direction, as if this were a natural expression of deference. On the edges of his sight, he watched the mirage float towards her.

He turned to get closer to it.

He faced Covenant in a way that allowed him to take two more steps, and remarked pointedly, 'You know, it just might turn out that that white gold of yours has been good for something after all.' Some of his excitement forced its way into his tone.

The next instant, he sprang into motion. He took three rapid strides, and threw himself at the roiling distortion in the air.

It tried to evade him, but he caught it in time. He hit it with a jarring impact, and toppled to the net with it in his arms.

It struggled – he could feel invisible arms and legs – but he kept his grip. He tightened his hold until the form stopped resisting and lay still. When he heaved himself to his feet, he lifted the light, limp weight easily in his arms.

'All right, my friend,' he gritted at it. 'Show yourself. Or shall I ask the High Lord to tickle your ribs with the Staff of Law?'

Covenant was staring at Troy as if the Warmark had lost his mind. But Lord Amatin watched him avidly, and the High Lord moved forward as if to support his threat.

A peal of high, young laughter rang out. 'Ah, very well,' said a bodiless voice bubbling with gaiety. 'I am captured. You have surprising vision. Release me – I will not escape.'

The air swirled suddenly, and Amok became visible in Troy's grasp. He was the same incongruously ancient youth who had appeared before the Council of Lords in Revelstone.

'Hail, High Lord!' he said cheerfully. When Troy let go of him, he bowed humorously to her, then turned and repeated his bow to his captor. 'Hail, Warmark! You are perceptive – but rough. Is this the hospitality of Revelwood?' Glee filled his voice, effaced any reproof in his words. 'Your strength was not needed, I am here.'

'By hell,' Covenant muttered. 'By hell.'

'Indeed?' said Amok with a boyish grin that seemed to light up the laughing curls of his hair. 'Well, that is not for me to say. But I am well made. You bear the white gold. It is for your sake that I have returned.'

All the people of Revelwood had surged to their feet when Amok appeared, and the Lorewardens now stood in a ready circle around the Warmark and his captive. Both Corimini and Asuraka were confusedly questioning the High Lord. But Elena deferred to Lord Amatin. Stepping into the circle, Amatin asked Amok, 'How so?'

Amok replied, 'Lord, the white gold surpasses my purpose. I felt the sign of readiness when the *krill* of Loric came to life. I went to Revelstone. There I learned that the *krill* was not awakened by the Lords of Kevin's Lore. I feared that I had erred. But now I have travelled the Land, and seen the peril. And I have learned of the white gold, which awakened Loric's *krill*. This shows the wisdom of my creation. Though the conditions of my life are not met, I see the need, and I appear.'

'Are you changed?' said Amatin. 'Will you give us your knowledge now?'

'I am who I am. I respect the white gold, but I am unchanged.'

'Who is he?' Corimini insisted.

By answering the Eldest, High Lord Elena provided Amatin with a moment in which to prepare herself. 'He is Amok, the waiting bearer of knowledge. He was made by High Lord Kevin to – to answer certain questions. It was Kevin's thought that when those who came after him had mastered the *krill*, they would be ready for Amok's knowledge. But we have not mastered the *krill*. We do not know the questions.'

After this, a breath of astonishment blew through the Loresraat. But Troy could see that the Lorewardens immediately understood the situation better than he did. Their eyes gleamed with possibilities he did not comprehend.

At a nod from Corimini, the two Elders, Asuraka and Drinishok, entered the circle and stood on either side of Lord Amatin, placing their knowledge at her service. She acknowledged them, then raised her studious face to Amok, and said, 'Stranger, who are you?'

'Lord, I am what you see,' Amok responded cryptically. 'Those who know me have no need for my name.'

'Who made you?'

'High Lord Kevin son of Loric son of Damelon son of Berek Heartthew the Lord-Fatherer.'

'Why were you made?'

'I wait. And I answer.' The boy's open grin seemed to mock the incorrectness of Amatin's questions.

Irritated by Amok's riddling, Drinishok interposed, 'Boy, do you bear knowledge that belongs to the Warlore?'

Amok laughed. 'Old man, I was old when the grandsire of your grandsire's grandsire was a babe. Do I appear to be a warrior?'

'I care nothing for age,' the Sword-Elder snapped. 'You behave as a child.'

'I am what I am. I behave as I was made to behave.'

When Lord Amatin spoke again, she emphasized her words intently. 'Amok, what are you?'

Without hesitation, Amok replied, 'I am the Seventh Ward of High Lord Kevin's Lore.'

His answer threw a stunned silence over the whole gathering. Both Elders gasped, and Corimini had to brace himself on Elena's shoulder. A burst of wild emotion shot across Elena's face. Mhoram's eyes crackled with sudden visionary fire. And Lord Amatin gaped – amazed or appalled at what she had uncovered. Even Troy, who had not devoted his whole life to the mysteries of the Wards, felt abruptly unbalanced, as if his precarious perch had been jolted by something inscrutable. Then a ragged cheer sprang up among the students. The Lorewardens pressed eagerly forward, as if they wanted to verify Amok's existence by touching him. And through the clamour, Troy heard High Lord Elena exclaim, 'By the Seven! We are saved!'

Covenant also heard her. 'Saved?' he rasped across the din. 'You don't even know what the Seventh Ward is!'

Elena ignored him. She beamed grateful congratulations to Lord Amatin, then raised her arms to quiet the assembly. When some degree of order had returned to the *viancome*, she said, 'Amok, you are indeed well made. You chose wisely in returning to us. Now the Despiser does not overpower us as much as he may think.'

With an effort, old Corimini forced himself to remember his long experience with the unattainability of the Wards. In a thin voice, he quavered, 'But still we do not know the questions to unlock this knowledge.'

'We will find them,' Elena responded. Sharp determination thrummed in her voice.

After a pause to steady herself, Lord Amatin returned to her enquiry. 'Amok, the Wards which we have found contain various knowledges on many subjects. It is so with the Seventh Ward?'

Amok seemed to think that this was a penetrating question. He bowed to her as seriously as his bubbling spirits permitted, and said, 'Lord, the Seventh Ward has many uses, but I am only one answer.'

'What answer are you?'

'I am the way and the door.'

'How so?'

'That is my answer.'

Lord Amatin looked towards Elena and Mhoram for suggestions, and Troy took the opportunity to ask, 'The way and the door to what?'

With a chuckle, Amok replied, 'Those who know me have no need for my name.'

'Yes, I remember,' Troy growled. 'And among those who do not know you, you are named Amok. Why don't you think of something else to say?'

'Think of some other question,' the youth retorted gaily.

Troy retreated, baffled, and after a moment Lord Amatin was ready to continue. 'Amok, knowledge is the way and door of power. The Earthpower answers those who know its name. How great is the power of the Seventh Ward?'

'It is the pinnacle of Kevin's Lore,' said Amok slyly, as if he were making a subtle joke.

'Can it be used to defeat the Despiser?'

'Power is power. Its uses are in the hands of the user.'

'Amok,' Amatin said, then hesitated. She seemed almost afraid of her next question. But she clenched her resolve, and spoke it. 'Does the Seventh Ward contain knowledge of the Ritual of Desecration?'

'Lord, Desecration requires no knowledge. It comes freely to any willing hand.'

The Lord sighed, then turned to Asuraka and asked the Staff-Elder for advice. Asuraka referred the question to Drinishok, but he was out of his element, and could offer her nothing. On an impulse, she turned to Corimini. The two conferred in hushed tones for a moment. When Asuraka returned to Amok, she said tentatively, 'Amok, the other Wards teach knowledge concerning power. Are you the power of the Seventh Ward?'

'I am the way and the door.'

'Do you bear the power itself within you?' she insisted.

For a moment, Amok appeared to study the legitimacy of this question. Then he said simply, 'No.'

'Are you a teacher?'

'I am the way – '

Suddenly Lord Amatin grasped a new idea, and interrupted Amok. 'You are a guide.'

'Yes.'

'You were created to teach us the location of some knowledge or power?'

'Ah, that may be as it happens. Much is taught, but few learn.'

'Where is this power?'

'Where all such powers should be – hidden.'

'What is the power?'

Laughing, the youth replied, 'There is a time for all things.' Then he added, 'Those who know me have no need of my name.'

Amatin sagged, and turned away towards the High Lord. Her thin face held a look of strain as she admitted defeat. Around her, the assembly of the Loresraat sighed as the people shared her disappointment. But the High Lord answered Amatin by stepping calmly forward, and planting the Staff of Law in front of Amok. In a voice soft and confident, she said, 'Amok, will you guide me?'

With an unexpected seriousness, Amok bowed. 'High Lord, yes. If the white gold permits.'

'Don't ask me for permission,' Covenant said quickly. But no one listened to him. The High Lord smiled and asked, 'Where will we go?'

The youth did not speak, but he gave a general nod towards the Westron Mountains.

'And when will we go?'

'Whenever the High Lord desires.' Throwing back his head, he began to laugh again as if he were releasing an overflow of high humour. 'Think of me, and I will join you.'

As he laughed, he flourished his arms intricately, and vanished. Either his power was stronger than before, or he moved more swiftly; Troy caught no last glimpse of him.

The Warmark found that he regretted Amok's appearance intensely.

Soon after that, the gathering of the Loresraat broke up. The Lorewardens and students of the Staff hurried away to begin analysing what had happened, and Drinishok ordered all his students and fellow teachers away to the practice fields. Elena, Mhoram, and Lord Amatin went with Corimini and Staff-Elder Asuraka to their main library. In moments, Troy, Covenant, and Bannor were the only people left in the bowl.

Troy felt that he should speak with Covenant; there were things that he needed to understand. But he feared that he would not be able to keep his temper, so he also moved away, leaving Bannor to help Covenant struggle off the net. He wanted to talk to the High Lord, ask her why she had made such a foolhardy offer to Amok. But he was not in command of his emotions. He climbed out of the *viancome*, and strode away along one of the boughs towards Drinishok's quarters.

In the Sword-Elder's larder, he ate a little bread and meat, and drank quantities of springwine in an effort to dissipate the dark sensation of foreboding which Amok had given him. The idea that Elena might wander off somewhere with the youth, hunting for a cryptic and probably useless power when she was desperately needed elsewhere, made him grind his teeth in frustration. His heart groaned with a prescience that told him he was going to lose her. The Land was going to lose her. Searching for balance, he consumed a great deal of springwine. But it did not steady him; his brain reeled as if dangerous winds were buffeting him.

Early in the afternoon, he went in search of the Lords, but one of the Lorewardens soon told him that they were closeted with Asuraka, studying the *lomillialor* communication rods. So he descended to the ground, whistled for Mehryl, and rode away from Revelwood with Ruel at his side. He wanted to visit the grave of the student who had summoned him to the Land.

Covenant had said, *It isn't you they've got faith in at all. It's the student who summoned you.* Troy needed to think about that. He could not simply shrug it away. One reason he distrusted Covenant was because the Unbeliever had first been called by Drool Rockworm at Lord Foul's behest. Did the nature of the summoner have any connection to the worth of the one summoned?

Furthermore, Covenant had referred to that student strangely, as if he knew something about the young man Troy did not know.

Troy went to the place of his summons hoping that its physical context, its concrete location in Trothgard, would ease his vague fears and forebodings. He needed to regain his self-confidence. He knew he could not challenge Elena's decision to follow Amok if he did not believe in himself.

But when he reached the site of the grave, he found Trell there. The big Gravelingas knelt by the grassy mound as if he were praying. When he heard Troy's approach, he raised his head suddenly, and his face was so swollen with grief that it struck Troy momentarily dumb. He could think of no reason why Trell Gravelingas should be here grieving.

Before Troy could collect his thoughts to ask for an explanation, Trell jumped up and hastened away towards his mount, which he had tethered nearby.

'Trell — !' Troy started to call after him, but Ruel interposed flatly, 'Warmark, let him go.'

Troy turned in surprise towards the Bloodguard. Ruel's visage was as passionless as ever, but something in the way his eyes followed Trell seemed to express an unwonted sympathy. Carefully Troy said, 'Why? I don't understand.'

'That you must ask the High Lord,' Ruel replied without inflection.

'I'm asking you!' the Warmark snapped before he could control his irritation.

'Nevertheless.'

With an effort, Troy mastered himself. Ruel's mien said as plainly as words that he was acting on the High Lord's instructions, and that nothing which did not threaten her life could induce him to disobey her. 'All right,' Troy said stiffly. 'I'll do that.' Turning Mehryl, he trotted after Trell's galloping mount back towards Revelwood.

But when he re-entered the Valley of Two Rivers and approached the Tree, he found Drinishok waiting impatiently for him. The Lords had announced that they would leave Revelwood the next morning, and the Sword-Elder wanted Troy to discuss the defence of the city with all the Lorewardens and students of the Sword. This was a responsibility which Troy could not ignore, so while his private fog turned to dusk and then to night blindness, he addressed the assembled discipline of the Sword. He did not even try to see what he was talking about; he went into the strategy of the Valley from memory.

But when he was done, he found that he had lost his chance to talk to the Lords. In the darkness, he seemed to lack courage as well as vision. After his lecture, he went to Drinishok's home, and shared a meal full of indigestible lumps of silence with the Sword-Elder. Then he went to bed early; he could not endure any more of the blurred half-sight of torches. Drinishok respected his mood, and left him alone. In blind isolation, he stared uselessly into the darkness, and tried to recover his balance. He felt certain that he was going to lose Elena.

He ached to talk to her, to dissuade her, cling to her. But the next morning, when all the riders gathered with their mounts just after dawn on the south side of the great Tree, he found that he could not confront the High Lord with his fears. Sitting regally on Myrha's back in the gleam of day, she had too much presence, too much personal authority. He could not deny or challenge her. And while she was surrounded by so many people, he could not ask her his questions about Trell. His apprehension was too personal to be aired so publicly. He strove to occupy his mind with other things until he got a chance to talk to someone.

Deliberately, he scanned the company of riders. Standing by their Ranyhyn behind the Lords were twenty Bloodguard – First Mark Morin, Terrel, Bannor, Ruel, Runnik, and fifteen others. Obviously, Koral would remain with Lord Amatin at Revelwood. In addition to them, the group included only five others: High Lord Elena, Lord Mhoram, Covenant, Troy, and Trell. When he saw the Gravelingas, Troy again felt a desire to speak to him. The unconcealed wound of Trell's expression was taut with suspense, as if he awaited some decision from Elena with a degree of agony that surprised Troy. But the Warmark refrained, despite his mounting anxiety. The High Lord had begun to address Lord Amatin and Eldest Corimini.

'My friends,' she said gravely. 'I leave Revelwood in your care. Ward it well! The Tree and the Loresraat are the two great achievements of the new Lords – two symbols of our service. If it may be

578

done, they must be preserved. Remember vigilance, and watch the Centre Plains. If war comes upon you, you must not be taken unaware. And remember that if Revelwood cannot be saved, the Lore still must be preserved, and Lord's Keep warned. The Loresraat and the Wards must find safety in Revelstone at need.

'Sister Amatin, these are great burdens. But I place them in your hands without fear. They do not surpass you. And the help of Corimini the Eldest, and of Asuraka and Drinishok the Elders, is beyond price. I do not believe that the Warward will fall in this war. But you must be prepared for all chances, even the worst. You will not fail. This trust becomes you.'

Lord Amatin blinked back a moment of tears, and bowed silently to the High Lord. Then Elena lifted her head to Revelwood, and projected her voice so that she could be heard in the Tree.

'Friends! Comrades! Proud people of the Land! There is war upon us. Together we confront the test of death. Now is the time of parting, when all the defenders of the Land must go to their separate tasks. Do not desire to change your lot for another's. All faith and service are equal, alike worthy and perilous, in this time of need. And do not grieve at parting. We go to the greatest glory of our age – we are honoured by the chance to give our utmost for the Land. This is the test of death, that at the last we may prove worthy of what we serve.

'Be of good heart. If the needs of this war go beyond your strength, do not despair. Give all your strength, and hold Peace, and do not despair. Hold courage and faith high! It is better to fall and die in Peace than to re-Desecrate the Land.

'My friends, I am honoured that I have shared life with you.'

High in Revelwood, a strident voice cried, 'Hail to the High Lord and the Staff of Law!' And all the people in the Tree and on the ground answered, 'Hail! Hail to the High Lord!'

Elena bowed deeply to Revelwood, spreading her arms wide in the traditional gesture of farewell. Then she turned Myrha towards the riders, and spoke to Lord Mhoram.

'Now, Mhoram, my most trusted friend, you must depart. You and Warmark Hile Troy must rejoin the Warward, to guide it into war. I have decided. I will leave you now, and follow Amok to the Seventh Ward of Kevin's Lore.'

In spite of himself, Troy groaned, and clutched at Mehryl's mane as if to keep himself from falling. But the High Lord took no notice of him. Instead, she said to Mhoram, 'You know that I do not do this to evade the burden of war. But you also know that you are the more experienced and ready in battle. And you know that the outcome of the war may allow us no second opportunity to discover this Ward. Yet the Ward may enable a victory which would other-wise be taken from us. I cannot choose otherwise.'

Lord Mhoram gazed at her intently for a time. When he finally spoke, his voice was thick with suppressed appeals. 'Beware, High Lord. Even the Seventh Ward is not enough.'

Elena met him squarely, but her own gaze appeared unfocused. The other dimension of her sight was so pronounced that she did not seem to see him at all. 'Perhaps it was not enough for Kevin Landwaster,' she replied softly, 'but it will suffice for me.'

'No!' Mhoram protested. 'The danger is too great. Either this power did not meet Kevin's need in any way, or its peril was so great that he feared to use it. Do not take this risk.'

'Have you seen it?' she asked. 'Do you speak from vision?'

With an effort, Mhoram forced himself to say, 'I have not seen it. But I feel it in my heart. There will be death because of it. People will be slain.'

'My friend, you are too careful of all risks but your own. If you held the Staff of Law in my place, you would follow Amok to the ends of the Earth. And people will still be slain. Mhoram, ask your heart – do you truly believe that the future of the Land can be won in war? It was not so for Kevin. I must not lose any chance which may teach me another way to resist the Despiser.'

Mhoram bowed his head, too moved to make any answer. In the silence, they melded their thoughts, and after a moment the strain in his face eased. When he looked up again, he directed his gaze explicitly towards Covenant and Troy. Softly, he said, 'Then – if you must go – please do not go alone. Take someone with you – someone who may be of service.'

For one wild instant, Troy thought that the High Lord was going to ask him to go with her. Despite his responsibilities to the Warward, his lips were already forming his answer – *Yes* – when she said, 'That is my desire. Ur-Lord Covenant, will you accompany me? I wish to share this quest with you.'

Awkwardly, as if her request embarrassed him, Covenant said, 'Do you really think I'm going to be of service?'

A gentle smile touched Elena's lips. 'Nevertheless.'

He stared into the expanse of her eyes for a moment. Then, abruptly, he looked away and shrugged. 'Yes. I'll come.'

Troy hardly heard the things that were said next – the last formal speeches by Elena and Corimini, the Loresraat's brief song of encouragement, the exchange of farewells. When the High Lord said a final word to him, he could barely bring himself to bow in answer. With his *Yes* frozen on his lips, he watched the end of the ceremonies, and saw Elena and Covenant ride away together westward, accompanied only by Bannor and First Mark Morin. He felt paralysed in the act of falling – crying, I'm going to lose you! Lord Mhoram came close to him, and spoke. But he did not move until he realized through his distress that Trell had not followed Covenant and the High Lord.

Suddenly, his restraint broke. He spun urgently towards Trell, turned in time to see the Gravelingas yank his heavy fists out of his hair, snatch up the reins of his horse, and start away at a gallop towards the ford of the Llurallin north of Revelwood.

Troy went after him. Mehryl flashed under the Tree, and caught up with Trell in the sunlight beyond the city. Troy ordered the Gravelingas to stop, but Trell ignored him. At once, the Warmark told Mehryl to halt Trell's mount. Mehryl gave one short, commanding whinny, and the horse stopped so sharply that Trell almost lost his seat.

When the Gravelingas forced his head up to meet Troy, his eyes ran with tears, and he panted as if he were being slowly suffocated. But Troy had no more time to spare for considerateness. 'What're you doing?' he rasped. 'Where're you going?'

'Revelstone,' croaked Trell. 'There is nothing for me here.'

'So? We're going south – don't you know that? You live in the South Plains, don't you? Don't you want to help defend your home?' This was not what Troy wanted to ask, but he had not found the words for his real question.'

'No.'

'Why not?'

'I cannot go back. She is there – I cannot bear it. After this!'

As Trell panted his answer, Lord Mhoram rode up to them. At once, he started to speak, but Troy cut him off with a savage gesture. 'She?' the Warmark demanded. 'Who? Your daughter?' When Trell nodded dumbly, Troy said, 'Wait a minute. Wait a minute.' Things he did not know buffeted him; he had to find answers. 'I don't understand. Why don't you go back home – to your daughter? She's going to need you.'

'*Melenkurion*!' Trell gasped. 'I cannot! How could I look into her face – answer questions – after this? Do not torment me!'

'Warmark!' Mhoram's voice was hard and dangerous – a warning, almost a threat. 'Let him be. Nothing that he can say will help you.'

'No!' Troy retorted. 'I've got to know. Trell, listen to me. I have got to know. Believe me, I understand how you feel about him.'

Trell no longer seemed to hear Troy. 'She chose!' he panted, 'chose!' He heaved the words between his clenched teeth as if they

581

were about to burst him. 'She chose him – him!'

'Trell, answer me. What were you doing out there yesterday? – at that grave? Trell!'

The word *grave* penetrated Trell's passion. Abruptly, he wrapped his arms around his chest, hunched forward. Through his tears, he glared at Troy. 'You are a fool!' he hissed. 'Blind! She wasted her life.'

'Wasted?' Troy gaped. 'Wasted?' *It's the student who summoned you.* Was Covenant right?

'Perhaps,' Lord Mhoram said grimly. This time his tone compelled Troy's attention. Troy stared at Mhoram with a gaze thick with dread. 'He has abundant reason to visit that grave,' the Lord went on. 'Atiaran Trell-mate is buried there. She died in the act which summoned you to the Land. She gave her life in an effort to regain ur-Lord Covenant – but she failed of her purpose. Your presence here is the outcome of her Peace-less grief and her hunger for retribution.'

Mhoram's explanation exceeded the limit of Trell's endurance. Pain convulsed his features. He struck his horse a fierce blow with his heels, and it sprang at once into a frightened gallop towards the Llurallin ford. But Troy did not even see him go. The Warmark turned sharply, and found that he could still discern Elena, Covenant, and the two Bloodguard riding westward out of the Valley. Amok was already with them, walking jauntily at the High Lord's side.

Atiaran Trell-mate? *Trell*-mate? She was his wife? He knew of Atiaran – he had heard too much talk about Covenant not to know that she was the woman who had guided the Unbeliever from Mithil Stonedown to Andelain and the Soulsease River. But he had not known that Trell was her husband. That had been kept from him.

Then he went a step further. Covenant had raped Trell's daughter – Atiaran's daughter – the daughter of the woman who –!

'Covenant! You bastard!' Troy howled. 'What have you done?' But he knew that the travellers could not hear him across the distance; the noise of the two rivers obliterated distant shouts. A stiff gust of helplessness knocked down his protest, so that his voice cracked and stumbled into silence.

It was no wonder that Trell could not return home, face his daughter. How could he tell her that the High Lord had chosen friendship rather than retribution for the man who had raped her? Troy did not understand how she could do such a thing to Trell.

Another moment passed before he grasped the rest of what Mhoram had said. *She died in the act* – Atiaran was his summoner, not some young ignorant or inspired student. That, too, had been kept from him. He was the result and consequence of her unanswerable pain.

It isn't you – Was Covenant right? Were all his plans only so much despair work, set in motion by the extravagance of Atiaran's death?

'Warmark.' Lord Mhoram's tone was stern. 'That was not well done. Trell's hurt is great enough.'

'I know,' Troy gritted over the aching of his heart. 'But why didn't you tell me? You knew about all this.'

'The Council decided together to withhold this knowledge from you. We saw only harm in the sharing of it. We wished to spare you pain. And we hoped that you would learn to trust ur-Lord Covenant.'

'You were dreaming,' Troy groaned. 'That bastard thinks this whole thing is some kind of mental game. All that Unbelieving is just a bluff. He thinks he can get away with anything. You can't trust him.' Grimly, he pushed the argument to its conclusion. 'And you can't trust me – or you would have told me all this before. She was trying to summon him. As far as you know, I'm just a surrogate.' He tried to sound lucid, but his voice shook.

'You misunderstand me,' Mhoram said carefully.

'No, I don't misunderstand.' He could feel deadly forces at work around him – choosing, manipulating, determining. He had to clench himself to articulate, 'Mhoram, something terrible is going to happen to her.'

He looked at the Lord, then turned away; he could not bear the compassion in Mhoram's gaze. Patting Mehryl's neck, he sent the Ranyhyn trotting around the east side of Revelwood. He avoided the waiting Lorewardens, avoided having to bid them farewell. Gesturing roughly for the Bloodguard and Lord Mhoram to follow him, he rode straight away from Revelwood towards the south ford.

He was looking forward to his war. He wanted to get to it in a hurry.

16

FORCED MARCH

Yet even in this mood, he could not cross the ford of the Rill out of Trothgard without regret. He loved the sunbright beauty of Revelwood, the uncomplex friendship of the Lorewardens; he did not want to lose them. But he did not look back. He could not understand why Elena had repudiated Trell Atiaran-mate's just rage and grief. And he sensed now, in a way more fundamental than he had ever seen it before, that he would have to prove himself in this war. He would have to prove that he was the fruit of hope, not of despair.

He would have to win.

If he did not, then he was more than a failure; he was an active evil – a piece of treachery perpetrated against the Land in defiance of his own love or volition – worse than Covenant, for Covenant at least tried to avoid the lie of being trusted. But he, Hile Troy, had deliberately sought trust, responsibility, command –

No, that thought was intolerable. He had to win, had to win.

When he had passed the crest of the south hill, he slowed Mehryl to a better travelling pace, and allowed Lord Mhoram and the remaining eighteen Bloodguard to catch up with him. Then he said through his teeth, biting down on his voice to avoid accusing Mhoram, 'Why is she taking him? He raped Trell's daughter.'

Mhoram responded gently, 'Warmark Troy, my friend, you must understand that the High Lord has little choice. The way of her duty is narrow, and beset with perils. She must seek out the Seventh Ward. And she must take ur-Lord Covenant with her – because of the white gold. With the Staff of Law, she must ensure that his ring does not fall into Lord Foul's hands. And if he turns against the Land, she must be near him – to fight him.'

Troy nodded to himself. That was reasoning he could comprehend. Abruptly, he shook himself, forced down his instinctive protest. With an effort, he unclenched his teeth, and sighed, 'I'll tell you something, Mhoram. When I'm done with this war – when I can look back and tell myself that poor Atiaran is satisfied – I'm going to take a vacation for a few years. I'm going to sit down in Andelain and not move a muscle until I get to see the Celebration of Spring. Otherwise I'm never going to be able to forgive that damn Covenant for being luckier than I am.' But he meant *luckier* in another way. Though he realized now that no other choice was possible, he ached to think that Elena had chosen Covenant, not him.

If Mhoram understood him, however, the Lord tactfully followed what he had said rather than what he meant. 'Ah, if we are victorious' – Mhoram was smiling, but his tone was serious – 'you will not be alone. Half the Land will be in Andelain when next the dark of the moon falls on the middle night of spring. Few who yet live have seen the Dance of the Wraiths of Andelain.'

'Well, I'm going to get there first,' Troy muttered, trying to sustain this conversation. But then he could not keep himself from reverting to the subject of the Unbeliever. 'Mhoram, don't you resent him? After what he's done?'

Evenly and openly, Lord Mhoram said, 'I have no special virtue to make me resent him. One must have strength in order to judge the weakness of others. I am not so mighty.'

This answer surprised Troy. For a moment, he stared at Mhoram, asking silently, Is that true? Do you believe that? But he could see that Mhoram did believe it. Baffled, Troy turned away.

Surrounded by the Bloodguard, he and Lord Mhoram followed a curve through the hills that took them generally east-southeast to intercept the Warward.

As the day passed, Troy was able to turn his thoughts more and more towards his marching army. Questions began to crowd his mind. Were the villages along the march able to provide enough food for the warriors? Was First Haft Amorine able to keep up the pace? Such concerns enabled him to put aside his foreboding, his aching sense of loss. He became another man – less the blind uncertain stranger to the Land, and more the Warmark of the Warward of the Lord's Keep.

The change steadied him. He felt more comfortable with this aspect of himself.

He wanted to hurry, but he resisted the temptation because he wanted to make this part of the journey as easy as possible for the Ranyhyn. Still, by the end of that day, the eighth since he had left Revelstone, he, Lord Mhoram, and the Bloodguard had left behind the reblooming health of Trothgard. Even at a pace which covered no more than seventeen leagues in a day, the land through which they rode changed rapidly. East and southeast of them was the more austere country of the Centre Plains. In this wide region the stern rock of the Earth seemed closer to the surface of the soil than in Trothgard. The Plains supported life without encouraging it, sustained people who were tough, hardy.

Most of the men and women who made up the Warward came from the villages of the Centre Plains. This was traditionally true – and for good reason. In all the great wars of the Land, the Despiser's armies had struck through the Centre Plains to approach Revelstone. Thus these Plains bore much of the brunt of Lord Foul's malice. The people of the Plains remembered this, and sent their sons and daughters to the Loresraat to be trained in the skills of the Sword.

As he made camp that night, Troy was intensely conscious of how personally his warriors depended on him. Their homes and families were at the mercy of his success or failure. At his command they were enduring the slow hell of this forced march.

And he knew that the war would begin within the next day. By that time, the vanguard of Lord Foul's army would reach the western end of the Mithil valley, and would encounter Hiltmark Quaan and the Lords Callindrill and Verement. He was sure of it; no later than the evening of the ninth day. Then men and women would begin to die – his warriors. Bloodguard would begin to die. He wanted to be with them, wanted to keep them alive, but he could not. And the march to Doom's Retreat would go on and on and on, grinding down the Warward like the millstone of an unanswerable need. Soon Troy stretched himself out in his blankets and pressed his face against the earth as if that were the only way he could keep his balance.

He spent most of the night reviewing every facet of his battle plan, trying to assure himself that he had not made any mistakes.

The next morning, he felt full of urgency, and he found that whenever he forgot himself he began to hurry Mehryl's pace. So he turned to Mhoram and asked the Lord to talk to him, distract him.

In response, the Lord slowly dropped into a musing, half-singing tone, and began to tell Troy about the various legended or potent parts of the Land which lay between them and Doom's Retreat. In particular, he narrated some of the old tales about the One Forest, the mighty wood which had covered the Land in an age that was ancient before Berek Halfhand's time, with its Forestals and its fierce foes, the Ravers. During the centuries when the trees were still awake, he said, the Forestals had cherished their consciousness and guided their defences against *turiya*, *moksha*, and *samadhi*. But now, if the old tales spoke truly, no active remnant or vestige of the One Forest and the Forestals remained in the Land, except the grim woods of Garroting Deep and Caerroil Wildwood. And none who entered Garroting Deep, for good or ill, ever returned.

This dark forest lay near the line of the Warward's march, beyond the Last Hills.

Then Troy talked for a while about himself and his reactions to the Land. He felt close to Mhoram, and this enabled him to discuss the way High Lord Elena personified his sense of the Land. Gradually, he relaxed, regained his ability to say to himself, It doesn't matter who summoned me. I am who I am. I'm going to do it.

So he was not just surprised when he and Mhoram caught up with the struggling march of the warriors by midafternoon. He was shocked.

The Warward was almost half a day's march behind schedule.

The warriors met him with a halting cheer that stumbled into silence as they realized that the High Lord was not with him. But Troy ignored them. Riding straight up to First Haft Amorine, he barked, 'You're slow! Speed up the beat! At this rate, we're going to be exactly one and a half days too late!'

The welcome on Amorine's face fell into chagrin, and she whirled away at once towards the drummers. With a wide, sighing groan of pain, the warriors stepped up their pace, hurried to the demand of the drums until they were half running. Then Warmark Troy rode up and down beside their ranks like a flail, enforcing the new rhythm with his angry presence. When he found one Eoward lagging slightly, he shouted into the young drummer's face, 'By God! I'm not going to lose this war because of you!' He clapped his beat by the shamed Warhaft's ear until the drummer copied it exactly.

Only after his dismay had subsided did he observe what nine days of hard marching had done to the Warward. Then he wished that he could recant his harshness. The warriors were suffering severely. Almost all of them limped in some way, pushed themselves unevenly against the nagging pain of cuts and torn muscles and bone bruises. Many were so tired that they had stopped sweating, and the overheated flush of their faces was caked with dust, giving them a yellow and demented look. More than a few bled at the shoulders from sores worn by the friction of their pack straps. Despite their doggedness, they marched raggedly, as if they could hardly remember the ranked order which had been trained into them ninety leagues ago at Revelstone.

And they were behind schedule. They were still one hundred and eighty leagues away from Doom's Retreat.

By the time they lurched and gasped their way into camp for the night, Troy was almost frantic for some way to save them. He sensed that bare determination would not be enough.

As soon as the accompanying Hirebrands and Gravelingases had started their campfires, Lord Mhoram went to do what he could for the Warward. He moved from Eoward to Eoward, helping the cooks. In each stewpot, his blue fire worked some effect on the food, enhanced it, increased its health and vitality. And when the meal was done, he walked through all the Warward, spreading the balm of his presence – talking to the warriors, helping them with their bruises and bandages, jesting with any who could muster the strength to laugh.

While the Lord did this, Troy met with his officers, the Hafts and Warhafts. After he had explained High Lord Elena's absence, he turned to the problem of the march. Painfully, he reviewed the circumstances which made this ordeal so imperative, so irretrievably necessary. Then he addressed himself to specific details. He organized a rotation schedule for the leather water jugs, so that they would be passed continuously through the ranks for the sake of the over-heated warriors. He made arrangements for the packs of the men and women with bleeding shoulders to be carried by the horses. He ordered all the mounted officers except the drummers to ride double, so that the most exhausted warriors could rest on horseback; and he told these officers to gather *aliantha* for the marchers as they rode. He assigned all scouting and water duties to the Bloodguard, thus freeing more horses to help the warriors. Then he sent the Hafts and Warhafts back to their commands.

When they were gone, First Haft Amorine came over to speak with him. Her blunt, dour face was charged with some grim statement, and he forestalled her quickly. 'No, Amorine,' he said, 'I am not going to put someone else in your place.' She tried to protest, and he hurried on more gently, 'I know I've made it sound as if I blame you because we're behind schedule. But that's just because I really blame myself. You're the only one for this job. The Warward respects you – just as it respects Quaan. The warriors trust your experience and honesty.' Glumly, he concluded, 'After all this, I'm not so sure how they feel about me.'

At once, her self-doubt vanished. 'You are the Warmark. Who has dared to question you?' Her tone implied that anyone who wanted to challenge him would have to deal with her first.

Her loyalty touched him. He was not entirely sure that he deserved it. But he intended to deserve it. Swallowing down his emotion, he replied, 'No one is going to question me as long as we keep up the pace. And we are going to keep it up.' To himself, he added, I promised Quaan. 'We're going to gain back the time we've lost – and we're going to do it here, in the Centre Plains. The terrain gets worse south of the Black River.'

The First Haft nodded as if she believed him.

After she had left him, he went to his blankets, and spent the night battering the private darkness of his brain in search of some alternative to his dilemma. But he could conceive nothing to eliminate the need for this forced march. When he slept, he dreamed of warriors shambling into the south as if it were an open grave.

The next morning, when the ranks of the Warward stirred, tensed weakly, lumbered into motion like a long dark groan across the Plains, Warmark Hile Troy marched with them. Eschewing his Ranyhyn, he started the beat of the drums, verified it, and moved to it himself. As he marched, he worked his way up and down among the Eoward, visiting every Eoman, encouraging every Warhaft by name, surprising the warriors out of their numb fatigue with his presence and concern – striving in spite of his own untrained physical condition to set an example that would be of some help to his army. At the end of the day in the ranks, he was so weary that he barely reached the small camp he shared with Lord Mhoram and First Haft Amorine before he mumbled something about dying and pitched into sleep. But the next day he hauled himself up and repeated his performance, hiding his pain behind the commiseration which he carried in one way or another to the Warriors of the Warward.

He marched with his army for four days across the Centre Plains. After each day at his cruel pace, he felt that he had passed his limit – that the whole forced march was impossible, and he must give it up. But each night Lord Mhoram helped cook the army's food, and then went among the warriors, sharing his courage with them. And twice during those four days the Warward came upon Bloodguard tending large caches of food – supplies prepared by the villagers of the Centre Plains. Fresh and abundant food had a surprising efficacy; it restored the fortitude of warriors who no longer believed in their ability to drive themselves forward. At the end of his fourth day on foot – the thirteenth day of the march – Troy finally allowed himself to think that the condition of the Warward had stabilized.

He had walked more than forty leagues.

Fearing to do anything which might damage his army's fragile balance, he planned to continue his own march. Both Mhoram and Amorine urged him to stop – they were concerned about his exhaustion, about his bleeding feet and unsteady gait – but he shrugged their arguments aside. In his heart, he was ashamed to ride when his warriors were suffering afoot.

But the next morning he tasted a worse shame. When the light of dawn woke him, he struggled out of his blankets to find Amorine standing before him. In a grim voice, she reported that the Warward had been attacked during the night.

Sometime after midnight, the Bloodguard scouts had reported that the tethered horses were being stalked by a pack of *kresh*. At once, the alarm spread throughout the camp, but only the mounted Hafts and Warhafts had been able to answer it swiftly. With the Bloodguard, they rushed to the defence of the horses.

They found themselves confronting a huge pack of the great yellow wolves – at least tenscore *kresh*. The Bloodguard on their Ranyhyn met the first brunt of the attack, but they were outnumbered ten to one. And the officers behind them were on foot. The scent of the *kresh* had panicked the horses, so that they could not be mounted, or herded out of danger. One Ranyhyn, five horses, and nearly a dozen Hafts and Warhafts were slain before Amorine and Lord Mhoram were able to mobilize their defence effectively enough to drive back the wolves.

And before the *kresh* were repelled, a score or more of them broke past the officers and charged into a part of the camp where some of the warriors, stunned by exhaustion, were still asleep. Ten of those men and women lay dead or maimed in their blankets after the Bloodguard and Mhoram had destroyed the wolves.

Hearing this, Troy became livid. Brandishing his fists in anger and frustration, he demanded, 'Why didn't you wake me?'

Without meeting his gaze, the First Haft said, 'I spoke to you, shook you, shouted in your ear. But I could not rouse you. The need was urgent, so I went to meet it.'

After that, Troy did no more marching. He did not intend to be betrayed by his weakness again. Astride Mehryl, he rode with Ruel along the track of the *kresh*; and when he had assured himself that the wolves were not part of a concerted army, he returned to take his place at the head of the Warward. From time to time, he cantered around his army as if he were prepared to defend it single-handed.

The *kresh* attacked again that night, and again the next night. But both times, Warmark Troy was ready for them. Though he was blind in the darkness, unable to fight, he studied the terrain and chose his campsites carefully before dusk. He made provision for the protection of the horses, planned his defences. Then he set ambushes of Bloodguard, archers, fire. Many *kresh* were killed, but his Warward suffered no more losses.

After that third assault, the wolves left him alone. But then he had other things to worry about. During the morning of the march's sixteenth day, a wall of black clouds moved out of the east towards the warriors. Before noon, gusts of wind reached them, ruffling their hair, riling the tall grass of the Plain. The wind stiffened as the outer edges of the storm drew nearer. Soon rain began to lick at them out of the darkening sky.

The intense blackness of the clouds promised a murderous downpour. It effectively blinded Troy. All the Hirebrands and Gravelingases lit their fires, to provide light to hold the Warward together against the force of the torrents. But the main body of the storm did not come that far west; it seemed to focus its centre on a point somewhere in the eastern distance, and when it had taken its position it remained stationary.

The warriors marched through the outskirts of the grim weather. The ragged and tormented rain which lashed at them out of the infernal depths of the storm did not harm them much, but their spirits suffered nevertheless. They all felt the ill force which drove the blast. They did not need Troy to tell them that it was almost certainly directed at Hiltmark Quaan's command.

By the time the storm had dissipated itself late the next day, Troy

ks to the roborant of the *rillinlure* and hurtloam, his
he call of dawn with renewed resolution in their eyes
g like strength in their limbs. When he climbed a
speak to them, they crowded around him, and gave a
ade his chest tight with pride. He wanted to embrace

he Warward with his back to the sunrise, and when he
n their faces through the mist, he began. 'My friends,'
'hear me! I'm going to go to Kevin's Watch to find out
s doing, so this will probably be my last chance to talk to
the fighting starts. And I want to give you fair warning.
taking it pretty easy for the past twenty-two days. But
ft part is over. We're going to have to start earning our
pay

d this bleak joke apprehensively. If the warriors under-
stoo, they might relax a bit, shed some of their pain and care,
drer to each other. But if they heard derogation in his words,
if re affronted by his grim humour — then they were lost to
hi

n immense relief and gratitude when he saw that many
iors smiled. A few even laughed aloud. Their response
el suddenly and beautifully in harmony with them — in
s army, the instrument of his will. At once, he was
n of his command.

went on, 'As you know, we're only five days from
. We have almost exactly forty-eight leagues left to
ou've already done, you should be able to do this in
till there are a few things I want to say about it.

uld know that you've already accomplished more
rmy in the history of the Land. No other Warward
this far this fast. So every one of you is already a
ging — facts are facts. You are already the best.

t, our job isn't done until we've won. That's why
m's Retreat. It's a perfect place for a trap — once
n handle an army five times our size. And just
pulling Foul's army south like this — we've
f Stonedowns and Woodhelvens in the Centre
, that means we've saved your homes.'

let his own confidence reach into the hearts
e said, 'But we have got to get to the Retreat
iltmark Quaan expects to find us. He and his
hell to give us these five more days. If we
fore they do, they will all die.

t I can tell you for a fact that the Hiltmark

had lost nearly one Eoman. Somewhere in the darkness and the fear of what assailed Quaan, almost a score of the least hardy warriors lost their courage; amid all the slipping and struggling of the Warward, they simply lay down in the mud and died.

But they were only eighteen. Close to sixteen thousand men and women survived the storm and marched on. And for the sake of the living, Warmark Troy steeled his heart against the dead. Riding Mehryl as if there were no limit to his courage, he led his army southward, southward, and did not let his crippling pace waver.

Then, three days later — the day after the full of the moon — the Warward had to swim the Black River.

This river formed the boundary between the Centre and South Plains. It flowed northeast out of the Westron Mountains, and joined the Mithil many scores of leagues in the direction of Andelain. Old legends said that when the Black River burst out from under the great cliff of Rivenrock, the eastward face of *Melenkurion* Skyweir, its water was as red as pure heart's-blood. But from Rivenrock the Black poured into the centre of Garroting Deep. Before it passed through the Last Hills into the Plains, it crossed the foot of Gallows Howe, the ancient execution mound of the Forestals. The water which the Warward had to cross was reddish-black, as if it were thick with a strange silt. In all the history of the Land, the Black River between the Last Hills and the Mithil had never tolerated a bridge or ford; it simply washed away every effort to make a way across it. The warriors had no choice but to swim.

As they climbed the south bank, they looked drained, as if some essential stamina or commitment had been sucked from their bones by the current's dark hunger.

Still they marched. The Warmark commanded them forward and they marched. But now they moved like battered empty hulks, driven by a meaningless wind over the trackless sargasso of the South Plains. At times, it seemed that only the solitary fire of Troy's will kept them stumbling, trudging ahead, striving.

And in the South Plains yet another difficulty awaited them. Here the terrain became rougher. In the southwest corner of the Centre Plains, only the thick curve of the Last Hills separated Garroting Deep from the Plains. But south of the Black River, these hills became mountains — a canted wedge of rugged peaks with its tip at the river, its eastern corner at the bottleneck of Doom's Retreat, and its western corner at Cravenshaw, where Garroting Deep opened into the Southron Wastes forty leagues southwest of Doom's Retreat. The line of the Warward's march took it deeper and deeper into the rough foothills skirting these mountains.

After two days of struggling with these hills, the warriors looked like reanimated dead. They were not yet lagging very far behind the pace, but clearly it was only a matter of time before they began to drop in their tracks.

As the sun began to set, covering Troy's sight with mist, the Warmark made his decision. The condition of the warriors wrung his heart; he felt his army had reached a kind of crisis. The Warward was still five days from Doom's Retreat, five terrible days. And he did not know where Quaan was. Without some knowledge of the Hiltmark's position and status, some knowledge of Lord Foul's army, Troy could not prepare for what lay ahead. And his army no longer appeared capable of any preparation.

The time had come for him to act.

Though the Warward was still a league away from the end of its scheduled march, he halted it for the night. And while the warriors shambled about the business of making camp, he called Lord Mhoram aside. In the dusk, he could hardly make out the Lord's features, but he concentrated on them with all his determination, strove to convey to Mhoram the intensity of his appeal. 'Mhoram,' he breathed, 'there has got to be something you can do for them. Something – anything to help pull them together. Something you can do with your staff, or sing, or put in the food, something. There has got to be!'

Lord Mhoram studied the Warmark's face closely. 'Perhaps,' he said after a moment. 'There is one aid which may have some effect against the touch of the Black River. But I have been loath to use it, for once it has been done it cannot be done again. We are yet long days from Doom's Retreat – and the need of the warriors for strength in battle will be severe. Should not this aid be kept until that time?'

'No.' Troy tried to make Mhoram hear the depth of his conviction. 'The time is now. They need strength now – in case they have to fight before they get to the Retreat. Or in case they have to run to get there in time. We don't know what's happening to Quaan. And after tonight you won't get another chance until after the fighting's already started.'

'How so?' the Lord asked carefully.

'Because I'm leaving in the morning. I'm going to Kevin's Watch – I want to get a look at Foul's army. I have to know exactly how much time Quaan is giving us. And you're coming with me. You're the one who knows how to use that High Wood communication rod.'

Mhoram appeared surprised. 'Leave the Warward?' he asked quickly, softly. 'Now? Is that wise?'

Troy was sure. 'I've got to do it. I've been – ignorant too long. Now I've got to know. From here on we can't afford to let Foul

surprise us. And I'm' – he grimac
who can see far enough to tell

After a moment, he added,
Even he needed to know what

Abruptly, the Lord passed a h
nodded. 'Very well. It will be do
given. Each of the Gravelingases be
hurtloam. And the Hirebrands have
name *rillinlure*. I had hoped to save
battle wounds. But they will be placed in
they will suffice.' Without further question,
his instructions to the Hirebrands and Gravelin

Soon these men were moving throughout the c
hurtloam or *rillinlure* in each cooking pot. Each pot
pinch; each warrior ate only a minute quantity. But th
and Gravelingases knew how to extract the most bene
wood dust and loam. With songs and invocations, the
gift to the warriors strong and efficacious. Shortly aft
warriors began to fall asleep; many of them simply
ground and lost consciousness. For the first time in
of the march, several of them smiled at their drea

When Mhoram returned to Warmark Troy af
almost smiling himself.

Then Troy began to give First Haft Amor
the battle of Doom's Retreat. After they ha
final stages of the march, they talked abo
of his assurances, she viewed that plac
of the Land, that was the place to w
hopes had been destroyed. Grim
which nested high in the sides
scree and boulders of the
defeated.

But Troy had never d
was an ideal place fo
could be lured into
beauty of it,' Tr
going to turn F
make it into
hand. Fou'
him. Bu'
to turn his
pace for five n

Amorine's blun
five days might be.

has already bought three of those five days for us. You all saw that storm six days ago. You know what it was – an attack on the Hiltmark's Eoward. That means that six days ago he was still holding Foul's army in the Mithil valley. And you know Hiltmark Quaan. You know he won't let a mere two days get between us and victory.

'It is going to be close. We're not going to get much rest. But once we're in the Retreat, I'm not afraid of the outcome.'

At this, the Hafts raised a cheer to answer Troy's bravado, and he stood silently in the ovation with his head bowed, accepting it only because the courage in the shout, the courage of his army, overwhelmed him. When the cheering subsided, and the Warward became silent again, he said thickly into the stillness, 'My friends, I'm proud of you all.'

Then he turned and almost ran from the hill.

Lord Mhoram followed him as he sprang onto Mehryl's back. Accompanied by Ruel, Terrel, and eight other Bloodguard, the two men galloped away from the Warward. Troy set a hard pace until his army was out of sight in the hills behind him. Then he eased Mehryl back to a gait which would cover the distance to Mithil Stonedown and the base of Kevin's Watch in three days. With Mhoram at his side, he cantered eastward over the rumpled Plains.

After a time, the Lord said quietly, 'Warmark Troy, you have moved them.'

'You've got it backward,' replied Troy in a voice gruff with emotion. 'They did it to me.'

'No, my friend. They have become very loyal to you.'

'They're loyal people. They – all right, yes, I know what you mean. They're loyal to me. If I ever let them down – if I even make any normal human mistakes – they're going to feel betrayed. I know. I've focused too much of their courage and hope on myself, on my plans. But if it gets them to Doom's Retreat in time, the risk'll be worth it.'

Lord Mhoram assented with a nod. After a pause, he said, 'But you have done your part. My friend, I must tell you this. When I first understood your intention to march towards Doom's Retreat at such a pace, I felt the task to be impossible.'

'Then why did you let me do it?' flared Troy. 'Why wait until now to say anything?'

'Ah, Warmark,' returned the Lord, 'everything that passes unattempted is impossible.'

At this, Troy turned on Mhoram. But when he met the Lord's probing gaze, he realized that Mhoram would not have raised such a question gratuitously. Forcing himself to relax, he said, 'You don't actually expect me to be satisfied with an answer like that.'

'No,' the Lord replied simply. 'I speak only to express my appreciation for what you have done. I trust you. I will follow your lead in this war into any peril.'

Abruptly, a rush of gratitude filled Troy's throat, and he had to clench his teeth to keep from grinning foolishly. To meet Mhoram's trust, he whispered, 'I won't let you down.'

But later, when his emotion had receded, he was disconcerted to remember how many such promises he had made. They seemed to expand with every new development in the march. His speech to the Warward was only one in a series of assertions. Now he felt that he had given his personal guarantee of success to practically the entire Land. He had manoeuvred himself into a corner – a place where defeat and betrayal became the same thing.

The simple thought of failure made his pulse labour vertiginously in his head.

If this was the kind of thinking that inspired Covenant's Unbelief, then Troy could see that it made a certain kind of sense. But he had a savage name for it; he called it *cowardice*. He forced the thought down, and turned his attention to the South Plains.

Away from the mountains, the terrain levelled somewhat and opened into broad stretches of sharp, hard grass mottled with swaths of grey bracken and heather turning purple in the autumn. It was not a generous land – Troy had been told that there were only five Stonedowns in all the South Plains – but its unprofligate health was vital and strong, like the squat, muscular people who lived with it. Something in its austerity appealed to him, as if the ground itself were appropriate for war. He rode it steadily, keeping a brisk pace while conserving Mehryl's strength for the hard run from Kevin's Watch to Doom's Retreat.

But the second night, his confidence suffered a setback. Soon after moonrise, Lord Mhoram sprang suddenly awake, screaming so vehemently that Troy's blood ran cold. Troy groped towards him through the darkness, but he struck the Warmark down with his staff, and started firing fierce blasts of power into the invulnerable heavens as if they were attacking him. A madness gripped him. He did not stop until Terrel caught his arms, shouted into his face, 'Lord! Corruption will see you!'

With an immense effort, Mhoram mastered himself, silenced his power.

Then Troy could see nothing. He had to wait in blind suspense until at last he heard Mhoram breathe, 'It is past. I thank you, Terrel.' The Lord sounded utterly weary.

Troy thronged with questions, but Mhoram either would not or could not answer them. The force of his vision left him dumb and quivering. He could barely compel his lips to form the few words he spoke to reassure Troy.

The Warmark was not convinced. He demanded a light. But when Ruel built up the campfire, Troy saw the garish heat of torment and danger in Mhoram's eyes. It stilled him, denied his offer of support or consolation. He was forced to leave the Lord alone in his cruel, oracular pain.

For the rest of the night, Troy lay awake, waiting anxiously. But when the dawn came and his sight returned, he perceived that Mhoram had weathered the crisis. The fever in his gaze had been replaced by a hard gleam like a warning that it was perilous to challenge him – a gleam that reminded Troy of that picture in the Hall of Gifts entitled 'Lord Mhoram's Victory'.

The Lord offered no explanation. In silence they rode away into the third day.

On the horizon ahead, Troy could make out the thin, black finger of Kevin's Watch, though the valley of Mithil Stonedown was still twenty-two leagues distant. After the strain of the night, he was under even more pressure than before to climb the Watch and see Lord Foul's army. In that sight he would find the fate of his battle plan. But he did not drive the Ranyhyn beyond their best travelling gait. So the valley was already full of evening shadows when he and Mhoram reached the Mithil River, and followed it upstream into the Southron Range.

Through his personal haze, he caught only one glimpse of Mithil Stonedown. From the top of a heavy stone bridge across the river, he looked southward along the east bank, and dimly made out a dark, round cluster of stone huts. Then the last penetration of his sight faded, and he had to ride into the village on trust.

When Troy and his companions had dismounted within the round, open centre of the Stonedown, Lord Mhoram spoke quietly to the people who came out to greet him. Soon the Stonedownors were joined by a group of five, bearing with them a wide bowl of graveling. They placed it on a dais in the centre of the circle, where its warm glow and fresh loamy smell spread all around them. The light enabled Troy to see dimly.

The group of five included three women and two men. Four of them were white-haired, aged, and dignified, but one man appeared just past middle age. His thick dark hair was streaked with grey, and over his short, powerful frame he wore a traditional brown Stonedownor tunic, with a curious pattern resembling crossed lightning on his shoulders. He had a permanently twisted bitter expression, as if something had broken in him early in life, turning all the tastes of his experience sour. But despite his bitterness and his relative youth, his companions deferred to him. He spoke first.

'Hail, Mhoram son of Variol, Lord of the Council of Revelstone. Hail, Warmark Hile Troy. Be welcome in Mithil Stonedown. I am Triock son of Thuler, first among the Circle of Elders of Mithil Stonedown. It is not our custom to question our guests before hospitality has cleansed the weariness of their way. But these are perilous times. A Bloodguard brought us tidings of war. What need calls you here?'

'Triock, your welcome honours us,' replied Lord Mhoram. 'And we are honoured that you know us. We have not met.'

'That is true, Lord. But I studied for a time in the Loresraat. The Lords, and the friends of the Lords' — he nodded to Troy — 'were made known to me.'

'Then, Triock, elders and people of Mithil Stonedown, I must tell you that there is indeed war upon the Land. The army of the Grey Slayer marches in the South Plains, to do battle with the Warward of Revelstone at Doom's Retreat. We have come so that Warmark Troy may climb Kevin's Watch, and study the movements of the foe.'

'He must have brave sight, if he can see so far — though it is said that High Lord Kevin viewed all the Land from his Watch. But that is not our concern. Please accept the welcome of Mithil Stonedown. How may we serve you?'

Smiling, Mhoram answered, 'A hot meal would be a rich welcome. We have eaten camp food for many days.'

At this, another of the elders stepped forward. 'Lord Mhoram, I am Terass Slen-mate. Our home is large, and Slen my husband is proud of his cooking. Will you eat with us?'

'Gladly, Terass Slen-mate. You honour us.'

'Accepting a gift honours the giver,' she returned gravely. Accompanied by the other elders, she led Mhoram and Troy out of the centre of the Stonedown. Her home was a wide, flat building which had been formed out of one prodigious boulder. Within, it was bright with graveling. After several ceremonious introductions, Troy and Lord Mhoram found themselves seated at a long stone table. The meal that Slen set before them did full justice to his pride.

When all the guests had eaten their fill, and the stoneware dishes and pots had been cleared away, Lord Mhoram offered to answer the questions of the elders. Terass began by asking generally about the war, but before she had gone far Triock interrupted her.

'Lord, what of High Lord Elena? Is she well? Does she fight in this war?'

Something abrupt in Triock's tone irritated Troy, but he left the answers to Mhoram. The Lord replied, 'The High Lord is well. She has uncovered knowledge of one of the hidden Wards of Kevin's Lore, and has gone in quest of the Ward itself.' He sounded cautious, as if he had some reason to distrust Triock.

'And what of Thomas Covenant the Unbeliever? The Bloodguard said that he has returned to the Land.'

'He has returned.'

'Ah, yes,' said Triock. He seemed aware of Mhoram's caution. 'And what of Trell Atiaran-mate? For many years he was the Gravelingas of Mithil Stonedown. How does he meet the need of this war?'

'He is in Revelstone, where his skills serve the defence of the Keep.'

At once, Triock's attitude changed. 'Trell is not with the High Lord?' he demanded sharply.

'No.'

'Why not?'

For a moment, Lord Mhoram searched Triock's face. Then he said as if he were taking a risk, 'Ur-Lord Thomas Covenant, Unbeliever and Ringthane, rides with the High Lord.'

'With her?' Triock cried, springing to his feet. 'Trell permitted this?' He glared bitterly at Mhoram, then spun away and flung out of the house.

His vehemence left an awkward silence in the room, and Terass spoke quietly to ease it. 'Please do not be offended, Lord. His life is full of trouble. It may be that you know part of his tale.'

Mhoram nodded, assured Terass that he was not offended. But Triock's conduct disturbed Warmark Troy; it reminded him vividly of Trell. 'I don't know,' he said bluntly. 'What business is the High Lord of his?'

'Ah, Warmark,' Terass said sadly, 'he would not thank me for speaking of it. I – '

A sharp glance from Mhoram silenced her. Troy turned towards Mhoram, but the Lord did not meet his gaze. 'Before ur-Lord Covenant's first summoning to the Land,' Mhoram said carefully, 'Triock was in love with the daughter of Trell and Atiaran.'

Troy barely restrained an ejaculation. He wanted to curse Covenant; there seemed to be no end to the damage Covenant had done. But he held himself back for the sake of his hosts. He scarcely heard Mhoram ask, 'Is Trell's daughter well? Is there any way in which I may help her?'

'No, Lord,' sighed Terass. 'The health of her body is strong, but her mind is unsteady. Always she has believed that the Unbeliever will come for her. She has asked the Circle of elders – asked permission to marry him. We can find no Healer able to touch this illness. I fear you would only turn her thoughts more towards him.'

Mhoram accepted her judgment morosely. 'I am sorry. This failure grieves me. But the Lords know only of one Unfettered Healer with power for such needs – and she left her home, and passed out of knowledge forty years ago, before the battle of Soaring Woodhelven. It humbles us to be of so little use for such needs.'

His words left behind a pall of silence in their wake. For a time like a muffled sigh, he stared at his clasped hands. But then, rousing himself from his reverie, he said, 'Elders, how will you meet the chance of war? Have you prepared?'

'Yes, Lord,' one of the other women replied. 'We have little cause to fear the destruction of our homes, so we will hide in the mountains if war comes. We have prepared food stores against that need. From the mountains, we will harass any who assail Mithil Stonedown.'

Mhoram nodded, and after a moment, Terass said, 'Lord, War-mark, will you spend the night with us? We will be honoured to provide beds for you. And perhaps you will be able to speak to the gathering of the people?'

'No,' said Troy abruptly. Then, hearing his discourtesy, he softened his tone. 'Thank you, but no. I need to get up to the Watch – as soon as possible.'

'What will you see? The night is dark. You may sleep in comfort here, and still climb to Kevin's Watch before morning.'

But Troy was adamant. His anger at Covenant only increased his impatience; he had a strong sense of pressure, of impending crisis. Lord Mhoram's polite, firm support soon satisfied the Stonedownors that this decision was necessary, and in a short time he and Troy were on their way. They accepted a pot of graveling from the elders to light their path, left all the Bloodguard except Terrel and Ruel to care for the Ranyhyn and watch over the valley, then started walking briskly along the Mithil into the night.

Troy could see nothing outside the primary glow of the graveling, but when he was sure he was out of earshot of the Stonedown, he said to Mhoram, 'You knew about Triock before tonight. Why didn't you tell me?'

'I did not know the extent of his distress. Why should I burden you? Yet now it is in my heart that I have treated him wrongly. I should have dealt with him openly, and trusted him to bear my words. My caution has only increased his pain.'

Troy took a different view. 'You wouldn't need to be cautious at all if it weren't for that damned Covenant.'

But Mhoram only walked on up the valley in silence.

Together they worked their way south into the foothills of the surrounding mountains, then doubled back northward, up the eastern slopes. On the mountainside, the trail was difficult. Terrel led Lord Mhoram, and Troy followed them with Ruel at his back. As he ascended the path, he could see nothing of his situation – for him, the glow of the graveling was encased in dark fog – but slowly he began to feel a change in the air. The warm autumn night of the South Plains turned cooler, rarer; it made his heart pound. By the time he had climbed a couple of thousand feet, he knew that he was moving into mountains which had already received their first winter snows.

Soon after that, he and his companions left the open mountainside and began to work upward through rifts and crevices and hidden valleys. When they reached open space again, they were on a ledge in a cliff face, moving eastward under the huge loom of a peak. This ledge took them to the base of the long, leaning stone shaft of the Watch. Then, clambering through empty air like solitary dream figures, they went up the exposed stair of the shaft. After another five hundred feet, they found themselves on the parapeted platform of Kevin's Watch.

Troy moved cautiously over the floor of the Watch, and seated himself with his back against the surrounding parapet. He knew from descriptions that he was on the tip of the shaft, poised four thousand feet directly above the foothills of a promontory in the Range, and he did not want to give his blindness a chance to betray him. Even sitting with solid stone between his back and the fall, he had an intense impression of abysses. His sense of ambience felt poignantly the absence of any comforting confines or enclosures or limits. This was like being cast adrift in the trackless heavens, and he reacted to it like a blind man – with fear, and a conviction of irremediable isolation. He placed the pot of graveling on the stone before him, so that he could at least vaguely see his three companions. Then he braced both arms against the stone beside him as if to keep himself from falling.

A slight breeze drifted onto the Watch from the towering mountain face south of it, and the air carried a foretaste of winter that made Troy shiver. As midnight passed through the darkness, he began to talk desultorily, as if to warm the vigil by the sound of his voice. His present sense of suspension, of voids, reminded him of his last moments in that world which Covenant insisted on calling 'real' – moments during which his apartment had been flame-gutted, forcing him to hang by failing fingers from his windowsill, with the long fall and smash on concrete hovering below him.

He talked erratically about that world until the vividness of the memory eased. Then he said, 'Friend Mhoram, remind me – remind me to tell you sometime how grateful I am – for everything.' He was embarrassed to say such things aloud, but these feelings were too important to be left unexpressed. 'You and Elena and Quaan and Amorine – you're all incredibly precious to me. And the Warward – I think I'd be willing to jump from here if the Warward needed it.'

He fell silent again, and time passed. Although he shivered in the chill breeze, his speech had steadied him. He tried to turn his thoughts to the fighting ahead, but the unknown sight crouched in the coming day dominated his brain, confusing all his anticipations and plans. And around him the blank night remained unchanged, as impenetrable as chaos. He needed to know where he stood. In the distance, he thought he heard dim hoof-beats. But none of his companions reacted to them; he could not be sure he had heard anything.

He needed to distract himself. Half to Mhoram, he growled, 'I hate dawns. I can cope with nights. They keep me – they're something I've had experience with, at least. But dawns! I can't stand waiting for what I'm going to see.' Then, abruptly, he asked, 'Is the sky clear?'

'It is clear,' Mhoram said softly.

Troy sighed his relief. For a moment, he was able to relax.

Silence encompassed the Watch again. The waiting went on. Gradually, Troy's shivering became worse. The stone he leaned against remained cold, impervious to his body warmth. He wanted to stand up and pace, but did not dare. Around him, Mhoram, Ruel, and Terrel stood as still as statues. After a while, he could no longer refrain from asking the Lord if he had received any messages from Elena. 'Has she tried to contact you? How is she doing?'

'No, Warmark,' Mhoram answered. 'The High Lord does not bear with her any of the *lomillialor* rods.'

'No?' The news dismayed Troy. Until this moment, he had not realized how much trust he had put in Mhoram's power to contact Elena. He wanted to know that she was safe. And as a last resort, he had counted on being able to summon her. But now she was as completely lost to him as if she were already dead. 'No?' He felt suddenly so blind that he could not see Mhoram's face, that he had never really seen Mhoram's face. 'Why?'

'The High Wood rods were only three. One went to Lord's Keep, and one stayed in Revelwood, so that the Loresraat and Revelstone could act together to defend themselves. One rod remained. It was given into my hands for use in this war.'

Troy's voice crackled with protest. 'What good is that?'

'At need I will be able to speak to Revelwood and Lord's Keep.'

'Oh, you fool.' Troy did not know whether he was referring to

Mhoram or himself. So many things had been kept from him. And yet he had never thought to ask who had the rods. He had been saving that whole subject until he saw Lord Foul's army, knew what help he would need. 'Why didn't you tell me?'

For answer, Mhoram only gazed at him. But through his haze, Troy could not read the Lord's expression. 'Why didn't you tell me?' he repeated more bitterly. 'How much else is there that you haven't told me?'

Mhoram sighed. 'As to the *lomillialor* – I did not speak because you did not ask. The rods are not a tool that you could use. They were made for the Lords, and we used them as we saw fit. It did not occur to us that your desires would be otherwise.'

He sounded withdrawn, weary. For the first time, Troy noticed how unresponsive the Lord had been all day. A fit of shivering shook him. That dream Mhoram had had last night – what did it mean? What did the Lord know that made him so unlike his usual self? Troy felt a sudden foretaste of dread. 'Mhoram,' he began, 'Mhoram – '

'Peace, Warmark,' the Lord breathed. 'Someone comes.'

At once, Troy heaved to his feet, and caught at Ruel's shoulder to anchor himself. Though he strained his ears, he could hear nothing but the low breeze. 'Who is it?'

For a moment, no one answered. When Ruel spoke, his voice sounded as distant and passionless as the darkness. 'It is Tull, who shared the mission of Korik to the Giants of Seareach.'

17

TULL'S TALE

Troy's heart lurched, and began to labour heavily. Tull! He could feel his pulse beating in his temples. Korik's mission! After the shock of Runnik's news, he had had repressed all thought of the Giants, refused to let himself think of them. He had concentrated on the war, concentrated on something he could do something about. But now his thoughts reeled. The Giants!

Almost instantly he began to calculate. He had been away from Revelstone for twenty-five days. The mission to Seareach had left eighteen days before that. That was almost enough time, almost enough. The Giants could not travel as fast as Bloodguard on Ranyhyn – but surely they would not be far behind. Surely –

Troy could understand how Tull had come here. It made sense. The other Bloodguard would be leading the Giants, and Tull had come ahead to tell the Warward that help was on the way. With war on the Land and Lord Foul marching, the Giants would not go to Revelstone, would not go north at all. They would go south, around Sarangrave Flat if not through it. The Bloodguard knew Troy's battle plan; they would know what to do. They would pick up the trail of Lord Foul's army above Landsdrop south of Mount Thunder, and would follow it – past Morinmoss, through the Mithil valley, then southwest towards Doom's Retreat. They would be hoping to attack Lord Foul's rear during the battle of the Retreat. And Tull, seeking to circumvent Lord Foul's army in search of the Warward, would naturally come south to skirt the Southron Range towards Doom's Retreat. That route would bring him almost to the doorstep of Mithil Stonedown. Surely – !

When Tull topped the stair and stepped onto the Watch, Troy was so eager that he jumped past all preliminary questions. 'Where are they?' The words came so rapidly that he could hardly articulate them. 'How far behind are they?'

In the dim light of the graveling, he was unable to make out Tull's face. But he could tell that the Bloodguard was not looking at him. 'Lord,' Tull said, 'I was charged by Korik to give my tidings to the High Lord. With Shull and Vale I was charged – ' For an instant, his flat voice faltered. 'But the Bloodguard in the Stonedown have told me that the High Lord has gone into the Westron Mountains with Amok. I must give my tidings to you. Will you hear?'

Even through his excitement, Troy sensed something strange in Tull's tone, something that sounded like pain. But he could not wait to hear it explained. Before Lord Mhoram could reply, Troy repeated, 'Where are they?'

'They?' said the Bloodguard.

'The Giants! How far behind are they?'

Tull turned deliberately away from him to face Lord Mhoram.

'We will hear you,' Mhoram said. His voice was tense with dread, but he spoke steadily, without hesitation. 'This war is in our hands. Speak, Bloodguard.'

'Lord, they – we could not – the Giants – ' Suddenly the habitual flatness of Tull's voice was gone. 'Lord!' The word vibrated with a grief so keen that the Bloodguard could not master it.

The sound of it stunned Troy. He was accustomed to the characteristic alien lack of inflection of all the Bloodguard. He had long since stopped expecting them to express what they felt – had virtually forgotten that they even had emotions. And he was not braced for grief; his anticipation of good news was so great that he could already taste it.

Instantly, before either he or Lord Mhoram could say anything, react at all, Terrel moved towards Tull. Swinging so swiftly that Troy hardly saw the blow, he struck Tull across the face. The hit resounded heavily in the empty air.

At once, Tull stiffened, came to attention. 'Lord,' he began again, and now his voice was as expressionless as the night, 'with Shull and Vale I was charged to bear tidings to the High Lord. Before the dawn of the twenty-fourth day of the mission – the dawn after the dark of the moon – we left *Coercri* and came south, as Korik charged us, seeking to find the High Lord in battle at Doom's Retreat. But because of the evil which is awake, we were compelled to journey on foot around the Sarangrave, and so twelve days were gone. We came too near to the Shattered Hills, and so Vale and Shull fell to the scouts and defenders of Corruption. But I endured. Borne by the Ranyhyn, I fled to Landsdrop and the Upper Land, following Corruption's army. Striving to pass around it, I rode through the hills to the Southron Range, and so came within hail of Mithil Stonedown – eight days in which the Ranyhyn has run without rest.

'Lord – ' Again he faltered, but at once he controlled himself. 'I must tell you of the mission to Seareach, and of the ill doom which has befallen The Grieve.'

'I hear you,' Mhoram said painfully. 'But forgive me – I must sit.' Like an old man, he lowered himself down his staff to rest with his back against the wall of the parapet. 'I lack the strength to stand for such tidings.'

Tull seated himself opposite the Lord across the graveling pot, and Troy sat down also, as if Tull's movement compelled him. The vestiges of his sight were locked on the Bloodguard.

After a moment, Mhoram said, 'Runnik came to us in Trothgard. He spoke of Hoerkin and Lord Shetra, and of the lurker of the Sarangrave. There is no need to speak of such things again.'

'Very well.' Tull faced the Lord, but his visage was shrouded in darkness. Troy could not see his eyes; he appeared to have no eyes, no mouth, no features. When he began his tale, his voice seemed to be the voice of the blind night.

But he told his tale clearly and coherently, as if he had rehearsed it many times during his journey from Seareach. And as he spoke, Troy was reminded that he was the youngest of the Bloodguard – a *Haruchai* no older than Troy himself. Tull had come to Revelstone to replace one of the Bloodguard who had been slain during Lord Mhoram's attempt to scout the Shattered Hills. So he was still new to the Vow. Perhaps that explained his unexpected emotion, and his ability to tell a tale in a way that his hearers could understand.

After the deaths of Lord Shetra and the Bloodguard Cerrin, there was rain in Sarangrave Flat all that day. It was cold and merciless, and it harmed the mission, for Lord Hyrim was sickened by the river water he had swallowed, and the rain made his sickness worse. And the Bloodguard could give him no ease – neither warmth nor shelter. In the capsizing of the raft, all the blankets had been lost. And the rank water of the Defiles Course did other damage: it spoiled all the food except that which had been kept in tight containers; it ruined the *lillianrill* rods, so that they had no more potency to burn against the rain; it even stained the clothing, so that Lord Hyrim's robe and the raiment of the Bloodguard became black.

Before the end of the day, the Lord was no longer strong enough to propel or steer the raft. Fever filled his eyes, and his lips were blue and trembling with cold. Sitting in the centre of the raft, he hugged his staff as if for warmth.

During the night he began to rant.

In a voice that bubbled through the water running down his face, he spoke to himself as to an adversary and tormentor, alternately cursing and pleading. At times, he wept like a child. His delirium was cruel to him, demeaning him as if he were without use or worth. And the Bloodguard could do nothing to succour him.

But at last before dawn the rain broke, and the sky became clear. Then Korik ordered the raft over to one bank. Though it was perilous to stop thus in darkness, he sent half the Bloodguard foraging into the jungle for firewood and *aliantha*.

After Sill fed him a handful of treasure-berries, the Lord rallied enough to call up a flame from his staff. With this, Korik started a fire, built it into a steady blaze near the centre of the raft. Then the steersmen pushed the raft out into the night, and the mission continued on its way.

In the course of that day, they slowly passed out of the Sarangrave. Across the leagues, the Defiles Course was now growing constantly wider and shallower, dividing into more channels as islets and mudbanks increased. These channels were treacherous – shallow, barred with mudbanks, full of rotten logs and stumps – and the effort of navigating them slowed the raft still more. And around it, the jungle gradually changed. The vegetation of the Sarangrave gave way to different kinds of growths: tall, dark trees with limbs that spread out widely above bare trunks, hanging mosses, ferns of all kinds, bushes that clung to naked rock with thin root-fingers and seemed to drink from the river through leaves and branches. Water snakes swam out of the path of the raft. And the stench of the Course slowly faded into a smell of accumulated wet decay and stagnation.

Thus the mission entered Lifeswallower, the Great Swamp.

As they moved, Korik kept the raft in the northern passages. In this way, he was able to begin travelling northeastward – towards Seareach – and to avoid the heart of Lifeswallower.

When night came, they were fortunate that the sky was clear; in that tortuous channel, starless darkness would have halted the mission altogether.

Yet they were still in one of the less difficult regions of Lifeswallower; water still flowed over the deep mud and silt. Eastward, in the heart of the Great Swamp, the water slowly sank into the ground, creating one continuous quagmire for scores of leagues in all directions, where the mud flowed and seethed almost imperceptibly.

But in other things they were not so fortunate. The fever now raged in Lord Hyrim. Though Sill had fed him with *aliantha*, and on water boiled clean, he was failing. Already he looked thinner, and he shook as if there were a palsy in his bones.

And without him – without the power of his staff – the mission could not escape Lifeswallower. The steersmen were forced to keep the raft where the water was deepest because the mud of the Swamp sucked at their poles. If the logs touched that clinging mud, the Bloodguard would be unable to pull the raft free.

Even in the centre of the channel, their progress was threatened by the peculiar trees of Lifeswallower. These trees the Giants called marshwaders. Despite their height, and the wide stretch of their limbs, their roots were not anchored in solid ground. Rather they held themselves erect in the mud, and they seemed to move with the submerged, subtle currents of the Swamp. Passages that looked open from a distance were closed when the raft reached them; channels appeared which had been invisible earlier. More than once trees moved towards each other as the raft passed between them, as if they sought to capture it.

All these things grew worse as the days passed. The level of the water in the channel was declining. As the mission moved north and east, more and more of the river was swallowed into the mire, and the raft sank towards the mud.

The Bloodguard could find no escape. Lifeswallower allowed them no opportunity to work their way northward to solid ground. Although they were always within half a league of the simple marsh which bordered the Swamp, they could not reach it. They thrust the raft along, laboured tirelessly day and night, paused only to collect *aliantha* and firewood. But they could not escape. They needed Lord Hyrim's power – and he was lost in delirium. His eyes were crusted as if with dried foam, and only the treasure-berries and boiled water which Sill forced into him kept him alive.

During the afternoon of the eighteenth day of the mission, the logs of the raft touched mud. Though thin water still gleamed among the trees, the raft no longer floated. The bog held it despite the best efforts of the steersmen, and drew it eastward deeper into the Swamp, moving with the slow current of the mire.

Korik could not see any hope. But Sill disagreed. He insisted that within Lord Hyrim's ill flesh an unquenched spirit survived. He felt it with his hand on the Lord's brow; something in Hyrim still resisted the fever. Through the long watch of the day, he nourished that spirit with treasure-berries and boiled, brackish water. And in the evening the Lord rallied. Some of the dry flush left his face; he began to sweat. As his chills faded, his breathing became easier. By nightfall he was sleeping quietly.

But it appeared that he had begun to recover too late. Deep in the dark night, the grip of the mud bore the raft into an open flat devoid of trees. There the current eddied, turned back on itself, formed a slow whirlpool just broad enough to catch all four sides of the raft and start sucking it down.

And the Bloodguard could do nothing. Here all strength and fidelity lost their worth; here no Vow had meaning. The mission was in Lord Hyrim's hands, and he was weak.

But when Korik wakened him, the Lord's eyes were lucid. He listened as Korik told him of the mission's plight. Then after a time, he said, 'How far must we go to escape?'

'A league, Lord.' Korik indicated the direction with a nod.

'So far? Friend Korik, some day you must tell me how we came to these straits.' Sighing, he pulled himself close to the fire and began eating the mission's store of *aliantha*. He made no attempt to rise until he had eaten it all.

Then, with Sill's help, he climbed to his feet on the slowly revolving raft, and moved into position. Bracing himself against the Bloodguard, he thrust his staff between the logs into the mud.

A snatch of song broke through his teeth; the staff began to pulse in his hands.

For a time, his exertions had no effect. Power mounted in his staff, grew higher at the command of his uncertain strength, but the raft still sank deeper into the Swamp. The stench of decay and death thickened. Lord Hyrim groaned at the strain, and summoned more of his strength. He began to sing aloud.

Blue sparks burst from the wood of his staff, ran down into the muck. With a loud sucking noise, the raft pulled free of the eddy, lumbered away. Swinging around the whirlpool, it started northward.

For a long time, Lord Hyrim kept the raft moving. Then he reached the marshwaders on the north side of the eddy. There the Bloodguard threw out *clingor* lines to the trees ahead, used the ropes to pull the raft along. At once, Hyrim dropped his power and slumped forward. Sill bore him back to the centre of the raft. As soon as he lay down by the embers of the fire, he was asleep.

But now the Bloodguard no longer needed his help. They cast out the *clingor* ropes and heaved on them, hauled the raft between the trees. Their progress was slow, but they did not falter. And when the mud became so thick that their ropes broke under the strain, they strung lines between the trees and left the raft. Sill carried Lord Hyrim lashed to his back, and moved through the mire by pulling himself along the lines while the other Bloodguard strung new ropes ahead and released the ones behind. Then, at last, in the light of dawn, the mud changed to soft wet clay, the trees gave way to stands of cane and marshgrass, and the Bloodguard began to feel solid ground with their bare toes.

Thus they came out into the wide belt of marsh that bordered Lifeswallower.

In the distance ahead, they could see the steep hills which formed the southern edge of Seareach.

The mission had lost three days.

Yet the Bloodguard did not begrudge Lord Hyrim the time to cook a hot meal from the last supplies. The Lord was worn and wasted; his once-round face had become as lean as a wolf's. He needed food and rest. And the mission would make good speed across Seareach towards *Coercri*. If necessary, the Bloodguard could carry Lord Hyrim.

When he had eaten, the Lord groaned to his feet, and started towards the hills. He set a slow pace; he was forced to rest long and often. The Bloodguard soon saw that at this rate they would need all day to cross the five leagues to the hills. But the Lord refused their offer of aid. 'Haste?' he said. 'I have no heart for haste.' And his voice had a bitterness which surprised them until Korik reminded them of what they had heard from Warhaft Hoerkin, and of what the Lord's response had been. Hyrim apparently believed Hoerkin's prophecy concerning the downfall of the Giants.

Yet the Lord laboured throughout the day to reach the hills, and the next day he strove to climb the hills as if he had changed during the night, recovered his sense of urgency. Rolling his eyes at the arduous slope, he pushed himself, laboured upward at the limit of his returning strength.

When at last he crested the hill, he and all the Bloodguard paused to look at Seareach.

The land which the Old Lords had given to the Giants for a home was wide and fair. Enclosed by hills on the south, mountains on the west, and the Sunbirth Sea on the east, it was a green haven for the shipwrecked voyagers. But although they used the Land – cultivated the rolling countryside with crops of all kinds, planted immense vineyards, grew whole forests of the special redwood and teak trees from which they crafted their huge ships – they did not people it. They were lovers of the sea, and preferred to make their dwelling places in the cliffs of the rocky coast, forty leagues east from where the mission now stood.

During the age of Damelon Giantfriend, when the Unhomed were more numerous, they had spread out along the coast, building homes and villages across the whole eastern side of Seareach. But their numbers had slowly declined, until now they were only a third of what they had once been. Yet they were a long-lived, story-loving, gay people and the lack of children hurt them cruelly. Out of slow loneliness, they had left their scattered homes in the north and south of Seareach, and had formed one community – a sea-cliff city where they could share their few children and their songs and their long tales. Despite their ancient custom of long names – names which told the tale of the thing named – they called their city simply *Coercri*, The Grieve. There they had lived since High Lord Kevin's youth.

Looking out over the land of the Giants, Lord Hyrim gave a low cry. 'Korik! Pray that Hoerkin lied! Pray that his message was a lie! Ah, my heart!' He clutched at his chest with both hands, and started down the soft slope into Seareach at a run.

Korik and Sill caught him swiftly, placed a hand under each of his arms. They bore him up between them so that he could move more easily. Thus the mission began its journey towards The Grieve.

Lord Hyrim ran that way for the rest of the day, resting only at moments when the pain in his chest became unendurable. And the Bloodguard knew that he had good reason. Lord Mhoram had said, *Twenty days.* This was the twentieth day of the mission.

The next dawn, when Lord Hyrim arose from his exhausted sleep, he spurned Korik and Sill, and ran alone.

His pace soon brought the mission to the westmost of the Giants' vineyards. Korik sent Doar and Shull through the rows, searching for some sign. But they reported that the Giants who had been working this vineyard had left it together in haste. The matter was clear. Giantish hoes and rakes as tall as men lay scattered among the vines with their blades and teeth still in the marks of their work, and several of the leather sacks in which the Giants usually carried their food and belongings had been thrown to the ground and abandoned. Apparently, the Unhomed had received some kind of signal, and had dropped their work at once to answer it.

Their footprints in the open earth of the vineyard ran in the direction of *Coercri*.

That day, the mission passed through vineyards, teak stands, fields. In all of them, the scattered tools and supplies told the same tale. But the next day came a rain which effaced the footprints and work signs. The Bloodguard were able to gain no more knowledge from such things.

During the night, the rain ended. In the slow breeze, the Bloodguard could smell sea salt. The clear sky appeared to promise a clear day, but the dawn of the twenty-third day had a red cast scored at moments with baleful glints of green, and it gave the Lord no relief. After he had eaten the treasure-berries Sill offered him, he did not arise. Rather, he wrapped his arms around his knees and bowed his head as if he were cowering.

For the sake of the mission, Korik spoke. 'Lord, we must go. The Grieve is near.'

The Lord did not raise his head. His voice was muffled between his knees. 'Are you impervious to fear? Do you not know what we will find? Or does it not touch you?'

'We are the Bloodguard,' Korik replied.

'Yes,' Lord Hyrim sighed. 'The Bloodguard. And I am Hyrim son of Hoole, Lord of the Council of Revelstone. I am sworn to the services of the Land. I should have died in Shetra's place. If I had her strength.'

Abruptly, he sprang to his feet. Spreading his arms, he cried in the words of the old ritual, "We are the new preservers of the Land – votaries of the Earthpower. Sworn and dedicate – dedicate – We will not rest – " ' But he could not complete it. '*Melenkurion*!' he moaned, clutching his black robe at his chest. '*Melenkurion* Skyweir! Help me!'

Korik was loath to speak, but the mission compelled him. 'If the Giants are to be aided, we must do it.'

'Aided?' Lord Hyrim gasped. 'There is no aid for them!' He stooped, snatched up his staff. For several shuddering breaths, he held it, gripped it as if to wrest courage from it. 'But there are other things. We must learn – The High Lord must be told what power performed this abomination!' His eyes had a shadow across them, and their lids were red as if with panic. Trembling, he turned and started towards *Coercri*.

Now the mission did not hasten. It moved cautiously towards the Sea, warding against an ambush. Yet the morning passed swiftly.

Before noon, the Bloodguard and the Lord reached the high lighthouse of The Grieve.

The lighthouse was a tall spire of open stonework that stood on the last and highest hill before the cliffs of the coast. The Giants had built it to guide their roving ships, and someone was always there to tend the focused light beam of the signal fire.

But as the Bloodguard crept up the hill towards the foot of the spire, they could see that the fire was dead. No gleam of light or wisp of smoke came from the cupola atop the tower.

They found blood on the steps of the lighthouse. It was dry and black, old enough to resist the washing of the rain.

At a command from Korik, Vale ran up the steep steps into the spire. The rest of the Bloodguard waited, looking out over *Coercri* and the Sunbirth Sea.

In the noon sun under a clear sky, the Sea was bright with dazzles, and out of sight below the rim of the cliff the waves made muffled thunder against the piers and levees of The Grieve.

There, like a honeycomb in the cliff, was the city of the Giants. All its homes and halls and passages, all its entrances and battlements, had been delved into the rock of the coast. And it was immense. It had halls where five hundred Giants could gather for their Giantclaves and their stories which consumed days in the telling; it had docks for eight or ten of the mighty Giant ships; it had hearths and homes enough for all the remnant of the Unhomed.

Yet it showed no sign of habitation. The back of The Grieve, the side facing inland, looked abandoned. Above it, an occasional gull screamed. And below, the Sea beat. But it revealed no life.

However, *Coercri* had been built to face the Sea. Still the Bloodguard hoped to find Giants there.

Then Vale came down out of the lighthouse. He spoke directly to Lord Hyrim. 'One Giant is there.' He indicated the cupola of the spire with a jerk of his head. 'She is dead.' After a moment, he said, 'She was killed. Her face and the top of her head are gone. Her brain is gone. Consumed.'

All the Bloodguard looked at Lord Hyrim.

He was staring at Vale with red in his eyes. His lean face was twisted. In his throat, he made a confused noise like a snarl. His knuckles were white on his staff. Without a word, he turned and started down towards the main entrance of The Grieve.

Then Korik gave his commands. Of the eleven Bloodguard, Vale, Doar, Shull, and two others he instructed to remain at the lighthouse, to watch, and to give warning if necessary, and to carry out the mission if the others fell. Three he sent northward to begin exploring *Coercri* from that end. And with Tull and Sill, he followed

Lord Hyrim. These three took the Lord away from the main entrance towards the south of the city.

Together, the four crept into The Grieve on its southern side.

The entrance they chose was a tunnel that led straight through the cliff, sloping slightly downward. They passed along it to its end, where it opened into a roofless rampart overhanging the Sea. From this vantage, they could see much of the city's cliff front. Ramparts like the one on which they stood alternately projected and receded along the wall of rock for several levels below them, giving the face of the city a knuckled appearance. They could see into many of the projections until the whole city passed out of sight north of them behind a bulge in the cliff. Down at sea level, just south of this bulge, was a wide levee between two long stone piers.

The levee and the piers were deserted. Nothing moved on any of the ramparts. Except for the noise of the Sea, the city was still.

But when Lord Hyrim opened a high stone door and entered the apartments beyond it, he found two Giants lying cold in a pool of dried blood. Both their skulls were broken asunder and empty, as if the bones had been blasted apart from within.

In the next set of rooms were three more Giants, and in the next set three more, one of them a child – all dead. They lay among pools of their blood, and the blood was spattered around as if someone had stamped through the pools while they were still fresh. All including the child had been slain by having their heads rent open.

But they were not decayed. They had not been long dead – not above three days.

'Three days,' Korik said.

And Lord Hyrim said bitterly, 'Three days.'

They went on with the search.

They looked into every apartment along the rampart until they were directly above the levee. In each set of rooms, they found one or two or three Giants, all slaughtered in the same way. And none but the youngest children showed any sign of resistance, of struggle. The few youngest bodies were contorted and frantic; all the rest lay as if they had been simply struck dead where they stood or sat.

When the searchers entered one round meeting hall, they discovered that it was empty. And the huge kitchen beyond it was also empty. The stove fires had fallen into ash, but the cooks had not been killed there.

The sight dismayed Lord Hyrim. Groaning, he said, 'They went to their homes to die! They knew their danger – and went to their homes to await it. They did not fight – or flee – or send for help. *Melenkurion abatha*! Only the children – What horror came upon them?'

The Bloodguard had no answer. They knew of no wrong potent enough to commit such a slaughter unresisted.

As he left the hall, Lord Hyrim wept openly.

From that rampart, he and the Bloodguard worked downward through the levels of *Coercri*. They took a crooked stairway which descended back into the cliff, then towards the Sea again. At the next level, they again went to look into the rooms. Here also the Giants were dead.

Everywhere it was the same. The Unhomed had gone to their private dwellings to die.

Then an urgency came upon the Bloodguard and the Lord. They began to hasten. The Lord leaped down the high stairs, ran along the ramparts to inspect the apartments. In their black garb, the four flew downward like the ravens of midnight, taking the tale of shed blood and blasted skulls.

When they were more than halfway down The Grieve, Korik stopped them. He had noticed a change in the air of the city. But the difference was subtle; for a moment, he could not identify it. Then he ran into the nearest apartment, hastened to the lone Giant dead in one of the back rooms, touched the pool of blood.

This Giant had been slain more recently; a few spots of the pool were still damp.

Perhaps the slayer was still in the city, stalking its last victims.

At once, Lord Hyrim whispered, 'We must reach the lowest level swiftly. If any Giants yet live, they will be there.'

Korik nodded. Tull sprinted to scout ahead as the others ran to the stairs and started down them. In each level, they stopped long enough to find one dead Giant, test the condition of the blood. Then they raced on downward.

The blood grew steadily damper. Two levels above the piers, they found a child whose flesh still retained a vestige of warmth.

They explored the next level more carefully. And in one room they discovered a Giant with the last blood still dripping from her riven skull.

With great caution, they crept down the final stairs.

The stairway opened on a broad expanse of rock, the base of the two piers and the head of the levee between them. The tide was low and quiet – the waves broke far down the levee – but still the sound filled the air. Even here, the Bloodguard and the Lord could not see beyond the great cliff-bulge just north of the piers. This bulge, and the outward bend of *Coercri's* southern tip, formed a shallow cove around the levee. The flat base of the city lay in the afternoon shadow of the cliff, and the unwarmed rock was damp with spray.

No one moved on the piers, or along the walkway which traversed the city from its southern end northward around the curve of the cliff.

Cut into the base of the cliff behind the walkway and the headrock of the piers were many openings. All had heavy stone doors to keep out the Sea in storms. But most of the doors were open. They led into workshops – high chambers where the Giants formed the planks and hawsers of their ships. Like the meeting halls and kitchens, these places were deserted. But, unlike the western vineyards and fields, the workshops had not been abandoned suddenly. All the tools hung in their racks on the walls; the tables and benches were free of work; even the floors were clean. The Giants labouring there had taken the time to put their shops in order before they went home to die.

But one smaller door near the south end of the headrock was tightly closed. Lord Hyrim tried to open it, but it had no handle, and he could not grip the smooth stone.

Korik and Tull approached it together. Forcing their fingers into one crack of the door, they heaved at it. With a scraping noise like a gasp of pain, it swung outward, admitting shadowy light to the chamber beyond.

The single room was bare; it contained nothing but a low bed against one side wall. It was lightless, and the air in it smelled stale.

On the floor against the back wall sat a Giant.

Even crouched with his knees drawn up before him, he was as tall as the Bloodguard. His staring eyes caught the light and gleamed.

He was alive. A shallow breath stirred in his chest, and a thin trail of saliva ran from the corner of his mouth into his grizzled beard.

But he made no move as the four entered the cell. No blink or flicker of his eyes acknowledged them.

Lord Hyrim rushed towards him gladly, then stopped when he saw the look of horror on the Giant's face.

Korik approached the Giant, touched one of the bare arms which gripped his knees. The Giant was not cold; he was not another Hoerkin.

Korik shook the Giant's arm but the Giant did not respond. He sat gaping blindly out of the doorway. Korik looked a question at the Lord. When Hyrim nodded, Korik struck the Giant across the face.

His head lurched under the blow, but it did not penetrate him. Without blinking, he raised his head again, resumed his stare. Korik prepared to strike again with more force, but Lord Hyrim stopped him. 'Do him no injury, Korik. He is closed to us.'

'We must reach him,' Korik said.

'Yes,' said Hyrim. 'Yes, we must.' He moved close to the Giant, and called, 'Rockbrother! Hear me! I am Hyrim son of Hoole, Lord of the Council of Revelstone. You must hear me. In the name of all the Unhomed – in the name of friendship and the Land – I adjure you! Open your ears to me!'

The Giant made no reply. The slow rate of his breathing did not vary; his white gaze did not falter.

Lord Hyrim stepped back, studied the Giant. Then he said to Korik, 'Free one of his hands.' He rubbed one heel of his staff, and when he took his hand away a blue flame sprang up on the metal. 'I will attempt the *caamora* – the fire of grief.'

Korik understood. The *caamora* was a ritual by which the Giants purged themselves of grief and rage. They were impervious to any ordinary fire, but the flames hurt them, and they used that pain at need to help them master themselves. Swiftly, Korik pried the Giant's right hand loose from its grip, pulled the arm back so that its hand was extended towards Lord Hyrim.

Moaning softly, 'Stone and Sea, Rockbrother! Stone and Sea!' the Lord increased the strength of his Lords-fire. He placed the flame directly under the Giant's hand, enveloped the fingers in fire.

At first, nothing happened; the ritual had no effect. The Giant's fingers hung motionless in the flame, and the flame did not consume them. But then they twitched, groped, clenched. The Giant pushed his hand farther into the fire, though his fingers were writhing in pain.

Abruptly, he drew a deep shuddering breath. His head snapped back, thudded against the wall, dropped forward onto his knees. Yet still he did not withdraw his hand. When he raised his head again, his eyes were full of tears.

Trembling, panting, he pulled back his hand. It was undamaged.

At once, Lord Hyrim extinguished his fire. 'Rockbrother,' he cried softly. 'Rockbrother. Forgive me.'

The Giant stared at his hand. Time passed as he became slowly aware of his situation. At last he recognized the Lord and the Bloodguard. Suddenly he flinched, jerked both hands to the sides of his head, gasped, 'Alive?' Before Lord Hyrim could answer, he went on, 'What of the others? My people?'

Lord Hyrim clutched his staff for support. 'All dead.'

'Ah!' the Giant groaned. His hands dropped to his knees, and he leaned his head back against the wall. 'Oh, my people!' The tears streamed down his cheeks like blood.

The Lord and the Bloodguard watched him in silence, waited for him. At last his grief eased, and his tears ceased. When he brought his head forward from the wall, he murmured as if in defeat, 'He has left me to the last.'

With a visible effort, Lord Hyrim forced himself to ask, 'Who is he?'

The Giant answered in misery, 'He came soon – he came soon after we had learned the fate of the three brothers – the brothers of one birth – Damelon Rockbrother's omen of the end. This spring – ah, was it so recent? It needs more time. There should be years given to it. There – ah, my people! This spring – this – we knew at last that the old slumbering ill of the Sarangrave was awake. We thought to send word to brave Lord's Keep – ' For a moment, he choked on the grief in his throat. 'Then we lost the brothers. Lost them. We arose to one sunrise, and they were gone.

'We did not send to the Lords. How could we bear to tell them that our hope was lost? No. Rather, we searched. From the Northron Climbs to the Spoiled Plains and beyond, we searched. We searched – through all the summer. Nothing. In despair, the searchers returned to The Grieve, *Coercri*, last home of the Unhomed.

'Then the last searcher returned – Wavenhair Haleall, whose womb bore the three. Because she was their mother, she searched when all the others had given up the search, and she was the last to return. She had journeyed to the Shattered Hills themselves. She called all the people together, and told us the fate of the three before she died. The wounds of the search – '

He groaned again. 'Now I am the last. Ah, my people!' As he cried out, he moved, shoved himself to his feet, stood erect against the wall. Towering over his hearers, he put back his head and began to sing the old song of the Unhomed.

> Now we are Unhomed,
>   bereft of root and kith and kin.
> From other mysteries of delight,
>   we set our sails to resail our track;
> but the winds of life blew not the way we chose,
> and the land beyond the Sea was lost.

It was long, like all Giantish songs. But he sang only a fragment of it. Soon he fell silent, and his chin dropped to his breast.

Again Lord Hyrim asked, 'Who is he?'

The Giant answered by resuming his tale. 'Then he came. Omen of the end and Home turned to misery and gall. Then we knew the truth. We had seen it before – in lighter times, when the knowledge might have been of some use – but we had denied it. We had seen our evil, and had denied it, thinking that we might find our way Home and escape it. Fools! When we saw him, we knew the truth.

Through folly and withering seed and passion and impatience for Home, we had become the thing we hate. We saw the truth in him. Our hearts were turned to ashes, and we went to our dwellings – these small rooms which we called homes in vain.'

'Why did you not flee?'

'Some did – some four or five who did not know the long name of despair – or did not hear it. Or they were too much like him to judge. The ill of the Sarangrave took them – they are no more.'

Compelled by the ancient passion of the Bloodguard, Korik asked, 'Why did you not fight?'

'We had become the thing we hate. We are better dead.'

'Nevertheless!' Korik said. 'Is this the fealty of the Giants? Does all promised faithfulness come to this? By the Vow, Giant! You destroy yourselves, and let the evil live! Even Kevin Landwaster was not so weak.'

In his emotion, he forgot caution, and all the Bloodguard were taken unaware. The sudden voice behind them was cold with contempt; it cut through them like a gale of winter. Turning, they found another Giant stood in the doorway. He was much younger than the Giant within, but he resembled the older Giant. The chief difference lay in the contempt that filled his face, raged in his eyes, twisted his mouth as if he were about to spit.

In his right hand, he clenched a hot green stone. It blazed with an emerald strength that shone through his fingers. As he gripped it, it steamed thickly.

He stank of fresh blood; he was spattered with it from head to foot. And within him, clinging to his bones, was a powerful presence that did not fit his form. It slavered from behind his eyes with a great force of malice and wrong.

'Hmm,' he said in a despising tone, 'a Lord and three Bloodguard. I am pleased. I had thought that my friend in the Sarangrave would take all like you – but I see I shall have that pleasure myself. Ah, but you are not entirely scathless, are you? Black becomes you. Did you lose friends to my friend?' He laughed with a grating sound, like the noise of boulders being crushed together.

Lord Hyrim stepped forward, planting his staff, said bravely, 'Come no closer, *turiya* Raver. I am Hyrim, Lord of the Council of Revelstone. *Melenkurion abatha! Duroc minas mill khabaal!* I will not let you pass.'

The Giant winced as Lord Hyrim uttered the Words of power. But then he laughed again. 'Hah! Little Lord! Is that the limit of your lore? Can you come no closer than that to the Seven Words? You pronounce them badly. But I must admit – you have recognized me. I am *turiya* Herem. But we have new names now, my brothers and

I. There is Fleshharrower, and Satansfist. And I am named Kinslaughterer.'

At this, the older Giant groaned heavily. The Raver glanced into the back of the cell, and said in a tone of satisfaction, 'Ah, there he is. Little Lord, I see that you have been speaking with Sparlimb Keelsetter. Did he tell you that he is my father? Father, why do you not welcome your son?'

The Bloodguard did not look at the older Giant. But they heard Keelsetter's pain, and understood it. Something within the Giant was breaking. Suddenly, he gave a savage roar. Leaping past the four, he attacked Kinslaughterer.

His fingers caught the Raver's throat. He drove him back out of the doorway onto the headrock of the piers.

Kinslaughterer made no attempt to break his father's hold. He resisted the impetus until his feet were braced. Then he raised the green stone, moved it towards Keelsetter's forehead. Both fist and stone passed through the older Giant's skull into his brain.

Keelsetter screamed. His hands dropped, his body went limp. He hung from the point of power which impaled his head.

Grinning ravenously, the Raver held his father there for a long moment. Then he tightened his fist. Deep emerald flashed; the stone blasted the front of Keelsetter's skull. He fell dead, pouring blood over the headrock.

Kinslaughterer stamped his feet in the spreading pool.

He appeared oblivious to the four, but he was not. As Korik and Tull started forward to attack him, he swung his arm, hurled a bolt of power at them. It would have slain them before they reached the doorway, but Lord Hyrim lunged, thrust up his staff between them. The end of his staff caught the bolt. It detonated with such force that it broke the staff in two, and flung the four humans against the back of the cell.

The impact made them unconscious.

Thus even the Vow could not preserve the Bloodguard from the extremity of their need.

Korik was the first to reawaken. Hearing returned before sight or touch, and he began to listen. In his ears, the noise of the Sea grew, became violent. But the sound was not the sound of waves in storm; it was more erratic, more vicious. When his sight was restored, he was surprised to find that he could see. He had expected the darkness of clouds.

But early starlight shone through the doorway from a clear night sky. Outside, the Sea thrashed and heaved across the piers and up the levee as if goaded by rowels. And along the sky lightning leaped, followed by such thunder that he felt the bursting in his chest.

Through the spray a high wind howled. And still the sky was clear.

There was a bayamo upon the Sea.

Then a different lightning struck upward into the heavens – a bolt as green as blazing emerald. It came from the levee. Looking through the darkness, Korik discerned the form of the Raver, Kinslaughterer. He stood down in the levee, so close to the tide that the waves broke against his knees. With his stone, he hurled green blasts into the sky, and shook his arms as if the windstorm were his to command.

On the levee behind him were three dead forms – the three Bloodguard whom Korik had sent to the northern end of the city.

For a time, Korik did not comprehend what Kinslaughterer was doing. But then he perceived that the seas out beyond the piers moved in consonance with Kinslaughterer's arms. As the Giant-Raver waved and gestured, they heaved and reared and broke and piled themselves together.

Farther away, the situation was worse. Slowly, with great pitchings and shudders, a massive wall of water rose out of the ocean. Kinslaughterer's green lightning glared across the face of it as it mounted, tossed its crest higher and higher. And as it grew, it moved towards the cliff.

The Raver was summoning a tsunami.

Korik turned to rouse his companions.

Sill and Tull were soon conscious and alert. But Lord Hyrim lay still, and blood trickled from the corner of his mouth. Swiftly, Sill ran his hands over the Lord's body, reported that Hyrim had several broken ribs, but no other injuries. Together, Korik and Sill chafed his wrists, slapped his neck. At last, his eyelids fluttered, and he awakened.

He was dazed. At first, he could not grasp Korik's tidings. But when he looked out into the night, he understood. Already, the mounting tidal wave appeared half as high as the cliff, and its writhing had a dark, ill cast. There was enough hatred concentrated in it to shatter The Grieve. When Lord Hyrim turned from it, his face was taut with terrible purpose.

He had to shout to make himself heard over the roar of waves and wind and thunder. 'We must stop him! He violates the Sea! If he succeeds – if he bends the Sea to his will – the Law that preserves it will be broken. It will serve the Despiser like another Raver!'

Korik answered, 'Yes!' There was a fury in the Bloodguard. They would have disobeyed any other decision.

Yet Sill remembered caution enough to say, 'He has the Illearth Stone.'

'No!' Lord Hyrim searched the floor for the pieces of his staff.

When he found them, he called for *clingor*. Tull gave him a length of line. He used it to lash the two pieces of his staff together, metal heels joined. Clutching this unwieldy instrument, he said, 'That is only a fragment of the Stone! The Illearth Stone itself – is much larger! But in our worst dreams we did not guess that the Despiser would dare cut pieces of the Stone for his servants. His mastery of it must – must be very great. Thus he is able to subdue Giants – the Ravers and the Stone together, the Stone empowering the Raver, and the Raver using the Stone! And the others – Fleshharrower, Satansfist – they also must possess fragments of the Stone. Do you hear, Korik?'

'I hear,' Korik replied. 'The High Lord will be warned.'

Lord Hyrim nodded. The pain in his ribs made him wince. But he thrust his way out of the cell into the howling wind. Korik, Sill, and Tull followed at once.

Ahead of them, Kinslaughterer laboured in an ecstasy of power. Though it was still some distance from the piers, the tsunami towered over him, dwarfed his stolen form. Now he was chanting to it, invoking it. His words cut through the tumult of the storm.

> Come, Sea!
> Obey me!
> Raise high!
> crash down!
> Break rock!
> break stone:
> crush heart:
> grind soul:
> rend flesh:
> crack whole!
> Eat dead
> for bread!
> Come, Sea!
> Obey me!

And the seas answered, piled still higher. Now the wave's crest frothed and lashed level with the upper ramparts of *Coercri*.

The Bloodguard wished to attack instantly, but Lord Hyrim held them back. So that he would not be heard by Kinslaughterer, he mouthed the words, 'I must strike the first blow.' Then he moved over the headrock as fast as his damaged chest permitted.

When the four started into the levee, the huge wall of water already appeared to be leaning over them. Only the might of Kinslaughterer's Stone kept it erect. As they approached, he was too consumed by the spectacle of his own power to sense them. But in the last moment, some instinct warned him. He spun suddenly, found Lord Hyrim within a few yards of him.

Roaring savagely, he raised his glowing fist to hurl a blast at the Lord.

But while the Raver cocked his arm, Lord Hyrim leaped the last distance towards him. With the lashed fragments of his staff, the Lord struck upward.

The metal heels hit Kinslaughterer's hand before his bolt was ready.

The two powers clashed in a blaze of green and blue. Kinslaughterer's greater force drove his might like lightning down the length of Lord Hyrim's arms into his head and body. The green fire burned within him, burned his brain and heart. When the flame ceased, he collapsed.

But the clash scorched Kinslaughterer's hand, and its recoil knocked his arms back. He lost the Stone. It fell, rolled away from him across the headrock.

At once, the three Bloodguard sprang; together they struck the Raver with all their strength. And in that assault their Vow at last found utterance. The Giant-Raver was dead before his form fell into the water.

Yet still for a long moment the Bloodguard hurled blows at him, driven by the excess of their rage and abomination. Then the splashing of salt water cooled them, and they perceived that the storm had begun to fade.

Without the compulsion of the Stone, the wind failed. The lightning stopped. After a few last tolls, the thunder fell away.

The tidal wave made a sound like an avalanche as it fell backward into the sea. Its spray wet the faces of the Bloodguard, and its waves broke over their thighs. Then it was gone.

Together, the three hastened back to Lord Hyrim.

He still clung to life, but he was almost at an end; the Raver's blast had burned him deeply. His eye sockets were empty, and from between his hollow lids a thin grey smoke rose up into the starlight. As Sill lifted him into a sitting position, his hands groped about him as if they were searching for his staff, and he said weakly, 'Do not — do not touch — take — '

He could not speak it. The effort burst his heart. With a groan, he died in Sill's arms.

For a time, the Bloodguard stood over him in silence, gave him what respect they could. But they had no words to say. Soon Korik went and took up Kinslaughterer's fragment of the Illearth Stone. Without a will to drive it, it was dull; it showed only fitful gleams in its core. But it hurt his hand with a deep and fiery cold. He clenched it in his fist.

'We will take it to the High Lord,' he said. 'Perhaps the other Ravers have such power. The High Lord may use this power to defeat them.'

Sill and Tull nodded. In the ruin of the mission, there was no other hope left to them.

'Then we sent homeward the bodies of our fallen comrades,' Tull said softly. 'There was no need for haste – we knew that their Ranyhyn could find a way in safety north of the Sarangrave. And when that task was done, we returned to the five who stood watch at the lighthouse. Two of them Korik charged to return to Lord's Keep with all possible speed, so that Revelstone might be warned. And because he judged that the war had already begun – that the High Lord would be marching in the South Plains with the Warward – I was charged, and Shull and Vale with me, to bear these tidings southward, the way I have come. With Sill and Doar, Korik undertook the burden of the Illearth Stone, so that it might be taken in safety to Revelstone for the Lords.'

At last the Bloodguard fell silent. For a long time, Troy sat gazing sightlessly at the stone before him. He felt deaf and numb – too shocked to hear the low breeze blowing around Kevin's Watch, too stunned to feel the chill of the mountain air. Dead? he asked silently. All dead? But it seemed to him that he felt nothing. In him there was a pain so deep that he was not conscious of it.

But in time he recollected himself enough to raise his head, look over at Lord Mhoram. He could see the Lord dimly. His forehead was tight with pain, and his eyes bled tears.

With an effort, Troy found his voice. It was husky with emotion as he asked, 'Is this what you saw – last night? Is this it?'

'No.' Mhoram's reply was abrupt. But it was not abrupt with anger; it was abrupt with the exertion of suppressing his sobs. 'I saw Bloodguard fighting in the service of the Despiser.'

There was a long and heartrending pause before Tull said through his teeth, 'That is impossible.'

'They should not have touched the Stone,' the Lord breathed weakly. 'They should not – !'

Troy wanted to question Mhoram, ask him what he meant. But then suddenly he realized that he was seeing more clearly. His fog was lifting.

At once, he rose to his knees, turned, braced his chest on the edge of the parapet. Instinctively, he tightened his sunglasses on his face.

Along the rim of the eastern horizon dawn had already begun.

18

DOOM'S RETREAT

Immediately, Troy jumped erect to face the sun.

His companions stood with him in tense silence, as if they intended to share what he would see. But he knew that even the Bloodguard could not match his mental sight. He paid no attention to them. All his awareness was consumed by the gradual revelations of the dawn.

At first, he could see only a fading grey and purple blankness. But then the direct rays of the sun caught the platform, and his surroundings began to lift their heads out of the mist. Above the long fall into shadow, he received his first visual sense of the wide open air in which Kevin's Watch stood as if on the tip of a dark finger accusing the heavens. In the west, across a distance too great for any sight but his, he saw sunlight touch the thin snowcaps of the mountain wedge which separated the South Plains from Garroting Deep. And as the sun climbed higher, he made out the long curve of peaks running south then west from the valley of Mithil Stonedown to Doom's Retreat.

Then the light reached down to the hills which formed the eastern border of the Plains between Kevin's Watch and Andelain. Now he could follow the whole course of the Mithil River northwest and then north until it joined the Black. He felt strangely elevated and mighty. His gaze had never comprehended so much before, and he understood how High Lord Kevin must have felt. Standing on the Watch was like being on the pinnacle of the Earth.

But the sun kept rising. Like a tide of illumination, it flooded across the Plains, washing away the last of blindness.

What he saw staggered him where he stood. Horror filled his eyes like the rush of an avalanche. It was worse than anything he could have imagined.

He made out the Warward first. His army had just begun to march; it crept south along the mountain wedge. He saw it as hardly more than a smudge in the foothills, but he could gauge its speed. It was still two days from Doom's Retreat.

Hiltmark Quaan's force was closer to him, and farther from the Retreat. But the horsemen were moving faster. He estimated their numbers instinctively, instantly; he knew at once that they had been decimated. More than a third of the two hundred Bloodguard were gone, and of Quaan's twelve Eoward less than six remained. They hurried raggedly, almost at a dead rout.

Raging at their heels came a vast horde of *kresh* – at least ten thousand of the savage yellow wolves. The mightiest of them, the most powerful two thousand, bore black riders – ur-viles. The ridden *kresh* ran in tight wedges, and the ur-vile loremasters at the wedge tips threw torrents of dark force at every rider who fell within their reach.

In an effort to control the pace, restrain it from utter flight, Eoman turned at intervals. Twenty or forty warriors threw themselves together at the yellow wall to slow the charge of the *kresh*. Troy could see flashes of blue fire in these sorties; Callindrill and Verement were alive. But two Lords were not enough. The riders were hopelessly outnumbered. And they were already well beyond the Mithil River in their race towards Doom's Retreat. Even if they ran no faster, they would reach the Retreat before the marching Warward.

Quaan had been unable to gain the last day that the marchers needed.

Yet even that was not the most crushing sight. Behind the wolves came the main body of Lord Foul's army. This body was closer than the others to Kevin's Watch, and Troy could see it with appalling clarity.

The Giant striding at its head was the least of its horrors. At the Giant's back marched immense ranks of Cavewights – at least twenty thousand of the strong, ungainly rock delvers. Behind them hurried an equal number of ur-viles, loping on all fours for better speed. Through their ranks, hundreds of fearsome, lionlike *griffins* alternately trotted and flew. And after the Demondim-spawn came a seething, grim army so huge that Troy could not even guess its numbers: humans, wolves, Waynhim, forest animals, creatures of the Flat, all radiating the fathomless blood-hunger which coerced them – many myriad of warped, rabid creatures, the perverted handiwork of Lord Foul and the Illearth Stone.

Most of this prodigious army had already crossed the Mithil in pursuit of Hiltmark Quaan and his command. It moved with such febrile speed that it was little more than three days from Doom's Retreat. And it was so mighty that no ambush, however well conceived, could hope to stand against it.

But there would be no ambush. The Warward did not know its peril and would not reach the Retreat in time.

Like jagged hunks of rock, these facts beat Warmark Troy to his knees. 'Dear God!' he breathed in anguish. 'What have I done?' The avalanche of revelations battered him down. 'Dear God. Dear God. What have I done?'

Behind him, Lord Mhoram insisted with mounting urgency, 'What is it? What do you see? Warmark, what do you see?' But Troy could not answer. His world was reeling around him. Through the vertigo of his perceptions, his clutching mind could grasp only one thought: this was his fault, all of it was his fault. The futility of Korik's mission, the end of the Giants, the inevitable slaughter of the Warward — everything was on his head. He had been in command. And when the debacle of his command was over, the Land would be defenceless. He had served the Despiser from the start without knowing it, and what Atiaran Trell-mate had given her life for was worse than nothing.

'Worse,' he gasped. He had condemned his warriors to death. And they were only the beginning of the toll Lord Foul would exact for his misjudgment. 'Dear God.' He wanted to howl, but his chest was too full of horror; it had no room for outcries.

He did not understand how the Despiser's army could be so big. It surpassed his most terrible nightmares.

Wildly, he surged to his feet. He tore at his breast, trying to wrest enough air from his unbreathable failure for just one cry. But he could not get it; his lungs were clogged with ruin. A sudden loud helplessness roared in his ears, and he pitched forward.

He did not realize that he had tried to jump until Terrel and Ruel caught his legs and hauled him back over the parapet.

Then he felt a burning in his cheeks. Lord Mhoram was slapping him. When he flinched, the Lord pulled close to him, shouted into his eyeless face, 'Warmark! Hile Troy! Hear me! I understand — the Despiser's army is great. And the Warward will not reach Doom's Retreat in time. I can help!'

Dumbly, instinctively, Troy tried to straighten his sunglasses on his face, and found that they were gone. He had lost them over the edge of Kevin's Watch.

'Hear me!' Mhoram cried. 'I can send word. If either Callindrill or Verement lives, I can be heard. They can warn Amorine.' He grabbed Troy's shoulders, and his fingers dug in, trying to gain a hold on Troy's bones. 'Hear! I am able. But I must have reason, hope. I cannot — if it is useless. Answer!' he demanded through clenched teeth. 'You are the Warmark. Find hope! Do not leave your warriors to die!'

'No,' Troy whispered. He tried to break away from Mhoram's grip, but the Lord's fingers were too strong. 'There's no way. Foul's army is too big.'

He wanted to weep, but Mhoram did not let him. 'Discover a

way!' the Lord raged. 'They will be slain! You must save them!'

'I can't!' Troy shouted in sudden anger. The stark impossibility of Mhoram's demand touched a hidden resource in him, and he yelled, 'Foul's army is too goddamn big! Our forces are going to get there too late! The only way they can stay alive just a little longer is to run straight through the Retreat and keep going until they drop! There's nothing out there − just Wastes, and Desert, and a clump of ruins, and − !'

Abruptly, his heart lurched. Kevin's Watch seemed to tilt under him, and he grabbed at Mhoram's wrists to steady himself. 'Sweet Jesus!' he whispered. 'There is one chance.'

'Speak it!'

'There's one chance,' Troy repeated in a tone of wonder. 'Jesus.' With an effort, he forced his attention into focus on Mhoram. 'But you'll have to do it.'

'Then I will do it. Tell me what must be done.'

For a moment longer, the sweet sense of reprieve amazed Troy, outweighing the need to act, almost dumbfounding him. 'It's going to be rough,' he murmured to himself. 'God! It's going to be rough.' But Mhoram's insistent grip held him. Speaking slowly to help himself collect his thoughts, he said, 'You're going to have to do it. There's no other way. But first you've got to get through to Callindrill or Verement.'

Lord Mhoram's piercing gaze probed Troy. Then Mhoram helped the Warmark to his feet. Quietly, the Lord asked, 'Do Callindrill and Verement live?'

'Yes. I saw their fire. Can you reach them? They don't have any of that High Wood.'

Mhoram smiled grimly. 'What message shall I give?'

Now Troy studied Mhoram. He felt oddly vulnerable without his sunglasses, as if he were exposed to reproach, even to abhorrence, but he could see Mhoram acutely. What he saw reassured him. The Lord's eyes gleamed with hazardous potentials, and the bones of his skull had an indomitable hue. The contrast to his own weakness humbled Troy. He turned away to look out over the Plains again. The ponderous movement of Lord Foul's hordes continued as before, and at the sight he felt a resurgence of panic. But he held onto his power of command, gripped it to keep his shame at bay. Finally, he said, 'All right. Let's get going. Tull, you'd better go back to the Stonedown. Have the Ranyhyn brought as far up the trail as possible. We've got a long run ahead of us.'

'Yes, Warmark.' Tull left the Watch soundlessly.

'Now, Mhoram. You had the right idea. Amorine has got to be warned. She has got to get to the Retreat ahead of Quaan.' It occurred to him that Quaan might not be alive, but he forced that fear down. 'I don't care how she does it. She's got to have that ambush ready when the riders arrive. If she doesn't – ' He had to lock his jaw to keep his voice from shaking. 'Can you communicate that?' He shuddered to think of the warriors' plight. After a twenty-five-day march, they would have to run the last fifty miles – only to learn that their ordeal was not done. Pushing himself around to face Mhoram, he demanded, 'Well?'

Mhoram had already taken the *lomillialor* rod from his robe, and was lashing it across his staff with a *clingor* thong. As he secured the rod, he said, 'My friend, you should leave the Watch. You will be safer below.'

Troy acquiesced without question. He gazed at the armies once more to be sure that he had gauged their relative speeds accurately, then wished Lord Mhoram good luck, and started the descent. The stairs felt slippery under his hands and feet, but he was reassured by Ruel's presence right below him. Soon he stood on the ledge at the base of the Watch, and stared up into the blue sky towards Lord Mhoram.

After a pause that seemed unduly long to Troy's quickening sense of urgency, he heard snatches of song from atop the shaft. The song mounted into the air, then abruptly fell silent. At once, flame erupted around Lord Mhoram. It engulfed the whole platform of the Watch, and it filled the air with an impression of reverberation, as if the cliff face echoed a protracted and inaudible shriek. The noiseless ululation made Troy's ears burn, made him ache to cover them and hide his head, but he forced himself to withstand it. He did not take his gaze off the Watch.

The echoing was mercifully brief. Moments after its last vibration had faded, Terrel came down the stair, half carrying Mhoram.

Troy was afraid that the Lord had damaged himself. But Mhoram only suffered from a sudden exhaustion – the price of his exertion. All his movements were weak, unsteady, and his face dripped with sweat, but he managed a faint smile for Troy. 'I would not care to be Callindrill's foe,' he said wanly. 'He is strong. He sends riders to Amorine.'

'Good.' Troy's voice was gruff with affection and relief. 'But if we don't get to Doom's Retreat before midafternoon tomorrow, it'll be wasted.'

Mhoram nodded. He braced himself on Terrel's shoulder, and stumbled away along the ledge with Troy and Ruel behind him.

They made slow progress at first because of Mhoram's fatigue, but before long they reached a small, pine-girdled valley plentifully grown with *aliantha*. A breakfast of treasure-berries rejuvenated

Lord Mhoram, and after that he moved more swiftly.

Behind Mhoram and Terrel, with Ruel at his back, Troy travelled on an urgent wind, a pressure for haste, that threatened to become a gale. He was eager to reach the Ranyhyn. When they met Tull and the other Bloodguard on their way up the trail, he mounted Mehryl at once, and hurried the Ranyhyn into a brisk trot back towards Mithil Stonedown.

He intended to ride straight past the village to the Plains, where the Ranyhyn could run. However, as he and his companions approached the Stonedown, he saw the Circle of elders waiting beside the trail. Reluctantly, he stopped and saluted them.

'Hail, Warmark Troy,' Terass Slen-mate replied. 'Hail, Lord Mhoram. We have heard some of the tidings of war, and know that you must make haste. But Triock son of Thuler would speak with you.'

As Terass introduced him, Triock stepped forward.

'Hail, elders of Mithil Stonedown,' Mhoram responded. 'Our thanks again for your hospitality. Triock son of Thuler, we will hear you. But speak swiftly – time presses heavily upon us.'

'It is no great matter,' said Triock stiffly. 'I wish only to seek pardon for my earlier conduct. I have reason for distress, as you know. But I kept my Oath of Peace at Atiaran Trell-mate's behest, at a time when I sorely wished to break it. I have no wish to dishonour her courage now.

'It was my hope that Trell Gravelingas would stay with the High Lord – to protect her.' He said this defiantly, as if he expected Mhoram to reprimand him. 'Now he is not with her – and I am not with her. My heart fears this. But if it were possible, I would take back my harshness to you.'

'There is no need for pardon,' Mhoram answered. 'My own weak faith provoked you. But I must tell you that I believe Thomas Covenant to be a friend of the Land. The burden of his crime hurts him. I believe he will seek atonement at the High Lord's side.'

He paused, and Triock bowed in a way that said he accepted the Lord's words without being convinced. Then Mhoram went on, 'Triock son of Thuler, please accept a gift from me – in the name of the High Lord, who is loved by all the Land.' Reaching into his robe, he brought out his *lomillialor* rod. 'This is High Wood, Triock. You have been in the Loresraat, and will know some of its uses, I will not use it again.' He said this with a resolution that surprised Troy. 'And you will have need of it. I am called seer and oracle – I speak from knowledge, though the need itself is closed to me. Please accept it – for the sake of the love we share – and as expiation for my doubt.'

Triock's eyes widened, and the twisting of his face relaxed briefly. Troy caught a glimpse of what Triock might have looked like if his life had not been blighted. In silence, he accepted the rod from Lord Mhoram's hands. But when he held the High Wood, his old bitterness gripped his features again, and he said dourly, 'I may find a use which will surprise you.' Then he bowed, and the other elders bowed with him, freeing Mhoram and Troy to be on their way.

Troy threw them a salute, and took his opportunity. He had no time to spare for Mhoram's strange gift, or for Triock's brooding promises. Instead, he clapped Mehryl with his heels, and led his companions out of the valley of Mithil Stonedown at a gallop.

In a short time, they rounded the western spur of the mountains, and swung out into the Plains. As Troy scanned his companions, he was surprised to see that Tull's mount could keep up the pace. This Ranyhyn had been ridden through danger at cruel speeds for the past eight days, and the strain had wounded its gait. But it was a Ranyhyn; its head was up, its eyes were proud, and its matted mane jumped on its neck like a flag gallantly struggling to unfurl. For a moment, Troy understood why the Ramen did not ride. But he made no concessions to the Ranyhyn's fatigue. Throughout the day, he kept his company running like rapid thunder into the west.

He ached to join his warriors, to share the fight and the desperation with them, to show them the one way in which they might be able to steal a victory out of the teeth of Lord Foul's army. Only an exigent need for sleep forced him to stop during part of the night.

Ruel awakened him before dawn, and he rode on again along the base of the Southron Range. When daylight returned his vision to him, he could see the cliffs near Doom's Retreat ahead. Now his direct route to the Retreat would take him angling rapidly closer to the vanguard of Lord Foul's army. But he kept his heading. Near that horde of *kresh* and ur-viles, he would find whatever was left of the mounted Eoward.

He caught sight of Quaan's force sooner than he had expected. The Hiltmark must have taken his riders on a southward curve towards the Retreat to keep their pursuers as far as possible from the march of the Warward. Shortly after noon, Troy and his companions crested a high foothill which enabled them to look some distance north into the Plains. And there, only a league away, they saw the tattered, fleeing remnant of Quaan's command.

At first, Troy felt a thrill of relief. He could see Hiltmark Quaan riding beside his standard-bearer among the warriors. At least sixscore Bloodguard galloped among the Eoward. And the blue robes of Callindrill and Verement were clearly visible through the dark surge of the retreat.

But then Troy perceived how the riders were moving. They were almost completely routed. In a tight mass like a swath of panic on the Plains, they pushed and jostled against each other, threw frantic glances behind them in ways that unbalanced their mounts, bristled with angry and fearful cries. Some of them whipped their horses.

Behind them, the *kresh* ran like a yellow gale scored with black.

Nevertheless, the distance between the warriors and the wolves remained constant. After a moment, Troy understood. Quaan's Eoward were struggling to match exactly the hunting pace of the *kresh*. The wolves themselves could not maintain a dead run. They were forced by the weight of their riders, and by the long distance of the chase, to travel at the swift, loping gait of a hunting pack. And Quaan's warriors fought to keep their flight almost directly under the noses of the wolves. In this way, they lured the *kresh* onward. With prey so near, the wolves could neither rest nor turn aside.

Quaan's strategy was cunning – cunning and fatal. The warriors also could not rest. They were vulnerable to every spurt of speed from the *kresh*. And any warrior who was unseated for any reason was instantly torn to pieces. Another Eoward had already been lost this way. But if Quaan could maintain these tactics, the marching Eoward would have until late afternoon to reach their positions in Doom's Retreat.

The Warmark did not bother to calculate the odds. He urged Mehryl ahead. At full stretch, the Ranyhyn raced to join Quaan.

When they saw Troy and Lord Mhoram, the warriors gave a raw, dry cheer. Quaan, Callindrill, and Verement dashed out towards the Warmark. But there was little joy in their reunion. The plight of the Eoward was desperate. When he drew close to them, Troy saw that most of the horses were virtually prostrate on their feet; only their fear of the wolves kept them up and running. And the warriors were in no better condition. They had ridden for days without proper food or sleep. None of them lacked injuries. The dust of the Plains clung to their faces and clotted their wounds, making the cuts and rents look like premature scars. Troy had to tear his aching gaze from them to salute the Hiltmark.

Through the thunder of the hooves, Quaan shouted, 'Hail, Warmark! Well met!' As Troy swung Mehryl into place beside him, he added, 'Not eight days, I fear!'

'Did you send word to Amorine?' Troy yelled.

'Yes!'

'Then it's all right! Seven will be enough!' He clapped the Hiltmark's shoulder, then slowed Mehryl, and dropped back among the warriors.

Immediately, dust and fear and tension swirled around him like the hot breath of the *kresh*. Now he could hear the hunting snarl of the wolves, and the roynish barking of the ur-viles. He felt their presence as if they were his fault — as if they had been created by his folly. Yet he forced himself to smile at his warriors, shout encouragement through the din. He could not afford self-recrimination. The burden of saving the Warward was on his shoulders now.

Moments later, a surge ran through the barking commands of the ur-viles. Troy guessed that the pursuers were about to attempt another spurt.

He looked ahead quickly towards the sheer cliffs of Doom's Retreat. They were no more than two leagues away. There the western tip of the Southron Range swung northward to meet the southeast corner of the mountain wedge which separated the South Plains from Garroting Deep, and between these two ranges was the defile of Doom's Retreat. The narrow canyon lay like a gash through the rock, and its crooked length provided the Land's only access to the Wastes and the Grey Desert.

Troy's gaze sprang to the mouth of the canyon.

The last marching Eoward were still arriving at the Retreat.

If they were not given more time, they would be caught outside the canyon by the *kresh*. Their ambush would fail.

The Warmark was moving too swiftly for hesitation. When he was sure that the Warward had seen Quaan's riders, he pushed Mehryl ahead, away from the *kresh*, and caught the Hiltmark's attention with a wave of his arm. Then he gave Quaan a hand signal which ordered the Eoward to turn and attack.

Quaan did not falter; he understood the need for the order. Despite the maimed condition of his command, he sent up a shrill, piercing whistle which drew the eyes of his officers towards him. With hand signals, he gave the Hafts and Warhafts their instructions.

Almost at once, the riders responded. The outer Eoward peeled back, and the warriors in the centre tried to turn where they were. Frantically, they fought their horses around to face the wolves.

Disaster struck the manoeuvre immediately. As soon as the riders stopped fleeing, *kresh* crashed in among them. The whole trailing edge of Quaan's command went down under the onslaught; and the ur-vile loremasters whirled their iron staves, throwing acid power gleefully over the fallen humans and horses. The screaming of the horses shot through the tumult of snarls and cries. Instantly, a wide swath of grey-green bracken turned blood-red.

But the abrupt profusion of corpses broke the charge of the *kresh*. Their leaders stopped to kill and tear and eat, and this threw the following wolves into confusion. Only the ur-vile wedges drove straight ahead, into the milling heart of the Eoward.

Bloodguard raced to the aid of the warriors. The three Lords threw themselves at the nearest ur-viles. Other warriors rallied and struck. And through the centre of the fight Warmark Troy charged like a madman, hacking at every wolf within reach.

For a time, the *kresh* were held. The warriors fought with a desperate fury, and the cool Bloodguard broke wolves in all directions. Working together, the Lords blasted one ur-vile wedge apart, then another. But that accounted for only a tenth of the mounted ur-viles. The others regrouped, began to restore order, coordination, to the *kresh*. Some of the horses lost their footing on the slick ground. Others went out of control with fear, threw their riders, and lost themselves in futile plunges among the wolves.

Troy saw that if any of the warriors were to survive this fight they would have to flee soon.

He battled his way towards the Lords. But suddenly a whole pack of *kresh* swirled about him. Mehryl spun, dodging the fangs and kicking. Troy fought as best he could, but Mehryl's whirling unbalanced him. Twice he almost lost his seat. A wolf leaped up at him, and he barely saved himself by jabbing his sword into its belly.

Then Ruel brought other Bloodguard to his aid. In a concerted charge, ten of them hammered into the pack, shattered it. Troy righted himself, tried uselessly to straighten his missing sunglasses, then cursed himself and sent Mehryl towards the Lords again.

As he moved, he snapped a glance at the Retreat. The last of the marchers were just disappearing down the canyon.

'Do something!' he howled when he neared Lord Mhoram. 'We're being slaughtered!'

Mhoram spun and shouted to Callindrill and Verement, then returned to the Warmark. 'On my signal!' he yelled over the din. 'Flee on my signal!' Without waiting for a reply, he pushed his Ranyhyn into a gallop and dashed towards the Retreat with the other Lords.

In a hundred yards, they separated. Verement stopped directly between the conflict and the Retreat, while Mhoram raced straight north and Callindrill ran south. When they were in a position, they formed a long line across the approach to Doom's Retreat.

They dismounted. Lord Verement held his staff upright on the ground in the centre as Mhoram and Callindrill whirled their staffs and shouted strange invocations through the noise of battle. While they prepared, Troy fought his way to Quaan's side, told him what Mhoram had said. The Hiltmark accepted it without pausing. They separated, battled away towards the flanks of the struggle, spreading the command.

Troy feared that Mhoram's call would come too late. The power of ninetyscore ur-viles rapidly organized the turbulent *kresh*. As the Eoward gathered themselves to flee, the ur-viles wrenched the *kresh* away from the tearing of carcasses, bunched them again into fighting wedges, and hurled them at the warriors.

In that instant, Lord Mhoram signalled with his staff.

The riders sent their horses running straight towards Doom's Retreat. They seemed to rush out from under the piled spring of the wolves. Once again, the trailing warriors crashed to the ground under a massive breaker of *kresh*. But this time the remaining riders did not fight back. They gave free rein to the fear of their horses, and fled.

The suddenness of their flight opened a gap between them and the wolves, and the gap widened slowly as the horses at last found release for all their accumulated dread. In moments, Troy and Quaan with the last three Eoward and little more than a hundred Bloodguard flashed by on either side of Lord Verement. As they passed him, he took his staff from where he had planted it in the line between Mhoram and Callindrill, caught it by one end with both hands, and cocked it behind his head.

Then the last rider had crossed the line.

Verement swung his staff and struck the ground of the line with all his might.

Instantly, a shimmering wall of force sprang up between Mhoram and Callindrill. When the first *kresh* charged it, it flared into brilliant blue flame, and hurled them back.

Seeing that the wall held, Lord Mhoram leaped onto the Ranyhyn, and sprinted after the warriors. Lord Verement followed as swiftly as his sturdy mustang could carry him. When they neared Troy and Quaan, Mhoram shouted, 'Make haste! The forbidding cannot hold! The ur-viles will break it! Flee!'

The warriors needed no urging, and Quaan dashed after them, stridently herding them towards the Retreat. Troy went with him. For a moment, Mhoram and Verement were right behind them. But suddenly the Lords stopped. At the same time, all the Bloodguard wheeled their Ranyhyn, and pounded back towards the forbidding.

Cursing in dismay, Troy turned to see what had happened.

Lord Callindrill was on the ground near the wall. Several badly wounded warriors had fallen from their mounts within yards of the blue fire, and Callindrill was trying to help them. Rapidly, he tore their clothing into strips, made tourniquets and bandages.

He did not look up to see his danger.

Already the ur-viles were preparing to fight the wall. They sent most of the riderless *kresh* running to pass around the ends of the fire. Three ur-vile wedges moved forward to attack. The rest retreated a short distance and began re-forming themselves into a huge, single wedge.

Troy kicked Mehryl into a gallop, and joined the Bloodguard following Mhoram and Verement.

Lord Mhoram was twenty yards ahead of Troy, but he could not reach Callindrill in time. The three ur-vile wedges near the fire attacked. They did not try to break the Lords' wall. Instead, the loremasters concentrated all their power in one place. With a harsh clang, they struck their iron staves together. A great spew of liquid force gushed from the impact, splashed into the forbidding fire, and passed through it.

In black, burning gouts, the corrosive fluid dropped towards Callindrill. It fell just short of him, did not touch him. But it hit the ground with a concussion that flung him and the injured warriors into the air like limp bundles.

When they flopped down again, they lay still.

At once, the three wedges hurried aside, and the new, single, massed wedge started lumbering towards the wall.

Simultaneously, the first *kresh* rounded both ends of the fire.

The next instant, Lord Mhoram threw himself from his Ranyhyn's back, landed beside Callindrill. A quick glance told him that the warriors were dead; the force of the concussion had killed them. He concentrated on Callindrill. Touching the Lord's chest with his hands, he confirmed what his eyes told him; life still flickered in Callindrill, but his heart was not beating.

Then Troy reached Mhoram's side, and the Bloodguard poised themselves to defend the Lords. On horseback, Verement worked at the wall of forbidding, tightened it against the assault of the wedge. But it could not withstand fifteen hundred ur-viles. The wedge moved slowly, but it was hardly twenty yards from the fire. And *kresh* poured around the ends of the wall now, pelting towards the Bloodguard and Lords. The Bloodguard moved out to meet the wolves, but a hundred Bloodguard could not hold back five thousand *kresh* for long.

'Flee!' Mhoram yelled. 'Go! Save yourselves! We must not all die here!'

But he did not wait to observe that no one obeyed him. Instead, he bent over the fallen Lord again. Holding his lower lip in his teeth, he massaged Callindrill's chest, hoping to renew his pulse. But his heart remained motionless.

Mhoram drew a sudden sharp breath, raised his fist, and hammered once with all his might on Callindrill's chest.

The blow jolted the Lord's heart. It lurched, stumbled, then broke into a limping beat.

Mhoram shouted for Morril. At once, the Bloodguard leaped down from his Ranyhyn, caught Callindrill in his arms, and sprang up again. Seeing this, Lord Verement broke away from the forbidding wall, started back towards Doom's Retreat. Mhoram and Troy mounted, surged away from the wall after him. The Bloodguard followed in a protective ring around the Lords.

A moment later, the massed ur-vile wedge hit the wall and tore it. Dark liquid power shredded the blue flame, ripped it into fragments and scattered it. Instantly, the rest of the *kresh* flooded after the escaping Ranyhyn. And the wolves pouring around the ends of the wall changed directions to intercept the riders.

But the Ranyhyn outdistanced them. The great horses of Ra pulled past Verement and thundered towards Doom's Retreat.

Ahead, under the late afternoon shadow of the cliffs, Hiltmark Quaan was urging the last of his warriors into the canyon.

Maddened by the escape of so many prey, the *kresh* howled with rage, and swung to converge on Lord Verement.

His mustang ran hard and bravely. But it was already exhausted; slowly the *kresh* gained on it. Before it had covered half the distance to the Retreat, Troy could see that it would lose the race.

He called for help, but the Bloodguard did not respond. Only Thomin, the Bloodguard personally responsible for Verement, remained behind. Incensed, Troy started to go back himself, but Mhoram stopped him by shouting, 'There is no need!'

Thomin waited until the last possible moment – until the *kresh* were raging at the heels of the mustang. Then he pulled the Lord onto his own Ranyhyn, and carried him away towards the Retreat.

Almost at once, the mustang fell screaming under an avalanche of wolves.

For an instant, the haze of the cliff shadow turned sickly red in Troy's sight. But then Mehryl's taut run bore him beyond the scream, took him straight towards the gap in the cliffs. He flashed into the deeper gloom of the defile. Except for the slit of light ahead, he could see nothing. The sharp change made him feel that he was foundering. The rumble of hooves pounded back at him from the cliffs, and behind the echo came the shrill croaking derision of the ravens. He felt waters of darkness closing over his head. When he broke out the end of the Retreat into the dim, late light of day, he was almost dazed with relief.

As he passed, First Haft Amorine gave a piercing shout, and thousands of warriors dashed away from the cliffs on either side of the gap. Despite the long fatigue which radiated from them, they ran with precision, took positions, formed an arc over the end of the canyon, sealing the trap.

Moments later, the first *kresh* came howling out of the Retreat and sprang at them. The whole arc of warriors staggered under the shock of impact. But Amorine had eighteen Eoward braced to meet the onslaught. The arc gave ground, but did not break.

With an effort, Troy brought himself under control. Over to one side, he could hear Lord Verement barking, 'Release me! Am I a child, that I must be carried?' Troy grinned grimly, then drew Mehryl up behind the arc so that he would be ready to help his warriors if the wolves outweighed them. He ached to see the outcome of the trap, but the darkness of the Retreat foiled his sight.

Soon, however, he could hear the sounds of combat echoing out of the defile. Over the noise of the embattled arc, he made out a sudden raw howl as the *kresh* in the Retreat found themselves attacked from above by twenty Eoward hidden in the canyon walls. At first, the howl contained surprise and ferocity, but no fear; the wolves did not understand their danger.

The ur-viles were wiser. Their commands cut stridently through the rage of the wolves. And soon the howling changed. To their dismay, the *kresh* began to understand the glee of the ravens. And the yammering of the ur-viles became fiercer, more desperate. In the narrow defile, they could not make effective use of their fighting wedges, and without that focus of power, they were vulnerable to arrows and spears and rockfalls. Caught in a seething, confused mass of wolves, the wedges began to collapse.

As the wedges crumbled, fear and uncertainty penetrated the wolves' fury for blood. In tattered bunches, the *kresh* broke away, tried to flee through the canyon. But the cramped panic of their numbers only hampered them, and made the ur-viles more vulnerable. And death rained down on them through the jeering of the ravens. In mad frenzy, wild to fight an enemy they could not reach, the *kresh* started to attack the ur-viles.

No wolves or ur-viles escaped. When the battle was done, the entire vanguard of Fleshharrower's army lay dead in Doom's Retreat.

For one moment, a hush fell over the battleground; even the ravens were silent. Then a hoarse cheer came echoing from the canyon. The Eoward sealing the end of the Retreat responded loudly. And the ravens began sailing down to the defile's floor, where they feasted on Demondim-spawn and *kresh*.

Slowly, Troy became aware that First Haft Amorine was at his side. When he turned to her, he felt that he was grinning insanely, but even without his sunglasses he did not care. 'Congratulations, Amorine,' he said. 'You've done well.' The evening fog on his sight was already so bad that he had to ask her about casualties.

'We have lost few warriors,' she replied with dour satisfaction. 'Your battle plan is a good one.'

But her praise only reminded him of the rest of Lord Foul's army, and of the ordeal still before the Warward. He shook his head. 'Not good enough.' But then, rather than explain what he meant, he said to her, 'First Haft, give my thanks to the warriors. Get them fed and settled for the night – there won't be any more fighting today. When they're taken care of, we'll have a council.'

Amorine's gaze showed that she did not understand his attitude, but she saluted without question, and moved away to carry out his orders. His blank mist swallowed her at once. Darkness blew about him as if it rode on the wind of the Warward's shouting. He called for Ruel, and asked the Bloodguard to guide him to Lord Mhoram.

They found Mhoram beside a small campfire under the lee of the westward mountains. He was tending Lord Callindrill. Callindrill had regained consciousness, but his skin was as pale as alabaster, and he looked weak. Mhoram cooked some broth over the campfire, and massaged Callindrill while the broth heated.

Lord Callindrill greeted the Warmark faintly, and Troy replied with pleasure. He was glad to see that Callindrill was not mortally injured; he was going to need the Lord. He was going to need every help or power that he could find.

But he had other things to consider before he began to think about his need for help. When he had assured himself that Lord Callindrill was on the way to recovery, he drew Mhoram away for a private talk.

He waited until they were beyond earshot of the Warward's camp. Then he sighed wearily, 'Mhoram, we're not finished. We can't stop here.' Without transition, as if he had not changed subjects, he went on, 'What are we going to do about Lord Verement? One of us has got to tell him – about Shetra. I'll do it if you want. I probably deserve it.'

'I will do it,' Mhoram murmured distantly.

'All right.' Troy felt acutely relieved to be free of that responsibility. 'Now, what about this – what Tull told us? I don't like the idea of telling everyone that – that the mission – ' He could not bring himself to say the words, *The Giants are dead.* 'I don't think the warriors will survive what's ahead if they know what happened to the mission. It's too much. Having three Giants taken over by Ravers is bad enough. And I'll have to tell them worse things than that myself.'

Softly, Mhoram breathed, 'They deserve to know the truth.'

'Deserve?' Troy's deep feeling of culpability flooded into anger.

'What they deserve is victory. By God, don't tell me what they deserve! It's a little late for you to start worrying about what they know or don't know. You've seen fit to keep secrets from me all along. God knows how many horrors you still haven't told me. Keep your mouth shut about this.'

'That choice was made by the Council. No one person has the right to withhold knowledge from another. No one is wise enough.' Mhoram spoke as if he were wrestling with himself.

'It's too late for that. If you want to talk about rights – you don't have the right to destroy my army.'

'My friend, have you – have you suffered – has the withholding of knowledge harmed you?'

'How should I know? Maybe if you had told me the truth – about Atiaran – we wouldn't be here now. Maybe I would have been afraid of the risk. You tell me if that's good or bad.' Then his anger softened. 'Mhoram,' he pleaded, 'they're right on the edge. I've already pushed them right to the edge. And we're not done. I just want to spare them something that will hurt so bad – '

'Very well,' Mhoram sighed in a tone of defeat. 'I will not speak of the Giants.'

'Thank you,' Troy said intensely.

Mhoram gazed at him searchingly, but through his darkness he could not read the Lord's expression. For a moment, he feared that Mhoram was about to tell him something, reveal the last mysteries of Trell and Elena and Covenant. He did not want to hear such things – not now, when he was already overburdened. But finally the Lord turned silently and started back towards Callindrill.

Troy followed him. But on the way he paused to speak with Terrel, who was the ranking Bloodguard. 'Terrel, I want you to send scouts out to the South Plains. I don't expect Foul's army before midday tomorrow, but we shouldn't take any chances – and the warriors are too tired. But there's one thing. If Foul or Fleshharrower or whoever is in command sends any scouts this way, make sure they know we're here. I don't want them to have any doubt about where to find us.'

'Yes, Warmark,' Terrel said, and stepped away to make the arrangements. Troy and Mhoram went on to their campfire.

They found Lord Verement feeding Callindrill. As he spooned the broth to Callindrill's lips, the hawk-faced Lord talked steadily in a low, exasperated tone, as if his pride were offended; but his movements were gentle, and he did not abandon the task to Mhoram. He hovered over Callindrill until the warm broth had restored a touch of colour to his pale cheeks. Then Verement stood up and rasped, 'You would be less foolhardy were you not Ranyhyn-borne. A lesser mount would teach you the limits of your own strength.'

This inverted repetition of Verement's old accusation against himself momentarily overcame Lord Mhoram. A moan escaped through his teeth, and his eyes filled with tears. For that moment, his courage seemed to fail him, and he reached towards Verement as if he were groping through blind grief. But then he caught himself, smiled crookedly at the rough look of surprise and concern on Verement's face. 'Come, my brother,' he murmured, 'I must speak with you.' Together, they walked away into the night, leaving Troy to watch over Callindrill.

In a wan voice, Callindrill asked, 'What has happened? What disturbs Mhoram?'

Sighing heavily, Troy seated himself beside the Lord. He was full of all the evil he had caused. He had to swallow several times before he could find his voice to say, 'Runnik came back from Korik's mission. Lord Shetra died in the Sarangrave.'

Then he was grateful that Callindrill did not speak. He did not think he could stand the reprimand of any more pain. They sat together in silence until Lord Mhoram returned alone.

Mhoram carried himself sorely, as if he had just been beaten with clubs. The flesh around his eyes was red and swollen, sorrowful. But his eyes themselves wielded a hot peril, and his glances were like spears. He said nothing about Lord Verement. Words were unnecessary; Mhoram's expression revealed how Verement took the news of his wife's death.

To steady himself, Mhoram set about preparing food for Troy and himself. Their meal passed under a shroud of gloom, but as he ate Lord Mhoram slowly mastered himself, relaxed the pain in his face. To match him, Warmark Troy grappled inwardly for the tone of confidence he would need when the council started. He did not want his doubt to show; he did not intend to make his army pay for his personal dilemmas and inadequacies. When Hiltmark Quaan approached the fire and announced that all the Hafts were ready, both Troy and Mhoram answered him resolutely, calmly.

The Lord threw a large pile of wood onto the fire while Quaan brought his officers into a wide circle around it. But despite the bright blaze of the fire, the Hafts looked hazy and insubstantial to Troy. For an irrational instant, he feared that they would break into illusions and disappear when he told them what they had to do. But he braced himself. Hiltmark Quaan and First Haft Amorine stood near him like pillars on one side, and Lord Mhoram watched him from the other. Clearing his throat, he opened the council.

'Well, we're here. In spite of everything, we've accomplished something that any of us would have said was impossible. Before we get into what's ahead, I want to thank you all for what you've done. I'm proud of you – more than I'll ever be able to say.'

As he spoke, he had to resist a temptation to duck his head as if he were ashamed of his uncovered eyelessness. Painfully, he wondered what effect this view of him would have on the Hafts. But he forced himself to hold his head up as he continued. 'But I have to tell you plainly – we haven't come near winning this war yet. We've made a good start, but it's only a start. Things are going to get worse –·' He lost his voice for a moment, and had to clench himself to recover it. 'It's not going to work out the way I planned. Hiltmark Quaan – First Haft Amorine – you've done everything you could do – everything I asked. But it's not going to work out the way I told you it would.

'But – first things first. We've got reports to make. Hiltmark, will you go first?'

Quaan bowed, and stepped forward into the circle. His square, white-haired visage was streaked with grime and blood and fatigue, but his open gaze did not falter. In blunt, unaffected language, he described all that had happened to his command since he had left Revelstone – raft ride and run to the Mithil valley, the blockade there, the progression of the battle as Fleshharrower, the corrupted Giant of whom Manethrall Rue had spoken, organized successive efforts to break the hold of the defenders. For five days, the Bloodguard, the warriors, and the two Lords withstood Cavewights, *kresh*, warped manlike creations of the Illearth Stone, ur-viles.

'But on the sixth day,' Quaan continued, 'Fleshharrower came against us himself.' Now his voice expressed the weariness of long fighting and lost warriors. 'With a power that I do not name, he called a great storm against us. Abominable creatures like those of which Manethrall Rue spoke fell upon us from the sky. They cast fear among our mounts, and we were driven back. Then Fleshharrower broke the forbidding, and sent *kresh* and ur-viles to pursue us. Time and again, we turned to fight, so that the enemy might be delayed – and time and again we were overmastered. Often we sent riders ahead to bear warning, but every messenger was slain – flocks of savage cormorants assailed them from the sky, and destroyed them all, though some of them were Bloodguard.

'Still we fought,' he concluded. 'At last we are here. But half the Bloodguard and eight of the Eoward were slain. And the horses have passed the end of their strength. Many will never bear riders again, and all need long days of rest. The battle which remains must be met afoot.'

When he finished, he returned to his place in the circle. His courage was evident, but as he moved, his square shoulders seemed already to be carrying all the weight they could bear. And because Troy could find no words for his respect and gratitude, he said nothing. Silently, he nodded to First Haft Amorine.

She described briefly the last few days of the Warward's march, then she reported on the present condition of the army. 'Water and *aliantha* are not plentiful here, beyond Doom's Retreat. The Warward carries food which may be stretched for five days or six – no more. The warriors themselves are sorely damaged by their march. Even the uninjured are crippled by exhaustion. Great numbers have wounds about their feet and shoulders – wounds which do not heal. Threescore of the weakest died during our last run to the Retreat. Many more will die if the Warward does not rest now.'

Her words made Troy groan inwardly; they were full of unintended reproaches. He was the Warmark. He had promised victory again and again to people who trusted him. And now – He felt a sharp desire to berate himself, tell the Hafts just how badly he had miscalculated. But before he could begin, Lord Callindrill spoke. The wounded Lord was supported by two Bloodguard, but he was able to make his weak voice heard.

'I must speak of the power which Hiltmark Quaan did not name. I still do not comprehend how the Despiser gained mastery over a Giant – it surpasses my understanding. But Fleshharrower is in truth a Giant, and he is possessed of a great power. He bears with him a fragment of the Illearth Stone.'

Lord Mhoram nodded painfully. 'Alas, my friends,' he said, 'this is a dark time for all the Land. Danger and death beset us on every hand, and ill defies all defence. Hear me, I know how this Giant – this Fleshharrower – has been turned against us. It is accomplished through the combined might of the Stone and the Ravers. Either alone would not suffice – the Giants are strong and sure. But together – ! Who in the Land could hope to endure? Therefore the Giant carries a fragment of the Illearth Stone, so that the Despiser's power will remain upon him, and the Raver will possess an added weapon. *Melenkurion abatha*! This is a great evil.'

For a moment, he stood silent as if in dismay, and distress filled the Hafts as they tasted the magnitude of the ill he described. But then he drew himself up, and his eyes flashed around the circle. 'Yet it is always thus with the Despiser. Let not the knowledge of this evil blind you or weaken you. Lord Foul seeks to turn all the good of the Land to harm and corruption. Our task is clear. We must find the strength to turn harm and corruption to good. For that reason we fight. If we falter now, we become like Fleshharrower – unwilling enemies of the Land.'

His stern words steadied the Hafts, helped them to recover their resolve. However, before he or Troy could continue, Lord Verement said harshly, 'What of the Giants, Mhoram? What of the mission? How many other souls have already been lost to the Despiser?'

Verement had entered the circle across from Troy while Lord Callindrill had been speaking. The cloud on Troy's sight prevented him from seeing Verement's expression, but when the Lord spoke his voice was raw with bitterness. 'Answer, Mhoram. Seer and oracle! Is Hyrim dead also? Do any Giants yet live?'

Troy felt Verement's bitterness as an attack on the Warward, and he used words like whips to strike back. 'That isn't our concern. There's nothing we can do about it. We're stuck here – we're going to live or die here! It doesn't matter what's happening anywhere else.' In his heart, he felt that he was betraying the Giants, but he had no choice. 'All we can do is fight! Do you hear me?'

'I hear you.' Lord Verement fell silent as if he understood Troy's vehemence, and the Warmark seized his chance to change the subject.

'All right,' he said to the whole circle. 'At least now we know where we stand. Now I'll tell you what we're going to do about it. I have a plan, and with Lord Mhoram's help I'm going to make it work.'

Bracing himself, he said bluntly, 'We're going to leave here. Fleshharrower and his army probably won't arrive before midday tomorrow. By that time, we will be long gone.'

The Hafts gaped and blinked momentarily as they realized that he was ordering another march. Then several of them groaned aloud, and others recoiled as if he had struck them. Even Quaan winced openly. Troy wanted to rush into explanations, but he contained himself until Amorine stepped forward and protested, 'Warmark, why will your former plan not suffice? The warriors have given their utmost to gain Doom's Retreat as you commanded. Why must we leave?'

'Because Foul's army is too goddamn big!' He did not want to shout, but for a while he could not stop himself. 'We've killed ten thousand *kresh* and a couple thousand ur-viles. But the rest of that army is still out there! It's not three times bigger than we are – or even five times bigger! Fleshharrower has twenty times our numbers, twenty! I've seen them.' With an effort, he caught hold of his pointless fury, jerked it down. 'My old plan was a good one while it lasted,' he went on. 'But it just didn't take into account that Foul's army might be so big. Now there's only two things that can happen. If that Giant sends his army in here just ten or twenty thousand at a time, the fight is going to last for weeks. But we've only got food for six days — we'll starve to death in here. And if he cuts through in one big blast, he'll get control of both ends of the Retreat. Then we'll be trapped, and he can pick us off in his own good time.

'Now listen to me!' he shouted again at the chagrined Hafts. 'I'm not going to let us get slaughtered as long as there is anything I can do to stop it — anything at all! And there is one thing, just one! I've got one more trick to play in this game, and I'm going to play it if I have to carry every one of you on my back!'

He glared around the circle, trying to fill his eyeless stare with authority, command, some kind of power that would make the Warward obey him. 'We will march at dawn tomorrow.'

Darkness shrouded the night, but in the firelight he could see Quaan's face. The old veteran was wrestling with himself, struggling to find the strength for this new demand. He closed his eyes briefly, and all the Hafts waited for him as if he had their courage in his hands, to uphold or deny as he saw fit. When he opened his eyes, his face seemed to sag with fatigue. But his voice was steady.

'Warmark, where will we march?'

'West for now,' Troy replied quickly. 'Towards those old ruins. It won't be too bad. If we handle things right, we can go slower than we have so far.'

'Will you tell us your plan?'

'No.' Troy was tempted to say, If I tell you, you'll be so horrified that you'll never follow me. But instead he added, 'I want to keep it to myself for a while — get it ready. You'll just have to trust me.' He sounded to himself like a man falling out of a tree, shouting to the people above him as he fell that he would catch them.

'Warmark,' Quaan said stiffly, 'you know that I will always trust you. We all trust you.'

'Yes, I know,' Troy sighed. A sudden weariness flooded over him, and he could barely hear his own voice. He had already fallen a long way since he had left Revelstone. Miscalculations denuded his ideas of all their vitality, divested them of their power to save. He wondered how many other things he would have torn from him before this war was done. A long moment passed before he could find enough energy to say, 'There's one more thing. It's got to be done — we don't have any choice any more. We've got to leave some people behind. To try to hold the Retreat — make Fleshharrower think we're still here — slow him down. It'll be suicide, so we'll need volunteers. Two or three Eoward should be enough to make it work.'

Quaan and Amorine took this stolidly; they were warriors familiar with this kind of thinking. But before Troy could say anything else, Lord Verement sprang into the circle. 'No!' he barked, striking the ground with his staff. 'None will be left behind. I forbid it!'

Now Troy could see him clearly. His lean face looked as sharp as if it had been taken to a grindstone, and his eyes flamed keenly. Troy's throat felt abruptly bone-dry. With difficulty, he said, 'Lord Verement, I'm sorry. I've got no choice. This march'll kill the warriors unless they can go more slowly. So somebody has got to gain them time.'

'Then I will do it!' Verement's tone was raw. 'I will hold Doom's Retreat. It is a fit place for me.'

'You can't,' Troy objected, almost stammering. 'I can't let you. I'll need you with me.' Unable to bear the force of Verement's gaze, he turned to Lord Mhoram for help.

'Warmark Troy speaks truly,' Mhoram said carefully. 'Death will not heal your grief. And you will be sorely needed in the days ahead. You must come with us.'

'By the Seven!' Verement cried. 'Do you not hear me? I have said that I will remain! Shetra my wife is lost! She whom I loved with all my strength, and yet did not love enough. *Melenkurion*! Do not speak to me of cannot or must! I will remain. No warriors will be left behind.'

Mhoram cut in, 'Lord Verement, do you believe that you are able to defeat Fleshharrower?'

But Verement did not reply to that question. 'Heal Callindrill,' he said harshly. 'I will require you both. And call the Bloodguard from the Plains. I start at dawn.' Then he swung away, and stalked out of the circle into the night.

His departure left Troy bewildered and exhausted. He felt that the burden of the Warward already clung to his shoulders, bent his back so that he moved as if he were decrepit. His confused fatigue made him unfit for speeches, and he dismissed the Hafts abruptly. As he did so, he felt that he was failing them – that they needed him to lead them, give them a strong figure around which they could rally. But he had no strength. He went to his blankets as if he hoped that some kind of fortitude would come to him in a dream.

He sank at once into exhaustion, and slept until sleep was no longer possible for him – until the sunrise above the mountains filled his brain with shapes and colours. When he arose, he discovered that he had slept through all the noise of the Warward as it broke camp and began its march. Already the last Eoward were shambling away from Doom's Retreat. They trudged as if they were maimed into the dry, heat-pale land of the Southron Wastes.

Cursing dully at his weakness, he grabbed a few bites of the food Ruel offered him, then hurried away towards the Retreat.

There he found Callindrill and Mhoram, with a small group of Bloodguard. On either side of the defile's southern end, the Lords had climbed as high as they could up the scree into the jumbled boulders piled against the canyon walls. From these positions, they plied their staffs in a way that cast a haze across the air between them.

Beyond them, in Doom's Retreat itself, Lord Verement clambered over the rocks and fallen shale. As he moved, he waved the fire of his staff like a torch against the darkness of the cliffs. Only Thomin accompanied him.

Troy looked closely at Callindrill. The wounded Lord looked wan and tired, and sweat glistened on his pale forehead, but he stood on his own, and wielded his staff firmly. Troy saluted him, then climbed the scree on the other side to join Lord Mhoram.

When he reached Mhoram, he sat and watched while the haze moved and took shape. It appeared to revolve slowly like a large wheel standing in the end of the Retreat. Its circumference fitted just within the scree and stone, so that it effectively blocked the canyon floor, and it turned as if it were hanging on a pivot between Mhoram and Callindrill. Beyond it, Troy could see only the empty Retreat – the raven-cleaned bones of the ur-viles and wolves – and the lone Lord struggling up and down the sides of the canyon with his flame bobbing like a will-o'-the-wisp.

Soon, however, both Mhoram and Callindrill ended their exertions. They planted their staffs like anchors in the edges of the haze, and leaned back to rest. Lord Mhoram greeted Troy tiredly.

After a moment's hesitation, Troy nodded towards Verement. 'What's he doing?'

Mhoram closed his eyes, and said as if he were answering Troy, 'We have made a Word of Warning.'

While he was thinking of ways to rephrase his question, Troy asked, 'What does it do?'

'It seals Doom's Retreat.'

'How will it work? I can see it. It won't take Fleshharrower by surprise.'

'Your sight is keen in some ways. I cannot see the Word.'

Awkwardly, Troy asked, 'Is there anyone still out there – besides Verement?'

'No. All the warriors have left. The scouts have been recalled. None may pass this way now without encountering the Word.'

'So he's committed himself – he's stuck out there.'

'Yes.' Mhoram bit at the word angrily.

Troy returned to his first question. 'What does he hope to gain? It's suicide.'

Mhoram opened his eyes, and Troy felt the force of the Lord's gaze. 'We will gain time,' Mhoram said. 'You spoke of a need for time.' Then he sighed and looked away down the canyon. 'And Lord Verement Shetra-mate will gain an end to anguish.'

Numbly, Troy watched Verement. The hawkish Lord did not look like a man in search of relief. He threw himself up and down in the tumbled edges of the defile, kicked his way through the shale and the fleshless bones and the watchful silence of the ravens, as if he were possessed. And he was exhausting himself. Already his stride was unsteady, and he had fallen several times. Yet he had covered less than a third of Doom's Retreat with the invisible skein of his fire. But some power, some relentless coercion of will, kept him going. Throughout the morning, he continued his weird progress along the canyon, stopping only at rare moments to accept water and treasure-berries from Thomin. By midmorning, he was half done.

Now, however, he could no longer keep up his pace. He had to lean on Thomin as he stumbled up into the rocks and down again, and his staff's fire guttered and smoked. A few ravens dropped out of their high nests and sailed around him as if to see how much longer he would endure. But he went on; the force which blazed in him did not waver.

In the end, he was compelled to leave the last few yards of the Retreat unwoven. Thomin pointed out to him the rising dust of Fleshharrower's approach. Shortly, the leading wave of yellow wolves came into view. Lord Verement dropped his task, straightened his shoulders; he gave Thomin one final order. Then he walked out of Doom's Retreat to meet the army of the Despiser.

The wide front of the wolves rushed towards him, suddenly eager for prey. But at the last they hesitated, halted. The unflinching challenge of his stance threw them into confusion. Though they snapped and snarled fiercely, they did not attack. They encircled the two men, and ran howling around them while the rest of the army made its approach.

Fleshharrower's army marched out of the northeast until the dark line of it filled the horizon, and the tramping of its myriad feet shook the ground. The Despiser's hordes seemed to cover the whole Plains, and their tremendous numbers dwarfed Lord Verement like an ocean. When the Giant came forward, kicked his way through the wolves to confront the Lord and his Bloodguard, his size alone made the two men appear puny and insignificant.

But when the Giant was within ten yards of him, Verement made a forbidding gesture. 'Come no closer, *moksha* Raver!' he shouted hoarsely. 'I know you, Jehannum Fleshharrower! Go back! Back to the evil which made you. I deny you passage – I, Verement Shetramate, Lord of the Council of Revelstone! You may not pass here!'

Fleshharrower stopped. 'Ah, a Lord,' he said, peering down at Verement as if the Lord were too tiny to be seen easily. 'I am amazed.' His face was twisted, and his leer gave him an expression of acute pain, as if his flesh could not disguise the hurt of the rabid presence within it. But his voice seemed to suck and cling in the air like quicksand. It held only derision and lust as he continued, 'Have you come to welcome me to the slaughter of your army? But of course you know it is too small to be called an army. I have fought and followed you from Andelain, but do not think that you have outwitted me. I know you seek to meet me in Doom's Retreat because your army is too weak to fight elsewhere. Perhaps you have come to surrender – to join me.'

'You speak like a fool,' Verement barked. 'No friend of the Land will ever surrender to you, or join you. Admit the truth, and go. Go, I say! *Melenkurion abatha!*' Abruptly, he caught his staff in both hands and raised it over his head. '*Duroc minas mill khabaal!* With all the names of the Earthpower, I command you! There is no victory for the Despiser here!'

As Verement shouted his Words, the Raver flinched. To defend himself, he thrust his hand into his leather jerkin, snatched out a smooth green stone that filled his fist. A lambent emerald flame played in its depths, and it steamed like boiling ice. He clenched it, made it steam more viciously, and exclaimed, 'Verement Shetramate, for a hundred leagues I have driven two Lords before me like ants! Why do you believe that you can resist me now?'

'Because you have killed Shetra my wife!' the Lord cried in rage. 'Because I have been unworthy of her all my life! Because I do not fear you, Raver! I am free of all restraint! No fear or love limits my strength! I match you hate for hate, *moksha* Raver! *Melenkurion abatha!*'

His staff whirled about his head, and a livid blue bolt of power sprang from the wood at Fleshharrower. Simultaneously, Thomin rushed forward with his fingers crooked like claws, threw himself at the Giant's throat.

Fleshharrower met the attack easily, disdainfully. He caught Verement's bolt on his Stone and held it burning there like a censer. Almost at once, the blue flame turned deep dazzling green, blazed up higher. And with his other hand, the Giant dealt Thomin a blow which sent him sprawling behind Verement.

Then Fleshharrower flung the fire back.

The Lord's fury never winced. Swinging his staff, he jabbed its metal end like a lance into the gout of power. Savage cracking noises came from the wood as it buckled and bent – but the staff held. Verement shouted mighty words over the flame, compelled it to his will again. Slowly the green burned blue on his staff. When he had mastered it, he hurled it again at the Raver.

Fleshharrower began to laugh. Verement's attack, multiplied by some of the Giant's own power, caught on the Stone as if the green rock were its wick. There it grew hungrily until the column of emerald fire reached high into the air.

Laughing, the Raver shot this fire towards Verement. It splintered his staff, flash-burned the pieces to cinders, deluged him. But then the flame bent itself to his form, gripped him, clung and crawled all over him like a corona. His arms dropped, his head fell forward until his chin touched his chest, his eyes closed; he hung in the fire as if he had been nailed there.

Triumphantly, Fleshharrower cried, 'Now, Verement Shetra-mate! Where is your defiance now?' For a moment, his derision scaled upward, echoed off the cliffs. Then he went on: 'Defeated, I see. But harken to me, puppet. It may be that I will let you live. Of course, to gain life you must change your allegiance. Repeat these words – "I worship Lord Foul the Despiser. He is the one word of truth."'

Lord Verement's lips remained clamped shut. Within the paralysing fire, his cheek muscles bulged as he set his jaws.

'Speak it!' Fleshharrower roared. With a jerk of the Stone, he tightened the corona around Verement. A gasp of agony tore the Lord's lips apart. He began to speak.

'I – worship – '

He went no further. Behind him, Thomin jumped to carry out his last duty. With one kick, the Bloodguard broke Lord Verement's back. Instantly, the Lord fell dead.

Thomin's face was taut with murder as he sprang again at Fleshharrower's throat.

This time, the Bloodguard's attack was so swift and ruthless that it broke past the Raver's defences. He caught Fleshharrower, dug his fingers into the Giant's neck. For a moment, the Giant could not tear him away. He ground his fingers into that thick throat with such passion that Fleshharrower could not break his hold.

But then the Raver brought the Stone to his aid. With one blast, he burned Thomin's bones to ash within him. The Bloodguard collapsed in a heap of structureless flesh.

Then for a time Fleshharrower seemed to go mad. Roaring like a cataclysm, he jumped and stamped on Thomin's form until the Bloodguard's bloody remains were crushed into the grass. And after that, he sent the vast hordes of his wolves howling into the gullet of Doom's Retreat. Driven by his fury, they ran blindly down the canyon, and hurtled into the Word of Warning.

The first wolf to touch the Word triggered it. In that instant, the piled rock within the walls seemed to blow apart. The power which Verement had placed there threw down the sloped sides of the defile. A deadly rain of boulders and shale fell into the canyon, crushing thousands of wolves so swiftly that the pack had time for only one yowl of terror.

When the dust blew clear, Fleshharrower could see that the Retreat was now blocked, crowded with crumbled rock and scree. An army might spend days struggling through the rubble.

The setback appeared to calm him. The hunger for vengeance did not leave his eyes, but his voice was steady as he shouted his commands. He called forward the *griffins*. Flying heavily with ur-viles on their backs, they went into the Retreat to fight Verement's Word. And behind them Fleshharrower sent his rock-wise Cavewights to clear the way for the rest of the army.

Compelled by his power, the creatures worked with headlong desperation. Many of the *griffins* were destroyed because they flew mindlessly against the Word. Scores of Cavewights killed each other in their frenzy to clear the debris from the canyon floor. But lore-wise ur-viles finally tore down the Word of Warning. And the Cavewights accomplished prodigious feats. Given sufficient time and numbers, they had the strength and skill to move mountains. Now they heaved and tore at the rubble. They worked through the night, and by dawn they had cleared a path ten yards wide down the centre of the Retreat.

Holding the Stone high, Fleshharrower led his army through the canyon. At the south end of the Retreat, he found the Warward gone. The last of his enemies – a small band of riders including two Lords – were galloping away out of reach. He howled imprecations after them, vowing that he would pursue them to the death.

But then his farseeing Giantish eyes made out the Warward, seven or eight leagues beyond the riders. He marked the direction of their march – saw where they were headed. And he began to laugh again. Peals of sarcasm and triumph echoed off the blank cliffs of Doom's Retreat.

The Warward marched towards Garroting Deep.

19

THE RUINS OF THE SOUTHRON WASTES

By the time Warmark Troy rode away from Doom's Retreat with the Lords Mhoram and Callindrill and a group of Bloodguard, he had put aside his enervation, his half-conscious yearning to hide his head. Gone, too, was the sense of horror which had paralysed him when Lord Verement died. He had pushed these things down during the dark night, while Mhoram and Callindrill fought to maintain the Word of Warning. Now he felt strangely cauterized. He was the Warmark, and he had returned to his work. He was thinking — measuring distances, gauging relative speeds, forecasting the Warward's attrition rate. He was in command.

He could see his army's need for leadership as clearly as if it were in some way atrocious. Ahead of him, the Warward had swung slightly south to avoid the immediate foothills of the mountains, and across this easier ground it moved at a pace which would cover no more than seven leagues a day. But still the conditions of the march were horrendous. His army was travelling into the dry half-desert of the Southron Wastes.

No vestige or hint of autumn ameliorated the arid breeze which blew northward off the parched, lifeless Grey Desert. Most of the grass had already failed, and the few rills and rivulets which ran down out of the mountains evaporated before they reached five leagues into the Wastes. And even south of the foothills the terrain was difficult — eroded and rasped and cut by long ages of sterile wind into jagged hills, gullies, arroyos. The result was a stark, heat-pale land possessed by a weird and unfriendly beauty. The Warward had to march over packed ground that felt as hard and hostile as rock underfoot, and yet sent up thick dust as if the soil were nothing but powder.

Within three leagues of the Retreat, Troy and his companions found the first dead warrior. The Woodhelvennin corpse lay contorted on the ground like a torture victim. Exhaustion blackened its lips and tongue, and its staring eyes were full of dust. Troy had a mad impulse to stop and bury the warrior. But he was sure of his calculations; in this acrid heat, the losses of the Warward would probably double every day. None of the living could afford the time or strength to care for the dead.

By the time the Warmark caught up with his army, he had counted ten more fallen warriors. Numbers thronged in his brain: eleven dead the first day, twenty-two the second, forty-four the third – six hundred and ninety-three human beings killed by the cruel demands of the march before he reached his destination. And God alone knew how many more – He found himself wondering if he would ever be able to sleep again.

But he forced himself to pay attention as Quaan and Amorine reported on their efforts to keep the warriors alive. Food was rationed; all water jugs were refilled at every stream, however small; every Haft and Warhaft moved on foot, so that their horses could carry the weakest men and women; Quaan's remaining riders also walked, and their damaged mounts bore packs and collapsed warriors; all scouting and water gathering were done by the Bloodguard. And every warrior who could go no farther was supplied with food, and ordered to seek safety in the mountains.

There was nothing else the commanders could do.

All this filled Troy with pain. But then Quaan described to him how very few warriors chose to leave the march and hide in the hills. That news steadied Troy; he felt it was both terrible and wonderful that so many men and women were willing to follow him to the utter end of his ideas. He mustered his confidence to answer Quaan's and Amorine's inevitable questions.

Quaan went bluntly to the immediate problem. 'Does Fleshharrower pursue us?'

'Yes,' Troy replied. 'Lord Verement gained us about a day. But that Giant is coming after us now – he's coming fast.'

Quaan did not need to ask what had happened to Lord Verement. Instead, he said, 'Fleshharrower will move swiftly. When will he overtake us?'

'Sometime tomorrow afternoon. Tomorrow evening at the latest.'

'Then we are lost,' said Amorine, and her voice shook. 'We can march no faster. The warriors are too weary to turn and fight. Warmark,' she implored, 'take this matter from me. Give the First Haft's place to another. I cannot bear – I cannot give these commands.'

He tried to comfort her with his confidence. 'Don't worry. We're not beaten yet.' But to himself he sounded more hysterical than confident. He had a sudden desire to scream. 'We won't have to march any faster than this. We're just going to turn south a fraction more, so that we'll reach that old ruined city – "Doriendor Corishev",

Mhoram calls it. We should get there before noon tomorrow.'

He felt that he was speaking too quickly. He forced himself to slow down while he explained his intentions. Then he was relieved to see dour approval in the faces of his officers. First Haft Amorine took a deep, shuddering breath as she caught hold of her courage again, and Quaan's eyes glinted with bloody promises for the enemy. Shortly, he asked, 'Who will command the Eoward which must remain?'

'Permit me,' Amorine said. 'I am at the end of my strength for this marching. I wish to fight.'

The Hiltmark opened his mouth to answer her, but Troy stopped them both with a gesture. For a moment, he juggled burdens mentally, seeking a point of balance. Then he said to Quaan, 'The Lords and I will stay behind with First Haft Amorine. We'll need eight Eoward of volunteers, and every horse that can still stand. The Bloodguard will probably stay with us. If we handle it right, most of us will survive.'

Quaan frowned at the decision. But his acceptance was as candid as his dislike. To Amorine, he said, 'We must find those who are willing, and prepare them today, so that tomorrow no time will be lost.'

In answer the First Haft saluted both Quaan and Troy, then rode away among the Warward. She carried herself straighter than she had for several days, and her alacrity demonstrated to Troy that he had made the correct choice. He nodded after her, sardonically congratulating himself for having done something right.

But Quaan still had questions. Shortly, he said, 'I ask your pardon, Warmark – but we have been friends, and I must speak of this. Will you not explain to me why we march now? If Doom's Retreat is not the battleground you desire, perhaps Doriendor Corishev will serve. Why must this terrible march continue?'

'No, I'm not going to explain. Not yet.' Troy kept his final plan to himself as if by silence and secrecy he could contain its terrors. 'And Doriendor Corishev won't serve. We could fight there for a day or two. But after that, Fleshharrower would surround us and just squeeze. We've got to do better than that.'

The Hiltmark nodded morosely. Troy's refusal saddened him like an expression of distrust. But he managed a wry smile as he said, 'Warmark, is there no end to your plans?'

'Yes,' Troy sighed. 'Yes, there is. And we're going to get there. After that, Mhoram is going to have to save us. He promised – '

Because he could not bear to face Quaan with his inadequacies, he turned away. Clapping Mehryl with his heels, he went in search of the Lords. He wanted to explain his intentions for Doriendor Corishev, and to find out what additional help Mhoram or Callindrill could give the Warward.

During the rest of that day and the next morning, he received regular reports from the Bloodguard on Fleshharrower's progress. The Giant-Raver's army was large and unwieldy; it had covered only nine leagues during the day after it traversed Doom's Retreat. But it did not halt during the dark night, and took only one short rest before dawn. Troy judged that the Giant would reach Doriendor Corishev by midafternoon.

That knowledge made him ache to drive the Warward faster. But he could not. Too many warriors left the army or died that night and the next morning. To his dismay, the attrition tripled. A litany of numbers ran through his brain: eleven, thirty-three, ninety-nine – at that rate, the march itself would claim four thousand and four victims by the end of six days. And lives would be lost in Doriendor Corishev. He needed complex equations to measure the plight of his army. He did not try to hurry it.

As a result, the warriors were only a league ahead of Fleshharrower when they started up the long slope towards the ruins of Doriendor Corishev. The ancient city sat atop a high hill under the perpetual frown of the mountains, and the hill itself crested a south-running ridge. The ruins were elevated on a line that separated, hid from each other, the east and west sides of the Southron Wastes. In past ages, when the city lived and thrived, it had commanded perfectly the northern edge of that region, and now the low, massive remains of fortifications testified that the inhabitants of the city had known the value of their position. According to the legends which had been preserved in Kevin's Lore, these people had been warlike; they had needed their strategic location. Lord Callindrill translated the name as 'masterplace' or 'desolation of enemies'.

The legends said that for centuries Doriendor Corishev had been the capital of the nation which gave birth to Berek Halfhand.

That was the age of the One Forest's dominion in the Land. Then there were no Wastes south of the mountains; the region was green and populous. But in time it became too populous. Groups of people from this southern country slowly moved up into the Land, and began to attack the Forest. At first, they only wanted timber for the civilization of Doriendor Corishev. Then they wanted fields for crops. Then they wanted homes. With the unconscious aid of other immigrants from the north, they eventually accomplished the maiming of the One Forest.

But that injury had many ramifications. On the one hand, the felling of the trees unbound the interdict which the Colossus of the

Fall had held over the Lower Land. The Ravers were unleashed – a release which led with deft inevitability to the destruction of Doriendor Corishev's monarchy in the great war of Berek Halfhand. And on the other hand, the loss of perhaps a hundred thousand square leagues of Forest altered the natural balances of the Earth. Every falling tree hammered home an ineluctable doom for the masterplace. As the trees died, the southern lands lost the watershed which had preserved them from the Grey Desert. Centuries after the ravage of the One Forest became irreversible, these lands turned to dry ruin.

But the city had been deserted since the time of Berek, the first Lord. Now, after millennia of wind and dust, nothing remained of the masterplace except the standing shards of its walls and buildings, a kind of group map formed by the bloodless stumps of its grandeur. Warmark Troy could have hidden his whole army in its labyrinthian spaces and ways. Behind fragmentary walls that reached meaning-lessly into the sky, the warriors could have fought guerrilla war for days against an army of comparable size.

Troy trusted that Fleshharrower knew this. His plans relied heavily on his ability to convince the Giant that the Warward chose to make its last stand in Doriendor Corishev, rather than under the certain death of Garroting Deep. He marched his army straight up the long hillside, and into the toothless gate of the masterplace. Then he took the warriors through the city and out its western side, where they were hidden from Fleshharrower by the ridge on which the city stood.

There he gave Quaan all the instructions and encouragement he could. Then he saluted the Hiltmark, and watched as the main body of the Warward marched away down the slope. When it was gone, he and his volunteers returned to the city with the two Lords, First Haft Amorine, all the Bloodguard, and every horse still strong enough to bear a rider.

Within the ruined walls, he addressed the eight Eoward that had offered to buy the Warward's escape from Doriendor Corishev. He had a taut, dry feeling in his throat as he began, 'You're all volunteers, so I'm not going to apologize for what we're doing. But I want you to be sure you know why we're doing it. I have two main reasons. First, we're going to give the rest of the warriors a chance to put some distance between them and Fleshharrower. Second, we're going to help squeeze out a victory in this war. I'm preparing a little surprise for Foul's army, and we're going to help make it work. Parts of that army move faster than others – but if they get too spread out, they won't all fall into my trap. So we're going to pull them together here.'

He paused to look over the warriors. They stood squarely before him with expressions coloured by every hue of grimness and fatigue and determination, and their very bones seemed to radiate mortality. At the sight, he began to understand Mhoram's statement that they deserved to know the truth; they were serving his commands with their souls. Roughly, he went on, 'But there's one more thing. Fleshharrower may be planning a surprise or two for us. Many of you were with Hiltmark Quaan during that storm – you know what I'm talking about. That Giant has power, and he intends to use it. We're going to give him a chance. We're hoping to be a target, so that whatever he does will hit us instead of the rest of the Warward. I think we can survive it – if we do things right. But it's not going to be easy.'

Abruptly, he turned to Amorine, and ordered her to deploy the Eoward in strategic positions throughout the east side of the masterplace. 'Make sure of your lines of retreat. I don't want people getting lost in this maze when it's time for us to pull out.' Then he spoke to the Bloodguard, asked them to scout beyond the city along the ridge. 'I've got to know right away if Fleshharrower tries to surround us.'

Terrel nodded, and a few of the Bloodguard rode away.

First Haft Amorine took her Eoward back across Doriendor Corishev. They left all their horses, including the Ranyhyn, at the west gate under the care of several Bloodguard.

Accompanied by the rest of the Bloodguard, Troy and the two Lords made their way on foot to the east wall.

While they passed through the ruins, Lord Mhoram asked, 'Warmark, do you believe that Fleshharrower will not attempt to surround us? Why would he do otherwise?'

'Instinct,' Troy replied curtly. 'I think he'll be very careful to let us escape on the west side. You heard him laugh – back at Doom's Retreat – when he saw where we were going. I think that what he really wants is to trap us against Garroting Deep. He's a Raver. He probably thinks the idea of using that Forest against us is hilarious.'

Then he was grateful that Mhoram refrained from asking him what his own ideas about Garroting Deep were. He did not want to think about that. Instead, he tried to concentrate on the layout of the city, so that he could find his way through it at night if necessary. But his heart was not in the task. Too many other anxieties occupied him.

When he reached the east wall, and climbed up on some rubble to peer over it, he saw Fleshharrower's army.

It approached like a great discoloration, a dark bruise, on the pale ground of the Wastes. Its front stretched away both north and south of the ruins. It was less than a league away.

And it was immense beyond comprehension. Troy could not imagine how Lord Foul had been able to create such an army.

It came forward until it reached the foot of the hill upon which Doriendor Corishev stood.

As he watched, Troy gripped the handle of his sword as if it were the only thing that kept him from panic. Several times, he reached up to adjust the sunglasses he no longer possessed. The movement was like an involuntary prayer of appeal. But neither of the Lords observed him. Their faces were set towards Fleshharrower.

Troy almost shouted with elation when the Giant-Raver stopped his army at the foot of the hill. The halt ran through his hordes like a shock, as if the force which drove them had struck a wall. The wolves smelled prey; they sent up a howl of frustration at the halt. Ur-viles barked furiously. Warped humans groaned, and Cavewights hopped hungrily from foot to foot. But Fleshharrower's command mastered them all. They spread out until they formed a ready arc around the entire eastern side of the hill, then set themselves to wait.

When he was satisfied with the position of his army, the Raver took a few steps up the hill, placed his fists on his hips, and shouted sardonically, 'Lords! Warriors! I know you hear me! Listen to my words! Surrender! You cannot escape – you are ensnared between the Desert and the Deep. I can eradicate you from the Earth with only a tenth of my strength. Surrender! If you join me, I may be merciful.' At the word *merciful*, a yammer of protest and hunger went up from his army. He waited for the outcry to pass before he continued: 'If not, I will destroy you! I will burn and blast your homes. I will make Revelwood a charnel, and use Revelstone for an offal ground. I will wreck and ravage the Land until Time itself breaks! Hear me and despair! Surrender or die!'

At this, an irresistible impulse caught hold of the Warmark; frustration and rage boiled up in him. Without warning, he leaped onto the wall. He braced his feet to steady himself, and raised his fists defiantly. 'Fleshharrower!' he shouted. 'Vermin! I am Warmark Hile Troy! I command here! I spit in your face, Raver! You're only a slave! And your master is only a slave! He's a slave to hunger, and he gnaws his worthlessness like an old bone. Go back! Leave the Land! We're free people. Despair has no power over us. But I'll teach you despair if you dare to fight me!'

Fleshharrower snapped an order. A dozen bowstrings thrummed; shafts flew past Troy's head as Ruel snatched him down from the wall. Troy stumbled as he landed, but Ruel upheld him. When the Warmark regained his balance, Mhoram said, 'You took a grave risk. What have you gained?'

'I've made him mad,' Troy replied unsteadily. 'This has got to be done right, and I'm going to do it. The madder he gets, the better off we are.'

'Are you so certain of what he will do?'

'Yes.' Troy felt an odd confidence, a conviction that he would not be proved wrong until the end. 'He's already doing it – he's stopped. If he's mad enough he'll attack us first himself. His army will stay stopped. That's what we want.'

'Then I believe that you have succeeded,' Lord Callindrill inserted quietly. He was gazing over the wall as he spoke. Mhoram and Troy joined him, and saw what he meant.

Fleshharrower had retreated until there was a flat space of ground between himself and the hill. Around him, the army shifted. Several thousand ur-viles moved to form wedges with their loremasters poised on both sides of the space. There they waited while the Giant-Raver marked out a wide circle in the dirt, using the tip of one of the loremasters' staves. Then Fleshharrower ordered all but the ur-viles away from the circle.

When the space was cleared, the loremasters began their work.

Chanting in arhythmic unison, like a mesmerized chorus of dogs, the ur-viles bent their might forward, into the hands of their loremasters. The loremasters thrust the points of their staves into the rim of Fleshharrower's circle, and began to rock the irons slowly back and forth.

A low buzzing noise became audible. The ur-viles were singing in their own roynish tongue, and their song made the flat, hard ground vibrate. Slowly, the buzz scaled upward, as if a swarm of huge, mad bees were imprisoned in the dirt. And the earth in the circle began to pulse visibly. A change like an increase of heat came over the rock and soil; hot, red gleams played through the circle erratically, and its surface seethed. The buzz became fiercer, sharper.

The process was slow, but its horrible fascination made it seem swift to the onlookers. As daylight started to fall out of the stricken sky, the buzz replaced it like a cry of pain from the ground itself. The Raver's circle throbbed and boiled as if the dirt within it were molten.

The sound tormented Troy; it clawed at his ears, crawled like lice over his flesh. Sweat slicked his eyeless brows. For a time, he feared that he would be compelled to scream. But at last the cry scaled past the range of his senses. He was able to turn away, rest briefly.

When he looked back towards the circle, he found that the ur-viles had withdrawn from it. Fleshharrower stood there alone. A demonic look clenched his face as he stared into the hot, red, boiling soil.

In his hands, he held one of the loremasters. It gibbered fearfully, clung to its stave, but it could not break his grip.

Laughing, Fleshharrower lifted the loremaster over his head and hurled it into the circle. As it hit the ground, its scream died in a flash of fire. Only its stave remained, slowly melting on the surface.

As the sun set, Fleshharrower began using his fragment of the Stone to reshape the molten iron, forge it into something new.

Softly, as if he feared that the Giant-Raver might hear him, Troy asked the Lords, 'What's this for? What's he doing?'

'He makes a tool,' Mhoram whispered, 'some means to increase or concentrate his power.'

The implications of that gave Troy a feeling of grim gratification. His strategy was justified at least to the extent that the main body of the Warward would be spared this particular attack. But he knew that such justification was not enough. His final play lay like a dead weight in his stomach. He expected to lose command of the Warward as soon as he revealed it; it would appal the warriors so much that they would rebel. After all his promises of victory, he felt like a false prophet. Yet his plan was the Warward's only hope, the Land's only hope.

He prayed that Lord Mhoram would be equal to it.

With the sunset, his sight failed. He was forced to rely on Mhoram to report the Raver's progress. In the darkness, he felt trapped, bereft of command. All that he could see was the amorphous, dull glow of the liquid earth. Occasionally, he made out flares and flashes of lurid green across the red, but they meant nothing to him. His only consolation lay in the fact that Fleshharrower's preparations were consuming time.

Along the wall on both sides of him, First Haft Amorine's Eoward kept watch over the Raver's labours. No one slept; the poised threat of Fleshharrower's army transfixed everyone. Moonrise did not ease the blackness; the dark of the moon was only three nights away. But the Raver's forgework was bright enough to pale the stars.

During the whole long watch, Fleshharrower never left his molten circle. Sometime after midnight, he retrieved his newly made sceptre, and cooled it by waving it in a shower of sparks over his head. Then he affixed his fragment of the Stone to its end. But when that was done, he remained by the circle. As night waned towards day, he gestured and sang over the molten stone, weaving incantations out of its hot power. It lit his movements luridly, and the Stone flashed across it at intervals, giving green glimpses of his malice.

But this was indistinct to Troy. He clung to his hope. In the darkness, his calculations were the only reality left to him, and he recited them like counters against the night. When the first slit of dawn touched him from the east, he felt a kind of elation.

Softly, he asked for Amorine.

'Warmark.' She was right beside him.

'Amorine, listen. That monster has made his mistake – he's wasted too much time. Now we're going to make him pay for it. Get the warriors out of here. Send them after the Warward. Whatever happens, that Giant won't get as many of us as he thinks. Just keep one warrior for every good horse we have.'

'Perhaps all should depart now,' she replied, 'before the Raver attacks.'

Troy grinned at the idea. He could imagine Fleshharrower's fury if the Giant's attack found Doriendor Corishev empty. But he knew that he had not yet gained enough time. He answered, 'I want to squeeze another half day out of him. With the Bloodguard and a couple hundred warriors, we'll be able to do it. Now get going.'

'Yes, Warmark.' She left his side at once, and soon he could hear most of the warriors withdrawing. He gripped the wall again, and stared away into the sunrise, waiting for sight.

Shortly, he became aware that the dry breeze out of the south was stiffening.

Then the haze faded from his mind. First he became able to see the ruined wall, then the hillside; finally he caught sight of the waiting army.

It had not moved during the night.

It did not need to move.

Fleshharrower still stood beside his circle. The fire in the ground had died, but before it failed, he had used it to wrap himself in a shimmering, translucent cocoon of power. Within the power, he was as erect as an icon. He held his sceptre rigidly above his head; he did not move; he made no sound. But when the sunlight touched him, the wind leaped suddenly into a hard blow like a violent exhalation through the teeth of the Desert. And it increased in ragged gusts like the leading edge of a sirocco.

Then a low cry from one of the warriors pulled Troy's attention away from Fleshharrower. Turning his head, he looked down the throat of the mounting gale.

From the southeast, where the Southron Range met the Grey Desert, a tornado came rushing towards Doriendor Corishev. Its undulating shaft ploughed straight across the Wastes.

It conveyed such an impression of might that several moments passed before Troy realized it was not the kind of whirlwind he understood.

It brought no rain or clouds with it; it was as dry as the Desert.

And it carried no dust or sand; it was as clean as empty air. It should not have been visible at all. But its sheer force made it palpable to Troy's sight. He could feel it coming. It was so vivid to him that at first he could not grasp the fact that the tornado was not moving with the wind.

The gale blew straight out of the south, tearing dust savagely from the ground as it came. And the tornado cut diagonally across it, ignored the wind to howl straight towards Doriendor Corishev.

Troy stared at it. Dust clogged his mouth, but he did not know this until he tried to shout something. Then, coughing convulsively, he wrenched himself away from the sight. At once, the sirocco hit him. When he stopped looking at the tornado, the force of the wind sent him reeling. Ruel caught him. He pivoted around the Bloodguard, and threw himself towards Lord Mhoram.

When he reached Mhoram, he shouted, 'What is it?'

'Creator preserve us!' Mhoram replied. The yowling wind whipped his voice from his lips, and Troy barely heard him. 'It is a vortex of trepidation.'

Troy tried to thrust his words past the wind to Mhoram's ears. 'What will it do?'

Shouting squarely into Troy's face, Mhoram answered, 'It will make us afraid!'

The next moment, he pulled at Troy's arm, and pointed upward, towards the top of the tornado. There a score of dark creatures flew, riding the upper reaches of the vortex.

The tornado had already covered more than half the distance to Doriendor Corishev, and Troy saw the creatures vividly. They were birds as large as *kresh*. They had clenched satanic faces like bats, wide eagle-wings, and massive barbed claws. As they flew, they called to each other, showing double rows of hooked teeth. Their wings beat with lust.

They were the most fearsome creatures Troy had ever seen. As he stared, he tried to rally himself against them – judge their speed, calculate the time left before their arrival, plan a defence. But they staggered his mind; he could not comprehend an existence which permitted them.

He struggled to move, regain his balance enough to tell himself that he was already tasting the vortex of trepidation. But he was paralysed. Voices shouted around him. He had a vague impression that Fleshharrower's hordes greeted the vortex with glee – or were they afraid of it, too? He could not tell.

Then Ruel grabbed his arm, snatched him away from the wall, shouted into his ear, 'Warmark, come! We must make a defence!'

Troy could not remember ever having heard a Bloodguard shout before. But even now Ruel's voice did not sound like panic. Troy felt that there was something terrible in such immunity. He tried to look around him, but the wind lashed so much dust across the ruins that all details were lost. Both Lords were gone. Warriors ran in all directions, stumbling against the wind. Bloodguard bobbed in and out of view like ghouls.

Ruel shouted at him again. 'We must save the horses! They will go mad with fear!'

For one lorn moment, Troy wished High Lord Elena were with him, so that he could tell her this was not his fault. Then, abruptly, he realized that he had made another mistake. If he were killed, no one would know how to save the Warward. His final plan would die with him, and every man and woman of his army would be butchered as a result.

The realization seemed to push him over an edge. He plunged to his knees. The sirocco and the dust were strangling him.

Ruel shouted, 'Warmark! Corruption attacks!'

At the word *Corruption*, a complete lucidity came over Troy. Fear filled all his thoughts with crystalline incisiveness. At once, he perceived that the Bloodguard was trying to undo him; Ruel's impenetrable fidelity was a deliberate assault upon his fitness for command.

The understanding made him reel, but he reacted lucidly, adroitly. He took one last look around him, saw one or two figures still surging back and forth through the livid anguish of the dust. Ruel was moving to capture him. Overhead, the dark birds dropped towards the ruins. Troy picked up a rock and climbed to his feet. When Ruel touched him, he suddenly gestured away behind the Bloodguard. Ruel turned to look. Troy hit him on the back of the skull with the rock.

Then the Warmark ran. He could not make progress against the wind, so he worked across it. The walls of buildings loomed out of the dust at him. He started towards a door.

Without warning, he stumbled into First Haft Amorine.

She caught at him, buffeted him with cries like fear. But she, too, was someone faithful, someone who threatened him. He lunged at her with his shoulder, sent her sprawling. Immediately, he dodged into the maze of the masterplace.

He fell several times as the wind sprang at him through unexpected gaps in the walls. But he forced himself ahead. The clarity of his terror was complete; he knew what he had to do.

After a swift, chaotic battle, he found what he needed. With a rush, he lurched out into the centre of a large, open space – the remains of one of Doriendor Corishev's meeting halls. In this unsheltered expanse, the force of the wind belaboured him venomously. He welcomed it. He felt a paradoxical glee of fear; his own terror delighted him. He stood like an exalted fanatic in the open space, and looked up to see how long he would have to wait.

When he glanced behind him, his heart leaped. One of the birds glided effortlessly towards him, as if it were in total command of the wind. It had a clear approach to him. The ease of its movement thrilled him, and he poised himself to jump into its jaws.

But as it neared him, he saw that it carried Ruel's crumpled body in its mighty talons. He could see Ruel's flat dispassionate features. The Bloodguard looked as if he had been betrayed.

A convulsion shook Troy. As the bird swooped towards him, he remembered who he was. The strength of terror galvanized his muscles; he snatched out his sword and struck.

His blow split the bird's skull. Its weight bowled him over. Green blood spewed from it over his head and shoulders. The hot blood burned him like a corrosive, and it smelled so thickly of attar that it asphyxiated him. With a choked cry, he clawed at his forehead, trying to tear the pain away. But the acid fire consumed his headband, burned through his skull into his brain. He lost consciousness.

He awoke to silence and the darkness of night.

After a long lapse of time like an interminable scream, he raised his head. The wind had piled dust over him, and his movements disturbed it. It filled his throat and mouth and lungs. But he bit back a spasm of coughing, and listened to the darkness.

All around him, Doriendor Corishev was as still as a cairn. The wind and the vortex were gone, leaving only midnight dust and death to mark their path. Silence lay over the ruins like a bane.

Then he had to cough. Gasping, retching, he pushed himself to his knees. He sounded explosively loud to himself. He tried to control the violence of his coughing, but he was helpless until the spasm passed.

As it released him, he realized that he was still clutching his sword. Instinctively, he tightened his grip on it. He cursed his night blindness, then told himself that the darkness was his only hope.

His face throbbed painfully, but he ignored it.

He kept himself still while he thought.

This long after the vortex, he reasoned, all his allies were either dead or gone. If the vortex and the birds had not killed them, they had been swept from the ruins by Fleshharrower's army. So they could not help him. He did not know how much of that army had stayed behind in the masterplace.

And he could not see. He was vulnerable until daylight. Only the darkness protected him; he could not defend himself.

His first reaction was to remain where he was, and pray that he was not discovered. But he recognized the futility of that plan. At best, it would only postpone his death. When dawn came, he would still be alone against an unknown number of enemies. No, his one chance was to sneak out of the city now and lose himself in the Wastes. There he might find a gully or hole in which to hide.

That escape was possible, barely possible, because he had one advantage; none of Fleshharrower's creatures except the ur-viles could move through the ruins at night as well as he. And the Raver would not have left ur-viles behind. They were too valuable. If Troy could remember his former skills — his sense of ambience, his memory for terrain — he would be able to navigate the city.

He would have to rely on his hearing to warn him of enemies.

He began by sliding his sword quietly into its scabbard. Then he started groping his way over the hot sand. He needed to verify where he was, and he knew only one way to do it.

Nearby, his hands found a patch of ground that felt burned. The dirt which stuck to his fingers reeked of attar. And in the patch, he located Ruel's twisted body. His sense of touch told him that Ruel was badly charred. The dark bird must have caught fire when it died, and burned away, leaving the Bloodguard's corpse behind.

The touch of that place nauseated him, and he backed away from it. He was sweating heavily. Sweat stung his burns. The night was hot; sunset had brought no relief to the ruins. Folding his arms over his stomach, he climbed to his feet.

Standing unsteadily in the open, he tried to clear his mind of Ruel and the bird. He needed to remember how to deal with blindness, how to orient himself in the ruins. But he could not determine which way he had come into this open place. Waving his arms before him, he went in search of a wall.

His feet distrusted the ground — he could not put them down securely — and he moved awkwardly. His sense of balance had deserted him. His face felt raw, and sweat seared his eye sockets. But he clenched his concentration, and measured the distance.

In twenty yards, he reached a wall. He touched it at an angle, promptly squared himself to it, then moved along it. He needed a gap which would permit him to touch both sides of the wall. Any discrepancy in temperature between the sides would tell him his directions.

After twenty more yards, he arrived in a corner. Turning at right angles, he followed this new wall. He kept himself parallel to it by brushing the stone with his fingers. Shortly, he stumbled into some rubble, and found an entryway.

The wall here was thick, but he could touch its opposite sides without stretching his arms. Both sides felt very warm, but he thought he discerned a slightly higher temperature on the side facing back into the open space. That direction was west, he reasoned; the afternoon sun would have heated the west side of a wall.

Now he had to decide which way to go.

If he went east, he would be less likely to meet enemies. Since they had not already found him, they might be past him, and their search would move from east to west after the Warward. But if any chance of help from his friends or Mehryl remained, it would be on the west side.

The dilemma seemed to have no solution. He found himself shaking his head and moaning through his teeth. At once, he stuffed his throat with silence. He decided to move west towards Mehryl. The added risk was preferable to a safe escape eastward – an escape which would leave him alone in the Southron Wastes, without food or water or a mount.

He leaned against the unnatural heat of the wall for a few moments, breathing deeply to steady himself. Then he stood up, grasped his sense of direction with all the concentration he could muster, and started walking straight out into the ruined hall.

His progress was slow. The uncertainty of his steps made him stagger repeatedly away from a true westward line. But he corrected the variations as best he could, and kept going. Without the support of a wall, his balance grew worse at every stride. Before he had covered thirty yards, the floor reeled around him, and he dropped to his knees. He had to clamp his throat shut to keep from whimpering.

When he regained his feet, he heard quiet laughter – first one voice, then several. It had a cruel sound, as if it were directed at him. It resonated slightly off the walls, so that he could not locate it, but it seemed to come from somewhere ahead.

He froze where he stood. Helplessly, he prayed that the darkness would cover him.

But a voice shattered that hope. 'Look here, brothers,' it said. 'A man – alone.' Its utterance was awkward, thick with slavering, but Troy could understand it. He could hear the malice in the low chorus of laughter which answered it.

Other voices spoke.

'A man, yes. Slayer take him!'

'Look. Such pretty clothes. An enemy.'

'Ha! Look again, fool. That is no man.'

'He has no eyes.'

'Is it an ur-vile?'

'No – a man, I say. A man with no eyes! Here is some sport, brothers.'

All the voices laughed again.

Troy did not stop to wonder how the speakers could see him. He turned, started to run back the way he had come.

At once, they gave pursuit. He could hear the slap of bare feet on stone, the sharp breathing. They overtook him swiftly. Something veered close to him, tripped him. As he fell, the running feet surrounded him.

'Go gently, brothers. No quick kill. He will be sport for us all.'

'Do not kill him.'

'Not kill? I want to kill. Kill and eat.'

'The Giant will want this one.'

'After we sport.'

'Why tell the Giant, brothers? He is greedy.'

'He takes our meat.'

'Keep this one for ourselves, yes.'

'Slayer take the Giant.'

'His precious ur-viles. When there is danger, men must go first.'

'Yes! Brothers, we will eat this meat.'

Troy heaved himself to his feet. Through the rapid chatter of the voices, he heard, *go first*, and almost fell again. If these creatures were the first of Fleshharrower's army to enter the masterplace – ! But he pushed down the implications of that thought, and snatched out his sword.

'A sword? Ho Ho!'

'Look, brothers. The man with no eyes wants to play.'

'Play!'

Troy heard the lash of a whip; cord flicked around his wrist. It caught and jerked, hauled him from his feet. Strong hands took his sword. Something kicked him in the chest, knocked him backward. But his breastplate protected him.

One of the voices cried, 'Slayer! My foot!'

'Fool!' came the answer. There was laughter.

'Kill him!'

A metallic weapon clattered against his breastplate, fell to the ground. He scrambled for it in the dust, but sudden hands shoved him away. He recoiled and got to his feet again.

He heard the whistle of the whip, and its cord lashed at his ankles. But this time he did not go down.

'Do not kill him yet. Where is the sport?'

'Make him play.'

'Yes, brothers. Play.'

'Play for us, man with no eyes.'

The whip burned around his neck. He staggered under the blow. The bewildering crossfire of voices went on.

'Play, Slayer take you!'

'Sport for us!'

'Why sport? I want meat. Blood-wet meat.'

'The Giant feeds us sand.'

'Play, I say! Are you blind, man with no eyes? Does the sun dazzle you?'

This gibe was met with loud laughter. But Troy stood still in his dismay. *The sun*? he thought numbly. Then he had chosen the wrong direction, east instead of west; he had walked right into these creatures. He wanted to scream. But he was past screaming. He could feel the light of his life going out. His hands shook as he tried to straighten his sunglasses.

'Dear God,' he groaned.

Numbly, as if he did not know what he was doing, he put his fingers to his lips and gave a shrill whistle.

The whip coiled around his waist and whirled him to the ground.

'Play!' the voices shouted raggedly together.

But when he stumbled to his feet again, he heard the sound of hooves. And a moment later, Mehryl's whinny cut through the gibbering voices. It touched Troy's heart like the call of a trumpet. He jerked up his head, and his ears searched, trying to locate the Ranyhyn.

The voices changed to shouts of hunger as the hooves charged.

'Ranyhyn!'

'Kill it!'

'Meat!'

Hands grabbed Troy. He grappled with a fist that held a knife. But then the noise of hooves rushed close to him. An impact flung his assailant away. He turned, tried to leap onto Mehryl's back. But he only put himself in Mehryl's path. The shoulder of the Ranyhyn struck him, knocked him down.

Then he could hear bare feet leaping to the attack. The whip cracked, knives swished. Mehryl was forced away from him. Hooves skittered on the stone as the Ranyhyn retreated. Howling triumphantly the creatures gave chase. The sounds receded.

Troy pushed himself to his feet. His heart thudded in his chest; pain throbbed sharply in his face. The noises of pursuit seemed to indicate that he was being left alone. But he did not move. Concentrating all his attention, he tried to hear over the beat of his pain.

For a long moment, the open space around him sounded empty, still. He waved his arms, and touched nothing.

But then he heard a sharp intake of breath.

He was trembling violently. He wanted to turn and run. But he forced himself to hold his ground. He concentrated, bent all his alertness towards the sound. In the distance, the other creatures had lost Mehryl. They were returning; he could hear them.

'But the near voice hissed, 'I kill you. You hurt my foot. Slayer take them! You are my meat.'

Troy could sense the creature's approach. It loomed out of the blankness like a faint pressure on his face. The rasp of its breathing grew louder. With every step, he felt its ambience more acutely.

The tension was excruciating, but he held himself still. He waited. Interminable time passed.

Suddenly, he felt the creature bunching to spring.

He snatched Manethrall Rue's cord from his belt, looped it around the neck of his attacker, and jerked as the creature hit him. He put all his strength into the pull. The creature's leap toppled him, but he clung to the cord, heaved on it. The creature landed on top of him. He threw his weight around, got himself onto the creature. He kept pulling. Now he could feel the limpness of the body under him. But he did not release his hold. Straining on the cord, he banged the creature's head repeatedly against the stone.

He was gasping for breath. Dimly, he could hear the other creatures charging him.

He did not release his hold.

Then power crackled through the air. Flame burst around him. He heard shouts, and the clash of swords. Bowstrings thrummed. Creatures screamed, ran, fell heavily.

A moment later, hands lifted Troy. Rue's cord was taken from his rigid fingers. First Haft Amorine cried, 'Warmark! Warmark! Praise the Creator, you are safe!' She was weeping with relief. People moved around him. He heard Lord Mhoram say, 'My friend, you have led us a merry chase. Without Mehryl's aid, we would not have found you in time.' The voice came disembodied out of the blankness.

At first, Troy could not speak. His heart struggled through a crisis. It made him gasp so hard that he could barely stand. He sounded as if he were trying to sob.

'Warmark,' Amorine said, 'what has happened to you?'

'Sun,' he panted, 'is – the sun – shining?' The effort of articulation seemed to impale his heart.

'Warmark? Ah, Warmark! What has been done to you?'

'The sun?' he retched out. He was desperate to insist, but he could only stamp his foot uselessly.

'The sun stands overhead,' Mhoram answered. 'We have survived the vortex and its creatures. But now Fleshharrower's army enters Doriendor Corishev. We must depart swiftly.'

'Mhoram,' Troy coughed hoarsely. 'Mhoram.' Stumbling forward, he fell into the Lord's arms.

Mhoram held him in a comforting grip. Without a word, the Lord supported him until some of his pain passed, and he began to breathe more easily. Then Mhoram said quietly, 'I see that you slew one of the Despiser's birds. You have done well, my friend. Lord Callindrill and I remain. Perhaps seventy of the Bloodguard survive. First Haft Amorine has preserved a handful of her warriors. After the passing of the vortex, all the Ranyhyn returned. They saved many horses. My friend, we must go.'

Some of Mhoram's steadiness reached Troy, and he began to regain control of himself. He did not want to be a burden to the Lord. Slowly, he drew back, stood on his own. Covering his burned forehead with his hands as if he were trying to hide his eyelessness, he said, 'I've got to tell you the rest of my plan.'

'May it wait? We must depart at once.'

'Mhoram,' Troy moaned brokenly, 'I can't see.'

20

GARROTING DEEP

Two days later – shortly after noon on the day before the dark of the moon – Lord Mhoram led the Warward to Cravenhaw, the south-most edge of Garroting Deep. In noon heat, the army had swung stumbling and lurching like a dying man around the foothills, and had marched northward to a quivering halt before the very lips of the fatal Deep. The warriors stood on a wide, grassy plain – the first healthy green they had seen since leaving the South Plains. Ahead was the Forest. Perhaps half a league away on either side, east and west, were mountains, steep and forbidding peaks like the jaws of the Deep. And behind was the army of *moksha* Fleshharrower.

The Giant-Raver drove his forces savagely. Despite the delay at Doriendor Corishev, he was now no more than two leagues away.

That knowledge tightened Lord Mhoram's cold, weary dread. He had so little time in which to attempt Warmark Troy's plan. From this position, there were no escapes and no hopes except the one Troy had envisioned. If Mhoram were not successful – successful soon! – the Warward would be crushed between the Raver and Garroting Deep.

Yet he doubted that he could succeed at all, regardless of the time at his disposal. In a year or a score of years, he might still fail. The demand was so great – Even the vortex of trepidation had not made him feel so helpless.

Yet he shuddered when he thought of the vortex. Although Troy had saved virtually all the Warward, the men and women who had remained in the masterplace had paid heavily for their survival. Something in Lord Callindrill had been damaged by Fleshharrower's attack. The strain of combat against bitter ill had humiliated him in some way, taught him a deep distrust of himself. He had not been able to resist the fear. Now his clear soft eyes were clouded, pained. When he melded his thoughts with Lord Mhoram, he shared knowledge and concern, but not strength; he no longer believed in his strength.

In her own way, First Haft Amorine suffered similarly. During the Raver's onslaught, she had held the collapsing remains of her command together by the simple force of her courage. She had taken the terror of her warriors upon herself. Every time one of them fell under the power of the vortex, or died in the talons of the birds, she had tightened her grip on the survivors. And after that, when the sirocco had passed, she began a frantic search for Warmark Troy. The perverted, man-like creatures that rushed into the ruins – some with claws for fingers, others with cleft faces and limbs covered with suckers, still others with extra eyes or arms, all of them warped in some way by the power of the Stone – steadily brought more and more of the city under their control. But she fought her way through them as if they were mere shades to haunt her while she hunted. The idea of following Mehryl was hers.

But the Warmark's blindness was too much for her. The cause of it was clear. The slain bird's corrosive blood had ravaged his face, and that burning had undone the Land's gift of sight. Neither of the Lords had any hurtloam, *rillinlure*, or other arts of healing with which to counteract the hurt. When she understood Troy's plight, she appeared to lose herself; independent will deserted her. Until she rejoined the Warward, she followed Lord Mhoram's requests and instructions blankly, like a puppet from which all authority had evaporated. And when she saw Hiltmark Quaan again, she transferred herself to him. As she told him of Troy's plan, she was so numb that she did not even falter.

The Warmark himself had said nothing more after describing his final strategy. He wrapped himself in his blindness and allowed Mhoram to place him on Mehryl's back. He did not ask about Fleshharrower's army, though only the speed of the Ranyhyn saved him and his companions from being trapped in the city. Despite the scream of frustration which roared after the riders, he carried himself like an invalid who had turned his face to the wall.

And Lord Mhoram also suffered. After the battle of the master-place, fatigue and dread had forced tenacious fingers into the crevices and crannies of his soul, so that he could not shake them off. Yet he helped the First Haft and Lord Callindrill as best he could. He knew that only time and victory could heal their wounds; but he absorbed those parts of their burdens which came within his reach, and gave back to them all the consolation he possessed.

There was nothing he could do to ease the shock which Amorine's report of the Warmark's final plan gave Quaan. As she spoke, the Hiltmark's concern for her gave way to a livid horror on behalf of the warriors. His expression flared, and he erupted, 'Madness! Every man and woman will be slain! Troy, what has become of you? By the Seven! Troy — Warmark!' — he hesitated awkwardly before uttering his thought — 'Do you rave? My friend,' he breathed gripping Troy's shoulders, 'how can you meditate such folly?'

Troy spoke for the first time since he had left Doriendor Corishev. 'I'm blind,' he said in a hollow voice, as if that explained everything. 'I can't help it.' He pulled himself out of Quaan's grasp, sat down near the fire. Locating the flames by their heat, he hunched towards them like a man studying secrets in the coals.

Quaan turned to Mhoram. 'Lord, do you accept this madness? It will mean death for us all — and destruction for the Land.'

Quaan's protest made the Lord's heart ache. But before he could find words for any answer, Troy spoke suddenly.

'No, he doesn't,' the Warmark said. 'He doesn't actually think I'm a Raver.' Inner pain made his voice harsh. 'He thinks Foul had a hand in summoning me — interfered with Atiaran somehow so that I showed up, instead of somebody else who might have *looked* less friendly.' He stressed the word *looked*, as if sight itself were inherently untrustworthy. 'Foul wanted the Lords to trust me because he knew what kind of man I am. Dear God! It doesn't matter how much I hate him. He knew I'm the kind of man who backs into corners

671

where just being fallible is the same thing as treachery.

'But you forget that it isn't up to me any more. I've done my part – I've put you where you haven't got any choice. Now Mhoram has got to save you. It's on his head.'

Quaan appeared torn between dismay for the Warward and concern for Troy. 'Even a Lord may be defeated,' he replied gruffly.

'I'm not talking about a Lord,' Troy rasped. 'I'm talking about Mhoram.'

In his weariness, Lord Mhoram ached to deny this, to refuse the burden. He said, 'Warmark, of course I will do all that lies within my strength. But if Lord Foul has chosen you for the work of our destruction – ah, then, my friend, all aid will not avail. The burden of this plan will return to you at the last.'

'No.' Troy kept his face towards the fire, as if here reliving the acid burn which had blinded him. 'You've given your whole life to the Land, and you're going to give it now.'

'The Despiser knows me well,' Mhoram breathed. 'He ridicules me in my dreams.' He could hear echoes of that belittling mirth, but he held them at a distance. 'Do not mistake me, Warmark. I do not flinch this burden. I accept it. On Kevin's Watch I made my promise – and you dared this plan because of that promise. You have not done ill. But I must speak what is in my heart. You are the Warmark. I believe that the command of this fate must finally return to you.'

'I'm blind. There's nothing more I can do. Even Foul can't ask any more of me.' The heat of the fire made the burn marks on his face lurid. He held his hands clasped together, and his knuckles were white.

In distress, Quaan gazed at Mhoram with eyes that asked if he had been wrong to trust Troy.

'No,' Lord Mhoram answered. 'Do not pass judgment upon this mystery until it is complete. Until that time, we must keep faith.'

'Very well,' Quaan sighed heavily. 'If we have been betrayed, we have no recourse now. To flee into the Desert will accomplish only death. And Cravenhaw is a place to fight and die like any other. The Warward must not turn against itself when the last battle is near. I will stand with Warmark Troy.' Then he went to his blankets to search for sleep among his fears. Amorine followed his example dumbly, leaving Callindrill and Mhoram with Troy.

Callindrill soon dropped into slumber. And Mhoram was too worn to remain awake. But Troy sat up by the embers of the campfire. As the Lord's eyes closed, Troy was still huddled towards the flames like a cold cipher seeking some kind of remission for its frigidity.

Apparently, the Warmark found an answer during the long watch. When Lord Mhoram awoke the next morning, he found Troy erect, standing with his arms folded across his breastplate. The Lord studied him closely, but could not discern what kind of answer Troy had discovered. Gently he greeted the blind man.

At the sound of Mhoram's voice, Troy turned. He held his head with a slight sideward tilt, as if that position helped him focus his hearing. The old half-smile which he had habitually worn during his years in Revelstone was gone, effaced from his lips. 'Call Quaan,' he said flatly. 'I want to talk to him.'

Quaan was nearby; he heard Troy, and approached at once.

Fixing the Hiltmark with his hearing, Troy said, 'Guide me. I'm going to review the Warward.'

'Troy, my friend,' Quaan murmured, 'do not torment yourself.'

Troy stood stiffly, rigid with exigency. 'I'm the Warmark. I want to show my warriors that blindness isn't going to stop me.'

Mhoram felt a hot premonition of tears, but he held them back. He smiled crookedly at Quaan, nodded his answer to the old veteran's question. Quaan saluted Troy, bravely ignoring the Warmark's inability to see him. Then he took Troy's arm, and led him away to the Eoward.

Lord Mhoram watched their progress among the warriors – watched Quaan's respectful pain guiding Troy's erect helplessness from Eoman to Eoman. He endured the sight as best he could, and blinked down his own heart hurt. Fortunately, the ordeal did not last long; Fleshharrower's pursuit did not allow Troy time for a full review of the Warward. Soon Mhoram was mounted on his Ranyhyn, Drinny son of Hynaril, and riding on towards Cravenhaw.

He spent most of that day watching over the Warmark. But the next morning, while the Warward made its final approach to Garroting Deep, he was forced to turn his attention to his task. He had to plan some way in which to keep his promise. He melded his thoughts with Lord Callindrill, and together they searched through their combined knowledges and intuitions for some key to Mhoram's dilemma. In his dread, he hoped to gain courage from the melding, but the ache of Callindrill's self-distrust denied him. Instead of receiving strength, Mhoram gave it.

With Callindrill's help, he prepared an approach to his task, arranged a series of possible answers according to their peril and likelihood of success. But by noon, he had found nothing definitive. Then he ran out of time. The Warward staggered to a halt at the very brink of Garroting Deep.

There, face-to-face with the One Forest's last remaining consciousness, Lord Mhoram began to taste the full gall of his inadequacy. The Deep's dark, atavistic rage left him effectless; he felt like a man with no fingers. The first trees were within a dozen yards of him.

Like irregular columns, they appeared suddenly out of the ground, with no shrubs or bushes leading up to them, and no underbrush cluttering the greensward on which they stood. They were sparse at first. As far back as he could see, they did not grow thickly enough to close out the sunlight. Yet a shadow deepened on them; mounting dimness spurned the sunlight. In the distance, the benighted will of the Forest became an almost tangible refusal of passage. He felt that he was peering into a chasm. The idea that any bargain could be made with such a place seemed to be madness, vanity woven of dream stuff. For a long time, he only stood before the Deep and stared, with a groan of cold dread on his soul.

But Troy showed no hesitation. When Quaan told him where he was, he swung Mehryl around and began issuing orders. 'All right, Hiltmark,' he barked, 'let's get ready for it. Food for everyone. Finish off the supplies, but make it fast. After that, move the warriors back beyond bowshot, and form an arc around Lord Mhoram. Make it as wide as possible, but keep it thick – I don't want Fleshharrower to break through. Lord Callindrill, I think you should fight with the Warward. And Quaan – I'll speak to the warriors while they're eating. I'll explain it all.'

'Very well, Warmark.' Quaan sounded distant, withdrawn into the recessed stronghold of his courage; and the lines of his face were taut with resolution. He returned Troy's blind salute, then turned and gave his own orders to Amorine. Together, they went to make the Warward's final preparations.

Troy pulled Mehryl around again. He tried to face Mhoram, but missed by several feet. 'Maybe you'd better get started,' he said. 'You haven't got much time.'

'I will wait until you have spoken to the Warward.' Sadly, Mhoram saw Troy grimace with vexation at the discovery that he had misjudged the Lord's position. 'I need strength. I must seek it awhile.'

Troy nodded brusquely, and turned away as if he meant to watch the Warward's preparations.

Together, they waited for Quaan's signal. Lord Callindrill remained with them long enough to say, 'Mhoram, the High Lord had no doubt of your fitness for the burden of these times. She is no ordinary judge of persons. My brother, your faith will suffice.' His voice was gentle, but it implicitly expressed his belief that his own faith did not suffice. When he walked away from the Deep to take his stand with the warriors, he left Mhoram wrestling with insistent tears.

A short time later, Quaan reported that the Warward was ready to hear Troy. The Warmark asked Quaan to guide him to a place from which he could speak, and they trotted away together. Lord Mhoram walked after them. He wished to hear the Warmark's speech.

Troy stopped within the wide-seated arc of warriors. He did not need to ask for silence. Except for the noises of eating, the warriors were still, too exhausted to talk. They had marched and ached in blank silence for the last three days, and now they chewed their food with a kind of aghast lifelessness, ate as if compelled by an old habit unassoiled by any remaining endurance, desire. Moving their jaws, staring out of moistureless eyes, they looked like dusty skeletons, bare, dry bones animated by some obsession not their own.

Mhoram could not hold back his tears. They ran down his jaw and spattered like warm pain on his hands where he held his staff.

Yet he was glad that Troy could not see what his plans had done to the Warward.

Warmark Hile Troy faced the warriors squarely, held up his head as if he were offering his burns for inspection. Sitting on Mehryl's back, he was stiff with discipline – a rigid refusal of his own abjection. As he began to speak, his voice was hoarse with conflicting impulses, but he grew steadier as he continued.

'Warriors!' he said abruptly. 'We are here. For victory or defeat, this is the end. Today the outcome of this war will be decided.

'Our position is desperate – but you know that. Fleshharrower is only a league away by now. We're caught between his army and Garroting Deep. I want you to know that this is not an accident. We didn't panic and run here out of fear. We didn't come here because Fleshharrower forced us. You aren't victims. We came here on my order. I made the decision. When I was on Kevin's Watch, I saw how big Fleshharrower's army is. It's so big that we wouldn't have had a chance in Doom's Retreat. So I made the decision. I brought us here.

'I believe we're going to win today. We are going to cause the destruction of that horde – I believe it. I brought you here because I believe it. Now let me tell you how we're going to do it.'

He paused for a moment, and became even stiffer, more erect, as he braced himself for what he had to say. Then he went on, 'We are going to fight that army here for one reason. Lord Mhoram needs time. He's going to make that plan of mine work – and we have to keep him safe until he's ready.

'When he's ready' – Troy seemed to clench himself – 'we're going to run like hell into Garroting Deep.'

If he expected an outcry, he was surprised; the warriors were too weak to protest. But a rustle of anguish passed among them, and Mhoram could see horror on many faces.

Troy went on promptly, 'I know how bad that sounds. No one has ever survived the Deep – no one has ever returned. I know all that. But Foul is hard to beat. Our only chance is something that seems impossible. I believe we won't be killed.

'While we fight, Lord Mhoram is going to summon Caerroil Wildwood, the Forestal. And Caerroil Wildwood is going to help us. He's going to give us free passage through Garroting Deep. He's going to defeat Fleshharrower's army.

'I believe this. I want you to believe it. It will work. The Forestal has no reason to hate us – you know that. And he has every reason to hate Fleshharrower. That Giant is a Raver. But the only way Caerroil Wildwood can get at Fleshharrower is to give us free passage. If we run into Garroting Deep, and Fleshharrower sees that we aren't harmed – then he'll follow us. He hates us and he hates the Deep too much to pass up a chance like this. It will work. The only problem is to summon the Forestal. And that is up to Lord Mhoram.'

He paused again, weighing his words before he said, 'Many of you have known Lord Mhoram longer than I have. You know what kind of man he is. He'll succeed. You know that.

'Until he succeeds, the only thing we have to do is fight – keep him alive while he works. That's all. I know how tough it's going to be for you. I – I hear how tired you are. But you are warriors. You will find the strength. I believe it. Whatever happens, I'll be proud to fight with you. And I won't be afraid to lead you into Garroting Deep. You are the true preservers of the Land.'

He stopped, waiting for some kind of answer.

The warriors gave no cheers or shouts or cries; the extravagant grip of their exhaustion kept them silent. But together they heaved themselves to their feet. Twelve thousand men and women stood to salute the Warmark.

He seemed to hear their movement and understand it. He saluted them at once, rigidly. Then he turned his proud Ranyhyn, and went trotting back towards where he had left Lord Mhoram.

He caught Mhoram by surprise, and the Lord failed to intercept him. He moved as if he were held erect by the stiffness of extreme need; his voice rocked as he said to the empty air where Mhoram had been, 'I hope you understand what'll happen if you fail. We won't have any choice. We'll still have to go into the Deep. And pray the Forestal doesn't kill us until Fleshharrower follows. We'll all die that way, but maybe the Raver will, too.'

Mhoram hastened towards Troy. But Terrel was closer to the Warmark, and he spoke before Mhoram could stop him. 'That we will not permit,' he said dispassionately. 'It is suicide. We do not speak of the Warward. But we are the Bloodguard. We will not permit the Lords to enact their own death. We failed to prevent High Lord Kevin's self-destruction. We will not fail again.'

'I hear you,' Mhoram replied sharply. 'But that moment has not yet come. First I must work.' Turning to Troy, he said, 'My friend, will you remain with me while I make this attempt? I need – I have need of support.'

Troy seemed to totter on Mehryl's back. But he caught hold of the Ranyhyn's mane, steadied himself. 'Just tell me if there's anything I can do.' He reached out his hand, and when Mhoram clasped it, he slipped down from Mehryl's back.

Mhoram gripped his hand for a moment, then released him. The Lord looked over at the Warward, saw that it was preparing to meet Fleshharrower's charge. He turned his attention to the Deep. Dread constricted his heart. He was afraid that Caerroil Wildwood would simply strike him where he stood for the affront of his call – strike all the army. But he was still his own master. He stepped forward, raised his staff high over his head, and began the ritual appeal to the woods.

Hail, Garroting Deep! Forest of the One Forest! Enemy of our enemies! Garroting Deep, hail! We are the Lords – foes to your enemies, and learners of the *lillianrill* lore. We must pass through!

'Harken Caerroil Wildwood! We hate the axe and flame which hurt you. Your enemies are our enemies. Never have we brought edge of axe or flame of fire to touch you – nor ever shall. Forestal, harken! Let us pass!'

There was no answer. His voice fell echoless on the trees and grass; nothing moved or replied in the dark depths. He strained his senses to listen and look for any sign, but none came. When he was sure of the silence, he repeated the ritual. Again there was no reply. After a third appeal, the silent gloom of the Deep seemed to increase, to grow more profound and ominous, as he beseeched it.

Through the Forest's unresponsiveness, he heard the first gleeful shout of Fleshharrower's army as it caught sight of the Warward. The hungry cry multiplied his dread; his knuckles whitened as he resisted it. Planting his staff firmly on the grass, he tried another approach.

While the sun arced through the middle of the afternoon, Lord Mhoram strove to make himself heard in the heart of Garroting Deep. He used every Forestal name which had been preserved in the lore of the Land. He wove appeals and chants out of every invocation or summoning known to the Loresraat. He bent familiar forms away from their accustomed usage, hoping that they would unlock the silence. He even took the Summoning Song which had called Covenant to the Land, altered it to fit his need, and sang it into the Deep. It had no effect. The Forest remained impenetrable, answerless.

And behind him the last battle of the Warward began. As Fleshharrower's hordes rushed at them, the warriors raised one tattered cheer like a brief pennant of defiance. But then they fell silent, saved the vestiges of their strength for combat. With their weapons ready, they faced the ravening that charged towards them out of the Wastes.

The Raver's army crashed murderously into them. Firing their arrows at close range, they attempted to crack the momentum of the charge. But the horde's sheer numbers swept over slain ur-viles and Cavewights and other creatures, trampled them underfoot, drove into the Warward.

Its front lines crumbled at the onslaught; thousands of ill beasts broke into its core. But Hiltmark Quaan rallied one flank, and First Haft Amorine shored up the other. For the first time since she had left Doriendor Corishev, she seemed to remember herself. Throwing off her enervation of will, she brought her Eoward to the aid of the front lines. And Lord Callindrill held his ground in the army's centre. Whirling his staff about his head, he rained blue fiery force in all directions. The creatures gave way before him; scores of unorganized ur-viles fell under his fire.

Then Quaan and Amorine reached him from either side.

From a place deep within them, beyond their most bereft exhaustion, the men and women of the Land brought up the strength to fight back. Faced with the raw malevolence of Lord Foul's perverse creations, the warriors found that they could still resist. Bone-deep love and abhorrence exalted them. Passionately, they hurled themselves at the enemy. Hundreds of them fell in swaths across the ground, but they threw back the Raver's first assault.

Fleshharrower roared his orders; the creatures drew back to regroup. Ur-viles hurried to form a wedge against Lord Callindrill, and the rest of the army shifted, brought Cavewights forward to bear the brunt of the next charge.

In an effort to disrupt these preparations, Quaan launched an attack of his own. Warriors leaped after the retreating beasts. Lord Callindrill and one Eoward ran to prevent the formation of the ur-vile wedge. For several furious moments, they threw the black Demondim-spawn into chaos.

But then the Giant-Raver struck, used his Stone to support the ur-viles. Several blasts of emerald fire forced Callindrill to give ground. At once, the wedge pulled itself together. The Eoward had to retreat.

It was a grim and silent struggle. After the first hungry yell of the attack, Fleshharrower's army fought with dumb maniacal ferocity. And the warriors had no strength for shouts or cries, only the tumult of feet, and the clash of weapons, and the moans of the maimed and dying, and the barking of orders, punctuated the mute engagement. Yet Lord Mhoram felt these clenched sounds like a deafening din; they seemed to echo off his dread. The effort to ignore the battle and concentrate on his work, squeezed sweat out of his bones, made his pulse hammer like a prisoner against his temples.

When traditional names and invocations failed to bring the Forestal, he began using signs and arcane symbols. He drew pentacles and circles on the grass with his staff, set fires burning within them, waved eldritch gestures over them. He murmured labyrinthian chants under his breath.

All were useless. The silence of the Deep's gloom sounded like laughter in his ears.

Yet the sounds of killing came steadily nearer. All the valiance of the warriors was not enough; they were driven back.

Troy heard the retreat also. At last he could no longer contain himself. 'Dear God, Mhoram!' he whispered urgently. 'They are being butchered.'

Mhoram spun on Troy, raging, 'Do you think I am unaware?' But when he beheld the Warmark, he stopped. He could see Troy's torment. The sting of sweat made the Warmark's burns flame garishly; they throbbed with pain. His hands groped aimlessly about him, as if he were lost. He was blind. For all his power to plan and conceive, he was helpless to execute even the simplest of his ideas.

Lord Mhoram wrenched his anger into another channel. With its strength, he made his decision.

'Very well, my friend,' he breathed heavily. 'There are other attempts to be made, but perhaps only one is perilous enough to have some hope of success. Stand ready. You must take my place if I fall. Legends say that the song I mean to sing is fatal.'

As he strode forward, he felt a new calm. Confronting his dread, he could see that it was only fear. He had met and mastered its kindred when a Raver had laid hands on him. And the knowledge he had gained then could save the Warward now. With peril in his eyes, he went towards the Deep until he was among the first trees. There he ignited his staff and raised it over his head, carefully holding it away from any of the branches. Then he began to sing.

The words came awkwardly to his lips, and the accents of the melody seemed to miss their beats. He was singing a song to which no former Lord had ever given utterance. It was one of the dark mysteries of the Land, forbidden because of the hazard it carried. Yet the words of the song were clear and simple. Their peril lay elsewhere. According to Kevin's Lore, they belonged like cherished treasure to the Forestals of the One Forest. The Forestals slew all mortals who profaned those words.

Nevertheless, Lord Mhoram lifted up his voice and sang them boldly.

> Branches spread and tree trunks grow
> > Through rain and heat and snow and cold:
> Though wide world's winds untimely blow,
> > And earthquakes rock and cliff unseal,
>
> My leaves grow green and seedlings bloom,
> > Since days before the Earth was old
> And Time began its walk to doom,
> > The Forests world's bare rock anneal,
>
> Forbidding dusty waste and death.
> > I am the Land's Creator's hold:
> I inhale all expiring breath.
> > And breathe out life to bind and heal.

As his singing faded into the distance, he heard the reply. Its music far surpassed his own. It seemed to fall from the branches like leaves bedewed with rare melody – to fall and flutter around him, so that he stared as if he were dazzled. The voice had a light, clear sound, like a splashing brook, but the power it implied filled him with awe.

> But axe and fire leave me dead.
> > I know the hate of hands grown bold.
> Depart to save your heart-sap's red:
> > My hate knows neither rest nor weal.

A shimmer of music rippled his sight. When it cleared, he saw Caerroil Wildwood walking towards him across the green sward.

The Forestal was a tall man with a long white beard and flowing white hair. He wore a robe of purest samite, and carried a gnarled wooden rod like a sceptre in the crook of one arm. A garland of purple and white orchids about his neck only heightened his austere dignity. He appeared out of the gloaming of the Deep as if he had stepped from behind a veil, and he moved like a monarch between the trees. They nodded to him as he passed. With every step, he scattered droplets of melody about him as if his whole person were drenched in song. His sparkling voice softened the severity of his mien. But his eyes were not soft. From under his thick white brows, a silver light shone from orbs without pupil or iris, and his glances had the force of physical impact.

Still humming the refrain of his song, he approached Lord Mhoram. His gaze held the Lord motionless until they were almost within arm's reach of each other. Mhoram felt himself being probed. The sound of music continued, and some time passed before he realized that the Forestal was speaking to him, asking him, 'Who dares taint my song?'

With an effort, Lord Mhoram set aside his awe to answer, 'Caerroil Wildwood, Forestal and servant of the Tree-soul, please pardon my presumption. I intend no offence or taint. But my need is urgent, surpassing both fear and caution. I am Mhoram son of Variol, Lord of the Council of Revelstone, and a defender of the Land in tree and rock. I seek a boon, Caerroil Wildwood.'

'A boon?' the Forestal mused musically. 'You bring a fire among my trees, and then ask a boon? You are a fool, Mhoram son of Variol. I make no bargains with men. I grant no boons to any creature with knowledge of blade or flame. Begone.' He did not raise his voice or sharpen his song, but the might of his command made Mhoram stagger.

'Forestal, hear me.' Mhoram strove to keep his voice calm. 'I have used this fire only to gain your notice.' Extinguishing his staff, he lowered it to the ground and gripped it as a brace against the Forestal's refusal. 'I am a Lord, a servant of the Earthpower. Since the Lords began, all have sworn all their might to the preservation of Land and Forest. We love and honour the wood of the world. I have done no harm to these trees – and never shall, though you refuse my boon and condemn the Land to fire and death.'

Humming as if to himself, Caerroil Wildwood said, 'I know nothing of Lords. They are nothing to me. But I know men, mortals. The Ritual of Desecration is not forgotten in the Deep.'

'Yet hear me, Caerroil Wildwood.' Mhoram could feel the sound of battle beating against his back. But he remembered what he had learned of the history of the One Forest, and remained steady, serene. 'I do not ask a boon for which I can make no return. Forestal, I offer you a Raver.'

At the word *Raver*, Caerroil Wildwood changed. The dewy glistening aura of his music took on an inflection of anger. His eyes darkened; their silver light gave way to thunderheads. Mist spread from his orbs, and drifted upward through his eyebrows. But he said nothing, and Mhoram continued.

'The people of the Land fight a war against the Despiser, the ancient tree ravager. His great army has driven us here, and the last battle now rages in Cravenhaw. Without your aid, we will surely be destroyed. But with our death, the Land becomes defenceless. Then the tree ravager will make war upon all the Forest – upon the trees in beautiful Andelain, upon slumbering Grimmerdhore and restless Morinmoss. In the end, he will attack the Deep and you. He must be defeated now.'

The Forestal appeared unmoved by this appeal. Instead of replying to it, he hummed darkly, 'You spoke of a Raver.'

'The army which destroys us even now is commanded by a Raver, one of the three decimators of the One Forest.'

'Give me a token that you speak the truth.'

Lord Mhoram did not hesitate. Though the ground he trod was completely trackless, unmapped by any lore but his own intuition, he answered promptly, 'He is *moksha* Raver, also named Jehannum and Fleshharrower. In ages long past, he and *turiya* his brother taught the despising of trees to the once-friendly Demondim. *Samadhi* his brother guided the monarch of Doriendor Corishev when that mad king sought to master the life and death of the One Forest.'

'*Moksha* Raver,' Caerroil Wildwood trilled lightly, dangerously. 'I have a particular hunger for Ravers.'

'Their might is greatly increased now. They share the unnatural power of the Illearth Stone.'

'I care nothing for that,' the Forestal replied almost brusquely. 'But you offered a Raver to me. How can that be done, when he defeats you even now?'

The sound of battle came inexorably nearer as the Warward was driven back. Lord Mhoram heard less combat and more slaughter with every passing moment. And he could feel Warmark Troy panting behind him. With all his hard-won serenity, he answered, 'That is the boon I ask, Caerroil Wildwood. I ask safe passage for all my people through Garroting Deep. This boon will deliver *moksha* Raver into your hands. He and all his army, all his ur-viles and Cavewights and creatures will be yours. When the Raver sees that we flee into the Deep and are not destroyed, he will follow. He will believe that you are weak – or that you have passed away. His hatred for us, and for the trees, will drive him and all his force into your demesne.'

A moment that throbbed urgently in Mhoram's ears passed while Caerroil Wildwood considered. The battle noise seemed to say that soon there would be nothing of the Warward left to save. But Mhoram faced the Forestal, and waited.

At last, the Forestal nodded. 'It is a worthy bargain,' he sang slowly. 'The trees are eager to fight again. I am prepared. But there is a small price to be paid for my help – and for the tainting of my song.'

The upsurge of Mhoram's hope suddenly gave way to fear, and he spun to try to stop Warmark Troy. But before he could shout a warning, Troy said fervidly, 'Then I'll pay it! I'll pay anything. My army is being slaughtered.'

Mhoram winced at the irrevocable promise, tried to protest. But the Forestal sang keenly, 'Very well. I accept your payment. Bring your army cautiously among the trees.'

Troy reacted instantly; he whirled, leaped for Mehryl's back. Some instinct guided him; he landed astride the Ranyhyn as securely as if he could see. At once, he went galloping towards the battle, yelling with all his strength, 'Quaan! Retreat! Retreat!'

The Warward was collapsing as he shouted. The ranks of the warriors were broken, and Fleshharrower's creatures ranged bloodily among them. More than two-thirds of the Eoward had already fallen. But something in Troy's command galvanized the warriors for a final exertion. Breaking away, they turned and ran.

Their sudden flight opened a brief gap between them and Fleshharrower's army. At once, Lord Callindrill set himself to widen the gap. Protected by a circle of Bloodguard, he unleashed a lightning fire that caught in the grass and crackled across the front of the foe. His blast did little damage, but it caused the Raver's forces to hesitate one instant in their pursuit. Using that instant, he followed the warriors. Together the survivors – hardly more than ten Eoward – ran straight towards Mhoram.

When he saw them coming, Lord Mhoram went out to meet Troy. He pulled the Warmark from Mehryl's back – it was not safe to ride under the branches of the Deep – took his arm, and guided him towards the trees. The fleeing warriors were almost on their heels when Mhoram and Troy strode into Garroting Deep.

Caerroil Wildwood had vanished, but his song remained. It seemed to resonate lightly off every leaf in the Forest. Mhoram could feel it piloting him, and he followed it implicitly. Behind him, he heard the warriors consummating their exhaustion in a last rush towards sanctuary or death. He heard Quaan shouting as if from a great distance that all survivors were now among the trees. But he did not look back. The Forestal's song exercised a fascination over him. Gripping Troy's arm and peering steadily ahead into the gloom, he moved at a brisk walk along the path of the melody.

With Callindrill, Troy, Quaan, Amorine, twoscore Bloodguard, all the Ranyhyn, and more than four thousand warriors, Lord Mhoram passed for a time out of the world of humankind.

Slowly, the music transmuted his conscious alertness, drew him into a kind of trance. He felt that he was still aware of everything, but that now nothing touched him. He could see the onset of evening in the altered dimness of the Deep, but he felt no passage of time. In openings between the trees, he could see the Westron Mountains. By the changing positions of the peaks, he could gauge his speed. He appeared to be moving faster than a galloping Ranyhyn. But he felt no exertion or strain of travel. The breath of the song wafted him ahead, as if he and his companions were being inhaled by the Deep. It was a weird, dreamy passage, a soul journey, full of speed he could not experience and events he could not feel.

Night came – the moon was completely dark – but he did not lose sight of his way. Some hint of light in the grass and leaves and song made his path clear to him, and he went on confidently, untouched by any need for rest. The Forestal's song released him from mortality, wrapped him in careless peace.

Sometime during the darkness, he heard the change of the song. The alteration had no effect on him, but he understood its meaning. Though the Forest swallowed every other sound, so that no howls or screams or cries reached his ears, he knew that Fleshharrower's army was being destroyed. The song described ages of waiting hate, of grief over vast tracts of kindred lost, ages of slow rage which climbed through the sap of the woods until every limb and leaf shared it, lived it, ached to act. And through that melodic narration came whispers of death as roots and boughs and trunks moved together to crush and rend.

Against the immense Deep, even Fleshharrower's army was small and defenceless – a paltry insult hurled against an ocean. The trees brushed aside the power of the ur-viles and the strength of the Cavewights and the mad, cornered, desperate fear of all the other creatures. Led by Caerroil Wildwood's song, they simply throttled the invaders. Flames were stamped out, blade wielders were slain, lore and force overwhelmed. Then the trees drank the blood and ate the bodies – eradicated every trace of the enemy in an apotheosis of ancient and exquisite fury.

When the song resumed its former placid wafting, it seemed to breathe grim satisfaction and victory.

Soon after that – Mhoram thought it was soon – a rumble like thunder passed over the woods. At first, he thought that he was hearing Fleshharrower's death struggle. But then he saw that the sound had an entirely different source. Far ahead and to the west, some terrible violence occurred in the mountains. Red fires spouted from one part of the range. After every eruption, a concussion rolled over the Deep, and a coruscating exhaust paled the night sky. But

Mhoram was immune to it. He watched it with interest, but the song wrapped him in its enchantments and preserved him from all care.

And he felt no concern when he realized that the Warward was no longer behind him. Except for Lord Callindrill, Troy, Amorine, Hiltmark Quaan and two Bloodguard, Terrel and Morril, he was alone. But he was not anxious; the song assuaged him with peace and trust. It led him onward and still onward through a measureless night into the dawn of a new day.

With the return of light, he found that he was moving through a woodland profuse with purple and white orchids. Their soft, pure colours fell in with the music as if they were the notes Caerroil Wildwood sang. They folded Mhoram closely in the consolation of the melody. With a wide, unconscious smile, he let himself go as if the current which carried him were an anodyne for all his hurts.

His strange speed was more apparent now. Already through gaps in the overhanging foliage, he could see the paired spires of *Melenkurion* Skyweir, the tallest peaks in the Westron Mountains. He could see the high, sheer plateau of Rivenrock as the struggle it concealed continued. Eruptions and muffled booms came echoing from the depths of the mountains, and red bursts of force struck the sky at irregular intervals. But still he was untouched. His speed, his exhilarating, easy swiftness, filled his heart with gay glee. He had covered thirty or forty leagues since entering the Deep. He felt ready to walk that way forever.

But the day passed with the same timeless evanescence that had borne him through the night. Soon the sun was close to setting, yet he had no sense of duration, no weary or hungry physical impression that he had travelled all day.

Then the song changed again. Gradually, it no longer floated him forward. The end of his wafting filled him with quiet sadness, but he accepted it. The thunders and eruptions of Rivenrock were now almost due southwest of him. He judged that he and his companions were nearing the Black River.

The song led him straight through the Forest to a high bald hill that stood up out of the woodland like a wen of barrenness. Beyond it, he could hear a rush of water – the Black River – but the hill itself caught his attention, restored some measure of his self-awareness. The soil of the hill was completely lifeless, as if in past ages it had been drenched with too much death ever to bloom again. And just below its crown on the near side stood two rigid trees like sentinels, witnesses, ten yards or more apart. They were as dead as the hill – blackened, bereft of limbs and leaves, sapless. Each dead trunk had only one bough left. Fifty feet above the ground, the trees reached towards each other, and their limbs interwove to form a crossbar between them.

This was Gallows Howe, the ancient slaying place of the Forestals. Here, according to the legends of the Land, Caerroil Wildwood and his brethren had held their assizes in the long-past ages when the One Forest still struggled for survival. Here the Ravers who had come within the Forestals' grasp had been executed.

Now *moksha* Fleshharrower hung from the gibbet. Black fury congested his face, his swollen tongue protruded like contempt between his teeth, and his eyes stared emptily. A rictus of hate strained and stretched all his muscles. His dying frenzy had been so extravagant that many of his blood vessels had ruptured, staining his skin with dark haemorrhages.

As Lord Mhoram gazed upward through the thickening dusk, he felt suddenly tired and thirsty. Several moments passed before he noticed that Caerroil Wildwood was nearby. The Forestal stood to one side of the hill, singing quietly, and his eyes shone with a red and silver light.

At Mhoram's side, Warmark Troy stirred as if he were awakening, and asked dimly, 'What is it? What do you see?'

Mhoram had to swallow several times before he could find his voice. 'It is Fleshharrower. The Forestal has slain him.'

A sharp intensity crossed Troy's face, as if he were straining to see. Then he smiled. 'Thank God.'

'It is a worthy bargain,' Caerroil Wildwood sang. 'I know that I cannot slay the spirit of a Raver. But it is a great satisfaction to kill the flesh. He is garroted.' His eyes flared redly for a moment, then faded towards silver again. 'Therefore do not think that I have rescinded my word. Your people are unharmed. The presence of so many faithless mortals disturbed the trees. To shorten their discomfort, I have sent your people out of Garroting Deep to the north. But because of the bargain, and the price yet to be paid, I have brought you here. Behold the retribution of the Forest.'

Something in his high clear voice made Mhoram shudder. But he remembered himself enough to ask, 'What has become of the Raver's Stone?'

'It was a great evil,' the Forestal hummed severely. 'I have destroyed it.'

Quietly, Lord Mhoram nodded. 'That is well.' Then he tried to focus his attention on the matter of Caerroil Wildwood's price. He wanted to argue that Troy should not be held to the bargain; the Warmark had not understood what was being asked of him. But while Mhoram was still searching for words, Terrel distracted him. Silently, the Bloodguard pointed away upriver.

The night was almost complete; only open starlight and the glow of Caerroil Wildwood's eyes illumined Gallows Howe. But when the Lord followed Terrel's indication, he saw two different lights. Far in the distance, Rivenrock's fiery holocaust was visible. The violence there seemed to be approaching its climacteric. The fires spouted furiously, and dark thunder rolled over the Deep as if great cliffs were cracking. The other light was much closer. A small, grave, white gleam shone through the trees between Mhoram and the river. As he looked at it, it moved out of sight beyond the Howe.

Someone was travelling through Garroting Deep along the Black River.

An intuition clutched Lord Mhoram, and at once he found that he was afraid. Glimpses and visions which he had forgotten during the past days returned to him. Quickly, he turned to the Forestal. 'Who comes? Have you made other bargains?'

'If I have,' sang the Forestal, 'they are no concern of yours. But these two pass on sufferance. They have not spoken to me. I allow them because the light they bear presents no peril to the trees – and because they hold a power which I must respect. I am bound by the Law of creation.'

'Melenkurion!' Mhoram breathed. 'Creator preserve us!' Catching hold of Troy's arm, he started up the bald hill. His companions hastened after him. He passed the gibbet, gained the crest of the Howe, and looked down beyond it at the river.

Two men climbed the hill towards him from the riverbank. One of them held a shining stone in his right hand, and supported his comrade with his left arm. They moved painfully, as if they ascended against a weight of barrenness. When they were near the hilltop, in full view of Mhoram's company, they stopped.

Slowly, Bannor held up the *orcrest* so that it lighted the crest of the Howe. With a nod, he acknowledged the Lords.

When Thomas Covenant realized that all the people on the hill were watching him, he pushed away from Bannor's support, stood on his own. The exertion cost him a sharp effort. As he stood, he wavered unsteadily. In the *orcrest* light, his forehead gleamed atrociously. His eyes held a sightless stare – a stare without object, and yet of such intensity that his eyes appeared to be crossed, as if he were so conscious of his own duplicities that he could not see singly. His hands clenched each other against his chest. But then a fierce blast from Rivenrock struck him, and he almost lost his balance. He was forced to reach his halfhand towards Bannor. The movement bared his left fist.

On his wedding finger, the argent ring throbbed hotly.

PART III

The Blood of the Earth

21

LENA'S DAUGHTER

Troy had called Thomas Covenant's Unbelief a bluff. But Covenant was not playing a mental game. He was a leper. He was fighting for his life.

Unbelief was his only defence against the Land, his only way to control the intensity, the potential suicide, of his response to the Land. He felt that he had lost every other form of self-protection. And without self-protection he would end up like the old man he had met in the leprosarium – crippled and fetid beyond all endurance. Even madness would be preferable. If he went mad, he would at least be insulated from knowing what was happening to him, blind and deaf and numb to the vulturine disease that gnawed his flesh.

Yet as he rode westward away from Revelwood with High Lord Elena, Amok, and the two Bloodguard, in quest of Kevin Landwaster's Seventh Ward, he knew that he was changing. By fits and starts, his ground shifted under him; some potent, subtle Earthpower altered his personal terrain. Unstable footing shrugged him towards a precipice. And he felt helpless to do anything about it.

The most threatening aspect of his immediate situation was Elena. Her nameless inner force, her ancestry, and her strange irrefusability both disturbed and attracted him. As they left the Valley of Two Rivers, he was already cursing himself for accepting her invitation. And yet she had the power to sway him. She tangled his emotions, and pulled unexpected strands of assent out of the knot.

This was not like his other acquiescences. When Lord Mhoram had asked him to go with the Warward, he had agreed because he completely lacked alternatives. He urgently needed to keep moving, keep searching for an escape. No similar reasoning vindicated him when the High Lord had asked him to accompany her. He felt that he was riding away from the crux of his dilemma, the battle against Lord Foul – evading it like a coward. But in the moment of decision he had not even considered refusing. And he sensed that she could draw him farther. Hopelessly, without one jot or tittle of belief to his name, he could be made to follow her, even if she went to attack the Despiser himself. Her beauty, her physical presence, her treatment of him, ate away portions of his armour, exposing his vulnerable flesh.

Travelling through the crisp autumn of Trothgard, he watched her alertly, timorously.

High and proud on the back of Myrha, her Ranyhyn, she looked like a crowned vestal, somehow both powerful and fragile – as if she could have shattered his bones with a glance, and yet would have fallen from her seat at the touch of a single hurled handful of mud. She daunted him.

When Amok appeared beside her as if concretized abruptly out of blank air, she turned to speak with him. They exchanged greetings, and bantered pleasantly like old friends while Revelwood fell into the distance behind them. Amok's reticence on the subject of his Ward did not prevent him from gay prolixity in other matters. Soon he was singing and talking happily as if his sole function were to entertain the High Lord.

As Amok whiled away the morning, Covenant gazed over the countryside around him.

The party of the quest rode easily up out of the lowlands of Trothgard. They travelled a few points south of westward, roughly paralleling the course of the Rill River towards the Westron Mountains. The western edge of Trothgard, still sixty or sixty-five leagues away, was at least three thousand feet higher than the Valley of Two Rivers, and the whole region slowly climbed towards the mountains. Already the High Lord's party moved into the gradual uprise. Covenant could feel their relaxed ascent as they rode through woodlands anademed in autumn, ablaze with orange, yellow, gold, red leaf-flames, and over lush grassy hillsides, where the scars of Stricken Stone's ancient wars had been effaced by thick heather and timothy like healthy new flesh over the wounds, green with healing.

He was barely able to sense the last hints of Trothgard's convalescence. Under the mantling growth of grass and trees, all the injuries of Kevin's last war had not been undone. From time to time, the riders passed near festering barren patches which still refused all repair, and some of the hills seemed to lie awkwardly, like broken bones imperfectly set. But the Lords had laboured to good effect. The air of Trothgard was tangy, animate, vital. Very few of the trees showed that their roots ran down into once-desecrated soil. The new Council of Lords had found a worthy way to spend their lives.

Because of what it had suffered, Trothgard touched Covenant's heart. He found that he liked it, trusted it. At times as the day passed into afternoon, he wished that he was not going anywhere. He wanted to roam Trothgard – destinationless, preferably alone –

without any thought of Wards or rings or wars. He would have welcomed the rest.

Amok seemed a fit guide for such sojourns. The bearer of the Seventh Ward moved with a sprightly, boyish stride which disguised the fact that the pace he set was not a lazy one. And his good spirits bubbled irrepressibly. He sang long songs which he claimed to have learned from the faery *Elohim* – songs so alien that Covenant could distinguish neither the words nor sentences, and yet curiously suggestive, so like moonlight in a forest, that they half entranced him. And Amok told intimate tales of the stars and heavens, describing merrily the sky dance as if he had pranced in it himself. His happy voice complemented the clear, keen evening air and the sunset conflagration of the trees, interwove his listeners like an incantation, a mesmerism.

Yet in the twilight of Trothgard, he disappeared suddenly, gestured himself out of visibility, leaving the High Lord's party alone.

Covenant was startled out of his reverie. 'Where – ?'

'Amok will return,' answered Elena. In the gloaming, he could not tell if she were looking at him or through him or into him or in spite of him. 'He has only left us for the night. Come, ur-Lord,' she said as she dropped lightly down from Myrha's back. 'Let us rest.'

Covenant followed her example, released his mount to Bannor's care. Myrha and the other two Ranyhyn galloped away, stretching their legs after a day's walking. Then Morin went to the Rill for water while Elena began to make camp. She produced a small urn of graveling, and used the fire-stones to cook a frugal meal for herself and Covenant. Her face followed the motion of her hands, but her vision's strange otherness was far distant, as if in the earthy light she read of events on the opposite edge of the Land.

Covenant watched her; in the performance of even the simplest chores she fascinated him. But as he studied her lithe form, her sure movements, her bifurcated gaze, he was trying to regain a grip on himself, trying to recover some sense of where he stood with her. She was a mystery to him. Out of all the strong and knowledgeable people of the Land, she had chosen him to accompany her. He had raped her mother – and still she had chosen him. In Glimmermere she had kissed – The memory made his heart hurt. She had chosen him. But not out of anger or desire for retribution – not for any reason that Trell would have approved. He could see in her smiles, hear in her voice, feel in her ambience that she intended him no harm. Then why? From what secret forgetfulness or passion did her desire for his company spring? He needed to know. And yet he was half afraid of the answer.

After supper, when he sat drinking his ration of springwine across the pot of graveling from Elena, he mustered his courage to question her. Both Bloodguard had withdrawn from the campsite, and he was relieved that he did not have to contend with them. Rubbing his fingers through his beard, remembering the peril of physical sensations, he began by asking her if she had learned anything from Amok.

She shook her head unconcernedly, and her hair haloed her head in the graveling light. 'We are surely several days from the location of the Seventh Ward. There will be time enough for the questioning of Amok.'

He accepted this, but it did not meet his need. Tightening his hold on himself, he asked her why she had chosen him.

She gazed at him or through him for several moments before she replied. 'Thomas Covenant, you know that I did not choose you. No Lord of Revelstone chose you. Drool Rockworm performed your first summoning, and he was guided by the Despiser. In that way, we are your victims, just as you are his. It may be as Lord Mhoram believes – perhaps the Land's Creator also chose. Or perhaps the dead Lords – perhaps High Lord Kevin himself wields some influence from beyond his lost grave. But I made no choice.' Then her tone changed, and she went on, 'Yet had I chosen – '

Covenant interrupted her. 'That isn't what I meant. I know why this is happening to me. It's because I'm a leper. A normal person would just laugh – No, what I meant is, why did you ask me to come with you – looking for the Seventh Ward? Surely there were other people you could have chosen.'

Gently, she returned, 'I do not understand this disease which causes you to be a – leper. You describe a world in which the innocent are tormented. Why are such things done? Why are they permitted?'

'Things aren't so different here. Or what did you think it was that happened to Kevin? But you're changing the subject. I want to know why you picked me.' He winced at the memory of Troy's chagrin when the High Lord had announced her choice.

'Very well, ur-Lord,' she said with a tone of reluctance. 'If this question must be answered, I will answer it. There are many reasons for my choice. Will you hear them?'

'Go ahead.'

'Ah, Unbeliever. At times I think that Warmark Troy is not so blind. The truth – you evade the truth. But I will give you my reasons. First, I prepare for the chances of the future. If at the last you should come to desire the use of your white gold, with the Staff of Law I am better able to aid you than any other. I do not know the wild magic's secret – but there is no more discerning tool than the Staff. And if at the last you should turn against the Land, with the Staff I will be able to resist you. We possess nothing else which can hope to stand against the power of white gold.

'But I seek other goals also. You are no warrior – and the Warward will meet great peril, where only power and skill in combat may hope to preserve life. I do not wish to risk your death. You must be given time to find your own reply to yourself. And for myself I seek companionship. Neither Warmark Troy nor Lord Mhoram can be spared from the war. Do you desire more explanation?'

He sensed the incompleteness of her response, and forced himself to pursue it despite his fear. With a grimace of distaste for the pervasive irrectitude of his conduct in the Land, he said deliberately, 'Companionship? After all I've done. You're remarkably tolerant.'

'I am not tolerant. I do not make choices without consulting my own heart.'

For a moment, he faced squarely the implications of what she said. It was what he had both wanted and feared to hear. But then a complex unwillingness, composed of sympathy and dread and self-judgment, deflected him. It made his voice rough as he said, 'You're breaking Trell's heart. And your mother's.'

Her face stiffened. 'Do you accuse me of Trell's pain?'

'I don't know. He would be following us if he had any hope left. Now he knows for sure that you're not even thinking about punishing me.'

He stopped, but the sight of the pain he had given her made him speak again, rush to answer replies, counter-accusations, that she had not uttered. 'As for your mother – I've got no right to talk. I don't mean about what I did to her. That's something I can at least understand. I was in such – penury – and she seemed so rich.

'No, I mean about the Ranyhyn – those Ranyhyn that went to Mithil Stonedown every year. I made a bargain with them. I was trying to find some solution – some way to keep myself from going completely insane. And they hated me. They were just like the Land – they were big and powerful and superior – and they loathed me.' He rasped that word *loathed*, as if he were echoing, *Leper outcast unclean!* 'But they reared to me – a hundred of them. They were driven –

'So I made a bargain with them. I promised that I wouldn't ride – wouldn't force one of them to carry me. And I made them promise – I was trying to find some way to keep all that size and power and health and fidelity from driving me crazy. I made them promise to answer if I ever called them. And I made them promise to visit your mother.'

'Their promise remains.' She said this as if it gave her a deep pride.

He sighed. 'That's what Rue said. But that's not the point. Do you see? I was trying to give her something, make it up to her somehow. But that doesn't work. When you've hurt someone that badly, you can't go around giving them gifts. That's arrogant and cruel.' His mouth twisted at the bitter taste of what he had done. 'I was really just trying to make myself feel better.

'Anyway, it didn't work. Foul can pervert anything. By the time I got to the end of the Quest for the Staff of Law, things were so bad that no bargain could have saved me.'

Abruptly, he ran out of words. He wanted to tell Elena that he did not accuse her, could not accuse her – and at the same time a part of him did accuse her. That part of him felt that Lena's pain deserved more loyalty.

But the High Lord seemed to understand this. Though her elsewhere gaze did not touch him, she replied to his thought. 'Thomas Covenant, you do not altogether comprehend Lena my mother. I am a woman – human like any other. And I have chosen you to be my companion on this quest. Surely my choice reveals my mother's heart as well as my own. I am her daughter. From birth I lived in her care, and she taught me. Unbeliever, she did not teach me any anger or bitterness towards you.'

'No!' Covenant breathed. 'No.' No! Not her, too! A vision of blood darkened his sight – the blood on Lena's loins. He could not bear to think that she had forgiven him, she!

He turned away. He felt Elena watching him, felt her presence reaching towards him in an effort to draw him back. But he could not face her. He was afraid of the emotions that motivated her; he did not even name them to himself. He lay down in his blankets with his back to her until she banked the graveling for the night and settled herself to sleep.

The next morning, shortly after dawn, Morin and Bannor reappeared. They brought Myrha and Covenant's mount with them. He roused himself, and joined Elena in a meal while the Bloodguard packed their blankets. And soon after they had started westward again, Amok became visible at the High Lord's side.

Covenant was in no mood for any more of Amok's spellbinding. And he had made a decision during the night. There was a risk he had to take – a dangerous gesture that he hoped might help him to recover some kind of integrity. Before the youth could begin, Covenant clenched himself to contain the sudden hammering of his heart, and asked Amok what he knew about white gold.

'Much and little, Bearer,' Amok answered with a laugh and a bow. 'It is said that white gold articulates the wild magic which destroys peace. But who is able to describe peace?'

Covenant frowned. 'You're playing word games. I asked you a straight question. What do you know about it?'

'Know, Bearer? That is a small word – it conceals the magnitude of its meaning. I have heard what I have been told, and have seen what my eyes have beheld, but only you bear the white gold. Do you call this knowledge?'

'Amok,' Elena came to Covenant's aid, 'is white gold in some way interwoven with the Seventh Ward? Is white gold the subject or key of that Ward?'

'Ah, High Lord, all things are interwoven.' The youth seemed to relish his ability to dodge questions. 'The Seventh Ward may ignore white gold, and the master of white gold may have no use for the Seventh Ward – yet both are power, forms and faces of the one Power of Life. But the Bearer is not my master. He shadows but does not darken me. I respect that which he bears, but my purpose remains.'

Elena's response was firm. 'Then there is no need to evade his questions. Speak of what you have heard and learned concerning white gold.'

'I speak after my fashion, High Lord. Bearer, I have heard much and learned little concerning white gold. It is the girding paradox of the arch of Time, the undisciplined restraint of the Earth's creation, the absent bone of the Earthpower, the rigidness of water and the flux of rock. It articulates the wild magic which destroys peace. It is spoken of softly by the *Bhrathair*, and named in awe by the *Elohim*, though they have never seen it. Great *Kelenbhrabanal* dreams of it in his grave, and grim Sandgorgons writhe in voiceless nightmare at the touch of its name. In his last days, High Lord Kevin yearned for it in vain. It is the abyss and the peak of destiny.'

Covenant sighed to himself. He had feared that he would receive this kind of answer. Now he would have to go further, push his question right to the edge of his dread. In vexation and anxiety he rasped, 'That's enough – spare me. Just tell me how white gold – ' For an instant he faltered. But the memory of Lena compelled him. ' – how to use this bloody ring.'

'Ah, Bearer,' Amok laughed, 'ask the Sunbirth Sea or *Melenkurion* Skyweir. Question the fires of Gorak Krembal, or the tinder heart of Garroting Deep. All the Earth knows. White gold is brought into use like any other power – through passion and mystery, the honest suoterfuge of the heart.'

'Hellfire,' Covenant growled in an effort to disguise his relief. He did not like to admit to himself how glad he was to remain ignorant on this subject. But that ignorance was vital to his self-defence. As long as he did not know how to use the wild magic, he could not be blamed for the fate of the Land. In a secret and perfidious part of his heart, he had risked his question only because he trusted Amok to give him an unrevealing answer. Now he felt like a liar. Even his attempts at integrity were flawed. But his relief was greater than his self-distaste.

That relief enabled him to change the subject, attempt a normal conversation with the High Lord. He felt as awkward as a cripple; he had not conversed casually with another person since before the onset of his leprosy. But Elena responded willingly, even gladly; she welcomed his attention. Soon he no longer had to search for leading questions.

For some time, their talk floated on the ambience of Trothgard. As they climbed westward through the hills and woodlands and moors, the autumn air grew crisper. Birds roved the countryside in deft flits and soars. The cheerful sunlight stretched as if it might burst at any moment into sparkles and gleams. In it, the fall colours became dazzling. And the riders began to see more animals — rabbits and squirrels, plump badgers, occasional foxes. The whole atmosphere seemed to suit High Lord Elena. Gradually, Covenant came to understand this aspect of Lordship. Elena was at home in Trothgard. The healing of Kurash Plenethor became her.

In the course of his questions, she avoided only one subject — her childhood experiences with the Ranyhyn. Something about her young rides and initiations was too private to be treated under the open sky. But on other topics she replied without constraint. She allowed herself to be led into talk of her years in the Loresraat, of Revelwood and Trothgard, of Revelstone and Lordship and power. He sensed that she was helping him, allowing him, cooperating, and he was grateful. In time, he no longer felt maimed during the pauses in their conversation.

The next day passed similarly. But the day after that, this unthreatened mood eluded him. He lost his facility. His tongue grew stiff with remembered loneliness, and his beard itched irritably, like a reminder of peril. It's impossible, he thought. None of this is happening to me. Deliberately, driven by his illness, and by all the survival disciplines he had lost, he raised the question of High Lord Kevin.

'I am fascinated by him,' she said, and the core of stillness in her voice sounded oddly like the calm in the eye of a storm. 'He was the highest of all Berek Heartthew's great line — the Lord most full of dominion in all the Land's known or legended history. His fidelity to the Land and the Earthpower knew neither taint nor flaw. His friendship with the Giants was a matter for a fine song. The Ranyhyn adored him, and the Bloodguard wove their Vow because of him. If he had a fault, it was in excessive trust – yet how can trust be counted for blame? At the first, it was to his honour that the Despiser could gain Lordship from him – Lordship, and access to his heart. Was not Fangthane witnessed and approved by the *orcrest* and *lomillialor* tests of truth? Innocence is glorified by its vulnerability.

'And he was not blind. In the awful secret of his doubt, he refused the summons which would have taken him to his death in Treacher's Gorge. In his heart-wrung foresight or prophecy, he made decisions which preserved the Land's future. He prepared his Wards. He provided for the survival of the Giants and the Ranyhyn and the Bloodguard. He warned the people. And then with his own hand he destroyed –

'Thomas Covenant, there are some who believe that the Ritual of Desecration expressed High Lord Kevin's highest wisdom. They are few, but eloquent. The common understanding holds that Kevin strove to achieve that paradox of purity through destruction – and failed, for he and all the works of the Lords were undone, yet the Despiser endured. But these few argue that the final despair or madness with which Kevin invoked the Ritual was a necessary sacrifice, a price to make possible ultimate victory. They argue that his preparations and then the Ritual – forcing both health and ill to begin their work anew – were enacted to provide us with Fangthane's defeat. In this argument, Kevin foresaw the need which would compel the Despiser to summon white gold to the Land.'

'He must have been sicker than I thought,' Covenant muttered. 'Or maybe he just liked desecrations.'

'Neither, I think,' she replied tartly, sternly. 'He was a brave and worthy man driven to extremity. Any mortal or unguarded heart may be brought to despair – for this reason we cling to the Oath of Peace. And for this same reason High Lord Kevin fascinates me. He avowed the Land, and defiled it – in the same breath affirmed and denounced.' Her voice rose on the inner wind of her emotion. 'How great must have been his grief? And how great his power had he only survived that last consuming moment – if, after beholding the Desecration, and hearing the Despiser's glee, he had lived to strike one more blow!

'Thomas Covenant, I believe that there is immeasurable strength in the consummation of despair – strength beyond all conceiving by an unholocausted soul. I believe that if High Lord Kevin could speak from beyond the grave, he would utter a word which would unmarrow the very bones of Lord Foul's Despite.'

'That's madness!' Covenant gasped thickly. Elena's gaze wavered on the edge of focus, and he could not bear to look at her. 'Do you think that some existence after death is going to vindicate you after you've simply extirpated life from the Earth? That was exactly Kevin's mistake. I tell you, he is roasting in hell!'

'Perhaps,' she said softly. To his surprise, the storm implied in her voice was gone. 'We will never possess such knowledge – and should not need it to live our lives. But I find a danger in Lord Mhoram's belief that the Earth's Creator has chosen you to defend the Land. It is in my heart that this does not account for you.

'However, I have thought at times that perhaps our dead live in your world. Perhaps High Lord Kevin now restlessly walks your Earth, searching a voice which may utter his word here.'

Covenant groaned; Elena's suggestion dismayed him. He heard the connection she drew between Kevin Landwaster and himself. And the implications of that kinship made his heart totter as if it were assailed by potent gusts of foreboding. As they rode onward, the new silence between them glistened like white eyes of fear.

This mood grew stronger through that day and the next. The magnitude of the issues at stake numbed Covenant; he did not have the hands to juggle them. He withdrew into silence as if it were a chrysalis, an armour for some special vulnerability or metamorphosis. An obscure impulse like a memory of his former days with Atiaran prompted him to drop away from Elena's side and ride behind her. At her back, he followed Amok into the upper reaches of Trothgard.

Then, on the sixth day, the thirteenth since he had left Revelstone, he came to himself again after a fashion. Scowling thunderously, he raised his head, and saw the Westron Mountains ranging above him. High Lord Elena's party was nearing the southwest corner of Trothgard, where the Rill River climbed up into the mountains; and already the crags and snows of the range filled the whole western sky. Trothgard lay unrolled behind him like the Lords' work exposed for review; it beamed in the sunlight as if it were confident of approbation. Covenant frowned at it still more darkly, and turned his attention elsewhere.

The riders moved near the rim of the canyon of the Rill. The low, incessant rush of its waters, unseen below the edge of the canyon, gave Trothgard a dimension of sound like a subliminal humming made by the mountains and hills. All the views had a new suggestiveness, a timbre of implication. It reminded Covenant that he was climbing into one of the high places of the Land – and he did not like high places. But he clenched his frown to anchor the involuntary reactions of his face, and returned to Elena's side. She gave him a smile which he could not return, and they rode on together towards the mountains.

Late that afternoon, they stopped, made camp beside a small pool near the edge of the canyon. Water came splashing out of the mountainside directly before them, and collected in a rocky basin before pouring over the rim towards the Rill. That pool could have served as a corner marker for Trothgard. Immediately south of it was the Rill's canyon; on the west, the mountains seemed to spring abruptly out of the ground, like a frozen instant of ambuscade; and Kurash Plenethor lay draped north-eastward across the descending terrain. The aggressive imminence of the mountains contrasted vividly with the quiet panoply of Trothgard – and that contrast, multiplied by the lambent sound of the unseen Rill, gave the whole setting a look of surprise, an aspect or impression of suddenness. The atmosphere around the pool carried an almost tangible sense of boundary.

Covenant did not like it. The air contained too much crepuscular lurking. It made him feel exposed. And the riders were not forced to stop there; enough daylight remained for more travelling. But the High Lord had decided to camp beside the pool. She dismissed Amok, sent the two Bloodguard away with the Ranyhyn and Covenant's horse, then set her pot of graveling on a flat rock near the pool, and asked Covenant to leave her alone so that she could bathe.

Snorting as if the very air vexed him, he stalked off into the lee of a boulder where he was out of sight of the pool. He sat with his back to the stone, hugged his knees, and gazed down over Trothgard. He found the woodland hills particularly attractive as the mountain shadow began to fall across them. The peaks seemed to exude an austere dimness which by slow degrees submerged Trothgard's lustre. Through simple size and grandeur, they exercised precedence. But he preferred Trothgard. It was lower and more human.

Then the High Lord interrupted his reverie. She had left her robe and the Staff of Law on the grass by her graveling. Wrapped only in a blanket and drying her hair with one corner of it, she came to join him. Though the blanket hung about her thickly, revealing even less of her supple figure than did her robe, her presence felt more urgent than ever. The simple movement of her limbs as she seated herself at his side exerted an unsettling influence over him. She demanded responses. He found that his chest hurt again, as it had at Glimmermere.

Striving to defend himself against an impossible tenderness, he flung away from the boulder, walked rapidly towards the pool. The

701

itching of his beard reminded him that he also needed a bath. The High Lord remained out of sight; Bannor and Morin were nowhere around. He dropped his clothes by the graveling pot, and went to the pool.

The water was as cold as snow, but he thrust himself into it like a man exacting penance, and began to scrub at his flesh as if it were stained. He attacked his scalp and cheeks until his fingertips tingled, then submerged himself until his lungs burned. But when he pulled himself out of the water and went to the graveling for warmth, he found that he had only aggravated his difficulties. He felt whetted, more voracious, but no cleaner.

He could not understand Elena's power over him, could not control his response. She was an illusion, a figment; he should not be so attracted to her. And she should not be so willing to attract him. He was already responsible for her; his one potent act in the Land had doomed him to that. How could she not blame him?

Moving with an intemperate jerkiness, he dried himself on one of the blankets, then draped it by the pot to dry, and began to dress. He put on his clothes fiercely, as if he were girding for battle – laced and hauled and zipped and buckled himself into his sturdy boots, his T-shirt, his tough, protective jeans. He checked to be sure that he still carried his penknife and Hearthrall Tohrm's *orcrest* in his pockets.

When he was properly caparisoned, he went back through the twilight towards the High Lord. He stamped his feet to warn her of his approach, but the grass absorbed his obscure vehemence, and he made no more noise than an indignant spectre.

He found her standing a short distance downhill from the boulder. She was gazing out over Trothgard with her arms folded across her chest, and did not turn towards him as he drew near. For a time, he stood two steps behind her. The sky was still too sun-pale for stars, but Trothgard lay under the premature gloaming of the mountains. In the twilight, the face of the Lords' promise to the Land was veiled and dark.

Covenant twisted his ring, wound it on his finger as if he were tightening it to the pitch of some outbreak. Water from his wet hair dripped into his eyes. When he spoke, his voice was harsh with frustration that he could neither relieve nor repress.

'Hellfire, Elena! I'm your father!'

She gave no sign that she had heard him, but after a moment she said in a low, musing tone, 'Triock son of Thuler would believe that you have been honoured. He would not utter it kindly – but his heart would speak those words, or hold that thought. Had you not been summoned to the Land, he might have wed Lena my mother. And he would not have taken himself to the Loresraat, for he had no yearning for knowledge – the stewardship of Stonedownor life would have sufficed for him. But had he and Lena my mother borne a child who grew to become High Lord of the Council of Revelstone, he would have felt honoured – both elevated and humbled by his part in his daughter.

'Hear me, Thomas Covenant. Triock Thuler-son of Mithil Stonedown is my true father – the parent of my heart, though he is not the sire of my blood. Lena my mother did not wed him, though he begged her to share her life with him. She desired no other sharing – the life of your child satisfied her. But though she would not share her life, he shared his. He provided for her and for me. He took the place of a son with Trell Lena's father and Atiaran her mother.

'Ah, he was a dour parent. His heart's love ran in broken channels – yearning and grief and, yes, rage against you were diminishless for him, finding new paths when the old were turned or dammed. But he gave to Lena my mother and to me all a father's tenderness and devotion. Judge of him by me, Thomas Covenant. When dreaming of you took Lena's thoughts from me – when Atiaran lost in torment her capacity to care for me, and called to herself all Trell her husband's attention – then Triock son of Thuler stood beside me. He is my father.'

Covenant tried to efface his emotions with acid. 'He should have killed me when he had the chance.'

She went on as if she had not heard him. 'He shielded my heart from unjust demands. He taught me that the anguishes and furies of my parents and their parents need not rack or enrage me – that I was neither the cause nor the cure of their pain. He taught me that my life is my own – that I could share in the care and consolation of wounds without sharing the wounds, without striving to be the master of lives other than my own. He taught me this – he who gave his own life to Lena my mother.

'He abhors you, Thomas Covenant. And yet without him as my father I also would abhor you.'

'Are you through?' Covenant grated through the clench of his teeth. 'How much more do you think I can stand?'

She did not answer aloud. Instead, she turned towards him. Tears streaked her cheeks. She was silhouetted against the darkening vista of Trothgard as she stepped up to him, slipped her arms about his neck, and kissed him.

He gasped, and her breath was snatched into his lungs. He was stunned. A black mist filled his sight as her lips caressed his.

Then for a moment he lost control. He repulsed her as if her breath carried infection. Crying, 'Bastard!' he swung, back-handed her face with all his force.

The blow staggered her.

He pounced after her. His fingers clawed her blanket, tore it from her shoulders.

But his violence did not daunt her. She caught her balance, did not flinch or recoil. She made no effort to cover herself. With her head high, she held herself erect and calm; naked, she stood before him as if she were invulnerable.

It was Covenant who flinched. He quailed away from her as if she appalled him. 'Haven't I committed enough crimes?' he panted hoarsely. 'Aren't you satisfied?'

Her answer seemed to spring clean and clear out of the strange otherness of her gaze. 'You cannot ravish me, Thomas Covenant. There is no crime here. I am willing. I have chosen you.'

'Don't!' he groaned. 'Don't say that!' He flung his arms about his chest as if to conceal a hole in his armour. 'You're just trying to give me gifts again. You're trying to bribe me.'

'No. I have chosen you. I wish to share life with you.'

'Don't!' he repeated. 'You don't know what you're doing. Don't you understand how desperately I – I – ?'

But he could not say the words, *need you*. He choked on them. He wanted her, wanted what she offered him more than anything. But he could not say it. A passion more fundamental than desire restrained him.

She made no move towards him, but her voice reached out. 'How can my love harm you?'

'Hellfire!' In frustration, he spread his arms wide like a man baring an ugly secret. 'I'm a leper! Don't you see that?' But he knew immediately that she did not see, could not see because she lacked the knowledge or the bitterness to perceive the thing he called *leprosy*. He hurried to try to explain before she stepped closer to him and he was lost. 'Look. Look!' He pointed at his chest with one accusing finger. 'Don't you understand what I'm afraid of? Don't you comprehend the danger here? I'm afraid I'll become another Kevin! First I'll start loving you, and then I'll learn how to use the wild magic or whatever, and then Foul will trap me into despair, and then I'll be destroyed. That's been his plan all along. Once I start loving you or the Land or anything, he can just sit back and laugh! Bloody hell, Elena! Don't you see it?'

Now she moved. When she was within arm's reach, she stopped, and stretched out her hand. With the tips of her fingers she touched his forehead as if to smooth away the darkness there. 'Ah, Thomas Covenant,' she breathed gently, 'I cannot bear to see you frown so. Do not fear, beloved. You will not suffer Kevin Landwaster's fate. I will preserve you.'

At her touch, something within him broke. The pure tenderness of her gesture overcame him. But it was not his restraint which broke; it was his frustration. An answering tenderness washed through him. He could see her mother in her, and at the sight he suddenly perceived that it was not anger which made him violent towards her, not anger which so darkened his love, but rather grief and self-despite. The hurt he had done her mother was only a complex way of hurting himself – an expression of his leprosy. He did not have to repeat that act.

It was all impossible, everything was impossible, she did not even exist. But at that moment he did not care. She was his daughter. Tenderly, he stooped, retrieved her blanket, wrapped it around her shoulders. Tenderly, he held her face in his hands, touched her sweet face with the impossible aliveness of his fingers. He stroked away the salt pain of her tears with his thumbs, and kissed her forehead tenderly.

22

ANUNDIVIAN YAJÑA

The next morning, they left Trothgard, and rode into the unfamiliar terrain of the mountains. Half a league into the range, Amok brought them to a bridge of native stone which spanned the narrowing river-gorge of the Rill. To ameliorate his own dread of heights as well as to steady his mount, Covenant led his horse across. The bridge was wide, and the Bloodguard bracketed him with their Ranyhyn; he had no difficulty.

From there, Amok guided the High Lord's party up into the recesses of the peaks.

Beyond the foothills, his path became abruptly demanding – precipitous, rugged, and slow. He was reduced to a more careful pace as he led the riders along valleys as littered and racked as wrecks – up treacherous slides and scree falls which lay against cliffs and cols and coombs as if regurgitated out of the mountain gut-rock – down ledges which traversed weathered stone fronts like scars. But he left no doubt that he knew his way. Time and again he walked directly to the only possible exit from a closed valley, or found the only horseworthy trail through a rockfall, or trotted without hesitation into a crevice which bypassed a blank peak. Through the rough-hewn bulk and jumble of the mountains, he led the High Lord with the obliqueness of a man threading an accustomed maze.

For the first day or so, his goal seemed to be simply to gain elevation. He took riders scrambling upward until the cold appeared to pour down on them from the ice tips of the tallest peaks. Thinner air gave Covenant visions of scaling some inaccessible and remorseless mountain, and he accepted a thick half-robe from Bannor with a shiver which was not caused by the chill alone.

But then Amok changed directions. As if he were finally satisfied by the icy air and the pitch of the mountain-scapes, he sought no more altitude. Instead, he began to follow the private amazement of his trail southward. Rather than plunging deeper into the Westron Mountains, he moved parallel to their eastern borders. By day, he guided his companions along his unmarked way, and at night he left them in sheltered glens and coombs and gorges, where there were unexpected patches of grass for the mounts, to deal as they saw fit with the exhilarating or cruel cold.

He did not seem to feel the cold himself. With his thin apparel fluttering against his limbs he strode ahead in unwearied cheerfulness, as if he were impervious to fatigue and ice. Often he had to hold himself back so that the Ranyhyn and Covenant's mustang could keep pace with him.

The two Bloodguard were like him – unaffected by cold or altitude. But they were *Haruchai*, born to these mountains. Their nostrils distended at the vapoury breath of dawn or dusk. Their eyes roamed searchingly over the sunward crags, the valleys occasionally bedizened with azure tarns, the hoary glaciers crouching in the highest cols, the snow-fed streams. Though they wore nothing but short robes, they never shivered or gasped at the cold. Their wide foreheads and flat cheeks and confident poise betrayed no heart upsurge, no visceral excitement. Yet there was something clear and passionate in their alacrity as they watched over Elena and Covenant and Amok.

Elena and Covenant were not so immune to the cold. Their susceptibility clung cunningly to them, made them eager for each new day's progress towards warmer southern air. But their blankets and extra robes were warm. The High Lord did not appear to suffer. And as long as she did not suffer, Covenant felt no pain. Discomfort he could ignore. He was more at peace than he had been for a long time.

Since they had left Trothgard – since he had made the discovery which enabled him to love her without despising himself – he had

706

put everything else out of his mind and concentrated on his daughter. Lord Foul, the Warward, even this quest itself, were insubstantial to him. He watched Elena, listened to her, felt her presence at all times. When she was in the mood to talk, he questioned her readily, and when she was not he gave her silence. And in every mood he was grateful to her, poignantly moved by the offer she had made – the offer he had refused.

He could not help being conscious of the fact that she was not equally content. She had not made her offer lightly, and seemed unwilling to understand his refusal. But the sorrow of having given her pain only sharpened his attentiveness towards her. He concentrated on her as only a man deeply familiar with loneliness could. And she was not blind to this. After the first few days of their mountain trek, she again relaxed in his company, and her smiles expressed a frankness of affection which she had not permitted herself before. Then he felt that he was in harmony with her, and he travelled with her gladly. At times he chirruped to his horse as if he enjoyed riding it.

But in the days that followed, a change slowly came over her – a change that had nothing to do with him. As time passed – as they journeyed nearer to the secret location of the Seventh Ward – she became increasingly occupied by the purpose of her quest. She questioned Amok more often, interrogated him more tensely. At times, Covenant could see in the elsewhere stare of her eyes that she was thinking of the war – a duty from which she had turned aside – and there were occasional lashes of urgency in her voice as she strove to ask the questions that would unlock Amok's mysterious knowledge.

This was a burden that Covenant could not help her bear. He knew none of the crucial facts himself. The days passed; the moon expanded to its full, then declined towards its last quarter, but she made no progress. Finally, his desire to assist her in some way led him to speak to Bannor.

In a curious way, he felt unsafe with the Bloodguard – not physically, but emotionally. There was a tension of disparity between himself and Bannor. The *Haruchai*'s stony gaze had the magisterial air of a man who did not deign to utter his judgment of his companions. And Covenant had other reasons to feel uncomfortable with Bannor. More than once, he had made Bannor bear the brunt of his own bootless outrage. But he had nowhere else to turn. He was entirely useless to Elena.

Since his days in Revelstone, he had been alert to a fine shade of discrepancy in the Bloodguard's attitude towards Amok – a discrepancy which had been verified but not explained in Revelwood.

However, he did not know how to approach the subject. Extracting information from Bannor was difficult; the Bloodguard's habitual reserve baffled enquiry. And Covenant was determined to say nothing which might sound like an offence to Bannor's integrity. Bannor had already proved his fidelity in the Wightwarrens under Mount Thunder.

Covenant began by trying to find out why the Bloodguard had seen fit to send only Bannor and Morin to protect the High Lord on her quest. He was acutely aware of his infacility as he remarked, 'I gather you don't think we're in any great danger on this trip.'

'Danger, ur-Lord?' The repressed lilt of Bannor's pronunciation seemed to imply that anyone protected by the Bloodguard did not need to think of danger.

'Danger,' Covenant repeated with a touch of his old asperity. 'It's a common word these days.'

Bannor considered for a moment, then said, 'These are mountains. There is always danger.'

'Such as?'

'Rocks may fall. Storms may come. Tigers roam these low heights. Great eagles hunt here. Mountains' — Covenant seemed to hear a hint of satisfaction in Bannor's tone — 'are perilous.'

'Then why — Bannor, I would really like to know why there are only two of you Bloodguard here.'

'Is there need for more?'

'If we're attacked — by tigers, or whatever? Or what if there's an avalanche? Are two of you enough?'

'We know mountains,' Bannor replied flatly. 'We suffice.'

This assertion was not one that Covenant could contradict. He made an effort to approach what he wanted to know in another way, though the attempt took him onto sensitive ground — terrain he would rather have avoided. 'Bannor, I feel as if I'm slowly getting to know you Bloodguard. I can't claim that I understand — but I can at least recognize your devotion. I know what it looks like. Now I get the feeling that something is going on here — something — inconsistent. Something I don't recognize.

'Here we are climbing through the mountains, where anything could happen. We're following Amok who knows where, even though we've got next to no idea what he's doing, never mind why he's doing it. And you're satisfied that the High Lord is safe when she's only got two Bloodguard to protect her. Didn't you learn anything from Kevin?'

'We are the Bloodguard,' answered Bannor stolidly. 'She is safe — as safe as may be.'

'Safe?' Covenant protested.

'A score or a hundredscore Bloodguard would not make her more safe.'

'I admire your confidence.'

Covenant winced at his own sarcasm, paused for a moment to reconsider his questions. Then he lowered his head as if he meant to batter Bannor's resistance down with his forehead, and said bluntly, 'Do you trust Amok?'

'Trust him, ur-Lord?' Bannor's tone hinted that the question was inane in some way. 'He has not led us into hazard. He has chosen a good way through the mountains. The High Lord elects to follow him. We do not ask for more.'

Still Covenant felt the lurking presence of something unexplained. 'I tell you, it doesn't fit,' he rasped in irritation. 'Listen. It's a little late in the day for these inconsistencies. I've sort of given up – they don't do me any good any more. If it's all the same to you, I'd rather hear something that makes sense.

'Bannor, you – Bear with me. I can't help noticing it. First there was something I don't understand, something – out of pitch – about the way you Bloodguard reacted to Amok when he came to Revelstone. You – I don't know what it was. Anyway, at Revelwood you didn't exactly jump to help Troy when he caught Amok. And after that – only two Bloodguard! Bannor, it doesn't make sense.'

Bannor was unmoved. 'She is the High Lord. She holds the Staff of Law. She is easily defended.'

That answer foiled Covenant. It did not satisfy him, but he could think of no way around it. He did not know what he was groping for. His intuition told him that his questions were significant, but he could not articulate or justify them in any utile way. And he reacted to Bannor's trenchant blankness as if it were some kind of touchstone, a paradoxically private and unavoidable criterion of rectitude. Bannor made him aware that there was something not altogether honest about his own accompaniment of the High Lord.

So he withdrew from Bannor, returned his attention to Elena. She had had no better luck with Amok, and her air of escape as she turned towards Covenant matched his. They rode on together, hiding their various anxieties behind light talk of mutual commiseration.

Then, during the eleventh evening of their sojourn in the mountains, she expressed an opinion to him. As if the guess were hazardous, she said, 'Amok leads us to *Melenkurion* Skyweir. The Seventh Ward is hidden there.' And the next day – the eighteenth since they had left Revelwood, and the twenty-fifth since the War Council of the Lords – the rhythm of their trek was broken.

The day dawned cold and dull, as if the sunlight were clogged with grey cerements. A troubled smell shrouded the air. Torn fragments of wind flapped back and forth across the camp as Elena and Covenant ate their breakfast, and far away they could hear a flat, detonating sound like the retort of balked canvas on unlashed spars. Covenant predicted a storm. But the First Mark shook his head in flat denial, and Elena said, 'This is not the weather of storms.' She glanced warily up at the peaks as she spoke. 'There is pain in the air. The Earth is afflicted.'

'What's happening?' A burst of wind scattered Covenant's voice, and he had to repeat his question at a shout to make himself heard. 'Is Foul going to hit us here?'

The wind shifted and lapsed; she was able to answer normally. 'Some ill has been performed. The Earth has been assaulted. We feel its revulsion. But the distance is very great, and time has passed. I feel no peril directed towards us. Perhaps the Despiser does not know what we do.' In the next breath, her voice hardened. 'But he has used the Illearth Stone. Smell the air! There has been malice at work in the Land.'

Covenant began to sense what she meant. Whatever amassed these clouds and roiled this wind was not the impassive natural violence of a storm. The air seemed to carry inaudible shrieks and hints of rot, as if it were blowing through the aftermath of an atrocity. And on a subliminal level, almost indiscernible, the high bluff crags seemed to be shuddering.

The atmosphere made him feel a need for haste. But though her face was set in grim lines, the High Lord did not hurry. She finished her meal, then carefully packed the food and graveling away before calling to Myrha. When she mounted, she summoned Amok.

He appeared before her almost at once, and gave her a cheerful bow. After acknowledging him with a nod, she asked him if he could explain the ill in the air.

He shook his head, and said, 'High Lord, I am no oracle.' But his eyes revealed his sensitivity to the atmosphere; they were bright, and a sharp gleam lurking behind them showed for the first time that he was capable of anger. A moment later, however, he turned his face away, as if he did not wish to expose any private part of himself. With a flourishing gesture, he beckoned for the High Lord to follow him.

Covenant swung into his mount's *clingor* saddle, and tried to ignore the brooding ambience around him. But he could not resist the impression that the ground under him was quivering. Despite all his recent experience, he was still not a confident rider – he could not shed his nagging distrust of horses – and he worried that he might fulfil the prophecy of his height fear by falling off his mount.

Fortunately, he was spared cliff ledges and exposed trails. For some time, Amok's path ran along the spine of a crooked rift between looming mountain walls. The enclosed valley did not challenge Covenant's uncertain horsemanship. But the muffled booming in the air continued to grow. As morning passed, the sound became clearer, echoed like brittle groans off the sheer walls.

Early in the afternoon, Amok led the riders around a final bend. Beyond it, they found an immense landslide. Great, scalloped wounds stood opposite each other high in the walls, and the jumbled mass of rock and scree which had fallen from both sides was piled up several hundred feet above the valley floor.

It completely blocked the valley.

This was the source of the detonations. There was no movement in the huge fall; it had an old look, as if its formation had been forgotten long ago by the mountains. But tortured creaks and cracks came from within it as if its bones were breaking.

Amok walked forward, but the riders halted. Morin studied the blockage for a moment, then said, 'It is impassable. It breaks. Perhaps on foot we might attempt it at its edges. But the weight of the Ranyhyn will begin a new fall.' Amok reached the foot of the slide, and beckoned, but Morin said absolutely, 'We must find another passage.'

Covenant looked around the valley. 'How long will that take?'

'Two days. Perhaps three.'

'That bad? You would think this trip wasn't long enough already. Are you sure that isn't safe? Amok hasn't made any mistakes yet.'

'We are the Bloodguard,' Morin said.

And Bannor explained, 'This fall is younger than Amok.'

'Meaning it wasn't here when he learned his trail? Damnation!' Covenant muttered. The landslide made his desire for haste keener.

Amok came back to them with a shade of seriousness in his face. 'We must pass here,' he said tolerantly, as if he were explaining something to a recalcitrant child.

Morin said, 'The way is unsafe.'

'That is true,' Amok replied. 'There is no other.' Turning to the High Lord, he repeated, 'We must pass here.'

While her companions had been speaking, Elena had gazed speculatively up and down the landfall. When Amok addressed her directly, she nodded her head, and responded, 'We will.'

Morin protested impassively, 'High Lord.'

'I have chosen,' she answered, then added, 'It may be that the Staff of Law can hold the fall until we have passed it.'

Morin accepted this with an emotionless nod. He took his mount trotting back away from the slide, so that the High Lord would have room in which to work. Bannor and Covenant followed. After a moment, Amok joined them. The four men watched her from a short distance.

She made no complex or strenuous preparations. Raising the Staff, she sat erect and tall on Myrha's back for a moment, faced the slide. From Covenant's point of view, her blue robe and the Ranyhyn's glossy coat met against the mottled grey background of scree and rubble. She and Myrha looked small in the deep sheer valley, but the conjunction of their colours and forms gave them a potent iconic appearance. Then she moved.

Singing a low song, she advanced to the foot of the slide. There she gripped the Staff by one end, and lowered the other to the ground. It appeared to pulse as she rode along the slide's front, drawing a line in the dirt parallel to the fall. She walked Myrha to one wall, then back to the other. Still touching the ground with the Staff, she returned to the centre.

When she faced the slide again, she lifted the Staff, and rapped once on the line she had drawn.

A rippling skein of verdigris sparks flowed up the fall from her line. They gleamed like interstices of power on every line or bulge of rock that protruded from the slope. After an instant, they disappeared, leaving an indefinite smell like the aroma of orchids in the air.

The muffled groaning of the fall faded somewhat.

'Come,' the High Lord said. 'We must climb at once. This Word will not endure.'

Briskly, Morin and Bannor started forward. Amok loped beside them. He easily kept pace with the Ranyhyn.

As he looked upward, Covenant felt nausea like a presage in his guts. His jaw muscles knotted apprehensively. But he slapped his mount with his heels, and rode at the moaning fall.

He caught up with the Bloodguard. They took positions on either side of him, followed Elena and Amok onto the slope.

The High Lord's party angled back and forth up the slide. Their climbing balanced the danger of delay against the hazard of a direct attack on the slope. Covenant's mustang laboured strenuously, and its struggles contrasted with the smooth power of the Ranyhyn. Their hooves kicked scuds of shale and scree down the fall, but their footing was secure, confident. There were no mishaps. Before long, Covenant stood on the rounded V atop the slide.

He was not prepared for what lay beyond the blockage. Automatically, he had expected the south end of the valley to resemble the north. But from the ridge of the landslide, he could see that the huge scalloped wounds above him were too big to be explained by the slide as it appeared from the north.

Somewhere buried directly below him, the valley floor plunged dramatically. The two avalanches had interred a precipice. The south face of the slide was three or four times longer than the north. Far below him, the valley widened into a grassy bottom featured by stands of pine and a stream springing from one of the walls. But to reach that alluring sight, he had to descend more than a thousand feet down the detonating undulation of the slide.

He swallowed thickly. 'Bloody hell. Can you hold that?'

'No,' Elena said bluntly. 'But what I have done will steady it. And I can take other action – if the need arises.'

With a sharp nod, she started Amok down the slope.

Bannor told Covenant to stay close behind him, then eased his Ranyhyn over the edge after Amok. For a moment, Covenant felt too paralysed by prophetic trepidation to move. His dry, constricted throat and awkward tongue could not form words. Hellfire, he muttered silently. Hellfire.

He abandoned himself, pushed his mustang after Bannor.

Part of him knew that Morin and then Elena followed him, but he paid no attention to them. He locked his eyes on Bannor's back and tried to cling there for the duration of the descent.

Before he had gone a hundred feet, the skittishness of his mount drove everything else from his mind. Its ears flinched as if it were about to shy at every new groan within the fall. He heaved and sawed at the reins in an effort to control the horse, but he only aggravated its distress. Faintly, he could hear himself mumbling, 'Help. Help.'

Then a loud boom like the crushing of a boulder shivered the air. A swath of slide jumped and shifted. The rubble under Covenant began to slip.

His mount tried to spring away from the shift. It shied sideways, and started straight down the slope.

Its lunge only precipitated the slide. Almost at once, the mustang was plunging in scree that poured over its knees.

It struggled to escape downward. Each heave increased the weight of rubble piling against it.

Covenant clung frantically to the *clingor* saddle. He fought to pull the horse's head aside, make his mount angle out of the slide's main force. But the mustang had its teeth on the bit now. He could not turn it.

Its next plunge buried it to its haunches in the quickening rush of rubble. Covenant could hear Elena shouting stridently. As she yelled,

Bannor's Ranyhyn sprang in front of him. Ploughing through the scree, it threw its weight against his mount. The impact almost unseated him, but it deflected his horse. Guided by Bannor, the Ranyhyn shoved against the horse, forced it to fight towards the cliff.

But the avalanche was already moving too heavily. A small boulder struck the mustang's rump; the horse fell. Covenant sprawled down the slope out of Bannor's reach. The rubble tumbled him over and over, but for a moment he managed to stay above it. He got his feet under him, tried to move across the slide.

Through the gathering roar of the fall, he heard Morin shout, 'High Lord!' The next instant, she flashed by him, riding Myrha straight down the outer edge of the slide. Fifty feet below him, she swung into the avalanche. With a wild cry, she whirled the Staff of Law and struck the fall.

Fire blazed up through the slide. Like a suddenly clenched fist, the rubble around Covenant stopped moving. His own momentum knocked him over, but he jumped up again in time to meet Bannor as the Bloodguard landed his Ranyhyn on the small patch of steady ground. Bannor caught Covenant with one hand, swung him across the Ranyhyn's back, charged away out of the slide.

When they reached the relatively still ground against the cliff wall, Covenant saw that Elena had saved him at the risk of herself. The stasis which she had applied to the slipping tons of the avalanche was not large enough to include her own position. And an instant later, that stasis broke. An extra breaker of rubble dropped towards her.

She had no second chance to wield the Staff. Almost at once, the wave of scree crashed over her and Myrha.

An instant later, she appeared downhill from Myrha. The Ranyhyn's great strength momentarily sheltered her.

But the fall piled against Myrha's chest. And Covenant's mustang, still madly fighting the slide, hurtled towards the Ranyhyn. Instinctively, Covenant tried to run back into the avalanche to help Elena. But Bannor held him back with one hand.

He started to struggle, then stopped as a long *clingor* rope flicked out over the slide and caught the High Lord's wrist. With his Ranyhyn braced against the wall below Covenant and Bannor, First Mark Morin flung out his line, and the adhesive leather snared Elena. She reacted immediately. 'Flee!' she yelled to Myrha, then clutched the Staff and heaved against the waist-deep flow of scree as Morin pulled her to safety.

Though the great mare was battered and bleeding, she had other intentions. With a tremendous exertion, she lunged out of the mustang's path. As the screaming horse tumbled past, she turned and caught its reins in her teeth.

For one intense moment, she held the mustang, hauled it to its feet, swung it in the direction of the wall.

Then the avalanche swept them down a steep bulge. The sudden plunge sank her. With a rushing cry, the weight of the landslide poured over her.

Somehow, the mustang kept its feet, struggled on down the slope. But Myrha did not reappear.

Covenant hugged his stomach as if he were about to retch. Below him, Elena cried, 'Myrha! Ranyhyn!' The passion in her voice appalled him. Several moments passed before he realized that his rescue had carried his companions more than two-thirds of the way down the slide.

'Come,' Bannor said flatly. 'The balance has broken. There will be more falls. We are imperilled here.' His efforts had not even quickened his breathing.

Numbly, Covenant sat behind Bannor as his Ranyhyn picked its way along the wall to the High Lord and Morin. Elena looked stricken, astonished with grief. Covenant wanted to throw his arms around her, but the Bloodguard gave him no chance. Bannor took him on down the slope, and Morin followed with the High Lord riding emptily at his back.

They found Amok awaiting them on the grass at the bottom of the valley. His eyes held something that resembled concern as he approached the High Lord and helped her to dismount. 'Pardon me,' he said quietly. 'I have brought you pain. What could I do? I was not made to be of use in such needs.'

'Then begone,' Elena replied harshly. 'I have no more use for you this day.'

Amok's gaze constricted as if the High Lord had hurt him. But he obeyed her promptly. With a bow and a wave, he wiped himself out of sight.

Dismissing him with a grimace, Elena turned towards the landslide. The piled rubble creaked and retorted more fiercely now, promising other slides at any moment, but she ignored the hazard to kneel at the foot of the scree. She bent forward as if she were presenting her back to a whip, and tears streaked her voice as she moaned, 'Alas, Ranyhyn! Alas, Myrha! My failure has slain you.'

Covenant hurried to her. He ached to throw his arms around her, but her grief restrained him. With an effort, he said, 'It's my fault. Don't blame yourself. I should know how to ride better.' Hesitantly, he reached out and stroked her neck.

His touch seemed to turn her pain to anger. She did not move, but she screamed at him, 'Let me be! This is indeed your doing. You should not have sent the Ranyhyn to Lena my mother.'

He recoiled as if she had struck him. At once, his own instinctive ire flamed. The panic of his fall had filled his veins with a tinder that burned suddenly. Her quick recrimination changed him in an instant. It was as if the peace of his past days had been transformed abruptly into umbrage and leper's vehemence. He was mute with outrage. Trembling, he turned and stalked away.

Neither Bannor nor Morin followed him. Already they were busy tending the cuts and abrasions of their Ranyhyn and his mustang. He strode past them, went on down the valley like a scrap of frail ire fluttering helplessly along the breeze.

After a while, the dull detonations of the landslide began to fade behind him. He kept on walking. The smell of the grass tried to beguile him, and within the pine stands a consoling susurrus and gloom, a soft, quiet, sweet rest, beckoned him. He ignored them, paced by with a jerky, mechanical stride. Thick anger roiled his brain, drove him forward. Again! he cried to himself. Every woman he loved – ! How could such a thing happen twice in the same life?

He went on until he had covered almost a league. Then he found himself beside a trilling stream. Here the bottom of the valley was uneven on both sides of the brook. He searched along it until he found a grass-matted gully from which he could see nothing of the valley's northward reach. There he threw himself down on his stomach to gnaw the old bone of his outrage.

Time passed. Soon shadows crossed the valley as the sun moved towards evening. Twilight began as if it were seeping out of the ground between the cliffs. Covenant rolled over on his back. At first, he watched with a kind of dour satisfaction as a darkness climbed the east wall. He felt ready for the isolation of night and loss.

But then the memory of Joan returned with redoubled force. It stung him into a sitting position. Once again, he found himself gaping at the cruelty of his delusion, the malice which tore him away from Joan – for what? Hellfire! he gasped. The gloaming made him feel that he was going blind with anger. When he saw Elena walking into the gully towards him, she seemed to move through a haze of leprosy.

He looked away from her, tried to steady his sight against the failing light on the eastern cliff; and while his face was averted, she approached, seated herself on the grass by his feet. He could feel her presence vividly. At first she did not speak. But when he still refused to meet her gaze, she said softly, 'Beloved. I have made a sculpture for you.'

With an effort, he turned his head. He saw her bent forward, with a hopeful smile on her lips. Both her hands extended towards him a white object that appeared to be made of bone. He paid no attention to it; his eyes slapped at her face as if that were his enemy.

In a tone of entreaty, she continued, 'I formed it for you from Myrha's bones. I cremated her – to do her what honour I could. Then from her bones I formed this. For you, beloved. Please accept it.'

He glanced at the sculpture. It caught his unwilling interest. It was a bust. Initially, it appeared too thick to have been made from any horse's bone. But then he saw that four bones had been in some way fused together and moulded. He took the work from her hands to view it more closely. The face interested him. Its outlines were less blunt than in other marrowmeld work he had seen. It was lean and gaunt and impenetrable – a prophetic face, taut with purpose. It expressed someone he knew, but a moment passed before he recognized the countenance. Then, gingerly, as if he feared to be wrong, he said, 'It's Bannor. Or one of the other Bloodguard.'

'You tease me,' she replied. 'I am not so poor a crafter.' There was a peculiar hunger in her smile. 'Beloved, I have sculpted you.'

Slowly, his ire faded. After all, she was his daughter, not his wife. She was entitled to any reproach that seemed fit to her. He could not remain angry with her. Carefully, he placed the bust on the grass, then reached out towards her and took her into his arms as the sun set.

She entered his embrace eagerly, and for a time she clung to him as if she were simply glad to put their anger behind them. But gradually he felt the tension of her body change. Her affection seemed to become grim, almost urgent. Something taut made her limbs hard, made her fingers grip him like claws. In a voice that shook with passion, she said, 'This also Fangthane would destroy.'

He lifted his cheek from her hair, moved her so that he could see her face.

That sight chilled him. Despite the dimness of the light, her gaze shocked him like an immersion in polar seas.

The otherness of her sight, the elsewhere dimension of its power, had focused, concentrated until it became the crux of something savage and illimitable. A terrible might raved out of her orbs. Though her gaze was not directed at him, it bored through him like an auger. When it was gone, it left a bloody weal across him.

It was a look of apocalypse.

He could not think of any other name for it but *hate*.

23

KNOWLEDGE

The sight sent him stumbling up the gully away from her. He had trouble keeping himself erect; he listed as if a gale had left him aground somewhere. He heard her low cry, 'Beloved!' but he could not turn back. The vision made his heart smoke like dry ice, and he needed to find a place where he could huddle over the pain and gasp alone.

For a time, smoke obscured his self-awareness. He ran into Bannor, and fell back as if he had smashed against a boulder. The impact surprised him, Bannor's flat mien had the force of a denunciation. Instinctively, he recoiled. 'Don't touch me!' He lurched off in another direction, stumbled through the night until he had placed a steep hill between himself and the Bloodguard. There he sat down on the grass, wrapped his arms around his chest, and made a deliberate effort to weep.

He could not do it. His weakness, his perpetual leprosy, dammed that emotional channel; he had spent too long unlearning the release of grief. And the frustration of failure made him savage. He brimmed with old, unresolved rage. Even in delusion, he could not escape the trap of his illness. Leaping to his feet, he shook his fists at the sky like a reefed and lonely galleon firing its guns in bootless defiance of the invulnerable ocean. Damnation!

But then his self-consciousness returned. His anger became bitterly cold as he bit off his shout, clamped shut that outlet for his fury. He felt that he was waking up after a blind sleep. Snarling extremely between his teeth, he stalked away towards the stream.

He did not bother to take off his clothes. Fiercely, he dropped flat on his face in the water as if he were diving for some kind of cauterization or release in the glacial frigidity of the brook.

He could not endure the cold for more than a moment; it burned over all his flesh, seized his heart like a convulsion. Gasping, he sprang up and stood shuddering on the rocky streambed. The water and the breeze sent a ravenous ache through his bones, as if cold consumed their marrow. He left the stream.

The next instant, he saw Elena's gaze again, felt it sear his memory. He halted. A sudden idea threw back the chill. It sprang practically full-grown into view as if it had been maturing for days in the darkness of his mind, waiting until he was ready.

He realized that he had access to a new kind of bargain – an arrangement or compromise distantly similar, but far superior, to the one which he had formed with the Ranyhyn. They were too limited; they could not meet his terms, fulfil the contract he had made for his survival. But the person with whom he could now bargain was almost ideally suited to help him.

It was just possible that he could buy his salvation from the High Lord.

He saw the difficulties at once. He did not know what the Seventh Ward contained. He would have to steer Elena's apocalyptic impulse through an unpredictable future towards an uncertain goal. But that impulse was something he could use. It made her personally powerful – powerful and vulnerable, blinded by obsession – and she held the Staff of Law. He might be able to induce her to take his place, assume his position as the onus of Lord Foul's machinations. He might be able to lead her extravagant passion to replace his white gold at the crux of the Land's doom. If he could get her to undertake the bitter responsibility which had been so ineluctably aimed at him, he would be free. That would remove his head from the chopping block of this delusion. And all he had to do in return was to place himself at Elena's service in any way which would focus rather than dissipate her inner drives – keep her under control until the proper moment.

It was a more expensive bargain than the one he had made with the Ranyhyn. It did not allow him to remain passive; it required him to help her, manipulate her. But it was justified. During the Quest for the Staff of Law, he had been fighting merely to survive an impossibly compelling dream. Now he understood his true peril more clearly.

So much time had passed since he had thought freedom possible that his heart almost stopped at the thrill of the conception. But after its first excitement, he found that he was shivering violently. His clothes were completely soaked.

Aching with every move, he started back towards the gully and the High Lord.

He found her sitting despondent and thoughtful beside a bright campfire. She wore one blanket over her robe; the others were spread out by the blaze for warmth. When he entered the gully, she looked up eagerly. He could not meet her eyes. But she did not appear to notice the chagrin behind his blue lips and taut forehead. Snatching up a warm blanket for him, she drew him close to the fire. Her few low comments were full of concern, but she asked him nothing until the flames had beaten back his worst shivers. Then, shyly, as if she were inquiring where she stood in relation to him, she reached up and kissed him.

He returned the caress of her lips, and the movement seemed to carry him over an inner hurdle. He found that he could look at her now. She smiled softly; the voracious power of her gaze was lost again in its elsewhere otherness. She appeared to accept his kiss at its surface valuation. She hugged him, then seated herself beside him. After a moment, she asked, 'Did it surprise you to learn that I am so vehement?'

He tried to excuse himself. 'I'm not used to such things. You didn't give me fair warning.'

'Pardon me, beloved,' she said contritely. Then she went on, 'Were you very dismayed – by what you have beheld in me?'

He thought for a while before he said, 'I think if you ever looked at me that way I would be as good as dead.'

'You are safe,' she assured him warmly.

'What if you change your mind?'

'Your doubt chastises me. Beloved, you are part of my life and breath. Do you believe that I could set you aside?'

'I don't know what to believe.' His tone expressed vexation, but he hugged her again to counteract it. 'Dreaming is like – it's like being a slave. Your dreams come out of all the parts of you that you don't have any control over. That's why – that's why madness is the only danger.'

He was grateful that she did not attempt to argue with him. When the shivering was driven from his bones, he became incontestably drowsy. As she put him to bed, wrapped him snugly in his blankets by the campfire, the only thing which kept him from trusting her completely was the conviction that his bargain contained something dishonest.

For the most part, he forgot that conviction during the next three days. His attention was clouded by a low fever which he seemed to have caught from his plunge in the stream. Febrile patches appeared on his obdurately pale cheeks; his forehead felt clammy with sweat and cold; and his eyes glittered as if he were in the grip of a secret excitement. From time to time, he dozed on the back of his battered mount, and awoke to find himself babbling deliriously. He could not always remember what he had said, but at least once he had insisted manically that the only way to stay well was to be perpetually awake. No antiseptic could cleanse the wounds inflicted in dreams. The innocent did not dream.

When he was not mumbling in half-sleep, he was occupied with the trek itself.

The High Lord's party was nearing some kind of destination.

The morning after the landslide had dawned into crisp sunshine – a clear vividness like an atonement for the previous day's distress. When Amok had appeared to lead the High Lord onward, Elena had whistled as if she were calling Myrha, and another Ranyhyn had answered the summons. Covenant had watched it gallop up the valley with amazement in his face. The fidelity of the Ranyhyn towards their own choices went beyond all his conceptions of pride or loyalty. The sight had reminded him of his previous bargain – a bargain which both Elena and Rue had said was still kept among the great horses. But then he had struggled up on his mustang, and other matters had intruded on his fever-tinged thoughts. He had retained barely enough awareness to place Elena's marrowmeld gift in Bannor's care.

After the riders had followed Amok out of the valley, Covenant caught his first glimpse of *Melenkurion* Skyweir. Though it was still many leagues almost due southeast of him, the high mountain lifted its twin, icebound peaks above the range's rugged horizon, and its glaciers gleamed blue in the sunlight as if the sky's azure feet were planted there. Elena's guess seemed correct: Amok's ragged, oblique trail tended consistently towards the towering Skyweir. It vanished almost immediately as Amok led the riders into the lee of another cliff, but it reappeared with increasing frequency as the day passed. By the following noon, it dominated the southeastern horizon.

But at night Covenant did not have the mountains veering around him. He could not see *Melenkurion* Skyweir. And after the evening meal, his fever abated somewhat. Freed from these demands and drains upon his weakened concentration, he came to some vague terms with his bargain.

It did not need her consent; he knew this, and berated himself for it. Once the thrill of hope had faded into fever and anxiety, he ached to tell her what he had been thinking. And her attentiveness to him made him ache worse. She cooked special healing broths and stews for him; she went out of her way to supply him with *aliantha*. But his emotions towards her had changed. There was cunning and flattery in his responses to her tenderness. He was afraid of what would happen if he told her his thoughts.

When he lay awake late at night, shivering feverishly, he had a bad taste of rationalization in his mouth. Then it was not embarrassment or trust which kept him from explaining himself. His jaws were locked by his clinging need for survival, his rage against his own death.

Finally, his fever broke. Late in the afternoon of the third day – the twenty-first since the High Lord's party had left Revelwood – a sudden rush of sweat poured over him, and a tight inner cord seemed to snap. He felt himself relaxing at last. That night, he fell asleep while Elena was still discussing the ignorance or failure of comprehension which kept her from learning anything from Amok.

A long, sound sleep restored his sense of health, and the next morning he was able to pay better attention to his situation. Riding at Elena's side, he scrutinized *Melenkurion* Skyweir. It stood over him like an aegis, shutting out the whole southeastern dawn. With a low surge of apprehension, he judged that the High Lord's party would probably arrive there before this day was done. Carefully, he asked her about the Skyweir.

'I can tell you little,' she replied. 'It is the tallest mountain known to the Land, and its name shares one of the Seven Words. But Kevin's Lore reveals little of it. Perhaps there is other knowledge in the other Wards, but the First and Second contain few hints or references. And in our age the Lords have gained nothing of their own concerning this place. None have come so close to the Skyweir since people returned to the Land after the Ritual of Desecration.

'It is in my heart that these great peaks mark a place of power – a place surpassing even Gravin Threndor. But I have no evidence for this belief apart from the strange silence of Kevin's Lore. *Melenkurion* Skyweir is one of the high places of the Land – and yet the First and Second Wards contain no knowledge of it beyond a few old maps, a fragment of one song, and two unexplained sentences which, if their translation is not faulty, speak of *command* and *blood*. So,' she said wryly, 'my failure to unlock Amok is not altogether surprising.'

This brought her back to a contemplation of her ignorance, and she lapsed into silence. Covenant tried to think of a way to help her. But the effort was like trying to see through a wall of stone; he had even less of the requisite knowledge. If he intended to keep his side of the bargain, he would have to do so in some other way.

He believed intuitively that his chance would come.

In the meantime, he settled himself to wait for Amok to bring them to the mountains.

Their final approach came sooner than he had expected. Amok took them down a long col between two blunt peaks, then into a crooked ravine that continued to descend while it shifted towards the east. By noon they had lost more than two thousand feet of elevation. There the ravine ended, leaving them on a wide, flat, barren plateau which clung to the slopes of the great mountain. The plateau ran east and south as far as Covenant could see around *Melenkurion* Skyweir. The flat ground looked like a setting, a base for the fifteen or twenty thousand feet of its matched spires. And east of the plateau were no mountains at all.

The Ranyhyn were eager for a run after long days of constricted climbing, and they cantered out onto the flat rock. With surprising fleetness, Amok kept ahead of them. He laughed as he ran, and even increased his pace. The Ranyhyn stretched into full stride, began to gallop in earnest, leaving Covenant's mustang behind. But still Amok's prancing step outran them. Gaily, he led the riders east and then south down the centre of the plateau.

Covenant followed at a more leisurely gait. Soon he was passing along the face of the first peak. The plateau here was several hundred yards wide, and it extended southward until it curved west out of sight beyond the base of the second peak. The spires joined each other a few thousand feet above the plateau, but the line of juncture between them remained clear, as if the two sides differed in texture. At the place where this line touched the plateau, a cleft appeared in the flat rock. This crevice ran straight across the plateau to its eastern edge.

Ahead of Covenant, the Ranyhyn had ended their gallop near the rim of the crevice. Now Elena trotted down its length towards the outer edge of the plateau. Covenant swung his mustang in that direction, and joined her there.

Together, they dismounted, and he lay down on his stomach to peer over the precipice. Four thousand feet below the sheer cliff, a dark, knotted forest spread out as far as he could see. The woods brooded over its rumpled terrain – a thick-grown old blanket of trees which draped the foot of the Westron Mountains as if to conceal, provide the solace of privacy for, a rigid and immediate anguish. And northeastward across this covered expanse ran the red-black line of the river which spewed from the base of the cleft. Inaudible in the distance, it came moiling out of the rock and slashed away through the heart of the forest. The river looked like a weal in the woods, a cut across the glowering green countenance. This scar gave the hurt, rigid face an expression of ferocity, as if it dreamed of rending limb from limb the enemy which had scored it.

Elena explained the view to Covenant. 'That is the Black River,' she said reverently. She was the first new Lord ever to see this sight. 'From this place, it flows a hundred and fifty leagues and more to join the Mithil on its way towards Andelain. Its spring is said to lie deep under *Melenkurion* Skyweir. We stand on Rivenrock, the eastern porch or portal of the great mountain. And below us is Garroting Deep, the last forest in the Land where a Forestal still walks – where the maimed consciousness of the One Forest still holds communion with itself.' For a moment, she breathed the brisk air. Then she added, 'Beloved, I believe that we are not far from the Seventh Ward.'

Pushing himself back from the edge, he climbed unsteadily to his feet. The breeze seemed to carry vertigo up at him from the precipice. He waited until he was several strides from the edge before he replied, 'I hope so. For all we know, that war could be over by now. If Troy's plans didn't work, Foul might be halfway to Revelstone.'

'Yes. I, too, have felt that fear. But my belief remains that the Land's future will not be won in war. And that battle is not in our hands. We have other work.'

Covenant studied the distance of her eyes, measuring the risk of offending her, then said, 'Has it occurred to you that you might not be able to unlock Amok?'

'Of course,' she returned sharply. 'I am not blind.'

'Then what will you do, if he doesn't talk?'

'I hold the Staff of Law. It is a potent key. When Amok has guided us to the Seventh Ward, I will not be helpless.'

Covenant looked away with a sour expression on his face. He did not believe that it would be that easy.

At Elena's side, he walked back along the crevice towards the two Bloodguard and Amok. The afternoon was not far gone, but already *Melenkurion* Skyweir's shadow stretched across Rivenrock. The shadow thickened the natural gloom of the cleft, so that it lay like a fault of darkness across the plateau. At its widest, it was no more than twenty feet broad, but it seemed immeasurably deep, as if it went straight down to the buried roots of the mountain. On an impulse, Covenant tossed a small rock into the cleft. It bounced from wall to wall on its way down; he counted twenty-two heartbeats before it fell beyond hearing. Instinctively, he kept himself a safe distance from the crevice as he went on towards Bannor and Morin.

The two Bloodguard had unpacked the food, and Covenant and Elena made a light meal for themselves. Covenant ate slowly, as if he were trying to postpone the next phase of the quest. He foresaw only three alternatives – up the mountain, down the crevice, across the cleft – and they all looked bad to him. He did not want to do any kind of climbing or jumping; the simple proximity of precipices made him nervous. But when he saw that the High Lord was waiting for him, he recollected the terms of his bargain. He finished what he was eating, and tried to brace himself for whatever Amok had in mind.

Gripping the Staff of Law firmly, Elena turned to her guide. 'Amok, we are ready. What should be done with the Ranyhyn? Will you have us ride or walk?'

'That is your choice, High Lord,' said Amok with a grin. 'If the Ranyhyn remain, they will not be needed. If they depart, you will be forced to resummon them.'

'Then we must walk to follow you now?'

'Follow me? I have said nothing of leaving this place.'

'Is the Seventh Ward here?' she asked quickly.

'No.'

'Then it is elsewhere.'

'Yes, High Lord.'

'If it is elsewhere, we must go to it.'

'That is true. The Seventh Ward cannot be brought to you.'

'To go to it, we must walk or ride.'

'That also is true.'

'Which?'

As he listened to this exchange, Covenant felt a quiet admiration for the way in which Elena tackled Amok's vagueness. Her past experience appeared to have taught her how to corner the youth. But with his next answer he eluded her.

'That is your choice,' he repeated. 'Decide and go.'

'Do you not lead us?'

'No.'

'Why not?'

'I act according to my nature. I do what I have been created to do.'

'Amok, are you not the way and the door of the Seventh Ward?'

'Yes, High Lord.'

'Then you must guide us.'

'No.'

'Why not?' she demanded again. 'Are you capricious?' Covenant heard a hint of desperation in her tone.

Amok replied in mild reproof, 'High Lord, I have been created for the purpose I serve. If I appear wilful, you must ask my maker to explain me.'

'In other words,' Covenant interjected heavily, 'we're stuck without the other four Wards. This is Kevin's way of protecting — whatever it is. Without the clues he planted with such cleverness in the other Wards, we're up against a blank wall.'

'The *krill* of Loric came to life,' said Amok. 'That is the appointed word. And the Land is in peril. Therefore I have made myself accessible. I can do no more. I must serve my purpose.'

The High Lord searched him for a moment, then said sternly, 'Amok, are my companions unsuitable to your purpose in some way?'

'Your companions must suit themselves. I am the way and the door. I do not judge those who seek.'

'Amok' — she hung fire, and her lips moved silently as if she were reciting a list of her choices – 'are there conditions to be met – before you can guide us onward?'

Amok bowed recognition of her question, and answered with a chuckle, 'Yes, High Lord.'

'Will you guide us to the Seventh Ward when the conditions are met?'

'That is the purpose of my creation.'

'What are your conditions?'

'There is only one. If you desire more, you must conceive them without my aid.'

'What is your condition, Amok?'

The youth gazed impishly askance at Elena. 'High Lord,' he said in a tone of soaring glee, 'you must name the power of the Seventh Ward.'

She gaped at him for an instant, then exclaimed, 'Melenkurion! You know I lack that knowledge.'

He was unmoved. 'Then perhaps it is well that the Ranyhyn have not departed. They can bear you to Revelstone. If you gain wisdom there, you may return. You will find me here.' With a bow of infuriating insouciance, he waved his arms and vanished.

She stared after him and clenched the Staff as if she meant to strike the empty air of his absence. Her back was to Covenant; he could not see what was happening to her face, but the tension of her shoulders made him fear that her eyes were drawing into focus. At that thought, blood pounded in his temples. He reached out, tried to interrupt or distract her.

His touch caused her to swing around towards him. Her face looked emaciated – her flesh was tight over the pale intensity of her skull – and she seemed astonished, as if she had just discovered her capacity for panic. But she did not move into his arms. She halted, deliberately closed her eyes. The bones of her jaw and cheeks and forehead concentrated on him.

He felt an abyss opening in his mind.

He did not comprehend the black, yawning sensation. Elena stood before him in the shadow of *Melenkurion* Skyweir like an icon of gleaming bone robed in blue; but behind her, behind the solid stone of Rivenrock, darkness widened like a crack across the cistern of his thoughts. The rift sucked at him; he was losing himself.

The sensation came from Elena.

Suddenly, he understood. She was attempting to meld her mind with his.

A glare of fear shot through the sable vertigo which drained him. It illuminated his peril; if he abandoned himself to the melding, she would learn the truth about him. He could not afford such a plunge, could never have afforded it. Crying, No! he recoiled, staggered back away from her within himself.

The pressure eased. He found that his body was also retreating. With an effort, he stopped, raised his head.

Elena's eyes were wide with disappointment and grief, and she leaned painfully on the Staff of Law. 'Pardon me, beloved,' she breathed. 'I have asked for more than you are ready to give.' For a moment, she remained still, gave him a chance to respond. Then she groaned, 'I must think,' and turned away. Supporting herself with the Staff, she moved slowly along the cleft towards the outer edge of the plateau.

Shaken, Covenant sat straight down on the rock, and caught his head in his hands. Conflicting emotions tore at him. He was dismayed by his narrow escape, and angry at his weakness. To save himself, he had hurt Elena. He thought that he should go to her, but something in the focused isolation of her figure warned him not to intrude. For a time, he gazed at her with an ache in his heart. Then he climbed to his feet, muttering at the needless air, 'He could've had the decency to tell us – at least before she lost her Ranyhyn.'

To his surprise, the First Mark answered, 'Amok acts according to the law of his creation. He cannot break that law merely to avoid pain.'

Covenant threw up his hands in disgust. Fulminating uselessly, he stalked away across the plateau.

He spent the remainder of the afternoon roving restlessly from place to place across Rivenrock, searching for some clue to the continuation of Amok's trail. After a while, he calmed down enough to understand Morin's comment on Amok. Morin and Bannor were the prisoners of their Vow; they could speak with authority about the exigencies of an implacable law. But if the Bloodguard sympathized with Amok, that was just one more coffin nail in the doom of the High Lord's quest.

Covenant's effectlessness was another such nail. He could hear the inflated fatuity of his bargain mocking him now. How could he help Elena? He did not even know enough to grasp the issues Amok raised. Though his disconsolate hiking covered a wide section of the plateau, he learned nothing of any significance. The barren stone was like his inefficacy – irreducible and binding. While the last sunlight turned to dust in the sky, he bent his steps towards the graveling glow which marked the High Lord's camp. He was brooding on the familiar idea that futility governed his very existence.

He found Elena beside her pot of graveling. She looked both worn and whetted, as if the pressure on her ground down her individuality, fitted her to the pattern of her Lord's duty. Resolution gleamed in the honed patina of her bones. She had accepted all the implications of her burden.

Covenant cleared his throat awkwardly. 'What have you got? Have you figured it out?'

In a distant voice, she asked, 'How great is your knowledge of Warmark Troy's battle plan?'

'I know generally what he's trying to do – nothing specific.'

'If his plan did not fail, the battle began yesterday.'

He considered for a moment, then inquired carefully, 'Where does that leave us?'

'We must meet Amok's condition.'

He gestured his incomprehension. 'How?'

'I don't know. But I believe that it may be done.'

'You're missing four Wards.'

'Yes,' she sighed. 'Kevin clearly intended that we should gain the Seventh Ward only after mastering the first Six. But Amok has already violated that intent. Knowing that we have not comprehended Loric's *krill*, he still returned to us. He saw the Land's peril, and returned. This shows some freedom – some discretion. He is not explicitly bound by his law at all points.'

She paused, and after a moment Covenant said, 'Offhand, I would say that makes him dangerous. Why would he drag us all the way out here when he knew we would get stuck – unless he was trying to distract you from the war?'

'Amok intends no betrayal. I hear no malice in him.'

To penetrate her abstraction, he snapped, 'You can be fooled. Or are you forgetting that Kevin even accepted Foul as a Lord?'

Steadily, Elena replied, 'Perhaps the first six Wards do not contain the name of this power. Perhaps they teach only the way in which Amok may be brought to speak its name himself.'

'In that case – '

'Amok guided us here because in some way it is possible for us to meet his condition.'

'But can you find the right questions?'

'I must. What other choice exists for me? I cannot rejoin the Warward now.'

Her voice had a dull finality, as if she were passing sentence on herself. Early the next morning, she called Amok.

He appeared, grinning boyishly. She gripped the Staff of Law in both hands and braced it on the rock before her.

In the dawn under *Melenkurion* Skyweir, they began to duel for access to the Seventh Ward.

For two days, High Lord Elena strove to wrest the prerequisite name from Amok. During the second day, a massive storm brooded on the southeastern horizon, but it did not approach Rivenrock, and everyone ignored it. While Covenant sat twisting his ring around his finger, or paced restlessly beside the combatants, or wandered muttering away at intervals to escape the strain, she probed Amok with every question she could devise. At times, she worked methodically; at others, intuitively. She elaborated ideas for his assent or denial. She forced him to recite his answers at greater and greater length. She led him through painstaking rehearsals of known ground, and launched him with all her accuracy towards the unknown. She built traps of logic for him, tried to fence him into contradictions. She sought to meld her mind with his.

It was like duelling with a pool of water. Every slash and counter of her questions touched him as if she had slapped a pond with the flat of her blade. His answers splashed at every inquiry. But when she strove to catch him on her need's point, she passed through him and left no mark. Occasionally he allowed himself a laughing riposte, but for the most part he parried her questions with his accustomed cheerful evasiveness. Her toil earned no success. By sunset, she was trembling with frustration and suppressed fury and psychic starvation. The very solidity of Rivenrock seemed to jeer at her.

In the evenings, Covenant comforted her according to the terms of his bargain. He said nothing of his own fears and doubts, his helplessness, his growing conviction that Amok was impenetrable; he said nothing about himself at all. Instead, he gave her his best attention, concentrated on her with every resource he possessed.

But all his efforts could not touch the core of her distress. She was learning that she did not suffice to meet the Land's need, and that was a grief for which there was no consolation. Late at night, she made muffled grating noises, as if she ground her teeth to keep herself from weeping. And in the morning of the third day – the thirty-second since she had left Revelstone – she neared the end of her endurance. Her gaze was starved and hollow, and it had an angle of farewell.

Thickly, Covenant asked her what she was going to do.

'I will appeal.' Her voice had a raw, flagellated sound. She looked as frail as a skeleton – mere brave, fragile bones standing in the path of someone who, for all his boyish gaiety, was as unmanageable as an avalanche. A presage like an alarm in his head told Covenant that her crisis was at hand. If Amok did not respond to her appeals, she might turn to the last resort of her strange inner force.

The violence of that possibility frightened him. He caught himself on the verge of asking her to stop, give up the attempt. But he remembered his bargain; his brain raced after alternatives.

He accepted her argument that the answer to Amok's condition must be accessible. But he believed that she would not find it; she was approaching the problem from the wrong side. Yet it seemed to be the only side. Kicking at the rubbish which clogged his mind, he tried to imagine other approaches.

While his thoughts scrambled for some kind of saving intuition, High Lord Elena took her stance, and summoned Amok. The youth appeared at once. He greeted her with a florid bow, and said, 'High Lord, what is your will today? Shall we set aside our sparring, and sing glad songs together?'

'Amok, hear me.' Her voice grated. Covenant could hear depths of self-punishment in her. 'I will play no more games of inquiry with you.' Her tone expressed both dignity and desperation. 'The need of the Land will permit no more delay. Already, there is war in the distance – bloodshed and death. The Despiser marches against all that High Lord Kevin sought to preserve when he created his Wards. This insisting upon conditions is false loyalty to his intent. Amok, I appeal. In the name of the Land, guide us to the Seventh Ward.'

Her supplication seemed to touch him, and his reply was inordinately grave. 'High Lord, I cannot. I am as I was made to be. Should I make the attempt, I would cease to exist.'

'Then teach us the way, so that we may follow it alone.'

Amok shook his head. 'Then also I would cease to exist.'

For a moment, she paused as if she were defeated. But in the silence, her shoulders straightened. Abruptly, she lifted the Staff of Law, held it horizontally before her like a weapon. 'Amok,' she commanded, 'place your hands upon the Staff.'

The youth looked without flinching into the authority of her face. Slowly, he obeyed. His hands rested lightly between hers on the rune-carved wood.

She gave a high, strange cry. At once, fire blossomed along the Staff; viridian flames opened from all the wood. The blaze swept over her hands and Amok's; it intensified as if it were feeding on their fingers. It hummed with deep power, and radiated a sharp aroma like the smell of duress.

'Kevin-born Amok!' she exclaimed through the hum. 'Way and door to the Seventh Ward! By the power of the Staff of Law – in the name of High Lord Kevin son of Loric who made you – I adjure you. Tell me the name of the Seventh Ward's power!'

Covenant felt the force of her command. Though it was not levelled at him – though he was not touching the Staff – he gagged over the effort to utter a name he did not know.

But Amok met her without blinking, and his voice cut clearly through the flame of the Staff. 'No, High Lord. I am impervious to compulsion. You cannot touch me.'

'By the Seven!' she shouted. 'I will not be denied!' She raged as if she were using a fury to hold back a scream. '*Melenkurion abatha!* Tell me the name!'

'No,' Amok repeated.

Savagely, she tore the Staff out of his hands. Its flame gathered, mounted, then sprang loudly into the sky like a bolt of thunder.

He gave a shrug, and disappeared.

For a long, shocked moment, the High Lord stood frozen, staring at Amok's absence. Then a shudder ran through her, and she turned towards Covenant as if she had the weight of a mountain on her shoulders. Her face looked like a wilderland. She took two tottering steps, and stopped to brace herself on the Staff. Her gaze was blank; all her force was focused inward, against herself.

'Failed,' she gasped. 'Doomed.' Anguish twisted her mouth. 'I have doomed the Land.'

Covenant could not stand the sight. Forgetting all his issueless thoughts, he hurried to say, 'There's got to be something else we can do.'

She replied with an appalling softness. Tenderly, almost caressingly, she said, 'Do you believe in the white gold? Can you use it to meet Amok's condition?' Her voice had a sound of madness. But the next instant, her passion flared outward. With all her strength, she pounded the Staff against Rivenrock, and cried, 'Then do so!'

The power she unleashed caused a wide section of the plateau to lurch like a stricken raft. The rock bucked and plunged; seamless waves of force rolled through it from the Staff.

The heaving knocked Covenant off his feet. He stumbled, fell towards the cleft.

Almost at once, Elena regained control over herself. She snatched back the Staff's power, shouted to the Bloodguard. But Bannor's reflexes were swifter. While the rock still pitched, he bounded surefootedly across it and caught Covenant's arm.

For a moment, Covenant was too stunned to do anything but hang limply in Bannor's grip. The High Lord's violence flooded through him, sweeping everything else out of his awareness. But then he noticed the pain of Bannor's grasp on his arm. He could feel something prophetic in the ancient strength with which Bannor clenched him, kept him alive. The Bloodguard had an iron grip, surer than the stone of Rivenrock. When he heard Elena moan, 'Beloved! Have I harmed you?' he was already muttering half aloud, 'Wait. Hold on. I've got it.'

His eyes were closed. He opened them, and discovered that Bannor was holding him erect. Elena was nearby; she flung her arms around him and hid her face in his shoulder. He said, 'I've got it.' She ignored him, started to mumble contrition into his shoulder. To stop her, he said sharply, 'Forget it. I must be losing my mind. I should have figured this out days ago.'

Finally she heard him. She released him and stepped back. Her ravaged face stiffened. She caught her breath between her teeth, pushed a hand through her hair. Slowly, she became a Lord again. Her voice was unsteady but lucid as she said, 'What have you learned?'

Bannor released Covenant also, and the Unbeliever stood wavering on his own. His feet distrusted the stone, but he locked his knees, and tried to disregard the sensation. The problem was in his brain; all his preconceptions had shifted. He wanted to speak quickly, ease Elena's urgent distress. But he had missed too many clues. He needed to approach his intuition slowly, so that he could pull all its strands together.

He tried to clear his head by shaking it. Elena winced as if he were reminding her of her outburst. He made a placating gesture towards her, and turned to confront the Bloodguard. Intently, he scrutinized the blank metal of their faces, searched them for some flicker or hue of duplicity, ulterior purpose, which would verify his intuition. But their ancient, sleepless eyes seemed to conceal nothing, reveal nothing. He felt an instant of panic at the idea that he might be wrong, but he pushed it down, and asked as calmly as he could, 'Bannor, how old are you?'

'We are the Bloodguard,' Bannor replied. 'Our Vow was sworn in the youth of Kevin's High Lordship.'

'Before the Desecration?'

'Yes, ur-Lord.'

'Before Kevin found out that Foul was really an enemy?'

'Yes.'

'And you personally, Bannor? How old are you?'

'I was among the first *Haruchai* who entered the Land. I shared in the first swearing of the Vow.'

'That was centuries ago.' Covenant paused before he asked, 'How well do you remember Kevin?'

'Step softly,' Elena cautioned. 'Do not mock the Bloodguard.'

Bannor did not acknowledge her concern. He answered the Unbeliever inflexibly, 'We do not forget.'

'I suppose not,' Covenant sighed. 'What a hell of a way to live.' For a moment, he gazed away towards the mountain, looking for courage. Then, with sudden harshness, he went on, 'You knew

Kevin when he made his Wards. You knew him and you remember. You were with him when he gave the First Ward to the Giants. You were with him when he hid the Second in those bloody catacombs under Mount Thunder. How many times did you come here with him, Bannor?'

The Bloodguard cocked one eyebrow fractionally. 'High Lord Kevin made no sojourns to Rivenrock or *Melenkurion* Skyweir.'

That answer rocked Covenant. 'None?' His protest burst out before he could stop it. 'Are you telling me you've never been here before?'

'We are the first Bloodguard to stand on Rivenrock,' Bannor replied flatly.

'Then how – ? Wait. Hold on.' Covenant stared dizzily, then hit his forehead with the heel of his hand. 'Right. If the Ward is some kind of natural phenomenon – like the Illearth Stone – if it isn't something he put here – Kevin wouldn't have to come here to know about it. Loric or somebody could have told him. Loric could have told anybody.'

He took a deep breath to steady himself. 'But everybody who might have known about it died in the Desecration. Except you.'

Bannor blinked at Covenant as if his words had no meaning.

'Listen to me, Bannor,' he went on. 'A lot of things are finally starting to make sense. You reacted strangely – when Amok turned up at Revelstone that first time. You reacted strangely when he turned up at Revelwood. And you let the High Lord herself follow him into the mountains with just two Bloodguard to protect her. Just two, Bannor! And when we end up stuck here on this godforsaken rock, Morin has the actual gall to apologize for Amok. Hellfire! Bannor, you should have at least told the High Lord what you know about this Ward. What kind of loyal do you think you are?'

Elena cautioned Covenant again. But her tone had changed; his thinking intrigued her.

'We are the Bloodguard,' Bannor said. 'You cannot raise doubt against us. We do not *know* Amok's intent.'

Covenant heard the slight stress which Bannor placed on the word *know*. To his own surprise, he felt a sudden desire to take Bannor at his word, leave what the Bloodguard *knew* alone. But he forced himself to ask, 'Know, Bannor? How can you not know? You've trusted him too much for that.'

Bannor countered as he had previously, 'We do not trust him. The High Lord chooses to follow him. We do not ask for more.'

'The hell you don't.' His effort of self-compulsion made him brutal. 'And stop giving me that blank look. You people came to the Land, and you swore a Vow to protect Kevin. You swore to preserve

733

him or at least give your lives for him and the Lords and Revelstone until Time itself came to an end, if not forever, or why are you bereft even of the simple decency of sleep? But that poor desperate man outsmarted you. He actively saved you when he destroyed himself and everything else he merely believed in. So there you were, hanging from your Vow in empty space as if all the reasons in the world had suddenly disappeared.

'And then! Then you get a second chance to do your Vow right when the new Lords come along. But what happens? Amok turns up out of nowhere, and there's a war on against Foul himself – and what do you do? You let this creation of Kevin's lead the High Lord away as if it were safe and she didn't have anything better to do.

'Let me tell you something, Bannor. Maybe you don't positively know Amok. You must have learned some kind of distrust from Kevin. But you sure as hell understand what Amok is doing. And you *approve!*' The abrupt ferocity of his own yell stopped him for an instant. He felt shaken by the moral judgments he saw in Bannor. Thickly, he continued, 'Or why are you risking her for the sake of something created by the only man who has ever succeeded in casting doubt on your incorruptibility?'

Without warning, Amok appeared. The youth's arrival startled Covenant, but he took it as a sign that he was on the right track. With a heavy sigh, he said, 'Why in the name of your Vow or at least simple friendship didn't you tell the High Lord about Amok when he first showed up?'

Bannor's gaze did not waver. In his familiar, awkward, atonal inflection, he replied, 'Ur-Lord, we have seen the Desecration. We have seen the fruit of perilous lore. Lore is not knowledge. Lore is a weapon, a sword or spear. The Bloodguard have no use for weapons. Any knife may turn and wound the hand which wields it. Yet the Lords desire lore. They do work of value with it. Therefore we do not resist it, though we do not touch it or serve it or save it.

'High Lord Kevin made his Wards to preserve his lore – and to lessen the peril that his weapons might fall into unready hands. This we approve. We are the Bloodguard. We do not speak of lore. We speak only of what we know.'

Covenant could not go on. He felt that he had already multiplied his offences against Bannor too much. And he was moved by what Bannor said, despite the Bloodguard's flat tone.

But Elena had learned enough to pursue his reasoning. Her voice was both quiet and authoritative as she said, 'First Mark – Bannor – the Bloodguard must make a decision now. Hear me. I am Elena, High Lord by the choice of the Council. This is a question of loyalty. Will you serve dead Kevin's wisdom, or will you serve me? In the past, you have served two causes, the dead and the living. You have served both well. But here you must choose. In the Land's need, there is no longer any middle way. There will be blood and blame upon us all if we allow Corruption to prevail.'

Slowly, Bannor turned towards the First Mark. They regarded each other in silence for a long moment. Then Morin faced the High Lord with a magisterial look in his eyes. 'High Lord,' he said, 'we do not know the name of the Seventh Ward's power. We have heard many names – some false, others dead. But one name we have heard only uttered in whispers by High Lord Kevin and his Council.

'That name is the *Power of Command*.'

When Amok heard the name, he nodded until his hair seemed to dance with glee.

24

DESCENT TO EARTHROOT

Covenant found that he was sweating. Despite the chill breeze, his forehead was damp. Moisture itched in his beard, and cold perspiration ran down his spine. Morin's submission left him feeling curiously depleted. For a moment, he looked up at the sun as if to ask it why it did not warm him.

Melenkurion's spires reached into the morning like fingers straining to bracket the sun. Their glaciered tips caught the light brilliantly; the reflected dazzle made Covenant's eyes water. The massive stone of the peaks intimidated him. Blinking rapidly, he forced his gaze back to High Lord Elena.

Through his sun blindness, he seemed to see only her brown, blonde-raddled hair. The lighter tresses gleamed as if they were burnished. But as he blinked, his vision cleared. He made out her face. She was vivid with smiles. A new thrill of life lit her countenance with recovered hope. She did not speak, but her lips formed the one word, *Beloved*.

Covenant felt that he had betrayed her.

Morin and Bannor stood almost shoulder to shoulder behind her. Nothing in the alert poise of their balance, or in the relaxed readiness of their arms, expressed any surprise or regret at the decision they had made. Yet Covenant knew they had fundamentally altered the character of their service to the Lords. He had exacted that from them. He wished he could apologize in some way which would have meaning to the Bloodguard.

But there was nothing he could say to them. They were too absolute to accept any gesture of contrition. Their solitary communion with their Vow left him no way in which to approach them. No apology was sufficient.

'The Power of Command,' he breathed weakly. 'Have mercy on me.' Unable to bear the sight of Elena's relieved, triumphant, grateful smile, or of Amok's grin, he turned away and walked wearily out across the plateau towards Rivenrock's edge as if his feet were trying to learn again the solidity of the stone.

He moved parallel to the cleft, but stayed a safe distance from it. As soon as he could see a substantial swath of Garroting Deep beyond the cliff edge, he stopped. There he remained, hoping both that Elena would come to him and that she would not.

The prevailing breeze from the Forest blew in his face, and for the first time in many days he was able to distinguish the tang of the season. He found that the autumn of the Land had turned its corner, travelled its annual round from joy to sorrow. The air no longer gleamed with abundance and fruition, with ripeness either glad or grim. Now the breeze tasted like the leading edge of winter – a sere augury, promising long nights and barrenness and cold.

As he smelled the air, he realized that Garroting Deep had no fall colour change. He could make out stark black stands where the trees had already lost their leaves, but no blazonry palliated the Deep's darkness. It went without transition or adornment from summer to winter. He sensed the reason with his eyes and nose; the old Forest's angry clench of consciousness consumed all its strength and will, left it with neither the ability nor the desire to spend itself in mere displays of splendour.

Then he heard footsteps behind him, and recognized Elena's tread. To forestall whatever she wanted to tell him or ask him, he said, 'You know, where I come from, the people who did this to a forest would be called pioneers – a very special breed of heroes, since instead of killing other human beings they concentrate on slaughtering nature itself. In fact, I know people who claim that all our social discomfort comes from the mere fact that we've got nothing left to pioneer.'

'Beloved,' she said softly, 'you are not well. What is amiss?'

'Amiss?' He could not bring himself to look at her. His mouth was full of his bargain, and he had to swallow hard before he could say, 'Don't mind me. I'm like that Forest down there. Sometimes I can't seem to help remembering.'

In the silence, he sensed how little this answer satisfied her. She cared about him, wanted to understand him. But the rebirth of hope had restored the urgency of her duty. He knew that she could not spare the time to explore him now. He nodded morosely as she said, 'I must go – the Land's need bears heavily upon me.' Then she added, 'Will you remain here – await my return?'

At last, he found the strength to turn and face her. He met the solemn set of her face, the displaced otherness of her gaze, and said gruffly, 'Stay behind? And miss risking my neck again? Nonsense. I haven't had a chance like this since I was in Mount Thunder.'

His sarcasm was sharper than he had intended, but she seemed to accept it. She smiled, touched him lightly on the arm with the fingers of one hand. 'Come then, beloved,' she said. 'The Bloodguard are prepared. We must depart before Amok places other obstacles in our way.'

He tried to smile in return, but the uncertain muscles of his face treated the attempt like a grimace. Muttering at his failure, he went with her back towards the Bloodguard and Amok. As they walked, he watched her sidelong, assessed her covertly. The strain of the past three days had been pushed into the background; her forthright stride and resolute features expressed new purpose, strength. The resurgence of hope enabled her to discount mere exhaustion. But her knuckles were tense as she gripped the Staff, and her head was thrust forward at a hungry angle. She made Covenant's bargain lie unquiet in him, as if he were an inadequate and unbinding grave.

In his mind, he could still feel Rivenrock heaving. He needed steadier footing; nothing would save him if he could not keep his balance.

Vaguely, he observed that the First Mark and Bannor were indeed ready to travel. They had bound all the supplies into bundles, and had tied these to their backs with *clingor* thongs. And Amok sparkled with eagerness; visions seemed to caper in his gay hair. The three of them gave Covenant an acute pang of unpreparedness. He did not feel equal to whatever lay ahead of the High Lord's party. A pulse of anxiety began to run through his weary mood. There was something that he needed to do; he needed to try to recover his integrity in some way. But he did not know how.

He watched as the High Lord bade farewell to the Ranyhyn. They greeted her gladly, stamping their feet and nickering in pleasure at the prospect of activity after three days of patient waiting. She embraced each of the great horses, then stepped back, gripped the Staff, and saluted them in the Ramen fashion.

The Ranyhyn responded by tossing their manes. They regarded her with proud, laughing eyes as she addressed them.

'Brave Ranyhyn – first love of my life – I thank you for your service. We have been honoured. But now we must go on foot for a time. If we survive our path, we will call upon you to carry us back to Revelstone – in victory or defeat, we will need the broad backs of your strength.

'For the present, be free. Roam the lands your hearts and hooves desire. And if it should come to pass that we do not call – if you return unsummoned to the Plains of Ra – then, brave Ranyhyn, tell all your kindred of Myrha. She saved my life in the landslide, and gave her own for a lesser horse. Tell all the Ranyhyn that Elena daughter of Lena, High Lord by the choice of the Council, and holder of the Staff of Law, is proud of your friendship. You are the Tail of the Sky, Mane of the World.'

Raising the Staff, she cried, 'Ranyhyn! Hail!'

The great horses answered with a whinny that echoed off the face of *Melenkurion* Skyweir. Then they wheeled and galloped away, taking with them Covenant's mustang. Their hooves clattered like a roll of fire on the stone as they swept northward and out of sight around the curve of the mountain.

When Elena turned back towards her companions, her sense of loss showed clearly in her face. In a sad voice, she said, 'Come. If we must travel without the Ranyhyn, then let us at least travel swiftly.'

At once, she turned expectantly to Amok. The ancient youth responded with an ornate bow, and started walking jauntily towards the place where the Skyweir's cliff joined the cleft of the plateau.

Covenant tugged at his beard, and watched hopelessly as Elena and Morin followed Amok.

Then, as abruptly as gasping, he exclaimed, 'Wait!' The fingers of his right hand tingled in his beard. 'Hang on.' The High Lord looked questioningly at him. He said, 'I need a knife. And some water. And a mirror, if you've got one – I don't want to cut my throat.'

Elena said evenly, 'Ur-Lord, we must go. We have lost so much time – and the Land is in need.'

'It's important,' he snapped. 'Have you got a knife? The blade of my penknife isn't long enough.'

For a moment, she studied him as if his conduct were a mystery. Then, slowly, she nodded to Morin. The First Mark unslung his bundle, opened it, and took out a stone knife, a leather waterskin, and a shallow bowl. These he handed to the Unbeliever. At once, Covenant sat down on the stone, filled the bowl, and began to wet his beard.

He could feel the High Lord's presence as she stood directly before him – he could almost taste the tension with which she held the Staff – but he concentrated on scrubbing water into his whiskers.

His heart raced as if he were engaged in something dangerous. He had a vivid sense of what he was giving up. But he was impelled by the sudden conviction that his bargain was false because it had not cost him enough. When he picked up the knife, he did so to seal his compromise with his fate.

Elena stopped him. In a low, harsh voice, she said, 'Thomas Covenant.'

The way she said his name forced him to raise his head.

'Where is the urgency in this?' She controlled her harshness by speaking quietly, but her indignation was tangible in her voice. 'We have spent three days in delay and ignorance. Do you now mock the Land's need? Is it your deliberate wish to prevent this quest from success?'

An angry rejoinder leaped to his lips. But the terms of his bargain required him to repress it. He bent his head again, splashed more water into his beard. 'Sit down. I'll try to explain.'

The High Lord seated herself cross-legged before him.

He could not comfortably meet her gaze. And he did not want to look at *Melenkurion* Skyweir; it stood too austerely, coldly, behind her. Instead, he watched his hands as they toyed with the stone knife.

'All right,' he said awkwardly. 'I'm not the kind of person who grows beards. They itch. And they make me look like a fanatic. They – So I've been letting this one grow for a reason. It's a way of proving – a way to demonstrate so that even somebody as thick-headed and generally incoherent as I am can see it – when I wake up in the real world and find that I don't have this beard I've been growing, then I'll know for sure that all this is a delusion. It's proof. Forty or fifty days' worth of beard doesn't just vanish. Unless it was never really there.'

She continued to stare at him. But her tone changed. She recognized the importance of his self-revelation. 'Then why do you now wish to cut it away?'

He trembled to think of the risks he was taking. But he needed freedom, and his bargain promised to provide it. Striving to keep the fear of discovery out of his voice, he told her as much of the truth as he could afford.

'I've made another deal – like the one I made with the Ranyhyn. I'm not trying to prove that the Land isn't real any more.' In the back of his mind, he pleaded, Please don't ask me anything else. I don't want to lie to you.

She probed him with her eyes. 'Do you believe, then – do you accept the Land?'

In his relief, he almost sighed aloud. He could look at her squarely to answer this. 'No. But I'm willing to stop fighting about it. You've done so much for me.'

'Ah, beloved!' she breathed with sudden intensity, 'I have done nothing – I have only followed my heart. Within my Lord's duty, I would do anything for you.'

He seemed to see her affection for him in the very hue of her skin. He wanted to lean forward, touch her, kiss her, but the presence of the Bloodguard restrained him. Instead, he handed her the knife.

He was abdicating himself to her, and she knew it. A glow of pleasure filled her face as she took the knife. 'Do not fear, beloved,' she whispered. 'I will preserve you.'

Carefully, as if she were performing a rite, she drew close to him and began to cut his beard.

He winced instinctively when the blade first touched him. But he gritted himself into stillness, locked his jaw, told himself that he was safer in her hands than in his own. He could feel the deadliness of the keen edge as it passed over his flesh – it conjured up images of festering wounds and gangrene – but he closed his eyes, and remained motionless.

The knife tugged at his beard, but the sharpness of the blade kept the pull from becoming painful. And soon her fingers found his knotted jaw muscle. She stroked his clenching to reassure him. With an effort, he opened his eyes. She met his gaze as if she were smiling through a mist of love. Gently, she tilted back his head, and cleaned the beard away from his neck with smooth, confident strokes.

Then she was done. His bared flesh felt vivid in the air, and he rubbed his face with his hands, relishing the fresh texture of his cheeks and neck. Again, he wanted to kiss Elena. To answer her smile, he stood up and said, 'Now I'm ready. Let's go.'

She grasped the Staff of Law, sprang lightly to her feet. In a tone of high gaiety, she said to Amok, 'Will you now lead us to the Seventh Ward?'

Amok beckoned brightly, as if he were inviting her to a game, and started once more towards the place where the cleft of Rivenrock vanished under *Melenkurion* Skyweir. Morin quickly repacked his bundle, and placed himself behind Amok; Elena and Covenant followed the First Mark; and Bannor brought up the rear.

In this formation, they began the last phase of their quest for the Power of Command.

They crossed the plateau briskly. Amok soon reached the juncture of cliff and cleft. There he waved to his companions, grinned happily, and jumped into the crevice.

Covenant gasped in spite of himself, and hurried with Elena to the edge. When they peered into the narrow blackness of the chasm, they saw Amok, standing on a ledge in the opposite wall. The ledge began fifteen or twenty feet below and a few feet under the overhang of the mountain. It was not clearly visible. The blank stone and shadowed dimness of the cleft formed a featureless abyss. Amok seemed to be standing on darkness which led to darkness.

'Hellfire!' Covenant groaned as he looked down. He felt dizzy already. 'Forget it. Just forget I ever mentioned it.'

'Come!' said Amok cheerfully. 'Follow!' His voice sounded over the distant, subterranean gush of the river. With an insouciant stride, he moved away into the mountain. At once, the gloom swallowed him completely.

Morin glanced at the High Lord. When she nodded, he leaped into the cleft, landed where Amok had been standing a moment before. He took one step to the side, and waited.

'Don't be ridiculous,' Covenant muttered as if he were talking to the dank, chill breeze which blew out of the crevice. 'I'm no Bloodguard. I'm just ordinary flesh and blood. I get dizzy when I stand on a chair. Sometimes I get dizzy when I just stand.'

The High Lord was not listening to him. She murmured a few old words to the Staff, and watched intently as it burst into flame. Then she stepped out into the darkness. Morin caught her as her feet touched the ledge. She moved past him, and positioned herself so that the light of the Staff illuminated the jump for Covenant.

The Unbeliever found Bannor looking at him speculatively.

'Go on ahead,' said Covenant. 'Give me time to get up my courage. I'll catch up with you in a year or two.' He was sweating again, and his perspiration stung the scraped skin of his cheeks and neck. He looked up at the mountain to steady himself, efface the effects of the chasm from his mind.

Without warning, Bannor caught him from behind, lifted him, and carried him to the cleft.

'Don't touch me!' Covenant spluttered. He tried to break free, but Bannor's grip was too strong. 'By hell! I – !' His voice scaled into a yell as Bannor threw him over the edge.

Morin caught him deftly, and placed him, wide-eyed and trembling, on the ledge at Elena's side.

A moment later, Bannor made the jump, and the First Mark passed Covenant and Elena to stand between her and Amok. Covenant watched their movements through a stunned fog. Numbly, he pressed his back against the solid stone, and stared into the chasm as if it were a tomb. Some time seemed to pass before he noticed the High Lord's reassuring hold on his arm.

'Don't touch me,' he repeated aimlessly. 'Don't touch me.'

When she moved away, he followed her automatically, turning

his back on the sunlight and open sky above the cleft.

He rubbed his left shoulder against the stone wall, and kept close to Elena, stayed near her light. The Staff's incandescence cast a viridian aura over the High Lord's party, and reflected garishly off the dark, flat facets of the stone. It illuminated Amok's path without penetrating the gloom ahead. The ledge – never more than three feet wide – moved steadily downward. Above it, the ceiling of the cleft slowly expanded, took on the dimensions of a cavern. And the cleft itself widened as if it ran towards a prodigious hollow in the core of *Melenkurion* Skyweir.

Covenant felt the yawning rent in the mountain rocks as if it were beckoning to him, urging him seductively to accept the drowsy abandon of vertigo, trust the chasm's depths. He pressed himself harder against the stone, and clung to Elena's back with his eyes. Around him, darkness and massed weight squeezed the edges of the Staff's light. And at his back, he could hear the hovering vulture wings of his private doom. Gradually, he understood that he was walking into a crisis.

Underground! he rasped harshly at his improvidence. He could not forget how he had fallen into a crevice under Mount Thunder. That experience had brought him face-to-face with the failure of his old compromise, his bargain with the Ranyhyn. Hellfire! He felt he had done nothing to ready himself for an ordeal of caves.

Ahead of him, the High Lord followed Morin and Amok. They adjusted themselves to her pace, and she moved as fast as she safely could on the narrow ledge. Covenant was hard pressed to keep up with her. Her speed increased his apprehension; it made him feel that the rift was spreading its jaws beside him. He laboured fearfully down the ledge. It demanded all his concentration.

He had no way to measure duration or distance – had nothing with which to judge time except the accumulation of his fear and strain and weariness – but gradually the character of the cavern's ceiling changed. It spread out like a dome. After a while, Elena's fire lit only one small arc of the stone. Around it, spectral shapes peopled the darkness. Then the rough curve of rock within the Staff's light became gnarled and pitted, like the slow clenching of a frown on the cave's forehead. And finally the frown gave way to stalactites. Then the upper air bristled with crooked old shafts and spikes – poised spears and misdriven nails – pending lamias – slow, writhed excrescences of the mountain's inner sweat. Some of these had flat facets which reflected the Staff's fire in fragments, casting it like a chiaroscuro into the recessed groins of the cavern. And others leaned towards the ledge as if they were straining ponderously to strike the heads of the human interlopers.

For some distance, the stalactites grew thicker, longer, more intricate, until they filled the dome of the cavern. When Covenant mustered enough fortitude to look out over the crevice, he seemed to be gazing into a blue-lit, black, inverted forest – a packed stand of gnarled and ominous old trees with their roots in the ceiling. They created the impression that it was possible, on the sole trail of the ledge, for him to lose his way.

The sensation excoriated his stumbling fear. When Elena came abruptly to a stop, he almost flung his arms around her.

Beyond her in the Staff's velure light, he saw that a massive stalactite had angled downward and attached itself to the lip of the ledge. The stalactite hit there as if it had been violently slammed into place. Despite its ancientness, it seemed to quiver with the force of impact. Only a straight passage remained between the stalactite and the wall.

Amok halted before this narrow gap. He waited until his companions were close behind him. Then, speaking over his shoulder in an almost reverential tone, he said, 'Behold Damelon's Door – entryway to the Power of Command. For this reason among others, none may approach the Power in my absence. The knowledge of this unlocking is contained in none of High Lord Kevin's Wards. And any who dare Damelon's Door without this unlocking will not find the Power. They will wander forever lorn and pathless in the wilderness beyond. Now hear me. Pass swiftly through the entryway when it is opened. It will not remain open long.'

Elena nodded intently. Behind her, Covenant braced 'imself on her shoulder with his right hand. He had a sudden inchoate feeling that this was his last chance to turn back, to recant or undo the decisions which had brought him here. But the chance – if it was a chance – passed as quickly as it had come. Amok approached the Door.

With slow solemnity, the youth extended his right hand, touched the blank plane of the gap with his index finger. In silence he held his finger at that point, level with his chest.

A fine yellow filigree network began to grow in the air. Starting from Amok's fingertip, the delicate web of light spread outward in the plane of the gap. Like a skein slowly crystallizing into visibility, it expanded until it filled the whole Door.

Amok commanded, 'Come,' and stepped briskly through the web.

He did not break the delicate strands of light. Rather, he disappeared as he touched them. Covenant could see no trace of him on the ledge beyond the Door.

Morin followed Amok. He, too, vanished as he came in contact with the yellow web.

Then the High Lord started forward. Covenant stayed with her. He kept his grip on her shoulder; he was afraid of being separated from her. Boldly, she stepped into the gap. He held her and followed. When he touched the glistening network, he winced, but he felt no pain. A swift tingling like an instant of ants passed over his flesh as he crossed the gap. He could feel Bannor close behind him.

He found himself standing in a place different from the one he had expected.

As he looked around him, the web faded, vanished. But the Staff of Law continued to burn. Back through the gap, he could see the ledge and the stalactites and the chasm. But no chasm existed on this side of Damelon's Door. Instead there stretched a wide stone floor in which stalactites and stalagmites stood like awkward colonnades, and a mottled ceiling hunched over the open spaces. Hushed stillness filled the air; a moment passed before Covenant realized that he could no longer hear the low background rumble of *Melenkurion* Skyweir's river.

With an encompassing gesture, Amok said formally, 'Behold the Audience Hall of Earthroot. Here in ages long forgotten the sunless lake would rise in season to meet those who sought its waters. Now, as the Earthpower fades from mortal knowledge, the Audience Hall is unwet. Yet it retains a power of mazement, to foil those who are unready in heart and mind. All who enter here without the proper unlocking of Damelon's Door will be forever lost to life and use and name.'

Grinning, he turned to Elena. 'High Lord, brighten the Staff for a moment.'

She seemed to guess his intention. She straightened as if she anticipated awe; eagerness seemed to gleam on her forehead. Murmuring ritualistically, she struck the Staff's heel on the stone. The Staff flared, and a burst of flame sprang towards the ceiling.

The result staggered Covenant. The surge of flame sparked a reaction in all the stalactites and stalagmites. They became instantly glittering and reflective. Light ignited on every column, resonated, rang in dazzling peals back and forth across the cave. It burned into his eyes from every side until he felt that he was caught on the clapper of an immense bell of light. He tried to cover his eyes, but the clangour went on in his mind. Gasping, searching blindly for support, he began to founder.

Then Elena silenced the Staff. The clamouring light faded away, echoed into the distance like the aftermath of a clarion. Covenant found that he was on his knees with his hands clamped over his ears. Hesitantly, he looked up. All the reflections were gone; the columns had returned to their former rough illustre. As Elena helped him to his feet, he was muttering weakly, 'By hell. By hell.' Even her fond face, and the flat, unamazed countenances of the Bloodguard, could not counteract his feeling that he no longer knew where he was. And when Amok led the High Lord's party onward, Covenant kept stumbling as if he could not find his footing on the stone.

After they left the perilous cavern, time and distance passed confusedly for him. His retinae retained a capering dazzle which disoriented him. He could see that the High Lord and Amok descended a slope which spread out beyond the range of the Staff's light like a protracted shore, a colonnaded beach left dry by the recession of a subterranean sea. But his feet could not follow their path. His eyes told him that Amok led them directly down the slope, but his sense of balance registered alterations in direction, changes in the pitch and angle of descent. Whenever he closed his eyes, he lost all impression of straightness; he reeled on the uneven surface of a crooked trail.

He did not know where or how far he had travelled when Elena stopped for a brief meal. He did not know how long the halt lasted, or what distance he walked when it was over. All his senses were out of joint. When the High Lord halted again, and told him to rest, he sank down against a stalagmite and went to sleep without question.

In dreams he wandered like one of the lorn who had improvidently braved Damelon's Door in search of Earthroot – he could hear shrill, stricken wails of loss as if he were crying for his companions, crying for himself – and he awoke to a complete confusion. The darkness made him think that someone had pulled the fuses of his house while he lay bleeding and helpless on the floor beside his coffee table. Numbly, he groped for the receiver of the telephone, hoping that Joan had not yet hung up on him. But then his fumbling fingers recognized the texture of stone. With a choked groan, he sprang to his feet in the midnight under *Melenkurion* Skyweir.

Almost at once, the Staff flamed. In the blue light, Elena arose to catch him with her free arm and clasp him tightly. 'Beloved!' she murmured. 'Ah, beloved. Hold fast. I am here.' He hugged her achingly, pressed his face into her sweet hair until he could still his pain, regain his self-command. Then he slowly released her. He strove to express his thanks with a smile, but it broke and fell into pieces in his face. In a raw, rasping voice, he said, 'Where are we?'

Behind him, Amok fluted, 'We stand in the Aisle of Approach. Soon we will gain Earthrootstair.'

'What' – Covenant tried to clear his head – 'what time is it?'

'Time has no measure under *Melenkurion* Skyweir,' the youth replied imperviously.

'Oh, bloody hell.' Covenant groaned at the echo he heard in Amok's answer. He had been told too often that white gold was the crux of the arch of Time.

Elena came to his relief. 'The sun has risen to midmorning,' she said. 'This is the thirty-third day of our journey from Revelstone.' As an afterthought, she added, 'Tonight is the dark of the moon.'

The dark of the moon, he muttered mordantly to himself. Have mercy — Terrible things happened when the moon was dark. The Wraiths of Andelain had been attacked by ur-viles — Atiaran had never forgiven him for that.

The High Lord seemed to see his thoughts in his face. 'Beloved,' she said calmly, 'do not be so convinced of doom.' Then she turned away and started to prepare a spare meal.

Watching her — seeing her resolution and personal force implicit even in the way she performed this simple task — Covenant clenched his teeth, and kept the silence of his bargain.

He could hardly eat the food she handed to him. The effort of silence made him feel ill; holding down his passive lie seemed to knot his guts, make sustenance unpalatable. Yet he felt that he was starving. To ease his inanition, he forced down a little of the dry bread and cured meat and cheese. The rest he returned to Elena. He felt almost relieved when she followed Amok again into the darkness.

He went dumbly after her.

Sometime during the previous day, the High Lord's party had left behind the Audience Hall. Now they travelled a wide, featureless tunnel like a road through the stone. Elena's light easily reached the ceiling and walls. Their surfaces were oddly smooth, as if they had been rubbed for long ages by the movement of something rough and powerful. This smoothness made the tunnel seem like a conduit or artery. Covenant distrusted it; he half expected thick, laval ichor to come rushing up through it. As he moved, he played nervously with his ring, as if that small circle were the binding of his self-control.

Elena quickened her steps. He could see in her back that she was impelled by her mounting eagerness for the Power of Command.

At last, the tunnel changed. Its floors swung in a tight curve to the left, and its right wall broke off, opening into another crevice. The rift immediately became a substantial gulf. The stone shelf of the road narrowed until it was barely ten feet wide, then divided into rude steep stairs as it curved downward. In moments, the High Lord's party was on a stairway which spiralled around a central shaft into the chasm.

Many hundreds of feet below them, a fiery red glow lit the bottom of the gulf. Covenant felt that he was peering into an inferno.

He remembered where he had seen such a light before. It was rocklight – radiated stone-shine like that which the Cavewights used under Mount Thunder.

The descent affected him like vertigo. Within three rounds of the shaft, his head was reeling. Only Elena's unwavering light, and his acute concentration as he negotiated the uneven steps, saved him from pitching headlong over the edge. But he was grimly determined not to ask either Elena or Bannor for help. He could afford no more indebtedness; it would nullify his bargain, tip the scales of payment against him. No! he muttered to himself as he lurched down the steps. No. No more. Don't be so bloody helpless. Save something to bargain with. Keep going. Distantly, he heard himself panting, 'Don't touch me. Don't touch me.'

A spur of nausea rowelled him. His muscles bunched as if they were bracing for a fall. But he hugged his chest, and clung to Elena's light for support. Her flame bobbed above her like a tongue of courage. Slowly its blue illumination took on a red tinge as she worked down towards the gulf's glow.

He made the descent grimly, mechanically, like a volitionless puppet stalking down the irregular steps of his designated end. Round by round, he approached the source of the rocklight. Soon the red illumination made the Staff's flame unnecessary, and High Lord Elena extinguished it. Ahead of her, Amok began to move more swiftly, as if he were impatient, jealous of all delays which postponed the resolution of his existence. But Covenant followed at his own pace, effectively unconscious of anything but the spiralling stairs and his imperious dizziness. He went down the last distance through a high wash of rocklight as numbly as if he were sleep-walking.

When he reached the flat bottom, he took a few wooden steps towards the lake, then stopped, covered his eyes against the deep, fiery, red light, and shuddered as if his nerves jangled on the edge of hysteria.

Ahead of him, Amok crowed jubilantly, 'Behold, High Lord! The sunless lake of Earthroot! Unheavened sap and nectar of great *Melenkurion* Skyweir, the sire of mountains! Ah, behold it. The long years of my purpose are nearly done.' His words echoed clearly away, as if they were seconded by scores of light crystal voices.

Drawing a tremulous breath, Covenant opened his eyes. He was standing on the gradual shore of a still lake which spread out before him as far as he could see. Its stone roof was high, hidden in shadows, but the lake was lit everywhere by rocklight burning in the immense pillars which stood up like columns through the lake – or like roots of the mountain reaching down to the water. These columns or roots were evenly spaced along and across the cavern; they were repeated regularly into the vast distance. Their rocklight, and the vibrant stillness of the lake, gave the whole place a cloistral air, despite its size. Earthroot was a place to make mere mortals humble and devout.

It made Covenant feel like a sacrilege in the sanctified and august temple of the mountains.

The lake was so still – it conveyed such an impression of weight, massiveness – that it looked more like fluid bronze than water, a liquid cover for the unfathomable abysses of the Earth. The rocklight gleamed on it as if it were burnished.

'Is this – ?' Covenant croaked, then caught himself as his question ran echoing lightly over the water, restating itself without diminishment into the distance. He could not bring himself to go on. Even the low shuffling of his boots on the stone echoed as if it carried some kind of prophetic significance.

But Amok took up the question gaily. 'Is the Power of Command here, in Earthroot?' The echoes laughed as he laughed. 'No. Earthroot but partakes. The heart of the Seventh Ward lies beyond. We must cross over.'

High Lord Elena asked the next question carefully, as if she, too, were timid in the face of the awesome lake. 'How?'

'High Lord, a way will be provided. I am the way and the door – I have not brought you to a pathless end. But the use of the way will be in your hands. This is the last test. Only one word am I permitted to say: do not touch the water. Earthroot is strong and stern. It will take no account of mortal flesh.'

'What must we do now?' she inquired softly to minimize the echoes.

'Now?' Amok chuckled. 'Only wait, High Lord. The time will not be long. Behold! Already the way approaches.'

He was standing with his back to the lake, but as he spoke he gestured behind him with one arm. As if in answer to this signal, a boat came into sight around a pillar some distance from the shore.

The boat was empty. It was a narrow wooden craft, pointed at both ends. Except for a line of bright reflective gilt along its gunwales and thwarts, it was unadorned – a clean, simple work smoothly formed of light brown wood, and easily long enough to seat five people. But it was unoccupied; no one rowed or steered it. Without making a ripple, it swung gracefully around the pillar, and glided shoreward. Yet in Earthroot's sacramental air, it did not seem strange; it was a proper and natural adjunct of the bronze lake. Covenant was not surprised to see that it carried no oars.

He watched its approach as if it were an instrument of dread. It made his wedding ring itch on his finger. He glanced quickly at his hand, half expecting to see that the band glowed or changed colour. The argent metal looked peculiarly vivid in the rocklight; it weighed heavily on his hand, tingled against his skin. But it revealed nothing. 'Have mercy,' he breathed as if he were speaking directly to the white gold. Then he winced as his voice tripped away in light echoes, spread by a multitude of crystal repetitions.

Amok laughed at him, and clear peals of glee joined the mimicry.

High Lord Elena was now too enrapt in Earthroot to attend Covenant. She stood on the shore as if she could already smell the Power of Command, and waited like an acolyte for the empty boat.

Soon the craft reached her. Silently, it slid its prow up the dry slope, and stopped as if it were ready, expectant.

Amok greeted it with a deep obeisance, then leaped lithely aboard. His feet made no sound as they struck the planks. He moved to the far end of the craft, turned, and seated himself with his arms on the gunwales, grinning like a monarch.

First Mark Morin followed Amok. Next, High Lord Elena entered the craft, and placed herself on a seat board near its middle. She held the Staff of Law across her knees. Covenant saw that his turn had come. Trembling, he walked down the shore to the wooden prow. Apprehension beat in his temples, but he repressed it. He clutched the gunwales with both hands, climbed into the craft. His boots thudded and echoed on the planks. As he sat down, he seemed to be surrounded by the clatter of unseemly burdens.

Bannor shoved the boat into the lake, and sprang immediately aboard. But by the time he had taken his seat, the boat had glided to a halt. It rested as if it were fused to the burnished water a few feet from shore.

For a moment, no one moved or spoke. They sat bated and hushed, waiting for the same force which had brought the boat to carry it away again. But the craft remained motionless – fixed like a censer in the red, still surface of the lake.

The pulse in Covenant's head grew sharper. Harshly, he defied the echoes. 'Now what do we do?'

To his surprise, the boat slid forward a few feet. But it stopped again when the repetitions of his voice died. Once again, the High Lord's party was held, trapped.

He stared about him in astonishment. No one spoke. He could see thoughts concentrate the muscles of Elena's back. He looked at Amok once, but the youth's happy grin so dismayed him that he tore his gaze away. The ache of his suspense began to seem unendurable.

Bannor's unexpected movement startled him. Turning, he saw that the Bloodguard had risen to his feet. He lifted his seat board from its slots.

For an oar! Covenant thought. He felt a sudden upsurge of excitement.

Bannor held the board in both hands, braced himself against the side of the boat, and prepared to paddle.

As the end of the board touched the water, some power grabbed it, wrenched it instantly from his grasp. It was snatched straight down into the lake. There was no splash or ripple, but the board vanished like a stone hurled into the depths.

Bannor gazed after it, and cocked one eyebrow as if he were speculating abstractly on the kind of strength which could so easily tear something away from a Bloodguard. But Covenant was not so calm. He gasped weakly, 'Hellfire.'

Again the boat moved forward. It coasted for several yards until the echoes of Covenant's amazement disappeared. Then it stopped, resumed its reverent stasis.

Covenant faced Elena, but he did not need to voice his question. Her face glowed with comprehension. 'Yes, beloved,' she breathed in relief and triumph. 'I see.' And as the boat once more began to glide over the lake, she continued, 'It is the sound of our voices which causes the boat to move. That is the use of Amok's way. The craft will seek its own destination. But to carry us it must ride upon our echoes.'

The truth of her perception was immediately apparent. While her clear voice cast replies like ripples over Earthroot, the boat slid easily through the water. It steered itself between the pillars as if it were pursuing the lodestone of its purpose. Soon it had passed out of sight of Earthrootstair. But when she stopped speaking – when the delicate echoes had chimed themselves into silence – the craft halted again.

Covenant groaned inwardly. He was suddenly afraid that he would be asked to talk, help propel the boat. He feared that he would give his bargain away if he were forced into any kind of extended speech. In self-defence, he turned the demand around before it could be directed at him. 'Well, say something,' he growled at Elena.

A light, ambiguous smile touched her lips – a response, not to him, but to some satisfying inner prospect. 'Beloved,' she replied softly, 'we will have no difficulty. There is much which has not been said between us. There are secrets and mysteries and sources of power in you which I perceive but dimly. And in some ways I have not yet spoken of myself. This is a fit place for the opening of hearts. I will tell you of that Ranyhyn-ride which took the young daughter of Lena from Mithil Stonedown into the Southron Range, and there at the great secret horserite of the Ranyhyn taught her – taught her many things.'

With a stately movement, she rose to her feet facing Covenant. She set the Staff of Law firmly on the planks, and lifted her head to the ceiling of Earthroot's cavern. 'Ur-Lord Thomas Covenant,' she said, and the echoes spread about her like a skein of gleaming rocklight, interweaving the burnished waters, 'Unbeliever and white gold wielder, Ringthane – beloved – I must tell you of this. You have known Myrha. In her youth, she came to Lena my mother, according to the promise of the Ranyhyn. She carried me away to the great event of my girlhood. Thus you were the unknowing cause. Before this war reaches its end for good or ill, I must tell you what your promises have wrought.'

Have mercy on me! he cried again in the obdurate incapacity of his heart. But he was too numb, too intimidated by the lake and the echoes, to stop her. He sat in mute dread, and listened as Elena told him the tale of her experience with the Ranyhyn. And all the time, the craft bore them on an oblique intimate course between the lake pillars, floated them on the resonances of her voice as if it were ferrying them to a terrible shore.

Her adventure had occurred the third time that Lena her mother had allowed her to ride a Ranyhyn. During the two previous annual visits to Mithil Stonedown, dictated by the Ranyhyn promise to Covenant Ringthane, the old horse from the Plains of Ra had rolled his eyes strangely at the little girl as Trell her grandfather had boosted her onto its broad back. And the next year young Myrha took the old stallion's place. The mare gazed at Elena with that look of deliberate intention which characterized all the Ranyhyn – and Elena, sensing the Ranyhyn's offer without understanding it, gladly gave herself up to Myrha. She did not look back as the mare carried her far away from Mithil Stonedown into the mountains of the Southron Range.

For a day and a night, Myrha galloped, bearing Elena far south along mountain trails and over passes unknown to the people of the Land. At the end of that time, they gained a high valley, a grassy glen folded between sheer cliffs, with a rugged, spring-fed tarn near its centre. This small lake was mysterious, for its dark waters did not reflect the sunlight. And the valley itself was wondrous to behold, for it contained hundreds of Ranyhyn – hundreds of proud, glossy, star-browed stallions and mares – gathered together for a rare and secret ritual of horses.

But Elena's wonder quickly turned to fear. Amid a chorus of wild, whinnied greetings, Myrha carried the little girl towards the lake, then shrugged her to the ground and dashed away in a flurry of hooves. And the rest of the Ranyhyn began to run around the valley. At first they trotted in all directions, jostling each other and sweeping by the child as if they were barely able to avoid crushing her. But gradually their pace mounted. Several Ranyhyn left the pounding mob to drink at the tarn, then burst back into the throng as if the dark waters roiled furiously in their veins. While the sun passed overhead, the great horses sprinted and bucked, drank at the tarn, rushed away to run again in the unappeasable frenzy of a dance of madness. And Elena stood among them, imperilled for her life by the savage flash and flare of hooves – frozen with terror. In her fear, she thought that if she so much as flinched she would be instantly trampled to death.

Standing there – engulfed in heat and thunder and abysmal fear as final as the end of life – she lost consciousness for a time. She was still standing when her eyes began to see again; she was erect and petrified in the last glow of evening. But the Ranyhyn were no longer running. They had surrounded her; they faced her, studied her with a force of compulsion in their eyes. Some were so close to her that she inhaled their hot, damp breath. They wanted her to do something – she could feel the insistence of their wills battering at her immobile fear. Slowly, woodenly, choicelessly, she began to move.

She went to the tarn and drank.

Abruptly, the High Lord dropped her narration, and began to sing – a vibrant, angry, and anguished song which cast ripples of passion across the air of Earthroot. For reasons at which Covenant could only guess instinctively, she broke into Lord Kevin's Lament as if it were her own private and immedicable threnody.

> Where is the power that protects
> beauty from the decay of life?
> preserves truth pure of falsehood?
> secures fealty from that slow stain of chaos
> which corrupts?
> How are we so rendered small by Despite?
> Why will the very rocks not erupt
> for their own cleansing,
> or crumble into dust for shame?

While echoes of the song's grief ran over the lake, she met Covenant's gaze for the first time since she had begun her tale.

'Beloved,' she said in a low, thrilling voice, 'I was transformed – restored to life. At the touch of those waters, the blindness or ignorance of my heart fell away. My fear melted, and I was joined to the communion of the Ranyhyn. In an instant of vision, I understood – everything. I saw that in honour of your promise I had been brought to the horserite of *Kelenbhrabanal*, Father of Horses – a Ranyhyn ritual enacted once each generation to pass on and perpetuate their great legend, the tale of mighty *Kelenbhrabanal*'s death in the jaws of Fangthane the Render. I saw that the turmoiled running of the Ranyhyn was their shared grief and rage and frenzy at the Father's end.

'For *Kelenbhrabanal* was the Father of Horses, Stallion of the First Herd. The Plains of Ra were his demesne and protectorate. He led the Ranyhyn in their great war against the wolves of Fangthane.

'But the war continued without issue, and the stench of shed blood and rent flesh became a sickness in the Stallion's nostrils. Therefore he made his way to Fangthane. He stood before the Render, and said, "Let this war end. I smell your hate – I know that you must have victims, else in your passion you will consume yourself. I will be your victim. Slaughter me, and let my people live in peace. Appease your hate on me, and end this war." And Fangthane agreed. So *Kelenbhrabanal* bared his throat to the Render's teeth, and soaked the earth with his sacrifice.

'But Fangthane did not keep his word – the wolves attacked again. The Ranyhyn were leaderless, heart-stricken. They could not fight well. The remnant of the Ranyhyn was compelled to flee into the mountains. They could not return to their beloved Plains until they had gained the service of the Ramen, and with that aid had driven the wolves away.

'Thus each generation of the Ranyhyn holds its horserite to preserve the tale of the Stallion – to hold pure in memory all their pride at his self-sacrifice, and all their grief at his death, and all their rage at the Despite which betrayed him. Thus they drink of the mind-uniting waters, and hammer out against the ground the extremity of their passion for one day and one night. And thus, when I had tasted the water of the tarn, I ran and wept and raged with them throughout the long exaltation of that night. Heart and mind and soul and all, I gave myself to a dream of Fangthane's death.'

Listening to her, clinging to her face with his eyes, Covenant felt himself knotted by the clench of unreleasable grief. She was the woman who had offered herself to him. He understood her passion now, understood the danger she was in. And her elsewhere glance was drawing into focus; already he could feel conflagrations blazing at the corners of her vision.

His dread of that focus gave him the impetus to speak. With his voice rent between fear and love, he wrenched out hoarsely, 'What I don't understand is what Foul gets out of all this.'

25

THE SEVENTH WARD

For a long moment, High Lord Elena gripped the Staff of Law and glared down at him. Focus crackled on the verge of her gaze; it was about to lash out and scourge him. But then she seemed to recollect who he was. Slowly, the passion dimmed in her face, went behind an inward veil. She lowered herself to her seat in the boat. Quietly, dangerously, she asked, 'All this? Do you ask what Lord Foul gains from what I have told you?'

He answered her with quivering promptitude. Careless now of the illimitable range of implications with which the echoes multiplied his voice, he hastened to explain himself, ameliorate at least in this way the falseness of his position.

'That, too. You said it yourself – that old, unsufferable bargain I made with the Ranyhyn put you – where you are. Never mind what I did to your mother. That, too. But it's really this time I'm thinking about. You summoned me, and we're on our way to the Seventh Ward – and I want to know what Foul gets out of it. He wouldn't waste a chance like this.'

'This is no part of his intent,' she replied coldly. 'The choice to summon you was mine, not his.'

'Right. That's the way he works. But what made you decide to summon me? – I mean aside from the fact that you were going to call me anyway at some time or other because I have the simple misfortune to wear a white gold wedding ring and have two fingers missing. What made you decide then – when you did?'

'*Dukkha* Waynhim gave us new knowledge of Fangthane's power.'

'New knowledge, by hell!' Covenant croaked. 'Do you think that was an accident? Foul released him.' He shouted the word *released*, and its echoes jabbered about him like dire significances. 'He released that poor suffering devil because he knew exactly what you would do about it. And he wanted me to be in the Land then, at that precise time, not sooner or later.'

The importance of what he was saying penetrated her; she began to hear him seriously. But her voice remained non-committal as she asked, 'Why? How are his purposes served?'

For a moment, he shied away from what he was thinking. 'How should I know? If I knew, I might be able to fight it somehow. Aside from the idea that I'm supposed to destroy the Land – ' But Elena's grave attention stopped him. For her sake, he mustered his courage. 'Well, look at what's happened because of me. I did something to Loric's *krill* – therefore Amok showed up – therefore you're going to try to unlock the Seventh Ward. It's as neat as clockwork. If you'd summoned me sooner, then when we got to this point you wouldn't be under such pressure to use lore you don't understand. And if all this had happened later, you wouldn't have come here at all – you would have been too busy fighting the war.

'As for me' – he swallowed and looked away for an instant, then took a step closer to the root of his bargain – 'this is the only way I can possibly get off the hook. If things had gone differently, there would have been a lot more pressure on me – from everywhere – to learn how to use this ring. And Joan – But this way you've been distracted – you're thinking about the Seventh Ward instead of wild magic or whatever. And Foul doesn't want me to learn what white gold is good for. I might use it against him.

'Don't you see it? Foul put us right where we are. He released *dukkha* so that we would be right here now. He must have a reason. He likes to destroy people through the things that make them hope. That way he can get them to desecrate – No wonder this is the dark of the moon.' He was poignantly conscious of the way in which he endangered his own cause as he concluded softly, 'Elena, the Seventh Ward might be the worst thing that has happened yet.'

But she had her answer ready. 'No, beloved. I do not believe it. High Lord Kevin formed his Wards in a time before his wisdom fell into despair. Fangthane's hand is not in them. It may be that the Power of Command is perilous – but it is not ill.'

Her statement did not convince him. But he did not have the heart to protest. The echoes placed too much stress on even his simplest words. Instead, he sat gazing morosely at her feet while he scratched at the itch of his wedding band. As the echoes died – as the boat slid gently to a stop in the water – he felt that he had missed a chance for rectitude.

For a time, no voice arose to move the boat. Covenant and Elena sat in silence, studying their private thoughts. But then she spoke again. Softly, reverently, she recited the words of Lord Kevin's Lament. The boat glided onward again.

Shortly the craft rounded another column, and Covenant found himself staring at a high, sparkling, silent waterfall ahead. Its upper reaches disappeared into the shadows of the cavern's ceiling. But the torrents which poured noiselessly down its ragged surface caught the fiery rocklight at thousands of bright points, so that the falls looked like a cascade of hot, rich, red gems.

The boat flowed smoothly on Elena's recitation towards a rock levee at one side of the waterfall, and slid up into place. At once, Amok leaped from the craft, and stood waiting for his companions on the edge of Earthroot. But for a moment they did not follow him. They sat spellbound by the splendour and silence of the falls.

'Come, High Lord,' the youth said. 'The Seventh Ward is nigh. I must bring my being to an end.' His tone matched the unwonted seriousness of his countenance.

Elena shook her head vaguely, as if she were remembering her limitations, her weariness and lack of knowledge. And Covenant covered his eyes to block out the disconcerting noiseless tumble and glitter of the falls. But then Morin stepped up onto the levee, and Elena followed him with a sigh. Gripping the gunwales with both hands, Covenant climbed out of the craft. When Bannor joined them, the High Lord's party was complete.

Amok regarded them soberly. He seemed to have aged during the boat ride. The cheeriness had faded from his face, leaving his ancient bones uncontradicted. His lips moved as if he wished to speak. But he said nothing. Like a man looking for support, he gazed briefly at each of his companions. Then he turned away, went with an oddly heavy step towards the waterfall. When he reached the first wet rocks, he scrambled up them, and stepped into the plunging water.

With his legs widely braced against the weight of the falls, he looked back towards his companions. 'Do not fear,' he said through the silent torrent. 'This is merely water as you have known it. Earthroot's potency springs from another source. Come.' With a beckoning gesture, he disappeared under the falls.

At this, Elena stiffened. The nearness of the Seventh Ward filled her face. Discarding her fatigue, she hastened behind Morin towards the waterfall.

Covenant followed her. Racked, weary, full of uncomprehending dread, he nevertheless could not hang back now. As Elena pushed through the cascade and passed out of sight, he thrust himself up the wet jumble of rocks, began to crouch towards the falls. Spray dashed into his face. The rocks were too slick for him; he was forced to crawl. But he kept moving to evade Bannor's help. Holding his breath, he burrowed into the water as if it were an avalanche.

It almost flattened him; it pounded him like the accumulated weight of his delusion. But as he propped himself up against it – as the falls drenched him, filled his eyes and mouth and ears – he felt some of its vitality. It attacked him like an involuntary ablution, a cleansing performed as the last prerequisite of the Power of Command. It scrubbed at him as if it meant to peel his bones. But the water force missed his face and chest. It laid bare all his nerves, but failed to purify the marrow of his unfitness. A moment later, he crawled raw and untransmogrified into the darkness beyond the waterfall.

Quivering, he shook his head, blew the water out of his mouth and nose. His hands told him that he was on flat stone, but it felt strange, both dry and slippery. It resisted solid contact with his palms. And he could see nothing, hear no scuffles or whispers from his companions. But his sense of smell reacted violently. He found himself in an air so laden with force that it submerged every other odour of his life. It swamped him like the stink of gangrene, burned him like the reek of brimstone, but it bore no resemblance to these or any other smells he knew. It was like the polished, massive expanse of Earthroot – like the immensity of the rocklit cavern – like the continual, adumbrated weight of the waterfall – like the echoes – like the deathless stability of *Melenkurion* Skyweir. It reduced his restless consciousness to the scale of mere brief flesh.

It was the smell of Earthpower.

He could not stand it. He was on his knees before it, with his forehead pressed against the cold stone and his hands clasped over the back of his neck.

Then he heard a low, flaring noise as Elena lit the Staff of Law. Slowly, he raised his head. The sting of the air filled his eyes with tears, but he blinked at them, and looked about him.

He was in a tunnel which ran straight and lightless away from the falls. Down its centre – out of the distance and into the falls – flowed a small stream less than a yard wide. Even in the Staff's blue light, the fluid of this stream was as red as fresh blood. This was the source of the smell – the source of Earthroot's dangerous potency. He could see its concentrated might.

He pushed to his feet, scrambled towards the tunnel wall; he wanted to get as far as possible from the stream. His boots slipped on the black stone floor as if it were glazed with ice. He had to struggle to keep his balance. But he reached the wall, pressed himself against it. Then he looked towards Elena.

She was gazing as if with bated breath down the tunnel. A rapt, exultant expression filled her face, and she seemed taller, elevated in stature by her grasp on the Staff of Law – as if the Staff's flame fed a fire within her, a blaze like a vision of victory. She looked like a priestess, an enactor of hallowed and effective rites, approaching the occult ground of her strength. The very gaps of her elsewhere gaze were crowded with exalted and savage possibilities. They made Covenant forget the uncomfortable power of the air, forget the tears which ran from his eyes like weeping, and step forward to warn her.

At once, he lost his footing, barely managed to avoid a fall. Before he could try again, he heard Amok say, 'Come. The end is at hand.' The youth's speech sounded as spectral as an invocation of the dead, and High Lord Elena started down the tunnel in answer to his summons. Quickly Covenant looked around, found Bannor behind him. He caught hold of Bannor's arm as if he meant to demand, Stop her! Don't you see what she's going to do? But he could not say it; he had made a bargain. Instead, he thrust away, tried to hurry after Elena.

He could find no purchase for his feet. His boots skidded off the stone; he seemed to have lost his sense of balance. But he scrabbled grimly onward. With an intense effort of will, he relaxed the force of his strides, pushed less sharply against the ground. As a result, he gained some control over his movements, contrived to keep pace with the High Lord.

But he could not catch her. And he could not watch where she was going; his steps required too much concentration. He did not look up until the assailing odour took a leap which almost reduced him to his knees again. Tears flooded his eyes so heavily that they felt irretrievably blurred, bereft of focus. But the smell told him that he had reached the spring of the red stream.

Through his tears, he could see Elena's flame guttering.

He squeezed the water out of his eyes, gained a moment in which to make out his surroundings. He stood behind Elena in a wider cave at the tunnel's end. Before him, set into the black stone end-wall like an exposed lode-facet, was a rough, sloping plane of wet rock. This whole plane shimmered; its emanations distorted his ineffectual vision, gave him the impression that he was staring at a mirage, a wavering in the solid stuff of existence. It confronted him like a porous membrane in the foundation of time and space. From top to bottom, it bled moisture which dripped down the slope, collected in a rude trough, and flowed away along the centre of the tunnel.

'Behold,' Amok said quietly. 'Behold the Blood of the Earth. Here I fulfil the purpose of my creation. I am the Seventh Ward of High Lord Kevin's Lore. The power to which I am the way and the door is here.' As he spoke, his voice deepened and emptied, grew older.

The weary burden of his years bent his shoulders. When he continued, he seemed conscious of a need for haste, a need to speak before his old immunity to time ran out.

'High Lord, attend. The air of this place unbinds me. I must complete my purpose now.'

'Then speak, Amok,' she replied. 'I hear you.'

'Ah, hear,' said Amok in a sad, musing tone, as if her answer had dropped him into a reverie. 'Where is the good of hearing, if it is not done wisely?' Then he recollected himself. In a stronger voice, he said, 'But hear, then, for good or ill. I fulfil the law of my creation. My maker can require no more of me.

'High Lord, behold the Blood of the Earth. This is the passionate and essential ichor of the mountain rock – the Earthpower which raises and holds peaks high. It bleeds here – perhaps because the great weight of *Melenkurion* Skyweir squeezes it from the dense rock – or perhaps because the mountain is willing to lay bare its heart's-blood for those who need and can find it. Whatever the cause, its result remains. Any soul who drinks of the EarthBlood gains the Power of Command.'

He met her intense gaze, and went on, 'The Power is rare and potent – and full of hazard. Once it has been taken in from the Blood, it must be used swiftly – lest its strength destroy the drinker. And none can endure more than a single draught – no mortal thew and bone can endure more than a single swallow of the Blood. It is too rare a fluid for any cup of flesh to hold.

'Yet such hazards do not explain why High Lord Kevin himself did not essay the Power of Command. For this Power is the power to achieve any desired act – to issue any command to the stone and soil and grass and wood and water and flesh of life, and see that command fulfilled. If any drinker were to say to *Melenkurion* Skyweir, "Crumble and fall," the great peaks would instantly obey. If any drinker were to say to the Fire-Lions of Mount Thunder, "Leave your bare slopes, attack and lay waste Ridjeck Thome," they would at once strive with all their strength to obey. This Power can achieve anything which lies within the scope of the commanded. Yet High Lord Kevin did not avail himself of it.

'I don't know all the purposes which guided his heart when he chose to leave the EarthBlood untasted. But I must explain if I can the deeper hazards of the Power of Command.'

Amok spoke in a tone of deepening, spectral hollowness, and Covenant listened desperately, as if he were clinging with raw, bruised fingers to the precipice of Amok's words. Hot things hammered in his veins, and tears like rivulets of fire ran unstanchably down his sweating cheeks. He felt that he was suffocating on the smell of EarthBlood. His ring itched horribly. He could not keep his balance; his footing constantly oozed from under him. Yet his perceptions went beyond all this. His flooded senses stretched as if they were at last thrusting their heads above water. As Amok spoke of deeper hazards, Covenant became aware of a new implication in the cave.

Through the brunt of the Blood, he began to smell something wrong, something ill. It crept insidiously across the whelming odour like an oblique defiance which seemed to succeed in spite of the immense force which it opposed, undercut, betrayed. But he could not locate its source. Either the Power of Command itself was in some way false, or the wrong was elsewhere, making itself apparent slowly through the dense air. He could not tell which.

No one else appeared to notice the subtle reek of ill. After a short, tired pause, Amok continued his explication.

'The first of these hazards – first, but perhaps not foremost – is the one great limit of the Power. It holds no sway over anything which is not a natural part of the Earth's creation. Thus it is not possible to Command the Despiser to cease his warring. It is not possible to Command his death. He lived before the arch of Time was forged – the Power cannot compel him.

'This alone might have given Kevin pause. Perhaps he did not drink of the Blood because he could not conceive how to levy any Command against the Despiser. But there is another and subtler hazard. Here any soul with the courage to drink may give a command – but there are few who can foresee the outcome of what they have enacted. When such immeasurable force is unleashed upon the Earth, any accomplishment may recoil upon its accomplisher. If a drinker were to Command the destruction of the Illearth Stone, perhaps the Stone's evil would survive uncontained to blight the whole Land. Here the drinker who is not also a prophet risks self-betrayal. Here are possibilities of Desecration which even High Lord Kevin in his despair left slumbering and untouched.'

The stench of wrong grew in Covenant's nostrils, but still he could not identify it. And he could not concentrate on it; he had a question which he fevered to ask Amok. But the tenebrous atmosphere clogged his throat, stifled him.

While Covenant struggled for breath, something happened to Amok. During his speech, his tone had become older and more cadaverous. And now, in the pause after his last sentence, he suddenly lurched as if some taut cord within him snapped. He staggered a step towards the trough of Blood. A moment passed before he could straighten his stance, raise his head again.

A look of fear or pain or grief widened his eyes, and around them lines of age spread visibly, as if his skin were being crumpled. The soft flesh of his cheeks eroded; grey ran through his hair. Like a dry sponge, he soaked up his natural measure of years. When he spoke again, his voice was weak and empty. 'I can say no more. My time is ended. Farewell, High Lord. Do not fail the Land.'

Convulsively, Covenant gasped out his question. 'What about the white gold?'

Amok answered across a great gulf of age, 'White gold exists beyond the arch of Time. It cannot be Commanded.'

Another inward snapping shook him; he jerked closer to the trough.

'Help him!' croaked Covenant. But Elena only raised the Staff of Law in a mute, fiery salute.

With an age-palsied exertion, Amok thrust himself erect. Tears ran through the wrinkled lattice of his cheeks as he lifted his face towards the roof of the cave, and cried in a stricken voice, 'Ah, Kevin! Life is sweet, and I have lived so short a time! Must I pass away?'

A third snapping shuddered him like an answer to his appeal. He stumbled as if his bones were falling apart, and tumbled into the trough. In one swift instant, the Blood dissolved his flesh and he was gone.

Covenant groaned helplessly, 'Amok!' Through the blur of his own ineffectual tears, he gaped at the red, flowing rill of EarthBlood. Imbalance poured into him from the stone, mounted in his muscles like vertigo. He lost all sense of where he was. To steady himself, he reached out to grasp Elena's shoulder.

Her shoulder was so hard and intense, so full of rigid purpose, that it felt like naked bone under the fabric of her robe. She was poised on the verge of her own climax; her passion was tangible to his touch.

It appalled him. Despite the dizziness which anchored his mind, he located the source of the nameless reek of wrong.

The ill was in Elena, in the High Lord herself.

She seemed unconscious of it. In a tone of barely controlled excitement, she said, 'Amok is gone – his purpose is accomplished. Now there must be no more delay. For the sake of all the Earth, I must drink and Command.' To Covenant's ears, she sounded rife with hungry conclusions – so packed with needs and duties and intents that she was about to shatter.

The realization caught him like a damp hand on the back of his neck, forced him inwardly to his knees. When she stepped out of his grasp, moved towards the trough of Blood, he felt that she had torn away his last defence. Elena! he wailed silently, Elena! His cries were cries of abjection.

For a moment, he knelt within himself as if he were in the grip of a vision. Dizzily, he saw all the manifest ways in which he was responsible for Elena – all the ways in which he had caused her to be who and what and where she was. His duplicity was the cause – his violence, his futility, his need. And he remembered the apocalypse hidden in her gaze. That was the ill. It made him shudder in anguish. He watched her through his blur of tears. When he saw her bend towards the trough, all of him leaped up in defiance of the slick rock, and he cried out hoarsely, 'Elena! Don't! Don't do it!'

The High Lord stopped. But she did not turn. The whole rigour of her back condensed into one question: *Why?*

'Don't you see it?' he gasped. 'This is all some plot of Foul's. We're being manipulated – *you're* being manipulated. Something terrible is going to happen.'

For a time, she remained silent while he ached. Then, in a tone of austere conviction, she said, 'I cannot let pass this chance to serve the Land. I am forewarned. If this is Fangthane's best ploy to defeat us, it is also our best means to strike at him. I do not fear to measure my will against his. And I hold the Staff of Law. Have you not learned that the Staff is unsuited to his hands? He would not have delivered it to us if it were in any way adept for his uses. No. The Staff warrants me. Lord Foul cannot contrive my vision.'

'Your vision!' Covenant extended his hands in pleading towards her. 'Don't you see what that is? Don't you see where that comes from? It comes from me – from that unholy bargain I made with the Ranyhyn. A bargain that failed, Elena!'

'Yet it would appear that you bargained better than you knew. The Ranyhyn kept their promise – they gave in return more than you could either foresee or control.' Her answer seemed to block his throat, and into his silence she said, 'What has altered you, Unbeliever? Without your help, we would not have gained this place. On Rivenrock you gave aid without stint or price, though my own anger imperilled you. Yet now you delay me. Thomas Covenant, you are not so craven.'

'Craven? Hellfire! I'm a bloody coward!' Some of his rage returned to him, and he spluttered through the sweat and tears that ran into his mouth, 'All lepers are cowards. We have to be!'

At last, she turned towards him, faced him with the focus, the blazing holocaust, of her gaze. Its force ripped his balance away from him, and he sprawled in fragments on the stone. But he pushed himself up again. Driven by his fear of her and for her, he dared to confront her power. He stood tenuously, and abandoned himself, took his plunge.

'Manipulation, Elena,' he rasped. 'I'm talking about manipulation. Do you understand what that means? It means using people. Twisting them to suit purposes they haven't chosen for themselves. Manipulation. Not Foul's – mine! I've been manipulating you, using you. I told you I'd made another bargain – but I didn't tell you what it is. I've been using – using you to get myself off the hook. I promised myself that I would do everything I could to help you find this Ward. And in return I promised myself that I would do everything I could to make you take my responsibility. I watched you and helped you so that when you got here you would look exactly like that – so you would challenge Foul yourself without stopping to think about what you're doing – so that whatever happens to the Land would be your fault instead of mine. So that I could escape! Hell and blood, Elena! Do you hear me? Foul is going to get us for sure!'

She seemed to hear only part of what he said. She bent her searing focus straight into him, and said, 'Was there ever a time when you loved me?'

In an agony of protest, he half screamed, 'Of course I loved you!' Then he mastered himself, put all his strength back into his appeal. 'It never even occurred to me that I might be able to use you until – until after the landslide. When I began to understand what you're capable of. I loved you before that. I love you now. I'm just an unconscionable bastard, and I used you, that's all. Now I regret it.' With all the resources of his voice, he beseeched her, 'Elena, please don't drink that stuff. Forget the Power of Command and go back to Revelstone. Let the Council decide what to do about all this.'

But the way in which her gaze left his face and burned around the walls of the cave told him that he had not reached her. When she spoke, she only confirmed his failure.

'I would be unworthy of Lordship if I failed to act now. Amok offered us the Seventh Ward because he perceived that the Land's urgent need surpassed the conditions of his creation. Fangthane is upon the Land now – he wages war now – Land and life and all are endangered now. While any power or weapon lies within my grasp, I will not permit him!' Her voice softened as she added, 'And if you have loved me, how can I fail to strive for your escape? You need not have bargained in secret. I love you. I wish to serve you. Your regret only strengthens what I must do.'

Swinging back towards the trough, she raised the Staff's guttering flame high over her head, and shouted like a war cry, *'Melenkurion abatha!* Ward yourself well, Fangthane! I seek to destroy you!'

Then she stooped to the EarthBlood.

Covenant struggled frantically in her direction, but his feet scattered out from under him again, and he went down with a crash like a shock of incapacity. As she lowered her face to the trough, he shouted, 'That's not a good answer! What happens to the Oath of Peace?'

But his cry did not penetrate her exaltation. Without hesitation, she took one steady sip of the Blood, and swallowed it.

At once, she leaped to her feet, stood erect and rigid as if she were possessed. She appeared to swell, expand like a distended icon. The fire of the Staff ran down the wood to her hands. Instantly, her whole arm burst into flame.

'Elena!' Covenant crawled towards her. But the might of her blue crackling blaze threw him back like a hard wind. He struck the tears from his eyes to see her more clearly. Within her enveloping fire, she was unharmed and savage.

While the flame burned about her, enfolded her from head to foot in fiery cerements, she raised her arms, lifted her face. For one fierce moment she stood motionless, trapped in conflagration. Then she spoke as if she were uttering words of flame.

'Come! I have tasted the EarthBlood! You must obey my will. The walls of death do not prevail. Kevin son of Loric! Come!'

No! howled Covenant, No! Don't! But even his inner cry was swamped by a great voice which shivered and groaned in the air so hugely that he seemed to hear it, not with his ears, but with the whole surface of his body.

'Fool! Desist!' Staggering waves of anguish poured from the voice. 'Do not do this!'

'Kevin, hear me!' Elena shouted back in a transported tone. 'You cannot refuse! The Blood of the Earth compels you. I have chosen you to meet my Command. Kevin, come!'

The great voice repeated, 'Fool! You know not what you do!'

But an instant later, the ambience of the cave changed violently, as if a tomb had opened into it. Breakers of agony rolled through the air. Covenant winced at every surge. He braced himself where he knelt, and looked up.

The spectre of Kevin Landwaster stood outlined in pale light before Elena.

He dwarfed her — dwarfed the cave itself. Momentarily upright and desolate, he was visible through the stone rather than within the cave. He towered over Elena as if he were part of the very mountain rock. He had a mouth like a cut, eyes full of the effects of Desecration, and on his forehead was a bandage which seemed to cover some mortal wound. 'Release me!' he groaned. 'I have done harm enough for one soul.'

'Then serve me!' she cried ecstatically up to him. 'I offer you a Command to redeem that harm. You are Kevin son of Loric, the waster of the Land. You have known despair to its dregs – you have tasted the full cup of gall. That is knowledge and strength which no one living can equal.

'High Lord Kevin, I Command you to battle and defeat Lord Foul the Despiser! Destroy Fangthane! By the Power of the EarthBlood, I Command you.'

The spectre stared aghast at her, and raised his fists as if he meant to strike her. 'Fool!' he repeated terribly.

The next instant, a concussion like the slamming of a crypt shook the cave. One last pulse of anguish pummelled the High Lord's party; Elena's flame was blown out like a weak candle; darkness flooded the cave.

Then Kevin was gone.

A long time passed. When Covenant regained consciousness, he rested wearily for a while on his hands and knees, glad of the darkness, and the reduced scale of the cave, and the spectre's absence. But eventually he remembered Elena. Pushing himself to his feet, he reached towards her with his voice. 'Elena? Come on. Elena? Let's get out of here.'

At first, he received no response. Then blue fire flared as Elena lit the Staff. She was sitting like a wreck on the floor. When she turned her wan, spent face towards him, he saw that her crisis was over. All the exaltation had been consumed by the act of Command. He went to her, helped her gently to her feet. 'Come on,' he said again. 'Let's go.'

She shook her head vaguely, and said in an exhausted voice, 'He called me a fool. What have I done?'

'I hope we never find out.' A rough edge of sympathy made him sound harsh. He wanted to care for her, and did not know how. To give her time and privacy to gather her strength, he stepped away. As he glanced dully around the cave, he noticed Bannor, noticed the faint look of surprise in Bannor's face. Something in that unfamiliar expression gave Covenant a twist of apprehension. It seemed to be directed at him. He probed for an explanation by asking, 'That was Kevin, wasn't it?'

Bannor nodded; the speculative surprise remained on his face.

'Well, at least it wasn't that beggar – At least now we know it wasn't Kevin who picked me for this.'

Still Bannor's gaze did not change. It made Covenant feel

uncomfortably exposed, as if there were something indecent about himself that he did not realize.

Confused, he turned back to the High Lord.

Suddenly, a silent blast like a howl of stone jolted the cave, made it tremble and jump like an earthquake. Covenant and Elena lost their footing, slapped against the floor. Morin's warning shout echoed flatly:

'Kevin returns!'

Then the buried tomb of the air opened again; Kevin's presence resonated against Covenant's skin. But this time the spectre brought with him a ghastly reek of rotten flesh and attar, and in the background of his presence was the deep rumble of rock being crushed. When Covenant raised his head from the bucking floor, he saw Kevin within the stone – furiously poised, fists cocked. Hot green filled the orbs of his eyes, sent rank steam curling up his forehead; and he dripped with emerald light as if he had just struggled out of a quagmire.

'Fool!' he cried in a paroxysm of anguish. 'Damned betrayer! You have broken the Law of Death to summon me – you have unleashed measureless opportunities for evil upon the Earth – and the Despiser mastered me as easily as if I were a child! The Illearth Stone consumes me. Fight, fool! I am Commanded to destroy you!'

Roaring like a multitude of fiends, he reached down and clutched at Elena.

She did not move. She was aghast, frozen by the result of her great dare.

But Morin reacted instantly. Crying, 'Kevin! Hold!' he sprang to her aid.

The spectre seemed to hear Morin – hear and recognize who he was. An old memory touched Kevin, and he hesitated. That hesitation gave Morin time to reach Elena, thrust her behind him. When Kevin threw off his uncertainty, his fingers closed around Morin instead of the High Lord.

He gripped the Bloodguard and heaved him into the air.

Kevin's arm passed easily through the rock, but Morin could not. He crashed against the ceiling with tremendous force. The impact tore him from Kevin's grasp. But that impact was sufficient. The First Mark fell dead like a broken twig.

The sight roused Elena. At once, she realized the danger. She whirled the Staff swiftly about her head. Its flame sprang into brilliance, and a hot blue bolt lashed straight at Kevin.

The blast struck him like a physical blow, drove him back a step through the stone. But he shrugged off its effects. With a deep snarl of pain, he moved forward, snatched at her again.

Shouting frantically, '*Melenkurion abatha!*' she met his attack with the Staff. Its fiery heel seared his palm.

Again he recoiled, gripping his scorched fingers and groaning.

In that momentary reprieve, she cried strange invocations to the Staff, and swung its blaze around her three times, surrounding herself with a shield of power. When the spectre grabbed for her once more, he could not gain a hold on her. He squeezed her shield, and his fingers dripped with emerald ill, but he could not touch her. Whenever he dented her defence, she healed it with the Staff's might.

Yelling in frustration and pain, he changed his tactics. He reared back, clasped his fists together, and hammered them at the floor of the cave. The stone jumped fiercely. The lurch knocked Covenant down, threw Bannor against the opposite wall.

A gasping shudder like a convulsion of torment shot through the mountain. The cave walls heaved; rumblings of broken stone filled the air; power blared.

A crack appeared in the floor directly under Elena. Even before she was aware of it, it started to open. Then, like ravenous jaws, it jerked wide.

High Lord Elena dropped into the chasm.

Kevin pounced after her, and vanished from sight. His howls echoed out of the cleft like the shrieking of a madman.

But even as they disappeared, their battle went on. Lords-fire spouted hotly up into the cave. The thunder of tortured stone pounded along the tunnel, and the cave pitched from side to side like a nausea in the guts of *Melenkurion* Skyweir. In his horror, Covenant thought that the whole edifice of the mountain was about to tumble.

Then he was snatched to his feet, hauled erect by Bannor. The Bloodguard gripped him with compelling fingers, and shouted at him through the tumult, 'Save her!'

'I can't!' The pain of his reply made him yell. Bannor's demand rubbed so much salt into the wound of his essential futility that he could hardly bear it. 'I cannot!'

'You must!' Bannor's grasp allowed no alternatives.

'How?' Waving his empty hands in Bannor's face, he cried, 'With these?'

'Yes!' The Bloodguard caught Covenant's left hand, forced him to look at it.

On his wedding finger, his ring throbbed ferally, pulsed with power and light like a potent instrument panting to be used.

For an instant, he gaped at the argent band as if it had betrayed him. Then forgetting escape, forgetting himself, forgetting even that he did not know how to exert wild magic, he pulled despairingly away from Bannor and stumbled towards the crevice. Like a man battering himself in armless impotence against a blank doom, he leaped after the High Lord.

26

GALLOWS HOWE

But he failed before he began. He did not know how to brace himself for the kind of battle which raged below him. As he passed the rim of the crevice, he was hit by a blast of force like an eruption from within the rift. He was defenceless against it; it snuffed out his consciousness like a frail flame.

Then for a time he rolled in darkness – ran in a blind, caterwauling void which pitched and broke over him until he staggered like a ship with sprung timbers. He was aware of nothing but the force which thrashed him. But something caught his hand, anchored him. At first he thought that the grip on his hand was Elena's – that she held him now as she had held him and kept him during the night after his summoning. But when he shook clear of the darkness, he saw Bannor. The Bloodguard was pulling him out of the crevice.

That sight – that perception of his failure – undid him. When Bannor set him on his feet, he stood listing amid the riot of battle – detonations, deep, groaning creaks of tormented stone, loud rockfalls – like an empty hulk, a cargoless hull sucking in death through a wound below its waterline. He did not resist or question as Bannor half carried him from the cave of the EarthBlood.

The tunnel was unlit except by the reflected glares of combat, but Bannor moved surely over the black rock. In moments, he brought his shambling charge to the waterfall. There he lifted the Unbeliever in his arms, and bore him like a child through the weight of the falls.

In the rocklight of Earthroot, Bannor moved even more urgently. He hastened to the waiting boat, installed Covenant on one of the seats, then leaped aboard as he shoved out into the burnished lake. Without hesitation, he began to recite something in the native tongue of the *Haruchai*. Smoothly, the boat made its way among the cloistral columns.

But his efforts did not carry the craft far. Within a few hundred yards, its prow began to tug against its intended direction. He stopped speaking, and at once the boat swung off to one side. Gradually, it gained speed.

It was in the grip of a current. Standing in the centre of Covenant's sightless gaze, Bannor cocked one eyebrow slightly, as if he perceived an ordeal ahead. For long moments, he waited for the slow increase of the current to reveal its destination.

Then in the distance he saw what caused the current. Far ahead of the craft, rocklight flared along a line in the lake like a cleft which stretched out of sight on both sides. Into this cleft Earthroot rushed and poured in silent cataracts.

He reacted with smooth efficiency, as if he had been preparing for this test throughout the long centuries of his service. First he snatched a coil of *clingor* from his pack; with it, he lashed Covenant to the boat. In answer to the vague question in Covenant's face, he replied, 'The battle of Kevin and the High Lord has opened a crevice in the floor of Earthroot. We must ride the water down, and seek an outlet below.' He did not wait for a response. Turning, he braced his feet, gripped one of the gilt gunwales, and tore it loose. With this long, curved piece of wood balanced in his hands for a steering pole, he swung around to gauge the boat's distance from the cataract.

The hot line of the crevice was less than a hundred yards away now, and the boat slipped rapidly towards it, caught in the mounting suction. But Bannor made one more preparation. Bending towards Covenant, he said quietly, 'Ur-Lord, you must use the *orcrest*.' His voice echoed with authority through the silence.

Covenant stared at him without comprehension.

'You must. It is in your pocket. Bring it out.'

For a moment, Covenant continued to stare. But at last the Bloodguard's command reached through his numbness. Slowly, he dug into his pocket, pulled out the smooth lucid stone. He held it awkwardly in his right hand, as if he could not properly grip it with only two fingers and a thumb.

The cataract loomed directly before the boat now, but Bannor spoke calmly, firmly. 'Hold the stone in your left hand. Hold it above your head, so that it will light our way.'

As Covenant placed the *orcrest* in contact with his troubled ring, a piercing silver light burst from the core of the stone. It flared along the gunwale in Bannor's hands, paled the surrounding rocklight. When Covenant numbly raised his fist, held the stone up like a torch, the Bloodguard nodded his approval. His face wore a look of satisfaction, as if all the conditions of his Vow had been fulfilled.

Then the prow of the boat dropped. Bannor and Covenant rode the torrent of Earthroot into the dark depths.

The water boiled and heaved wildly. But one end of the crevice opened into other caverns. The cataracts turned as they fell, and thrashed through the crevice as if it were an immense chute or channel. By the *orcrest* light, Bannor saw in time which way the water poured. He poled the boat so that it shot downward along the torrent.

After that, the craft hurtled down the frenetic water-course in a long nightmare of tumult, jagged rocks, narrows, sudden heart-stopping falls, close death. The current tumbled, thundered, raced from cavern to cavern through labyrinthian gaps and tunnels and clefts in the fathomless bowels of *Melenkurion* Skyweir. Many times the craft disappeared under the fierce roil of the rush, but each time its potent wood – wood capable of withstanding Earthroot – bore it to the surface again. And many times Bannor and Covenant foundered in cascades that crashed onto them from above, but the water did not harm them – either it had lost its strength in the fall, or it was already diluted by other buried springs and lakes.

Through it all, Covenant held his *orcrest* high. Some last uncon-scious capacity for endurance kept his fingers locked and his arm raised. And the stone's unfaltering fire lighted the boat's way, so that, even in the sharpest hysteria of the current, Bannor was able to steer, avoid rocks and backwaters, fend around curves – preserve himself and the Unbeliever. The torrent's violence soon splintered his pole, but he replaced it with the other gunwale. When that was gone, he used a seat board as a rudder.

Straining and undaunted, he brought the voyage through its final crisis.

Without warning, the boat shot down a huge flow into a cavern that showed no exit. The water frothed viciously, seeking release, and the air pressure mounted, became more savage every instant. A swift eddy caught the craft, swung it around and under the massive pour of water.

Helplessly, the boat was driven down.

Bannor clawed his way to Covenant. He wrapped his legs around Covenant's waist, snatched the *orcrest* from him. Clutching the stone as if to sustain himself with it, Bannor clamped his other hand over Covenant's nose and mouth.

He held that position as the boat sank.

The plunging weight of water thrust them straight under. Pressure squeezed them until Bannor's eyes pounded in their sockets, and his ears yowled as if they were about to rupture. He could feel Covenant screaming in his grasp. But he held his grip in the extremity of the last faithfulness – clung to the bright strength of the *orcrest* with one hand, and kept Covenant from breathing with the other.

Then they were sucked into a side tunnel, an outlet. Immediately, all the pressure of the trapped air and water hurled them upward. Covenant went limp; Bannor's lungs burned. But he retained enough alertness to swing himself upright as the water burst free. In a high, arching spout, it carried the two men into the cleft of Rivenrock, and sent them shooting out into the open morning of the Black River and Garroting Deep.

For a moment, sunshine and free sky and forest reeled around Bannor, and flares of released pressure staggered across his sight. Then the fortitude of his Vow returned. Wrapping both arms around Covenant, he gave one sharp jerk which started the Unbeliever's lungs working again.

With a violent gasp, Covenant began breathing rapidly, feverishly. Some time passed before he showed any signs of consciousness, yet all the while his ring throbbed as if it were sustaining him. Finally, he opened his eyes, and looked at Bannor.

At once, he started to struggle weakly in his *clingor* bonds. Bannor appeared to him like one of the djinn who watches over the accursed. But then he lapsed. He recognized where he was – how he had arrived there – what he had left behind. He went on staring nakedly while Bannor untied the lines which lashed him to the boat.

Over the Bloodguard's shoulder, he could see the great cliff of Rivenrock – and behind it *Melenkurion* Skyweir – shrinking as the boat scudded downriver. From the cleft, turgid black smoke broke upward in gouts sporadically emphasized by battle flashes deep within the mountains. Muffled blasts of anguish rent the gut-rock, wreaking havoc in the very grave of the ages. Covenant felt he was floating away on a wave of ravage and destruction.

Fearfully, he looked down at his ring. To his dismay, he found that it still throbbed like an exclamation of purpose. Instinctively, he clasped his right hand over it, concealed it. Then he faced forward in the boat, turned away from Bannor and Rivenrock as if to protect his shame from scrutiny.

He sat huddled there, weak and staring dismally, throughout the swift progress of the day. He did not speak to Bannor, did not help him bail out the boat, did not look back. The current spewing from Rivenrock raised the Black River to near-flood levels, and the light Earthroot craft rode the rush intrepidly between glowering walls of forest. The morning sun glittered and danced off the dark water into Covenant's eyes – but he stared at it without blinking, as if even the protective reflex of his eyelids were exhausted. And after that, nothing interfered with his sightless vision. The sodden food which Bannor offered to him he ate automatically, with his left hand concealed between his thighs. Midday and afternoon passed unrecognized, and when evening came he remained crouched on his seat, clenching his ring against his chest as if to protect himself from some final stab of realization.

Then, as dusk thickened about him, he became aware of the music. The air of the Deep was full of humming, of voiceless song – an eldritch melody which seemed to arise like passion from the faint throats of all the leaves. It contrasted sharply with the distant, storming climacteric of *Melenkurion* Skyweir, the song of violence which beat and shivered out of Rivenrock. Gradually, he raised his head to listen. The Deep song had an inflection of sufferance, as if it were deliberately restraining a potent melodic rage, sparing him.

In the light of the *orcrest*, he saw that Bannor was guiding the boat towards a high, treeless hill which rose against the night sky close to the south bank. The hill was desolate, bereft of life, as if its capacity to nourish even the hardiest plants had been irremediably scalded out of it. Yet it seemed to be the source of the Deep's song. The melody which wafted riverward from the hill sounded like a host of gratified furies.

He regarded the hill incuriously. He had no strength left to care about such places. All his waning sanity was focused on the sounds of battle from *Melenkurion* Skyweir – and on the grip which concealed his ring. When Bannor secured the boat, and took hold of his right elbow to help him ashore, Covenant leaned on the Bloodguard and followed his guidance woodenly.

Bannor went to the barren hill. Without question, Covenant began to struggle up it.

Despite his weariness, the hill impinged upon his awareness. He could feel its deadness with his feet as if he were shambling up a corpse. Yet it was eager death; its atmosphere was thick with the slaughter of enemies. Its incarnate hatred made his joints ache as he climbed it. He began to sweat and tremble as if he were carrying the weight of an atrocity on his shoulders.

Then, near the hilltop, Bannor stopped him. The Bloodguard lifted the *orcrest*. In its light, Covenant saw the gibbet beyond the crest of the hill. A Giant dangled from it. And between him and the gibbet – staring at him as if he were a concentrated nightmare – were people, people whom he knew.

Lord Mhoram stood there erect in his battled-grimed robe. He clasped his staff in his left hand, and his lean face was taut with vision. Behind him were Lord Callindrill and two Bloodguard. The Lord had a dark look of failure in his soft eyes. Quaan and Amorine were with him. And on Mhoram's right, supported by the Lord's right hand, was Hile Troy.

Troy had lost his sunglasses and headband. The eyeless skin of his skull was knotted as if he were straining to see. He cocked his head, moved it from side to side to focus his hearing. Covenant understood intuitively that Troy had lost his Land-born sight.

With these people was one man whom Covenant did not know. He was the singer – a tall, white-haired man with glowing silver eyes, who hummed to himself as if he were dewing the ground with melody. Covenant guessed without thinking that he was Caerroil Wildwood, the Forestal of Garroting Deep.

Something in the singer's gaze – something severe, yet oddly respectful – recalled the Unbeliever to himself. At last he perceived the fear in the faces watching him. He pushed himself away from Bannor's support, took the weight of all his burdens on his own shoulders. For a moment, he met the trepidation before him with a glare so intense that it made his forehead throb. But then, as he was about to speak, a fierce detonation from Rivenrock shook his bones, knocked him off balance. When he reached towards Bannor, he exposed the shame of his ring.

Facing Mhoram and Troy as squarely as he could, he groaned, 'She's lost. I lost her.' But his face twisted, and the words came brokenly between his lips, like fragments of his heart.

His utterance seemed to pale the music, making the muffled clamour from Rivenrock louder. He felt every blast of the battle like an internal blow. But the deadness under his feet became more and more vivid to him. And the gibbeted Giant hung before him with an immediacy he could not ignore. He began to realize that he was facing people who had survived ordeals of their own. He flinched, but did not fall, when their protests began – when Troy gave a strangled cry, 'Lost? Lost?' and Mhoram asked in a stricken voice, 'What has happened?'

Under the night sky on the lifeless hilltop – lit by the stars, and the twin gleams of Caerroil Wildwood's eyes, and the *orcrest* fire – Covenant stood braced on Bannor like a crippled witness against himself, and described in stumbling sentences High Lord Elena's plight. He made no mention of the focus of her gaze, her consuming passion. But he told all the rest – his bargain, Amok's end, the summoning of Kevin Landwaster, Elena's solitary fall. When he was done, he was answered by an aghast silence that echoed in his ears like a denunciation.

'I'm sorry,' he concluded into the stillness. Forcing himself to drink the bitter dregs of his personal inefficacy, he added, 'I loved her. I would have saved her if I could.'

'Loved her?' Troy murmured. 'Alone?' His voice was too disjointed to register the degree of his pain.

Lord Mhoram abruptly covered his eyes, bowed his head.

Quaan, Amorine, and Callindrill stood together as if they could not endure what they had heard alone.

Another blast from Rivenrock shivered the air. It snatched Mhoram's head up, and he faced Covenant with tears streaming down his cheeks. 'It is as I have said,' he breathed achingly. 'Madness is not the only danger in dreams.'

At this, Covenant's face twisted again. But he had nothing more to say; even the release of assent was denied him. However, Bannor seemed to hear something different in the Lord's tone. As if to correct an injustice, he went to Mhoram. As he moved, he took from his pack Covenant's marrowmeld sculpture.

He handed the work to Mhoram. 'The High Lord gave it to him as a gift.'

Lord Mhoram gripped the bone sculpture tightly, and his eyes shone with sudden comprehension. He understood the bond between Elena and the Ranyhyn; he understood what the giving of such a gift to Covenant meant. A gasp of weeping swept over his face. But when it passed, it left his self-mastery intact. His crooked lips took on their own humane angle. When he turned to Covenant again, he said gently, 'It is a precious gift.'

Bannor's unexpected support, and Mhoram's gesture of conciliation, touched Covenant. But he had no strength to spare for either of them. His gaze was fixed on Hile Troy.

The Warmark winced eyelessly under repeated blows of realization, and within him a gale brewed. He seemed to see Elena in his mind – remember her, taste her beauty, savour all the power of sight which she had taught him. He seemed to see her useless, solitary end. 'Lost?' he panted as his fury grew. 'Lost? Alone?'

All at once, he erupted. With a livid howl, he raged at Covenant. 'Do you call that love?! Leper! Unbeliever!' – he spat the words as if they were the most damning curses he knew – 'This is all just a game for you! Mental tricks. Excuses. You're a leper! A moral leper! You're too selfish to love anyone but yourself. You have the power for everything, and you won't use it. You just turned your back on her when she needed you. You – despicable – leper! Leper!' He shouted with such force that the muscles of his neck corded. The veins in his temples bulged and throbbed as if he were about to burst with execration.

Covenant felt the truth of the accusation. His bargain exposed him to such charges, and Troy hit the heart of his vulnerability as if some prophetic insight guided his blindness. Covenant's right hand twitched in a futile fending motion. But his left clung to his chest as if to localize his shame in that one place. When Troy paused to gather himself for another assault, Covenant said weakly, 'Unbelief has got nothing to do with it. She was my daughter.'

'What?'

'My daughter.' Covenant pronounced it like an indictment. 'I raped Trell's child. Elena was his granddaughter.'

'Your daughter.' Troy was too stunned to shout. Implications like glimpses of depravity rocked him. He groaned as if Covenant's crimes were so multitudinous that he could not hold them all in his mind at one time.

Mhoram spoke to him carefully. 'My friend – this is the knowledge which I have withheld from you. The withholding gave you unintended pain. Please pardon me. The Council feared that this knowledge would cause you to abominate the Unbeliever.'

'Damn right,' Troy panted. 'Damn right.'

Suddenly, his accumulated passion burst into action. Guided by a sure instinct, he reached out swiftly, snatched away Lord Mhoram's staff. He spun once to gain momentum, and levelled a crushing blow with the staff at Covenant's head.

The unexpectedness of the attack surpassed even Bannor. But he recovered, sprang after Troy, jolted him enough to unbalance his swing. As a result, only the heel of the staff clipped Covenant's forehead. But that sent him tumbling backward down the hill.

He caught himself, got to his knees. When he raised a hand to his head, he found that he was bleeding profusely from a wound in the centre of his forehead.

He could feel old hate and death seeping into him from the blasted earth. Blood ran down his cheeks like spittle.

The next moment, Mhoram and Quaan reached Troy. Mhoram tore the staff from his grasp; Quaan pinned his arms. 'Fool!' the Lord rasped. 'You forget the Oath of Peace. Loyalty is due!'

Troy struggled against Quaan. Rage and anguish mottled his face. 'I haven't sworn any Oath! Let go of me!'

'You are the Warmark of the Warward,' said Mhoram dangerously. 'The Oath of Peace binds. But if you cannot refrain from murder for that reason, refrain because the Despiser's army is destroyed. Fleshharrower hangs dead on the gibbet of Gallows Howe.'

'Do you call that victory? We've been decimated! What good is a victory that costs so much?' Troy's fury rose like weeping. 'It would have been better if we'd lost! Then it wouldn't have been such a waste!' The passion in his throat made him gasp for air as if he were asphyxiating on the reek of Covenant's perfidy.

But Lord Mhoram was unmoved. He caught Troy by the breastplate and shook him. 'Then refrain because the High Lord is not dead.'

'Not?' Troy panted. 'Not dead?'

'We hear her battle even now. Do you not comprehend the sound? Even as we listen, she struggles against dead Kevin. The Staff sustains her – and he has not the might she believed of him. But the proof of her endurance is here, in the Unbeliever himself. She is his summoner – he will remain in the Land until her death. So it was when Drool Rockworm first called him.'

'She's still fighting?' Troy gaped at the idea. He seemed to regard it as the conclusive evidence of Covenant's treachery. But then he turned to Mhoram and cried, 'We've got to help her!'

At this, Mhoram flinched. A wave of pain broke through his face. In a constricted voice, he asked, 'How?'

'How?' Troy fumed. 'Don't ask me how. *You're* the Lord! We have got to help her!'

The Lord pulled himself erect, clenched his staff for support. 'We are fifty leagues from Rivenrock. A night and a day would pass before any Ranyhyn could carry us to the foot of the cliff. Then Bannor would be required to guide us into the mountain in search of the battle. Perhaps the effects of the battle have destroyed all approaches to it. Perhaps they would destroy us. Yet if we gained the High Lord, we would have nothing to offer her but the frail strength of two Lords. With the Staff of Law, she far surpasses us. How can we help her?'

They faced each other as if they met mind to mind across Troy's eyelessness. Mhoram did not falter under the Warmark's rage. The hurt of his inadequacy showed clearly in his face, but he neither denied nor cursed at his weakness.

Though Troy trembled with urgency, he had to take his demand elsewhere.

He swung towards Covenant. 'You!' he shouted stridently. 'If you're too much of a coward to do anything yourself, at least give me a chance to help her! Give me your ring! – I can feel it from here. Give it to me! Come on, you bastard. It's her only chance.'

Kneeling on the dead, sabulous dirt of the Howe, Covenant looked up at Troy through the blood in his eyes. For a time, he was unable to answer. Troy's adjuration seemed to drop on him like a rockfall. It swept away his last defence, and left bare his final shame. He should have been able to save Elena. He had the power; it pulsed like a wound on his wedding finger. But he had not used it. Ignorance was no excuse. His claim of futility no longer covered him.

The barren atmosphere of the Howe ached in his chest as he climbed to his feet. Though he could hardly see where he was going, he started up the hill. The exertion made his head hurt as if there were splinters of bone jabbing his brain, and his heart quivered. A silent voice cried out to him, No! No! But he ignored it. With his halfhand, he fumbled at the ring. It seemed to resist him – he had trouble gripping it – but as he reached Troy he finally tore it from his finger. In a wet voice, as if his mouth were full of blood, he said, 'Take it. Save her.' He put the band in Troy's hand.

The touch of the pulsing ring exalted Troy. Clenching his fingers around it, he turned, ran fearlessly to the hillcrest. He searched quickly with his ears, located the direction of Rivenrock, faced the battle. Like a titan, he swung his fist at the heavens; power flamed from the white gold as if it were answering his passion. In a livid voice, he cried, 'Elena! Elena!'

Then the tall white singer was at his side. The music took on a forbidding note that spread involuntary stasis like a mist over the hilltop. Everyone froze, lost the power of movement.

In the stillness, Caerroil Wildwood lifted his gnarled sceptre. 'No,' he trilled. 'I cannot permit this. It is a breaking of Law. And you forget the price that is owed to me. Perhaps when you have gained an incondign mastery over the wild magic, you will use it to recant the price.' With his sceptre, he touched Troy's upraised fist; the ring dropped to the ground. As it fell, all the heat and surge of its power faded. It looked like mere metal as it struck the lifeless earth, rolled lightly along the music, and stopped near Covenant's feet.

'I will not permit it,' the singer continued. 'The promise is irrevocable. In the names of the One Tree and the One Forest – in the name of the unforgiving Deep – I claim the price of my aid.' With a solemn gesture like the sound of distant horns, he touched his sceptre to Troy's head. 'Eyeless one, you have promised payment. I claim your life.'

Lord Mhoram strove to protest. But the singer's stasis held him. He could do nothing but watch as Troy began to change.

'I claim you to be my disciple,' the singer hummed. 'You shall be Caer-Caveral, my help and hold. From me you shall learn the work of a Forestal, root and branch, seed and sap and leaf and all. Together we will walk the Deep, and I will teach you the songs of the trees, and the names of all the old, brave, wakeful woods, and the ancient forestry of thought and mood. While trees remain, we will steward together, cherishing each new sprout, and wreaking wood's revenge on each hated human intrusion. Forget your foolish friend. You cannot succour her. Caer-Caveral, remain and serve!'

The song moulded Troy's form. Slowly, his legs grew together. His feet began to send roots into the soil. His apparel turned to thick dark moss. He became an old stump with one last limb upraised. From his fist green leaves uncurled.

Softly, the singer concluded, 'Together we will restore life to Gallows Howe.' Then he turned towards the Lords and Covenant. The silver brilliance of his eyes increased, dimming even the *orcrest* fire; and he sang in a tone of dewy freshness:

> Axe and fire leave me dead.
> I know the hate of hands grown bold.
> Depart to save your heart-sap's red:
> My hate knows neither rest nor weal.

As the words fluted through them, he disappeared into the music as if he had wrapped it about him and passed beyond the range of sight. But the warning melody lingered behind him like an echo in the air, repeating his command and repeating it until it could not be forgotten.

Gradually, like figures lumbering stiffly out of a dream, the people on the hilltop began to move again. Quaan and Amorine hastened to the mossy stump. Grief filled their faces. But they had endured too much, struggled too hard, in their long ordeal. They had no strength left for horror or protest. Amorine stared as if she could not comprehend what had happened, and tears glistened in Quaan's old eyes. He called, 'Hail, Warmark!' But his voice sounded weak and dim on the Howe, and he said no more.

Behind them, Lord Mhoram sagged. His hands trembled as he held up his staff in mute farewell. Lord Callindrill joined him, and they stood together as if they were leaning on each other.

Covenant dropped numbly to his knees to pick up his ring.

He reached for it like an acolyte bending his forehead to the ground, and when his fingers closed on it, he slid it into place on his wedding finger. Then, with both hands, he tried to wipe the blood out of his eyes.

But as he made the attempt, a blast from Rivenrock staggered the air. The mountain groaned as if it were grievously wounded. The concussion threw him on his face in the dirt. Blackness filled the remains of his sight as if it were flooding into him from the barren Howe. And behind it he heard the blast howling like the livid triumph of fiends.

A long tremor passed through the Deep, and after it came an extended shattering sound, as if the whole cliff of Rivenrock were crumbling. People moved; voices called back and forth. But Covenant could not hear them clearly. His ears were deluged by tumult, a yammering, multitudinous yell of glee. And the sound came closer. It became louder and more immediate until it overwhelmed his eardrums, passed beyond the range of physical perception and shrieked directly into his brain.

After that, voices reached him obscurely, registered somehow through his overdriven hearing.

Bannor said, 'Rivenrock bursts. There will be a great flood.'

Lord Callindrill said, 'Some good will come of it. It will do much to cleanse the Wightwarrens under Mount Thunder.'

Lord Mhoram said, 'Behold – the Unbeliever departs. The High Lord has fallen.'

But these things surpassed him; he could not hold onto them. The black dirt of Gallows Howe loomed in his face like an incarnation of midnight. And around it, encompassing it, consuming both it and him, the fiendish scream scaled upward, filling his skull and chest and limbs as if it were grinding his very bones to powder. The howl overcame him, and he answered with a cry that made no sound.

27

LEPER

The shriek climbed, became louder as it grew more urgent and damaging. He could feel it breaking down the barriers of his comprehension, altering the terrain of his existence. Finally he seemed to shatter against it; he fell against it from a great height, so that he broke on its remorseless surface. He jerked at the force of the impact. When he lay still again, he could feel the hardness pressing coldly against his face and chest.

Gradually, he realized that the surface was damp, sticky. It smelled like clotting blood.

That perception carried him across a frontier. He found that he could distinguish between the flat, bitter, insulting shriek outside and the ragged hurt inside his head. With an agonizing effort, he moved one hand to rub the caked blood out of his eyes. Then, tortuously, he opened them.

His vision swam into focus like a badly smeared lens, but after a while he began to make out pieces of where he was. There was plenty of soulless yellow light. The legs of the sofa stood a few feet away across the thick defensive carpet. He was lying prostrate on the floor beside the coffee table as if he had fallen off a catafalque.

With his left hand, he clutched something hard to his ear, something that shrieked brutally.

When he shifted his hand, he discovered that he was holding the receiver of the telephone. From it came the shriek – the piercing wail of a phone left off its hook. The phone itself lay on the floor just out of reach.

A long, dumb moment passed before he regained enough of himself to wonder how long ago Joan had hung up on him.

Groaning, he rolled to one side and looked up at a wall clock. He could not read it; his eyes were still too blurred. But through one window he could see the first light of an uncomfortable dawn. He had been unconscious for half the night.

He started to his feet, then slumped down again while pain rang in his head. He feared that he would lose consciousness once more. But after a while, the noise cleared, faded into the general scream of the phone. He was able to get to his knees.

He rested there, looking about him at the controlled orderliness of his living room. Joan's picture and his cup of coffee stood just where he had left them on the table. The jolt of his head on the table edge had not even spilled the coffee.

The sanctuary of the familiar place gave him no consolation. When he tried to concentrate on the room's premeditated neatness, his gaze kept sliding back to the blood – dry, almost black – which crusted the carpet. That stain violated his safety like a chancre. To get away from it, he gripped himself and climbed to his feet.

The room reeled as if he had fallen into vertigo, but he steadied himself on the padded arm of the sofa, and after a moment he regained most of his balance. Carefully, as if he were afraid of disturbing a demon, he placed the receiver back on its hook, then sighed deeply as the shriek was chopped out of the air. Its echo continued to ring in his left ear. It disturbed his equilibrium, but he ignored it as best he could. He began to move through the house like a blind man, working his way from support to support – sofa to doorframe to kitchen counter. Then he had to take several unbraced steps to reach the bathroom, but he managed to cross the distance without falling.

He propped himself on the sink, and rested again.

When he had caught his breath, he automatically ran water and lathered his hands – the first step in his rite of cleansing, a vital part of his defence against a relapse. For a time, he scrubbed his hands without raising his head. But at last he looked into the mirror.

The sight of his own visage stopped him. He gazed at himself out of raw, self-inflicted eyes, and recognized the face that Elena had sculpted. She had not placed a wound on the forehead of her carving, but his cut only completed the image she had formed of him. He could see a gleam of bone through the caked black blood which darkened his forehead and cheeks, spread down around his eyes, emphasizing them, shadowing them with terrible purposes. The wound and the blood on his grey, gaunt face made him look like a false prophet, a traitor to his own best dreams.

Elena! he cried thickly. What have I done?

Unable to bear the sight of himself, he turned away and glanced numbly around the bathroom. In the fluorescent lighting, the porcelain of the tub and the chromed metal of its dangerous fixtures glinted as if they had nothing whatever to do with weeping. Their blank superficiality seemed to insist that grief and loss were unreal, irrelevant.

He stared at them for a long time, measuring their blankness. Then he limped out of the bathroom. Grimly, deliberately, he left his forehead uncleaned, untouched. He did not choose to repudiate the accusation written there.

THE POWER THAT PRESERVES

Be true, Unbeliever

1

THE DANGER IN DREAMS

Thomas Covenant was talking in his sleep. At times he knew what he was doing; the broken pieces of his voice penetrated his stupor dimly, like flickers of innocence. But he could not rouse himself – the weight of his exhaustion was too great. He babbled like millions of people before him, whole or ill, true or false. But in his case there was no one to hear. He would not have been more alone if he had been the last dreamer left alive.

When the shrill demand of the phone cut through him, he woke up wailing.

For a moment after he threw himself upright in bed, he could not distinguish between the phone and his own flat terror; both echoed like torment through the fog in his head. Then the phone rang again. It pulled him sweating out of bed, compelled him to shamble like a derelict into the living room, forced him to pick up the receiver. His numb, disease-cold fingers fumbled over the black plastic, and when he finally gained a grip on it, he held it to the side of his head like a pistol.

He had nothing to say to it, so he waited in blankness for the person at the other end of the line to speak.

A woman's voice asked uncertainly, 'Mr Covenant? Thomas Covenant?'

'Yes,' he murmured, then stopped, vaguely surprised by all the things he had with that one word admitted to be true.

'Ah, Mr Covenant,' the voice said. 'Megan Roman calling.' When he said nothing, she added with a touch of acerbity, 'Your lawyer. Remember?'

But he did not remember, he knew nothing about lawyers. Numb mist confused all the links of his memory. Despite the metallic distortion of the connection, her voice sounded distantly familiar; but he could not identify it.

She went on, 'Mr Covenant, I've been your lawyer for two years now. What's the matter with you? Are you all right?'

The familiarity of her voice disturbed him. He did not want to remember who she was. Dully, he murmured, 'It doesn't have anything to do with me.'

'Are you kidding? I wouldn't have called if it didn't have to do with you. I wouldn't have anything to do with it if it weren't your business.' Irritation and discomfort scraped together in her tone.

'No.' He did not want to remember. For his own benefit, he strained to articulate. 'The Law doesn't have anything to do with me. She broke it. Anyway. I – It can't touch me.'

'You better believe it can touch you. And you better listen to me. I don't know what's wrong with you, but – '

He interrupted her. He was too close to remembering her voice. 'No,' he said again. 'It doesn't bind me. I'm – outside. Separate. It can't touch me. Law is – ' he paused for a moment, groped through the fog for what he wanted to say – 'not the opposite of Despite.'

Then in spite of himself he recognized her voice. Through the disembodied inaccuracy of the phone line, he identified her.

Elena.

A sickness of defeat took the resistance out of him.

She was saying, ' – what you're talking about. I'm your lawyer, Megan Roman. And if you think the law can't touch you, you'd better listen to me. That's what I'm calling about.'

'Yes,' he said hopelessly.

'Listen, Mr Covenant.' She gave her irritation a free hand. 'I don't exactly like being your lawyer. Just thinking about you makes me squirm. But I've never backed down on a client before, and I don't mean to start with you. Now pull yourself together and listen to me.'

'Yes.' Elena? he moaned dumbly. Elena? What have I done to you?

'All right. Here's the situation. That – unfortunate escapade of yours – Saturday night – has brought matters to a head. It – Did you have to go to a nightclub, Mr Covenant? A nightclub, of all places?'

'I didn't mean it.' He could think of no other words for his contrition.

'Well, it's done now. Sheriff Lytton is up in arms. You've given him something he can use against you. He spent Sunday evening and this morning talking to a lot of people around here. And the people he talked to talked to other people. The township council met at noon.

'Mr Covenant, this probably wouldn't have happened if everyone didn't remember the last time you came to town. There was a lot of talk then, but it'd calmed down for the most part. Now it's stirred up again. People want action.

'The council intends to give them action. Our scrupulous local government is going to have your property rezoned. Haven Farm will probably be zoned industrial. Residential use will be prohibited.

Once that's done, you can be forced to move. You'll probably get a fair price for the Farm – but you won't find any other place to live in this county.'

'It's my fault,' he said. 'I had the power, and I didn't know how to use it.' His bones were full to the marrow with old hate and death.

'What? Are you listening to me? Mr Covenant, you're my client – for whatever that's worth. I don't intend to stand by and let this happen to you. Sick or not, you've got the same civil rights as anyone else. And there are laws to protect private citzens from – persecution. We can fight. Now I want – ' against the metallic background noise of the phone, he could hear her gathering her courage – 'I want you to come to my office. Today. We'll dig into the situation – arrange to appeal the decision, or file suit against it – something. We'll discuss all the ramifications, and plan a strategy. All right?'

The sense of deliberate risk in her tone penetrated him for a moment. He said, 'I'm a leper. They can't touch me.'

'They'll throw you out on your ear! Damn it, Covenant – you don't seem to understand what's going on here. You are going to lose your home. It can be fought – but you're the client, and I can't fight it without you.'

But her vehemence made his attention retreat. Vague recollections of Elena swirled in him as he said. 'That's not a good answer.' Absently, he removed the receiver from his ear and returned it to its cradle.

For a long time, he stood gazing at the black instrument. Something in its irremediable pitch and shape reminded him that his head hurt.

Something important had happened to him.

As if for the first time, he heard the lawyer saying, *Sunday evening and this morning.* He turned woodenly and looked at the wall clock. At first he could not bring his eyes into focus on it; it stared back at him as if it were going blind. But at last he made out the time. The afternoon sun outside his windows confirmed it.

He had slept for more than thirty hours.

Elena? he thought. That could not have been Elena on the phone. Elena was dead. His daughter was dead. It was his fault.

His forehead began to throb. The pain rasped his mind like a bright, brutal light. He ducked his head to try to evade it.

Elena had not even existed. She had never existed. He had dreamed the whole thing.

Elena! he moaned. Turning, he wandered weakly back towards his bed.

As he moved, the fog turned crimson in his brain.

When he entered the bedroom, his eyes widened at the sight of his pillow; and he stopped. The pillowcase was stained with black splotches. They looked like rot, some species of fungus gnawing away at the white cleanliness of the linen.

Instinctively, he raised a hand to his forehead. But his numb fingers could tell him nothing. The illness that seemed to fill the whole inside of his skull began laughing. His empty guts squirmed with nausea. Holding his forehead in both hands, he lurched into the bathroom.

In the mirror over the sink, he saw the wound on his forehead.

For an instant, he saw nothing of himself but the wound. It looked like leprosy, like an invisible hand of leprosy clenching the skin of his forehead. Black crusted blood clung to the ragged edges of the cut, mottling his pale flesh like deep gangrene; and blood and fluid seeped through cracks in the heavy scabs. He seemed to feel the infection festering its way straight through his skull into his brain. It hurt his gaze as if it already reeked of disease and ugly death.

Trembling fiercely, he spun the faucets to fill the sink. While water frothed into the basin, he hurried to lather his hands.

But when he noticed his white gold ring hanging loosely on his wedding finger, he stopped. He remembered the hot power which had pulsed through that metal in his dream. He could hear Bannor, the Bloodguard who had kept him alive, saying, *Save her! You must!* – hear himself reply, *I cannot!* He could hear Hile Troy's shout, *Leper! You're too selfish to love anyone but yourself.* He winced as he remembered the blow which had laid open his forehead.

Elena had died because of him.

She had never existed.

She had fallen into that crevice, fighting desperately against the spectre of mad Kevin Landwaster, whom she had Commanded from his grave. She had fallen and died. The Staff of Law had been lost. He had not so much as lifted his hand to save her.

She had never even existed. He had dreamed her while he lay unconscious after having hit his head on the edge of the coffee table.

Torn between conflicting horrors, he stared at his wound as if it were an outcry against him, a two-edged denunciation. From the mirror it shouted to him that the prophecy of his illness had come to pass.

Moaning, he pushed away, and rushed back towards the phone. With soapy, dripping hands, he fumbled at it, struggled to dial the number of Joan's parents. She might be staying with them. She had been his wife, he needed to talk to her.

But half-way through the number, he threw down the receiver.

In his memory, he could see her standing chaste and therefore merciless before him. She still believed that he had refused to talk to her when she had called him Saturday night. She would not forgive him for the rebuff he had helplessly dealt her.

How could he tell her that he needed to be forgiven for allowing another woman to die in his dreams?

Yet he needed someone – needed someone to whom he could cry out, Help me!

He had gone so far down the road to a leper's end that he could not pull himself back alone.

But he could not call the doctors at the leprosarium. They would return him to Louisiana. They would treat him and train him and counsel him. They would put him back into life as if his illness were all that mattered, as if wisdom were only skin-deep – as if grief and remorse and horror were nothing but illusions, tricks done with mirrors, irrelevant to chrome and porcelain and clean, white, stiff hospital sheets and fluorescent lights.

They would abandon him to the unreality of his passion.

He found that he was gasping hoarsely, panting as if the air in the room were too rancid for his lungs.

He needed – needed.

Dialling convulsively, he called Information and got the number of the nightclub where he had gone drinking Saturday night.

When he reached that number, the woman who answered the phone told him in a bored voice that Susie Thurston had left the nightclub. Before he could think to ask, the woman told him where the singer's next engagement was.

He called Information again, then put a long-distance call through to the place where Susie Thurston was now scheduled to perform. The switchboard of this club connected him without question to her dressing-room.

As soon as he heard her low, waifish, voice, he panted thickly, 'Why did you do it? Did he put you up to it? How did he do it? I want to know – '

She interrupted him roughly. 'Who are you? I don't know what the hell you're talking about. Who do you think you are? I didn't do nothing to you.'

'Saturday night. You did it to me Saturday night.'

'Buster, I don't know you from Adam, I didn't do nothing to you. Just drop dead, will you? Get off my phone.'

'You did it Saturday night. He put you up to it. You called me "Berek".' Berek Halfhand – the long-dead hero in his dream. The people in his dream, the people of the Land, had believed him to be

789

Berek Halfhand reborn – believed that because leprosy had claimed the last two fingers of his right hand. 'That crazy old beggar told you to call me Berek, and you did it.'

She was silent for a long moment before she said, 'Oh, it's you. You're the guy – the people at the club said you were a leper.'

'You called me Berek,' Covenant croaked as if he were strangling on the sepulchral air of the house.

'A leper,' she breathed. 'Oh, hell! I might've kissed you. Buster, you sure had me fooled. You look a hell of a lot like a friend of mine.'

'Berek,' Covenant groaned.

'What – "Berek"? You heard me wrong. I said, "Berrett". Berrett Williams is a friend of mine. He and I go 'way back. I learned a lot from him. But he was three-quarters crocked all the time. Anyway, he was sort of a clown. Coming to hear me without saying a thing about it is the sort of thing he'd do. And you looked – '

'He put you up to it. That old beggar made you do it. He's trying to do something to me.'

'Buster, you got leprosy on the brain. I don't know no beggars. I got enough useless old men of my own. Say, maybe you are Berrett Williams. This sounds like one of his jokes. Berrett, damn you, if you're setting me up for something – '

Nausea clenched in Covenant again. He hung up the phone and hunched over his stomach. But he was too empty to vomit; he had not eaten for forty-eight hours. He gouged the sweat out of his eyes with his numb fingertips, and dialled Information again.

The half-dried soap on his fingers made his eyes sting and blur as he got the number he wanted and put through another long-distance call.

When the crisp voice said, 'Department of Defence,' he blinked at the moisture which filled his eyes like shame, and responded, 'Let me talk to Hile Troy.' Troy had been in his dream, too. But the man had insisted that he was real, an inhabitant of the real world, not a figment of Covenant's nightmare.

'Hile Troy? One moment, sir.' Covenant heard the riffling of pages briefly. Then the voice said, 'Sir, I have no listing for anyone by that name.'

'Hile Troy,' Covenant repeated. 'He works in one of your – in one of your think tanks. He had an accident. If he isn't dead, he should be back to work by now.'

The military voice lost some of its crispness. 'Sir, if he's employed here as you say – then he's security personnel. I couldn't contact him for you, even if he were listed here.'

'Just get him to the phone,' Covenant moaned. 'He'll talk to me.'

'What is your name, sir?'

'He'll talk to me.'

'Perhaps he will. I still need to know your name.'

'Oh, hell!' Covenant wiped his eyes on the back of his hand, then said abjectly, 'I'm Thomas Covenant.'

'Yes, sir. I'll connect you to Major Rolle. He may be able to help you.'

Then the line clicked into silence. In the background, Covenant could hear a running series of metallic snicks like the ticking of a deathwatch. Pressure mounted in him. The wound on his forehead throbbed like a scream. He clasped the receiver to his head, and hugged himself with his free arm, straining for self-control. When the line came to life again, he could hardly keep from howling at it.

'Mr Covenant?' a bland, insinuating voice said. 'I'm Major Rolle. We're having trouble locating the person you wish to speak to. This is a large department – you understand. Could you tell me more about him?'

'His name is Hile Troy. He works in one of your think tanks. He's blind.' The words trembled between Covenant's lips as if he were freezing.

'Blind, you say? Mr Covenant, you mentioned an accident. Can you tell me what happened to this Hile Troy?'

'Just let me speak to him. Is he there or not?'

The major hesitated, then said, 'Mr Covenant, we have no blind men in this department. Could you give me the source of your information? I'm afraid you're the victim of – '

Abruptly, Covenant was shouting, raging. 'He fell out of a window when his apartment caught fire, and he was killed! He never even existed!'

With a savage heave, he tore the phone cord from its socket, then turned and hurled it at the clock on the living-room wall. The phone struck the clock and bounced to the floor as if it were impervious to injury, but the clock shattered and fell in pieces.

'He's been dead for days! He never existed!'

In a paroxysm of fury, he lashed out and kicked the coffee table with one numb booted foot. The table flipped over, broke the frame of Joan's picture as it jolted across the rug. He kicked it again, breaking one of its legs. Then he knocked over the sofa, and leaped past it to the bookcases. One after another, he heaved them to the floor.

In moments, the neat leper's order of the room had degenerated into dangerous chaos. At once, he rushed back to the bedroom. With stumbling fingers, he tore the penknife out of his pocket, opened it, and used it to shred the bloodstained pillow. Then, while the feathers settled like guilty snow over the bed and bureaux, he thrust the knife back into his pocket and slammed out of the house.

He went down into the woods behind Haven Farm at a run, hurrying towards the secluded hut which held his office. If he could not speak of his distress, perhaps he could write it down. As he flashed along the path, his fingers were already twitching to type out: Help me help help help! But when he reached the hut, he found that it looked as if he had already been there. Its door had been torn from its hinges, and inside the hulks of his typewriters lay battered amid the litter of his files and papers. The ruin was smeared with excrement, and the small rooms stank of urine.

At first, he stared at the wreckage as if he had caught himself in an act of amnesia. He could not remember having done this. But he knew he had not done it; it was vandalism, an attack on him like the burning of his stables days or weeks ago. The unexpected damage stunned him. For an odd instant, he forgot what he had just done to his house. I am not a violent man, he thought dumbly. I'm not.

Then the constricted space of the hut seemed to spring at him from all the walls. A suffocating sensation clamped his chest. For the third time, he ached to vomit, and could not.

Gasping between clenched teeth, he fled into the woods.

He moved aimlessly at first, drove the inanition of his bones as fast as he could deep into the woodland with no aim except flight. But as sunset filled the hills, cluttered the trails with dusk, he bent his steps towards the town. The thought of people drew him like a lure. While he stumbled through the twilit spring evening, odd, irrational surges of hope jabbed his heart. At erratic intervals, he thought that the mere sight of a forthright, unrecriminating face would steady him, bring the extremities of his plight back within his grasp.

He feared to see such a face. The implicit judgement of its health would be beyond his endurance.

Yet he jerked unevenly on through the woods like a moth fluttering in half-voluntary pursuit of immolation. He could not resist the cold siren of people, the allure and pain of his common mortal blood! Help! He winced as each cruel hope struck him. Help me!

But when he neared the town – when he broke out of the woods in back of the scattered old homes which surrounded like a defensive perimeter the business core of the small town – he could not muster the courage to approach any closer. The bright-lit windows and porches and driveways seemed impassable: he would have to brave too much illumination, too much exposure, to reach any door, whether or not it would welcome him. Night was the only cover he had left for his terrible vulnerability.

Whimpering in frustration and need, he tried to force himself forward. He moved from house to house, searching for one, any one, which might offer him some faint possibility of consolation. But the lights refused him. The sheer indecency of thrusting himself upon unwitting people in their homes joined his fear to keep him back. He could not impose on the men and women who lived in sanctuary behind the brightness. He could not carry the weight of any more victims.

In this way – dodging and ducking around the outskirts of the community like a futile ghost, a ghoul impotent to horrify – he passed the houses, and then returned as he had come, made his scattered way back to Haven Farm like a dry leaf, brittle to the breaking point, and apt for fire.

At acute times during the next three days, he wanted to burn his house down, put it to the torch – make it the pyre or charnel of his uncleanness. And in many less savage moods, he ached to simply slit his wrists – open his veins and let the slow misery of his collapse drain away. But he could not muster the resolution for either act. Torn between horrors, he seemed to have lost the power of decision. The little strength of will that remained to him he spent in denying himself food and rest.

He went without food because he had fasted once before, and that hunger had helped to carry him through a forest of self-deceptions to a realization of the appalling thing he had done to Lena, Elena's mother. Now he wanted to do the same; he wanted to cut through all excuses, justifications, digressions, defences, and meet his condition on its darkest terms. If he failed to do this, then any conclusion he reached would be betrayed from birth, like Elena, by the inadequacy of his rectitude or comprehension.

But he fought his bone-deep need for rest because he was afraid of what might happen to him if he slept. He had learned that the innocent did not sleep. Guilt began in dreams.

Neither of these abnegations surpassed him. The nausea lurking constantly in the pit of his stomach helped him to keep from food. And the fever of his plight did not let him go. It held and rubbed him like a harness: he seemed to have the galls of it on his soul. Whenever the penury of his resources threatened him, he gusted out of his house like a lost wind, and scudded through the hills for miles up and down the wooded length of Righters Creek. And when he could not rouse himself with exertion, he lay down across the broken furniture in his living room, so that if he dozed he would be too uncomfortable to rest deeply enough for dreams.

In the process, he did nothing to care for his illness. His VSE – the Visual Surveillance of Extremities on which his struggle against leprosy depended – and other self-protective habits he neglected as if they had lost all meaning for him. He did not take the medication which had at one time arrested the spreading of his disease. His forehead festered; cold numbness gnawed its slow way up the nerves of his hands and feet. He accepted such things, ignored his danger. It was condign; he deserved it.

Nevertheless, he fell into the same fey mood every evening. In the gloom of twilight, his need for people became unendurable; it drew him spitting and gnashing his teeth to the outer darkness beyond the home lights of the town. Night after night he tried to drive himself to the door of a home, any home. But he could not raise his courage high enough to accost the lights. People within a stone's throw of him remained as unattainable as if they occupied another world. Each night he was thrown back for companionship on the unrelieved aspect of his own weakness – and on the throbbing ache which filled his skull as the infection in his forehead grew.

Elena had died because of him. She was his daughter, and he had loved her. Yet he had trapped her into death.

She had never even existed.

He could find no answer to it.

Then, Thursday night, the pattern of his decline was broken for him. In the process of his futile ghosting, he became aware of sounds on the dark breeze. A tone rose and fell like a voice in oratory, and between its stanzas he heard singing. Disembodied in the darkness, the voices had a tattered, mournful air, like an invitation to a gathering of damned souls – verses and chorus responding in dolour to each other. Elena had been a singer, daughter of a family of singers. Fumbling his way through the benighted outskirts of the town, he followed the reft sorrow of the music.

It led him past the houses, around the town, down the road to the barren field which served as a parade ground whenever the town celebrated a patriotic occasion. A few people were still hurrying towards the field as if they were late, and Covenant avoided them by staying off the road. When he reached the parade ground, he found that a huge tent had been erected in its centre. All the sides of the tent were rolled up, so that the light of pressure lanterns shone vividly from under the canvas.

People filled the tent. They were just sitting down on benches after singing, and during the movement, several ushers guided the latecomers to the last empty seats. The benches faced in tight rows towards a wide platform at the front of the tent, where three men sat. They were behind a heavy pulpit, and behind them stood a makeshift altar, hastily hammered together out of pine boards, and bleakly adorned by a few crooked candles and a dull, battered gold cross.

As the people settled themselves on the benches, one of the men on the platform – a short fleshy man dressed in a black suit and a dull white shirt – got to his feet and stepped to the pulpit. In a sonorous, compelling voice, he said, 'Let us pray.'

All the people bowed their heads. Covenant was on the verge of turning away in disgust, but the quiet confidence of the man's tone stayed him. He listened unwillingly as the man folded his hands on the pulpit and prayed gently:

'Dear Jesus, our Lord and Saviour – please look down on the souls that have come together here. Look into their hearts, Lord – see the pain, and the hurt, and the loneliness, and the sorrow – yes, and the sin – and the hunger for You in their hearts. Comfort them, Lord. Help them, heal them. Teach them the peace and the miracle of prayer in Thy true name. Amen.'

Together, the people responded, 'Amen.'

The man's voice tugged at Covenant. He heard something in it that sounded like sincerity, like simple compassion. He could not be sure; he seemed to have learned what little he knew about sincerity in dreams. But he did not move away. Instead, while the people raised their heads from prayer, he moved cautiously forward into the light, went close enough to the tent to read a large sign posted at the side of the road. It said:

The EASTER HEALTH Crusade–
Dr B. Sam Johnson
revivalist and healer
tonight through Sunday
only.

On the platform, another man approached the pulpit. He wore a clerical collar, and a silver cross hung from his neck. He pushed his heavy glasses up on his nose, and beamed out over the people. 'I'm pleased as punch,' he said, 'to have Dr Johnson and Matthew Logan here. They're known everywhere in the state for their rich ministry to the spiritual needs of people like us. I don't need to tell you how much we need reviving here – how many of us need to recover that healing faith, especially in this Easter season. Dr Johnson and Mr Logan are going to help us return to the matchless Grace of God.'

The short man dressed in black stood up again and said, 'Thank you, sir.' The minister hesitated, then left the pulpit as if he had been dismissed – cut off in the opening stages of a fulsome introduction – and Dr Johnson went on smoothly: 'My friends, here's my dear brother in Christ, Matthew Logan. You've heard his wonderful, wonderful singing. Now he'll read the Divine Word of God for us. Brother Logan.

As he stepped to the pulpit, Matthew Logan's powerful frame towered over Dr Johnson. Though he seemed to have no neck at all, the head resting on his broad shoulders was half a yard above his partner's. He flipped authoritatively through a massive black Bible on the pulpit, found his place, and bowed his head to read as if in deference to the Word of God.

He began without introduction:

'"But if you will not hearken to me, and will not do all these commandments, but break my covenant, I will do this to you: I will appoint over you sudden terror, consumption, and fever that waste the eyes and cause life to pine away. And you shall sow your seed in vain, for your enemies shall eat it; those who hate you shall rule over you, and you shall flee when none pursues you. I will make your heavens like iron and your earth like brass; and your strength shall be spent in vain, for your land shall not yield its increase, and the trees of the land shall not yield their fruit.

'"Then if you walk contrary to me, and will not hearken to me, I will bring more plagues upon you, sevenfold as many as your sins. And I will let loose the wild beasts among you, which shall rob you of your children, and destroy your cattle, and make you few in number, so that your ways shall become desolate. I also will walk contrary to you, and I will bring a sword upon you, and shall execute vengeance for the covenant; and if you gather within your cities I will send pestilence among you, and you shall be delivered into the hand of the enemy."'

As Matthew Logan rolled out the words, Covenant felt their spell falling on him. The promise of punishment caught at his heart; it snared him as if it had been lying in ambush for his grey, gaunt soul. Stiffly, involuntarily, he moved towards the tent as the curse drew him to itself.

'"And if in spite of this you will not hearken to me, but walk contrary to me, then I will walk contrary to you in fury, and chastise you myself sevenfold for your sins. You shall eat the flesh of your sons, and you shall eat the flesh of your daughters. My soul will abhor you. I will lay your cities waste. I will scatter you among the nations, and I will unsheathe the sword after you; and your land shall be a desolation, and your cities shall be a waste.

'"Then the land shall pay for its sabbaths as long as it lies desolate."'

Covenant ducked under an edge of the canvas and found himself standing beside an usher at the rear of the tent. The usher eyed him distrustfully, but made no move to offer him a seat. High on the platform at the other end, Matthew Logan stood like a savage patriarch levelling retribution at the bent, vulnerable heads below him. The curse gathered a storm in Covenant, and he feared that he would cry out before it ended. But Matthew Logan stopped where he was and flipped through the Bible again. When he found his new place, he read more quietly:

'"Whoever, therefore, eats the bread or drinks the cup of the Lord in an unworthy manner will be guilty of profaning the body and blood of the Lord. Anyone who eats and drinks without discerning the body eats and drinks judgement upon himself. That is why many of you are weak and ill, and some have died. But if we judged ourselves truly, we should not be judged. But when we are judged by the Lord, we are chastened so that we may not be condemned along with the world."'

Slapping the Bible closed, he returned stolidly to his seat.

At once, Dr B. Sam Johnson was on his feet. Now he seemed to bristle with energy; he could not wait to begin speaking. His jowls quivered with excitement as he addressed his audience.

'My friends, how marvellous are the Words of God! How quick to touch the heart. How comforting to the sick, the downtrodden, the weak. And how easily they make even the purest of us squirm. Listen, my friends! Listen to the Word of the Apocalypse:

'"To the thirsty I will give water without price from the fountain of the water of life. He who conquers shall have this heritage, and I will be his God and he shall be my son. But as for the cowardly, the unbelievers, the polluted, as for murderers, fornicators, sorcerers, idolaters, and all liars, their lot shall be in the lake that burns with fire and brimstone, which is the second death."

'Marvellous, marvellous Words of God. Here in one short passage we hear the two great messages of the Bible, the Law and the Gospel, the Old Covenant and the New. Brother Logan read to you first from the Old Testament, from the twenty-sixth chapter of Leviticus. Did you hear him, my friends? Did you listen with all the ears of your heart? That is the voice of God, Almighty God. He doesn't mince words, my friends. He doesn't beat around the bush. He doesn't hide things in fine names and fancy language. No! He says, if you sin, if you break My Law, I will terrify you and make you sick. I will make the land barren and attack you with plagues and pestilence. And if you still sin, I will make cannibals and cripples out of you. "Then the land shall pay for its sabbaths as long as it lies desolate."

'And do you know what the Law is, my friends? I can summarize it for you in the Words of the Apocalypse. "Thou shalt not be cowardly, or unbelieving, or polluted." Never mind murder, fornication, sorcery, idolatry, lies. We're all *good* people here. We don't do things like *that*. But have you ever been afraid? Have you ever faltered just a bit in your faith? Have you ever failed to keep yourself clean in heart and mind? "Then the land shall pay for its sabbaths as long as it lies desolate." The Apostle Paul calls a spade a spade. He says, "That is why many of you are weak and ill, and some have died." But Jesus goes further. He says, "Depart from me, you cursed, into the eternal fire prepared for the devil and his angels."

'Do I hear you protesting? Do I hear some of you saying to yourselves, "No one can be that good. I'm human. I can't be perfect." You're right! Of course, you're right. But the Law of God doesn't care for your excuses. If you're lame, if you've got arthritis, if you're going blind or your heart is failing, if you're crippled, if you've got multiple sclerosis or diabetes or any other of those fancy names for sin, you can be sure that the curse of God is on you. But if you're healthy, don't think you're safe! You're just lucky that God hasn't decided to "walk contrary to you in fury". You can't be perfect, my friends. And the Law doesn't care how hard you tried. Instead of telling yourself what a valiant try you made, listen to the Bible. The Old Covenant says to you as plain as day, "The leper who has the disease shall wear torn clothes and let the hair of his head hang loose, and he shall cover his upper lip and cry, 'Unclean, unclean.'"'

He held his audience in the palm of his hand now. The orotund resonance of his voice swept them all together in one ranked assembly of mortality and weakness. Even Covenant forgot himself, forgot that he was an intruder in this canvas tabernacle; he heard so many personal echoes and gleams in the peroration that he could not resist it. He was willing to believe that he was accursed.

'Ah, my friends,' Dr Johnson went on smoothly, 'it's a dark day for us when illness strikes, when pain or dismemberment or bereavement afflict us, and we can no longer pretend we're clean. But I haven't told you about the Gospel yet. Do you remember Christ saying, "He who loses his life for my sake shall find it"? Did you hear Paul say, "When we are judged by the Lord, we are chastened so that we may not be condemned along with the world"? Did you hear the writer of the Apocalypse say, "He who conquers shall have this heritage, and I will be his God and he shall be my son"? There's another side, my friends. The Law is only half of God's holy message. The other half is chastening, heritage, forgiveness, healing — the Mercy that matches God's Righteousness. Do I have to remind you that the Son of God healed everyone who asked Him? Even lepers? Do I have to remind you that He hung on a cross erected in the midst of misery and shame to pay the price of our sin for us? Do I have to remind you that the nails tore His hands and feet? That the spear pierced His side? That He was dead for three days? Dead and in hell?

'My friends, He did it for only one reason. He did it to pay for all our cowardly, unbelieving, unclean sabbaths, so that we could be healed. And all you have to do to get healed is to believe it, and accept it, and love Him for it. All you have to do is say with the man whose child was dying, "I believe; help my unbelief!" Five little words, my friends. When they come from the heart, they're enough to pay for the whole Kingdom of Righteousness.'

As if on cue, Matthew Logan stood up and began singing in soft descant, 'Blessed assurance, Jesus is mine.' Against this background, Dr Johnson folded his hands and said, 'My friends, pray with me.'

At once, every head in the audience dropped. Covenant, too, bowed. But the wound on his forehead burned extravagantly in that postion. He looked up again as Dr Johnson said, 'Close your eyes, my friends. Shut out your neighbours, your children, your parents, your mate. Shut out every distraction. Look inward, my friends. Look deep inside yourselves, and see the sickness there. Hear the voice of God saying, "Thou are weighed in the balance, and found wanting." Pray with me in your hearts.

'Dear holy Jesus, Thou art our only hope. Only Thy Divine Mercy can heal the disease which riddles our courage, rots the fibre of our faith, dirties us in Thy sight. Only Thou canst touch the sickness which destroys the peace, and cure it. We lay bare our hearts to Thee, Lord. Help us to find the courage for those five difficult, difficult words, "I believe; help my unbelief!" Dear Lord, please give us the courage to be healed.'

Without a break, he raised his arms over the audience and continued, 'Do you feel His spirit, my friends? Do you feel it in your hearts? Do you feel the finger of His Righteousness probing the sick spot in your soul and body? If you do, come forward now, and let me pray for health with you.'

He bowed his head in silent supplication while he waited for the repentant to heed his call. But Covenant was already on his way down the aisle. The usher made a furtive movement to stop him, then backed off as several members of the audience looked up. Covenant stalked feverishly the length of the tent, climbed the rough wooden steps to the platform, and stopped facing Dr Johnson. His eyes glistened as he said in a raw whisper, 'Help me.'

The man was shorter than he had appeared to be from the audience. His black suit was shiny, and his shirt soiled from long use. He had not shaved recently; stiff, grizzled whiskers roughened his jowls and cheeks. His face wore an uncertain aspect – almost an expression of alarm – as Covenant confronted him, but he quickly masked it with blandness, and said in a tone of easy sonority, 'Help you, son? Only God can help you. But I will joyfully add my prayers to the cry of any contrite heart.' He placed a hand firmly on Covenant's shoulder. 'Kneel, son, and pray with me. Let's ask the Lord for help together.'

Covenant wanted to kneel, wanted to submit to the commanding spell of Dr Johnson's hand and voice. But his knees were locked with urgency and inanition. The pain in his forehead flamed like acid gnawing at his brain. He felt that if he bent at all he would collapse completely. 'Help me,' he whispered again. 'I can't stand it.'

Dr Johnson's face became stern at Covenant's resistance. 'Are you repentant, son?' he asked gravely. 'Have you found the sick spot of sin in your soul? Do you truly ache for Almighty God's Divine Mercy?'

'I am sick,' Covenant responded as if he were answering a litany. 'I have committed crimes.'

'And do you repent? Can you say those five difficult words with all the honest pain of your heart?'

Covenant's jaw locked involuntarily. Through clenched teeth, he said as if he were whimpering. 'Help my unbelief.'

'Son, that's not enough. You know that's not enough.' Dr Johnson's sternness changed to righteous judgement. 'Do not dare to mock God. He will cast you out for ever. Do you believe? Do you believe in God's own health?'

'I do -' Covenant struggled to move his jaw, but his teeth clung together as if they had been fused by despair – 'I do not believe.'

Behind him, Matthew Logan stopped singing his descant. The abrupt silence echoed in Covenant's ears like ridicule. Abjectly, he breathed, 'I'm a leper.'

He could tell by the curious, expectant faces in the first rows of the audience that the people had not heard him, did not recognize him. He was not surprised; he felt that he had been altered past all recognition by his delusions. And even in his long-past days of health he had never been associated with the more religious townspeople. But Dr Johnson heard. His eyes bulged dangerously in their sockets, and he spoke so softly that his words barely reached Covenant. 'I don't know who put you up to this but you won't get away with it.'

With hardly a pause, he began speaking for the people in the tent again. 'Poor man, you're delirious. That cut is infected, and it's given you a bad fever.' His public voice was redolent with sympathy. 'I grieve for you, son. But it will take a great power of prayer to clear your mind so that the voice of God can reach you. Brother Logan, would you take this poor sick man aside and pray with him? If God blesses your efforts to lift his fever, he may yet come to repentance.'

Matthew Logan's massive hands closed like clamps on Covenant's biceps. The fingers ground into him as if they meant to crush his bones. He found himself propelled forward, almost carried down the steps and along the aisle. Behind him, Dr Johnson was saying, 'My friends, will you pray with me for this poor suffering soul? Will you sing and pray for his healing with me?'

In a covered whisper, Matthew Logan said near Covenant's ear, 'We haven't taken the offering yet. If you do anything else to interrupt, I'll break both your arms.'

'Don't touch me!' Covenant snarled. The big man's treatment tapped a resource of rage which had been dammed in him for a long time. He tried to struggle against Logan's grasp. 'Get your hands off me.'

Then they reached the end of the aisle and ducked under the canvas out into the night. With an effortless heave, Brother Logan threw Covenant from him. Covenant stumbled and fell on the bare dirt of the parade ground. When he looked up, the big man was standing with fists on hips like a dark colossus between him and the light of the tent.

Covenant climbed painfully to his feet, pulled what little dignity he could find about his shoulders, and moved away.

As he shambled into the darkness, he heard the people singing, 'Blessed Assurance'. And a moment later, a pathetic childish voice cried, 'Lord, I'm lame! Please heal me!'

Covenant dropped to his knees and retched dryly. Some time passed before he could get up again and flee the cruel song.

He went homeward along the main road, defying the townspeople to hurt him further. But all the businesses were closed, and the street was deserted. He walked like a flicker of darkness under the pale yellow streetlamps, past the high, belittling giant-heads on the columns of the courthouse – made his way unmolested out the end of town towards Haven Farm.

The two miles to the Farm passed like all his hikes – measured out in fragments by the rhythm of his strides, a scudding, mechanical rhythm like the ticking of overstressed clockwork. The mainspring of his movement had been wound too tight; it was turning too fast, rushing to collapse. But a change had taken place in the force which drove him.

He had remembered hate.

He was spinning wild schemes for vengeance in his head when he finally reached the long driveway leading into Haven Farm. There in the cold starlight he saw a heavy sack sitting by his mailbox. A moment passed before he remembered that the sack contained food; the local grocery store delivered to him twice a week rather than face the risk that he might choose to do his shopping in person; and yesterday – Wednesday – had been one of the delivery days. But he had been so occupied with his restless fasting that he had forgotten.

He picked up the sack without stopping to wonder why he bothered, and carried it down the driveway towards his house.

But when he looked into the sack in the bright light of his kitchen, he found he had decided to eat. Vengeance required strength; there was nothing he could do to strike back against his tormentors if he were too weak to hold himself erect. He took a package of buns from the sack.

The wrapping of the buns had been neatly cut on one side, but he ignored the thin slit. He tore off the plastic and threw it aside. The buns were dry and stiff from their exposure to the air. He took one and held it in the palm of his hand, gazed down at it as if it were a skull he had robbed from some old grave. The sight of the bread sickened him. Part of him longed for the clean death of starvation, and he felt that he could not lift his hand, could not complete his decision of retribution.

Savagely, he jerked the bun to his mouth and bit into it.

Something sharp caught between his lower lip and upper gum. Before he could stop biting, it cut him deeply. A keen shard of pain stabbed into his face. Gasping, he snatched back the bun.

It was covered with blood. Blood ran like saliva down his chin.

When he tore open the bun with his hands, he found a tarnished razor blade in it.

At first, he was too astonished to react. The rusty blade seemed beyond comprehension; he could hardly believe the blood that smeared his hands and dropped to the floor from his jaw. Numbly, he let the bun fall from his fingers. Then he turned and made his way into the littered wreckage of his living room.

His eyes were irresistibly drawn to Joan's picture. It lay face up under the remains of the coffee table, and the glass of its frame was webbed with cracks. He pushed the table aside, picked up the picture. Joan smiled at him from behind the cracks as if she had been caught in a net of mortality and did not know it.

He began to laugh.

He started softly, but soon scaled upward into manic howling. Water ran from his eyes like tears, but still he laughed, laughed as if he were about to shatter. His bursts spattered blood over his hands and Joan's picture and the ruined room.

Abruptly, he threw down the picture and ran from it. He did not want Joan to witness his hysteria. Laughing madly, he rushed from the house into the woods, determined even while he lost control of himself to take his final breakdown as far away from Haven Farm as possible.

When he reached Righters Creek, he turned and followed it upstream into the hills, away from the dangerous lure of people as fast as his numb, awkward feet could carry him – laughing desperately all the while.

Some time during the night, he tripped; and when he found himself on the ground, he leaned against a tree to rest for a moment. At once, he fell asleep, and did not awaken until the morning sun was shining full in his face.

For a time, he did not remember who or where he was. The hot white light of the sun burned everything out of his mind; his eyes were so dazzled that he could not make out his surroundings. But when he heard the thin, wordless cry of fear, he began to chuckle. He was too weak to laugh loudly, but he chuckled as if that were the only thing left in him.

The thin cry repeated itself. Inspired by it, he managed a fuller laugh, and started to struggle to his feet. But the effort weakened him. He had to stop laughing to catch his breath. Then he heard the cry again, a child's shriek of terror. Supporting himself on the tree, he looked around, peering through his sun blindness at the dim shapes of the woods.

Gradually, he became able to see. He was perched high on a hill in the woods. Most of the branches and bushes were bursting with green spring leaves. A few yards from him, Righters Creek tumbled gaily down the rocky hillside and wandered like a playful silver trail away among the trees. Most of the hill below him was free of brush because of the rockiness of the soil; nothing obscured his downward view.

An odd splotch of colour at the bottom of the hill caught his attention. With an effort, he focused his eyes on it. It was cloth, a light blue dress worn by child – a little girl perhaps four or five years old. She stood half turned towards him, with her back pressed against the black, straight trunk of a tall tree. She seemed to be trying to push herself into the wood, but the indifferent trunk refused to admit her.

She was screaming continuously now, and her cries begged at the anguish in his mind. As she yelled, she stared in unmasked terror at the ground two or three feet in front of her. For a moment, Covenant could not see what she was looking at. But then his ears discerned the low buzzing noise, and he picked out the ominous brown shaking of the rattle.

The timber rattler was coiled less than a yard from the girl's bare legs. Its head bobbed as if it were searching for the perfect place to strike.

He recognized her terror now. Before the shout had a chance to burst past his blood-caked lips, he pushed himself away from the tree and started running down the hill.

The slope seemed interminably long, and his legs were hardly strong enough to sustain him. At each downward plunge, his muscles gave, and he almost fell to his knees. But the child's irrefusable fear held him up. He did not look at the snake. He fixed his eyes on her bare shins, concentrated himself on the importance of reaching her before the rattler's fangs jabbed into her flesh. The rest of her was blurred in his sight, as if she did not exist apart from her peril.

With each shrill cry, she begged him to hurry.

But he was not watching his footing. Before he had covered half the distance, he tripped — pitched headlong down the hill, tumbled and bounced over the rough rocks. For an instant, he protected himself with his arms. But then his head smacked against a broad facet of stone in the hillside.

He seemed to fall into the stone, as if he were burying his face in darkness. The hard surface of it broke over him like a wave; he could feel himself plunging deep into the rock's granite essence.

No! he cried. No! Not now!

He fought it with every jot of his strength. But it surpassed him. He sank into it as if he were drowning in stone.

2

VARIOL-SON

High Lord Mhoram sat in his private chambers deep in Revelstone. The unadorned gut-rock walls around him were warmly lit by small urns of graveling in each corner of the room, and the faint aroma of newly broken earth from the lore-glowing stones wrapped comfortably around him. But still he could feel the preternatural winter which was upon the Land. Despite the brave hearth fires set everywhere by the Hirebrands and Gravelingases of Lord's Keep, a bitter chill seeped noticeably through the mountain granite of the city. High Lord Mhoram felt it. He could sense its effect on the physical mood of the great Giant-wrought Keep. On an almost subliminal level, Revelstone was huddling against the cold.

Already, the first natural turnings of winter towards spring were a full cycle of the moon late. The middle night of spring was only fourteen days away, and still ice clung to the Land.

Outside the wedge-shaped mountain plateau of the Keep, there was not much snow; the air was too cold for snow. It blew at Revelstone on a jagged, uncharacteristic wind out of the east, kicking a thin skiff of snow across the foothills of the plateau, blinding all the windows of the Keep under deep inches of frost and immobilizing with ice the lake at the foot of Furl Falls. Mhoram did not need to smell the Despite which hurled that wind across the Land to know its source.

It came from Ridjeck Thome, Foul's Creche.

As the High Lord sat in his chambers, with his elbows braced on the stone table and his chin propped on one palm, he was aware of that wind hissing through the background of his thoughts. Ten years ago, he would have said that it was impossible; the natural weather patterns of the Land could not be so wrenched apart. Even five years ago, after he had had time to assess and reassess the loss of the Staff of Law, he would have doubted that the Illearth Stone could make Lord Foul so powerful. But now he knew better, understood more.

High Lord Elena's battle with dead Kevin Landwaster had taken place seven years ago. The Staff of Law must have been destroyed in that struggle. Without the Staff's innate support for the natural order of the Earth, one great obstacle was gone from the path of the Despiser's corrupting power. And the Law of Death had been broken; Elena had summoned Old Lord Kevin from beyond the grave. Mhoram could not begin to measure all the terrible implications of that rupture.

He blinked, and his gold-flecked eyes shifted into focus on the carving which stood on the table two feet from the flat blade of his nose. The bone of the carving gleamed whitely in the light of the fire-stones. It was a marrowmeld sculpture, the last of Elena's *anundivian yajña* work. Bannor of the Bloodguard had preserved it, and had given it to Mhoram when they had come together on Gallows Howe in Garroting Deep. It was a finely detailed bust, a sculpting of a lean, gaunt, impenetrable face, and its lines were tense with prophetic purpose. After Mhoram and the survivors of the Warward had returned to Revelstone from Garroting Deep, Bannor had explained the history of the bone sculpture.

In fact, he had explained it in unaccustomed detail. His habitual Bloodguard reticence had given way almost to prolixity; and the fullness of his description had provided Mhoram with a first hint of the fundamental alteration which had taken place in the Bloodguard. And in turn that description had led circuitously to the great change in Mhoram's own life. By a curious logic of its own, it had put an end to the High Lord's power of prevision.

He was no longer seer and oracle to the Council of Lords. Because of what he had learned, he caught no more glimpses of the future in dreams, read no more hints of distant happenings in the dance of the fire. The secret knowledge which he had gained so intuitively from the marrowmeld sculpture had blinded the eyes of his prescience.

It had done other things to him as well. It had afflicted him with more hope and fear than he had ever felt before. And it had partly estranged him from his fellow Lords; in a sense, it had estranged him from all the people of Revelstone. When he walked the halls of the Keep, he could see in the sympathy and pain and doubt and wonder of their glances that they perceived his separateness, his voluntary isolation. But he suffered more from the breach which now obtained between him and the other Lords – Callindrill Faermate, Amatin daughter of Matin, Trevor son of Groyle, and Loerya Trevor-mate. In all their work together, in all the intercourse of their daily lives, even in all the mind melding which was the great strength of the new Lords, he was forced to hold that sickening hope and fear apart, away from them. For he had not told them his secret.

He had not told them, though he had no justification for his silence except dread.

Intuitively, by steps which he could hardly articulate, Elena's marrowmeld sculpture had taught him the secret of the Ritual of Desecration.

He felt that there was enough hope and fear in the knowledge to last him a lifetime.

In the back of his mind, he believed that Bannor had wanted him to have this knowledge and had not been able to utter it directly. The Bloodguard Vow had restricted Bannor in so many ways. But during the single year of his tenure as First Mark, he had expressed more than any Bloodguard before him his solicitude for the survival of the Lords.

High Lord Mhoram winced unconsciously at the memory. The secret he now held had been expensive in more ways than one.

There was hope in the knowledge because it answered the quintessential failure which had plagued the new Lords from the beginning – from the day in which they had accepted the First Ward of Kevin's Lore from the Giants, and had sworn the Oath of Peace. If it were used, the knowledge promised to unlock the power which had remained sealed in the Wards despite the best efforts of so many generations of Lords and students at the Loresraat. It promised mastery of Kevin's Lore. It might even show ur-Lord Thomas Covenant how to use the wild magic in his white gold ring.

But Mhoram had learned that the very thing which made Kevin's Lore powerful for good also made it powerful for ill. If Kevin son of Loric had not had that particular capacity for power, he would not have been able to Desecrate the Land.

If Mhoram shared his knowledge, any Lord who wished to reinvoke the Ritual would not be forced to rely upon an instinctive distrust of life.

That knowledge violated the Oath of Peace. To his horror, Mhoram had come to perceive that the Oath itself was the essential blindness, the incapacity which had prevented the new Lords from penetrating to the heart of Kevin's Lore. When the first new Lords, and all the Land with them, had taken the Oath, articulated their highest ideal and deepest commitment by forswearing all violent, destructive passions, all human instincts for murder and ravage and contempt – when they had bound themselves with the Oath, they had unwittingly numbed themselves to the basic vitality of the Old Lords' power. Therefore High Lord Mhoram feared to share his secret. It was a strength which could only be used if the wielders denied the most basic promise of their lives. It was a weapon which could only be used by a person who had cast down all defences against despair.

And the temptation to use the weapon would be strong, perhaps irrefusable. Mhoram did not need oracular dreams to foresee the peril which Lord Foul the Despiser was preparing for the defenders of the Land. He could feel it in the frigid winter wind. And he knew that Trothgard was already under attack. The siege of Revelwood was under way even while he sat in his private quarters, staring morosely at a marrowmeld sculpture.

He could taste in his own mouth the desperation which had led High Lord Kevin to Kiril Threndor and the Ritual of Desecration. Power was dreadful and treacherous. When it was not great enough to accomplish its wielder's desires, it turned against the hands which held it. High Lord Elena's fate only repeated the lesson of Kevin Landwaster; he had possessed far more power than the new Lords could ever hope for, now that the Staff of Law was gone; and all his might had achieved nothing but his own ineluctable despair and the ruin of the Land. Mhoram feared to share that danger by revealing his secret. He was appalled to think he was in such peril himself.

Yet this withholding of knowledge ran against every grain of his character. He believed intensely that the refusal to share knowledge demeaned both the denier and the denied. By keeping the secret to himself, he prevented Callindrill and Amatin and Trevor and Loerya and every Lorewarden or student of the Staff from finding within themselves the strength to refuse Desecration; he placed himself falsely in the position of a judge who had weighed them and found them wanting. For this reason ten years ago he had argued passionately against the Council's decision to withhold from Hile Troy the knowledge of Elena's parentage. That decision had lessened Troy's control over his own fate. Yet how could he, Mhoram, bear the responsibility of sharing his secret if that sharing led to the Land's destruction? Better that the evil should be done by the Despiser than by a Lord.

When he heard the abrupt knock at his door, he said, 'Enter,' at once. He was expecting a message, and he knew from the sound of the knock who his visitor was. He did not look up from his contemplation of the sculpture as Warmark Quaan strode into the chamber and presented himself at the table.

But Quaan remained silent, and Mhoram sensed that the old Warmark was waiting to meet his gaze. With an inward sigh, the High Lord raised his head. In Quaan's age- and sun-weathered face, he read that the news was not what they had hoped it would be.

Mhoram did not offer Quaan a seat; he could see that the Warmark preferred to stand. They had sat together often enough in the past. After all the experiences they had shared, they were old comrades – though Quaan, who was twenty years younger than Mhoram, looked twenty years older. And the High Lord frequently found Quaan's blunt, soldierly candour soothing. Quaan was a follower of the Sword who had no desire to know any secrets of the Staff.

Despite his seventy years, Quaan carried proudly the insignia of his office: the yellow breastplate with its twin black diagonal slashes, the yellow headband, and the ebony sword. His gnarled hands hung up at his sides as if they were ready to snatch up weapons at any moment. But his pale eyes were disquieted.

Mhoram met the Warmark's gaze steadily and said, 'Well, my friend?'

'High Lord,' Quaan said brusquely, 'the Loresraat has come.'

Mhoram could see that the Warmark had more to say than this. His eyes asked Quaan to continue.

'All the Lorewardens and students have made the journey from Trothgard safely,' Quaan responded. 'The libraries of the Loresraat and the Wards have been brought here intact. All the visitors and those made homeless by the march of Satansfist's army through the Centre Plains have come seeking sanctuary. Revelwood is besieged.'

He stopped again, and Mhoram asked quietly, 'What word do the Lorewardens bring of that army?'

'It is – vast, High Lord. It assaults the Valley of Two Rivers like a sea. The Giant-Raver Satansfist bears with him the – the same power which we saw in Fleshharrower at the battle of Doriendor Corishev. He easily overcame the river fords of the Rill and Llurallin. Revelwood will soon fall to him.'

The High Lord put a measure of sternness in his voice to counter Quaan's dismay. 'We were forewarned, Warmark. When the Giant-Raver and his horde climbed Landsdrop to the north of the Plains of Ra, the Ramen sent word to us. Therefore the Loresraat has been preserved.'

Quaan braced one hand on his sword and said, 'Lord Callindrill has remained in Revelwood.'

Mhoram winced in painful surprise.

'He has remained to defend the tree city. With him are five Eoward commanded by Hiltmark Amorine – also Sword-Elder Drinishok and Staff-Elder Asuraka.'

After the first jolt of the news, the High Lord's gold-flecked irises concentrated dangerously. 'Warmark, the Council commanded that Revelwood should be defended only by those of the *lillianrill* who could not bear to abandon it. The Council commanded that the battle for the Land should take place here – ' he slapped the table with his palm – 'where we can exact the greatest possible price for our lives.'

'You and I are not at Revelwood,' Quaan replied bluntly. 'Who there could command Lord Callindrill to turn aside from his purpose? Amorine could not – you know this. They are bound together by the costs they bore at Doriendor Corishev. Nor could she leave him alone. Nor could she refuse the aid of the Elders.'

His voice was sharp in Hiltmark Amorine's defence, but he stopped when Mhoram with a distracted gesture waved all questions of anger aside. They remained together in silence for a moment. The High Lord felt an aching anticipation of grief, but he forced it down. His eyes wandered back to the bust on the table. Softly, he said, 'Has this word been given to Faer Callindrill-mate?'

'Corimini the Eldest of the Loresraat went to her at once. Callindrill studied with him, and he has known them both for many years. He apologized for not first paying his respects to the High Lord.'

Mhoram shrugged away the need for any apology. His helplessness to reach Callindrill hurt him. He was six days from Revelwood by horse. And he could not call upon the Ranyhyn. The Despiser's army had effectively cut Revelstone off from the Plains of Ra; any Ranyhyn that tried to answer a summons would almost certainly be slaughtered and eaten. All the High Lord could do was wait – and pray that Callindrill and his companions fled Revelwood before Satansfist encircled them. Two thousand warriors and the Hiltmark of the Warward, two of the leaders of the Lorewardens, one Lord – it was a terrible price to pay for Callindrill's bravado.

But even as he thought this, Mhoram knew that Callindrill was not acting out of bravado. The Lord simply could not endure the thought that Revelwood might perish. Mhoram privately hoped Satansfist would let the tree stand – use it rather than destroy it. But Callindrill had no such hope. Ever since he had faltered during the battle of Doriendor Corishev, he had seen himself as a man who had disgraced his Lord's duty, failed to meet the challenge of the Land's need. He had seen himself as a coward. And now Revelwood, the fairest work of the new Lords, was under attack. Mhoram sighed again, and gently touched the bone of the marrowmeld with his fingers.

In the back of his mind, he was readying his decision.

'Quaan, my friend,' he mused grimly, 'what have we accomplished in seven years?'

As if this signalled an end to the formal side of their conversation, Quaan lowered himself into a chair opposite Mhoram, and allowed his square shoulders to sag fractionally. 'We have prepared for the siege of Revelstone with all our strength. We have restored the Warward somewhat – the ten Eowards which survived have been increased to twenty-five. We have brought the people of the Centre Plains here, out of Satansfist's way. We have stored food, weapons, supplies. The Grey Slayer will require more than a sea of ur-viles and Cavewights to break our hold here.'

'He has more, Quaan.' Mhoram continued to stroke the strangely revealing face of the *anundivian yajña* bust. 'And we have lost the Bloodguard.'

'Through no fault of ours.' Quaan's pain at the loss made him sound indignant. He had fought side-by-side with the Bloodguard more than any other warrior in the Land. 'We could not have known at that time, when the mission to Seareach was given to Korik and the Bloodguard, that the Grey Slayer would attack the Giants with the Illearth Stone. We could not have known that Korik would defeat a Raver and would attempt to bring a piece of the Stone here.'

'We could not have known,' Mhoram echoed hollowly. After all, the end of his oracular dreams was not a great loss. Despite the myriad terrors he had beheld, he had not glimpsed or guessed at Lord Foul's attack on the Giants in time. 'My friend, do you remember what Bannor told us concerning this sculpture?'

'High Lord?'

'He reported that Elena daughter of Lena carved it of Thomas Covenant, Unbeliever and white gold wielder – and that ur-Lord Covenant mistook it for the face of a Bloodguard.' Bannor had also reported that Covenant had forced him to tell Elena the name of the Power hidden in the Seventh Ward, so that she could meet the conditions for approaching that Power. But Mhoram was interested for a moment in the resemblance which High Lord Elena had worked into her carving. That had been the starting point, the beginning from which he had travelled to reach his secret knowledge. 'She was a true Craftmaster of the bone-sculpting skill. She would not unwittingly have made such confusion possible.'

Quaan shrugged.

Mhoram smiled fondly at the Warmark's unwillingness to hazard opinions beyond his competence. 'My friend,' he said, 'I saw the resemblance, but could not decipher it. Ahanna daughter of Hanna aided me. Though she does not know the marrowmeld skill, she has an artist's eye. She perceived the meaning which Elena made here.

'Quaan, the resemblance is that both ur-Lord Covenant the Unbeliever and Bannor of the Bloodguard require absolute answers to their own lives. With the Bloodguard it was their Vow. They demanded of themselves either pure, flawless service for ever or no service at all. And the Unbeliever demands – '

'He demands,' Quaan said sourly, 'that his world is real and ours is not.'

Another smile eased Mhoram's sombreness, then faded. 'This demand for absolute answers is dangerous. Kevin, too, required either victory or destruction.'

The Warmark met Mhoram's gaze grimly for a moment before he said, 'Then do not resummon the Unbeliever. High Lord, he will lay waste the Land to preserve his "real" world.'

Mhoram cocked an eyebrow at Quaan, and his crooked lips tightened. He knew that the Warmark had never trusted Covenant, yet in this time of crisis any doubt was more important, less answerable. But before he could reply, urgent knuckles pounded at his door. The tight voice of a sentry hissed, 'High Lord, come swiftly! High Lord.'

Immediately, Mhoram stood and moved towards the door. As he strode, he banished all his reveries, and brought his sense into focus on the ambience of Revelstone, searching it for the cause of the sentry's distress.

Quaan, reaching the door a step ahead of him, thrust it open. Mhoram hastened out into the bright, round courtyard.

The whole high cavern of the court was clearly illuminated by the pale-yellow light which shone up through the stone floor, but Mhoram did not need to look up to any of the projecting coigns in the cavern walls to see why the sentry had called him. Lord Amatin stood in the centre of the floor's inextinguishable light. She faced him with her back to her own chambers, as if she had been on her way towards him when the distress had come upon her.

In her hands she gripped the *lomillialor* communication rod which the Loresraat had given to Revelstone seven years ago.

She looked like a dark shadow against the bright floor, and in her hands the High Wood burned flamelessly, like a slit opening into a furnace. Small cold balls of sparks dropped in spurts from the wood. Mhoram understood instantly that she was receiving a message from whomever it was who held the other communication rod, the one at Revelwood.

He snatched up his long, iron-heeled staff from its tripod outside his door and strode across the courtyard to Amatin. He knew from experience that the sending or receiving of *lomillialor* messages was an exhausting ordeal. Amatin would want his help. She was not physically strong, and knew it; when word of the Despiser's army had reached the Lords, she had transferred to Callindrill her responsibility for Revelwood – hers because of her passionate love for lore – because she believed she lacked the sheer bodily toughness to endure prolonged strain. Yet hidden within her slight waifish frame and grave eyes was a capacity for knowledge, a devotion to study, which no other Lord could match. The High Lord had often thought that she was better equipped and less likely to uncover his secret than anyone else in the Land.

Now, silhouetted by the bright floor of the courtyard, she looked thin and frail – a mere image cast by the power in her hands. Her whole body trembled, and she held the *lomillialor* rod at arm's length as if to keep it as far from herself as possible without releasing it. She started to speak before Mhoram reached her.

'Asuraka,' she gasped. 'Asuraka speaks.' Her voice juddered like a branch in a high wind. 'Satansfist. Fire. Fire! The tree! Ahh!' As she panted the words, she stared at Mhoram in wide dismay as if through him she could see flames chewing at the trunks of Revelwood.

Mhoram stopped within reach of the High Wood and planted his staff like a command on the floor. Pitching his voice to penetrate her transfixion, he said, 'Hold fast, Amatin. I hear.'

She ducked her head, trying to avoid what she saw, and words spattered past her lips as if someone had hurled a heavy boulder into the waters of her soul. 'Fire! The bark burns. The wood burns. The Stone! Leaves, roots, fibres are consumed. Callindrill fights. Fights!

Screams – the warriors scream. The south hall burns! Ah, my home!'

Grimly, Mhoram clenched his fist around the centre of the *lomillialor* rod. The power of the message stung him, jolted him from head to foot, but he gripped the smooth wood and forced the strength of his will into it. Through it, he reached Amatin, steadied her; and with her support he reversed the flow of power through the High Wood for an instant. Against the flood of Asuraka's emotion, he hissed towards her, 'Flee!'

The Staff-Elder heard. Through Amatin's lips, she cried back, 'Flee? We cannot flee! Revelwood dies under us. We are surrounded. All the outer branches burn. Two trunks are aflame to their tops. Screams! Screams. Lord Callindrill stands in the *viancome* and fights. The central trunks burn. The net of the *viancome* burns. Callindrill!'

'Water!' Mhoram dashed his words at Asuraka through the communication rod. 'Call the rivers! Flood the valley!'

For a moment, the pressure from Asuraka sagged, as if she had turned away from her rod. Mhoram breathed urgently, 'Asuraka! Staff-Elder!' He feared that she had fallen in the fire. When she resumed her message, she felt distant, desolate.

'Lord Callindrill called the rivers – earlier. Satansfist turned the flood aside. He – the Illearth Stone – ' A new note of horror came into the weak voice which shuddered between Amatin's lips. 'He resurrected the old death of Kurash Plenethor. Blasted rock and blood and bones and burned earth rose up through the ground. With old waste he walled Revelwood, and turned the water. How is it possible? Is Time broken? With one stroke of the Stone centuries of healing are rent asunder.'

Suddenly, Amatin stiffened in one shrill cry: 'Callindrill!'

The next instant, the *lomillialor* fell silent; the power dropped from it like a stricken bird. Lord Amatin staggered, almost fell to her knees. Mhoram caught her forearm to help her to keep her feet.

In the abrupt silence, the courtyard felt as dead and cold as a tomb. The atmosphere flocked with echoes of anguish like the noiseless beating of black wings. Mhoram's knuckles where he gripped his staff were strained and white.

Then Amatin shuddered, took hold of herself. The High Lord stepped back and made himself aware of the other people in the court. He could feel their presences. Quaan stood a few paces behind him, and several sentries were scattered around the rim of the shining floor. A handful of spectators watched fearfully from the railed coigns in the walls of the cavity. But the High Lord turned from them all to his left, where Corimini the Eldest of the Loresraat stood with Faer Callindrill-mate. The Eldest held each of Faer's shoulders with an old wrinkled hand. Tears glistened under his heavy eyelids, and his long white beard quivered in grief. But Faer's bluff face was as blank and pale as bone sculpture.

'Is he dead, then, High Lord?' she asked softly.

'Death reaps the beauty of the world,' replied Mhoram.

'He burned.'

'Satansfist is a Raver. He hates all green growing things. I was a fool to hope that Revelwood might be spared.'

'Burned,' she repeated.

'Yes, Faer.' He could find no words adequate for the ache in his heart. 'He fought to preserve Revelwood.'

'High Lord, there was doubt in him — here.' She pointed to her bosom. 'He forgot himself.'

Mhoram heard the truth in her voice. But he could not let her bare statement pass. 'Perhaps. He did not forget the Land.'

With a low moan, Lord Amatin turned and hastened painfully back to her chambers. But Faer paid no attention to her. Without meeting Mhoram's intent gaze, she asked, 'Is it possible?'

He had no answer for that question. Instead, he replied as if she had repeated Asuraka's cry. 'The Law of Death has been broken. Who can say what is possible now?'

'Revelwood,' groaned Corimini. His voice trembled with age and sorrow. 'He died bravely.'

'He forgot himself.' Faer moved out of the Eldest's hands as if she had no use for his consolation. Turning away from the High Lord, she walked stiffly back to her rooms. After a moment, Corimini followed, blinking uselessly against his tears.

With an effort, Mhoram loosened his grip on his staff, flexed his clawed fingers.

Firmly, deliberately, he made his decision.

His lips were tight and hard as he faced Quaan. 'Summon the Council,' he said as if he expected the Warmark to protest. 'Invite the Lorewardens, and any of the *rhadhamaerl* and *lillianrill* who desire to come. We can no longer delay.'

Quaan did not mistake Mhoram's tone. He saluted the High Lord crisply, and at once began shouting orders to the sentries.

Mhoram did not wait for the Warmark to finish. Taking his staff in his right hand, he strode off the bright floor and down the hallway which separated the apartments of the Lords from the rest of Revelstone. He nodded to the guards at the far end of the hall, but he did not stop to answer their enquiring faces. Everybody he encountered had felt the disturbance of Revelstone's ambience, and their eyes thronged with anxiety. But he ignored them. They would have their answers soon enough. Sternly, he began to climb up through the levels of Lord's Keep towards the Close.

Haste mounted around him as word of Asuraka's message spread through the walls of the city. The usual busyness of life which pulsed in the rock, concerting the rhythms of the Keep's inhabitants, gave way to an impression of focus, as if Revelstone itself were telling the people what had happened and how to respond. In this same way, the mountain rock had helped to order the lives of its denizens for generations, centuries.

Deep in his aching heart, Mhoram knew that even this rock could come to an end. In all the ages of its existence, it had never been besieged. But Lord Foul was powerful enough now. He could tear these massive walls down, reduce the Land's last bastion to rubble. And he would begin the attempt soon.

This, at least, Callindrill had understood clearly. The time had come for desperate hazards. And the High Lord was full to bursting with the damage Satansfist had already done in his long march from Ridjeck Thome. He had chosen his own risk.

He hoped to turn the breaking of the Law of Death to the Land's advantage.

He found himself hurrying, though he knew he would have to wait when he reached the Close. The pressure of decision impelled him. Yet when Trell hailed him from a side passage, he stopped at once, and turned to meet the approach of the big Gravelingas. Trell Atiaran-mate had claims which Mhoram could neither deny nor evade.

Trell was traditionally dressed as a Stonedownor – over his light brown pants he wore a short tunic with his family symbol, a white leaf pattern, woven into its shoulders – and he had the broad, muscular frame which characterized the people of the rock villages; but the Stonedownors were usually short, and Trell was tall. He created an impression of immense physical strength, which was only augmented by his great skill in the *rhadhamaerl* lore.

He approached the High Lord with his head lowered in an attitude of shyness, but Mhoram knew that it was not embarrassment which caused Trell to avoid meeting the eyes of other people. Another explanation glowered behind the thick intensity of Trell's red and grey beard and the graveling ruddiness of his features. Involuntarily, Mhoram shivered as if the wind of winter had found its way through Revelstone to his heart.

Like the other *rhadhamaerl*, Trell had given his whole life to the service of stone. But he had lost his wife and daughter and granddaughter because of Thomas Covenant. The simple sight of Covenant seven years ago had driven him to damage the rock of the Keep; he had gouged his fingers into the granite as if it were nothing more than stiff clay.

He avoided other people's eyes in an effort to conceal the conflicting hate and hurt which knotted themselves within him.

He usually kept to himself, immersing himself in the stone labours of the Keep. But now he accosted the High Lord with an air of grim purpose.

He said, 'You go to the Close, High Lord.' Despite the severity of his mien, his voice held an odd note of supplication.

'Yes,' Mhoram answered.

'Why?'

'Trell Atiaran-mate, you know why. You are not deaf to the Land's need.'

Flatly, Trell said, 'Do not.'

Mhoram shook his head gently. 'You know that I must make this attempt.'

Trell pushed this statement aside with a jerk of his shoulders, and repeated, 'Do not.'

'Trell, I am High Lord of the Council of Revelstone. I must do what I can.'

'You will denounce – you will denounce the fall of Elena my daughter's daughter.'

'Denounce?' Trell's assertion surprised the High Lord. He cocked an eyebrow and waited for the Gravelingas to explain.

'Yes!' Trell averred. His voice sounded awkward, as if in the long, low, subterranean songs of his *rhadhamaerl* service he had lost his familiarity with human speech; and he looked as if he were resisting an impulse to shout. 'Atiaran my wife said – she said that it is the responsibility of the living to justify the sacrifices of the dead. Otherwise their deaths have no meaning. You will undo the meaning Elena earned. You must not – approve her death.'

Mhoram heard the truth in Trell's words. His decision might well imply an affirmation, or at least an acceptance, of Elena's fall under *Melenkurion* Skyweir; and that would be bitter bread for Trell's distress to swallow. Perhaps this explained the inchoate fear which he sensed behind Trell's speech. But Mhoram's duty to the Land bound him straitly. So that Trell could not mistake him, he said, 'I must make this attempt.' Then he added gently, 'High Lord Elena broke the Law of Death. In what way can I approve?'

Trell's gaze moved around the walls, avoiding the face of the High Lord, and his heavy hands clutched his hips as if to prevent themselves from striking out – as if he did not trust what his hands might do if he failed to hold them down. 'Do you love the Land?' he said in a thick voice. 'You will destroy it.'

Then he met Mhoram's gaze, and his sore eyes gleamed with moist fire. 'It would have been better if I had – ' abruptly, his hands tore loose from his sides, slapped together in front of him, and his shoulders hunched like a strangler's – 'crushed Lena my own daughter at birth.'

'No!' Mhoram affirmed softly. 'No.' He yearned to put his arms around Trell, to console the Gravelingas in some way. But he did not know how to untie Trell's distress; he was unable to loosen his own secret dilemma. 'Hold Peace, Trell,' he murmured. 'Remember the Oath.' He could think of nothing else to say.

'Peace?' Trell echoed in ridicule or grief. He no longer seemed to see the High Lord. 'Atiaran believed in Peace. There is no Peace.' Turning vaguely from Mhoram, he walked away down the side passage from which he had come.

Mhoram stared after him down the passage for a long moment. Duty and caution told him that he should have warriors assigned to watch the Gravelingas. But he could not bear to torment Trell with such an expression of distrust; that judgement might weaken the last clutch of Trell's self-control. And he, Mhoram, had seen men and women rise to victory from anguish as bad as Trell's.

Yet the Gravelingas had not looked like a man who could wrest new wholeness out of the ruins of his old life. Mhoram was taking a grave risk by not acting in some way. As he started again towards the Close, the weight of his responsibilities bore heavily on him. He did not feel equal to the multitude of dooms he carried.

The Lords possessed nothing of their own with which to fight the long cruel winter that fettered the Land.

He strode down a long, torchlit corridor, climbed a spiral stairway, and approached one of the Lords' private entrances to the Close. Outside the door, he paused to gauge the number of people who had already gathered for the Council, and after a moment he heard Lord Amatin coming up the stair behind him. He waited for her. When she reached the landing where he stood, he saw that her eyes were red-rimmed, her forlorn mouth aggravated by tension. He was tempted to speak to her now, but he decided instead to deal with her feelings before the Council. If he were ever to reveal his secret knowledge, he would first have to prepare the ground for it. With a quiet, sympathetic smile, he opened the door for her and followed her into the Close.

From the door, he and Amatin went down the steps to the Lords' table, which stood below the level of the tiered galleries in the high, round council hall. The hall was lit by four huge, lore-burning *lillianrill* torches set into the walls above the galleries, and by an open pit of graveling in the base of the Close, below and within the wide C of the table. Stone chairs for the Lords and their special guests waited around the outer edge of the table, facing in towards the open floor and the graveling pit; and at the head of the table was the high-backed seat of the High Lord.

On the floor of the Close beside the graveling pit was a round stone table with a short silver sword stabbed half-way to the hilt in its centre. This was the *krill* of Loric, left where Covenant had driven it seven years ago. In that time, the Lords had found no way to remove it from the stone. They left it in the Close so that anyone who wished to study the *krill* could do so freely. But nothing had changed except the clear white gem around which the guards and haft of the two-edge blade were forged.

When Mhoram and Callindrill had returned from their plunge into Garroting Deep, they had found the gem lightless, dead. The hot fire which Covenant had set within it had gone out.

It stood near the graveling like an icon of the Lords' futility, but Mhoram kept his thoughts away from it. He did not need to look around to learn who was already present in the Close; the perfect acoustics of the hall carried every low noise and utterance to his ears. In the first row of the gallery, above and behind the seats of the Lords, sat warriors, Hafts of the Warward, occupying the former places of the Bloodguard. The two Hearthralls, Tohrm the Gravelingas and Borillar the Hirebrand, sat with Warmark Quaan in their formal positions high in the gallery behind the High Lord's chair. Several Lorewardens had taken seats in tiers above the table; the weary dust of their flight from Revelwood was still on them, but they were too taut with the news of the tree's fall to miss the Council. And with them were virtually all the *lillianrill* of Lord's Keep. The burning of a tree struck at the very hearts of the Hirebrands, and they watched the High Lord's approach with pain in their eyes.

Mhoram reached his seat but did not sit down immediately. As Lord Amatin moved to her place on the right side of the table, he felt a sharp pang at sight of the stone seat which Callindrill should have filled. And he could sense the remembered presence of the others who had occupied the High Lord's chair; Variol, Prothall, Osondrea, and Elena among the new Lords, Kevin, Loric, and Damelon of the Old. Their individual greatness and courage humbled him, made him realize how small a figure he was to bear such losses and duties. He stood on the brink of the Land's doom without Variol's foresight or Prothall's ascetic strength or Osondrea's dour intransigence or Elena's fire; and he had not power enough to match the frailest Lord in the weakest Council led by Kevin or Loric or Damelon or Berek Heartthew the Lord-Fatherer. Yet none of the remaining Lords could take his place. Amatin lacked physical toughness. Trevor did not believe in his own stature; he felt that he was not the equal of his fellow Lords. And Loerya was torn between her love for the Land and her desire to protect her own family. Mhoram knew that more than once she had almost asked him to release her from her Lordship, so that she could flee with her daughters into the relative sanctuary of the Westron Mountains.

With Callindrill gone, High Lord Mhoram was more alone than he had ever been before.

He had to force himself to pull out his chair and sit down.

He waited for Trevor and Loerya in a private reverie, gathering his fortitude. Finally, the main doors of the Close opened opposite him, and the two Lords started down the broad steps, accompanying Eldest Corimini. He moved with slow difficulty, as if the end of Revelwood had exhausted the last elasticity of his thews, leaving him at the mercy of his age; and Trevor and Loerya supported him gently on either side. They helped him to a chair down the table from Amatin, then walked around and took their places on the High Lord's left.

When they were seated, the Close grew quiet. All talking stopped, and after a brief shuffle of feet and positions, silence filled the warm yellow light of the torches and graveling. Mhoram could hear nothing but the low susurration of hushed breathing. Slowly, he looked around the table and the galleries. Every eye in the chamber was on him. Stiffening himself, he placed his staff flat on the table before him, and stood up.

'Friends and servants of the Land,' he said steadily, 'be welcome to the Council of Lords. I am Mhoram son of Variol, High Lord by the choice of the Council. There are dire matters upon us, and we must take action against them. But first we must welcome the Lorewardens of the Loresraat. Corimini, Eldest of the Loresraat, be at home in Lord's Keep with all your people. You have brought the great school of lore safely to Revelstone. How may we honour you?'

Corimini rose infirmly to his feet as if to meet the High Lord's salutation, but the diffusion of his gaze showed that his mind was elsewhere. 'Faer,' he began in a tremulous old voice, 'Faer begs me to apologize for the absence of Callindrill her husband. He will be unable to attend the Council.' Dislocation gathered in his tone while he spoke, and his voice trailed off as if he had forgotten what he meant to say. Slowly, his thoughts slipped out of contact with his situation. As he stood before the Council, the power of the lore which had preserved him for so long from the effects of age seemed to fail within him. After a moment, he sat down, murmuring aimlessly to himself, wandering in his mind like a man striving to comprehend a language he no longer knew. At last he found the word, 'Revelwood.' He repeated it several times, searching to understand it. Softly he began to weep.

Tears burned the backs of Mhoram's eyes. With a quick gesture he sent two of the Lorewardens to Corimini's aid. They lifted him from his seat and bore him between them up the stairs towards the high wooden doors. 'Take him to the Healers,' Mhoram said thickly. 'Find Peace for him. He has served the Land with courage and devotion and wisdom for more years than any other now living.'

The Lords came to their feet, and at once all the people in the Close stood. Together, they touched their right hands to their hearts, then extended the palms towards Corimini in a traditional salute. 'Hail, Corimini,' they said, 'Eldest of the Loresraat. Be at Peace.'

The two Lorewardens took Corimini from the Close, and the doors shut behind them. Sadly, the people in the galleries reseated themselves. The Lords looked towards Mhoram with mourning in their eyes, and Loerya said stiffly, 'This is an ill omen.'

Mhoram gripped himself with a stern hand. 'All omens are ill in these times. Despite is abroad in the Land. For that reason we are Lords. The Land would not require us if there were no harm at work against it.'

Without meeting Mhoram's gaze, Amatin replied, 'If that is our purpose, then we do not serve it.' Her anger and pain combined to give her a tone of defiance. She held her palms flat on the table and watched them as if she were trying to push them through the stone. 'Only Callindrill of all the Lords lifted his hand in Revelwood's defence. He burned in my place.'

'No!' the High Lord snapped at once. He had hoped to deal with the issues before the Council on other terms, but now that Amatin had spoken, he could not back away. 'No, Lord Amatin. You cannot take upon your shoulders responsibility for the death of Callindrill Faer-mate. He died in his own place, by his own choice. When you believed that you were no longer the Lord best suited to watch over Revelwood, you expressed your belief to the Council. The Council accepted your belief and asked Lord Callindrill to take that burden upon himself.

'At the same time, the Council decided that the defenders of the Land should not spend themselves in a costly and bootless battle for Revelwood.' As he spoke, the tightness around his eyes expressed how hard, how poignantly hard, that decision had been to make. 'The home of the Loresraat was not made for war, and could not be well defended. The Council decided for the sake of the Land that we must save our strength, put it to its best use here. Callindrill chose – ' the authority of Mhoram's tone faltered for an instant –

'Lord Callindrill Faer-mate chose otherwise. There is no blame for you in this.'

He saw the protest in her eyes and hastened to answer her. He did not want to hear her thought uttered aloud. 'Further, I tell you that there is no blame for us in the wisdom or folly, victory or defeat, of the way we have elected to defend the Land. We are not the Creators of the Earth. Its final end is not on our heads. We are creations, like the Land itself. We are accountable for nothing but the purity of our service. When we have given our best wisdom and our utterest strength to the defence of the Land, then no voice can raise accusation against us. Life or death, good or ill – victory or destruction – we are not required to solve these riddles. Let the creator answer for the doom of his creation.'

Amatin stared at him hotly, and he could feel her probing the estranged, secret place in his heart. Speaking barely above a whisper, she said, 'Do you blame Callindrill then? There is no "best wisdom" in his death.'

The misdirection of her effort to understand him pained the High Lord, but he answered her openly. 'You are not deaf to me, Lord Amatin. I loved Callindrill Faer-mate like a brother, I have no wisdom or strength or willingness to blame him.'

'You are the High Lord. What does your wisdom teach you?'

'I am the High Lord,' Mhoram affirmed simply. 'I have no time for blame.'

Abruptly, Loerya joined the probing. 'And if there is no Creator? Or if the creation is untended?'

'Then who is there to reproach us? We provide the meaning of our own lives. If we serve the Land purely to the farthest limit of our abilities, what more can we ask of ourselves?'

Trevor answered, 'Victory, High Lord. If we fail, the Land itself reproaches us. It will be made waste. We are its last preservers.'

The force of this thrust smote Mhoram. He found that he still lacked the courage to retort nakedly, *Better failure than desecration.* Instead, he turned the thrust with a wry smile and said, 'The last, Lord Trevor? No. The *Haruchai* yet live within their mountain fastness. In their way, they know the name of the Earthpower more surely than any Lord. Ramen and Ranyhyn yet live. Many people of the South and North Plains yet live. Many of the Unfettered yet live. Caerroil Wildwood, Forestal of Garroting Deep, has not passed away. And somewhere beyond the Sunbirth Sea is the homeland of the Giants – yes, and of the *Elohim* and *Bhrathair*, of whom the Giants sing. They will resist Lord Foul's hold upon the Earth.'

'But the Land, High Lord! The Land will be lost! The Despiser will rack it from end to end.'

At once, Mhoram breathed intensely, 'By the Seven! Not while one flicker of love or faith remains alive!'

His eyes burned into Trevor's until the Lord's protest receded. Then he turned to Loerya. But in her he could see the discomfortable fear for her daughters at work, and he refrained from touching her torn feelings. Instead, he looked towards Amatin and was relieved to see that much of her anger had fallen away. She regarded him with an expression of hope. She had found something in him that she needed. Softly, she said, 'High Lord, you have discovered a way in which we may act against this doom.'

The High Lord tightened his hold upon himself. 'There is a way.' Raising his head, he addressed all the people in the Close. 'My friends, Satansfist Raver has burned Revelwood. Trothgard is now in his hands. Soon he will begin to march upon us. Scant days remain before the siege of Revelstone begins. We can no longer delay.' The gold in his eyes flared as he said, 'We must attempt to summon the Unbeliever.'

At this, a stark silence filled the Close. Mhoram could feel waves of surprise and excitement and dread pouring down on him from the galleries. Warmark Quaan's passionate objection struck across his shoulders. But he waited in the silence until Lord Loerya found her voice to say, 'That's impossible. The Staff of Law has been lost. We have no means for such a summoning.' The soft timbre of her voice barely covered its hard core.

Still Mhoram waited, looking towards the other Lords for answers to Loerya's claim. After a long moment, Trevor said hesitantly, 'But the Law of Death has been broken.'

'And if the Staff has been destroyed,' Amatin added quickly, 'then the Earthpower which it held and focused has been released upon the Land. Perhaps it is accessible to us.'

'And we must make the attempt,' said Mhoram. 'For good or ill, the Unbeliever is inextricably linked to the Land's doom. If he is not here, he cannot defend the Land.'

'Or destroy it!' Quaan rasped.

Before Mhoram could respond, Hearthrall Borillar was on his feet. He said in a rush, 'The Unbeliever will save the Land.'

Quaan growled, 'This is odd confidence, Hearthrall.'

'He will save,' Borillar said as if he were surprised at his own temerity. Seven years ago, when he had met Covenant, he had been the youngest Hirebrand ever to take the office of Hearthrall. He had been acutely aware of his inexperience, and he was still deferential – a fact which amused his friend and fellow Hearthrall, Tohrm. 'When I met the Unbeliever, I was young and timid – afraid.' Tohrm grinned impishly at the implication that Borillar was no longer young and timid. 'Ur-Lord Covenant spoke kindly to me.'

He sat down again, blushing in embarrassment. But no one except Tohrm smiled, and Tohrm's smile was always irrepressible. It expressed only amused fondness, not mockery. The pitch of Borillar's conviction seemed to reproach the doubts in the Close. When Lord Loerya spoke again, her tone had changed. With a searching look at the young Hearthrall, she said, 'How shall we make this attempt?'

Mhoram gravely nodded his thanks to Borillar, then turned back to the Lords. 'I will essay the summoning. If my strength fails, aid me.' The Lords nodded mutely. With a final look around the Close, he sat down, bowed his head, and opened his mind to the melding of the Lords.

He did so, knowing that he would have to hold back part of himself, prevent Trevor and Loerya and Amatin from seeing into his secret. He was taking a great risk. He needed the consolation, the sharing of strength and support, which a complete mind melding could give; yet any private weakness might expose the knowledge he withheld. And in the melding his fellow Lords could see that he did withhold something. Therefore it was an expensive rite. Each meld drained him because he could only protect his secret by giving fortitude rather than receiving it. But he believed in the meld. Of all the lore of the new Lords, only this belonged solely to them; the rest had come to them through the Wards of Kevin Landwaster. And when it was practised purely, melding brought the health and heart of any Lord to the aid of all the others.

As long as the High Lord possessed any pulse of life or thew of strength, he could not refuse to share them.

At last, the contact was broken. For a moment, Mhoram felt that he was hardly strong enough to stand; the needs of the other Lords, and their concern for him, remained on his shoulders like an unnatural burden. But he understood himself well enough to know that in some ways he did not have the ability to surrender. Instead, he had an instinct for absolute exertions which frightened him whenever he thought of the Ritual of Desecration. After a momentary rest, he rose to his feet and took up his staff. Bearing it like a standard, he walked around the table to the stairs and started down towards the open floor around the graveling pit.

As Mhoram reached the floor, Tohrm came down out of the gallery to join him. The Gravelingas's eyes were bright with humour, and he grinned as he said, 'You will need far sight to behold the Unbeliever.' Then he winked as if this were a jest. 'The gulf between worlds is dark, and darkness withers the heart. I will provide more light.'

The High Lord smiled his thanks, and the Hearthrall stepped briskly to one side of the graveling pit. He bent towards the fire-stones, and at once seemed to forget the other people in the Close. Without another look at his audience, he softly began to sing.

In a low rocky language known only to those who shared the *rhadhamaerl* lore, he hymned an invocation to the fire-stones, encouraging them, stoking them, calling to life their latent power. And the red-gold glow of the graveling reflected like a response from his face. After a moment, Mhoram could see the brightness growing. The reddish hue faded from the gold; the gold turned purer, whiter, hotter, and the new-earth aroma of the graveling rose up like incense in the Close.

In silence, the three Lords stood, and the rest of the people joined them in a mute expression of respect for the *rhadhamaerl* and the Earthpower. Before them, the radiance of the pit mounted until Tohrm himself was pale in the light.

With a slow, stately movement, High Lord Mhoram lifted his staff, held it in both hands level with his forehead.

The summoning song of the Unbeliever began to run in his mind as he focused his thoughts on the power of his staff. One by one, he eliminated the people in the Close, and then the Close itself, from his awareness. He poured himself into the straight, smooth wood of his staff until he was conscious of nothing but the song and the light – and the illimitable implications of the Earthpower beating like ichor in the immense mountain-stone around him. Then he gathered as many strands of the pulse as he could hold together in the hands of his staff, and rode them outward through the warp and weft of Revelstone's existence. And as he rode, he sang to himself:

> There is wild magic graven in every rock,
> contained for white gold to unleash or control –
> gold, rare metal, not born of the Land,
> nor ruled, limited, subdued
> by the Law with which the Land was created –
> but keystone rather, pivot, crux
> for the anarchy out of which Time was made.

The strands carried him out through the malevolent wind, so that his spirit shivered against gusts of spite; but his consciousness passed beyond them swiftly, passed beyond all air and wood and water and stone until he seemed to be spinning through the quintessential fabric of which actuality was made. For an interval without dimension in time and space, he lost track of himself. He felt that he was floating beyond the limits of creation. But the song and the light held him, steadied him. Soon his thoughts pointed like a compass to the lodestone of the white gold.

Then he caught a glimpse of Thomas Covenant's ring. It was unmistakable; the Unbeliever's presence covered the chaste circlet like an aura, bound it, sealed up its power. And the aura itself ached with anguish.

High Lord Mhoram reached towards that presence and began to sing:

> Be true, Unbeliever –
> Answer the call.
> Life is the Giver:
> Death ends all.
> The promise is truth,
> And banes disperse
> With promise kept:
> But soul's deep curse
> On broken faith
> And faithless thrall,
> For doom of darkness
> Covers all.
> Be true, Unbeliever –
> Answer the call,
> Be true.

He caught hold of Covenant with his song and started back towards the Close.

The efficacy of the song took much of the burden from him, left him free to return swiftly to himself. As he opened his eyes to the dazzling light, he almost fell to his knees. Sudden exhaustion washed over him; he felt severely attenuated, as if his soul had been stretched to cover too great a distance. For a time, he stood strengthless, even forgetting to sing. But the other Lords had taken up the song for him, and in the place of his power their staffs vitalized the summoning.

When his eyes regained their sight, he beheld Thomas Covenant, Unbeliever and white gold wielder, standing half-substantial in the light before him.

But the apparition came no closer, did not incarnate itself. Covenant remained on the verge of physical presence; he refused to cross over. In a voice that barely existed, he cried, 'Not now! Let me go!'

The sight of the Unbeliever's suffering shocked Mhoram. Covenant was starving, he desperately needed rest, he had a deep and seriously untended wound on his forehead. His whole body was bruised and battered as if he had been stoned, and one side of his mouth was caked with ugly blood. But as bad as his physical injuries were, they paled beside his psychic distress. Appalled resistance oozed from him like the sweat of pain, and a fierce fire of will held him unincarnate. As he fought the completion of his summoning, he reminded Mhoram forcibly of *dukkha*, the poor Waynhim upon which Lord Foul had practised so many torments with the Illearth Stone. He resisted as if the Lords were coercing him into a vat of acid and virulent horror.

'Covenant!' Mhoram groaned. 'Oh, Covenant.' In his fatigue, he feared that he would not be able to hold back his weeping. 'You are in hell. Your world is a hell.'

Covenant flinched. The High Lord's voice seemed to buffet him physically. But an instant later he demanded again, 'Send me back! She needs me!'

'We need you also,' murmured Mhoram. He felt frail, sinewless, as if he lacked the thews and ligaments to keep himself erect. He understood now why he had been able to summon Covenant without the Staff of Law, and that understanding was like a hole of grief knocked in the side of his being. He seemed to feel himself spilling away.

'She needs me!' Covenant repeated. The effort of speech made blood trickle from his mouth. 'Mhoram, can't you hear me?'

That appeal touched something in Mhoram. He was the High Lord; he could not, must not, fall short of the demands placed upon him. He forced himself to meet Covenant's feverish gaze.

'I hear you, Unbeliever,' he said. His voice became stronger as he spoke. 'I am Mhoram son of Variol, High Lord by the choice of the Council. We need you also. I have summoned you to help us face the Land's last need. The prophecy which Lord Foul the Despiser gave you to pronounce upon the Land has come to pass. If we fall, he will have the command of life and death in his hand, and the universe will be a hell for ever. Ur-Lord Covenant, help us! It is I, Mhoram son of Variol, who beseech you.'

The words struck Covenant in flurries. He staggered and quailed under the sound of Mhoram's voice. But his aghast resistance did not falter. When he regained his balance, he shouted again, 'She needs me, I tell you! That rattlesnake is going to bite her! If you take me now, I can't help her.'

In the back of his mind, Mhoram marvelled that Covenant could so grimly deny the summoning without employing the power of his ring. Yet that capacity for refusal accorded with Mhoram's secret knowledge. Hope and fear struggled in the High Lord, and he had difficulty keeping his voice steady.

'Covenant – my friend – please hear me. Hear the Land's need in my voice. We cannot hold you. You have the white gold – you have the power to refuse us. The Law of Death does not bind you. Please hear me. I will not require much time. After I have spoken, if you still choose to depart – I will recant the summoning. I will – I will tell you how to make use of your white gold to deny us.'

Again, Covenant recoiled from the assault of sound. But when he had recovered, he did not repeat his demand. Instead, he said harshly, 'Talk fast. This is my only chance – the only chance to get out of a delusion is at the beginning. I've got to help her.'

High Lord Mhoram clenched himself, mustered all his love and fear for the Land, put it into his voice. 'Ur-Lord, seven years have passed since we stood together on Gallows Howe. In that time we have recovered from some of our losses. But since – since the Staff of Law was lost – the Despiser has been much more free. He has built a new army as vast as the sea, and has marched against us. Already he has destroyed Revelwood. Stansfist Raver has burned Revelwood and slain Lord Callindrill. In a very few days, the siege of Lord's Keep will begin.

'But that does not complete the tale of our trouble. Seven years ago, we might have held Revelstone against any foe for seasons together. Even without the Staff of Law, we might have defended ourselves well. But – my friend, hear me – we have lost the Bloodguard.'

Covenant cowered as if he were being pounded by a rock-fall, but Mhoram did not stop. 'When Korik of the Bloodguard led his mission to the Giants of Seareach, great evils claimed the lives of the Lords Hyrim and Shetra. Without them – ' Mhoram hesitated. He remembered Covenant's friendship with the Giant, Saltheart Foamfollower. He could not bear to torment Covenant by telling him of the Giants' bloody fate. 'Without them to advise him, Korik and two comrades captured a fragment of the Illearth Stone. He did not recognize his danger. The three Bloodguard bore the fragment with them, thinking to carry it to Lord's Keep.

'But the Illearth Stone is a terrible wrong in the Land. The three Bloodguard were not forewarned – and the Stone enslaved them. Under its power, they bore their fragment to Foul's Creche. They believed that they would fight the Despiser. But he made them his own.' Again, Mhoram forbore to tell the whole story. He could not say to Covenant that the Bloodguard Vow had been subtly betrayed by the breaking of the Law of Death – or that the fine metal of the Bloodguard rectitude had been crucially tarnished when Covenant had forced Bannor to reveal the name of the Power of Command. 'Then he – ' Mhoram still winced whenever he remembered what had happened – 'he sent the three to attack Revelstone. Korik, Sill and Doar marched here with green fire in their eyes and Corruption in their hearts. They killed many farmers and warriors before we comprehended what had been done to them.

'Then First Mark Bannor and Terrel and Runnik of the Bloodguard went to do battle with the three. They slew Korik and Sill and Doar their comrades, and brought their bodies to the Keep. In that way, we found – ' Mhoram swallowed thickly – 'we found that Lord Foul had cut off the last two fingers from the right hand of each of the three.'

Covenant cried out in pain, but Mhoram drove his point home hoarsely. 'He damaged each Bloodguard to resemble you.'

'Stop!' Covenant groaned. 'Stop. I can't stand it.'

Still the High Lord continued. 'When First Mark Bannor saw how Korik and his comrades had been corrupted despite their Vow, he and all the Bloodguard abandoned their service. They returned to the mountain home of the *Haruchai*. He said that they had been conquered by Corruption, and could no longer serve any Vow.

'My friend, without them – without the Staff of Law – without any immense army of dour-handed allies – we will surely fall. Only the wild magic can now come between us and Lord Foul's hunger.'

As Mhoram finished, Covenant's eyes looked as bleak as a wilderland. The heat of his fever seemed to make any tears impossible. His resistance sagged briefly, and for an instant he almost allowed his translation into the Close to be completed. But then he raised his head to look at other memories. His refusal stiffened; he moved back until he almost vanished in the bright graveling light. 'Mhoram, I can't,' he said as distantly as if he were choking. 'I can't. The snake – That little girl is all alone. I'm responsible for her. There's no one to help the child but me.'

From high in the opposite gallery, Mhoram felt a surge of anger as Quaan's old indignation at Covenant flared into speech. 'By the Seven!' he barked. 'He speaks of responsibility.' Quaan had watched himself become old and helpless to save the Land, while Covenant neither aged nor acted. He spoke with a warrior's sense of death, a warrior's sense of the value in sacrificing a few lives to save money. 'Covenant, you are responsible for us!'

The Unbeliever suffered under Quaan's voice as he did under Mhoram's, but he did not turn to face the Warmark. He met Mhoram's gaze painfully and answered, 'Yes, I know. I know. I am – responsible. But she needs me. There's no one else. She's part of my world, my real world. You're – not so real now. I can't give you anything now.' His face twisted frantically, and his resistance mounted until it poured from him like agony. 'Mhoram, if I don't get back to her she is going to die.'

828

The desolate passion of Covenant's appeal wrung Mhoram. Unconsciously, he gnawed his lips, trying to control with physical pain the strain of his conflicting compassions. His whole life, all his long commitments, seemed rent within him. His love for the Land urged him to deny the Unbeliever, to struggle now as if he were wrestling for possession of Covenant's soul. But from the same wellspring of his self arose an opposite urge, a refusal to derogate Covenant's sovereignty, Covenant's right to choose his own fate. For a time, the High Lord hesitated, trapped in the contradiction. Then slowly he lifted his head and spoke to the people in the Close as well as to Thomas Covenant.

'No one may be compelled to fight the Despiser. He is resisted willingly, or not at all. Unbeliever, I release you. You turn from us to save life in your own world. We will not be undone by such motives. And if darkness should fall upon us, still the beauty of the Land endures. If we are a dream – and you the dreamer – then the Land is imperishable, for you will not forget.

'Be not afraid, ur-Lord Thomas Covenant. Go in Peace.'

He felt a pressure of protest from Lord Loerya and some of the other spectators, but he overruled them with a commanding gesture. One by one, the Lords withdrew the power of their staffs while Tohrm lowered the graveling fire. Covenant began to fade as if he were dissolving in the abyss beyond the arch of Time.

Then High Lord Mhoram recollected his promise to reveal the secret of the wild magic. He did not know whether or not Covenant could still hear him, but he whispered after the fading form, '*You* are the white gold.'

A moment later, he knew that the Unbeliever was gone. All sense of resistance and power had left the air, and the light of the graveling had declined to a more normal level. For the first time since the summoning began, Mhoram saw the shapes and faces of the people around him. But the sight did not last. Tears blinded him, and he leaned weakly on his staff as if only its stern wood could uphold him.

He was full of grief over the strange ease with which he had summoned the Unbeliever. Without the Staff of Law, he should not have been able to call Covenant alone; yet he had succeeded. He knew why. Covenant had been so vulnerable to the summons because he was dying.

Through his sorrow, he heard Trevor say, 'High Lord – the *krill* – the gem of the *krill* came to life. It burned as it did when the Unbeliever first placed it within the table.'

Mhoram blinked back his tears. Leaning heavily on his staff, he moved to the table. In its centre, Loric's *krill* stood like a dead cross

— as opaque and fireless as if it had lost all possibility of light. A rage of grief came over Mhoram. With one hand, he grasped the hilt of the silver sword.

A fleeting blue gleam flickered across the gem, then vanished.

'It has no life now,' he said dully.

Then he left the Close and went to the sacred enclosure to sing for Covenant and Callindrill and the Land.

3

THE RESCUE

A cold wind blew through Covenant's soul as he struggled up out of the rock. It chilled him as if the marrow of his bones had been laid bare to an exhalation of cruel ice — cruel and sardonic, tinged with that faint yet bottomless green travail which was the antithesis of green things growing. But slowly it left him, slid away into another dimension. He became more conscious of the stone. Its granite impenetrability thickened around him; he began to feel that he was suffocating.

He flailed his arms and legs, tried to reach towards the surface. But for a time he could not even be sure that his limbs were moving. Then a series of jolts began to hurt his joints. He sensed through his elbows and knees that he was thrashing against something hard.

He was pounding his arms and legs at the hillside. Behind the muffled thuds and slaps he made, he could hear running water. The sun shone objectively somewhere beyond him. He jerked up his head.

At first, he could not orient himself. A stream splashed vividly across his sight; he felt that he was peering at it from above, that the slope down which it ran was canted impossibly under him. But at last he realized that he was not looking downward. He lay horizontally across the slope. The hill rose above him on the right, dropped away on the left.

He turned his head to search for the girl and the snake.

His eyes refused to focus. Something pale gleamed in front of his face, prevented him from seeing down the hill.

A thin, childish voice near him said, 'Mister? Are you okay, mister? You fell down.'

He was trying to see too far away. With an effort, he screwed his gaze closer, and at last found himself staring from a distance of a few inches at a bare shin. In the sunlight, it gleamed as pure and pale as if it had been anointed with chrism. But already it showed a slight swelling. And in the centre of the swelling were two small red marks like paired pin-pricks.

'Mister?' the child said again. 'Are you okay? The snake bit me. My leg hurts.'

The frigid winter he had left behind seemed to leap at him from the depths of his mind. He began to shiver. But he forced himself to disregard the cold, bent all his attention towards those two red fang marks. Without taking his eyes off them, he climbed into a sitting position. His bruises groaned at him, and his forehead throbbed sickly, but he ignored all the pain, discounted it as if it had nothing to do with him. His trembling hands drew the little girl towards him.

Snakebite, he thought numbly. How do you treat snakebite?

'All right,' he said, then stopped. His voice shook unreassuringly, and his throat felt too dry to be controlled. He did not seem to know any comforting words. He swallowed hoarsely and hugged the child's thin bones to his chest. 'All right. You're going to be all right. I'm here. I'll help you.'

He sounded grotesque to himself — ghoulish and useless. The cut in his lip and gum interfered with his articulation. But he ignored that, too. He could not afford the energy to worry about such things. A haze of fever parched his thoughts, and he needed all his strength to fight it, recollect the treatment for snakebite.

He stared at the fang marks until he remembered. Stop the circulation, he said to himself as if he were stupid. Cut. Get out the poison.

Jerking himself into movement, he fumbled for his penknife.

When he got it out, he dropped it on the ground beside him, and hunted through the debris which littered his brain for something which he could use as a tourniquet. His belt would not do, he had no way to fasten it tightly enough. The child's dress had no belt. Her shoelaces did not look long enough.

'My leg hurts,' she said plaintively. 'I want my mommy.'

'Where is she?' muttered Covenant.

'That way.' She pointed vaguely downstream. 'A long way. Daddy spanked me and I snuck away.'

Covenant clutched the girl with one arm to keep her from moving, and thus hasten the spread of the venom. With his free hand, he tore at the lace of his left boot. But it was badly frayed and snapped in his hand. Hellfire! he groaned in chagrin. He was taking too long. Trembling, he started on the right bootlace.

After a moment, he succeeded in removing it intact.

'All right,' he said unclearly. 'I've got – got to do something about that bite. First I have to tie off your leg – so the poison won't spread. Then I have to cut your leg a little. That way the poison can get out, and it won't hurt you so much.' He strove to sound calm. 'Are you brave today?'

She replied solemnly, 'Daddy spanked me and I didn't cry. I ran away.' He heard no trace of her earlier terror.

'Good girl,' he mumbled. He could not delay any longer; the swelling over her skin had increased noticeably, and a faint, blackish hue had started to stain her pale flesh. He wrapped his bootlace around her wounded leg above the knee.

'Stand on your other leg, so this one can relax.'

When she obeyed, he pulled the lace tight until she let out a low gasp of pain. Then he tied it off. 'Good girl,' he said again. 'You're very brave today.'

With uncertain hands, he picked up his penknife and opened it.

For a time, he quailed at the prospect of cutting her. He was shivering too badly; the sun's warmth went nowhere near the chill in his bones. But the livid fang marks compelled him. Gently, he lifted the child and seated her on his lap. With his left hand, he raised her leg until its swelling was only ten or twelve inches from his face. His penknife he gripped inadequately with the two fingers and thumb of his right hand.

'If you don't look, you might not even feel it,' he said, and hoped he was not lying.

She acted as if the mere presence of an adult banished all her fears. 'I'm not afraid,' she replied proudly. 'I'm brave today.' But when Covenant turned so that his right shoulder came between her face and the sight of her leg, she caught her hands in his shirt and pressed her face against him.

In the back of his mind, he could hear Mhoram saying, *We have lost the Bloodguard. Lost the Bloodguard. Lost. Oh, Bannor!* he moaned silently. Was it that bad?

He clenched his teeth until his jaws ached, and the wound on his forehead pounded. The pain steadied him. It held him like a spike driven through his brain, affixing him to the task of the fang marks.

With an abrupt movement, he slashed twice, cut an X across the swelling between the two red marks.

The child let out a cry, and went rigid, clinging to him fervidly.

For an instant he stared in horror at the violent red blood which welled out of the cuts and ran across the pale leg. Then he dropped the knife as if it had burned him. Gripping her leg in both hands, he bent his mouth to the fang marks and sucked.

The strain of stretching his lips tight over her shin made his mouth sting, and his blood mingled with hers as it trickled across the darkening stain of the swelling. But he ignored that as well. With all his strength, he sucked at the cuts. When he stopped to breathe, he rubbed the child's leg, trying to squeeze all of her blood towards the cuts. Then he sucked again.

A nauseating dizziness caught hold of his head and made it spin. He stopped, afraid that he would faint. 'All right,' he panted. 'I'm finished. You're going to be all right.' After a moment, he realized that the child was whimpering softly into the back of his shoulder. Quickly, he turned, put his arms around her, hugged her to him. 'You're going to be all right,' he repeated thickly. 'I'll take you to your mommy now.' He did not believe that he had the strength to stand, much less to carry her any distance at all.

But he knew that she still needed treatment; he could hardly have removed all the venom. And the cuts he had inflicted would have to be tended. She could not afford his weakness. With an effort that almost undid him, he lurched painfully to his feet, and stood listing on the hillside as if he were about to capsize.

The child sniffed miserably in his arms. He could not bear to look at her, for fear that she would meet his gaze with reproach. He stared down the hill while he struggled to scourge or beg himself into a condition of fortitude.

Through her tears, the child said, 'Your mouth's bleeding.'

'Yes, I know,' he mumbled. But that pain was no worse than the ache in his forehead, or the hurt of his bruises. And all of it was only pain. It was temporary; it would soon fall under the pall of his leprosy. The ice in his bones made him feel that the numbness of his hands and feet was already spreading. Pain was no excuse for weakness.

Slowly, he unlocked one knee, let his weight start forward. Like a poorly articulated puppet, he lumbered woodenly down the hillside.

By the time he reached the tree – it stood black and straight like a signpost indicating the place where the child had been bitten – he had almost fallen three times. His boots were trying to trip him; without laces to hold them to his feet, they cluttered every step he took. For a moment, he leaned against the tree, trying to steady himself. Then he kicked off his boots. He did not need them. His feet were too numb to feel the damage of hiking barefoot.

'You ready?' he breathed. 'Here we go.' But he was not sure he made any sound. In the fever which clouded his thoughts, he found himself thinking that life was poorly designed; burdens were placed on the wrong people. For some obscure reason, he believed that in Bannor's place he could have found some other answer to Korik's

833

corruption. And Bannor would have been equal many times over to the physical task of saving this child.

Then he remembered that Mhoram had not told him any news of the Giants in connection with Korik's mission. Sparked by the association, a vision of Gallows Howe cut through his haze. He saw again a Giant dangling from the gibbet of the Forestal.

What had happened to the Giants?

Gaping mutely as if the woods and the stream and the little girl in his arms astonished him, he pushed away from the black tree and began shambling along Righters Creek in the general direction of the town.

As he moved, he forced open his caked lips to cry aloud, 'Help!'

The child had said that her parents were a long way away, but he did not know what distances meant to her. He did not know whether or not her parents were anywhere near the Creek. He did not even know how far he was from Haven Farm; the whole previous night was a blank hurt in his mind. But the banks of the stream offered him the most accessible route towards town, and he could think of nothing to do but move in that direction. The girl's pain was increasing. Her leg was blacker every time he looked at it, and she winced and whimpered at every jolt of his stiff stride. At intervals she moaned for her parents, and every moan made him gasp out like the jab of a goad, 'Help!'

But his voice seemed to have no authority, no carrying power; it dropped into silence after him like a stillborn. And the effort of shouting aggravated the injury to his mouth. Soon he could feel his lip swelling like the girl's leg, growing dark and taut and heavy with pain. He hugged her closer to him and croaked in grim, forlorn insistence, 'Help! Help me!'

Gradually, the heat of the sun made him sweat. It stung his forehead until his eyes blurred. But it did not touch the cold in his bones. His shivering mounted. Dizziness dismembered his balance, made him reel through the woods as if he were being driven by a tattered gale. Whenever he stepped on a pointed rock or branch, it gouged far enough up into his arches to hurt him. Several times his joints folded sharply, and he plunged to his knees. But each time, the dark wound he carried pulled him upright again, and sent him forward, mumbling past his thick lip, 'Help me.'

His own swelling seemed to take over his face like a tumour. Hot lances of pain thrust from it through his head every time the ground jarred him. As time passed, he could feel his heart itself trembling, quivering between each beat as it laboured to carry the strain. The haze of his fever thickened until at odd moments he feared that he had lost his sight. In the blur, he quailed away from the dazzles of sunlight which sprang at him off the stream; but when the creek passed through shadows, it looked so cool and healing that he could hardly restrain himself from stumbling into it, burying his face in its anodyne.

Yet all the while he knew he could not deviate from the strait path of his trek. If he failed to find help for the child, then everything he had already done for her would be useless, bereft of meaning. He could not stop. Her wound would not tolerate his futility. He saw too much of his lost son Roger in her bare skin. Despite the nails of pain which crucified him, he lurched onward.

Then in the distance he heard shouts, like people wailing for someone lost. He jerked to a swaying halt on stiff legs, and tried to look around. But he seemed to have lost control of his head. It wobbled vainly on his neck, as if the weight of his swelling threw it out of joint, and he was unable to face it in the direction of the shouts.

In his arms the girl whimpered pitifully, 'Mommy. Daddy.'

He fought his black tight pain to frame the word, *Help*. But no sound came between his lips. He forced his vocal cords to make some kind of noise.

'Help me.'

It was no louder than a whisper.

A sound like hoarse sobs shook him, but he could not tell whether they came from him or from the girl. Weakly, almost blindly, he straightened his arms, lifted the child outward as if he were offering her to the shouts.

They became a woman's voice and took on words. 'Karen! Here she is! Over here! Oh, Karen, my baby!' Running came towards him through the leaves and branches; it sounded like the blade of a winter wind cutting at him from the depths of his fever. At last he was able to see the people. A woman hurried down the side of a hill, and a man ran anxiously after her. 'Karen!' the woman cried.

The child reached out towards the woman and sobbed, 'Mommy! Mommy!'

An instant later, the burden was snatched from Covenant's arms. 'Karen. Oh, my baby,' the woman moaned as she hugged the child. 'We were so frightened. Why did you run away? Are you all right?' Without a glance at Covenant, she said, 'Where did you find her? She ran away this morning, and we've been frightened half to death.' As if this needed some explanation, she went on, 'We're camping over there a ways. Dave has Good Friday off, and we decided to camp out. We never thought she would run away.'

835

The man caught up with her, and she started speaking to the child again. 'Oh, you naughty, naughty girl. Are you all right? Let me look at you.'

The girl kept sobbing in pain and relief as the woman held her at arm's length to inspect her. At once, the woman saw the tourniquet and the swelling and the cuts. She gave a low scream, and looked at Covenant for the first time.

'What happened?' she demanded. 'What've you done to her?' Suddenly, she stopped. A look of horror stretched her face. She backed away towards the man, and screamed at him, 'Dave! It's that leper! That Covenant!'

'What?' the man gasped. Righteous indignation rushed up in him. 'You bastard!' he spat belligerently, and started towards Covenant.

Covenant thought that the man was going to hit him; he seemed to feel the blow coming at him from a great distance. Watching it, he lost his balance, stumbled backward a step, and sat down heavily. Red pain flooded across his sight. When it cleared, he was vaguely surprised to find that he was not being kicked. But the man had stopped a dozen feet away, he stood with his fists clenched, trying not to show that he was afraid to come closer.

Covenant struggled to speak, explain that the child still needed help. But a long, stunned moment passed before he was able to dredge words past his lips. Then he said in a tone of detachment completely at variance with the way he looked and felt, 'Snakebite. Timber rattler. Help her.'

The effort exhausted him; he could not go on. He lapsed into silence, and sat still as if he were hopelessly waiting for an avalanche to fall on him. The man and woman began to recede from him, lose solidity, as if they were dissolving in the acid of his prostration. Vaguely, he heard the child moan, 'The snake bit me, Mommy. My leg hurts.'

He realized that he still had not seen the child's face. But he had lost his chance. He had exercised too strenuously with snake venom in his blood. By degrees, he was slipping into shock.

'All right, Mhoram,' he mumbled wanly. 'Come and get me. It's over now.'

He did not know whether he had spoken aloud. He could not hear himself. The ground under him had begun to ripple. Waves rolled through the hillside, tossing the small raft of hard soil on which he sat. He clung to it as long as he could, but the earthen seas were too rough. Soon he lost his balance and tumbled backward into the ground as if it were an undug grave.

4

SIEGE

Twelve days after the last charred trunks of Revelwood were consumed, reduced to ashes and trampled underfoot, Satansfist Raver, the right hand of the Grey Slayer, brought is vast, dolorous army to the stone gates of Lord's Keep. He approached slowly, though his hordes tugged forward like leashed wolves; he restrained the ravening of the ur-viles and Cavewights and creatures he commanded so that all the inhabitants of Trothgard, and of the lands between Revelwood and the North Plains, would have time to seek safety in the Keep. This he did because he wished all the humans he meant to slay to be gathered in one place. Every increase in the Keep's population would weaken its endurance by eating its stores of food. And crowds of people would be more susceptible than trained warriors or Lords to the fear he bore.

He was sure of the outcome of his siege. His army was not as immense as the one which *moksha* Fleshharrower his brother had lost in Garroting Deep. In order to secure his hold upon the regions he had already mastered, he had left scores of thousands of his creatures behind along the Roamsedge River, throughout the valley which formed the south border of Andelain, and across the Centre Plains. But the Despiser had lost little more than a third of his forces in that earlier war. And instead of wolves and *kresh* and unwieldy *griffins*, Satansfist had with him more of the lore-cunning, roynish, black, eyeless ur-viles, and more of the atrocious creatures which Lord Foul had raised up from the Great Swamp, Lifeswallower, from Sarangrave Flat, from the Spoiled Plains and the bosque of the Ruinwash – raised up and demented with the power of the Illearth Stone. In addition, the Giant-Raver had at his back a power of which the Lords of Revelstone had no conception. Therefore he was willing to prolong his approach to the Keep, so that he could hasten its eventual and irreparable collapse.

Then, early on the twelfth day, a sky-shaking howl shot through his hordes as they caught their first sight of the mountain plateau of Revelstone. Thousands of his creatures started to rush madly towards it through the foothills, but he knocked them back with the flail of his power. Ruling his army with a green scourge, he spent the whole day making his approach, placing his forces in position. When daylight at last drained away into night, his army was wrapped around the entire promontory of Revelstone, from the westmost edge of its south wall to the cliffs of the plateau on the northwest. His encampment locked the Keep in a wide, round formation, sealing it from either flight or rescue, from forages for food or missions to unknown allies. And that night, Satansfist feasted on the flesh of prisoners who had been captured during his long march from Landsdrop.

If any eyes in Revelstone had been able to penetrate the unbroken mass of clouds which frowned now constantly over the Land, they would have seen that this night was the dark of the moon on the middle night of spring. The Despiser's preternatural winter had clenched the Land for forty-two days.

Satansfist had followed precisely the design which his master had given him for his march through the Upper Land.

The next morning, he went to face the watchtower which fronted the long walls of Revelstone at their wedge point. He paid no attention to the intricate Giantish labour which had produced the pattern of coigns and oriels and walks and battlements in the smooth cliff-walls; that part of him which could have responded to the sight had long ago been extinguished by the occupying Raver. Without a second glance at the walls, or at the warriors who sentried the crenellated parapets, he strode around the promontory until he stood before the great stone gates in the base of the tower on its southeast side – the only entrance into Lord's Keep.

He was not surprised to find that the gates were open. Though the Giantish passion for stonework had been quelled in his blood, he retained his knowledge of the Keep. He knew that as long as those massive, interlocking gates remained intact, they could close upon command, trapping anyone who dared enter the tunnel under the tower. While in the tunnel, attackers would be exposed to counter-attack from defensive windows built into the roof of the passage. And beyond the tunnel was nothing but a courtyard, open only to the sky, and then another set of gates even stronger than the first. The tower itself could not be entered except by suspended crosswalks from the main Keep, or through two small doors from the courtyard. Lord's Keep had been well made. The Giant-Raver did not accept the dare of the open gates.

Instead, he placed himself just close enough to the tower to taunt skilled archers, and shouted up at the stone walls in a voice that vibrated with malice and glee. 'Hail, Lords! Worthy Lords! Show yourselves, Lordlings! Leave off cowering in your useless warrens, and speak with me. Behold! I come courteously to accept your surrender!'

There was no answer. The tower, only half as high as the main Keep behind it, stood with its windows and battlements as silent as if it were uninhabited. A whimpering growl passed among the army as the creatures begged for a chance to charge through the open gates.

'Hear me, little Lords!' he shouted. 'See the toils of my strength wrapped around you. I hold your last lives in the palm of my hand. There is no hope for you unless you surrender yourselves and all to the mercy of the Despiser.' Jeering barks from the ur-viles greeted this, and Satansfist grinned. 'Speak, Lordlings! Speak or die!'

A moment later two figures appeared atop the tower – one a warrior and the other a blue-robed Lord whom Satansfist recognized. At first they ignored the Giant. They went to the flagpoles, and together raised High Lord's Furl, the azure oriflamme of the Council. Only after it was fluttering defiantly in the gelid wind did they step to the parapet and face Satansfist.

'I hear you!' the Lord snapped. 'I hear you, *samadhi* Raver. I know you, Sheol Satansfist. And you know me. I am Mhoram son of Variol, High Lord by the choice of the Council. Depart, Raver! Take your ill hordes with you. You have touched me. You know that I will not be daunted.'

Fury glinted in the Giant's eyes at the memory Mhoram invoked, but he placed his hand over the livid fragment of the Stone hidden under his jerkin, and gave Mhoram a sarcastic bow. 'I know you, Mhoram,' he replied. 'When I placed my hand upon you in the labyrinth of Kurash Qwellinir, I knew you. You were too blind with folly and ignorance to feel a wise despair. Therefore I permitted your life – so that you would live to better knowledge. Are you yet blind? Have you no eyes to see that your effectless end at my hand is as sure as the arch of Time? Have you forgotten the Giants? Have you forgotten the Bloodguard? In the name of the Despiser, I will certainly crush you where you cower!'

'Empty words,' Mhoram retorted. 'Bravado is easily uttered – but you will find it difficult of proof. *Melenkurion abatha!* Raver, begone! Return to your forsaken master before the Creator forgets restraint, and wreaks a timeless vengeance upon you.'

The Giant laughed harshly. 'Do not comfort yourself with lies, Lordling. The arch of Time will be broken if the Creator seeks to strike through it – and then Lord Foul the Despiser, Satansheart and Soulcrusher, Corruption and Render, will be unloosed upon the universe! If the Creator dares to lift his hand, my brothers and I will feast upon his very soul! Surrender, fool! Learn to be daunted while grovelling may still preserve your life. Perhaps you will be permitted to serve me as my hand slave.'

'Never!' High Lord Mhoram cried boldly. 'We will never bow to you while one pulse of faith still beats in the Land. The Earthpower is yet strong to resist you. We will seek it until we have found the means to cast down you and your master and all his works. Your victories are hollow while one soul remains with breath enough to cry out against you!' Raising his staff, he whirled it so that blue fire danced in the air about his head. 'Begone, *samadhi* Raver! *Melenkurion abatha! Duroc minas mill khabaal!* We will never surrender!'

Below him, Satansfist flinched under the power of the words. But an instant later, he sprang forward, snatching at his jerkin. With his piece of the Illearth Stone clenched and steaming in his fist, he hurled a gout of emerald force up at the High Lord. At the same time, hundreds of creatures broke from their ranks and charged towards the open gates.

But Mhoram deflected the blast with his staff, sent it into the air over his head, where his own fiery power attacked it and consumed it. Then he ducked behind the concealment of the parapet. Over his shoulder, he called to Warmark Quaan, 'Seal the gates! Order the archers to slay any creatures which gain the courtyard. We cannot deal gently with this foe.'

Quaan was already on his way down the stairs into the complex passages of the tower, shouting orders as he ran to oversee the fray. Mhoram looked downward to assure himself that Satansfist had not passed through the gates. Then he hastened after Quaan.

From the highest of the crosswalks above the courtyard, he surveyed the skirmish. Strong Woodhelvennin archers drove their shafts into the milling creatures from the battlements on both sides of the court, and the sound of weapons echoed out of the tunnel. In moments, the fighting would be done. Gritting his teeth over the shed blood, Mhoram left the conclusion of the skirmish in Quaan's competent hands, and crossed the wooden span to the main Keep, where his fellow Lords awaited him.

As he met the sombre eyes of Trevor, Loerya and Amatin, a sudden weariness came over him. Satansfist's threats came so close to the truth. He and his companions were inadequate for the task of using even those few powers and mysteries which they possessed. And he was no nearer to a resolution of his secret knowledge than he had been when he had summoned and lost Thomas Covenant. He sighed, allowed his shoulders to sag. To explain himself, he said, 'I had not thought there were so many ur-viles in all the world.' But the words were only tangential to what he felt.

Yet he could not afford such weariness. He was the High Lord. Trevor, Loerya and Amatin had their own uncertainties, their own needs, which he could not refuse; he had already done them enough damage in the private dilemma of his heart. Drawing himself erect, he told them what he had seen and heard of the Raver and Lord Foul's army.

When he was done, Amatin smiled wryly. 'You affronted *samadhi* Raver. That was boldly done, High Lord.'

'I did not wish to comfort him with the thought that we believe him safe.'

At this, Loerya's gaze winced. 'Is he safe?' she asked painfully.

Mhoram hardened. 'He is not safe while there is heart or bone or Earthpower to oppose him. I only say that I know not how he may be fought. Let him discover my ignorance for himself.'

As she had so often in the past, Loerya once again attempted to probe his secret. 'Yet you have touched Loric's *krill* and given it life. Your hand drew a gleam of blue from the gem. Is there no hope in this? The legends say that the *krill* of Loric Vilesilencer was potent against the peril of the Demondim.'

'A gleam,' Mhoram replied. Even in the privacy of his own knowledge, he feared the strange power which had enabled him to spark the *krill*'s opaque jewel. He lacked the courage to explain the source of his strength. 'What will that avail?'

In response, Loerya's face thronged with demands and protests, but before she could voice them, a shout from the courtyard drew the Lords' attention downward. Warmark Quaan stood on the flagstones amid the corpses. When Mhoram answered him, he saluted mutely with his sword.

Mhoram returned the salute, acknowledging Quaan's victory. But he could not keep the hue of sadness from his voice as he said, 'We have shed the first blood in this siege. Thus even those who oppose ill must wreak harm upon the victims of ill. Bear their bodies to the upland hills and burn them with purging fires, so that their flesh may recover its innocence in ashes. Then scatter their ashes over Furl Falls, as a sign to all the Land that we abhor the Despiser's wrong, not the slaves which he has made to serve his wrong.'

The Warmark scowled, loath to honour his enemies with such courtesy. But he promptly gave the orders to carry out Mhoram's instructions. Sagging again, Mhoram turned back to his fellow Lords. To forestall any further probing, he said, 'The Giant knows he cannot breach these walls with swords and spears. But he will not stand idle, waiting for hunger to do his work. He is too avid for blood. He will attempt us. We must be prepared. We must stand constant watch within the tower – to counter any force which he may bring against us.'

Lord Trevor, eager for any responsibility which he believed to be within his ability, said, 'I will watch.'

With a nod, Mhoram accepted. 'Summon one of us when you are weary. And summon us all when Satansfist chooses to act. We must see him at work, so that we may learn our defence.' Then he turned to a warrior standing nearby. 'Warhaft, bear word to the Hearthralls Tohrm and Borillar. Ask the Hirebrands and Gravelingases of Lord's Keep to share the watch of the Lords. They also must learn our defence.'

The warrior saluted and walked briskly away. Mhoram placed a hand on Trevor's shoulder, gripped it firmly for a moment. Then, with one backward look at the winter-stricken sky, he left the balcony and went to his chambers.

He intended to rest, but the sight of Elena's marrowmeld sculpture standing restlessly on his table disturbed him. It had the fantastic, vulnerable look of a man, chosen to be a prophet, who entirely mistakes his errand – who, instead of speaking to glad ears the words of hope with which he was entrusted, spends his time preaching woe and retribution to a wilderland. Looking at the bust, Mhoram had to force himself to remember that Covenant had rejected the Land to save a child in his own world. And the Unbeliever's ability to refuse help to tens of thousands of lives – to the Land itself – for the sake of one life was a capacity which could not be easily judged. Mhoram believed that large balances might be tipped by the weight of one life. Yet the face of the sculpture seemed at this moment taut with misapprehended purpose – crowded with all the people who would die so that one young girl might live.

As he gazed at this rendition of Covenant's face, High Lord Mhoram experienced again the sudden passion which had enabled him to draw a gleam from Loric's *krill*. Danger filled his eyes, and he snatched up the sculpture as if he meant to shout at it. But then the hard lines of his mouth bent, and he sighed at himself. With conflicting intensities in his face, he bore the *anundivian yajña* work to the Hall of Gifts, where he placed it in a position of honour high on one of the rude, rootlike pillars of the cavern. After that, he returned to his chambers and slept.

He was awakened shortly after noon by Trevor's summons. His dreamless slumber vanished instantly; and he was on his way out of his rooms before the young warrior who brought the message was able to knock a second time. He hastened up out of the recesses of Revelstone towards the battlements over the gates of the main Keep, where he chanced upon Hearthrall Tohrm. Together, they crossed to the tower and climbed the stairs to its top. There they found Trevor Loerya-mate with Warmark Quaan and Hirebrand Borillar.

Quaan stood between the Lord and the Hearthrall like an anchor to their separate tensions. Trevor's whole face was clenched white with apprehension, and Borillar's hands trembled on his staff with mixed dread and determination; but Quaan held his arms folded across his chest and frowned stolidly downward as if he had lost the capacity to be surprised by anything any servant of the Grey Slayer did. As the High Lord joined them, the old Warmark pointed with one tanned, muscular arm, and his rigid finger guided Mhoram's eyes like an accusation to a gathering of ur-viles before the gates of the tower.

The ur-viles were within arrow reach, but a line of red-eyed Cavewights bearing wooden shields protected them by intercepting the occasional shafts which Quaan's warriors loosed from the windows of the tower. Behind this cover, the ur-viles were building.

They worked with deft speed, and their construction quickly took shape in their midst. Soon Mhoram saw that they were making a catapult.

Despite the freezing ire of Foul's wind, his hands began to sweat on his staff. As the ur-viles looped heavy ropes around the sprocketed winches at the back of the machine, lashed the ropes to the stiff throwing-arm, and sealed with flashes of black power a large, ominous iron cup to the end of the arm, he found himself tensing, calling all his lore and strength into readiness. He knew instinctively that the attackers did not intend to hurl rocks at Revelstone.

The Demondim-spawn worked without instructions from Satansfist. He watched from a distance, but neither spoke nor moved. A score of them clambered over the catapult – adjusting, tightening, sealing it – and High Lord Mhoram marvelled grimly that they could build so well without eyes. But they showed no need for eyes, noses were as discerning as vision. In a short time the finished catapult stood erect before Revelstone's tower.

Then barking shouts chorused through the encampment, and a hundred ur-viles ran forward to the machine. On either side, a score of them formed wedges to concentrate their power and placed themselves so that their loremaster stood at the winches. Using their iron staves, the two loremasters began turning the sprockets, thus tightening the ropes and slowly bending the catapult's arm backward. The catapult dwarfed the creatures, but by focusing their strength in wedges, they were able to crank the winches and bend the arm. And while this was being done, the other ur-viles came together and made an immense wedge behind the catapult. Against the background of the frozen snow-scud, they looked like a spear point aimed at the heart of the Keep.

With part of his mind, Mhoram observed that Lord Amatin now stood beside him. He glanced around for Loerya and saw her on a balcony of the main Keep. He waved his approval to her; if any holocaust struck the watchtower, all the Lords would not be lost. Then he cocked an eyebrow at Quaan, and when the Warmark nodded to indicate that the warriors were ready for any sudden orders, High Lord Mhoram returned his attention to the ur-viles.

As the arm of the catapult was drawn back, Gravelingas Tohrm knelt at the parapet, spreading his arms and pressing his palms against the slow curve of the wall. In a dim, alien voice, he began to sing a song of granite endurance to the stone.

Then the arm reached its fullest arc. Quivering as if it were about to splinter, it strained towards the tower. At once, it was locked into place with iron hooks. Its wide cup had been brought down to chest level directly in front of the loremaster who apexed the largest wedge.

With a ringing clang, the loremaster struck its stave against the cup. Strength surged through scores of black shoulders; they emanated power as the loremaster laboured over the cup. And thick, cruel fluid, as fiery as the vitriol which consumes flesh and obsidian and teak alike, splashed coruscating darkly from the stave into the waiting cup.

The High Lord had seen human bodies fall into ash at the least touch of fluid like that. He turned to warn Quaan. But the old Warmark needed no warning: he also had watched warriors die in Demondim acid. Before Mhoram could speak, Quaan was shouting down the stairwell into the tower, ordering his warriors away from all exposed windows and battlements.

At Mhoram's side, Lord Amatin's slight form began to shiver in the wind. She held her staff braced before her as if she were trying to ward the cold away.

Slowly, the loremaster's fluid filled the cup. It splashed and spouted like black lava, throwing midnight sparks into the air; but the lore of the ur-viles contained it, held its dark force together, prevented it from shattering the catapult.

Then the cup was full.

The ur-viles did not hesitate. With a hoarse, hungry cry, they knocked free the restraining hooks.

The arm arced viciously forward, slapped with flat vehemence against the stop at the end of its throw.

A black gout of vitriol as large as a Stonedownor home sprang through the air and crashed against the tower a few dozen feet below the topmost parapet.

As the acid struck stone, it erupted. In lightless incandescence, it burned at the mountain rock like the flare of a dark sun. Tohrm cried out in pain, and the stone's agony howled under Mhoram's feet. He leaped forward. With Trevor and Amatin beside him, he called blue Lords-fire from his staff and flung it down against the vitriol.

Together, the three staffs flamed hotly to counter the acid. And because the ur-viles could not replenish it, it fell apart in moments – dropped like pieces of hate from the wall, and seared the ground before it was extinguished.

It left behind a long scar of corrosion in the stone. But it had not broken through the wall.

With a groan, Tohrm sagged away from the parapet. Sweat ran down his face, confusing his tears so that Mhoram could not tell whether the Gravelingas wept from pain or grief or rage. *'Melenkurion abatha!'* he cried thickly. 'Ah, Revelstone!'

The ur-viles were already cranking their catapult into position for another throw.

For an instant, Mhoram felt stunned and helpless. With such catapults, so many thousands of ur-viles might be able to tear Lord's Keep down piece by piece, reduce it to dead rubble. But then his instinct for resistance came to life within him. To Trevor and Amatin he snapped, 'Those blasts must not touch the Keep. Join me. We will shape a Forbidding.'

Even as they moved away from him on either side to prepare between them as wide a defence as possible, he knew that these tactics would not suffice. Three Lords might be able to deflect the greatest harm of a few attacks, but they could not repulse the assault of fifteen or twenty thousand ur-viles. 'Tohrm!' he commanded sharply. 'Borillar!'

At once, Hearthrall Tohrm began calling for more Gravelingases. But Borillar hesitated, searching around him uncertainly as if the urgency of the situation interfered with his thinking, hid his own lore from him.

'Calmly, Hirebrand,' Mhoram said to steady him. 'The catapults are of wood.'

Abruptly, Borillar spun and dashed away. As he passed Warmark Quaan, he cried, 'Archers!' Then he was yelling towards the main Keep, 'Hirebrands! Bring *lor-liarill!* We will make arrows!'

In a dangerously short time, the ur-viles had cocked their machine, and were filling its cup with their black vitriol. They fired their next throw scant moments after Tohrm's *rhadhamaerl* reinforcements had positioned themselves to support the stone.

At Mhoram's command, the Lords struck against the arcing gout of acid before it reached the tower. Their staffs flashed as they threw up a wall of fire across the acid's path.

The fluid hit their fire with a force which shredded their Forbidding. The black acid shot through their power to slam against the tower wall. But the attack had spent much of its virulence. When it reached the stone, Tohrm and his fellow Gravelingases were able to withstand it.

It shattered against the strength which they called up in the rock, and fell flaming viciously to the ground, leaving behind dark stains on the wall but no serious damage.

Tohrm turned to meet High Lord Mhoram's gaze. Hot anger and exertion flushed the Hearthrall's face, but he bared his teeth in a grin which promised much for the defence of Revelstone.

Then three of Quaan's archers joined the Lords, followed closely by two Hirebrands. The archers were tall Woodhelvennin warriors, whose slimness of form belied the strength of their bows. Warmark Quaan acknowledged them, and asked Borillar what he wanted them to do. In response, Borillar accepted from the Hirebrands six long, thin arrows. These were deliberately rune-carved, despite their slenderness; their tips were sharpened to keen points; and their ends were fletched with light brown feathers. The Hearthrall gave two of them to each archer, saying as he did so, 'This is *lor-liarill*, the rare wood called by the Giants of Seareach "Gildenlode". They – '

'We are Woodhelvennin,' the woman who led the archers said bluntly. '*Lor-liarill* is known to us.'

'Loose them well,' returned Borillar. 'There are no others prepared. Strike first at the Cavewights.'

The woman looked at Quaan to see if he had any orders for her, but he waved her and her companions to the parapet. With smooth competence, the three archers nocked arrows, bent bows, and took aim at the catapult

Already, the ur-viles had pulled back its arm, and were busy rabidly refilling its iron cup.

Through his teeth, Quaan said, 'Strike now.'

Together, three bowstrings thrummed.

Immediately, the defending Cavewights jerked up their shields, caught the arrows out of the air.

The instant the arrows bit wood, they exploded into flames. The force of their impact spread fire over the shields, threw blazing shreds and splinters down on to the Cavewights. Yelping in surprise and pain, the dull-witted, gangling creatures dropped their shields and jumped away from the fire.

At once, the archers struck again. Their shafts sped through the air and hit the catapult's throwing-arm, just below the cup. The *lor-liarill* detonated instantly, setting the black acid afire. In sudden conflagration, the fluid's power smashed the catapult, scattered blazing wood in all directions. A score of ur-viles and several Cavewights fell, and the rest went scrambling beyond arrow range, leaving the pieces of the machine to burn themselves out.

With a fierce grin, the Woodhelvennin woman turned to Borillar and said, 'The *lillianrill* make dour shafts, Hearthrall.'

Borillar strove to appear dispassionate, as if he were accustomed to such success, but he had to swallow twice before he could find his voice to say, 'So it would appear.'

High Lord Mhoram placed a hand of praise on the Hearthrall's shoulder. 'Hirebrand, is there more *lor-liarill* which may be formed into such arrows?'

Borillar nodded like a veteran. 'There is more. All the Gildenlode keels and rudders which were made for the Giants – before – That wood may be reshaped.'

'Ask the Hirebrands to begin at once,' said Mhoram quietly.

Smiling broadly, Tohrm moved to stand beside Borillar. 'Hearthrall, you have outdone me,' he said in a teasing tone. 'The *rhadhamaerl* will not rest until they have found a way to match this triumph of yours.'

At this, Borillar's dispassion broke into a look of wide pleasure. Arm in arm, he and Tohrm left the tower, followed by the other Hirebrands and Gravelingases.

After bowing under a few curt words of praise from Quaan, the archers left also. He and the three Lords were left alone on the tower, gazing sombrely into each other's eyes.

Finally, Quaan spoke the thought that was in all their faces. 'It is a small victory. Larger catapults may strike from beyond the reach of arrows. Larger wedges may make power enough to breach the walls. If several catapults are brought to the attack together, we will be sorely pressed to resist even the first throws.'

'And the Illearth Stone has not yet spoken against us,' Mhoram murmured. He could still feel the force which had rent his defence tingling in his wrists and elbows. As an afterthought, he added, 'Except in the voice of this cruel wind and winter.'

For a moment, he melded his mind with Trevor and Amatin, sharing his strength with them, and reminding them of their own resources. Then, with a sigh, Lord Amatin said, 'I am of Woodhelvennin blood. I will assist Hearthrall Borillar in the making of these shafts. It will be slow work, and many of the *lillianrill* have other tasks.'

'And I will go to Tohrm,' Trevor said. 'I have no lore to match the *rhadhamaerl*. But it may be that a counter to this Demondim-bane can be found in the fire-stones.'

Mhoram approved silently, put his arm around the two Lords and hugged them. 'I will stand watch,' he said, 'and summon Loerya when I am weary.' Then he sent Quaan with them from the tower, so that the Warmark could ready his warriors for all the work they might have to do if the walls were harmed. Alone, the High Lord stood and faced the dark encampment of Satansfist's hordes – stood below the snapping Furl, which was already ragged in the sharp wind, planted the iron heel of his staff on the stone, and faced the encircling enemy as if his were the hand which held the outcome of the siege.

In the grey dimness towards evening, the ur-viles built another catapult. Beyond the reach of arrows, they constructed a stronger machine, one capable of throwing their power across the additional ground. But High Lord Mhoram summoned no aid. When the black spew of corrosion was launched, it had farther to travel; it was beyond the command of its makers for a longer time. Mhoram's blue power lashed out at it as it reached the top of its arc. A fervid lightning of Lords-fire bolted into the vitriol, weakened its momentum, caused it to fall short. Splashing angrily, effectlessly, it crashed to the earth, and burned a morbid hole like a charnel pit in the frozen dirt.

The ur-viles withdrew, returned to the garish watch fires which burned throughout the army for the sake of the misborn creatures that needed light. After a time, Mhoram rubbed the strain from his forehead, and called Lord Loerya to take his place.

During the blind night, three more catapults were built in the safety of distance, then brought forward to attack Revelstone. None of them assaulted the tower; two of them threw at the walls of the main Keep from the north, one from the south. But each time the defenders were able to react quickly. The loremasters' exertion of power as they cocked the machines radiated a palpable impression up at the battlements, and this emanation warned the Keep of each new assault. Archers waiting with *lor-liarill* arrows raced to respond.

They gained light to aim with by driving arrows into the ground near the catapults; in the sudden revealing fires, they destroyed two of the new threats as they had destroyed the first. But the third remained beyond bowshot, and attacked the south wall from a position out of Loerya's reach. Yet this assault was defeated also. In a moment of inspiration, the Haft commanding the archers ordered them to direct their shafts at the acid as it arced towards the Keep. The archers fired a dozen shafts in rapid succession into the gout of fluid, and succeeded in breaking it apart, so that it spattered against the stone in weaker pieces and did little harm.

Fortunately, there were no more attacks that night. All the new Gildenlode arrows had been used, and the process of making more was slow and difficult. Throughout the next day also there were no attacks, though the sentries could see ur-viles building catapults in the distance. No move was made against Revelstone until deep in the chattering darkness of midnight. Then alarms rang through the Keep, calling all its defenders from their work or rest. In the wind-torn light of arrows aflame like torches in the frozen earth, the Lords and Hirebrands and Gravelingases and warriors and Lorewardens saw ten catapults being cranked into position beyond the range of the archers.

Orders hummed through the stone of the Keep. Men and women dashed to take their places. In moments, a Lord or a team of defenders stood opposite each catapult. As the cups were filled, Revelstone braced itself for the onslaught of power.

At the flash of a dank green signal from Satansfist, the ten catapults threw.

The defence outlined Revelstone in light, cast so much bright orange, yellow and blue fire from the walls that the whole plateau blazed in the darkness like a conflagration of defiance. Working together from the tower, Mhoram and Amatin threw bolts of power which cast down two of the vitriol attacks. From the plateau atop Revelstone, the Lords Trevor and Loerya used their advantage of height to help them each deflect one cupful of corrosion into the ground.

Two of the remaining attacks were torn apart by Hearthrall Borillar's arrows. Using a piece of *orcrest* given to them by Hearthrall Tohrm, and a *lomillialor* rod obtained from Lord Amatin, teams of Lorewardens erected barriers which consumed most of the virulence in two assaults, prevented them from doing any irrecoverable damage.

Gravelingases met the last two throws of the ur-viles. With one partner, Tohrm had positioned himself on a balcony directly in front of one catapult. They stood on either side of a stone vat of graveling, and sang a deep *rhadhamaerl* song which slowly brought their mortal flesh into harmony with the mounting radiance of the fire-stones. While the ur-viles filled the cup of the machine, Tohrm and his companion thrust their arms into the graveling, pushed their lore-preserved hands deep among the fire-stones near the sides of the vat. There they waited in the golden heat, singing their earthish song until the catapult threw and the vitriol sprang towards them.

In the last instant, they heaved a double armful of graveling up at the black gout. The two powers collided scant feet above their heads, and the force of the impact knocked them flat on the balcony. The wet corrosion of the acid turned the graveling instantly to cinders, but in turn the *rhadhamaerl* might of the fire-stones burned away the acid before the least drop of it touched Tohrm or Revelstone.

The other pair of Gravelingases were not so successful. They mistimed their countering heave, and as a result their graveling only stopped half the vitriol. Both men died in fluid fire which destroyed a wide section of the balcony.

But instead of striking again, launching more attacks to wear down the defences of the Keep, the ur-viles abandoned their catapults and withdrew – apparently satisfied with what they had learned about Revelstone's mettle.

High Lord Mhoram watched them go with surprise in his face and cold dread in his heart. Surely the ur-viles had not been intimidated by the defence. If Satansfist chose now to change his tactics, it was because he had measured the weakness of Revelstone, and knew a better way to capitalize on it.

The next morning, Mhoram saw the commencement of Satansfist's new strategy but for two days after that he did not comprehend it. The Raver's hordes moved closer to Revelstone, placed themselves hardly a hundred yards from the walls, and faced the plateau as if they expected its defenders to leap willingly into their jaws. The ur-viles moved among the slavering creatures and Cavewights, and formed scores of wedges which seemed to point towards the very heart of Revelstone. And behind them Satansfist stood in a broad piece of open ground, openly wielding his Stone for the first time. But he launched no physical onslaught, offered the Keep no opportunity to strike or be stricken. Indeed, his creatures dropped to their hands and knees, and glared hungrily at Revelstone like crouching preyers. The ur-vile loremasters set the tips of their staves in the ground, began a barking ululation or invocation which carried in shreds to the Keep through the tearing wind. And *samadhi* Raver, Sheol and Satansfist, squeezed his fragment of the Illearth Stone so that it ran with steam like boiling ice.

As Mhoram watched, he could feel the upsurge of power on all sides; the exertion of might radiated at him until the skin of his cheeks stung under it, despite the raw chill of the wind. But the besiegers took no other action. They held their positions in fierce concentration, scowling murderously as if they were envisioning the blood of their victims.

Slowly, tortuously, they began to have an effect upon the ground of the foothills. From the unflickering green blaze of the Stone, a rank emerald hue spread to the dirt around Satansfist's feet and throbbed in the soil. It encircled him, pulsing like a fetid heart, then sent crooked offshoots like green veins through the ground towards Revelstone. These grew with each savage throb, branched out until they reached the backs of the crouching hordes. At that point, red pain sickly tinged with green blossomed from the embedded tips of the loremasters' staves. Like Satansfist's emerald, the ill red grew in the ground like arteries or roots of hurt. It shone through the grey ice on the earth without melting it, and expanded with each throb of *samadhi*'s central power until all of Revelstone was ringed in pulsing veins.

The process of this growth was slow and deadly; by nightfall, the red-green harm was not far past the feet of the ur-viles; and after a long, lurid darkness, dawn found the veins just half-way to the walls. But it was implacable and sure. Mhoram could conceive no defence against it because he did not know what it was.

During the next two days, the dread of it spread over Lord's Keep. People began to talk in whispers. Men and women hurried from place to place as if they feared that the city stone were turning against them. Children whimpered inexplicably, and winced at the sight of well-known faces. A thick atmosphere of fear and incomprehension hovered in Revelstone like the spread wings of an alighting vulture. Yet Mhoram did not grasp what was being done to the city until the evening of the third day. Then by chance he approached Warmark Quaan unseen and unheard, and at the touch of his hand on Quaan's shoulder, the Warmark reeled away in panic, clawing at his sword. When his eyes finally recognized the High Lord, his face filled with a grey ash of misery, and he trembled like an overwhelmed novice.

With a groan of insight, Mhoram understood Revelstone's plight. Dread of the unknown was only the surface of the peril. As he threw his arms around Quaan's trembling, he saw that the red-green veins of power in the ground were not a physical danger; rather, they were a vehicle for the raw emotional force of the Despiser's malice — a direct attack on the Keep's will, a corrosive hurled against the moral fabric of Revelstone's resistance.

Fear was growing like a fatal disease in the heart of Lord's Keep. Under the influence of those lurid veins, the courage of the city was beginning to rot.

It had no defence. The *lillianrill* and *rhadhamaerl* could build vast warming fires within the walls. The Lorewardens could sing in voices that shook helplessly brave songs of encouragement and victory.

The Warward could drill and train until the warriors had neither leisure nor stamina for fear. The Lords could flit through the city like blue ravens, carrying the light of courage and support and intransigence wherever they went, from grey day to blind night to grey day again. The Keep was not idle. As time dragged its dread-aggravated length along, moved through its skeletal round with an almost audible clatter of fleshless bones, everything that could be done was done. The Lords took to moving everywhere with their staffs alight, so that their bright azure could resist the erosion of Revelstone's spirit. But still the veined, bloody harm in the ground multiplied its aegis over the city. The malignance of tenscore thousand evil hearts stifled all opposition.

Soon even the mountain rock of the plateau seemed to be whimpering in silent fear. Within five days, some families locked themselves in their rooms and refused to come out; they feared to be abroad in the city. Others fled to the apparent safety of the upland hills. Mad fights broke out in the kitchens, where any cook or food handler could snatch up a knife to slash at sudden gusts of terror. To prevent such outbursts, Warmark Quaan had to station Eoman in every kitchen and refectory.

But though he drove them as if he had a gaunt spectre of horror clinging to his shoulders, he could not keep even his warriors from panic. This fact he was finally forced to report to the High Lord, and after hearing it, Mhoram went to stand his watch on the tower. Alone there, he faced the night which fell as heavily as the scree of despair against the back of his neck, faced the unglimmering emerald loathsomeness of the Stone, faced the sick, red-green veined fire – and hugged his own dread within the silence of his heart. If he had not been so desperate, he might have wept in sympathy for Kevin Landwaster, whose dilemma he now understood with a keenness that cut him to the bone of his soul.

Some time later – after darkness had added all its chill to Lord Foul's winter, and the watch fires of the encampment had paled to mere sparks beside *samadhi* Raver's loud, strong lust for death, Loerya Trevor-mate came to the tower, bearing with her a small pot of graveling which she placed before her when she sat on the stone, so that the glow lit her drawn face. The uplift of her visage cast her eyes into shadow, but still Mhoram could see that they were raw with tears.

'My daughters – ' her voice seemed to choke her – 'my children – they – You know them, High Lord,' she said as if she were pleading. 'Are they not children to make a parent proud?'

'Be proud,' Mhoram replied gently. 'Parents and children are a pride to each other.'

'You know them, High Lord,' she insisted. 'My joy in them has been large enough to be pain. They – High Lord, they will no longer eat. They fear the food – they see poison in the food. This evil maddens them.'

'We are all maddened, Loerya. We must endure.'

'How endure? Without hope – ? High Lord, it were better if I had not borne children.'

Gently, quietly, Mhoram answered a different question. 'We cannot march out to fight this evil. If we leave these walls, we are ended. There is no other hold for us. We must endure.'

In a voice suffused with weeping, Loerya said, 'High Lord, summon the Unbeliever.'

'Ah, sister Loerya – that I cannot do. You know I cannot. You know that I chose rightly when I released Thomas Covenant to the demands of his own world. Whatever other follies have twisted the true course of my life, that choice was not folly.'

'Mhoram!' she beseeched thickly.

'No, Loerya, think what you ask. The Unbeliever desired to save a life in his world. But time moves in other ways there. Seven and forty years have passed since he came first to Revelstone, yet in that time he has not aged even three cycles of the moon. Perhaps only moments have gone by for him since his last summoning. If he were called again now, perhaps he would still be prevented from saving the young child who needs him.'

At the mention of a child, sudden anger twisted Loerya's face. 'Summon him!' she hissed. 'What are his nameless children to me? By the Seven, Mhoram! Summon – !'

'No.' Mhoram interrupted her, but his voice did not lose its gentleness. 'I will not. He must have the freedom of his own fate – it is his right. We have no right to take it from him – no, even the Land's utterest need does not justify such an act. He holds the white gold. Let him come to the Land if he wills. I will not gainsay the one true bravery of my unwise life.'

Loerya's anger collapsed as swiftly as it had come. Wringing her hands over the graveling as if even the hope of warmth had gone out of them, she moaned, 'This evening my youngest – Yolenid – she is hardly more than a baby – she shrieked at the sight of me.' With an effort, she raised her streaming eyes to the High Lord, and whispered, 'How endure?'

Though his own heart wept for her, Mhoram met her gaze. 'The alternative is Desecration.' As he looked into the ragged extremity of her face, he felt his own need crying out, uging him to share his perilous secret. For a moment that made his pulse hammer apprehensively in his temples, he knew that he would answer Loerya if she asked him. To warn her, he breathed softly, 'Power is a dreadful thing.'

A spark of inchoate hope lit her eyes. She climbed unsteadily to her feet, brought her face closer to his and searched him. The first opening of a meld drained the surface of his mind. But what she saw or felt in him stopped her. His cold doubt quenched the light in her eyes, and she receded from him. In an awkward voice that carried only a faint vibration of bitterness, she said, 'No, Mhoram. I will not ask. I trust you or no one. You will speak when your heart is ready.'

Gratitude burned under Mhoram's eyelids. With a crooked smile, he said, 'You are courageous, sister Loerya.'

'No.' She picked up her graveling pot and moved away from him. 'Though it is no fault of theirs, my daughters make me craven.' Without a backward glance, she left the High Lord alone in the lurid night.

Hugging his staff against his chest, he turned and faced once more the flawless green wrong of the Raver's Stone. As his eyes met that baleful light, he straightened his shoulders, drew himself erect, so that he stood upright like a marker or witness to Revelstone's inviolate rock.

5

LOMILLIALOR

The weight of mortality which entombed Covenant seemed to press him deeper and deeper into the obdurate stuff of the ground. He felt that he had given up breathing – that the rock and soil through which he sank sealed him off from all respiration – but the lack of air gave him no distress; he had no more need for the sweaty labour of breathing. He was plunging irresistibly, motionlessly downward, like a man falling into his fate.

Around him, the black earth changed slowly to mist and cold. It lost none of its solidity, none of its airless weight, but its substance altered, became by gradual increments a pitch-dark fog as massive and unanswerable as the pith of granite. With it, the cold increased. Cold and winter and mist wound about him like cerements.

He had no sense of duration, but at some point he became aware of a chill breeze in the mist. It eased some of the pressure on him, loosened his cerements. Then an abrupt rift appeared some distance away. Through the gap, he saw a fathomless night sky, unredeemed by any stars. And from the rift shone a slice of green light as cold and compelling as the cruellest emerald.

The cloud rift rode the breeze until it crossed over him. As it passed, he saw standing behind the heavy clouds a full moon livid with green force, an emerald orb radiating ill through the heavens. The sick green light caught at him. When the rift which exposed it blew by him and away into the distance, he felt himself respond. The authority, the sovereignty, of the moon could not be denied; he began to flow volitionlessly through the mist in the wake of the rift.

But another force intervened. For an instant, he thought he could smell the aroma of a tree's heart sap, and pieces of song touched him through the cold: *be true . . . answer . . . soul's deep curse . . .*

He clung to them, and thier potent appeal anchored him. The darkness of the mist locked around him again, and he went sinking in the direction of the song.

Now the cold stiffened under him, so that he felt he was descending on a slab, with the breeze blowing over him. He was too chilled to move, and only the sensation of air in his chest told him that he was breathing again. His ribs and diaphragm worked, pumped air in and out of his lungs automatically. Then he noticed another change in the mist. The blank, wet, blowing night took on another dimension, an outer limit; it gave the impression that it clung privately to him, leaving the rest of the world in sunlight. Despite the cloud, he could sense the possibility of brightness in the cold breeze beyond him. And the frigid slab grew harder and harder under him, until he felt he was lying on a catafalque with a cairn of personal darkness piled over him.

The familiar song left him there. For a time, he heard nothing but the hum of the breeze and the hoarse, lisping sound made by his breath as it laboured past his swollen lip and gum. He was freezing slowly, sinking into icy union with the stone under his back. Then a voice near him panted, 'By the Seven! We have done it.'

The speaker sounded spent with weariness and oddly echoless, forlorn. Only the hum of the wind supported his claim to existence; without it, he might have been speaking alone in the uncomprehended ether between the stars.

A light voice full of glad relief answered, 'Yes, my friend. Your lore serves us well. We have not striven in vain these three days.'

'My lore and your strength. And the *Lomillialor* of High Lord Mhoram. But see him. He is injured and ill.'

'Have I not told you that he also suffers?'

The light voice sounded familiar to Covenant. It brought the sunshine closer, contracted the mist until it was wholly within him, and he could feel cold brightness on his face.

'You have told me,' said the forlorn man. 'And I have told you that I should have killed him when he was within my grasp. But all my acts go astray. Behold – even now the Unbeliever comes dying to my call.'

The second speaker replied in a tone of gentle reproof, 'My friend, you – '

But the first cut him off. 'This is an ill-blown place. We cannot help him here.'

Covenant felt hands grip his shoulders. He made an effort to open his eyes. At first he could see nothing; the sunlight washed everything out of his sight. But then something came between him and the sun. In its shadow, he blinked at the blur which marred all his perceptions.

'He awakens,' the first voice said. 'Will he know me?'

'Perhaps not. You are no longer young, my friend.'

'Better if he does not,' the man muttered. 'He will believe that I seek to succeed where I once failed. Such a man will understand retribution.'

'You wrong him. I have known him more closely. Do you not see the greatness of his need for mercy?'

'I see it. And I also know him. I have lived with Thomas Covenant in my ears for seven and forty years. He receives mercy even now, whether or not he comprehends it.'

'We have summoned him from his rightful world. Do you call this mercy?'

In a hard voice, the first speaker said, 'I call it mercy.'

After a moment, the second sighed. 'Yes. And we could not have chosen otherwise. Without him, the Land dies.'

'Mercy?' Covenant croaked. His mouth throbbed miserably.

'Yes!' the man bending over him averred. 'We give you a new chance to resist the ill which you have allowed upon the Land.'

Gradually, Covenant saw that the man had the square face and broad shoulders of a Stonedownor. His features were lost in shadow, but woven into the shoulders of his thick, fur-lined cloak was a curious pattern of crossed lightning – a pattern Covenant had seen somewhere before. But he was still too bemused with fog and shock to trace the memory.

He tried to sit up. The man helped him, braced him in that position. For a moment, his gaze wandered. He found that he was on a circular stone platform edged by a low wall. He could see nothing but sky beyond the parapet. The cold blue void held his eyes as if it were beckoning to him; it appealed to his emptiness. He had to wrestle his gaze into focus on the Stonedownor.

From this angle, the sun illuminated the man's face. With his grey-black hair and weathered cheeks, he appeared to be in his mid-sixties, but age was not his dominant feature. His visage created a self-contradictory impression. He had a hard bitter mouth which had eaten sour bread for so long that it had forgotten the taste of sweetness, but his eyes were couched in fine lines of supplication, as if he had spent years looking skyward and begging the sun not to blind him. He was a man who had been hurt and had not easily borne the cost.

As if the words had just penetrated through his haze, Covenant heard the man say, *Should have killed him.* A man wearing a pattern of crossed lightning on his shoulders had once tried to kill Covenant – and had been prevented by Atiaran Trell-mate. She had invoked the Oath of Peace.

'Triock?' Covenant breathed hoarsely. 'Triock?'

The man did not flinch from Covenant's aching gaze. 'I promised that we would meet again.'

Hellfire, Covenant groaned to himself. Hell and blood. Triock had been in love with Lena daughter of Atiaran before Covenant had ever met her.

He struggled to get to his feet. In the raw cold, his battered muscles could not raise him; he almost fainted at the exertion. But Triock helped him, and someone else lifted him from behind. He stood wavering, clinging helplessly to Triock's support, and looked out beyond the parapet.

The stone platform stood in empty air as if it were afloat in the sky, riding the hum of the breeze. In the direction Covenant faced, he could see straight to the farthest horizon, and that horizon was nothing but a sea of grey clouds, a waving, thick mass of blankness like a shroud over the earth. He wobbled a step closer to the parapet, and saw that the deep flood covered everything below him. The platform stood a few hundred feet above the clouds as if it were the only thing in the world on which the sun still shone.

But a promontory of mountains jutted out of the grey sea on his left. And when he peered over his shoulder past the man who supported him from behind, he found another promontory towering over him on that side; a flat cliff-face met his view, and on either side of it a mountain range strode away into the clouds.

He was on Kevin's Watch again, standing atop a stone shaft which joined that cliff-face somewhere out of sight below him.

For a moment, he was too surprised to be dizzy. He had not expected this; he had expected to be recalled to Revelstone. Who in the Land besides the Lords had the power to summon him? When he had known Triock, the man had been a Cattleherd, not a wielder of lore. Who but the Despiser could make such a summons possible?

Then the sight of the long fall caught up with him, and vertigo took the last strength from his legs. Without the hands which held him, he would have toppled over the parapet.

'Steady, my friend,' Triock's companion said reassuringly. 'I will not release you. I have not forgotten your dislike of heights.' He turned Covenant away from the wall, supporting him easily.

Covenant's head rolled loosely on his neck, but when the Watch stopped reeling around him, he forced himself to look toward Triock. 'How?' he mumbled quickly. 'Who — where did you get the power?'

Triock's lips bent in a hard smile. To his companion, he said, 'Did I not say that he would understand retribution? He believes that even now I would break my Oath for him.' Then he directed the bitterness of his mouth at Covenant. 'Unbeliever, you have earned retribution. The loss of High Lord Elena has caused — '

'Peace, my friend,' the other man said. 'He has pain enough for the present. Tell him no sad stories now. We must bear him to a place where we may succour him.'

Again, Triock looked at Covenant's injuries. 'Yes,' he sighed wearily. 'Pardon me, Unbeliever. I have spent seven and forty years with people who cannot forget you. Be at rest — we will preserve you from harm as best we may. And we will answer your questions. But first we must leave this place. We are exposed here. The Grey Slayer has many eyes, and some of them may have seen the power which summoned you.'

He slid a smooth wooden rod under his cloak, then said to his companion, 'Rockbrother, you can bear the Unbeliever down this stair? I have rope if you desire it.'

His companion laughed quietly. 'My friend, I am a Giant. I have not lost my footing on stone since the first sea voyage of my manhood. Thomas Covenant will be secure with me.'

A *Giant*? Covenant thought dumbly. For the first time, he noticed the size of the hands which supported him. They were twice as big as his. They turned him lightly, lifted him into the air as if he were weightless.

He found himself looking up into the face of Saltheart Foamfollower.

The Giant did not appear to have changed much since Covenant had last seen him. His short, stiff iron beard was greyer and longer, and deep lines of care furrowed his forehead, on which the mark of the wound he had received at the battle of Soaring Woodhelven was barely visible; but his deep-set eyes still flashed like enthusiastic gems from under the massive fortification of his brows, and his lips curled wryly around a smile of welcome. Looking at him, Covenant could think of nothing except that he had not said goodbye to the Giant when they had parted in Treacher's Gorge. Foamfollower had befriended him – and he had not even returned that friendship to the extent of one farewell. Shame pushed his eyes from Foamfollower's face. He glanced down the Giant's gnarled, oaklike frame. Then he saw that Foamfollower's heavy leather jerkin and leggings were tattered and rent, and under many of the tears were battle scars, both old and new. The newest ones hurt him as if they had been cut into his own flesh.

'Foamfollower,' he croaked. 'I'm sorry.'

The Giant replied gently, 'Peace, my friend. All that is past. Do not condemn yourself.'

'Hellfire.' Covenant could not master his weakness. 'What's happened to you?'

'Ah, that is a long tale, full of Giantish episodes and apostrophes. I will save it until we have taken you to a place where we may aid you. You are ill enough to bandy stories with death itself.'

'You've been hurt,' Covenant went on. But the intensity of Foamfollower's eyes stopped him.

In mock sternness, the Giant commanded, 'Be silent, Unbeliever. I will listen to no sad stories in this place.' Gently, he cradled the wounded man in his arms, then said to Triock, 'Follow carefully, Rockbrother. Our work has only begun. If you fall, I will be hard pressed to catch you.'

'Look to yourself,' Triock replied gruffly. 'I am not unaccustomed to stone – even stone as chill as this.'

'Well, then. Let us make what haste we can. We have endured much to come so far, you and I. We must not lose the ur-Lord now.'

Without waiting for an answer, he started down the rude stair of Kevin's Watch.

Covenant turned his face to the Giant's breast. The breeze had a high lonely sound as it rustled past the cliff and eddied around Foamfollower; it reminded Covenant that the Watch stood more than four thousand feet above the foothills. But Foamfollower's heart beat with forthright confidence, and his arms felt unbreakable. At each downward step, a slight jolt passed through him, as if that foot had locked itself to the stair stone. And Covenant no longer possessed even strength enough for fear. He rode numbly in the Giant's hold until the hum of the wind increased, and Foamfollower dropped one step at a time into the cold sea of clouds.

In moments, the sunlight was gone as if it had been irretrievably lost. The wind took on a raw, dry, cutting edge, too chill to be softened by moisture. Covenant and Foamfollower descended through dim vistaless air as icy as polar mist – cloud as thick and thetic as a fist clenched around the world. Under its pressure, Covenant felt icicles crawling up his spine towards the last warmth of life left in him.

Then they reached the ledge at the base of Kevin's Watch. The precipice loomed darkly beside them as Foamfollower turned to the right and moved out along the ledge, but he stepped securely, as if he had no conception of falling. And shortly he left the exposed cliff-face, began to clamber along the trail into the mountains. After that, the last tension faded from the background of Covenant's mind. His weakness opened in him like a funeral lily, and the mist drew him into a wan, slumberous daze.

For some time he lost track of where Foamfollower was going. He seemed to feel himself bleeding away into the grey air. Tranquillity like the peace of ice surrounded his heart. He no longer understood what Foamfollower was talking about when the Giant whispered urgently, 'Triock, he fails. We must aid him now or not at all.'

'Yes,' Triock agreed. He called commandingly, 'Bring blankets and graveling! He must have warmth.'

'That will not suffice. He is ill and injured. He must have healing.'

Triock snapped, 'I see him. I am not blind.'

'Then what can we do? I am helpless here – the Giants have no lore for cold. We suffer little from it.'

'Rub his limbs. Put your strength into him. I must think.'

Something rough began to batter Covenant, but the ice in him was impervious to it. Vaguely, he wondered why Foamfollower and Triock would not let him sleep.

'Is there no hurtloam here?' asked the Giant.

'At one time there was,' Triock responded distantly. 'Lena – Lena healed him in this same place – when he first came to the Land. But I am not a *rhadhamaerl* – I do not feel the secret flavours and powers of the Earth. And it is said that the hurtloam has – retreated – that it has hidden itself to escape the ill which is upon the Land. Or that this winter has slain it. We cannot succour him in any way.'

'We must help him. His very bones freeze.'

Covenant felt himself being shifted, felt blankets being wrapped around him. In the background of his haze, he thought he saw the kind yellow light of graveling. That pleased him; he could rest better if the grey fog did not dominate everything.

After a moment, Triock said uncertainly, 'It is possible that the power of the High Wood can help him.'

'Then begin!' the Giant urged.

'I am no Hirebrand. I have no *lillianrill* lore – I have only studied this matter in the Loresraat for a year – after High Lord Mhoram gave the *lomillialor* to me. I cannot control its power.'

'Nevertheless! You must make the attempt.'

Triock protested. 'The High Wood test of truth may quench the last flicker within him. Hale and whole, he might fail such testing.'

'Without it he will surely die.'

Triock snarled under his breath, then said grimly, 'Yes. Yes, Rockbrother. You outsee me. Keep life within him. I must prepare.'

In a mood of sadness, Covenant saw that the yellow light was receding into grey around him. He did not know how he could bear to lose it. Raw, reviling fog had no right to outweigh graveling in the balance of the Land. And there was no more hurtloam. No more hurtloam, he repeated with an unexpected pang. His sorrow turned to anger. By hell! Foul, he grated mutely, you can't do this. I won't let you. The hate for which he had been groping a night and a world earlier began to return to him. With the strength of anger, he prised his eyes open.

Triock was standing over him. The Stonedownor held his *lomillialor* rod as if he meant to drive it like a spike between Covenant's eyes. In his hands, the white wood shone hotly, and steam plumed from it into the chill air. A smell of wood sap joined the loamy odour of the graveling.

Muttering words that Covenant could not understand, Triock brought the rod down until its end touched the infected fever in his forehead.

At first, he felt nothing from the contact; the *lomillialor* pulsed effectlessly on his wound as if he were immune to it. But then he was touched from another direction. An exquisite ache of heat cut through the ice in his left palm, spreading from the ring he wore. It sliced into him, then moved up through his wrist. It hurt him as if it were flaying cold and flesh off his bones, but the pain gave him a kind of savage pleasure. Soon his whole left arm was livid with excruciation. And under the heat his bruises reawoke, came back from the dead.

When the hold of the ice had been broken that far, it began to give way in other places. Warmth from the blankets reached towards his battered ribs. The joints of his legs throbbed as if they had been kicked into consciousness. In moments, his forehead remembered its anguish.

Then Triock transferred the tip of the High Wood from his forehead to the tight black swelling on his lip. At once, agony erupted within him, and he plunged into it as if it were solace.

He returned to consciousness slowly, but when he opened his eyes he knew that he had become steadier. His wounds were not healed; both his forehead and mouth ached like goads embedded in his flesh, and his body moaned with bruises. But the ice no longer gnawed his bones. The swelling of his lip was reduced, and his sight had improved, as if the lenses of his eyes had been cleaned. Yet he felt a private grief at the numbness which clung to his hands and feet. His dead nerves had not yet rediscovered the health which he had learned to expect from the Land.

But he was alive – he was in the Land – he had seen Foamfollower. He set aside the distress of his nerves for another time, and looked around him.

He lay in a small, sheer valley nestled among the mountains behind Kevin's Watch. While he had been unconscious, the enshrouding sea of clouds had receded a few hundred feet, and now light snow filled the air like murmuring. Already an inch of it blanketed him. Something in the timbre of the snow gave him the impression that the time was late afternoon. But he was not concerned about time. He had been in this valley once before, with Lena.

The memory of it contrasted starkly with what he saw. It had been a quiet, grassy place girdled with pines like tall sentinels guarding its quietude and a sprightly brook flowing down its centre. But now only bare, wasted earth showed through the thickening snow. The pines had been stripped naked and splintered by more winter than they could survive; and instead of water, a weal of ice ran through the valley like a scar already old.

Covenant wondered painfully how long this weather would last.

The implications of that question made him shiver, and he fought his tired frame into a sitting position so that he could lean closer to the pot of graveling. As he did so, he saw three figures sitting around another pot a short distance away. One of them observed his movement and spoke to the others. At once Triock stood and strode towards Covenant. He squatted near the Unbeliever, and studied him gravely before saying, 'You have been grievously ill. My lore does not suffice to heal you. But I see that you are no longer dying.'

'You saved me,' Covenant said as bravely as he could through the pain of his mouth and his inanition.

'Perhaps. I am unsure. The wild magic has been at work in you.' Covenant stared, and Triock went on: 'It appeared that the *lomillialor* drew a response from the white gold of your ring. With that power, you surpass any test of truth I might give.'

My ring, Covenant thought dully. But he was not ready to deal with that idea, and he set it aside also. 'You saved me,' he repeated. 'There are things I need to know.'

'Let them be. You must eat now. You have not taken food for

many days.' He looked around through the snow, then said, 'Saltheart Foamfollower brings you *aliantha*.'

Covenant heard heavy feet moving across the frozen ground. A moment later Foamfollower knelt with a quiet smile beside him. Both his hands were full of viridian treasure-berries.

Covenant looked at the *aliantha*. He felt he had forgotten what to do with them: he had been hungry for so long that hunger had become a part of him. But he could not refuse the offer behind the Giant's kind smile. Slowly, he reached out a numb hand and took one of the treasure-berries.

When he slipped it past his lip and bit into it, the tangy salt-peach flavour which blossomed in his mouth seemed to refute all his reasons for fasting. And as he swallowed, he could feel nourishment rushing eagerly into him. He spat the seed into his palm; as if he were completing a ritual, he dropped it over his shoulder. Then he began to eat rapidly, wolfishly.

He did not stop until Foamfollower's hands were empty. Sighing as if he longed for more, he sowed the last seed behind him.

The Giant nodded approval and seated himself in a more relaxed position near the graveling. Triock followed his example. When they were both looking at him, Covenant said softly, 'I won't forget this.' He could not think of any other way to express his thanks.

Triock frowned sharply. He asked Foamfollower, 'Does he threaten us now?'

The Giant's cavernous eyes searched Covenant's face. He smiled wanly as he replied, 'The Unbeliever has a mournful turn of speech. He does not threaten – he does not threaten us.'

Covenant felt a surge of grim gratitude for Foamfollower's understanding. He tried to smile in return, but the tightness of his lip prevented him. He winced at the effort, then pulled his blankets more closely around him. He sensed a depth of cold answers behind the questions he needed to ask.

But he did not know how to ask them. Triock's bitter mouth and Foamfollower's scars intruded between him and his summoners; he feared that he was to blame for the tales they might tell him if he asked. Yet he had to know the answers, had to know where he stood. The first outlines of purpose were taking shape within him. He could not forget how this valley had looked when he had first seen it. And Mhoram had pleaded with him for help.

Lamely, he began, 'I didn't expect to turn up here. I thought Mhoram was going to call me back. But even he doesn't have the Staff of Law. How – how did you do it?'

Triock answered in stiff tones, 'Mhoram son of Variol, seer and oracle to the Council of Lords, came to Mithil Stonedown before the last war – the battle against Fleshharrower Raver. At that time, he gave to me the *lomillialor* rod which I have used today – and for the past three days. Because of this gift I journeyed to the Loresraat, to study the uses of the High Wood. There I learned of High Lord Elena's fall – I – '

He paused for a moment to lash down his passion, then went on. 'In the years which followed, I waited for the reason of High Lord Mhoram's gift to be made plain. During that time, I fought with my people against the marauders of the Grey Slayer. Then the Giant Saltheart Foamfollower joined us, and we fought together through the South Plains. While winter increased upon the Land, we attacked and ran and attacked again, doing what damage we could to our vast foe. But at last word came to us that Revelwood had fallen – that great Revelstone itself was besieged. We left our battles, and returned to Mithil Stonedown and Kevin's Watch. With the *lomillialor* of High Lord Mhoram, and the strength of Saltheart Foamfollower, and the lore I brought from the Loresraat, we laboured for three days, and in the end brought you to the Land. It was not easily done.'

Triock's flint voice sparked visions of desperation in Covenant's mind. To resist them, control them until he was ready for them, he asked, 'But how? I thought only the Staff of Law – '

'Much has been broken by the fall of High Lord Elena,' Triock retorted. 'The Land has not yet tasted all the consequences of that evil. But the Staff made possible certain expressions of power – and limited others. Now that limit is gone. Do you not feel the malice of this winter?'

Covenant nodded with an ache in his eyes. His responsibility for Elena's end stung him, goaded him to ask another kind of question. 'That doesn't tell me why you did it. After Lena – and Elena – and Atiaran – ' he could not bring himself to be more specific – 'and everything – you've got less reason than anyone in the world to want me back. Even Trell – Maybe Foamfollower here can forget, but you can't. If you were thinking it any louder, I could taste it.'

Bitterness clenched Triock's jaws, but his reply was sharp and ready, as if he had whetted it many times. 'Yet Foamfollower is persuasive. The Land is persuasive. The importance which the Lorewardens see in you is persuasive. And Lena daughter of Atiaran still lives in Mithil Stonedown. In her last years, Atiaran Trell-mate said often that it is the duty of the living to make meaningful the sacrifices of the dead. But I wish to find meaning for the sacrifices of those who live. After – after the harm which you wrought upon Lena – she hid herself so that the harm would not be known – so that you would be left free to bear your prophecy to the Lords. That sacrifice requires meaning, Unbeliever.'

In spite of himself, in spite of his own expectations of hostility and recrimination, Covenant believed Triock. Elena had warned him; she had described the size of Triock's capabilities. Now he wondered where Triock found his strength. The man had been an unambitious Cattleherd. The girl he loved had been raped, and her bastard daughter had grown up to love the rapist. Yet because of them he had gone to the Loresraat, studied dangerous lore for which he had no desire or affinity. He had become a guerrilla fighter for the Land. And now he had summoned Covenant at the command of the Land's need and his own harsh sense of mercy. Thickly, Covenant muttered, 'You've kept your Oath.' He was thinking, I owe you for this, too, Foul.

Abruptly, Triock got to his feet. The lines around his eyes dominated his face as he scrutinized Covenant. In a low voice, he said, 'What will you do?'

'Ask me later.' Covenant was ashamed that he could not match Triock's gaze. 'I'm not ready yet.' Instinctively, he clasped his right hand over his ring, hiding it from consideration.

'There is time,' murmured Foamfollower. 'You have a great need for rest.'

Triock said, 'Choose soon. We must be on our way at dawn.' Then he moved brusquely away through the mounting snow towards his two companions by the second pot of graveling.

'He is a good man,' Foamfollower said softly. 'Trust him.'

Oh, I trust him, Covenant thought. How can I help it?

Despite the warmth of the blankets, he began to shiver again.

As he leaned still closer to the glowing fire-stones he noticed the look of concern on Foamfollower's face. To forestall any expression of anxiety which would remind him how little he deserved the Giant's concern, he said hastily, 'I still don't know what's happened to you. The Giants were – I don't know what happened to them. And you – You've been outrageously hacked upon.' In an effort to probe Foamfollower, he went on: 'I'll tell you something funny. I was afraid of what you might do – after all that business in Treacher's Gorge. I was afraid you might go back to your people – and convince them to stop fighting, give it up. What do you think? Have I finally succeeded in telling you a story you can laugh at?'

But he saw poignantly that he had not. Foamfollower bowed his head, covered his face with one hand. For a moment, the muscles of his shoulders tensed as if with his fingers he was squeezing the bones of his countenance into an attitude which he could not achieve in any other way. 'Joy is in the ears that hear,' he said in a voice muffled by his hand. 'My ears have been too full of the noise of killing.'

Then he raised his head, and his expression was calm. Only a smouldering deep within the caves of his eyes revealed that he was hurt. 'I am not yet ready to laugh over this matter. Were I able to laugh, I would not feel so – driven to slay Soulcrusher's creatures.'

'Foamfollower,' Covenant murmured again, 'what's happened to you?'

The Giant gestured helplessly with both hands, as if he could not conceive any way to tell his story. 'My friend, I am what you see. Here is a tale which lies beyond even my grasp, and I am a Giant – though you will remember that my people considered me uncommonly brief of speech. Stone and Sea! Covenant, I know not what to say. You know how I fought for the Quest for the Staff of Law. When Damelon Giantfriend's prophecy for my people came to pass, I found that I could not give up this fighting. I had struck blows which would not stop. Therefore I left Seareach, so that I would at least serve the Land with my compulsion.

'But I did not go to the Lords. In my thoughts, the great rare beauty of Revelstone, Giant-wrought Lord's Keep, daunted me. I did not wish to stand in those brave halls while Soulcrusher's creatures raved in the Land. For that reason, I fight, and spend my days with people who fight. From the Northron Climbs to the Last Hills I have struck my blows. When I met Triock son of Thuler and his companions – when I learned that he holds a limb of the High Wood, descendant of the One Tree from which the Staff of Law was made – I joined him. In that way, I garnered my scars, and at last came here.'

'You've been around humans too long,' muttered Covenant. 'You haven't told me anything. What? How – ? I don't know where to begin.'

'Then do not begin, my friend. Rest.' Foamfollower reached out and gently touched Covenant's shoulder. 'You also have been too long among – people of another world. You need days of rest which I fear you will not receive. You must sleep.'

To his surprise, Covenant found that he was capable of sleep. Warm drowsiness seeped into him from the blankets and the graveling light, spread outward from the *aliantha* in his blood. Tomorrow he would know better what questions to ask. He lay back on the cold ground and pulled the blankets about his ears.

But as Foamfollower adjusted his blankets for him, he asked, 'How much longer is this winter going to last?'

'Peace, my friend,' Foamfollower replied. 'The Land's spring should have been born three full moons ago.'

A shudder of ice ran through Covenant. Bloody hell, Foul! he gritted. Hellfire!

But in his reclining position he could not resist his long weariness. He fell asleep almost at once, thinking, Hellfire. Hell and blood.

He lay in red, visionless slumber until some time after dark he seemed to hear voices that awakened him slightly. Disembodied in his grogginess, they spoke across him as if he were a prostrate corpse.

'You told him little of the truth,' Triock said.

And Foamfollower answered, 'He has pain enough for one heart. How could I tell him?'

'He must know. He is responsible.'

'No. For this he is not responsible.'

'Still he must know.'

'Even stone may break when it is too heavily burdened.'

'Ah, Rockbrother. How will you justify yourself if he turns against the Land?'

'Peace, my friend. Do not torment me. I have already learned that I cannot be justified.'

Covenant listened incomprehendingly. When the voices drifted out of his awareness, he sank into wild dreams of purpose and savage restitution.

6

THE DEFENCE OF MITHIL STONEDOWN

Later, he was shaken awake by Foamfollower. The Giant nudged his shoulder until he started up out of his blankets into the darkness. In the dim light of half covered graveling pots, he could see that the snow had stopped, but dawn was still some time away. Night locked the valley full of black air.

He dropped back into his blankets, muttering groggily, 'Go away. Let me sleep.'

Foamfollower shook him again. 'Arise, ur-Lord. You must eat now. We will depart soon.'

'Dawn,' Covenant said. The stiff soreness of his lip made him mumble as if the numbness of his hands and feet had spread to his tongue. 'He said dawn.'

'Yeurquin reports watch fires approaching Mithil Stonedown from the South Plains. They will not be friendly – few people of the south dare show light at night. And someone climbs towards us from the Stonedown itself. We will not remain here. Arise.' He lifted Covenant into a sitting position, then thrust a flask and bowl into his hands. 'Eat.'

Sleepily, Covenant drank from the stone flask, and found that it contained water as icy as melted snow. The chill draught jolted him towards wakefulness. Shivering, he turned to the bowl. It contained unleavened bread and treasure-berries. He began to eat quickly to appease the cold water in his stomach.

Between bites, he asked, 'If whatever they are – marauders – are coming, aren't we safe here?'

'Perhaps. But the Stonedownors will fight for their homes. They are Triock's people – we must aid them.'

'Can't they just hide in the mountains – until the marauders go away?'

'They have done so in the past. But Mithil Stonedown has been attacked many times. The Stonedownors are sick at the damage done to their homes in these attacks. This time, they will fight.'

Covenant emptied the bowl, and forced himself to drink deeply from the flask. The chill of the water made his throat ache.

'I'm no warrior.'

'I remember,' Foamfollower said with an ambiguous smile, as if what he remembered did not accord with Covenant's assertion. 'We will keep you from harm.'

He took the flask and bowl and stowed them in a large leather sack. Then from it he pulled out a heavy sheepskin jacket, which he handed to Covenant. 'This will serve you well – though it is said that no apparel or blaze can wholly refute the cold of this winter.' As Covenant donned the jacket, the Giant went on, 'I regret that I have no better footwear for you. But the Stonedownors wear only sandals.' He took from his sack a pair of thick sandals and passed them to Covenant.

When Covenant pushed back his blankets, he saw for the first time the damage he had done to his feet. They were torn and bruised from toe to heel; dry, caked blood covered them in blotches; and the remains of his socks hung from his ankles like the ragged frills of a jester. But he felt no pain; the deadness of his nerves reached deeper than those injuries. 'Don't worry about it,' he rasped as he pulled the socks from his ankles. 'It's only leprosy.'

He snatched the sandals from Foamfollower, jammed them on to his feet, and tied their thongs behind his heels. 'One of these days I'll figure out why I bother to protect myself at all.' But he knew why; his inchoate purpose demanded it.

'You ought to visit my world,' he growled only half to the Giant. 'It's painless. You won't feel a thing.'

Then Triock hailed them. Foamfollower got swiftly to his feet. When Covenant climbed from the blankets, Foamfollower picked them up and pushed them into his sack. With the sack in one hand and the graveling pot in the other, he went with Covenant towards the Stonedownor.

Triock stood with three companions near the narrow ravine which was the outlet of the valley. They spoke together in low, urgent tones until Foamfollower and Covenant joined them. Then Triock said rapidly, 'Rockbrother, our scouts have returned from the Plains. Slen reports that — ' Abruptly he stopped himself. His mouth bent into a sardonic smile, and he said, 'Pardon me. I forget my courtesy. I must make introductions.

He turned to one of his companions, a stocky old man breathing hoarsely in the cold. 'Slen Terass-mate, here is ur-Lord Thomas Covenant, Unbeliever and white gold wielder. Unbeliever, here is Slen, the rarest cook in all the South Plains. Terass his wife stands among the Circle of elders of Mithil Stonedown.'

Slen gave Covenant a salute which he returned awkwardly, as if the steaming of his breath and the numbness of his hands prevented him from grace. Then Triock turned to his other companions. They were a man and a woman who resembled each other like twins. They had an embattled look, as if they were familiar with bloodshed and killing at night, and their brown eyes blinked at Covenant like the orbs of people who had lost the capacity to be surprised. 'Here are Yeurquin and Quirrel,' said Triock. 'We have fought together from the first days of this attack upon the Land.

'Unbeliever, when the Giant and I heard the word of Revelstone's siege, we were at work harrying a large band of the Slayer's creatures in the centre of the South Plains. We fled from them at once, taking care to hide our trail so that they would not follow. And we left scouts to keep watch on the band. Now the scouts have returned to say that at first the band hunted us without success. But two days ago they turned suddenly and hastened straight away towards the Mithil valley.'

Triock paused grimly, then said, 'They have felt the power of our works upon Kevin's Watch. *Melenkurion!* Some creature among them has eyes.'

'Therefore we are not safe here,' Foamfollower said to Covenant. 'If they have truly seen the power of the High Wood, they will not rest until they have captured it for Soulcrusher — and slain its wielder.'

Slen coughed a gout of steam. 'We must go. We will be assailed at daybreak.'

With a sharp nod, Triock agreed. 'We are ready.' He glanced towards Foamfollower and Covenant. 'Unbeliever, we must travel afoot. The days of horseback sojourning are gone from the Land. Are you able?'

Covenant shrugged the question away. 'It's a little late for us to start worrying about what I can or can't do. Foamfollower can carry me easily enough – if I slow you down.'

'Well then.' Triock tightened his cloak, then picked up the graveling pot and held it over his head so that it lighted the ravine ahead of him. 'Let us go.'

Quirrel strode briskly ahead of them into the darkness of the ravine, and Triock preceded Slen after her. At a gesture from the Giant, Covenant followed Slen. Foamfollower came behind him with the other graveling pot, and Yeurquin brought up the rear of the group.

Before he had worked his way twenty yards down the ravine, Covenant knew that he was not yet strong enough to travel. Lassitude clogged his muscles, and what little energy he had he needed to defend himself from the penetrating cold. At first he resolved to endure despite his weakness. But by the time he had hauled himself half-way up the rift which led to the mountainside overlooking Mithil Stonedown, he understood that he could not go on without help. If he were to accomplish the purpose which grew obscurely in the back of his mind, he would have to learn how to accept help.

He leaned panting against the stone. 'Foamfollower.'

The Giant bent near him. 'Yes, my friend.'

'Foamfollower – I can't make it alone.'

Chuckling gently, Foamfollower said, 'Nor can I. My friend, there is comfort – in some companionships.' He lifted Covenant effortlessly into his arms, carried him in a half-sitting position so that Covenant could see ahead. Though he only needed one arm to bear Covenant's weight, he put the graveling pot into Covenant's hands. The warm light revealed that Foamfollower was grinning as he said, 'This is hazardous for me. It is possible that being of use may become a dangerous habit.'

Gruffly, Covenant muttered, 'That sounds like something I might say.'

Foamfollower's grin broadened. But Triock threw back a warning scowl, and the Giant made no other response.

Moments later, Triock covered his graveling pot. At a nod from Foamfollower, Covenant did the same. The Giant placed the urn in his sack. Without any light to give them away, the group climbed out of the rift on to the exposed mountainside high above the Mithil valley.

Under the heavy darkness, they could see nothing below them but the distant watch fires smouldering like sparks in cold black tinder. Covenant could not gauge how far away the fires were, but Foamfollower said tightly, 'It is a large band. They will gain the Stonedown by dawn – as Slen said.'

'Then we must make haste,' snapped Triock. He swung away to the left, moving swiftly along the unlit ledge.

The Giant followed at once, and his long strides easily matched Triock's trotting pace. Soon they had left the ledge, crossed from it to more gradual slopes as their trail worked downward into the valley. Slowly, Covenant could feel the air thickening. With the warmth of the graveling pot resting against his chest, he began to feel stronger. He made an effort to remember what this trail had looked like in the spring, but no memories came; he could not escape the impression of bare bleakness which shone through the night at him. He sensed that if he could have seen the unrelieved rock faces of the mountains, or the imposed lifelessness of the foothills, or the blasted tree trunks, or the Mithil River writhing in ice, he would have been dismayed. He was not yet ready for dismay.

Ahead of him, Triock began to run.

Foamfollower's jogging shook other thoughts out of Covenant's mind, and he began to concentrate in earnest on the gloomy night. By squinting grotesquely, he found that he could adjust his sight somewhat to the dark; apparently his eyes were remembering their Land-born penetration. As Foamfollower hurried him down the trail, he made out the high loom of the mountains on his left and the depth of the valley on his right. After a while, he caught vague, pale glimpses of the ice-gnarled river. Then the trail neared the end of the valley, and swung down in a wide arc towards the Mithil. When Foamfollower had completed the turn, Covenant saw the first dim lightening of dawn behind the eastern peaks.

Their pace became more urgent. As dawn leaked into the air, Covenant could see shadowy clouts of snow jumping from under the beat of Triock's feet. Foamfollower's strong respiration filled his ears, and behind it at odd intervals he heard the river straining in sharp creaks and groans against the weight of its own freezing. He began to feel a need to get down from the Giant's arms, either to separate himself from this urgency or to run towards it on his own.

Then Quirrel slowed abruptly and stopped. Triock and Foamfollower caught up with her, found her with another Stonedownor woman. The woman whispered quickly, 'Triock, the people are ready. Enemies approach. They are many, but the scouts saw no Cavewights or ur-viles. How shall we fight them?'

As she spoke, Covenant dropped to the ground. He stamped his feet to speed the circulation in his knees and stepped close to Triock so that he could hear what was said.

'Someone among them has eyes,' Triock responded. 'They hunt the High Wood.'

'So say the elders.'

'We will use it to lure them. I will remain on this side of the Stonedown – away from them, so that they must search all the homes to find me. The houses will disrupt their formations, come between them. The Stonedown itself and surprise will aid us. Tell the people to conceal themselves on this side – behind the walls, in the outer houses. Go.'

The woman turned and ran towards the Stonedown. Triock followed her more slowly, giving instructions to Quirrel and Yeurquin as he moved. With Foamfollower at his side, Covenant hurried after them, trying to figure out how to keep himself alive when the fighting started. Triock seemed sure that the marauders were after the *lomillialor*, but Covenant had other ideas. He was prepared to believe that this band of Foul's creatures had come for him and the white gold.

He panted his way up a long hill behind Triock, and when they topped it, he found himself overlooking the crouched stone shapes of the village. In the unhale dawn, he made out the rough, circular configuration of the Stonedown; its irregular houses, most of them flat-roofed and single-storeyed, stood facing inward around its open centre, the gathering place for its people.

In the distance, near the mouth of the valley, were the fires of the marauders. They moved swiftly, as if they had the scent of prey in their nostrils.

Triock stopped for a moment to peer through the gloom towards them. Then he said to Foamfollower, 'If this goes astray, I leave the High Wood and the Unbeliever in your care. You must do what I cannot.'

'It must not go astray,' Foamfollower replied. 'We cannot allow it. What is there that I could do in your stead?'

Triock jerked his head towards Covenant. 'Forgive him.'

Without waiting for an answer, he started at a lope down the hill.

Covenant rushed to catch up with him, but his dead feet slipped so uncertainly through the snow that he could not move fast enough. He did not overtake Triock until they were almost at the bottom of the hill. There Covenant grabbed his arm, stopped him, and panted steamily into his face, 'Don't forgive me. Don't do any more violence to yourself for me. Just give me a weapon so I can defend myself.'

Triock struck Covenant's hand away. 'A weapon, Unbeliever?' he barked. 'Use your ring.' But a moment later he controlled himself, fought down his bitterness. Softly, he said, 'Covenant, perhaps one day we will come to comprehend each other, you and I.' Reaching into his cloak, he drew out a stone dagger with a long blade, and handed it to Covenant gravely, as if they were comrades. Then he hastened away to join the people scurrying towards their positions on the outskirts of the village.

Covenant regarded the knife as if it were a secret asp. For a moment, he was uncertain what to do with it; now that he had a weapon, he could not imagine using it. He had had other knives, the implications of which were ambiguous. He looked questioningly up at Foamfollower, but the Giant's attention was elsewhere. He was staring intently towards the approach of the fires, and his eyes held a hot, enthusiastic gleam, as if they reflected or remembered slaughter. Covenant winced inwardly. He passed the knife back and forth between his hands, almost threw it away, then abruptly opened his jacket and slid the blade under his belt.

'Now what?' he demanded, trying to distract Foamfollower's stare. 'Do we just stand here, or should we start running around in circles?'

The Giant looked down sharply and his face darkened. 'They fight for their homes,' he said dangerously. 'If you cannot aid, at least forbear to ridicule.' With a commanding gesture, he strode away between the nearest houses.

Groaning at the Giant's unfamiliar ire, Covenant followed him into the Stonedown. Most of the people had stopped moving now and were stealthily crouched behind the houses around that side of the village. They seemed to ignore Covenant, and he went by them after Foamfollower as if he were on his way to bait their trap for the marauders.

Foamfollower halted at the back of one of the inner houses. It was flat-roofed, like most of the buildings around it, and its stone eaves reached as high as the Giant's throat. When Covenant joined him, he picked up the Unbeliever and tossed him lightly on to the roof.

Covenant landed face down in the snow. At once, he lurched sputtering to his knees, and turned angrily back towards the Giant.

'You will be safer here,' Foamfollower said. He nodded towards a neighbouring house. 'I will ward you from here. Stay low. They are almost upon us.'

Instinctively, Covenant dropped to his belly.

As if on signal, he felt a hushed silence spring up around him. No sound touched the Stonedown except the low, dislocated whistle of the wind. He felt acutely exposed on the roof. But even this height made him dizzy; he could not look or jump down. Hastily, he skittered back from the edge, then froze as he heard the noise he made. Though his movements were muffled by the snow, they sounded as loud as betrayal in the stillness. For a moment, he could not muster the courage to turn around. He feared to find cruel faces leering at him over the roof edge.

But slowly the apprehension beating in his temples eased. He began to curse himself. Spread-eagled on the roof, he worked slowly around until he was facing in towards the centre of the Stonedown.

Across the valley, light bled into the air through the grey packed clouds. The clouds shut out any other sky completely, and under their cold weight the day dawned bleak and cheerless, irremediably aggrieved. The sight chilled Covenant more than black night. He could see now more clearly than he had from Kevin's Watch that this shrouded, constant gloom was unnatural, wrong – the pall of Lord Foul's maddest malice. And he was aghast at the power it implied. Foul had the might to distort the Earth's most fundamental orders. It would not exhaust him to crush one ineffectual leper. Any purpose to the contrary was mere witless buffoonery.

Covenant's hand moved towards the knife as if its stone edge could remind him of fortitude, tighten the moorings of his endurance. But a distant, clashing sound, uncertain in the wind, cast all other thoughts from his mind. After straining his ears briefly, he knew that he was hearing the approach of the marauders.

He began to shiver as he realized that they were making no effort to move quietly. The whole valley lay open before them, and they had the hungry confidence of numbers; they came up along the river clattering their weapons, defying the Stonedownors to oppose them. Cautiously, Covenant slid into a better position to see over the edge of the roof. His muscles trembled, but he locked his jaws, pressed himself flat in the snow, and peered through the dim air towards the centre of the village with an intensity of concentration that made his head ache.

Soon he heard guttural shouts and the clang of iron on stone as the marauders rushed to search the first houses. Still he could see nothing; the roofline of the village blocked his view. He tried to keep his breathing low, so that exhaled vapour would not obscure his sight or reveal his position. When he turned his head to look in other directions, he found that he was clenching fistfuls of snow, squeezing them into ice. He opened his hands, forced his fingers to unclaw themselves, then braced his palms flat on the stone so that he would be ready to move.

The loud approach spread out over the far side of the village and began to move inward, working roughly parallel to the river. Instead of trying to surround and trap the Stonedownors, the marauders were performing a slow sweep of the village; disdaining surprise, they manoeuvred so that the people would be forced to flee towards the narrow end of the valley. Covenant could think of no explanation for these tactics but red-eyed confidence and contempt. The marauders wanted to drive the people into the final trap of the valley's end, thus prolonging and sharpening the anticipated slaughter. Such malicious surety was frightening, but Covenant found relief in it. It was not an approach designed to capture something as reputedly powerful as white gold.

But he soon learned another explanation. As he strained his eyes to peer through the dawn, he saw a sharp flash of green light from the far side of the village. It lasted only an instant, and in its wake a crumbling noise filled the air – a noise like the sound of boulders crushing each other. It startled him so much that he almost leaped to his feet to see what had happened. But he caught himself when he saw the first creatures enter the centre of the Stonedown.

Most of them were vaguely human in outline. But their features were tormented, grotesquely arranged, as if some potent fist had clenched them at birth, twisting them beyond all recognition. Eyes were out of place, malformed; noses and mouths bulged in skin that was contorted like clay which had been squeezed between strong fingers; and in some cases all the flesh of face and scalp oozed fluid as if the entire head were a running sore. And the rest of their forms were no healthier. Some had backs bent at demented angles, others bore extra arms or legs, still others wore their heads between their shoulder blades or in the centre of their chests. But one quality they shared: they all reeked of perversion as if it were the very lifeblood of their existence; and a hatred of everything hale or well curdled their sight.

Naked except for food sacks and bands to hold weapons, they came snarling and spitting into the open core of Mithil Stonedown. There they stopped until the shouts of their fellows told them that the first half of the village was under their control. Then a tall figure with a knuckled face and three massive arms barked a command to the marauders behind her. In response, a group moved into the open circle, bringing with it three prodigious creatures unlike the others.

These three were as blind and hairless as if they had been spawned from ur-viles, but they had neither ears nor noses. Their small heads sat necklessly on their immense shoulders. At the bottom of trunks as big as hogsheads, their short legs protruded like braces, and their heavy arms were long enough to reach the ground. From shoulder to fingertip, the inner surfaces of their arms were covered with suckers. Together, they seemed to ripple in Covenant's sight, as if within them they carried so much ill might that his unwarped eyes could not discern their limits.

On command, the marauders led the three to a house at the edge of the circle. They were positioned around the building, and at once they moved close to the walls, spread their arms to their fullest extent, gripped the flat rock with their suckers.

Hoarse, growling power began to mount between them. Their might reached around the house and tightened slowly like a noose.

Covenant watched them in blank dismay. He understood the marauders' tactics now; the band attacked as it did to protect these three. With a stink of attar, their power increased, tightened, growled, until he could see a hawser of green force running through them and around the house, squeezing it in implacable fury. He thought that he should shout to the Stonedownors, warn them of the danger. But he was dry-mouthed and frozen with horror. He hardly knew that he had risen to his hands and knees to gain a better view of what was happening.

Moments passed. Tension crackled in the air as the stone of the house began to scream silently under the stress. Covenant gaped at it as if the mute rock were crying out to him for help.

Then the noose exploded in a flash of green force. The house crumbled inward, fell into itself until all its rooms and furnishings were buried in rubble. Its three destroyers stepped back and searched blindly around them for more stone to crush.

Abruptly, a woman screamed – a raw shout of outrage. Covenant heard her running between the houses. He leaped to his feet and saw a fleet, white-haired woman dash past the eaves of his roof with a long knife clenched in both hands. In an instant, she had raced beyond him towards the centre of the Stonedown.

At once he went after her. With two quick steps, he threw himself like a bundle of disjointed limbs towards the next roof. He landed off balance, fell, and slid through the snow almost up to the edge of the house. But he picked himself up and moved back to get a running start towards the next roof.

From that position, he saw the woman rush into the open circle. Her scream had alerted the marauders, but they were not ready for the speed with which she lunged herself at them. As she sprang, she stabbed the long knife with all her strength, drove it hilt-deep into the breast of the three-armed creature which had been commanding the assault.

The next instant, another creature grabbed her by the hair and flung her back. She lost her knife, fell out of Covenant's sight in front of one of the houses. The marauders moved after her, swords upraised.

Covenant leaped for the next roof. He kept his balance as he landed this time, ran across the stone, and leaped again. Then he fell skidding on the roof of the house which blocked the woman from his sight. He had too much momentum now; he could not stop. In a cloud of snow, he toppled over the edge and slammed heavily to the ground beside the woman.

The impact stunned him. But his sudden appearance had surprised the attackers, and the nearest creature recoiled several steps, waving its sword defensively as if Covenant were a group of warriors. In the interval, he shook red mist from his eyes, and got gasping to his feet.

The marauders whirled their weapons, dropped into fighting crouches. But when they saw that they were theatened by only one half-stunned man, some of them spat hoarse curses at him and others began to laugh malevolently. Sheathing their weapons, several of them moved forward with an exaggerated display of caution to capture Covenant and the old woman. At this, other creatures jeered harshly, and more came into the circle to see what was happening.

Covenant's gaze dashed in all directions, hunting for a way of escape. But he could find nothing; he and the woman were alone against more than a score of the misborn creatures.

The marauders' breathing did not steam in the cold air. Though they wore nothing to protect their flesh from the cold, they seemed horribly comfortable in the preternatural winter.

They approached as if they meant to eat Covenant and the woman alive.

The woman hissed at them in revulsion, but he paid no attention to her. All of him was concentrated on escape. An odd memory tugged at the back of his mind. He remembered a time when Mhoram had made even powerless white gold useful. As the creatures crept hooting towards him, he suddenly brandished his ring and sprang forward a step, shouting, 'Get back, you bloody bastards, or I'll blast you where you stand!'

Either his shout or the sight of his ring startled them; they jumped back a few paces, grabbing at their weapons.

In that instant, Covenant snatched up the woman's hand and fled. Pulling her after him, he raced to the corner of the house, swung sharply around it, and sped as fast as he could away from the open ground. He lost his hold on the woman almost at once; he could not grip her securely with his half-fingerless hand. But she was running on her own now. In a moment, she caught up with him and took hold of his arm, helped him make the next turn.

Roaring with fury, the marauders started in pursuit. But when they entered the lane between the houses, Foamfollower dived from a rooftop and crashed headlong into them like a battering ram. Constricted by the houses on either side, they could not evade him; he hit them squarely, breaking the ones nearest him and bowling the others back into the centre of the Stonedown.

Then Triock, Quirrel and Yeurquin led a dozen Stonedownors into the village across the roofs. Amid the confusion caused by the Giant's attack, the defenders fell on to the marauders like a rain of swords and javelins. Other people ran forward to engage the creatures that were still hunting among the houses. In moments, fighting raged throughout the Stonedown.

But Covenant did not stop; drawing the woman with him, he fled until he was past the last buildings. There he lengthened his stride, intending to run as far as he could up the valley. But Slen intercepted him. Panting hoarsely, Slen snapped at the woman, 'Fool! You have lost sense altogether.' Then he tugged at Covenant. 'Come. Come.'

Covenant and the woman followed him away from the river along an unmarked path into the foothills. A few hundred yards above the village, they came to a jumble of boulders – the ancient remains of a rockfall from the mountains. Slen took a cunning way in among the boulders and soon reached a large, hidden cave. Several Stonedownors stood on guard at the cave mouth, and within it the children and the ill or infirm huddled around graveling bowls.

Covenant was tempted to enter the cave and share its sanctuary. But near its mouth was a high, sloped heap of rock with a broad crown. He turned and climbed the rocks to find out if he could see the Stonedown from its top. The white-haired woman ascended lightly behind him; soon they stood together, looking down at the battle of Mithil Stonedown.

The altitude of his position surprised him. He had not realized that he had climbed so high. Vertigo made his feet suddenly slippery, and he recoiled from the sight. For a moment, the valley reeled around him. He could not believe that a short time ago he had been leaping across rooftops; the mere thought of such audacity seemed to sweep his balance away, leaving him at the mercy of the height. But the woman caught hold of him, supported him. And his urgent need to watch the fighting helped him to resist his dizziness. Clinging half-consciously to the woman's shoulder, he forced himself to peer downward.

At first, the cloud-locked dimness of the day obscured the battle, prevented him from being able to distinguish what was happening. But as he concentrated he made out the Giant.

Foamfollower dominated the mêlée in the Stonedown's centre. He waded hugely through the marauders, heaved himself from place to place. Swinging his mighty fists like cudgels he chopped creatures down, pounded them out of his way with blows which appeared powerful enough to tear their heads off. But he was sorely outnumbered. Though his movement prevented the marauders from hitting him with a concerted attack, they were armed and he was not. As Covenant watched, several of the creatures succeeded in knocking Foamfollower towards one of the rock destroyers.

The soft, glad tone of the woman's voice jarred painfully against his anxiety. 'Thomas Covenant, I thank you,' she said. 'My life is yours.'

Foamfollower! Covenant cried silently. 'What?' He doubted that the woman had actually spoken. 'I don't want your life. What in hell possessed you to run out there, anyway?'

'That is unkind,' she replied quietly. 'I have waited for you. I have ridden your Ranyhyn.'

The meaning of what she said did not penetrate him. 'Foamfollower is getting himself killed down there because of you.'

'I have borne your child.'

What?

Without warning, her words hit him in the face like ice water. He snatched his hand from her shoulder, jerked backward a step or two across the rock. A shift in the wind brought the clamour of battle up to him in tatters, but he did not hear it. For the first time, he looked at the woman.

She appeared to be in her mid-sixties – easily old enough to be his mother. Lines of groundless hope marked her pale skin around the blue veins in her temples, and the hair which plumed her head was no longer thick. He saw nothing to recognize in the open expectancy of her mouth, or in the bone-leanness of her body, or in her wrinkled hands. Her eyes had a curious, round, misfocused look, like the confusion of madness.

But for all their inaccuracy, they were spacious eyes, like the eyes of the women she claimed for her mother and daughter. And woven into the shoulders of her long blue robe was a pattern of white leaves.

'Do you know me, Thomas Covenant?' she said gently. 'I have not changed. They all wish me to change – Triock and Trell my father and the Circle of elders, all wish me to change. But I do not. Do I appear changed?'

'No,' Covenant panted. With sour nausea in his mouth, he understood that he was looking at Lena, the woman he had violated with his lust – mother of the woman he had violated with his love –

recipient of the Ranyhyn-boon he had instigated when he had violated the great horses with his false bargains. Despite her earlier fury, she looked too old, too fragile, to be touched. He forced out the words as if they appalled him. 'No – change.'

She smiled with relief. 'I am glad. I have striven to hold true. The Unbeliever deserves no less.'

'Deserves,' Covenant croaked helplessly. The battle noises from Mithil Stonedown taunted him again. 'Hellfire.'

He coerced himself to meet her gaze, and slowly her smile turned to a look of concern. She moved forward, reached out to him. He wanted to back away, but he held still as her fingertips lightly touched his lip, then stroked a cool line around the wound on his forehead. 'You have been harmed,' she said. 'Does the Despiser dare to assault you in your own world?'

He felt that he had to warn her away from him, the misfocus of her gaze showed that she was endangered by him. Rapidly, he whispered, 'Atiaran's judgement is coming true. The Land is being destroyed, and it's my fault.'

Her fingers caressed him as if they were trying to smooth a frown from his brow. 'You will save the Land. You are the Unbeliever – the new Berek Halfhand of our age.'

'I can't save anything – I can't even help those people down there. Foamfollower is my friend, and I can't help him. Triock – Triock has earned anything I can do, and I can't – '

'Were I a Giant,' she interrupted with sudden vehemence, 'I would require no aid in such a battle. And Triock – ' She faltered unexpectedly, as if she had stumbled over an unwonted perception of what Triock meant to her. 'He is a Cattleherd – content. He wishes – But I am unchanged. He – '

Covenant stared at the distress which strained her face. For an instant, her eyes seemed to be on the verge of seeing clearly, and her forehead tightened under the imminence of cruel facts. 'Covenant?' she whispered painfully. 'Unbeliever?'

'Yes. I know.' Covenant mumbled in spite of himself. 'He would consider himself lucky if he got killed.' As tenderly as he could, he reached out and drew her into his arms.

At once she embraced him, clung convulsively to him while a crisis within her crested, receded. But even as he gave her what comfort he could with his arms, he was looking back towards the Stonedown. The shouts and cries and clatter of the fighting outweighed his own torn emotions, his conflicting sympathy for and horror of Lena. When she stepped back from him, he had to force himself to meet the happiness which sparkled in her mistaken eyes.

'I am so glad – my eyes rejoice to behold you. I have held – I have desired to be worthy. Ah, you must meet our daughter. She will make you proud.'

Elena! Covenant groaned thickly. They haven't told her – she doesn't understand – Hellfire.

For a moment, he ached under his helplessness, his inability to speak. But then a hoarse shout from the Stonedown rescued him. Looking down, he saw people standing in the centre of the village with their swords and spears upraised. Beyond them, the surviving marauders had fled for their lives towards the open plains. A handful of the defenders gave savage pursuit, harried the creatures to prevent as many as possible from escaping.

Immediately, Covenant started down the rocks. He heard Lena shout word of the victory to Slen and the other people at the mouth of the cave, but he did not wait for her or them. He ran down out of the foothills as if he too were fleeing – fleeing from Lena, or from his fear for Foamfollower, he did not know which. As swiftly as he could without slipping in the snow, he hurried towards Mithil Stonedown.

But when he dashed between the houses and stumbled in among the hacked corpses, he lurched to a halt. All around him the snow and stone were spattered with blood – livid incarnadine patches, heavy swaths of red-grey serum diseased by streaks of green. Stonedownors – some of them torn limb from limb – lay confused amid the litter of Lord Foul's creatures. But the perverse faces and forms of the creatures were what drew Covenant's attention. Even in death, they stank of the abomination which had been practised upon them by their maker, and they appalled him more than ur-viles or *kresh* or discoloured moons. They were so entirely the victims of Foul's contempt. The sight and smell of them made his guts heave. He dropped to his knees in the disfigured snow and vomited as if he were desperate to purge himself of his kinship with these creatures.

Lena caught up with him. When she saw him, she gave a low cry and flung her arms around him. 'What is wrong?' she moaned. 'Oh, beloved, you are ill.'

Her use of the word *beloved* stung him like acid flung from the far side of Elena's lost grave. It drove him reeling to his feet. Lena tried to help him, but he pushed her hands away. Into the concern of her face, he cried, 'Don't touch me. Don't.' Jerking brokenly, his hands gestured at the bodies around him. 'They're lepers. Lepers like me. This is what Foul wants to do to everything.' His mouth twisted around the words as if they shared the gall of his nausea.

Several Stonedownors had gathered near him. Triock was among them. His hands were red, and blood ran from a cut along the line of his jaw, but when he spoke, he only sounded bitterer, harder. 'It boots nothing to say that they have been made to be what they are. Still they shed blood – they ravage – they destroy. They must be prevented.'

'They're like me.' Covenant turned panting towards Triock as if he meant to hurl himself at the Stonedownor's throat. But when he looked up he saw Foamfollower standing behind Triock. The Giant had survived a fearsome struggle. The muscles of his arms quivered with exhaustion. His leather jerkin hung from his shoulders in shreds, and all across his chest were garish red sores – wounds inflicted by the suckers of the rock destroyers. But a sated look glazed his deepset eyes, and the vestiges of a fierce grin clung to his lips.

Covenant struggled for breath in the bloody air of the Stonedown. The sight of Foamfollower triggered a reaction he could not control. 'Get your people together,' he rasped at Triock. 'I've decided what I'm going to do.'

The hardness of Triock's mouth did not relent, but his eyes softened as he searched Covenant's gaze. 'Such choices can wait a little longer,' he replied stiffly. 'We have other duties. We must cleanse Mithil Stonedown – rid our homes of this stain.' Then he turned and walked away.

Soon all the people who were whole or strong enough were at work. First they buried their fallen friends and kindred in honourable rocky cairns high in the eastern slopes of the valley. And when that grim task was done, they gathered together all the creature corpses and carted this hacked and broken rubble downriver across the bridge to the west bank of the Mithil. There they built a pyre like a huge warning blaze to any marauders in the South Plains and burned the dead creatures until even the bones were reduced to white ash. Then they returned to the Stonedown. With clean snow, they scrubbed it from rim to centre until all the blood and gore had been washed from the houses and swept from the ground of the village.

Covenant did not help them. After his recent exertions, he was too weak for such labour. But he felt cold, upright and passionate, ballasted by the new granite of his purpose. He went with Lena, Slen and the Circle of elders to the banks of the river, and there helped treat the injuries of the Stonedownors. He cleaned and bound wounds, removed slivers of broken weapons, amputated mangled fingers and toes. When even the elders faltered, he took the blue-hot blade and used it to clean the sores which covered Foamfollower's chest and back. His fingers trembled at the task, and his halfhand slipped on the knife's handle, but he pressed fire into the Giant's oaken muscles until all the sucker wounds had been seared.

Foamfollower took a deep breath that shuddered with pain, and said, 'Thank you, my friend. That is a grateful fire. You have made it somewhat like the *caamora*.' But Covenant threw down the blade without answering, and went to plunge his shaking hands into the icy waters of the Mithil. All the while, a deep rage mounted within him, grew up his soul like slow vines reaching towards savagery.

Later, when all the wounded had been given treatment, Slen and the elders cooked a meal for the whole village. Sitting in the new cleanliness of the open centre, the people ate hot savoury stew with unleavened bread, cheese, and dried fruit. Covenant joined them. Throughout the meal, Lena tended him like a servant. But he kept his eyes down, stared at the ground to avoid her face and all other faces; he did not wish to be distracted from the process taking place within him. With cold determination, he ate every scrap of food offered to him. He needed nourishment for his purpose.

After the meal, Triock made new arrangements for the protection of the Stonedown. He sent scouts back out to the Plains, designed tentative plans against another attack, asked for volunteers to carry word of the rock-destroying creatures to the Stonedown's nearest neighbours, thirty leagues away. Then at last he turned to the matter of Covenant's decision.

Yeurquin and Quirrel sat down on either side of Triock as he faced the village. Before he began, he glanced at Foamfollower, who stood nearby. Obliquely, Covenant observed that in the place of his ruined jerkin Foamfollower now wore an armless sheepskin cloak. It did not close across his chest, but it covered his shoulders and back like a vest. He nodded in response to Triock's mute question, and Triock said, 'Well then. Let us delay no longer.' In a rough, sardonic tone, he added, 'We have had rest enough.

'My friends, here is ur-Lord Thomas Covenant, Unbeliever and white gold wielder. For good or ill, the Giant and I have brought him to the Land. You know the lore which has been abroad in the Land since that day seven and forty years ago when the Unbeliever first came to Mithil Stonedown from Kevin's Watch. You see that he comes in the semblance of Berek Halfhand, Heartthew and Lord-Fatherer, and bears with him the talisman of the wild magic which destroys peace. You have heard the ancient song:

> And with the one word of truth or treachery,
> he will save or damn the Earth
> because he is mad and sane,
> cold and passionate,
> lost and found.

He is among us now so that he may fulfil all his prophecies.

'My friends, a blessing in the apparel of disease may still right wrongs. And teachers in any other garb remain accursed. I know not whether we have wrought life or death for the Land in this matter. But many brave hearts have held hope in the name of the Unbeliever. The Lorewardens of the Loresraat saw omens of good in the darkest deeds which cling to Covenant's name. And it was said among them that High Lord Mhoram does not falter in his trust. Each of you must choose your own faith. I choose to support the High Lord's trust.'

'I, also,' said Foamfollower quietly. 'I have known both Mhoram son of Variol and Thomas Covenant.'

Omens, hell! Covenant muttered to himself. Rape and betrayal. He sensed that Lena was gathering herself to make some kind of avowal. To prevent her, he pushed glaring to his feet. 'That's not all,' he grated. 'Tamarantha and Prothall and Mhoram and who knows how many others thought that I was chosen for this by the Creator or whoever's responsible in the end. Take consolation in that if you can. Never mind that it's just another way of saying I chose myself. The idea itself isn't so crazy. Creators are the most helpless people alive. They have to work through unsufferable – they have to work through tools as blunt and misbegotten and useless as myself. Believe me, it's easier just to burn the world down, reduce it to innocent or clean or at least dead ash. Which may be what I'm doing. How else could I – ?'

With an effort, he stopped himself. He had already iterated often enough the fundamental unbelief with which he viewed the Land; he had no reason to repeat that it was a delusion spawned by his abysmal incapacity for life. He had gone beyond the need for such assertions. Now he had to face their consequences. To begin, he broached a tangent for what was in his heart. 'Did any of you see a break in the clouds – some time – maybe a couple of nights ago?'

Triock stiffened. 'We saw,' he said gruffly.

'Did you see the moon?'

'It was full.'

'It was green!' Covenant spat. His vehemence cracked his swollen lip, and a trickle of blood started down his chin. He scrubbed the blood away with his numb fingers, steadied himself on the stone visage of his purpose. Ignoring the stares of the Stonedownors, he went on, 'Never mind. Never mind that. Listen. I'll tell you what we're going to do. I'll tell you what you're going to do.'

He met Triock's gaze. Triock's lips were white with tension, but his eyes crouched in their sockets as if they ached to flinch away from what they beheld. Covenant scowled into them. 'You're going to find some way to let Mhoram know I'm here.'

For an instant, Triock gaped involuntarily. Then he drew himself up as if he were about to start yelling at Covenant. Seeing this, Foamfollower interposed, 'Ur-Lord, do you know what you ask? Revelstone is three hundred leagues distant. In the best of times, even a Giant could not gain the high halls of Lord's Keep in less than fifteen days.'

'And the Plains are aswarm with marauders!' barked Triock. 'From here to the joining of the Black and Mithil rivers, a strong band might fight and dodge its way in twenty days. But beyond – in the Centre Plains – are the fell legions of the Grey Slayer. All the Land from Andelain to the Last Hills is under their dominion. With twenty thousand warriors, I could not battle my way even to the Soulsease River in twice or ten times fifty days.'

Covenant began, 'I don't give a bloody damn what – '

Flatly, Quirrel interrupted him, 'Further, you must not call upon the Ranyhyn for aid. The creatures of the Grey Slayer prize Ranyhyn-flesh. The Ranyhyn would be taken and eaten.'

'I don't care!' Covenant fumed. 'It doesn't matter what you think is possible or impossible. Everything here is impossible. If we don't start doing the impossible now, it'll be too late. And Mhoram has got to know.'

'Why?' Anger still crackled in Triock's voice, but he was watching Covenant closely now, scrutinizing him as if he could see something malignant growing behind Covenant's belligerence.

Under Triock's gaze, Covenant felt too ashamed to admit that he had already refused a summons from Mhoram. He could taste the outrage with which all the Stonedownors would greet such a confession. Instead, he replied, 'Because it will make a difference to him. If he knows where I am – if he knows what I'm doing – it'll make a difference. He'll know what to do.'

'What can he do? Revelstone is besieged by an army as unanswerable as the Desert. High Lord Mhoram and all the Council are prisoners in Lord's Keep. We are less helpless than they.'

'Triock, you're making a big mistake if you ever assume that Mhoram is helpless.'

'The Unbeliever speaks truly,' Foamfollower said. 'The son of Variol is a man of many resources. Much that may appear impossible is possible for him.'

At this Triock looked at his hands, then nodded sharply. 'I hear you. The High Lord must be told. But still I know not how such a thing may be accomplished. Much which may appear possible to

Giants and white gold wielders is impossible for me.'

'You've got one of those *lomillialor* rods,' rasped Covenant. 'They were made for communication.'

Triock growled in exasperation, 'I have told you that I lack the lore for such work. I did not study the speaking of messages in the Loresraat.'

'Then learn. By hell! Did you expect it to be easy? Learn!' Covenant knew how unfairly he was treating Triock, but the exigency of his purpose countenanced neither consideration nor failure.

For a long moment, Triock glared miserably at Covenant, and his hands twitched with anger and helplessness. But then Quirrel whispered to him and his eyes widened hopefully. 'Perhaps,' he murmured. 'Perhaps it may be done.' He made an effort to steady himself, forced a measure of calmness into his face. 'It is said – ' he swallowed thickly – 'it is said that an Unfettered One lives in the mountains which protect the South Plains from Garroting Deep. Uncertain word of such a One has been whispered among the Southron villages for – many years. It is said that he studies the slow breathing of the mountains – or that he gazes constantly across Garroting Deep in contemplation of *Melenkurion* Skyweir – or that he lives in a high place to learn the language of the wind. If such a One lives – if he may be found – perhaps he can make use of the High Wood as I cannot.'

A rustle of excitement ran through the circle at this idea. Triock took a deep breath and nodded to his companions. 'I will make this attempt.' Then a sardonic hue coloured his voice. 'If it also goes astray, I will at least know that I have striven to fulfil your choices.

'Unbeliever, what word shall I send to High Lord Mhoram and the Council of Revelstone?'

Covenant looked away, raised his face to the leaden sky. Snow had started to fall in the valley; a scattering of flakes drifted on the breeze like instants of mist, dimming the day even further. They had an early look about them, as if they presaged a heavy fall. For a moment, Covenant watched them tumble through the Stonedown. He was acutely conscious of Triock's question. It confronted him starkly, challenged the untried mettle of his purpose. And he feared to answer it. He feared to hear himself say things which were so insane. When he returned his gaze to the waiting Stonedownors, he replied obliquely, seeking fuel for his courage.

'Foamfollower, what happened to your people?'

'My friend?'

'Tell me what happened to the Giants.'

Foamfollower squirmed at Covenant's scowl. 'Ah, ur-Lord, there is no need for such stories now. They are long in the telling, and would better suit another time. The present is full.'

'Tell me!' Covenant hissed. 'Bloody hell, Foamfollower! I want to know it all! I need – everything, every damned despicable thing that Foul – '

Without warning, Triock interrupted him, 'The Giants have returned to their Home beyond the Sunbirth Sea.'

Covenant whirled towards Triock. The lie in his words was so palpable that it left Covenant gasping, and around him the Stone-downors gaped at Triock. But Triock met Covenant's aghast stare without flinching. The cut along his jaw emphasized his determination. In a hard, steady voice that cut through Covenant's superficial ire to the rage growing within him, Triock said, 'We have sworn the Oath of Peace. Do not ask us to feed your hate. The Land will not be served by such passions.'

'It's all I've got!' Covenant answered thickly. 'Don't you understand? I don't have anything else. Nothing! All by itself, it has got to be enough.'

Gravely, almost sorrowfully, Triock said, 'Such a foe cannot be fought with hate. I know. I have felt it in my heart.'

'Hellfire, Triock! Don't preach at me. I'm sick to death of being victimized. I'm sick of walking meekly or at least quietly and just putting my head on the block. I am going to fight this.'

'Why?' Triock asked in a restrained voice. 'What will you fight for.'

'Are you deaf as well as blind?' Covenant wrapped his arms around his chest to steady himself. 'I hate Foul. I've had all I can stand of – '

'No. I am neither deaf nor blind. I see and hear that you intend to fight. What will you fight for? There is matter enough to occupy your hate in your own world. You are in the Land now. What will you fight for?'

Hell and blood! Covenant shouted silently. How much of me do you want? But Triock's question threw him back upon himself. He could have replied: I hate Foul because of what he's doing to the Land. But that sounded like a disclaimer of responsibility, and he was too angry to deny his own convictions. He was too angry, also, to give Triock any comforting answer. In a brittle voice, he said, 'I'm going to do it for myself. So that I can at least believe in me before I lose my mind altogether.'

This response silenced Triock, and after a moment Foamfollower asked painfully, 'My friend, what will you do with your passion?'

Snow slowly thickened in the air. The flakes danced like motes of obscurity across Covenant's vision, and the strain of his fierce stare

887

made his unhealed forehead throb as if his skull were crippled with cracks. But he did not relent, could not relent now. 'There's only one good answer to someone like Foul.' Yet in spite of his anger, he found that he could not meet Foamfollower's gaze.

'What answer?'

Involuntarily, Covenant's fingers bent into claws. 'I'm going to bring Foul's Creche down around his ears.'

He heard the surprise and incredulity of the Stonedownors, but he ignored them. He listened only to Foamfollower as the Giant said, 'Have you learned then how to make use of the white gold?'

With all the intensity of conviction he could muster, Covenant replied, 'I'll find a way.'

As he spoke, he believed himself. Hatred would be enough. Foul could not take it from him, could not quench it or deflect its aim. He, Thomas Covenant, was a leper; he alone in all the Land had the moral experience or training for this task. Facing between Foamfollower and Triock, addressing them both, he said, 'You can either help me or not.'

Triock met him squarely. 'I will not aid you. I will undertake to send word of you to High Lord Mhoram – but I will not share in this defamation of Peace.'

'It is the wild magic, Triock,' Foamfollower said as if he were pleading on Covenant's behalf, 'the wild magic which destroys Peace. You have heard the song. White gold surpasses all Oaths.'

'Yet I will retain my own. Without the Oath, I would have slain the Unbeliever seven and forty years ago. Let him accept that, and be content.'

Softly, the Giant said, 'I hear you, my friend. You are worthy of the Land you serve.' Then he turned to Covenant. 'Ur-Lord, permit me to accompany you. I am a Giant – I may be of use. And I – I yearn to strike closer blows against the Soulcrusher who so appalled my kindred. And I know the peril. I have seen the ways in which we become what we hate. Permit me.'

Before Covenant could reply, Lena jumped to her feet. 'Permit me also!' she cried excitedly.

'Lena!' Triock protested.

She paid no attention to him. 'I wish to accompany you. I have waited so long. I have striven to be worthy. I have mothered a High Lord and ridden a Ranyhyn. I am young and strong. Ah, I yearn to share with you. Permit me, Thomas Covenant.'

The wind hummed softly between the houses, carrying the snow like haze into Covenant's eyes. The flakes flicked cold at his sore lip, but still he nodded his approval of the gathering flurries. A good snowfall would cover his trail. The snow muffled the sounds of the village, and he seemed to be speaking to himself as he said, 'Let's get going. I've got debts to pay.'

7

MESSAGE TO REVELSTONE

Though his jaws ached with protests, Triock gave the orders which sent several of his comrades hurrying to collect supplies for Covenant, Foamfollower and Lena. In that moment, the giving of those orders seemed to be the hardest thing he had ever done. The restraint which had allowed Covenant to live seven and forty years ago paled by comparison. The exertions which had brought Covenant to the Land now lost their meaning. Lena Atiaran-daughter's desire to accompany the Unbeliever turned all Triock's long years of devotion to dust and loss, and all his lavish love had been wasted.

Yet he could not refuse her – would not, though he had the authority to do so. He was one of Mithil Stonedown's Circle of elders, and by old Stonedown tradition, even marriages and long journeys were subject to the approval of the Circle. Furthermore, he was the acknowledged leader of Mithil Stonedowns's defence. He could have commanded Lena to stay at home, and if his reasons were valid, all the Stonedown would have fought to keep her.

His reasons were valid. Lena was old, half confused. She might hamper Covenant's movements; she might even risk his life again, as she had so recently. She would be in danger from all the enemies between Mithil Stonedown and Foul's Creche. Covenant was the one man responsible for her condition, the man who had permanently warped the channel of her life. And he, Triock son of Thuler – he loved her.

Yet he gave the orders. He had never loved Lena in a way which would have enabled him to control her. At one time, he had been ready to break his Oath of Peace for her, but throughout most of his life now he had kept it for her. He had done his utmost to raise her daughter free of shame and outrage. He could not begin now to refuse the cost of a love to which he had so entirely given himself.

Once that ordeal was over, he grew somewhat calmer. In the back of his heart, he believed that if there were any hope for the Land in Thomas Covenant, it depended upon Covenant's responses to Lena. Then his chief bitterness lay in the fact that he himself could not accompany Covenant, could not go along to watch over Lena. He had his own work to do, work which he acknowledged and approved. Through the yearning clench of his jaws, he told himself that he would have to rely on Saltheart Foamfollower.

With a brusque movement, he pushed the grey snow out of his eyes and looked toward the Giant. Foamfollower met his gaze, came over to him, and said, 'Be easy at heart, my friend. You know that I am not an inconsiderable ally. I will do all I can for both.'

'Take great care,' Triock breathed through his teeth. 'The eyes which saw our work upon Kevin's Watch are yet open. We did not close them in this battle.'

Foamfollower studied this thought for a moment, then said, 'If that is true, then it is you who must take the greater care. You bear your High Wood into the hazard of the South Plains.'

Triock shrugged. 'High Wood or white gold – we must all tread cunningly. I can send none of my people with you.'

With a nod of approval, the Giant said, 'I would refuse if they were offered. You will need every sword. The mountains where you will seek this Unfettered One are many leagues distant, and you will be required to fight much of your way.'

The clench of Triock's teeth made his voice rasp harshly. 'I take none but Quirrel and Yeurquin with me.'

Foamfollower started to protest, but Triock cut him off. 'I need the speed of few companions. And Mithil Stonedown stands now in its gravest peril. For the first time, we have given open battle to the marauders. With the power we revealed on Kevin's Watch, and the strength of our victory here, we have declared beyond question that we are not mere vagabond warriors, seeking refuge in lifeless homes. We have defended our Stonedown – we are an unbeaten people. Therefore the enemy will return against us with a host to dwarf this last band. No, Rockbrother,' he concluded grimly, 'every war-ready hand must remain to hold what we have won – lest our foes break upon the Stonedown with a wave and leave not one home standing.'

After a moment, Foamfollower sighed. 'I hear you. Ah, Triock – these are grave times indeed. I will rest easier when my friend Mhoram son of Variol has received word of what we do.'

'You believe I will succeed?'

'Who can if you cannot? You are hardy and knowledgeable, familiar with plains and mountains – and marauders. You have accepted the need, though your feet yearn to follow other paths. Those who pursue their heart's desire risk more subtle failures and treacheries. In some ways, it is well to leave your soul's wish in other hands.' He spoke musingly, as if in his thoughts he were comparing Triock's position with his own. 'You can accomplish this message purely.'

'I reap one other blessing also,' Triock returned through a mouthful of involuntary gall. 'The burden of mercy falls on your shoulders. Perhaps you will bear it more easily.'

Foamfollower sighed again, then smiled gently. 'Ah, my friend, I know nothing of mercy. My own need for it is too great.'

The sight of Foamfollower's smiling regret made Triock wish that he could protest against what the Giant said. But he understood only too well the complex loss and rue which weighed on Foamfollower. Instead, he returned the best smile he could manage and saluted Foamfollower from the bottom of his heart. Then he turned away to make his own preparations for travel.

In a short time, he packed blankets, an extra cloak, a small stoneware pot of graveling, supplies of dried meat, cheese and fruit, and a knife to replace the one he had given Covenant, in a knapsack. He took only a few moments to whet his sword, and to secure his *lomillialor* rod in the tunic belt under his cloak. Yet when he returned to the open centre of the Stonedown, he found Covenant, Foamfollower and Lena ready to depart. Lena carried her own few belongings in a pack like his; Foamfollower had all the supplies for the three of them in his leather sack, which he slung easily over his shoulder; and Covenant's wounded face held a look of intentness or frustration, as if only the hurt on his mouth kept him from complaining impatiently. In that look, Triock caught a glimpse of how fragile Covenant's avowed hatred was. It did not appear to be a sustaining passion. Triock shivered. A foreboding distrust told him that Thomas Covenant's resolve or passion would not suffice.

But he clenched the thought to himself as he returned Foamfollower's final salute. There was nothing he could say. And a moment later, the Giant and his two companions had disappeared northward between the houses. Their footmarks filled with snow and faded from sight until Mithil Stonedown seemed to retain no record of their passing.

Gruffly, Triock said to Yeurquin and Quirrel, 'We also must depart. We must leave this valley while the snow holds.'

His two friends nodded without question. Their faces were empty of expression; they looked like people from whom combat had drained all other considerations — carried their short javelins as if the killing of enemies were their sole interest. From them, Triock drew a kind of serenity. He was no High Wood wielder to them, no bearer of burdens which would have bent the back of a Lord. He was only a man, fighting as best he could for the Land, without pretensions to wisdom or prophecy. This was a proper role for a Cattleherd in times of war, and he welcomed it.

Girded by the readiness of his companions, he went to the other elders and spent a short time discussing with them Mithil Stonedown's precautions against future attacks. Then he left his home to them and went out into the snow again as if it were the duty of his life.

Flanked by Quirrel and Yeurquin, he left the village by the northward road, and crossed without stealth the stone bridge to the western side of the valley. He wanted to make good time while the snow cover lasted, so he stayed on the easiest route until he neared the end of the horn of mountains which formed the Mithil valley's western wall. At that point, he moved off the road and started up into the foothills that clung around the tip of the horn.

He intended to skirt the peaks west and south almost as far as Doom's Retreat, then swing northwest towards the isolated wedge of mountains which defended the South Plains from Garroting Deep. He could not take the straight march westward. In the open Plains, he would certainly encounter marauders, and when he did, he would have to flee wherever they chased him. So he chose the rugged terrain of the foothills. The higher ground would give him both a vantage from which to watch for enemies and a cover in which to hide from them.

Yet, as he plodded upward through the snow, he feared the choice he had made. In the foothills, he would need twenty days to reach those mountains beyond Doom's Retreat; twenty days would be lost before he could begin to search for the Unfettered One. In that time, Covenant and his companions might travel all the way to Landsdrop or beyond. Then any message which the High Lord might receive would be too late; Covenant would be beyond any hand but the Grey Slayer's.

With that dread in his heart, he began the arduous work of rounding the promontory.

He and his comrades had reached the first lee beyond the horn when the snowfall ended, late that afternoon. There he ordered a halt. Instead of running the risk of being seen – brown against the grey slush of the snow – he made camp and let the long weariness which had been his constant companion since he first began fighting lull him to sleep.

Some time after nightfall, Yeurquin awakened him. They moved on again, chewing strips of dried meat to keep some warmth in their bones, and washing the salt from their throats with mouthfuls of the unsavoury snow. In the cloud-locked darkness, they made slow progress. And every league took them farther from the hills they knew most intimately. After a tortuous and unsuccessful effort to scale one bluff slope, Triock cursed the dreary clasp of the sky and turned to descend towards easier ground nearer the Plains.

For most of the night, they travelled the lower hillsides, but when they felt dawn crouching near, they climbed again to regain their vantage. They pushed upward until they gained a high ridge from which they could see a long stretch of the way they had come. There they stopped. During the grey seepage of day into the air, they opened their smokeless graveling pots and cooked one hot meal. When they were done, they waited until the wind had obliterated all their tracks. Then they set watches, slept.

They followed this pattern for two more days – down out of the foothills at dusk, long, dark nighttrek, back towards higher ground at dawn for one hot meal and sleep – and during these three days, they saw no sign of any life, human or animal, friend or foe, anywhere; they were alone in the cold grey world and the forlorn wind. Trudging as if they were half crippled by the snow, they pressed themselves through the chapped solitude towards Doom's Retreat. Aside from the unpredictably crisp or muffled noises of their own movement, they heard nothing but the overstressed cracklings of the ice and the scrapings of the wind, fractured in their ears by the rumpled hills.

But in the dawn of the fourth day, while they watched the wind slowly filling the footmarks of their trail, they saw a dull, ugly, yellow movement cross one rib of the hills below them and come hunting upward in their direction. Triock counted ten in the pack.

'*Kresh*!' Yeurquin spat under his breath.

Quirrel nodded. 'And hunting us. It must be that they passed downwind of us during the night.'

Triock shivered. The fearsome yellow wolves were not familiar to the people of the South Plains; until the last few years, the *kresh* had lived primarily in the regions north of Ra, foraging into the North Plains when they could not get Ranyhyn-flesh. And many thousands of them had been slain in the great battle of Doom's Retreat. Yet they soon replenished their numbers, and now scavenged in every part of the Land where the hand of the Lords no longer held sway. Triock had never had to fight *kresh*, but he had seen what they could do. A year ago, one huge pack had annihilated the whole population of Gleam Stonedown, in the crystal hills near the joining of the Black and Mithil rivers; and when Triock had walked through the deserted village, he had found nothing but rent clothes and splinters of bone.

893

'*Melenkurion*!' he breathed as he gauged the speed of the yellow wolves. 'We must climb swiftly.'

As his companions slung their packs, he searched the terrain ahead for an escape or refuge. But despite their roughness, the hills and slopes showed nothing which the wolves might find impassable; and Triock knew of no defensible caves or valleys this far from Mithil Stonedown.

He turned upward. With Quirrel and Yeurquin behind him, he started along a ridge of foothills towards the mountains.

In the lee of the ridge, the snow was not thick. They made good speed as they climbed and scrambled towards the nearest mountain flank. But it rose sheerly out of the hillslope ahead, preventing escape in that direction. When the western valley beside the ridge rose up towards the mountain, Triock swung to the right and ran downward, traversed the valley, lunged through the piled snow towards the higher ground on the far side.

Before he and his companions reached the top, the leading *kresh* crested the ridge behind them and gave out a ferocious howl. The sound hit Triock between his shoulder blades like the flick of a flail. He stopped, whirled to see the wolves rushing like yellow death along the ridge hardly five hundred yards from him.

The sight made the skin of his scalp crawl, and his cold-stiff cheeks twitched as if he were trying to bare his teeth in fear. Without a word, he turned and attacked the climb again, threw himself through the snow until his pulse pounded and he seemed to be surrounded by his own gasping.

When he gained the ridge top, he paused long enough to steady his gaze, then scanned the terrain ahead. Beyond this rib of the foothills, all the ground in a wide half-circle reaching to the very edge of the mountains fell steeply away into a deep valley. The valley was roughly conical in shape, open to the plains only through a sheer ravine on its north side. It offered no hope to Triock's searching eyes. But clinging to the mountain edge beyond a narrow ledge along the lip of the valley was a broken pile of boulders, the remains of an old rockfall. Triock's attention leaped to see if the boulders could be reached along the ledge.

'Go!' Quirrel muttered urgently. 'I will hold them here.'

'Two javelins and one sword,' Triock panted in response. 'Then they will outweigh us seven to two. I prefer you alive.' Pointing, he said, 'We must cross that ledge to the rocks. There we can strike at the *kresh* from above. Come.'

He started forward again, driving his tired legs as fast as he could, and Quirrel and Yeurquin followed on his heels. When they reached the rough ground where the ridge blended into the cliff, they clambered through it towards the ledge.

At the ledge, Triock hesitated. The lip of the valley was packed in snow, and he could not tell how much solid rock was hidden under it. But the *kresh* were howling up the hill behind him; he had no time to scrape the snow clear. Gritting his teeth, he pressed himself against the cliff and started outward.

His feet felt the slickness of the ledge. Ice covered the rock under the snow. But he had become accustomed to ice in the course of this preternatural winter. He moved with small, unabrupt steps, did not let himself slip. In moments, Quirrel and Yeurquin were on the ledge as well, and he was half-way to his destination.

Suddenly, a muffled boom like the snapping of old bones echoed off the cliff. The ledge jerked. Triock scrambled for handholds in the rock, and found none. He and his comrades were too far from safety at either end of the ledge.

An instant later, it fell under their weight. Plunging like stones in an avalanche, they tumbled helplessly down the steep side of the valley.

Triock tucked his head and knees together and rolled as best he could. The snow protected him from the impacts of the fall, but it also gave way under him, prevented him from stopping or slowing himself. He could do nothing but hug himself and fall. Dislodged by the collapse of the ledge, more snow slid into the valley with him, adding its weight to his momentum as if it were hurling him at the bottom. In wild vertigo, he lost all sense of how far he had fallen or how far he was from the bottom. When he hit level ground, the force of the jolt slammed his breath away, left him stunned while snow piled over him.

For a time, he lay smothered under the snow, but as the dizziness relaxed in his head, he began to recover. He thrust himself to his hands and knees. Gasping, he fought the darkness which swarmed his sight like clouds of bats rushing at his face. 'Quirrel!' he croaked. 'Yeurquin!'

With an effort, he made out Quirrel's legs protruding from the snow a short distance away. Beyond her, Yeurquin lay on his back. A bloody gash on his temple marred the blank pallor of his face. Neither of them moved.

Abruptly, Triock heard the scrabbling of claws. A savage howl like a tantara of victory snatched his gaze away from Quirrel and Yeurquin, made him look up towards the slope of the valley.

The *kresh* were charging furiously down towards him. They had chosen a shallower and less snowbound part of the ridge side, and were racing with rapacious abandon towards their fallen prey. Their leader was hardly a dozen yards from Triock.

He moved instantly. His fighting experience took over, and he reacted without thought or hesitation. Snatching at his sword, he heaved erect, presented himself as a standing target to the first wolf. Fangs bared, red eyes blazing, it leaped for his throat. He ducked under it, twisted, and wrenched his sword into its belly.

It sailed past him and crashed into the snow, lay still as if it were impaled on the red trail of its blood. But its momentum had torn his sword from his cold hand.

He had no chance to retrieve his weapon. Already the next wolf was gathering to spring at him.

He dived out from under its leap, rolled heels over head, snapped to his feet holding his *lomillialor* rod in his hands.

The rod was not made to be a weapon; its shapers in the Loresraat had wrought that piece of High Wood for other purposes. But its power could be made to burn, and Triock had no other defence. Crying the invocation in a curious tongue understood only by the *lillianrill*, he swung the High Wood over his head and chopped it down on the skull of the nearest wolf.

At the impact, the rod burst into flame like a pitch-soaked brand, and all the wolf's fur caught fire as swiftly as tinder.

The flame of the rod lapsed immediately, but Triock shouted to it and hacked at a *kresh* bounding at his chest. Again the power flared. The wolf fell dead in screaming flames.

Another and another Triock slew. But each blast, each unwonted exertion of the High Wood's might, drained his strength. With four *kresh* sizzling in the snow around him, his breath came in ragged heaves, gasps of exhaustion veered across his sight, and fatigue clogged his limbs like iron fetters.

The five remaining wolves circled him viciously.

He could not face them all at once. Their yellow fur bristled in violent smears across his sight; their red and horrid eyes flashed at him above their wet chops and imminent fangs. For an instant, his fighting instincts faltered.

Then a weight of compact fury struck him from behind, slammed him face down in the trampled snow. The force of the blow stunned him, and the weight on his back pinned him. He could do nothing but hunch his shoulders against the rending poised over the back of his neck.

But the weight did not move. It lay as inert as death across his shoulder blades.

His fingers still clutched the *lomillialor*.

With a convulsive heave, he rolled to one side, tipped the heavy fur off him. It smeared him with blood – blood that ran, still pulsing, from the javelin which pierced it just behind its foreleg.

Another javelined *kresh* lay a few paces away.

The last three wolves dodged and feinted around Quirrel. She stood over Yeurquin, whirling her sword and cursing.

Triock lurched to his feet.

At the same time, Yeurquin moved, struggled to get his legs under him. Despite the wound on his temple, his hands pulled instinctively at his sword.

The sight of him made the wolves hesitate.

In that instant, Triock snatched a javelin from the nearest corpse and hurled it with the strength of triumph into the ribs of another *kresh*.

Yeurquin was unsteady on his feet; but with one lumbering hack of his sword, he managed to disable a wolf. It lurched away from him on three legs, but he caught up with it and cleft its skull.

The last *kresh* was already in full flight. It did not run yipping, with its tail between its legs, like a thrashed cur; it cut straight towards the narrow outlet of the valley as if it knew where allies were and intended to summon them.

'Quirrel!' Triock gasped.

She moved instantly. Ripping her javelin free of the nearest wolf, she balanced the short shaft across her palm, took three quick steps, and lofted it after the running *kresh*. The javelin arched so high that Triock feared it would fall short, then plunged sharply downward and caught the wolf in the back. The beast collapsed in a rolling heap, flopped several times across the snow, throwing blood in all directions, quivered, and lay still.

Triock realized dimly that he was breathing in rough sobs. He was so spent that he could hardly retain his grip on the *lomillialor*. When Quirrel came over to him, he put his arms around her, as much to gain strength from her as to express his gratitude and comradeship. She returned the clasp briefly, as if his gesture embarrassed her. Then they moved towards Yeurquin.

Mutely, they inspected and tended Yeurquin's wound. Under other circumstances, Triock would not have considered the hurt dangerous; it was clean and shallow, and the bone was unharmed. But Yeurquin still needed time to rest and heal – and Triock had no time. The plight of his message was now more urgent than ever.

He said nothing about this. While Quirrel cooked a meal, he retrieved their weapons, then buried all the *kresh* and the blood of battle under mounds of grey snow. This would not disguise what had happened from any close inspection, but Triock hoped that a chance enemy passing along the rim of the valley would not be attracted to look closer.

When he was done, he ate slowly, gathering his strength, and his eyes jumped around the valley as if he expected ur-viles or worse to rise up suddenly from the ground against him. But then his mouth locked into its habitual dour lines. He made no concessions to Yeurquin's injury; he told his companions flatly that he had decided to leave the foothills and risk cutting straight west towards the mountains where he hoped to find the Unfettered One. For such a risk, the only possibility of success lay in speed.

With their supplies repacked and their weapons cleaned, they left the valley through its narrow northward outlet at a lope.

They travelled during the day now for the sake of speed. Half dragging Yeurquin behind them, Triock and Quirrel trotted doggedly due west, across the cold-blasted flatland towards the eastmost outcropping of the mountains. As they moved, Triock prayed for snow to cover the trail.

By the end of the next day, they caught their first glimpses of the great storm which brooded for more than a score of leagues in every direction over the approaches to Doom's Retreat.

North of that defile through the mountains, the parched ancient heat of the Southron Wastes met the Grey Slayer's winter, and the result was an immense storm, rotating against the mountain walls which blocked it on the south and west. Its outer edges concealed the forces which raged within, but even from the distance of a day's hard travelling, Triock caught hints of hurricane conditions: cycling winds that ripped along the ground as if they meant to lay bare the bones of the earth; snow as thick as night; gelid air cold enough to freeze blood in the warmest places of the heart.

It lay directly across his path.

Yet he led Quirrel and Yeurquin towards it for another day, hurried in the direction of the storm's core until its outer winds were tugging at his garments, and its first snows were packing wetly against his windward side. Yeurquin was in grim condition – blood oozed like exhaustion through the overstrained scabs of his wound, and the tough fibre of his stamina was frayed and loosened like a breaking rope. But Triock did not turn aside. He could not attempt to skirt the storm, could not swing north towards the middle of the South Plains to go around. During the first night after the battle with the *kresh*, he had seen watch fires northeast of him. They were following him. He had studied them the next night, and had perceived that they were moving straight towards him, gaining ground at an alarming rate.

898

Some enemy had felt his exertion of the *lomillialor*. Some enemy knew his scent now and pursued him like mounting furore.

'We cannot outrun them,' Quirrel observed grimly as they huddled together under the lip of the storm to rest and eat.

Triock said nothing. He could hear Covenant rasping, *If we don't start doing the impossible. Doing the impossible.*

A moment later, she sniffed the wind. 'And I do not like the taste of this weather. There is a blizzard here – a blast raw enough to strike the flesh from our limbs.'

The impossible, Triock repeated to himself. He should have said to the Unbeliever, 'I was born to tend cattle. I am not a man who does impossible things.' He was tired and cold and unwise. He should have taken Lena and led his people towards safety deep in the Southron Range, should have chosen to renew the ancient exile rather than allow one extravagant stranger to bend all Mithil Stonedown to the shape of his terrible purpose.

Without looking at him, Quirrel said, 'We must separate.'

'Separate,' Yeurquin groaned hollowly.

'We must confuse the trail – confuse these – ' she spat fiercely along the wind – 'so that you may find your way west.'

Impossible. The word repeated itself like a weary litany in Triock's mind.

Quirrel raised her eyes to face him squarely. 'We must.'

And Yeurquin echoed, 'Must.'

Triock looked at her, and the wrinkles around his eyes winced as if even the skin of his face were afraid. For a moment, his jaw worked soundlessly. Then he grimaced. 'No.'

Quirrel tightened in protest, and he forced himself to explain. 'We would gain nothing. They do not follow our trail – they could not follow a trail so swiftly. Your trails would not turn them aside. They follow the spoor of the High Wood.'

'That cannot be,' she replied incredulously. 'I sense nothing of it from an arm's reach away.'

'You have no eyes for power. If we part, you will leave me alone against them.'

'Separate,' Yeurquin groaned again.

'No!' Anger filled Triock's mouth. 'I need you.'

'I slow you,' the injured man returned emptily, fatally. His face looked pale and slack, frost-rimed, defeated.

'Come!' Triock surged to his feet, quickly gathered his supplies and threw his pack over his shoulders, then stalked away across the wind in the direction of the storm's heart. He did not look behind him. But after a moment Quirrel caught up with him on the right,

899

and Yeurquin came shambling after him on the left. Together, they cut their way into the blizzard.

Before they had covered a league, they were stumbling against wind and snow as if the angry air were assaulting them with fine granite chips of cold. Snow piled against them, and the wind tore through their clothes as if the fabric were thinner than gauze. And in another league, they lost the light of day; the mounting snow flailed it out of the air. Quirrel tried to provide some light by uncovering a small urn of graveling, but the wind snatched the firestones from the urn, scattered them like a brief burning plume of gems from her hands. When they were gone, Triock could hardly make out her form huddled dimly near him, too cold even to curse what had happened. Yeurquin had dropped to the ground when they had stopped, and already he was almost buried in snow. Ahead of them – unmuffled now by the outer winds – Triock could see something of the rabid howl and scourge of the storm itself, the hurricane or blizzard shrieking at the violence of the forces which formed it.

Its fury slammed against his senses like the crumbling of a mountain. Peering at it, he knew that there was nothing erect within it, no beast or man or Giant or tree or stone; the maelstroming winds had long since levelled everything which had dared raise its head above the battered line of the ground. Triock had to protect his eyes with his hands. *Impossible* was a pale word to describe the task of walking through that storm. But it was his only defence against pursuit.

With all the strength he could muster, he lifted Yeurquin and helped the injured man lurch onward.

Black wind and sharp snow clamped down on him, stamped at him, slashed sideways to cut his legs from under him. Cold blinded him, deafened him, numbed him; he only knew that he had not lost his companions because Quirrel clutched the back of his cloak and Yeurquin sagged with growing helplessness against him. But he himself was failing, and could do nothing to prevent the loss. He could hardly breathe; the wind ripped past him so savagely that he caught only inadequate pieces of it. Yeurquin's weight seemed unendurable. He jerked woodenly to a halt. Out of a simple and unanswerable need for respite, he pushed Yeurquin away, forced him to support himself.

Yeurquin reeled, tottered a few steps along the wind, and abruptly vanished – disappeared as completely as if a sudden maw of the blizzard had swallowed him.

'Yeurquin!' Triock screamed. 'Yeurquin!'

He dashed after his friend, grappling, groping frantically for him.

For an instant, a dim shape scudded away just beyond his reach. 'Yeurquin!' Then it was gone, scattered into the distance like a handful of brittle leaves on the raving wind

He ran after it. He was hardly conscious of Quirrel's grip on his cloak, or of the wind yammering at his back, impelling him southward, away from his destination. Fear for Yeurquin drove every other thought from his mind. Suddenly he was no longer the bearer of impossible messages for the Lords. With a rush of passion, he became mere Triock son of Thuler, the former Cattleherd who could not bear to abandon a friend. He ran along the wind in search of Yeurquin as if his soul depended on it.

But the snow struck at his back like one vicious blow prolonged into torment; the wind yelped and yowled in his numb ears, unmoored his bearings; the cold sucked the strength out of him, weakened him as if it frosted the blood in his veins. He could not find Yeurquin. He had rushed past his friend unknowing in the darkness – or Yeurquin had somewhere found the strength to turn to one side against the wind – or the injured man had simply fallen and disappeared under the snow. Triock shouted and groped and ran, and encountered nothing but the storm. When he tried to turn his head towards Quirrel, he found that inches of ice had already formed on his shoulders, freezing his neck into that one strained position. His very sweat turned to ice on him. He could not resist the blast. If he did not keep stumbling tortuously before the wind, he would fall and never rise again.

He kept going until he had forgotten Yeurquin and Covenant and messages, forgotten everything except the exertion of his steps and Quirrel's grim grasp on his cloak. He had no conception of where he was going; he was not going anywhere except along the wind, always along the wind. Gradually the storm became silent around him as the crusting snow froze over his ears. Leagues passed unnoticed. When the ground abruptly canted upward under him, he fell to his hands and knees. A wave of numbness and lassitude ran through him as if it were springing from the frostbite in his hands and feet.

Something shook his head, something was hitting him on the side of his head. At first, the ice protected him, then it broke away with a tearing pain as if it had taken his ear with it. The howling of wind demons rushed at him, and he almost did not hear Quirrel shout, 'Hills! Foothills! Climb! Find shelter!'

He was an old man, too old for such labour.

He was a strong Stonedown Cattleherd, and did not intend to die frozen and useless. He lumbered to his feet, struggled upwards.

Leaning weakly back against the wind, he ascended the ragged slope. He realized dimly that both wind and snow were less now. But still he could see nothing; now the storm itself was wrapped in night. When the slope became too steep for the wind to push him up it, he turned to the side which offered the least resistance and went on, lumbering blindly through kneedeep snow, letting the blizzard guide him wherever it chose.

Yet in spite of the night and the storm, his senses became slowly aware of looming rock walls. The wind lost its single fury, turned to frigid gusts and eddies, and he limped between sheer, close cliffs into a valley. But the disruption of the storm's force came too late to save him. The valley floor lay waist-deep in heavy grey snow, and he was too exhausted to make much headway against it. Once again, he found he was supporting a comrade; Quirrel hung from his shoulders like spent mortality. Soon he could go no farther. He fell into a snowbank, gasping into the snow, 'Fire. Must – fire.'

But his hands were too frozen, his arms were too locked in ice. He could not reach his *lomillialor* rod, could never have pulled flame from it. Quirrel had already lost her graveling. And his was in his pack. It might as well have been lost also; he could not free his shoulders from the pack straps. He tried to rouse Quirrel, failed. The lower half of her face was caked in ice, and her eyelids fluttered as if she were going into shock.

'Fire,' Triock rasped. He was sobbing and could not stop. Frustration and exhaustion overwhelmed him. The snow towered above him as if it would go on for ever.

Tears froze his eyes shut, and when he pried them open again, he saw a yellow flame flickering its way towards him. He stared at it dumbly. It bobbed and weaved forward as if it were riding the wick of an invisible candle until it was so close to his face that he could feel its warm radiance on his eyeballs. But it had no wick. It stood in the air before his face and flickered urgently, as if it were trying to tell him something.

He could not move; he felt that ice and exhaustion had already frozen his limbs to the ground. But when he glanced away from the flame, he saw others, three or four more, dancing around him and Quirrel. One of them touched her forehead as if it were trying to catch her attention. When it failed, it flared slightly, and at once all the flames left, scurried away down the valley. Triock watched them go as if they were his last hope.

Then the cold came over him like slumber, and he began to lose consciousness. Unable to help himself, he sagged towards night. The cold and the snow and the valley faded and were replaced by vague faces – Lena, Elena, Atiaran, Trell, Saltheart Foamfollower, Thomas Covenant. They all regarded him with supplication, imploring him to do something. If he failed, their deaths would have no meaning. 'Forgive me,' he breathed, speaking especially to Covenant. 'Forgive.'

'Perhaps I shall,' a distant voice replied. 'It will not be easy – I do not desire these intrusions. But you bear a rare token. I see that I must at least help you.'

Struggling, Triock turned his sight outward again. The air over his head was bright with dancing flames, each no larger than his hand. And among them stood a tall man dressed only in a long robe the colour of granite. He met Triock's gaze awkwardly, as if he were unaccustomed to dealing with eyes other than his own. But when Triock croaked, 'Help,' he replied quickly, 'Yes. I will help you. Have no fear.'

Moving decisively, he knelt, pulled open Triock's cloak and tunic, and placed one warm palm on his chest. The man sang softly to himself, and as he did so, Triock felt a surge of heat pour into him. His pulse steadied almost at once; his breathing unclenched; with wondrous speed, the possibility of movement returned to his limbs. Then the man turned away to help Quirrel. By the time Triock was on his feet among the bobbing flames, she had regained consciousness.

He recognized the flames now; he had heard of them in some of the happiest and saddest legends of the Land. They were Wraiths. As he shook his head clear of ice, he heard through the gusting wind snatches of their light crystal song, music like the melody of perfect quartz. They danced about him as if they were asking him questions which he would never be able to understand or answer, and their lights bemused him, so that he stood entranced among them.

The tall man distracted him by helping Quirrel to her feet. Surrounded by Wraiths, he raised her, supported her until she could stand on her own. Then for a moment he looked uncomfortably back and forth between her and Triock. He seemed to be asking himself if he could justify leaving them there, not helping them further. Almost at once, however, he made his decision. The distant roar of the blizzard rose and fell as if some hungry storm-animal strove to gain access to the valley. He shivered and said, 'Come. Foul's winter is no place for flesh and blood.'

As the man turned to move towards the upper end of the valley, Triock said abruptly, 'You are One of the Unfettered.'

'Yes. Yet I aid you.' His voice vanished as soon as it appeared on the tattered wind. 'I was once Woodhelvennin. The hand of the Forest is upon me. And you – ' he was thrusting powerfully away through the snow as if he had been companionless for so long that he had forgotten how people listen – 'bear *lomillialor*.'

Triock and Quirrel pushed after him. His gait was strong, unweary, but by following his path through the drifts, they were able to keep up with him. The Wraiths lighted their way with crystal music until Triock felt that he was moving through a pocket of Andelain, a brief eldritch incarnation of clean light and warmth amid the Grey Slayer's preternatural malevolence. In the dancing encouragement of the flames, he was able to disregard his great fatigue and followed the Unfettered One's song:

> Lone
> Unfriended
> Bondless
> Lone –
> Drink of loss until 'tis done:
> 'Til solitude has come and gone,
> And silence is communion –
> And yet
> Unfriended
> Bondless
> Lone.

Slowly, they worked their way up to the end of the valley. It was blocked by a huge litter of boulders, but the Unfettered One led them along an intricate path through the rocks. Beyond, they entered a sheer ravine which gradually closed over their heads until they were walking into a black cave lit only by the flickering of the Wraiths. In time, the crooked length of the cave shut out all the wind and winter. Warmth grew around Triock and Quirrel, causing their garments to drip thickly. And ahead they saw more light.

Then they reached the cave end, the Unfettered One's home. Here the cave expanded to form a large chamber, and all of it was alive with light and music, as scores of Wraiths flamed and curtsied in the air. Some of them cycled through the centre of the chamber, and others hung near the black walls as if to illuminate inscriptions on the gleaming facets of the stone. The floor was rude granite marked by lumps and projecting surfaces which the Unfettered one clearly used as chairs, tables, bed. But the walls and ceiling were as black as obsidian, and they were covered with reflective irregular planes like the myriad fragments of a broken mirror in which the Wraith light would have dazzled the beholders if the surfaces had not been made of black stone. As it was, the chamber was warm and evocative; it seemed a fit place for a seer to read the writing graved within the heart of the mountain.

At the mouth of the chamber, Triock and Quirrel shed their packs and cloaks, opened their ice-stiff inner garments to the warmth. Then they took their first clear look at their rescuer. He was bald except for a white fringe at the back of his head, and his mouth hid in a gnarled white beard. His eyes were so heavily couched in wrinkles that he seemed to have spent generations squinting at illegible communications; and this impression of age was both confirmed by the old pallor of his skin and denied by the upright strength of his frame. Now Triock could see that his robe had been white at one time. It had gained its dull granite colour from long years of contact with the cave walls.

In his home, he seemed even more disturbed by the Stonedownors. His eyes flicked fearful and surprised glances at them – not as if he considered them evil, but rather as if he distrusted their clumsiness, as if his life lay in fragile sections on the floor and might be broken by their feet.

'I have little food,' he said as he watched the puddles which Triock and Quirrel left behind. 'Food also – I have no time for it.' But then an old memory seemed to pass across his face – a recollection that the people of the Land did not treat their guests in this way. Triock felt suddenly sure that the One had been living in this cave before he, Triock, was born. 'I am not accustomed,' the man went on as if he felt he should explain himself. 'One life does not suffice. When I found I could not refuse succour to the Wraiths – much time was lost. They repay me as they can, but much – much – How can I live to the end of my work? You are costly to me. Food itself is costly.'

As Triock recovered himself in the cave's mouth, he remembered his message to the Lords, and his face tightened into its familiar frown. 'The Grey Slayer is costly,' he replied grimly.

His statement disconcerted the Unfettered One. 'Yes,' he mumbled. Bending quickly, he picked up a large flask of water and a covered urn containing dried fruit. 'Take all you require,' he said as he handed these to Triock. 'I have – I have seen some of the Despiser's work. Here.' He gestured vaguely at the walls of his cave.

There was little fruit in the urn, but Triock and Quirrel divided it between them. As he munched his share, Triock found he felt a great deal better. Although the meagre amount of food hardly touched his hunger, his skin seemed to be absorbing nourishment as well as warmth from the Wraith light. And the radiance of the flames affected him in other ways also. Gradually the numbness of frostbite faded from his fingers and toes and ears; blood and health flowed back into them as if they had been treated with hurtloam. Even the habitual sourness which galled his mouth seemed to decline.

But his mission remained clear to him. When he was sure that

Quirrel had regained her stability, he asked her to go a short way out of the tunnel to stand guard.

She responded tightly, 'Will pursuit come even here?'

'Who can say?' The Unfettered One did not appear to be listening, so Triock went on: 'But we must have this One's aid – and I fear he will not be persuaded easily. We must not be surprised here with the message unattempted.'

Quirrel nodded, approving his caution though she clearly believed that no pursuit could have followed them through the blizzard. Without delay, she collected her cloak and weapons and moved away down the cave until she was out of sight beyond the first bend.

The Unfettered One watched her go with a question in his face.

'She will stand guard while we talk,' Triock answered.

'Do we require guarding? There are no ill creatures in these mountains – in this winter. The animals do not intrude.'

'Foes pursue me,' said Triock. 'I bear my own ill – and the Land's need.' But there he faltered and fell silent. For the first time, he realized the immensity of his situation. He was face to face with an Unfettered One and Wraiths. In this cave, accompanied by dancing flames, the One studied secret lores which might have amazed even the Lords. Awe crowded forward in Triock; his own audacity daunted him. 'Unfettered One,' he mumbled, 'lore-servant – I do not intrude willingly. You are beyond me. Only the greatness of the need drives – '

'I have saved your life,' the One said brusquely. 'I know nothing of other needs.'

'Then I must tell you.' Triock gathered himself and began, 'The Grey Slayer is abroad in the Land – '

The tall man forestalled him. 'I know my work. I was given the Rites of Unfettering when Tamarantha was Staff-Elder of the Loresraat, and know nothing else. Except for the intrusion of the Wraiths – except – which I could not refuse – I have devoted my meagre flesh here, so that I might work my work and see what no eyes have seen before. I know nothing else – no, not even how the Wraiths came to be driven from Andelain, though they speak of ur-viles and – Such talk intrudes.'

Triock was amazed. He had not known that Tamarantha Variolmate had ever been Staff-Elder of the Loresraat, but such a time must have been decades before Prothall became High Lord at Revelstone. This Unfettered One must have been out of touch with all the Land for the past four- or five-score years. Thickly, awfully, Triock said, 'Unfettered One, what is your work?'

A grimace of distaste for explanations touched the man's face. 'Words – I do not speak of it. Words falter.' Abruptly, he moved to the wall and touched one of the stone facets gently, as if he were caressing it. 'Stone is alive. Do you see it? You are Stonedownor — do you see it? Yes, alive — alive and alert. Attentive. Everything — everything which transpires upon or within the Earth is seen — beheld — by the Earthrock.' As he spoke, enthusiasm came over him. Despite his awkwardness, he could not stop once he had begun. His head leaned close to the stone until he was peering deeply into its flat blackness. 'But the — the process — the action of this seeing is slow. Lives like mine are futilely swift — Time — time! — is consumed as the seeing spreads — from the outer surfaces inward. And this time varies. Some veins pass their perception in to the mountain roots in millennia. Others require millennia of millennia.

'Here — ' he gestured around him without moving from where he stood — 'can be seen the entire ancient history of the Land. For one whose work is to see. In these myriad facets are a myriad perceptions of all that has occurred. All!

'It is my work to see — and to discover the order — and to preserve — so that the whole life of the Land may be known.'

As he spoke, a tremor of passion shook the Unfettered One's breathing.

'Since the coming of the Wraiths, I have studied the fate of the One Forest. I have seen it since the first seed grew to become the great Tree. I have seen its awakening — its awareness — the peaceful communion of its Land-spanning consciousness. I have seen Forestals born and slain. I have seen the Colossus of the Fall exercise its interdict. The band of the Forest is upon me. Here — ' His hands touched the facet into which he stared as if the stone were full of anguish — 'I see men with axes — men of the ground with blades formed from the bones of the ground — I see them cut — !'

His voice trembled vividly. 'I am Woodhelvennin. In this rock I see the desecration of trees. You are Stonedownor. You bear a rare fragment of High Wood, precious *lomillialor*.'

Suddenly, he turned from the wall and confronted Triock with a flush of urgent fervour, almost of desperation, in his old face. 'Give it to me!' he begged. 'It will help me see.' He came forward until his eager hands nearly touched Triock's chest. 'My life is not the equal of this rock.'

Triock did not need to think or speak. If Covenant himself had been standing at his back, he would not have acted differently; he could not distrust an Unfettered One any more than he could have distrusted a Lord. Without hesitation, he drew out the High Wood rod and placed it in the tall man's hands. Then, very quietly, he said, 'The foes who pursue me also seek this *lomillialor*. It is a perilous thing I have given you.'

The One did not appear to hear him. As his fingers closed on the wood, his eyes rolled shut, and a quiver passed through his frame; he seemed to be drinking in the High Wood's unique strength through his hands.

But then he turned outward again. With several deep breaths he steadied himself until he was gazing calmly into Triock's face.

'Perilous,' he said. 'I hear you. You spoke of the Land's need. Do you require aid to fight your foes?'

'I require a message.' All at once, Triock's own urgency came boiling up in him, and he spouted, 'The whole Land is at war! The Staff of Law has been lost again, and with it the Law of Death has been broken! Creatures that destroy stone have attacked Mithil Stonedown. Revelstone itself is besieged! I need – !'

'I hear you,' the tall man repeated. His earlier awkwardness was gone; possession of the High Wood seemed to make him confident, capable. 'Do not fear. I have found that I must help you also. Speak your need.'

With an effort, Triock wrenched himself into a semblance of control. 'You have heard the Wraiths,' he rasped. 'They spoke to you of ur-viles – and white gold. The bearer of that white gold is a stranger to the Land, and he has returned. The Lords do not know this. They must be told.'

'Yes.' The One held Triock's hot gaze. 'How?'

'The Loresraat formed this High Wood so that messages may be spoken through it. I have no lore for such work. I am a Stonedownor, and my hands are not apt for wood. I – '

But the Unfettered One accepted Triock's explanation with a wave of his hand. 'Who,' he asked, 'who in Revelstone can hear such speaking.'

'High Lord Mhoram.'

'I do not know him. How can I reach him? I cannot direct my words to him if I do not know him.'

Inspired by urgency, Triock answered, 'He is the son of Tamarantha Variol-mate. You have known Tamarantha. The thought of her will guide you to him.'

'Yes,' the One mused. 'It is possible. I have – I have not forgotten her.'

'Tell the High Lord that Thomas Covenant has returned to the Land and seeks to attack the Grey Slayer. Tell him that Thomas Covenant has sworn to destroy Foul's Creche.'

The One's eyes widened at this. But Triock went on: 'The message must be spoken now. I have been pursued. A blizzard will not prevent any eyes which could see the High Wood in my grasp.'

'Yes,' the tall man said once more. 'Very well I will begin. Perhaps it will bring this intrusion to an end.'

He turned as if dismissing Triock from his thoughts, and moved into the centre of his cave. Facing the entrance of the chamber, he gathered the Wraiths around him so that he was surrounded in light, and held the *lomillialor* rod up before his face with both hands. Quietly, he began to sing – a delicate, almost wordless melody that sounded strangely like a transposition, a rendering into human tones, of the Wraith song. As he sang, he closed his eyes, and his head tilted back until his forehead was raised towards the ceiling.

'Mhoram,' he murmured through the pauses in his song. 'Mhoram. Son of Variol and Tamarantha. Open your heart to hear me.'

Triock stared at him, tense and entranced.

'Tamarantha-son, open your heart. Mhoram.'

Slowly, power began to gleam from the core of the smooth rod.

The next instant, Triock heard feet behind him. Something about them, something deadly and abominable, snatched his attention, spun him towards the entrance to the chamber.

A voice as harsh as the breaking of stone grated, 'Give it up. He cannot open his heart to you. He is caught in our power and will never open his heart again.'

Yeurquin stood just within the cave, eyes exalted with madness.

The sight stunned Triock. Yeurquin's frozen apparel had been partially torn from him, and wherever his flesh was bare the skin hung in frostbitten tatters. The blizzard had clawed his face and hands to the bone. But no blood came from his wounds.

He bore Quirrel in his arms. Her head dangled abjectly from her broken neck.

When he saw Yeurquin, the Unfettered One recoiled as if he had been struck – reeled backward and staggered against the opposite wall of the cave, gaping in soundless horror.

Together, the Wraiths fled, screaming.

'Yeurquin.' The death and wrong which shone from the man made Triock gag. He croaked the name as if he were strangling on it. 'Yeurquin?'

Yeurquin laughed with a ragged, nauseating sound. In gleeful savagery, he dropped Quirrel to the floor and stepped past her. 'We meet at last,' he rasped to Triock. 'I have laboured for this encounter. I think I will make you pay for that labour.'

'Yeurquin?' Staggering where he stood, Triock could see that the man should have been dead; the storm damage he had suffered was too great for anyone to survive. But some force animated him, some ferocity that relished his death kept him moving. He was an incarnated nightmare.

The next moment, the Unfettered One mastered his shock, rushed forward. Wielding the *lomillialor* before him like a weapon, he cried hoarsely, '*Turiya* Raver! Tree foe! I know you – I have seen you. *Melenkurion abatha!* Leave this place. Your touch desecrates the very Earth.'

Yeurquin winced under the flick of the potent words. But they did not daunt him. 'Better dead feet like mine than idiocy like yours,' he smirked. 'I think I will not leave this place until I have tasted your blood, Unfettered wastrel. You are so quick to give your life to nothing. Now you will give it to me.'

The One did not flinch. 'I will give you nothing but the *lomillialor* test of truth. Even you have cause to fear that, *turiya* Raver. The High Wood will burn you to the core.'

'Fool!' the Raver laughed. 'You have lived here so long that you have forgotten the meaning of power!'

Fearlessly, he started towards the two men.

With a sharp cry, Triock threw off his stunned dismay. Sweeping his sword from its scabbard, he sprang at the Raver.

Yeurquin knocked him effortlessly aside, sent him careening to smack his head against the wall. Then *turiya* closed with the Unfettered One.

Pain slammed through Triock, flooded his mind with blood. Gelid agony shrieked in his chest where the Raver had struck him. But for one moment, he resisted unconsciousness, lurched to his feet. In torment, he saw *turiya* and the Unfettered One fighting back and forth, both grasping the High Wood. Then the Raver howled triumphantly. Bolts of sick, red-green power shot up through the Unfettered One's arms and shattered his chest.

When Triock plunged into darkness, the Raver had already started to dismember his victim. He was laughing all the while.

8

WINTER

With snow swirling around him like palpable mist, Thomas Covenant left Mithil Stonedown in the company of Saltheart Foamfollower and Lena daughter of Atiaran. The sensation of purpose ran high in him – he felt that all his complex rages had at last found an effective focus – and he strode impatiently northward along the snow-clogged road as if he were no longer conscious of his still-unhealed forehead and lip, or of the damaged condition of his feet, or of fatigue. He walked leaning ahead into the wind like a fanatic.

But he was not well, could not pretend for any length of time that he was well. Snowflakes hurried around him like subtle grey chips of Lord Foul's malice, seeking to drain the heat of his life. And he felt burdened by Lena. The mother of Elena his daughter stepped proudly at his side as if his companionship honoured her. Before he had travelled half a league towards the mouth of the valley, his knees were trembling, and his breath scraped unevenly past his sore lip. He was forced to stop and rest.

Foamfollower and Lena regarded him gravely, concernedly. But his former resolution to accept help had deserted him; he was too angry to be carried like a child. He rejected with a grimace the tacit offer in Foamfollower's eyes.

The Giant also was not well – his wounds gave him pain – and he appeared to understand the impulse behind Covenant's refusal. Quietly, he asked, 'My friend, do you know the way – ' he hesitated as if he were searching for a short name – 'the way to Ridjeck Thome, Foul's Creche?'

'I'm leaving that to you.'

Foamfollower frowned. 'I know the way – I have it graven in my heart past all forgetting. But if we are separated – '

'I don't have a chance if we're separated,' Covenant muttered mordantly. He wished that he could leave the sound of leprosy out of his voice, but the malady was too rife in him to be stifled.

'Separated? Who speaks of separation?' Lena protested before Foamfollower could reply. 'Do not utter such things, Giant. We will not be separated. I have preserved – I will not part from him. You are old, Giant. You do not remember the giving of life to life in love – or you would not speak of separation.'

In some way, her words twisted the deep knife of Foamfollower's hurt. 'Old, yes.' Yet after a moment he forced a wry grin on to his lips. 'And you are altogether too young for me, fair Lena.'

Covenant winced for them both. Have mercy on me, he groaned. Have mercy. He started forward again, but almost at once he tripped on a snow-hidden roughness in the road.

Lena and Foamfollower caught him from either side and upheld him.

He looked back and forth between them. 'Treasure-berries. I need *aliantha*.'

Foamfollower nodded and moved away briskly, as if his Giantish instincts told him exactly where to find the nearest *aliantha*. But Lena retained her hold on Covenant's arm. She had not pulled the hood of her robe over her head, and her white hair hung like wet snow. She was gazing into Covenant's face as if she were famished for the sight of him.

He endured her scrutiny as long as he could. Then he carefully removed his arm from her fingers and said, 'If I'm going to survive this, I'll have to learn to stand on my own.'

'Why?' she asked. 'All are eager to aid – and none more eager than I. You have suffered enough for your aloneness.'

Because I'm all I have, he answered. But he could not say such a thing to her. He was terrified by her need for him.

When he did not reply, she glanced down for a moment, away from the fever of his gaze, then looked up again with the brightness of an idea in her eyes. 'Summon the Ranyhyn.'

The Ranyhyn?

'They will come to you. They come to me at your comamnd. It has hardly been forty days since they last came. They come each year on – ' she faltered, looked around at the snow with a memory of fear in her face – 'on the middle night of spring.' Her voice fell until Covenant could hardly hear her. 'This year the winter cold in my heart would not go away. The Land forgot spring – forgot – Sunlight abandoned us. I feared – feared that the Ranyhyn would never come again – that all my dreams were folly.

'But the stallion came. Sweat and snow froze in his coat, and ice hung from his muzzle. His breath steamed as he asked me to mount him. But I thanked him from the bottom of my heart and sent him home. He brought back such thoughts of you that I could not ride.'

Her eyes had left his face, and now she fell silent as if she had forgotten why she was speaking. But when she raised her head, Covenant saw that her old face was full of tears. 'Oh, my dear one,' she said softly, 'you are weak and in pain. Summon the Ranyhyn and ride them as you deserve.'

'No, Lena.' He could not accept the kind of help the Ranyhyn would give him. He reached out and awkwardly brushed at her tears. His fingers felt nothing. 'I made a bad bargain with them. I've made nothing but bad bargains.'

'Bad?' she asked as if he amazed her. 'You are Thomas Covenant the Unbeliever. How could any doing of yours be bad?'

Because it let me commit crimes.

But he could not say that aloud either. He reacted instead as if she had struck the touchstone of his fury.

'Listen, I don't know who you think I am these days; maybe you've still got Berek Halfhand on the brain. But I'm not him – I'm not any kind of hero. I'm nothing but a broken-down leper, and I'm doing this because I've had it up to here with being pushed around.

With or without your company I'm going to start getting even regardless of any misbegotten whatever that tries to get in my way. I'm going to do it my own way. If you don't want to walk, you can go home.'

Before she had a chance to respond, he turned away from her in shame, and found Foamfollower standing sadly beside him. 'And that's another thing,' he went on almost without pause. 'I have also had it with your confounded misery. Either tell me the truth about what's happened to you or stop snivelling.' He emphasized his last two words by grabbing treasure-berries from the Giant's open hands. 'Hell and blood! I'm sick to death of this whole thing.' Glaring up at the Giant's face, he jammed *aliantha* into his mouth, chewed them with an air of helpless belligerence.

'Ah, my friend,' Foamfollower breathed. 'This way that you have found for yourself is a cataract. I have felt it in myself. It will bear you to the edge in a rush and hurl you into abysses from which there is no recovery.'

Lena's hands touched Covenant's arm again, but he threw them off. He could not face her. Still glaring at Foamfollower, he said, 'You haven't told me the truth.' Then he turned and stalked away through the snow. In his rage, he could not forgive himself for being so unable to distinguish between hate and grief.

Treasure-berries supplied by both Foamfollower and Lena kept him going through most of the afternoon. But his pace remained slow and ragged. Finally his strength gave out when Foamfollower guided him off the road and eastward into the foothills beyond the mouth of the valley. By then, he was too exhausted to worry about the fact that the snowfall was ending. He simply lumbered into the lee of a hill and lay down to sleep. Later, in half-conscious moments, he discovered that the Giant was carrying him, but he was too tired to care.

He awoke some time after dawn with a pleasant sensation of warmth on his face and a smell of cooking in his nostrils. When he opened his eyes, he saw Foamfollower crouched over a graveling pot a few feet away, preparing a meal. They were in a small ravine. The leaden skies clamped over them like a coffin lid, but the air was free of snow. Beside him Lena lay deep in wary slumber.

Softly, Foamfollower said, 'She is no longer young. And we walked until near dawn. Let her sleep.' With a short gesture around the ravine, he went on: 'We will not be easily discovered here. We should remain until nightfall. It is better for us to travel at night.' He smiled faintly. 'More rest will not harm you.'

'I don't want to rest,' Covenant muttered, though he felt dull with fatigue. 'I want to keep moving.'

'Rest,' Foamfollower commanded. 'You will be able to travel more swiftly when your health has improved.'

Covenant acquiesced involuntarily. He lacked the energy to argue. While he waited for the meal, he inspected himself. Inwardly, he felt steadier; some of his self-possession had returned. The swelling of his lip had receded, and his forehead no longer seemed feverish. The infection in his battered feet did not appear to be spreading.

But his hands and feet were as numb as if they were being gradually gnawed off his limbs by frostbite. The backs of his knuckles and the tops of his arches retained some sensitivity, but the essential deadness was anchored in his bones. At first he tried to believe that the cause actually was frostbite. But he knew better. His sight told him clearly that it was not ice which deadened him.

His leprosy was spreading. Under Lord Foul's dominion – under the grey malignant winter – the Land no longer had the power to give him health.

Dream health! He knew that it had always been a lie, that leprosy was incurable because dead nerves could not be regenerated, that the previous impossible aliveness of his fingers and toes was the one incontrovertible proof that the Land was a dream, a delusion. Yet the absence of that health staggered him, dismayed the secret, yearning recusancy of his immedicable flesh. Not any more, he gaped dumbly. Now he had been bereft of that, too. The cruelty of it seemed to be more than he could bear.

'Covenant?' Foamfollower asked anxiously. 'My friend?'

Covenant gaped at the Giant as well, and another realization shook him. Foamfollower was closed to him. Except for the restless grief which crouched behind the Giant's eyes, Covenant could see nothing of his inner condition, could not see whether his companion was well or ill, right or wrong. His Land-born sight or penetration had been truncated, crippled. He might as well have been back in his own blind, impervious, superficial world.

'Covenant?' Foamfollower repeated.

For a time, the fact surpassed Covenant's comprehension. He tested – yes, he could see the interminable corruption eating its ill way towards his wrists, towards his heart. He could smell the potential gangrene in his feet. He could feel the vestiges of poison in his lip, the residual fever in his forehead. He could see the hints of Lena's age, Foamfollower's sorrow. He could taste the malevolence which hurled this winter across the Land – that he could perceive without question. And he had surely seen the ill in the marauders at Mithil Stonedown.

But that was no feat; their wrong was written on them so legibly that even a child could read it. Everything else was essentially closed to him. He could not discern Foamfollower's spirit, or Lena's cofusion, or the snow's falseness. The stubbornness which should have been apparent in the rocky hillsides above him was invisible. Even this rare gift which the Land had twice given him was half denied him now.

'Foamfollower.' He could hardly refrain from moaning. 'It's not coming back. I can't – this winter – it's not coming back.'

'Softly, my friend. I hear you. I – ' a wry smile bent his lips – 'I have seen what effect this winter has upon you. Perhaps I should be grateful that you cannot behold its effect upon me.'

'What effect?' Covenant croaked.

Foamfollower shrugged as if to deprecate his own plight. 'At times – when I have been too long unsheltered in this wind – I find I cannot remember certain precious Giantish tales. My friend, Giants do not forget stories.'

'Hell and blood.' Covenant's voice shook convulsively. But he neither cried out nor moved from his blankets. 'Get that food ready,' he juddered. 'I've got to eat.' He needed food for strength. His purpose required strength.

There was no question in him about what he meant to do. He was shackled to it as if his leprosy were an iron harness. And the hands that held the reins were in Foul's Creche.

The stew which Foamfollower handed to him he ate severely, tremorously. Then he lay back in his blankets as if he were stretching himself on a slab, and coerced himself to rest, to remain still and conserve his energy. When the warm stew, and the long debt of recuperation he owed to himself, sent him drifting towards slumber, he fell asleep still glowering thunderously at the bleak, grey, cloud-locked sky.

He awoke again towards noon and found Lena yet asleep. But she was nestling against him now, smiling faintly at her dreams. Foamfollower was no longer nearby.

Covenant glanced around and located the Giant keeping watch up near the head of the ravine. He waved when Covenant looked towards him. Covenant responded by carefully extricating himself from Lena, climbing out of his blankets. He tied his sandals securely on to his numb feet, tightened his jacket, and went to join the Giant.

From Foamfollower's position, he found that he could see over the rims of the ravine into its natural approaches. After a moment, he asked quietly, 'How far did we get?' His breath steamed as if his mouth were full of smoke.

'We have rounded the northmost point of this promontory,' Foamfollower replied. Nodding back over his left shoulder, he continued, 'Kevin's Watch is behind us. Through these hills we can gain the Plains of Ra in three more nights.'

'We should get going,' muttered Covenant. 'I'm in a hurry.'

'Practise patience, my friend. We will gain nothing if we hasten into the arms of marauders.'

Covenant looked around, then asked, 'Are the Ramen letting marauders get this close to the Ranyhyn? Has something happened to them?'

'Perhaps. I have had no contact with them. But the Plains are threatened along the whole length of the Roamsedge and Landrider rivers. And the Ramen spend themselves extravagantly to preserve the great horses. Perhaps their numbers are too few for them to ward these hills.'

Covenant accepted this as best he could. 'Foamfollower,' he murmured, 'whatever happened to all that Giantish talk you used to be so famous for? You haven't actually told me what you're worried about. Is it those "eyes" that saw you and Triock summon me? Every time I ask a question, you act as if you've got lockjaw.'

With a dim smile, Foamfollower said, 'I have lived a brusque life. The sound of my own voice is no longer so attractive to me.'

'Is that a fact?' Covenant drawled. 'I've heard worse.'

'Perhaps,' Foamfollower said softly. But he did not explain.

The Giant's reticence made Covenant want to ask more questions, attack his own ignorance somehow. He was sure that the issues at stake were large, that the things he did not yet know about the Land's doom were immensely important. But he remembered the way in which he had extracted information from Bannor on the plateau of Rivenrock. He could not forget the consequences of what he had done. He left Foamfollower's secrets alone.

Down the ravine from him, Lena's slumber became more restless. He shivered to himself as she began to flinch from side to side, whimpering under her breath. An impulse urged him to go to her, prevent her from thrashing about for fear that she might break her old frail bones; but he resisted. He could not afford all that she wanted to mean to him.

Yet when she jerked up and looked frantically around her, found that he was gone from her side – when she cried out piercingly, as if she had been abandoned – he was already halfway down the ravine towards her. Then she caught sight of him. Surging up from her blankets, she rushed to meet him, threw herself into his arms. There she clung to him so that her sobs were muffled in his shoulder.

With his right hand – its remaining fingers as numb and awkward as if they should have been amputated – he stroked her thin white hair. He tried to hold her consolingly to make up for his utter lack of comfortable words. Slowly, she regained control of herself. When he eased the pressure of his embrace, she stepped back. 'Pardon me, beloved,' she said contritely. 'I feared that you had left me. I am weak and foolish, or I would not have forgotten that you are the Unbeliever. You deserve better trust.'

Covenant shook his head dumbly, as if he wished to deny everything and did not know where or how to begin.

'But I could not bear to be without you,' she went on. 'In deep nights – when the cold catches at my breast until I cannot keep it out – and the mirror lies to me, saying that I have not kept myself unchanged for you – I have held to the promise of your return. I have not faltered, no! But I learned that I could not bear to be without you – not again. I have learned – I have – But I could not bear it – to sneak alone into the night and crouch in hiding as if I were ashamed – not again.'

'Not again,' Covenant breathed. In her old face he could see Elena clearly now, looking so beautiful and lost that his love for her wrenched his heart. 'As long as I'm stuck in this thing – I won't go anywhere without you.'

But she seemed to hear only his proviso, not his promise. With anguish in her face, she asked, 'Must you depart?'

'Yes.' The stiffness of his mouth made it difficult for him to speak gently; he could not articulate without tearing at his newly formed scabs. 'I don't belong here.'

She gasped at his words as if he had stabbed her with them. Her gaze fell away from his face. Panting, she murmured, 'Again! I cannot – cannot – Oh, Atiaran my mother! I love him. I have given my life without regret. When I was young, I ached to follow you to the Loresraat – to succeed so boldly that you could say, "There is the meaning of my life, there in my daughter." I ached to marry a Lord. But I have given – '

Abruptly, she caught the front of Covenant's jacket in both hands, pulled herself close to him, thrust her gaze urgently at his face. 'Thomas Covenant, will you marry me.'

Covenant gaped at her in horror.

The excitement of the idea carried her on in a rush. 'Let us marry! Oh, dearest one, that would restore me. I could bear any burden. We do not need the permission of the elders – I have spoken to them many times of my desires. I know the rites, the solemn promises – I can teach you. And the Giant can witness the sharing of our lives.' Before Covenant could gain any control over his face, she was pleading with him. 'Oh, Unbeliever! I have borne your daughter, I have ridden the Ranyhyn that you sent to me. I have waited – ! Surely I have shown the depth of my love for you. Beloved, marry me. Do not refuse.'

Her appeal made him cringe, made him feel grotesque and unclean. In his pain, he wanted to turn his back on her, push her from him and walk away. Part of him was already shouting, You're crazy, old woman! It's your daughter I love! But he restrained himself. With his shoulders hunched like a strangler's to choke the violence of his responses, he gripped Lena's wrists and pulled her hands from his jacket. He held them up so that his fingers were directly in front of her face. 'Look at my hands,' he rasped. 'Look at my fingers.'

She stared at them wildly.

'Look at the sickness in them. They aren't just cold – they're sick, numb with sickness almost all the way across my palms. That's my disease.'

'You are closed to me,' she said desolately.

'That's leprosy, I tell you! It's there – even if you're blind to it, it's there. And there's only one way you can get it. Prolonged exposure. You might get it if you stayed around me long enough. And children – what's marriage without children?' He could not keep the passion out of his voice. 'Children are even more susceptible. They get it more easily – children and – and old people. When I get wiped out of the Land the next time, you'll be left behind, and the only absolutely guaranteed legacy you'll have from me is leprosy. Foul will make sure of it. On top of everything else, I'll be responsible for contaminating the entire Land.'

'Covenant – beloved,' Lena whispered. 'I beg you. Do not refuse.' Her eyes swam with tears, torn by a cruel effort to see herself as she really was. 'Behold I am frail and faulty. I have neither worth nor courage to preserve myself alone. I have given – Please, Thomas Covenant.' Before he could stop her, she dropped to her knees. 'I beg – do not shame me in the eyes of my whole life.'

His defensive rage was no match for her. He snatched her up from her knees as if he meant to break her neck, but then he held her tenderly, put all the gentleness of which he was capable into his face. For an instant, he felt he had in his hands proof that he – not Lord Foul – was responsible for the misery of the Land. And he could not accept that responsibility without rejecting her. What she asked him to do was to forget –

He knew that Foamfollower was watching him. But if Triock and Mhoram and Bannor had been behind him as well – if even Trell and Atiaran had been present – he would not have changed his answer.

'No, Lena,' he said softly. 'I don't love you right – I don't have the right kind of love to marry you. I'd only be cheating you. You're beautiful – beautiful. Any other man wouldn't wait for you to ask

918

him. But I'm the Unbeliever, remember? I'm here for a reason.' With a sick twisting of his lips that was as close as he could come to a smile, he finished, 'Berek Halfhand didn't marry his Queen, either.'

His words filled him with disgust. He felt that he was telling her a lie worse than the lie of marrying her – that any comfort he might try to offer her violated the severe truth. But as she realized what he was saying, she caught hold of the idea and clasped it to her. She blinked rapidly at her tears, and the harsh effort of holding her confusion at bay faded from her face. In it place, a shy smile touched her lips. 'Am I your Queen then, Unbeliever?' she asked in a tone of wonder.

Roughly, Covenant hugged her so that she could not see the savagery which white-knuckled his countenance. 'Of course.' He forced up the words as if they were too thick for his aching throat. 'No one else is worthy.'

He held her, half fearing she would collapse if he let her go, but after a long moment, she withdrew from his embrace. With a look that reminded him of her sprightly girlhood, she said, 'Let us tell the Giant,' as if she wished to announce something better than a betrothal.

Together, they turned and climbed arm in arm up the ravine toward Saltheart Foamfollower.

When they reached him, they found that his buttressed visage was still wet with weeping. Grey ice sheened his face, hung like beads from his stiff beard. His hands were gripped and straining across his knees. 'Foamfollower,' Lena said in surprise, 'this is a moment of happiness. Why do you weep?'

His hands jerked up to scrub away the ice, and when it was gone, he smiled at her with wonderful fondness. 'You are too beautiful, my Queen,' he told her gently. 'You surpass me.'

His response made her shine with pleasure. For a moment, her old flesh blushed youthfully, and she met the Giant's gaze with joy in her eyes. Then a recollection started her. 'But I am remiss. I have been asleep, and you have not eaten. I must cook for you.' Turning lightly, she scampered down the ravine towards Foamfollower's supplies.

The Giant glanced up at the chill sky, then looked at Covenant's gaunt face. His cavernous eyes glinted sharply as if he understood what Covenant had been through. As gently as he had spoken to Lena, he asked, 'Do you now believe in the Land?'

'I'm the Unbeliever. I don't change.'

'Do you not?'

'I am going to – ' Covenant's shoulders hunched – 'exterminate Lord Foul the bloody Despiser. Isn't that enough for you?'

'Oh, it is enough for me,' Foamfollower said with sudden vehemence. 'I require nothing more. But it does not suffice for you. What do you believe – what is your faith?'

'I don't know.'

Foamfollower looked away again at the weather. His heavy brows hid his eyes, but his smile seemed sad, almost hopeless. 'Therefore I am afraid.'

Covenant nodded grimly, as if in agreement.

Nevertheless, if Lord Foul had appeared before him at that moment, he, Thomas Covenant, Unbeliever and leper, would have tried to tear the Despiser's heart out with his bare hands.

He needed to know how to use the white wild magic gold.

But there were no answers in the meal Lena cooked for him and Foamfollower, or in the grey remainder of the afternoon, which he spent huddled over the fire-stones with Lena resting drowsily against him, or in the dank, suffering twilight that finally brought his waiting to an end. When Foamfollower led the way eastward out of the ravine, Covenant felt that he understood nothing but the wind which blew through him like scorn for the impotence of sunlight and warmth. And after that he had no more time to think about it. All his attention was occupied with the work of stumbling numbly through the benighted hills.

Travelling was difficult for him. His body's struggle to recover from injury and inanition drained his strength; the bitter cold drained his strength. He could not see where to place his feet, could not avoid tripping, falling, bruising himself on insensate dirt and rock. Yet he kept going, pushed himself after Foamfollower until the sweat froze on his forehead and his clothing grew crusted with stains of ice. His resolve held him. In time, he even became dimly grateful that his feet were numb, so that he could not feel the damage he was doing to himself.

He had no sense of duration or progress; he measured out the time in rest halts, in *aliantha* unexpectedly handed to him out of the darkness by Foamfollower. Such things sustained him. But eventually he stopped rubbing the ice from his nose and lips, from his forehead and his fanatical beard; he allowed the grey cold to hang like a mask on his features, as if he were becoming a creature of winter. And he stumbled on in the Giant's wake.

When Foamfollower stopped at last, shortly before dawn, Covenant simply dropped to the snow and fell asleep.

Later, the Giant woke him for breakfast, and he found Lena sleeping beside him, curled against the cold. Her lips were faintly tinged with blue, and she shivered from time to time, unable to get warm. Her years showed clearly now in the lines of her face and in the frail, open-mouthed rise and fall of her breathing. Covenant roused her carefully, made her eat hot food until her lips lost their cold hue and the veins in her temples became less prominent. Then, despite her protests, he put her down in blankets and lay beside her until she went back to sleep.

Some time later, he roused himself to finish his own breakfast. Calculating backward, he guessed that the Giant had been without rest for at least the last three days and nights. So he said abruptly, 'I'll let you know when I can't stay awake any more,' took the graveling pot, and moved off to find a sheltered place where he could keep watch. There he sat and watched daylight ooze into the air like seepage through the scab of an old wound.

He awoke later in the afternoon to find Foamfollower sitting beside him, and Lena preparing a meal a short distance away. He jerked erect, cursing inwardly. But his companions did not appear to have suffered from his dereliction. Foamfollower met his gaze with a smile and said, 'Do not be alarmed. We have been safe enough – though I was greatly weary and slept until mid-day. There is a deer run north of us, and some of the tracks are fresh. Deer would not remain here in the presence of marauder spoor.'

Covenant nodded. His breath steamed heavily in the cold. 'Foamfollower,' he muttered, 'I am incredibly tired of being so bloody mortal.'

But that night he found the going easier. In spite of the encroaching numbness of his hands and feet, some of his strength had returned. And as Foamfollower led him and Lena eastward, the mountains moved away from them on the south, easing the ruggedness of the hills. As a result, he was better able to keep up the pace.

Yet the relaxation of the terrain caused another problem. Since they were less protected from the wind, they often had to walk straight into the teeth of Lord Foul's winter. In that wind, Covenant's inmost clothing seemed to turn to ice, and he moved as if he were scraping his chest raw like a penitent.

Still, he had enough stamina left at the end of the night's march to take the first watch. The Giant had chosen to camp in a small hollow sheltered on the east by a low hill; and after they had eaten, Foamfollower and Lena lay down to sleep while Covenant took a position under a dead, gnarled juniper just below the crown of the knoll. From there, he looked down at his companions, resting as if they trusted him completely. He was determined not to fail them again.

Yet he knew, could not help knowing, that he was poorly equipped for such duty. The wintry truncation of his senses nagged at him as if it implied disaster – as if his inability to see, smell, hear peril would necessarily give rise to peril. And he was not mistaken. Though he was awake, almost alert – though the day had begun, filling the air with its grey, cold sludge – though the attack came from the east, upwind from him – he felt nothing until too late.

He had just finished a circuit of the hilltop, scanning the terrain around the hollow, and had returned to sit in the thin shelter of the juniper, when at last he became aware of danger. Something imminent ran along the wind; the atmosphere over the hollow became suddenly intense. The next instant, dark figures rose up out of the snow around Foamfollower and Lena. As he tried to shout a warning, the figures attacked.

He sprang to his feet, raced down into the hollow. Below him, Foamfollower surged to his knees, throwing dark brown people aside. With a low cry of anger, Lena struggled against the weight of the attackers who pinned her in her blankets. But before Covenant could get to her, someone hit him from behind, knocked him headlong into the snow.

He rolled, got his feet under him, but immediately arms caught him around the chest above the elbows. His own arms were trapped. He fought, threw himself from side to side, but his captor was far too strong; he could not break the grip. Then a flat, alien voice said into his ear, 'Remain still or I will break your back.'

His helplessness infuriated him. 'Then break it,' he panted under his breath as he struggled. 'Just let her go.' Lena was resisting frantically, yelping in frustration and outrage as she failed to free herself.

'Foamfollower!' Covenant shouted hoarsely.

But he saw in shocked amazement that the Giant was not fighting. His attackers stood back from him, and he sat motionless, regarding Covenant's captor gravely.

Covenant went limp with chagrin.

Roughly, the attackers pulled Lena from her blankets. They had already lashed her wrists with cords. She still struggled, but now her only aim seemed to be to break loose so that she could run to Covenant.

Then Foamfollower spoke. Levelly, dangerously, he said, 'Release him.' When the arms holding Covenant did not loosen, the Giant went on: 'Stone and Sea! You will regret it if you have harmed him. Do you not know me?'

'The Giants are dead,' the voice in Covenant's ear said dispassionately. 'Only Giant-Ravers remain.'

'Let me go!' Lena hissed. 'Oh, look at him, you fools! *Melenkurion abatha!* Is he a Raver?' But Covenant could not tell whether she referred to Foamfollower or himself.

His captor ignored her. 'We have seen – I have seen The Grieve. I have made that journey to behold the work of the Ravers.'

A shadow tightened in Foamfollower's eyes, but his voice did not flicker. 'Distrust me, then. Look at him, as Lena daughter of Atiaran suggests. He is Thomas Covenant.'

Abruptly, the strong arms spun Covenant. He found himself facing a compact man with flat eyes and a magisterial mien. The man wore nothing but a thin, short, vellum robe, as if he were impervious to the cold. In some ways he had changed; his eyebrows were stark white against his brown skin; his hair had aged to a mottled grey; and deep lines ran like the erosion of time down his cheeks past the corners of his mouth. But still Covenant recognized him.

He was Bannor of the Bloodguard.

9

RAMEN COVERT

The sight of him stunned Covenant. Lithe, loam-coloured forms, some wearing light robes shaded to match the grey-white snow, moved closer to him as if to verify his identity; a few of them muttered, 'Ringthane', in tense voices. He hardly saw them. 'But Mhoram said – '

But Mhoram had said that the Bloodguard were lost.

'Ur-Lord Covenant.' Bannor inclined his head in a slight bow. 'Pardon my error. You are well disguised.'

'Disguised?' Covenant had no conception of what Bannor was talking about. Mhoram's pain had carried so much conviction. Numbly, he glanced downward as if he expected to find two fingers missing from Bannor's right hand.

'A Stonedownor jacket. Sandals. A Giant for a companion.' Bannor's impassive eyes held Covenant's face. 'And you stink of infection. Only your countenance may be recognized.'

'Recognized.' Covenant could not stop himself. He repeated the word because it was the last thing Bannor had said. Fighting for self-control, he croaked, 'Why aren't you with the Lords?'

'The Vow was Corrupted. We no longer serve the Lords.'

Covenant gaped at this answer as if it were nonsense. Confusion befogged his comprehension. Had Mhoram said anything like this?

He found that his knees were trembling as if the ground under him had shifted. *No longer serve the Lords*, he repeated blankly. He did not know what the words meant.

But then the sounds of Lena's struggle penetrated him. 'You have harmed him,' she gasped fiercely. 'Release me!'

He made an effort to pull himself together. 'Let her go,' he said to Bannor. 'Don't you understand who she is?'

'Did the Giant speak truly?'

'What? Did he what?' Covenant almost lapsed back into his stupor at the jolt of this distrust. But for Lena's sake he took a deep breath, resisted. 'She is the mother of High Lord Elena,' he grated. 'Tell them to let her go.'

Bannor glanced past Covenant at Lena, then said distantly, 'The Lords spoke of her. They were unable to heal her.' He shrugged slightly. 'They were unable to heal many things.'

Before Covenant could respond, the Bloodguard signalled to his companions. A moment later, Lena was at Covenant's side. From somewhere in her robes, she produced a stone knife and brandished it between Bannor and Covenant. 'If you have harmed him,' she fumed, 'I will take the price of it from your skin, old man.'

The Bloodguard cocked an eyebrow at her. Covenant reached for her arm to hold her back, but he was still too staggered to think of a way to calm her, reassure her. 'Lena,' he murmured ineffectively, 'Lena.' When Foamfollower joined them, Covenant's eyes appealed to the Giant for help.

'Ah, my Queen,' Foamfollower said softly. 'Remember your Oath of Peace.'

'Peace!' Lena snapped in a brittle voice. 'Speak to them of Peace. They attacked the Unbeliever.'

'Yet they are not our enemies. They are the Ramen.'

She jerked incredulously to face the Giant. 'Ramen? The tenders of the Ranyhyn?'

Covenant stared as well. Ramen? He had unconsciously assumed that Bannor's companions were other Bloodguard. The Ramen had always secretly hated the Bloodguard because so many Ranyhyn had died while bearing the Bloodguard in battle. Ramen and Bloodguard? The ground seemed to lurch palpably under him. Nothing was as he believed it to be; everything in the Land would either astound or appal him, if only he were told the truth.

'Yes,' Foamfollower replied to Lena. And now Covenant recognized the Ramen for himself. Eight of them, men and women, stood around him. They were lean, swift people, with the keen faces of hunters, and skin so deeply tanned from their years in the open air that even this winter could not pale them. Except for their scanty robes, their camouflage, they dressed in the Ramen fashion as Covenant remembered it – short shifts and tunics which left their legs and arms free; bare feet. Seven of them had the cropped hair and roped waists characteristic of Cords; and the eighth was marked as a Manethrall by the way his fighting thong tied his long black hair into one strand, and by the small, woven circlet of yellow flowers on the crown of his head.

Yet they had changed; they were not like the Ramen he had known forty-seven years ago. The easiest alteration for him to see was in their attitude towards him. During his first visit to the Land, they had looked at him in awed respect. He was the Ringthane, the man to whom the Ranyhyn had reared a hundred strong. But now their proud, severe faces regarded him with asperity backed by ready rage, as if he had violated their honour by committing some nameless perfidy.

But that was not the only change in them. As he scrutinized the uncompromising eyes around him, he became conscious of a more significant difference, something he could not define. Perhaps they carried themselves with less confidence or pride; perhaps they had been attacked so often that they had developed a habitual flinch; perhaps this ratio of seven Cords to one Manethrall, instead of three or four to one, as it should have been, indicated a crippling loss of life among their leaders, the teachers of the Ranyhyn-lore. Whatever the reason, they had a haunted look, an aspect of erosion, as if some subliminal ghoul were gnawing at the bones of their courage. Studying them, Covenant was suddenly convinced that they endured Bannor, even followed him, because they were no longer self-sure enough to refuse a Bloodguard.

After a moment, he became aware that Lena was speaking more in confusion than in anger now. 'Why did you attack us? Can you not recognize the Unbeliever? Do you not remember the Rockbrothers of the Land? Can you not see that I have ridden Ranyhyn?'

'Ridden!' spat the Manethrall.

'My Queen,' Foamfollower said softly, 'the Ramen do not ride.'

'As for Giants,' the man went on, 'they betray.'

'Betray?' Covenant's pulse pounded in his temples, as if he were too close to an abyss hidden in the snow.

'Twice now Giants have led Fangthane's rending armies north of the Plains of Ra. These "Rockbrothers" have sent fangs and claws in scores of thousands to tear the flesh of Ranyhyn. Behold!' With a swift tug, he snatched his cord from his hair and grasped it taut like a garotte. 'Every Ramen cord is black with blood.' His knuckles tightened as if he were about to leap at the Giant. 'Manhome is abandoned. Ramen and Ranyhyn are scattered. Giants!' He spat again as if the very taste of the word disgusted him.

'Yet you know me,' Foamfollower said to Bannor. 'You know that I am not one of the three who fell to the Ravers.'

Bannor shrugged noncommittally. 'Two of the three are dead. Who can say where those Ravers have gone?'

'I am a Giant, Bannor!' Foamfollower insisted in a tone of supplication, as if that fact were the only proof of his fidelity. 'It was I who first brought Thomas Covenant to Revelstone.'

Bannor was unmoved. 'Then how is it that you are alive?'

At this, Foamfollower's eyes glinted painfully. In a thin tone, he said, 'I was absent from *Coercri* – when my kindred brought their years in Seareach to an end.'

The Bloodguard cocked an eyebrow, but did not relent. After a moment, Covenant realized that the resolution of this impasse was in his hands. He was in no condition to deal with such problems, but he knew he had to say something. With an effort, he turned to Bannor. 'You can't claim you don't remember me. You probably have nightmares about me, even if you don't ever sleep.'

'I know you, ur-Lord Covenant.' As he spoke, Bannor's nostrils flared as if they were offended by the smell of illness.

'You know me, too,' Covenant said with mounting urgency to the Manethrall. 'Your people call me Ringthane. The Ranyhyn reared to me.'

The Manethrall looked away from Covenant's demanding gaze, and for an instant the haunted look filled his face like an ongoing tragedy. 'Of the Ringthane we do not speak,' he said quietly. 'The Ranyhyn have chosen. It is not our place to question the choices of the Ranyhyn.'

'Then back off!' Covenant did not intend to shout, but he was too full of undefined fears to contain himself. 'Leave us alone! Hellfire! We've got enough trouble as it is.'

His tone brought back the Manethrall's pride. Severely, the man asked, 'Why have you come?'

'I haven't "come". I don't want to be here at all.'

'What is your purpose?'

In a voice full of mordant inflections, Covenant said, 'I intend to pay a little visit to Foul's Creche.'

His words jolted the Cords, and their breath hissed through their teeth. The Manethrall's hands twitched on his weapon.

A flare of savage desire widened Bannor's eyes momentarily. But his flat dispassion returned at once. He shared a clear glance with the Manethrall, then said, 'Ur-Lord, you and your companions must accompany us. We will take you to a place where more Ramen may give thought to you.'

'Are we your prisoners?' Covenant glowered.

'Ur-Lord, no hand will be raised against you in my presence. But these matters must be given consideration.'

Covenant glared hard into Bannor's expressionlessness, then turned to Foamfollower. 'What do you think?'

'I do not like this treatment,' Lena interjected. 'Saltheart Foamfollower is a true friend of the Land. Atiaran my mother spoke of all Giants with gladness. And you are the Unbeliever, the bearer of white gold. They show disrespect. Let us leave them and go our way.'

Foamfollower replied to them both, 'The Ramen are not blind. Bannor is not blind. They will see me more clearly in time. And their help is worth seeking.'

'All right,' Covenant muttered. 'I'm no good at fighting anyway.' To Bannor, he said stiffly, 'We'll go with you.' Then, for the sake of everything that had happened between himself and the Bloodguard, he added, 'No matter what else is going on here, you've saved my life too often for me to start distrusting you now.'

Bannor gave Covenant another fractional bow. At once, the Manethrall snapped a few orders to the Cords. Two of them left at a flat run towards the northeast, and two more moved off to take scouting positions on either side of the company, while the rest gathered small knapsacks from hiding places around the hollow. Watching them, Covenant was amazed once again how easily, swiftly, they could disappear into their surroundings. Even their footprints seemed to vanish before his eyes. By the time Foamfollower had packed his leather sack, they had effaced all signs of their presence from the hollow. It looked as untroubled as if they had never been there.

Before long, Covenant found himself trudging between Lena and Foamfollower in the same general direction taken by the two runners. The Manethrall and Bannor strode briskly ahead of them, and the three remaining Cords marched at their backs like guards. They seemed to be moving openly, as if they had no fear of enemies. But twice when he looked back Covenant saw the Cords erasing the traces of their passage from the grey drifts and the cold ground.

The presence of those three ready garottes behind him only aggravated his confusion. Despite his long experience with hostility, he was not prepared for such distrust from the Ramen. Clearly, important events had taken place – events of which he had no conception. His ignorance afflicted him with a powerful sense that the fate of the Land was moving towards a crisis, a fundamental concatenation in which his own role was beclouded, obscure. The facts were being kept from him. This feeling cast the whole harsh edifice of his purpose into doubt, as if it were erected on slow quicksand. He needed to ask questions, to get answers. But the unspoken threat of those Ramen ropes disconcerted him. And Bannor – ! He could not frame his questions, even to himself.

And he was tired. He had already travelled all night, had not slept since the previous afternoon. Only four days had passed since his summoning. As he laboured to keep up the pace, he found that he lacked the strength of concentration to think.

Lena was in no better condition. Although she was healthier than he, she was old, and not hardened to walking. Gradually, he became as worried about her as he was weary himself. When she began to droop against him, he told Bannor flatly that he would have to rest.

They slept until mid-afternoon, then travelled late into the night before camping again. And the next morning, they were on their way before dawn. But Covenant and Lena did better now. The food which the Ramen gave them was hot and nourishing. And soon after grey dim day had shambled into the laden air, they reached the edge of the hills, came in sight of the Plains of Ra. At this point, they swung northward, staying in the rumbled terrain of the hills-edge rather than venturing into the bleak, winter-bitten openness of the Plains. But still they found the going easier. In time, Covenant recovered enough to begin asking questions.

As usual, he had trouble talking to Bannor. The Bloodguard's unbreachable dispassion daunted him, often made him malicious or angry through simple frustration; such reticence seemed outrageously immune from judgement – the antithesis of leprosy. Now all the Bloodguard had abandoned the Lords, Revelstone, death refusal. Lord's Keep would fall without them. And yet Bannor was here, living and working with the Ramen. When Covenant tried to ask questions, he felt that he no longer knew the man to whom he spoke.

Bannor met his first tentative enquiries by introducing Covenant to the Ramen – Manethrall Kam, and his Cords, Whane, Lal and Puhl – and by assuring him that they would reach their destination by evening the next day. He explained that this band of Ramen was a scouting patrol responsible for detecting marauders along the western marge of Ra; they had found Covenant and his companions by chance rather than by design. When Covenant asked about Rue, the Manethrall who had brought word of Fleshharrower's army to Revelstone seven years ago, Bannor replied flatly that she had died soon after her return home. But after that, Covenant had to wrestle for what he wanted to know.

At last he could find no graceful way to frame his question. 'You left the Lords,' he rasped awkwardly. 'Why are you here?'

'The Vow was broken. How could we remain?'

'They need you. They couldn't need you more.'

'Ur-Lord, I say to you that the Vow was broken. Many things were broken. You were present. We could not – ur-Lord, I am old now. I, Bannor, First Mark of the Bloodguard. I require sleep and hot food. Though I was bred for mountains, this cold penetrates my bones. I am no fit server for Revelstone – no, nor for the Lords, though they do not equal High Lord Kevin who went before them.'

'Then why are you here? Why didn't you just go home and forget it?'

Foamfollower winced at Covenant's tone, but Bannor replied evenly, 'That was my purpose – when I departed Lord's Keep. But I found I could not forget. I had ridden too many Ranyhyn. At night I saw them – in my dreams they ran like clear skies and cleanliness. Have you not beheld them? Without Vows or defiance of death, they surpassed the faith of the Bloodguard. Therefore I returned.'

'Just because you were addicted to Ranyhyn? You let the Lords and Revelstone and all go to hell and blood, but you came here because you couldn't give up riding Ranyhyn?'

'I do not ride.'

Covenant stared at him.

'I have come to share the work of the Ramen. A few of the *Haruchai* – I know not how many – a few felt as I did. We had known Kevin in the youth of his glory, and could not forget. Terrel is here, and Runnik. There are others. We teach our skills to the Ramen, and learn from them the tending of the great horses. Perhaps we will learn to make peace with our failure before we die.'

Make peace, Covenant groaned. Bannor! The very simplicity of the Bloodguard's explanation dismayed him. So all those centuries of untainted and sleepless service came to this.

He asked Bannor no more questions; he was afraid of the answers.

For the rest of that day, he fell out of touch with his purpose. Despite the concern and companionship of Foamfollower and Lena, he walked between them in morose separateness. Bannor's words had numbed his heart. And he slept that night on his back with his eyes upward, as if he did not believe that he would ever see the sun again.

But the next morning he remembered. Shortly after dawn, Manethrall Kam's party met another Cord. The man was on his way to the edge of the Plains, and in his hands he carried two small bouquets of yellow flowers. The grey wind made their frail petals flutter pathetically. After saluting Manethrall Kam, he strode out into the open, shouted shrilly against the wind in a language Covenant could not understand. He repeated his shout, then waited with his hands extended as if he were offering flowers to the wind.

Shortly, out of the shelter of a frozen gully came two Ranyhyn, a stallion and a mare. The stallion's chest was scored with fresh claw-marks, and the mare had a broken, hollow look, as if she had just lost her foal. Both were as gaunt as skeletons; hunger had carved the pride from their shoulders and haunches, exposed their ribs, given their emaciated muscles an abject starkness. They hardly seemed able to hold up their heads. But they nickered to the Cord. With a stumbling gait, they trotted forward, and began at once to eat the flowers he offered them. In three bites the food was gone. He hugged them quickly, then turned away with tears in his eyes.

Without a word, Manethrall Kam gave the Cord the bedraggled circlet from his hair, so that each of the Ranyhyn could have one more bite. 'That is *amanibhavam*, the healing grass of Ra,' he explained stiffly to Covenant. 'It is a hardy grass, not so easily daunted by this winter as the Render might wish. It will keep life in them – for another day.' As he spoke, he glared redly into Covenant's face, as if the misery of these two horses were the Unbeliever's doing. With a brusque nod towards the Cord feeding the Ranyhyn, he went on: 'He walked ten leagues today to bring even this much food to them.' The haunted erosion filled his face; he looked like the victim of a curse. Painfully, he turned and strode away again northward, along the edges of the Plains.

Covenant remembered; he had no trouble remembering his purpose now. When he followed the Manethrall, he walked as if he were fighting the deadness of his feet with outrage.

In the course of that day, he saw a few more Ranyhyn. Two were uninjured, but all were gaunt, weak, humbled. All had gone a long way down the road towards starvation.

The sight of them wore heavily upon Lena. There was no confusion in the way she perceived them, no distortion or inaccuracy. Such vision consumed her. As time passed, her eyes sank back under her brows, as if they were trying to hide in her skull, and dark circles like bruises grew around the orbs. She stared brittlely about her as if even Covenant were dim in her gaze – as if she beheld nothing but the protruding ribs and fleshless limbs of Ranyhyn.

Covenant held her arm as they walked, guided and supported her as best he could. Weariness gradually became irrelevant to him; even the keen wind, flaying straight towards him across the Plains, seemed to lose its importance. He stamped along behind Kam like a wild prophet, come to forge the Ramen to his will.

They reached the outposts of Kam's destination by mid-afternoon. Ahead of them, two Cords abruptly stepped out of a barren copse of wattle, and saluted Manethrall Kam in the Ramen fashion, with their hands raised on either side of their heads and their palms open, weaponless. Kam returned the bow, spoke to the two briefly in a low, aspirated tongue, then motioned for Covenant, Lena and Foamfollower to continue on with him. As they moved back into the hills, he told them, 'My Cords were able to summon only three other Manethralls. But four will be enough.'

'Enough?' Covenant asked.

'The Ramen will accept a judgement made by four Manethralls.'

Covenant met Kam's glare squarely. A moment later, the Manethrall turned away with an oddly daunted air, as if he had remembered that Covenant's claim on him came from the Ranyhyn. Hurrying now, he led his company upward with the grey wind cutting at their backs.

They climbed across two steep bluffs which gave them a panoramic view of the Plains. The hard open ground lay ruined below them, scorched with winter and grey snow until it looked maimed and lifeless. But Manethrall Kam moved rapidly onward, ignoring the sight. He took his companions past the bluffs down into a valley cunningly hidden among rough knolls and hilltops. This valley was largely sheltered from the wind, and faint, cultivated patches of unripe *amanibhavam* grew on its sides. Now Covenant remembered what he had heard about *amanibhavam* during his previous visit to the Plains of Ra. This grass, which held such a rare power of healing horses, was poisonous to humans.

Aside from the grass, the valley contained nothing but three dead copses leaning at various points against the steepest of the slopes. Manethrall Kam walked directly towards the thickest one. As he approached, four Cords stepped out of the wood to meet him. They had a tense, frail air about them which made Covenant notice how young they were; even the two older girls seemed to have had their Cording thrust unready upon them. They saluted Kam nervously, and when he had returned their bow, they moved aside to let him enter the copse.

Covenant followed Bannor into the wood and found that at its back was a narrow rift in the hillside. The rift did not close, but its upper reaches were so crooked that Covenant could not see out the top. Under his feet, a layer of damp, dead leaves muffled his steps; he passed in silence like a shadow between the cold stone walls. A smell of musty age filled his nostrils, as if the packed leaves had been rotting in the rift for generations; and despite their wetness, he felt dim warmth radiating from them. No one spoke. Gripping Lena's chill fingers in his numb hand, he moved behind Bannor as the cleft bent irregularly from side to side on its way through the rock.

Then Manethrall Kam stopped. When Covenant caught up with

him, he said softly, 'We now enter the secret places of a Ramen covert. Be warned, Ringthane. If we are not taught to trust you and your companions, you will not leave this place. In all the Plains of Ra and the surrounding hills, this is the last covert.

'At one time, the Ramen held several such hidden places of refuge. In them the Manethralls tended the grievous wounds of the Ranyhyn and trained Cords in the secret rites of their Maneing. But one by one in turn each covert – ' Kam fixed Covenant with a demon-ridden gaze – 'has been betrayed. Though we have preserved them with our utterest skill, *kresh* – ur-viles – Cavewights – ill flesh in every shape – all have found our hidden coverts and ravaged them.' He studied the Ringthane as if he were searching for some sign which would brand Covenant as the betrayer. 'We will hold you here – we will kill your companions – rather than permit treachery to this place.'

Without allowing Covenant time to reply, he turned on his heel and stalked around another bend in the cleft.

Covenant followed, scowling stormily. Beyond the bend, he found himself in a large chamber. The air was dim, but he could see well enough to discern several Ranyhyn standing against the walls. They were eating scant bundles of grass, and in this closed space the sharp aroma of the *amanibhavam* made his head ring. All of them were injured – some so severely that they could hardly stand. One had lost the side of its face in a fight, another still bled from a cruel fretwork of claw-marks in its flanks, and two others had broken legs which hung limply, with excruciating bone-splinters tearing the skin.

As he stared gauntly at them, they became aware of him. A restless movement passed through them, and their heads came up painfully, turning soft, miserable eyes towards him. For a long moment, they looked at him as if they should have been afraid but were too badly hurt for fear. Then, in agony, even the horses with broken legs tried to rear.

'Stop it. Stop.' Covenant hardly knew that he was moaning aloud. His hands flinched in front of his face, trying to ward off an abominable vision. 'I can't stand it.'

Firmly, Bannor took his arm and drew him past the chamber into another passage through the rock.

After a few steps, his legs failed him. But Bannor gripped him, bore him up. Clutching with useless fingers at the Bloodguard's shoulders, he pulled himself around until he was facing Bannor. 'Why? ' he panted, into Bannor's flat visage. 'Why did they do that?'

Bannor's face and voice revealed nothing. 'You are the Ringthane. They have made promises to you.'

'Promises.' Covenant rubbed a hand over his eyes. The promises of the Ranyhyn limped across his memory. 'Hell and blood.' With an effort, he pushed away from Bannor. Bracing himself against the wall of the crevice, he clenched his trembling fists as if he were trying to squeeze steadiness out of them. His fingers ached for the Despiser's throat. 'They should be killed!' he raged thickly. 'They should be put out of their misery! How can you be so cruel?'

Manethrall Kam spat, 'Is that how it is done in your world, Ringthane?'

But Bannor replied evenly, 'They are the Ranyhyn. Do not presume to offer them kindness. How can any human decide the choices of death and pain for them?'

At this, Foamfollower reached out and touched Bannor's shoulder in a gesture of respect.

Covenant's jaw muscles jumped as he bit his shouts into silence. He followed the Giant's gesture, turned, and looked greyly up at Foamfollower. Both the Giant and Bannor had witnessed his bargain with the Ranyhyn forty-seven years ago, when the great horses had first reared to him; Bannor and Foamfollower and Mhoram and Quaan might be the last remaining survivors of the Quest for the Staff of Law. But they were enough. They could accuse him. The Ramen could accuse him. He still did not know all the things of which they could accuse him.

His wedding band hung loosely on his ring finger; he had lost weight, and the white gold dangled as if it were meaningless. He needed its power. Without power, he was afraid to guess at the things which were being kept from him.

Abruptly, he stepped up to Kam, jabbed the Manethrall's chest with one stiff finger. 'By hell,' he muttered into Kam's glare, 'if you're only doing this out of pride, I hope you rot for it. You could have taken them south into the mountains – you could have saved them from this. Pride isn't a good enough excuse.'

Again the ghoul-begotten hurt darkened Kam's gaze. 'It is not pride,' he said softly. 'The Ranyhyn do not choose to go.'

Without wanting to, Covenant believed him. He could not doubt what he saw in the Manethrall. He drew back, straightened his shoulders, took a deep breath. 'Then you'd better help me. Trust me whether you want to or not. I hate Foul just as much as you do.'

'That may be,' Kam replied, recovering his severity. 'We will not contradict the Ranyhyn concerning you. I saw – I would not have believed if I had not seen. To rear! Hurt as they are! You need not fear us. But your companions are another matter. The woman – ' he made an effort to speak calmly – 'I do not distrust. Her love for the Manes is in her face. But this Giant – he must prove himself.'

'I hear you, Manethrall,' said Foamfollower quietly. 'I will respect your distrust as best I can.'

Kam met the Giant's look, then glanced over at Bannor. The Bloodguard shrugged impassively. Kam nodded and led the way farther down the cleft.

Before following, Covenant regained his grip on Lena's hand. She did not raise her head, and in the gloom he could see nothing of her eyes but the bruises under them. 'Be brave,' he said gently as he could. 'Maybe it won't all be this bad.' She made no response, but when he drew her forward she did not resist. He kept her at his side, and soon they stepped together out of the far end of the passage.

The cleft opened into a hidden valley which seemed spacious after the constriction of its approach. Over a flat floor of packed dirt the sheer walls rose ruggedly to a narrow swath of evening sky. The valley itself was long and deep; its crooked length formed a vague S, ending in another crevice in the hills. Battered rock pillars and piles stood against the walls in several places, and in the corners and crannies around these immense stones, sheltered from any snowfall through the open roof, were Ramen tents – the nomadic homes of individual families. They seemed pitifully few in the canyon.

Manethrall Kam had announced himself with a shout as he entered the valley, and when Covenant and Lena caught up with him, dozens of Ramen were already moving towards them from the tents. Covenant was struck by how much they all shared Kam's haunted air. In sharp contrast to the Ranyhyn, they were not ill-fed. The Ramen were renowned for their skill as hunters, and clearly they were better able to provide more meat for themselves than grass for the horses. Nevertheless they were suffering. Every one of them who was not either a child or infirm wore the apparel of a Cord, though even Covenant's untrained and superficial eyes could see how unready some were for the work and risk of being Cords. This fact confirmed his earlier guess that the Ramen population had been dangerously reduced, by winter or war. And they all had Kam's driven, sleepless aspect, as if they could not rest because their dreams were fraught with horror.

Now Covenant knew intuitively what it was. All of them, even the children, were haunted by the bloody visage of Ranyhyn extermination. They were afraid that the meaning, the reason, of their entire race would soon be eradicated utterly from the Land. The Ramen had always lived for the Ranyhyn, and now they believed they would only survive long enough to see the last Ranyhyn slaughtered. As long as the great horses refused to leave the Plains, the Ramen were helpless to prevent that end.

Only their stubborn, fighting pride kept them from despair.

They met Covenant, Lena and the Giant with silence and hollow stares: Lena hardly seemed to notice them, but Foamfollower gave them a bow in the Ramen style, and Covenant took his example, though the salute exposed his ring for all to see.

Several Cords murmured at the sight of the white gold, and one of the Manethralls said grimly, 'It is true, then. He has returned.' When Kam told them what the wounded Ranyhyn had done, some recoiled in pained amazement, and others muttered angrily under their breath. Yet they all bowed to Covenant; the Ranyhyn had reared to him, and the Ramen could not refuse him welcome.

Then the Winhomes, the Ramen who were too young or too old or too crippled to be Cords, moved away, and the three Manethralls Kam had mentioned earlier came forward to be introduced. When they had given their names, Manethrall Jain, the grim woman who had just spoken, asked Kam, 'Was it necessary to admit the Giant?'

'He's my friend,' Covenant said at once. 'And Bannor knows he can be trusted, even if the Bloodguard are too thickheaded to say such things out loud. I wouldn't be here if it weren't for Saltheart Foamfollower.'

'You honour me too much,' Foamfollower said wryly.

The Manethralls weighed Covenant's words as if his speech had more than one meaning. But Bannor said, 'Saltheart Foamfollower shared the Quest for the Staff of Law with High Lord Prothall, ur-Lord Covenant, and Manethrall Lithe. At that time, he was worthy of trust. But I have seen many trusts fall into corruption. Perhaps nothing of the old Giantish faith remains.'

'You don't believe that,' Covenant snapped.

Bannor raised one eyebrow. 'Have you seen The Grieve, ur-Lord? Has Saltheart Foamfollower told you what occurred in the Seareach home of the Giants?'

'No.'

'Then you have been too quick with your trust.'

Covenant tightened his grip on himself. 'Why don't you tell me about it?'

'That is not my place. I do not offer to guide you to Ridjeck Thome.'

Covenant started to protest, but Foamfollower placed a restraining hand on his shoulder. In spite of the conflicting emotions which knotted the Giant's forehead, smouldered dangerously in his cavernous eye-sockets, his voice was steady as he said, 'Is it the Ramen custom to keep their guests standing cold and hungry after a long journey?'

Kam spat on the ground, but Manethrall Jain replied tautly, 'No, that is not our custom. Behold.' She nodded towards the head of the canyon, where the Winhomes were busy around a large fire under the overhang of one of the pillars. 'The food will be prepared soon. It is *kresh* meat, but you may eat it in safety – it has been cooked many times.' Then she took Lena's arm and said, 'Come. You have suffered at the sight of the Ranyhyn. Thus you share our pain. We will do what we can to restore you.' As she spoke, she guided Lena towards the fire.

Covenant was seething with frustration and dread, but he could not refuse the warmth of the campfire; his flesh needed it too badly. His fingertips and knuckles had a frostbitten look in addition to their sick numbness, and he knew that if he did not tend his feet soon he would be in danger of blood poisoning and gangrene. The effort of self-command hurt him, yet he followed Lena and Jain to the fire. As quietly as he could, he asked one of the Winhomes for hot water in which to bathe his feet.

Despite his numbness, the soaking of his feet gave him relief. The hot water helped the fire's warmth thaw out his bones. And his feet were not as badly damaged as he had feared they would be. Both were swollen with infection, but the harm was no worse than it had been several days ago. For some reason, his flesh was resisting the illness. He was glad to discover that he was in no immediate danger of losing his feet.

A short time later, the food was ready. Kam's seven Cords sat cross-legged around the fire with the four Manethralls, Bannor, Foamfollower, Lena and Covenant, and the Winhomes set dry, brittle banana leaves in front of them as plates. Covenant found himself positioned between Lena and Bannor. A lame man muttering dimly to himself served the three of them stew and hot winter potatoes. Covenant did not relish the idea of eating *kresh* – he expected to find the meat rank and stringy – but it had been cooked so long, with such potent herbs, that only a faint bitterness remained. And it was hot. His appetite for heat seemed insatiable. He ate as if he could see long days of cold, scarce provender ahead of him.

He had good reason. Without help, he and his companions would not be able to find enough food for the journey to Foul's Creche. He seemed to remember having heard somewhere that *aliantha* did not grow in the Spoiled Plains. The hostility of the Ramen boded ill for him in more ways than one.

Though he was afraid of it, he knew he would have to penetrate to the bottom of that hostility.

He looked for an antidote to fear in food, but while he chewed and thought, he was interrupted by a strange man who strode unexpectedly into the covert. The man entered at the far end of the canyon, and moved directly, deliberately, towards the seated men and women. His dress vaguely resembled that of the Ramen; he used the same materials to make his thin shirt and pants, his cloak. But he wore the cloak hanging from his shoulders in a way that affected his freedom of movement more than any Ramen would have tolerated. And he bore no cords anywhere about him. Instead of a Ramen garotte, he carried a short spear like a staff in one hand; and under his belt he wore a sharp wooden stave.

Despite the directness with which he approached, he created an impression of uncomfortable daring, as if he had some reason to believe that the Ramen might jeer at him. His gaze flicked fearfully about him, jumping away from rather than towards what he saw.

He had an air of blood about him that Covenant could not explain. He was clean, uninjured; neither spear nor spike showed recent use. Yet something in him spoke of blood, of killing and hunger. As the man reached the fire, Covenant realized that all the Ramen were sitting stiffly in their places – not moving, not eating, not looking at the stranger. They knew this man in a way that gave them pain.

After a moment, the man said aggressively, 'Do you eat without me? I, too, need food.'

Manethrall Jain's eyes did not raise themselves from the ground. 'You are welcome, as you know. Join us or take what food you require.'

'Am I so welcome? Where are the salutes and words of greeting? Pah! You do not even gaze at me.'

But when Kam glared up from under his angry brows at the stranger, the man winced and looked away.

Jain said softly, 'You have drunk blood.'

'Yes!' the man barked rapidly. 'And you are offended. You understand nothing. If I were not the best runner and Ranyhyn-tender in the Plains of Ra, you would slay me where I stand without a moment's concern for your promises.'

Darkly, Kam muttered, 'We are not so swift to forget promises.'

The stranger took no notice of Kam's assertion. 'Now I see guests among you. The Ringthane himself. And a Giant – ' he drawled acerbically – 'if my eyes do not mistake. Are Ravers also welcome?'

Covenant was surprised to hear Bannor speaking before either Jain or Kam could reply. 'He is Saltheart Foamfollower.' The Bloodguard's alien inflection carried an odd note of intensity, as if he were communicating a crucial fact.

'Saltheart Foamfollower!' the stranger jeered. But he did not meet the Giant's gaze. 'Then you are already certain that he is a Raver.'

Kam said, 'We are uncertain.'

Still the man ignored him. 'And the Ringthane – the tormentor of horses. Does he also Rave? He holds his proper place – at the right hand of a Bloodguard. This is a proud feast – all the cruellest foes of the Ranyhyn together. And welcome!'

At this, Jain's tone tightened. 'You are also welcome. Join us – or take what food you require and go.'

A Winhome moved hesitantly towards the stranger, carrying a leaf laden with food. He caught it from her hands brusquely. 'I will go. I hear your heart deny your words. I am not proud or welcome enough to eat with such as these.' At once, he turned sarcastically on his heel, strode back the way he had come. Moments later, he had left the covert as abruptly as he had entered.

Covenant stared uncomprehendingly after him, then looked towards the Manethralls for some explanation. But they sat glowering at their food as if they could not meet either his eyes or each other's. Foamfollower also showed no understanding of what had happened. Lena had not noticed it; she was half asleep where she sat. Covenant turned to Bannor.

The Bloodguard faced Covenant's question squarely, answered it with the same dispassionate intensity. 'He is Pietten.'

'Pietten,' Covenant repeated dismally. And Foamfollower echoed thickly, 'Pietten!'

'He and the Heer Llaura were saved by the Quest for the Staff of Law at the battle of Soaring Woodhelven. Do you remember? Llaura and the child Pietten were damaged – '

'I remember,' Covenant answered bitterly. 'The ur-viles did something to them. They were used to bait the trap. She – she – ' The memory appalled him. Llaura had been horribly abused, and all her great courage had not sufficed to overcome what had been done to her. And the child, Pietten – the child, too, had been abused.

Across Covenant's dismay, Foamfollower said, 'We bore both Heer Llaura and Pietten to the Plains of Ra and Manhome.' Covenant remembered that the Giant had carried Pietten in his arms. 'There, at the request of the Ringthane and – and myself – the Ramen took Llaura and Pietten into their care.'

Bannor nodded. 'That is the promise of which he spoke.'

'Llaura?' asked Covenant weakly.

'While Pietten was yet young she died. The harm done to her cut short her years.'

'And Pietten?' Foamfollower pursued. 'What did the ur-viles do to him?'

Manethrall Kam broke his silence to mutter, 'He is mad.'

But Jain countered grimly, 'He is the best runner and Ranyhyn-tender in the Plains of Ra – as he said.'

'He serves the Ranyhyn,' Bannor added. 'He cares for them as entirely as any Manethrall. But there is – ' he searched briefly for a description – 'a ferocity in his love. He – '

'He liked the taste of blood,' Covenant interrupted. In his memory, he could see Pietten – hardly more than four years old – under the crimson light of the sick moon. Pietten had smeared his hands on the bloody grass, then licked his fingers and smiled.

Bannor agreed with a nod.

'He licks the wounds of the Ranyhyn to clean them!' Kam snapped in horror.

'Because of his great skill with the Ranyhyn,' Bannor went on, 'and because of old promises made in the days of the Quest, the Ramen share their lives and work with him. But he is feared for his wildness. Therefore he lives alone. And he abuses the Ramen as if they have outcast him.'

'Yet he fights,' Jain breathed a moment later. 'I have seen that spear slay three *kresh* in their very death hold on a Ranyhyn.'

'He fights,' Kam murmured. 'He is mad.'

Covenant took a deep breath as if he were trying to inhale courage. 'And we're responsible – Foamfollower and I – we're the ones who gave him to you, so we're responsible. Is that it?'

At the sound of his voice, Lena stirred, blinked wearily, and Foamfollower said, 'No, my friend.'

But Manethrall Jain answered in a haunted voice, 'The Ranyhyn have chosen you. We do not ask you to save them.'

And Kam added, 'You may call that pride if you wish. The Ranyhyn are worthy of all pride.'

'And the responsibility is mine,' Foamfollower said in a tone of pain that made Covenant's hearing ache. 'The blame is mine. For after the battle of Soaring Woodhelven – when all the Quest knew that some nameless harm had been done to the child – it was I who denied to him that hurtloam which might have healed him.'

This also Covenant remembered. Stricken by remorse for all the Cavewights he had slain, Foamfollower had used the last of the hurtloam to ease one of the wounded creatures rather than to treat Pietten. In protest against the Giant's self-judgement, Covenant said, 'You didn't *deny* it. You – '

'I did not *give* it.' Foamfollower's response was as final as an axe.

'Oh, hell!' Covenant glared around the group, searching for some way in which to grasp the situation. But he did not find it.

He had unintentionally roused Lena. She pulled herself erect, and asked, 'Beloved, what is amiss?'

Covenant took her hand in his numb fingers. 'Don't worry about it. I'm just trying to figure out what's going on here.'

'My Queen,' Foamfollower interposed. He wiped his mouth, set aside the leaves which had held his meal, then climbed to his feet. Towering over the circle of Ramen, he stepped forward to stand beside the fire. 'My Queen, our difficulty is that the Ramen misdoubt me. They have spoken their respect for you, Lena Atiaran-daughter, and their acceptance of ur-Lord Thomas Covenant, Unbeliever and Ringthane. But me they distrust.'

Lena looked up at him. 'Then they are fools,' she said with dignity.

'No.' Foamfollower smiled wanly. 'It is true that I have been a guest at Manhome, and a companion of Manethrall Lithe on the Quest for the Staff of Law. And it is true that Bannor of the Bloodguard has known me. We fought together at the battle of Soaring Woodhelven. But they are not fools. They suffer a doom of Giants, and their distrust must be respected.'

He turned to the four Manethralls. 'Yet, though I acknowledge your doubt, it is hard for me to bear. My heart urges me to leave this place where I am not trusted. You could not easily stop me. But I do not go. My thoughts urge me to turn to my friend Thomas Covenant. Perhaps he would compel you to accept me. But I do not ask this of him. I must bring your acceptance upon myself. I will strive to meet your doubt – so that the enemies of the Despiser, Soulcrusher and Fangthane, may not be divided against themselves. Ask anything that you require.'

The Manethralls looked sharply at each other, and Covenant felt the atmosphere over the gathering tighten. The Giant's face was ominously calm, as if he recognized a personal crisis and understood how to meet it. But Covenant did not understand. The hostility of the Ramen continued to amaze him. He ached to jump to the Giant's defence.

He refrained because he saw why Foamfollower wanted to prove himself – and because he had a fascinated, fearful desire to see how the Giant would do it.

After a wordless consultation with the other Manethralls, Jain got to her feet and confronted Foamfollower across the fire. Unbidden, Bannor joined her. They regarded the Giant gravely for a long moment. Then Jain said, 'Saltheart Foamfollower, the Render is cunning in malice. To discover him in all his secret treacheries requires an equal cunning. The Ramen have no such cunning. How is it possible for us to test you?'

'Enquire of my past,' Foamfollower responded evenly. 'I was absent from Giant-wrought *Coercri* when the Ravers put their hands upon my kindred. Since that time, I have roved the Land, striking – slaying marauders. I have fought at the side of the Stonedownors in defence of their homes. I – '

'They had creatures which destroyed stone!' Lena cut in with sudden vehemence. 'Their great, cruel arms tore our homes to rubble. Without the Giant's strength, we could not have preserved one rock upright.'

'Lena.' Covenant wanted to applaud, cheer her affirmation, but he stopped her gently, squeezed her arm until she turned her angry gaze towards him. 'He doesn't need our help,' he said as if he were afraid her ire might break the frail bones of her face. 'He can answer for himself.'

Slowly, her anger turned to pain. 'Why do they torment us? We seek to save the Ranyhyn also. The Ranyhyn trust us.'

Covenant steadied her as best he could. 'They've suffered. They've got to answer for themselves too.'

'I also shared somewhat in the returning of Thomas Covenant to the Land,' Foamfollower continued. 'He would not sit here now, purposing to aid the Land, had I not given of my strength.'

'That does not suffice,' said Jain sternly. 'The Render would not hesitate to kill his own for the sake of a larger goal. Perhaps you served the Stonedownors and the summoning so that this white gold might fall into Fangthane's hands.'

'And you have not given an account of The Grieve,' Bannor's voice was soft, withdrawn, as if the question he raised were perilous.

But Foamfollower turned such issues aside with a jerk of his massive head. 'Then discount my past — discount the scars of risk which cover my flesh. It is possible that I am a tool of the Despiser. Enquire of what you see. Behold me. Do you truly believe that a Raver might disguise himself within me?'

'How can we answer?' Jain muttered. 'We have never seen you hale.'

But Foamfollower was facing Bannor now, addressing his question to the Bloodguard.

Evenly, objectively, Bannor replied, 'Giant, you do not appear well. Many things are obscured in this winter — but you do not appear well. There is a lust in you that I do not comprehend. It has the look of Corruption.'

The Manethralls nodded in sharp agreement.

'Bannor!' Foamfollower breathed intently. His stiff calm broke momentarily, and a pang of anguish twisted his countenance. 'Do not damn me with such short words. It may be that I too much resemble Pietten. I have struck blows that I cannot call back or prevent. And you have seen — there is the blood of Giants upon my head.'

The blood of Giants? Covenant moaned. Foamfollower!

The next instant, Foamfollower regained mastery of himself. 'But you have known me, Bannor. You can see that it is not my intent to serve the Despiser. I could not – !' The words ripped themselves savagely past his lips.

'I have known you,' Bannor agreed simply. 'In what way do I know you now?'

The Giant's hands twitched as if they were eager for a violent answer, but he kept his steadiness. Without dropping Bannor's gaze, he knelt by the fire. Even then he was taller than Bannor or Manethrall Jain. His muscles tensed as he leaned forward, and the orange firelight echoed dangerously out of the dark caves of his eyes.

'You have seen the *caamora*, Bannor,' he said tightly, 'the Giantish ritual fire of grief. You have seen its pain. I am not prepared – this is not my time for such rituals. But I will not withdraw until you acknowledge me, Bannor of the Bloodguard.'

He did not release Bannor's eyes as he thrust both his fists into the hottest coals of the campfire.

The Cords gasped at the sight, and the other Manethralls jumped up to join Jain. Covenant followed as if the Giant had snatched him erect.

Foamfollower was rigid with agony. Though the flames did not consume his flesh, they tortured him horrendously. The muscles of his forehead bulged and worked as if they were tearing his skull apart; the thews of his neck stood out like cables; sweat oozed like blood down his fire-hot cheeks; his lips drew back into a white snarl across his teeth. But his gaze did not waver. In anguish he kept up the demand of his pain.

Bannor stared back with a look of magisterial indifference on his alien mien.

The Cords were appalled. They gaped sickly at Foamfollower's hands. And the Manethralls painfully, fearfully, watched Bannor and the Giant, measuring the test of will between them. But Lena gave a low cry and hid her face in Covenant's shoulder.

Covenant, too, could not bear to see Foamfollower's hurt. He turned on Bannor and gasped into the Bloodguard's ear, 'Give it up! Admit you know him. Hellfire! Bannor – you bloody egomaniac! You're so proud – after the Bloodguard failed you can't stand to admit there might be any faithfulness left anywhere. It's you or nothing. But he's a Giant, Bannor!' Bannor did not move, but a muscle quivered along his jaw. 'Wasn't Elena enough for you?' Covenant hissed. 'Are you trying to make *another* Kevin out of him?'

For an instant, Bannor's white eyebrows gathered into a stark frown. Then he said flatly, 'Pardon me, Saltheart Foamfollower. I trust you.'

Foamfollower withdrew his hands. They were rigid with pain, and he hugged them to his chest, panting hoarsely.

Bannor turned to Covenant. Something in his pose made Covenant flinch as if he expected the Bloodguard to strike him. 'You also caused the fall of High Lord Elena,' Bannor said brittlely. 'You compelled us to reveal the unspoken name. Yet you did not bear the burden of that name yourself. Therefore the Law of Death was broken, and Elena fell. I did not reproach you then, and do not now. But I say to you: beware, ur-Lord Covenant! You hold too many dooms in your unwell hands.'

'I know that,' muttered Covenant. He was shaking so badly that he had to keep both arms around Lena to support himself. 'I know that. It's the only thing I know for sure.' He could not look at Foamfollower; he was afraid of the Giant's pain, afraid that the Giant might resent his intervention. Instead, he held on to Lena while his reaction to the strain surged into anger.

'But I've had enough of this.' His voice was too violent, but he did not care. He needed some outlet for his passion. 'I'm not interested in asking for help any more. Now I'm going to *tell* you what to do. Manethrall Lithe promised that the Ramen would do whatever I wanted. You care about promises – you keep this one. I want food, all we can carry. I want guides to take us to Landsdrop as fast as possible. I want scouts to help us get across the Spoiled Plains.' Words tumbled through his teeth faster than he could control them. 'If Foamfollower's been crippled – By hell, you're going to make it up to him!'

'Ask for the moon,' Manethrall Kam muttered.

'Don't tempt me!' Hot shouts thronged in his throat like fire; he whirled to fling flames at the Manethralls. But their haunted eyes stopped him. They did not deserve his rage. Like Bannor and Foamfollower, they were the victims of the Despiser – the victims of the thing he, Thomas Covenant, had not done, had been unwilling or unable to do, for the Land. Again, he could feel the ground on which he stood tremoring.

With an effort, he turned back to Bannor, met the Bloodguard's ageing gaze. 'What happened to Elena wasn't your fault at all,' he mumbled. 'She and I – did it together. Or I did it to her.' Then he pushed himself to go to Foamfollower.

But as he moved, Lena caught his arm, swung him around. He had been bracing himself on her without paying any attention to her: now she made him look at her. 'Elena – my daughter – what has happened to her?' Horror crackled in her eyes. The next instant, she was clawing at his chest with desperate fingers. 'What has happened to her?'

Covenant stared at her. He had half forgotten, he had not wanted to remember that she knew nothing of Elena's end.

'He said she fell!' she cried at him. 'What have you done to her?'

He held her at arm's length, backed away from her. Suddenly everything was too much for him. Lena, Foamfollower, Bannor, the Ramen – he could not keep a grip on it all at once. He turned his head towards Foamfollower, ignored Lena, and looked dumbly to the Giant for help. But Foamfollower did not even see Covenant's stricken, silent plea. He was still wrapped in his own pain, struggling to flex his racked fingers. Covenant lowered his head and turned back towards Lena as if she were a wall against which he had to batter himself.

'She's dead,' he said thickly. 'It's my fault – she wouldn't have been in that mess if it hadn't been for me. I didn't save her because I didn't know how.'

He heard shouts behind him, but they made no impression on him. He was watching Lena. Slowly the import of his words penetrated her. 'Dead,' she echoed emptily. 'Fault.' As Covenant watched her, the light of consciousness in her eyes seemed to falter and go out.

'Lena,' he groaned. 'Lena!'

Her gaze did not recognize him. She stared blankly through him as if her soul had lapsed within her.

The shouting behind him mounted. A voice nearby gasped out, 'We are betrayed! Ur-viles and Cavewights – ! The sentries were slain.'

The urgency in the voice reached him. He turned dully. A young Cord almost chattering with fear stood before the Manethralls and Bannor. Behind her, in the entrance to the covert, fighting had already begun. Covenant could hear the shouts and groans of frantic hand-to-hand combat echoing out of the rift.

The next instant, a tight pack of Cavewights burst into the canyon, whirling huge broadswords in their powerful, spatulate hands. With a shrill roar, they charged the Ramen.

Before Covenant could react, Bannor caught hold of him and Lena, began to drag them both towards the other end of the valley. 'Flee,' he said distinctly as he impelled them forward. 'The Giant and I will prevent pursuit. We will overtake you – as soon as may be. Flee north, then east.'

The cliffs narrowed until Covenant and Lena stood in the mouth of another cleft through the hills. Bannor thrust them in the direction of the dark crevice. 'Make haste. Keep to the left.' Then he was gone, running towards the battle.

Half unconsciously, Covenant checked to be sure that he still had

Triock's knife under his belt. Part of him yearned to run after Bannor, to throw himself like Bannor into the absolution of the fray – to seek forgiveness.

Clutching hard at Lena's arm, he drew her with him into the cleft.

10

PARIAH

After the first bend, even the trailing light of the campfires was cut off, and he could see nothing. Lena moved like a puppet in his grasp – empty and unadept. He wanted her to hold on to him, so that he would have both hands free; but when he wrapped her fingers around his arm, they slipped limply off again. He was forced to grope ahead with his left hand, and retain her with his maimed right. His numbness made him feel at every moment that he was about to lose her.

The shouting pursued him along the crevice furiously, trying to keep himself from being frantic.

When the rift divided, he followed the left wall. In a few steps, this crevice became so narrow that he had to move along it sideways, pulling Lena after him. Then it began to descend. Soon it was so steep that the mouldering leaves and loam of the floor occasionally shifted under their feet. There the rift became a tunnel. The stone sealed over their heads, while the floor levelled until the ceiling was so close that it made Covenant duck for fear he might crack open his skull. The utter lightlessness of the passage dismayed him. He felt that he was groping his way blindly into the bowels of the earth, felt at every step that the tunnel might pitch him into a chasm. He no longer heard any sound from the canyon; his own loud scrabbling filled his ears. Yet he did not stop. The pressure of his urgency, the pressure of the blind stone impending over the back of his neck, compelled him onward.

Still Lena gave no sign of life. She stumbled, moved at his pull, bumped dumbly against the walls of the tunnel; but her arm in his grasp was inert. He could not even hear her breathing. He tugged her after him as if she were a mindless child.

At last the tunnel ended. Without warning, the stone vanished, and Covenant blundered into a thicket. The stems and branches lashed at him as if he were an enemy. Protecting his eyes with his forearm, he thrust ahead until he found himself on open ground, sweating in the teeth of the wind.

The night was as dank and bitter as ever, but after the pitch blackness of the tunnel he found that he could see vaguely. He and Lena stood below a high, looming bluff. Thickets and brush covered most of its base, but beyond them the ground sloped down barrenly towards the Plains of Ra.

He paused in the scything wind and tried to take stock of the situation. The tunnel from this side was well disguised by the thickets and underbrush, but still the Ramen should have posted sentries here. Where were they? He saw no one, heard nothing but the wind.

He was tempted to call out, but the frigid emptiness of the night restrained him. If the Ramen were defeated, the marauders would have no difficulty following him through the tunnel; Cavewights and ur-viles could take such passages in the dark gleefully. Ur-viles might already be watching him from the thicket.

North, then east, Bannor had said. He knew he had to start moving. But he had no supplies – no food, no bedding, no fire. Even if he were not pursued, he could hardly hope to survive in this cold. If Bannor and the Giant did not come soon, he and Lena were finished.

But Bannor had said that they would overtake him. It's too late, he muttered to steady his resolve, it's too late to start worrying about the impossible. It's all been impossible from the beginning. Just get going. At least get her out of this wind.

He put Lena on his left, wrapped his arm around her, and started north across the preternatural current of the winter.

He hurried as much as possible, supporting Lena, glancing fearfully back over his shoulder to see if they were being followed. When he reached a break in the hills on his left, he faced a difficult decision: Bannor and Foamfollower would locate him more easily if he stayed on the edge of the Plains, but if he moved up among the hills he would have a better chance of finding shelter and *aliantha*. After a painful moment, he chose the hills. He would have to trust the hunting skills of his friends; Lena was his first concern.

He laboured strenuously up through the break, half carrying his companion. Once he had passed beyond the first crests, he found a shallow valley running roughly northward which provided some cover from the wind. But he did not stop; he was not far enough from the tunnel. Instead, he took Lena along the valley and into the hills beyond it.

On the way, he stumbled by chance into a battered *aliantha*. It had few berries, but its presence there reassured him somewhat. He ate two berries himself, then tried to get Lena to take the others. But she neither saw the *aliantha* nor heard his demands; all her outer senses were blank.

He ate the rest of the treasure-berries so that they would not be wasted, then left the bush behind and took Lena along and out of the valley. For a long time after that, he could not find an easy way through the hills. He struggled generally northward, searching for usable valleys or paths, but the terrain turned him insistently east, downhill towards the plains. Now the sweat was freezing his beard again, and his muscles slowly stiffened against the icy cut of the wind. Whenever the wind hit Lena directly, she trembled. At last her need for shelter became imperative in his mind. When he saw a darker shadow which looked like a gulley in the wasteland below him, he gave up on the hills and went down to it.

It had not deceived him. It was a dry arroyo with sheer sides. In places its walls were more than ten feet high. He took Lena down an uneven slope into the gulley, then guided her under the lee of the opposite wall and seated her with her back against the packed dirt.

As he peered at her through the darkness, her condition scared him. She shivered constantly now, and her skin was cold and clammy. Her face held no recognition, no awareness of where she was or what was happening to her. He chafed her wrists roughly, but her arms remained limp, as if the cold had unmarrowed her bones. 'Lena,' he called to her hesitantly, then with more force. 'Lena!' She did not answer. She sat slack against the wall as if she had decided to freeze to death rather than acknowledge the fact that the man she loved was a murderer.

'Lena!' he begged gruffly. 'Don't make me do this. I don't want to do it again.'

She did not respond. The irregular moan and catch of her breathing gave no indication that she had heard him. She looked as brittle as frostbitten porcelain.

With a fierce grimace clenched on his face, he drew back his halfhand and struck her hard across the side of her head for the second time in his life.

Her head snapped soddenly to the side, swung back towards him. For an instant, her breath shuddered in her lungs, and her lips trembled as if the air hurt her mouth. Then suddenly her hands leaped out like claws. Her nails dug into the flesh of his face around his eyes. She gripped him there, gouging him, poised ready to tear his eyes out.

A sharp nausea of fear wrenched his guts, made him flinch. But he did not back away.

After a moment, she said starkly, 'You slew Elena my daughter.'

'Yes.'

Her fingers tightened. 'I could blind you.'

'Yes.'

'Are you afraid?'

'I'm afraid.'

Her fingers tightened again. 'Then why do you not resist?' Her nails drew blood from his left cheek.

'Because I've got to talk to you – about what happened to Elena. I've got to tell you what she did – and what I did – and why I did it. You won't listen unless you decide – '

'I will not listen at all!' Her voice shook with weeping. Savagely, she snatched back her hand and returned his blow, struck his cheek with all her strength. The sting brought water to his eyes. When he blinked them clear, he saw that she had clamped her hands to her face to keep herself from sobbing aloud.

Awkwardly, he put his arms around her. She did not resist. He held her firmly while she wept, and after a time she moved her head, pressed her face into his jacket. But soon she stiffened and withdrew. She wiped her eyes, averting her face as if she were ashamed of a momentary weakness. 'I do not want your comfort, Unbeliever. You have not been her father. It is a father's place to love his daughter, and you did not love her. Do not mistake my frail grief – I will not forget what you have done.'

Covenant hugged himself in an effort to contain his hurt. 'I don't want you to forget.' For that moment, he would have been willing to lose his eyes if the pain of blindness could have enabled him to weep. 'I don't want anyone to forget.'

But he was too barren for tears; the water which blurred his sight did not come from his heart. Roughly, he forced himself to his feet. 'Come on. We'll freeze to death if we don't get moving.'

Before she could respond, he heard feet hit the ground behind him. He whirled, waving his hands to ward off an attack. A dark figure stood opposite him in the gulley. It was wrapped in a cloak; he could not discern its outlines. But it carried a spear like a staff in its right hand.

'Pah!' the figure spat out. 'You would be dead five times if I had not chosen to watch over you.'

'Pietten?' Covenant asked in surprise. 'What're you doing here?' Lena was at his side, but she did not touch him.

'You are stupid as well as unskilled,' rasped Pietten. 'I saw at once that the Ramen would not defend you. I took the task upon myself. What folly made you deliver yourself into their hands?'

'What happened in the fight?' Questions rushed up in Covenant.

'What happened to Bannor and Foamfollower? Where are they?'

'Come!' the Woodhelvennin snapped. 'Those wormspawn are not far behind. We must move swiftly if you wish to live.'

Covenant stared. Pietten's attitude unnerved him. For an instant, his jaw worked uselessly. Then he repeated with a note of desperation in his voice, 'What happened to Bannor and Foamfollower?'

'You will not see them again.' Pietten sounded scornful. 'You will see nothing again unless you follow me now. You have no food and no skill. Remain here, and you will be dead before I have gone a league.' Without waiting for answer, he turned and trotted away along the gulley.

Covenant hesitated indecisively while contradictory fears clamoured at him. He did not want to trust Pietten. His instincts shouted loudly, He drinks blood! Foul did something to him and he likes the taste of blood! But he and Lena were too helpless. They could not fend for themselves. Abruptly, he took Lena's arm and started after Pietten.

The Ramen-trained Woodhelvennin allowed Covenant and Lena to catch up with him, but then he set a pace for them which kept Covenant from asking any questions. Travelling swiftly, he guided them northward out of the arroyo into the open Plains, hastened them along like a man with a goal clearly visible before him. When they showed signs of tiring, he irritably found *aliantha* for them. But he revealed no weariness himself; he moved strongly, surely, revelling in the flow of his strides. And from time to time he grinned jeeringly at Covenant and Lena, mocking them for their inability to match him.

They followed him as if they were entranced, spellbound to him by the harsh winter and their extreme need. Covenant maintained the pace doggedly, and Lena laboured at his side, spurning his every effort to help her. Her new, grim independence seemed to sustain her; she covered nearly two leagues before she began to weaken. Then, however, her strength rapidly deserted her.

Covenant was deeply tired himself, but he ached to aid her. When she stumbled for the third time, and could hardly regain her feet, he demanded breathlessly across the wind, 'Pietten, we've got to rest. We need fire and shelter.'

'You are not hardy, Ringthane,' Pietten gibed. 'Why do so many people fear you?'

'We can't go on like this.'

'You will freeze to death if you stop here.'

Painfully, Covenant mustered the strength to shout, 'I know that! Are you going to help us or not?'

Pietten's voice sounded oddly cunning as he replied, 'We will be safer – beyond the river. It is not far.' He hurried on before Covenant could question him.

Covenant and Lena made the effort to follow him and found that he had spoken the truth. Soon they reached the banks of a dark river flowing eastward out of the hills. It lay forbiddingly across their way like a stream of black ice, but Pietten jumped into it at once and waded straight to the opposite bank. The current was stiff, but did not reach above his knees.

Cursing, Covenant watched him go. His weariness multiplied his distrust; his instinctive leper's caution was yowling inside him like a wounded animal. He did not know this river, but he guessed it was the Roamsedge, Ra's northern boundary. He feared that Bannor and Foamfollower would not expect him to leave the Plains – if they were still alive.

But he still had no choice. The Woodhelvennin was their only chance.

'Will you halt there?' Pietten scoffed at them from the far bank. 'Halt and die.'

Hellfire! Covenant snarled to himself. He took Lena's arm despite her angry efforts to pull away, and went down the bank into the river.

His feet felt nothing of the cold, but it burned like numb fire into his lower legs. Before he had waded a dozen yards, his knees hurt as if his calves were being shredded by the river. He tried to hurry, but the speed of the current and the unevenness of the river bottom only made him trip and stagger brokenly. He clung to Lena's arm and ploughed onward with his gaze fixed on the bank ahead.

When he stumbled up out of the river, his legs ached as if they had been maimed. 'Damn you, Pietten,' he muttered. 'Now we have got to have a fire.'

Pietten bowed sardonically. 'Whatever you command, Ringthane.' Turning on his heel, he ran lightly away into the low hills north of the river like a sprite enticing them to perdition.

Covenant lumbered in pursuit, and when he crested the hill, he saw that Pietten had already started a fire in the hollow beyond it. Flames crackled in a dry patch of brambles and bushes. As Covenant and Lena descended towards it, the fire spread, jumping fiendishly higher and higher as it ran through the dead wood.

They hastened fervidly to the blaze. Lena's legs gave way at the last moment, and she fell to her knees as if that were the only way she could prevent herself from leaping into the flames. And Covenant spread his arms to the heat, stood on the very verge of the fire and threw open his jacket like an acolyte embracing vision. For long moments they neither spoke nor moved.

But when the warmth melted the ice to make itself felt against Covenant's forehead, started to draw the moisture in steam from his clothes, he stepped back a pace and looked about him.

Pietten was leering at him mercilessly.

He felt suddenly trapped, cornered; for reasons that he could not name, he knew he was in danger. He looked quickly towards Lena. But she was absorbed in the fire, oblivious. Unwillingly he met Pietten's gaze again. That stare held him like the eyes of a snake, trying to paralyse him. 'That was a damn stupid thing to do.' He indicated the fire with a jerk of one hand. 'A fire this big will throw light over the hill. We'll be seen.'

'I know.' Pietten licked his lips.

'You know,' Covenant muttered mordantly. 'Did it occur to you that this could bring a pack of marauders down on us?' He snarled the words thoughtlessly, but as soon as he had spoken them, they sent a stammer of fear through him.

'Are you not grateful?' Pietten grinned maliciously. 'You command fire – fire I provide. Is that not how men show their devotion to the Ringthane?'

'What are we going to do if we're attacked? She and I are in no condition to fight.'

'I know.'

'You know,' Covenant repeated. The upsurge of his trepidation almost made him stutter.

'But no marauders will come,' the Woodhelvennin went on immediately. 'I hate them. Pah! They slay Ranyhyn.'

'What do you mean, they won't come? You said – ' he searched his memory – 'you said they weren't far behind. How in hell do you expect them to miss us in all this light?'

'I do not want them to miss us.'

'What!' The fear taking shape within him made him shout. 'Hellfire! Make sense!'

'Ringthane,' Pietten shot back with sudden vehemence, 'this night I will complete the whole sense of my life!'

The next instant he had returned to scorn. 'I desire them to find us, yes! I desire them to see this blaze and come. Land friends – horse servants – pah! They torment the Ranyhyn in the name of faith. I will teach them faith.' Covenant felt Lena jump to her feet behind him; he could sense the way she focused herself on Pietten. In the warmth of the fire, he finally noticed what had caught her attention. It was the smell of blood. 'I desire the Giant my benefactor and Bannor the Bloodguard to stand upon this hillside and witness my faith.'

'You said that they are dead!' Lena hissed. 'You said that we would not see them again.'

At the same time, Covenant croaked, 'It was you!' His apprehension burst into clarity. 'You did it.' In the lurid light of the fire, he caught his first glimpse of his plight. 'You're the one who betrayed all those coverts!'

Lena's movement triggered him into movement. He was one step ahead of her as she threw herself at Pietten.

But Pietten was too swift for them. He aimed his spear and braced himself to impale the first attack.

Covenant leaped to a stop. Grappling frantically, he caught Lena, held her from hurling herself on to Pietten's weapon. She struggled for one mute, furious moment, then became still in his grasp. Her bedraggled white hair hung across her face like a fringe of madness. Grimly, he set her behind him.

He was trembling, but he forced himself to face Pietten. 'You want them to watch while you kill us.'

Pietten laughed sourly. 'Do they not deserve it?' His eyes flashed as if a lightning of murder played behind them. 'If I could have my wish, I would place the entire Ramen nation around this hollow so that they might behold my contempt for them. Ranyhyn servants! Pah! They are vermin.'

'Render!' Lena spat hoarsely.

With his left hand, Covenant held her behind him. 'You betrayed those coverts – you betrayed them all. You're the only one who could have done it. You killed the sentries and showed those marauders how to get in. No wonder you stink of blood.'

'It pleases me.'

'You betrayed the Ranyhyn!' Covenant raged. 'Injured Ranyhyn got slaughtered!'

At this, Pietten jerked forward, brandished his spear viciously. 'Hold your tongue, Ringthane!' he snapped. 'Do not question my faith. I have fought – I would slay any living creature that raised his hands against the Ranyhyn.'

'Do you call that faith? There were injured Ranyhyn in that covert, and they were butchered!'

'They were murdered by Ramen!' Pietten retorted redly. 'Vermin! They pretend service to the Ranyhyn, but they do not take the Ranyhyn to the safety of the south. I hold no fealty for them.' Lena tried to leap at Pietten again, but Covenant restrained her. 'They are like you – and that Giant – and the Bloodguard! Pah! You feast on Ranyhyn-flesh like jackals.'

With an effort, Covenant made Lena look at him. 'Go!' he whispered rapidly. 'Run. Get out of here. Get back across the river – try to find Bannor or Foamfollower! He doesn't care about you. He won't chase you. He wants me.'

Pietten cocked his spear. 'If you take one step to flee,' he grated, 'I will kill the Ringthane where he stands and hunt you down like a wolf.'

The threat carried conviction. 'All right,' Covenant groaned to Lena. 'All right.' Glowering thunderously, he swung back towards Pietten. 'Do you remember ur-viles, Pietten? Soaring Woodhelven? Fire and ur-viles? They captured you. Do you remember?'

Pietten stared back like lightning.

'They captured you. They did things to you. Just as they did to Llaura. Do you remember her? They hurt her inside so that she had to help trap the Lords. The harder she tried to break free, the worse the trap got. Do you remember? It's just like that with you. They hurt you so that you would – destroy the Ranyhyn. Listen to me! Foul knew when he started this war that he wouldn't be able to crush the Ranyhyn unless he found some way to betray the Ramen. So he hurt you. He made you do what he wants. He's using you to butcher the Ranyhyn! And he's probably given you special orders about me. What did he tell you to do with my ring?' He hurled the words at Pietten with all his strength. 'How many bloody times have you been to Foul's Creche since this winter started?'

For a moment, Pietten's eyes lost their focus. Dimly, he murmured, 'I must take it to him. He will use it to save the Ranyhyn.' But the next instant, white fury flared in him again. 'You lie! I love the Ranyhyn! You are the butchers, you and those vermin!'

'That isn't true. You know it isn't true.'

'Is it not?' Pietten laughed desperately. 'Do you think I am blind, Ringthane? I have learned much in – in my journeys. Do you think the Ramen hold the Ranyhyn here out of love?'

'They can't help it,' Covenant replied. 'The Ranyhyn refuse to go.'

Pietten did not hear him. 'Do you think the Bloodguard are here out of love? You are a fool! Bannor is here because he has caused the deaths of so many Ranyhyn that he has become a betrayer. He needs to betray, as he did the Lords. Oh, he fights – he has always fought. He hungers to see every Ranyhyn slain in spite of his fighting so that his need will be fed. Pah!'

Covenant tried to interrupt, protest, but Pietten rushed on: 'Do you think the Giant is here out of love? You are anile – sick with trust. Foamfollower is here because he has betrayed his people. Every last Giant, every man, woman and child of his kindred, lies dead and mouldered in Seareach because he abandoned them! He fled rather than defend them. His very bones are made of treachery, and he is here because he can find no one else to betray. All his other companions are dead.'

Foamfollower! Covenant cried in stricken silence. All dead? Foamfollower!

'And you, Ringthane – you are the worst of all. You surpass my contempt. You ask what I remember.' His spear point waved patterns of outrage at Covenant's chest. 'I remember that the Ranyhyn reared to you. I remember that I strove to stop you. But you had already chosen to betray them. You bound them with promises – promises which you knew they could not break. Therefore the Ranyhyn cannot seek the safety of the mountains. They are shackled by commitments which you forced from them, you! You are the true butcher, Ringthane, I have lived my life for the chance to slay you.'

'No,' Covenant gasped. 'I didn't know.' But he heard the truth in Pietten's accusation. Waves of crime seemed to spread from him in all directions. 'I didn't know.'

Bannor? he moaned. Foamfollower? A livid orange mist filled his sight like the radiance of brimstone. How could he have done so much harm? He had only wanted to survive – had only wanted to extract survival from the raw stuff of suicide and madness. The Giants! – lost like Elena. And now the Ranyhyn were being driven down the same bloody road. Foamfollower? Did I do this to you? He knew that he was defenceless, that he could have done nothing to ward off a spear thrust. But he was staring into the abyss of his own actions and could not look away.

'We're the same,' he breathed without knowing what he was saying. 'Foul and I are the same.'

Then he became aware that hands were pulling at him. Lena had gripped his jacket and was shaking him as hard as she could. 'Is it true?' she shouted at him. 'Are they dying because you made them promise to visit me each year?'

He met her eyes. They were full of firelight; they compelled him to recognize still another of his crimes. In spite of his peril, he could not refuse her the truth.

'No.' His throat was clogged with grief and horror. 'That's only part – Even if they went into the mountains, they could still reach you. I – I – ' his voice ached thickly – 'I made them promise to save me – if I ever called them. I did it for myself.'

Pietten laughed.

A cry of fury and despair tore between her lips. With the strength of revulsion, she thrust Covenant from her, then started to run out of the hollow.

'Stop!' Pietten barked after her. 'You cannot escape!' He turned as she ran, following her with the tip of his spear.

In the instant that Pietten cocked his arm to throw, Covenant charged. He got his hands on the spear, heaved his weight against Pietten, tried to tear the spear away. Pietten recoiled a few steps under the onslaught. They wrestled furiously. But the grip of Covenant's halfhand was too weak. With a violent wrench, Pietten twisted the spear free.

Covenant grappled for Pietten's arms. Pietten knocked him back with the butt of the spear and stabbed its point at him. Covenant threw himself to the side, managed to avoid the thrust. But he landed heavily on one foot, with the ankle bent under his weight.

Bones snapped. He heard them retorting through his flesh as he crashed to the ground, heard himself scream. Agony erupted in his leg. But he made himself roll, trying to evade the jabs of the spear.

As he flopped on to his back, he saw Pietten standing over him with the spear clenched like a spike in both hands.

Then Lena slammed into the Woodhelvennin. She launched her slight form at him with such ferocity that he fell under her, lost his grip on the spear. It landed across Covenant.

He grabbed it, tried to lever himself to his feet with it. But the pain in his ankle held him down as if his foot had been nailed to the ground. 'Lena!' he shouted wildly. 'No!'

Pietten threw her off him with one powerful sweep of his arm. She sprang up again and pulled a knife out of her robe. Rage contorted her fragile face as she hacked at Pietten.

He evaded her strokes, backed away quickly for an instant to gather his balance. Then, fiercely, he grinned.

'No!' Covenant shrieked.

When Lena charged again, Pietten caught her knife wrist neatly and turned the blade away from him. Slowly, he twisted her arm, forcing her down. She hammered at him with her free hand, but he held her. She could not resist his strength. She fell to her knees.

'The Ranyhyn!' she gasped to Covenant. 'Call the Ranyhyn!'

'Lena!' Using the spear, he lunged to his feet, fell, tried to crawl forward.

Slowly, inexorably, Pietten bent her backward until she lay writhing on the ground. Then he pulled his sharp wooden stave from his belt. With one savage blow he stabbed her in the stomach, spiked her to the frozen earth.

Horror roared in Covenant's head. He seemed to feel himself shattering; stricken with pain, he lost consciousness momentarily.

When he opened his eyes, he found Pietten standing in front of him.

Pietten was licking the blood off his hand.

Covenant tried to raise the spear, but Pietten snatched it from him. 'Now, Ringthane!' he cried ecstatically. 'Now I will slay you. Kneel there – grovel before me. Bring my dreams to life. I will be fair – I will allow you a chance. From ten paces I will hurl my spear. You may dodge – if your ankle permits. Do so. I relish it.'

With a grin like a snarl on his face, he strode away, turned and balanced the spear on his palm. 'Do you not choose to live?' he jeered. 'Kneel, then. Grovelling becomes you.'

Numbly, as if he did not know what he was doing, Covenant raised the two fingers of his right hand to his mouth and let out a weak whistle.

A Ranyhyn appeared instantly over the hillcrest and came galloping down into the hollow. It was miserably gaunt, reduced by the long winter to such inanition that only its chestnut coat seemed to hold its skeleton together. But it ran like indomitable pride straight towards Covenant.

Pietten did not appear to see it coming. He was in a personal trance, exalted by blood. Obliviously, he drew back his arm, bent his body until his muscles strained with passion – obliviously he launched the spear like a bolt of retribution at Covenant's heart.

The Ranyhyn veered, flashed between the two men, then fell tumbling like a sack of dismembered bones. When it came to rest on its side, both men saw Pietten's spear jutting from its bloodstained coat.

The sight struck Pietten like a blast of chaos. He gaped at what he had done in disbelief, as if it were inconceivable, unendurable. His shoulders sagged, eyes stared widely. He seemed to lack language for what he saw. His lips fumbled over meaningless whimpers, and the muscles of his throat jerked as if he could not swallow. If he saw Covenant crawling terribly towards him, he gave no sign. His arms dangled at his sides until Covenant reared up in front of him on one leg and drove a sharp Stonedownor knife into his chest with both hands.

Covenant delivered the blow like a double fistful of hate. Its momentum carried him forward, and he toppled across Pietten's corpse. Blood pumping from around the blade scored his jacket, slicked his hands, stained his shirt. But he paid no attention to it. That one blow seemed to have spent all his rage. He pushed himself off the body, and crawled away towards Lena, dragging his broken ankle like a millstone of pain behind him.

When he reached her, he found that she was still alive. The whole front of her robe was soaked, and blood coughed thinly between her lips; but she was still alive. He gripped the spike to draw it out. But the movement drew a gasp of pain from her. With an effort, she opened her eyes. They were clear, as if she were finally free of the confusion which had shaped her life. After a moment, she recognized Covenant, and tried to smile.

'Lena,' he panted. 'Lena.'

'I love you,' she replied in a voice wet with blood. 'I have not changed.'

'Lena.' He struggled to return her smile, but the attempt convulsed his face as if he were about to shriek.

Her hand reached towards him, touched his forehead as if to smooth away his scowl. 'Free the Ranyhyn,' she whispered.

The plea took her last strength. She died with blood streaming between her lips.

Covenant stared at it as if it were vituperation. His eyes had a feverish cast, a look of having been blistered from within. Now words came to his mind, but he knew what had happened. Rape, treachery, now murder – he had done them all, he had committed every crime. He had broken the promise he had made after the battle of Soaring Woodhelven, when he swore that he would not kill again. For a long moment, he regarded his numb fingers as if they were things of no importance. Only the blood on them mattered. Then he pushed himself away from Lena. Crawling like an abject passion, he moved towards the Ranyhyn.

Its muzzle was frothed with pain, and its sides heaved horridly. But it watched Covenant's approach steadily, as if for the first time in its life it was not afraid of the bearer of white gold. When he reached it, he went directly to its wound. The spear was deeply embedded; at first he did not believe he could draw it out. But he worked at it with his hands, digging his elbows into the Ranyhyn's panting ribs. At last the shaft tore free. Blood pulsed from the wound, yet the horse lurched to its feet, stood wavering weakly on splayed legs, and nuzzled him as if to tell him that it would live.

'All right,' he muttered, speaking half to himself. 'Go back. Go – tell all the others. Our bargain is over. No more bargains. No more – ' The fire was falling into embers, and his voice faded as if he were losing strength along with it. Dark fog blew into him along the wind. But a moment later, he rallied. 'No more bargains. Tell them.'

The Ranyhyn stood as if it were unwilling to leave him.

'Go on,' he insisted thickly. 'You're free. You've got to tell them. In the – in the name of *Kelenbhrabanal*, Father of Horses. Go.'

At the sound of that name, the Ranyhyn turned painfully and started to limp out of the hollow. When it reached the crest of the hill, it stopped and faced him once more. For an instant, he thought he could see it silhouetted against the night, rearing. Then it was gone.

He did not wait, did not rest. He was past taking any account of the cost of his actions. He caught up Pietten's spear and used it as a staff to hold himself erect. His ankle screamed at him as it dragged the ground, but he set his teeth and struggled away from the fire. As soon as he left the range of its warmth, his wet clothing began to freeze.

He had no idea where he was headed, but he knew he had to go. On each breath that panted through his locked teeth, he whispered *hate* as if it were a question.

11

THE RITUAL OF DESECRATION

After Loerya left him, High Lord Mhoram stayed on the tower for the rest of the night. He kept himself warm against the bitter wind by calling up a flow of power through his staff from time to time and watched in silent dread as the pronged veins of malice in the ground pulsed at Revelstone like sick, green-red lava oozing its way into the Keep's courage. The ill might which spread from *samadhi* Raver's Stone and the staves of the ur-viles lit the night garishly; and at irregular intervals, fervid sparks writhed upward when the attack met resistance in the rock of the foothills.

Though it moved slowly, the hungry agony of the attack was now only scant yards from Revelstone's walls. Through his feet, Mhoram could feel the Keep moaning in silent immobility, as if it ached to recoil from the leering threat of those veins.

But that was not why Mhoram stood throughout the long night exposed to the immedicable gall of the wind. He could have sensed the progress of the assault from anywhere in the Keep, just as he did not need his eyes to tell him how close the inhabitants of the city were to gibbering collapse. He watched because it was only by beholding Satansfist's might with all his senses, perceiving it with all its resources in all its horror, that he could deal with it.

When he was away from the sight, dread seemed to fall on him from nowhere, adumbrate against his heart like the knell of an unmotivated doom. It confused his thoughts, paralysed his instincts. Walking through the halls of Revelstone, he saw faces grey with inarticulate terror, heard above the constant, clenched mumble of sobs children howling in panic at the sight of their parents, felt the rigid moral exhaustion of the stalwart few who kept the Keep alive – Quaan, the three Lords, most of the Lorewardens, *lillianrill* and *rhadhamaerl*. Then he could hardly master the passion of his futility, the passion which urged him to strike at his friends because it blamed him for failing the Land. A wild hopelessness moved in him, shouldered its way towards the front of his responses. And he alone of all the Lords knew how to make such hopelessness bear fruit.

But alone on the watchtower, with Satansfist's army revealed below him, he could clarify himself, recognize what was being done to Revelstone. The winter and the attack assumed a different meaning. He no longer accused himself; he knew then that no one could be blamed for being inadequate in the face of such unanswerable malevolence. Destruction was easier than preservation, and when destruction had risen high enough, mere men and women could not be condemned if they failed to throw back the tide. Therefore he was able to resist his own capacity for desecration. His eyes burned like yellow fury at the creeping attack, but he was searching for defences.

The aspect of the assault which most daunted him was its unwavering ferocity. He could see that the ur-viles maintained their part of the power by rotating their positions, allowing each wedge and loremaster to rest in turn. And he knew from experience that Lord Foul's strength – his own prodigious might making use of the Illearth Stone – was able to drive armies mad, push them to greater savagery than their flesh could bear. But Satansfist was only one Giant, one body of mortal thew and bone and blood. Even a Giant-Raver should not have been able to sustain such an extravagant exertion for so long.

In addition, while *samadhi* concentrated on his attack, he might reasonably have been expected to lose some of his control over his army. Yet the whole horde, legion after legion, remained poised around Revelstone. Each creature in its own way bent the lust of its will at the Keep. And the emerald expenditure of *samadhi*'s strength never blinked. Clearly, Lord Foul supported his army and its commander with might so immense that it surpassed all Mhoram's previous conceptions of power.

He could see no hope for Revelstone anywhere except in the cost of that unwavering exertion. The defenders would have to hope and pray that Satansfist's aegis broke before they did. If they could not contrive to endure the Raver's attack, they were doomed.

When Mhoram returned to the hollow stone halls in the first, grey, dim ridicule of dawn, he was ready to strive for that endurance. The hushed, tight wave of panic that struck him as he strode

959

down the main passage into the Keep almost broke his resolve. He could feel people grinding their teeth in fear behind the walls on either side of him. Shouts reached him from a far gallery; two parties had banded together to defend themselves from each other. Around a bend he surprised a hungry group that was attempting to raid one of the food storerooms; the people believed that the cooks in the refectories were preparing poison.

His anger blazed up in him, and he surged forward, intending to strike them where they stood in their folly. But before he reached them, they fell into panic and fled from him as if he were a ghoul. Their retreat left two of Quaan's warriors standing guard in front of the storeroom as if they were watching each other rather than the supplies. Even these two regarded Mhoram with dread.

He mastered himself, forced a smile on to his crooked lips, said a few encouraging words to the guards. Then he hastened away.

He saw now that Revelstone was at the flash point of crisis. To help it, he had to provide the city with something more than moments of temporary aid. Grimly, he ignored the other needs, the multitudes of fear, which cut at his awareness. As he strode along passages and down stairways, he used his staff to summon Hearthrall Tohrm and all the Gravelingases. He put his full authority into the command, so that as many *rhadhamaerl* as possible might resist their panic and answer.

When he reached the bright floor of the courtyard around which the Lords' chambers were situated, he felt a brief surge of relief to see that Tohrm and a dozen Gravelingases were already there, and more were on their way. Soon a score of the *rhadhamaerl* – nearly all the Keep's masters of stone-lore – stood on the shining rock, waiting to hear him.

For a moment, the High Lord gazed at the men, wincing inwardly at their misery. They were Gravelingases of the *rhadhamaerl*, and were being hurt through the very stone around them. Then he nodded sharply to himself. This was the right place for him to begin; if he could convince these men that they were able to resist Satansfist's ill, they would be able to do much for the rest of the city.

With an effort that strained the muscles of his face, he smiled for them. Tohrm answered with an awkward grin which quickly fell into apprehension again.

'Gravelingases,' Mhoram began roughly, 'we have spent too long each of us alone enduring this ill in small ways. We must put our strength together to form a large defence.'

'We have obeyed your orders,' one man muttered sullenly.

'That is true,' Mhoram returned. 'Thus far we have all given our strength to encourage the people of Revelstone. You have kept your graveling fires bright, as I commanded. But wisdom does not always come swiftly. Now I see with other eyes. I have listened more closely to the voice of the Keep. I have felt the rock itself cry out against this evil. And I say now that we must resist in other ways if Revelstone is to endure.

'We have mistaken our purpose. The Land does not live for us — we live for the Land. Gravelingases, you must turn your lore to the defence of the stone. Here, in this place — ' he touched the radiant floor with the heel of his staff — 'slumbers power that perhaps only a *rhadhamaerl* may comprehend. Make use of it. Make use of any possible lore — do here together whatever must be done. But find some means to seal the heartrock of Revelstone against this blight. The people can provide for themselves if Revelstone remains brave.'

As he spoke, he realized that he should have understood these things all along. But the fear had numbed him, just as it had icebound the Gravelingases. And like him they now began to comprehend. They shook themselves, struck their hands together, looked around them with preparations rather than dread in their eyes. Tohrm's lips twitched with their familiar grin.

Without hesitation, High Lord Mhoram left the Gravelingases alone to do their work. As he walked along the tunnel away from the courtyard, he felt like a man who had discovered a new magic.

He directed his steps towards one of the main refectories, whose chief cook he knew to be a feisty, food-loving man not prone to either awe or fear; and as he moved, he sent out more summonses, this time calling his fellow Lords and Hearthrall Borillar's Hirebrands. Amatin and Trevor answered tensely, and Borillar sent a half-timid sign through the walls. But a long moment passed before Loerya answered, and when her signal came it was torpid, as if she were dazed with dismay. Mhoram hoped that the *rhadhamaerl* could make themselves felt soon, so that people like Loerya might not altogether lose heart; and he climbed up through the levels of the Keep towards the refectory as if he were surging through viscous dread.

But as he neared the kitchen, he saw a familiar figure dodge away into a side passage, obviously trying to avoid him. He swung around the corner after the man, and came face to face with Trell Atiaran-mate.

The big man looked feverish. His greying beard seemed to bristle hotly, his sunken cheeks were flushed, and his dull, hectic eyes slid away from Mhoram's gaze in all directions, as if he could not control their wandering. He stood under Mhoram's scrutiny as if he might break and run at any moment.

'Trell Gravelingas,' Mhoram said carefully, 'the other *rhadhamaerl* are at work against this ill. They need your strength.'

Trell's gaze flickered once across Mhoram's face like a lash of anger. 'You wish to preserve Revelstone so that it will be intact for the Despiser's use.' He filled the word *intact* with so much bitterness that it sounded like a curse.

At the accusation, Mhoram's lips tightened. 'I wish to preserve the Keep for its own sake.'

The roaming of Trell's eyes had an insatiable cast, as if they were afraid of going blind. 'I do not work well with others,' he said dimly after a moment. Then, without transition, he became urgent. 'High Lord, tell me your secret.'

Mhoram was taken aback. 'My secret?'

'It is a secret of power. I must have power.'

'For what purpose?'

At first, Trell squirmed under the question. But then his gaze hit Mhoram again. 'Do you wish Revelstone intact?' Again, *intact* spat like gall past his lips. He turned sharply and strode away.

For an instant, Mhoram felt a cold hand of foreboding on the back of his neck, and he watched Trell go as if the big Gravelingas trailed plumes of calamity. But before he could grasp the perception, Revelstone's ambience of dread clouded it, obscured it. He did not dare give Trell his secret knowledge. Even a Gravelingas might be capable of invoking the Ritual of Desecration.

With an effort, he remembered his purpose, and started again towards the refectory.

Because he had been delayed, all the people he had summoned were waiting for him. They stood ineffectively among the forlorn tables in the great, empty hall, and watched his approach with trepidation, as if he were a paradoxically fatal hope, a saving doom. 'High Lord,' the chief cook began at once, quelling his fear with anger, 'I cannot control these useless sheep disguised as cooks. Half have deserted me, and the rest will not work. They swing knives and refuse to leave the corners where they hide.'

'Then we must restore their courage.' Despite the scare Trell had given him, Mhoram found that he could smile more easily. He looked at the Lords and Hirebrands. 'Do you not feel it?'

Amatin nodded with tears in her eyes. Trevor grinned.

A change was taking place under their feet.

It was a small change, almost subliminal. Yet soon even the Hirebrands could feel it. Without either heat or light, it warmed and lit their hearts.

On a barely palpable level, the rock of Revelstone was remembering that it was obdurate granite, not susceptible sandstone.

Mhoram knew that this change could not be felt everywhere in the Keep – that all the strength of the *rhadhamaerl* would never suffice to throw back the lurid dread of Satansfist's attack. But the Gravelingases had made a start. Now anyone who felt the alteration would know that resistance was still possible.

He let his companions taste the granite for a moment. Then he began the second part of his defence. He asked Hearthrall Borillar for all the healing wood essence – the *rillinlure* – he could provide, and sent the other Hirebrands to help the chief cook begin working again. 'Cook and do not stop,' he commanded. 'The other refectories are paralysed. All who seek food must find it here.'

Borillar was doubtful. 'Our stores of *rillinlure* will be swiftly consumed in such quantities of food. None will remain for the future of this siege.'

'That is as it must be. Our error has been to conserve and portion our strength against future perils. If we fail to endure this assault, we will have no future.' When Borillar still hesitated, Mhoram went on: 'Do not fear, Hearthrall. Satansfist himself must rest after such an exertion of power.'

After a moment, Borillar recognized the wisdom of the High Lord's decision. He left to obey, and Mhoram turned to the other Lords. 'My friends, to us falls another task. We must bring the people here so that they may eat and be restored.'

'Send the Warward,' said Loerya. Her pain at being away from her daughters was plainly visible in her face.

'No. Fear will cause some to resist with violence. We must call them, make them wish to come. We must put aside our own apprehension, and send a call like a melding through the Keep, so that the people will choose to answer.'

'Who will defend Revelstone – while we work here?' Trevor asked.

'The peril is here. We must not waste our strength on useless watching. While this attack continues, there will be no other. Come. Join your power to mine. We, the Lords, cannot permit the Keep to be thus broken in spirit.'

As he spoke, he drew a fire bright and luminescent from his staff. Tuning it to the ambience of the stone, he set it against one wall so that it ran through the rock like courage, urging all the people within its range to lift up their heads and come to the refectory.

At his back, he felt Amatin, Trevor, then Loerya following his example. Their Lords-fire joined his; their minds bent to the same task. With their help, he pushed dread away, shared his own indomitable conviction, so that the appeal which radiated from them into Revelstone carried no flaw or dross of fear.

Soon people began to answer. Hollow-eyed like the victims of nightmares, they entered the refectory – accepted steaming trays from the chief cook and the Hirebrands – sat at the tables and began to eat. And when they had eaten, they found themselves ushered to a nearby hall where the Lorewardens enjoined them to sing boldly in the face of defeat:

> Berek! Earthfriend! – help and weal,
> Battle-aid against the foe!
>   Earth gives and answers Power's peal,
>   Ringing, Earthfriend! help and heal!
> Clean the Land from bloody death and woe!

More and more people came, drawn by the music, and the Lords, and the reaffirmation of Revelstone's granite. Supporting each other, carrying their children, dragging their friends, they fought their fear and came because the deepest impulses of their hearts responded to food, music, *rillinlure*, rock – to the Lords and the life of Revelstone.

After the first influx, the Lords took turns resting so that fatigue would not make their efforts waver. When the *rillinlure* gave out, the Hirebrands provided special fires for the returning cooks, and joined their own lore to the call of the Lords. Quaan's warriors gave up all pretence of guarding the walls, and came to help the cooks – clearing tables, cleaning pots and trays, carrying supplies from the storerooms.

Now the city had found a way to resist the dread, and it was determined to prevail. In all, less than half of Revelstone's people responded. But they were enough. They kept Lord's Keep alive when the very air they breathed reeked with malice.

For four days and four nights, High Lord Mhoram did not leave his post. He rested and ate to sustain himself, but he stayed at his station by the refectory wall. After a time, he hardly saw or heard the people moving around him. He concentrated on the stone, wrought himself to the pitch of Revelstone, to the pulse of its existence and the battle for possession of its life rock. He saw as clearly as if he were standing on the watchtower that Satansfist's livid power oozed close to the outer walls and then halted – hung poised while the Keep struggled against it. He heard the muffled groaning of the rock as it fought to remember itself. He felt the exhaustion of the Gravelingases. All these things he took into himself, and against the Despiser's wrong he placed his unbreaking will.

And he won.

Shortly before dawn on the fifth day, the onslaught broke like a tidal wave collapsing out to sea under its own weight. For a long stunned moment, Mhoram felt jubilation running through the rock under his feet and could not understand it. Around him, people gaped as if the sudden release of pressure astounded them. Then, swept together by a common impulse, he and everyone else dashed towards the outer battlements to look at the siege.

The ground below them steamed and quivered like wounded flesh, but the malevolence which had stricken it was gone. Satansfist's army lay prostrate from over-exertion in its encampments. The Giant-Raver himself was nowhere to be seen.

Over all its walls from end to end, Revelstone erupted in the exultation of victory. Weak, hoarse, ragged, starving voices cheered, wept, shouted raucous defiance as if the siege had been beaten. Mhoram found his own vision blurred with relief. When he turned to go back into the Keep, he discovered Loerya behind him, weeping happily and trying to hug all three of her daughters at once. At her side, Trevor crowed, and tossed one of the girls giggling into the air.

'Rest now, Mhoram,' Loerya said through her joy. 'Leave the Keep to us. We know what must be done.'

High Lord Mhoram nodded his mute gratitude and went wearily away to his bed.

Yet even then he did not relax until he had felt the Warward resume its defensive stance – felt search parties hunting through the Keep for the most blighted survivors of the assault – felt order slowly reform the city like a mammoth being struggling out of chaos. Only then did he let himself flow with the slow pulse of the gut-rock and lose his burdens in sleep – secure in the confidence of stone.

By the time he awoke the next morning, Lord's Keep had been returned as much as possible to battle-readiness. Warmark Quaan brought a tray of breakfast to him in his private quarters, and reported the news of the city to him while he ate.

Thanks to its training, and to exceptional service by some of the Hafts and Warhafts, the Warward had survived essentially unscathed. The Gravelingases were exhausted, but well. The Lorewardens and Hirebrands had suffered only chance injuries from panic-stricken friends. But the people who had not answered the Lords' summons had not fared so well. Search parties had found several score dead, especially in ground-level apartments near the outer walls. Most of these people had died of thirst, but some were murdered by their fear-mad friends and neighbours. And of the hundreds of other survivors, four- or fivescore appeared irreparably insane.

After the search had ended, Lord Loerya had taken to the Healers all those who were physically and mentally damaged, as well as those who seemed to remember having committed murder. She was assisting the Healers now. In other ways, Revelstone was swiftly recovering. The Keep was intact.

Mhoram listened in silence, then waited for the old Warmark to continue. But Quaan fell studiously silent, and the High Lord was forced to ask, 'What of the Raver's army?'

Quaan spat in sudden vehemence. 'They have not moved.'

It was true. Satansfist's hordes had retreated to their encampment and fallen into stasis as if the force which animated them had been withdrawn.

In the days that followed, they remained essentially still. They moved enough to perform the bare functions of their camp. They received dark supply wains from the south and east. From time to time, an indefinite flicker of power ran among them – a half-hearted whip keeping surly beasts under control. But none of them approached within hailing distance of the Keep. *Samadhi* Raver did not show himself. Only the unbroken girdle of the siege showed that Lord Foul had not been defeated.

For five days – ten – fifteen – the enemy lay like a dead thing around Revelstone. At first, some of the more optimistic inhabitants of the city argued that the spirit of the attackers had been broken. But Warmark Quaan did not believe this, and after one long look from the watchtower, Mhoram agreed with his old friend.

Satansfist was simply waiting for Revelstone to eat up its supplies, weaken itself, before he launched his next assault.

As the days passed, High Lord Mhoram lost his capacity to rest. He lay tense in his chambers and listened to the mood of the city turn sour.

Slowly, day by day, Lord's Keep came to understand its predicament. The Giants who had delved Revelstone out of the mountain rock thousands of years ago, in the age of Damelon, had made it to be impregnable; and all its inhabitants had lived from birth with the belief that this intention had succeeded. The walls were granite, and the gates, unbreakable. In a crisis the fertile upland plateau could provide the Keep with food. But the Despiser's unforeseen, unforeseeable winter had laid the upland barren; crops and fruit could not grow, cattle or other animals could not live, in the brazen wind. And the storerooms had already supplied the city since the natural onset of winter.

For the first time in its long history, Revelstone's people saw that they might starve.

In the initial days of waiting, the Lords began a stricter rationing of the supplies. They reduced each person's daily share of food until everyone in Revelstone felt hungry all the time. They organized the refectories more stringently, so that food would not be wasted. But these measures were palpably inadequate. The city had many thousand inhabitants, even on minimal rations they consumed large portions of the stores every day.

Their earlier elation ran out of them like water leaking into parched sand. The wait became first stupefying, then heavy and ominous, like pent thunder, then maddening. And High Lord Mhoram found himself yearning for the next attack. He could fight back against an attack.

Gradually, the cold grey days and suspense began to weaken the Keep's discretion, its pragmatic sense. Some of the farmers – people whose lifework had been taken from them by the winter – crept out to the upland hills around Glimmermere, sneaking as if they were ashamed to be caught planting futile rows of seeds in the frozen earth.

Lord Trevor began to neglect some of his duties. At odd times, he forgot why he had become a Lord, forgot the impulse which had made him a Lord in defiance of his lack of belief in himself; and he shirked normal responsibilities as if he were inexplicably afraid of failure. Loerya his wife remained staunch in her work, but she became distracted, almost furtive, as she moved through the Keep. She often went hungry so that her daughters could have more food. Whenever she saw the High Lord, she glared at him with a strange resentment in her eyes.

Like Loerya, Lord Amatin grew slowly distant. At every free moment she plunged into a feverish study of the First and Second Wards, searching so hard for the unlocking of mysteries that when she went back to her public duties her forehead looked as sore as if she had been battering it against her table.

Several Hirebrands and Gravelingases took to carrying fire with them wherever they went, like men who were going incomprehensibly blind. And on the twentieth day of the waiting, Warmark Quaan abruptly reversed all his former decisions; without consulting any of the Lords, he sent a party of scouts out of the Keep towards Satansfist's camp. None of them returned.

Still the Raver's army lay like dormant chains, constricting the heart of Revelstone.

Quaan berated himself to the High Lord. 'I am a fool,' he articulated severely, 'an old fool. Replace me before I am mad enough to send the Warward itself out to die.'

'Who can replace you?' Mhoram replied gently. 'It is the Despiser's purpose to make mad all the defenders of the Land.'

Quaan looked around him as if to measure with his eyes the chill of Revelstone's travail. 'He will succeed. He requires no weapon but patience.'

Mhoram shrugged. 'Perhaps. But I think it is an unsure tactic. Lord Foul cannot foretell the size of our stores – or the extent of our determination.'

'Then why does he wait?'

The High Lord did not need to be a seer to answer this question. '*Samadhi* Raver awaits a sign – perhaps from us – perhaps from the Despiser.'

Glowering at the thought, Quaan went back to his duties. And Mhoram returned to a problem which had been nagging at him. For the third time, he went in search of Trell.

But once again he could not locate the tormented Gravelingas. Trell must have secreted himself somewhere. Mhoram found no trace, felt no emanation, and none of the other *rhadhamaerl* had seen the big Stonedownor recently. Mhoram ached at the thought of Trell in hiding, gnawing in cataleptic isolation the infested meat of his anguishes. Yet the High Lord could not afford either the time or the energy to dredge all Revelstone's private places for the sake of one embittered Gravelingas. Before he had completed even a cursory search, he was distracted by a group of Lorewardens who had decided to go and negotiate a peace with the Raver. Once again, he was compelled to put aside the question of Trell Atiaran-mate.

On the twenty-fourth day, Lord Trevor forsook his duties altogether. He sealed himself in his study like a penitent, and refused all food and drink. Loerya could get no response from him, and when the High Lord spoke to him, he said nothing except that he wished his wife and daughters to have his ration of food.

'Now even I am a cause of pain to him,' Loerya murmured with hot tears in her eyes. 'Because I have given some of my food to my daughters, he believes that he is an insufficient husband and father, and must sacrifice himself.' She gave Mhoram one desperate glance, like a woman trying to judge the cost of abdication, then hurried away before he could reply.

On the twenty-fifth day, Lord Amatin strode up to Mhoram and demanded without preface or explanation that he reveal to her his secret knowledge.

'Ah, Amatin,' he sighed, 'are you so eager for burdens?'

She turned at once and walked fragilely away as if he had betrayed her.

When he went to stand his solitary watch on the tower, a dull vermeil mood was on him, and he felt that he had in fact betrayed her; he had withheld dangerous knowledge from her as if he judged her unable to bear it. Yet nowhere in his heart could he find the courage to give his fellow Lords the key to the Ritual of Desecration. That key had a lurid, entrancing weight. It urged him to rage at

Trevor, pummel the pain from Loerya's face, shake Amatin's frail shoulders until she understood, call down fire from the hidden puissance of the skies on Satansfist's head – and refused to let him speak.

On the twenty-seventh day, the first of the storerooms was emptied. Together, the chief cook and the most experienced Healer reported to Mhoram that the old and infirm would begin to die of hunger in a few days.

When he went to his chambers to rest, he felt too cold to sleep. Despite the warm graveling, Lord Foul's winter reached through the stone walls at him as if the grey, unfaltering wind were tuned to his most vulnerable resonances. He lay wide-eyed on his pallet like a man in a fever of helplessness and imminent despair.

The next night he was snatched off his bed shortly after midnight by the sudden thrill of trepidation which raced through the walls like a flame in the extreme tinder of the Keep's anticipation. He was on his way before any summons could reach him; with his staff clenched whitely in his hand, he hastened towards the highest eastward battlements of the main Keep. He focused on Quaan's dour presence, found the Warmark on a balcony overlooking the watchtower and the night soot of Satansfist's army.

As Mhoram joined him, Quaan pointed one rigid arm like an indictment away towards the east. But the High Lord did not need Quaan's gesture; the sight seemed to spring at him out of the darkness like a bright abomination on the wind.

Running from the east towards Revelstone was a rift in the clouds, a break that stretched out to the north and south as far as Mhoram could see. The rift appeared wide, assertive, but the clouds behind it were as impenetrable as ever.

It was so clearly visible because through it streamed light as green as the frozen essence of emerald.

Its brightness made it seem swift, but it moved like a slow, ineluctable tide across the ice-blasted fields beyond the foothills. Its green, radiant swath swept like a blaze of wrong over the ground, igniting invisible contours into brilliance and then quenching them again. Mhoram watched it in stunned silence as it lit the Raver's army and rushed on into the foothills of the plateau. Like a tsunami of malignant scorn, it rolled upward and broke across the Keep.

People screamed when they saw the full emerald moon leering evilly at them through the rift. The High Lord himself flinched, raising his staff as if to ward off a nightmare. For a horrific moment while the rift moved, Lord Foul's moon dominated the clear, starless abysm of the sky like an incurable wound, a maiming of the very

Law of the heavens. Emerald radiance covered everything, drowned every heart and drenched Revelstone's every upraised rock in thetic, green defeat.

Then the rift passed; sick light slid away into the west. Lord's Keep sank like a broken sea-cliff into irreparable night.

'Melenkurion!' Quaan panted as if he were suffocating. *'Melenkurion!'*

Slowly, Mhoram realized that he was grimacing like a cornered madman. But while the darkness crashed and echoed around him, he could not relax his features; the contortion clung to his face like the grin of a skull. A long, taut time seemed to pass before he thought to peer through the night at Satansfist's army.

When at last he compelled himself to look, he saw that the army had come to life. It sloughed off its uneasy repose and began to seethe, bristling in the darkness like reanimated lust.

'Ready the Warward,' he said, fighting an unwonted terror in his rough voice. 'The Raver has been given his sign. He will attack.'

With an effort, Warmark Quaan brought himself back under control and left the balcony, shouting orders as he moved.

Mhoram hugged his staff to his chest and breathed deeply, heavily. At first, the air shuddered in his lungs, and he could not pull the grimace off his face. But slowly he untied his muscles, turned his tension into other channels. His thoughts gathered themselves around the defence of the Keep.

Calling on the Hearthralls and the other Lords to join him, he went to the tower to watch what *samadhi* Raver was doing.

There, in the company of the two shaken sentries, he could follow the Raver's movements. Satansfist held his fragment of the Illearth Stone blazing aloft, an oriflamme of gelid fire, and its stark green illumination revealed him clearly as he moved among his forces, barking orders in a hoarse, alien tongue. Without haste he gathered ur-viles about him until their midnight forms spread out under his light like a lake of black water. Then he forged them into two immense wedges, one on either side of him, with their tips at his shoulders, facing Revelstone. In the garish Stone light, the loremasters looked like roynish, compact power, fatal and eager. Waves of other creatures fanned out beyond them on either side as they began to approach the Keep.

Following the Raver's fire, they moved deliberately straight out of the southeast towards the knuckled and clenched gates at the base of the watchtower.

High Lord Mhoram tightened his grip on his staff and tried to prepare himself for whatever might happen.

At his back, he felt Lord Amatin and Hearthrall Borillar arrive, followed shortly by Tohrm and then Quaan. Without taking his eyes off Satansfist's approach, the Warmark reported.

'I have ordered two Eoward into the tower. More would serve no purpose – they would block each other. Half are archers. They are good warriors,' he added unnecessarily, as if to reassure himself, 'and all their Hafts and Warhafts are veterans of the war against Fleshharrower.'

'The archers bear *lor-liarill* shafts. They will begin at your signal.'

Mhoram nodded his approval. 'Tell half the archers to strike when the Raver enters arrow range. Hold the rest for my signal.'

The Warmark turned to deliver these instructions, but Mhoram abruptly caught his arm. A chill tightened the High Lord's scalp as he said, 'Place more archers upon the battlements above the court of the Gilden. If by some great ill Satansfist breaches the gates, the defenders of the tower will require aid. And – stand warriors ready to cut loose the crosswalks from the Keep.'

'Yes, High Lord.' Quaan was a warrior and understood the necessity for such orders. He returned Mhoram's grip firmly, like a clasp of farewell, then left the top of the tower.

'Breach the gates?' Borillar gaped as if the mere suggestion amazed him. 'How is it possible?'

'It is not possible,' Tohrm replied flatly.

'Nevertheless we must prepare.' Mhoram braced his staff on the stone like a standard, and watched *samadhi* Sheol's approach.

No one spoke while the army marched forward. It was already less than a hundred yards below the gates. Except for the dead rumble of its myriad feet on the frozen ground, it moved in silence, as if it were stalking the Keep – or as if in spite of their driven hunger many of its creatures themselves dreaded what Satansfist meant to do.

Mhoram felt that he had only moments left. He asked Amatin if she had seen either Trevor or Loerya.

'No.' Her whispered answer had an empty sound, like a recognition of abandonment.

Moments later, a flight of arrows thrummed from one of the upper levels of the tower. They were invisible in the darkness, and Satansfist gave no sign that he knew they had been fired. But the radiance of the Illearth Stone struck them into flame and knocked them down before they were within thirty feet of him.

Another flight, and another, had no effect except to light the front of the Raver's army, revealing in lurid green and orange the deadly aspect of its leaders.

Then *samadhi* halted. On either side of him, the ur-viles trembled.

He coughed his orders. The wedges tightened. Snarling, the Cave-wights and other creatures arranged themselves into formation, ready to charge.

Without haste or hesitation, the Giant-Raver clenched his fist, so that iridescent steam plumed upward from his fragment of the Stone.

Mhoram could feel the Stone's power mounting, radiating in tumid waves against his face.

Abruptly, a bolt of force lashed from the Stone and struck the ground directly before one of the loremasters. The blast continued until the soil and rock caught fire, burned with green flames, crackled like firewood. Then *samadhi* moved his bolt, drew it over the ground in a wide, slow arc towards the other loremaster. His power left behind a groove that flamed and smouldered, flared and groaned in earthen agony.

When the arc was complete, it enclosed Satansfist from side to side – a half-circle of emerald coals standing in front of him like a harness anchored by the two ur-vile wedges.

Remembering the vortex of trepidation with which Fleshharrower had attacked the Warward at Doriendor Corishev, Mhoram strode across the tower and shouted up at the Keep, 'Leave the battlements! All but the warriors must take shelter! Do not expose yourselves lest the sky itself assail you!' Then he returned to Lord Amatin's side.

Below him, the two great loremasters raised their staves and jabbed them into the ends of the arc. At once, Demondim vitriol began to pulse wetly along the groove. The green flames turned black; they bubbled, spattered, burst out of the arc as if Satansfist had tapped a vein of EarthBlood in the ground.

By the time Warmark Quaan had returned to the tower, Mhoram knew that *samadhi* was not summoning a vortex. The Raver's exertion was like nothing he had ever seen before. And it was slower than he had expected it to be. Once the ur-viles had tied themselves to the arc, Satansfist started to work with his Stone. From its incandescent core, he drew a fire that gushed to the ground and poured into the groove of the arc. This force combined with the black fluid of the ur-viles to make a mixture of ghastly potency. Soon black-green snake-tongues of lightning were flicking into the air from the whole length of the groove, and these bursts carried to the onlookers a gut-deep sense of violation, as if the rocky founda-tions of the foothills were under assault – as if the Despiser dared traduce even the necessary bones of the Earth.

Yet the power did nothing except grow. Tongues of lightning leaped higher, joined together, became gradually but steadily more brilliant and wrong. Their violence increased until Mhoram felt that the nerves of his skin and eyes could endure no more – and went on increasing. When dawn began to bleed into the night at Satansfist's back, the individual tongues had merged into three continuous bolts striking without thunder into the deepest darkness of the clouds.

The High Lord's throat was too dry; he had to swallow roughly several times before he could muster enough moisture to speak. 'Hearthrall Tohrm – ' still he almost gagged on the words – 'they will attack the gates. This power will attack the gates. Send any Gravelingases who will go to the aid of the stone.'

Tohrm started at the sound of his name, then hurried away as if he were glad to remove himself from the baleful glare of the arc.

While grey daylight spread over the siege, the three unbroken bolts jumped and gibbered maniacally, raged at the silent clouds, drew closer to each other. Behind them, the army began to howl as the pressure became more and more unendurable.

Lord Amatin dug her thin fingers into the flesh of Mhoram's arm. Quaan had crossed his arms over his chest, and was straining against himself to keep from shouting. Borillar's hands scrubbed fervidly over his features in an effort to erase the sensation of wrong. His staff lay useless at his feet. The High Lord prayed for them all and fought his dread.

Then, abruptly, the Raver whirled his Stone and, roaring, threw still more power into the arc.

The three great columns of lightning sprang together, became one.

The earth shook with thunder in answer to that single, prodigious bolt. At once, the lightning vanished, though *samadhi* and the urviles did not withdraw their power from the arc.

The thunder continued, tremors jolted the ground. In moments, the tower was trembling as if its foundations were about to crack open and swallow it.

Immensely, tortuously, the ground of the foothills began to shift. It writhed, jerked, cracked; and through the cracks, stone shapes thrust upward. To his horror, Mhoram saw the forms of humans and Giants and horses rip themselves out of the earth. The forms were blunt, misshapen, insensate, they were articulated stone, the ancient fossilized remains of buried bodies.

The memory of Asuraka's cry from Revelwood echoed in Mhoram's ears. *He resurrected the old death*!

By hundreds and then thousands, the stone shapes heaved up out of the ground. Amid the colossal thunder of the breaking earth, they thrust free of their millennia-long graves and lumbered blindly towards the gates of Revelstone.

'Defend the tower!' Mhoram cried to Quaan. 'But do not waste lives. Amatin! Fight here! Flee if the tower falls. I go to the gates.'

But when he spun away from the parapet, he collided with Hearthrall Tohrm. Tohrm caught hold of him, stopped him. Yet in spite of the High Lord's urgency, a long moment passed before Tohrm could bring himself to speak.

At last he wrenched out, 'The tunnel is defended.'

'Who?' Mhoram snapped.

'The Lord Trevor ordered all others away. He and Trell Gravelingas support the gates.'

'*Melenkurion*!' Mhoram breathed. '*Melenkurion abatha*!' He turned back to the parapet.

Below him, the dead, voiceless shapes had almost reached the base of the tower. Arrows flew at them from hundreds of bows, but the shafts glanced uselessly off the earthen forms and fell flaming to the ground without effect.

He hesitated, muttering to himself in extreme astonishment. The breaking of the Law of Death had consequences beyond anything he had imagined. Thousands of the gnarled shapes were already massed and marching, and at every moment thousands more struggled up from the ground, writhed into motion like lost souls and obeyed the command of Sheol Satansfist's power.

But then the first shape set its hands on the gates, and High Lord Mhoram sprang forward. Whirling his staff, he sent a blast down the side of the tower, struck the dead form where it stood. At the impact of his Lords-fire, it shattered like sandstone and fell into dirt.

At once, he and Lord Amatin set to work with all their might. Their staffs rang and fired, rained blue strength like hammer blows down on the marching shapes. And every blow broke the dead into sand. But every one that fell was replaced by a score of others. Across all the terrain between the watchtower and Satansfist's arc, the ground heaved and buckled, pitching new forms into motion like being dredged up from the bottommost muck of a lifeless sea. First one by one, then by tens, scores, fifties, they reached the gates and piled against them.

Through the stone, Mhoram could feel the strain on the gates mounting. He could feel Trevor's fire and Trell's mighty subterranean song supporting the interlocked gates, while hundreds, thousands, of the blind, mute forms pressed against them, crushed forward in lifeless savagery like an avalanche leaping impossibly up out of the ground. He could feel the groaning retorts of pressure as if the bones of the tower were grinding together. And still the dead came, shambling out of the earth until they seemed as vast as the Raver's army and as irresistible as a cataclysm. Mhoram and Amatin broke hundreds of them and had no effect.

Behind the High Lord, Tohrm was on his knees, sharing the tower's pain with his hands and sobbing openly, 'Revelstone! Oh, Revelstone, alas! Oh, Revelstone, Revelstone!'

Mhoram tore himself away from the fighting, caught hold of Tohrm's tunic, hauled the Hearthrall to his feet. Into Tohrm's broken face, he shouted, 'Gravelingas! Remember who you are! You are the Hearthrall of Lord's Keep.'

'I am nothing!' Tohrm wept. 'Ah! the Earth – !'

'You are Hearthrall and Gravelingas! Hear me – I, High Lord Mhoram, command you. Study this attack – learn to know it. The inner gates must not fall. The *rhadhamaerl* must preserve Revelstone's inner gates!'

He felt the change in the attack. Satansfist's Stone now threw bolts against the gates. Amatin tried to resist, but the Raver brushed her efforts aside as if they were nothing. Yet Mhoram stayed with Tohrm, focused his strength on the Hearthrall until Tohrm met the demand of his eyes and hands.

'Who will mourn the stone if I do not?' Tohrm moaned.

Mhoram controlled his desire to yell. 'No harm will receive its due grief if we do not survive.'

The next instant, he forgot Tohrm, forgot everything except the silent screams that detonated through him from the base of the tower. Over Trell's shrill rage and the vehemence of Trevor's fire, the gates shrieked in agony.

A shattering concussion convulsed the stone. The people atop the tower fell, tumbled across the floor. Huge thunder like a howl of victory crashed somewhere between earth and sky, as if the very firmament of existence had been rent asunder.

The gates split inward.

Torrents of dead stone flooded into the tunnel under the tower.

Mhoram was shouting at Quaan and Amatin, 'Defend the tower!' The shaking subsided, and he staggered erect. Pulling Tohrm with him, he yelled, 'Come! Rally the Gravelingases! The inner gates must not fall.' Though the tower was still trembling, he started towards the stairs.

But before he could descend, he heard a rush of cries, human cries. An anguish like rage lashed through the roiling throng of his emotions. 'Quaan!' he roared, though the old Warmark had almost caught up with him. 'The warriors attack!' Quaan nodded bitterly as he reached Mhoram's side. 'Stop them! They cannot fight these dead. Swords will not avail.'

With Tohrm and Quaan, the High Lord raced down the stairs, leaving Amatin to wield her fire from the edge of the parapet.

Quaan went straight down through the tower, but Mhoram took

Tohrm out over the courtyard between the tower and the Keep on the highest crosswalk. From there, he saw that Trell and Lord Trevor had already been driven back out of the tunnel. They were fighting for their lives against the slow, blind march of the dead. Trevor exerted an extreme force like nothing Mhoram had ever seen in him before, battering the foremost attackers, breaking them rapidly, continuously, into sand. And Trell wielded in both hands a massive fragment of one gate. He used the fragment like a club with such ferocious strength that even shapes vaguely resembling horses and Giants went down under his blows.

But the two men had no chance. Swords and spears and arrows had no effect on the marching shapes; scores of warriors who leaped into the tunnel and the courtyard were simply crushed underfoot; and the cries of the crushed were fearful to hear. While Mhoram watched, the dead pushed Trell and Trevor back past the old Gilden tree towards the closed inner gates.

Mhoram shouted to the warriors on the battlements below him, commanding them to stay out of the courtyard. Then he ran across to the Keep and dashed down the stairways towards the lower levels. With Tohrm behind him, he reached the first abutment over the inner gates in time to see Cavewights spill through the tunnel, squirming their way among the dead to attack the side doors which provided the only access to the tower.

Some of them fell at once with arrows in their throats and bellies, and others were cut down by the few warriors in the court who had avoided being crushed. But their thick, heavy jerkins protected them from most of the shafts and swords. With their great strength and their knowledge of stone, they threw themselves at the doors. And soon the gangrel creatures were swarming through the tunnel in large numbers. The High Lord saw that the warriors alone could not keep *samadhi*'s creatures out of the tower.

For a harsh moment, he pushed Trevor and Trell, Cavewights, warriors, animated dead earth from his mind, and faced the decision he had to make. If Revelstone were to retain any viable defence, either the tower or the inner gates must be preserved. Without the gates, the tower might still restrict Satansfist's approach enough to keep Revelstone alive; without the tower, the gates could still seal out Satansfist. Without one or the other, Revelstone was defeated. But Mhoram could not fight for both, could not be in both places at once. He had to choose where to concentrate the Keep's defence.

He chose the gates.

At once, he sent Tohrm to gather the Gravelingases. Then he turned to the battle of the courtyard. He ignored the Cavewights, focused instead on the shambling dead as they trampled the Gilden tree and pushed Trell and Trevor back against the walls. Shouting to the warriors around him for *clingor*, he hurled his Lords-fire down at the faceless shapes, battered them into sand. Together, he and Trevor cleared a space in which the trapped men could make their escape.

Almost immediately, the sentries brought two tough *clingor* lines, anchored them, tossed them down to Trevor and Trell. But in the brief delay, a new wave of Cavewights rode into the courtyard on the shoulders of the dead and joined the assault on the doors. With a nauseating sound like the breaking of bones, they tore the doors off the hinges, tossed the stone slabs aside, and charged roaring into the tower. They were met instantly by staunch, dour-handed warriors, but the momentum and strength of the Cavewights carried them inward.

When he saw the doors broken, Trell gave a cry of outrage, and tried to attack the Cavewights. Slapping aside the *clingor* line, he rushed the dead as if he believed he could fight his way through them to join the defence of the tower. For a moment, his granite club and his *rhadhamaerl* lore broke passage for him, and he advanced a few steps across the court. But then even his club snapped. He went down under the prodigious weight of the dead.

Trevor sprang after him. Aided by Mhoram's fire, the Lord reached Trell. One of the dead stamped a glancing blow along his ankle, but he ignored the pain, took hold of Trell's shoulders, dragged him back.

As soon as he was able to regain his feet, Trell pushed Trevor away and attacked the insensate forms with his fists.

Trevor snatched up one of the *clingor* lines and whipped it several times around his chest. Then he pounced at Trell's back. With his arms under Trell's, he gripped his staff like a bar across Trell's chest, and shouted for the warriors to pull him up. Instantly, ten warriors caught the line and hauled. While Mhoram protected the two men, they were drawn up the wall and over the parapet of the abutment.

With a sickening jolt, the dead thudded against the inner gates.

Amid the cries of battle from the tower, and the mute pressure building sharply against the gates, High Lord Mhoram turned his attention to Trell and Lord Trevor.

The Gravelingas struggled free of Trevor's hold and the hands of the warriors, thrust himself erect, and faced Mhoram as if he meant to leap at the High Lord's throat. His face flamed with exertion and fury.

'Intact!' he rasped horribly. 'The tower lost – intact for Sheol's use! Is that your purpose for Revelstone? Better that we destroy it ourselves!'

Swinging his powerful arms to keep anyone from touching him, he spun wildly and lurched away into the Keep.

Mhoram's gaze burned dangerously, but he bit his lips, kept himself from rushing after the Gravelingas. Trell had spent himself extravagantly, and failed. He could not be blamed for hating his inadequacy; he should be left in peace. But his voice had sounded like the voice of a man who had lost all peace for ever. Torn within himself, Mhoram sent two warriors to watch over Trell, then turned towards Trevor.

The Lord stood panting against the back wall. Blood streamed from his injured ankle; his face was stained with the grime of battle, and he shuddered as the effort of breathing racked his chest. Yet he seemed unconscious of his pain, unconscious of himself. His eyes gleamed with eldritch perceptions. When Mhoram faced him he gasped, 'I have felt it, I know what it is.'

Mhoram shouted for a Healer, but Trevor shrugged away any suggestion that he needed help. He met the High Lord like a man exalted, and repeated, 'I have felt it, Mhoram.'

Mhoram controlled his concern. 'Felt it?'

'Lord Foul's power. The power which makes all this possible.'

'The Stone – ' Mhoram began.

'The Stone does not suffice. This weather – the speed with which he became so mighty after his defeat in Garroting Deep – the force of this army, though it is so far from his command – these dead shapes, compelled from the very ground by power so vast – !

'The Stone does not suffice. I have felt it. Even Lord Foul the Despiser could not become so much more unconquerable in seven short years.'

'Then how?' the High Lord breathed.

'This weather – this winter. It sustains and drives the army – it frees Satansfist – it frees the Despiser himself for other work – the work of the Stone. The work of these dead. Mhoram, do you remember Drool Rockworm's power over the weather – and the moon?'

Mhoram nodded in growing amazement and dread.

'I have felt it. Lord Foul holds the Staff of Law.'

A cry tore itself past Mhoram's lips, despite his instantaneous coviction that Trevor was right. 'How is it possible? The Staff fell with High Lord Elena under *Melenkurion* Skyweir.'

'I do not know. Perhaps the same being who slew Elena bore the Staff to Foul's Creche – perhaps it is dead Kevin himself who wields the Staff on Foul's behalf, so that the Despiser need not personally use a power not apt for his control. But I have felt the Staff, Mhoram – the Staff of Law beyond all question.'

Mhoram nodded, fought to contain the amazed fear that seemed to echo illimitably within him. The Staff! Battle raged around him; he could afford neither time nor strength for anything but the immediate task. Lord Foul held the Staff! If he allowed himself to think about such a thing, he might lose himself in panic. Eyes flashing, he gave Trevor's shoulder a hard clasp of praise and comradeship, then turned back towards the courtyard.

For a moment, he pushed his perceptions through the din and clangour, bent his senses to assess Revelstone's situation. He could feel Lord Amatin atop the tower, still waging her fire against the dead. She was weakening – her continuous exertions had long since passed the normal limits of her stamina – yet she kept her ragged blaze striking downward, fighting as if she meant to spend her last pulse or breath in the tower's defence. And her labour had its effect. Though she could not stop even a tenth of the shambling shapes, she had now broken so many of them that the unbound sand clogged the approaches to the tunnel. Fewer of the dead could plough forward at one time; her work, and the constriction of the tunnel, slowed their march, slowed the multiplication of their pressure on the inner gates.

But while she strove, battle began to mount up through the tower towards her. Few Cavewights now tried to enter through the doors. Their own dead blocked the corridors; and while they fought for access, they were exposed to the archers of the Keep. But enemies were breaching the tower somehow; Mhoram could hear loud combat surging upward through the tower's complex passages. With an effort, he ignored everything else around him, concentrated on the tower. Then through the hoarse commands, the clash of weapons, the raw cries of hunger and pain, the tumult of urgent feet, he sensed Satansfist's attack on the outer wall of the tower. The Raver threw fierce bolts of Illearth power at the exposed coigns and windows, occasionally at Lord Amatin herself; and under the cover of these blasts, his creatures threw up ladders against the wall, swarmed through the openings.

In the stone under his feet, High Lord Mhoram could feel the inner gates groaning.

Quickly, he turned to one of the warriors, a tense Stonedownor woman. 'Go to the tower. Find Warmark Quaan. Say that I command him to withdraw from the tower. Say that he must bring Lord Amatin with him. Go.'

She saluted and ran. A few moments later, he saw her dash over the courtyard along one of the crosswalks.

By that time, he had already returned to the battle. With Lord Trevor working doggedly at his side, he renewed his attack on the earthen pressure building against Revelstone's inner gates. While the supportive power of the Gravelingases vibrated in the stone under him, he gathered all his accumulated ferocity and drove it at the crush of dead. Now he knew clearly what he hoped to achieve; he wanted to cover the flagstones of the courtyard with so much sand that the blind, shambling shapes would have no solid footing from which to press forward. Trevor's aid seemed to uplift his effectiveness, and he shattered dead by tens and scores until his staff hummed in his hands and the air around him became so charged with blue force that he appeared to emanate Lords-fire.

Yet while he laboured, wielded his power like a scythe through Satansfist's ill crop, he kept part of his attention cocked towards the crosswalks. He was watching for Quaan and Amatin.

A short time later, the first crosswalk fell. The battered remnant of an Eoman dashed along it out of the tower, rabidly pursued by Cavewights. Archers sent the Cavewights plunging to the courtyard, and as soon as the warriors were safe, the walk's cables were cut. The wooden span swung clattering down and crashed against the wall of the tower.

The tumult of battle echoed out of the tower. Abruptly, Warmark Quaan appeared on one of the upper spans. Yelling stridently to make himself heard, he ordered all except the two highest crosswalks cut.

Mhoram shouted up to the Warmark, 'Amatin!'

Quaan nodded, ran back into the tower.

The next two spans fell promptly, but the sentries at the third waited. After a moment, several injured warriors stumbled out on to the walk. Supporting each other, carrying the crippled, they struggled towards the Keep. But then a score of Stone-born creatures charged madly out of the tower. Defying arrows and swords, they threw the injured off the span and rushed on across the walk.

Grimly, deliberately, the sentries cut the cables.

Every enemy that appeared in the doorways where the spans had been was killed or beaten back by a hail of fiery arrows. The higher crosswalks fell in swift succession. Only two remained for the survivors in the tower.

Now Lord Trevor was panting dizzily at the High Lord's side, and Mhoram himself felt weak with strain. But he could not afford to rest. Tohrm's Gravelingases would not be able to hold the gates alone.

Yet his flame lost its vehemence as the urgent moments passed. Fear for Quaan and Amatin disrupted his concentration. He wanted intensely to go after them. Warriors were escaping constantly across the last two spans, and he watched their flight with dread in his throat, aching to see their leaders.

One more span went down.

He stopped fighting altogether when Quaan appeared alone in the doorway of the last crosswalk.

Quaan shouted across to the Keep, but Mhoram could not make out the word. He watched with clenched breath as four warriors raced towards the Warmark.

Then a blue-robed figure moved behind Quaan – Amatin. But the two made no move to escape. When the warriors reached them, they both disappeared back into the tower.

Stifling in helplessness, Mhoram stared at the empty doorway as if the strength of his desire might bring the two back. He could hear the Raver's hordes surging constantly upward.

A moment later, the four warriors reappeared. Between them they carried Hearthrall Borillar.

He dangled in their hands as if he were dead.

Quaan and Amatin followed the four. When they all had gained the Keep, the last crosswalk fell. It seemed to make no sound amid the clamour from the tower.

A mist passed across Mhoram's sight. He found that he was leaning heavily on Trevor; while he gasped for breath, he could not stand alone. But the Lord upheld him. When his faintness receded, he met Trevor's gaze and smiled wanly.

Without a word, they turned back to the defences of the gates.

The tower had been lost, but the battle was not done. Unhindered now by Amatin's fire, the dead were slowly able to push a path through the sand. The weight of their assault began to mount again. And the sensation of wrong that they sent shuddering through the stone increased. The High Lord felt Revelstone's pain growing around him until it seemed to come from all sides. If he had not been so starkly confronted with these dead, he might have believed that the Keep was under attack at other points as well. But the present need consumed his attention. Revelstone's only hope lay in burying the gates with sand before they broke.

He sensed Tohrm's arrival behind him, but did not turn until Quaan and Lord Amatin had joined the Hearthrall. Then he dropped his power and faced the three of them.

Amatin was on the edge of prostration. Her eyes ached in the waifish pallor of her face; her hair stuck to her face in sweaty strands. When she spoke, her voice quivered. 'He took a bolt meant for me. Borillar – he – I did not see *samadhi*'s aim in time.'

A moment passed before Mhoram found the self-mastery to ask quietly, 'Is he dead?'

'No. The Healers – he will live. He is a Hirebrand – not defenceless.'

She dropped to the stone and slumped against the wall as if the thews which held her up had snapped.

'I had forgotten he was with you,' Mhoram murmured. 'I am ashamed.'

'*You* are ashamed!' The rough croak of Quaan's voice caught at Mhoram's attention. The Warmark's face and arms were smeared with blood, but he appeared uninjured. He could not meet Mhoram's gaze. 'The tower – lost!' He bit the words bitterly. 'It is I who am ashamed. No Warmark would permit – Warmark Hile Troy would have found a means to preserve it.'

'Then find a means to aid us,' Tohrm groaned. 'These gates cannot hold.'

The livid desperation in his tone pulled all the eyes on the abutment towards him. Tears streamed down his face as if he would never stop weeping, and his hands flinched distractedly in front of him, seeking something impossible in the air, something that would not break. And the gates moaned at him as if they were witnessing to the truth of his distress.

'We cannot,' he went on. 'Cannot. Such force! May the stones forgive me! I am – we are unequal to this stress.'

Quaan turned sharply on his heel and strode away, shouting for timbers and Hirebrands to shore up the gates.

But Tohrm did not seem to hear the Warmark. His wet gaze held Mhoram as he whispered, 'We are prevented. Something ill maims our strength. We do not comprehend – High Lord, is there other wrong here? Other wrong than weight and dead violence? I hear – all Revelstone's great rock cries out to me of evil.'

High Lord Mhoram's senses veered, and he swung into resonance with the gut-rock of the Keep as if he were melding himself with the stone. He felt all the weight of *samadhi*'s dead concentrated as if it were impending squarely against him; he felt his own soul gates groaning, detonating, cracking. For an instant, like an ignition of prophecy, he became the Keep, took its life and pain into himself, experienced the horrific might which threatened to rend it – and something else, too, something distant, private, terrible. When he heard frantic feet clattering towards him along the main hall, he knew that Tohrm had glimpsed the truth.

One of the two men Mhoram had sent to watch over Trell dashed forward, jerked to a halt. His face was as white as terror, and he could hardly thrust words stuttering through his teeth.

'High Lord, come! He! – the Close! Oh, help him!'

Amatin covered her head with her arms as if she could not bear any more. But the High Lord said, 'I hear you. Remember who you are. Speak clearly.'

The man gulped sickly several times. 'Trell – you sent – he immolates himself. He will destroy the Close.'

A hoarse cry broke from Tohrm, and Amatin gasped, *'Melenkurion!'* Mhoram stared at the warrior as if he could not believe what he had heard. But he believed it; he felt the truth of it. He was appalled by the dreadful understanding that this knowledge also had come too late. Once again, he had failed of foresight, failed to meet the needs of the Keep. Spun by irrefusable exigencies, he wheeled on Lord Trevor and demanded, 'Where is Loerya?'

For the first time since his rescue, Trevor's exaltation wavered. He stood in his own blood as if his injury had no power to hurt him, but the mention of his wife pained him like a flaw in his new courage. 'She,' he began, then stopped to swallow thickly. 'She has left the Keep. Last night – she took the children upland – to find a place of hiding. So that they would be safe.'

'By the Seven!' Mhoram barked, raving at all his failures rather than at Trevor. 'She is needed!' Revelstone's situation was desperate, and neither Trevor nor Amatin were in any condition to go on fighting. For an instant, Mhoram felt that the dilemma could not be resolved, that he could not make these decisions for the Keep. But he was Mhoram son of Variol, High Lord by the choice of the Council. He had said to the warrior: *Remember who you are.* He had said it to Tohrm. He was High Lord Mhoram, incapable of surrender. He struck the stone with his staff so that its iron heel rang, and sprang to his work.

'Lord Trevor, can you hold the gates?'

Trevor met Mhoram's gaze. 'Do not fear, High Lord. If they can be held, I will hold them.'

'Good.' The High Lord turned his back on the courtyard. 'Lord Amatin – Hearthrall Tohrm – will you aid me?'

For answer, Tohrm met the outreach of Amatin's arm and helped her to her feet.

Taking the fear-blanched warrior by the arm, Mhoram hastened away into the Keep.

As he strode through the halls towards the Close, he asked the warrior to tell him what had happened. 'He – it – ' the man stammered. But then he seemed to draw a measure of steadiness from Mhoram's grip. 'It surpassed me, High Lord.'

'What has happened?' repeated Mhoram firmly.

'At your command, we followed him. When he learned that we did not mean to leave him, he reviled us. But his cursing showed us a part of the reason for your command. We were resolved to obey you. At last he turned from us like a broken man and led us to the Close.

'There he went to the great graveling pit and knelt beside it. While we watched over him from the doors, he wept and prayed, begging. High Lord, it is in my heart that he begged for peace. But he found no peace. When he raised his head, we saw – we saw abomination in his face. He – the graveling – flame came from the fire-stones. Fire sprang from the floor. We ran down to him. But the flames forbade us. They consumed my comrade. I ran to you.'

The words chilled Mhoram's heart, but he replied to meet the pain and faltering in the warrior's face. 'His Oath of Peace was broken. He lost self-trust, and fell into despair. This is the shadow of the Grey Slayer upon him.'

After a moment, the warrior said hesitantly, 'I have heard – it is said – is this not the Unbeliever's doing?'

'Perhaps. In some measure, the Unbeliever is Lord Foul's doing. But Trell's despair is also in part my doing. It is Trell's own doing. The Slayer's great strength is that our mortal weakness may be so turned against us.'

He spoke as calmly as he could, but before he was within a hundred yards of the Close, he began to feel the heat of the flames. He had no doubt that this was the source of the other ill Tohrm had sensed. Hot waves of desecration radiated in all directions from the council chamber. As he neared the high wooden doors, he saw that they were smouldering, nearly aflame, and the walls shimmered as if the stone were about to melt. He was panting for breath, wincing against the heat, even before he reached the open doorway and looked down into the Close.

An inferno raged within it. Floors, tables, seats – all burned madly, sprouted roaring flames like a convulsion of thunder. Heat scorched Mhoram's face, crisped his hair. He had to blink tears away before he could peer down through the conflagration to its centre.

There Trell stood in the graveling pit like the core of a holocaust, bursting with flames and hurling great gouts of fire at the ceiling with both fists. His whole form blazed like incarnated damnation, white-hot torment striking out at the stone it loved and could not save.

The sheer power of it staggered Mhoram. He was looking at the onset of a Ritual of Desecration. Trell had found in his own despair the secret which Mhoram had guarded so fearfully, and he was using that secret against Revelstone. If he were not stopped, the gates would only be the first part of the Keep to break, the first and least link in a chain of destruction which might tear the whole plateau to rubble.

He had to be stopped. That was imperative. But Mhoram was not a Gravelingas, had no stone-lore to counter the might which made this fire possible. He turned to Tohrm.

'You are of the *rhadhamaerl*!' he shouted over the raving of the fire. 'You must silence this flame!'

'Silence it?' Tohrm was staring, aghast, into the blaze; he had the stricken look of a man witnessing the ravage of his dearest love. 'Silence it?' He did not shout; Mhoram could only comprehend him by reading his lips. 'I have no strength to equal this. I am a Gravelingas of the *rhadhamaerl* – not Earthpower incarnate. He will destroy us all.'

'Tohrm!' the High Lord cried. 'You are the Hearthrall of Lord's Keep! You or no one can meet this need!'

Tohrm mouthed soundlessly. 'How?'

'I will accompany you! I will give you my strength – I will place all my power in you!'

The Hearthrall's eyes rolled fearfully away from the Close and hauled themselves by sheer force of will into focus on the High Lord's face.

'We will burn.'

'We will endure!'

Tohrm met Mhoram's demand for a long moment. Then he groaned. He could not refuse to give himself for the sake of the Keep's stone. 'If you are with me,' he said silently through the roar.

Mhoram whirled to Amatin. 'Tohrm and I will go into the Close. You must preserve us from the fire. Put your power around us – protect us.'

She nodded, distractedly, pushed a damp strand of hair out of her face. 'Go,' she said weakly. 'Already the table melts.'

The High Lord saw that she was right. Before their eyes, the table slumped into magma, poured down to the lowest level of the Close and into the pit around Trell's feet.

Mhoram called his power into readiness and rested the shaft of his staff on Tohrm's shoulder. Together they faced the Close, waited while Amatin built a defence around them. The sensation of it swarmed over their skin like hiving insects, but it kept back the heat.

When she signalled to them, they started down into the Close as if they were struggling into a furnace.

Despite Amatin's protection, the heat slammed into them like the fist of a cataclysm. Tohrm's tunic began to scorch. Mhoram felt his own robe blackening. All the hair on their heads and arms shrivelled. But the High Lord put heat out of his mind; he concentrated on his staff and Tohrm. He could feel the Hearthrall singing now, though he heard nothing but the deep, ravenous howl of the blaze. Tuning his power to the pitch of Tohrm's song, he sent all his resources running through it.

The savage flames backed slightly away from them as they moved, and patches of unburned rock appeared like stepping-stones under Tohrm's feet. They walked downward like a gap in the hell of Trell's rage.

But the conflagration sealed behind them instantly. As they drew farther from the doors, Amatin's defence weakened; distance and flame interfered. Mhoram's flesh stung where his robe smouldered against it, and his eyes hurt so badly that he could no longer see. Tohrm's song became more and more like a scream as they descended. By the time they reached the level of the pit, where Loric's *krill* still stood embedded in its stone, Mhoram knew that if he did not take his strength away from Tohrm and use it for protection they would both roast at Trell's feet.

'Trell!' Tohrm screamed soundlessly. 'You are a Gravelingas of the *rhadhamaerl*! Do not do this!'

For an instant, the fury of the inferno paused. Trell looked at them, seemed to see them, recognize them.

'Trell!'

But he had fallen too far under the power of his own holocaust. He pointed a rigid, accusing finger, then stooped to the graveling and heaved a double armful of fire at them.

At the same moment, a thrill of strength ran through Mhoram. Amatin's protection steadied, stiffened. Though the force of Trell's attack knocked Tohrm back into Mhoram's arms, the fire did not touch them. And Amatin's sudden discovery of power called up an answer in the High Lord. With a look like joy gleaming in his eyes, he swept aside all his self-restraints and turned to his secret understanding of desecration. That secret contained might – might which the Lords had failed to discover because of their Oath of Peace – might which could be used to preserve as well as destroy. Despair was not the only unlocking emotion. Mhoram freed his own passion and stood against the devastation of the Close.

Power coursed vividly in his chest and arms and staff. Power made even his flesh and blood seem like invulnerable bone. Power shone out from him to oppose Trell's ill. And the surge of his strength restored Tohrm. The Hearthrall regained his feet, summoned his lore; with all of his and Mhoram's energy, he resisted Trell.

Confronting each other, standing almost face to face, the two Gravelingases wove their lore-secret gestures, sang their potent *rhadhamaerl* invocations. While the fire raged as if Revelstone were about to crash down upon them, they commanded the blaze, wrestled will against will for mastery of it.

Tohrm was exalted by Mhoram's support. With the High Lord's power resonating in every word and note and gesture, renewing him, fulfilling his love for the stone, he bent back the desecration. After a last convulsive exertion, Trell fell to his knees, and his fire began to fail.

It ran out of the Close like the recession of a tide – slowly at first, then faster, as the force which had raised it broke. The heat declined; cool fresh air poured around Mhoram from the airways of the Keep. Sight returned to his scorched eyes. For a moment, he feared that he would lose consciousness in relief.

Weeping with joy and grief, he went to help Tohrm lift Trell Atiaran-mate from the graveling pit. Trell gave no sign that he felt them, knew in any way that they were present. He looked around with hollow eyes, muttering brokenly, 'Intact. There is nothing intact. Nothing.' Then he covered his head with his arms and huddled into himself on the floor at Mhoram's feet, shaking as if he needed to sob and could not.

Tohrm met Mhoram's gaze. For a long moment, they looked into each other's faces, measuring what they had done together. Tohrm's features had the burned aspect of a wilderland, a place that would never grin again. But his emotion was clear and clean as he murmured at last, 'We will grieve for him. The *rhadhamaerl* will grieve. The time has come for mourning.'

From the top of the stairs, an excited voice cried, 'High Lord! The dead! They have all fallen into sand! Satanfist has exhausted this attack. The gates hold!'

Through his tears, Mhoram looked around the Close. It was badly damaged. The Lords' table and chairs had melted, the steps were uneven, and most of the lower tiers had been misshaped by the fire. But the place had survived. The Keep had survived. Mhoram nodded to Tohrm. 'It is time.'

His sight was so blurred with tears that he seemed to see two blue-robed figures moving down the stairs towards him. He blinked his tears away, and saw that Lord Loerya was with Amatin.

Her presence explained the protection which had saved him and Tohrm; she had joined her strength to Amatin's.

When she reached him, she looked gravely into his face. He searched her for shame or distress but saw only regret. 'I left them with the Unfettered One at Glimmermere,' she explained quietly. 'Perhaps they will be safe. I returned – when I found courage.'

Then something at Mhoram's side caught her attention. Wonder lit her face, and she turned him so that he was looking at the table which held Loric's *krill*.

The table was intact.

In its centre, the gem of the *krill* blazed with a pure white fire, as radiant as hope.

Mhoram heard someone say, 'Ur-Lord Covenant has returned to the Land.' But he could no longer tell what was happening around him. His tears seemed to blind all his senses.

Following the light of the gem, he reached out his hand and clasped the *krill*'s haft. In its intense heat, he felt the truth of what he had heard. The Unbeliever had returned.

With his new might, he gripped the *krill* and pulled it easily from the stone. Its edges were so sharp that when he held the knife in his hand he could see their keenness. His power protected him from the heat.

He turned to his companions with a smile that he felt like a ray of sunshine on his face.

'Summon Lord Trevor,' he said gladly. 'I have – a knowledge of power that I wish to share with you.'

12

AMANIBHAVAM

Hate.

It was the only thought in Covenant's mind. The weight of things he had not known crushed everything else.

Hate.

He clung to the unanswered question as he pried himself with the spear up over the rim of the hollow and hobbled down beyond the last ember-light of Pietten's fire.

Hate.

His crippled foot dragged along the ground, grinding the splintered bones of his ankle together until beads of excruciation burst from his pores and froze in the winter wind. But he clutched the shaft of the spear and lurched ahead, down that hillside and diagonally up the next. The wind cut against his right cheek, but he paid no attention to it; he turned gradually towards the right because of the steepness of the hill, not because he had any awareness of direction. When the convolution of the next slope bent him northward again, away from the Plains of Ra and his only friends, he followed it, tottered down it, fluttering in the wind like a maimed wildman, thinking only:

Hate.

Atiaran Trell-mate had said that it was the responsibility of the living to make meaningful the sacrifices of the dead. He had a whole Land full of death to make meaningful. Behind him, Lena lay slain in her own blood, with a wooden spike through her belly. Elena was buried somewhere in the bowels of *Melenkurion* Skyweir, dead in her private apocalypse because of his manipulations and his failures. She had never even existed. Ranyhyn had been starved and slaughtered. Bannor and Foamfollower might be dead or in despair. Pietten and Hile Troy and Trell and Triock were all his fault. None of them had ever existed. His pain did not exist. Nothing mattered except the one absolute question.

He moaned deep in his throat, 'Hate?'

Nothing could have any meaning without the answer to that question. Despite its multitudinous disguises, he recognized it as the question which had shaped his life since the day he had first learned that he was subject to the law of leprosy. Loathing, self-loathing, fear, rape, murder, leper outcast unclean,– they were all the same thing. He hobbled in search of the answer.

He was totally alone for the first time since the beginning of his experiences in the Land.

Sick grey dawn found him labouring vaguely northeastward – poling himself feverishly with the spear, and shivering in the bitter ague of winter. The dismal light seemed to rouse parts of him. He plunged into the shallow lee of a hillside and tried to take the measure of his situation.

The shrill wind gibed around him as he plucked with diseased and frozen fingers at his pants leg. When he succeeded in moving the fabric, he felt a numb surprise at the dark discoloration of his flesh above the ankle. His foot sat at a crooked angle on his leg, and through the crusted blood he could see slivers of bone protruding against the thongs of his sandals.

The injury looked worse than it felt. Its pain grated in his knee joint dully, gouged aches up through his thigh to his hip, but the ankle itself was bearable. Both his feet had been frozen senseless by the cold. And both were jabbed and torn and painlessly infected like the feet of a pilgrim. He thought blankly that he would probably lose the broken one. But the possibility carried no weight with him, it was just another part of his experience that did not exist.

There were things that he should have been doing for himself, but he had no idea what they were. He had no conception of anything except the central need which drove him. He lacked food, warmth, knowledge of where he was or where he was going. Yet he was already urgent to be moving again. Nothing but movement could keep his lifeblood circulating – nothing but movement could help him find his answer.

No tentative or half-unready answer would satisfy his need.

He levered himself up, then slipped and fell, crying out unconsciously at the unfelt pain. For a moment, the winter roared in his ears like a triumphant predator. His breathing rasped him as if claws of cold had already torn his air passages and lungs. But he braced the spear on the hard earth again, and climbed up it hand over hand until he was erect. Then he lurched forward once more.

He forced himself up the hill and beyond it to a low ridge lying across his way like a minor wall. His arms trembled at the strain of bearing his weight, and his hands slipped repeatedly on the smooth shaft of the spear. The ascent almost defeated him. When he reached the top, air whooped brokenly in and out of his frostbitten lungs, and icy vertigo made the whole winterscape cant raggedly from side to side. He rested, leaning on the spear. His respiration was so difficult that he thought the frozen sweat and vapour on his face might be suffocating him. But when he tried to break it, it tore away like a protective scab, hurting his skin, exposing new nerves to the cold. He let the rest of his frozen mask remain, and stood panting until at last his vision began to clear.

The hard barren region ahead of him was so dreary, so wilderlanded by Foul's cruelty, that he could hardly bear to look at it. It was grey cold and dead from horizon to horizon under the grey dead clouds – not the soft comfortable grey of twilit illusions, of unstark colours blurring like consolation or complacency into each other, but rather the grey of disconsolation and dismay, paradoxically dull and raw, numb and poignant, a grey like the ashen remains of colour and sap and blood and bone. Grey winds drove grey cold over the grey frozen hills; grey snow gathered in thin drifts under the lees of the grey terrain; grey ice underscored the black, brittle, leafless branches of the trees barely visible in the distance on his left, and stifled the grey, miserable current of the river almost out of sight on his right; grey numbness clutched at his flesh and soul. Lord Foul the Despiser was everywhere.

Then for a time he remembered his purpose. He set his ice-muzzled teeth into the teeth of the cold and hobbled down from the ridge straight towards the source of the winter. Half blinded by the opposition of the wind, he stumped unheeding past slight shelters and straggling *aliantha*, thrust his tattered way among the hills, dragging his frozen foot like an accusation he meant to bring against the Despiser.

But gradually the memory faded, lapsed from his consciousness like everything else except his reiterating interrogation of hate. Some inchoate instinct kept him from wending downward towards the river, but all other sense of direction deserted him. With the wind angling against his right cheek, he struggled slowly upward, upward, as if it were only in climbing that he could keep himself erect at all.

As the morning passed, he began to fall more often. He could no longer retain his grip on the spear; his hands were too stiff, too weak, and a slick sheen of ice sweat made the spear too slippery. Amid the crunch of ice and his own panting cries, he slipped repeatedly to the ground. And after several convulsive efforts to go on, he lay face down on the ruined earth with his breath rattling in his throat, and tried to sleep.

But before long he moved again. Sleep was not what he wanted; it had no place in the one focused fragment of his consciousness. Gasping thickly, he levered himself to his knees. Then, with an awkward abruptness, as if he were trying to take himself by surprise, he put weight on his broken ankle.

It was numb enough. Pain jabbed the rest of his leg, and his foot twisted under him. But his ankle was numb enough.

Ignoring the fallen spear, he heaved erect, tottered – and limped extremely into motion again.

For a long time, he went on that way, jerking on his broken ankle like a badly articulated puppet commanded by clumsy fingers. He continued to fall; he was using two hunks of ice for feet, and could not keep his balance when the hillsides became too steep. And these slopes grew gradually worse. For some reason, he tended unevenly to his left, where the ground rose up to meet black trees; so more and more often he came to ascents and descents that affected him like precipices, though they might have seemed slight enough to a healthy traveller. He went up them on hands and knees, clawing against the hard ground for handholds, and plunged rolling helplessly down them like one of the damned.

But after each fall he rested prone in the snow like a penitent, and after each rest he staggered or crawled forward once more, pursuing his private and inevitable apotheosis, though he was entirely unable to meet it.

As the day waned into afternoon, his falls came more and more often. And after falling he lay still and listened to the air sob in and out of his lungs as if the breaking of his ankle had fractured some essential bone in him, some obdurate capacity for endurance – as if at last numbness failed him, proved in some way inadequate, leaving him at the mercy of his injury. By degrees he began to believe that after all his dream was going to kill him.

Some time in the middle of the afternoon, he slipped, rolled, came to rest on his back. He could not muster the strength to turn over. Like a pinned insect, he struggled for a moment, then collapsed into prostrate sleep – trapped there between the iron heavens and the brass earth.

Dreams roiled his unconsciousness, giving him no consolation. Again and again, he relived the double-fisted blow with which he had stabbed Pietten. But now he dealt that fierce blow at other hearts – Llaura, Manethrall Rue, Elena, Joan, the woman who had been killed protecting him at the battle of Soaring Woodhelven – why had he never asked anyone her name? In dreams he slew them all. They lay around him with gleams of light shining keenly out of their wounds like notes in an alien melody. The song tugged at him, urged – but before he could hear it, another figure hove across his vision, listing like a crippled frigate. The man was dressed in misery and violence. He had blood on his hands and the love of murder in his eyes, but Covenant could not make out his face. Again he raised the knife, again he drove it with all his might into that vulnerable breast. Only then did he see that the man was himself.

He lurched as if the blank sky had struck him, and flopped over on to his chest to hide his face, conceal his wound.

When he remembered the snow in which he lay, he got quavering to his feet and limped on into the late afternoon.

Before long, he came to a hillside he could not master. He flung himself at it, limped and crawled at it as hard as he could. But he was exhausted and crippled. He turned left and stumbled along the slope, seeking a place where he could ascend, but then inexplicably he found himself rolling downward. When he tumbled to a stop at the bottom, he rested for a while in confusion. He must have crossed the top without knowing it. He hauled himself up again, gasping, and went on.

The next hill was no better. But he had to master it. When he could not drive himself upward any farther, he turned to the left again, always left and up, though for some strange reason this seemed to take him down towards the river.

After a short distance he found a trail in the snow.

Part of him knew that he should be dismayed, but he felt only relief, hope. A trail meant that someone had passed this way – passed recently, or the wind would have effaced the marks. And that someone might help him.

He needed help. He was freezing, starving, failing. Under its crust of scab and ice, his ankle was still bleeding. He had reached the infinitude of his impotence, his inefficacy, the point beyond which he could not keep going, could not believe, envision, hope that continuation, life, was possible. He needed whoever or whatever had made that trail to decide his fate for him.

He followed it to the left, downward, into a hollow between hills. He kept his eyes on the trail immediately before him, fearing to look up and find that the maker of the trail was out of sight, out of reach. He saw where the maker had fallen, shed blood, rested, limped onward. Soon he met the next hill and began crawling up it along the crawling trail. He was desperate – alone and impoverished as he had never before been in the Land.

But at last he recognized the truth. When the trail turned, crawled away to the left, fell back down the hillside, he could no longer deny that he had been following himself, that the trail was his own, a circle between hills he could not master.

With a thick moan, he passed the boundary. His last strength fell out of him. Keen gleams winked across the dark gulf behind his closed eyes, but he could not answer them. He fell backward, slid down the hill into a low snowdrift.

Yet even then his ordeal continued. His fall uncovered something in the snow. While he lay gasping helplessly, felt his heart tremble towards failure in his chest, a smell intruded on him. Despite the cold, it demanded his notice, it rose piquant and seductive in his face, ran into him on every breath, compelled him to respond. He propped himself up on quivering arms, and wiped the snow away with dead fingers.

He found grass growing under the snowdrift. Somehow its potent life refused to be quenched; even a few yellow flowers blossomed under the weight of the snow. And their sharp aroma caught hold of him. His hands were useless for plucking, so he knocked some of the ice from around his mouth. Then he lowered his face to the grass, tore up blades with his teeth and ate them.

As he swallowed the grass, its juice seemed to flow straight to his muscles like the energy of madness. The suddenness of the infusion caught him unawares. As he bent for a fourth bite, a convulsion came over him, and he collapsed into a rigid fetal position while raw power raged through his veins.

For an instant, he screamed in agony. But at once he passed beyond himself into a bleak wilderland where nothing but winter and wind and malice existed. He felt Lord Foul's preternatural assault on a level that was not sight or hearing or touch, but rather a compaction of all his senses. The nerves of his soul ached as if they had been laid bare to the livid ill. And in the core of this perception, a thought struck him, stabbed into him as if it were the spear point of the winter. He identified the thing he did not understand.

It was *magic*.

A suggestion of keen gleams penumbraed the thought, then receded. Magic: eldritch power, theurgy. Such a thing did not exist, could not exist. Yet it was part of the Land. And it was denied to him. The thought turned painfully in him as cruel hands twisted the spear.

He had heard Mhoram say, *You are the white gold*. What did that mean? He had no power. The dream was his, but he could not share its life-force. Its life-force was what proved it to be a dream. Magic: power. It sprang from him, and he could not touch it. It was impossible. With the Land's doom locked in the irremediable white gold circle of his ring, he was helpless to save himself.

Gripped by an inchoate conviction, where prophecy and madness became indistinguishable, he flung himself around the contradiction and tried to contain it, make it all one within him.

But then it faded in a scatter of keen alien gleaming. He found himself on his feet without any knowledge of how he had climbed erect. The gleam danced about his head like silent melody. The wild light of the grass played through his veins and muscles, elevating inanition and cold to the stature of gaunt priests presiding over an unholy sacrifice. He laughed at the immense prospect of his futility. The folly of his attempts to survive alone amused him.

He was going to die a leper's death.

His laughter scaled up into high gibbering mirth. Stumbling, limping, falling, lurching up and limping again, he followed the music towards the dark trees.

He laughed every time he fell, unable to contain the secret humour of his distress; the frozen agony grinding in his ankle drew shrill peals from him like screams. But though he was impatient now for the end, eager for any blank damnable repose, still the keen gleams carried him along. Advancing and receding, urging, sprinkling his way like glaucous petals of ambergris, they made him rise after each fall and continue towards the outskirts of the forest.

After a while, he began to think that the trees were singing to him. The gleams which fraught the air fell about him in alien intervals, like moist, blue-green shines of woodsong. But he could neither see nor hear them; they were apparent only to the restless energy in his veins. When in his wildness he tried to pluck them as if they were *aliantha*, they strewed themselves beyond his reach, enticing him on and on again after each fall until he found himself among the first winter-black trunks.

As he wended through the marge of the forest, he felt an unexpected diminution of the cold. Daylight was dying out of the ashen sky behind him, and ahead lay nothing but the brooding gloom of the forest depths. Yet the winter seemed to ease rather than sharpen with the coming of night. Shambling onward, he soon discovered that the snow thinned as he moved deeper among the trees. In a few places, he even saw living leaves. They clung grimly to the branches, and the trees in turn clung to each other, interwove their branches and leaned on each other's shoulders like staunch, broad, black-wounded comrades holding themselves erect together. Through the thinning snow, animal tracks made light whorls that dizzied him when he tried to follow them. And the air grew warmer.

Gradually, a dim light spread around him. For a time, he did not notice it to wonder what it was; he walked like a ruin along the alien spangles, and did not see the pale ghost-like expanding. But then a wet strand of moss struck his face, and he jerked into awareness of his surroundings.

The tree trunks were glowing faintly, like moonlight mystically translated out of the blind sky into the forest. They huddled around him in stands and stretches and avenues of gossamer illumination; they were poised on all sides like white eyes, watching him. And through their branches hung draped, dangled curtains and hawsers of moist black moss.

Then, in his madness, fear came upon him like a shout of ancient forestial rage, springing from the unavenged slaughter of the trees; and he turned to flee. Wailing lornly, he slapped the moss away from him and tried to run. But his ankle buckled under him at every stride. And the music held him. Its former allure became a command, swinging him against his will so that his panic itself, his very flight, drove him deeper among the trees and the moss and the light. He had lost all possession of himself. The strength of the grass capered in him like poison; the gleams danced through their blue-green intervals, guiding him. He fled like the hunted, battering and recoiling against trunks, tangling himself in moss, tearing his hair in fear. Animals scampered out of his wailing path, and his ears echoed to the desolate cries of owls.

He was soon exhausted. His flesh could not bear any more. As his wailing turned to frenzy in his throat, a large hairy moth the size of a cormorant suddenly fluttered out of the branches, veered erratically, and crashed into him. The impact knocked him to the ground in a pile of useless limbs. For a moment, he thrashed weakly. But he could not regain his breath, steady himself, rise. After a brief struggle, he collapsed on the warm turf and abandoned himself to the forest.

For a time, the gleaming hovered over him as if it were curious about his immobility. Then it spangled away into the depth of the trees, leaving him clapped in dolorous dreams. While he slept, the light mounted until the trunks seemed to be reaching towards him with their illumination, seeking a way to absorb him, rid the ground of him, efface him from the sight of their hoary rage. But though they glowered, they did not harm him. And before long a feathery scampering came through the branches and the moss. The sound seemed to reduce the trees to baleful insentience; they withdrew their threatening as a host of spiders began to drop lightly on to Covenant's still form.

Guided by gleams, the spiders swarmed over him as if they were searching for a vital spot to place their stings. But instead of stinging him, they gathered around his wounds; working together, they started to weave their webs over him wherever he was hurt.

In a short time, both his feet were thickly wrapped in pearl-grey webs. The bleeding of his ankle was staunched, and its protruding bone-splinters were covered with gentle protection. A score of the spiders draped his frostbitten cheeks and nose with their threads, while others bandaged his hands, and still others webbed his forehead, though no injury was apparent there. Then they all scurried away as quickly as they had come.

He slept on. His dreams racked him at odd moments, but for the most part he lay still, and so his ragged pulse grew steadier, and the helpless whimper faded from his breathing. In his grey webs, he looked like a cocooned wreck in which something new was aborning.

Much later that night, he stirred and found the keen gleams peering at him again through his closed eyelids. He was still far from consciousness, but the notes of the melody roused him enough to hear feet shuffling towards him across the grass. 'Ah, mercy,' an old woman's voice sighed over him, 'mercy. So peace and silence come to this. I left all thought of such work — and yet my rest comes to this. Have mercy.'

Hands cleared the gentle bindings from his head and face.

'Yes I see — for this reason the Forest called me from my old repose. Injured — cold-ill. And he has eaten *amanibhavam*. Ah, mercy. How the world intrudes, when even Morinmoss bestirs itself for such things as this. Well, the grass has kept life in him, whatever its penalty. But I mislike the look of his thoughts. He will be a sore trial to me.'

Covenant heard the words, though they did not penetrate the cold centre of his sleep. He tried to open his eyes, but they kept themselves closed as if out of fear of what he might see. The old woman's hands as they searched him for other injuries filled him with loathing; yet he lay still, slumberous, shackled in mad dreams. He had no volition with which to oppose her. So he lurked within himself, hid from her until he could spring and strike her down and free himself.

'Mercy,' she mumbled on to herself, 'mercy, indeed. Cold-ill and broken-minded. I left such work. Where will I find the strength for it?' Then her deft fingers bared his left hand, and she gasped, '*Melenkurion!* White gold? Ah, by the Seven! How has such a burden come to me?'

The need to protect his ring from her drew him closer to consciousness. He could not move his hand, could not even clench his fist around the ring, so he sought to distract her.

'Lena,' he croaked through cracked lips, without knowing what he said. 'Lena? Are you still alive?'

With an effort he pried open his eyes.

13

THE HEALER

Still sleep shrouded his sight; at first he saw nothing except the compact, baleful light of the trees. But his ring was in danger from her. He was jealous of his white gold. Sleep or no sleep, he did not mean to give it up. He strove to focus his eyes, strove to come far enough out of hiding to engage her attention.

Then a soft stroke of her hand swept the cobwebs from his eyebrows, and he found that he could see her.

'Lena?' he croaked again.

She was a dusky, loamy woman, with hair like tangled brown grass, and an old face uneven and crude in outline, as if it had been inexpertly moulded in clay. The hood of a tattered fallow-green cloak covered the crown of her head. And her eyes were the brown of soft mud, an unexpected and suggestive brown, as if the silt of some private devotion filled her orbs, effaced her pupils — as if the black, round nexus between her mind and the outside world were something that she had surrendered in exchange for the rare, rich loam of power. Yet there was no confidence, no surety in her gaze as she regarded him; the life which had formed her eyes was far behind her. Now she was old, timorous. Her voice rustled like the creaking of antique parchment as she asked, 'Lena?'

'Are you still alive?'

'Am I – ? No, I am not your Lena. She is dead – if the look of you tells any truth. Mercy.'

Mercy, he echoed soundlessly.

'This is the doing of the *amanibhavam*. Perhaps you have preserved your life in eating it – but surely you know that it is poison to you, a food too potent for human flesh.'

'Are you still alive?' he repeated with cunning in his throat. Thus he disguised himself, protected that part of him which had come out of hiding and sleep to ward his ring. Only the damaged state of his features kept him from grinning at his own slyness.

'Perhaps not,' she sighed. 'But let that pass. You have no knowledge of what you say. You are cold-ill and poison-mad – and – and there is a sickness in you that I do not comprehend.'

'Why aren't you dead?'

She brought her face close to his, and went on: 'Listen to me. I know that the hand of confusion is upon you – but listen to me. Hear and hold my words. You have come in some way into Morinmoss Forest. I am – a Healer, an Unfettered One who turned to the work of healing. I will help you – because you are in need, and because the white gold reveals that great matters are afoot in the Land – and because the Forest found its voice to summon me for you, though that also I do not comprehend.'

'I saw him kill you.' The raw croak of Covenant's voice sounded like horror and grief, but in his depths he hugged himself for glee at his cunning.

She drew back her head but showed no other reaction to what he had said. 'I came to this place – from my life – because the Forest's unquiet slumber met my own long ache for repose. I am a Healer, and Morinmoss permits me. Yet now it speaks – Great matters, indeed. Ah, mercy. It is in my heart that the Colossus itself – Well, I wander. I have made my home here for many years. I am accustomed to speak only for my own pleasure.'

'I saw.'

'Do you not hear me?'

'He stabbed you with a wooden spike. I saw the blood.'

'Mercy! Is your life so violent then? Well, let that pass also. You do not hear me – you have fallen too far into the *amanibhavam*. But violent or not I must aid you. It is well that my eyes have not forgotten their work. I see that you are too weak to harm me, whatever your purpose.'

Weak, he echoed to himself. What she said was true; he was too frail even to clench his fist for the protection of his wedding band.

'Have you come back to haunt me?' he gasped. 'To blame me?'

'Speak if you must,' she said in a rustling tone, 'but I cannot listen. I must be about my work.' With a low groan, she climbed to her feet and moved stiffly away from him.

'That's it,' he continued, impelled by his grotesque inner glee. 'That's it, isn't it? You've come back to torture me. You're not satisfied that I killed him. I put that knife all the way into his heart but you're not satisfied. You want to hurt me some more. You want me to go crazy thinking about all the things I'm guilty of. I did Foul's work for him, and you came to torture me for it. You and your blood! Where were you when it would have made a difference what happens to me? Why didn't you try to get even with me after I raped you? Why wait until now? If you'd made me pay for what I did then, maybe I would have figured out what's going on before this. All that generosity – ! It was cruel. Oh, Lena! I didn't even understand what I'd done to you until it was too late, too late, I couldn't help myself. What are you waiting for? Torture me! I need pain!'

'You need food,' the Healer muttered as if he had disgusted her. With one hand she fixed his jaw in an odd compelling grip while the other placed two or three treasure-berries in his mouth. 'Swallow the seeds. They, too, will sustain you.'

He wanted to spit out the *aliantha*, but her grip made him chew in spite of himself. Her other hand stroked his throat until he swallowed, then fed him more of the berries. Soon she had coerced him to eat several mouthfuls. He could feel sustenance flowing into him, yet for some reason it seemed to feed his deep slumber rather than his cunning. Before long he could not remember what he had been saying. An involuntary drowsiness shone into him from the trees. He was unable to resist or comply when the Healer lifted him from the grass.

Grunting at the strain, she raised his limp form until he was half erect in her arms. Then she leaned him against her back with his arms over her shoulders, and gripped his upper arms like the handles of a burden. His feet dragged behind him; he dangled on her squat shoulders. But she bore his weight, carried him like a dead sack into the pale white night of Morinmoss.

While he drowsed, she took him laboriously farther and farther into the secret depths of the Forest. And as they left its borders behind, they passed into warmer air and greater health – a region where spring had not been quenched by Lord Foul's winter. Leaves multiplied and spread out around bird nests to cloak the branches; moss and grass and small woodland animals increased among the trees. A defying spirit was abroad in this place – resisting cold, nourishing growth, affirming Morinmoss's natural impulse towards buds and new sap and arousal. It was as if the ancient Forestals had returned, bringing with them the wood's old knowledge of itself.

Yet even in its secret heart Morinmoss was not impervious to the Despiser's fell influence. Temperatures rose above the freezing point, but failed to climb any higher. The leaves had no spring profusion; they grew thinly, in dark bitter greens rather than in hale verdancy. The animals wore their winter coats over bones that were too gaunt for the true spring. If a Forestal had indeed returned to Morinmoss, he lacked the potency of his olden predecessors.

No, it was more likely that the monolithic Colossus of the Fall had shrugged off its brooding slumber to take a hand in the defences of the Forest. And it was more likely still that Caerroil Wildwood was reaching out from his fastness in Garroting Deep, doing what he could across the distance to preserve old Morinmoss.

Nevertheless, this lessening of winter was a great boon to the trees, and to the denizens of the Forest. It kept alive many things which might have been among the first to die when Lord Foul interdicted spring. For that reason among others, the Unfettered Healer trudged onwards with Covenant on her back. The defying spirit had not only tolerated both her and him; it had summoned her to him. She could not refuse. Though she was old, and found Covenant painfully heavy, she sustained herself by sucking moisture from the moss, and plodded under him towards her home among the secrets of the Forest.

The tree shine had lapsed into dim grey dawn before her journey ended at a low cave in the bank of a hill. Thrusting aside the moss which curtained its small entrance, she stooped and dragged Covenant behind her into the modest single chamber of her dwelling.

The cave was not large. It was barely deep enough for her to stand erect in its centre, and its oval floor was no more than fifteen feet wide. But it was a cosy home for one person. It had comfort enough in the soft loam of its walls and its bed of piled dry leaves. It was warm, protected from the winter. And when other lights were withdrawn, it was lit in ghostly filigree by the tree roots which held its walls and ceiling. In its underground safety, her small cookfire was not a threat to the Forest.

In addition to the low embers which awaited her against one wall, she possessed a pot of graveling. Dropping Covenant wearily on the bed, she opened the graveling and used some of its heat to resurrect her fire. Then she set her stiff old bones on the floor and rested for a long time.

It was nearly mid-morning when her fire threatened to die out.

Sighing dryly, she roused herself to stoke up a blaze and cook a hot meal for herself. This she ate without a glance at Covenant. He was in no condition for solid food. She cooked and ate to gather strength for herself, because her peculiar power of healing required strength – so much strength that she had exhausted her reserves of courage before reaching middle age, and had left her work to rest in Morinmoss for the remainder of her days. Decades – four or five, she no longer knew – had passed since she had fled; and during that time she had lived in peace and reticence among the seasons of the Forest, believing that the ordeals of her life were over.

Yet now even Morinmoss had bestirred itself to bring her work back to her. She needed strength. She forced herself to eat a large meal, then rested again.

But at last she rallied herself to begin the task. She set her pot of fire-stones on a shelf in the wall so that its warm yellow light fell squarely over Covenant. He was still asleep, and this relieved her; she did not want to face either his mad talk or his resistance. But she was made afraid once again by the extent of his sickness. Something bone-deep had hold of him, something she could not recognize or understand. In its unfamiliarity, it reminded her of old nightmares in which she had terrified herself by attempting to heal the Despiser.

The acute fracture of his ankle she did understand; his cold-bitten and battered hands and feet were within her experience, and she saw that they might even heal themselves, if he were kept warm for a long convalescence; his cheeks and nose and ears, his cracked lips with the odd scar on one side, his uncleanly healed forehead, all did not challenge her. But the damage the *amanibhavam* had done to his mind was another matter. It made his sleeping eyes bulge so feverishly in their sockets that through their lids she could read every flick and flinch of his wild dreams; it knuckled his forehead in an extreme scowl of rage or pain; it locked his hands into awkward fists, so that even if she had dared to touch his white gold she could not have taken it from him. And his essential sickness was still another matter. She caught glimpses of the way in which it was interwoven with his madness. She dreaded to touch that ill with her power.

To steady herself, she hummed an old song under her breath:

> When last comes to last,
> I have little power:
> I am merely an urn.
> I hold the bone-sap of myself,
> and watch the marrow burn.

When last comes to last,
   I have little strength:
   I am only a tool.
I work its work; and in its hands
   I am the fool.

When last comes to last,
   I have little life.
   I am simply a deed:
an action done while courage holds:
   A seed.

While she strove to master her faintheartedness, she made preparations. First she cooked a thin broth, using hot water and a dusty
powder which she took from a leather pouch among her few
belongings. This she fed to Covenant without awakening him. It
deepened his repose, made rest and unconsciousness so thick in him
that he could not have struggled awake to save his own life. Then,
when he was entirely unable to interfere with her, she began to strip
off his attire.

Slowly, using her own hesitation to enhance the thoroughness of
her preparations, she removed all his raiment and bathed him from
head to foot. After cleaning away the cobwebs and grime and old
sweat and encrusted blood, she explored him with her hands, probed
him gently to assure herself that she knew the full extent of his
hurts. The process took time, but it was done too soon for her
unready courage.

Still hesitating, she unwrapped from her belongings one of her
few prized possessions – a long, cunningly woven white robe, made
of a fabric both light and tough, easy to wear and full of warmth. It
had been given to her decades ago by a great weaver from Soaring
Woodhelven, whose life she had saved at severe cost to herself. The
memory of his gratitude was precious to her, and she held the robe
for a long time in hands that trembled agedly. But she was old now,
old and alone; she had no need of finery. Her tattered cloak would
serve her well enough as either apparel or cerement. With an
expansive look in her loamy eyes, she took the robe to Covenant
and dressed him tenderly in it.

The effort of moving his limp form shortened her breathing, and
she rested again, muttering out of old habit, 'Ah, mercy, mercy. This
is work for the young – for the young. I rest and rest, but I do not
become young. Well, let that pass. I did not come to Morinmoss in
search of youth. I came because I had lost heart for my work. Have I
not found it again – in all this time? Ah, but time is no Healer. The

body grows old – and now cruel winter enslaves the world – and the heart does not renew itself. Mercy, mercy. Courage belongs to the young, and I am old – old.

'Yet surely great matters are afoot – great and terrible. White gold! – by the Seven! White gold. And this winter is the Despiser's doing, though Morinmoss resists. Ah, there are terrible purposes – The burden of this man was put upon me by a terrible purpose. I cannot – I must not refuse. Must not! Ah, mercy, but I am afraid. I am old – I have no need to fear – no, I do not fear death. But the pain. The pain. Have mercy – have mercy upon me. I lack the courage for this work.'

Yet Covenant lay on her bed like an irrefusable demand moulded of broken bone and blood and mind, and after she had dozed briefly, she came back to herself. 'Well that too I must set aside. Complaint also is no Healer. I must set it aside, and work my work.'

Stiffly, she got to her feet, went to the far end of the cave to her supplies of firewood. Even now, she hoped in her heart that she would find she did not have enough wood; then she would need to hunt through the Forest for fallen dead branches and twigs before she could begin her main task. But her woodpile was large enough. She could not pretend that it justified any further delay. She carried most of the wood to her cookfire and faced the commencement of her ordeal.

First she took her graveling pot from the shelf above Covenant and made a place for it in the centre of the fire, so that its heat and light were added to the core of the coals. Then, panting already at the thought of what she meant to do, she began to build up the fire. She stoked it, concentrated it with dry hard wood, until its flames mounted towards the cave's ceiling and its heat drew sweat from her old brows. And when the low roar of its blaze sucked at the air, causing the moss curtains over the entrance to flutter in the draught, she returned to the pouch of powder from which she had made the broth. With her fist clenched in the pouch, she hesitated once more, faltering as if the next step constituted an irretrievable commitment. 'Ah, mercy,' she breathed brittlely to herself. 'I must remember – remember that I am alone. No one else will tend him – or me. I must do the work of two. For this reason eremites do not Heal. I must do the work.'

Panting in dismay at her own audacity, she threw a small quantity of the powder into the high fire.

At once, the blaze began to change. The flames did not die down, but they muted themselves, translated their energy into a less visible form. Their light turned from orange and red and yellow to brown, a steadily deepening brown, as if they sprang now from thick loam rather than from wood. And as the brightness of the fire dimmed, a rich aroma spread into the cave. It tasted to the Healer like the breaking of fresh earth so that seeds could be planted – like the lively imminence of seeds and buds and spring – like the fructifying of green things which had germinated in healthy soil. She could have lost herself in that brown fragrance, forgetful of Lord Foul's winter and the sick man and all pain. But it was part of her work. Through her love for it, it impelled her to Covenant's side. There she planted her feet and took one last moment to be sure of what she meant to do.

His hands and feet and face she would not touch. They were not crucial to his recovery, not worth what they would cost her. And the sickness in his mind was too complex and multifarious to undertake until he was physically whole enough to bear the strain of healing. So she bent her loamy gaze towards his broken ankle.

As she concentrated on that injury, the light of the fire became browner, richer, more potent and explicit, until it shone like the radiance of her eyes between her face and his ankle. The rest of the cave fell into gloom; soon only the link of sight between her attention and his pain retained illumination. It stretched between them, binding them together, gradually uniting their opposed pieces of need and power. Amid the heat and fragrancy of the fire, they became like one being, annealed of isolation, complete.

Blindly, tremulously, as if she were no longer aware of herself, she placed her hands on his ankle, explored it with her touch until she unconsciously knew the precise angle and acuteness of its fracture. Then she withdrew.

Her power subsumed her, made her independent flesh seem transient, devoid of significance; she became an involuntary vessel for her work, anchor and source of the bond which made her one with his wound.

When the bond grew strong enough, she retreated from him. Without volition or awareness, she stooped and picked up the smooth heavy stone which she used as a pestle; without volition or awareness, she held it like a weighty gift in both hands, offering it to Covenant. Then she raised it high over her head.

She blinked, and the brown link of oneness trembled.

With all her strength, she swung the stone down, slammed it against her own ankle.

The bones broke like dry wood.

Pain shot through her – pain like the splintering of souls, hers and his. She shrieked once and crumpled to the floor in a swoon.

Then time passed for her in a long agony that shut and sealed every other door of her mind. She lay on the floor while the fire died into dim embers, and the aroma of spring turned to dust in the air, and the ghostly fibres of the roots shone and waned. Nothing existed for her except the searing instant in which she had matched Covenant's pain – the instant in which she had taken all their pain, his and hers, upon herself. Night passed and came again; still she lay crumpled. Her breathing gasped hoarsely between her flaccid lips, and her heart fluttered along the verges of extinction. If she could have regained consciousness long enough to choose to die, she would have done so gladly, eagerly. But the pain sealed her within herself and had its way with her until it became all she knew of life or death.

Yet at last she found herself thinking that it had never been this bad when she was younger. The old power had not altogether failed her, but her ordeals at their worst had never been like this. Her body was racked with thirst and hunger. And this, too, was not as it had ever been before. Where were the people who should have watched over her – who should have at least given her water so that she did not die of thirst before the agony passed? Where were the family or friends who brought the ill and injured to her, and who gladly did all they could to aid the healing?

In time, such questions led her to remember that she was alone, that she and the sick man were both untended. He, too, had been without food or water during the whole course of her ordeal; and even if her power had not failed, he was in no condition to endure such privation. He might be dead in spite of what she had survived for him.

With an effort that made her old body tremble exhaustedly, she raised herself from the floor.

On her hands and knees she rested, panting heavily. She needed to gather the feeble remnant of herself before she faced the sick man. Miserable tasks awaited her if he were dead. She would have to struggle through the Despiser's winter to take that white gold ring to the Lords of Revelstone. And she would have to live with the fact that her agony had been the agony of failure. Such possibilities daunted her.

Yet she knew that even this delay might make the difference, might prove fatal. Groaning, she tried to stand up.

Before she could get her legs under her, movement staggered towards her from the bed. A foot kicked her to the floor again. The sick man lumbered past her and thrashed through the curtain of moss while she sprawled on the packed earth.

The surprise of the blow hurt her more than the kick itself; the man was far too weak to do her any real harm. And his violence rekindled some of her energy. Panting blunt curses to herself, she stumbled stiffly upright and limped out of the cave after him.

She caught up with him within twenty feet of the cave's mouth. The gleaming pale gaze of the tree trunks had stopped his flight. He reeled with fear whimpering in his throat, as if the trees were savage beasts crouched and waiting for him.

'You are ill,' the Healer muttered wearily. 'Understand that if you understand nothing else. Return to the bed.'

He veered around to face her. 'You're trying to kill me.'

'I am a Healer. I do not kill.'

'You hate lepers, and you're trying to kill me.' His eyes bulged insanely in his haggard face. 'You don't even exist.'

She could see that inanition had only aggravated his *amanibhavam* confusion and his inexplicable sickness; they had become so dominant that she could no longer tell them apart. And she was too weak to placate him; she had no strength to waste on words or gentleness which would not reach him. Instead, she simply stepped closer to him and jabbed her rigid fingers into his stomach.

While he fell gagging to the grass, she made her way to the nearest *aliantha*.

It was not far from the entrance to her cave, but her fatigue was so extreme that she nearly swooned again before she could pluck and eat a few of the treasure-berries. However, their tangy potency came to her aid as soon as she swallowed them. Her legs steadied. After a moment, she was able to throw the seeds aside and pick more berries.

When she had eaten half the ripe fruit, she picked the rest and took it back to Covenant. He tried to crawl away from her, but she held him down and forced him to eat. Then she went to a large sheet of moss hanging nearby, where she drank deeply of its rich green moisture. This refreshed her, gave her enough strength to wrestle the sick man back into the cave and control him while she put him back to sleep with a pinch of her rare powder.

Under other circumstances, she might have pitied the turgid panic with which he felt himself lapsing into helplessness again. But she was too weary – and too full of dread for the work she had yet to do. She did not know how to console him and made no attempt. When he fell into uneasy slumber, she only muttered, 'Mercy', over him, and turned away.

She wanted to sleep, too, but she was alone and had to bear the burden of care herself. Groaning at the unwieldiness of her old joints, she built another fire from the graveling and started a meal for herself and the sick man.

While the food heated, she inspected his ankle. She nodded dully when she saw that it was as whole as her own. Already his pale scars were fading. Soon his bones would be as well and sturdy as if they had never been fractured. Looking at the evidence of her power, she wished that she could take pleasure in it. But she had lost decades ago her capacity to be pleased by the results of her anguish. She knew with certainty that if she had comprehended when she was young what her decisions would cost, she would never have taken the Rites of Unfettering, never have surrendered to the secret power yearning for birth within her.

But power was not so easily evaded. Costs could not be known until they came to full fruition, and by that time the power no longer served the wielder. Then the wielder was the servant. No escape, no peace or reticence, could then evade the expense, and she could take no pleasure in healing. With the work she had yet to do lying stricken before her, she had no more satisfaction than choice.

Yet as she resumed her cooking, she turned her back on regret. 'Let it pass,' she murmured dimly. 'Let it pass. Only let it be done purely – without failure.' At least the work which remained would be a different pain altogether.

When the food was ready, she fed herself and Covenant, then gave him more of the soporific broth, so that he would not arise to strike her again. Then she banked her cookfire, pulled her tattered cloak tightly around her, and went agedly to sleep leaning against the pile of leaves that had been her bed.

In the days that followed, she rested, tended Covenant's madness, and tried to remember courage. His need made her heart quail in her old bosom. Even in his slumber she could see that his mind was being eaten away by its ingrown torments. As his body regained its strength, her potions slowly lost their ability to control the restlessness of his dream-ridden sleep. He began to flail his arms and jabber deliriously, like a man snared in the skein of a nightmare. At unexpected moments, his ring gave out white gleams of passion; and when by chance the Healer saw them squarely, they seemed to pierce her like a voice of misery, beseeching her to her work.

The Forest itself echoed his distress. Its mood bent in towards her like a demand, a compulsion as unmistakable as the summons which had called her to him in the beginning. She did not know why Monrinmoss cared; she only felt its caring brush her cheek like the palm of authority, warning her. He needed to be healed. If it were not done in time, the essential fabric of his being would rot beyond all restitution.

At last she became aware of time; she felt in the brightness of the tree shine that somewhere behind the impenetrable clouds moved a dark moon, readying itself for a new phase of the Despiser's power. She forced herself to unclench her hesitations, one by one, and to face her work again.

Then she built her high blaze for the second time and made ready her rare powder. While the hard wood took fire, she set both water and food on the shelf above Covenant so that if he regained consciousness before she did, he would not have to search for what he needed. A fatal mood was on her, and she did not believe she would survive. 'Mercy,' she muttered as the fire mounted, 'mercy.' She uttered the word as if she were seeking a benediction for herself.

Soon the flames filled her cave with light and heat, flushing the withered skin of her cheeks. The time had come; she could feel the power limping in her like a sere lover, oddly frail and masterful, yearning for its chance to rise up once more and take her – yearning, and yet strangely inadequate, old, as if it could no longer match what it remembered of its desires. For a moment, her blood deserted her; weakness filled all her muscles, so that the leather pouch fell from her fingers. But then she stooped to regain it, thrust her trembling hand into it, threw its dust into the fire as if that gesture were her last, best approximation of courage.

As the potent aroma of the dust spread its arms, took all the air of the cave into its embrace, began its slow transubstantiation of the firelight, she stood near Covenant's head and locked her quavering knees. Staring brownly at his forehead while the heat and illumination of the blaze came into consonance with her attention, she passed beyond the verges of volition and became once more the vessel of her power. Around her the cave grew dim as the rich loamy light of the bond wove itself between her pupilless orbs and his sick, mad mind. And before her Covenant tensed, stiffened – eyes staring gauntly, neck corded, knuckles white – as if her power clutched his very soul with fear.

Trembling, she reached out her hands, placed her palms flat against the gathered thunder of his forehead.

The next instant, she recoiled as if he had scalded her. 'No!' she cried. Horror flooded her, she foundered in it. 'You ask too much!' Deep within her, she fought to regain her self-command, fought to thrust down the power, deny it, return to herself so that she would not be destroyed. 'I cannot heal this!' But the man's madness came upon her as if he had reached out and caught her wrists. Wailing helplessly, she returned to him, replaced her palms on his forehead.

The terror of it rushed into her, filled her until it burst between her lips like a shriek. Yet she could not withdraw. His madness pounded through her as she sank into it, trying not to see what lay at its root. And when at last it made her see, forced her to behold

1008

itself, the leering disease of its source, she knew that she was ruined. She wrenched her seared hands from his head and went hunting, scrabbling frantically among her possessions.

Still shrieking, she pounced upon a long stone cooking knife, snatched it up, aimed it at his vulnerable heart.

He lay under the knife like a sacrifice defiled with leprosy.

But before she could stab out his life, consummate his unclean pain in death, a host of glaucous, alien gleams leaped like music into the air around her. They fell on her like dew, clung to her like moist melody, stayed her hand; they confined her power and her anguish, held all things within her until her taut, soundless cry imploded. They contained her until she broke under the strain of things that could not be contained. Then they let her fall.

Gleaming like the grief of trees, they sang themselves away.

14

ONLY THOSE WHO HATE

Covenant first awoke after a night and a day. But the stupor of essential sleep was still on him, and he only roused himself at the behest of a nagging thirst. When he sat up in the bed of leaves, he found a water jug on a shelf by his head. He drank deeply, then saw that a bowl of fruit and bread also occupied the shelf. He ate, drank again, and went back to sleep as soon as he had stretched himself out among the warm dry leaves once more.

The next time, he came languorously out of slumber amid the old gentle fragrance of the bed. When he opened his eyes, he discovered that he was looking up through a dim gloom of daylight at the root-woven roof of a cave. He turned his head, looked around the earthen walls until he located the moss-hung entrance which admitted so little light. He did not know where he was, or how he had come here, or how long he had slept. But his ignorance caused him no distress. He had recovered from fear. On the strength of unknown things which lay hidden behind the veil of his repose, he felt sure that he had no need to fear.

That feeling was the only emotion in him. He was calm, steady, and hollow – empty and therefore undisturbed – as if the same cleansing or apotheosis which had quenched his terror had also drained every other passion from him. For a time, he could not even remember what those passions had been; between him and his past lay nothing but sleep and an annealed gulf of extravagant fear.

Then he caught the first faint scent of death in the air. It was not urgent, and he did not react to it immediately. While he took its measure, made sure of it, he stretched his sleep-stiff muscles, feeling the flex of their revitalization. Whatever had brought him to this place had happened so long ago that even his body appeared to have forgotten it. Yet his recovery gave him little satisfaction. He accepted it with complete and empty confidence, for reasons that were hidden from him.

When he was ready, he swung his feet off the bed and sat up. At once, he saw the old brown woman lying crumpled on the floor. She was dead with an outcry still rigid on her lips and a blasted look in the staring loam of her eyes. In the dim light, she seemed like a racked mound of earth. He did not know who she was – he gazed at her with an effort of recollection and could not remember ever having seen her before – but she gave him the vague impression that she, too, had died for him.

That's enough, he said dimly to himself. Other memories began to float to the surface like the dead seaweed and wreckage of his life. This must not happen again.

He looked down at the unfamiliar white robe for a moment, then pushed the cloth aside so that he could see his ankle.

It was broken, he thought in hollow surprise. He could remember breaking it; he could remember wrestling with Pietten, falling – he could remember using Pietten's spear to help him walk until the fracture froze. Yet now it showed no sign of any break. He tested it against the floor, half expecting its wholeness to vanish like an illusion. He stood up, hopped from foot to foot, sat down again. Muttering dully to himself, By hell, by hell, he gave himself his first VSE in many days.

He found that he was more healed than he would have believed possible. The damage which he had done to his feet was almost completely gone. His gaunt hands flexed easily – though they had lost flesh, and his ring hung loosely on his wedding finger. Except for a faint numbness at their tips, his ears and nose had recovered from frostbite. His very bones were full of deep, sustaining warmth.

But other things had not changed. His cheeks felt as stiff as ever. Along his forehead was the lump of a badly healed scar; it was tender to the touch, as if beneath the surface it festered against his skull. And his disease still gnawed its way remorselessly up the nerves of his hands and feet. His fingers were numb to the palms, and only the tops of his feet and the backs of his heels remained sensitive. So the fundamental condition of his existence remained intact. The law of his leprosy was graven within him, carved with the cold chisel of death as if he were made of dolomite or marble rather than bone and blood and humanity.

For that reason he remained unmoved in the hollow centre of his healing. He was a leper and had no business exposing himself to the risks of passion.

Now when he looked back at the dead woman, he remembered what he had been doing before the winter had reft him of himself; he had been carrying a purpose of destruction and hate eastward, towards Foul's Creche. That purpose now wore the aspect of madness. He had been mad to throw himself against the winter alone, just as he had been mad to believe that he could ever challenge the Despiser. The path of his past appeared strewn with corpses, the victims of the process which had brought him to that purpose – the process of manipulation by which Lord Foul sought to produce the last fatal mistake of a direct challenge. And the result of that mistake would be a total victory for the Despiser.

He knew better now. The fallen woman taught him a kind of wisdom. He could not challenge the Despiser for the same reason that he could not make his way through the Despiser's winter alone: the task was impossible, and mortal human beings accomplished nothing but their own destruction when they attempted the impossible. A leper's end – prescribed and circumscribed for him by the law of his illness – awaited him not far down the road of his life. He would only hasten his journey towards that end if he lashed himself with impossible demands. And the Land would be utterly lost.

Then he realized that his inability to remember what had brought him to this place, what had happened to him in this place, was a great blessing, a giving of mercy so clear that it amazed him. Suddenly he understood at least in part why Triock had spoken to him of the *mercy* of new opportunities – and why Triock had refused to share his purpose. He put that purpose aside and looked around the cave for his clothes.

He located them in a heap against one wall, but a moment later he had decided against them. They seemed to represent participation in something that he now wished to eschew. And this white robe was a gift which the dead woman had given him as part and symbol of her larger sacrifice. He accepted it with calm, sad, hollow gratitude.

But he had already started to don his sandals before he realized how badly they reeked of illness. In days of walking, his infection had soaked into the leather, and he was loath to wear the unclean stench. He tossed the sandals back among his discarded apparel. He had come barefoot into this dream, and knew that he would go barefoot and sole-battered out of it again, no matter how he tried to protect himself. In spite of his reawakening caution, he chose not to worry about his feet.

The faint attar of death in the air reminded him that he could not remain in the cave. He drew the robe tight around him and stooped through the entrance to see if he could discover where he was.

Outside, under the grey clouds of day, the sight of the Forest gave him another surge of empty surprise. He recognized Morinmoss; he had crossed this wood once before. His vague knowledge of the Land's geography told him in general terms where he was, but he had no conception of how he had come here. The last thing in his memory was the slow death of Lord Foul's winter.

There was little winter to be seen here. The black trees leaned against each other as if they were rooted interminably in the first grey verges of spring; but the air was brisk rather than bitter, and tough grass grew sufficiently over the clear ground between the trunks. He breathed the Forest smells while he examined his unreasoning confidence, and after a moment he felt sure that Morinmoss also was something he should not fear.

When he turned to re-enter the cave, he had chosen at least the first outlines of his new road.

He did not attempt to bury the woman; he had no digging tool and no desire to offer any injury to the soil of the Forest. He wore her robe in part to show his respect for her, but he could not think of any other gesture to make towards her. He wanted to apologize for what he was doing – for what he had done – but had no way to make her hear him. At last he placed her on her bed, arranged her stiff limbs as best he could to give her an appearance of dignity. Then he found a sack among her possessions and packed into it all the food he could find.

After that, he drank the last of her water and left behind the jug to save weight. With a pang of regret, he also left behind the pot of graveling; he knew he would want its warmth, but did not know how to tend it. The knife which lay oddly in the centre of the floor he did not take because he had had enough of knives. Remembering Lena, he lightly kissed the woman's cold, withered cheek. Then he shrugged his way out of the cave, muttering, as if the word were a talisman he had learned from her sacrifice, 'Mercy'.

He strode away into the day of his new comprehension.

He did not hesitate over the choice of directions. He knew from past experience that the terrain of Morinmoss sloped generally downward from northwest to southeast, towards the Plains of Ra. He followed the slope with his sack over his shoulder and his heart hollow — steady because it was full of lacks, like the heart of a man who had surrendered himself to the prospect of a colourless future.

Before he had covered two leagues, daylight began to fail in the air, and night fell from the clouds like rain. But Morinmoss roused itself to light his way. And after his long rest, he did not need sleep. He slowed his pace so that he could move without disturbing the dark moss, and went on while the Forest grew lambent and restless around him. Its ancient uneasiness, its half-conscious memory of outrage and immense bereavement, was not directed at him — the perennial mood of the trees almost seemed to stand back as he passed, allowing him along his way — but he felt it nonetheless, heard it muttering through the breeze as if Morinmoss were breathing between clenched teeth. His senses remained truncated, winter-blurred, as they had been before his crisis with Pietten and Lena, but still he could perceive the Forest's sufferance of him. Morinmoss was aware of him and made a special exertion of tolerance on his behalf.

Then he remembered that Garroting Deep also had not raised its hand against him. He remembered Caerroil Wildwood and the Forestal's unwilling disciple. Though he knew himself suffered, permitted, he murmured, 'Mercy', to the pale, shining trunks and strove to move carefully, avoiding anything which might give offence to the trees.

His caution limited his progress, and when dawn came he was still wending generally southeast within the woods. But now he was re-entering the demesne of winter. Cold snapped in the air, and the trees were bleak. Grass had given way to bare ground. He could see the first thin skiffs of snow through the gloom ahead of him. And as dawn limped into ill day, he began to learn what a gift the white robe was. Its lightness made it easy to wear, yet its special fabric was warm and comfortable, so that it held out the harshness of the wind. He considered it a better gift than any knife or staff or *orcrest*-stone, and he kept it sashed gratefully around him.

Once the tree shine had subsided into daylight, he stopped to rest and eat. But he did not need much rest, and after a frugal meal he was up and moving again. The wind began to gust and flutter around him. In less than a league, he left the last black shelter of the Forest, and went out into Foul's uninterrupted spite.

The wilderness of snow and cold that met his blunt senses seemed unchanged. From the edges of the Forest, the terrain continued to slope gradually downward, through the shallow rumpling of old hills, until it reached the dull river flowing miserably into the north-east. And across his whole view, winter exerted its grey ruination. The frozen ground slumped under the ceaseless rasp of the wind and the weight of the snowdrifts until it looked like irreparable disconsolation or apathy, an abdication of loam and intended verdancy. In spite of his white robe and his recovered strength, he felt the cut of the cold, and he huddled into himself as if the Land's burden were on his shoulders.

For a moment he peered through the wind with moist eyes to choose his direction. He did not know where he was in relation to the shallows where he had crossed the river. But he felt sure that this river was in fact the Roamsedge, the northern boundary of the Plains of Ra. And the terrain off to his left seemed vaguely familiar. If his memory of the Quest for the Staff of Law did not delude him, he was looking down at the Roamsedge Ford.

Leaning against the wind, limping barefoot over the brutalized ground, he made for the Ford as if it were the gateway to his altered purpose.

But the distance was greater than it had appeared from the elevation of the Forest, and his movements were hampered by wind and snow and hill slopes. Noon came before he reached the last ridge west of the Ford.

When his gaze passed over the top of the ridge and down towards the river crossing, he was startled to see a man standing on the bank.

The man's visage was hidden by the hood of a Stonedownor cloak, but he faced squarely towards Covenant with his arms akimbo as if he had been impatiently awaiting the Unbeliever's arrival for some time. Caution urged Covenant to duck out of sight. But almost at once the man gestured brusquely, barking in tones that sounded like a distortion of a voice Covenant should have been able to recognize, 'Come, Unbeliever! You have no craft for hiding or flight. I have watched your approach for a league.'

Covenant hesitated, but in his hollow surety he was not afraid. After a moment, he shrugged, and started towards the Ford. As he moved down the hillside, he kept his eyes on the waiting man and searched for some clue to the man's identity. At first he guessed that the man represented a part of his lost experience in the Forest and the woman's cave – a part he might never be able to comprehend or evaluate. But then his eyes made out the pattern woven into the shoulders of the Stonedownor cloak. It was a pattern like crossed lightning.

'Triock!' he gasped under his breath. Triock?

He ran over the hard ground, hurried up to the man, caught him by the shoulders. 'Triock.' An awkward thickness in his throat constricted his voice. 'Triock? What are you doing here? How did you get here? What happened?'

As Covenant panted questions at him, the man averted his face so that the hood sheltered his features. His hands leaped to Covenant's wrists, tore Covenant's hands off his shoulders as if their touch were noxious to him. With unmistakable ire, he thrust Covenant away from him. But when he spoke, his barking tone sounded almost casual.

'Well, ur-Lord Covenant, Unbeliever and white gold wielder.' He invested the titles with a sarcastic twang. 'You have not come far in so many days. Have you rested well in Morinmoss?'

Covenant stared and rubbed his wrists; Triock's anger left a burning sensation in them, like a residue of acid. The pain gave him an instant of doubt, but he recognized Triock's profile beyond the edge of the hood. In his confusion, he could not think of a reason for the Stonedownor's belligerence. 'What happened?' he repeated uncertainly. 'Did you get in touch with Mhoram? Did you find that Unfettered One?'

Triock kept his face averted. But his fingers flexed and curled like claws, hungry for violence.

Then a wave of sorrow effaced Covenant's confusion. 'Did you find Lena?'

With the same hoarse casualness, Triock said, 'I followed you because I did not trust your purpose – or your companions. I see that I have not misjudged.'

'Did you find Lena?'

'Your vaunted aim against the Despiser is expensive in companions as well as in time. How was the Giant persuaded from your side? Did you leave him – ' he sneered – 'among the perverse pleasures of Morinmoss?'

'Lena?' Covenant insisted thickly.

Triock's hands jerked to his face as if he meant to claw out his eyes. His palms muffled his voice, made it sound more familiar. 'With a spike in her belly. And a man slain at her side.' Fierce trembling shook him. But abruptly he dropped his hands, and his tone resumed its mordant insouciance. 'Perhaps you will ask me to believe that they slew each other.'

Through his empty sorrow, Covenant replied, 'It was my fault. She tried to save me. Then I killed him.' He felt the incompleteness of this, and added, 'He wanted my ring.'

'The fool!' Triock barked sharply. 'Did he believe he would be permitted to keep it?' But he did not give Covenant time to respond. Quietly again, he asked, 'And the Giant?'

'We were ambushed. He stayed behind – so that Lena and I could get away.'

A harsh laugh spat between Triock's teeth. 'Faithful to the last,' he gibed. The next instant, a wild sob convulsed him as if his self-control had snapped – as if a frantic grief had burst the bonds which held it down. But immediately he returned to sarcasm. Showing Covenant a flash of his teeth, he sneered, 'It is well that I have come.'

'Well?' Covenant breathed. 'Triock, what happened to you?'

'Well, forsooth.' The man sniffed as if he were fighting tears. 'You have lost much time in that place of harm and seduction. With each passing day, the Despiser grows mightier. He straitly binds – ' His teeth grinned at Covenant under the shadow of his hood. 'Thomas Covenant, your work must be no longer delayed. I have come to take you to Ridjeck Thome.'

Covenant gazed intensely at the man. A moment passed while he tested his hollow core and found that it remained sure. Then he bent all his attention towards Triock, tried to drive his truncated sight past its limits, its superficiality, so that he might catch some glimpse of Triock's inner estate. But the winter, and Triock's distraction, foiled him. He saw the averted face, the rigid flex and claw of the fingers, the baring of the white wet teeth, the turmoil, but he could not penetrate beyond them. Some stark travail was upon the Stonedownor. In sympathy and bafflement and self-defence, Covenant said, 'Triock, you've got to tell me what happened.'

'Must I?'

'Yes.'

'Do you threaten me? Will you turn the wild magic against me if I refuse?' Triock winced as if he were genuinely afraid, and an oddly craven grimace flicked like a spasm across his lips. But then he shrugged sharply and turned his back, so that he was facing straight into the wind. 'Ask, then.'

Threaten? Covenant asked Triock's hunched shoulders. No, no. I don't want it to happen again. I've done enough harm.

'Ask!'

'Did you – ' he could hardly get the words through his clogged throat – 'did you find that Unfettered One?'

'Yes!'

'Did he contact Mhoram?'

'No!'

'Why not?'

'He did not suffice!'

The bitterness of the words barked along the bitter wind, and Covenant could only repeat, 'Triock, what happened?'

'The Unfettered One lacked strength to match the *lomillialor*. He took it from me and could not match it. Yeurquin and Quirrel were lost – more companions lost while you dally and falter!'

Both lost.

1016

'I didn't – How did you find me?'

'This is expensive blood, Covenant. When will it sate you?'

Sate me? Triock! The question hurt him, but he endured it. He had long ago lost the right to take umbrage at anything Triock might say. With difficulty, he asked again, 'How did you find me?'

'I waited! Where else could you have gone?'

'Triock.' Covenant covered himself with the void of his calm and said, 'Triock, look at me.'

'I do not wish to look at you.'

'Look at me!'

'I have no stomach for the sight.'

'Triock!' Covenant placed his hand on the man's shoulder.

Instantly, Triock spun and struck Covenant across the cheek.

The blow did not appear powerful; Triock swung shortly, as if he were trying to pull back his arm. But force erupted at the impact, threw Covenant to the ground several feet away. His cheek stung with a deep pain like vitriol that made his eyes stream. He barely saw Triock flinch, turn and start to flee, then catch himself and stop, waiting across the distance of a dozen yards as if he expected Covenant to hurl a spear through his back.

The pain roared like a rush of black waters in Covenant's head, but he forced himself to sit up, ignored his burning cheek, and said quietly, 'I'm not going to Foul's Creche.'

'Not?' Surprise spun Triock to face Covenant.

'No.' Covenant was vaguely surprised by his own certitude. 'I'm going to cross the river – I'm going to try to go south with the Ramen. They might – '

'You dare?' Triock yelled. He seemed livid with fury, but he did not advance towards Covenant. 'You cost me my love! My comrades! My home! You slay every glad face of my life! And then you say you will deny the one promise which might recompense? Unbeliever! Do you think I would not kill you for such treachery?'

Covenant shrugged. 'Kill me if you want to. It doesn't make any difference.' The pain in his face interfered with his concentration, but still he saw the self-contradiction behind Triock's threat. Fear and anger were balanced in the Stonedownor, as if he were two men trapped between flight and attack, straining in opposite directions. Somewhere amid those antagonists was the Triock Covenant remembered. He resisted the roaring in his head and tried to explain so that this Triock might understand.

'The only way you can kill me is if I'm dying in my own world. You saw me – when you summoned me. Maybe you could kill me. But if I'm really dying, it doesn't matter whether you kill me or not.

I'll get killed somehow. Dreams are like that.

'But before you decide, let me try to tell you why – why I'm not going to Foul's Creche.'

He got painfully to his feet. He wanted to go to Triock, look deeply into the man's face, but Triock's conflicting passions kept him at a distance.

'I'm not exactly innocent. I know that. I told you it was my fault, and it is. But it isn't *all* my fault. Lena and Elena and Atiaran – and Giants and Ranyhyn and Ramen and Bloodguard – and you – it isn't all my fault. All of you made decisions for yourselves. Lena made her own decision when she tried to save me from punishment – after I raped her. Atiaran made her own decision when she helped me get to Revelstone. Elena made her own decision when she drank the EarthBlood. You made your own decision – you decided to be loyal to the Oath of Peace. None of it is entirely my doing.'

'You talk as if we exist,' Triock growled bitterly.

'As far as my responsibility goes, you do. I don't control my nightmares. Part of me – the part that's talking – is a victim, as you are. Just less innocent.

'But Foul has arranged it all. He – or the part of me that does the dreaming – has been arranging everything from the beginning. He's been manipulating me, and I finally figured out why. He wants this ring – he wants the wild magic. And he knows – knows! – that if he can get me feeling guilty and responsible and miserable enough I'll try to fight him on his own ground – on his own terms.

'I can't win a fight like that. I don't know how to win it. So he wants me to do it. That way he ends up with everything. And I end up like any other suicide.

'Look at me, Triock! Look! You can see that I'm diseased. I'm a leper. It's carved into me so loud anybody could see it. And lepers – commit suicide easily. All they have to do is forget the law of staying alive. That law is simple, selfish, practical caution. Foul's done a pretty good job of making me forget it – that's why you might be able to kill me now if you want to. But if I've got any choice left, the only way I can use it is by remembering who I am. Thomas Covenant, leper. I've got to give up these impossible ideas of trying to make restitution for what I've done. I've got to give up guilt and duty, or whatever it is I'm calling responsibility these days. I've got to give up trying to make myself innocent again. It can't be done. It's suicide to try. And suicide for me is the only absolute, perfect way Foul can win. Without it, he doesn't get the wild magic, and it's just possible that somewhere, somehow, he'll run into something that can beat him.

'So I'm not going – I am not going to Foul's Creche. I'm going to do something simple and selfish and practical and cautious instead. I'm going to take care of myself as a leper should. I'll go into the Plains – I'll find the Ramen. They'll take me with them. The Ranyhyn – the Ranyhyn are probably going south already to hide in the mountains. The Ramen will take me with them. Mhoram doesn't know I'm here, so he won't be expecting anything from me.

'Please understand, Triock. My grief for you is – it'll never end. I loved Elena, and I love the Land. But if I can just keep myself alive the way I should – Foul can't win. He can't win.'

Triock met this speech queerly across the distance between them. His anger seemed to fade, but it was not replaced by understanding. Instead, a mixture of cunning and desperation gained the upper hand on his desire to flee, so that his voice held a half-hysterical note of cajolery as he said, 'Come, Unbeliever – do not take this choice hastily. Let us speak of it calmly. Let me urge – ' he looked around as if in search of assistance, then went on hurriedly – 'you are hungry and worn. That Forest has exacted a harsh penance – I see it. Let us rest here for a time. We are in no danger. I will build a fire – prepare food for you. We will talk of this choice while it may still be altered.'

Why? Covenant wanted to ask. Why have you changed like this? But he already knew too many explanations. And Triock bustled away promptly in search of firewood as if to forestall any questions. The land on this side of the Roamsedge had been wooded at one time, and before long he had collected a large pile of dead brush and bushes, which he placed in the shelter of a hill a short distance from the Ford. All the time, he kept his face averted from Covenant.

When he was satisfied with his quantity of wood, he stooped in front of the pile with his hands hidden as if for some obscure reason he did not want Covenant to see how he started the fire. As soon as flames had begun to spread through the brush, he positioned himself on the far side of the fire and urged Covenant to approach its warmth.

Covenant acquiesced gladly enough. His robe could not keep the cold out of his hands and feet; he could hardly refuse a fire. And he could hardly refuse Triock's desire to discuss his decision. His debt to Triock was large – not easily borne. He sat down within the radiant balm of the fire opposite Triock and silently watched him prepare a meal.

As he worked, Triock mumbled to himself in a tone that made Covenant feel oddly uncomfortable. His movements seemed awkward, as if he were trying to conceal arcane gestures while he handled the food. He avoided Covenant's gaze, but whenever Covenant looked away, he could feel Triock's eyes flick furtively over him and flinch away. He was startled when Triock said abruptly, 'So you have given up hate.'

'Given up – ?' He had not thought of the matter in those terms before. 'Maybe I have. It doesn't seem like a very good answer. I mean, aside from the fact that there's no room for it in – in the law of leprosy. Hate, humiliation, revenge – I make a mistake every time I let them touch me. I risk my life. And love, too, if you want to know the truth. But aside from that. It doesn't seem that I could beat Foul that way. I'm just a man. I can't hate – for ever – as he can. And – ' he forced himself to articulate a new perception – 'my hate isn't pure. It's corrupt because part of me always hates me instead of him. Always.'

Triock placed a stoneware pot of stew in the fire to cook and said in a tone of eerie conviction, 'It is the only answer. Look about you. Health, love, duty – none suffice against this winter. Only those who hate are immortal.'

'Immortal?'

'Certainly. Death claims all else in the end. How else do the Despiser and – and his – ' he said the name as if it dismayed him – 'Ravers endure? They hate.' In his hoarse, barking tone, the word took on a wide range of passion and violence, as if indeed it were the one word of truth and transcendence.

The savour of the stew began to reach Covenant. He found that he was hungry – and that his inner quiescence covered even Triock's queer asseverations. He stretched out his legs, reclined on one elbow. 'Hate,' he sighed softly, reducing the word to manageable dimensions. 'Is that it, Triock? I think – I think I've spent this whole thing – dream, delusion, fact, whatever you want to call it – I've spent it all looking for a good answer to death. Resistance, rape – ridicule – love – hate? Is that it? Is that your answer?'

'Do not mistake me,' Triock replied. 'I do not hate death.'

Covenant gazed into the dance of the fire for a moment and let the aroma of the stew remind him of deep, sure, empty peace. Then he said as if he were completing a litany, 'What do you hate?'

'I hate life.'

Brusquely, Triock spooned stew into bowls. When he handed a bowl around the fire to Covenant, his hand shook. But as soon as he had returned to his hooded covert beyond the flames, he snapped angrily, 'Do you think I am unjustified? You, Unbeliever?'

No. No. Covenant could not lift up his head against the accusation in Triock's voice. Hate me as much as you need to, he breathed into the crackling of the fire and the steaming stew. I don't want anyone else to sacrifice himself for me. Without looking up, he began to eat.

The taste of the stew was not unpleasant, but it had a disconcerting under-flavour which made it difficult to swallow. Yet once a mouthful had passed his throat, he found it warm and reassuring. Slowly, drowsiness spread outward from it. After a few moments, he was vaguely surprised to see that he had emptied the bowl.

He put it aside and lay down on his back. Now the fire seemed to grow higher and hotter, so that he only caught glimpses of Triock watching him keenly through the weaving spring and crackle of the flames. He was beginning to rest when he heard Triock say through the fiery veil, 'Unbeliever, why do you not resume your journey to Foul's Creche? Surely you do not believe that the Despiser will permit your flight – after he has striven so to bring about this confrontation of which you speak.'

'He won't want me to get away,' Covenant replied emptily, surely. 'But I think he's too busy doing other things to stop me. And if I can slip through his fingers just once, he'll let me go – at least for a while. I've – I've already done so much for him. The only thing he still wants from me is the ring. If I don't threaten him with it, he'll let me go while he fights the Lords. And then he'll be too late. I'll be gone as far as the Ranyhyn can take me.'

'But what of this – this Creator – ' Triock spat the word – 'who they say also chose you? Has he no hold upon you?'

Sleepiness only strengthened Covenant's confidence. 'I don't owe him anything. He chose me for this – I didn't choose it or him. If he doesn't like what I do, let him find someone else.'

'But what of the people who have died and suffered for you?' Triock's anger returned, and he ripped the words as if they were illustrations of meaning which he tore from the walls of a secret Hall of Gifts deep within him. 'How will you supply the significance they have earned from you? They have lost themselves in bootless death if you flee.'

I know, Covenant sighed to the sharp flames and the wind. We're all futile, alive or dead. He made an effort to speak clearly through his coming sleep. 'What kind of significance will it give them if I commit suicide? They won't thank me for throwing away – something that cost them so much. While I'm alive – ' he lost the thought, then recovered it – 'while I'm alive, the Land is still alive.'

'Because it is your dream!'

Yes. For that reason among others.

Covenant experienced a moment of stillness before the passion of Triock's response penetrated him. Then he hauled himself up and peered blearily through the fire at the Stonedownor. Because he could think of nothing else to say, he murmured, 'Why don't you get some rest? You probably exhausted yourself waiting for me.'

'I have given up sleep.'

Covenant yawned. 'Don't be ridiculous. What do you think you are? A Bloodguard?'

In answer, Triock laughed tautly, like a cord about to snap.

The sound made Covenant feel that something was wrong, that he should not have been so irresistibly sleepy. He should have had the strength to meet Triock's distress responsibly. But he could hardly keep his eyes open. Rubbing his stiff face, he said, 'Why don't you admit it? You're afraid I'll sneak off as soon as you stop watching me.'

'I do not mean to lose you now, Thomas Covenant.'

'I wouldn't – do that to you.' Covenant blinked and found his cheek resting against the hard ground. He could not remember having reclined. Wake up, he said to himself without conviction. Sleep seemed to be falling on him out of the greyness of the sky. He mumbled, 'I still don't know how you found me.' But he was asleep before the sound of his voice reached his ears.

He felt he had been unconscious for only a moment when he became aware on a half-subliminal level of darknesses thronging towards him out of the winter, as abysmal as death. Against them came faint alien gleams of music which he recognized and did not remember. They melodied themselves about him in blue-green intervals that he could neither hear nor see. They appeared weak, elusive, like voices calling to him across a great distance. But they were insistent; they nudged him, sang to him, plied him towards consciousness. Through his uncomprehending stupor, they danced a blind, voiceless warning of peril.

To his own surprise, he heard himself muttering: He drugged me. By hell! that crazy man drugged me. The assertion made no sense. How had he arrived at such a conclusion? Triock was an honest man, frank and magnanimous in grief – a man who clove to mercy and peace despite their cost to himself.

He drugged me.

Where had that conviction come from? Covenant fumbled with numb fingers through his unconsciousness, while an unshakable sense of peril clutched his heart. Darkness and harm crowded towards him. Behind his sleep – behind the glaucous music – he seemed to see Triock's campfire still burning.

How did he light that fire?

How did he find me?

The urgent gleams were trying to tell him things he could not hear. Triock was a danger. Triock had drugged him. He must get up and flee – flee somewhere – flee into the Forest.

He struggled into a sitting position, wrenched his eyes open. He faced the low campfire in the last dead light of evening. Winter blew about him as if it were salivating gall. He could smell the approach of snow; already a few fetid flakes were visible at the edges of the firelight. Triock sat cross-legged opposite him, stared at him out of the smouldering abomination of his eyes.

In the air before Covenant danced faint glaucous gleams, fragments of inaudible song. They were shrill with insistence: flee! flee!

'What is it?' He tried to beat off the clinging hands of slumber. 'What are they doing?'

'Send it away,' Triock answered in a voice full of fear and loathing. 'Rid yourself of it. He cannot claim you now.'

'What is it?' Covenant lurched to his feet and stood trembling, hardly able to contain the panic in his muscles. 'What's happening?'

'It is the voice of a Forestal.' Triock spoke simply, but every angle of his inflection expressed execration. He jumped erect and balanced himself as if he meant to give chase when Covenant began to run. 'Garroting Deep has sent Caer-Caveral to Morinmoss. But he cannot claim you. I can – ' his voice shook – 'I cannot permit it.'

'Claim? Permit?' The peril gripping Covenant's heart tightened until he gasped. Something in him that he could not remember urged him to trust the gleams. 'You drugged me!'

'So that you would not escape!' White, rigid fear clenched Triock, and he stammered through drawn lips, 'He urges you to destroy me. He cannot reach far from Morinmoss, but he urges – the white gold – ! Ah!' Abruptly, his voice sharpened into a shriek. 'Do not toy with me! I cannot – ! Destroy me and have done! I cannot endure it!'

The cries cut through Covenant's own dread. His distress receded, and he found himself grieving for the Stonedownor. Across the urging of the gleams, he breathed thickly, 'Destroy you? Don't you know that you're safe from me? Don't you understand that I haven't got one godforsaken idea how to use this – this white gold? I couldn't hurt you if that were my heart's sole desire.'

'What?' Triock howled. 'Still? Have I feared you for nothing?'

'For nothing,' groaned Covenant.

Triock gaped bleakly out from under his hood, then threw back his head and began to laugh. Mordant glee barked through his teeth, making the music shiver as if its abhorrence were no less than his. 'Powerless!' he laughed. 'By the mirth of my master! Powerless!'

Chuckling savagely, he started towards Covenant.

At once, the silent song rushed gleaming between them. But Triock advanced against the lights. 'Begone!' he growled. 'You also will pay for your part in this.' With a deft movement, he caught one spangle in each fist. Their wailing shimmered in the air as he crushed them between his fingers.

Ringing like broken crystal, the rest of the music vanished.

Covenant reeled as if an unseen support had been snatched away. He flung up his hands against Triock's approach, stumbled backward. But the man did not touch him. Instead, he stamped one foot on the hard ground. The earth bucked under Covenant, stretched him at Triock's feet.

Then Triock threw off his hood. His visage was littered with broken possibilities, wrecked faiths and loves, but behind his features his skull shone with pale malice. The backs of his eyes were as black as night, and his teeth gaped as if they were hungry for the taste of flesh. Leering down at Covenant, he smirked. 'No, groveller. I will not strike you again. The time for masquerading has ended. My master may frown upon me if I harm you now.'

'Master?' Covenant croaked.

'I am *turiya* Raver, also called Herem – and Kinslaughterer – and Triock.' He laughed again grotesquely. 'This guise has served me well, though "Triock" is not pleased. Behold me, groveller! I need no longer let his form and thoughts disguise me. You are powerless. Ah, I savour that jest! So now I permit you to know me as I am. It was I who slew the Giants of Seareach – I who slew the Unfettered One as he sought to warn that fool Mhoram – I who have captured the white gold! Brothers! I will sit upon the master's right hand and rule the universe!'

As he gloated, he reached into his cloak and drew out the *lomillialor* rod. Brandishing it in Covenant's face, he barked, 'Do you see it? High Wood! I spit on it. The test of truth is not a match for me.' Then he gripped it between his hands as if he meant to break it, and shouted quick cruel words over it. It caught fire, blazed for an instant in red agony, and fell into cinders.

Gleefully, the Raver snarled at Covenant, 'Thus I signal your doom, as I was commanded. Breathe swiftly, groveller. There are only moments left to you.'

Covenant's muscles trembled as if the ground still pitched under him, but he braced himself, struggled to his feet. He felt stunned with horror, helpless. Yet in the back of his mind he strained to find an escape. 'The ring,' he panted. 'Why don't you just take the ring?'

A black response leaped in Triock's eyes. 'Would you give it to me?'

'No!' He thought desperately that if he could goad Triock into some act of power, Caer-Caveral's glaucous song might return to aid him.

'Then I will tell you, groveller, that I do not take your ring because the command of my master is too strong. He does not choose that I should have such power. In other times, he did not bind us so

1024

straitly, and we were free to work his will in our several ways. But he claims – and – I obey.'

'Try to take it!' Covenant panted. 'Be the ruler of the universe yourself. Why should he have it?'

For an instant, he thought he saw something like regret in Triock's face. But the Raver only snarled, 'Because the Law of Death has been broken, and he is not alone. There are eyes of compulsion upon me even now – eyes which may not be defied.' His leer of hunger returned. 'Perhaps you will see them before you are slain – before my brother and I tear your living heart from you and eat it in your last sight.'

He laughed harshly, and as if in answer the darkness around the campfire grew thicker. The night blackened like an accumulation of spite, then drew taut and formed discrete figures that came forward. Covenant heard their feet rustling over the cold ground. He whirled, and found himself surrounded by ur-viles.

When their eyeless faces felt his stricken stare, they hesitated for an instant. Their wide, drooling nostrils quivered as they tasted the air for signs of power, evidence of wild magic. Then they rushed forward and overwhelmed him.

Livid red blades wheeled above him like the shattering of the heavens. But instead of stabbing him, they pressed flat against his forehead. Red waves of horror crashed through him. He screamed once and went limp in the grasp of the ur-viles.

15

'LORD MHORAM'S VICTORY'

The exertion of hauling the dead forms from the ground and throwing them at Revelstone had exhausted *samadhi* Satansfist, drained him until he could no longer sustain that expenditure of force. He had seen High Lord's Furl torn from its flagpole atop the tower by his Cavewights. He knew he had met at least part of his master's objective in this assault. While his forces held the tower – while tons of sand blocked the inner gates of the Keep – while winter barrened the upland plateau above Revelstone – the Lords and all their people were doomed. They could not feed themselves within those stone walls indefinitely. If last came to last, the Giant-Raver knew that he could through patience alone make the great Keep into one reeking tomb or crypt. He let his dead collapse into sand.

Yet his failure to burst those inner gates enraged him, made him pant for recompense even though he lacked the strength to assail the walls himself. He was a Raver, insatiable for blood despite the mortal limits of the Giantish body he occupied. And other things compelled him also. There was an implacable coercion in the wind, a demand which brooked no failure, however partial or eventually meaningless.

As the dead fell apart, Satansfist ordered his long-leashed army to the attack.

With a howl that shivered the air, echoed savagely off the carven walls, beat against the battlements like an ululation of fangs and claws and hungry blades, the Despiser's hordes charged. They swept up through the foothills like a shrill grey flood and hurled themselves at Revelstone.

Lord Foul's Stone-spawned creatures led the attack − not because they were effective against granite walls and abutments, but because they were expendable. The Raver's army included twice a hundred thousand of them, and more arrived every day, marching to battle from Foul's Creche through the Centre Plains. So *samadhi* used them to absorb the defence of the Keep, thus protecting his Cavewights and ur-viles. Thousands of perverted creatures fell with arrows, spears, javelins jutting from them, but many many thousands more forged ahead. And behind them came the forces which knew how to damage Revelstone.

In moments, the charge hit. Rabid, rockwise Cavewights found crafty holds in the stone, vaulted themselves up on to the lowest battlements and balconies. Mighty ur-vile wedges used their black vitriol to wipe clear the parapets above them, then pounced upward on sturdy wooden ladders brought to the walls by other creatures. Within a short time, Revelstone was under assault all along its south and north faces.

But the ancient Giants who made Lord's Keep had built well to defend against such an attack. Even the lowest parapets were high off the ground; they could be sealed off, so that the attackers were denied access to the city; they were defended by positions higher still in the walls. And Warmark Quaan had drilled the Warward year after year, preparing it for just this kind of battle. The prearranged defences of the Keep sprang into action instantly as alarms sounded throughout the city. Warriors left secondary tasks and ran to the battlements; relays formed to supply the upper defences with arrows and other weapons; concerted Eoman charged the Cavewights and ur-viles which breached the lower abutments. Then came Lorewardens, Hirebrands, Gravelingases. Lorewardens repulsed the attacks with songs of power, while Hirebrands set fire to the ladders, and Gravelingases braced the walls themselves against the strength of the Cavewights.

As he commanded the struggle from a coign in the upper walls, Quaan soon saw that his warriors could have repulsed this assault if they had not been outnumbered thirty or more to one – if every life in his army had not been so vital, and every life in the Raver's so insignificant. But the Warward was outnumbered; it needed help. In response to the fragmentary reports which reached him from the Close – reports of fire and power and immense relief – he sent an urgent messenger to summon the Lords to Revelstone's aid.

The messenger found High Lord Mhoram in the Close, but Mhoram did not respond to Quaan's call. It only reached the outskirts of his mind, and he held it gently distant, away from himself. When he heard one of the guards explain to the messenger what had transpired in the fire-ruined Close, he let his own awareness of the battle slip away – let all thought of the present danger drop from him, and gave himself to the melding of the Lords.

They sat on the slumped floor around the gaveling pit with their staffs on the stone before them – Trevor and Loerya on Mhoram's left, Amatin on his right. In his trembling hands, the *krill* blazed in hot affirmation of white gold. Yet he barely saw the light; his eyes were heat-scorched, and he was blinded by tears of release that would not stop. Through the silent contact of the meld, he spread strength about him, and shared knowledge which had burdened him more than he had ever realized. He told his fellow Lords how he had been able to remove the *krill* from its stone rest, and why now it did not burn his vulnerable flesh.

He could feel Amatin shrink from what he said, feel Trevor shake with a pain that only in part came from his injury, feel Loerya appraise his communication as she might have appraised any new weapon. To each of them, he gave himself; he showed them his conviction, his understanding, his strength. And he held the proof in his hands, so that they could not doubt him. With such evidence shining amid the ravage of the Close, they followed the process which had led him to his secret knowledge and shared the dismay which had taught him to keep it secret.

Finally, Lord Amatin framed her question aloud. It was too large for silence; it required utterance, so that Revelstone itself could hear it. She swallowed awkwardly, then floated words in the untarnished acoustics of the chamber. 'So it is we – we ourselves who have – for so many generations the Lords themselves have inured themselves to the power of Kevin's Lore.'

'Yes, Lord,' Mhoram whispered, knowing that everyone in the Close could hear him.

'The Oath of Peace has prevented – '

'Yes, Lord.'

Her breathing shuddered for a moment. 'Then we are lost.'

Mhoram felt the lorn dilemma in her words and stood up within himself, pulling the authority of His Lordship about his shoulders. 'No.'

'Without power, we are lost,' she countered. 'Without the Oath of Peace, we are not who we are, and we are lost.'

'Thomas Covenant has returned,' responded Loerya.

Brusquely, Amatin put this hope aside. 'Nevertheless. Either he has no power, or his power violates the Peace with which we have striven to serve the Land. Thus also we are lost.'

'No,' the High Lord repeated. 'Not lost. We – and ur-Lord Covenant – must find the wisdom to attain both Peace and power. We must retain our knowledge of who we are, or we will despair as Kevin Landwaster despaired, in Desecration. Yet we must also retain this knowledge for the Land. Perhaps the future Lords will find that they must turn from Kevin's Lore – that they must find lore of their own, lore which is not so apt for destruction. We have no time for such a quest. Knowing the peril of this power, we must cling to ourselves all the more, so that we do not betray the Land.'

His words seemed to ring in the Close, and time passed before Amatin said painfully, 'You offer us things which contradict each other, and tell us that we must preserve both, achieve both together. Such counsel is easily spoken.'

In silence, the High Lord strove to share with her his sense of how the contradiction might be mastered, made whole; he let his love for the Land, for Revelstone, for her, flow openly into her mind. And he smiled as he heard Lord Trevor say slowly, 'It may be done. I have felt something akin to it. What little strength I have returned to me when the Keep's need became larger for me than my fear of the Keep's foe.'

'Fear,' Loerya echoed in assent.

And Mhoram added, 'Fear – or hatred.'

A moment later, Amatin began to weep quietly in comprehension. With Loerya and Trevor, Mhoram wrapped courage around her and held her until her dread of her own danger, her own capacity to Desecrate the Land, relaxed. Then the High Lord put down the *krill* and opened his eyes to the Close.

Dimly, blurrily, his sight made out Hearthrall Tohrm and Trell.

Trell still huddled within himself, shirking the horror of what he had done. And Tohrm cradled his head, commiserating in *rhadhamaerl* grief with the torment of soul which could turn a Gravelingas against beloved stone. They were silent, and Mhoram gazed at them as if he were to blame for Trell's plight.

But before he could speak, another messenger from Warmark Quaan arrived in the Close, demanded notice. When the High Lord looked up at him, the messenger repeated Quaan's urgent call for help.

'Soon,' Mhoram sighed, 'soon. Tell my friend that we will come when we are able. The Lord Trevor is wounded. I am – ' with a brief gesture, he indicated the scalded skin of his head – 'the Lord Amatin and I must have food and rest. And the Lord Loerya – '

'I will go,' Loerya said firmly. 'I have not yet fought as I should for Revelstone.' To the messenger, she responded, 'Take me to the place of greatest need, then carry the High Lord's reply to Warmark Quaan.' Moving confidently, as if the new discovery of power answered her darkest doubts, she climbed the stairs and followed the warrior away towards the south wall of the Keep.

As she departed, she sent the guards to call the Healers and bring food. The other Lords were left alone for a short time, and Tohrm took that opportunity to ask Mhoram what was to be done with Trell.

Mhoram gazed around the ruined galleries as if he were trying to estimate the degree to which he had failed Trell. He knew that generations of *rhadhamaerl* work would be required to restore some measure of the chamber's useful rightness, and tears blurred his vision again as he said to Tohrm, 'The Healers must work with him. Perhaps they will be able to restore his mind.'

'What will be the good? How will he endure the knowledge of what he has done?'

'We must help him to endure. I must help him. We must attempt all healing, no matter how difficult. And I who have failed him cannot deny the burden of his need now.'

'Failed him?' Trevor asked. The pain of his injury had drawn the blood from his face, but he had not lost the mood which had inspired him to bear such a great share of the Keep's defence. 'In what way? You did not cause his despair. Had you treated him with distrust, you would have achieved nothing but the confirmation of his distress. Distrust – vindicates itself.'

Mhoram nodded. 'And I distrusted – I distrusted all. I kept knowledge secret even while I knew the keeping wrong. It is fortunate that the harm was no greater.'

'Yet you could not prevent – '

'Perhaps. And perhaps – if I had shared my knowledge with him, so that he had known his peril – known – Perhaps he might have found the strength to remember himself – remember that he was a Gravelingas of the *rhadhamaerl*, a lover of stone.'

Tohrm agreed stiffly, and his sympathy for Trell made him say, 'You have erred, High Lord.'

'Yes, Hearthrall,' Mhoram replied with deep gentleness in his voice. 'I am who I am – both human and mortal. I have – much to learn.'

Tohrm blinked fiercely, ducked his head. The tautness of his shoulders looked like anger, but Mhoram had shared an ordeal with the Hearthrall, and understood him better.

A moment later, several Healers hurried into the Close. They brought with them two stretchers, and carefully bore Trell away in one. Lord Trevor they carried in the other, peremptorily ignoring his protests. Tohrm went with Trell. Soon Mhoram and Amatin were left with the warrior who brought their food, and a Healer who softly applied a soothing ointment to the High Lord's burns.

Once Mhoram's hurts had been treated, he dismissed the warrior and the Healer. He knew that Amatin would want to speak with him, and he cleared the way for her before he began to eat. Then he turned to the food. Through his weariness, he ate deliberately, husbanding his strength so that when he was done he would be able to return to his work.

Lord Amatin matched his silence; she seemed to match the very rhythm of his jaws, as if his example were her only support in the face of a previously unguessed peril. Mhoram sensed that her years of devotion to Kevin's Wards had left her peculiarly unprepared for what he had told her; her trust in the Lore of the Old Lords had been exceedingly great. So he kept silent while he ate; and when he was done, he remained still, resting himself while he waited for her to speak what was in her heart.

But her question, when it came, took a form he had not anticipated. 'High Lord,' she said with a covert nod towards the *krill*, 'if Thomas Covenant has returned to the Land – who summoned him? How was that call performed? And where is he?'

'Amatin – ' Mhoram began.

'Who but the Despiser could do such a thing?'

'There are – '

'And if this is not Lord Foul's doing, then where has Covenant appeared? How can he aid us if he is not here?'

'He will not aid us.' Mhoram spoke firmly to stop the tumble of her questions. 'If there is help to be found in him, it will be aid for the Land, not aid for us against this siege. There are other places from which he may serve the Land – yes, and other summoners also. We and Lord Foul are not the only powers. The Creator himself may act to meet this need.'

Her waifish eyes probed him, trying to locate the source of his serenity. 'I lack your faith in this Creator. Even if such a being lives, the Law which preserves the Earth precludes – Do not the legends say that if the Creator were to break the arch of Time to place his hand upon the Earth, then the arch and all things in it would come to an end, and the Despiser would be set free?'

'That is said,' Mhoram affirmed. 'I do not doubt it. Yet the doom of any creation is upon the head of its Creator. Our work is enough for us. We need not weary ourselves with the burden of gods.'

Amatin sighed. 'You speak with conviction, High Lord. If I were to say such things, they would sound glib.'

'Then do not say them. I speak only of what gives me courage. You are a different person and will have a different courage. Only remember that you are a Lord, a servant of the Land – remember the love that brought you to this work, and do not falter.'

'Yes, High Lord,' she replied, looking intensely into him. 'Yet I do not trust this power which makes Desecration possible. I will not hazard it.'

Her gaze turned him back to the *krill*. Its white gem flamed at him like the light of a paradox, a promise of life and death. Slowly, he reached out and touched its hilt. But his exaltation had faded, and the *krill*'s heat made him withdraw his hand.

He smiled crookedly. 'Yes,' he breathed as if he were speaking to the blade, 'it is a hazard. I am very afraid.' Carefully, he took a cloth from within his robe; carefully, he wrapped the *krill* and set it aside until it could be taken to a place where the Lorewardens could study it. Then he glanced up and saw that Amatin was trying to smile also.

'Come, sister Amatin,' he said to her bravery, 'we have delayed our work too long.'

Together, they made their way to the battle, and with Lord Loerya they called fire from their staffs to throw back the hordes of the Despiser.

The three were joined late in the afternoon by a bandaged and hobbling Trevor. But by that time, Revelstone had survived the worst frenzy of Satansfist's assault. The Lords had given the Warward the support it needed. Under Quaan's stubborn command, the warriors held back the onslaught. Wherever the Lords worked, the casualties among the defenders dropped almost to nothing, and the losses of the attackers increased vastly. In this kind of battle, the ur-viles could not focus their power effectively. As a result, the Lords were able to wreak a prodigious ruin among the Cavewights and other creatures. Before the shrouded day had limped into night, *samadhi* Raver called back his forces.

But this time he did not allow the Keep to rest. His attacks began again shortly after dark. Under the cover of cold winter blackness, ur-viles rushed forward to throw liquid vehemence at the battlements, and behind them tight companies of creatures charged, carrying shields and ladders. Gone now was the haphazard fury of the assault, the unconcerted wild attempt to breach the whole Keep at once. In its place were precision and purpose. Growling with hunger, the hordes shaped themselves to the task of wearing down Revelstone as swiftly and efficiently as possible.

In the days that followed, there was no let to the fighting. Satansfist controlled his assaults so that his losses did not significantly outrun the constant arrival of his reinforcements; but he exerted pressure remorselessly, allowing the warriors no respite in which to recover. Despite Quaan's best efforts to rotate his Eoman and Eoward, so that each could rest in turn, the Warward grew more and more weary – and weary warriors were more easily slain. And those who fell could not be replaced.

But the Warward did not have to carry the burden of this battle alone. Gravelingases and Hirebrands and Lorewardens fought as well. People who had no other urgent work – homeless farmers and Cattleherds, artists, even older children – took over supporting tasks; they supplied arrows and other weapons, stood sentry duty, ran messages. Thus many Eoman were freed for either combat or rest. And the Lords rushed into action whenever Quaan requested their aid. They were potent and compelling; in their separate ways, they fought with the hard strength of people who knew themselves capable of Desecration and did not intend to be driven to that extreme.

Thus Lord's Keep endured. Eoman after Eoman fell in battle every day; food stores shrank; the Healers' supplies of herbs and poultices dwindled. Strain carved the faces of the people, cut away comfortable flesh until their skulls seemed to be covered by nothing but pressure and apprehension. But Revelstone protected its inhabitants, and they endured.

At first, the Lords concentrated their attention on the needs of the battle. Instinctively, they shied away from their dangerous knowledge. They spent their energy in work and fighting, rather than in studying last resorts. But when the continuous adumbrations of assault had echoed through the Keep for six days, High Lord Mhoram found that he had begun to dread the moment when Satansfist would change his tactics – when the Raver and his master were ready to use the Stone and the Staff again. And during the seventh night, Mhoram's sleep was troubled by dim dreams like shadows of his former visionary nightmares. Time and again, he felt that he could almost hear somewhere in the depths of his soul the sound of an Unfettered One screaming. He awoke in an inchoate sweat, and hastened upland to see if anything had happened to the Unfettered One of Glimmermere.

The One was safe and well, as were Loerya's daughters. But this did not relieve Mhoram. It left a chill in the marrow of his bones like an echo of winter. He felt sure that someone, somewhere, had been slain in torment. Straightening himself against the shiver of dread, he called the other Lords to a Council, where for the first time he raised the question of how their new knowledge could be used against the Despiser.

His question sparked unspoken trepidations in them all. Amatin stared widely at the High Lord, Trevor winced, Loerya studied her hands – and Mhoram felt the acuteness of their reaction as if they were saying, *Do you think then that we should repeat the work of Kevin Landwaster?* But he knew they did not intend that accusation. He waited for them, and at last Loerya found her voice. 'When you defended the Close – you worked against another's wrong. How will you control this power if you initiate it?'

Mhoram had no answer.

Shortly, Trevor forced himself to add, 'We have nothing through which we could channel such might. It is in my heart that our staffs would not suffice – they would not be strong enough to control power of that extent. We lack the Staff of Law, and I know of no other tool equal to this demand.'

'And,' Amatin said sharply, 'this knowledge in which you dare to put your faith did not suffice for High Lord Kevin son of Loric. It only increased the cost of his despair. I have – I have given my life to his Lore, and I speak truly. Such power is a snare and a delusion. It cannot be controlled. It strikes the hand that wields it. Better to die in the name of Peace than to buy one day of survival at the cost of such peril!'

Again, Mhoram had no answer. He could not name the reasons behind his question. Only the cold foreboding in his bones impelled him, told him that unknown horrors stalked the Land in places far distant from Revelstone. When Amatin concluded grimly, 'Do you fear that ur-Lord Covenant may yet Desecrate us?' he could not deny that he was afraid.

So the Council ended without issue, and the Lords went back to the defence of the Keep.

Still the fighting went on without surcease. For four more days, the Lords wielded their staff fire with all the might and cunning they

1033

could conceive – and the Warward drove itself beyond its weariness as if it could not be daunted – and the other people of Revelstone did their utmost to hurl Cavewights, ur-viles, Stonespawn, from the walls. But Satansfist did not relent. He pressed his assault as if his losses were meaningless, spent whole companies of his creatures to do any kind of damage to the city, however small. And the accumulating price that Lord's Keep paid for its endurance grew more terrible day by day.

During the fifth day, Mhoram withdrew from the battle to inspect the condition of the city. Warmark Quaan joined him, and when they had seen the fatal diminishment of the stores, had taken the toll of lost lives, Quaan met Mhoram's gaze squarely and said with a tremor in his brusque voice, 'We will fall. If this Raver does not raise another finger against us, still we will fall.'

Mhoram held his old friend's eyes. 'How long can we hold?'

'Thirty days – at most. No more. Forty – if we deny food to the ill, and the injured, and the infirm.'

'We will not deny food to any who yet live.'

'Thirty, then. Less, if my warriors lose strength and permit any breach of the walls.' He faltered and his eyes fell. 'High Lord, does it come to this? Is this the end – for us – for the Land?'

Mhoram put a firm hand on Quaan's shoulder. 'No, my friend. We have not come to the last of ourselves. And the Unbeliever – Do not forget Thomas Covenant.'

That name brought back Quaan's war-hardness. 'I would forget him if I could. He will – '

'Softly, Warmark,' Mhoram interrupted evenly. 'Do not be abrupt to prophesy doom. There are mysteries in the Earth of which we know nothing.'

After a moment, Quaan murmured, 'Do you yet trust him?'

The High Lord did not hesitate. 'I trust that Despite is not the sum of life.'

Quaan gazed back into this answer as if he were trying to find its wellspring. Some protest or plea moved in his face; but before he could speak, a messenger came to recall him to the fighting. At once, he turned and strode away.

Mhoram watched his stern back for a moment, then he stirred himself to visit the Healers. He wanted to know if any progress had been made with Trell Atiaran-mate.

In the low groaning hall which the Healers had made into a hospital for the hundreds of injured men and women, Mhoram found the big Gravelingas sprawled like a wreck on a pallet in the centre of the floor. A fierce brain-fever had wasted him. To Mhoram's cold dread, he looked like the incarnated fate of all

Covenant's victims – a fleshless future crouched in ambush for the Land. The High Lord's hands trembled. He did not believe he could bear to watch that ineluctable ravage happen.

'At first, we placed him near the wall,' one of the attendants said softly, 'so that he would be near stone. But he recoiled from it in terror. Therefore we have laid him here. He does not recover – but he no longer shrieks. Our efforts to succour him are confounded.'

'Covenant will make restitution,' Mhoram breathed in answer, as if the attendant had said something else. 'He must.'

Trembling, he turned away, and tried to find relief for his dismay in the struggle of Revelstone.

The next night, *samadhi* changed his tactics. Under cover of darkness, a band of Cavewights rushed forward and clambered up on to one of the main battlements, and when warriors ran out to meet the attack, two ur-vile wedges hidden in the night near the walls swiftly formed Forbiddings across the ends of the battlement, thus trapping the warriors, preventing any escape or rescue. Two Eoman were caught and slaughtered by the ur-viles before Lord Amatin was able to break down one of the Forbiddings.

The same pattern was repeated simultaneously at several points around the Keep.

Warmark Quaan had lost more than eightscore warriors before he grasped the purpose of these tactics. They were not intended to break into Revelstone, but rather to kill defenders.

So the Lords were compelled to bear the brunt of defending against these new assaults; a Forbidding was an exercise of power which only they were equipped to counter. As long as darkness covered the approach of the ur-viles, the attacks continued, allowing the Lords no chance to rest. And when dawn came, Sheol Satansfist resumed the previous strategy of his assault.

After four nights of this, Mhoram and his comrades were near exhaustion. Each Forbidding cost two of them an arduous exertion; one Lord could not counteract the work of three- or fivescore ur-viles swiftly enough. As a result, Amatin was now as pale and hollow-eyed as an invalid; Loerya's once-sturdy muscles seemed to hang like ropes of mortality on her bones; and Trevor's eyes flinched at everything he saw, as if even in the deepest safety of the Keep he was surrounded by ghouls. Mhoram himself felt that he had a great weight leaning like misery against his heart. They could all taste the accuracy of Quaan's dire predictions, and they were sickening on the flavour.

During a brief moment of dazed half-sleep late that fourth night, the High Lord found himself murmuring, 'Covenant, Covenant,' as if he were trying to remind the Unbeliever of a promise.

But the next morning the attacks stopped. A silence like the quietude of open graves blew into Revelstone on the wind. All the creatures had returned to their encampment, and in their absence Revelstone panted and quivered like a scourged prisoner between lashes. Mhoram took the opportunity to eat, but he put food into his mouth without seeing it and chewed without tasting it. In the back of his mind, he was trying to measure the remnant of his endurance. Yet he responded immediately when a message hastened up to him, informed him that *samadhi* Raver was approaching the Keep alone.

Protected by flanks of archers, from any attack by the enemy occupying the tower, Mhoram and the other Lords went to one of the high balconies near the eastward point of the Keep and faced Satansfist.

The Giant-Raver approached sardonically, with a swagger and confidence and a spring of contempt in his stride. His huge fist gripped his fragment of the Stone, and it steamed frigidly in the freezing air. He stopped just beyond effective bow range, leered up at the Lords, and shouted stertorously, 'Hail, Lords! I give you greeting! Are you well?'

'Well!' Quaan grated under his breath. 'Let him come five paces nearer, and I will show him "well".'

'My master is concerned for you!' *samadhi* continued. 'He fears that you have begun to suffer in this unnecessary conflict!'

The High Lord's eyes glinted at this gibe. 'Your master lives for the suffering of others! Do you wish us to believe that he has eschewed Despite?'

'He is amazed and saddened that you resist him. Do you still not see that he is the one word of truth in this misinformed world? His is the only strength – the one right. The Creator of the Earth is a being of disdain and cruelty! All who are not folly-blind know this. All who are not cowards in the face of the truth know that Lord Foul is the only truth. Has your suffering taught you nothing? Has Thomas Covenant taught you nothing? Surrender, I say! Give up this perverse and self-made misery – surrender! I swear to you that you will stand as my equals in the service of Lord Foul!'

In spite of his mordant sarcasm, the Raver's voice carried a strange power of persuasion. The might of the Stone was in his words, compelling his hearers to submit. As *samadhi* spoke, Mhoram felt that the flesh of his resistance was being carved away, leaving his bare bones exposed to the winter. His throat ached at the taste of abdication, and he had to swallow heavily before he could reply.

'*Samadhi* Sheol,' he croaked, then swallowed again and focused all his skeletal resolve in his voice. '*Samadhi* Sheol! You mock us, but we are not mocked. We are not blind – we see the atrocity which underlies your persuasion. Begone! Foul-chattel! Take this army of torment and despication -- return to your master. He has made your suffering -- let him take joy in it while he can. Even as we stand here, the days of his might are numbered. When his end comes upon him, be certain he will do nothing to preserve your miserable being. Begone, Raver! I have no interest in your cheap taunts.'

He hoped that the Raver would react with anger, do something which would bring him within reach of the archers. But Satansfist only laughed. Barking with savage glee, he turned away and gave a shout that sent his forces forward to renew their assault.

Mhoram turned also, pulled himself painfully around to face his fellow Lords. But they were not looking at him. They were intent on a messenger who stood trembling before them. Fear-sweat slicked his face despite the cold, and the muscles of his throat locked, clenched him silent. Mutely, he reached into his tunic, brought out a cloth bundle. His hands shook as he unwrapped it.

After a febrile moment, he exposed the *krill*.

Its gem was as dull as death.

Mhoram thought he heard gasps, groans, cries, but he could not be sure. Dread roared in his ears, made other sounds indistinguishable. He snatched up the *krill*. Staring aghast at it, he fell to his knees, plunged as if his legs had broken. With all the force of his need, he thrust his gaze into the gem, tried to find some gleam of life in it. But the metal was cold to his touch, and the edges of the blade were dull. Blind, lustreless winter filled the farthest depths of the jewel.

The hope of the wild magic was lost. Covenant was gone.

Now Mhoram understood why the Raver had laughed.

'Mhoram?'

'High Lord.'

'Mhoram!'

Supplications reached towards him, asking him for strength, begging him, requiring. He ignored them. He shrugged off the hands of melding which plucked at his mind. The prophecy of his dread had come to pass. He had nothing left with which to answer supplications.

'Ah, High Lord!'

There were tears and despair in the appeals, but he had nothing left with which to answer.

He was only dimly aware that he rose to his feet, returned the *krill* to the messenger. He wanted it removed from his sight as if it were a treacher, yet that feeling occupied only a distant portion of him. With the rest, he tightened his frail blue robe as if he were still fool enough to believe it could protect him from the cold, and walked numbly away from the battlement. The short, stiff shock of his hair, newly grown after the fire in the Close, gave him a demented aspect. People came after him, beseeching, requiring, but he kept up his wooden pace, kept ahead of them so that he would not have to see their needy faces.

He gave no thought to where he was going until he reached a fork in the passage. There, the weight of decision almost crushed him to his knees again – left and down into the Keep, or right and out towards the upland plateau. He turned to the right because he could not bear the unintended recrimination of Revelstone – and because he was a man who already knew that he had no choice.

When he started up the long ascending road, the people behind him slowed, let him go. He heard them whispering:

'He goes to the Unfettered One – to the interpreter of dreams.'

But that was not where he was going; he had no questions to ask an oracle. Oracles were for people to whom ambiguous visions could make a difference, but now the only things which could make a difference to High Lord Mhoram son of Variol were things which would give him courage.

In a stupor of dread, he climbed out into the wind which scythed across the open plateau. Above its chill ululations, he could hear battle crashing against the walls of the Keep, waves of assailants hurling themselves like breakers against a defiant and ultimately frangible cliff. But he put the sound behind him; it was only a symbol, a concentration, of the whole Land's abominable doom. Without Thomas Covenant – ! Mhoram could not complete the thought. He walked up through the barren hills away from Revelstone, up towards the river and northward along it, with an abyss in his heart where the survival of the Land should have been. This, he told himself, was what Kevin Landwaster must have felt when Lord Foul overwhelmed Kurash Plenethor, making all responses short of Desecration futile. He did not know how the pain of it could be endured.

After a time, he found himself standing cold in the wind on a hill above Glimmermere. Below him, the rare, potent waters of the lake lay unruffled despite the buffeting of the wind. Though the skies above it were as grey as the ashes of the world's end, it seemed to shine with remembered sunlight. It reflected cleanly the hills and the distant mountains, and through its purity he could see its fathomless, rocky bottom.

He knew what he would have to do; he lacked courage, not comprehension. The last exactions of faith lay unrolled before him in his dread like the map of a country which no longer existed. When he stumbled frozenly down towards the lake, he did so because he had nowhere else to turn. There was Earthpower in Glimmermere. He placed his staff on the bank, stripped off his robe, and dropped into the lake, praying that its icy waters would do for him what he could not do for himself.

Though he was already numb with cold, the water seemed to burn instantly over all his flesh, snatch him out of his numbness like a conflagration in his nerves. He had had no thought of swimming when he had slipped into the depths, but the force of Glimmermere triggered reactions in him, sent him clawing up towards the surface. With a whooping gasp, he broke water, sculled for a moment to catch his breath against the fiery chill, then struck out for the bank where he had left his robe.

Climbing out on to the hillside, he felt aflame with cold, but he compelled himself to remain naked while the wind made ice of the water on his limbs and dried him. Then he pulled his robe urgently over his shoulders, hugged his staff to his chest so that its heat warmed him where he most needed warming. His feverish chill took some time to pass, and while he waited, he braced himself, strove to shore up his heart against the obstacles and the dismay which awaited him.

He had to do something which was obviously impossible. He had to slay *samadhi* Satansfist.

He would need help.

Putting grimly aside all his former scruples, he turned to the only possible source of help — the only aid whose faithfulness matched his need. He raised one cold hand to his lips and whistled shrilly three times.

The turbulent wind seemed to snatch the sound to pieces, tatter it instantly. In a place where echoes were common, his call disappeared without resonance or answer, the wind tore it away as if to undo his purpose, make him unheard. Nevertheless he summoned his trust, pried himself up the hillside to stand waiting on the vantage of the crest. A suspense like the either/or of despair filled him, but he faced the western mountains as if his heart knew neither doubt nor fear.

Long moments which sharpened his suspense to the screaming point passed before he saw a dull brown movement making its way towards him out of the mountains. Then his soul leaped up in spite of its burdens, and he stood erect with the wind snapping in his ears so that his stance would be becoming to the Ranyhyn that was answering his call.

The wait nearly froze the blood in his veins, but at last the Ranyhyn reached the hills around Glimmermere, and nickered in salutation.

Mhoram groaned at the sight. In order to answer his call, the Ranyhyn must have left the Plains of Ra scores of days ago – must have fled Satansfist's army to run straight across the Centre Plains into the Westron Mountains, then found its pathless way among the high winter of the peaks northward to the spur of the range which jutted east and ended in the plateau of Revelstone. The long ordeal of the mountain trek had exacted a severe price from the great stallion. His flesh hung slack over gaunt ribs, he stumbled painfully on swollen joints, and his coat had a look of ragged misery. Still Mhoram recognized the Ranyhyn, and greeted him with all the respect his voice could carry:

'Hail, Drinny, proud Ranyhyn! Oh, bravely done! Worthy son of a worthy mother. Tail of the Sky, Mane of the World, I am – ' a clench of emotion caught his throat, and he could only whisper – 'I am honoured.'

Drinny made a valiant effort to trot up to Mhoram, but when he reached the High Lord he rested his head trembling on Mhoram's shoulder as if he needed the support in order to keep his feet. Mhoram hugged his neck, whispered words of praise and encouragement in his ear, stroked his ice-clogged coat. They stood together as if in their differing weaknesses they were making promises to each other. Then Mhoram answered the nudging of Drinny's unquenchable pride by springing on to the Ranyhyn's back. Warming the great horse with his staff, he rode slowly, resolutely, back towards Revelstone.

The ride took time – time made arduous and agonizing by the frailty of Drinny's muscles, his painful, exhausted stumbling. When they passed down through the hills, Mhoram's own weariness returned, and he remembered his inadequacy, his stupefying dread. But he had placed his feet on the strait path of his faith; now he held the Ranyhyn between his knees and bound himself in his determination not to turn aside. Drinny had answered his call. While his thoughts retained some vestige of Glimmermere's clarity, he made his plans.

Then at last his mount limped down into the wide tunnel which led into Lord's Keep. The clop of hooves echoed faintly against the smooth stone walls and ceiling – echoed and scurried ahead of the High Lord like a murmurous announcement of his return. Soon he could feel the voices of the Keep spreading word of him, proclaiming that he had come back on a Ranyhyn. People left their work and hastened to the main passage of the tunnel to see him. They lined his way, muttered in wonder or pain at the sight of the Ranyhyn, whispered intently to each other about the look of focused danger which shone in his eyes. Down into the Keep he rode as if he were borne on a low current of astonishment and hope.

After he had ridden a few hundred yards along the main way of Revelstone, he saw ahead of him the other leaders of the city – the Lords Trevor, Amatin and Loerya, Warmark Quaan, the two Hearthralls, Tohrm and Borillar. They awaited him as if they had come out together to do him honour. When the Ranyhyn stopped before them, they saluted the High Lord and his mount mutely, lacking words for what they felt.

He gazed back at them for a moment, studied them. In their separate ways, they were all haggard, needy, stained with battle. Quaan in particular appeared extravagantly worn. His bluff old face was knotted into a habitual scowl now, as if only the clench of constant belligerence held the pieces of his being together. And Amatin, too, looked nearly desperate, her physical slightness seemed to drain her moral stamina. Borillar's face was full of tears that Mhoram knew came from the loss of Thomas Covenant. Trevor and Loerya supported each other, unable to remain upright alone. Of them all, only Tohrm was calm, and his calm was the steadiness of a man who had already passed through his personal crisis. Nothing could be worse for him than the stone Desecration he had experienced in the Close – experienced and mastered. The others met Mhoram with concentrated hope and dismay and suspense and effectlessness in their faces – expressions which begged to know what this returning on a Ranyhyn meant.

He nodded to their silent salute, then dropped heavily from Drinny's back and moved a step or two closer to them. On the only level for which he had sufficient strength – the level of his authority – he answered them. He spoke softly, but his voice was raw with peril. 'Hear me. I am Mhoram son of Variol, High Lord by the choice of the Council. I have taken my decision. Hear me and obey. Warmark Quaan, Drinny of the Ranyhyn must be given care. He must be fed and healed – he must be returned swiftly to his strength. I will ride him soon.

'Lords, Hearthralls, Warmark – the watchtower of Revelstone must be regained. The gates of the Keep must be cleared. Do it swiftly. Warmark, ready the horses of the Warward. Prepare all mounted warriors and as many unmounted as you deem fit – prepare them to march against *samadhi* Satansfist. We strike as soon as our way has been made clear.'

He could see that his commands stunned them, that they were appalled at the mad prospect of attacking the Raver's army. But he did not offer them any aid, any reassurance. When the time came for the certain death of his purpose, he hoped to leave behind him men and women who had proved to themselves that they could meet extreme needs – leaders who had learned that they could do without him.

Yet he could not refuse to explain the reason for his commands. 'My friends,' he went on with the rawness livid in his tone, 'the light of the *krill* has failed. You know the meaning of this. Thomas Covenant has left the Land – or has fallen to his death – or has been bereft of his ring. Therein lies our sole hope. If the Unbeliever lives – and while the wild magic has not been brought into use against us – we can hope that he will regain his ring.

'We must act on this hope. It is small – but all hopes are small in this extremity. It is our work to redeem victory from the blood and havoc of despair. We must act. Surely the Despiser knows that ur-Lord Covenant has lost the white gold – if it has been lost and not withdrawn from the Land or captured. Therefore his thoughts may be turned from us for a time. In that time we may have some hope of success against *samadhi* Raver. And if Lord Foul seeks to prevent the Unbeliever's recovery of his ring, we may give a distant aid to ur-Lord Covenant by requiring the Despiser to look towards us again.'

He could not bear to watch the aghast supplications which wrung the faces of his friends. He put his arm over Drinny's neck and concluded as if he were speaking to the Ranyhyn, 'This choice is mine. I will ride against Satansfist alone if I must. But this act must be made.'

At last, Amatin found herself to gasp, '*Melenkurion! Melenkurion abatha!* Mhoram, have you learned nothing from Trell Atiaran-mate – from the Bloodguard – from Kevin Landwaster himself? You beg yourself to become a Desecrator. In this way, we learn to destroy that which we love!'

High Lord Mhoram's reply had the sting of authority. 'Warmark, I will take no warrior with me who has not accepted this hazard freely. You must explain to the Warward that the light of Loric's *krill* has failed.'

He ached to rush to his friends, ached to throw his arms around them, hug them, show them in some way his love and his terrible need for them. But he knew himself; he knew he would be utterly unable to leave them if they did not first show their independence to themselves and him by meeting alone his extreme demands. His own courage hung too much on the verge of faltering; he needed some demonstration from them to help him follow the strait line of faith. So he contained himself by hugging Drinny tightly for a moment, then turned on his heel and walked stiffly away to his private chambers.

He spent the next days alone, trying to rest – searching himself for some resource which would enable him to bear the impossibility and the uselessness of his decision. But a fever was on his soul. The foundation of serenity which had sustained him for so long seemed to have eroded. Whether he lay on his bed, or ate, or paced his chambers, or studied, he could feel a great emptiness in the heart of the Keep where the *krill*'s fire should have been. He had not realized how much that white blaze had taught him to rely on the Unbeliever. Its quenching left him face to face with futile death – death for himself, for Drinny, for any who dared follow him – death that could only be trusted to foreshorten Revelstone's survival. So he spent large stretches of the time on his hands and knees on the floor, probing through the stone in an effort to sense how his commands were being met.

Without difficulty he read the preparations of the Warward. The few hundred horses which had been stabled in the Keep were being made ready. The duty rotations of the warriors were changed so that those who chose to follow the High Lord could rest and prepare. And as a result, the burden of resisting *samadhi*'s attacks fell on fewer shoulders. Soon the defence took on a febrile pitch which matched Mhoram's own fever. His commands had hastened the Warward's ineluctable decline into frenzy and desperation. He ground his teeth on that pain and hunted elsewhere in the city for the Lords.

He found that Lord Amatin had retreated to the isolation of the Loresraat's libraries, but Trevor, Loerya and Hearthrall Tohrm were active. Together, Lord Trevor and Tohrm went down into one of the unfrequented caverns directly under the tower. There they combined their lore in a rite dangerously similar to Trell's destruction of the Close, and sent a surge of heat up through the stone into the passages of the tower. They stoked the heat for a day, raised it against the enemy until the Cavewights and creatures began to abandon the tower.

And when the lowest levels were empty, Lord Loerya led several Eoman in an assault. Under cover of darkness, they leaped from the main Keep into the sand, crossed the courtyard, and entered the tower to fight their way upward. By the dawn of the third day, they were victorious. Makeshift crosswalks were thrown up over the courtyard, and hundreds of archers rushed across to help secure the tower.

Their success gave Mhoram a pride in them that eased his distress for a time. He doubted that the tower could be held for more than a day or two, but a day or two would be enough, if the rest of his commands were equally met.

Then, during the third day, Amatin returned to work. She had spent the time in an intense study of certain arcane portions of the Second Ward which High Lord Mhoram himself had never grasped, and there she had found the rites and invocations she sought. Armed with that knowledge, she went to the abutments directly above the courtyard, made eldritch signs and symbols on the stone, wove rare gestures, chanted songs in the lost language of the Old Lords – and below her the sandy remains of the dead slowly parted. They pulled back far enough to permit the opening of the gates, far enough to permit an army to ride out of Revelstone.

Her achievement drew Mhoram from his chambers to watch. When she was done, she collapsed in his arms, but he was so proud of her that his concern was dominated by relief. When the Healers assured him she would soon recover if she were allowed to rest, he left her and went to the stables to see Drinny.

He found a Ranyhyn that hardly resembled the ragged, worn horse he had ridden into Revelstone. Good food and treatment had rekindled the light in Drinny's eyes, renewed his flesh, restored elasticity to his muscles. He pranced and nickered for Mhoram as if to show the High Lord he was ready.

Such things rejuvenated Mhoram. Without further hesitation, he told Warmark Quaan that he would ride out against the Raver the next morning.

But late that night, while Trevor, Loerya and Quaan all struggled against a particularly fierce flurry of onslaughts, Lord Amatin came up to Mhoram's rooms. She did not speak, but her wan, bruised aspect caught at his heart. Her labours had done something to her; in straining herself so severely, she had lost her defences, left herself exposed to perils and perceptions for which she was neither willing nor apt. This vulnerability gave her a look of abjection, as if she had come to cast herself at Mhoram's feet.

Without a word, she raised her hands to the High Lord. In them she held the *krill* of Loric.

He accepted it without dropping his gaze from her face. 'Ah, sister Amatin,' he breathed gently, 'you should rest. You have earned – '

But a spasm of misery around her eyes cut him off. He looked down, made himself look at the *krill*.

Deep in its gem, he saw faint glimmerings of emerald.

Without a word, Amatin turned and left him alone with the knowledge that Covenant's ring had fallen into the power of the Despiser.

When he left his rooms the next morning, he looked like a man who had spent the night wrestling in vain against his own damnation. His step had lost its conviction; he moved as if his very bones were loose and bending. And the dangerous promise of his gaze had faded, leaving his eyes dull, stricken. He bore the *krill* within his robe, and could feel Lord Foul's sick emerald hold upon it growing. Soon, he knew, the cold of the green would begin to burn his flesh. But he was past taking any account of such risks. He dragged himself forward as if he were on his way to commit a perfidy which appalled him.

In the great entrance hall a short distance within Revelstone's still-closed gates, he joined the warriors. They were ranked by Eoman, and he saw at a glance that they numbered two thousand: one Eoward on horseback and four on foot – a third of the surviving Warward. He faltered at the sight; he had not expected to be responsible for so many deaths. But the warriors hailed him bravely, and he forced himself to respond as if he trusted himself to lead them. Then he moved in anguish to the forefront, where Drinny awaited him.

The Lords and Warmark Quaan were there with the Ranyhyn, but he passed by them because he could not meet their eyes, and tried to mount. His muscles failed him; he was half paralysed by dread and could not leap high enough to gain Drinny's back. Shaking on the verge of an outcry, he clung to the horse for support, and besearched himself for the serenity which had been his greatest resource.

Yet he could not make the leap; Drinny's back was too high for him. He ached to ask for help. But before he could force words through his locked throat, he felt Quaan behind him, felt Quaan's hand on his shoulder. The old Warmark's voice was gruff with urgency as he said, 'High Lord, this risk will weaken Revelstone. A third of the Warward – two thousand lives wasted. High Lord – why? Have you become like Kevin Landwaster? Do you wish to destroy that which you love?'

'No!' Mhoram whispered because the tightness of his throat blocked any other sound. With his hands, he begged Drinny for strength. 'I do not – I do not forget – I am the High Lord. The path of faith is clear. I must follow it – because it is not despair.'

'You will teach us despair – if you fail.'

Mhoram heard the pain in Quaan's voice, and he compelled himself to answer. He could not refuse Quaan's need; he was too weak, but he could not refuse. 'No. Lord Foul teaches despair. It is an easier lesson than courage.' Slowly, he turned around, met first Quaan's gaze, then the eyes of the Lords. 'An easier lesson,' he repeated. 'Therefore the counsels of despair and hate can never triumph over Despite.'

But his reply only increased Quaan's pain. While knuckles of distress clenched Quaan's open face, he moaned brokenly, 'Ah, my

Lord. Then why do you delay? Why do you fear?'

'Because I am a mortal, weak. The way is only clear – not sure. In my time, I have been a seer and oracle. Now I – I desire a sign. I require to see.'

He spoke simply, but almost at once his mortality, his weakness, became too much for him. Tears blurred his vision. The burden was not one that he could bear alone. He opened his arms and was swept into the embrace of the Lords.

The melding of their minds reached him, poured into him on the surge of their united concern. Folded within their arms and their thoughts, he felt their love soothe him, fill him like water after a long thirst, feed his hunger. Throughout the siege, he had given them his strength, and now they returned strength to him. With quiet diffidence, Lord Trevor restored his crippled sense of endurance in service – a fortitude which came, not from the server, but from the preciousness of the thing served. Lord Loerya shared with him her intense instinct for protection, her capacity for battle on behalf of children – loved ones who could not defend themselves. And Lord Amatin, though she was still frail herself, gave him the clear, uncluttered concentration of her study, her lore-wisdom – a rare gift which for his sake she proffered separate from her distrust of emotion.

In such melding, he began to recover himself. Blood seemed to return to his veins; his muscles uncramped; his bones remembered their rigor. He accepted the Lords deep into himself, and in response he shared with them all the perceptions which made his decision necessary. Then he rested on their love and let it assuage him.

His appetite for the meld seemed to have no bottom, but after a time the contact was interrupted by a strident voice so full of strange thrills that none of the Lords could refuse to hear it. A sentry raced into the hall clamouring for their attention, and when they looked at her she shouted, 'The Raver is attacked! His army – the encampment – ! It is under attack. By Waynhim! They are few – few – but the Raver had no defences on that side, and they have already done great damage. He has called his army back from Revelstone to fight them!'

High Lord Mhoram whirled away, ordering the Warward to readiness as he moved. He heard Warward Quaan echo his commands. A look full of dire consequences for the Raver passed between them; then Quaan leaped on to his own horse, a tough, mountain-bred mustang. To one side among the warriors, Mhoram saw Hearthrall Borillar mounting. He started to order Borillar down; Hirebrands were not fighters. But then he remembered how much

1046

hope Borillar had placed in Thomas Covenant, and left the Hearthrall alone.

Loerya was already on her way to aid the defences of the tower, keep it secure so that the Warward would be able to re-enter Revelstone. Trevor had gone to the gates. Only Amatin remained to see the danger shining in Mhoram's eyes. She held him briefly, then released him, muttering, 'It would appear that the Waynhim have made the same decision.'

Mhoram spun and leaped lightly on to Drinny's back. The Ranyhyn whinnied; peals of pride and defiance resounded through the hall. As the huge gates opened outward on the courtyard, Mhoram sent Drinny forward at a canter.

The Warward started into motion behind him, and at its head High Lord Mhoram rode out to war.

In a moment, he flashed through the gates, across the courtyard between steep banks of sand and earth, into the straight tunnel under the tower. Drinny stretched jubilantly under him, exalted by health and running and the scent of battle. As Mhoram passed through the splintered remains of the outer gates, he had already begun to outdistance the Warward.

Beyond the gates, he wheeled Drinny once, gave himself an instant in which to look back up at the lofty Keep. He saw no warriors in the tower, but he sensed them bristling behind the fortifications and windows. The bluff stone of the tower, with Revelstone rising behind it like the prow of a great ship, answered his gaze in granite permanence as if it were a prophecy by the old Giants – a cryptic perception that victory and defeat were human terms which had no meaning in the language of mountains.

Then the riders came cantering through the throat of the tower, and Mhoram turned to look at the enemy. For the first time, he saw *samadhi*'s army from ground level. It stood blackly in the bleak winterscape around him like a garotte into which he had prematurely thrust his neck. Briefly, he remembered other battles – Kiril Threndor, Doom's Retreat, Doriendor Corishev – as if they had been child's play, mere shadows cast by the struggle he now faced. But he pushed them out of his mind, bent his attention towards the movements in the foothills below him.

As the sentry had said, Revelstone's attackers were pelting furiously back towards their encampment. It was only a few hundred yards distant, and Mhoram could see clearly why *samadhi*'s forces had been recalled. The Giant-Raver was under assault by a tight wedge of ten or fifteenscore Waynhim.

Satansfist himself was not their target, though he fought against them personally with feral blasts of green. The Waynhim struck against the undefended rear of the encampment in order to destroy its food supplies. They had already incinerated great long troughs of the carrion and gore on which Lord Foul's creatures fed; and while they warded off the scourge of Satansfist's Stone as best they could, they assailed other stores, flash-fired huge aggregations of hacked dead flesh into cinders.

Even if they had faced the Raver alone, they would have had no chance to survive. With his Giantish strength and his fragment of the Illearth Stone – with the support of the Staff of Law – he could have beaten back ten or fifteen thousand Waynhim. And he had an army to help him. Hundreds of ur-viles were nearly within striking distance, thousands of other creatures converged towards the fighting from all directions. The Waynhim had scant moments of life left.

Yet they fought on, resisted *samadhi*'s emerald ill with surprising success. Like the ur-viles, they were Demondimspawn – masters of a dark and potent lore which no Lord had ever touched. And they had not wasted the seven and forty years since they had gone into hiding. They had prepared themselves to resist Despite. Yelping rare words of power, gesturing urgently, they shrugged off the Raver's blasts, and continued to destroy every trough and accumulation of food they could reach.

All this High Lord Mhoram took in almost instantly. The raw wind hurt his face, made his eyes burn, but he thrust his vision through the blur to see. And he saw that, because of the Waynhim, he and the Warward had not yet been noticed by Satansfist's army.

'Warmark,' he snapped, 'we must aid the Waynhim! Give the commands.'

Rapidly, Quaan barked his instructions to the mounted warriors and the Hafts of the four unmounted Eoward as they came through the tunnel. At once, a hundred riders positioned themselves on either side of the High Lord. The remaining two hundred fell into ranks behind him. Without breaking stride, the unmounted warriors began to run.

Mhoram touched Drinny and started at a slow gallop straight down through the foothills towards the Raver.

Some distant parts of the encampment saw the riders before they had covered a third of the distance. Hoarse cries of warning sprang up on all sides; ur-viles, Cavewights, Stonemade creatures which had not already been ordered to the Giant-Raver's aid, swept like a ragged tide at the Warward. But the confusion around the Waynhim prevented Satansfist's immediate forces from hearing the alarm. The

Raver did not turn his head. Revelstone's counterattack was nearly upon him before he saw his danger.

In the last distance, Warmark Quaan shouted an order, and the riders broke into full gallop. Mhoram had time for one final look at his situation. The forces around *samadhi* were still locked in their concentration on the Waynhim. The Raver's reinforcements were long moments away. If Quaan's warriors could hit hard enough, break through towards the Waynhim fast enough, the unmounted Eoward might be able to protect their rear long enough for them to strike once at the Raver and withdraw. That way, some of the warriors might survive to return to the Keep.

Mhoram sent Drinny forward at a pace which put him among the first riders crashing into Satansfist's unready hordes.

They impacted with a shock that shook the High Lord in his seat. Horses plunged, hacked with their hooves. Swords were brandished like metal lightning. Shrieks of surprised pain and rage shivered the air as disorganized ranks of creatures went down under the assault. Heaving their mounts forward, the warriors cut their way in towards the Raver.

But thousands of creatures milled between them and Satansfist. Though the hordes were in confusion, the sheer weight of their numbers slowed the Warward's charge.

Seeing this, Quaan gave new orders. On his command, the warriors flanking Mhoram turned outward on either side, cleared a space between them for the riders behind the High Lord. These Eoman sprinted forward. When they reached Mhoram, he called up the power of his staff. Blue fire raged ahead of him like the point of a lance, piercing the wall of enemies as he led the second rush of riders deeper into the turmoil of the Raver's army.

For a moment, he thought they might succeed. The warriors with him hacked their way swiftly through the enemy. And ahead of them, Satansfist turned from the Waynhim to meet this new threat. The Raver howled orders to organize his army, turned his forces against the Warward, surged a few furious strides in that direction. Mhoram saw the distance shorten. He wielded his Lords-fire fiercely, striving to reach his foe before the impossible numbers of the enemy broke his momentum.

But then the riders ploughed into an obstacle. A band of Cavewights had had time to obey the Raver's commands; they had lined themselves across the path of the Warward, linked their strong earth-delvers' arms, braced themselves. When the riders plunged forward, they crashed into the creatures.

The strength of the Cavewights was so great that their line held. Horses were thrown down. Riders tumbled to the ground, both before and beyond the wall. The charge of the Warward was turned against itself as the horses which followed stumbled and trampled among the leaders.

Only Mhoram was not unhorsed. At the last instant, Drinny gathered himself, leaped; he hurdled the line easily, kicking at the heads of the Cavewights as he passed.

With the riders who had been thrown beyond the wall, Mhoram found himself faced by a massing wedge of ur-viles.

The Cavewights cut him off from the Warward. And the falling of the horses gave *samadhi*'s creatures a chance to strike back. Before Quaan could organize any kind of assault on the Cavewights, his warriors were fighting for their lives where they stood.

Wheeling Drinny, Mhoram saw that he would get no help from the riders. But if he went back to them, fought the wall himself, the ur-viles would have time to complete their wedge; they would have the riders at their mercy.

At once, he sent the warriors with him to attack the Cavewights. Then he flung himself like a bolt of Lords-fire at the ur-viles.

He was only one man against several hundred of the black, roynish creatures. But he had unlocked the secret of High Lord Kevin's Lore; he had learned the link between power and passion; he was mightier than he had ever been before. Using all the force his staff could bear, he shattered the formation like a battering ram, broke and scattered ur-viles like rubble. With Drinny pounding, kicking, slashing under him, he held his staff in both hands, whirled it about him, sent vivid blasts blaring like the blue fury of the cloud-damned heavens, shouting in a rapture of rage like an earthquake. And the ur-viles staggered as if the sky had fallen on them, collapsed as if the ground had bucked under their feet. He fired his way through them like a titan, and did not stop until he had reached the bottom of a low hollow in the hills.

There he spun, and discovered that he had completely lost the Warward. The riders had been thrown back; in the face of insuperable odds, Quaan had probably taken them to join the unmounted warriors so that they could combine their strength in an effort to save the High Lord.

On the opposite rim of the hollow, Satansfist stood glaring down at Mhoram. He held his Stone cocked to strike, and the mad lust of the Raver was in his Giantish face. But he turned away without attacking, disappeared beyond the rim as if he had decided that the Waynhim were a more serious threat than High Lord Mhoram.

'Satansfist!' Mhoram yelled. '*Samadhi* Sheol! Return and fight me! Are you craven, that you dare not risk a challenge?'

As he shouted, he hit Drinny with his heels, launched the

Ranyhyn in pursuit of Satansfist. But in the instant that his attention was turned upward, the surviving ur-viles rallied. Instead of retreating to form a wedge, they flung themselves at him. He could not swing his staff; ravenous black hands clutched at him, clawed his arms, caught hold of his robe.

Drinny fought back, but he succeeded only in pulling himself out from under the High Lord. Mhoram lost his seat and went down under a pile of rabid black bodies.

Blood-red Demondim blades flared at him. But before any of the eldritch knives could bite his flesh, he mustered an eruption of force which blasted the ur-viles away. Instantly, he was on his feet again, wielding his staff, crushing every creature that came near him — searching fervidly for his mount.

The Ranyhyn was already gone, driven out of the hollow.

Suddenly, Mhoram was alone. The last ur-viles fled, leaving him with the dead and dying. In their place came a fatal silence that chilled his blood. Either the fighting had ended, or the livid wind carried all sounds away; he could hear nothing but the low cruel voice of Lord Foul's winter, and his own hoarse respiration.

The abrupt absence of clamour and turmoil kept him still also. He wanted to shout for Quaan but could not raise his voice through the horror in his throat — wanted to whistle for Drinny, but could not bring himself to break the awful quietude. He was too astonished with dread.

The next instant, he realized that the Raver had trapped him. He sprang into a run, moving away from the Warward, towards the Waynhim, hoping that this choice would take the trap by surprise.

It was too complete to be surprised. Before he had gone a dozen yards, creatures burst into view around the entire rim of the hollow. Hundreds of them let him see them; they stood leering down at him, pawing the ground hungrily, slavering at the anticipated taste of his blood and bones. The wind bore their throaty lust down to him as if they gave tongue to the animating spirit of the winter.

He was alone against them.

He retreated to the centre of the hollow, hunted swiftly around the rim for some gap or weakness in the surrounding horde. He found none. And though he sent his perceptions ranging as far as he could through the air, he discovered no sign of the Warward; if the warriors were still alive, still fighting, they were blocked from his senses by the solid force of the trap.

As he grasped the utterness of his plight, he turned inward, retreated into himself as if he were fleeing. There he looked the end of all his hopes and all his Landservice in the face, and found that its scarred, terrible visage no longer appalled him. He was a fighter, a man born to fight for the Land. As long as something for which he could fight remained, he was impervious to terror. And something did remain; while he lived, at least one flame of love for the Land still burned. He could fight for that.

His crooked lips stretched into an extreme and perilous grin; hot, serene triumph shone in his eyes. 'Come, then!' he shouted. 'If your master is too much a coward to risk himself against me, then come for me yourselves! I do not wish to harm you, but if you dare me, I will give you death!'

Something in his voice halted them momentarily. They hesitated, moiling uneasily. But almost at once the grip of their malice locked like jaws. At the harsh shout of a command, they started down towards him from all sides like an avalanche.

He did not wait for them. He swung in the direction Satansfist had taken, intending to pursue the Raver as far as his strength would carry him. But some instinct or intuition tugged him at the last instant, deflected him to one side. He turned and met that part of the avalanche head-on.

Now the only thing which limited his might was his staff itself. That wood had been shaped by people who had not understood Kevin's Lore; it was not formed to bear the force he now sent blazing through it. But he had no margin for caution. He made the staff surpass itself, sent it bucking and crackling with power to rage against his assailants. His flame grew incandescent, furnace-hot; in brilliance and coruscation it sliced through his foes like a scythe of sun-fire.

In moments, their sheer number filled all his horizons, blocked everything but their dark assault out of his awareness. He saw nothing else, felt nothing but huge waves of misshapen fiends that sought to deluge him, knew nothing but their ravening lust for blood and his blue, fiery passion. Though they threw themselves at him in scores and hundreds, he met them, cut them down, blasted them back. Wading through their corpses as if they were the very sea of death, he fought them with fury in his veins, indomitability in his bones, extravagant triumph in his eyes.

Yet they outweighed him. They were too many. Any moment now, one of them would drive a sword into his back, and he would be finished. Through the savage clash of combat, he heard a high, strange cry of victory, but he hardly knew that he had made it himself.

Then, unexpectedly, he glimpsed the light of fire through a brief gap in his attackers. It disappeared instantly, vanished as if it had never happened. But he had recognized it. He shouted again and began to fight towards it. Ignoring the danger at his back, he reaped a break in the avalanche ahead. There he saw the fire again.

It was the blaze of a Hirebrand.

On the rim of the hollow, Hearthrall Borillar and the last of the Waynhim fought together against Mhoram's foes. Borillar used his flaming staff like a mace, and the Waynhim supported him with their own powers. Together they struggled impossibly to rescue the High Lord.

At the sight of them, Mhoram faltered; he could see immense monsters rising up to smite them, and their peril interrupted his concentration. But he recovered, surged towards them, driving his staff until it screamed in his hands.

Too many creatures were pressed between him and his rescuers; he could not reach them in time. While he fought slipping and ploughing through the blood, he saw Borillar slain, saw the formation of the Waynhim broken, scattered. He almost fell himself under his inability to help them.

But with their deaths they had purchased a thinning in the flood of attackers at that point. Through that thinning came Drinny of the Ranyhyn, bucking and charging to regain his rider.

His violent speed carried him down into the hollow. He crashed through creatures, leaped over them, hacked them out of his way. Before they could brace themselves to meet him, Drinny had reached the High Lord.

Mhoram sprang on to the Ranyhyn's back. From that vantage, he brought his power down on the heads of his assailants, while Drinny kicked and plunged back up the hillside. In moments, they crested the rim and broke into clearer ground beyond it.

As he guided Drinny ahead, Mhoram caught a glimpse of the Warward. It had rallied around Quaan and was struggling in the High Lord's direction. The riders charged to break up the ranks of the enemy, then the other warriors rushed to take advantage of the breach. But they were completely engulfed – a small, valiant island in the sea of Satansfist's army. Their progress was tortuous, their losses atrocious. High Lord Mhoram knew of only one effective way to help them, and he took Drinny towards it without an instant of hesitation.

Together, they pursued *samadhi* Raver.

Satansfist was only fifty yards away. He stood on a knoll from which he could direct the battle. And he was alone; all his forces were engaged elsewhere. He towered atop the hill like a monolith of hatred and destruction, wielding his army with the force of green ill.

Holding his staff ready, Mhoram sent the Ranyhyn lunging straight into the teeth of the winter – straight at *samadhi*. When he was scant strides away from his foe, he cried his challenge:

'*Melenkurion abatha! Duroc minas mill khabaal!*'

With all his strength, he levelled a blast of Lords-fire at the Raver's leering skull.

Satansfist knocked the attack down as if it were negligible; disdainfully, he slapped Mhoram's blue out of the air with his Stone and returned a bolt so full of cold emerald force that it scorched the atmosphere as it moved.

Mhoram sensed its power, knew that it would slay him if it struck. But Drinny dodged with a fleet, fluid motion which belied the wrenching change of his momentum. The bolt missed, crashed instead into the creatures pursuing the High Lord, killed them all.

That gave Mhoram the instant he needed. He corrected Drinny's aim, cocked his staff over his shoulder. Before *samadhi* could unleash another blast, the High Lord was upon him.

Using all Drinny's speed, all the strength of his body, all the violated passion of his love for the Land, Mhoram swung. His staff caught Satansfist squarely across the forehead.

The concussion ripped Mhoram from his seat like a dry leaf in the wind. His staff shattered at the blow, exploded into splinters, and he hit the ground amid a brief light rain of wood slivers. He was stunned. He rolled helplessly a few feet over the frozen earth, could not stop himself, could not regain his breath. His mind went blank for an instant, then began to ache as his body ached. His hands and arms were numb, paralysed by the force which had burned through them.

Yet even in his daze, he had room for a faint amazement at what he had done.

His blow had staggered Satansfist, knocked him backward. The Giant-Raver had fallen down the far side of the knoll.

With a gasp, Mhoram began to breathe again. Spikes of sensation dug into his arms; dazzling pain filled his vision. He tried to move, and after a moment succeeded in rolling on to his side. His hands hung curled on the ends of his wrists as if they were crippled, but he shifted his shoulder and elbow, turned himself on to his stomach, then levered himself with his forearms until he gained his knees. There he rested while the pain of returning life stabbed its way down into his fingers.

The sound of heavy steps, heavy breathing, made him look up.

Samadhi Sheol stood over him.

Blood poured from Satansfist's forehead into his eyes, but instead of blinding him, it seemed only to enrich his raving ferocity. His lips were contorted with a paroxysm of savage glee; ecstatic rage shone on his wet teeth. In the interlocked clasp of his fists, the Illearth Stone burned and fumed as if it were on the brink of apotheosis.

Slowly, he raised the Stone over Mhoram's head like an axe.

Transfixed, stunned – as helpless as a sacrifice – Mhoram watched his death rise and poise above him.

In the distance, he could hear Quaan shouting wildly, uselessly, 'Mhoram! Mhoram!' On the ground nearby, Drinny groaned and strove to regain his feet. Everywhere else there was silence. The whole battle seemed to have paused in midblow to watch Mhoram's execution. And he could do nothing but kneel and regret that so many lives had been spent for such an end.

Yet when the change of the air came an instant later, it was so intense, so vibrant and thrilling, that it snatched him to his feet. It made Satansfist arrest his blow, gape uncomprehendingly into the sky, then drop his fists and whirl to shout strident curses at the eastern horizon.

For that moment, Mhoram also only gaped and gasped. He could not believe his senses, could not believe the touch of the air on his cold-punished face. He seemed to be tasting something which had been lost from human experience.

.Then Drinny lurched up, braced himself on splayed legs, and raised his head to neigh in recognition of the change. His whinny was weak and strained, but it lifted Mhoram's heart like the trumpets of triumph.

While he and Satansfist and all the armies stared at it, the wind faltered. It limped, spurting and fluttering in the air like a wounded bird, then fell lifeless to the ground.

For the first time since Lord Foul's preternatural winter had begun, there was no wind. Some support or compulsion had been withdrawn from *samadhi* Satansfist.

With a howl of rage, the Raver spun back towards Mhoram. 'Fool!' he screamed as if the High Lord had let out a shout of jubilation. 'That was but one weapon of many! I will yet drink your heart's blood to the bottom!' Reeling under the weight of his fury, he lifted his fists again to deliver the executing blow.

But now Mhoram felt the fire which burned against his flesh under his robe. In a rush of exaltation, he understood it, grasped its meaning intuitively. As the Stone reached its height over his head, he tore open his robe and grasped Loric's *krill*.

Its gem blazed like a hot white brazier in his hands. It was charged to overflowing with echoes of wild magic; he could feel its keenness as he gripped its hilt.

It was a weapon strong enough to bear any might.

His eyes met Satansfist's. He saw dismay and hesitation clashing against the Raver's rage, against *samadhi* Sheol's ancient malice and the supreme confidence of the Stone.

Before Satansfist could defend himself, High Lord Mhoram sprang up and drove the *krill* deep into his bosom.

The Raver shrieked in agony. With Mhoram hanging from the blade in his chest, he flailed his arms as if he could not find anything to strike, anywhere to exert his colossal outrage. Then he dropped to his knees.

Mhoram planted his feet on the ground and braced himself to retain his grip on the *krill*. Through the focus of that blade, he drove all his might deeper and deeper towards the Giant-Raver's heart.

Yet *samadhi* did not die. Faced with death, he found a way to resist. Both his fists clenched the Stone only a foot above the back of Mhoram's neck. With all the rocky, Giantish strength of his frame, he began to squeeze.

Savage power steamed and pulsed like the beating of a heart of ice — a heart labouring convulsively, pounding and quivering to carry itself through a crisis. Mhoram felt the beats crash against the back of his spine. They kept Satansfist alive while they strove to quench the power which drove the *krill*.

But Mhoram endured the pain, did not let go; he leaned his weight on the blazing blade, ground it deeper and still deeper towards the essential cords of *samadhi*'s life. Slowly, his flesh seemed to disappear, fade as if he were being translated by passion into a being of pure force, of unfettered spirit and indomitable will. The Stone hammered at his back like a mounting cataclysm, and Satansfist's chest heaved against his hands in great, ragged, bloody gasps.

Then the cords were cut.

Pounding beyond the limits of control, the Illearth Stone exploded, annihilated itself with an eruption that hurled Mhoram and Satansfist tumbling inextricably together from the knoll. The blast shook the ground, tore a hole in the silence over the battle. One slow instant of stunned amazement gripped the air, then vanished in the dismayed shrieks of the Despiser's army.

Moments later, Warmark Quaan and the surviving remnant of his mounted Eoward dashed to the foot of the knoll. Quaan threw himself from his horse and leaped to the High Lord's side.

Mhoram's robe draped his bloodied and begrimed form in tatters; it had been shredded by the explosion. His hands as they gripped the *krill* were burned so badly that only black rags of flesh still clung to his bones. From head to foot, his body had the look of pain and brokenness. But he was still alive, still breathing faintly, fragilely.

Fear, weariness, hesitation dropped off Quaan as if they were meaningless. He took the *krill*, wrapped it, and placed it under his belt, then with celerity and care lifted the High Lord in his arms. For an instant, he looked around. He saw Drinny nearby, shaking his head and mane to throw off the effects of the blast. He saw the

Despiser's army seething in confusion and carnage. He hoped that it would fall apart without the Raver's leadership and coercion. But then he saw also that the ur-viles were rallying, taking charge of the creatures around them, reorganizing the hordes.

In spite of the High Lord's weight, Quaan ran and vaulted on to Drinny's back. Shouting to the Warward, 'Retreat! Return to the Keep! The Grey Slayer has not lost his hold!' he clapped Drinny with his heels and took the Ranyhyn at a full gallop towards the open gates of Revelstone.

16

COLOSSUS

There were gaps in the darkness during which Covenant knew dimly that rank liquids were being forced into him. They nourished him despite their rancid taste; his captors were keeping him alive. But between these gaps nothing interrupted his bereavement, his loss of everything he could grasp or recognize. He was dismembered from himself. The shrill vermilion nail of pain which the ur-viles had driven through his forehead impaled his identity, his memory and knowledge and awareness. He was at the nadir – captured, conquered, bereft – and only that iron stab in his forehead stood between him and the last numbness of the end.

So when he began to regain consciousness, he jerked towards it like a half-buried corpse, striving to shift the weight which enfolded him like the ready arms of his grave. Cold ebbed into him from the abyss of the winter. His heart laboured, shuddering ran through him like a crisis. His hands clutched uselessly at the frozen dirt.

Then rough hands flopped him on to his back. A grim visage advanced, receded. Something struck his chest. He gasped at the force of the blow. Yet it helped him; it seemed to break him free of imminent hysteria. He began to breathe more easily. In a moment, he became aware that he was beating the back of his head against the ground. With an effort, he stopped himself. Then he concentrated on trying to see.

He wanted to see, wanted to find some answer to the completeness of his loss. And his eyes were open – must have been open, or he would not have been able to perceive the shadowy countenance snarling over him. Yet he could not make it out. His eyeballs were dry and blind; he saw nothing but cold, universal grey smeared around the more compact grey of the visage.

'Up, Covenant,' a harsh voice rasped. 'You are of no use as you are.'

Another blow knocked his head to the side. He lurched suddenly. Through the pain in his cheek, he felt himself gaping into the raw wind. He blinked painfully at the dryness of his eyes, and tears began to resolve his blindness into shapes and spaces.

'Up, I say!'

He seemed to recognize the voice without knowing whose it was. But he lacked the strength to turn his head for another look. Resting on the icy ground, he blinked until his sight came into focus on a high, monolithic fist of stone.

It was perhaps twenty yards from him and forty feet tall – an obsidian column upraised on a plinth of native rock, and gnarled at its top into a clench of speechless defiance. Beyond it he could see nothing; it stood against a background of clouds as if it were erect on the rim of the world. At first, it appeared to him a thing of might, an icon of Earthpower upthrust or set down there to mark a boundary against evil. But as his vision cleared, the stone seemed to grow shallow and slumberous; blank; while he blinked at it, it became as inert as any old rock. If it still lived, he no longer had the eyes to see its life.

Slowly, fragments of other senses returned to him. He discovered that he could hear the wind hissing ravenously past him like a river thrashing across rapids; and behind it was a deep, muffled booming like the thunder of a waterfall.

'Up!' the harsh voice repeated. 'Must I beat you senseless to awaken you?'

Mordant laughter echoed after the demand as if it were a jest.

Abruptly, the rough hands caught hold of his robe and yanked him off the ground. He was still too weak to carry his own weight, too weak even to hold up his head. He leaned against the man's chest and panted at his pain, trying with futile fingers to grasp the man's shoulders.

'Where – ?' he croaked at last. 'Where – ?'

The laughter ridiculed him again. Two unrecognizable voices were laughing at him.

'Where?' the man snapped. 'Thomas Covenant, you are at my mercy. That is the only *where* which signifies.'

Straining, Covenant heaved up his head and found himself staring miserably into Triock's dark scowl.

Triock? He tried to say the name, but his voice failed him.

'You have slain everything that was precious to me. Think on that, Unbeliever — ' he invested the title with abysms of contempt — 'if you require to know where you are.'

Triock?

'There is murder and degradation in your every breath. Ah! you stink of it!' A spasm of revulsion knotted Triock's face, and he dropped Covenant to the ground again.

Covenant landed heavily amid sarcastic mirth. He was still too dazed to collect his thoughts. Triock's disgust affected him like a command; he lay prostrate with his eyes closed, trying to smell himself.

It was true. He stank of leprosy. The disease in his hands and feet reeked, gave off a rotten effluvium out of all proportion to the physical size of his infection. And its message was unmistakable. The ordure in him, the putrefaction of his flesh, was spreading — expanding as if he were contagious, as if at last even his body had become a violation of the fundamental health of the Land. In some ways, this was an even more important violation than the Despiser's winter — or rather his stench was the crown of the wind, the apex of Lord Foul's intent. That intent would be complete when his illness became part of the wind, when ice and leprosy together extinguished the Land's last vitality.

Then, in one intuitive leap, he understood his sense of bereavement. He identified his loss. Without looking to verify the perception, he knew that his ring had been taken from him; he could feel its absence like destitution in his heart.

The Despiser's manipulations were complete. The coercion and subterfuge which had shaped Covenant's experiences in the Land had borne fruit. Like a Stone-warped tree, they had fructified to produce this unanswerable end. The wild magic was now in Lord Foul's possession.

A wave of guilt rushed through Covenant. The enormity of the disaster he had precipitated upon the Land appalled him. His chest locked in a clench of sorrow, and he huddled on the verge of weeping.

But before he could release his pain, Triock was at him again. The Stonedownor gripped the shoulders of his robe, shook him until his bones rattled. 'Awaken!' Triock rasped viciously. 'Your time is short. My time is short. I do not mean to waste it.'

For a moment, Covenant could not resist; inanition and unconsciousness and grief crippled him. But then Triock's gratuitous violence struck sparks into the forgotten tinder of Covenant's rage. Anger galvanized him, brought back control to his muscles. He twisted in Triock's grip, got an arm and a leg braced on the ground.

Triock released him, and he climbed unevenly to his feet, panting, 'Hell and blood! Don't touch me, you – Raver!'

Triock stepped forward as Covenant came erect and stretched him in the dirt again with one sharp blow. Standing over Covenant, he shouted in a voice full of outrage, 'I am no Raver! I am Triock son of Thuler! – the man who loved Lena Atiaran-child – the man who took the part of a father for Elena daughter of Lena because you abandoned her! You cannot deny any blow I choose to strike against you!'

At that, Covenant heard laughter again, but he still could not identify its source. Triock's blow made the pain in his forehead roar; the noise of the hurt confused his hearing. But when the worst of the sound passed, his eyes seemed to clear at last. He forced himself to look up steadily into Triock's face.

The man had changed again. The strange combination of loathing and hunger, of anger and fear, was gone; the impression he had created that he was using his own anguish cunningly was gone. In the place of such distortion was an extravagant bitterness, a rage not controlled by any of his old restraints. He was himself and not himself. The former supplication of his eyes – the balance and ballast of his long acquaintance with gall – had foundered in passion. Now his brows clenched themselves into a knot of violence above the bridge of his nose; the pleading lines at the corners of his eyes had become as deep as scars; and his cheeks were taut with grimaces. Yet something in his eyes themselves belied the focus of his anger. His orbs were glazed and milky, as if they were blurred by cataracts, and they throbbed with a vain intensity. He looked as if he were going blind.

The sight of him made Covenant's own rage feel incondign, faulty. He was beholding another of his victims. He had no justification for anger. 'Triock!' he groaned, unable to think of any other response. 'Triock!'

The Stonedownor paused, allowed him a chance to regain his feet, then advanced threateningly.

Covenant retreated a step or two. He needed something to say, something that could penetrate or deflect Triock's bitterness. But his thoughts were stunned; they groped ineffectually, as if they had been rendered fingerless by the loss of his ring. Triock swung at him. He parried the blow with his forearms, kept himself from being knocked down again. Words – he needed words.

'Hellfire!' he shouted because he could not find any other reply. 'What happened to your Oath of Peace?'

'It is dead,' Triock growled hoarsely. 'It is dead with a spike of wood in its belly!' He swung again, staggered Covenant. 'The Law of Death is broken, and all Peace has been laid waste.'

Covenant regained his balance and retreated farther. 'Triock!' he gasped. 'I didn't kill her. She died trying to save my life. She knew it was my fault, and she still tried to save me. She would fight you now if she saw you like this! What did that Raver do to you?'

The Stonedownor advanced with slow ferocity.

'You're not like this!' Covenant cried. 'You gave your whole life to prove you're not like this!'

Springing suddenly, Triock caught Covenant by the throat. His thumbs ground into Covenant's windpipe as he snarled, 'You have not seen what I have seen!'

Covenant struggled, but he had no strength to match Triock's. His fingers clawed and clutched, and had no effect. The need for air began to hum in his ears.

Triock released one hand, cocked his fist deliberately, and hit Covenant in the centre of his wounded forehead. He pitched backward, almost fell. But hands caught him from behind, yanked him upright, put him on his feet – hands that burned him like the touch of acid.

He jerked away from them, then whirled to see who had burned him. Fresh blood ran from his yammering forehead into his eyes, clogged his vision, but he gouged it away with numb fingers, made himself see the two figures that had caught him.

They were laughing at him together. Beat for beat, their ridicule came as one, matched each other in weird consonance; they sounded like one voice jeering through two throats.

They were Ramen.

He saw them in an instant, took them in as if they had been suddenly revealed out of midnight by a flash of dismay. He recognized them as two of Manethrall Kam's Cords, Lal and Whane. But they had changed. Even his truncated vision could see the alteration which had been wrought in them, the complete reversal of being which occupied them. Contempt and lust submerged the former spirit of their health. Only the discomfortable spasms which flicked their faces, and the unnecessary violence of their emanations, gave any indication that they had ever been unlike what they were now.

'Our friend Triock spoke the truth,' they said together, and the unharmonized unison of their voices mocked both Covenant and Triock. 'Our brother is not with us. He is at work in the destruction of Revelstone. But Triock will take his place – for a time. A short time. We are *turiya* and *moksha*, Herem and Jehannum. We have come to take delight in the ruin of things we hate. You are nothing to us now, groveller – Unbeliever.' Again they laughed, one spirit or impulse uttering contempt through two throats. 'Yet you – and our friend Triock – amuse us while we wait.'

But Covenant hardly heard them. An instant after he comprehended what had happened to them, he saw something else, something that almost blinded him to the Ravers. Two other figures stood a short distance behind Whane and Lal.

The two people he had most ached to see since he had regained himself in Morinmoss: Saltheart Foamfollower and Bannor.

The sight of them filled him with horror.

Foamfollower wore a host of recent battle-marks among his older scars, and Bannor's silvering hair and lined face had aged perceptibly. But all that was insignificant beside the grisly fact that they were not moving.

They did not so much as turn their heads towards Covenant. They were paralysed, clenched rigid and helpless, by a green force which played about them like a corona, enveloped them in coercion. They were as motionless as if even pulse and respiration had been crushed out of them by shimmering emerald.

And if they had been able to look at Covenant, they would not have seen him. Their eyes were like Triock's, but much more severely glazed. Only the faintest outlines of pupil and iris were visible behind the white blindness which covered their orbs.

Bannor! Covenant cried. Foamfollower! Ah!

While his body swayed on locked joints, he cowered inwardly. His arms covered his head as if to protect it from an axe. The plight of Bannor and Foamfollower dealt him an unendurable shock. He could not bear it. He quailed where he stood as if the ground were heaving under him.

Then Triock caught hold of him again. The Stonedownor bent him to the dirt, hunched furiously over him to pant, 'You have not seen what I have seen. You do not know what you have done.'

Weak, ringless, and miserable though he was, Covenant still heard Triock, heard the whelming passion with which Triock told him that even now he did not know the worst, had not faced the worst. And that communication made a difference to him. It pushed him deep into his fear, down to a place in him which had not been touched by either capture or horror. It drove him back to the calm which had been given to him in Morinmoss. He seemed to remember a part of himself that had been hidden from him. Something had been changed for him in the Forest, something which could not be taken away. He caught hold of it, immersed himself in the gift.

A moment later, he raised his head as if he had come through a dark gulf of panic. He was too weak to fight Triock; he had lost his ring; blood streamed from his damaged forehead into his eyes. But he was no longer at the mercy of fear.

Blinking rapidly to clear his vision, he gasped up at Triock, 'What's happened to them?'

'You have not seen!' Triock roared. Once more, he raised his fist to hammer the Unbeliever's face. But before he could strike, a low voice commanded simply, 'Stop.'

Triock jerked, struggling to complete his blow.

'I have given you time. Now I desire him to know what I do.'

The command held Triock; he could not strike. Trembling, he wrenched away from Covenant, then spun back to point lividly towards the stone column and shout, 'There!'

Covenant lurched to his feet, wiped his eyes.

Midway between him and the upreared fist of stone stood Elena!

She was robed in radiant green velure, and she bore herself proudly, like a queen. She seemed swathed in an aura of emeralds; her presence sparkled like gems when she smiled. At once, without effort or assertion, she showed that she was the master of the situation. The Ravers and Triock waited before her like subjects before their liege.

In her right hand she held a long staff. It was metal-shod at both ends, and between its heels it was intricately carved with the runes and symbols of theurgy.

The Staff of Law.

But the wonder of its appearance there meant nothing to Covenant compared with the miracle of Elena's return. He had loved her, lost her. Her death at the hands of dead Kevin Landwaster had brought his second sojourn in the Land to an end. Yet she stood now scarcely thirty feet from him. She was smiling.

A thrill of joy shot through him. The love which had tormented his heart since her fall rushed up in him until he felt he was about to burst with it. Blood streamed from his eyes like tears. Joy choked him so that he could not speak. Half blinded, half weeping, he shrugged off his travail and started towards her as if he meant to throw himself down before her, kiss her feet.

Before he had crossed half the distance, she had made a short gesture with the Staff, and at once a jolt of force hit him. It drove the air from his lungs, pitched him to his hands and knees on the hard ground.

'No,' she said softly, almost tenderly. 'All your questions will be answered before I slay you, Thomas Covenant, ur-Lord and Unbeliever – beloved.' On her cold lips, the word *beloved* impugned him. 'But you will not touch me. You will come no closer.'

A great weight leaned against his shoulders, held him to the ground. He retched for air, but when he gasped it into his lungs, it hurt him as if he were inhaling disease. The atmosphere around him reeked with her presence. She pervaded the air like rot. On a scale that dwarfed him, she smelled as he did – smelled like – leprosy.

He forced up his head, gaped gasping at her from under the streaming spike of his wound.

With a smile like a smirk or leer, she extended her left hand towards him and opened it, so that he could see lying in her palm his white gold wedding band.

Elena! he retched voicelessly. Elena! He felt that he was being crushed under a burden of inpenetrable circumstance. In supplication and futility, he reached towards her, but she only laughed at him quietly, as if he were a masque of impotence enacted for her pleasure.

A moment passed before his anguish permitted him to see her clearly, and while he grovelled without comprehension, she shone defiantly before him like a soul of purest emerald. But slowly he recovered his vision. Like a reborn phoenix, she flourished in green loveliness. Yet in some way she reminded him of the spectre of Kevin Landwaster – a spirit dredged out of its uneasy grave by commands of irrefusable cruelty. Her expression was as placid as power could make it; she radiated triumph and decay. But her eyes were completely lightless, dark. It was as if the strange bifurcation, the dualness, of her sight had gone completely to its other pole, away from the tangible things around her. She seemed not to see where or who she was, what she did; her gaze was focused elsewhere, on the secret which compelled her.

She had become a servant of the Despiser. Even while she stood there with the Staff and the ring in her hands, Lord Foul's eyes held her like the eyes of a serpent.

In her violated beauty, Covenant beheld the doom of the Land. It would be kept fair, so that Lord Foul could more keenly relish its ravishment – and it would be diseased to the marrow.

'Elena,' he panted, then paused, gagging at the reek of her. 'Elena. Look at me.'

With a disdainful toss of her head, she turned away from him, moved a step or two closer to the stone pillar. 'Triock,' she commanded lightly, 'answer the Unbeliever's questions. I do not wish him to be in ignorance. His despair will make a pretty present for the master.'

At once, Triock strode stiffly forward, and stood so that Covenant could see him without fighting the pressure which held him to the ground. The Stonedownor's scowl had not changed, not abated one muscle or line of its vehemence, but his voice carried an odd undertow of grief. He began roughly, as if he were reading an indictment: 'You have asked where you are. You are at Landsdrop. Behind you lies the Fall of the River Landrider and the northmost reach of the Southron Range. Before you stands the Colossus of the Fall.'

Covenant panted at this information as if it interfered with his ragged efforts to breathe.

'Perhaps the Lords – ' Triock hissed the word *Lords* in rage or desperation – 'have spoken to you of the Colossus. In ages long past, it uttered the power of the One Forest to interdict its enemies the three Ravers from the Upper Land. The Colossus has been silent for millennia – silent since men broke the spirit of the Forest. Yet you may observe that *turiya* and *moksha* do not approach the stone. While one Forestal still lives in the remnants of the Forest, the Colossus may not be altogether undone. Thus it remains a thorn in the Despiser's mastery.

'It is now Elena's purpose to destroy this stone.'

Behind Covenant, both Ravers growled with pleasure at the thought.

'This has not been possible until now. Since this war began, Elena has stood here with the Staff of Law in support of the master's armies. With the Staff's power, she has held this winter upon the Land, thus freeing the master for other war work. This place was chosen for her so that she would be ready if the Colossus awoke – and so that she could destroy it if it did not awaken. But it has resisted her.' The hardness in his voice sounded almost like rage at Elena. 'There is Earthpower in it yet.

'But with the Staff and the wild magic, she will be capable. She will throw the rubble of the Colossus from its cliff. And when you have seen that no ancient bastion, however Earthpowerful and incorruptible, can stand against a servant of the master – then Elena Foul-wife will slay you where you kneel in your despair. She will slay us all.' With a jerk of his head, he included Bannor and Foamfollower.

In horrific unison, the Ravers laughed.

Covenant writhed under the pressure which held him. 'How?'

His question could have meant many things, but Triock understood him. 'Because the Law of Death has been broken!' he rasped. Fury flamed in his voice; he could no longer contain it. He watched Elena as she moved gracefully towards the Colossus, preparing herself to challenge it, and his voice blared after her as if he were striving in spite of her coercion to find some way to restrain her. Clearly, he knew how he was being compelled, what was being done to him, and the knowledge filled him with torment. 'Broken!'

he repeated, almost shouting. 'When she employed the Power of Command to bring Kevin Landwaster back from his grave, she broke the Law which separates life from death. She made it possible for the master to call her back in her turn – and with her the Staff of Law. Therefore she is his servant. And in her hands, the Staff serves him – though he would not use it himself, lest he share the fate of Drool Rockworm. Thus all Law is warped to his will!

'Behold her, Thomas Covenant! She is unchanged. Within her still lives the spirit of the daughter of Lena. Even as she readies herself for this destruction, she remembers what she was and hates what she is.' His chest heaved as if he were strangling on bitterness. 'That is the master's way. She is resurrected so that she may participate in the ruin of the Land – the Land she loves!'

He no longer made any pretence of speaking to Covenant; he hurled his voice at Elena as if his tone were the only part of him still able to resist her. 'Elena Foul-wife – ' he uttered the name with horror – 'now holds the white gold. She is more the master's servant than any Raver. In the hands of *turiya* or *moksha*, that power would breed rebellion. With wild magic, any Raver would throw down the master if he could, and take a new seat in the thronehall of Ridjeck Thome. But Elena will not rebel. She will not use the wild magic to free herself. She has been commanded from the dead, and her service is pure!'

He raged the word *pure* at her as if it were the worst affront he could utter. But she was impervious to him, secure in power and triumph. She only smiled faintly, amused by his ranting, and continued to make her preparations.

With her back to Covenant and Triock, she faced the monolith. It towered over her as if it were about to fall and crush her, but her stance admitted to no possibility of danger. With the Staff and the ring, she was superior to every power in the Land. In radiance and might, she raised her hands, holding up the Staff of Law and the white gold. Her sleeves fell from her arms. Exulting and exalted, she began to sing her attack on the Colossus of the Fall.

Her song hurt Covenant's ears, exacerbating his raw helplessness. He could not bear the intent, and could not oppose it; her interdict kept him on his knees like fetters of humiliation. Though he was only a dozen yards from her, he could not reach her, could not interfere with her purpose.

His thoughts raced madly, scrambled for alternatives. He could not abide the destruction of the Colossus. He had to find another answer.

'Foamfollower!' he croaked in desperation. 'I don't know what's happening to you – I don't know what's being done to you. But you've got to fight it! You're a Giant! You've got to stop her! Try to stop her! Foamfollower! Bannor!'

The Ravers met his plea with sardonic jeers, and Triock rasped without taking his eyes off Elena, 'You are a fool, Thomas Covenant. They cannot help you. They are too strong to be mastered – as I have been mastered – and too weak to be masters. Therefore she has imprisoned them by the power of the Staff. The Staff crushes all resistance. Thus it is proven that Law does not oppose Despite. We are all mastered beyond redemption.'

'Not you!' Covenant responded urgently. He fought the pressure until he feared his lungs would break, but he could not free himself. Without his ring, he felt as crippled as if his arms had been amputated. Without it, he weighed less than nothing in the scales of the Land's fate. 'Not you!' he gasped again. 'I can hear you, Triock! You! She isn't afraid of you – she isn't holding you. Triock! Stop her!'

Again the Ravers laughed. But this time Covenant heard the strain in their voices. Heaving against his captivity, he managed to wrench his head around far enough to look at Whane and Lal.

They still stood a safe distance from the Colossus. Neither made any move to help Covenant or oppose Elena. Both went on chuckling as if they could not help themselves. Yet their exertion was unmistakable. They were white-lipped and rigid, beads of effort ran down their faces. With all the long pride of their people, the Ramen were struggling to break free.

And behind them, Foamfollower and Bannor strove for freedom also. Somehow, both of them had found the strength to move slightly. Foamfollower's head was bowed, and he clenched his face with one hand as if he were trying to alter the shape of his skull. Bannor's fingers clawed at his sides; his face grew taut, baring his teeth. Urgently, desperately, they fought Elena's power.

Their ordeal felt terrible to Covenant – terrrible and hopeless. Like the Ramen, they were beyond the limits of what they could do. Pressure mounted in them, radiated from them. It was so acute that Covenant feared their hearts would rupture. And they had no chance of success. The power of the Staff increased to crush every extravagance of their self-expenditure.

Their futility hurt Covenant more than his own. He was accustomed to impotence, inured to it, but Bannor and Foamfollower were not. The stark vision of their defeat almost made him cry out in anguish. He wanted to shout to them, beg them to stop before they drove themselves soul-mad.

But the next instant a surge of new hope shot through him as he suddenly understood what they were doing. They knew they could not escape, were not trying to escape. They fought towards another goal. Elena was paying no attention to them; she concentrated on preparing for the destruction of the Colossus. So she was not actively exerting herself to imprison them. She had simply left her compulsion in the air and turned her back.

Foamfollower and Bannor were drawing on this compulsion, using it – using it up. As the Giant and the Bloodguard strained for freedom, strove with all their personal might, Triock jerked his head from side to side, quivered in a fever of passion, snapped his jaws as if he were trying to tear hunks of domination out of the air – and began to move towards Elena.

The Ravers made no attempt to stop him. They could not; the struggles of the Ramen gave them no leeway in which to act.

Triock strained as he moved as if his bones were being torn asunder, and he quavered imploringly again and again, 'Elena? Elena?' But he moved; he advanced step by step towards her.

Covenant watched him in an agony of suspense.

Before he came within arm's reach of her, she said severely, 'Stop.'

Swaying in a gale of conflicting demands, Triock halted.

'If you resist me one more step,' she grated, 'I will tear your heart from your pathetic old body and feed it to Herem and Jehannum while you observe them and beg me to let you die.'

Triock was weeping now, shaking with importunate sobs. 'Elena? Elena?'

Without even glancing at him, she resumed her song.

But the next instant, something snatched at her attention, spun her away from the Colossus. Her face pointed lividly towards the west. Surprise and anger contorted her features. For a moment, she stared in speechless indignation at the intrusion.

Then she brandished the Staff of Law. 'The Lords strike back!' she howled furiously. '*Samadhi* is threatened! They dare!'

Covenant gaped at the information, at her knowledge of the siege of Revelstone. But he had no time to assimilate it.

'Foul's blood!' she raged. 'Blast them, Raver!' Immense forces gathered in the Staff, mounting to be hurled across the distance to *samadhi* Sheol's aid.

For that instant, she neglected her compulsion of the people around her.

The blindness lost its hold on Bannor and Foamfollower. They trotted, lurched, started into motion. The Ravers tried to react, but could not move quickly enough against the resistance of the Ramen.

Covenant felt the pressure on his back ease. At once, he rolled out from under it. Springing to his feet, he launched himself towards Elena.

But Triock was the only one close enough to her to take advantage of her lapse. With a wild cry, he chopped both fists down at her left hand.

His hands passed through her spectral flesh and struck the ring. The unexpectedness of the blow tore the solid band from her surprised fingers. It dropped free.

He dived after it, got one hand on it, flicked it away towards Covenant as his body slapped the hard ground.

Elena's reaction came instantly. Before Triock could roll, try to evade her, she stabbed the Staff down at him, hit him in the centre of his back. Power flared through him, shattering his spine.

Almost in the same motion, she swung the Staff up again, caught it in a combat grip as she whirled to face Covenant.

His start towards her almost made him miss the ring. It went past him on one side, but he skidded and pounced on it, scooped it up before she could stop him. With his wedding band clenched in his fist, he braced himself to meet her attack.

She regarded him momentarily, then chose not to exert herself against him. With one wave of the Staff, she reimprisoned Foam-follower and Bannor, quenched the rebellion of the Ramen. Then she dropped her guard as if she no longer needed it. Her voice shook with anger, but she was steady as she said, 'It will not avail him. He knows not how to awaken its might. Herem, Jehannum – I leave him to you.'

In horrid unison, the two Ravers snarled their satisfaction, their hunger for him. Together, they moved slowly towards him.

He was caught between them and Elena.

So that he would not lose his ring again, he pushed it on to his wedding finger. He had lost weight; his fingers were gaunt, and the ring hung on him insecurely, as if it might fall off at any moment. Yet his need for it had never been greater. He clenched his fist around it and retreated before the advance of the Ravers.

In the back of his mind, he was sure that Triock was not dead. Triock was his summoner; he would disappear from the Land as soon as the Stonedownor died. But Triock surely had only moments of life left. Without knowing how to do it, Covenant wanted to make those moments count.

He backed away from the Ravers, towards Elena. She stood at rest near the Colossus, observing him. Glee and anger were balanced in her face. The Ravers came at him step by slow step, with their arms extended hungrily, sarcastically, inviting him to abandon resistance and rush into the oblivion of their grasp.

They advanced; he retreated; she stood where she was, defying him to touch her. His ring hung lifeless on his finger as if it were a thing of metal and futility, nothing more – a talisman devoid of meaning in his hands. A rising tide of protest filled him with ineffectual curses.

Hellfire. Hellfire. Hell and blood!

Impulsively, without knowing why he did it, he shrieked into the grey wind, 'Forestal! Help me!'

At once, the clenched crown of the Colossus burst into flame. For an instant while Herem and Jehannum yowled, the monolith blazed with verdant fire – a conflagration the colour of leaves and grass flourishing, green that had nothing in common with Lord Foul's emerald Illearth Stone. Raw, fertile aromas crackled in the air like violent spring.

Abruptly, two bolts of force raged out of the blaze, sprang like lightning at the Ravers. In a coruscating welter of sparks and might, the bolts struck the chests of Lal and Whane.

The monolith's power flamed at their hearts until the mortal flesh of the Ramen was incinerated, flash-burned into nothingness. Then the bolts dropped, the conflagration vanished.

Herem and Jehannum were gone.

The sudden blast and vanishing of the fire staggered Covenant. Forgetting his peril, he stared dumbly about him. The Ramen were dead. More blood, more lives sacrificed to his impotence. He wanted to cry out, No!

Some instinct warned him. He ducked, and the Staff of Law hissed past his head.

He jumped away, turned, caught his balance. Elena was advancing towards him. She held the Staff poised in both hands. Her face was full of murder.

She could have felled him with an exertion of the Staff's might, ravaged him where he stood by unleashing her power against him. But she was too mad with rage for such fighting. She wanted to crush him physically, beat him to death with the strength of her own arms. As he faced her, she gestured towards Foamfollower and Bannor without even glancing in their direction. They crumpled like puppets with cut strings, fell on their faces and lay still. Then she raised the Staff over his head like an axe and hacked at Covenant.

With a desperate fling of his arm, he deflected the Staff so that it slammed against his right shoulder rather than his head. The force of the blow seemed to paralyse his whole right side, but he grappled for the Staff with his left hand, caught hold of it, prevented her from snatching it back for another strike.

Quickly, she shifted her hands on the Staff and threw her weight on to the wood to take advantage of his defence. Bearing down on his shoulder, she drove him to his knees.

He braced his numb arm on the ground and strained to resist her, tried to get his feet under him. But he was too weak. She changed the direction of her pressure so that it jammed squarely against his throat. He had to fight the Staff with both hands to keep his larynx from being crushed. Slowly, almost effortlessly, she bent him back.

Then she had him flat on the ground. He pushed against the Staff with all his waning strength, but he could not stop her. His breathing was cut off. His bloodied eyes throbbed in their sockets as he stared at her ferocity.

Her gaze was focused on him as if he were food for the rankest hunger of her ill soul. Through it, he seemed to see the Despiser slavering in triumph and scorn. And yet her eyes showed something else as well. Triock had told the truth about her. Behind the savagery of her glare, he felt the last unconquerable core of her sobbing with revulsion.

He lacked the strength to save himself. If he could have hated her, met her fury with fury, he might have been capable of one convulsive heave, one thrust to buy himself another moment or two of life. But he could not. She was his daughter, he loved her. He had put her where she was as surely as if he had been a conscious servant of the Despiser all along. She was about to kill him, and he loved her. The only thing left for him was to die without breaking faith with himself.

He used his last air and his last resistance to croak, 'You don't even exist.'

His words inflamed her like an ultimate denial. In mad fury, she eased the pressure for an instant while she gathered all her force, all her strength, and all the power of the Staff, for one crush which would eradicate the offence of his life. She took a deep breath as if she were inhaling illimitable might, then threw her weight and muscle and power, her very Foul-given existence, through the Staff at his throat.

But his hands were clenched on the Staff. His ring pressed the wood. When her force touched his white gold, the wild magic erupted like an uncapped volcano.

His senses went blank at the immensity of the blast. Yet not one flame or thrust of it touched him; all the detonation went back through the Staff at Elena.

It did not hurl her off him; it was not that kind of power. But it tore through the rune-carved wood of the Staff like white sun-fire, rent the Staff fibre from fibre as if its Law were nothing but a shod bundle of splinters. A sharp riving shook the atmosphere, so that even the Colossus seemed to recoil from this unleashing of power.

The Staff of Law turned to ash in dead Elena's hands.

At once, the wind lurched as if the eruption of wild magic were an arrow in its bosom. With flutters and gusts and silent cries, it tumbled to the ground, came to an end as if the raw demon of winter had been stricken out of the air with one shaft.

A whirl of force sprang up around Elena, mounted like a wind devil with her in its centre. Her death had come back for her; the Law she had broken was sucking her out of life again. As Covenant watched – stunned and uncomprehending, almost blinded by his reprieve – she began to dissipate. Particle by particle, her being vanished into the gyre, fled into dissolution. But while she faded and failed, lost her ill existence, she found the solidity for one final cry.

'Covenant,' she called like a lorn voice of desolation. 'Beloved! Strike a blow for me!'

Then she was gone, reabsorbed into death. The gyre grew pale, paler, until it had disappeared in unruffled air.

Covenant was left alone with his victims.

Involuntarily, through means over which he had no control, he had saved himself – and had allowed his friends to be struck down. He felt chastened, frail, as devoid of victory as if he had actively slain the woman he loved.

So many people had sacrificed themselves.

He knew that Triock was still alive, so he climbed painfully to his feet and stumbled over to the fallen Stonedownor. Triock's breathing rattled like blood in his throat; he would be dead soon. Covenant seated himself on the ground and lifted Triock so that the man's head rested on his lap.

Triock's face was disfigured by the force which had smashed him. His charred skin peeled off his skull in places, and his eyes had been seared. From the slack dark hole of his mouth came faint plumes of smoke like the fleeing wisps of his soul.

Covenant hugged Triock's head with both arms and began to weep.

After a time, the Stonedownor sensed in some way who held him. Through the death thickening in his gullet, he struggled to speak. 'Covenant.'

His voice was barely audible, but Covenant fought back his tears to respond, 'I hear you.'

'You are not to blame. She was – flawed from birth.'

That was as far as his mercy could go. After one final wisp, the smoke faded away. Covenant held him, and knew he had no pulse or breath of life left.

He understood that Triock had forgiven him. The Stonedownor was not to blame if his gift gave no consolation. In addition to everything else, Covenant was responsible for the flaw of Elena's birth. She was the daughter of a crime which could never be undone. So he could do nothing but sit with Triock's unanswerable head in his lap, and weep while he waited for the reversal of his summons, the end which would reave him of the Land.

But no end came. In the past, he had always begun to fail as soon as his summoner died; but now he remained. Moments passed, and still he was undiminished. Gradually, he realized that this time he would not disappear, that for reasons he did not understand, he had not yet lost his chance.

He did not have to accept Elena's fate. It was not the last word – not yet.

When Bannor and Foamfollower stirred, groaned, began to regain consciousness, he made himself move. Carefully, deliberately, he took his ring from his wedding finger and placed it on the index finger of his halfhand, so that it would be less likely to slip off.

Then, amid all his grief and regret, he stood up on bones that could bear anything, and hobbled over to help his friends.

17

THE SPOILED PLAINS

Bannor recovered more quickly than Foamfollower. In spite of his advancing age, the toughness of the *Haruchai* was still in him; after Covenant had chafed his wrists and neck for a moment, he shrugged off his unconsciousness and became almost instantly alert. He met Covenant's teary gaze with characteristic dispassion, and together they went to do what they could for the Giant.

Foamfollower lay moaning on the ground in a fever of revulsion. Spasms bared his teeth, and his massive hands thrashed erratically against his chest as if he were trying to smite some fatal spot of wrong in himself. He seemed in danger of harming himself. So Bannor sat on the ground at the Giant's head, braced his feet on Foamfollower's shoulders, and caught his flailing arms by the wrists. Bannor held the Giant's arms still while Covenant sat on Foamfollower's chest and slapped his snarling face.

After a moment of resistance, Foamfollower let out a roar. Wrenching savagely, he heaved Bannor over Covenant's head, knocked the Unbeliever off his chest, and lurched panting to his feet.

Covenant retreated from the threat of Foamfollower's fists. But as the Giant blinked and panted, he recovered himself, recognized his friends. 'Covenant?' he gritted. 'Bannor?' as if he feared they were Ravers.

'Foamfollower,' Covenant responded thickly. Tears of relief streamed down his gaunt cheeks. 'You're all right.'

Slowly, Foamfollower relaxed as he saw that his friends were unmastered and whole. 'Stone and Sea!' he gasped weakly, shuddering as he breathed. 'Ah! My friends – have I harmed you?'

Covenant could not answer; he was choked with fresh weeping. He stood where he was and let Foamfollower watch his tears; he had no other way to tell the Giant how he felt. After a moment, Bannor replied for him, 'We are well – as well as may be. You have done us no injury.'

'And the – the spectre of High Lord Elena? The Staff of Law? How is it that we yet live?'

'Gone.' Covenant fought to control himself. 'Destroyed.'

Foamfollower's face was full of sympathy. 'Ah, no, my friend,' he sighed. 'She is not destroyed. The dead cannot be destroyed.'

'I know. I know that.' Covenant gritted his teeth, hugged his chest, until he passed the crest of his emotion. Then it began to subside, and he regained some measure of steadiness. 'She's just dead – dead again. But the Staff – it was destroyed. By wild magic.' Half fearing the reaction of his friends to this information, he added, 'I didn't do it. It wasn't my doing. She – ' He faltered. He had heard Mhoram say, *You are the white gold*. How could he be sure now what was or was not his doing?

But his revelation only drew a strange glint from Bannor's flat eyes. The *Haruchai* had always considered weapons unnecessary, even corruptive. Bannor found satisfaction rather than regret in the passing of the Staff. And Foamfollower shrugged the explanation aside, as if it were unimportant compared to his friend's distress. 'Ah, Covenant, Covenant,' he groaned. 'How can you endure? Who can withstand such things?'

'I'm a leper,' Covenant responded. He was surprised to hear himself say the word without bitterness. 'I can stand anything. Because I can't feel it.' He gestured with his diseased hands because his tears so obviously contradicted him. 'This is a dream. It can't touch me. I'm – ' he grimaced, remembering the belief which had first led Elena to break the Law of Death – 'numb.'

Answering tears blurred Foamfollower's cavernous eyes. 'And you are very brave,' he said in a thick voice. 'You are beyond me.'

The Giant's grief almost reopened Covenant's weeping. But he steadied himself by thinking of the questions he would have to ask, the things he would have to say. He wanted to smile for Foamfollower, but his cheeks were too stiff. Then he felt he had been caught in the act of a perennial failure, a habitual inadequacy of response. He was relieved to turn away when Bannor called their attention to the weather.

Bannor made him aware of the absence of wind. In his struggle with Elena, he had hardly noticed the change. But now he could feel the stillness of the atmosphere like a palpable healing. For a time, at least, Lord Foul's gelid frenzy was gone. And without the wind to drive it, the grey cloud-cover hung sullen and empty overhead, like a casket without a corpse.

As a result, the air felt warmer. Covenant half expected to see dampness on the ground as the hard earth thawed, half expected spring to begin on the spot. In the gentle stillness, the sound of the waterfall reached him clearly.

Bannor's perceptions went further, he sensed something Covenant had missed. After a moment, he took Covenant and Foamfollower to the Colossus to show them what he had found.

From the obsidian monolith came a soft emanation of heat.

This warmth held the true promise of spring; it smelled of buds and green grass, of *aliantha* and moss and forest-loam. Under its influence, Covenant found that he could relax. He put aside misery, fear, unresolved need, and sank down gratefully to sit with his back against the soothing stone.

Foamfollower hunted around the area until he located the sack of provisions he had carried with him from the Ramen covert. He took out food and his pot of graveling. Together, he, Bannor and Covenant ate a silent meal under the fist of the Colossus as if they were sharing a communion – as if they accepted the stone's warmth and shelter to do it honour. They had no other way to express their thanks.

Covenant was hungry; he had had nothing but Demondim-drink to sustain him for days. Yet he ate the food, absorbed the warmth, with a strange humility, as if he had not earned them, did not deserve them. He knew in his heart that the destruction of the Staff purchased nothing more than a brief respite for the Land, a short delay in the Despiser's eventual triumph. And that respite was not his doing. The reflex which had triggered the white gold was surely as unconscious, as involuntary, as if it had happened in his sleep. And yet another life had been spent on his account. That knowledge humbled him. He fed and warmed himself because all his work had yet to be done, and no other being in the Land could do it for him.

When the frugal meal was finished, he began his task by asking his companions how they had come to the Colossus.

Foamfollower winced at the memory. He left the telling of it to Bannor's terseness. While Bannor spoke, the Giant cleaned and tended Covenant's forehead.

In short sentences, Bannor indicated that the Ramen had been able to defeat the attack on their covert, thanks to the Giant's prodigious aid. But the battle had been a long and costly one and the night was gone before Bannor and Foamfollower could begin to search for Covenant and Lena. ('Ur-viles!' Foamfollower muttered at Covenant's injury. 'This will not heal. To make you captive, they put their mark upon you.') The Manethralls permitted only two Cords, Whane and Lal, to aid in the search. For during the night, a change had come over the Ranyhyn. To the surprise and joy of the Ramen, the great horses had unexpectedly started south towards the sanctuary of the mountains. The Ramen followed at once. Only their mixed awe and concern for the Ringthane induced them to give Bannor and Foamfollower any aid at all.

So the four of them began the hunt. But they had lost too much time; wind and snow had obscured the trail. They lost it south of the Roamsedge and could find no trace of Covenant. At last they concluded that he must have gained other aid to take him eastward. Together the four made what haste they could towards the Fall of the River Landrider.

The journey was made slow and arduous by *kresh* packs and marauders, and the four feared that Covenant would have left the Upper Land days ago. But when they neared the Colossus, they came upon a band of ur-viles accompanied by the Raver, Herem-Triock. Then the four were dismayed to see that the band bore with it the Unbeliever, prostrate as if he were dead.

The four attacked, slew the ur-viles. But they could not prevent the call which Herem sent. And before they could defeat Herem, rescue Covenant, and retrieve the ring, that call was answered by the dead Elena, wielding the Staff of Law. She mastered the four effortlessly. Then she gave Whane to Herem, so that Triock's anguish would be more poignant. When Jehannum came to her, that Raver entered Lal. Covenant knew the rest.

Bannor and Foamfollower had seen no sign of Lena. They did not know what had delayed Covenant's arrival at Landsdrop.

As Bannor finished, Foamfollower growled in angry disgust, 'Stone and Sea! She has made me unclean. I must bathe — I will need a sea to wash away this coercion.'

Bannor nodded, 'I, also.'

But neither of them moved, though the River Landrider was nearby beyond a low line of hills. Covenant knew they were holding themselves at his disposal; they seemed to sense that he needed them. And they had questions of their own. But he felt unready for the things he would have to say. After a silence, he asked painfully, 'Triock summoned me – and he's dead. Why am I still here?'

Foamfollower mused briefly, then said, 'Perhaps because the Law of Death has been broken – perhaps it was that Law which formerly sent you from the Land when your summoner died. Or perhaps it is because I also had a hand in this call.'

Yes, Covenant sighed to himself. His debt to Triock was hardly less than what he owed Foamfollower.

He could not shirk the responsibility any longer, he forced himself to describe what had happened to Lena.

His voice was dull as he spoke of her – an old woman brought to a bloody and graveless end because in her confusion she clung to the man who had harmed her. And her death was only the most recent tragedy in her family. First and last, her people had borne the brunt of him: Trell Gravelingas, Atiaran Trell-mate, High Lord Elena, Lena herself – he had ruined them all. Such things altered him, made a different man of him. That made it possible for him to ask another question after he had told all he knew of his own tale.

'Foamfollower – ' he framed his enquiry as carefully as he could – 'it's none of my business. But Pietten said some terrible things about you. Or he meant them to be terrible. He said – ' But he could not say the words. No matter how he uttered them, they would sound like an accusation.

The Giant sighed, and his whole frame sagged. He studied his intertwined hands as if somewhere in their clasped gentleness and butchery were a secret he could not unclose, but he no longer evaded the question. 'He said that I betrayed my kinfolk – that the Giants of Seareach died to the last child at the hands of *turiya* Raver because I abandoned them. It is true.'

Foamfollower! Covenant moaned. My friend! Sorrow welled up in him, almost made him weep again.

Abstractedly, Bannor said, 'Many things were lost in The Grieve that day.'

'Yes.' Foamfollower blinked as if he were trying to hold back tears, but his eyes were dry, as parched as a wilderland. 'Yes – many things. Among them I was the least.

'Ah, Covenant, how can I tell you of it? This tongue has no words long enough for the tale. No word can encompass the love for a lost homeland, or the anguish of diminishing seed, or the pride – the pride in fidelity – That fidelity was our only reply to our extinction. We could not have borne our decline if we had not taken pride.

'So my people – the Giants – I also, in my own way – the Giants were filled with horror – with abhorrence so deep that it numbed the very marrow of their bones – when they saw their pride riven – torn from them like rotten sails in the wind. They foundered at the sight. They saw the portent of their hope of Home – the three brothers – changed from fidelity to the most potent ill by one small stroke of the Despiser's evil. Who in the Land could hope to stand against a Giant-Raver? Thus the Unhomed became the means to destroy that to which they had held themselves true. And in horror at the naught of their fidelity, their folly practised through long centuries of pride, they were transfixed. Their revulsion left no room in them for thought or resistance or choice. Rather than behold the most of their failure – rather than risk the chance that more of them would be made Soulcrusher's servants – they – they elected to be slain.

'I also – in my way, I was horrified as well. But I had already seen what they had not, until that moment. I had seen myself become what I hated. Alone of all my kindred, I was not surprised. It was not the vision of a Giant-Raver which horrified me. It was my – my own people.

'Ah! Stone and Sea! They appalled me. I stormed at them – I ran through The Grieve like a dark sea of madness, howling at their abandonment, raging to strike one spark of resistance in the drenched tinder of their hearts. But they – they put away their tools, and banked their fires, and made ready their homes as if in preparation for departure – ' Abruptly, his suppressed passion broke into a cry. 'My people! I could not bear it! I fled them with abjection crowding at my heart – fled them lest I, too, should fall into their dismay. Therefore they were slain. I who might have fought the Raver deserted them in the deepest blackness of their need.' Unable to contain himself any longer, he heaved to his feet. His raw, scourged voice rasped thickly in his throat. 'I am unclean. I must – wash.'

Holding himself stiffly upright, he turned and lumbered away towards the river.

The helplessness of Covenant's pain came out as anger. His own voice shook as he muttered to Bannor, 'If you say one word to blame him, I swear – '

Then he stopped himself. He had accused Bannor unjustly too often in the past; the Bloodguard had long ago earned better treatment than this from him. But Bannor only shrugged. 'I am a *Haruchai*,' he said. 'We also are not immune. Corruption wears many

1078

faces. Blame is a more enticing face than others, but it is none the less a mask for the Despiser.'

His speech made Covenant look at him closely. Something came up between them that had never been laid to rest, neither on Gallows Howe nor in the Ramen covert. It wore the aspect of habitual Bloodguard distrust, but as he met Bannor's eyes, Covenant sensed that the issue was a larger one.

Without inflection, Bannor went on: 'Hate and vengeance are also masks.'

Covenant was struck by how much the Bloodguard had aged. His mortality had accelerated. His hair was the same silver as his eyebrows; his skin had a sere appearance, as if it had started to wither; and his wrinkles looked oddly fatal, like gullies of death in his countenance. Yet his steady dispassion seemed as complete as ever. He did not look like a man who had deserted his sworn loyalty to the Lords.

'Ur-Lord,' he said evenly, 'what will you do?'

'Do?' Covenant did his best to match the Bloodguard, though he could not look at Bannor's aging without remorse. 'I still have work to do. I've got to go to Foul's Creche.'

'For what purpose?'

'I've got to stop him.'

'High Lord Elena also strove to stop him. You have seen the outcome.'

'Yes.' Covenant did full justice to Bannor's statement. But he did not falter. 'I've got to find a better answer than she did.'

'Do you make this choice out of hate?'

He met the question squarely. 'I don't know.'

'Then why do you go?'

'Because I must.' That *must* carried the weight of an irrefusable necessity. The escape he had envisioned when he had left Morinmoss did not suffice. The Land's need held him like a harness. 'I've done so many things wrong. I've got to try to make them right.'

Bannor considered this for a moment, then asked bluntly, 'Do you know then how to make use of the wild magic?'

'No,' Covenant answered. 'Yes.' He hesitated, not because he doubted his reply, but because he was reluctant to say it aloud. But his sense of what was unresolved between him and Bannor had become clearer; something more than distrust was at stake. 'I don't know how to call it up, do anything with it. But I know how to trigger it.' He remembered vividly how Bannor had compelled him to help High Lord Prothall summon the Fire-Lions of Mount Thunder. 'If I can get to the Illearth Stone – I can do something.'

The Bloodguard's voice was hard. 'The Stone corrupts.'

'I know.' He understood Bannor's point vividly. 'I know. That's why I have to get to it. That's what this is all about – everything. That's why Foul has been manipulating me. That's why Elena – why Elena did what she did. That's why Mhoram trusted me.'

Bannor did not relent. 'Will it be another Desecration?'

Covenant had to steady himself before he could reply. 'I hope not. I don't want it to be.'

In answer, the Bloodguard got to his feet. Looking soberly down at the Unbeliever, he said, 'Ur-Lord Covenant, I will not accompany you for this purpose.'

'Not?' Covenant protested. In the back of his mind, he had been counting on Bannor's companionship.

'No. I no longer serve Lords.'

More harshly than he intended, Covenant rasped, 'So you've decided to turn your back?'

'No.' Bannor denied the charge flatly. 'What help I can, I will give. All the Bloodguard knowledge of the Spoiled Plains, of Kurash Qwellinir and Hotash Slay, I will share with you. But Ridjeck Thome, Corruption's seat – there I will not go. The deepest wish of the Bloodguard was to fight the Despiser in his home, pure service against Corruption. This desire misled. I have put aside such things. My proper place now is with Ranyhyn and their Ramen, in the exile of the mountains.'

Covenant seemed to hear an anguish behind the inflectionless tone of the speech – an anguish that hurt him in the same way that this man always hurt him. 'Ah, Bannor,' he sighed. 'Are you so ashamed of what you were?'

Bannor cocked a white eyebrow at the question, as if it came close to the truth. 'I am not shamed,' he said distinctly. 'But I am saddened that so many centuries were required to teach us the limits of our worth. We went too far, in pride and folly. Mortal men should not give up wives and sleep and death for any service – lest the fact of failure become too abhorrent to be endured.' He paused almost as if he were hesitating, then concluded, 'Have you forgotten that High Lord Elena carved our faces as one in her last marrowmeld work?'

'No.' Bannor had moved him. His response was both an assertion and a promise. 'I will never forget.'

Bannor nodded slowly. Then he said, 'I, too, must wash,' and strode away towards the river without a backward glance.

Covenant watched him go for a moment, then leaned his head back against the warmth of the Colossus and closed his sore eyes. He knew that he should not delay his departure any longer, that he increased his risk every moment he remained where he was. Lord Foul was certain to know what had happened; he would feel the sudden destruction of the Staff, and would search until he found the explanation, perhaps by compelling Elena once more out of her death to answer his questions. Then preparations would be made against the Unbeliever, Foul's Creche would be defended; hunting parties would be sent out. Any delay might mean defeat.

But Covenant was not ready. He still had one more confession to make – the last and hardest thing he would have to tell his friends. So he sat absorbing the heat of the Colossus like sustenance while he waited for Bannor and Foamfollower to return. He did not want to carry the weight of any more dishonesty with him when he left the place where Triock had died.

Bannor was not gone long. He and Foamfollower returned dripping to dry themselves in the heat of the stone. Foamfollower had regained his composure. His teeth flashed through his stiff wet beard as if he were eager to be on his way – as if he were ready to fight his way through a sea of foes for one chance to strike a blow at the Despiser. And Bannor stood dourly at the Giant's side. They were equals, despite the difference in size. They both met Covenant's gaze when he looked up at them. For an odd moment he felt torn between them, as if they represented the opposing poles of his dilemma.

But odder than this torn feeling was the confidence which came with it. In that fleeting moment, he seemed to recognize where he stood for the first time. While the impression lasted, his fear or reluctance or uncertainty dropped from him. 'There's one more thing,' he said to both his friends at once, 'one more thing I've got to tell you.'

Then, because he did not want to see their reactions until he had given them the whole tale, he sat gazing into the lifeless circle of his ring while he described how High Lord Mhoram had summoned him to Revelstone, and how he had refused.

He spoke as concisely as he could without minimizing the plight of Revelstone as he had seen it then, or the danger of the little girl for whom he had denied Mhoram's appeal, or the hysteria which had been on him when he had made his choice. He found as he spoke that he did not regret the decision. It seemed to have nothing to do with either his regret or his volition; he simply could not have chosen otherwise. But the Land had many reasons for regret – a myriad reasons, one for every life which had been lost, one for every day which had been added to the winter, because he had not given himself and his ring into Mhoram's hands. He explained what he had done so that Bannor and Foamfollower at least would not be able to reproach him for dishonesty.

When he was done, he looked up again. Neither Bannor nor

Foamfollower met his eyes at first; in their separate ways, they appeared upset by what they had heard. But finally Bannor returned Covenant's gaze and said levelly, 'A costly choice, Unbeliever. Costly. Much harm might have been averted – '

Foamfollower interrupted him. 'Costly! Might!' A fierce grin stretched his lips, echoed out of his deep eyes. 'A child was saved! Covenant – my friend – even reduced as I am, I can hear joy in such a choice. Your bravery – Stone and Sea! It astounds me.'

Bannor was not swayed. 'Call it bravery, then. It is costly nonetheless. The Land will bleed under the expense for many years, whatever the outcome of your purpose in Foul's Creche.'

Once again, Covenant was forced to say, 'I know.' He knew with a vividness that felt terrible to him. 'I couldn't do anything else. And – and I wasn't ready then. I'm ready now – readier.' I'll never be ready, he thought. It's impossible to be ready for this. 'Maybe I can do something now that I couldn't do then.'

Bannor held his eyes for another moment, then nodded brusquely. 'Will you go now?' he asked without expression. 'Corruption will be ahunt for you.'

Covenant sighed, and pushed himself to his feet. 'Yes.' He did not want to leave the comfort of the Colossus. 'Ready or not. Let's get on with it.'

He walked between Bannor and Foamfollower, and they took him up the last of the hills to a place where he could look down the cliff of Landsdrop to the Spoiled Plains.

The precipice seemed to leap out from behind the hills as if it had been hiding in ambush for Covenant – abruptly, he found himself looking over the edge and down two thousand feet – but he gripped the arms of his friends on either side and breathed deeply to hold back his vertigo. After a moment, the suddenness of the view faded, and he began to notice details.

At the base of the hill on his right, the River Landrider swooped downward in a final rush to pour heavily over the lip of Landsdrop. The tumult of its roar was complex. In this region, the cliff broke into four or five ragged stairs, so that the waterfall went down by steps, all pounding simultaneously, anharmonically. From the bottom of the Fall, it angled away southeastward into the perpetual wasteland of the Spoiled Plains.

'There,' said Bannor, 'there begins its ordeal. There the Landrider becomes the Ruinwash, and flows polluted towards the Sea. It is a murky and repelling water, unfit for use by any but its own unfit denizens. But it is your way for a time. It will provide a path for you through much of these hazardous Plains. And it will place you south of Kurash Qwellinir.

'You know – ' he nodded to Foamfollower – 'that the Spoiled Plains form a wide deadland around the promontory of Ridjeck Thome, where Foul's Creche juts into the Sea. Within that deadland lies Kurash Qwellinir, the Shattered Hills. Some say that these Hills were formed by the breaking of a mountain – others, that they were shaped from the slag and refuse of Corruption's war caverns, furnaces, breeding dens. However they were made, they are a maze to bewilder the approach of any foe. And within them lies Gorak Krembal – Hotash Slay. From Sea-cliff to Sea-cliff about the promontory, it defends Corruption's seat with lava, so that none may pass that way to gain the one gateless maw of the Creche.

'Corruption's creatures make their way to and from Ridjeck Thome through tunnels which open in secret places among Kurash Qwellinir. But it is in my heart that such an approach will not avail you. I do not doubt that a Giant may find a tunnel within the maze. But on that road all Corruption's defending armies stand before you. You cannot pass.

'I will tell you of a passage through the Shattered Hills on their southward side. The narrowest point of Hotash Slay is there, where the lava pours through a gash in the cliff into the Sea. A Giant may find crossing in that place.' He spoke as if he were discussing a convenient path among mountains, not an approach to the Corrupter of the Bloodguard. 'In that way, it may be that you will take Ridjeck Thome by surprise.'

Foamfollower absorbed this information, and nodded. Then he listened closely while Bannor detailed his route through the maze of Kurash Qwellinir. Covenant tried to listen also, but his attention wandered. He seemed to hear Landsdrop calling to him. Imminent vertigo foiled his concentration. Elena, he breathed to himself. He called her up in his mind, hoping that her image would steady him. But the emerald radiance of her fate made him wince and groan.

No! he averred into the approach of dizziness. It doesn't have to be that way. It's my dream. I can do something about it.

Foamfollower and Bannor were looking at him strangely. His fingers gripped them feebly, urgently. He could not take his eyes off the waterfall's rush. It called him downward like the allure of death.

He took a deep breath. Finger by finger, he forced himself to release his friends. 'Let's get going,' he murmured. 'I can't stand any more waiting.'

The Giant hefted his sack. 'I am ready,' he said. 'Our supplies are scant – but we have no recourse. We must hope for *aliantha* on the Lower Land.'

Without looking away from the Fall, Covenant addressed Bannor. He could not ask the Bloodguard to change his decision, so he said,

'You'll bury Triock? He's earned a decent grave.'

Bannor nodded, then said, 'I will do another thing also.' He reached one hand into his short robe and drew out the charred metal heels of the Staff of Law. 'I will bear these to Revelstone. When the time of my end comes upon me, I will return to the mountain home of the *Haruchai*. On the way, I will visit Revelstone – if the Lords and Lord's Keep still stand. I know not what value may remain in this metal, but perhaps the survivors of this war will find some use for it.'

Thank you, Covenant whispered silently.

Bannor put the bands away and bowed once briefly to Covenant and Foamfollower. 'Look for help wherever you go,' he said. 'Even in the Spoiled Plains, Corruption is not entirely master.' Before they could reply, he turned and trotted away towards the Colossus. As he passed over the hilltop, his back told them as clearly as speech that they would never see him again.

Bannor! Covenant groaned. Was it that bad? He felt bereft, deserted, as if half his support had been taken away.

'Gently, my friend,' Foamfollower breathed. 'He has turned his back on vengeance. Two thousand years and more of pure service were violated for him – yet he chooses not to avenge them. Such choices are not easily made. They are not easily borne. Retribution – ah, my friend, retribution is the sweetest of all dark sweet dreams.'

Covenant found himself still staring at the waterfall. The complex plunge of the river had a sweetness all its own. He shook himself. 'Hellfire.' The emptiness of his curses seemed appropriate to his condition. 'Are we going to do it or aren't we?'

'We will go.' Covenant felt the Giant's gaze on him without meeting it. 'Covenant – ur-Lord – there is no need for you to endure this descent. Close your eyes, and I will bear you as I did from Kevin's Watch.'

Covenant hardly heard himself answer, 'That was a long time ago.' Vertigo was beginning to reel in his head. 'I've got to do this for myself.' For a moment, he let slip his resistance and almost fell to his knees. As the suction tugged at his mind, he comprehended that he would have to go into it rather than away from it, that the only way to master vertigo was to find its centre. Somewhere in the centre of the spinning would be an eye, a core of stability. 'Just go ahead – so you can catch me.' Only in the eye of the whirl could he find solid ground.

Foamfollower regarded him dubiously, then started down to the edge of the cliff near the Fall. With Covenant limping in his wake, he went to the rim, glanced down to pick the best place for a descent, then lowered himself out of sight over the edge.

Covenant stood for a moment teetering on the lip of Landsdrop.

the Fall yawed abysmally from side to side; it beckoned to him like relief from delirium. It was such an easy answer. As his vertigo mounted, he did not see how he could refuse it.

But its upsurge made his pulse hammer in his wounded forehead. He spun around that pain as if it were a pivot, and found that the seductive panic of the plunge was fading. The simple hope that vertigo had a firm centre seemed to make his hope come true. The whirl did not stop, but its hold on him receded, withdrew into the background. Slowly, the pounding in his forehead eased.

He did not fall.

He felt as weak as a starving penitent – hardly able to carry his own weight. But he knelt on the edge, lowered his legs over the rim. Clinging to the top of the cliff with his arms and stomach, he began to hunt blindly for footholds. Soon he was crawling backward down Landsdrop as if it were the precipice of his personal future.

The descent took a long time, but it was not particularly difficult. Foamfollower protected him all the way down each stage of the broken cliff. And the steeper drops were moderated by enough ledges and cracks and hardy scrub brush to make that whole stretch of the cliff passable. The Giant had no trouble finding a route Covenant could manage, and Covenant eventually gained a measure of confidence, so that he was able to move with less help down the last stages to the foothills.

When at last he reached the lower ground, he took his drained nerves straight to the pool at the foot of the Fall and dropped into the chill waters to wash away the accumulated sweat of his fear.

While Covenant bathed, Foamfollower filled his water jug and drank deeply at the pool. This might be the last safe water they would find. Then the Giant set out the graveling for Covenant. As the Unbeliever dried himself, he asked Foamfollower how long their food supplies would last.

The Giant grimaced. 'Two days. Three or four, if we find *aliantha* a day or two into the Spoiled Plains. But we are far from Foul's Creche. Even if we were to run straight into Soulcrusher's arms, we would have three or four foodless days within us before he made sustenance unnecessary.' Then he grinned. 'But it is said that hunger teaches many things. My friend, a wealth of wisdom awaits us on this journey.'

Covenant shivered. He had had some experience with hunger. And now the possibility of starvation lay ahead of him; his forehead had been reinjured; he would have to walk a long distance on bare feet. One by one, the conditions of his return to his own life were being met. As he tightened the sash of his robe, he muttered sourly,

'I heard Hyrim say once that wisdom is only skin-deep. Or something like that. Which means that lepers must be the wisest people in the world.'

'Are they?' the Giant asked. 'Are you wise, Unbeliever?'

'Who knows? If I am – wisdom is overrated.'

At this, Foamfollower's grin broadened. 'Perhaps it is – perhaps it is. My friend, we are the two wisest hearts in the Land – we who march thus weaponless and unredeemed into the very bosom of the Despiser. Verily, wisdom is like hunger. Perhaps it is a very fine thing – but who would willingly partake of it?'

Despite the absence of the wind, the air was still wintry. Knuckles of ice clenched the rocky borders of the pool where the spray of the Fall had frozen, and Foamfollower's breath plumed wetly in the humid air. Covenant needed to move to warm himself, keep up his courage. 'It's not fine,' he grated, half to himself. 'But it's useful. Come on.'

Foamfollower repacked his graveling, then swung the sack on to his shoulder, and led Covenant away from Landsdrop along the river.

Night stopped them when they had covered only three or four leagues. But by that time they had left behind the foothills and the last vestiges of the un-Spoiled flatland which had at one time, ages ago in the history of the Earth, stretched from the Southron Wastes north to the Sarangrave and Lifeswallower, the Great Swamp. They were down in the bosque of the Ruinwash.

Grey, brittle, dead brush and trees – cottonwoods, junipers, once-beautiful tamarisks – stood up out of the dried mud on both sides of the stream, occupying ground which had once been part of the riverbed. But the Ruinwash had shrunk decades or centuries ago, leaving partially fertile mud on either side – mud in which a scattering of tough trees and brush had eked out a bare existence until Lord Foul's preternatural winter had blasted them. As darkness soaked into the air as if it were oozing out of the ground, the trees became spectral shapes of forbidding which made the bosque almost impassable. Covenant resigned himself to camping there for the night, though the dried mud had an old, occluded reek, and the river made a slithering noise like an ambush in its course. He knew that he and Foamfollower would be safe if they travelled at night, but he was weary and did not believe the Giant could find his way in the cloud-locked dark.

Later, however, he found that the river gave off a light like lambent verdigris; the whole surface of the water glowed dimly. This light came, not from the water, but from the hot eels which flicked back and forth across the current. They had a hungry aspect, and their jaws were rife with teeth. Yet they made it possible for him and Foamfollower to resume their journey.

Even in the cynosural eel light, they did not go much farther. The destruction of the Staff had changed the balance of Lord Foul's winter, without the wind to hold them, the massed energies of the clouds recoiled. In the deeper chill of darkness, they triggered rain out of the blind sky. Soon torrents fell through the damaged grasp of the clouds, crashed straight down on to the Lower Land as if the vaulting which held up the heavens had broken. Under those conditions, Foamfollower could not find his way. He and Covenant had no choice but to huddle together for warmth in the mud and try to sleep while they waited.

With the coming of dawn, the rain stopped, and Covenant and Foamfollower went on along the Ruinwash in the blurred light of morning. During that day, they saw the last of the *aliantha*; as they penetrated into the Spoiled Plains, the mud became too dead for treasure-berries. The travellers kept themselves going on scant shares of their dwindling supplies. At night, the rains came again, soaking them until they seemed to have its dankness in the marrow of their bones.

The next day, an eagle spotted them through a gap in the grey trees. It cycled twice close over their heads, then soared away, screaming in mockery like a voice from the dead, 'Foamfollower! Kinabandoner!'

'They're after us,' said Covenant.

The Giant spat violently. 'Yes. They will hunt us down.' He found a smooth stone the size of Covenant's two fists and carried it with him to throw at the eagle if it returned.

It did not come back that day, but the next – after another torrential downpour avalanched the Plains as if the cloud lid over the Land were a shattered sea – Lord Foul's bird circled them twice, morning and afternoon. The first time, it taunted them until Foamfollower had hurled all the stones he could find nearby, then it slashed close to bark scornfully, 'Kinabandoner! Groveller!'

The second time, Foamfollower kept one stone hidden. He waited until the eagle had swooped lower to jeer, then threw at it with deadly force. It survived by breaking the blow with its wings, but it flew limping away, barely able to stay aloft.

'Make haste,' Foamfollower growled. 'That ill bird has been guiding the pursuit towards us. It is not far off.'

At the best pace Covenant could manage on his numb, battered feet, he pushed ahead through the bosque.

They stayed under tree cover as much as possible to ward against spying birds. This caution slowed them somewhat, but the largest drag on their progress was Covenant's weariness. His injury and the ordeal of the Colossus appeared to have drained some essential resilience out of him. He got little sleep in the cold wet nights, and he felt that he was slowly starving on his share of the food. In dogged silence he shambled along league after league as if his fear of the hunt were the only thing that kept him moving. And that evening, in the gloaming verdigris of the eel fire, he consumed the last of Foamfollower's supplies.

'Now what?' he muttered vaguely when he was done.

'We must resign ourselves. There is no more.'

Ah, hell! Covenant groaned to himself. He remembered vividly what had happened to him in the woods behind Haven Farm, when his self-imposed inanition had made him hysterical. The memory filled him with cold dread.

In turn, that dread called up other memories — recollections of his ex-wife, Joan, and his son, Roger. He felt an urge to tell Foamfollower about them, as if they were spirits he could exorcise by simply saying the right thing about them to the right person. But before he could find the words, his thoughts were scattered by the first attack of the hunt.

Without warning, a band of apelike creatures came crashing through the bosque from the south side of the Ruinwash. Voiceless, like the rush of a nightmare, they broke through the brittle wood and the eel light. They threw themselves from the low bank and heaved across the current towards their prey.

Either they did not know their danger, or they had forgotten it. Without one shout or cry, they all vanished under a sudden, hot, seething of blue-green iridescence. None of them reappeared.

At once, Covenant and Foamfollower started on their way again. While the crepuscular light lasted, they put as much distance as possible between themselves and the place of the attack.

A short time later the rain began. It fell on them like the collapse of a mountain, made the whole night impenetrable. They were forced to stop. They hunched together like waifs under the scant, leafless shelter of a tree, trying to sleep and hoping that the hunt could not follow them in this weather.

After a while, Covenant dozed. He was hovering near the true depths of sleep when Foamfollower shook him awake.

'Listen!'

Covenant could hear nothing but the uninterrupted smash of the rain.

The Giant's ears were keener. 'The Ruinwash rises! There will be a flood.'

Straggling like blind men, thrashing their way against unseen trees and brush, slipping through water that already reached above their ankles, they tried to climb out of the bosque towards higher ground. After a long struggle, they worked clear of the old riverbed. But the water continued to mount, and the terrain did not. Now beyond the rain, Covenant could hear the deeper roar of the flood; it seemed to tower above them in the night. He was stumbling knee-deep in muddy water, and could see no way to save himself.

But Foamfollower dragged him onward. Some time later, they waded into an erosion gully. Its walls were slick, and the water poured down through it like flowing silt, but the Giant did not hesitate. He attached Covenant to him with a short *clingor* line and began to forge up the gully.

Covenant clung to Foamfollower for a distance that seemed as long as leagues. But at last he could feel that they were climbing. The walls of the gully narrowed. Foamfollower used his hands to help him ascend.

When they reached an open hillside where the flow of water hardly covered their feet, they stopped. Covenant sank exhausted into the mud. The rain faltered to an end, and he went numbly to sleep until another cold grey dawn smeared its way across the clouds from the east.

At last he rubbed the caked fatigue out of his eyes and sat up. Foamfollower was gazing at him with amusement. 'Ah, Covenant,' the Giant said, 'we are a pair. You are so bedraggled and sober – And I fear my own appearance is not improved.' He struck a begrimed pose. 'What is your opinion?'

For a moment, Foamfollower looked as gay and carefree as a playing child. The sight gave Covenant a pang. How long had it been since he had heard the Giant laugh? 'Wash your face,' he croaked with as much humour as he could manage. 'You look ridiculous.'

'You honour me,' Foamfollower returned. But he did not laugh. As his amusement faded, he turned away and splashed a little water on his face to clean it.

Covenant followed his example, though he was too tired to feel dirty. He drank three swallows from the jug for breakfast, then pried himself unsteadily to his feet.

In the distance, he could see a few treetops sticking out of the broad brown swath of the flood. No other signs remained visible to mark the bosque of the Ruinwash.

Opposite the flood, in the direction he and Foamfollower would now have to take, lay a long ridge of hills. They piled in layers above him until they seemed almost as high as mountains, and their scarred sides looked as desolate as if their very roots had been dead for aeons.

He groaned at the prospect. His worn flesh balked. But he had no choice; the lowlands of the Ruinwash were no longer passable.

With nothing to sustain them but frugal rations of water, he and the Giant began to climb.

The ascent was shallower than it had appeared. If Covenant had been well fed and healthy, he would not have suffered. But in his drained condition, he could hardly drag himself up the slopes. The festering wound on his forehead ached like a heavy burden attached to his skull, pulling him backward. The thick humid air seemed to clog his lungs. From time to time, he found himself lying among the stones and could not remember how he had lost his feet.

Yet with Foamfollower's help he kept going. Late that day, they crested the ridge of hills, started their descent.

Since leaving the Ruinwash, they had seen no sign of pursuit.

The next morning, after a night's rain as ponderous and rancid as if the clouds themselves were stagnant, they moved down out of the hills. As Covenant's gaunt flesh adjusted to hunger, he grew steadier – not stronger, but less febrile. He made the descent without mishap, and from the ridge he and Foamfollower travelled generally eastward out into the barren landscape.

After a foodless and dreary noon, they came to an eerie wilderness of thorns. It occupied the bottom of a wide lowland; for nearly a league, dead thorn-trees with limbs like arms and grey barbs as hard as iron stood in their way. The whole bottom looked like a ruined orchard where sharp spikes and hooks had been grown for weapons; the thorns stood in crooked rows as if they had been planted there so that they could be tended and harvested. Here and there, gaps appeared in the rows, but from a distance Covenant could not see what caused them.

Foamfollower did not want to cross the valley. Higher ground bordered the thorn wastes on both sides, and the barren trees offered no concealment; while they were down in the bottom, they could be easily seen. But again they had no choice. The wastes extended far to the north and south. They would need time to circumvent the thorns – time in which hunger could overcome them, pursuit overtake them.

Muttering to himself, Foamfollower scanned all the terrain as far as he could see, searching for any sign of the hunt. Then he led Covenant down the last slope into the thorns.

They found that the lowest branches of the trees were six or seven feet above the ground. Covenant could move erect along the crooked rows of trunks, but Foamfollower had to crouch or bend almost double to keep the barbs from ripping open his torso and head. He risked injury if he moved too quickly. As a result, their progress through the wastes was dangerously slow.

Thick dust covered the ground under their feet. All the rain of the past nights seemed to have left this valley untouched. The lifeless dirt faced the clouds as if years of torrents could never assuage the thirst of its ancient ruin. Choking billows rose up from the strides of the travellers, filled their lungs and stung their eyes – and plumed into the sky to mark their presence as clearly as smoke.

Soon they came to one of the gaps in the thorns. To their surprise, they found that it was a mud pit. Damp clay bubbled in a small pool. In contrast to the dead dust all around it, it seemed to be seething with some kind of muddy life, but it was as cold as the winter air. Covenant shied away from it as if it were dangerous, and hurried on through the thorns as fast as Foamfollower could go.

They were half-way to the eastern edge of the valley when they heard a hoarse shout of discovery in the distance behind them. Whirling, they saw two large bands of marauders spring out of different parts of the hills. The bands came together as they charged in among the thorn-trees, howling for the blood of their prey.

Covenant and Foamfollower turned and fled.

Covenant sprinted with the energy of fear. In the first surge of flight, he had room in his mind for nothing but the effort of running, the pumping of his legs and lungs. But shortly he realized that he was pulling away from Foamfollower. The Giant's crouched stance cramped his speed; he could not use his long legs effectively without tearing his head off among the thorns. 'Flee!' he shouted at Covenant. 'I will hold them back!'

'Forget it!' Covenant slowed to match the Giant's pace. 'We're in this together.'

'Flee!' Foamfollower repeated, flailing one arm urgently as if to hurl the Unbeliever ahead.

Instead of answering, Covenant rejoined his friend. He heard the savage outcry of the pursuit as if it were clawing at his back, but he stayed with Foamfollower. He had already lost too many people who were important to him.

Abruptly, Foamfollower lurched to a halt. 'Go, I say! Stone and Sea!' He sounded furious. 'Do you believe I can bear to see your purpose fail for my sake?'

Covenant wheeled and stopped. 'Forget it,' he panted again. 'I'm good for nothing without you.'

Foamfollower spun to look at the charging hunters. 'Then you must find the way of your white gold now. They are too many.'

'Not if you keep moving! By hell! We can still beat them.'

The Giant swung back to face Covenant. For an instant, his muscles bunched to carry him forward again. But then he went rigid; his head jerked up. He stared hotly through the branches into the distance past Covenant's head.

A new dread seized Covenant. He turned, followed the Giant's gaze.

There were ur-viles on the eastern slope of the valley. They rushed in large numbers towards the wastes as if they were swarming, and as they moved, they coalesced into three wedges. Covenant could see them clearly through the thorns. When they reached the bottom, they halted, wielded their staves. All along the eastern edge of the forest, they set fire to the dead trees.

The thorns flared instantly. Flames leaped up with a roar, spread rapidly through the branches from tree to tree. Each trunk became a torch to light its neighbours. In moments, Covenant and Foamfollower were cut off from the east by a wall of conflagration.

Foamfollower snatched his gaze back and forth between the fire and the charging hunters, and his eyes shot gleams of fury like battle-lust from under his massive brows. 'Trapped!' he shouted as if the impossibility of the situation outraged him. But his anger had a different meaning. 'They have erred! I am not so vulnerable to fire. I can break through and attack!'

'I'm vulnerable,' Covenant replied numbly. He watched the Giant's rising rage with a nausea of apprehension in his guts. He knew what his response should have been. Foamfollower was far better equipped than he to fight the Despiser. He should have said, Take my ring and go. You can find a way to use it. You can get past those ur-viles. But his throat would not form the words. And the fear that Foamfollower would ask for his wedding band churned in him, inspired him to find an alternative. He croaked, 'Can you swim in quicksand?'

The Giant stared at him as if he had said something incomprehensible.

'The mud pits! We can hide in one of them — until the fire passes. If you can keep us from drowning.'

Still Foamfollower stared. Covenant feared that the Giant was too far gone in rage to understand what he said. But a moment later Foamfollower took hold of himself. With a sharp convulsion of will, he mastered his desire to fight. 'Yes!' he snapped. 'Come!' At once, he scuttled away towards the fire.

They raced to find a pool of the bubbling clay near the fire before the hunters caught up with them. Covenant feared that they would be too late; even through the wild roar of the fire, he could hear his pursuers howling. But the blaze moved with frightful rapidity. While the creatures were still several hundred yards distant, he slapped into the heat of the flames and veered aside, searching for one of the pits.

He could not find one. The rush of heat stung his eyes, half blinded him. He was too close to the fire. It chewed its way through the treetops towards him like a world-devouring beast. He called to Foamfollower, but his voice made no sound amid the tumult of the blaze.

The Giant caught his arm, snatched him up. Running crouched like a cripple, he headed towards a pool directly under the wall of flame. The twigs and thorns nearest the pit were already bursting into hot orange flower as if they had been brought back to life by fire.

Foamfollower leaped into the mud.

His impetus carried them in over their heads, but with the prodigious strength of his legs he thrust them to the surface again. The mounting heat seemed to scorch their faces instantly. But Covenant was more afraid of the mud. He thrashed frantically for a moment, then remembered that the swiftest way to die in quicksand was to struggle. Straining against his instinctive panic, he forced himself limp. At his back, he felt Foamfollower do the same. Only their heads protruded from the mud.

They did not sink. The fire swept over them while they floated, and long moments of pain seared Covenant's face as he hung in the wet clay, hardly daring to breathe. His intense helplessness seemed to increase as the fire passed.

When the flames were gone, he and Foamfollower would be left floating in mire to defend themselves as best they could against three wedges of ur-viles without so much as moving their arms.

He tried to draw a large enough breath to shout to Foamfollower. But while he was still inhaling, hands deep in the mud pit caught his ankles and pulled him down.

18

THE CORRUPT

He struggled desperately, trying to regain the surface. But the mud clogged his movements, sucked at his every effort, and the hands on his ankles tugged him downward swiftly. He grappled towards

Foamfollower, but found nothing. Already, he felt he was far beneath the surface of the pit.

He held his breath grimly. His obdurate instinct for survival made him keep on fighting though he knew that he could never float to the surface from this cold depth. Straining against the mud, he bent, worked his hands down his legs in an effort to reach the fingers which held him. But he could not find them. They pulled him downward – he felt their wet clench on his ankles – but his own hands passed through where those hands should have been, must have been.

In his extremity, he seemed to feel the white gold pulsing for an instant. But the pulse gave him no sensation of power, and it disappeared as soon as he reached towards it with his mind.

The air in his lungs began to fail. Red veins of light intaglioed the insides of his eyelids. He began to cry wildly, Not like this! Not like this!

The next moment, he felt that he had changed directions. While his lungs wailed, the hands pulled him horizontally, then began to take him upward. With a damp sucking noise, they heaved him out of the mud into dank, black air.

He snatched at the air in shuddering gasps. It was stale and noisome, like the air in a wet crypt, but it was life, and he gulped it greedily. For a long moment, the red blazonry in his brain blinded him to the darkness. But as his respiration subsided into dull panting, he squeezed his eyes free of mud and blinked them open, tried to see where he was.

The blackness around him was complete.

He was lying on moist clay. When he moved, his left shoulder touched a muddy wall. He got to his knees and reached up over his head; an arm's length above him, he found the ceiling. He seemed to be against one wall of a buried chamber in the clay.

A damp voice near his ear said, 'He cannot see.' It sounded small and frightened but the surprise of it startled him, made him jerk away and slip panting against the wall.

'That is well,' another timorous voice responded. 'He might harm us.'

'It is not well. Provide light for him.' This voice seemed more resolute, but it still quavered anxiously.

'No! No, no,' Covenant could distinguish eight or ten speakers protesting.

The sterner voice insisted. 'If we did not intend to aid him, we should not have saved him.'

'He may harm us!'

'It is not too late. Drown him.'

'No.' The sterner voice stiffened. 'We chose this risk.'

'Oh! If the Maker learns – !'

'We chose, I say! To save and then slay – that would surely be Maker-work. Better that he should harm us. I will – ' the voice hesitated fearfully – 'I will provide light myself if I must.'

'Stand ready!' speakers chorused, spreading an alarm against Covenant.

A moment later, he heard an odd slippery noise like the sound of a stick being thrust through mud. A dim red glow the colour of rocklight opened in the darkness a few feet from his face.

The light came from a grotesque figure of mud standing on the floor of the chamber. It was about two feet tall, and it faced him like a clay statue formed by the unadept hands of a child. He could discern awkward limbs, vague misshapen features, but no eyes, ears, mouth, nose. Reddish pockets of mud in its brown form shone dully, giving off a scanty illumination.

He found that he was in the end of a tunnel. Near him was a wide pit of bubbling mud, and beyond it the walls, floor and ceiling came together, sealing the space. But in the opposite direction the tunnel stretched away darkly.

There, at the limit of the light, stood a dozen or more short clay forms like the one in front of him.

They did not move, made no sound. They looked inanimate, as if they had been left behind by whatever creature had formed the tunnel. But the tunnel contained no one or nothing else that might have spoken. Covenant gaped at the gnarled shapes, and tried to think of something to say.

Abruptly, the mud pit began to seethe. Directly in front of Covenant, several more clay forms hopped suddenly out of the mire, dragging two huge feet with them. The glowing shape quickly retreated down the tunnel to make room for them. In an instant, they had heaved Foamfollower out on to the floor of the tunnel and had backed away from him to join the forms which stood watching Covenant.

Foamfollower's Giantish lungs had sustained him; he needed no time at all to recover. He flung himself around in the constricted space and lurched snarling towards the clay forms with rage in his eyes and one heavy fist upraised.

At once, the sole light went out. Amid shrill cries of fear, the mud creatures scudded away down the tunnel.

'Foamfollower!' Covenant shouted urgently. 'They saved us!'

He heard the Giant come to a stop, heard him panting hoarsely. 'Foamfollower,' he repeated. 'Giant!'

Foamfollower breathed deeply for a moment, then said, 'My

friend?' In the darkness, his voice sounded cramped, too full of suppressed emotions. 'Are you well?'

'Well?' Covenant felt momentarily unbalanced on the brink of hysteria. But he steadied himself. 'They didn't hurt me. Foamfollower – I think they saved us.'

The Giant panted a while longer, regaining his self-command. 'Yes,' he groaned. 'Yes. Now I have taught them to fear us.' Then, projecting his voice down the tunnel, he said, 'Please pardon me. You have indeed saved us. I have little restraint – yes, I am quick to anger, too quick. Yet without purposing to do so you wrung my heart. You took my friend and left me. I feared him dead – despair came upon me. Bannor of the Bloodguard told us to look for help wherever we went. Fool that I was, I did not look for it so near to Soulcrusher's demesne. When you took me also, I had no thought left but fury. I crave your pardon.'

Empty silence answered him out of the darkness.

'Ah, hear me!' he called intently. 'You have saved us from the hands of the Despiser. Do not abandon us now.'

The silence stretched, then broke. 'Despair is Maker-work,' a voice said. 'It was not our intent.'

'Do not trust them!' other voices cried. 'They are hard.'

But the shuffling noise of feet came back towards Covenant and Foamfollower, and several of the clay forms lit themselves as they moved, so that the tunnel was filled with light. The creatures advanced cautiously, stopped well beyond the Giant's reach. 'We also ask your pardon,' said the leader as firmly as it could.

'Ah, you need not ask,' Foamfollower replied. 'It may be that I am slow to recognize my friends – but when I have recognized them, they have no cause to fear me. I am Saltheart Foamfollower, the –' he swallowed as if the words threatened to choke him – 'the last of the Seareach Giants. My friend is Thomas Covenant, ur-Lord and bearer of the white gold.'

'We know,' the leader said. 'We have heard. We are the *jheherrin* – the *aussat jheherrin Befylam*. The Maker-place has no secret that the *jheherrin* have not heard. You were spoken of. Plans were made against you. The *jheherrin* debated and chose to aid you.'

'If the Maker learns,' a voice behind the leader quavered, 'we are doomed.'

'That is true. If he guesses at our aid, he will no longer suffer us. We fear for our lives. But you are his enemies. And the legends say –'

Abruptly, the leader stopped, turned to confer with the other *jheherrin*. Covenant watched in fascination as they whispered together. From a distance, they all looked alike, but closer inspection revealed that they were as different as the claywork of different children. They varied in size, shape, hue, timidity, tone of voice. Yet they shared an odd appearance of unsolidity. They bulged and squished when they moved as if they were only held together by a fragile skin of surface tension – as if any jar or blow might reduce them to amorphous wet mud.

After a short conference, the leader returned. Its voice quivered as if it were afraid of its own audacity as it said, 'Why have you come? You dare – What is your purpose?'

Foamfollower answered grimly, so that the *jheherrin* would believe him, 'It is our purpose to destroy Lord Foul the Despiser.'

Covenant winced at the bald statement. But he could not deny it. How else could he describe what he meant to do?

The *jheherrin* conferred again, then announced rapidly, anxiously, 'It cannot be done. Come with us.'

The suddenness of this made it sound like a command, though the leader's voice was too tremulous to carry much authority. Covenant felt impelled to protest, not because he had any objection to following the *jheherrin*, but because he wanted to know why they considered this task impossible. But they forestalled him by the celerity of their withdrawal; before he could frame a question, half the lights were gone and the rest were going.

Foamfollower shrugged and motioned Covenant ahead of him down the tunnel. Covenant nodded. With a groan of weariness, he began to crouch along behind the *jheherrin*.

They moved with unexpected speed. Bulging and oozing at every step, they half trotted and half poured their way down the tunnel. Covenant could not keep up with them. In his cramped crouch, his lungs ached on the stale air, and his feet slipped erratically in the slimy mud. Foamfollower's pace was even slower, the low ceiling forced him to crawl. But some of the *jheherrin* stayed behind with them, guiding them past the bends and intersections of the passage. And before long the tunnel began to grow larger. As the number and complexity of the junctions increased, the ceiling rose. Soon Covenant was able to stand erect, and Foamfollower could move at a crouch. Then they travelled more swiftly.

Their journey went on for a long time. Through intricate clusters of intersections where tunnels honeycombed the earth, and the travellers caught glimpses of other creatures, all hastening the same way, through mud so wet and thick that Covenant could barely wade it and shiny coal-lodes reflecting the rocklight of the *jheherrin* garishly, they tramped for leagues with all the speed Covenant could muster. But that speed was not great, and it became steadily less as the leagues passed. He had been two days without food and closer to ten without adequate rest. The caked mud throbbed like fever on his forehead. And the numbness in his hands and feet – a lack of sensation which had nothing to do with the cold – was spreading.

Yet he trudged on. He was not afraid that he would cripple himself; in his weariness, that perpetual leper's dread had lost its power over him. Feet, head, hunger – the conditions for his return to his own world were being met. It was not the fear of leprosy which drove him. He had other motivations.

The conditions of the trek gradually improved. Rock replaced the mud of the tunnel; the air grew slowly lighter, cleaner; the temperature moderated. Such things helped Covenant keep going. And whenever he faltered, Foamfollower's concern and encouragement steadied him. League after league, he went on as if he were trying to erase the troublesome numbness of his feet on the bare rock.

At last he lapsed into somnolence. He took no more notice of his surroundings or his guides or his exhaustion. He did not feel the hand Foamfollower placed on his shoulder from time to time to direct him. When he found himself unexpectedly stationary in a large, rocklit cavern full of milling creatures, he stared at it dumbly as if he could not imagine how he had arrived there.

Most of the creatures stayed a safe distance from him and Foamfollower, but a few dragged themselves forward, carrying bowls of water and food. As they approached, they oozed with instinctive fear. Nevertheless, they came close enough to offer the bowls.

Covenant reached out to accept, but the Giant stopped him.

'Ah, *jheherrin*,' Foamfollower said in a formal tone, 'your hospitality honours us. If we could, we would return honour to you by accepting. But we are not like you – our lives are unalike. Your food would do us harm rather than help.'

This speech roused Covenant somewhat. He made himself look into the bowls and found that Foamfollower was right. The food had the appearance of liquefied marl, and it reeked of old rot, as if dead flesh had mouldered in it for centuries.

But the water was fresh and pure. Foamfollower accepted it with a bow of thanks, drank deeply, then handed it to Covenant.

For the first time, Covenant realized that Foamfollower's sack had been lost in the thorn wastes.

The rush of cold water into his emptiness helped him shake off more of his somnolence. He drank the bowl dry, savouring the purity of the water as if he believed he would never taste anything clean again. When he returned it to the waiting, trembling *jheherrin*, he did his best to match Foamfollower's bow.

Then he began to take stock of his situation. The cavern already held several hundred creatures, and more were arriving constantly.

Like the *jheherrin* who had rescued him, they all appeared to be made of animated mud. They were grotesquely formed, like monsters ridiculed for their monstrosity; they lacked any sense organs that Covenant could recognize. Yet he was vaguely surprised to see that they came in several different types. In addition to the short erect forms he had first seen, there were two or three distinct beast-shapes, which looked like miserably failed attempts to mould horses, wolves, Cavewights in mud, and one oddly serpentine group of belly crawlers.

'Foamfollower?' he murmured. A painful intuition twisted in him. 'What are they?'

'They name themselves in the tongue of the Old Lords,' Foamfollower replied carefully, as if he were skirting something dangerous, 'according to their shapes. Those who rescued us are the *aussat Befylam* of the *jheherrin*. Other *Befylam* you see – the *fael Befylam* – ' he pointed to the crawlers – 'and the *roge* – ' he indicated the Cavewight-like creatures. 'I have heard portions of their talk as we marched,' he explained. But he did not continue.

Covenant felt nauseated by the thrust of his guess. He insisted, 'What are they?'

Under the mud which darkened his face, Foamfollower's jaw muscles knotted. His voice quivered slightly as he said, 'Ask them. Let them speak of it if they will.' He stared around the cavern, did not meet Covenant's gaze.

'We will speak,' a cold dusky voice said. One of the *fael jheherrin Befylam* crawled a short distance towards them. It slopped wetly over the rock as it moved, and when it halted, it lay panting and gasping like a landed fish. Resolution and fear opposed each other in every heave of its length. But Covenant was not repelled. He felt wrung with pity for all the *jheherrin*. 'We will speak,' the crawler repeated. 'You are hard – you threaten us all.'

'They will destroy us,' a host of voices whimpered.

'But we have chosen to aid.'

'The choice was not unopposed!' voices cried.

'We have chosen. You are – the legend says – ' It faltered in confusion. 'We accept this risk.' Then a wave of misery filled its voice. 'We beg you – do not turn against us.'

Evenly, firmly, Foamfollower said, 'We will never willingly harm the *jheherrin*.'

A silence like disbelief answered him from every part of the cavern. But then a few voices said in a tone of weary self-abandonment, 'Speak, then. We have chosen.'

The crawler steadied itself. 'We will speak. We have chosen. White gold human, you ask what we are. We are the *jheherrin* – the soft

1099

ones – Maker-work.' As it spoke, the rocklight pulsed in the air like sorrow.

'The Maker labours deep in the fastness of his home, breeding armies. He takes living flesh as you know living flesh, and works his power upon it, shaping power and malice to serve his own. But his work does not always grow to his desires. At times the result is weakness rather than strength. At times his making is blind – or crippled – or stillborn. Such spawn he casts into a vast quagmire of fiery mud to be consumed.'

A vibration of remembered terror filled the cavern.

'But there is another potency in that abysm. We are not slain. In agony we become the *jheherrin* – the soft ones. We are transformed. From the depths of the pit we crawl.'

'We crawl,' voices echoed.

'In lightless combs lost even to the memory of the Maker – '

'Lost.'

' – we supplicate our lives.'

'Lives.'

'From the mud of the thorn wastes to the very walls of the Maker-place, we wander in soil and fear, searching – '

'Searching.'

' – listening – '

'Listening.'

' – waiting.'

'Waiting.'

'The surface of the Earth is denied to us. We would perish in dust if the light of the sun were to touch us. And we cannot delve – we cannot make new tunnels to lead us from this place. We are soft.'

'Lost.'

'And we dare not offend the Maker. We live in sufferance – he smiles upon our abjection.'

'Lost.'

'Yet we retain the shapes of what we were. We are – ' the voice shuddered as if it feared it would be stricken for its audacity – 'not servants of the Maker.'

Hundreds of the *jheherrin* gasped in trepidation.

'Many of our combs border the passages of the Maker. We search the walls and listen. We hear – the Maker has no secret. We heard his enmity against you, his intent against you. In the name of the legend, we debated and chose. Any aid that could be concealed from the Maker, we choose to give.'

As the crawler finished, all the *jheherrin* fell silent, and watched Covenant while he groped for a response. Part of him wanted to weep, to throw his arms around the monstrous creatures and weep.

But his purpose was rigid within him. He felt that he could not bend to gentleness without breaking. To destroy Lord Foul, he grated silently. Yes! 'But you,' he responded harshly, 'they said it's impossible. Cannot be done.'

'Cannot,' the crawler trembled. 'The passages of the Maker under Kurash Qwellinir are guarded. Kurash Qwellinir itself is a maze. The fires of Gorak Krembal ward the Maker-place. His halls swarm with malice and servants. We have heard. The Maker has no secret.'

'Yet you aided us.' The Giant's tone was thoughtful. 'You have dared the Maker's rage. You did not do this for any small reason.'

'That is true.' The speaker seemed afraid of what Foamfollower might say next.

'Surely there are other aids which you can give.'

'Yes – yes. Of Gorak Krembal we do not speak – there is nothing. But we know the ways of Kurash Qwellinir. And – and in the Maker-place also – there is something. But – ' The speaker faltered, fell silent.

'But,' Foamfollower said steadily, 'such aid is not the reason for the aid you have already given. I am not deaf or blind, *jheherrin*. Some other cause has led you to this peril.'

'The legend – ' gulped the speaker, then slithered away to confer with the creatures behind it. An intensely whispered argument followed, during which Covenant tried to calm his sense of impending crisis. For some obscure reason, he hoped that the creatures would refuse to speak of their legend. But when the crawler returned to them, Foamfollower said deliberately, 'Tell us.'

A silence of dread echoed in the cavern, and when the speaker replied fearfully, 'We will,' a chorus of shrieks pierced the air. Several score of the *jheherrin* fled, unable to bear the risk. 'We must. There is no other way.'

The crawler approached a few feet, then slumped wetly on the floor, gasping as if it could not breathe. But after a moment, it lifted up its quavering voice and began to sing. The song was in an alien tongue that Covenant did not comprehend, and its pitches were made so uncertain by fear that he could not discern the melody. Yet – more in the way the *jheherrin* listened than in the song itself – he sensed something of its potency, its attractiveness for the creatures. Without understanding anything about it, he was moved.

It was a short song, as if long ages of grim or abject use had reduced it to its barest bones. When it was done, the speaker said weakly, 'The legend. The one hope of the *jheherrin* – the sole part of our lives that is not Maker-work, the sole purpose. It tells that the distant forebears of the *jheherrin*, the un-Maker-made, were themselves Makers. But they were not seedless as he is – as we are. They were not driven to breed upon the flesh of others. From their bodies came forth young who grew and in turn made young. Thus the world was constantly renewed, in firmness and replenishment. Such things cannot be imagined.

'But the Makers were flawed. Some were weak, some blind, others incautious. Among them the Maker was born, seedless and bitter, and they did not see or fear what they had done. Thus they fell into his power. He captured them and took them to the deep fastnesses of his home, and used them to begin the work of forming armies.

'We are the last vestige of these flawed un-Maker-made. Their last life is preserved in us. In punishment for their flaws, we are doomed to crawl the combs in misery and watchfulness and eternal fear. Mud is our sun and blood and being, our flesh and home. Fear is our heritage, for the Maker could bring us to an end with one word, living as we do in the very shadow of his home. But we are watchful in the name of our one hope. For it is said that some un-Maker-made are still free of the Maker – that they still bring forth young from their bodies. It is said that when the time is ready, a young will be birthed without flaw – a pure offspring impervious to the Maker and his making – unafraid. It is said that this pure one will come bearing tokens of power to the Maker's home. It is said that he will redeem the *jheherrin* if they prove – if he finds them worthy – that he will win from the Maker their release from fear and mud – if – if – ' The crawler could not go on. Its voice stumbled into silence, left the cavern aching for a reply to fill the void of its misery.

But Covenant could not bend without breaking. He felt all the attention of the *jheherrin* focused on him. He could feel them voicelessly asking him, imploring, 'Are you that pure one? If we help you, will you free us?' But he could not give them the answer they wanted. Their living death deserved the truth from him, not a false hope.

Deliberately, he sacrificed their help. His voice was harsh; he sounded angry as he said, 'Look at me. You know the answer. Under all this mud, I'm sick – diseased. And I've done things – I'm not pure. I'm corrupt.'

One last pulse of silence met his denial – one still moment while the intent, tremulous hope around him shattered. Then a shrill wail of despair tore through the multitude of the *jheherrin*. All the light vanished at once. Shrieking in darkness, like desolated ghouls, the creatures ran.

Foamfollower caught hold of Covenant to protect him against the attack. But the *jheherrin* did not attack; they fled. The sound of their movement rushed through the cavern like a loud wind of loss, and died away. Soon the silence returned, fell limp at the feet of Covenant and Foamfollower like empty cerements, the remains of a violated grave.

Covenant's chest shook with dry spasms like sobs, but he clenched himself into union with the silence. He could not bend; he would break if the rictus of his determination were forced to bend. Foul! he jerked. Foul! You're too cruel.

He felt the attempted consolation of the Giant's hand on his shoulder. He wanted to respond, wanted to utter in some way the violence of his resolve. But before he could speak, the silence seemed to flow and concentrate itself into the sound of soft weeping.

The sound grew on him as he listened. Forlorn and miserable, it rose up into the darkness like irremediable grief, made the hollow air throb. He yearned to go to the weeper, yearned to comfort it in some way. But when he moved, it found words to halt him, desolate accusation, 'Despair is Maker-work.'

'Forgive me,' Covenant groaned. 'How could I lie to you?' He searched for the right reply, then said on intuition, 'But the legend hasn't changed. I haven't touched the legend. I don't deny your worth. You are worthy. I'm just – not the pure one. He hasn't come yet. I don't have anything to do with your hope.'

The weeper did not answer: Its sobs ached on in the air; having started, its old unanodyned misery could not stop. But after a moment it brought up a glimmer of rocklight. Covenant saw that it was the crawler who had spoken for the *jheherrin*.

'Come,' it wept. 'Come.' Shaking with sorrow, it turned and crept out of the cavern.

Covenant and the Giant followed without hesitation. In the presence of the creature's grief, they silently accepted whatever it intended for them.

It led them back into the combs – away from their earlier route, upward through a complex chain of tunnels. Soon the rock walls had become cold again, and the air began to smell faintly of brimstone. A short time later – little more than half a league from the cavern – their guide halted.

They kept themselves a respectful distance from the creature and waited while it tried to control its sobs. Its dim, rocklit struggle was painful to watch, but they contained their own emotions, waited. Covenant was prepared to allow the creature any amount of time. Patience seemed to be the only thing he could offer the *jheherrin*.

It did not keep them waiting long. Forcing down its grief, it said thickly, 'This tunnel – it ends in Kurash Qwellinir. At every turn choose – the way towards the fire. You must pass a passage of the Maker. It will be guarded. Beyond it take each turn away from the fire. You will find Gorak Krembal. You cannot cross — you must cross it. Beyond it is the rock of the Maker-place.

'Its mouth is guarded, but has no gate. Within it swarms — But there are secret ways — the Maker has secret ways, which his servants do not use. Within the mouth is a door. You cannot see it. You must find it. Press once upon the centre of the lintel. You will find many ways and hiding places.'

The crawler turned and began to shuffle back down the tunnel. Its light flickered and went out, leaving Covenant and Foamfollower in darkness. Out of the distance of the hollow comb, the creature moaned, 'Try to believe that you are pure.' Then the sound of its grief faded, and it was gone.

After a long moment of silence, Foamfollower touched Covenant's shoulder. 'My friend — did you hear it well? It has given us precious aid. Do you remember all it said?'

Covenant heard something final in the Giant's tone. But he was too preoccupied with the bitter rictus of his own intent to ask what that tone signified. 'You remember it,' he breathed stiffly. 'I'm counting on you. You must get me there.'

'My friend — Unbeliever,' the Giant began dimly, then stopped, let drop whatever he had been about to say. 'Come, then.' He steered Covenant by the shoulder. 'We will do what we can.'

They climbed on up the tunnel. It made two sharp turns and began to ascend steeply, narrowing as it rose. Soon Covenant was forced to his hands and knees by the angle of the cold stone slope. With Foamfollower breathing close behind him, helping him with an occasional shove, he pulled and scraped upward, kept on scrambling while the rock grew more and more constricted.

Then the tunnel ended in a blank wall. Covenant searched around with his numb hands. He found no openings — but he could not touch the ceiling. When he looked upward, he saw a faint window of red light out of reach above his head.

By pressing against each other, he and Foamfollower were able to stand in the end of the tunnel. The dim opening was within the stretch of Foamfollower's arms. Carefully, he lifted Covenant, boosted him through the window.

Covenant climbed into a vertical slit in the rock. Crawling along its floor, he went forward and looked out around its edges into what appeared to be a short, roofless corridor. Its walls were sheer stone, scores of feet high. It looked as if it had been rough-adzed out of raw, black, igneous rock — a passage leading senselessly from one blank wall to another. But as his eyes adjusted to the light, he discerned intersections at both ends of the corridor.

The light came from the night sky. Along one rim of the walls was a dull red glow – the shine of a fire in the distance. The air was acrid and sulphurous; if it had not been cold, Covenant would have guessed that he was already near Hotash Slay.

When he was sure that the corridor was empty, he called softly to Foamfollower. With a leap, the Giant thrust his head and shoulders through the opening into the slit, then squirmed up the rest of the way. In a moment, he was at Covenant's side.

'This is Kurash Qwellinir,' he whispered as he looked around, 'the Shattered Hills. If I have not lost all my reckoning, we are far from the passage which Bannor taught us. Without the aid of the *jheherrin*, we would be hard pressed to find our way.' Then he motioned for Covenant to follow him. 'Stay at my back. If we are discovered, I must know where you are.'

Gliding forward as smoothly as if he were rested and eager for stealth, he started towards the fiery glow, and Covenant limped along behind him on bare numb feet. Near the end of the corridor, they pressed themselves cautiously against one wall. Covenant held his breath while Foamfollower peered around the corner. An instant later, the Giant signalled. They both hurried into the next passage, taking the turn towards the red sky-shine.

This second corridor was longer than the first. The ones beyond it were crooked, curved; they reversed directions, twisted back on themselves, writhed their way through the black, rough rock like tormented snakes. Covenant soon lost all sense of progress. Without the instructions of the *jheherrin*, he would have attempted to recover lost ground, correct apparent errors. Once again he realized how much his survival had from the beginning depended on other people. Atiaran, Elena, Lena, Bannor, Triock, Mhoram, the *jheherrin* – he would have arrived nowhere, done nothing, without them. In return for his brutality, his raging and incondign improvidence, they had kept him alive, given him purpose. And now he was wholly dependent upon Saltheart Foamfollower.

It was not a good omen for a leper.

He trudged on under the aegis of dolorous portents. His wound felt like a weight under which he could no longer lift up his head, the brimstone air seemed to sap the strength from his lungs. In time he began to feel numb and affectless, as if he were wandering in confusion.

Yet he noticed the increase of light near a sharp turn in one corridor. The brightening was brief – it opened and shut like a door – but it plunged him into alertness. He dogged the Giant's feet like a shadow as they approached the corner.

They heard guttural voices from beyond the turn. Covenant flinched at the thought of pursuit, then steadied himself. The voices lacked the urgency or stealth of hunting.

Foamfollower put his head to the corner, and Covenant crouched under him to look as well.

Beyond it, the corridor opened into a wide area faintly lit by two small stones of rocklight, one near each entrance to the open space. Against the far wall mid-way between the two stones stood a dark band of half-human creatures. Covenant counted ten of them. They held spears and stood in relaxed or weary postures, talking to each other in low rough voices. Then five of them turned to the wall behind them. A section of the stone opened, letting out a stream of red light. Covenant glimpsed a deep tunnel behind the opening. The five creatures passed through the entrance and closed the stone behind them. The door closed so snugly that no crack or gleam of light revealed the tunnel's existence.

'Changing the watch,' Foamfollower breathed. 'We are fortunate that the light warned us.'

With the door closed, the guards placed themselves against the darkness of the wall where they were nearly invisible, and fell silent.

Covenant and Foamfollower backed a short distance away from the corner. Covenant felt torn; he could not think of any way past the guards, yet in his fatigue he dreaded the prospect of hunting through the maze for another passage. But Foamfollower showed no hesitation. He put his mouth to Covenant's ear and whispered grimly, 'Stay hidden. When I call, cross this open space and turn away from Hotash Slay. Wait for me beyond one turn.'

Trepidation beat in Covenant's head. 'What are you going to do?'

The Giant grinned. But his mud-dark face held no humour, and his eyes glinted hungrily. 'I think I will strike a blow or two against these Maker-work creatures.' Before Covenant could respond, he returned to the corner.

With both hands, Foamfollower searched the wall until he found a protruding lump of stone. His great muscles strained momentarily, and the lump came loose in his hands.

He sighted for an instant past the turn, then lofted the stone. It landed with a loud clatter in the far corridor.

One guard snapped a command to the others. Gripping their spears, they started towards the noise.

Foamfollower gave them a moment in which to move. Then he launched himself at them.

Covenant jumped to the corner, saw Foamfollower charge the guards. They were looking the other way. Foamfollower's long legs crossed the distance in half a dozen silent strides. They only caught a glimpse of him before he fell on them like the side of a mountain.

They were large, powerful fighters. But he was a Giant. He dwarfed them. And he took them by surprise. One blow, two, three – in instant succession, he crushed three of them, skull or chest, and sprang at the fourth.

The creature dodged backward, tried to use its spear. Foamfollower tore the spear from its hands and broke the guard's head with one slap of the shaft.

But that took an instant too long; it allowed the fifth guard to reach the entrance of the tunnel. The door sprang open. Light flared. The guard disappeared down the bright stone throat.

Foamfollower wheeled to the opening. In his right hand, he balanced the spear. It looked hardly larger than an arrow in his fist, but he cocked it over his shoulder like a javelin, and flung it at the fleeing guard.

A strangled shout of pain echoed from the tunnel.

The Giant whirled towards Covenant. 'Now!' he barked. 'Run!'

Covenant started forward, impelled by the Giant's urgency; but he could not run, could not force his limbs to move that fast. His friend transfixed him. Foamfollower stood in the vivid rocklight with blood on his hands, and he was grinning. Savage delight corrupted his bluff features; glee flashed redly from the caves of his eyes.

'Foamfollower?' Covenant whispered as if the name hurt his throat. 'Giant?'

'Go!' the Giant shouted, then turned back to the tunnel. With one sweep of his arm, he slammed the stone door shut.

Covenant stood blinking in the relative darkness and watched as Foamfollower snatched up the three remaining spears, took them to the doorway, then broke them in pieces and jammed the pieces into the cracks of the door to wedge it shut.

When he was done, he started away from the wall. Only then did he realize that Covenant had not obeyed him. At once, he pounced on the Unbeliever, caught him by the arm. 'Fool!' he snapped, swinging Covenant towards the far passage. 'Do you mock me?' But his hand was slick with blood. He lost his hold, accidentally sent Covenant reeling to jolt heavily against the stone.

Covenant slumped down the wall, gasping to regain his breath. 'Foamfollower – what's happened to you?'

Foamfollower reached him, gripped his shoulders, shook him. 'Do not mock me. I do such things for you!'

'Don't do them for me,' Covenant protested. 'You're not doing them for me.'

With a snarl, the Giant picked up Covenant. 'You are a fool if you believe we can survive in any other way.' Carrying the Unbeliever under his arm like an obdurate child, he loped into the maze towards Hotash Slay.

Now he turned away from the fiery sky-glow at every intersection. Covenant flopped in his grasp, demanding to be put down; but Foamfollower did not accede until he had put three turns and as many switchbacks behind him. Then he stopped and set Covenant on his feet.

Covenant staggered, regained his balance. He wanted to shout at the Giant, rage at him, demand explanations. But no words came. In spite of himself, he understood Saltheart Foamfollower. The last of the Unhomed had struck blows which could not be called back or stopped; Covenant could not pretend that he did not understand. Yet his heart cried out. He needed some other answer to his own extremity.

A moment passed before he heard the sound that consumed Foamfollower's attention. But then he caught it – a distant, reiterated boom like the impact of a battering ram on stone. He guessed what it was; the Despiser's creatures were trying to break out of their tunnel into the maze. An instant later, he heard a sharp, splintering noise and shouts.

The Giant put a hand on his shoulder. 'Come.'

Covenant broke into a run to keep pace with Foamfollower's trot. Together, they hurried through the corridors.

They discarded all caution now, made no attempt to protect themselves from what might lie ahead. At every junction of the maze, they swung away from the mounting red glow, and in every curve and switchback of the corridors, they moved closer to the fire, deeper into the thick, acrid atmosphere of Gorak Krembal. Covenant felt heat in the air now, a dry, stifling heat like the windless scorching of a desert. As it grew, it sent rivulets of sweat running down his back. He panted hoarsely on the air, stumbled across the rough rock, kept running. At odd intervals, he could hear shouts of pursuit echoing over the walls of Kurash Qwellinir.

Whenever he tripped, the Giant picked him up and carried him a short way. This happened more and more often. His fatigue and inanition affected him like vertigo. In his falls, he battered himself until he felt benumbed with bruises from head to foot.

When he reached it, the change was so sudden that it almost flattened him. One moment he was lurching through a blind series of corridors, the next he was out on the shores of Hotash Slay.

He slapped into the heat and light of the lava and stopped. The Hills ended sharply; he found himself on a beach of dead ash ten yards from a moiling red river of molten stone.

Under the blank dome of night, Hotash Slay curved away from

him out of sight on both sides. It bubbled and seethed, sent up flaring spouts of lava and brimstone into the air, swirled as if it were boiling where it stood rather than flowing. Yet it made no sound; it hit Covenant's ears, silent, as if he had been stricken deaf. He felt that he was suffocating on hot sulphur, but the lava seethed weirdly across his gaze as if it were inaudible – a nightmare manifestation, impossibly vivid and unreal.

At first, it dominated his sight, stretched from this ashen shore to the farthest limit of any horizon. But when he blinked back the damp heat-blur from his eyes, he saw that the lava was less than fifty yards wide. Beyond it, he could make out nothing but a narrow marge of ash. The hot red light cast everything else into darkness, made the night on the far side look as black and abysmal as the open throat of hell.

He groaned at that prospect, at the thought of Foul's Creche standing murderous and hidden beyond this impassable fire. Here all his purpose and pain came to nothing. Hotash Slay could not be crossed. Then a burst of echoed yelps jerked him around. He expected to see creatures pouring out of the maze.

The sound died again as the pursuit charged into less resonant corridors. But it could not be far behind them. 'Foamfollower!' Covenant cried, and his voice cracked with fear despite his efforts to control it. 'What do we do?'

'Listen to me!' Foamfollower said. A fever of urgency was on him. 'We must cross now – before we are seen. If you are seen – if Soulcrusher knows that you have crossed – he will hunt for you on the far side. He will capture you.'

'Cross?' Covenant gaped. 'Me?'

'If we are not seen, he will not guess what we have done. He will judge that you are elsewhere in the maze – he will hunt you there, not on the promontory of Ridjeck Thome.'

'Cross that? Are you crazy? What do you think I am?' He could not believe what he was hearing. In the past, he had assumed that he and Foamfollower would somehow get beyond Hotash Slay, but he had made that assumption because he had not visualized this moat of lava around Foul's dwelling place, had not conceived the true immensity of the obstacle. Now he saw his folly. He felt that if he went two steps closer to the lava, his skin would begin to char.

'No,' replied Foamfollower. His voice was full of fatality. 'I have striven to prepare myself. It may be that in doing this I will anneal the long harm of my life before I die. My friend, I will bear you across.'

At once, he lifted Covenant into the air, placed him sitting upon his broad shoulders.

'Put me down!' Covenant protested. 'What the hell are you doing?'

The Giant swung around to face the fiery liquefaction of the stone. 'Do not breathe!' he barked fiercely. 'My strength will help you to endure the heat, but it will sear your lungs if you breathe!'

'Damnation. Giant! Put me down! You're going to kill us!'

'I am the last of the Giants,' Foamfollower grated. 'I will give my life as I choose.'

Before Covenant could say another word, Foamfollower sprinted down the ashen beach towards the lava of Hotash Slay.

From the last edge of the shore, he leaped mightily out over the molten stone. As his feet touched the lava, he began to run with all his great Giantish strength towards the far shore.

The swift blast of heat almost snuffed out Covenant's consciousness. He heard a distant wailing, but moments passed before he realized that it came from his throat. The fire blinded him, wiped everything but red violence out of his sight. It tore at him as if it were flailing the flesh from his bones.

But it did not kill him. Endurance flowed into him from the Giant. And his ring ached on his halfhand as if it were absorbing his torment, easing the strain on his flesh.

He could feel Foamfollower sinking under him. The lava was thicker than mud or quicksand, but with each stride the Giant fell deeper into it. By the time his long surging strides had covered half the distance, he was in over his thighs. Yet he did not falter. Agony shot up through his shoulders at Covenant. Still he thrust himself forward, stretching every sinew past all limits in his effort to reach the far bank.

Covenant stopped wailing to hold his breath, though Foamfollower's pain seemed to burn him worse than the heat of the lava. He tried to grasp the white gold with his mind, pull strength from it to aid the Giant. But he could not tell whether or not he succeeded. The red fire blinded his perceptions. In another two strides, Foamfollower had sunk to his waist. He gripped Covenant's ankles, boosted him up so that the Unbeliever was standing on his shoulders. Covenant wavered on that heaving perch, but Foamfollower's hold on his ankles was as strong as iron, kept him erect.

Two more strides – the lava reached Foamfollower's chest. He mastered his pain for one instant to gasp out over the silent fire, 'Remember the *jheherrin*!' then he began to howl, driven beyond his endurance by red molten agony.

Covenant could see nothing, did not know how far they had come. Reeling over the lava, he held his breath, kept himself from joining Foamfollower's terrible scream. The Giant went on, propelled himself with his tortured legs as if he were treading water.

But finally he floundered to a stop. The weight and pain of the lava halted him. He could not wade any farther.

With one last, horrific exertion, he thrust himself upward, reared back, concentrated all his strength on his shoulders. Heaving so hard that he seemed to tear his arms from their sockets, he hurled Covenant towards the bank.

Covenant arched through the blazing light for an instant, clenched himself against the sudden pain of incineration.

He landed on dead cinders five feet from the edge of Hotash Slay. The ashes crunched under him, gave slightly, absorbed some of the impact. Gasping for breath, he rolled, staggered to his knees. He could not see; he was blind with tears. He gouged water out of his eyes with numb fingers, blinked furiously, forced his vision into focus.

Ten or more yards out in the lava, he saw one of Foamfollower's hands still above the surface. It clenched uselessly for a moment, trying to find a grip on the brimstone air. Then it followed the Giant into the molten depths.

Foamfollower! Covenant cried soundlessly. He could not find enough air to scream aloud. Foamfollower!

The heat beat back at him furiously. And through the pounding blaze came dim shouts – the approaching clamour of pursuit.

Before we are seen, Covenant remembered dumbly. Foamfollower had done this for him so that he would not be seen – so that Foul would not know that he had crossed Hotash Slay. He wanted to kneel where he was until he dissolved in heat and grief, but he stumbled to his feet.

Foamfollower! My friend!

Lumbering stiffly, he turned his back on the lava as if it were the grave of all his victims, and moved away into darkness.

After a short distance, he crossed a low, barren ridge, fell into the shallow gully beyond it. At once, a landfall of weariness buried him, and he abandoned himself to sleep. For a long time, he lay in his own night, dreaming of impossible sunlight.

19

RIDJECK THOME

He awoke with the acrid taste of brimstone in his mouth, and ashes in his heart. At first, he could not remember where he was; he could not identify the ruined ground on which he lay, or the rasp of sulphur in his throat, or the sunless sky; he could not recollect the cause of his loneliness. How could anyone be so alone and still go on breathing? But after a time he began to notice a smell of sweat and disease under the brimstone. Sweat, he murmured. Leprosy. He remembered.

Frailly, he levered himself into a sitting position in the gully, then leaned his back against one crumbling wall and tried to grasp his situation.

His thoughts hung in tatters from the spars of his mind, shredded by a gale of inanition and loss. He knew that he was starving. That's right, he said to himself. That's the way it was. His feet were battered, scored with cuts, and his forehead hurt as if a spike had been driven through his skull. He nodded in recognition. That's right. That's the way it was. But his dirty skin was not burned, and his mud-stained robe showed no signs of heat damage. For a while he sat without moving, and tried to understand why he was still alive.

Foamfollower must have saved him from the heat by exerting power through him, in the same way that the Giants propelled boats by exerting power through Gildenlode rudders. He shook his head at Foamfollower's valour. He did not know how he could go on without the help of a friend.

Yet he shed no tears over the Giant. He felt barren of tears. He was a leper and had no business with joy or grief. None, he claimed flatly. The crisis at the Colossus had taken him beyond himself, drawn responses from him which he did not properly possess. Now he felt that he had returned to his essential numbness, regained the defining touchstone of his existence. He was done pretending to be anything more than what he was.

But his work was not done. He needed to go on, to confront the Despiser – to complete, if he could, the purpose which had brought him here. All the conditions of his release from the Land had not yet been fulfilled. For good or ill, he would have to bring Lord Foul's quest for white gold to an end.

And he would have to do it as Bannor and Foamfollower would have done it – dispassionately and passionately, fighting and refusing to fight, both at once – because he had learned one more reason why he would have to seek out the Despiser. Surrounded in his mind by all his victims, he found that there was only one good answer still open to him.

That answer was a victory over Despite.

Only by defeating Lord Foul could he give meaning to all the lives which had been spent in his name, and at the same time preserve himself, the irremediable fact of who he was.

Thomas Covenant: Unbeliever. Leper.

Deliberately, he looked at his ring. It hung loosely on his emaciated finger – dull, argent, and intractable. He groaned, and started to wrestle himself to his feet.

He did not know why he was still in the Land after Foamfollower's death – and did not care. Probably the explanation lay somewhere in the breaking of the Law of Death. The Despiser could do anything. Covenant was prepared to believe that in Lord Foul's demesne all the former Law of the Earth had been abrogated.

He began to make his way up the far side of the gully. He had no preparations to make, no supplies or plans or resources to get ready – no reason why he should not simply begin his task. And the longer he delayed, the weaker he would become.

As he neared the crest of the hill, he raised his head to look around.

There he got his first sight of Foul's Creche.

It stood perhaps half a league away across a cracked, bare lowland of dead soil and rock, a place which had lain wrecked and riven for so long that it had forgotten even the possibility of life. From the vantage of the hill – the last elevation between him and Foul's Creche – he could see that he was at the base of Ridjeck Thome's promontory. Several hundred yards away from him on either side, the ground fell off in sheer cliffs which drew closer to each other as they jutted outward until they met at the tip of the promontory. In the distance, he heard waves thundering against the cliffs, and far beyond the lips of the wedge he could see the dark, grey-green waters of the Sea.

But he gave little attention to the landscape. His eyes were drawn by the magnet of the Creche itself. He had guessed from what he had heard that most of Lord Foul's home lay underground, and now he saw that this must be true. The promontory rose to a high pile of rock at its tip, and there the Creche stood. Two matched towers, as tall and slender as minarets, rose several hundred feet into the air, and between them at ground level was the dark open hole of the single entrance. Nothing else of the Despiser's abode was visible. From windows atop the towers, Lord Foul or his guards could look outward beyond the promontory, beyond Hotash Slay, beyond even the Shattered Hills, but the rest of his demesne – his breeding dens, storehouses, power works, barracks, thronehall – had to be underground, delved into the rock, accessible only through that one mouth and the tunnels hidden among Kurash Qwellinir.

Covenant stared across the promontory; and the dark windows of the towers gaped blindly back at him like soulless eyes, hollow and abhorred. At first, he was simply transfixed by the sight, stunned to find himself so close to such a destination. But when that emotion faded, he began to wonder how he could reach the Creche without being spotted by sentries. He did not believe that the towers would be as empty as they appeared. Surely the Despiser would not leave any approach unwatched. And if he waited for dark to conceal him, he might fall off a cliff or into one of the cracks.

He considered the problem for some time without finding any answer. But at last he decided that he would have to take his chances. They were no more impossible than they had ever been. And the ground he had to cross was blasted and rough, scarred with slag pits, ash heaps, crevices; he would be able to find cover for much of the distance.

He began by returning to the gully and following it south until it began to veer down towards the cliff. He could hear and see the ocean clearly now, though the lava's brimstone still overwhelmed any smell of salt in the air; but he took notice of it only to avoid the danger of the cliff. From there he climbed the hill again, and peered over it to study the nearby terrain.

To his relief, he saw more gullies. From the base of the hill, they ran like a web of erosion scars over that part of the lowland. If he could get into them without being seen, he would be safe for some distance.

He congratulated himself grimly on the filthiness of his robe, which blended well into the ruined colours of the ground. For a moment, he gathered his courage, steadied himself. Then he sprinted, tumbled down the last slope, rolled into the nearest gully.

It was too shallow to allow him to move erect, but by alternately crawling and crouching, he was able to work his way into the web. After that, he made better progress.

But beyond the heat of Hotash Slay, the air turned cold and wet like an exhalation from a dank crypt; it soaked into him despite his robe, made his sweat hurt like ice on his skin, drained his scant energies. The ground was hard, and when he crawled, his knees felt muffled ill beating up through the rock. Hunger ached precipitously within him. But he drove himself onward.

Beyond the gullies, he moved more swiftly for a time by limping between slag pits and ash heaps. But after that he came to a flat, shelterless stretch riddled with cracks and crevices. Through some he could hear the crashing of the Sea; from others came rank blasts of air, ventilation for the Creche. He had to scuttle unprotected across the flat, now running between wide gaps in the ground, now throwing himself in dizzy fear over cracks across his path. When at last he reached the foot of the rugged, upraised rock which led to the towers, he dropped into the shelter of a boulder and lay there, gasping, shivering in the damp cold, dreading the sound of guards.

But he heard no alarms, no shout or rush of pursuit – nothing but his own hoarse respiration, the febrile pulse of his blood, the pounding of the waves. Either he had not been seen or the guards were preparing to ambush him. He mustered the vestiges of his strength and began to clamber up through the rocks.

As he climbed, he grew faint. Weakness like vertigo filled his head, made his numb hands powerless to grasp, his legs powerless to thrust. Yet he went on. Time and again, he stopped with his heart lurching because he had heard – or thought he had heard – some clink of rock or rustle of apparel which said that he was being stalked. Still he forced himself to continue. Dizzy, weak, alone, trembling, vulnerable – he was engaged in a struggle that he could understand. He had come too far for any kind of surrender.

Now he was so high that he could seldom hide completely from the towers. But the angle was an awkward one for any guards that might have been at the windows. So as he gasped and scraped up the last ascents, he worried less about concealment. He needed all his attention, energy, just to move his hands and feet, lift his body upward, upward.

At last he neared the top. Peering through a gap between two boulders, he caught his first close look at the mouth of Foul's Creche.

It was smooth and symmetrical, unadorned, perfectly made. The round opening stood in a massive abutment of wrought stone – a honed and polished fortification which cupped the entrance as if it led to a sacred crypt. Its sheen echoed the clouded sky exactly, reflected the immaculate grey image of the parapets.

One figure as tall as a Giant stood before the cave. It had three heads, three sets of eyes so that it could watch in all directions, three brawny legs forming a tripod to give it stability. Its three arms were poised in constant readiness. Each held a gleaming broadsword, each was protected with heavy leather bands. A long leather buckler girded its torso. At first, Covenant saw no movement to indicate that the figure was alive. But then it blinked, drew his attention to its fetid yellow eyes. They roamed the hilltop constantly, searching for foes. When they flicked across the gap through which he peered, he recoiled as if he had been discovered.

But if the figure saw him, it gave no sign. After a moment, he calmed his apprehension. The warder was not placed to watch any part of the promontory except the last approaches to the cave; virtually all his trek from Hotash Slay had been out of the figure's line of sight. So he was safe where he crouched. But if he wanted to enter Foul's Creche, he would have to pass that warder.

He had no idea how to do so. He could not fight the creature. He could not think of any way to trick it. And the longer he waited for some kind of inspiration, the larger his fear and weakness became.

Rather than remain where he was until he paralysed himself, he squirmed on his belly up through the boulders to the fortification on one side of the entrance. Hiding behind the parapet almost directly below and between the twin towers, he clenched himself to quiet his breathing, and tried to muster his courage for the only approach he could conceive – drop over the parapet into the entryway and try to outrun the warder. He was so close to the figure now that he felt sure it could smell his sweat, hear the reel of his dizziness and the labour of his heart.

Yet he could not move. He felt utterly exposed to the towers, though he was out of sight of the windows; yet he could not make himself move. He was afraid. Once he showed himself – once the warder saw him – Foul's Creche would be warned. All Foamfollower's effort and sacrifice, all the aid of the *jheherrin*, would be undone in an instant. He would be alone against the full defences of Ridjeck Thome.

Damnation! he panted to himself. Come on, Covenant! You're a leper – you ought to be used to this by now.

Foul's Creche was a big place. If he could get past the warder, he might be able to avoid capture for a while, might even be able to find the secret door of which the *jheherrin* had spoken. This *if* was no greater than any other. He was trapped between mortal inadequacy and irrefusable need; he had long ago lost the capacity to count costs, measure chances.

He braced his hands on the stone, breathed deeply for a moment.

Before he could move, something crashed into him, slammed him down. He struggled, but a grip as hard as iron locked his arms behind his back. Weight pinned his legs. In fury and fear, he tried to yell. A hand clamped over his face.

He was helpless. His attacker could have broken his back with one swift wrench. But the hands only held him still – asserting their mastery over him, waiting for him to relax, submit.

With an effort, he forced his muscles to unclench.

The hand did not uncover his mouth, but he was suddenly flipped on to his back.

He found himself looking up into the warm, clean face of Saltheart Foamfollower.

The Giant made a silencing gesture, then released him.

At once, Covenant flung his arms around Foamfollower's neck, hugged him, clung to his strong neck like a child. A joy like sunrise washed the darkness out of him, lifted him up into hope as if it were the pure, clear dawn of a new day.

Foamfollower returned the embrace for a moment, then disentangled it and moved stealthily away. Covenant followed, though his eyes were so full of tears that he could hardly see where he was going. The Giant led him from the abutment to the far side of one of the towers. There they were hidden from the warder, and the rumble of the waves covered their voices. Grinning happily, Foamfollower whispered, 'Please pardon me. I hope I have not harmed you. I have been watching for you, but did not see you. When you gained the parapet, I could not call without alerting that Foul-spawn. And I feared that in your surprise, you might betray your presence.'

Covenant blinked back his tears. His voice shook with joy and relief as he said, 'Pardon you? You scared me witless.'

Foamfollower chuckled softly, hardly able to contain his own pleasure. 'Ah, my friend, I am greatly glad to see you once again. I feared I had lost you in Hotash Slay – feared you had been taken prisoner – feared – ah! I had a host of fears.'

'I thought you were dead.' Covenant sobbed once, then caught hold of himself, steadied himself. Brusquely, he wiped his eyes so that he could look at the Giant.

Foamfollower appeared beautifully healthy. He was naked – he had lost his raiment in the fires of the Slay – and from head to foot his flesh was clean and well. The former extremity of his gaze had been replaced by something haler, something serene; his eyes gleamed with laughter out of their cavernous sockets. The alabaster strength of his limbs looked as solid as marble; and except for a few recent scrapes received while scrambling from Hotash Slay to the Creche, even his old battle-scars were gone, effaced by a fire which seemed to have refined him down to the marrow of his bones. Nothing about him showed that he had been through agony.

Yet Covenant received an impression of agony, of a transcending pain which had fundamentally altered the Giant. Somehow in Hotash Slay, Foamfollower had carried his most terrible passions through to their apocalypse.

Covenant steadied himself with sea air, and repeated, 'I thought you were dead.'

The Giant's happiness did not falter. 'As did I. This outcome is an amazement to me, just as it is to you. Stone and Sea! I would have sworn that I would die. Covenant, the Despiser can never triumph entirely over a world in which such things occur.'

That's true, Covenant said to himself. In that kind of world. Aloud, he asked, 'But how – how did you do it? What happened?'

'I am not altogether certain. My friend, I think you have not forgotten the Giantish *caamora*, the ritual fire of grief. Giantish flesh is not harmed by ordinary fire. The pain purges, but does not burn. In that way the Unhomed from time to time found relief from the extravagance of their hearts.

'In addition – it will surprise you to hear that I believe your wild magic succoured me in some degree. Before I threw you from my shoulders, I felt – some power sharing strength with me, just as I shared strength with you.'

'Hellfire.' Covenant gaped at the blind argent band on his finger. Hellfire and bloody damnation. Again he remembered Mhoram's assertion, *You are the white gold*. But still he could not grasp what the High Lord had meant.

'And – in addition,' the Giant continued, 'there are mysteries alive in the Earth of which Lord Foul, Satansheart and Soulcrusher, does not dream. The Earthpower which spoke to befriend Berek Halfhand is not silent now. It speaks another tongue, perhaps – perhaps its ways have been forgotten by the people who live upon the Earth – but it is not quenched. The Earth could not exist if it did not contain good to match such banes as the Illearth Stone.'

'Maybe,' Covenant mused. He hardly heard himself. The thought of his ring had triggered an entirely different series of ideas in him. He did not want to recognize them, hated to speak of them, but after a moment he forced himself to say, 'Are you – are you sure you haven't been – resurrected – like Elena?'

A look of laughter brightened the Giant's face. 'Stone and Sea! That has the sound of the Unbeliever in it.'

'Are you sure?'

'No, my friend,' Foamfollower chuckled. 'I am not sure. I neither know nor care. I am only glad that I have been given one more chance to aid you.'

Covenant consumed Foamfollower's answer, then found his

response. He did his best to measure up to the Giant as he said, 'Then let's do something about it while we still can.'

'Yes.' Gravity slowly entered Foamfollower's expression, but it did not lessen his aura of ebullience and pain. 'We must. At our every delay, more lives are lost in the Land.'

'I hope you have a plan.' Covenant strove to repress his anxiety. 'I don't suppose that warden is just going to wave us through if we ask it nicely.'

'I have given some thought to the matter.' Carefully, Foamfollower outlined the results of his thinking.

Covenant considered for a moment, then said, 'That's all very well. But what if they know we're coming? What if they're waiting for us – inside there?'

The Giant shook his head, and explained that he had spent some time listening through the rock of the towers. He had heard nothing which would indicate an ambush, nothing to show that the towers were occupied at all. 'Perhaps Soulcrusher truly does not believe that he can be approached in this way. Perhaps this warder is the only guard. We will soon know.'

'Yes, indeed,' Covenant muttered. 'Only I hate surprises. You never know when one of them is going to ruin your life.'

Grimly, Foamfollower replied, 'Perhaps now we will be able to return a measure of ruin to the ruiner.'

Covenant nodded. 'I certainly hope so.'

Together, they crept back towards the entrance, then separated. Following the Giant's instructions, Covenant worked his way down among the boulders and rubble, trying to get as close as he could to the front of the cave without being seen. He moved with extreme caution, took a circuitous route. When he was done, he was still at least forty yards from the abutment. The distance distressed him, but he could find no alternative. He was not trying to sneak past the warder; he only wanted to make it hesitate.

Come on, Covenant, he snarled. Get on with it. This is no place for cowards.

He took a deep breath, cursed himself once more as if this were his last chance, and stepped out of his hiding place.

At once, he felt the warder's gaze spring at him, but he tried to ignore it, strove to pick his way up towards the cave with at least a semblance of nonchalance. Gripping his hands behind him, whistling tunelessly through his teeth, he walked forward as if he expected free admittance to Foul's Creche.

He avoided the warder's stare. That gaze felt hot enough to lay bare his purpose, expose him for what he was. It made his skin crawl with revulsion. But as he passed from the rubble on to the polished stone apron of the entryway, he forced himself to look into the figure's face.

Involuntarily, he faltered, stopped whistling. The yellow ill of the warder's gaze smote him with chagrin. Those eyes seemed to know him from skin to soul, seemed to know everything about him and hold everything they knew in the utterest contempt. For a fraction of an instant, he feared that this being was the Despiser himself. But he knew better. Like so many of the marauders, this creature was made of warped flesh – a victim of Lord Foul's Stonework. And there was uncertainty in the way it held itself.

Feigning cockiness, he strode up the apron until he was almost within sword reach of the warder. There he stopped, deliberately scrutinized the figure for a moment. When he had surveyed it from head to foot, he met its powerful gaze again, and said with all the insolence he could muster, 'Don't tell Foul I'm here. I want to surprise him.'

As he said *surprise him*, he suddenly snatched his hands from behind his back. With his ring exposed on the index finger of his right hand, he lunged forward as if to attack the warder with a blast of wild magic.

The warder jumped into a defensive stance. For an instant, all three of its heads turned towards Covenant.

In that instant, Foamfollower came leaping over the abutment above the entrance to the Creche.

The warder was beyond his reach; but as he landed, he dived forward, rolled at it, swept its feet from under it. It went down in a whirl of limbs and blades.

At once, he straddled it. It was as large as he, perhaps stronger. It was armed. But he hammered it so mightily with his fists, pinned it so effectively with his body, that it could not defend itself. After he dealt it a huge two-fisted blow at the base of its necks, it went limp.

Quickly, he took one of its swords to behead it.

'Foamfollower!' Covenant protested.

Foamfollower thrust himself up from the unconscious figure, faced Covenant with the sword clenched in one fist.

'Don't kill it.'

Panting slightly at his exertion, the Giant said, 'It will alert the Creche against us when it recovers.' His expression was grim, but not savage.

'There's been enough killing,' Covenant replied thickly. 'I hate it.'

For a moment, Foamfollower held Covenant's gaze. Then he threw back his head and began to laugh.

Covenant felt suddenly weak with gratitude. His knees almost buckled under him. 'That's better,' he mumbled in relief. Leaning against one wall of the entry, he rested while he treasured the Giant's mirth.

Shortly, Foamfollower subsided. 'Very well, my friend,' he said quietly. 'The death of this creature would gain time for us – time in which we might work our work and then seek to escape. But escape has never been our purpose.' He dropped the sword across the prostrate warder. 'If its unconsciousness allows us to reach our goal, we will have been well enough served. Let escape fend for itself.' He smiled wryly, then went on: 'However, it is in my heart that I can make a better use of this buckler.' Bending over the warder, he stripped off its garment, and used the leather to cover his own nakedness.

'You're right,' Covenant sighed. He did not intend to escape. 'But there's no reason for you to get yourself killed. Just help me find that secret door – then get out of here.'

'Abandon you?' Foamfollower adjusted the ill-fitting buckler with an expression of distaste. 'How could I leave this place? I will not attempt Hotash Slay again.'

'Jump into the Sea – swim away – I don't know.' A sense of urgency mounted in him; they could not afford to spend time debating at the very portal of Foul's Creche. 'Just don't make me responsible for you too.'

'On the contrary,' the Giant replied evenly, 'it is I who am responsible for you. I am your summoner.'

Covenant winced. 'I'm not worried about that.'

'Nor am I,' Foamfollower returned with a grin. 'But I mislike this talk of abandonment. My friend – I am acquainted with such things.'

They regarded each other gravely; and in the Giant's gaze Covenant saw as clearly as words that he could not take responsibility for his friend, could not make his friend's decisions. He could only accept Foamfollower's help and be grateful. He groaned in pain at the outcome he foresaw. 'Then let's go,' he said dismally. 'I'm not going to last much longer.'

In answer, the Giant took his arm, supported him. Side by side, they turned towards the dark mouth of the cave.

Side by side, they penetrated the gloom of Foul's Creche.

To their surprise, the darkness vanished as if they had passed through a veil of obscurity. Beyond it, they found themselves in the narrow end of an egg-shaped hall. It was coldly lit from end to end as if green sea-ice were aflame in its walls; the whole place seemed on the verge of bursting into frigid fire.

Involuntarily, they paused, stared about them. The hall's symmetry and stonework were perfect. At its widest point, it opened into matched passages which led up to the towers, and the floor of its opposite end sank flawlessly down to form a wide, spiral stairway into the rock. Everywhere the stone stretched and met without seams, cracks, junctures; the hall was as smoothly carved, polished, and even, as unblemished by ornament, feature, error, as if the ideal conception of its creator had been rendered into immaculate stone without the interference of hands that slipped, minds that misunderstood. It was obviously not Giant-work; it lacked anything which might intrude on the absolute exaction of its shape, lacked the Giantish enthusiasm for detail. Instead, it seemed to surpass any kind of mortal craft. It was preternaturally perfect.

Covenant gaped at it. While Foamfollower tore himself away to begin searching the side walls for the door of which the *jheherrin* had spoken, Covenant moved out into the hall, wandered as if aimlessly towards the great stairway. There was old magic here, might treasured by hate and hunger; he could feel it in the ceremental light, in the sharp cold air, in the immaculate walls. This fiery, frigid place was Lord Foul's home, seat and root of his power. The whole soulless demesne spoke of his suzerainty, his entire and inviolate rule. This empty hall alone made mere gnats and midges out of his enemies. Covenant remembered having heard it said that Foul would never be defeated while Ridjeck Thome still stood. He believed it.

When he reached the broad spiral of the stairway, he found that its open centre was like a great well, curving gradually back into the promontory as it descended. The stair itself was large enough to carry fifteen or twenty people abreast. Its circling drew his gaze down into the bright hole until he was leaning out from the edge to peer as far as he could; and its symmetry lent impetus to the surge of his vertigo, his irrational love and fear of falling.

But he had learned the secret of that dizziness and did not fall. His eyes searched the stairwell. And a moment later, he saw something which shook away his dangerous fascination.

Running soundlessly up out of the depths was a large band of ur-viles.

He pulled himself backward. 'You better find it fast,' he called to Foamfollower. 'They're coming.'

Foamfollower did not interrupt his scrutiny of the walls. As he searched the stone with his hands and eyes, probed it for any sign of a concealed entrance, he muttered, 'It is well hidden. I do not know how it is possible for stone to be so wrought. My people were not children in this craft, but they could not have dreamed such walls.'

'They had too many nightmares of their own,' gritted Covenant. 'Find it! Those ur-viles are coming fast.' Remembering the creature

1122

that had caused his fall in the catacombs under Mount Thunder, he added, 'They can smell white gold.'

'I am a Giant,' answered Foamfollower. 'Stonework is in the very blood of my people. This doorway cannot be concealed from me.'

Then his hands found a section of the wall which felt hollow. Swiftly, he explored the section, measured its dimensions, though no sign of any door was visible in that immaculate wall.

When he had located the entrance as exactly as possible, he pressed once on the centre of its lintel.

Glimmering with green tracery, the lintel appeared in the blank wall. Doorposts spread down from it to the floor as if they had at that instant been created out of the rock, and between them the door swung noiselessly inward.

Foamfollower rubbed his hands in satisfaction. Chuckling, 'As you commanded, ur-Lord,' he motioned for Covenant to precede him through the doorway.

Covenant glanced toward the stairs, then hastened into the small chamber beyond the door. Foamfollower came behind him, ducking for the lintel and the low ceiling of the chamber. At once, he closed the door, watched it dissolve back into featureless stone. Then he went ahead of Covenant to the corridor beyond the chamber.

This passage was as bright and cold as the outer hall. Foamfollower and Covenant could see that it sloped steeply downward, straight into the depths of the promontory. Looking along it, Covenant hoped that it would take him where he needed to go; he was too weak to sneak all through the Creche hunting for his doom.

Neither of them spoke; they did not want to risk being heard by the ur-viles. Foamfollower glanced at Covenant, shrugged once, and started down into the tunnel.

The low ceiling forced Foamfollower to move in a crouch, but he travelled down the corridor as swiftly as he could. And Covenant kept pace with him by leaning against the Giant's back and simply allowing gravity to pull his strengthless legs from stride to stride. Like twins, brothers connected to each other despite all their differences by a common umbilical need, they crouched and shambled together through the rock of Ridjeck Thome.

As they descended, Covenant fell several times. His sense of urgency, his fear, grew in the constriction of the corridor; but it drained rather than energized him, left him as slack as if he had already been defeated. Livid cold drenched him, soaked into his bones like the fire of an absolute chill, surrounded him until he began to feel strangely comfortable in it – comfortable and drowsy, as if, like an exhausted sojourner, he were at last arriving home, sinking down before his rightful hearth. Then at odd moments he caught glimpses of the spirit of this place, the uncompromising flawlessness which somehow gave rise to, affirmed, the most rabid and insatiable malice. In this air, contempt and comfort became the same thing. Foul's Creche was the domain of a being who understood perfection – a being who loathed life, not because it was any threat to him, but because its mortal infestations offended the defining passion of his existence. In those glimpses, Covenant's numb, lacerated feet seemed to miss the stone, and he fell headlong at Foamfollower's back.

But they kept moving, and at last they reached the end of the tunnel. It opened into a series of unadorned, unfurnished apartments – starkly exact and symmetrical – which showed no sign that they had ever been, or ever would be, occupied by anyone. Yet the cold, green light shone everywhere, and the air was as sharp as ice crystals. Foamfollower's sweat formed a cluster of emeralds in his beard, and he was shivering, despite his normal immunity to temperature.

Beyond the apartments, they found a chain of stairs which took them downward through blank halls, empty caverns large enough to house the most fearsome banes, uninhabited galleries where an orator could have stormed at an audience of thousands. Here again they found no sign of any occupation. All this part of the Creche was for Lord Foul's private use; no ur-viles or other creatures intruded, had ever intruded. Foamfollower hastened Covenant through the eerie perfection. Down they went, always down, seeking the depths in which Lord Foul would cherish the Illearth Stone. And around them, the ancient ill of Ridjeck Thome grew heavier and more dolorous at each deeper level. In time, Foamfollower became too cold to shiver; and Covenant shambled along at his side as if only an insistent yearning to find the Creche's chilliest place, the point of absolute ice, kept him from falling asleep where he was.

The instinct which took them downward at every opportunity did not mislead them. Gradually, Foamfollower began to sense the location of the Stone; the radiance of that bane became palpable to his sore nerves.

Eventually, they reached a landing in the wall of an empty pit. There he found another hidden door. Foamfollower opened it as he had the first one, and ducked through it into a high round hall. After Covenant had stumbled across the sill, Foamfollower closed the door and moved warily out into the centre of the hall.

Like the other halls the Giant had seen, this one was featureless except for its entrances. He counted eight large doorways, each perfectly spaced around the wall, perfectly identical to the others, each sealed shut with heavy stone doors. He could sense no life anywhere near him, no activity beyond any of the doors. But all his nerves shrilled in the direction of the Stone.

'There,' Foamfollower breathed softly, pointing at one of the entrances. 'There is the thronehall of Ridjeck Thome. There Soulcrusher holds the Illearth Stone.'

Without looking at his friend, he went over to the door, placed his hands on it to verify his perception. 'Yes,' he whispered. 'It is here.' Dread and exultation wrestled together in him. Moments passed before he realized that Covenant had not answered him.

He pressed against the door to measure its strength. 'Covenant,' he said over his shoulder, 'my friend, the end is near. Cling to your courage for one moment longer. I will break open this door. When I do, you must run at once into the thronehall. Go to the Stone – before any power intervenes.' Still Covenant did not reply. 'Unbeliever! We are at the end. Do not falter now.'

In a ghastly voice, Covenant said, 'You don't need to break it down.'

Foamfollower whirled, springing away from the door.

The Unbeliever stood in the centre of the hall. He was not alone.

An ur-vile loremaster stood before him, slavering from its gaping nostrils. In its hands, it held chains, shackles.

As Foamfollower watched in horror, it locked the shackles on to Covenant's wrists. Leading him by the chain, it took him to the door of the thronehall.

The Giant started towards his friend. But Covenant's terrible gaze stopped him. In the dark, starved bruises of Covenant's eyes, he read something that he could not answer. The Unbeliever was trying to tell him something, something for which he did not have words. Foamfollower had studied the injury which other ur-viles had done to Covenant, but he could not fathom the depth of a misery which could make a man surrender to Demondim-spawn.

'Covenant!' he cried in protest.

Deliberately, Covenant's gaze flicked away from the Giant – bored intensely into him and then jumped away, pulling Foamfollower's eyes with it.

The Giant turned in spite of himself, and saw another Giant standing across the hall from him. The newcomer's fists were clenched on his hips, and he was grinning savagely. Foamfollower recognized him at once; he was one of the three brothers who had fallen victim to the Ravers. Like Elena, this tormented soul had been resurrected to serve Soulcrusher.

Before Foamfollower could react, the door to the thronehall opened then closed behind Covenant.

At the same time, all the other doors leaped open, pouring Stone-made monsters into the hall.

20

THE UNBELIEVER

Foamfollower wheeled around, saw that he had been surrounded. Scores of creatures had entered the hall, they were more than enough to deluge him, bury him under their weight if they did not choose to slay him with their weapons. But they did not attack. They spread out along the wall, bunched in tight formations before the doors, so that he could not escape. There they stopped. With the doors closed behind them, they stood leaning eagerly forward as if they yearned to hack him to pieces. But they left him to the dead Giant.

Foamfollower swung back to face the spectre.

It advanced slowly, jeering at him with its malevolent grin. 'Greetings, Foamfollower,' it spat. 'Kinabandoner. Comrade! I have come to congratulate you. You serve the master well. Not content merely to desert our people in their time of doom, so that our entire race was extirpated from the Land, you have now delivered this groveller and his effectless white gold into the hands of the Despiser, Satansheart and Soulcrusher. Oh, well done! I give you greeting and praise, comrade!' It ejaculated the word *comrade* as if it were a supreme affront. 'I am Kinslaughterer. It was I who slew – adult and child – every Giant in The Grieve. Behold the fruit of your life, Kinabandoner. Behold and despair!'

Foamfollower retreated a few steps, but his eyes did not for an instant quail from the dead Giant.

'Retribution!' Kinslaughterer sneered. 'I see it in your face. You do not think of despair – you are too blind to perceive what you have done. By the master! You do not even think of your despicable friend. You have retribution in your heart, comrade! You behold me, and believe that if all else in your life fails, you have now at least been made able to exact vengeance for your loss. For your crime! Kinabandoner, I see it in you. It is the dearest desire of your heart to rend me limb from limb with your own hands. Fool! Do I have the appearance of one who fears you?'

While he held the spectre's gaze, Foamfollower gauged his position, measured distances around him. Kinslaughterer's words affected him. In them, he saw the sweetness of retribution. He knew the fury of killing, the miserable, involuntary delight of crushing flesh with his hands. He quivered as if he were eager, poised the gnarled might of his muscles for a leap.

'Attempt me, then,' the dead Giant went on. 'Unleash the lust which fills you. Do you believe you can vindicate yourself against me? Are you so blind? Comrade! There is nothing that justifies you. If you shed blood enough to wash the Land from east to west, you cannot wash out the ill of yourself. Imbecile! Anile fool! If the master did not control you, you would do his work for him so swiftly that he would be unable to take pleasure in it. Come then, comrade! Attempt me. I am slain already. How will you bring me to death again?'

'I will attempt it,' Foamfollower grated softly, 'in my own way.' The spectre's unnecessary goading told him what he needed to know. The creatures could have slain him at any time – yet they waited while Kinslaughterer strove to provoke him. Therefore Soulcrusher still had something to gain from him; therefore Covenant was still alive, still unbeaten. Perhaps Lord Foul hoped to use Foamfollower himself against the Unbeliever.

But Foamfollower had survived the *caamora* of Hotash Slay. He poised himself, his whole body tensed. Yet when he sprang suddenly into motion, he did not attack Kinslaughterer. Straining mightily, thrusting with all the power of his legs, he launched himself at the guards before the door of the thronehall.

They ducked under the suddenness of his assault. He dived headlong over them, forearms braced, so that his entire force struck the doors.

They had not been made to withstand such an impact. With a sharp cry of splintering stone, they burst inward.

Foamfollower fell in a flurry of door shards, somersaulted, snapped to his feet in the thronehall of Ridjeck Thome.

The room was a wide round hall like the one he had just left, but it had fewer doors, and its ceiling was far higher, as if to accommodate the immense powers which occupied it. Opposite Foamfollower was the great throne itself. On a low mound against the far wall, old grisly rock had been upreared to form the Despiser's seat in the shape of jaws, raw hooked teeth bared to grip and tear. It and its base were the only things he had seen in Foul's Creche which were not perfectly carved, utterly polished. It appeared to have been irremediably crippled, grotesqued, by the age-long weight of Lord Foul's malice. It looked like a prophecy or foretaste of ultimate doom for all Ridjeck Thome's immaculate rock.

Set into the floor directly before it was the Illearth Stone.

The Stone was not as large as Foamfollower had expected it to be; it did not appear so big or heavy that he could not have lifted it in his arms. Yet its radiance staggered him like the blow of a prodigious fist. It was not extremely bright – its illumination in the thronehall was only a little stronger than the light elsewhere – but it blazed in its setting like an incarnation of absolute cold. It pulsed like a mad heart, sent out unfetterable gouts or flares of force, radiated violently its power for corruption. Foamfollower slammed into the glare and stopped as if he could already feel the gelid emerald turning his skin to ice.

He stared at the Stone for a moment, horrified by its strength. But then his staggered senses became aware of another might in the thronehall. This power seemed oddly subdued in comparison to the Stone. But it was only subtler, more insidious – not weaker. As Foamfollower turned towards it, he knew that it was the Stone's master.

Lord Foul.

He located the Despiser more by tactile impression than by sight. Lord Foul was essentially invisible, though he cast an impenetrable blankness in the air like the erect shadow of a man – a shadow of absence rather than presence which showed where he would have been if he had been physically corporeal – and around the shadow shone a penumbra of glistening green. From within it, he reeked of attar.

He stood to one side of the Stone, with his back to the door and the Giant. And before him, facing Foamfollower, was Thomas Covenant.

They were alone; after delivering Covenant, the ur-vile had left the thronehall.

Covenant seemed unaware of the chains shackling his wrists. He did not appear to be struggling at all. He was already in the last stages of starvation and cold. Pain dripped like dank sweat down his emaciated cheeks; and his gaunt, desolate eyes met Lord Foul as if the Despiser's power were clenched in the ugly wound on his forehead.

Neither of them took any notice of Foamfollower's loud entrance; they were concentrated on each other to the exclusion of everything else. Some interchange had taken place between them – something Foamfollower had missed. But he saw the result. Just as he focused his attention on Lord Foul and Covenant, the Despiser raised one penumbral arm and struck Covenant across the mouth.

With a roar, Foamfollower charged to his friend's aid.

Before he had taken two strides, an avalanche of creatures rushed through the shattered doorway and fell on him. They pounded him to the floor, pinned him under their weight, secured his limbs. He fought wildly, extravagantly, but his opponents were many and strong. They mastered him in a moment. They dragged him to the side wall and fettered him there with chains so massive that he could not break them. When the creatures left him, hurried out of the thronehall, he was helpless.

The dead Giant was not with them. Already it had served or failed its purpose; it had been banished again.

He had been placed in a position where he could watch Lord Foul and Covenant – where their conflict would be enacted with him as its audience.

As soon as the creatures had departed, the Despiser turned towards him for the first time. When the gleaming green penumbra had shifted itself to face him, he saw the Despiser's eyes. They were the only part of Lord Foul that was visible within his aura.

He had eyes like fangs, carious and yellow – fangs so vehement in malice that they froze Foamfollower's voice, gagging him on the encouragement he had tried to shout for Covenant's sake.

'Be silent,' Lord Foul said venomously, 'or I will roast you before your time.'

Foamfollower obeyed without volition. He gaped as if he were choking on ice and watched with helpless passion in his throat.

The Despiser's eyes blinked in satisfaction. He turned his attention back to Covenant.

Covenant had been knocked from his feet by Lord Foul's blow, and he knelt now with his shackled hands covering his face in a gesture of the most complete abjection. His fingers seemed entirely numb; they pressed blindly against his face, as incapable as dead sticks of exploring his injury, of even identifying the dampness of his blood. But he could feel the disease gnawing at his nerves as if Lord Foul's presence amplified it, made the senseless erosion tangible; and he knew that his leprosy was in full career now, that the fragile arrest on which his life depended had been broken. Illness reached down into his soul like tendrils of affectlessness, searching like tree roots in a rock for cracks, flaws, at which the rock could be split asunder. He was as weak and weary as any nightmare could make him without causing the labour of his heart to stop.

But when he lowered his bloodied hands – when the swift poison of Foul's touch made his lip blacken and swell so acutely that he could no longer bear to touch it – when he looked up again towards the Despiser, he was not abject. He was unbeaten.

Damn you, he muttered dimly. Damn you. It's not that easy.

Deliberately, he closed the fingers of his halfhand around his ring.

The Despiser's eyes raged at him, but Lord Foul controlled himself to say in a sneering, fatherly tone, 'Come, Unbeliever. Do not prolong this unpleasantness. You know that you cannot stand against me. In my own name I am wholly your superior. And I possess the Illearth Stone. I can blast the moon in its course, compel the oldest dead from their deep graves, spread ruin at my whim. Without effort I can tear every fibre of your being from its moor and scatter the wreck of your soul across the heavens.'

Then do it, Covenant muttered.

'Yet I choose to forbear. I do not purpose harm against you. Only place your ring in my hand, and all your torment will be at an end. It is a small price to pay, Unbeliever.'

It's not that easy.

'And I am not powerless to reward you. If you wish to share my rule over the Land, I will permit you. You will find I am not an uncongenial master. If you wish to preserve the life of your friend Foamfollower, I will not demur — though he has offended me.' Foamfollower thrashed in his chains, struggled to protest, but he could not speak. 'If you wish health, that also I can and will provide. Behold!'

He waved one penumbral arm, and a ripple of distortion passed over Covenant's senses. At once, feeling flooded back into his hands and feet; his nerves returned to life in an instant. While they flourished, all his distress — all pain and hunger and weakness — sloughed off him. His body seemed to crow with triumphant life.

He was unmoved. He found his voice, breathed wearily through his teeth. 'Health isn't my problem. You're the one who teaches lepers to hate themselves.'

'Groveller!' Lord Foul snapped. Without transition, Covenant became leprous and starved again. 'You are on your knees to me! I will make you plead for the veriest fragments of life! Do lepers hate themselves? Then they are wise. I will teach you the true stature of hatred!'

For a moment, the Despiser's own immitigable hate gouged down at Covenant from his carious eyes, and Covenant braced himself for an onslaught. But then Lord Foul began to laugh. His scorn shone from him, shook the air of the thronehall like the sound of great boulders crushing each other, made even the hard stone of the floor seem as insidious as a quagmire. And when he subsided, he said, 'You are a dead man before me, groveller — as crippled of life as any corpse. Yet you refuse me. You refuse health, mastery, even friendship. I am interested – I am forbearant. I will allow you time to think better of your madness. Tell me why you are so rife with folly.'

Covenant did not hesitate. 'Because I loathe you.'

'That is no reason. Many men believe that they loathe me because they are too craven to despise stupidity, foolhardiness, pretension, subservience. I am not misled. Tell me why, groveller.'

'Because I love the Land.'

'Oh, forsooth!' Lord Foul jeered. 'I cannot believe that you are so anile. The Land is not your world – it has no claim upon your small fidelity. From the first, it has tormented you with demands you could not meet, honour you could not earn. You portray yourself as a man who is faithful unto death in the name of a fashion of apparel or an accident of diet – loyal to filthy robes and sand. No, groveller. I am unconvinced. Again, I say, tell me why.' He pronounced his *why* as if with that one syllable he could make Covenant's entire edifice founder.

The Land is beautiful, Covenant breathed to himself. You're ugly. For a time, he felt too weary to respond. But at last he brought out his answer.

'Because I don't believe.'

'No?' the Despiser shouted with glee. 'Still?' His laughter expressed perfect contempt. 'Groveller, you are pathetic beyond price. Almost I am persuaded to keep you at my side. You would be a jester to lighten my burdens.' Still he catechized Covenant. 'How is it possible that you can loathe or love where you do not believe?'

'Nevertheless.'

'How is it possible to disbelieve where you loathe or love?'

'Still.'

Lord Foul laughed again. 'Do my ears betray me? Do you – after my Enemy has done all within his power to sway you – do you yet believe that this is a dream?'

'It isn't real. But that doesn't matter. That's not important.'

'Then what is, groveller?'

'The Land. You.'

Once more, the Despiser laughed. But his mirth was short and vicious now; he sounded disturbed, as if there were something in Covenant which he could not understand. 'The Land and Unbelief,' he jeered. 'You poor, deranged soul! You cannot have both. They preclude each other.'

But Covenant knew better; after all that he had been through, he knew better. Only by affirming them both, accepting both poles of the contradiction, keeping them both whole, balanced, only by steering himself not between them but with them, could he preserve them both, preserve both the Land and himself, find the place where the parallel lines of his impossible dilemma met. The eye of the paradox. In that place lay the reason why the Land had happened to him. So he said nothing as he stared up at the blank shadow and the emerald aura and the incalculable might of the Despiser. But in himself, he gritted, No they don't, Foul. You're wrong. It's not that easy. If it were easy, I would have found it long ago.

'But I grow weary of your stupid assertions,' Lord Foul went on after a moment. 'My patience is not infinite. And there are other questions I wish to ask. I will set aside the matter of your entry into my demesne. It is a small matter, easily explained. In some manner unknown to me, you suborned a number of my chattel, so that twice I received false reports of your death. But set it aside. I will flay the very souls from their bones, and learn the truth. Answer this question, groveller.' He moved closer to Covenant, and the intensity of his voice told Covenant that the Despiser had reached the heart of his probing. 'This wild magic is not a part of your world. It violates your Unbelief. How can you use this power in which you do not believe?'

There Covenant found the explanation of Lord Foul's forbearance. The Despiser had spent his time interrogating Covenant rather than simply ripping the fingers off his hand to take the ring because he, Lord Foul, feared that Covenant had secretly mastered the wild magic – that he had concealed his power, risked death in the Spoiled Plains and Hotash Slay and Kurash Qwellinir, permitted himself to be taken captive, so that he could surprise the Despiser, catch Lord Foul from a weak or blind side.

Foul had reason for this fear. The Staff of Law had been destroyed.

For an instant, Covenant thought he might use this apprehension to help himself in some way. But then he saw that he could not. For his own sake, so that his defence would not be flawed by his old duplicity, he told the truth.

'I don't know how to use it.' His voice stumbled thickly past his swollen lip. 'I don't know how to call it up. But I know it is real in the Land. I know how to trigger it. I know how to bring this bloody icebox down around your ears.'

The Despiser did not hesitate, doubt. He seemed to expand in Covenant's sight as he roared savagely, 'You will trigger nothing! I have endured enough of your insolence. Do you say that you are a leper? I will show you leprosy!'

Power swarmed around Covenant like a thousand thousand mad wasps. Before him the Despiser's blank shadow grew horribly, swept upward larger and larger until it dwarfed Covenant, dwarfed Foam-follower, dwarfed the thronehall itself; it filled the air, the hall, the entire Creche. He felt himself plunging into the abyss of it. He cried out for help, but no help came. Like a stricken bird, he plummeted downward. The speed of his fall roared in his ears as if it were trying to suck him out of himself. He could sense the rock on which he would be shattered, unutterably far below him.

In the void, an attar-laden voice breathed, 'Worship me and I will save you.'

Giddy terror-lust rushed up in him. A black whirlwind hurled him at the rock as if all the puissance of the heavens had come to smash him against the unbreakable granite of his fate. Despite screamed in his mind, demanding admittance, demanding like the suicidal paradox of vertigo to overwhelm him. But he clung to himself, refused. He was a leper; the Land was not real; this was not the way he was going to die.

He clenched his fist on the ring with all the frail strength of his arm.

At the crash of impact, pain detonated in his skull. Incandescent agony yowled and yammered through his head, shredded him like claws ferociously tearing the tissue of his brain. Foul rode the pain as if it were a tidal wave, striving to break down or climb over the seawall of his will. But he was too numb to break. His hands and feet were blind, frozen; his forehead was already inured to harm; and the black swelling in his lip was familiar to him. The green, ghastly cold could not bend the rigor of his bones. Like a dead man, he was stiff with resistance.

Lord Foul tried to enter him, tried to merge with him. The offer was seductively sweet – a surcease from pain, a release from the long unrest which he had miscalled his life. But he was harnessed to himself in a way that allowed no turning aside, no surrender. He was Thomas Covenant, Unbeliever and leper. He refused.

Abruptly, his pain fell into darkness. Harm, injury, crushing, assault – all turned to ashes and blew away on windless air. In their place came his own numbness, his irreparable lack of sensation. In the great, unillumined abyss, he found that he could see himself.

He was standing nowhere, surrounded by nothing; he was staring as if in dumb incomprehension at his hands.

At first they seemed normal. They were as gaunt as sticks, and the two missing digits of his right hand gave him a sense of loss, unwholeness, that made him groan. But his ring was intact; it hung inertly on his index finger, an argent circle as perfect and inescapable as if it had some meaning.

But as he watched, dim purple spots began to appear on his hands – on his fingers, the backs of his knuckles, the heels of his palms. Slowly, they spread and started to suppurate; they bulged slightly like blisters, then opened to show abscesses under his skin. Fluid oozed from the sores as they grew and spread. Soon both his hands were covered with infection.

They became gangrenous, putrescent; the cloying stench of live, rotten flesh poured from them like the effluvium of some gnawing fungus, noisome and cruel. And under the infection, the bones of his fingers began to gnarl. Unmarrowed, flawed by rot, stressed by tendons whose nerves had died, leaving them perpetually taut, perpetually clenched against each other, the bones twisted, broke, and froze at crooked angles. In the rot and the disease, his hands maimed themselves. And the black, sick swelling of gangrene began to eat its way up his wrists.

The same pressures, the same fetid and uncontrollable tension of muscles and thews − bereft of volition by the rot in his nerves − bowed his forearms so that they hung grotesquely from his elbows. Then pus began to blossom like sweat from the abscessed pores of his upper arms. When he twitched his robe aside, he found that his legs were already contorted to the knees.

The assault horrified him, buried him in misery and self loathing. He was wearing his own future, the outcome of his illness − the destination of the road down which every leper fared who did not either kill himself or fight hard enough to stay alive. He was seeing the very thing which had first determined him to survive, all those long months ago in the leprosarium, but now it was upon him, virulent and immedicable. His leprosy was in full rank flower, and he had nothing left for which to fight.

Nevertheless he was on his home ground. He knew leprosy with the intimacy of a lover; he knew that it could not happen so swiftly, so completely. It was not real. And it was not all of him. This heinous and putrescent gnawing was not the sum total of his being. Despite what the doctors said − despite what he saw in himself − he was more than that, more than just a leper.

No, Foul! he panted bitterly. It's not that easy.

'Tom. Tom!' a stricken voice cried. It was familiar to him − a voice as known and beloved as health. 'Give it up. Don't you see what you're doing to us?'

He looked up, and saw Joan standing before him. She held their infant son, Roger, in her hands, so that the child was half extended like an offering towards him. Both of them appeared just as they had been when he had last seen them, so long ago; Joan had the same look of torn grief in her face, the expression that begged him to understand why she had already decided to divorce him. But she was inexplicably naked. His heart wept in him when he saw the lost love of her loins, the unwillingness of her breasts, the denied treasure of her face.

As he gazed at her, purple stains began to show through the warmth of her skin. Abscesses suppurated on her breasts: sickness oozed from her nipples like milk.

Roger was pulling pathetically in her hands. When he turned his helpless infant head towards his father, Covenant saw that his eyes were already glazed and cataractal, half blinded by leprosy. Two dim magenta spots tainted his cheeks.

Foul! Covenant shrieked. Damn you!

Then he saw other figures pressing forward behind Joan. Mhoram was there; Lena and Atiaran were there; Bannor and Hile Troy were there. Mhoram's whole face had fallen into yellow rot and running chancrous sores; his eyes cried out through the infection as if they were drowning in a quagmire of atrocious wrong. All Lena's hair had fallen out, and her bald scalp bristled with tubercular nodules. Atiaran's eyes were drowning in milky blindness. The grotesque gnarling of Bannor's limbs entirely crippled him. Troy's eyeless face was one puckered mass of gangrene, as if the very brain within his skull were festering.

And behind these figures stood more of the people Covenant had known in the Land. All were mortally ill, rife and hideous with leprosy. And behind them crowded multitudes more, numberless victims – all the people of the Land stricken and destitute, abominable to themselves, as ruined as if Covenant had brought a plague of absolute virulence among them.

At the sight of them, he erupted. Fury at their travail spouted up in him like lava. Volcanic anger, so long buried under the weight of his complex ordeal, sent livid, fiery passion geysering into the void.

Foul! he screamed. Foul! You can't do this!

'I will do it,' came the mocking reply. 'I am doing it.'

Stop it!

'Give me the ring.'

Never!

'Then enjoy what you have brought to pass. Behold! I have given you companions. The solitary leper has remade the world in his own image, so that he will not be alone.'

I won't let you!

The Despiser laughed sardonically. 'You will aid me before you die.'

'Never! Damn you! Never!'

Fury exalted Covenant – fury as hot as magma. A rage for lepers carried him beyond all his limits. He took one last look at the victims thronging innumerably before him. Then he began to struggle for freedom like a newborn man fighting his way out of an old skin.

He seemed to be standing in the nowhere nothingness of the

abyss, but he knew that his physical body still knelt on the floor of the thronehall. With a savage effort of will, he disregarded all sensory impressions, all appearances that prevented him from perceiving where he was. Trembling, jerking awkwardly, he levered his gaunt frame to its feet. The eyes of his body were blind, still caught in Lord Foul's control, but he grated fiercely. 'I see you, Foul.' He did not need eyes. He could sense with the nerves of his stiff cheeks the emanations of power around him.

He took three lumbering, tottering steps, and felt Foul suddenly surge towards him, rush to stop him. Before the Despiser could reach him, he raised his hands and fell fists first at the Illearth Stone.

The instant his wedding band struck the Stone, a hurricane of might exploded in his hand. Gales of green and white fire blasted through the air, shattered it like a bayamo. The veil of Lord Foul's assault was shredded in a moment and blown away. Covenant found himself lying on the floor with a tornado of power gyring upward from his halfhand.

He heaved to his feet. With one flex of his arms, he freed his wrists as if the shackles were a skein of lies.

Foul's penumbral shadow crouched in battle-readiness across the Stone from him. The Despiser brandished his carious eyes as if he were frantic to drive them into Covenant's heart. 'Fool!' he howled shrilly. 'Groveller! It is I who rule here! Alone I am your rightful master – and I command the Stone! I will destroy you. You will not so much as touch me!'

As he yelled, he threw out a flare of force which struck Covenant's hand, embedded itself deep in the core of his ring. Amid its raging gale, the white gold was altered. Cold ill soaked into the metal, forced itself into the ring until all the argent had been violated by green. Again, Covenant felt himself falling out of the thronehall.

Without transition, he found himself on Kevin's Watch. He stood on the stone platform like a titan, and with his malefic band he alone levied a new Ritual of Desecration upon the Land. All health withered before him. Great Gilden trees splintered and broke. Flowers died. *Aliantha* grew barren and became dust. Soil turned to sand. Rivers ran dry. Stonedowns and Woodhelvens were overthrown. Starvation and homelessness slew every shape of life that walked upon the earth. He was the Lord of a ruin more absolute than any other, a desolation utterly irreparable.

Never!

With one violent thrust of his will, he struck the green from his ring and returned to the thronehall. His wedding band was immaculate silver, and the slashing wind of its power was wild beyond all emerald mastery.

He almost laughed. The Stone could not corrupt him; he was already as fundamentally diseased as any corruption could make him.

To the Despiser, he rasped, 'You've had your chance. You've used your filthy power. Now it's my turn. You can't stop me. You've broken too many Laws. And I'm outside the Law. It doesn't control wild magic – it doesn't control me. But it was the only thing that might have stopped me. You could have used it against me. Now it's just me – it's my will that makes the difference.' He was panting heavily; he could not find enough air to support the extremity of his passion. 'I'm a leper, Foul. I can stand anything.'

At once, the Despiser attacked him. Foul put his hands on the Illearth Stone, placed his power on the pulsing heart of its violence. He sent green might raving at Covenant.

It fell on him like the collapse of a mountain, piled on to him like tons of wrecked stone. At first he could not focus the ring on it, and it drove him staggering backward. But then he found his error. He had tried to use the wild magic like a tool or weapon, something which could be wielded. But High Lord Mhoram had told him, *You are the white gold.* It was not a thing to be commanded, employed well or ill as skill or awkwardness allowed. Now that it was awake, it was a part of him, an expression of himself. He did not need to focus it, aim it; bone and blood, it arose from his passion.

With a shout, he threw back the attack, shattered it into a million droplets of rank fever.

Again Lord Foul struck. Power that fried the air between them sprang at Covenant, strove to interrupt the white, windless gale of the ring. Their conflict coruscated through the thronehall like a mad gibberish of lightning, green and white blasting, battering, devouring each other like all the storms of the world gone insane.

Its sheer immensity daunted Covenant, tried like a landslide to sweep the feet of his resolve from under him. He was unacquainted with power, unadept at combat. But his rage for lepers, for the Land, for the victims of Despite, kept him upright. And his Unbelief enabled him. He knew more completely than any native of the Land could have known that Lord Foul was not unbeatable. In this manifestation, Despite had no absolute reality of existence. The people of the Land would have failed in the face of Despite because they were convinced of it. Covenant was not. He was not overwhelmed; he did not believe that he had to fail. Lord Foul was only an externalized part of himself – not an immortal, not a god. Triumph was possible.

So he threw himself heart and soul and blood and bone into the battle. He did not think of defeat; the personal cost was irrelevant.

Lord Foul beat him back until he was pressed to the wall at Foamfollower's side. The savagery of the Stone made a holocaust around him, tore every last flicker of warmth from the air, shot great lurid icicles of hatred at him. But he did not falter. The wild magic was passionate and unfathomable, as high as Time and as deep as Earth – raw power limited only by the limits of his will. And his will was growing, raising its head, blossoming on the rich sap of rage. Moment by moment, he was becoming equal to the Despiser's attack.

Soon he was able to move. He forged away from the wall, waded like a strong man through the tempest towards his enemy. White and green blasts scalded the atmosphere; detonations of savage lightning shattered against each other. Lord Foul's fiery cold and Covenant's gale tore at each other's throats, rent each other, renewed themselves and tore again. In the virulence of the battle, Covenant thought that Ridjeck Thome would surely come crashing down. But the Creche stood; the thronehall stood. Only Covenant and Lord Foul shook in the thunderous silence of the power storm.

Abruptly, he succeeded in driving Lord Foul back from the Stone. At once, his own fire blazed higher. Without direct contact, the Despiser's control over his emerald bane was less perfect. His exertions became more frenzied, erratic. Unmastered force rocked the throne, tore ragged hunks of stone from the ceiling, cracked the floor. He was screaming now in a language Covenant could not understand.

The Unbeliever grabbed his opportunity. He moved forward, rained furious gouts and bolts of wild magic at the Despiser, then suddenly began to form a wall of might between Lord Foul and the Stone. Lord Foul shrieked, tried frantically to regain the Stone. But he was too late. In an instant, Convenant's force had surrounded Lord Foul.

With all the rage of his will, he pressed his advantage. He pounced like a hawk, clenched power around the Despiser. Whitely, brutally, he began to penetrate the penumbra.

Lord Foul's aura resisted with shrieks and showers of sparks. It was tough, obdurate; it shed Covenant's feral bolts as if they were mere show, incandescent child's play. But he refused to be denied. The dazzling of his wild magic flung shafts and quarrels of might at the emerald glister of the aura until one prodigious blast pierced it.

It ruptured with a shock which jarred the thronehall like an earth tremor. Waves of concussion pealed at Covenant's head, hammered at his sore and feverish skull. But he clung to his power, did not let his will wince.

The whole penumbra burst into flame like a skin of green tinder, and as it burned it tore, peeled away, fell in hot shreds and tatters to the floor.

Within Covenant's clench, Lord Foul the Despiser began to appear. By faint degrees, he became material, drifted from corporeal absence to presence. Perfectly moulded limbs, as pure as alabaster, grew slowly visible – an old, grand, leonine head, magisterially crowned and bearded with flowing white hair – an enrobed, dignified trunk, broad and solid with strength. Only his eyes showed no change, no stern, impressive surge of incarnation; they lashed constantly at Covenant like fangs wet with venom.

When he was fully present, Lord Foul folded his arms on his chest and said harshly, 'Now you do in truth see me, groveller.' His tone gave no hint of fear or surrender. 'Do you yet believe that you are my master? Fool! I grew beyond your petty wisdom or belief long before your world's babyhood. I tell you plainly, groveller – Despite such as mine is the only true fruit of experience and insight. In time you will not do otherwise than I have done. You will learn contempt for your fellow beings – for the small malices which they misname their loves and beliefs and hopes and loyalties. You will learn that it is easier to control them than to forbear – easier and better. You will not do otherwise. You will become a shadow of what I am – you will be a despiser without the courage to despise. Continue, groveller. Destroy my work if you must – slay me if you can – but make an end! I am weary of your shallow misperception.'

In spite of himself, Covenant was moved. Lord Foul's lordly mien, his dignity and resignation, spoke more vividly than any cursing or defiance. Covenant saw that he still had answers to find, regardless of all he had endured.

But before he could respond, try to articulate the emotions and intuitions which Lord Foul's words called up in him, a sudden clap of vehemence splintered the silence of the thronehall. A great invisible door opened in the air at his back; without warning, strong presences, furious and abhorring, stood behind him. The violence of their emanations almost broke his concentrated hold on Lord Foul.

He clenched his will, steadied himself to face a shock, and turned.

He found himself looking up at tall figures like the one he had seen in the cave of the EarthBlood under *Melenkurion* Skyweir. They towered above him, grisly and puissant; he seemed to see them through the stone rather than within the chamber.

They were the spectres of the dead Lords. He recognized Kevin Landwaster son of Loric. Beside Kevin stood two other livid men whom he knew instinctively to be Loric Vilesilencer and Damelon Giantfriend. There were Prothall, Osondrea, a score of men and women Covenant had never met, never heard named. With them was Elena daughter of Lena. And behind and above them all rose another figure, a dominating man with hot prophetic eyes and one halfhand: Berek Earthfriend, the Lord-Fatherer.

In one voice like a thunder of abomination – one voice of outrage that shook Covenant to the marrow of his bones – they cried, 'Slay him! It is within your power. Do not heed his treacherous lies. In the name of all Earth and health, slay him!'

The intensity of their passion poured at him, flooded him with their extreme desire. They were the sworn defenders of the Land. Its glory was their deepest love. Yet in one way or another, Lord Foul had outdone them all, seen them all taken to their graves while he endured and ravaged. They hated him with a blazing hate that seemed to overwhelm Covenant's individual rage.

But instead of moving him to obey, their vehemence washed away his fury, his power for battle. Violence drained out of him, giving place to sorrow for them – a sorrow so great that he could hardly contain it, hardly hold back his tears. They had earned obedience from him; they had a right to his rage. But their demand made his intuitions clear to him. He remembered Foamfollower's former lust for killing. He still had something to do, something which could not be done with rage. Anger was only good for fighting, for resistance. Now it could suborn the very thing he had striven to achieve.

In a voice thick with grief, he answered the Lords, 'I can't kill him. He always survives when you try to kill him. He comes back stronger than ever the next time. Despite is like that. I can't kill him.'

His reply stunned them. For a moment, they trembled with astonishment and dismay. Then Kevin asked in horror, 'Will you let him live?'

Covenant could not respond directly, could not give a direct answer. But he clung to the straight path of his intuition. For the first time since his battle with the Despiser had begun, he turned to Saltheart Foamfollower.

The Giant stood chained to the wall, watching avidly everything that happened. The bloody flesh of his wrists and ankles showed how hard he had tried to break free, and his face looked as if it had been wrung dry by all the things he had been forced to behold. But he was essentially unharmed, essentially whole. Deep in his cavernous eyes, he seemed to understand Covenant's dilemma. 'You have done well, my dear friend,' he breathed when Covenant met his gaze. 'I trust whatever choice your heart makes.'

'There's no choice about it,' Covenant panted, fighting to hold

1140

back his tears. 'I'm not going to kill him. He'll just come back. I don't want that on my head. No, Foamfollower – my friends. It's up to you now. You – and them.' He nodded towards the livid, spectral Lords. 'Joy is in the ears that hear – remember? You told me that. I've got joy for you to hear. Listen to me. I've beaten the Despiser – this time. The Land is safe – for now. I swear it. Now I want – Foamfollower!' Involuntary tears blurred his sight. 'I want to laugh. Take joy in it. Bring some joy into this bloody hole. Laugh!' He swung back to shout at the Lords. 'Do you hear me? Let Foul alone! Heal yourselves!'

For a long moment that almost broke his will, there was no sound in the thronehall. Lord Foul blazed contempt at his captor; the Lords stood aghast, uncomprehending; Foamfollower hung in his chains as if the burden were too great for him to bear.

'Help me!' Covenant cried.

Then slowly his plea made itself felt. Some prophecy in his words touched the hearts that heard him. With a terrible effort, Saltheart Foamfollower, the last of the Giants, began to laugh.

It was a gruesome sound at first; writhing in his fetters, Foam-follower spat out the laugh as if it were a curse. On that level, the Lords were able to share it. In low voices, they aimed bursts of contemptuous scorn, jeering hate, at the beaten Despiser. But as Foamfollower fought to laugh, his muscles loosened. The constriction of his throat and chest relaxed, allowing a pure wind of humour to blow the ashes of rage and pain from his lungs. Soon something like joy, something like real mirth, appeared in his voice.

The Lords responded. As it grew haler, Foamfollower's laugh became infectious; it drew the grim spectres with it. They began to unclench their hate. Clean humour ran through them, gathering momentum as it passed. Foamfollower gained joy from them, and they began to taste his joy. In moments, all their contempt or scorn had fallen away. They were no longer laughing to express their outrage at Lord Foul; they were not laughing at him at all. To their own surprise, they were laughing for the pure joy of laughter, for the sheer satisfaction and emotional ebullience of mirth.

Lord Foul cringed at the sound. He strove to sustain his defiance, but could not. With a cry of mingled pain and fury, he covered his face and began to change. The years melted off his frame. His hair darkened, beard grew stiffer; with astonishing speed, he was becoming younger. And at the same time he lost solidity, stature. His body shrank and faded with every undone age. Soon he was a youth again, barely visible.

Still the change did not stop. From a youth he became a child, growing steadily younger as he vanished. For an instant, he was a loud infant, squalling in his ancient frustration. Then he disappeared altogether.

As they laughed, the Lords also faded. With the Despiser vanquished, they went back to their natural graves – ghosts who had at last gained something other than torment from the breaking of the Law of Death. Covenant and Foamfollower were left alone.

Covenant was weeping out of control now. The exhaustion of his ordeal had caught up with him. He felt too frail to lift his head, too weary to live any longer. Yet he had one more thing to do. He had promised that the Land would be safe. Now he had to ensure its safety.

'Foamfollower?' he wept. 'My friend?' With his voice, he begged the Giant to understand him; he lacked the strength to articulate what he had to do.

'Do not fear for me,' Foamfollower replied. He sounded strangely proud, as if Covenant had honoured him in some rare way. 'Thomas Covenant, ur-Lord and Unbeliever, brave white gold wielder – I desire no other end. Do whatever you must, my friend. I am at Peace. I have beheld a marvellous story.'

Covenant nodded in the blindness of his tears. Foamfollower could make his own decisions. With the flick of an idea, he broke the Giant's chains, so that Foamfollower could at least attempt to escape if he chose. Then all Covenant's awareness of his friend became ashes.

As he shambled numbly across the floor, he tried to tell himself that he had found his answer. The answer to death was to make use of it rather than fall victim to it – master it by making it serve his goals, beliefs. This was not a good answer. But it was the only answer he had.

Following the nerves of his face, he reached towards the Illearth Stone as if it were the fruit of the tree of knowledge of life and death.

As soon as he touched it, his ring's waning might reawoke. Immense white-green fire pillared upward, towered out of the Stone and his ring like a pinnacle tall enough to pierce the heavens. As he felt its power tearing through the battered hull or conduit of his being, he knew that he had found his fire, the fire for which he was apt like autumn leaves or a bad manuscript. In the heart of the whirling gale, the pillar of force, he knelt beside the Stone and put his arms around it like a man embracing immolation. New blood from his poisoned lip ran down his chin, dripped into the green and was vaporized.

With each moment, the conjunction of the two powers produced more and more might. Like a lifeless and indomitable heart of fury, the Illearth Stone pulsed in Covenant's arms, labouring in mindless, automatic reflex to destroy him rather than be destroyed. And he hugged it to his breast like a chosen fate. He could not slay the Corruption, but he could at least try to break this corruptive tool; without it, any surviving remnant of the Despiser would have to work ages longer to regain his lost power. Covenant embraced the Stone, gave himself to its fire, and strove with the last tatters of his will to tear it asunder.

The green-white, white-green holocaust grew until it filled the thronehall, grew until it hurricaned up through the stone out of the bowels of Ridjeck Thome. Like fighters locked mortally at each other's throats, emerald and argent galed and blasted, gyring upwards at velocities which no undefended granite could withstand. In long pain, the roots of the promontory trembled. Walls bent; great chunks of ceiling fell; weaker stones melted and ran like water.

Then a convulsion shook the Creche. Gaping cracks shot through the floors, sped up the walls, as if they were headlong in mad flight. The promontory itself began to quiver and groan. Muffled detonations sent great clouds of debris up through the cracks and crevices. Hotash Slay danced in rapid spouts. The towers leaned like willows in a bereaving wind.

With a blast that jolted the Sea, the whole centre of the promontory exploded into the air. In a rain of boulders, Creche fragments as large as homes, villages, the wedge split open from tip to base. Accompanied by cataclysmic thunder, the rent halves toppled in ponderous, monumental agony away from each other into the Sea.

At once, ocean crashed into the gap from the east, and lava poured into it from the west. Their impact obscured in steam and fiery sibilation the seething cauldron of Ridjeck Thome's collapse, the sky-shaking fury of sea and stone and fire – obscured everything except the power which blazed from the core of the destruction.

It was green-white, savage, wild – mounting hugely towards its apocalypse.

But the white dominated and prevailed.

21

LEPER'S END

In that way, Thomas Covenant kept his promise.

For a long time afterward, he lay in a comfortable grave of oblivion; buried in utter exhaustion, he floated through darkness – the disengaged no-man's-land between life and death. He felt that he was effectively dead, insensate as death. But his heart went on beating as if it lacked the wit or wisdom to stop when it had no more reason to go on. Raggedly, fraily, it kept up his life.

And deep within him – in a place hidden somewhere, defended, inside the hard bone casque of his skull – he retained an awareness of himself. That essential thing had not yet failed him, though it seemed to be soaking slowly away into the warm soft earth of his grave.

He wanted rest; he had earned rest. But the release which had brought him to his present dim peace had been too expensive. He could not approve.

Foamfollower is dead, he murmured silently.

There was no escape from guilt. No answer covered everything. For as long as he managed to live, he would never be clean.

He did not think that he could manage to live very long.

Yet something obdurate argued with him. That wasn't your fault, it said. You couldn't make his decisions for him. Beyond a certain point, this responsibility of yours is only a more complex form of suicide.

He acknowledged the argument. He knew from experience that lepers were doomed as soon as they began to feel that they were to blame for contracting leprosy, were responsible for being ill. Perhaps guilt and mortality, physical limitation, were the same thing in the end – facts of life, irremediable, useless to protest. Nevertheless Foamfollower was gone, and could never be restored. Covenant would never hear him laugh again.

'Then take peace in your other innocence,' said a voice out of the darkness. 'You did not choose this task. You did not undertake it of your own free will. It was thrust upon you. Blame belongs to the chooser, and this choice was made by one who elected you without your knowledge or consent.'

Covenant did not need to ask who was speaking; he recognized the voice. It belonged to the old beggar who had confronted him before his first experience in the Land – the old man who had urged him to keep his wedding band, and had made him read a paper on the fundamental question of ethics.

Dimly, he replied, 'You must have been sure of yourself.'

'Sure? Ah, no. There was great hazard – risk for the world which I made – risk even for me. Had my enemy gained the white wild magic gold, he would have unloosed himself from the Earth – destroyed it so that he might hurl himself against me. No, Thomas Covenant. I risked my trust in you. My own hands were bound. I could not touch the Earth to defend it without thereby undoing what I meant to preserve. Only a free man could hope to stand against my enemy, hope to preserve the Earth.'

Covenant heard sympathy, respect, even gratitude in the voice. But he was unconvinced. 'I wasn't free. It wasn't my choice.'

'Ah, but you were – free of my suasion, my power, my wish to make you my tool. Have I not said that the risk was great? Choiceless, you were given the power of choice. I elected you for the Land but did not compel you to serve my purpose in the Land. You were free to damn Land and Earth and Time and all, if you chose. Only through such a risk could I hope to preserve the rectitude of my creation.'

In his darkness, Covenant shrugged. 'I still wasn't free. That singer – who called me Berek. That revival. The kid who got herself snakebit. Maybe you left me free in the Land, but you didn't leave me alone in my own life.'

'No,' the voice responded softly. 'I had no hand in those chances. Had I done anything at all to shape you, you would have been my tool – effectless. Without freedom, you could not have mastered my enemy – without independence – without the sovereignty of your own allegiance. No, I risked too much when I spoke to you once. I interfered in no other way.'

Covenant did not like to think that he had been so completely free to ruin the Land. He had come so close! For a while, he mused numbly to himself, measuring the Creator's risk. Then he asked, 'What made you think I wouldn't just collapse – wouldn't give up in despair?'

The voice replied promptly. 'Despair is an emotion like any other. It is the habit of despair which damns, not the despair itself. You were a man already acquainted with habit and despair – with the Law which both saves and damns. Your knowledge of your illness made you wise.'

Wise, Covenant murmured to himself. Wisdom. He could not

understand why his witless heart went on beating.

'Further, you were in your own way a creator. You had already tasted the way in which a creator may be impotent to heal his creation. It is oft-times this impotence which teaches a creation to despair.'

'What about the creator? Why doesn't he despair?'

'Why should he despair? If he cannot bear the world he has made he can make another. No, Thomas Covenant.' The voice laughed softly, sadly. 'Gods and creators are too powerful and powerless for despair.'

Yes, Covenant said with his own sadness. But then he added almost out of habit, It's not that easy. He wanted the voice to go away, leave him alone with his oblivion. But though it was silent, he knew it had not left him. He drifted along beside it for a time, then gathered himself to ask, 'What do you want?'

'Thomas Covenant – ' the voice was gentle – 'my unwilling son, I wish to give you a gift – a guerdon to speak my wordless gratitude. Your world runs by Law, as does mine. And by any Law I am in your debt. You have retrieved my Earth from the brink of dissolution. I could give you precious gifts a dozen times over, and still not call the matter paid.'

A gift? Covenant sighed to himself. No. He could not demean himself or the Creator by asking for a cure to leprosy. He was about to refuse the offer when a sudden excitement flashed across him. 'Save the Giant,' he said. 'Save Foamfollower.'

In a tone of ineffable rue, the voice answered, 'No, Thomas Covenant – I cannot. Have I not told you that I would break the arch of Time if I were to put my hand through it to touch the Earth? No matter how great my gratitude, I can do nothing for you in the Land or upon that Earth. If I could, I would never have permitted my enemy to do so much harm.'

Covenant nodded; he recognized the validity of the answer. After a moment of emptiness, he said, 'Then there's nothing you can do for me. I told Foul I don't believe in him. I don't believe in you either. I've had the chance to make an important choice. That's enough. I don't need any gifts. Gifts are too easy – I can't afford them.'

'Ah! but you have earned – '

'I didn't earn anything.' Faint anger stirred in him. 'You didn't give me a chance to earn anything. You put me in the Land without my approval or consent – even without my knowledge. All I did was see the difference between health and – disease. Well, it's enough for me. But there's no particular virtue in it.'

Slowly, the voice breathed, 'Do not be too quick to judge the makers of worlds. Will you ever write a story for which no character will have cause to reproach you?'

'I'll try,' said Covenant. 'I'll try.'

'Yes,' the voice whispered. 'Perhaps for you it is enough. Yet for my own sake I wish to give you a gift. Please permit me.'

'No.' Covenant's refusal was weary rather than belligerent. He could not think of anything he would be able to accept.

'I can return you to the Land. You could live out the rest of your life in health and honour, as befits a great hero.'

'No.' Have mercy on me. I couldn't bear it. 'That's not my world. I don't belong there.'

'I can teach you to believe that your experiences in the Land have been real.'

'No.' It's not that easy. 'You'll drive me insane.'

Again the voice was silent for a while before it said in a tone made sharp by grief, 'Very well. Then hear me, Thomas Covenant, before you refuse me once more. This I must tell you.

'When the parents of the child whom you saved comprehended what you had done, they sought to aid you. You were injured and weak from hunger. Your exertions to save the child had hastened the poison in your lip. Your condition was grave. They bore you to the hospital for treatment. This treatment employs a thing which the Healers of your world name "anti-venin". Thomas Covenant, this antivenin is made from the blood of horses. Your body loathes – you are allergic to the horse serum. It is a violent reaction. In your weak state, you cannot survive it. At this moment, you stand on the threshold of your own death.

'Thomas Covenant – hear me.' The voice breathed compassion at him. 'I can give you life. In this time of need, I can provide to your stricken flesh the strength it requires to endure.'

Covenant did not answer for some time. Somewhere in his half-forgotten past, he had heard that some people were allergic to rattlesnake antivenin. Perhaps the doctors at the hospital should have tested for the allergy before administering the full dosage; probably he had been so far gone in shock that they had not had time for medical niceties. For a moment, he considered the thought of dying under their care as a form of retribution.

But he rejected the idea, rejected the self-pity behind it. 'I'd rather survive,' he murmured dimly. 'I don't want to die like that.'

The voice smiled. 'It is done. You will live.'

By force of habit, Covenant said, 'I'll believe it when I see it.'

'You will see it. But there is first one other thing that you will see.

1147

You have not asked for this gift, but I give it to you whether or not you wish it. I did not ask your approval when I elected you for the Land, and do not ask now.'

Before Covenant could protest, he sensed that the voice had left him. Once again, he was alone in the darkness. Oblivion swaddled him so comfortably that he almost regretted his decision to live. But then something around him or in him began to change, modulate. Without sight or hearing or touch, he became aware of sunlight, low voices, a soft warm breeze. He found himself looking down as if from a high hill at Glimmermere.

The pure waters of the lake reflected the heavens in deep burnished azure, and the breeze smelled gently of spring. The hills around Glimmermere showed the scars of Lord Foul's preternatural winter. But already grass had begun to sprout through the cold-seared ground, and a few tough spring flowers waved bravely in the air. The stretches of bare earth had lost their grey, frozen deadness. The healing of the Land had begun.

Hundreds of people were gathered around the lake. Almost immediately, Covenant made out High Lord Mhoram. He stood facing east across Glimmermere. He bore no staff. His hands were heavily bandaged. On his left were the Lords Trevor and Loerya, holding their daughters, and on his right was Lord Amatin. All of them seemed solemnly glad, but Mhoram's serene gaze outshone them, testified more eloquently than they could to the Land's victory.

Behind the Lords stood Warmark Quaan and Hearthrall Tohrm – Quaan with the Hafts of his Warward, and Tohrm with all the Hirebrands and Gravelingases of Lord's Keep. Covenant saw that Trell Atiaran-mate was not among them. He understood intuitively; Trell had carried his personal dilemma to its conclusion, and was either dead or gone. Again, the Unbeliever found that he could not argue away his guilt.

All around the lake beyond the Lords were Lorewardens and warriors. And behind them were the survivors of Revelstone – farmers, Cattleherds, horse-tenders, cooks, artisans, Craftmasters – children and parents, young and old – all the people who had endured. They did not seem many, but Covenant knew that they were enough; they would be able to commence the work of restoration.

As he watched, they drew close to Glimmermere and fell silent. High Lord Mhoram waited until they were all attentive, ready. Then he lifted up his voice.

'People of the Land,' he said firmly, 'we are gathered here in celebration of life. I have no long song to sing. I am weak yet, and none of us is strong. But we live. The Land has been preserved. The mad riot and rout of Lord Foul's army shows us that he has fallen. The fierce echo of battle within the *krill* of Loric shows us that the white gold has done combat with the Illearth Stone, and has emerged triumphant. That is cause enough for celebration. Enough? My friends, it will suffice for us and for our children, while the present age of the Land endures.

'In token of this, I have brought the *krill* to Glimmermere.' Reaching painfully into his robe, he drew out the dagger. Its gem showed no light or life. 'In it, we see that ur-Lord Thomas Covenant, Unbeliever and white gold wielder, has returned to his world, where a great hero was fashioned for our deliverance.

'Well, that is as it must be, though my heart regrets his passing. Yet let none fear that he is lost to us. Did not the old legends say that Berek Halfhand would come again? And was not that promise kept in the person of the Unbeliever? Such promises are not made in vain.

'My friends – people of the Land – Thomas Covenant once enquired of me why we so devote ourselves to the Lore of High Lord Kevin Landwaster. And now, in this war, we have learned the hazard of that Lore. Like the *krill*, it is a power of two edges, as apt for carnage as for preservation. Its use endangers our Oath of Peace.

'I am Mhoram son of Variol, High Lord by the choice of the Council. I declare that from this day forth we will not devote ourselves to any Lore which precludes Peace. We will gain lore of our own – we will strive and quest and learn until we have found a lore in which the Oath of Peace and the preservation of the Land live together. Hear me, you people! We will serve Earthfriendship in a new way.'

As he finished, he lifted the *krill* and tossed it high into the air. It arced glinting through the sunlight, struck water in the centre of Glimmermere. When it splashed the potent water, it flared once, sent a burn of white glory into the depths of the lake. Then it was gone for ever.

High Lord Mhoram watched while the ripples faded. Then he made an exultant summoning gesture, and all the people around Glimmermere began to sing in celebration:

> Hail, Unbeliever! Keeper and Covenant,
> Unoathed truth and wicked's bane,
> Ur-Lord Illender, Prover of Life:
> Hail! Covenant!
> Dour-handed wild magic wielder,
> Ur-Earth white gold's servant and Lord –

Yours is the power that preserves.
Sing out, people of the Land –
Raise obeisance!
Hold honour and glory high to the end of days:
Keep clean the truth that was won!
Hail, Unbeliever!
Covenant!
Hail!

They raised their staffs and swords and hands to him, and his vision
blurred with tears. Tears smeared Glimmermere out of focus until it
became only a smudge of light before his face. He did not want to
lose it. He tried to clear his sight, hoping that the lake was not gone.
But then he became conscious of his tears. Instead of wetting his
cheeks, they ran from the corners of his eyes down to his ears and
neck. He was lying on his back in comfort. When he refocused his
sight, pulled it into adjustment like the resolution of a lens, he found
that the smear of light before him was the face of a man.

The man peered at him for a long moment, then withdrew into a
superficial haze of fluorescence. Slowly, Covenant realized that there
were gleaming horizontal bars on either side of the bed. His left wrist
was tied to one of them, so that he could not disturb the needle in
his vein. The needle was connected by a clear tube to an IV bottle
above his head. The air had a faint patina of germicide.

'I wouldn't have believed it if I hadn't seen it,' the man said. 'That
poor devil is going to live.'

'That's why I called you, doctor,' the woman said. 'Isn't there
anything we can do?'

'Do?' the doctor snapped.

'I didn't mean it like that,' the woman replied defensively. 'But
he's a leper! He's been making people in this town miserable for
months. Nobody knows what to do about him. Some of the other
nurses want – they want overtime pay for taking care of him. And
look at him. He's so messed up. I just think it would be a lot better
for everyone – if he – '

'That's enough.' The man was angry. 'Nurse, if I hear another
word like that out of you, you're going to be looking for a new job.
This man is ill. If you don't want to help people who are ill, go find
yourself some other line of work.'

'I don't mean any harm,' the nurse huffed as she left the room.

After she was gone, Covenant lost sight of the doctor for a while,
he seemed to fade into the insensitive haze of the lighting. Covenant
tried to take stock of his situation. His right wrist was also tied, so
that he lay in the bed as if he had been crucified. But the restraints

did not prevent him from testing the essential facts about himself. His feet were numb and cold. His fingers were in the same condition – numb, chill. His forehead hurt feverishly. His lip was taut and hot with swelling.

He had to agree with the nurse; he was in rotten shape.

Then he found the doctor near him again. The man seemed young and angry. Another man entered the room, an older doctor whom Covenant recognized as the one who had treated him during his previous stay in the hospital. Unlike the younger man, this doctor wore a suit rather than a white staff jacket. As he entered, he said, 'I hope you've got good reason for calling me, I don't give up church for just anyone – especially on Easter.'

'This is a hospital,' the younger man growled, 'not a bloody revival. Of course I've got good reason.'

'What's eating you? Is he dead?'

'No. Just the opposite – he's going to live. One minute he's in allergic shock, and dying from it because his body's too weak and infected and poisoned to fight back – and the next – Pulse firm, respiration regular, pupillary reactions normal, skin tone improving. I'll tell you what it is. It's a goddamn miracle, that's what it is.'

'Come, now,' the older man murmured. 'I don't believe in miracles – neither do you.' He glanced at the chart, then listened to Covenant's heart and lungs for himself. 'Maybe he's just stubborn.' He leaned close to Covenant's face. 'Mr Covenant,' he said, 'I don't know whether you can hear me. If you can, I have some news which may be important to you. I saw Megan Roman yesterday – your lawyer. She said that the township council has decided not to rezone Haven Farm. The way you saved that little girl – well, some people are just a bit ashamed of themselves. It's hard to take a hero's home away from him.

'Of course, to be honest, I should tell you that Megan performed a little legerdemain for you. She's a sharp lawyer, Mr Covenant. She thought the council might think twice about evicting you if it knew that a national news magazine was going to do a human interest story on the famous author who saves children from rattlesnakes. None of our politicians were very eager for headlines like "Town Ostracizes Hero". But the point is that you'll be able to keep Haven Farm.'

The older man receded. After a moment, Covenant heard him say to the other doctor, 'You still haven't told me why you're in such high dudgeon.'

'It's nothing,' the younger man replied as they left the room. 'One of our Florence Nightingales suggested that we should kill him off.'

'Who was it? I'll get the nursing superintendent to transfer her.

We'll get decent care for him from somewhere.'

Their voices drifted away, left Covenant alone in his bed.

He was thinking dimly, A miracle. That's what it was.

He was a sick man, a victim of Hansen's disease. But he was not a leper – not just a leper. He had the law of his illness carved in large, undeniable letters on the nerves of his body; but he was more than that. In the end, he had not failed the Land. And he had a heart which could still pump blood, bones which could still bear his weight; he had himself.

Thomas Covenant; Unbeliever.

A miracle.

Despite the stiff pain in his lip, he smiled at the empty room. He felt the smile on his face, and was sure of it.

He smiled because he was alive.

GLOSSARY

Acence: a Stonedownor, sister of Atiaran
ahamkara: Hoerkin, 'the Door'
Ahanna: painter, daughter of Hanna
aliantha: treasure-berries
amanibhavam: horse-healing grass, poisonous to men
Amatin: a Lord, daughter of Matin
Amok: mysterious guide and servant to ancient Lore
Amorine: First Haft, later Hiltmark
anundivian yajña: 'lost' Ramen craft of bone-sculpting
Asuraka: Staff-Elder of the Loresraat
Atiaran Trell-mate: a Stonedownor, mother of Lena
aussat Befylam: child-form of the *jheherrin*

Banas Nimoram: the Celebration of Spring
Bann: a Bloodguard, assigned to Lord Trevor
Bannor: a Bloodguard, assigned to Thomas Covenant
Baradakas: a Hirebrand of Soaring Woodhelven
Berek Halfhand: Heartthew, founder of the Line of Lords, first of the Old Lords
Bhrathair: a people met by the wandering Giants
Birinair: a Hirebrand; later a Hearthrall of Lord's Keep
Bloodguard: the defenders of the Lords
bone-sculpting: ancient Ramen craft, marrowmeld
Borillar: a Hirebrand and Hearthrall of Lord's Keep
Brabha: a Ranyhyn, Korik's mount

caamora: Giantish ordeal of grief by fire
Caer-Caveral: apprentice Forestal of Morinmoss Forest
Caerroil Wildwood: Forestal of Garroting Deep
Callindrill Faer-mate: a Lord
Cavewights: evil creatures existing under Mount Thunder
Celebration of Spring: the Dance of the Wraiths of Andelain on the dark of the moon in the middle night of spring
Cerrin: a Bloodguard, assigned to Lord Shetra
Circle of elders: Stonedown leaders

clingor: adhesive leather

Close, the: council chamber of Lord's Keep

Colossus, the: ancient stone figure guarding the Upper Land

Cord: second Ramen rank

Cording: ceremony of becoming a Cord

Corimini: Eldest of the Loresraat

Corruption: Bloodguard name for Lord Foul

Creator, the: legendary Timelord and Landsire, enemy of Lord Foul

Crowl: a Bloodguard

Damelon Giantfriend: Old High Lord, son of Berek Halfhand

Dance of the Wraiths: Celebration of Spring

Demondim: spawners of ur-viles and Waynhim

Desolation, the: era of ruin in the Land, after the Ritual of Desecration

Despiser, the: Lord Foul

Despite: Power of Evil

dharmakshetra: 'to brave the enemy', Waynhim name

diamondraught: Giantish liquor

Doar: a Bloodguard

Drinishok: Sword-Elder of the Loresraat

Drinny: a Ranyhyn, Lord Mhoram's mount, foal of Hynaril

Drool Rockworm: a Cavewight, later leader of the Cavewights, finder of the Staff of Law

dukkha: 'victim', Waynhim name

Dura Fairflank: a mustang, Thomas Covenant's mount

Earthfriend: title first given to Berek Halfhand

Earthpower, the: the source of all power in the Land

Elena: High Lord during first attack by Lord Foul; daughter of Lena

Elohim: people met by the wandering Giants

Eoman: twenty warriors plus a Warhaft

Eoward: twenty Eoman plus a Haft

fael Befylam: serpent-form of the *jheherrin*

Faer: mate of Lord Callindrill

Fangthane the Render: Ramen name for Lord Foul

Fire-Lions: fire-flow of Mount Thunder

fire-stones: graveling

First Haft: third-in-command of the Warward

First Mark: the Bloodguard commander

First Ward of Kevin's Lore: primary knowledge left by Lord Kevin

Fleshharrower: a Giant-Raver, Jehannum, *moksha*

Forbidding: a repelling force, a wall of power

Forestal: a protector of the Forests of the Land
Foul's Creche: the Despiser's home
Furl Falls: waterfall at Revelstone
Furl's Fire: warning fire at Revelstone

Gallows Howe: place of execution in Garroting Deep
Garth: Warmark of the Warward of Lord's Keep
Gay: a Winhome of the Ramen
Giantclave: Giantish conference
Giants: the Unhomed, ancient friends of the Lords
Gilden: a maple-like tree with golden leaves
Gildenlode: a power-wood formed from Gilden trees
Glimmermere: a lake on the upland above Revelstone
Gorak Krembal: Hotash Slay
Grace: a Cord of the Ramen
graveling: fire-stones, made to glow by stone-lore
Gravelingas: a master of stone-lore
Gravin Threndor: Mount Thunder
Grey Slayer: plains name for Lord Foul
Grieve, The: *Coercri*, Giant city
griffin: lionlike beast with wings

Haft: commander of an Eoward
Haruchai, the: original race of the Bloodguard
Healer: a physician
Hearthrall of Lord's Keep: a steward responsible for light, warmth
    and hospitality
Heart of Thunder: cave of power in Mount Thunder
Heartthew: Berek Halfhand
heartwood chamber: Woodhelven meeting place
Heer: leader of a Woodhelven
Herem: a Raver, Kinslaughterer, *turiya*
High Lord: leader of the Council of Lords
High Lord's Furl: banner of the High Lord
High Wood: *lomillialor*, offspring of the One Tree
Hile Troy: Warmark of High Lord Elena's Warward
Hiltmark: second-in-command of the Warward
Hirebrand: a master of wood-lore
Hoerkin: a Warhaft
Home: original homeland of the Giants
Howor: a Bloodguard, assigned to Lord Loerya
Hurn: a Cord of the Ramen
hurtloam: a healing mud

Huryn: a Ranyhyn, Terrel's mount
Hynaril: a Ranyhyn, mount of Tamarantha and Mhoram
Hyrim: a Lord, son of Hoole

Illearth Stone: stone found under Mount Thunder, source of evil power
Imoiran Tomal-mate: a Stonedownor
Irin: a warrior of the Third Eoman of the Warward

Jain: a Manethrall of the Ramen
Jehannum: a Raver, Fleshharrower, *moksha*
jheherrin: soft ones, living by-products of Foul's misshaping

Kam: a Manethrall of the Ramen
Kelenbhrabanal: Father of Horses in Ranyhyn legends
Kevin Landwaster: son of Loric Vilesilencer, last High Lord of the Old Lords
Kevin's Lore: knowledge of power left by Kevin in the Seven Wards
Kinslaughterer: a Giant-Raver, Herem, *turiya*
Kiril Threndor: chamber of power deep under Mount Thunder, Heart of Thunder
Koral: a Bloodguard, assigned to Lord Amatin
Korik: a Bloodguard, a commander of the original *Haruchai* army
kresh: savage, giant, yellow wolves
krill, the: enchanted sword of Loric, a mystery to the New Lords, wakened to power by Thomas Covenant
Kurash Plenethor: region once called Stricken Stone and later Trothgard
Kurash Qwellinir: the Shattered Hills

Lal: a Cord of the Ramen
Land, the: generally, area found on the Map
Law of Death, the: the separation of the living and the dead
Lena: a Stonedownor, daughter of Atiaran and Trell; mother of Elena
Lifeswallower: the Great Swamp
lillianrill: wood-lore, or masters of wood-lore
Lithe: a Manethrall of the Ramen
Llaura: Heer of Soaring Woodhelven
Loerya Trevor-mate: a Lord
lomillialor: High Wood, a wood of power
Lord: master of the Sword and Staff parts of Kevin's Lore

Lord-Fatherer: Berek Halfhand
Lord Foul: the enemy of the Land
'Lord Mhoram's victory': a painting by Ahanna
Lords-fire: staff fire used by the Lords
Lord's Keep: Revelstone
loremaster: ur-vile leader
Loresraat: Trothgard school at Revelwood where Kevin's Lore is
    studied
Lorewarden: teacher at the Loresraat
loreworks: Demondim power laboratory
Loric Vilesilencer: Old High Lord, son of Damelon Giantfriend
lor-liarill: Gildenlode
Lower Land, the: land east of Landsdrop

Maker, the: *jheherrin* name for Lord Foul
Maker-place: Foul's Creche
Malliner: Woodhelven Heer, son of Veinnin
Mane: a Ranyhyn
Maneing: ceremony of becoming a Manethrall
Manethrall: highest Ramen rank
Manhome: main dwelling place of the Ramen
Marny: a Ranyhyn, Tuvor's mount
marrowmeld: bone-sculpting
Mehryl: a Ranyhyn, Hile Troy's mount
Melenkurion abatha: phrase of invocation or power
Mhoram: a Lord, later High Lord, son of Variol
moksha: a Raver, Jehannum, Fleshharrower
Morin: First Mark of the Bloodguard, commander in original *Haru-
    chai* army
Morril: a Bloodguard, assigned to Lord Callindrill
Murrin Odona-mate: a Stonedownor
Myrha: a Ranyhyn, Elena's mount

Oath of Peace: oath by the people of the Land against needless
    violence
Odona Murrin-mate: a Stonedownor
Old Lords: Lords prior to the Ritual of Desecration
Omournil: Woodhelven Heer, daughter of Mournil
One Forest, the: ancient forest which covered most of the Land
One Tree, the: mystic tree from which the Staff of Law was made
orcrest: a stone of power
Osondrea: a Lord, later High Lord, daughter of Sondrea

Padrias: Woodhelven Heer, son of Mill
Peak of the Fire-Lions: Mount Thunder
Pietten: Woodhelven child damaged by Lord Foul's minions, son of Soranal
Porib: a Bloodguard
Power of Command: Seventh Ward of Kevin's Lore
Pren: a Bloodguard
Prothall: High Lord, son of Dwillian
Puhl: a Cord of the Ramen

Quaan: Warhaft of the Third Eoman of the Warward, later Hiltmark, then Warmark
Quest, the: the search to rescue the Staff of Law
Quirrel: a Stonedownor, companion of Triock

Ramen: people who serve the Ranyhyn
Ranyhyn: the great, free horses of the Plains of Ra
Ravers: Lord Foul's three ancient servants
Revelstone: Lord's Keep, mountain city of the Lords
Revelwood: seat of the Loresraat
rhadhamaerl: stone-lore or masters of stone-lore
Ridjeck Thome: Foul's Creche
rillinlure: healing wood dust
Ringthane: Ramen name for Thomas Covenant
Rites of Unfettering: the ceremony of becoming Unfettered
Ritual of Desecration: act of despair by which High Lord Kevin destroyed the Old Lords and ruined most of the Land
Rockbrother, Rocksister: terms of affection between men and Giants
roge Befylam: Cavewight-form of the *jheherrin*
Rue: a Manethrall, formerly named Gay
Ruel: a Bloodguard, assigned to Hile Troy
Runnik: a Bloodguard
Rustah: a Cord of the Ramen

sacred enclosure: Vespers hall at Revelstone
Saltheart Foamfollower: a Giant, friend of Thomas Covenant
samadhi: a Raver, Sheol, Satansfist
Sandgorgons: monsters described by the Giants
Satansfist: a Giant-Raver, Sheol, *samadhi*
Satansheart Soulcrusher: Giantish name for Lord Foul
Seven Wards, the: collection of knowledge left by Lord Kevin
Seven Words, the: power-words
Sheol: a Raver, Satansfist, *samadhi*
Shetra Verement-mate: a Lord

Shull: a Bloodguard
Sill: a Bloodguard, assigned to Lord Hyrim
Slen Terass-mate: a Stonedownor
Soranal: Woodhelven Heer, son of Thiller
Soulcrusher: Giantish name for Lord Foul
Sparlimb Keelsetter: a Giant, father of triplets
springwine: a mild, refreshing liquor
Staff, the: a branch of Kevin's Lore studied at the Loresraat
Staff of Law, the: formed by Berek from the One Tree
Stonedown: a stone-village
Stonedownor: one who lives in a stone-village
Stricken Stone: region of Trothgard before renovation
suru-pa-maerl: a stone craft
Sword, the: a branch of Kevin's Lore studied at the Loresraat
Sword-Elder: chief Lorewarden of the Sword at the Loresraat

Tamarantha Variol-mate: a Lord, daughter of Enesta
Terass Slen-mate: an elder of Mithil Stonedown, daughter of Annoria
Terrel: a Bloodguard, assigned to Lord Mhoram, a commander of
    the original *Haruchai* army
test of truth, the: test of veracity by *lomillialor* or *orcrest*
Thew: a cord of the Ramen
Thomin: a Bloodguard, assigned to Lord Verement
Tohrm: a Gravelingas and Hearthrall of Lord's Keep
Tomal: a Stonedownor craftmaster
treasure-berries: *aliantha*, nourishing fruit found throughout the
    Land
Trell Atiaran-mate: Gravelingas of Mithil Stonedown, father of Lena
Trevor Loerya-mate: a Lord
Triock: a Stonedownor, son of Thuler
Tull: a Bloodguard
turiya: a Raver, Herem, Kinslaughterer
Tuvor: First Mark of the Bloodguard, a commander of the original
    Haruchai army

Unbeliever, the: Thomas Covenant
Unfettered, the: lore-students freed from conventional responsi-
    bilities
Unhomed, the: the Giants
upland: plateau above Revelstone
Upper Land: land west of Landsdrop
ur-Lord: title given to Thomas Covenant
ur-viles: Demondim-spawn, evil creatures of power

Vailant: former High Lord

Vale: a Bloodguard

Valley of Two Rivers: site of Revelwood

Variol Farseer Tamarantha-mate: a Lord, later High Lord, son of Pentil, father of Mhoram

Verement Shetra-mate: a Lord

viancome: meeting place at Revelwood

Viles: sires of the Demondim

Vow, the: Bloodguard oath of service to the Lords

Ward: a unit of Kevin's Lore

Warhaft: commander of an Eoman

Warlore: 'Sword' knowledge in Kevin's Lore

Warmark: commander of the Warward

Warrenbridge: entrance to the catacombs under Mount Thunder

Warward, the: army of Lord's Keep

Wavenhair Haleall: a Giant, wife of Sparlimb Keelsetter, mother of triplets

Waynhim: tenders of the Waymeets, Demondim-spawn but opponents of the ur-viles

Whane: a Cord of the Ramen

Wightwarren: home of the Cavewights under Mount Thunder

Winhome: lowest Ramen rank

Woodhelven: wood-village

Woodhelvennin: inhabitants of a wood-village

Word of Warning: a powerful, destructive forbidding

Wraiths of Andelain: creatures of living light that perform the Dance at the Celebration of Spring

Yeurquin: a Stonedownor, companion of Triock

Yolenid: daughter of Loerya

STEPHEN DONALDSON

THE CHRONICLES OF THOMAS COVENANT

The First Chronicles of Thomas Covenant the Unbeliever
1. Lord Foul's Bane
2. The Illearth War
3. The Power That Preserves

'Something entirely out of the ordinary . . . you'll want to go straight through *Lord Foul's Bane*, *The Illearth War* and *The Power That Preserves* at one sitting.' *The Times*

'The Thomas Covenant saga is a remarkable achievement which will certainly find a place on the small list of true classics.' *Washington Post*

'Donaldson's epic is the most original fantasy since *Lord of the Rings* and an outstanding novel to boot.' *Time Out*

The Second Chronicles of Thomas Covenant
1. The Wounded Land
2. The One Tree
3. White Gold Wielder

'An irresistible epic . . . imagination, heroism and excitement, made all the more real by Donaldson's deft handling of the rich history of the Land.' *Chicago Daily News*

'*The Wounded Land* is a deeper . . . richer world than that presented in the previous volumes. Donaldson is extending himself, creating a fuller, more mature world of imagination.' *Seattle Post-Intelligencer*

'Donaldson has a vivid and unrestrained imagination . . . he writes well and wields symbols powerfully.' *Washington Post*

STEPHEN DONALDSON

REAVE THE JUST
and Other Tales

The world-renowned author of the *Thomas Covenant* trilogies returns to mainstream fantasy after more than ten years – with a brand-new collection of stories.

Here are tales rich with exotic atmosphere, mysticism and menace, including 'The Djinn Who Watches Over the Accursed', an unnerving fable about a reckless adulterer; 'The Killing Stroke', in which martial-arts masters fight as champions in a great mind-battle between mages; 'Penance', a haunting story of a vampire who roams a battlefield, searching for the dying; and 'Reave the Just', which demonstrates that neither brute force nor alchemy can contend with the power of suggestion.

Spellbinding, unpredictable and always entertaining, this new collection displays the remarkable imagination and extraordinary range of a writer at the height of his powers, and confirms Stephen Donaldson's position as a master of modern fantasy.

'If there is any justice in the literary world, Donaldson will earn the right to stand shoulder to shoulder with Tolkien.'
Time Out

'A writer of central significance as an author of demanding and exploratory fantasy.' JOHN CLUTE

'The most individual of the Tolkien successors.' *Guardian*

'Comparable to Tolkien at his best.' *Washington Post*

ISBN 0 00 651171 6

Daggerspell

Volume I of The Epic Deverry Series

Katharine Kerr

Enter a fantastical world where even death itself is cowed by the powers of passion and high magic.

In a world outside reality, the flickering spirit of a young girl hovers between the incarnations, knowing neither her past nor her future. But in the temporal world there is one who knows and waits: Nevyn, the wandering sorcerer. On a bloody day long ago he relinquished the maiden's hand in marriage – and so forged a terrible bond of destiny between three souls that would last through three generations. Now Nevyn is doomed to follow them across the plains of time, never resting until he atones for the tragic wrong of his youth . . .

Here in this newly revised edition comes the incredible novel that began one of the best-loved fantasy series of recent years. From long-standing fans to those who have yet to experience the series, *Daggerspell* is a rare and special treat.

0 00 648224 4

Talon of the Silver Hawk

Conclave of Shadows: Book One

Raymond E. Feist

Four days and four nights Kieli has waited upon the remote mountain peak of Shatana Higo for the gods to grant him his manhood name.

Exhausted and despairing, he is woken by the sharp claws of a rare silver hawk piercing his arm, though later he is not sure if it ever happened.

Devastation greets Kieli on his return home. His village is being burned, his people slaughtered. Although it means certain death, Kieli throws himself into the battle . . . and survives.

A distant voice echoes in his mind: *Rise up and be a talon for your people . . .*

Now he is Talon of the Silver Hawk, and he must avenge the murder of his people, at whatever cost.

'Feist writes fantasy of epic scope, fast-moving action and vivid imagination'   *Washington Post*

ISBN: 0-00-716185-9

The Redemption of Althalus

David and Leigh Eddings

From the modern masters of fantasy a stand-alone epic
on the grandest scale set in a new magical world.

Althalus, burglar, armed robber, is paid to steal a book by a
sinister stranger named Ghend. Althalus sets off to the House at
the End of the World where the book is kept. There, in the same
room as the book Ghend described, he finds a talking cat. What
he can't find when he turns around is the door by which he
entered.

By the time he sets out again, Althalus can read. He's read the
book and discovered that the evil god Daeva is trying to unmake
the world. The cat, whom Althalus calls Emerald, is in fact the
god's sister, and she needs Althalus to prevent Daeva returning
them all to primordial chaos. Althalus will teach her what she
needs to know, which is how to lie, cheat and steal – 'Whatever
works,' Emerald reflects.

Althalus is the first and foremost of a band of colourful helpers
who will battle Daeva and his bizarre, deadly minions. The
existence of the world hangs in the balance in this glorious epic
fantasy.

0 00 651483 9

Assassin's Apprentice

Book One of The Farseer Trilogy

Robin Hobb

A glorious classic fantasy combining the magic of Le Guin with the epic mastery of Tolkien

Fitz is a royal bastard, cast out into the world with only his magical link with animals for solace and companionship.

But when Fitz is adopted into the royal household, he must give up his old ways and learn a new life: weaponry, scribing, courtly manners; and how to kill a man secretly. Meanwhile, raiders ravage the coasts, leaving the people Forged and soulless. As Fitz grows towards manhood, he will have to face his first terrifying mission, a task that poses as much risk to himself as it does to his target: for Fitz is a threat to the throne . . . but he may also be the key to the future of the kingdom.

'Refreshingly original' JANNY WURTS

'I couldn't put this novel down' *Starburst*

ISBN: 0-00-648009-8

To Ride Hell's Chasm

Janny Wurts

A compelling standalone tale on an epic scale, filled with intrigue, adventure and dark magic.

When Princess Anja fails to appear at her betrothal banquet, the tiny, peaceful kingdom of Sessalie is plunged into intrigue. Charged with recovering the distraught King's beloved daughter is Mykkael, the rough-hewn newcomer who has won the post of Captain of the Garrison. A scarred veteran with a deadly record of field warfare, his 'interesting' background and foreign breeding are held in contempt by court society.

As the princess's trail vanishes outside the citadel's gates, anxiety and tension escalate. Mykkael's investigations lead him to a radical explanation for the mystery, but he finds himself under suspicion from the court factions. Can he convince them in time of his dramatic theory: that the resourceful, high-spirited princess was not taken by force, but fled the palace to escape a demonic evil?

'Janny Wurts writes with an astonishing energy . . . it ought to be illegal for one person to have so much talent'

STEPHEN R DONALDSON

'One to skive off work for' *Starburst*

'An absorbing read . . . set in a delightful world'

Dreamwatch

ISBN 0-00-710111-2